COOS COOPERATIVE

P9-CJC-426

3 2881 00915045 4

DISCARD

Carrion Comfort

HAZEL M. LEWIS LIBRARY
POWERS, OREGON 97466

Also by Dan Simmons

Drood
The Terror
A Winter Haunting
Children of the Night
Summer of Night
Song of Kali

Ilium
Olympos

Hyperion
The Fall of Hyperion
Endymion
The Rise of Endymion

World's Enough and Time
Lovedeath
Fires of Eden
The Hollow Man
Summer Sketches
Prayers to Broken Stones
Entropy's Bed at Midnight
Phases of Gravity

Darwin's Blade
The Crook Factory

Hardcase
Hard Freeze
Hard as Nails

DISCARD

HAZEL M. LEWIS LIBRARY
POWERS, OREGON 97466

DAN SIMMONS

Carrion Comfort

THOMAS DUNNE BOOKS
ST. MARTIN'S GRIFFIN
NEW YORK

This is a work of fiction. All of the characters, organizations, and events portrayed in this novel are either products of the author's imagination or are used fictitiously.

THOMAS DUNNE BOOKS.
An imprint of St. Martin's Press.

CARRION COMFORT. Copyright © 1989 by Dan Simmons. All rights reserved. Printed in the United States of America. For information, address St. Martin's Press, 175 Fifth Avenue, New York, N.Y. 10010.

www.thomasdunnebooks.com
www.stmartins.com

Library of Congress Cataloging-in-Publication Data

Simmons, Dan.
  Carrion comfort / Dan Simmons. — 1st St. Martin's Griffin ed.
    p. cm.
  ISBN 978-0-312-56707-1
  1. Vampires—Fiction.   2. Psychic ability—Fiction.   I. Title.

  PS3569.I47292C37 2009
  813'.54—dc22

                                        2009031308

First published in United States by Dark Harvest

First St. Martin's Griffin Edition: December 2009

10 9 8 7 6 5 4 3 2 1

This is for Ed Bryant

ACKNOWLEDGMENTS

Any book which successfully makes the Long Crossing to publication has been assisted by more minds and hands than the author's alone, but a novel of this size and scope accrues more debts than most. I would like to acknowledge with thanks some of those individuals who helped *Carrion Comfort* defy tempest and tides and storms at sea to reach safe harbor at last:

Dean R. Koontz, whose kind encouragement was as perfectly timed as it was generous.

Richard Curtis, whose persistence and professionalism are appreciated.

Paul Mikol, whose taste is impeccable and whose friendship is prized.

Brian Thomsen, whose love of chess and respect for history is appreciated.

Simon Hawke, Armorer in the tradition of Geoffrey Boothroyd.

Arleen Tennis, typist *extraordinaire*, for those hot summer days spent dealing with the next-to-last versions of the revised revisions.

Claudia Logerquist, for patiently reminding me that umlauts and diacritics shouldn't be sprinkled randomly, like salt.

Wolf Blitzer of the *Jerusalem Post*, for his help in tracking down the best falafel stand in Haifa.

Ellen Datlow, who said there couldn't be a sequel to the novella.

And very special thanks must go to . . .

Kathy Sherman, who enthusiastically entered into artistic collaboration on short notice and even shorter wages.

My daughter Jane, whose patient wait for Dad to "finish his scary book" has stretched across two-thirds of her lifetime.

Karen, who couldn't wait to see what happened next.

And finally, most sincerely, thanks to Edward Bryant, the gentleman and fine writer to whom this book is dedicated.

INTRODUCTION TO THE TWENTIETH ANNIVERSARY EDITION OF *CARRION COMFORT*

by Dan Simmons

Reader, I hate to be the one to break it to you, but blood-drinking, form-shifting, bat-flying, kill-with-a-stake-in-the-heart, walking-undead vampires aren't real. They're purely fictional constructs. You'll have to trust me on this. I've stalked Vlad Tsepes to his birthplace (in Sighisoara) and grave site on Snagov Island (it was empty) and tumbledown castle (the real one that the Romanians won't talk about, not the tourist trap one at Castle Bran) in Romania and Transylvania and the Carpathian mountains and, I regret to be the one to inform you, Dracula and his blood-slurping ilk are make-believe.

But mind vampires are real.

Few if any of us get through life without being preyed upon by more than one mind vampire. Even children are not exempt from falling victim to these foul fiends.

Mind vampires feed on violence, but the ultimate violence for them is the imposition of their will over yours. I long ago discovered that such an exercise of will and control of one person over another *is* a form of violence, and one we can all gain an unholy taste for if we're allowed to.

As adults, we suffer such mind-vampire attacks in almost all of our jobs—some petty, power-mad manager making our work harder and daily life miserable, some administrator or supervisor who revels in exercising arbitrary power over us and then lapping up the violence of that power as if it were warm blood—and we also encounter mind vampires in our daily lives, on the highways, in public places, in politics, and, sadly, in too many of our personal relationships.

No one carries scars on their necks from actual blood-drinking vampires, but all of us have psychic mind-vampire scars that heal slowly, if at all. And once invited into our lives, a mind vampire can return whenever he or she or it wants. And they do. Always.

Odds are great that you've met one of the rarest and most dangerous of the mind vampires that live among us, a seemingly normal human being with the Ability, and, if you have, odds are almost 100 percent that this mind vampire has used that unholy Ability to bend your will and to drink from your soul.

•
* * *

I hadn't planned to write an introduction for this Twentieth Anniversary Edition of my 1989 novel *Carrion Comfort* and, as things have worked out, I have a single day in which to write this. But I welcome the opportunity. With that brief amount of time, this introduction may contain something that most writers, including me, try to avoid in introductions—brutal honesty.

I almost never write about the *writing* side of my novels or stories in any introductions I do (and I tend to avoid introductions in the first place), and even on those rare occasions when I've commented on the creative side of writing, I've *always* avoided the business-anecdote side of any novel's history. But in this case, my epic tale of mind vampires living among us and the oddly (or absurdly) epic tale of the writing, sale, editorial struggle, and publishing nightmare of the original versions of *Carrion Comfort* overlap and interact in a way that might almost be described as metaphorical.

There's an ugly spiderweb in this true telling that is both fact and metaphor, and being enmeshed like a fly in a deadly spider's web is very much the experience too many of us have felt when encountering those real mind vampires of which I speak. *Carrion Comfort* started as my second attempt at a novel and it ended as an epic, personality-defining, life- and career-determining struggle with real mind vampires.

So with little art and less polishing, but with a rather unusual level of authorial honesty, I'm going to tell you the true tale of the creation of *Carrion Comfort* and the mind-vampirish spiderweb of nightmare that this book led me into over a period of several wonderful and intensely painful years.

Carrion Comfort is the only published piece I've done based on a dream image.

Now, it's rumored that some writers base their fiction on dreams, although I haven't met many of those writers. (I tend to hang around professionals, who tend not to depend upon dreams, drugs, or inspirations.) Many readers and nonliterary sorts just assume that we writers are constantly finding inspiration in our dreams, but save for the occasional vivid image, dreams are an unreliable energy source for plotting and tale-telling and I for one have never depended on them.

But with *Carrion Comfort*, the seed crystal came from a dream. In truth, it was just a dream fragment—a little disconnected dream-vignette—that got me hooked. No plot, not even a nonsensical dream plot, just an image.

I dreamt I was watching as an elderly woman ran through a dark forest. The trees were close together and the old woman was not moving quickly— she was too old to move very quickly—but she was obviously fleeing something. And that something was making a terrifying roar of a noise. It seemed to be twilight in the dream, after sunset or just before dawn, and the forest was thick and dark and filled with that growing unearthly roar as the old woman fled. And then I saw that the roar was coming from a large, black helicopter moving sideways above the trees. The helicopter was obviously hunting for the fleeing old woman and as I watched her I had the sudden impression that she was not a victim, not a persecuted innocent soul, but something both more or less than human and that those unseen killers in the helicopter *should* find her and *should* kill her. I had no idea what made this kindly faced elderly woman a monster, but I was certain— in the dream—that she was and that she must be destroyed.

And then I awoke.

This dream happened sometime in the summer of 1982, when I was writing my first novel, *Song of Kali*. It had nothing to do with the novel so I filed the image away and forgot it for the time being. In those years I was a full-time school teacher so I had to write any novels I might have in mind during my less-than-three-month summer vacations. It's good training for a future full-time novelist who will spend the rest of his life under constant deadlines.

I'd begun writing professionally the year before, in 1981, just *after* I'd given up my dream of writing for publication. When my wife told me that year that she was pregnant, I'd given up my brief (three-year) struggle to get published. As a swan song, I went off to a summer writers' workshop just to hear some writers that I'd always enjoyed, George R. R. Martin being one of them. But one had to submit a piece of fiction even to attend this writers' workshop so I paid my dues that way. And then I met Harlan Ellison who critiqued that short story I'd had to submit amid a day of Ellisonian critiquing that none of us there will ever forget.

That encounter with Harlan has, in its own modest circles, become something of a legend (you can find it in both Harlan's and my introductions to my first collection of short fiction, *Prayers to Broken Stones*) and I admit it can be inspiring to young writers who think it will take a miracle to get them published. Harlan, in his unique monster/mentor way, was that miracle for me.

After he told me at that workshop that I had no choice, that I was that rarest of things—*a writer*—and would always be so whether I disciplined myself to write for publication or not, I went back to work writing even while I continued to teach. That fall of 1981 I sold a story to *OMNI*. Also that year, before the story was published in *OMNI*, I was informed that the story I'd dragged to the workshop where I met Harlan, "The River Styx Runs Upstream," had tied for first place in *Twilight Zone Magazine*'s first short-story contest for previously unpublished writers. Harlan, it turns out, was one of the four judges—the others being Carol Serling (wife of the late Rod Serling), Robert (*Psycho*) Bloch, and Richard Matheson— and if Harlan hadn't disqualified himself when he saw my name and story, I would have won the thing outright rather than tied. The *Twilight Zone Magazine* editor at the time said that they'd received more than fifteen thousand story entries in that contest.

It seems that people were hungry to be published. And they still are.

So in the spring of 1982 my contest story "The River Styx Runs Up-stream" appeared in *Twilight Zone Magazine* and weeks later another story, "Eyes I Dare Not Meet in Dreams," (which later became the source for my novel *The Hollow Man*) appeared in *OMNI*.

That summer of 1982 I wrote my first novel, *Song of Kali*, which was to become the first first-novel ever to win the World Fantasy Award. That autumn, retrieving the memory of the frightening old lady fleeing the helicopter in the forest, I wrote my novelette or novella (I always forget the precise length of those forms) "Carrion Comfort" and sold it to *OMNI*. I believe it was the first two-part continued piece of fiction published in *OMNI* up to that time.

There was no forest and no helicopter in the tale yet—the original story was set in Melanie Fuller's house in Charleston, S.C., over one weekend reunion for the old mind vampires—but at least I'd discovered why the old woman in the forest in my dream seemed so frightening to me. She was a mind vampire.

Life was rich. In February of 1982, on the same day that my first published story appeared in the *Twilight Zone Magazine*, our daughter Jane was born. That summer I wrote *Song of Kali* and delivered it to my new agent and friend, Richard Curtis, and while no one wanted to buy the novel, that wasn't my problem. I trusted Richard to—someday—find a home for it. Meanwhile, I was still a sixth-grade teacher who loved and celebrated teaching as much as I always had. I wrote short fiction in the evenings, in the early mornings, on weekends, and—especially—during those wonderful summer vacations that school teachers receive as a bonus.

By 1984, *Song of Kali* still hadn't sold—its view of Calcutta and tragic tone actively frightened away publishers—but I'd earned a new day job of working with three other teachers to design a new K–6 gifted/talented program for our huge school district. The job was staggering in both scope and our own expectations (two of the four teachers on special assignment to design the program and identify students out of a K–6 population of thousands and then write the curriculum and then *teach it* literally had nervous breakdowns and left teaching over the next year) but the other survivor, Frank, and I pressed on and created the program called APEX, Advanced Programs for Excellence. [The the school board demanded an acronym and weren't amused at my suggestions of GANDALF (Gifted and Able Learners Forum) or LPOP (Little Program on the Prairie.)]

APEX was designed to serve thousands of high-end kids, both on the kindergarten through sixth-grade level in nineteen scattered elementary schools and (most excitingly) on the third-grade to sixth-grade level at the APEX Center where a round robin of new courses appeared every eight weeks. Any child in the district that met the age requirements could apply and take the half-hour DAT (Demonstrated Ability Task) that was the key to finding those kids who could work from three to fifteen years above "grade level" in those areas—literature, history, science, art, music, "show-biz," math, oceanography, biology, social studies, etc.—and every eight weeks or so another several hundred self-selected students came flowing into a whole new roster of APEX Center courses. A few kids qualified for all five mornings of APEX courses and were receiving several years' worth of truly differentiated gifted/talented advanced programming in eight weeks of long morning sessions and some astounding independent work between those sessions.

One of my courses was Carl Sagan's *Cosmos*, using curriculum written for college-level courses but also more extensive curriculum I'd written for it, all on the post–high school science level, all for a class of powerfully capable fifth- and sixth-graders who were *never* labeled gifted or talented or anything else. In what I believe to this day was the most successful advanced-learning G/T program in the nation, the hundreds upon hundreds of students flowing through APEX Center produced work, projects, and levels of thinking that would astound even master teachers around the nation.

Designing and administering and teaching APEX was the most creative thing I'd done in my life to that point and now—after publishing twenty-seven books—I still rate it as the single most successful creative thing I've done. For three years I was putting in a hundred hours of work a week on APEX—meetings, constantly reviewing and applying research in the field, writing advanced curriculum, designing new courses, designing the all-important Designated Ability Tasks that found these kids, training others to do such design, training others in the group holistic assessment the DAT's required, in-servicing more than eight hundred teachers on gifted/talented issues and classroom teaching options, carrying out all the administrative duties that flow from running a program serving thousands of kids in a constantly revolving basis, meeting with parent groups and others . . . and all through that period, I didn't begrudge the constant overtime one bit. It was exhilarating. Given the quality of kids I was honored to work with and the unparalleled height of our goals and expectations met, it was the teacher equivalent of mainlining heroin. I loved it.

In 1985, I received a phone call at my APEX office from my agent Richard Curtis. *Song of Kali* had finally sold. After being "Almost, not quite" rejected by Doubleday and Random House and Bantam and many other houses, a new publishing house called Bluejay Books, begun by a certain James Frenkel, was willing to take the risk on this dangerous tale by this unknown novelist. Bluejay would pay me $5,000 for the book.

When I got home that evening, Karen and I literally danced around the kitchen in joy. Three-year-old Jane, lifted up first by Karen and then by me, was part of the dance, whether she wanted to be or not. Life, I thought, doesn't get much better than this.

The tease on the back of the 1990 Warner paperback of *Carrion Comfort* says it all and should have been a premonition and a warning to me in 1985—

All humans feed on violence. But only those with the Ability have tasted the ultimate power.

Ordinary vampires possess the body. But only those who use the living can violate the soul.

They gather their strength through the years. They plot their unholy games. They war among themselves. And the victor will stand alone against a world without defenses.

Mind vampires, you see, have infinite patience. They will wait and wait and wait and wait and then strike when you least expect them.

Song of Kali didn't sell that many copies but it received some critical attention and eventually it would be nominated for (and win) the World Fantasy Award.

This time the Great News from my agent was that Jim Frenkel wanted a second book from me. Knowing that the dream of the old woman in the forest, now recognized as the vampire Melaine Fuller in my long story, was still haunting me—the theme of people exerting their will over others without their permission has haunted me my entire life—I proposed a large novel also titled *Carrion Comfort*.

James Frenkel agreed. This time, Bluejay Books would pay me an astounding $25,000 with half paid upon signing the contract. For Karen and me (and little Jane) who'd always survived on a single teacher's salary, this was fantastic. This time the three of us danced not only in the kitchen but right through the tiny living room of our house and out the front door.

And then I got to work writing *Carrion Comfort*, the epic novel. (I had warned Jim Frenkel from the beginning that it would be a large, large book. I was young, at least as a writer, and I had a lot to say about violence and about those who impose their will on us. The tale would begin with the Holocaust and work its way right up into the violence of the terrible 1980s, a decade that began with the murder of John Lennon, as well as the shooting of the pope and the American president.)

Reader, which is the worst mind vampire you've ever encountered?

Was it a pettifogging boss who made your employment a living hell as he or she got off on exerting control over you in your work or profession, ruining your own pleasure in that work?

Was it a lover who turned the most sacred things in life into tools of leverage over your heart and mind and life and emotions?

Was it someone you were sure would be your mentor who turned out to be a monster?

Was it one of your own children who devoted his or her young life to controlling *your* life with demands and confrontations and scenes and tantrums?

Or was it someone you would never have expected to be of the mind-vampire variety—the lurker in the shadows, the stranger soul-drainer hiding and gathering its strength while it waited for you to enter its web?

I had less than a year to write *Carrion Comfort* in 1985–1986. For an eager young novelist, it seemed plenty of time.

I was still working eighty and more hours a week on APEX, of course, but that was no problem. Evenings, weekends, watching TV with Karen and little Jane, going to movies, outings, trips, everything disappeared. I wrote the first draft longhand on yellow legal pads late into the night. In the morning I rose early—I often had to leave to supervise the APEX buses of kids before 6:30 A.M. and classes started shortly after 7 A.M.—and would madly type up the chapters finished the night before. My big expenditure at that time was a used and repaired IBM Selectric typewriter purchased from a rental place. It was a huge decision to spend that much money on technology, but my old, small Olivetti typewriter just couldn't keep up with the demands of typing out multiple drafts of what became a fifteen-hundred-plus-page mega-novel.

The story for *Carrion Comfort* was so complex—at least for me—and the cast of characters so large, that for the first and only time in my writing career, the walls of my tiny extra-bedroom-turned-office were covered with long strips of brown paper on which I'd tracked the actions, interactions, and ultimate fates of the many characters in lines of different-colored magic marker. Melanie Fuller, I remember, was red. Saul Laski was blue. Nina Drayton was a brief yellow. Tony Harod was a billious green. The Oberst, Willi, was a thick Nazi black. Up and down all my study's walls ran a riot of dozens of colored lines, crossing, crisscrossing, with scribbled notes at the junctions and important points. Sometimes the lines terminated with a terrible suddenness where the character died. The ceiling-to-floor strips of scribbled butcher paper looked like a seismometer's readout run amuck.

All around me, day after day through that autumn and winter and spring, were growing stacks of filled yellow legal pads, taller stacks of reference books and maps, and growing mountains of multiple-typed drafts of *Carrion Comfort*. From time to time I kept Jim Frenkel apprised of how large the book was going to be. "No problem," was the only response I got from my publisher-editor.

The book was due in the autumn of 1986. That summer, I hired our APEX secretary, Arleen, to work for me from her own home, daily typing up my revised revisions of the retyped and revised chapters I continued to churn out. I not only had fifty or sixty legal pads filled with scribbles and X-outs and revisions now, I also had four or more two-and-a-half-foot-tall heaps of my own typed manuscripts.

That summer I worked between sixteen and twenty hours a day on *Carrion Comfort*. Jane would come in to play on the floor of the study to be close to me, if she could find a bare spot on the floor of the tiny room. Karen would say good night to me at ten or eleven P.M., knowing that I would be working another four or five hours into the quiet night. Every day Arleen would bring back typed pages of the next-to-final-draft, minus the last few hundred pages I was still writing, and I'd scribble more revisions on them and send them back to her while I continued to write the new pages longhand. It was exhausting chaos. It was madness. I loved it.

Karen and I were concerned about the expense of hiring Arleen as a typist, but we reassured ourselves. That $12,500 half of the payment upon signing was a fortune. And half of the other $12,500 would be ours upon acceptance, the final $6,250 upon publication of the hardcover early in 1987. So what if I had to pay the entire first half of the advance out in typewriter purchase, typist's fees, and magic markers? We had a book to finish!

Late that summer, I finished *Carrion Comfort*. One thousand five hundred and thirty-four pages. The last I'd heard from James Frenkel and Bluejay weeks and weeks before, when I'd told him the final length of the opus, was—"That's long, but don't worry. We can handle it in one book." (Frenkel hadn't read a page of it, but he liked the verbal updates on the story.)

In the last days of my theoretical summer vacation before I went back to the eighty-to-hundred hours a week APEX teaching, I was spending days and nights madly typing up the last draft of some chapters. Arleen— much more speedily—typed up other chapters I gave her. We finished the day before school started again. I took the day off and went up to our town's little public swimming pool with Karen and Jane. Lying in the end-of-summer sunlight (I was as pale as a grub), I looked around at the other families and swimmers and thought *This—these few hours—is my summer vacation.*

It had been worth it.

Just as I was ready to send *Carrion Comfort* to Frenkel, I learned two things: my first novel, *Song of Kali*, had been nominated as one of the six finalists for the World Fantasy Award. And Bluejay Books had gone bankrupt.

"When shall we three meet again . . . ?" asked one of the three witches or Wyrd Sisters in Shakespeare's *Macbeth*. The witch might have been talking about the three major parts of the human brain.

Decades ago, Paul MacLean, then chief of the Laboratory of Brain Evolution and Behavior of the National Institute of Mental Health, forwarded his theory of the human "triune brain." The theory has been contested, debated, confirmed, and denied, but the essential anatomic and evolutionary facts of it are clear enough:

Our brains evolved over hundreds of millions of years, through a multitude of earlier species, and consist today of three major elements—the most recent and advanced and outward-lying neocortex, which we share (in size and near complexity) with certain advanced primates and whales and dolphins; the limbic system—so-called because there lies the control of our limbs among other things—which we share with all other mammals and partially with reptiles; and—most deeply buried—the reptilian complex, also called the R-complex, which evolved hundreds of millions of years ago and was *all* that the brains of early reptiles and dinosaurs had to work with.

Imagine a modern iPod that had to be built around (and depend upon) an old Commodore 64 that, in turn, had to be built around and depend upon (in all its actions and computations) a rusty abacus with only a few dull (but absolutely imperative) beads on its wires.

The R-complex reptile brain concerns itself with territoriality, with ritual and repetition, with fight or flight decisions, with rage, with violence, with aggression, and with hierarchy.

Always with hierarchy.

Carl Sagan reminded us that the term "cold-blooded killer" is almost certainly accurate, since so much of extreme human violence is a surrender to the constant reptilian aggressive-hierarchical kill-or-be-killed urgings of the R-complex at the base of the root of our brains. Machiavelli's advice to the Prince, when all language and higher brain-function manipulations of others failed, was "knowingly to adopt the beast."

The ancient Greeks never dreamt of equality and fraternity. Their view of the world was of a constant *agon* (yes, the root word for "agony")—an endless competition to separate everyone and everything in the world into the three categories of *less than, more than,* or *equal to.*

But the R-complex reptile brain—present in all of us, always dominant in the mind vampires among us—knows no *"equal to."* It allows only for the dinosaur-predator hierarchical imperative of *greater than* or *lesser than* and it will kill you, if need be, to establish itself in the former category.

In the modern human brain, the neocortex makes up about 85 percent of our brain mass, but much evidence suggests that the majority of our individual behavior, our social systems, our political systems, our sexual behavior, our bureaucratic behavior, and our endless wars are controlled by the reptile brain in us.

As G. K. Chesterton once wrote: "You can free things from alien or accidental laws of their own nature. . . . Do not go about . . . encouraging triangles to break out of the prison of their three sides. If a triangle breaks out of its three sides, its life comes to a lamentable end."

As a teacher (including as a BOCES-trained "resource room" teacher in New York state, assigned to test, diagnose, and remediate learning disabilities), I worked with children with borderline autism and psychotic children exhibiting such behavior as hebephrenic schizophrenia. As a classroom teacher for eighteen years, I worked with severely emotionally disturbed children, including two who were sociopaths.

All children, especially younger children, when left to their own devices, show frequent and deep ritualistic behavior. With the mentally retarded and emotionally disturbed, this ritualistic behavior was often visible as what we called *perseveration*—the inability to stop a behavior, such as fanning a hand in front of one's eyes or constant rocking or humming. With autistic children, the ritualistic behavior could become elaborate—homemade cardboard "machines" and string "wires" that had to go everywhere with the child just, he thought, to keep himself alive.

With all children in their natural state, the ritualistic behavior—most clearly among boys but more covertly among girls—included a constant sorting of themselves into hierarchies of acceptance and inclusion, with the losers being miserable and lonely as outsiders.

The neocortex in children is still developing and incomplete in its control.

The reptile brain is very alive in children. And sometimes it is frightening to watch it in action.

Montaigne, in his *Essays* (II-8) once wrote—"*. . . most commonly, we find ourselves more taken with the running up and down, the games, and the puerile simplicities of our children than we do, afterwards, with their most complete actions; as if we had loved them for our sport, like monkeys, not as men.*"

But it's not monkeys that a trained eye will see when watching children playing among themselves. It's male and female velociraptors.

Mind vampires may be an evolutionary example of arrested neocortal natal development combined with rare frontal-lobe overdevelopment that creates neuron spin axis perpendicular to physical polar magnetic field axis differing their brains as a form of crude holographic *generator* rather than a mere wave-front collapsing interferometer, as is the case of the rest of us. The R-complex in mind vampires, in other words, can *project* sheer force of will to the more passive neocortical, limbic, and R-complexes of other minds, although whether on the electromagnetic spectrum or via some other range of energy is unknown at this time.

The advanced neocortex in the mind vampires we encounter is merely along for the ride. Mind vampires can speak words fluidly and feign altruism and social niceties, but all a mind vampire (as is true with any sociopath) really knows is fight or flight, ascendancy or submission, and hierarchy and control.

And violence. Always violence.

The violence of their will over yours. And they live to control you.

In October of 1986 I went to Providence, Rhode Island, to attend the twelfth annual World Fantasy Convention there. I hadn't attended many SF or fantasy conventions before this. Not only had I not had time to go to many conventions, I couldn't afford the travel.

Karen and I couldn't afford the flight from Colorado to Rhode Island in

1986, either, but people associated with the convention had been "strongly urging me to attend" for some weeks now and my agent and other writers explained to me that this could be shorthand that my novel had won the World Fantasy Award and that the organizers wanted me there to pick up the award. I'd never received a writing award in person before. (I'd watched on TV as actor Jack Klugman, an old friend of Rod Serling's, had accepted my *Rod Serling Memorial Award* from host Mike Douglas for my cowinning the *Twilight Zone Magazine* short story contest. Someone from the magazine had phoned me and told me to turn on the TV about thirty minutes before the presentation. When I finally received the award in the mail a month or so later, it had been so poorly wrapped that one end of the gilded frame had been knocked off. The ink the judges had signed their names in—Harlan Ellison, Carol Serling, Robert Bloch, Richard Matheson (three of these people writer-heroes of mine)—had simply disappeared after being exposed to sunlight.)

So we wanted to go to Providence in October of 1986 but we couldn't afford for both of us to travel there. Reluctantly (on both our parts), Karen stayed home with four-year-old Jane while I took one business day leave from work to fly out there for the weekend.

I took the final version of *Carrion Comfort* with me. It weighed more than my suitcase.

What had happened after Bluejay Books went bankrupt was that my manuscript, even though no one at Bluejay had read it, had become one of the "assets"—like office furniture and typewriters—that were parceled out to creditors when Jim Frenkel's company went belly up. I like to think that Jim worked hard to find a good home for the few literary properties he hadn't got around to publishing, including *Carrion Comfort*.

At any rate, a large publisher that shall remain nameless (for reasons that will become obvious) had taken possession of the yet-to-be-delivered *Carrion Comfort*. My agent assured me that this was an improvement, since the larger publisher would have a larger print run of the book and insure a better distribution. Also, he said, this World Fantasy Awards Banquet would be a wonderful opportunity for me to meet my new publisher and—even more important—my new editor.

This thought did excite me. Publisher Frenkel had been my ad hoc editor for *Song of Kali*, but the editing—as with the copyediting—had been light and cursory and mostly my responsibility. By 1986 I'd published enough short fiction to have worked with such fine editors as Ellen Datlow at *OMNI* and Shawna McCarthy at *Asimov's Science Fiction* magazine, but I'd not yet worked hand-in-hand with an editor on a book-length project and I was looking forward to the experience.

I arrived in Providence very doubtful that *Song of Kali* was really going to win the award, despite the eagerness of the presenters to have me there. There was more than the fact that no first novel had ever won the

World Fantasy Award in that award's history. The other nominees that year were Clive Barker's *The Damnation Game*, Peter Carey's *Illywhacker*, Lisa Goldstein's *The Dream Years*, Paul Hazel's *Winterking*, and Anne Rice's *The Vampire Lestat*. How on earth could *Song of Kali*, which had only a very few thousand copies of the hardback even published and distributed, even have been read by many people?

But the trip was worth it for me, award or no award, just to meet my new editor and to deliver the completed manuscript of *Carrion Comfort* to its new owners.

My editor and I met in the bar of the Providence Biltmore Hotel on the day before the awards banquet. I'd already met my new publisher and liked him a lot.

I remember physically presenting the giant box of manuscript, so similar to Spalding Gray's giant, heavily strapped monster of his endless but unfinished novel that sat on the table with him in his funny-sad film monologue "Monster in a Box."

My new editor was a woman, just turned twenty-one years old, and only just appointed to her position as chief editor in the new "horror" section of the publishing house. I won't give her name.

I had very little to say during that first hour-long meeting in the bar of the Biltmore in Providence, Rhode Island. When my new editor asked me what I did other than write, I explained about my teaching career and the APEX program I ran.

"Oh, gifted-talented programs," she said with a dismissive wave of her pale hand. "I was in many of those."

I explained how we never labeled any kid as "gifted," only provided very high level instruction in the many fields in which advanced kids needed them.

"They told my mother that I was gifted at a very young age," said my editor with another whisk of that pale hand. "We gifted people know we're gifted."

And then I listened.

"I'm not going to be a passive editor," said my new editor. "Nor will I be kind or gentle. We'll consider this your *first* novel. You're going to receive page after page of my comments. Single-spaced. I won't let anything slide."

"Goo—" I said. There was supposed to be a "d" on the end of that word, but before I could finish the syllable, I was listening again.

"I'm going to create a new dynasty of horror fiction with this house," my editor said. "A sort of empire. I'm going to raise the bar all across the field. I haven't seen this book of yours, we didn't buy this book of yours, so it'll just have to measure up—after my editing—or it won't be on the list."

"Goo—" I said.

"I know the general idea of your book . . . sort of a ripoff of Robinson's

The Power . . . but I'm not convinced that the premise can support a manuscript of *that* size." She gave my giant box of pages a baleful, critical look.

I couldn't say "Good" or even "Goo—" to that, so I said nothing.

"We'll see if it measures up," she said. And then I drank my Coke while she told me about the gifted programs she'd been in at school and about her meteoric rise in the publishing business.

My wife Karen was at the banquet after all when *Song of Kali* won the World Fantasy Award the next day. After I'd left, she'd borrowed money from her brother for the ticket fare. I loved having her there when *Song of Kali* was announced the winner.

And now I'm going to write about something that will make Karen hit me with a closed fist.

As a matter of policy, I don't write about people's negative appearances (especially women's), even in my fiction. (Except for certain monsters.) I'm living proof that people can't really help their appearance in most cases—their looks, their weight, the occasional gaffes on wardrobe.

But at that awards banquet in 1986, my new editor sitting with us became a living metaphor for the next eighteen months of my life—some of the worst months I've ever had—and *that* metaphor, sadly, deserves the telling.

My new editor was short and overweight and very, very pale, all of which is irrelevant save for her choice of apparel that afternoon. She was wearing tiny black bikini underpants and a black bra and no slip or other undergarments, and I can report this because her "gown" that day was a sort of black-mesh body stocking with large open diamonds everywhere. It reminded me of a fish net that my dad and I used when fishing in the Illinois River or on Minnesota lakes when I was a small kid. (Once a large-diameter eel I caught oozed right through the large net openings, but I didn't notice because, thinking I'd hooked a giant snake, I'd turned around and started running full speed in the opposite direction. My dad caught me by the back of my belt as I left the boat that time and swung me back in, even as the eel oozed back into the river through the net.)

Anyway, such a garment could be mildly disconcerting at the best of times, but in this case the mesh-bodystocking dress-thing was far too small for her and her pale flesh was oozing out through the black-mesh diamonds everywhere.

Trying not to be a sexist jerk through my adult years, I'm pretty good at maintaining eye contact with women no matter what the reality is before the eye-gaze line, but this black-mesh spiderweb gown all but defeated my efforts. There was no aspect of sexiness involved. It was as if my new editor had been caught in a spider's web that was contracting, closing, tightening, and squeezing its occupant to death. All I could think at the time was—*That has to be uncomfortable.*

Later, I realized that the black web she wore that day was a metaphor. But not for her, for me.

And that particular web would continue to tighten around me for many months to come.

When Karen and I returned from Providence that autumn I told her about the major editing and revision job ahead. We decided that I should do the most I could do to help the editor with the big job on *Carrion Comfort* that obviously lay ahead of us.

Because the last few hours of my long, long APEX day consisted of visiting one or more of the nineteen schools we supervised services in, I was able to arrange to go "half time" for the next semester starting in January of 1987. What that really meant was that I was still putting in about eight hours a day and eighty hours a week on APEX, but would go *half pay* in order to gain a couple of hours for myself on weekday afternoons. I would use that time working on the revision suggestions on *Carrion Comfort* that would be coming from my new publisher and editor before Christmas of 1986.

Karen and I couldn't really afford this half-pay situation—my salary was still our primary income, we had a four-year-old daughter and a two-year-old mortgage on a tiny house we'd been brave enough to purchase when it looked as if writing novels would be augmenting my teaching salary—but it seemed like the right thing to do. Besides, we told each other, there's that $6,500 jackpot of half of the remaining half of the advance we'd be receiving when I finished the rewrites to my new editor's satisfaction and, somewhere far, far beyond that, an equal amount upon publication.

So, shocking my teaching colleagues and the school-district brass, I took the half pay for 90 percent APEX work situation to gain those two or three hours each late workday. My editor's "extensive revision suggestions" were promised to arrive before Thanksgiving.

But they didn't arrive before Thanksgiving of 1986. Nor before Christmas.

I continued teaching full-time on half pay and waiting.

The revision suggestions didn't arrive by Easter of 1987. Nor by April or early May.

Finally, close to the end of the regular school year (for which I'd done almost full work for half pay), the letters (this was pre-e-mail, remember) from my editor began pouring in.

She lived up to her word: the pages were single-spaced and many. The first revision-suggestion letter ran to something like sixteen pages.

But the revision suggestions were almost impossible to decode. They contradicted each other. Most of all, I understood at once, she wanted *Carrion Comfort* much *shorter*, and I certainly understood the publisher's need for that. It was a very long book, difficult to produce at that length. Although when I spoke to Robert R. "Rick" McCammon, publisher of the equally huge horror hit, *Swan Song*, about this time, Rick said that unit cost on a large book, beyond about five hundred pages, wasn't that great. He said that publishers were simply wary of such a large novel, unless Stephen King had written it (and they'd had Steve cut more than sixty thousand words of *The Stand*.)

At any rate, I wrestled with the contradictory suggestions, trying to cut *Carrion Comfort* while keeping the soul of the book intact, but it wasn't really possible. The next twenty-page editorial missive would arrive and now my editor was telling me—"Cut out all the Holocaust stuff. It's not really germane to the real story and just slows things down."

Not germane to the real story?

To me, the Holocaust aspect of the novel *was* the real story.

I'd been deeply interested in—"obsessed by" is not too strong a phrase—the impact of the Holocaust since I was in high school. In college I'd done independent research, in German, on the creation and deployment of the *Einsatzgruppen*, the so-called "Special Action Groups," made up largely of former policeman, civil servants, and even teachers, responsible for the mass shootings of Jews on the Eastern Front.

How could some of the most presumably civilized people in an advanced civilization in the modern age be turned to such barbarism?

To me, the Holocaust—with Germany's unholy mating of the power of a modern industrial state with all its bureaucratic and technological means with the goal of genocide—was nothing less than the apotheosis of evil in our time. It was, without doubt, the central fact and lesson of the twentieth century.

And it was the guts and sinew and soul of *Carrion Comfort*.

"Cut it," wrote my editor when I explained this.

I worked through the summer trying to rewrite and shorten and placate without eviscerating or emasculating the book. Nothing pleased my editor. After nine months of this, I felt as if I were the one caught in an ever-tightening web.

The editorial suggestions kept coming.

By summer of 1987, the new editorial suggestion was—"Rewrite it as two books."

I might have done that if I could, but the break between the two would have been artificial and false. It would have felt like one of the old Saturday movie serials from the era before me, one which always ended in a fake cliff-hanger. I simply couldn't do it.

At the end of the summer of 1987, events threw a new curve at me.

The school district administrators in order to show (in their words) that "*all teachers were interchangeable*" and "*it doesn't take a gifted person to teach gifted kids*" announced that they were going to rotate APEX designers/curriculum writers/coordinators/teachers back to the regular classroom and select their successors more or less at random.

I loved teaching. I'd loved teaching in the regular classroom. But I knew a simple secret that the district administrators didn't—namely that it *did* require gifted people to teach profoundly gifted kids (and to write the appropriate curriculum for them)—so I knew that APEX, the most profoundly creative and successful thing I'd ever accomplished, would die when they brought in teachers not able or willing to put in the time and creativity to keep it going.

So Karen and I made perhaps the riskiest and boldest decision of our life together: I would resign from teaching and write full-time. True, we didn't seem any closer to that elusive $6,500 for the accepted *Carrion Comfort* than we'd been a year earlier and my constant rewritings to please the unpleasable female editor were keeping me from beginning other novels or even writing many short stories, but if I were to *write full-time*. . . .

It was an insane choice. So we made it. That autumn, for the first time since I'd gone off to kindergarten in 1953, I didn't go to school come September. It was, to put it mildly, a traumatic separation.

And into September and October the waiting for clear editorial direction went on. It began to dawn on me that this new publisher had little or no vested interest in *Carrion Comfort*; they hadn't selected it, hadn't paid for it, but had merely inherited it as a sort of payment from a defunct, short-lived house that owed them money. Nor did the young editor who'd sent me so many (incomprehensible, undo-able) single-space pages over the last fourteen months have much vested interest in *Carrion Comfort*. Her job was to remake the entire field of horror fiction and make her house the preeminent purveyor of the new genre, not "fix" this long, sprawling almost-unknown writer's huge manuscript.

In late October of 1987, I panicked. Even though school had started more than two months earlier, I flew out to Massachussetts—one of the few states that takes gifted/talented education seriously—and looked for G/T-coordinator jobs in the Boston area. The competition for such jobs there was cutthroat. Teachers and administrators with Ph.D.'s routinely competed for such positions

After getting three offers of coordinator positions in districts around Boston, I returned to Colorado. Karen and I decided that since it seemed that I *could* get better employment than my old teaching job if necessary, I should defer that lifeboat for now and concentrate on getting *Carrion Comfort* published and on writing more novels.

We began living on our meager savings and then on our PERA—teacher retirement money. I remember the early winter day when we celebrated, dancing around as if I'd sold another book, when I found a couple of hundred dollars of mine in old Missouri and New York teacher retirement funds.

In the truest sense, we were eating our seed corn.

Early in 1988, more than eighteen months after the editorial relationship began, my editor sent me her final suggestion on the matter— "*Keep the title* Carrion Comfort, *throw everything else out. Start over from scratch.*"

That was it.

I'd wasted a year and a half of my writing time and lost half of my teacher's pay and left my real profession. For nothing.

I called my agent Richard Curtis and said that I was going to buy my book back from this publisher. I didn't have any money at the moment, but I was making arrangements to sell our house so that I could write a check to buy the book back and. . . .

Richard explained that I wouldn't be writing any check. He'd arrange the buy-back contract for *Carrion Comfort* so that the bulk of the $12,500 we'd repay would come only after I found a new publisher for the book.

It was a temporary relief.

Of course, I didn't believe I'd ever find a new publisher for the book.

Dalton Trumbo, author of the ultimate antiwar novel and movie *Johnny Got His Gun*, didn't live to finish his last novel, *Night of the Aurochs*.

Trumbo was born in 1905 and grew up in Grand Junction, Colorado, a town I know pretty well. Inspired by a newspaper article about a British officer who was horribly disfigured in the Great War, Trumbo managed to get *Johnny Got His Gun* published in 1939. (Ironically, *Johnny Got His Gun*, perhaps the most unrelenting antiwar novel to that time or since, was most popular in Japan right before World War II, even as that nation gave itself up totally to militarism and aggression. Perhaps for this reason, Trumbo himself later said that he was happy his little book had gone out of print by the time the United States entered the war. He then wrote the script for *Thirty Seconds Over Tokyo*, the story of Jimmy Dolittle's April 1942 raid, starring Spencer Tracy and Van Johnson.)

In 1943, Trumbo joned the Communist Party but was soon too busy to go to meetings or take any active role. That didn't help when he refused to testify in front of the House Un-American Activities Committee and he became one of the infamous "Hollywood Ten." In 1950 he went to jail for a year.

There are only two things that I imagine I have in common with Dalton Trumbo. First, we were both fast writers. (He churned out *Roman Holiday* using writer Ian McLellan Hunter as a "front" name and Hunter won an Oscar for the script. Trumbo went on to write *Spartacus*, *Exodus*, *Papillon*, and many other award-winning movies under his own name.) The second thing I believe Trumbo and I had in common was a fascination with the kind of evil and violence that comes from exerting one's will over another person.

Trumbo's unfinished *Night of the Aurochs*, which was published posthumously and that I read only after writing *Carrion Comfort*, was his attempt to explain the darkest parts of human nature that led to the Holocaust (and to the inevitable future Holocausts we're hurtling toward). Aurochs were a now-extinct shaggy, stupid, wild European ox.

Night of the Aurochs is written, at least partially, in the form of a first-person autobiography of a young Nazi named Grieban who eventually becomes the commandant at Auschwitz.

Grieban, as is true of most monsters, does not consider himself a monster. Much of his first-person narrative is an attempt to defend the Third Reich's Final Solution as something no more sinister than the Confederate States attempt to prevent racial miscegenation. He sees himself as a sort of Robert E. Lee in the cause of defending racial purity.

In truth, of course, Grieban is a mind vampire. It's not racial purity that he seeks, but power over other people. And nowhere in the recent history of our species has the scourge of mind vampirism spread so quickly and completely as it did in Europe from 1936 to 1945.

It's been decades since I've read *Night of the Aurochs* but I remember one scene early on where Grieban, narrating, tells of the time when he is a young teenager and he takes his innocent, blonde, Aryan, sweet little female cousin out into the woods. Once there, Grieban realizes he has total control over his little eight- or nine-year-old cousin.

Crouch, he orders her. Frightened, she crouches. Take your underpants off, he orders her. She complies. Now, pee, he commands.

Eventually, terrified, she does.

Grieban is sexually excited as he watches his little girl-cousin urinate in front of him, not because of her exposure, but because of his power over her. He realizes then that under the right circumstances, a person can make other people *do anything you want them to*. The idea excites him to orgasm, both then and later in Auschwitz.

It's a sick idea. It's also—I believe—an important truth.

Absolute power does more than corrupt us absolutely, it gives us the blood-power taste of total control. Such control is more addicting than heroin. It is the addiction of mind vampirism.

When I read the unfinished first draft that was Trumbo's *Night of the Aurochs*, I knew that it had been worth it to write and to fight for *Carrion Comfort*, even if my own book would never be published.

When I realized that my editor and publisher in 1986–1987 were never going to get around to figuring out or publishing my novel, I got busy.

Even before arranging to buy back *Carrion Comfort* from them, I'd started writing my brains out. The hardest part that first solo autumn of 1987 was simply realizing that I was technically *unemployed*. The thought made me crazy. I'd worked my way through college and graduate school and worked as a teacher ever since. The idea of having no job to go off to, no income to depend on—none at all—was terrifying. (Karen remained calmer than I did, even as we ate up our last seed corn in terms of our PERA retirement money. Knowing that there are fewer than five hundred full-time writers—writers who actually make a living just on their writing of fiction—out of a population of 300 *million* Americans, she still remained confident that things would work out for my writing career and us. Or at least she said she did . . . and she convinced me.)

With Richard Curtis looking for another publisher who might want a thousand page (in print) major horror novel about violence from a relatively unknown writer, I simply kept writing new fiction.

I wrote *Phases of Gravity*, a novel about the philosophical and epistemological midlife crisis of a former Apollo astronaut who'd walked on the moon but realized now that it had felt like just another simulation.

I wrote the SF novel *Hyperion*—an expansive, big-canvas, Jack Vance-ish science fiction tale written in the decade when SF had gotten small and tight and noir and cyberpunkish.

I knew that the full tale of *Hyperion* would be another fifteen-hundred-page book but I decided never to go through that struggle for publication again, at least not until I had some clout behind me as a writer to get it published in one volume. I immediately began the second part of the tale in a "sequel" I called *The Fall of Hyperion*.

I wrote two more stories for *OMNI* and four stories for a three-writer anthology from Dark Harvest Press called *Night Visions 5*—an anthology I shared with two guys named George R. R. Martin and Stephen King.

And while I was writing, both *Hyperion* and *Phases of Gravity* sold to Bantam, the former as an SF novel and the latter as a mainstream novel, the first in a new series of "near-SF-mainstream" books under an imprint they were calling Spectra. (They later rebadged *Phases of Gravity*, perhaps the favorite novel I've written, as SF, but it isn't.)

And then . . . *Carrion Comfort* sold.

The advance was low, not enough to pay back the publisher I'd taken the book away from, but I could make up the difference now with money from the other advances. The new publisher was a specialty, limited-edition publisher—Dark Harvest Press, the guys who'd sandwiched my three stories in between George Martin's and Steve King's—and the press run for *Carrion Comfort* would be small, only about three thousand hardcovers total.

I didn't care. It would be *published*. Finally.

Again, there was no real editing or copyediting. I remember the total copyediting suggestions of the two guy-publishers: change "mantle" to "mantel," and drop the "e" in "adrenaline." (Actually, "adrenalin" would have worked.)

They sent me proof pages with three days to copyedit *Carrion Comfort* myself when I was writing the final pages of *Hyperion*. It was a mess.

Then they showed me the only artist they could afford—for cover, color frontispiece, and about ten interior illustrations. (Illustrations for *Carrion Comfort*? The idea struck me as odd, but it *was* a limited-edition volume and I knew nothing about such things.) But I did know that I didn't like the artist's work.

So with about five weeks to go before the art deadline, I got a local artist friend Kathy—Kathleen McNeil Sherman—to do the cover, frontispiece, and ten interior pieces with me.

For some reason, Kathy and I decided on scratchboard as our common technique. Now, scratchboard is fun—it's working on a large, inked panel with a razor blade, simply scratching away the highlights and crosshatchings and stuff to expose the white beneath the black ink. But it's a tricky technique working in reverse like that, rather like backing a car and trailer down a curved alley, and neither Kathy nor I had worked in it for many years. It made it more fun.

And it *was* fun. After fifteen hours a day of working on my new novel upstairs, I'd go down into our little basement to the jury-rigged drawing board I'd cobbled together and scratch away on the interior illustrations for *Carrion Comfort*.

For the cover, I did the drawing and Kathy laid down the oil paint. I did the frontispiece with scatchboard and colored ink.

The illustrations—at least *my* contributions—were crude, but strangely powerful. Or at least satisfying. (For those readers who might want to see this original *Carrion Comfort* cover and some of these scratchboard illustrations, please feel free to visit my Website at dansimmons.com and specifically this URL for the artwork—http://dansimmons.com/art/dan_art3.htm.)

When *Carrion Comfort* finally came out, we invited the two publishers, Paul and Scott, to our publication party. Since Paul and Scott refused to fly, they drove from Chicago to Colorado to help us celebrate. Our tiny little house had about sixty guests in it and it was crowded. Karen arranged to have a cake made with the *Carrion Comfort* cover replicated perfectly in colored frosting. I'd just invested in a small black-and-white photocopy machine (to save in copying the final MSS, even though it took me many hours to copy my long manuscripts one page at a time) and I remember we had a party game where the writers, artists, friends, publishers, and other guests went alone into my little study and came out with a work of photocopy "art" to be judged later, after we'd had a few more drinks.

And I remember that our seven-year-old daughter Jane, who'd been watching the party from the staircase until then, won the voting by popular acclaim with her photocopy of "Teddy," her teddy bear.

It was a good day. It was a good year.

As the years passed, I watched a strange thing happen to my early chosen field of horror. My former editor lived up to her goal of creating an "empire" of horror fiction. She and other editors working for other publishers simply published so much of the stuff, under the assumption that readers couldn't get enough of it (since they seemed not to be able to get enough of Stephen King's work, was the reasoning, or Dean Koontz's) that after a few years Gresham's Law kicked. The bad drove out the good. The market was oversaturated. The readers were first satiated and then wary as they realized the low quality that was being sold in such vast quantities.

I watched horror all but die as a genre for a while. Some chains eliminated the "Horror" section of their bookstores. Many writers of horror in the late 1980s and early 1990s—myself included—moved on to other things.

When horror finally returned as a viable category, it did so through the work of a few excellent writers who helped redefine the genre yet again.

Thanks to the friendship of Herb Yellin, the publisher of the private Lord John Press (beautiful books, beautifully made, for collectors, featuring authors of personal interest to Herb), I once spent an evening in L.A. with Herb and his old friends Robert (*Psycho*) Bloch, the comedian/radio star Stan Freberg (author and voice of the hit 1960s comedy LP *The United States of America*), and Ray Bradbury. Yellin and Bloch and Freberg and Bradbury were old friends and had been meeting one night a month to chew the fat for decades.

It was a totally unforgettable night.

Robert Bloch warned me before the talking started that once it started I wouldn't be hearing from him again, and he was correct. (I loved Robert Bloch.) Freberg and Bradbury held the floor all night, late into the night, and the topic they stumbled across that night was "Mentors in Our Lives Who Were Also the Monsters in Our Lives."

For Freberg, it was his boss Bob Clampett when he wrote and puppeteered for the Emmy Award–winning TV show puppet show *Time for Beany* in the early 1950s. Clampett was so cheap that he'd put his writers to work in "a friend's car" along the curb in L.A. only for Freberg and the other writer to discover that it had been a stranger's car. Once Clampett set them up in their new "writing office" in an empty house up on blocks and Stan Freberg and his equally underpaid writing partner Daws Butler, to save money, moved into the house to live there, despite the fact that it had no electricity or running water.

And then one morning they woke up to find their "office" and home being moved down the street to its new location.

But Freberg's ultimate mentor/monster was the Broadway impresario David Merrick, and the tales of that love/hate relationship made me cry with laughter one minute and simply cry the next.

Then Ray Bradbury joined in to discuss his ultimate mentor/monster, John Huston.

In 1953, the young and rather innocent SF writer had been in Long Beach looking for dinosaur books with his friend Ray Harryhausen when he got word that Huston wanted to talk to him. The next day Ray went to the hotel in L.A. where Huston was staying and was flabbergasted to learn that the director had chosen young Bradbury—who'd never done a screenplay—to write Huston's screen adaptation of *Moby Dick*. And John Huston insisted that Bradbury and his wife come to Huston's estate in Ireland to write the script.

Bradbury admitted to Mr. Huston that he'd never been able to read the whole book. "Well, go home tonight and read it and come back tomorrow and tell me you'll help me kill that goddamned whale," boomed John Huston as only John Huston could boom.

The next hour or two of Bradbury's tale, liberally added to and heckled by Stan Freberg, was one of the funniest/saddest things I'd ever heard, perhaps equaled only by Freberg's tales of his relationship with David Merrick.

Bradbury described how Huston would bait and parody the innocent young writer, embarrassing him in front of the famous people who trooped through Huston's Irish estate. One night it would be famous writers and directors at the long table, the next night Lauren Bacall and Humphrey Bogart, but when Huston drank, he got mean.

"I had a habit of blessing people when we part," said Bradbury that night in L.A. "I still do, I guess. But one night outside an Irish pub, I gave the blessing sign to friends that were leaving and Huston just rounded on me and screamed, '*Who do you think you are, the fucking bloody pope? STOP IT!*'"

When the torment reached its climax, Bradbury and his wife would secretly phone for a taxi, order it to meet them at the end of the estate's long driveway after dark, and reserve tickets home on the next flight back to America. To hell with "*Moby Dick.*" No one deserved this kind of abuse.

But, as mentor/monsters tend to do, Huston always sensed young Bradbury's breaking point.

That night in L.A. I watched Bradbury act out that night almost more than forty years earlier when Ray and his wife tried to rush through dinner, despite the famous faces at the table, so they could sneak their luggage out to the taxi and escape. But then—and Bradbury could perform a perfect John Houston booming voice—Huston hushed the table and announced, "There's much talent here tonight, but only one genius at our table. I want to introduce you to that genius. This young man wrote an incredible storrrrreee about a lighthouse and a foghorn and a DINE-OH-SAURRRR."

And then John Huston acted out the entire tale of Bradbury's story "The Foghorn," becoming the lighthouse keepers, the bellowing foghorn, and the bellowing DINE-OH-SAURRRR. At the end, Huston made young Bradbury stand for the applause of all the people at the table.

And then Ray Bradbury and his wife Maggie (Marguerite) went back upstairs and unpacked their bags and cancelled the taxi and cancelled the flight back to America.

This mentor/monster dance went on for eight months.

I had a mentor after all, although he was invisible to me at the time.

It turns out, I discovered later, that a certain Dean Koontz had been one of the five judges for the 1986 World Fantasy Award. (Ellen Datlow had been another.) Koontz had seen something in *Song of Kali* and had bent the arms of a few of the other judges to read the huge tome and take it seriously, even though some were reluctant to give the prestigious award to a first-time novelist.

Then, even as *Carrion Comfort* was appearing in its brief hardcover stint as a special edition from Dark Harvest . . . (one young speculator in California sold his mother's insurance so that he could buy up one thousand copies of the book—a full one third of the print run, but I got him back for it. Besides throwing him and his lackeys out of an Orange County bookstore when he dragged in all one thousand copies for me to sign, I later learned from a friend that the fellow had fallen behind on his payments on the California storage shed where he stored the one thousand volumes, waiting for them to reach a certain high collector's price before selling, and the storage owner seized them . . . and sold them at cover price. I bought as many as I could. But I digress.) . . . even as the Dark Harvest hardcover of *Carrion Comfort* was quickly appearing and disappearing, Dean Koontz, totally without my knowledge (I'd never met him), was convincing Warner Books to publish it as a nine-hundred-plus-page, small-print paperback.

The paperback came out in 1990, the same year as my Bantam Doubleday Dell novel *The Fall of Hyperion*, my long novella *Entropy's Bed at Midnight* from Lord John's Press, and my first collection of short fiction, *Prayers to Broken Stones*. (I told you I was keeping busy.)

Finally, thanks to the efforts of a bestselling writer I hadn't yet met and had never spoken to, simply because he thought it was a book worth reading, readers could find and read *Carrion Comfort* . . . in its complete form.

When shall we three meet again?
In thunder, lightning, or in rain?

When the hurlyburly's done,
When the battle's lost and won.

That will be ere the set of sun.

Reader, I hope you enjoy this Twentieth Anniversary Edition of *Carrion Comfort*. I wish you good luck in avoiding the real mind vampires in this life who wish to play with you as if they were the cat and you a ball of yarn. And, finally, Reader, I wish you luck in vanquishing the monsters you do have to meet . . . and in celebrating the mentors who have and will again fill your life with unanticipated joy.

—DAN SIMMONS
Colorado, July 2009

"Not, I'll not, carrion comfort, Despair, not feast on thee;
Not untwist—slack they may be—these last strands of man
In me or, most weary, cry I can no more . . ."

—GERARD MANLEY HOPKINS

PROLOGUE

Chelmno, 1942

S aul Laski lay among the soon-to-die in a camp of death and thought about life. Saul shivered in the cold and dark and forced himself to remember details of a spring morning—golden light touching the heavy limbs of willows by the stream, a field of white daisies beyond the stone buildings of his uncle's farm.

The barracks was silent except for an occasional rasping cough and the furtive burrowings of Musselmänner, the living dead, vainly seeking warmth in the cold straw. Somewhere an old man coughed in a wracking spasm which signaled the end of a long and hopeless struggle. The old one would be dead by morning. Or even if he survived the night, he would miss the morning roll call in the snow, which meant that he would be dead before morning ended.

Saul curled away from the glare of the searchlight pouring in through frosted panes and pressed his back against the wooden mortises of his bunk. Splinters scraped at his spine and ribs through the thin cloth he wore. His legs began to shake uncontrollably as the cold and fatigue worked at him. Saul clutched at his thin thighs and squeezed until the shaking stopped.

I will live. The thought was a command, an imperative he drove so deep into his consciousness that not even his starved and sore-ridden body could defy his will.

When Saul had been a boy a few years earlier, an eternity earlier, and his Uncle Moshe had promised to take him fishing at his farm near Cracow, Saul had taught himself the trick of imagining, just before he fell asleep, a smooth, oval rock upon which he wrote the hour and minute at which he wished to awake. Then, in his mind's eye, he would drop the rock into a clear pond and watch it settle into the depths. Invariably, he would awake the next morning at the precise moment, alert, alive, breathing in the cool morning air and savoring the predawn silence in that fragile interval before his brother and sisters woke to break the perfection.

I will live. Saul squeezed his eyes shut and watched the rock sink into clear water. His body began to shake again and he pressed his back more firmly against the rough angle of boards. For the thousandth time he tried to nestle more deeply in his depression of straw. It had been better when old Mr. Shistruk and young Ibrahim had shared the bunk with him but Ibrahim had been shot at the mine works and Mr. Shistruk had sat down two days before at the quarry and refused to rise even when Gluecks, the

1

head of the SS guards, had released his dog. The old man had waved his bony arm almost merrily, a weak farewell to the staring prisoners, in the five seconds before the German shepherd ripped his throat out.

I will live. The thought had a rhythm to it that went beyond the words, beyond language. The thought set a counterpoint to everything Saul had seen and experienced during his five months in the camp. *I will live.* The thought pulsed with a light and warmth which partially offset the chill, vertiginous pit which threatened to open wider inside him and consume him. The Pit. Saul had seen the Pit. With the others he had shoveled cold clods of black soil over the warm bodies, some still writhing, a child feebly moving its arm as if waving to a welcoming relative in a train station or stirring in its sleep, shoveled the dirt and spread the lime from bags too heavy to lift while the SS guard sat dangling his legs over the edge of the Pit, his hands soft and white on the black steel barrel of the machine-pistol, a piece of plaster on his rough cheek where he had cut himself shaving, the cut already healing while naked white forms stirred feebly as Saul poured dirt into the Pit, his eyes red-rimmed from the cloud of lime hanging like a chalky fog in the winter air.

I will live. Saul concentrated on the strength of that cadence and ignored his shaking limbs. Two levels above him, a man sobbed in the night. Saul could feel the lice crawling up his arms and legs as they sought the center of his fading warmth. He curled into a tighter ball, understanding the imperative which drove the vermin, responding to the same mindless, illogical, incontestable command to continue.

The stone dropped deeper into the azure depths. Saul could make out the rough letters as he balanced on the edge of sleep. *I will live.*

Saul's eyes snapped open as a thought chilled him more deeply than did the wind whistling through ill-fitted window frames. *It was the third Thursday of the month.* Saul was almost sure it was the third Thursday. *They* came on the third Thursday. But not always. Perhaps not this Thursday. Saul pulled his forearms in front of his face and curled into an even tighter fetal position.

He was almost asleep when the barracks door crashed open. There were five of them—two Waffen-SS guards with submachine guns, a regular army noncom, Lieutenant Schaffner, and a young Oberst whom Saul had never seen before. The Oberst had a pale, Aryan face with a strand of blond hair falling across his brow. Their hand torches played over the rows of shelflike bunks. Not a man stirred. Saul could feel the silence as eighty-five skeletons held their breath in the night. He held his breath.

The Germans took five strides into the barracks, the cold air billowing ahead of them, their massive forms silhouetted against the open door while their breath hung in icy clouds around them. Saul pulled himself even deeper into the brittle straw.

"*Du!*" came the voice. The torch beam had fallen on a capped and striped figure crouched in the depths of a lower bunk six rows from Saul.

"Komm! Schnell!" When the man did not move the SS guards dragged him roughly into the aisle. Saul heard bare feet scraping on the floor. *"Du, raus!"* And again. *"Du!"* Now three Musselmänner stood like weightless scarecrows before the massive silhouettes. The procession stopped four bunks from Saul's row. The SS guards turned away to play their lights up and down the center row of bunks. Red eyes reflected back like startled rats staring from half-opened coffins.

I will live. For the first time it was a prayer rather than an imperative. They had never taken more than four men from a single barracks.

"Du." The man with the hand torch had turned and was shining the light full in Saul's face. Saul did not move. He did not breathe. The universe consisted of the back of his own hand centimeters in front of his face. The skin there was white, grub white, and flaking in spots. The hairs on the back of his hand were very dark. Saul stared at them with a deep sense of awe. The torch beam made the flesh of his hand and arm seem almost transparent. He could see the layers of muscle, the elegant pattern of tendons, the blue veins softly pulsing to the wild beating of his heart.

"Du, raus." Time slowed and pivoted. All of Saul's life, every second, every ecstasy and banal, forgotten afternoon, had led to this instant, this intersection. Saul's lips cracked open in a mirthless grin. He had long ago decided that they would not take him into the night. They would have to kill him here, in front of the others. If nothing else, he would dictate to his murderers the time of his murder. A great calm descended over him.

"Schnell!" One of the SS men screamed at him and both stepped forward. Saul was blinded by the light, smelled wet wool and the sweet scent of schnapps on the man's breath, felt the cold air against his face. His skin contracted waiting for their rough hands to fall on him.

"Nein!" snapped the young Oberst. Saul saw him only as a black simulacrum of a man against the white glare of light. *"Zurücktreten!"* The Oberst took one step forward as the SS men stepped quickly back. Time seemed frozen as Saul stared up at the dark shape. No one spoke. The fog of their breath hung around them.

"Komm!" said the Oberst softly. It was not a command. It was said softly, almost lovingly, the way one would call a favorite dog or urge one's infant to take his first tottering steps. *"Komm her!"*

Saul gritted his teeth and closed his eyes. He would bite them when they came. He would go for their throats. He would chew and rip and tear at veins and cartilage until they would have to shoot, they would have to fire, they would have to fire, they would be forced to. . . .

"Komm!" The Oberst tapped his knee lightly. Saul's lips drew back in a snarl. He would leap at the fuckers, tear the motherfucking son of a bitch's fucking throat open in front of the others, rip his fucking bowels out of his. . . .

"Komm!" Saul felt it then. Something *hit* him. None of the Germans had moved, not so much as an inch, but something struck Saul a terrible

blow at the base of the spine. He screamed. Something hit him and then it *entered* him.

Saul felt the intrusion as sharply as if someone had rammed a steel rod up his anus. Yet nothing had touched him. No one had come close to him. Saul screamed again and then his jaws were clamped shut by some invisible force.

"Komm her, Du Jude!"

Saul *felt* it. Something was *in* him, ramming his back straight, causing his arms and legs to spasm wildly. *In* him. He felt something close on his brain like a vise, squeezing, squeezing. He tried to scream but *it* would not let him. He flopped wildly on the straw, nerves misfiring, urinating down his own pant leg. Then he arched wildly and his body flopped out onto the floor. The guards stepped back.

"Steh auf!" Saul's back arched again so violently that it threw him up on his knees. His arms shook and waved of their own volition. He could *feel* something in his mind, a cold presence wrapped in a blazing corona of pain. Images danced before his eyes.

Saul stood up.

"Geh!" There was heavy laughter from one of the SS men, the smell of wool and steel, the distant feel of cold splinters underfoot. Saul lurched toward the open door and the white glare beyond. The Oberst followed quietly behind, calmly slapping a glove against one thigh. Saul stumbled down the outside stairs, almost fell, was righted by an invisible hand that squeezed his brain and sent fire and needles racing through every nerve. Barefooted, not feeling the cold, he led the procession across the snow and frozen mud toward the waiting lorry.

I will live thought Saul Laski, but the magical cadence shredded and fled before a gale of silent, icy laughter and a will much greater than his own.

BOOK ONE
Openings

ONE

Charleston
Friday, Dec. 12, 1980

Nina was going to take credit for the death of that Beatle, John. I thought that was in very bad taste. She had her scrapbook laid out on my mahogany coffee table, newspaper clippings neatly arranged in chronological order, the bald statements of death recording all of her Feedings. Nina Drayton's smile was as radiant as ever, but her pale blue eyes showed no hint of warmth.

"We should wait for Willi," I said.

"Of course, Melanie. You're right, as always. How silly of me. I know the rules." Nina stood and began walking around the room, idly touching the furnishings or exclaiming softly over a ceramic statuette or piece of needlepoint. This part of the house had once been the conservatory, but now I used it as my sewing room. Green plants still caught the morning light. The sunlight made it a warm, cozy place in the daytime, but now that winter had come the room was too chilly to use at night. Nor did I like the sense of darkness closing in against all those panes of glass.

"I love this house," said Nina. She turned and smiled at me. "I can't tell you how much I look forward to coming back to Charleston. We should hold all of our reunions here."

I knew how much Nina loathed this city, this house.

"Willi would be hurt," I said. "You know how he likes to show off his place in Beverly Hills. And his new girlfriends."

"And boyfriends," said Nina and laughed. Of all the changes and darkenings in Nina, her laugh has been least affected. It was still the husky but childish laugh that I had first heard so long ago. It had drawn me to her then—one lonely, adolescent girl responding to the warmth of another like a moth to a flame. Now it only served to chill me and put me even more on my guard. Enough moths had been drawn to Nina's flame over the many decades.

"I'll send for tea," I said.

Mr. Thorne brought the tea in my best Wedgwood china. Nina and I sat in the slowly moving squares of sunlight and spoke softly of nothing important; mutually ignorant comments on the economy, references to books which the other had not got around to reading, and sympathetic murmurs about the low class of persons one meets while flying these days. Someone peering in from the garden might have thought they were seeing an aging but attractive niece visiting her favorite aunt. (I draw the line at suggesting that anyone would mistake us for mother and daughter.) People usually consider me a well-dressed if not stylish person. Heaven knows I have paid enough to have the wool skirts and silk blouses mailed from Scotland and France. But next to Nina I always felt dowdy. This day she wore an elegant, light blue dress which must have cost several thousand dollars if I had identified the designer correctly. The color made her complexion seem even more perfect than usual and brought out the blue of her eyes. Her hair had gone as gray as mine, but somehow she managed to get away with wearing it long and tied back with a single barrette. It looked youthful and chic on Nina and made me feel that my short, artificial curls were glowing with a blue rinse.

Few would suspect that I was four years younger than Nina. Time had been kind to her. And she had Fed more often.

She set down her cup and saucer and moved aimlessly around the room again. It was not like Nina to show such signs of nervousness. She stopped in front of the glass display case. Her gaze passed over the Hummels, the pewter pieces, and then stopped in surprise.

"Good heavens, Melanie. A pistol! What an odd place to put an old pistol."

"It's an heirloom," I said. "Quite expensive. And you're right, it *is* a silly place to keep it. But it's the only case I have in the house with a lock on it and Mrs. Hodges often brings her grandchildren when she visits . . ."

"You mean it's *loaded*?"

"No, of course not," I lied. "But children should not play with such things . . ." I trailed off lamely. Nina nodded but did not bother to conceal the condescension in her smile. She went to look out the south window into the garden.

Damn her. It said volumes about Nina Drayton that she did not recognize that pistol.

On the day he was killed, Charles Edgar Larchmont had been my beau for precisely five months and two days. There had been no formal announcement, but we were to be married. Those five months had been a microcosm of the era itself—naive, flirtatious, formal to the point of preciosity, and romantic. Most of all romantic. Romantic in the worst sense of the word; dedicated to saccharine or insipid ideals that only an adolescent—or an adolescent society—would strive to maintain. We were children playing with loaded weapons.

Nina, she was Nina Hawkins then, had her own beau—a tall, awkward, but well-meaning Englishman named Roger Harrison. Mr. Harrison had met Nina in London a year earlier during the first stages of the Hawkins's Grand Tour. Declaring himself smitten—another absurdity of those childish times—the tall Englishman had followed her from one European capital to another until, after being firmly reprimanded by Nina's father (an unimaginative little milliner who was constantly on the defensive about his doubtful social status), Harrison returned to London to "settle his affairs" only to show up some months later in New York just as Nina was being packed off to her aunt's home in Charleston in order to terminate yet another flirtation. Still undaunted, the clumsy Englishman followed her south, ever mindful of the protocols and restrictions of the day.

We were a gay group. The day after I met Nina at Cousin Celia's June Ball, the four of us were taking a hired boat up the Cooper River for a picnic on Daniel Island. Roger Harrison, serious and solemn on every topic, was a perfect foil for Charles's irreverent sense of humor. Nor did Roger seem to mind the good-natured jesting since he was soon joining in the laughter with his peculiar *haw-haw-haw*.

Nina loved it all. Both gentlemen showered attention on her and while Charles never failed to show the primacy of his affection for me, it was understood by all that Nina Hawkins was one of those young women who invariably becomes the center of male gallantry and attention in any gathering. Nor were the social strata of Charleston blind to the combined charm of our foursome. For two months of that now distant summer, no party was complete, no excursion adequately planned, and no occasion considered a success unless we four merry pranksters were invited and had chosen to attend. Our happy dominance of the youthful social scene was so pronounced that Cousins Celia and Loraine wheedled their parents into leaving two weeks early for their annual August sojourns in Maine.

I am not sure when Nina and I came up with the idea of the duel. Perhaps it was during one of the long, hot nights when the other "slept over"—creeping into the other's bed, whispering and giggling, stifling our laughter when the rustling of starched uniforms betrayed the presence of our colored maids moving through the darkened halls. In any case, the idea was the natural outgrowth of the romantic pretensions of the time. The picture of Charles and Roger actually dueling over some abstract point of honor related to *us* thrilled both of us in a physical way which I recognize now as a simple form of sexual titillation.

It would have been harmless except for our Ability. We had been so successful in our manipulation of male behavior—a manipulation which was both expected and encouraged in those days—that neither of us had yet suspected that there lay anything beyond the ordinary in the way we could translate our whims into other people's actions. The field of parapsychology did not exist then: or rather, it existed only in the rappings and knockings of parlor game séances. At any rate, we amused ourselves with whispered fantasies for several weeks and then one of us—or perhaps both of us—used the Ability to translate the fantasy into reality.

In a sense it was our first Feeding.

I do not remember the purported cause of the quarrel, perhaps some deliberate misinterpretation of one of Charles's jokes. I can not recall who Charles and Roger arranged to have serve as seconds on that illegal outing. I do remember the hurt and confused expression on Roger Harrison's face during those few days. It was a caricature of ponderous dullness, the confusion of a man who finds himself in a situation not of his making and from which he cannot escape. I remember Charles and his mercurial swings of mood—the bouts of humor, periods of black anger, and the tears and kisses the night before the duel.

I remember with great clarity the beauty of that morning. Mists were floating up from the river and diffusing the rays of the rising sun as we rode out to the dueling field. I remember Nina reaching over and squeezing my hand with an impetuous excitement that was communicated through my body like an electric shock.

Much of the rest of that morning is missing. Perhaps in the intensity of that first, subconscious Feeding I literally lost consciousness as I was engulfed in the waves of fear, excitement, pride . . . of *maleness* . . . that was emanating from our two beaus as they faced death on that lovely morning. I remember experiencing the shock of realizing *this is really happening* as I shared the tread of high boots through the grass. Someone was calling off the paces. I dimly recall the weight of the pistol in my hand . . . Charles's hand I think, I will never know for sure . . . and a second of cold clarity before an explosion broke the connection and the acrid smell of gunpowder brought me back to myself.

It was Charles who died. I have never been able to forget the incredible quantities of blood which poured from the small, round hole in his breast. His white shirt was crimson by the time I reached him. There had been no blood in our fantasies. Nor had there been the sight of Charles with his head lolling, mouth dribbling saliva onto his bloodied chest while his eyes rolled back to show the whites like two eggs embedded in his skull. Roger Harrison was sobbing as Charles breathed his final, shuddering gasps on that field of innocence.

I remember nothing at all about the confused hours which followed. It was the next morning that I opened my cloth bag to find Charles's pistol lying with my things. Why would I have kept that revolver? If I had wished to take something from my fallen lover as a sign of remembrance, why that alien piece of metal? Why pry from his dead fingers the symbol of our thoughtless sin?

It said volumes about Nina that she did not recognize that pistol.

"Willi's here."

It was not Mr. Thorne announcing the arrival of our guest but Nina's "amanuensis," the loathsome Miss Barrett Kramer. Kramer's appearance was as unisex as her name; short cropped, black hair, powerful shoulders, and a blank, aggressive gaze which I associated with lesbians and criminals. She looked to be in her mid-thirties.

"Thank you, Barrett, dear," said Nina.

I went to greet Willi, but Mr. Thorne had already let him in and we met in the hallway.

"Melanie! You look marvelous! You grow younger each time I see you. Nina!" The change in Willi's voice was evident. Men continued to be over-powered by their first sight of Nina after an absence. There were hugs and kisses. Willi himself looked more dissolute than ever. His alpaca sports coat was exquisitely tailored, his turtleneck sweater successfully concealed the eroded lines of his wattled neck, but when he swept off his jaunty sportscar cap the long strands of white hair he had brushed forward to hide his en-croaching baldness were knocked into disarray. Willi's face was flushed with excitement, but there was also the telltale capillary redness about the nose and cheeks which spoke of too much liquor, too many drugs.

"Ladies, I think you've met my associates . . . Tom Reynolds and Jensen Luhar?" The two men added to the crowd in my narrow hall. Mr. Reynolds was thin and blond, smiling with perfectly capped teeth. Mr. Luhar was a gigantic Negro, hulking forward with a sullen, bruised look on his coarse face. I was sure that neither Nina nor I had encountered these specific catspaws of Willi's before.

"Why don't we go into the parlor?" I suggested. It was an awkward pro-cession ending with the three of us seated on the heavily upholstered chairs surrounding the Georgian tea table which had been my grand-mother's. "More tea, please, Mr. Thorne." Miss Kramer took that as her cue to leave, but Willi's two pawns stood uncertainly by the door, shifting from foot to foot and glancing at the crystal on display as if their mere proximity could break something. I would not have been surprised if that had proven to be the case.

"Jensen!" Willi snapped his fingers. The Negro hesitated and then brought forward an expensive leather attaché case. Willi set it on the tea table and clicked the catches open with his short, broad fingers. "Why don't you two see Miz Fuller's man about getting something to drink?"

When they were gone Willi shook his head and smiled at Nina. "Sorry about that, love."

Nina put her hand on Willi's sleeve. She leaned forward with an air of expectancy. "Melanie wouldn't let me begin the Game without you. Wasn't that *awful* of me to want to start without you, Willi dear?"

Willi frowned. After fifty years he still bridled at being called Willi. In Los Angeles he was Big Bill Borden. When he returned to his native Germany—which was not often because of the dangers involved—he was once again Wilhelm von Borchert, lord of dark manor, forest, and hunt. But Nina had called him Willi when they had first met in 1925, in Vienna, and Willi he had remained.

"You begin, Willi," said Nina. "You go first."

I could remember the time when we would have spent the first few days of our reunion in conversation and catching up with each other's lives. Now there was not even time for small talk.

Willi showed his teeth and removed news clippings, notebooks, and a stack of cassettes from his briefcase. No sooner had he covered the small table with his material than Mr. Thorne arrived with the tea and Nina's scrapbook from the sewing room. Willi brusquely cleared a small space.

At first glance one might see certain similarities between Willi Borchert and Mr. Thorne. One would be mistaken. Both men tend to the florid, but Willi's complexion was the result of excess and emotion: Mr. Thorne had known neither of these for many years. Willi's balding was a patchy, self-consciously concealed thing—a weasel with the mange—while Mr. Thorne's bare head was smooth and unwrinkled. One could not imagine Mr. Thorne ever having *had* hair. Both men had gray eyes—what a novelist would call cold, gray eyes—but Mr. Thorne's eyes were cold with indifference, cold with a clarity coming from an absolute absence of troublesome emotion or thought. Willi's eyes were the cold of a blustery North Sea winter and were often clouded with shifting curtains of the emotions that controlled him—pride, hatred, love of pain, the pleasures of destruction. Willi never referred to his use of the Ability as Feedings—I was evidently the only one who thought in those terms—but Willi sometimes talked of the Hunt. Perhaps it was the dark forests of his homeland that he thought of as he stalked his human quarry through the sterile streets of Los Angeles. Did Willi dream of the forest? I wondered. Did he look back to green wool hunting jackets, the applause of retainers, the gouts of blood from the dying boar? Or did Willi remember the slam of jackboots on cobblestones and the pounding of his lieutenants' fists on doors? Perhaps Willi still associated his Hunt with the dark European night of the oven which he had helped to oversee.

I called it Feeding. Willi called it the Hunt. I had never heard Nina call it anything.

"Where is your VCR?" asked Willi. "I have put them all on tape."

"Oh, Willi," said Nina in an exasperated tone. "You know Melanie. She's *so* old-fashioned. She wouldn't have a video player."

"I don't even have a television," I said. Nina laughed.

"Goddamn it," muttered Willi. "It doesn't matter. I have other records here." He snapped rubber bands from around the small, black notebooks. "It just would have been better on tape. The Los Angeles stations gave much coverage to the Hollywood Strangler and I edited in the . . . Ach! Never mind." He tossed the videocassettes into his briefcase and slammed the lid shut.

"Twenty-three," he said. "Twenty-three since we met twelve months ago. It doesn't seem that long, does it?"

"Show us," said Nina. She was leaning forward and her blue eyes seemed very bright. "I've been curious since I saw the Strangler interviewed on *Sixty Minutes*. He was yours, Willi? He seemed so . . ."

"*Ja, ja*, he was mine. A nobody. A timid little man. He was the gardener of a neighbor of mine. I left him alive so the police could question him, erase any doubts. He will hang himself in his cell next month after the press loses interest. But this is more interesting. Look at this." Willi slid across several glossy black and white photographs. The NBC executive had murdered the five members of his family and drowned a visiting soap opera actress in his pool. He had then stabbed himself repeatedly and written 50 SHARE in blood on the wall of the bathhouse.

"Reliving old glories, Willi?" asked Nina. "'Death to the Pigs' and all that?"

"No, goddamn it. I think it should receive points for irony. The girl had been scheduled to drown on the program. It was already in the script outline."

"Was he hard to Use?" It was my question. I was curious despite myself.

Willi lifted one eyebrow. "Not really. He was an alcoholic and heavily into cocaine. There was not much left. And he hated his family. Most people do."

"Most people in California, perhaps," said Nina primly. It was an odd comment from Nina. Her father had committed suicide by throwing himself in front of a trolley car.

I asked, "Where did you make contact?"

"A party. The usual place. He bought the coke from a director who had ruined one of my . . ."

"Did you have to repeat the contact?"

Willi frowned at me. He kept his anger under control, but his face grew redder. "*Ja, ja.* I saw him twice more. Once I just watched from my car as he played tennis."

"Points for irony," said Nina. "But you lose points for repeated contact. If he was as empty as you say, you should have been able to Use him after only one touch. What else do you have?"

He had his usual assortment. Pathetic skid row murders. Two domestic slayings. A highway collision which turned into a fatal shooting. "I was in the crowd," said Willi. "I made contact. He had a gun in the glove compartment."

"Two points," said Nina.

Willi had saved a good one for last. A once famous child star had suffered a bizarre accident. He had left his Bel Air apartment while it filled with gas and then returned to light a match. Two others had died in the ensuing fire.

"You get credit only for him," said Nina.

"*Ja, ja.*"

"Are you sure about this one? It *could* have been an accident . . ."

"Don't be ridiculous," snapped Willi. He turned toward me. "*This* one was very hard to Use. Very strong. I blocked his memory of turning on the gas. Had to hold it away for two hours. Then forced him into the room. He struggled not to strike the match."

"You should have had him use his lighter," said Nina.

"He didn't smoke," growled Willi. "He gave it up last year."

"Yes." Nina smiled. "I seem to remember him saying that to Johnny Carson." I could not tell if Nina was jesting.

The three of us went through the ritual of assigning points. Nina did most of the talking. Willi went from being sullen to expansive to sullen again. At one point he reached over and patted my knee as he laughingly asked for help. I said nothing. Finally he gave up, crossed the parlor to the liquor cabinet, and poured himself a tall glass of bourbon from Father's decanter. The evening light was sending its final, horizontal rays through the stained glass panels of the bay windows and it cast a red hue on Willi as he stood next to the oak cupboard. His eyes were small red embers in a bloody mask.

"Forty-one," said Nina at last. She looked up brightly and showed the calculator as if it verified some objective fact. "I count forty-one points. What do you have, Melanie?"

"*Ja*," interrupted Willi. "That is fine. Now let us see your claims, Nina." His voice was flat and empty. Even Willi had lost some interest in the Game.

Before Nina could begin, Mr. Thorne entered and motioned that dinner was served. We adjourned to the dining room, Willi pouring himself another glass of bourbon and Nina fluttering her hands in mock frustration at the interruption of the Game. Once seated at the long, mahogany table, I worked at being a hostess. From decades of tradition, talk of the Game was banned from the dinner table. Over soup we discussed Willi's new movie and the purchase of another store for Nina's line of boutiques. It seemed that Nina's monthly column in *Vogue* was to be discontinued but that a newspaper syndicate was interested in picking it up.

Both of my guests exclaimed over the perfection of the baked ham, but I thought that Mr. Thorne had made the gravy a trifle too sweet. Darkness had filled the windows before we finished our chocolate mousse. The refracted light from the chandelier made Nina's hair dance with highlights while I feared that mine glowed more blue than ever.

Suddenly there was a sound from the kitchen. The huge Negro's face appeared at the swinging door. His shoulder was hunched against white hands and his expression was that of a querulous child.

". . . the hell you think we are sittin' here like . . ." The white hands pulled him out of sight.

"Excuse me, ladies." Willi dabbed linen at his lips and stood up. He still moved gracefully for all of his years.

Nina poked at her chocolate. There was one sharp, barked command from the kitchen and the sound of a slap. It was the slap of a man's hand—hard and flat as a small caliber rifle shot. I looked up and Mr. Thorne was at my elbow, clearing away the dessert dishes.

"Coffee, please, Mr. Thorne. For all of us." He nodded and his smile was gentle.

Franz Anton Mesmer had known of it even if he had not understood it. I suspect that Mesmer must have had some small touch of the Ability. Modern pseudo-sciences have studied it and renamed it, removed most of its power, confused its uses and origins, but it remains the shadow of what Mesmer discovered. They have no idea of what it is like to Feed.

I despair at the rise of modern violence. I truly give in to despair at times, that deep, futureless pit of despair which Hopkins called carrion comfort. I watch the American slaughterhouse, the casual attacks on popes, presidents, and uncounted others, and I wonder if there are many more out there with the Ability or if butchery has simply become the modern way of life.

All humans feed on violence, on the small exercises of power over another, but few have tasted—as we have—the ultimate power. And without that Ability, few know the unequaled pleasure of taking a human life. Without the Ability, even those who do feed on life cannot savor the flow of emotions in stalker and victim, the total exhilaration of the attacker who has moved beyond all rules and punishments, the strange, almost sexual submission of the victim in that final second of truth when all options are canceled, all futures denied, all possibilities erased in an exercise of absolute power over another.

I despair at modern violence. I despair at the impersonal nature of it and the casual quality which has made it accessible to so many. I had a television set until I sold it at the height of the Vietnam War. Those sanitized snippets of death—made distant by the camera's lens—meant nothing to me. But I believe it meant something to these cattle which surround me. When the war and the nightly televised body counts ended, they demanded more, *more*, and the movie screens and streets of this sweet and dying nation have provided it in mediocre, mob abundance. It is an addiction I know well.

They miss the point. Merely observed, violent death is a sad and sullied tapestry of confusion. But to those of us who have Fed, death can be a *sacrament*.

"My turn! My turn!" Nina's voice still resembled that of the visiting belle who had just filled her dance card at Cousin Celia's June Ball.

We had returned to the parlor, Willi had finished his coffee and requested a brandy from Mr. Thorne. I was embarrassed for Willi. To have one's closest associates show any hint of unplanned behavior was certainly a sign of weakening Ability. Nina did not appear to have noticed.

"I have them all in order," said Nina. She opened the scrapbook on the now empty tea table. Willi went through them carefully, sometimes asking a question, more often grunting assent. I murmured occasional agreement although I had heard of none of them. Except for the Beatle, of course. Nina saved that for near the end.

"Good God, Nina, that was you?" Willi seemed near anger. Nina's Feedings had always run to Park Avenue suicides and matrimonial disagreements ending in shots fired from expensive, small calibered ladies' guns. This type of thing was more in Willi's crude style. Perhaps he felt that his territory was being invaded. "I mean . . . you were risking a lot, weren't you? It's so . . . damn it . . . so *public*."

Nina laughed and set down the calculator. "Willi, *dear*, that's what the Game is *about*, is it not?"

Willi strode to the liquor cabinet and refilled his brandy snifter. The wind tossed bare branches against the leaded glass of the bay window. I do not like winter. Even in the South it takes its toll on the spirit.

"Didn't this guy . . . whatshisname . . . buy the gun in Hawaii or someplace?" asked Willi from across the room. "That sounds like his initiative to me. I mean, if he was *already* stalking the fellow . . ."

"Willi, dear," Nina's voice had gone as cold as the wind that raked the branches, "no one said he was *stable*. How many of yours are stable, Willi? But I made it *happen*, darling. I chose the place and the time. Don't you see the irony of the *place*, Willi? After that little prank on the director of that witchcraft movie a few years ago? It was straight from the script . . ."

"I don't know," said Willi. He sat heavily on the divan, spilling brandy on his expensive sports coat. He did not notice. The lamplight reflected from his balding skull. The mottles of age were more visible at night and his neck, where it disappeared into his turtleneck, was all ropes and tendons. "I don't know." He looked up at me and smiled suddenly, as if we shared a conspiracy. "It could be like that writer fellow, eh, Melanie? It could be like that."

Nina looked down at the hands on her lap. The well-manicured fingers were white at the tips.

The Mind Vampires. That's what the writer was going to call his book. I sometimes wonder if he really would have written anything. What was his name? Something Russian.

Willi and I received the telegram from Nina: COME QUICKLY. YOU ARE NEEDED. That was enough. I was on the next morning's flight to New York. The plane was a noisy, propeller-driven Constellation and I spent much of the flight assuring the oversolicitous stewardess that I needed nothing, that, indeed, I felt fine. She obviously had decided that I was someone's grandmother who was flying for the first time.

Willi managed to arrive twenty minutes before me. Nina was distraught and as close to hysteria as I had ever seen her. She had been at a party in lower Manhattan two days before—she was not so distraught that she forgot to tell us what important names had been there—when she found herself sharing a corner, a fondue pot, and confidences with a young writer. Or rather, the writer was sharing confidences. Nina described him as a scruffy sort, wispy little beard, thick glasses, a corduroy sports coat worn over an old plaid shirt—one of the type invariably sprinkled around successful parties of that era according to Nina. She knew enough not to call him a beatnik for that term had just become passé, but no one had yet heard the term hippie and it wouldn't have applied to him anyway. He was a writer of the sort that barely ekes out a living, these days at least, by selling blood and doing novelizations of television series. Alexander something.

His idea for a book—he told Nina that he had been working on it for some time—was that many of the murders then being committed were actually the result of a small group of psychic killers—he called them *mind vampires*—who used others to carry out their grisly deeds. He said that a paperback publisher had already shown interest in his outline and would offer him a contract tomorrow if he would change the title to *The Zombie Factor* and put in more sex.

"So what?" Willi had said to Nina in disgust. "You have me fly across the continent for this? I might buy that idea to produce myself."

That turned out to be the excuse we used to interrogate this Alexander Somebody when Nina threw an impromptu party the next evening. I did not attend. The party was not overly successful according to Nina, but it gave Willi the chance to have a long chat with the young, would-be novelist. In the writer's almost pitiable eagerness to do business with Bill Borden, producer of *Paris Memories, Three On a Swing*, and at least two other completely forgettable Technicolor features touring the drive-ins that summer, he revealed that the book consisted of a well-worn outline and a dozen pages of notes. However, he was sure that he could do a "treatment" for Mr. Borden in five weeks, perhaps three weeks if he was flown out to Hollywood to get the proper creative stimulation.

Later that evening we discussed the possibility of Willi simply buying an option on the treatment, but Willi was short on cash at the time and Nina was insistent. In the end, the young writer opened his femoral artery with a Gillette blade and ran screaming into a narrow Greenwich Village side street to die. I don't believe that anyone ever bothered to sort through the clutter and debris of his remaining notes.

"It could be like that writer, *ja*, Melanie?" Willi patted my knee. I nodded. "He was mine," continued Willi, "and Nina tried to take credit. Remember?"

Again I nodded. Actually he had not been Nina's or Willi's. I had avoided the party so I could make contact later without the young man noticing he was being followed. I did so easily. I remember sitting in an overheated little delicatessen across the street from the apartment building. It was not at all difficult. It was over so quickly that there was almost no sense of Feeding. Then I was aware once again of the sputtering radiators and the smell of salami as people rushed to the door to see what the screaming was about. I remember finishing my tea slowly so that I did not have to leave before the ambulance was gone.

"Nonsense," said Nina. She busied herself with her little calculator. "How many points?" She looked at me. I looked at Willi.

"Six," he said with a shrug. Nina made a small show of totaling the numbers.

"Thirty-eight," she said and sighed theatrically. "You win again, Willi. Or rather, you beat *me* again. We must hear from Melanie. You've been so quiet, dear. You must have some surprise for us."

"Yes," said Willi, "it is your turn to win. It has been several years."

"None," I said. I had expected an explosion of questions, but the silence was broken only by the ticking of the clock on the mantelpiece. Nina was looking away from me, at something hidden by the shadows in the corner.

"None?" echoed Willi.

"There was . . . one," I said at last. "But it was by accident. I came across them robbing an old man behind . . . it was by accident."

Willi was agitated. He stood up, walked to the window, turned a straight-backed old chair around and straddled it, arms folded. "What does this mean?"

"You're quitting the Game?" asked Nina as she turned to look at me. I let the question serve as the answer.

"Why?" snapped Willi. In his excitement it came out with a hard "V."

If I had been raised in an era when young ladies were allowed to shrug, I would have done so then. As it was, I contented myself with running my fingers along an imaginary seam on my skirt. Willi had asked the question, but I stared straight into Nina's eyes when I finally answered. "I'm tired. It's been too long. I guess I'm getting old."

"You'll get a lot *older* if you do not Hunt," said Willi. His body, his voice, the red mask of his face, everything signaled great anger just kept in check. "My God, Melanie, you *already* look older! You look terrible. This is *why* we Hunt, woman. Look at yourself in the mirror! Do you want to die an old woman just because you're tired of using *them*? Acch!" Willi stood and turned his back on us.

"Nonsense!" Nina's voice was strong, confident, in command once more. "Melanie's *tired*, Willi. Be nice. We all have times like that. I remember how *you* were after the war. Like a whipped puppy. You wouldn't even go outside your miserable little flat in Baden. Even after we helped you get to New Jersey you just sulked around feeling sorry for yourself. Melanie *made up* the Game to help you feel better. So quiet! *Never* tell a lady who feels tired and depressed that she looks terrible. Honestly, Willi, you're such a *Schwächsinniger* sometimes. And a crashing boor to boot."

I had anticipated many reactions to my announcement, but this was the one I feared the most. It meant that Nina had also tired of the Game. It meant that she was ready to move to another level of play. It had to mean that.

"Thank you, Nina, darling," I said. "I knew you would understand."

She reached across and touched my knee reassuringly. Even through my wool skirt I could feel the cold of her white fingers.

My guests would not stay the night. I implored. I remonstrated. I pointed out that their rooms were ready, that Mr. Thorne had already turned down the quilts.

"Next time," said Willi. "Next time, Melanie, my little love. We'll make a weekend of it as we used to. A week!" Willi was in a much better mood since he had been paid his thousand dollar "prize" by each of us. He had sulked, but I had insisted. It soothed his ego when Mr. Thorne brought in a check already made out to William D. Borden.

Again I asked him to stay, but he protested that he had a midnight flight to Chicago. He had to see a prizewinning author about a screenplay. Then he was hugging me good-bye, his companions were in the hall behind me, and I had a brief moment of terror.

But they left. The blond young man showed his white smile and the Negro bobbed his head in what I took as a farewell. Then we were alone. Nina and I were alone.

Not quite alone. Miss Kramer was standing next to Nina at the end of the hall. Mr. Thorne was out of sight behind the swinging door to the kitchen. I left him there.

Miss Kramer took three steps forward. I felt my breath stop for an instant. Mr. Thorne put his hand on the swinging door. Then the husky little brunette went to the hall closet, removed Nina's coat, and stepped back to help her into it.

"Are you sure you won't stay?"

"No, thank you, darling. I've promised Barrett that we would drive to Hilton Head tonight."

"But it's late . . ."

"We have reservations. Thank you, anyway, Melanie. I *will* be in touch."

"Yes."

"I mean it, dear. We must talk. I understand *exactly* how you feel, but you have to remember that the Game is still important to Willi. We'll have to find a way to end it without hurting his feelings. Perhaps we could visit him next spring in Karinhall or whatever he calls that gloomy old Bavarian place of his. A trip to the Continent would do wonders for you, dear."

"Yes."

"I *will* be in touch. After this deal with the new store is settled. We need to spend some time together, Melanie . . . just the two of us . . . like old times." Her lips kissed the air next to my cheek. She held my forearms tightly for a few seconds. "Good-bye, darling."

"Good-bye, Nina."

I carried the brandy glass to the kitchen. Mr. Thorne took it in silence.

"Make sure the house is secure," I said. He nodded and went off to check the locks and alarm system. It was only nine forty-five, but I was very tired. *Age*, I thought. I went up the wide staircase—perhaps the finest feature of the house—and dressed for bed. It had begun to storm and the sound of the cold raindrops on the window carried a sad rhythm to it.

Mr. Thorne looked in as I was brushing my hair and wishing it were longer. I turned to him. He reached into the pocket of his dark vest. When his hand emerged, a slim blade flicked out. I nodded. He palmed the blade shut and closed the door behind him. I listened to his footsteps recede down the stairs to the chair in the front hall where he would spend the night.

I believe that I dreamed of vampires that night. Or perhaps I was thinking about them just prior to falling asleep and a fragment had stayed with me until morning. Of all of mankind's self-inflicted terrors, of all their pathetic little monsters, only the myth of the vampire had any vestige of dignity. Like the humans it fed on, the vampire responded to its own dark compulsions. But unlike its petty human prey, the vampire carried out its sordid means to the only possible ends which could justify such actions— the goal of literal immortality. There was a nobility there. And a sadness.

Willi was right—I had aged. The past year had taken a greater toll than the preceding decade. But I had not Fed. Despite the hunger, despite the aging reflection in the mirror, despite the dark compulsion which had ruled our lives for so many years, *I had not Fed*.

I fell asleep trying to remember the details of Charles's face.

I fell asleep hungry.

TWO

Beverly Hills
Saturday, Dec. 13, 1980

The front lawn of Tony Harod's home featured a large circular fountain into which a sculpture of a cloven-hoofed satyr urinated while staring down the canyon toward Hollywood with a perpetual grimace which might be interpreted as either pained aversion or sneering contempt. Those who knew Tony Harod had no doubt as to which expression was the more appropriate.

The home had once belonged to a silent-screen actor who, in the prime of his career and after much struggle, had made the difficult transition to talking pictures only to die of throat cancer three months after his first talkie opened at Graumann's Chinese Theater. His widow refused to leave the sprawling estate and stayed on for thirty-five years as a de facto mausoleum caretaker, frequently sponging off old Hollywood acquaintances and previously spurned relatives in order to pay the taxes. When she died in 1959 the home was purchased by a scriptwriter who had done three of the five Doris Day romance-comedies released by then. The writer complained about the gone-to-seed garden and a bad smell in the second-floor study. Eventually the writer went deep into debt and blew his brains out in the potting shed, to be discovered the next day by a gardener who did not report the death for fear of being revealed to be an illegal alien. The corpse of the screenwriter was discovered again twelve days later by a lawyer for the Screenwriters' Guild who had come out to discuss their upcoming defense in a plagiarism suit.

Subsequent owners of the house included a famous actress who resided there for the three-month interregnum between her fifth and sixth marriage, a special effects technician who died in a 1976 commissary fire, and an oil sheik who painted the satyr pink and gave it a Jewish name. The sheik was assassinated in 1979 by his brother-in-law while passing through Riyadh on pilgrimage and Tony Harod bought the estate four days later.

"It's fucking wonderful," Harod had told the realtor as they stood on the flagstone path and stared up at the urinating satyr. "I'll take the place." An hour later he handed over a check for $600,000 in down payment. He had not yet been inside the house.

Shayla Berrington knew the stories about Tony Harod's impulsive acts. She knew about the time Harod had insulted Truman Capote in front of two hundred guests and about the scandal in 1978 when he and one of Jimmy Carter's closest aides almost had been arrested for the possession of narcotics. No one had gone to jail, nothing had been proven, but it had been rumored that Harod had set the hapless Georgian up as a prank. Shayla leaned over to catch sight of the satyr as her chauffeur-driven Mercedes glided up the curved drive toward the main house. She was acutely aware that her mother was not with her. Also missing on this particular outing were Loren (her agent), Richard (her mother's agent), Cowles (her chauffeur/bodyguard), and Estaban (her hairdresser). Shayla was seventeen years old, a successful model for nine years and a movie star for the past two, but as the Mercedes came to a stop in front of the elaborately carved front doors of Harod's house, she felt like nothing so much as a fairy-tale princess who had been compelled to visit a fierce ogre.

No, not an ogre, thought Shayla. *What did Norman Mailer call Tony Harod after Stephen and Leslie's party last spring? A malignant little troll. I must pass through this malignant little troll's cave before finding the treasure.*

Shayla felt tension pull at her neck muscles as she rang the bell. She consoled herself with the knowledge that Mr. Borden would be there. She liked the aged producer with his Old World courtliness and pleasant hint of accent. Shayla felt the tension rise again as she thought of her mother's reaction if the older woman ever discovered that Shayla had secretly arranged such a meeting. Shayla was about to turn and leave when the door swung wide.

"Ah, Miss Berrington, I presume." Tony Harod stood in the doorway wearing a velvet robe. Shayla stared at him and wondered if he wore anything under the robe. A few gray hairs were visible in the black mat on his bare chest.

"How do you do," Shayla said and followed her would-be associate producer into the foyer. At first glance Tony Harod was not an obvious candidate for trolldom. He was slightly shorter than average—Shayla was 5'11", tall even for a model, and Harod could not have stood more than 5'7"—and his long arms and oversize hands seemed out of proportion as they hung from his thin, almost boyish frame. His hair was very dark and clipped so short that black bangs curled down over his high, pale forehead. Shayla thought that perhaps the first hint of the hidden troll was the sallowness to his skin that seemed more appropriate to a denizen of some sooty, northeastern city than to a twelve-year resident of Los Angeles. Harod's face was sharp-boned, sharp-edged, and not softened by a sardonic slash of a mouth that seemed filled with too many small teeth and a quick, pink tongue that moved constantly to moisten his thin lower lip. His eyes were set deep and looked vaguely bruised, but it was the intensity of that shadowed gaze which made Shayla inhale deeply and pause in the tiled entryway. Shayla was sensitive to eyes—her own had helped make her what she was—and she had never encountered a stare which struck her quite like Tony Harod's. Languid, heavy-lidded, almost unfocused in their mocking disinterest, Harod's small, brown eyes seemed to project a power and a challenge quite in contrast to the rest of his appearance.

"Come on in, kid. Jesus, where's your entourage? I didn't think you went anywhere without a mob that'd make Napoleon's Grand Army look like a rump session of Richard Nixon's fan club."

"Pardon me?" said Shayla and immediately regretted it. Too much was riding on this meeting for her to get behind on points.

"Forget it," said Harod and stood back to look at her. He jammed his hands in the pockets of his robe but not before Shayla had time to notice extraordinarily long, pale fingers. She thought of Gollum in *The Hobbit*.

"Christ, you're fucking beautiful," said the little man. "I knew you were a knockout, but you're even more impressive in real life. You must drive the beachboys apeshit."

Shayla stiffened. She had been prepared to suffer some boorishness, but she had been raised to abhor obscenities. "Is Mr. Borden here yet?" she asked coldly.

Harod smiled but shook his head. "Afraid not," he said. "Willi had to go visit some old friends back East . . . somewhere in the South . . . Bogsville or Redneck Beach or someplace."

Shayla hesitated. She had thought herself well-prepared to make the deal she wanted with Mr. Borden and his associate producer, but the thought of dealing just with Tony Harod made her shudder. She would have made some excuse then and left, but the movement was preempted by the appearance of a beautiful woman.

"Ms. Berrington, allow me to introduce my assistant, Maria Chen," said Harod. "Maria, this is Shayla Berrington, a very talented young actress who may be the star of our new film."

"How do you do, Miss Chen." Shayla took the measure of the older woman. In her thirties, her Oriental ancestry apparent only in the beautifully sculpted cheekbones, a raven richness of hair, and the slightest turn of the eye, Maria Chen could easily have been a model herself. The slight tension, so natural between two striking women being introduced, was immediately dissipated by the warmth of the older woman's smile.

"Ms. Berrington, it's a great pleasure to meet you." Chen's handshake was firm and pleasant. "I've been a great admirer of your ad work for some time. You have a rare quality. I think the Avedon spread in *Vogue* was magnificent."

"Thank you, Miss Chen."

"Please call me Maria." She smiled, brushed back her hair, and turned to Harod. "The pool is at the proper temperature. I've arranged to hold all calls for the next forty-five minutes."

Harod nodded. "Since my accident on the Ventura Freeway last spring I find it helpful to spend some time in the Jacuzzi each day," he said. He smiled thinly as he saw her hesitate. "Pool rule, suits required." Harod unbelted his robe to show a pair of red trunks with his initials mono-grammed in gold. "Shall Maria show you to a changing room or would you prefer to discuss the film at some future date when Willi can be here?"

Shayla thought quickly. She doubted if she could keep such a deal se-cret from Loren and her mother for long. This might be her only chance to get the movie on her own terms. "I didn't bring a suit," she said.

It was Maria Chen who laughed and said, "No problem there. Tony has suits for all shapes and sizes of guests. He even keeps several for his elderly aunt when she visits."

Shayla joined in the laughter. She followed the other woman down a long hallway, through a room filled with comfortable sectionals which was dominated by a large television viewing screen, past shelves filled with electronic video equipment, and then down another short hall into a cedar-lined dressing room. Wide drawers slid out to reveal men's and women's swimsuits of various styles and colors.

"I'll let you change," said Maria Chen.

"Will you be joining us?"

"Perhaps later. I have to finish typing some of Tony's correspondence. Enjoy the water . . . and Ms. Berrington . . . don't mind Tony's manner. He's a bit rough sometimes, but he's very fair."

Shayla nodded as Maria Chen closed the door. Shayla looked through the stacks of bathing suits. The styles varied from skimpy French bikinis to strapless maillots to conservative two-piece suits. Tags bore the names Gottex, Christian Dior, and Cole. Shayla chose an orange bandeau that was less than outrageous but cut high enough to show off her thighs and long legs to best advantage. She knew from experience how well her small, firm breasts would show and how there would be just a hint of nipple swelling the thin lycra fabric. The color would complement the green in her hazel eyes.

Shayla went out another door and emerged into a greenhouse setting enclosed on three sides by curved walls of glass where a proliferation of tropical plants caught the light. The fourth wall held yet another large projection screen next to the door. Muted classical music came from un-seen speakers. It was very humid. Shayla could see a much larger pool sparkling outside in the morning light. Inside, Tony Harod reclined in the shallow end of the spa and sipped at a tall drink. Shayla felt the hot, moist air press on her like a damp blanket.

"What kept you, kid? I started without you."

Shayla smiled and sat on the edge of the small pool. She remained about five feet from Harod—not so far as to convey insult, not so close as to suggest intimacy. She kicked idly at the frothing water, lifting her legs with her feet extended so as to best display her calf and thigh muscles.

"Let's get to it, shall we?" suggested Harod. He showed his thin, faintly mocking smile and his tongue darted out to wet his lower lip.

"I shouldn't even be here," Shayla said softly. "My agent handles this kind of thing. And I always consult with Mother before deciding on any new project . . . even a weekend modeling assignment. I came today only because Mr. Borden asked me to. He's been very nice to us since . . ."

"Yeah, yeah, he's crazy about you too," interrupted Harod and set his drink on the tile. "Here's the deal. Willi's bought the rights to a paperback best-seller called *The White Slaver*. It's a piece of formulized shit written for illiterate fourteen-year-olds and the kind of lobotomized housewife that lines up to buy the new Harlequin romances each month. Jack-off material for intellectual quadriplegics. Naturally it sold about three million copies. We got the rights before it was published. Willi has someone at Ballantine who tips him off when one of these concoctions of puréed batshit promises to be a sleeper."

"You make it sound very attractive," Shayla said softly.

"Fucking right. Of course the movie will throw out most of the book—keep the rough story line and the cheap sex. But we'll have good people working on it. Michael May-Dreinen's already started work on the script and Schubert Williams has agreed to direct."

"Schu Williams?" Shayla was startled. Williams had just finished directing George C. Scott in a much-touted film for MGM. She looked down at the bubbling surface of the pool. "I'm afraid it doesn't sound like something we'd be interested in," said Shayla. "My mother . . . that is, we've been very careful as to the type of vehicle we've chosen in which to start my film career."

"Uh-huh," said Harod and drained the last of his drink. "Two years ago you starred in *Shannerly's Hope* with Ryan O'Neal. Dying kid meets a dying conman in a Mexican laetrile clinic. Together they give up their search for false cures and find real happiness in the few weeks left to them. *Jee-juz-fucking-Christ*. And I quote Charles Champlin, 'The previews alone for this saccharine abomination would be sufficient to send diabetics into seizure.'"

"The distribution and promotion were poor and . . ."

"You'd better be damned glad of that, kiddo. Then last year your mom got you into Wise's *East of Happiness*. You were going to be another Julie Andrews in that cheap-shit rip-off of *The Sound of Mucus*. Only you weren't—and this isn't the flower child sixties, it's the mean-assed eighties and I'm not your agent or anything, Ms. Berrington, but I'd say that Momma and the crew have poled you pretty far up shit creek as far as your film career goes. They're trying to turn you into a Marie Osmond type . . . yeah, yeah, I know you're a member of the Church of the L.D.S. . . . so what? You were a class act on the cover of *Vogue* and *Seventeen* and now you're close to pissing it all away. They're trying to sell you as a twelve-year-old ingenue and it's too late for that kind of shit."

Shayla did not move. Her mind was racing, but she could think of nothing to say. Her impulse was to tell this malignant little troll to drop dead, but no words came and she continued to sit on the edge of the bubbling pool. Her future depended upon the next few minutes and her mind was a muddle.

Harod climbed out of the water and padded across the tiles to a wet bar set back among the ferns. He poured a tall glass of grapefruit juice and looked back at Shayla. "Want anything, kid? I've got everything here. Even some Hawaiian punch if you're feeling especially Mormon today."

Shayla shook her head.

The producer dropped back into the Jacuzzi and rested the glass on his chest. He glanced up at a mirror on one wall and nodded almost imperceptibly. "All right," he said. "Let's talk about *The White Slaver* or whatever it ends up being called."

"I don't think that we would be interested . . ."

"You'll get four hundred thousand dollars up front," said Harod, "plus a percentage of the picture . . . which you'll never see, bookkeeping being what it is. What you'll really get out of it is a name you can bank at any studio in town. This thing's going to be a fucking firecracker, kid. Trust me. I can smell big box office before the second draft of the treatment gets typed. This is big."

"I'm afraid not, Mr. Harod. Mr. Borden said that if I wasn't interested after hearing the initial proposal that we could . . ."

"Shooting starts in March," said Harod. He took a long sip and closed his eyes. "Schu figures about twelve weeks so count on twenty. Location shots'll include Algiers, Spain, a few days in Egypt, and about three weeks in Pinewood Studios for the palace stuff on the big soundstage there."

Shayla stood up. Water glistened on her legs. She put her hands on her hips and glared at the ugly little man in the pool. Harod did not open his eyes.

"You're not *listening*, Mr. Harod," she snapped. "I said no. No, I will not do your picture. I haven't even seen the *script*. Well, you can take your *White Slaver* or whatever it is and . . . and . . ."

"And shove it up my ass?" Harod opened his eyes. Shayla was reminded of a lizard awakening. The water frothed around Harod's pale chest.

"Good-bye, Mr. Harod," said Shayla Berrington and turned on her heel. She had taken three steps when Harod's voice stopped her.

"Afraid of the nude scenes, kid?"

She hesitated, then continued walking.

"Afraid of the nude scenes," repeated Harod and this time it was not a question.

Shayla was almost to the door when she whirled around. Her hands clawed at the air. "I haven't even seen the script!" Her voice broke and she was amazed to find herself near tears.

"Sure, there are some nude scenes," continued Harod as if she had not spoken. "And one love scene that'll make the little teeny-boppers cream their pants. We could use a body-double . . . but we won't have to. You can do it, kiddo."

Shayla shook her head. She felt a rising fury that was beyond words. She turned and reached blindly for the doorknob.

"Stop." Tony Harod's voice was softer than ever. Almost inaudible. But there was something in it that stopped her more surely than a scream. Cold fingers seemed to curl around her neck.

"Come here."

Shayla turned and walked toward him. Harod lay with his long-fingered hands crossed over his chest. His eyes were only slightly opened—moist, heavy-lidded—a crocodile's lazy gaze. Part of Shayla's mind screamed in panic and protest while another part merely watched in growing wonder.

"Sit down."

She sat on the edge of the pool three feet from him. Her long legs dropped into the Jacuzzi. White foam splashed her tan thighs. She felt distant from her own body, staring down at herself with an almost clinical detachment.

"As I was saying, you can do it, kid. Jesus, there's a little of the exhibitionist in all of us. Only you'll be paid a fat fortune to do what you want to do anyway."

As if fighting a terrible torpor, Shayla raised her head and looked into Tony Harod's eyes. In the dappled light, his irises appeared to have opened so far as to leave only black holes in his pale face.

"Like now," Harod said softly, so very softly. Perhaps he did not speak at all. The words seemed to slide into place in Shayla's brain, cold coins tumbling into dark water. "It's really quite warm in here. You don't need that suit. Do you? Of course not."

Shayla stared. Distantly, far back in the tunnel of her mind, she was a small child on the verge of tears. She watched in quiet surprise as her arm rose and her right hand slowly loosened the top of the bandeau and slid under the elastic. She tugged lightly and the lycra slid lower on her side, pulling tighter against the swell of her breasts. She pulled again on the right side. The fabric cut across her just above the nipple. She could see the faint red line fading where the elastic had pressed against her. She looked at Tony Harod.

Harod smiled ever so slightly and nodded.

As if given permission, Shayla pulled the suit down sharply. Her breasts bobbed softly as they came free of the orange fabric. She was very white there with only a few freckles dotting the tender skin. Her nipples were taut, rising quickly in the cool air. The areolae were brown and very wide, and were outlined by a few dark hairs which Shayla found too beautiful to pluck. No one knew that. Not even her mother. Shayla had not allowed anyone, not even Avedon, to photograph her breasts.

She looked back at Harod but his face was only a pale blur. The room seemed to tilt and spin around her. The noise of the pool recycler grew louder until it throbbed in her ears. At the same time, Shayla felt something stir inside her. A pleasant warmth began to fill her. It was as if someone had reached directly into her brain to softly stroke at the pleasure center there as surely as palm and fingers would stroke the soft mound between her legs. Shayla gasped and arched involuntarily.

"It's really quite warm," said Tony Harod.

Shayla ran her hands over her face, touched her eyelids with something akin to wonder, and then ran her palms down her neck, across her collarbone, and stopped with her fingers pressing flat against her chest where the pale flesh began. She could feel her pulse fluttering in her throat like a caged bird. Then she slid her hands lower, arching again as her palms slid across her suddenly painfully sensitive nipples, lifting her breasts as Dr. Kemmerer had taught her when she was fourteen, but not examining them, merely pressing, pressing against herself with a pleasurable pressure that made her want to scream.

"There's really no need for a suit at all," whispered Harod. *Did* he whisper? Shayla was confused. She was looking right at him and his lips had not moved. His slight smile showed small teeth like sharp, white stones.

It did not matter. Nothing mattered to Shayla except getting free of the clinging maillot. She pulled the material lower, tugged it over the slight swell of her belly, and raised her buttocks to slide the elastic from under her. Then the suit was only a clinging fold of fabric on one leg and she kicked it free. She looked down at herself, at the inward curving arc of thigh and the vertical, not quite V-shaped line of pubic hair that rose toward the demarcation of her tan. For a second she was dizzy again, this time with a distant sense of shock, but then she felt the stroking begin inside her once again and she leaned back on her elbows.

The Jacuzzi frothed warm water at her thighs. She raised a hand and slowly traced a blue vein where it pulsed under the white skin of her breast. The slightest touch brought fire to her flesh. The soft mounds of her breasts seemed to contract and grow heavier at the same instant. The noise of the pool seemed to synchronize and then syncopate with her thudding heartbeat. She raised her right knee and dropped her hand to the inside of her leg. Her own palm slid higher, disturbing the water droplets that gleamed on the thin, golden hairs of her upper legs. Warmth infused her, filled her, controlled her. Her vulva pulsed with a pleasure she had known only in that guilty twilight before sleep, known before only with a filter of shame now missing, and never known with this overwhelming sense of heat and urgency. Shayla's fingers found the moistened folds of her labia and she parted them with a soft gasp.

"Too warm for a suit," said Tony Harod. "For either of us." He took a final sip of his grapefruit juice, hoisted himself up on the tile, and set the glass far back from the edge of the pool.

Shayla slid around, feeling the cool tiles under her hip. Her long hair tumbled around her face as she crawled forward, her mouth open slightly, using her elbows for leverage. Harod was leaning back on his elbows with his feet kicking idly at the water. Shayla paused and looked up at him. Inside her mind the stroking intensified, found her core, and slid slowly along it in teasing strokes. Her senses registered only the ebb and flow of oiled friction. Shayla gasped and involuntarily clenched her thighs together as wave after wave of preliminary orgasm rippled through her. The whispering grew louder in her mind, a teasing sibilance which seemed to be part of the pleasure.

Shayla's breasts touched the floor as she leaned forward and tugged down Tony Harod's swim shorts in a frenzied motion that was somehow both violent and graceful. She pulled the bunched fabric down over his knees and into the water. Black hair marched down from his belly. His penis was pale and flaccid, slowly stirring in its nest of dark hair.

She looked up and saw that his smile was gone. Harod's eyes were perforations in a pale mask. There was no warmth there. No excitement. There was only the intense concentration of a predator gazing at its kill. Shayla did not care. She did not know what she saw. She knew only that the stroking in her mind had intensified, going beyond ecstasy into pain. Pure pleasure flooded her nervous system like a drug.

Shayla laid her cheek against Harod's thigh and reached for his penis with her right hand. He idly batted her hand away. Shayla bit into her lip and moaned. Her mind was a maelstrom of sensation which registered only the goadings of passion and pain. Her legs twitched in random spasms and she writhed against the edge of the pool. Shayla moved her lips along the salty expanse of Harod's thigh. She tasted her own blood while she reached to cup Harod's testicles in her palm. The little man raised his right leg and gently pushed her sideways into the pool. Shayla continued clinging to his legs, straining against him, making small noises while her mouth and hands sought him.

Maria Chen entered, plugged a telephone into a wall outlet, and set it on the floor near Harod. "It's Washington," she said, glanced once at Shayla, and walked out.

The warmth and friction left Shayla's mind and body with a cold suddenness that made her cry out in pain. She stared blindly for a second and then pushed herself backward in the foaming pool. She began trembling violently and covered her upper body with her arms.

"Harod here," said the producer. He rose, took three steps, and slipped into his terry-cloth robe. Shayla watched with bruised disbelief as his pale loins were covered. She began to shake even more violently then. Chills coursed through her. She raked at her hair with her fingernails and lowered her face to the foaming water.

"Yes?" said Harod. "Goddammit to goddamn hell. When? Are they sure he was on board? *Fuck.* Yeah. Both of them? What about the other one . . . whatshername? *Fuck!* No, no, I'll take care of it. No. I said *I'll* take care of it. Yeah. No, make it two days. Yeah, I'll be there." Harod slammed the receiver down, strode to a wicker chair, and threw himself into it.

Shayla reached as far as she could and pulled the wadded maillot into the pool. Still shaking, nausea making her dizzy, she squatted in the bubbling water to pull on the suit. She was sobbing without being aware of it. *This is a nightmare* was the thought that echoed through her spinning mind.

Harod picked up a remote control and clicked it at the large video projection screen set into one wall. Instantly the screen lit with an image of Shayla Berrington sitting on the edge of a small pool. She looked to one side, stared vacantly, smiled as if enjoying a dream, and began pulling down the elastic of her swimsuit. Her breasts were pale, the nipples erect, the areolae large and visibly brown even in the poor light. . . .

"No!" screamed Shayla and beat at the water.

Harod turned his head and seemed to notice her for the first time. His thin lips twisted into a simulacrum of a smile. "I'm afraid our plans have changed a bit," he said softly. "Mr. Borden won't be involved in this particular film. I'll be the sole producer."

Shayla stopped her frantic slapping at the water. Her hair hung across her face in moist strands. Her mouth was open and strings of saliva hung from her chin. Except for her uncontrolled sobs, the only sound was the purr of the pool recycler.

"We'll keep to the original shooting schedule," Harod said almost absently. He glanced up at the big screen. Shayla Berrington was crawling naked across dark tiles. The naked torso of a man came into view. The camera zoomed in on Shayla's face as she rubbed her cheek against a hairy white thigh. Her eyes were glazed with passion and her mouth pulsed roundly like that of a fish. "I'm afraid Mr. Borden won't be producing any more films with us," said Harod. His head rotated toward her and the black beacons of his eyes blinked slowly. "From here on out it's just you and me, kid."

Harod's lips twitched and Shayla could see the small teeth. They looked very white and sharp. "I'm afraid Mr. Borden won't be producing any more films with anyone." Harod turned his gaze back to the screen. "Willi's dead," he said softly.

THREE

Charleston
Saturday, Dec. 13, 1980

I awoke to bright sunlight through branches. It was one of those crystalline, warming winter days which makes living in the South so much less depressing than merely surviving a Yankee winter. I could see the green palmettos above red rooftops. I had Mr. Thorne open the window a crack when he brought in my breakfast tray. As I sipped my coffee I could hear children playing in the courtyard. Years ago Mr. Thorne would have brought the morning paper with the tray, but I had long since learned that to read about the follies and scandals of the world was to desecrate the morning. In truth, I was growing less and less interested in the affairs of men. I had done without a newspaper, telephone, or television for twelve years and had suffered no ill effects unless one were to count a growing self-contentment as an ill thing. I smiled as I remembered Willi's disappointment at not being able to play his videocassettes. He was such a child.

"It is Saturday, is it not, Mr. Thorne?" At his nod I gestured for the tray to be taken away. "We will go out today," I said. "A walk. Perhaps a trip to the Fort. Then dinner at Henry's and home. I have arrangements to make."

Mr. Thorne hesitated and half stumbled as he was leaving the room. I paused in the act of belting my robe. It was not like Mr. Thorne to commit an ungraceful movement. I realized that he too was getting old. He straightened the tray and dishes, nodded his head, and left for the kitchen.

I would not let thoughts of aging disturb me on such a beautiful morning. I felt charged with a new energy and resolve. The reunion the night before had not gone well, but neither had it gone as badly as it could have. I had been honest with Nina and Willi about my intention of quitting the Game. In the weeks and months to come, they—or at least Nina—would begin to brood over the ramifications of that, but by the time they chose to react, separately or together, I would be long gone. Already I had new (and old) identities waiting for me in Florida, Michigan, London, southern France, and even in New Delhi. Michigan was out for the time being. I had grown unused to the harsh climate. New Delhi was no longer the hospitable place for foreigners it had been when I resided there briefly before the war.

Nina had been right about one thing—a return to Europe would be good for me. Already I longed for the rich light and cordial *savoir vivre* of the villagers near my old summer house outside of Toulon.

The air outside was bracing. I wore a simple print dress and my spring coat. The trace of arthritis in my right leg had bothered me coming down the stairs, but I used my father's old walking stick as a cane. A young Negro servant had cut it for Father the summer we moved from Greenville to Charleston. I smiled as we emerged into the warm air of the courtyard.

Mrs. Hodges came out of her doorway into the light. It was her grandchildren and their friends who were playing around the dry fountain. The courtyard had been shared by the three brick buildings for two centuries. Only my home had not been parceled into expensive town houses or apartments.

"Good morning, Miz Fuller."

"Good morning, Mrs. Hodges. A beautiful day."

"It is that. Are you off shopping?"

"Just for a walk, Mrs. Hodges. I'm surprised that Mr. Hodges isn't out. He always seems to be working in the yard on Saturdays."

Mrs. Hodges frowned as one of the little girls ran between us. Her friend came squealing after her, sweater flying. "Oh, George is at the Marina already."

"In the daytime?" I had often been amused by Mr. Hodges's departure for work in the evening; his security guard uniform neatly pressed, gray hair jutting out from under his cap, black lunch pail gripped firmly under his arm. Mr. Hodges was as leathery and bowlegged as an aged cowboy. He was one of those men who was always on the verge of retiring but who probably realized that to be inactive would be a form of death sentence.

"Oh yes. One of those colored men on the day shift down at the storage building quit and they asked George to fill in. I told him that he was too old to work four nights a week and then go back on the weekend, but you know George."

"Well, give him my best," I said. The girls running around the fountain made me nervous.

Mrs. Hodges followed me to the wrought-iron gate. "Will you be going away for the holidays, Miz Fuller?"

"Probably, Mrs. Hodges. Most probably." Then Mr. Thorne and I were out onto the sidewalk and strolling toward the Battery. A few cars drove slowly down the narrow streets, tourists staring at the houses of our Old Section, but the day was serene and quiet. I saw the masts of the yachts and sailboats before we came in sight of the water as we emerged onto Broad Street.

"Please acquire tickets for us, Mr. Thorne," I said. "I believe I would like to see the Fort."

As is typical of most people who live in close proximity to a popular tourist attraction, I had not taken notice of it for many years. It was an act of sentimentality to visit the Fort now. An act brought on by my increasing acceptance of the fact that I would have to leave these parts forever. It is one thing to plan a move; it is something altogether different to be faced with the imperative reality of it.

There were few tourists. The ferry moved away from the marina and into the placid waters of the harbor. The combination of warm sunlight and the steady throb of the diesel caused me to doze briefly. I awoke as we were putting in at the dark hulk of the island fort.

For a while I moved with the tour group, enjoying the catacomb silences of the lower levels and the mindless singsong of the young woman from the Park Service. But as we came back to the museum with its dusty dioramas and tawdry little trays of slides, I climbed the stairs back to the outer walls. I motioned for Mr. Thorne to stay at the top of the stairs and moved out onto the ramparts. Only one other couple—a young pair with a baby in an uncomfortable-looking papoose carrier and a cheap camera— were in sight along the wall.

It was a pleasant moment. A midday storm was coming in from the west and it set a dark backdrop to the still-sunlit church spires, brick towers, and bare branches of the city. Even from two miles away I could see the movement of people strolling along the Battery walkway. The wind was blowing in ahead of the dark clouds and tossing whitecaps against the rocking ferry and wooden dock. The air smelled of river and winter and rain by nightfall.

It was not hard to imagine that day long ago. The shells had dropped onto the fort until the upper layers were little more than protective piles of rubble. People had cheered from the rooftops behind the Battery. The bright colors of dresses and silk parasols must have been maddening to the Yankee gunners. Finally one had fired a shot above the crowded rooftops. The ensuing confusion must have been amusing from this vantage point.

A movement on the water caught my attention. Something dark was sliding through the gray water; something dark and shark-silent. I was jolted out of thoughts of the past as I recognized it as a Polaris submarine, old but obviously still operational, slipping through the dark water without a sound. Waves curled and rippled over the porpoise-smooth hull, sliding to either side in a white wake. There were several men on the dark tower. They were muffled in heavy coats with hats pulled low. An improbably large pair of binoculars hung from the neck of one man whom I assumed to be the captain. He pointed at something beyond Sullivan's Island. I stared at him. The periphery of my vision began to fade as I made contact across the water. Sounds and sensations came to me as from a distance.

Tension. The pleasure of salt spray, breeze from the north-northwest. Anxiety of the sealed orders below. Awareness of the sandy shallows just coming into sight on the port side.

I was startled as someone came up behind me. The dots flickering at the edge of my vision fled as I turned.

Mr. Thorne was there. At my elbow. Unbidden. I had opened my mouth to command him back to the top of the stairs when I saw the cause of his coming closer. The youth who had been taking pictures of his pale wife was now walking toward me. Mr. Thorne moved to intercept him.

"Hey, excuse me, ma'am. Would you or your husband mind taking our picture?"

I nodded and Mr. Thorne took the proferred camera. It looked minuscule in his long-fingered hands. Two snaps and the couple was satisfied that their presence there was documented for posterity. The young man grinned idiotically and bobbed his head. Their baby began to cry as the cold wind blew in. I looked back to the submarine, but already it had passed on, its gray tower a thin stripe connecting the sea and sky.

We were almost back to town, the ferry was swinging in toward the slip, when a stranger told me of Willi's death.

"It's awful, isn't it?" The garrulous old woman had followed me out onto the exposed section of deck. Even though the wind had grown uncomfortably chilly and I had moved twice to escape her mindless chatter, the foolish woman had obviously chosen me as her conversational target for the final stages of the tour. Neither my reticence nor Mr. Thorne's glowering presence had discouraged her. "It must have been terrible," she continued. "In the dark and all."

"What was that?" A dark premonition prompted my question.

"Why, the airplane crash. Haven't you heard about it? It must have been awful, falling into the swamp and all. I told my daughter this morning. . . ."

"What airplane crash? When?" The old woman cringed a bit at the sharpness of my tone, but the vacuous smile stayed on her face.

"Why, last night. This morning. I told my daughter . . ."

"*Where?* What aircraft?" Mr. Thorne came closer as he heard the tone of my voice.

"The one last night," she quavered. "The one from Charleston. The paper in the lounge told all about it. Isn't it terrible? Eighty-five people. I told my daughter . . ."

I left her there by the railing. There was a crumpled newspaper near the snack bar and under the four-word headline were the sparse details of Willi's death. Flight 417, bound for Chicago, had left Charleston International Airport at 12:18 A.M. Twenty minutes later the aircraft had exploded in midair not far from the city of Columbia. Fragments of fuselage and parts of bodies had fallen into Congaree Swamp where night fishermen had found them. There had been no survivors. The FAA, NTSB, and FBI were investigating.

There was a loud rushing in my ears and I had to sit down or faint. My hands were clammy against the green vinyl upholstery. People moved past me on their way to the exits.

Willi was dead. Murdered. Nina had killed him. For a few dizzy seconds I considered the possibility of a conspiracy, an elaborate ploy by Nina and Willi to confuse me into thinking that only one threat remained. But no. There would be no reason. If Nina had included Willi in her plans, there would be no need for such absurd machinations.

Willi was dead. His remains were spread over a smelly, obscure marsh-land. It was all too easy to imagine his last moments. He would have been leaning back in first-class comfort, a drink in his hand, perhaps whisper-ing to one of his loutish companions. Then the explosion. Screams. Sud-den darkness. A brutal tilting and the final fall to oblivion. I shuddered and gripped the metal arm of the chair.

How had Nina done it? Almost certainly not one of Willi's entourage. It was not beyond Nina's powers to Use Willi's own cat's-paws, especially in light of his failing Ability, but there would have been no reason to do so. She could have Used anyone on that flight. It *would* have been difficult. The elaborate step of preparing the bomb, the supreme effort of blocking all memory of it, and the almost unbelievable feat of Using someone even as we sat together drinking coffee and brandy. But Nina could have done it. Yes. She *could* have. And the timing. The timing could mean only one thing.

The last of the tourists had filed out of the cabin. I felt the slight bump that meant we had tied up to the dock. Mr. Thorne stood by the door.

Nina's timing meant that she was attempting to deal with both of us at once. She obviously had planned it long before the reunion and my timo-rous announcement of withdrawal. How amused Nina must have been. No wonder she had reacted so generously! Yet she had made one great mistake. By dealing with Willi first Nina had banked everything on my not hearing the news before she could turn on me. She knew that I had no access to daily news and only rarely left the house anymore. Still, it was unlike Nina to leave anything to chance. Was it possible that she thought that I had lost the Ability completely and that Willi was the greater threat?

I shook my head as we emerged from the cabin into the gray afternoon light. The wind sliced at me through my thin coat. The view of the gang-plank was blurry and I realized that tears had filled my eyes. For Willi? He had been a pompous, weak old fool. For Nina's betrayal? Perhaps it was only the cold wind.

The streets of the Old Section were almost empty of pedestrians. Bare branches clicked together in front of the windows of fine homes. Mr. Thorne stayed by my side. The cold air sent needles of arthritic pain up my right leg to my hip. I leaned more heavily upon Father's walking stick.

What would her next move be? I stopped. A fragment of newspaper, tumbled by the wind, wrapped itself around my ankle and then blew on.

How would she come at me? Not from a distance. She was somewhere in town. I knew that. While it was possible to Use someone from a large distance, it would involve great rapport, an almost intimate knowledge of that person, and if contact were lost it would be difficult if not impossible to reestablish it at a distance. None of us had known why this was so. It did not matter now. But the thought of Nina still here, nearby, made my heart begin to thud.

Not from a distance. Whoever she Used would come at me. I would see my assailant. If I knew Nina at all, I knew that. Certainly Willi's death had been the least personal Feeding imaginable, but that had been a mere technical operation. Nina obviously had decided to settle old scores with *me* and Willi had become an obstacle to her, a minor but measurable threat which had to be eliminated before she could proceed. I could easily imagine that in Nina's own mind her choice of death for Willi would be interpreted as an act of compassion, almost a sign of affection. Not so with me. I felt that Nina would want me to know, however briefly, that she was behind the attack. In a sense her own vanity would be my warning. Or so I hoped.

I was tempted to leave immediately. I could have Mr. Thorne get the Audi out of storage and we could be beyond Nina's influence in an hour—away to a new life within a few more hours. There were important items in the house, of course, but the funds that I had stored elsewhere would be enough to replace most of them. It would be almost welcome to leave everything behind with the discarded identity that had accumulated them.

No. I could not leave. Not yet.

From across the street the house looked dark and malevolent. Had *I* closed those blinds on the second floor? There was a shadowy movement in the courtyard and I saw Mrs. Hodges's granddaughter and a friend scamper from one doorway to another. I stood irresolutely on the curb and tapped Father's stick against a black-barked tree. It was foolish to dither so—I knew it was—but it had been a long time since I had been forced to make a decision under stress.

"Mr. Thorne, please go in to check the house. Look in each room. Return quickly."

A cold wind came up as I watched Mr. Thorne's black coat blend into the gloom of the courtyard. I felt terribly exposed standing there alone. I found myself glancing up and down the street, looking for Miss Kramer's dark hair, but the only sign of movement was a young woman pushing a perambulator far down the street.

The blinds on the second floor shot up and Mr. Thorne's face stared out whitely for a minute. Then he turned away and I remained staring at the dark rectangle of window. A shout from the courtyard startled me, but it was only the little girl—what was her name?—calling to her friend. Kathleen, that was it. The two sat on the edge of the fountain and opened a box of animal crackers. I stared intently at them and then relaxed. I even managed to smile a little at the extent of my paranoia. For a second I considered Using Mr. Thorne directly, but the thought of being helpless on the street dissuaded me. When one is in complete contact, the senses still function but are a distant thing at best.

Hurry. The thought was sent almost without volition. Two bearded men were walking down the sidewalk on my side of the street. I crossed to stand in front of my own gate. The men were laughing and gesturing at each other. One looked over at me. *Hurry.*

Mr. Thorne came out of the house, locked the door behind him, and crossed the courtyard toward me. One of the girls said something to him and held out the box of crackers, but he ignored her. Across the street, the two men continued on. Mr. Thorne handed me the large front door key. I dropped it in my coat pocket and looked sharply at him. He nodded. His placid smile unconsciously mocked my consternation.

"You're sure?" I asked. Again the nod. "You checked all of the rooms?" Nod. "The alarms?" Nod. "You looked in the basement?" Nod. "No sign of disturbance?" Mr. Thorne shook his head.

My hand went to the metal of the gate, but I hesitated. Anxiety filled my throat like bile. I was a silly old woman, tired and aching from the chill, but I could not bring myself to open that gate.

"Come." I crossed the street and walked briskly away from the house. "We will have dinner at Henry's and return later." Only I was not walking toward the old restaurant; I was heading away from the house in what I inwardly knew was a blind, directionless panic. It was not until we reached the waterfront and were walking along the Battery wall that I began to calm down. No one else was in sight. A few cars moved along the street, but to approach us someone would have to cross a wide, empty space. The gray clouds were quite low and blended with the choppy, white-crested waves in the bay.

The open air and fading evening light served to revive me and I began to think more clearly. Whatever Nina's plans had been, they had almost certainly been thrown into disarray by my day-long absence. I doubted if Nina would stay if there was the slightest risk to herself. No, she would almost certainly be returning to New York by plane even as I stood shivering on the Battery walk. In the morning I would receive a telegram. I could almost imagine the precise wording. MELANIE. ISN'T IT TERRIBLE ABOUT WILLI? TERRIBLY SAD. CAN YOU TRAVEL WITH ME TO THE FUNERAL? LOVE, NINA.

I began to realize that my hesitation had come from a desire to return to the warmth and comfort of my home as much as anything else. I simply had been afraid to shuck off this old cocoon. I could do so now. I would wait in a safe place while Mr. Thorne returned to the house to pick up the one thing I could not leave behind. Then he would get the car out of storage and by the time Nina's telegram arrived I would be far away. It would be *Nina* who would be starting at shadows in the months and years to come. I smiled and began to frame the necessary commands.

"Melanie."

My head snapped around. Mr. Thorne had not spoken in twenty-eight years. He spoke now.

"Melanie." His face was distorted in a rictus grin that showed his back teeth. The knife was in his right hand. The blade flicked out as I stared. I looked into his empty gray eyes and I knew.

"Melanie."

The long blade came around in a powerful arc. I could do nothing to stop it. It cut through the fabric of my coat sleeve and continued into my side. But in the act of turning, my purse had swung with me. The knife tore through the leather, ripped through the jumbled contents, pierced my coat, and drew blood above my lowest left rib. The purse had saved my life.

I raised Father's heavy walking stick and struck Mr. Thorne squarely in his left eye. He reeled but did not make a sound. Again he swept the air with the knife, but I had taken two steps back and his vision was clouded. I took a two-handed grip on the cane and swung again, bringing the stick down in an awkward chop. Incredibly, it again found the eye socket. I took three more steps back.

Blood streamed down the left side of Mr. Thorne's face and the damaged eye protruded onto his cheek. The rictus grin remained, his head came up, he raised his left hand slowly, plucked out the eye with a soft snapping of a gray cord, and threw it into the water of the bay. He came toward me. I turned and ran.

I *tried* to run. The ache in my right leg slowed me to a walk after twenty paces. Fifteen more hurried steps and my lungs were out of air, my heart threatening to burst. I could feel a wetness seeping down my left side and there was a tingling—like an ice cube held against the skin—where the knife blade had touched me. One glance back showed me that Mr. Thorne was striding toward me faster than I was moving. Normally he could have overtaken me in four strides. It is hard to make someone run when you are Using them. Especially when that person's body is reacting to shock and trauma. I glanced back . . . again, almost slipping on the slick pavement, Mr. Thorne was grinning widely. Blood poured from the empty socket and stained his teeth. No one else was in sight.

Down the stairs, clutching at the rail so as not to fall. Down the twisting walk and up the asphalt path to the street. Pole lamps flickered and came on as I passed. Behind me Mr. Thorne took the steps in two jumps. I thanked God that I had worn low-heeled shoes for the boat ride as I hurried up the path. What would an observer think seeing this bizarre, slow motion chase between two old people? There were no observers.

I turned onto a side street. Closed shops, empty warehouses. Going left would take me to Broad Street, but to the right, half a block away, a lone figure had emerged from a dark storefront. I moved that way, no longer able to run, close to fainting. The arthritic cramps in my leg hurt more than I could ever have imagined and threatened to collapse me on the sidewalk. Mr. Thorne was twenty paces behind me and quickly closing the distance.

The man I was approaching was a tall, thin Negro wearing a brown nylon jacket. He was carrying a box of what looked like framed, sepia photographs. He glanced at me as I approached and then looked over my shoulder at the apparition ten steps behind.

"Hey!" The man had time to shout the single syllable and then I reached out with my mind and *shoved*. He twitched like a poorly handled marionette. His jaw dropped, his eyes glazed over, and he lurched past me just as Mr. Thorne reached for the back of my coat.

The box flew into the air and glass shattered on the brick sidewalk. Long, brown fingers reached for a white throat. Mr. Thorne backhanded him away, but the Negro clung tenaciously and the two swung around like awkward dance partners. I reached the opening to an alley and leaned my face against the cold brick to revive myself. The effort of concentration while Using this stranger did not afford me the luxury of resting even for a second. I watched the clumsy stumblings of the two tall men and resisted an absurd impulse to laugh.

Mr. Thorne plunged the knife into the other's stomach, withdrew it, plunged it in again. The Negro's fingernails were clawing at Mr. Thorne's good eye now. Strong teeth were snapping in search of Mr. Thorne's jugular. I distantly sensed the cold intrusion of the blade for a third time, but the heart was still beating and he was still usable. The man jumped, scissoring his legs around Mr. Thorne's middle while his jaws closed on his muscular throat. Fingernails raked bloody streaks across white skin. The two went down in a tumble.

Kill him. Fingers groped for an eye, but Mr. Thorne reached up with his left hand and snapped his thin wrist. Limp fingers continued to flail. With a tremendous exertion, Mr. Thorne lodged his forearm against the other's chest and lifted him bodily above him like a child being tossed above his reclining father. Teeth tore away a piece of flesh, but there was no vital damage. Mr. Thorne brought the knife between them, up, left, then right. He severed half the Negro's throat with the second swing and blood fountained over both of them. The smaller man's legs spasmed twice, Mr. Thorne threw him to one side, and I turned and walked quickly down the alley.

Out into the light again, the fading evening light, and I realized that I had run myself into a dead end. Backs of warehouses and the windowless, metal side of the Battery Marina pushed right up against the waters of the bay. A street wound away to the left, but it was dark, deserted, and far too long to try. I looked back in time to see the black silhouette enter the alley behind me.

I tried to make contact, but there was nothing there. Nothing. Mr. Thorne might as well have been a hole in the air. I would worry later how Nina had done this thing.

The side door to the marina was locked. The main door was almost a hundred yards away and also would be locked. Mr. Thorne emerged from the alley and swung his head left and right in search of me. In the dim light his heavily streaked face looked almost black. He began lurching toward me.

I raised Father's walking stick, broke the lower pane of the window, and reached in through the jagged shards. If there was a bottom or top bolt I was dead. There was a simple doorknob lock and cross bolt. My fingers slipped on the cold metal, but the bolt slid back as Mr. Thorne stepped up on the walk behind me. Then I was inside and throwing the bolt.

It was very dark. Cold seeped up from the concrete floor and there was the sound of many small boats rising and falling at their moorings. Fifty yards away, light spilled out of the office windows. I had hoped there would be an alarm system, but the building was too old and the marina too cheap to have one. I began to walk toward the light as Mr. Thorne's forearm shattered the remaining glass in the door behind me. The arm withdrew. A tremendous kick broke off the top hinge and splintered wood around the bolt. I glanced at the office, but only the sound of a radio talk show came out of the impossibly distant door. Another kick.

I turned to my right and jumped the three feet to the bow of a bobbing inboard cruiser. Five steps and I was in the small, covered space which passed for a forward cabin. I closed the flimsy access panel behind me and peered out through the streaked Plexiglas.

Mr. Thorne's third kick sent the door flying inward, dangling from long strips of splintered wood. His dark form filled the doorway. Light from a distant streetlight glinted off the blade in his right hand. *Please. Please hear the noise.* But there was no movement from the office, only the metallic voices from the radio. Mr. Thorne took four paces, paused, and stepped down onto the first boat in line. It was an open outboard and he was back up on the concrete in six seconds. The second boat had a small cabin. There was a ripping sound as Mr. Thorne kicked open the tiny hatch door and then he was back up on the walkway. My boat was the eighth in line. I wondered why he couldn't just hear the wild hammering of my heart.

I shifted position and looked through the starboard port. The murky Plexiglas threw the light into streaks and patterns. I caught a brief glimpse of white hair through the window and the radio was switched to another station. Loud music echoed in the long room. I slid back to the other porthole. Mr. Thorne was stepping off the fourth boat.

I closed my eyes, forced my ragged breathing to slow, and tried to remember countless evenings watching a bowlegged old figure shuffle down the street. Mr. Thorne finished his inspection of the fifth boat, a longer cabin cruiser with several dark recesses, and pulled himself back onto the walkway.

Forget the coffee in the thermos. Forget the crossword puzzle. Go look!

The sixth boat was a small outboard. Mr. Thorne glanced at it but did not step onto it. The seventh was a low sailboat, mast folded down, canvas stretched across the cockpit. Mr. Thorne's knife slashed through the thick material. Blood-streaked hands pulled back the canvas like a shroud being torn away. He jumped back to the walkway.

Forget the coffee! Go look! Now!

Mr. Thorne stepped onto the bow of my boat. I felt it rock to his weight. There was nowhere to hide, only a tiny storage locker under the seat, much too small to squeeze into. I untied the canvas strips that held the seat cushions to the bench. The sound of my ragged breathing seemed to echo in the little space. I curled into a fetal position behind the cushion as Mr. Thorne's legs moved past the starboard port. *Now.* Suddenly his face filled the Plexiglas strip not a foot from my head. His impossibly wide grimace grew even wider. *Now.* He stepped into the cockpit.

Now. Now. Now.

Mr. Thorne crouched at the cabin door. I tried to brace the tiny louvred door with my legs, but my right leg would not obey. Mr. Thorne's fist slammed through the thin wooden strips and grabbed my ankle.

"Hey there!"

It was Mr. Hodges's shaky voice. His flashlight bobbed in our direction.

Mr. Thorne shoved against the door. My left leg folded painfully. Mr. Thorne's left hand firmly held my ankle through the shattered slats while the hand with the knife blade came through the opening hatch.

"Hey—" cried Mr. Hodges and then my mind shoved. Very hard. The old man stopped. He dropped the flashlight and unfastened the safety strap over the grip of his revolver.

Mr. Thorne slashed the knife back and forth. The cushion was almost knocked out of my hands as shreds of foam filled the cabin. The blade caught the tip of my little finger as the knife swung back again.

Do it. Now. Do it.

Mr. Hodges gripped the revolver in both hands and fired. The shot went wide in the dark as the sound echoed off concrete and water. *Closer, you fool. Move!* Mr. Thorne shoved again and his body squeezed into the open hatch. He released my ankle to free his left arm, but almost instantly his hand was back in the cabin, grasping for me. I reached up and turned on the overhead light. Darkness stared at me from his empty eye socket. Light through the broken shutters spilled yellow strips across his ruined face. I slid to the left, but Mr. Thorne's hand, which had my coat, was pulling me off the bench. He was on his knees, freeing his right hand for the knife thrust.

Now! Mr. Hodges's second shot caught Mr. Thorne in the right hip. He grunted as the impact shoved him backward into a sitting position. My coat ripped and buttons rattled on the deck.

The knife slashed the bulkhead near my ear before it pulled away.

Mr. Hodges stepped shakily onto the bow, almost fell, and inched his way around the starboard side. I pushed the hatch against Mr. Thorne's arm, but he continued to grip my coat and drag me toward him. I fell to my knees. The blade swung back, ripped through foam, and slashed at my coat. What was left of the cushion flew out of my hands. I had Mr. Hodges stop four feet away and brace the gun on the roof of the cabin.

Mr. Thorne pulled the blade back and poised it like a matador's sword. I could sense the silent screams of triumph that poured out over the stained teeth like a noxious vapor. The light of Nina's madness burned behind the single, staring eye.

Mr. Hodges fired. The bullet severed Mr. Thorne's spine and continued on into the port scupper. Mr. Thorne arched backward, splayed out his arms, and flopped onto the deck like a great fish that had just been landed. The knife fell to the floor of the cabin while stiff, white fingers continued to slap nervelessly against the deck. I had Mr. Hodges step forward, brace the muzzle against Mr. Thorne's temple just above the remaining eye, and fire again. The sound was muted and hollow.

There was a first-aid kit in the office bathroom. I had the old man stand by the door while I bandaged my little finger and took three aspirin.

My coat was ruined and blood had stained my print dress. I had never cared very much for the dress—I thought it made me look dowdy—but the coat had been a favorite of mine. My hair was a mess. Small, moist bits of gray matter flecked it. I splashed water on my face and brushed my hair as best I could. Incredibly, my tattered purse had stayed with me although many of the contents had spilled out. I transferred keys, billfold, reading glasses, and Kleenex to my large coat pocket and dropped the purse behind the toilet. I no longer had Father's walking stick, but I could not remember where I had dropped it.

Gingerly, I removed the heavy revolver from Mr. Hodges's grip. The old man's arm remained extended, fingers curled around air. After fumbling for a few seconds I managed to click open the cylinder. Two unfired cartridges remained. The old fool had been walking around with all six chambers loaded! *Always leave an empty chamber under the hammer.* That is what Charles had taught me that gay and distant summer so long ago when such weapons were merely excuses for trips to the island for target practice punctuated by the shrill shrieks of our nervous laughter as Nina and I allowed ourselves to be held, arms supported, bodies shrinking back into the firm support of our so-serious tutors' arms. *One must always count the cartridges*, lectured Charles as I half swooned against him, smelling the sweet, masculine shaving soap and tobacco smell rising from him on that warm, bright day.

Mr. Hodges stirred slightly as my attention wandered. His mouth gaped open and his dentures hung loosely. I glanced at the worn leather belt, but there were no extra bullets there and I had no idea where he kept any. I probed, but there was little left in the old man's jumble of thoughts except for a swirling, loop-taped replay of the muzzle being laid against Mr. Thorne's temple, the explosion, the . . .

"Come," I said. I adjusted the glasses on Mr. Hodges's vacant face, returned the revolver to the holster, and let him lead me out of the building. It was very dark out. We moved from streetlight to streetlight. We had gone six blocks before the old man's violent shivering reminded me that I had forgotten to have him put on his coat. I tightened my mental vise and he quit shaking.

The house looked just as it had . . . my God . . . only forty-five minutes earlier. There were no lights. I let us into the courtyard and searched my overstuffed coat pocket for the key. My coat hung loose and the cold night air nipped at me. From behind lighted windows across the courtyard came the laughter of little girls and I hurried so that Kathleen would not see her grandfather entering my house. Mr. Hodges went in first with the revolver extended. I had him switch on the light before I entered.

The parlor was empty, undisturbed. The light from the chandelier in the dining room reflected off polished surfaces. I sat down for a minute on the Williamsburg reproduction chair in the hall to let my heart rate return to normal. I did not have Mr. Hodges lower the hammer on the still-raised pistol. His arm began to shake from the strain of holding it. Finally I rose and we moved down the hall toward the conservatory.

Miss Kramer exploded out of the swinging door from the kitchen with the heavy iron poker already coming down in an arc. The gun fired harmlessly into the polished floor as the old man's arm snapped from the impact. The gun fell from limp fingers as Miss Kramer raised the poker for a second blow.

I turned and ran back down the hallway. Behind me I heard the crushed-melon sound of the poker contacting Mr. Hodges's skull. Rather than run into the courtyard I went up the stairway. A mistake. Miss Kramer bounded up the stairs and reached the bedroom door only a few seconds after me. I caught one glimpse of her widened, maddened eyes and of the upraised poker before I slammed and locked the heavy door. The latch clicked just as the brunette on the other side began to throw herself against the wood. The thick oak did not budge. Then I heard the concussion of metal against the door and frame. Again. Again.

Cursing my stupidity I turned to the familiar room, but there was nothing there to help me, not even a telephone. There was not so much as a closet to hide in, only the antique wardrobe. I moved quickly to the window and threw up the sash. My screams would attract attention but not before that monstrosity had gained access. She was prying at the edges of the door now. I looked out, saw the shadows in the window across the way, and did what I had to do.

Two minutes later I was barely conscious of the wood around the latch giving way. I distantly heard the grating of the poker as it pried away the recalcitrant metal plate. The door swung inward.

Miss Kramer was covered with sweat. Her mouth hung slack and drool slid from her chin. Her eyes were not human. Neither she nor I heard the soft tread of sneakers on the stair behind her.

Keep moving. Lift it. Pull it back—all the way back. Use both hands. Aim it.

Something warned Miss Kramer. Warned Nina, I should say, for there was no more Miss Kramer. The brunette turned to see little Kathleen standing on the top stair, her grandfather's heavy weapon aimed and cocked. The other girl was in the courtyard shouting for her friend.

This time Nina knew she had to deal with the threat. Miss Kramer hefted the poker and turned into the hall just as the pistol fired. The recoil tumbled Kathleen backward down the stairs as a red corsage blossomed above Miss Kramer's left breast. She spun but grasped the railing with her left hand and lurched down the stairs after the child. I released the ten-year-old just as the poker fell, rose, fell again. I moved to the head of the stairway. I had to *see.*

Miss Kramer looked up from her grim work. Only the whites of her eyes were visible in her spattered face. Her masculine shirt was soaked with her own blood but still she moved, functioned. She picked up the gun in her left hand. Her mouth opened wider and a sound emerged like steam leaking from an old radiator.

"Melanie . . . Melanie . . ." I closed my eyes as the thing started up the stairs for me.

Kathleen's friend came in through the open door with her small legs pumping. She took the stairs in six jumps and wrapped her thin, white arms around Miss Kramer's neck in a tight embrace. The two went over backward, across Kathleen, all the way down the wide stairs to the polished wood below.

The girl appeared to be little more than bruised. I went down and moved her to one side. A blue stain was spreading along one cheekbone and there were cuts on her arms and forehead. Her blue eyes blinked uncomprehendingly.

Miss Kramer's neck was broken. I picked up the pistol on the way to her and kicked the poker to one side. Her head was at an impossible angle, but she was still alive. Her body was paralyzed, urine already stained the wood, but her eyes still blinked and her teeth clicked together obscenely. I had to hurry. There were adult voices calling from the Hodges's town house. The door to the courtyard was wide open. I turned to the girl. "Get up." She blinked once and rose painfully to her feet.

I shut the door and lifted a tan raincoat from the coatrack. It took only a minute to transfer the contents of my pockets to the raincoat and to discard my ruined spring coat. Voices were calling in the courtyard now.

I kneeled down next to Miss Kramer and seized her face in my hands, exerting strong pressure to keep the jaws still. Her eyes had rolled upward again, but I roughly shook her head until the irises were visible. I leaned forward until our cheeks were touching. My whisper was louder than a shout.

"I'm coming for you, Nina."

I dropped her head onto the wood and walked quickly to the conservatory, my sewing room. I did not have time to get the key from upstairs so I raised a Windsor side chair and smashed the glass of the cabinet. My coat pocket was barely large enough.

The girl remained standing in the hall. I handed her Mr. Hodges's pistol. Her left arm hung at a strange angle and I wondered if she had broken something after all. There was a knock at the door and someone tried the knob.

"This way," I whispered and led the girl into the dining room. We stepped across Miss Kramer on the way, walked through the dark kitchen as the pounding grew louder, and then were out, into the alley, into the night.

There were three hotels in this part of the Old Section. One was an expensive but modern motor hotel some ten blocks away, comfortable but commercial. I rejected it immediately. The second was a small but homey lodging house only a block from my home. It was a pleasant but nonexclusive little place, exactly the type I would choose when visiting another town. I rejected it also. The third was two and a half blocks farther on, an old Broad Street mansion, done over into a small hotel, expensive antiques in every room, absurdly overpriced. I hurried there. The girl moved quickly at my side. The pistol was still in her hand, but I had her remove her sweater and carry it over the weapon. My leg ached and I frequently leaned on the girl as we hurried down the street.

The manager of the Mansard House recognized me. His eyebrow went up a fraction of an inch as he noticed my disheveled appearance. The girl stood ten feet away in the foyer, half hidden in the shadows.

"I'm looking for a friend of mine," I said brightly. "A Mrs. Drayton."

The manager started to speak, paused, frowned without being aware of it, and tried again. "I'm sorry. No one under that name is registered here."

"Perhaps she registered under her maiden name," I said. "Nina Hawkins. She's an older woman but very attractive. A few years younger than me. Long gray hair. Her friend may have registered for her . . . an attractive young, dark-haired lady named Barrett Kramer . . ."

"No, I'm sorry," said the manager in a strangely flat tone. "No one under that name has registered here. Would you like to leave a message in case your party does arrive later?"

"No," I said. "No message."

I brought the girl into the lobby and we turned down a corridor leading to the rest rooms and side stairs. "Excuse me, please," I said to a passing porter. "Perhaps you can help me."

"Yes, ma'am." He stopped, annoyed, brushed back his long hair. It would be tricky. If I was not to lose the girl I would have to act quickly.

"I'm looking for a friend," I said. "An older lady but quite attractive. Blue eyes. Long gray hair. She travels with a young woman with dark, curly hair."

"No, ma'am. No one like that is registered here."

I reached out and took his forearm. I released that girl and focused on the boy. "Are you sure?"

"Mrs. Harrison," he said. His eyes looked past me. "Room 207. North front."

I smiled. *Mrs. Harrison*. Good God, what a fool Nina was. Suddenly the girl let out a small whimper and slumped against the wall. I made a quick decision. I like to think that it was compassion, but I sometimes remember that her left arm was useless.

"What's your name?" I asked the child, gently stroking her bangs. Her eyes moved left and right in confusion. "Your *name*," I prompted.

"Alicia." It was only a whisper.

"All right, Alicia. I want you to go home now. Hurry but don't run."

"My *arm* hurts," she said. Her lips began to quiver. I touched her forehead again and *pushed*.

"You're going home," I said. "Your arm does not hurt. You won't remember anything. This is like a dream that you will forget. Go home. Hurry but do not run." I took the pistol from her but left it wrapped in the sweater. "Bye, bye, Alicia."

She blinked and crossed the lobby to the doors. I looked both ways and handed the gun to the bellhop. "Put it under your vest," I said.

"Who is it?" Nina's voice was light.

"Albert, ma'am. The porter. Your car's out front and I'm ready to carry your bags down."

There was the sound of a lock clicking and the door opened the width of a still-secured chain. Albert blinked in the glare and smiled shyly, brushed his hair back. I pressed against the wall.

"Very well." She undid the chain and moved back. She had already turned and was latching her suitcase when I stepped into the room.

"Hello, Nina," I said softly. Her back straightened, but even that move was graceful. I could see the imprint on the bedspread where she had been lying. She turned slowly. She was wearing a pink dress I had never seen before.

"Hello, Melanie." She smiled. Her eyes were the softest, purest blue I had ever seen. I had the porter bring Mr. Hodges's gun out and aim it. His arm was steady. He pulled back the hammer until it locked in place. Nina folded her hands in front of her. Her eyes never left mine.

"Why?" I asked.

Nina shrugged ever so slightly. For a second I thought she was going to laugh. I could not have borne it had she laughed—that husky, childlike laugh which had touched me so many times. Instead she closed her eyes. Her smile remained.

"Why Mrs. Harrison?" I asked.

"Why, darling, I felt I owed him *something*. I mean, poor Roger. Did I ever tell you how he died? No, of course I didn't. And you never asked, Melanie dear." Her eyes opened. I glanced at the porter, but his aim was steady. It remained for him only to exert a little more pressure on the trigger.

"He *drowned*, darling," said Nina. "Poor Roger threw himself from that steamship—what was its name?—the one that was taking him back to England. So strange. And he had just written me a letter promising marriage. Isn't that a *terribly* sad story, Melanie? Why do you think he did a thing like that? I guess we'll never know, will we?"

"I guess we never will," I said. I silently ordered the porter to pull the trigger.

Nothing.

I looked quickly to my right. The young man's head was turning toward me. *I had not made him do that.* The stiffly extended arm began to swing my direction. The pistol moved smoothly like the tip of a weathervane swinging in the wind.

No! I strained until the cords in my neck stood out. The turning slowed but did not stop until the muzzle was pointing at my face. Nina laughed now. The sound was very loud in the little room.

"Good-bye, Melanie *dear*," said Nina and laughed again. She laughed and nodded at the porter. I stared into the black hole as the hammer fell.

On an empty chamber. And another. And another.

"Good-bye, Nina," I said as I pulled Charles's long pistol from my raincoat pocket. The explosion jarred my wrist and filled the room with blue smoke. A small hole, smaller than a dime but as perfectly round, appeared in the precise center of Nina's forehead. For the briefest second she remained standing as if nothing had happened. Then she fell backward, recoiled from the high bed, and dropped face forward onto the floor.

I turned to the porter and replaced his useless weapon with the ancient but well-maintained revolver. For the first time I noticed that the boy was not much younger than Charles had been. His hair was almost exactly the same color. I leaned forward and kissed him lightly on the lips.

"Albert," I whispered, "there are four cartridges left. One must always count the cartridges, mustn't one? Go to the lobby. Kill the manager. Shoot one other person, the nearest. Put the barrel in your mouth and pull the trigger. If it misfires, pull it again. Keep the gun concealed until you are in the lobby."

We emerged into general confusion in the hallway.

"Call for an ambulance!" I cried. "There's been an accident. Someone call for an ambulance!" Several people rushed to comply. I swooned and leaned against a white-haired gentleman. People milled around, some peering into the room and exclaiming. Suddenly there was the sound of three gunshots from the lobby. In the renewed confusion I slipped down the back stairs, out the fire door, into the night.

FOUR

Charleston
Tuesday, Dec. 16, 1980

Sheriff Bobby Joe Gentry rocked back in his chair and took another sip from his can of RC Cola. His feet were propped up on his cluttered desk and the leather of his gunbelt creaked as he settled his considerable bulk more comfortably into his chair. The office was small, enclosed by a cinderblock wall and by ancient wooden partitions which separated it from the noise and bustle of the rest of the County Building. The paint peeling from the old wood was a different shade of institutional green than the paint peeling from the rough cinderblock. The office was filled to overflowing with sheriff's massive desk, three tall file cabinets, a long table stacked with books and folders, a blackboard, cluttered shelves hung on wall brackets, and two dark, wooden chairs as littered with files and loose papers as the desk.

"I don't believe there's much more I can do down here," said Agent Richard Haines. The FBI man had cleared away some folders and was perched on the edge of the table. The crease along his gray trouser leg was knife-sharp.

"Nope," agreed Sheriff Gentry. He belched softly and rested the soft drink can on his knee. "I don't reckon there is much reason to hang around. Might as well head home."

The two law enforcement officers seemed to have little in common. Gentry was only in his mid-thirties, but his tall frame was already sagging to fat. His belly strained at his gray uniform shirt and hung down over his belt as if conforming to some cartoon caricature. His face was florid and faintly freckled. Despite the receding hairline and double chin, Gentry had the open, friendly, vaguely mischievous sort of look in which the outline of the boy was still visible in the face of the man.

Sheriff Gentry's voice was soft and set into a good-old-boy drawl that had recently become more familiar to Americans through a proliferation of thousands of CB radios, countless country-western songs, and a seemingly endless series of Burt Reynolds drive-in features. Gentry's open shirt, straining belly, and lazy drawl matched the general sense of amiable sloppiness suggested by his cluttered office, but there was a quick lightness, almost a grace, to the large man's movements which did not fit the image.

Special Agent Richard M. Haines of the Federal Bureau of Investigation was more consistent in looks and temperament. Haines was a good decade older than Gentry, but he looked younger. He wore a light gray, three-piece summer suit and beige shirt from Jos. A. Bank. His burgundy, silk foulard tie was number 280235 from the same catalog. His hair was cut moderately short, carefully combed, with only a trace of gray showing at the temples. Haines had a square, sober, regularly featured face to match his lean physique. He worked out four times a week to keep his belly flat and firm. His voice was also flat and firm, deep but unaccented. It was as if the late J. Edgar Hoover had designed Haines as a mold for all of his agents.

There was more than a difference in appearance separating the two men. Richard Haines had put in three years of mediocre undergraduate work at Georgetown University before he had been recruited for the Bureau. His FBI training had completed his education.

Bobby Joe Gentry had graduated from Duke University with dual art and history majors before going on to Northwestern to receive a Master's degree in history. Gentry had been introduced to police work through his Uncle Lee, a county sheriff near Spartanburg, who hired Bobby Joe as a part-time deputy in the summer of 1967. A year later Bobby Joe received his Master's degree and sat in a Chicago park and watched the police rage out of control, clubbing and beating antiwar demonstrators who had been dispersing peacefully.

Gentry returned home to the South, spent two years teaching at Morehouse College in Atlanta, and then took a job as a security guard while working on a book about the Freedman's Bureau and its role during Reconstruction. The book was never finished, but Gentry found himself enjoying the routine security work although it was a constant problem to keep his weight within required limits. In 1976 he moved to Charleston and joined the police force as a patrol officer. A year later he turned down an offer to fill in for a year as an associate professor of history at Duke. Gentry enjoyed the routine of police work, the daily contacts with drunks and crazies, and the sense that no day on the job was quite like any other. A year later he surprised himself by running for sheriff of Charleston County. He proceeded to surprise quite a few other people by being elected. A local columnist wrote that Charleston was a strange town, a town in love with its own history, and that the thought of an historian serving as sheriff had caught the public imagination. Gentry did not consider himself an historian. He considered himself a cop.

". . . if you won't be needing me then," said Haines.

"Mmmhh? What's that?" asked Gentry. His attention had wandered. He crushed the empty can and tossed it into the wastebasket, where it struck other crumpled cans and rebounded to the floor.

"I said I thought I'd check with Gallagher and then fly back to Washington tonight if you won't be needing me. We'll be in touch through Terry and the FAA team."

"Yeah, sure," said Gentry. "Well, we sure do appreciate your help, Dick. You 'n' Terry know more about this stuff than our whole department put together."

Haines rose to leave just as the sheriff's secretary stuck her head in the door. The woman had a hairdo twenty years out of date and rhinestone glasses on a chain. "Sheriff, that New York psychiatrist fellow is here."

"Shoot, I damn near forgot," said Gentry and struggled to his feet. "Thanks, Linda Mae. Tell him to come in, would you please?"

Haines moved toward the door. "Well, Sheriff, you have my number if anything . . ."

"Dick, would you-all do me a favor and sit in on this? I forgot this fellow was coming, but he may give us some information on the Fuller thing. He called yesterday. Said he was Mrs. Drayton's psychiatrist, was in town on a business trip. Would you mind waitin' a few more minutes? I could have Tommy run you over to the motel in one of the units after if you got to hurry to catch a plane or something."

Haines smiled and held his hand palm outward. "No hurry, Sheriff. Be happy to hear what the psychiatrist has to say." The FBI agent moved to one of the two chairs and lifted a white McDonald's bag out of the way.

"Thanks, Dick, really 'preciate it," said Gentry and mopped his face. He walked to the door just as there was a knock and a small, bearded man in a corduroy sports coat entered.

"Sheriff Gentry?" The psychiatrist pronounced the name with a hard "G."

"I'm Bobby Joe Gentry." The sheriff's huge hands closed around the other man's proferred hand. "You're Dr. Laski, right?"

"Saul Laski." The psychiatrist was of normal height but seemed dwarfed next to Gentry's bulk. He was a thin man with a high, pale brow, a salt and pepper tangle of beard, and sad, brown eyes that seemed older than the rest of him. His glasses were held together by a strip of masking tape on one hinge.

"This here's Special Agent Richard Haines of the Federal Bureau of Investigation," said Gentry with a wave. "Hope you don't mind, I asked Dick to be here. He was visitin' anyway and I figured he could probably ask more intelligent questions 'n I could."

The psychiatrist nodded at Haines. "I did not know that the Bureau became involved in local murders," said Laski. His voice was soft, the English accented only slightly, the syntax and pronunciation carefully controlled.

"Normally we don't," said Haines. "However, there are several factors in . . . ah . . . this situation which . . . ah . . . might fall under the Bureau's mandate."

"Oh? How so?" asked Laski.

Haines crossed his arms and cleared his throat. "Kidnapping for one,

Doctor. Also, the violation of one or more of the victims' civil rights. Also, we are offering the aid of our forensic experts to the local law enforcement agencies."

"And Dick's down here 'cause of that plane that got blown to bits," said Gentry. "Hey, sit down, Doctor. Sit down. Here, let me move that crap." He transferred some magazines, folders, and Styrofoam coffee cups to the table and went around to his own chair. "Now, you said on the phone yesterday that you might be able to help in this multiple murder business."

"The New York tabloids are calling it the Mansard House Murders," said Laski. He absently pushed his glasses up on the bridge of his nose.

"Yeah?" said Gentry. "Well, hell, that's better 'n the Charleston Massacre, I guess, though it isn't too accurate. Most of the folks weren't even *in* the Mansard House. I still think it's an awful lot of noise about nine people gettin' killed. I imagine that more 'n that get shot on a slow night in New York."

"Yes, perhaps," said Laski, "but the range of victims and murder suspects is not as . . . ah . . . fascinating as in this instance."

"You got me there," said Gentry. "We'd sure 'preciate it if you could shed some light on this mess, Doctor Laski."

"I would be very pleased to help. Unfortunately, I have little to offer."

"You were Mrs. Drayton's psychiatrist?" asked Haines.

"Ah yes, in a manner of speaking." Saul Laski paused and tugged at his beard. His eyes seemed very large and heavy-lidded, as if he had not slept well for a long time. "I have seen Mrs. Drayton only three times, the last time in September. She came up to me after a talk I gave at Columbia in August. We had two . . . ah . . . sessions after that."

"But she *was* a patient of yours?" Haines's voice had taken on the flat insistence of a prosecuting attorney.

"Technically, yes," said Laski. "However, I do not actually have a practice. I teach at Columbia, you see, and occasionally do consulting work at the clinic there . . . students that the resident psychologist, Ellen Hightower, feels would benefit by seeing a psychiatrist. And the occasional faculty member . . ."

"So Mrs. Drayton was a *student?*"

"No. No, I do not believe so," said Laski. "She occasionally audited a few graduate courses and attended the evening seminars, such as mine. She . . . ah . . . she expressed interest in a book I had written . . ."

"*The Pathology of Violence,*" said Sheriff Gentry.

Laski blinked and adjusted his glasses. "I do not remember mentioning the title of my book when I spoke to you yesterday, Sheriff Gentry."

Gentry folded his hands on his stomach and grinned. "You didn't, Professor. I read it last spring. Read it twice, to tell the truth. I didn't recognize your name until just now. I think it's a goddamned brilliant book. You oughtta read it, Dick."

"I am amazed you found a copy," said the psychiatrist. He swiveled toward the FBI agent. "It is a rather pedantic view of certain case histories. Only two thousand copies are printed. By Academy Press. Most of the copies sold were used in courses in New York and California."

"Dr. Laski thinks that some people are receptive to . . . what did you call it, sir? A climate of violence. That's it, isn't it?" asked Gentry.

"Yes."

"And that other people . . . or places . . . or times . . . sort of program these receptive folks into behaving in ways that otherwise would be unthinkable to them. 'Course that's just my simple-minded synopsis."

Laski blinked again at the sheriff. "A very astute synopsis," he said.

Haines stood and walked over to lean against a file cabinet. He crossed his arms and frowned slightly. "Wait a minute, we're getting lost here. So Mrs. Drayton came to you . . . was interested in this book . . . and then became your patient. Right?"

"I agreed to meet with her in a professional capacity, yes."

"And did you also have a personal relationship with her?"

"No," said Laski. "I met her only three times. Once for a few minutes after my talk on violence in the Third Reich and twice more—two one-hour sessions—at the clinic."

"I see," said Haines, although from his voice it was clear that he did not, "and you think that there was something that came out of these sessions that can help us clear up the current situation?"

"No," said Laski. "I am afraid not. Without breaking confidentiality, I can say that Mrs. Drayton had concerns about her relationship with her father, who died many years ago. I see nothing in our discussions that might shed light on the details of her murder."

"Mmmm," said Haines and returned to his chair. He glanced at his watch.

Gentry smiled and opened the door. "Linda Mae! Darling, would you bring us some coffee? Thank ya, darling."

"Doctor Laski, you may be aware that we are aware of who murdered your patient," said Haines. "What we lack at the moment is a motive."

"Ah yes," said Laski. He brushed at his beard. "It was a local young man, was it not?"

"Albert LaFollette," said Gentry. "He was a nineteen-year-old bellhop down to the hotel."

"And there is no doubt about his involvement?"

"Not a whole hell of a lot," said Gentry. "According to five witnesses we got, Albert came out of the elevator, walked over to the counter, and shot his boss, Kyle Anderson, he was manager of the Mansard House, shot his boss in the heart. Put the revolver right up to the man's chest. We got the powder burns on the suit. The boy was carryin' a Colt. 45 single action. No cheap reproduction, either, Doctor, but a real, genuine, serial-number-from-Mr.-Colt's-factory *pistola*. A real antique. So the kid sets this piece against Kyle's chest and pulls the trigger. Doesn't say anything according to our witnesses. Then he turns and shoots Leonard Whitney square in the face."

"Who is Mr. Whitney?" asked the psychiatrist.

It was Haines who cleared his throat and answered. "Leonard Whitney was a visiting businessman from Atlanta. He had just come out of the hotel's restaurant when he was shot. As far as we can tell, he had no connection to any of the other victims."

"Yeah," said Gentry. "So then young Albert puts the gun in his own mouth and squeezes the trigger. None of our five witnesses did a damn thing to interfere with any of this. 'Course, it was over in a few seconds."

"And this was the same weapon used to kill Mrs. Drayton."

"Yup."

"Were there witnesses to that shooting?"

"Not quite," said Gentry. "But a couple of folks saw Albert get onto the elevator. They remember him because he was headin' away from the room where the shouting was coming from. Someone'd just discovered Mrs. Drayton after the shooting. Funny thing, though, none of the folks remember seeing the revolver in the boy's hand. That's not unusual, though. You could probably carry a hog leg into a crowd 'n' no one'd take notice."

"Who was it that first saw Mrs. Drayton's body?"

"We're not sure," said the sheriff. "There was a lot of confusion up there and then the fun began in the lobby."

"Doctor Laski," said Haines, "if you cannot help us with any information about Mrs. Drayton, I'm not sure how useful all of this is." The FBI agent was obviously ready to terminate the interview, but he was interrupted by the secretary who bustled in with coffee. Haines set his Styrofoam cup on the file cabinet. Laski smiled gratefully and sipped at the lukewarm brew. Gentry's coffee came in a large white mug that said BOSS on the side. "Thank you, Linda Mae."

Laski shrugged slightly. "I wished only to offer any help that I could," he said softly. "I realize that you gentlemen are extraordinarily busy. I will not take up any more of your time." He set the coffee cup on the desk and rose to his feet.

"Whoa!" cried Bobby Joe Gentry. "Since you're here, I want to get your ideas on a coupla things." He turned to Haines. "The professor here was a consultant for the NYPD during that Son-of-Sam stuff a coupla years ago."

"Just one of many," said Laski. "We helped to put together a personality profile on the murderer. In the end, that was largely irrelevant. The killer was apprehended through fairly straightforward police work."

"Yeah," said Gentry. "But you wrote a book on this kind of mass murder stuff. Dick an' me sure'd like your opinion on this mess." He rose and walked over to a long chalkboard. There was a piece of brown wrapping paper attached with masking tape. Gentry flipped up the paper to reveal a board covered with chalky diagrams and scrawled names and times. "You probably read about the rest of our little cast of characters here."

"Some," said Laski. "The New York papers gave special attention to Nina Drayton, the little girl, and her grandfather."

"Yes, Kathy," said Gentry. He rubbed a knuckle on the board next to her name. "Kathleen Marie Eliot. Ten years old. I saw her fourth grade school picture yesterday. Cute. Lot nicer to look at than the crime scene photos over in the file there." Gentry paused and rubbed at his cheeks. Laski took another sip of coffee and waited. "We got four basic scenes here," said the sheriff and tapped at a street diagram. "One citizen killed here in broad daylight on Calhoun Street. Another one dead here a block or so away in the Battery Marina. Three bodies in the Fuller residence here . . ." He tapped at a neat little square in which three "X's" clustered together. "And our grand finale with four dead here at the Mansard House."

"Is there a common thread?" asked Laski.

"That's the hell of it," sighed Gentry. "There is and there ain't, if you take my meaning." He waved at the column of names. "Mr. Preston here, he's the black gentleman found slashed to death on Calhoun, he's been a local photographer and merchant in the Old Section for twenty-six years. We're working under the assumption that he was an innocent bystander, killed by the next corpse we got here . . ."

"Karl Thorne," Laski read from the list.

"The missing woman's servant," said Haines.

"Yeah," said Gentry, "but despite what was on his driver's license, his name wasn't Thorne. Or Karl. Fingerprint identification we got back from InterPol today says that he used to be known as Oscar Felix Haupt, a cheap little Swiss hotel thief. He disappeared from Berne in 1953."

"Good heavens," muttered the psychiatrist, "do they usually keep fingerprints of ex-hotel thieves on file for so long?"

"Haupt was more than that," interjected Haines. "It seems that he was the prime suspect in a rather lurid 1953 murder case involving a French baron visiting a spa. Haupt disappeared shortly after that. The Swiss police thought at the time that Haupt had been murdered, probably by European syndicate types."

"Guess they were wrong," said Sheriff Gentry.

"What made you query InterPol?" asked Laski.

"Just a hunch," said Gentry and looked back at the chalkboard. "OK, we got Karl Oscar Felix Thorne-Haupt dead here at the marina and if the craziness had stopped there we could've cobbled together some motive . . . boat theft, maybe . . . the bullet in Haupt's brain came from the night watchman's gun, a thirty-eight. Problem is, Haupt was all beat to hell besides being shot twice. There were two kinds of bloodstains on his clothes, besides his own, I mean, and samples of skin and tissue under his fingernails that pretty well cinches that he was Mr. Preston's assailant."

"Most confusing," said Saul Laski.

"Ah, Professor, you ain't seen nothin' yet." Gentry rapped his knuckles next to three more names: Barrett Kramer, George Hodges, Kathleen Marie Eliot. "You know this lady, Professor?"

"Barrett Kramer?" echoed Laski. "No. I read her name in the paper, but other than that I don't recognize it."

"Ah, well. Worth a try. She was Mrs. Drayton's traveling companion. 'Executive assistant,' I think the New York people who claimed Mrs. Drayton's body called her. Woman in her mid-thirties. Brunette. Sort of a muscular build?"

"No," said Laski, "I do not remember her. She did not come with Mrs. Drayton to either of the sessions. She may have been at my lecture on the evening I met Mrs. Drayton, but I did not notice her."

"Hokay. Well, we got Miss Kramer who was shot by Mr. Hodges's S&W thirty-eight. Only the coroner's pretty sure that that didn't kill her. She appears to have broken her neck in a fall down the stairs at the Fuller house. She was still breathin' when the paramedics got there but was pronounced dead at Emergency. No brain waves or something.

"Now, the damn thing is, forensic evidence suggests that poor old Mr. Hodges didn't even shoot the lady. He was found *here*"—Gentry tapped another diagram—"in the hallway of the Fuller house. His revolver was found *here*, on the floor of Mrs. Drayton's room at Mansard House. So what do we have here? Eight victims, nine if you count Albert LaFollette, five weapons . . ."

"Five weapons?" asked Laski. "Excuse me, Sheriff. I did not mean to interrupt."

"No, hell, that's OK. Yeah, five weapons that we know about. The old forty-five that Albert used, Hodges's thirty-eight, a knife found near Haupt's body, and a goddamned fireplace poker that the Kramer woman used to kill the little girl."

"Barrett *Kramer* used to kill the little girl?"

"Uh-huh. At least her fingerprints were all over the goddamned thing and the girl's blood was all over Kramer."

"That is still only four weapons," said Laski.

"Umm, oh, yeah, there's also a wooden walking stick we found at the back door of the marina. There was blood on it."

Saul Laski shook his head and looked over at Richard Haines. The agent had his arms crossed and was staring at the chalkboard. He looked very tired and very disgusted.

"A real can of worms, huh, Professor?" finished Gentry. He walked back to his chair and collapsed into it with a sigh. He leaned back and took a sip of cold coffee from the large mug. "Any theories?"

Laski smiled ruefully and shook his head. He stared intently at the chalkboard as if trying to memorize the information there. After a minute he scratched at his beard and said softly, "No theories, I am afraid, Sheriff. But I do have to ask the obvious question."

"What's that?"

"Where is Mrs. Fuller? The lady whose house was the scene of such carnage?"

"*Miz* Fuller," corrected Gentry. "From what the neighbors tell us, she was one of Charleston's grand old spinsters. And that title of Miz has been used around here for almost two hundred years, Professor. And to answer your question—there's no sign of Miz Melanie Fuller. There was one report that an unidentified older woman was seen in the upstairs hall at the hotel right after the shooting of Mrs. Drayton, but no one's confirmed that it was Miz Fuller. We have a three-state alert out for the lady, but not a word so far."

"She would seem to be the key," suggested Laski diffidently.

"Uh-huh. Maybe. Then again, her torn-up purse was found stuffed behind the toilet down at the Battery Marina. Bloodstains on it matched those on Karl-Oscar's made-in-Paris switchblade."

"My God," breathed the psychiatrist. "There's no sense to it."

There was a moment of silence and then Haines stood. "Perhaps it is simpler than it appears," he said and tugged at his cuffs. "Mrs. Drayton was visiting Mrs. Fuller . . . excuse me, Miz Fuller . . . the day before the murders. Fingerprints in the house confirm that she was there and a neighbor saw her enter on Friday evening. Mrs. Drayton had the poor judgment to hire this Barrett Kramer as an assistant. Kramer was wanted in Philadelphia and Baltimore for charges dating back to 1968."

"What kind of charges?" asked Laski.

"Vice and narcotics," snapped the agent. "So somehow Miss Kramer and Fuller's man—this Thorne—meet to plot against their elderly employers. After all, Mrs. Drayton's estate is said to come to almost two million dollars and Mrs. Fuller had a healthy bank account here in Charleston."

"But how could they have . . ." began the psychiatrist.

"Just a minute. So Kramer and Thorne—Haupt, whatever—murder your Mrs. Fuller and dispose of her body . . . the harbor patrol is searching the bay right now. Only her neighbor, the old security guard, interrupts their plans. He shoots Haupt and returns to the Fuller home only to encounter Kramer there. The old man's granddaughter sees him across the courtyard and rushes over in time to become a victim with him. Albert LaFollette, another conspirator, panics when Kramer and Haupt don't show up, kills Mrs. Drayton, and runs amok."

Gentry pivoted back and forth in his chair, his hands clasped over his stomach. He was smiling slightly. "What about Joseph Preston, the photographer?"

"As you said, an innocent bystander," replied Haines. "He may have seen where Haupt dumped the old lady's body. There's no doubt that the kraut killed him. The skin and tissue samples under Preston's fingernails match up perfectly with the claw marks on Haupt's face. What was left of Haupt's face."

"Yeah, what about his eye?" asked Gentry.

"His eye? Whose eye?" The psychiatrist looked from the sheriff to the FBI man.

"Haupt's," answered Gentry. "It's missing. Someone did a job on the left side of his face with a club."

Haines shrugged. "It's still the only scenario that makes any sense. We have two employees, ex-felons, who work for two rich old ladies. Their attempted kidnapping or murder or whatever backfires and ends up as a chain of killings."

"Yeah," said Gentry. "Maybe."

In the silence that followed, Saul Laski could hear laughter from the other offices in the County Building. Somewhere outside a siren howled and then fell into silence.

"What do you think, Professor? Any other ideas?" asked Gentry.

Saul Laski slowly shook his head. "I find it most baffling."

"What about the idea in your book of a 'resonance of violence'?" asked Gentry.

"Mmmm," said Laski, "this was not exactly the kind of situation I had in mind. There certainly appears to be a chain of violence, but I fail to see the catalyst."

"Catalyst?" repeated Haines. "What the hell are we talking about here?"

Gentry set his feet up on the desk and mopped at his neck with a red bandanna. "Dr. Laski's book talked about situations that program people into murder."

"I don't get it," said Haines. "What do you mean, 'program'? You mean that old liberal argument about poverty and social conditions causing crime?" It was apparent by the tone of the agent's voice what he thought of that point of view.

"Not at all," said Laski. "It was my hypothesis that there are some situations, conditions, institutions, even individuals, which set up a stress response in others that will culminate in violence, even homicide, when there seems to be no immediate causal relationship."

The FBI agent frowned. "I still don't get it."

"Hell," said Sheriff Gentry, "you seen our holding tank back there, Dick? No? Jeez, you gotta look into it before you leave. We painted it pink last August. We call it the Pepto-Bismol Hilton. But the damned thing works. Violent incidents have been down about sixty percent since we slopped that paint on and we haven't exactly been getting a better brand of clientele. Of course, that's sort of the opposite of what you're talking about, isn't it, Professor?"

Laski adjusted his glasses. As he raised his hand, Gentry caught a glimpse of faded blue numbers tattooed on his forearm just above the wrist. "Yes, but aspects of the same theory may apply," said the psychiatrist. "Color-environment studies have shown measurable attitudinal and behavioral changes in subjects. The reasons for the decrease in violent incidents in such an environment are vague, at best, but the empirical data stand . . . as you yourself attested, Sheriff . . . and seem to imply a modification of psycho-physiological response simply through altering the color variable. My thesis suggests that some of the less comprehensible incidents of violent crime are the result of a more complex series of stimulus factors."

"Uh-huh," said Haines. He glanced at his watch and looked at Gentry. The sheriff was sitting comfortably with his feet propped on his desk. Irritated, Haines brushed imaginary lint from his gray slacks. "I'm afraid I don't see how this can help us, Dr. Laski," said the agent. "Sheriff Gentry is dealing with a messy series of murders here, not some lab mice that will run through a maze for him."

Laski nodded and shrugged slightly. "I was visiting," he said. "I decided to tell the sheriff of my association with Mrs. Drayton and to offer any assistance I could give. I realize that I must be taking up precious time of yours. Thank you for the coffee, Sheriff."

The psychiatrist stood and moved toward the door.

"Thanks for your help, Professor," said Gentry and blew his nose into his red handkerchief. He rubbed the cloth back and forth as if to scratch an itch. "Oh, there is one other question I meant to ask."

Laski turned with one hand on the doorknob and waited.

"Dr. Laski, do you think that these murders might have been the result of some quarrel between the old ladies—Nina Drayton and Melanie Fuller, I mean? Could they possibly have set this whole thing in motion?"

Laski's face was without expression. The sad eyes blinked. "It's possible, but that does not explain the murders at the Mansard House, does it?" he said.

"No, no it sure doesn't," agreed Gentry and took a final swipe at his nose with the handkerchief. "All right. Well, thanks, Professor. We surely appreciate your checkin' in with us. If you remember anything else about Mrs. Drayton that might give us a lead into the why's and wherefore's of this mess, please give us a call, collect, OK?"

"Certainly," said the psychiatrist. "Good luck, gentlemen."

Haines waited until the door was closed. "We should run a check on Laski," he said.

"Mmm," said Gentry. He was holding his empty coffee mug and turning it slowly in his hands. "Already did. He's who he says he is, all right."

Haines blinked. "You checked up on him *before* he came in today?"

Gentry grinned and set the mug down. "After his call yesterday. I mean, it's not like we got so many suspects that I'd be wastin' my time making a phone call to New York."

"I'll have the Bureau check his whereabouts for the period commencing with . . ."

"Giving a lecture at Columbia," interrupted Gentry. "Saturday night. Was part of a public forum on street violence. There was a reception afterward that lasted 'til after eleven. I talked to the dean."

"Nonetheless," said Haines, "I'll check his file. The part about Nina Drayton coming to him for therapy just didn't ring true."

"Yeah," said Gentry, "I'd appreciate it if you'd do that, Dick."

The FBI man picked up his raincoat and briefcase. He paused when he looked at the sheriff. Gentry's hands were clasped so tightly together that the fingers were white. There was anger approaching rage in the usually jovial blue eyes. Gentry looked up at him.

"Dick, I'm going to need all the help I can get on this thing."

"Of course."

"I mean it," said Gentry and lifted a pencil with both hands. "Nobody gets away with committing nine goddamn murders in my county. Somebody set this shit into motion and I'm going to find out who."

"Yes," said Haines.

"I'm going to find out who," continued Gentry. He looked up. His eyes were cold. The pencil snapped in his fingers without him noticing. "And then I'm going to get them, Dick. I will. I swear I will."

Haines nodded, said good-bye, and left. Gentry stared for a long time at the green door after the FBI man was gone. Eventually he looked down at the splintered pencil in his hand. He did not smile. Slowly, carefully, he proceeded to snap the pencil into smaller and smaller fragments.

Haines took a cab to his hotel, packed, paid his bill, and took the same cab to Charleston International Airport. He was early. After checking his luggage, he strolled up and down the concourse, bought a *Newsweek*, and passed up several kiosk phone stands to stop finally at a series of phone booths set back in a side corridor. He punched in a number with a Washington area code.

"The number you have reached is temporarily out of service," said a recorded woman's voice. "Please try again or contact a Bell area service representative."

"Haines, Richard M.," said the FBI man. He glanced over his shoulder as a woman and child passed on their way to the rest room. "Coventry. Cable. I was trying to reach 779–491."

There was a click, a slight buzz, and then the hum of another recording device. "This office is closed for inventory until further notice. If you wish to leave a message, please wait until the tone. There is no time limit." There was a half minute of silence followed by a soft chime.

"This is Haines. I'm just leaving Charleston. A psychiatrist named Saul Laski showed up today to talk to Gentry. Laski says that he works at Columbia. He wrote a book called the *Pathology of Violence*. Academy Press. He says that he met three times with Nina Drayton in New York.

He denies knowing Barrett Kramer, but he may be lying. Laski has a concentration camp tattoo on his arm. Serial number 4490182.

"Also, Gentry ran a make on Karl Thorne and knows that he was really a Swiss thief named Oscar Felix Haupt. Gentry's a slob, but he's not stupid. He seems to have a bug up his ass about this whole thing.

"My report will be in by tomorrow. In the meantime, I recommend that surveillance be initiated on Laski and Sheriff Gentry. You might consider canceling both these gentlemen's policies as a precaution. I will be home by eight P.M. tonight and will await further instructions. Haines. Cable. Coventry."

Agent Richard Haines hung up, picked up his briefcase, and moved quickly to join the throng headed for the departure gates.

Saul Laski left the County Building and walked to the side street where his rented Toyota was parked. It was raining lightly. Despite the drizzle, Saul was struck by how warm the air was. The temperature had to be in the low 60s. When he had left New York the day before snow had been falling and the temperature had been hovering in the 20s for days.

Saul sat in the car and watched raindrops streak the windshield. The car smelled of new upholstery and someone's cigar. He began to tremble in spite of the warm air. The trembling turned to shaking. Saul gripped the steering wheel tightly until the shaking left his upper body and became a tense quivering in his legs. He took a firm grip on the muscles in his thighs and thought about other things; about spring, about a quiet lake he had discovered in the Adirondacks the summer before, about an abandoned valley he had come across in the Sinai where sandblasted Roman columns stood alone against shale cliffs.

After a few minutes Saul started the car and drove aimlessly through rain-slickened streets. There was little traffic. He considered driving out Route 52 to his motel. Instead he turned back south on East Bay Drive, toward the Old Section of Charleston.

The Mansard House was marked by an arched green awning which stretched to the curb. Saul glanced quickly at the dark entrance beneath and drove on. Three blocks farther he turned right onto a narrow residential street. Wrought-iron fences separated yards and courtyards from the brick sidewalks. Saul slowed, counted softly to himself, watched for house numbers.

Melanie Fuller's home was dark. The courtyard was empty and the house which bordered it to the north looked closed up with heavy shutters sealed across the windows. There was a chain and padlock on the courtyard gate. The padlock looked new.

Saul turned left at the next street and then left again, almost returning to Broad Street before finding a parking place behind a delivery truck. It was raining harder now. Saul pulled a white tennis hat from the backseat, tugged it far down over his forehead, and pulled up the collar of his corduroy sports coat.

The alley ran through the center of the block and was bordered by tiny garages, thick foliage, high fences, and countless trash cans. Saul counted houses as he had while driving but still had to check for the two dead-looking palmettos near the south bay window to make sure that he had the right house. He strolled with his hands in his pockets, knowing he was conspicuous in the narrow alley, unable to do anything about it. Rain continued to fall. The gray afternoon was sliding into the dimness of a winter evening. He would not have much more than a half hour of light. Saul took three deep breaths and walked up the ten-foot-long driveway that ended at what once must have been a small carriage house. The windows were painted black, but it was obvious that the structure had never been used as a garage. The back fence was high steel mesh, interlaced with vines and the sharp branches of a thick hedge. A lower gate, once part of a black iron fence, was chained and padlocked. A yellow ribbon of plastic wrapped alongside the chain read NO TRESPASSING BY ORDER OF CHARLESTON COUNTY SHERIFF'S OFFICE.

Saul hesitated. The only sound was the fusillade of rain on the slate roof of the carriage house and water dripping from the kudzu. He reached up, took a grip on the high fence, got his left foot up onto a crossbar of the gate, balanced precariously a moment above the rusted iron spikes, and then dropped down onto flagstone in the backyard.

Crouching there a second, fingers splayed against the wet stone, his right leg cramping, Saul listened to the pounding of his heart and to the sudden yapping of a small dog from some nearby yard. The barking stopped. Saul moved quickly past flowers and a tilted birdbath to a wooden back porch which obviously had been added long after the brick house had been built. The rain, the dimming light, and the dripping hedges seemed to muffle distant sounds and amplify every step and noise of Saul's. He could see plants behind panes of glass to his left where a remodeled conservatory extended into the garden. He tried the screen door to the porch. It opened with a rusty sigh and Saul stepped into the darkness.

The space was long and narrow and smelled of mold and decaying earth. Saul could see the dark silhouettes of empty clay pots set along shelves against the brick of the house. The inner door, massive, inset with lead-paned glass and beautiful moldings, was securely locked. Saul knew that there would be several locks. He also was sure that the old woman would have had some sort of alarm system, but he felt equally certain that it would have been an internal alarm, not connected to the police station.

But what if the police hooked it up? Saul shook his head and crossed the dark space to peer through narrow windows behind a shelf. The pale white hulk of a refrigerator was visible. Suddenly there came a distant rumble of thunder and the rain redoubled its assault on the rooftops and hedges. Saul moved pots, setting them on empty counter spaces and brushing black soil from his hands, and then took down a three-foot section of shelving. The windows above the rough counter were securely latched from the inside. Saul crouched there, pressed his fingers against the glass for a second, and then turned to find the largest and heaviest of the clay pots.

The shattering glass sounded very loud to Saul, louder than the thunderclaps which followed hard on the strobic reflections of lightning that turned the unbroken panes of glass into mirrors. Saul swung again, shattered the bearded silhouette of his own reflection as well as a muntin, tapped out the clinging shards of glass, and groped in the darkness for the latch. The sudden, childish thought of a hand touching his own made his neck go cold. He found a chain and tugged. The window swung outward. He squeezed in, stepped down onto Formica and broken glass, and jumped heavily onto the tile floor of the kitchen.

There were sounds in the old house. Water coursed through rain gutters just outside the windows. The refrigerator made some internal adjustment with a thump that made Saul's heart leap into his throat. He noted that the power must still be on. Somewhere there was a faint scratching, as of fingernails on glass.

Three swinging doors opened from the kitchen. Saul chose the one straight ahead of him and emerged into a long hallway. Even in the dim light he could see where the darkly polished floor had been splintered a few paces from the kitchen door. He paused at the base of the wide stairway, half expecting to see chalked silhouettes of bodies on the floor as in the American detective films he was so fond of. There were none. There was merely a wide stain discoloring the wood near the first step. Saul glanced down another short hall to the foyer and then moved into a large but overfurnished room which looked to be a parlor furnished from the previous century. Light filtered through stained glass panels at the top of a wide bay window. A clock on the mantel stood frozen at 3:26. The heavy upholstered furniture and tall cabinets filled with crystal and china seemed to have absorbed all of the oxygen in the room. Saul tugged at his collar and gave the parlor a quick inspection. The room *smelled*. It reeked of age and polish and a bitter talcum and decaying meat scent which Saul had always associated with his ancient Aunt Danuta and her small apartment in Cracow. Danuta had been one hundred and three when she died.

A dining room sat empty on the other side of the entrance hall. An elaborate chandelier tinkled slightly to Saul's footfalls. The entrance foyer held an empty hat rack and two black canes propped against the wall. A truck moved slowly by outside and the house trembled.

The conservatory, located behind the dining room, was much lighter than the rest of the house. Saul felt exposed standing in it. The rain had stopped and he could see the roses rising from the wet greenery in the garden. It would be dark in a very few minutes.

A beautiful cabinet had been smashed open. The polished cherry was splintered and broken glass still littered the floor. Saul stepped gingerly across to it and crouched. A few statuettes and pewter plates sat over-turned on the middle shelf.

Saul stood and looked around. A sense of panic was rising in him for no apparent reason. The odor of dead meat seemed to have followed him into the room. He found his right hand clasping and unclasping spasmodically. He could leave now, go directly into the kitchen through the swinging door, and be over the gate in two minutes.

Saul turned and went down the dark hallway to the stairway. The ban-ister was smooth and cool to his touch. Despite a small, circular window on the wall opposite the stairs, darkness seemed to rise like cold air and settle on the landing ahead of him. He paused at the top. A door to the right had been all but ripped from its hinges. Pale splinters hung like torn sinews from the frame. Saul forced himself to enter the bedroom. It smelled like a meat locker weeks after the electricity had failed. A tall wardrobe stood in one corner like an overstuffed coffin set on end. Heavy drapes covered windows that looked out onto the courtyard. An expen-sive antique ivory brush and comb set lay perfectly centered on an old dressing table. The mirror was faded and stained. The high bed was neatly made.

Saul had turned to leave when he heard the sound.

He froze in mid-step, hands rising involuntarily into fists. There was nothing but the smell of rotting meat. He was ready to move again, ready to ascribe the noise to water in the clogged rain gutters outside, when he heard it once more, more clearly now.

There were footsteps downstairs. Softly but with a deliberate, relent-less care, they began to ascend the stairs.

Saul pivoted and took four steps to the large wardrobe. The door made no noise as he opened it and slipped inside between the clinging wool of old lady's garments. There was a violent thudding in his ears. The warped doors would not close completely and the crack in front of him showed a thin vertical line of gray light bisected by the dark horizontal of the bed.

The footsteps climbed the last of the stairs, hesitated for a long silence, and then entered the room. They were very soft.

Saul held his breath. The wool and mothball smell mixed with the stink of rotted meat in his nostrils and threatened to suffocate him. The heavy dresses and scarves clung to him, reached for his shoulders and throat.

Saul could not tell if the footsteps had receded or not, so loud was the buzzing in his ears. Claustrophobic panic claimed him. He could not fo-cus on the thin slit of light. He remembered the soil falling on upturned faces, the pale white stirrings of an arm against the tumble of black dirt, the white plaster on a stubbled cheek and the negligent weight of leg, gray wool black in the winter light, hanging over the Pit where white limbs pushed like slow maggots up through the black dirt . . .

Saul gasped out a breath. He struggled against the clinging wool and reached to push open the wardrobe door.

His hand never touched it. Before he could move, the door was jerked open roughly from the other side.

FIVE

Washington, D.C.
Tuesday, Dec. 16, 1980

Tony Harod and Maria Chen flew into Washington's National Airport, rented a car, and drove directly to Georgetown. It was early afternoon. The Potomac looked gray and sluggish as they crossed the Mason Memorial Bridge. Bare trees threw thin shadows on the Mall. Wisconsin Avenue was not crowded.

"Here," said Harod. Maria turned onto M Street. The expensive town houses seemed to huddle together in the weak winter light. The house they sought was similar to many others on the street. There was a no-parking zone in front of the pale yellow garage door. A couple passed, both swathed in heavy fur, a quivering poodle straining at the leash.

"I'll wait," said Maria Chen.

"No," said Harod. "Drive around. Come by here at ten-minute intervals."

She hesitated a moment when Harod got out and then she drove off, pulling out in front of a chauffeur-driven limousine.

Harod ignored the front door of the town house and approached the garage. A metal panel flipped up to reveal a thin slot and four unmarked plastic buttons. Harod removed an undersized credit card from his wallet and fitted it into the slot. There was a click. He stood close to the wall and pressed the third button four times and then three others. The garage door clanked up. Harod retrieved his card and entered.

When the door lowered behind him it was very dark in the empty space. Harod smelled no hint of oil or gasoline, only cold concrete and the resin scent of two-by-fours. He took three steps to the center of the garage and stood still, making no effort to find a door or a light switch. There was a soft electric whir and Harod knew that the wall-mounted video camera had scanned him and was tracking to make sure that no one else had entered. He assumed that the camera was fitted with infrared or light-enhancing lenses. He really didn't give a damn.

A door clicked open. Harod moved toward the light and stepped up into an empty room which, judging from the electrical and plumbing outlets, originally had been planned as a laundry room. Another video camera perched over a second door swiveled to lock on him as he entered. Harod unzipped his leather bomber jacket.

"Please remove your dark glasses, Mr. Harod." The voice came from a standard home intercom panel on the wall.

"Up your ass," Harod said pleasantly and removed his aviator sunglasses. He was putting them back on when the door opened and two tall men in dark suits entered. One was bald and massive, the stereotyped image of a bouncer or bodyguard. The other was taller, slim, dark, and infinitely more threatening in some indefinable way.

"Would you raise your arms please, sir?" asked the heavy one.

"Would you go fuck yourself for a quarter?" asked Harod. He hated being touched by men. He hated the thought of touching *them*. The two waited patiently. Harod lifted his arms. The heavy man patted him down professionally, impersonally, and nodded to the dark man.

"Right this way, Mr. Harod." The thin man led him through the door, through an unused kitchen, down a bright hallway past several empty, unfurnished rooms, and stopped at the bottom of a staircase. "It's the first room on the left, Mr. Harod," he said and pointed upstairs. "They have been waiting for you."

Harod said nothing and climbed the stairs. The floors were light oak, polished to a high gloss. His boots on the stairs sent echoes through the house. The building smelled of new paint and emptiness.

"Mr. Harod, so glad you could make it." Five men sat on folding chairs set in a not-quite-closed circle. The room may have been meant as a master bedroom or large study. The floors were bare, the louvred shutters were white, and the fireplace was cold. Harod knew the men—or at least their names. From left to right they were known as Trask, Colben, Sutter, Barent, and Kepler. They wore expensive, conservatively tailored suits and sat in almost identical postures, backs straight, legs crossed, arms folded. Three of them had briefcases set near them. Three wore glasses. All five were white. They ranged in age from the late forties to the early sixties, with Barent being the oldest. Colben was almost bald, but the other four appeared to share the same Capitol Hill barber. Trask had been the one who spoke. "You're late, Mr. Harod," he added.

"Yeah," said Tony Harod and stepped closer. There was no chair set out for him. He took off his leather jacket and held it over his shoulder by one finger. He was wearing a bright red silk shirt, open down the front to show off a shark tooth's medallion on a gold chain, black corduroy pants set off by a large, gold R2-D2 belt buckle given to him by George Lucas, and heavy chukka boots with massive heels. "The flight was late."

Trask nodded. Colben cleared his throat as if he were about to speak but contented himself with repositioning his horn-rimmed glasses.

"So what do we know?" asked Harod. Not waiting for an answer he went to the closet, removed a metal folding chair, and set it down backward in the cusp of the circle. He straddled it and laid his jacket across the top. "Is there anything new?" he asked. "Or did I make this fucking trip for nothing?"

"We were about to ask *you*," said Barent. His voice was refined and well-modulated. There was a hint of both Eastern Shore and England in the vowels. Barent was obviously not a man who ever had to raise his voice to be heard. He was being listened to now.

Harod shrugged. "I gave one of the eulogies at Willi's memorial service," he said. "Forest Lawn. Very sad. About two hundred of Hollywood's famous showed up to pay their respects. Ten or fifteen of 'em had actually *met* Willi."

"His house," Barent said patiently. "Did you search his house as requested?"

"Yeah."

"And?"

"And nothing," said Harod. His mouth had become a thin line in the pale face. The muscles at the corners of his mouth, so often expressive of sarcasm and cruel humor, were pulled tight with strain. "I only had a couple of hours. I spent half of that chasing out some of Willi's old lover boys who had keys and who'd come back like vultures to pick at the bones of his estate . . ."

"Had they been Used?" Colben asked. There was anxiety in his voice.

"No, I don't think so. Willi was losing his power, remember. Maybe he used a little conditioning with them. Stroked them a little. I doubt if he even did that though. He didn't have to, what with his money and his in at the studios."

"The search," said Barent.

"Yeah. So I had about an hour. Tom McGuire, Willi's lawyer, is an old friend of mine and let me go through the papers in Willi's safe and desk. There wasn't much. Some film and literary properties. A few stocks, but not what you'd call a portfolio. Willi tended to stick to the film industry in his investments. A lot of business letters, but almost nothing personal. His will was read yesterday, you know. I got the house . . . if I pay the fucking taxes. Most of the money was tied up in projects. He left the rest of his bank account to the Hollywood A.S.P.C.A."

"The A.S.P.C.A.?" repeated Trask.

"You bet your ass. Old Willi was an animal freak. He was always complaining about the way they were used in films and lobbying for stricter laws and shop rules protecting horses in stunts and all that crap."

"Go on," said Barent. "There were no papers which might indicate Willi's past?"

"No."

"And nothing to indicate his Ability?"

"No. Nothing."

"And no mention of any of us?" asked Sutter.

Harod sat up straight. "Of course not. You know Willi didn't know anything about the Club."

Barent nodded and steepled his fingers. "There is no chance of that, Mr. Harod?"

"No chance."

"Yet he was aware of your Ability?"

"Well, yes, I mean, of course. But you agreed years ago that we'd let him know about that. You said that when you told me to get to know him."

"Yes."

"And besides, Willi always thought my Ability was weak and unreliable compared to his. Because I didn't need to Use anyone all the way like he did and because . . . because of my own preferences . . ."

"Not to Use men," said Trask.

"Because of my own preferences," said Harod. "What the fuck did Willi know? He looked down at me even when he'd lost everything but the power to keep Reynolds and Luhar, his two stroke-addicts, in line. He wasn't even successful at that half the time."

Barent nodded again. "So you do not believe that he was capable of Using people to cancel others any longer?"

"Christ no," said Harod. "Not really. He might've been able to use his two goons or one of his lover boys, but he wasn't stupid enough to do that."

"And you let him travel to Charleston for this . . . mmm . . . reunion with the two women?" asked Kepler.

Harod gripped the back of his chair through the leather jacket. "What do you mean, 'let him'? Hell, yes, I let him. My job was to watch him, not limit his travel. Willi traveled all over the world."

"And what do you think he did at these reunions?" asked Barent.

Harold shrugged. "Talk over old times. Chew the fat with those two other has-beens. For all I know, he was still banging the old crones. How the fuck should I know? He usually only stayed away two or three days. It was never a problem."

Barent turned to Colben and made a gesture. The bald man unclasped his briefcase and removed a brown, wire-bound booklet that looked like someone's photo album. He carried it across the circle to Harod.

"What the shit is this?"

"Look at it," ordered Barent.

Harold flipped through the album, quickly at first, then very slowly. He read several of the news clippings all the way through. When he was finished he took off his dark glasses. No one spoke. A horn blasted somewhere on M Street.

"It's not Willi's," said Harod.

"No," said Barent. "It belonged to Nina Drayton."

"Incredible. Jesus-fucking-incredible. It can't be real. The old broad must've been senile, delusions of grandeur. Wishing it was like the good old days."

"No," said Barent. "It appears that she was present at most of the appropriate times. They quite probably are hers."

"Holy shit," said Harod. He put his glasses on and massaged his cheeks. "How'd you get this? Her New York apartment?"

"No," Colben answered. "We had someone in Charleston last Saturday because of Willi's plane crash. He was able to retrieve this from Nina Drayton's belongings at the coroner's office before the local authorities had an opportunity to see it."

"You're sure?" asked Harod.

"Yes."

"The question is," said Barent, "were the three still playing some variant of their old Vienna Game? And if so, did your friend Willi have any similar documents in his possession?"

Harod shook his head but said nothing.

Colben removed a dossier from his briefcase. "Nothing conclusive has been found in the remains of the aircraft. Of course, few recognizable items have been found at all. More than half of the bodies remain to be recovered. Those which have been pulled out of the swamp are generally too fragmented to be identified quickly. It was a very powerful explosion. The swampy conditions hinder recovery. It is a difficult situation for investigators."

"Which one of the old bitches was responsible?" asked Harod.

"We are not sure," said Colben. "It doesn't appear, however, that Willi's friend Mrs. Fuller survived the weekend. She is the logical candidate."

"What a shitty way for Willi to die," Harod said to no one in particular.

"If, indeed, he did die," said Barent.

"What?" Harod leaned back. His legs straightened and his heels made black marks on the oak floor. "You think he didn't? You think he wasn't aboard?"

"The ticket agent remembers Willi and his two friends boarding," said Colben. "They were arguing, Willi and his black colleague."

"Jensen Luhar," said Harod. "That brainless asshole."

Barent said, "But there is no guarantee that they remained on board. The ticket agent was called away from the boarding area for a few minutes prior to the sealing of the aircraft."

"But there's nothing to suggest that Willi *wasn't* aboard," pressed Harod.

Colben put away the dossier. "No. However, until we find Mr. Borden's body, we cannot safely assume that he has been . . . ah . . . neutralized."

"Neutralized," repeated Harod.

Barent stood and went to the window. He pulled aside the tab curtains that hung above the white shutters. His skin looked porcelain-smooth in the indirect light. "Mr. Harod, is there any possibility that Willi von Borchert knew about the Island Club?"

Harod's head snapped back as if he had been slapped. "No. Absolutely not."

"You are sure?"

"Positive."

"You never mentioned it? Not even indirectly?"

"Why the fuck would I do that? No, goddammit, Willi didn't know a thing about it."

"You are sure of this?"

"Willi was an old man, Barent. I mean *old*. He was half crazy because he couldn't Use people anymore. Especially Use them to kill. That's *kill*, Colben, k-i-l-l, not neutralize or cancel policies or terminate with extreme prejudice or any of your other fucking agency euphemisms. Willi *killed* to stay young and he couldn't do it anymore and the poor old fart was drying up like a prune left out in the sun. If he'd known about your goddamn Island Club he would've crawled here on his knees to beg you to be let in."

"It's your Island Club, too, Harod," said Barent.

"Yeah, so I hear. Only I haven't been there yet so I wouldn't know."

Barent said, "You will be invited for the second week this summer. The first week is not the . . . ah . . . necessary one, is it?"

"Maybe not. But I guess I'd like to rub elbows with the rich and powerful. Not to mention do a little stroking of my own."

Barent laughed. Several of the others followed his lead. "My God, Harod," Sutter said, "don't you get enough of that out in Tinsel Town?"

"Besides," said Trask, "wouldn't you find it a bit difficult? I mean, given our guest list for the first week . . . I mean, in light of your *preferences*."

Harod turned and looked at the man. Harod's eyes had become thin slits in a pale mask. He spoke very slowly, each word clicking into place like shotgun shells going into a chamber. "You know what I *meant*. Don't fuck with me."

"Yes," said Barent. His voice was soothing, the British accent more audible. "We know what you meant, Mr. Harod. And this may be your year for it. Do you know who will be on the Island this coming June?"

Harod shrugged and turned his gaze away from Colben. "The usual bunch of boys eager for summer camp, I suppose. I'd imagine Henry the K will be there again. Maybe an ex-president."

"*Two* ex-presidents," said Barent with a smile. "And the chancellor of West Germany. But that is not so important. We will have the *next* president."

"The *next* president? Jesus Christ, didn't you just put one in?"

"Yes, but he is *old*," said Trask and the others laughed as if it were a favorite in-joke.

"Seriously," said Barent, "this is your year, Mr. Harod. When you help us clear up the details of this Charleston mess, nothing will remain in your way to full membership."

"What details?"

"First, help us ascertain that William D. Borden a.k.a. Herr Wilhelm von Borchert is dead. We will continue our own inquiries. Perhaps his body will be recovered soon. You may help us simply by eliminating other possibilities if any arise."

"All right. What else?"

"Second, carry out a much more thorough search of Mr. Borden's estate before anymore . . . ah . . . vultures descend. Make sure that he has left absolutely nothing which could embarrass anyone."

"I'm flying back tonight," said Harod. "I'll go back to Willi's place in the morning."

"Excellent. Third, and finally, we would like your assistance in dealing with this final Charleston detail."

"What's that?"

"The person who killed Nina Drayton and who almost certainly is responsible for the death of your friend Willi. Melanie Fuller."

"You think she's still alive?"

"Yes."

"And you want me to help find her?"

"No," said Colben. "We'll find her."

"What if she's left the country? I would if I were her."

"We will find her," said Colben.

"If you don't want me to find her, what do you want me to do?"

"We want you to be present when she is apprehended," said Colben. "We want you to cancel her policy."

"Neutralize her," said Trask with a thin smile.

"Terminate her with extreme prejudice," said Kepler.

Harod blinked and looked to the window where Barent stood. The tall man turned and smiled. "It is time to pay your dues, Mr. Harod. We will find the lady for you. Then we want you to kill the meddling bitch."

Harod and Maria Chen had to fly out of Dulles International in order to get a direct flight to Los Angeles before the Red Eye Special. The flight was delayed twenty minutes by mechanical problems. Harod badly wanted a drink. He hated to fly. He hated to put himself at anyone's mercy and that was precisely what flying always had meant to him. He knew the statistics which showed how safe it was to fly. They meant nothing to him. He had clear images of wreckage strewn across several acres, of twisted pieces of metal still white-hot from flame, of bits of bodies lying pink and red in the grass like slices of salmon drying in the sun. *Poor Willi*, he thought.

"Why don't they serve the fucking drinks *before* takeoff, when we need them?" he said. Maria Chen smiled.

The runway lights were on by the time they finally rolled into their takeoff run, but once above the solid layer of clouds there were a few final minutes of sunlight. Harod opened his briefcase and removed a heavy stack of scripts. There were five possible screenplays on his lap. Two were too long, over 150 pages, so he tossed those back into his briefcase unread. One had an unreadable first page so he set it aside. He was eight pages into the fourth manuscript when the stewardess approached to get their drink orders.

"Vodka on the rocks," said Harod. Maria Chen declined a drink.

Harod looked up at the young stewardess when she returned with his drink. It was his opinion that one of the most asinine acts in corporate history occurred when airlines surrendered to sex discrimination charges and began hiring men as stewards. Even the stewardesses seemed older and homelier to Harod these days. Not this one. She was young and well-scrubbed-looking, not the usual airlines mannequin, and pleasingly sexy in a peasant girl way. She looked Scandinavian. She had blond hair, blue eyes, and lightly flushed cheeks replete with freckles. Her breasts were full, perhaps too full for her height, and they pressed nicely against her gold and blue blazer.

"Thank you, my dear," said Harod as she set his glass on the small tray in front of him. He touched her hand as she straightened up. "What's your name?"

"Kristen." She smiled, but the effect was offset by the speed with which she had pulled her hand away. "My friends call me Kris."

"Well, Kris, sit down here a second." Harod patted the wide arm of his chair. "Let's talk a minute."

Kristen smiled again, but it was a perfunctory smile, almost mechanical. "I'm sorry, sir. We're running behind schedule and I have to get the meals ready."

"I'm reading a movie script here," said Harod. "I'll probably end up producing it. There's a part in here that sounds like it was written for a beautiful little Mädchen like you."

"Thanks, but I really have to help Laurie and Curt with the meals."

Harold grasped her wrist as she started to leave. "Would it kill you to bring me another vodka and ice before you get it on with Curt and Laurie?"

She pulled her arm away slowly, obviously resisting the temptation to rub the wrist that he had squeezed tightly. She did not smile.

The second drink had not come by the time a smiling Laurie delivered Harod's dinner of steak and lobster. He did not eat it. It was dark outside and the port running lights were blinking redly at the end of the wing. Harod switched on an overhead reading light but finally put away the screenplay. He watched as Kristen moved efficiently to and fro. It was Curt who cleared away Harod's untouched meal. "Care for some more coffee, sir?"

Harod said nothing. He watched as the blond stewardess bantered with a businessman and brought a pillow for a sleepy five-year-old two rows in front of Harod.

"Tony," began Maria Chen.

"Shut up," said Harod.

He waited until Curt and Laurie were busy elsewhere and Kristen was alone near the forward rest room. Then Harod rose. The girl turned in the aisle to let him squeeze by but otherwise did not seem to notice him.

The rest room was unoccupied. Harod stepped in and then opened the door to peer back around the corner.

"Excuse me, miss?"

"Yes?" Kristen looked up from stowing trays.

"The water doesn't seem to be running in here."

"No water pressure?"

"No water at all," said Harod. He stepped aside to let her enter. Over his shoulder he could see the first-class passengers listening to music on their earphones, reading, or dozing. Only Maria Chen was looking their way.

"It seems to be running all right now," said the stewardess. Harod stepped in behind her and slid the bolt into place. Kristen straightened and turned. Harod gripped her upper arm before she spoke.

Stay quiet. Harod brought his face close to hers. The compartment was very small and the vibration of the jet engines pulsed through the bulkheads and metal counter.

The girl's eyes opened wide and she parted her lips to speak, but Harod *pushed* and she said nothing. He stared into her eyes so fiercely that the force of his gaze was much more intense than the pressure of his hand on her arm. Harod felt resistance and pushed against it. He sensed the current of her thoughts and pushed even more strongly, forcing his way like a man wading upstream. Harod felt her squirm, physically at first and then in the confines of her mind. He pinned her straining consciousness as firmly as he had once pinned his cousin Elizabeth in a wrestling match when they were children, Harod accidentally ending up on top, holding her arms by the wrists, forcing them against the ground, his lower body between her legs, between her thighs, resisting her straining, thrusting pelvis with the friction of his weight, embarrassed and excited by his sudden erection and by the vain and violent struggles of his helpless captive.

Stop it. Kristen's resistance slackened and slid aside. To Harod it was like the shocking, penultimate warmth when physically entering a woman. There was a sudden calm and an almost alarming looseness as his will expanded into her mind. Her sense of self dimmed like a dying light. Harod let it dim. He made no effort to slide along the warp and weave of her thoughts to the warm pleasure center at her core. He did not take time to stroke her. Harod was not interested in her pleasure, only her submission.

Do not move. Harod brought his face even closer. There was a faint golden down on Kristen's flushed cheeks. Her eyes were very wide, very blue, the pupils fully dilated. Her lips were moist and open. Harod ran his mouth across hers, bit softly at her full lower lip, and then inserted his tongue.

Kristen did not stir except for a slight exhalation which might have been a sigh or moan or scream had she been free. She tasted of peppermint. Harod bit her lower lip again, sharply this time, and then pulled his face back and smiled. The tiniest drop of blood left her lip and moved slowly to her chin. Her eyes stared past Harod, through him, passive, passionless, but behind them there was a flicker of fright like the half-perceived motion of a caged animal behind cold bars.

Harod released her arm and drew his palm across her cheek. He savored the helpless twistings of her will, the firm sureness of his own control. Her panic filled his nostrils like a powerful perfume. He ignored the pleading undertones of her writhing and followed well-trod paths of darkness to the motor center of her mind. He shaped and molded her consciousness as surely as strong hands could knead soft dough. She sighed again.

Stand still. Harod tugged off her blazer and let it fall crumpled on the counter behind her. The tiny cabin resonated to his heavy breathing and to the throb of the engines. The plane banked slightly and Harod was thrown against her, thighs touching. His excitement added to his power over her.

Stay silent. She was wearing a silk scarf of red and blue airline colors tucked inside her beige blouse. Harod ignored the scarf and unbuttoned the blouse with sure fingers. She began to tremble when he roughly pulled the blouse loose from the elastic of her skirt, but he tightened his mental grip and she stopped.

Kristen wore a plain white bra. Her breasts were pale and heavy, rounded above the white curve of fabric. Harod felt the inevitable tenderness well up inside of him, the wave of love and loss he never failed to feel. It did not interfere with his control.

The young woman's mouth moved slightly. Saliva and blood trembled on her lower lip.

Don't move. Harod tugged the blouse off her shoulders and let it hang from her limp arms. Her fingers twitched. He unhooked her bra and tugged it up. Harod opened his leather jacket and unbuttoned his own shirt in order to rub his chest against her. Her breasts were even larger than he had thought, heavy against him, the skin so vulnerably white and nipples so delicately pink and undeveloped that Harod felt his throat tighten with the force of his love for her.

Shut up, shut up, shut up. Stand still, bitch. The plane banked more steeply to the left. Harod leaned against her, his weight on her, and rubbed himself against the soft curve of her belly.

There was noise in the corridor. Someone tried the lock. Harod bunched up her skirt and forced it up over her wide thighs to her lips. Her panty hose tore as he roughly tugged them down, trapped them with one foot, moved her left leg aside with his knee to free her of them. She wore white bikini underpants under the panty hose. There was more soft, golden down on her thighs. Her legs felt smooth and firm beyond belief. Harod closed his eyes in gratitude.

"Kristen? You there?" It was the steward's voice. The lock rattled again. "Kristen? It's Curt."

Harod pulled her white pants down and opened his trousers. He was painfully erect. He touched her lower belly just above the line of pubic hair and the contact made him tremble. The plane pitched to turbulence. Somewhere a chime sounded urgently. Harod gripped her buttocks, moved her legs apart, and slid up and into her as the aircraft began to shudder violently. He felt the edge of the sink beneath his fingers as her weight settled backward on his hands. There was a second of dry resistance and then, for the second time, the overwhelming sensation of surrendering warmth. Harod moved roughly against her. The shark tooth's medallion bounced against her flattened breasts.

"Kristen? What the hell's wrong? We've got some weather here. Kristen?" The plane lurched to the right. The sink and countertop vibrated. Harod thrust, lifted her weight against him, thrust again.

"Are you hunting for the stewardess?" Maria Chen's voice came through the thin door. "She was helping an older lady who was ill . . . quite ill, I'm afraid."

There was an unintelligible murmur. Sweat glistened between Kristen's breasts. Harod held her to him more tightly, squeezing her, seizing her in the tightening vise of his will, inside her, feeling himself entering and withdrawing through the rough reflection of her thoughts, tasting the salt of her flesh and the brine fear of her panic, moving her in response like a great, soft puppet, feeling the orgasm building in her, no, in him, the two streams of thought and sensation cascading into one dark cauldron of physical response.

"I'll certainly tell her," said Maria Chen. There was a soft tap on the door inches from Harod's face.

Harod strained, exploded, felt the medallion cut into both of them, and buried his chin in the hollow at the side of her neck. The girl's head was arched back. Her mouth was open in a silent scream and her eyes stared fixedly at the low ceiling.

The plane bounced and slewed. Harod kissed the sweat on her throat and stooped to retrieve her skirt. His fingers shook as he buttoned her blouse. Her panty hose were torn in several pieces. He stuffed them in the pocket of his jacket and brushed at the wrinkles in her skirt. Her legs seemed tan enough to hide the absence of stockings.

Harod gradually relaxed the pressure. Her thoughts were a jumble, memories confused with dreams. Harod let her bend over the sink as he slid open the bolt.

"Seat belt sign is on, Tony." Maria Chen's thin form filled the door.

"Yeah."

"What?" said Kristen vacantly. Her eyes had not yet focused. "What?" She lowered her face to the steel basin and vomited quietly.

Maria stepped in and held the girl's shoulders. When she was done, Maria dabbed at her face with a wet towel. Harod stood in the corridor, bracing himself against the door frame as the aircraft pitched like a small ship on a rough sea.

"What?" asked Kristen and looked blankly at Maria Chen. "I don't . . . why am I . . . remember?"

Maria looked at Harod while she stroked the girl's forehead. "You'd better go sit down, Tony. You'll get in trouble for not having your seat belt fastened."

Harod returned to his seat and pulled out the script he had been reading. Maria Chen joined him a moment later. The turbulence abated. Up front, Curt's worried voice could be heard above the engines.

"I don't know," came Kristen's dulled response. "I don't know." Harod ignored them and made notes in the margins of the manuscript. A few minutes later he looked up to see Maria Chen looking at him. He smiled, the muscles at the corners of his mouth twisting down. "I don't like waiting for my second drink," he said softly.

Maria Chen turned away and looked out at darkness and the blinking light pulsing red at the end of the wing.

Early the next morning Tony Harod drove to Willi's house. The guard at the gate recognized Harod's car from a distance and had the gate open by the time the red Ferrari rolled to a stop.

"Good morning, Chuck."

"Morning, Mr. Harod. Not used to seeing you out here so early."

"Me either, Chuck. Gotta go through more business papers. Trying to untangle the finances for some new projects Willi got us into. Especially a thing called *The White Slaver*."

"Yessir, read about that in the trades."

"Security staying on here, Chuck?"

"Yessir, at least until the auction next month."

"McGuire paying you?"

"Yessir. Comes out of the estate."

"Yeah. See you around, Chuck. Don't take any wooden tokens."

"You too, Mr. Harod."

He pulled away with a satisfying rumble and accelerated up the long driveway. The morning sun created a stroboscope effect through the line of poplars along the drive. Harod swung the car around the dry fountain in front of the main entrance and parked near the west wing where Willi had his offices.

Bill Borden's Bel Air home looked like a palace transported north from some banana republic. Acres of stucco and red tile and multi-paned windows caught the morning light. Gates opened into courtyards which were bordered by covered porches which abutted open, airy rooms, which were connected by tiled corridors to other courtyards. The house appeared to have been added onto for several generations rather than constructed in the hot summer of 1938 for a minor movie mogul who died three years later while watching daily rushes.

Harod used his key to let himself into the west wing. Venetian blinds sent yellow stripes across the carpet of the secretaries' office. The room was neat, the typewriters covered, desktops cleared. Harod felt an unexpected twinge when he thought of the usual chaos of phone calls and office noise that had reigned there. Willi's office was two doors down, past the conference room.

Harod pulled a slip of paper out of his pocket and opened the safe. He placed the color-coded files and folded documents on the center of Willi's wide, white desk. He unlocked the file cabinet and sighed. It would be a long morning.

Three hours later Harod stretched, yawned, and pushed the chair back from the cluttered desk. There was nothing in William Borden's papers that would embarrass anyone except a few deadbeats and devotees of quality in the cinema. Harod stood and shadowboxed at the wall. His Adidas running shoes made him feel light and agile. He wore a light blue jogging suit, unzipped at the wrists and ankles. He was hungry. Moving lightly, his sneakers making a soft noise on tile, Harod went up the west wing corridor, across a courtyard with a fountain, down the length of a covered terrace large enough to host a Screen Actors' Guild convention, and into the kitchen through the south door. There was still food in the refrigerator. He had uncorked a magnum of champagne and was spreading mayonnaise on a slice of French bread when he heard a noise. Still carrying the champagne bottle, he went through the huge dining room into the living room.

"Hey, what the fuck are you doing?" shouted Harod. Twenty-five feet away, a man was bent over rummaging through the shelves where Willi kept his videotape library. The man stood up quickly, his upper torso throwing a shadow on the twelve-foot screen in the corner.

"Oh, it's you," said Harod. The young man was one of Willi's boyfriends whom Harod and Tom McGuire had chased off a few days earlier. He was very young, very blond, and sported the kind of perfect tan which very few people in the world could afford to maintain. The boy was over six feet tall and wore only tight cutoffs and sneakers. His bare upper body rippled with muscle. The deltoids and pectorals alone testified to hundreds of hours spent pressing weights and wrestling with a Universal machine. His stomach looked to Harod like someone smashed rocks on it regularly.

"Yeah, it's me." Harod thought that the kid's voice sounded more like that of a marine D.I. than a Malibu beach fairy. "Wanta make something out of it?"

Harod sighed tiredly and took a long pull of champagne. He wiped his mouth. "Get the hell out of here, kid. You're trespassing."

The tanned-Cupid face curled into a pout. "Oh yeah, who says? Bill was a good friend of mine."

"Uh-huh."

"I have a right to be here. We shared a meaningful relationship."

"Yeah, that and a jar of K-Y jelly," said Harod. "Now get the fuck out of here before you get thrown out."

"Yeah, who's gonna throw me out?"

"Me," said Harod.

"You and who else?" The boy rose to his full height and rippled his muscles. Harod couldn't tell if he was seeing biceps or triceps; they all seemed to flow together like gerbils humping under a tight tarp.

"Me and the cops," Harod said and crossed to a desk phone near the sectional.

"Oh yeah?" The kid pulled the receiver out of Harod's left hand and then jerked the cord out of the phone. Not content with that, he grunted and ripped the fifteen-foot cord out of the wall.

Harod shrugged and set down the champagne bottle. "Calm down, Brucie. They're more phones. Willi had lots and lots of phones."

The boy took three quick steps and was in front of Harod, blocking him. "Not so fast, motherfucker."

"Motherfucker? Jeez, I haven't heard that since I graduated from Evanston High School. Got any others like that, Brucie?"

"Don't call me Brucie, shithead."

"Now that one I've heard," said Harod and went to step around him. The boy set three fingers against Harod's chest and shoved. Harod bounced off the arm of the sectional. The kid jumped back and went into a crouch, arms at odd angles. "Karate?" said Harod. "Hey, there's no need to get physical here." There was the slightest hint of a quaver in his voice.

"Shithead," said the kid. "Asshole motherfucker."

"Uh-oh, repeating yourself. Sign of age," said Harod and turned to run. The boy jumped forward. Harod completed his turn, the magnum of champagne suddenly in his hand again. The bottle made a heavy arc which terminated on the kid's left temple. The bottle did not break. There was a dull thwump sounding like nothing so much as a large bell being struck by a dead cat and the boy went down on his right knee, head hanging. Harod stepped forward and made a field goal attempt with the imaginary ball contacted directly under the point of the kid's heavy jaw.

"Argh!" yelled Tony Harod and grabbed at his Adidas running shoe. He hopped on his left foot while the boy levitated backward, bounced off the thick cushions of the sectional, and landed on both knees in front of Harod like a penitent sinner. Harold swung a heavy Mexican lamp off the end table into the handsome face. Unlike the bottle, the lamp shattered quite satisfactorily. So did the boy's nose and other less prominent structures. He went over sideways into the thick carpet like a scuba diver going off a raft.

Harod stepped over him and went to a kitchen phone. "Chuck? This is Tony Harod. Put Leonard on the front gate and bring your car up to the house, will you? Willi left some garbage here that has to be taken out to the dump."

HAZEL M. LEWIS LIBRARY
POWERS, OREGON 97466

Later, after Willi's boyfriend had been driven away to the emergency room and Harod had finished his second helping of champagne and paté on French bread, he wandered back to Willi's video library. There were more than three hundred tapes shelved there. Some were copies of Willi's early triumphs—such cinema masterpieces as *Three On a Swing, Beach Party Creature*, and *Paris Memories*. Shelved nearby were the eight films which Harod had coproduced with Willi, including *Prom Massacre, The Children Died*, and two of the *Walpurgis Night* sequels. Also on the shelves were old favorites from the late show screen tests, outtakes, a pilot, and three episodes of Willi's abortive entry into TV sitcoms—"His and Hers"— a complete collection of Jerry Damiano X-rated films, some new studio releases, and a miscellaneous collection of other cassettes. The boyfriend had pulled out several tapes and Harod kneeled to look at these. The first one was labeled only *A&B*. Harod switched on the projection unit and popped the cassette into the VCR. Computer-lettered titles read: "Alexander and Byron 4/23."

The opening shots were of Willi's large swimming pool. The camera panned right, past the waterfall to the open door of Willi's bedroom. A thin young man in red bikini trunks bounced out into the light. He waved at the camera in the best home-movie style and stood uncomfortably by poolside, looking a bit, Harod thought, like an anemic, flat-chested version of Venus on the Half Shell. Suddenly the muscled boyfriend emerged from the shadows. He was wearing even briefer red trunks and he immediately went into a series of muscleman poses. The slim youth— Alexander?—mimed his appreciation. Harod knew that Willi had owned a good microphone system for his home video outfit, but this particular excursion into cinema verité was as silent as an early Chaplin two-reeler.

The boyfriend finished his demonstration with a torso-twisting finale. Alexander was on his knees by this time, a worshiper at the feet of Adonis. As Adonis held his final pose, the worshiper reached up and pulled down his deity's bikini pants. The kid's tan *was* perfect. Harod switched off the VCR.

"Byron?" muttered Harod. "Jesus." He walked back to the wall of shelves. It took fifteen minutes, but Harod finally found what he was looking for. Labeled "In the Event of My Death," it had been filed between *In Cold Blood* and *In the Heat of the Night*. Harod sat on an ottoman and turned the cassette over and over in his hands. There was an emptiness in his gut and he had the urge to go straight out the door and drive away. He set the cassette in place, hit the play button, and leaned forward.

"Hello, Tony," said Willi, "greetings from the grave." His image was larger than life-size. He was sitting in a webbed chair near his pool. Palm leaves stirred to the breeze behind him, but no one else, not even a servant, was visible in the shot. Willi's white hair was combed forward, but Harod could see the sunburn on the bald spots. The old man was wearing a loose, flowered Hawaiian shirt and baggy green shorts. His knees were

HAZEL M. LEWIS LIBRARY
POWERS, OREGON 97466

white. Harod's heart hammered at his ribs. "If you've found this tape," said Willi's image, "then I must assume that some unfortunate event has taken me from you. I trust that you, Tony, are the first to find this . . . mmm . . . final testament and that you are watching alone."

Harod made a tight fist. He could not tell precisely when the tape had been made, but it looked recent.

"I trust you have taken care of any unfinished business we might have had," said Willi. "I know that the production company will be in good hands. Relax, my friend, if you have had the will read already, do not worry. There are no surprise codas in this tape. The house is yours. This is a friendly visit between two old friends, *ja*?"

"Fuck," hissed Harod. There were goose bumps rising along his arms.

". . . enjoy the house," Willi was saying. "I know that you never especially admired it, but it should be easily convertible to investment capital should the need arise. Maybe you could use it for our little *White Slaver* project, no?"

The tape was *very* recent. Harod shivered in spite of the warm day.

"Tony, I have very little to say to you. You would agree that I have treated you like a son, *nicht wahr?* Well, if not a son, then perhaps a favorite nephew. This is despite the fact that you have not always been as honest with me as you could have been. You have friends that you have not told me about . . . is this not true? Ah, well, no friendship is perfect, Tony. Perhaps I have not told you everything there is to know about my friends. We must live our own lives, yes?"

Harod sat upright, very still, scarcely breathing.

"It does not matter now," said Willi and looked away from the camera to squint at the motes of light dancing on the pool. "If you are seeing this tape, I must be gone. No one lives forever, Tony. You will understand this when you reach my age . . ." Willi looked back into the camera lens. "*If* you reach my age." He smiled. The dentures were perfect. "Just three more things I want to say, Tony. First, I regret that you never learned to play chess. You know how much it meant to me. It is more than a game, my friend. *Ja*, it is much more than a game. You once said that you had no time for such games when you had a life to lead. Well, there is always time to learn, Tony. Even a dead man could help you learn. *Zweitens*, second, I must tell you that I have always detested the name Willi. Should we meet in the afterlife, Tony, I would ask that you address me differently. Herr von Borchert would be acceptable. Or Der Meister. Do you *believe* in an afterlife, Tony? I do. I am sure that one exists. How do you picture such a place, eh? I have always imagined paradise as a wonderful island on which all of one's needs are met, where there are many interesting people to converse with, and where one could Hunt to his heart's content. A pleasant picture, no?"

Harod blinked. He had often read the term "break out in a cold sweat" but had never experienced it before. He did so now.

"Finally, Tony, I must ask. What kind of name is Harod, eh? You say you are from Midwestern Christian stock and you certainly invoke the name of Christus frequently enough, but I think maybe the name Harod has other origins, yes? I think maybe my dear nephew is a Jew. Ah, well, it does not matter now. We can speak of it should we meet again in paradise. Meanwhile, there is more to this tape, Tony. I have added a few excerpts from the news. You might find them enlightening even though you do not usually have time for such things. Good-bye, Tony. Or rather, *Auf Wiedersehn.*" Willi waved at the camera. The tape blanked for a few seconds and then cut to a five-month-old local news report on the capture of the Hollywood Strangler. More news fragments followed, covering a year's selection of random murders. Twenty-five minutes later the tape ended and Harod turned off the VCR. He sat for a long time holding his head in his hands. Finally he rose, removed the cassette, put it in his jacket pocket, and left.

He drove hard going home, taking the long way, slamming the car up through the gears, entering the Hollywood Freeway at better than 80 miles per hour. No one stopped him. His jogging suit was wet with perspiration when he pulled up his own drive and slid to a stop under the baleful glare of his satyr.

Harod went to the bar near the Jacuzzi and poured a tall glass of vodka. He drank it in four swallows and took the cassette out of his pocket. He tugged the tape loose and unrolled it onto the floor, tearing the ends loose from the plastic reels in the cassette. It took several minutes to burn the entire tape in the old barbecue pit on the terrace beyond his pool. A melted residue remained in the ashes. Harod smashed the empty cassette repeatedly against the stone chimney of the barbecue until the plastic was shattered. He tossed the broken cassette into the Dumpster next to the cabana and went back inside to have another vodka, mixed with Rose's lime juice this time.

Harod stripped and lay back in the Jacuzzi. He was almost asleep when Maria Chen entered with the day's mail and his dictation recorder.

"Leave it there," he said and went back to dozing. Fifteen minutes later he opened his eyes and began sorting through the day's stack of envelopes, occasionally dictating notes or brief replies into the Sony. Four new scripts had arrived. Tom McGuire had sent a mass of paperwork relating to acquiring Willi's house, arranging for the auction, and paying taxes. There were three invitations to parties and Harod made a note to consider one of them. Michael May-Dreinan, a cocky young writer, had sent a scribbled note complaining that Schubert Williams, the director, was already rewriting Dreinan's screenplay and the *goddamn thing wasn't even* finished *yet.* Would Harod *please* intervene? Otherwise, he, Dreinan, would quit the project. Harod tossed the note aside and dictated no response.

The final letter was in a small, pink envelope postmarked in Pacific Palisades. Harod tore it open. The stationery matched the envelope and was softly perfumed. The handwriting was tight and heavily slanted with childish circles above the "i's."

Dear Mr. Harod,

I do not know what came over me last Saturday. I will never understand it. But I do not blame you and I forgive you even if I cannot forgive myself.

Today Loren Sayles, my agent, received a packet of contractual forms relating to your film proposal. I told Loren and my mother that there has been a mistake. I told them that I had spoken to Mr. Borden about the film just prior to his death but that no commitment had been made.

I cannot be associated with such a project at this point in my career, Mr. Harod. I am *sure* you can understand my situation. This does not mean that we may not work together on some other film venture in the future. I trust that you understand this decision and would remove any obstacles—or any embarrassing details—which might damage such a future relationship.

I know that I can depend upon you to do the right thing in this situation, Mr. Harod. You mentioned last Saturday that you are aware that I am a member of the Church of Jesus Christ of the Latter Day Saints. You must also understand that my faith is very strong and that my commitment to the Lord and to His Laws must come before all other considerations.

I pray—and know in my heart—that God will help you see the proper course of action in this situation.

Yours most sincerely,
Shayla Berrington

Harod put the scented stationery back in the envelope. *Shayla Berrington*. He had almost forgotten about her. He picked up the tiny recorder and spoke into the built-in mike on the end. "Maria, letter to Tom McGuire. Dear Tom. I'll get this legal stuff out of the way as soon as I can. Proceed with the auction as outlined. New paragraph. Very happy to hear that you enjoyed the X-rated outtakes I sent you for Cal's birthday party. I thought you guys might get a kick out of them. I'm sending you another tape that you might like. Don't ask me any questions, just enjoy. Feel free to make as many copies as you like. Maybe Marv Sandborne and the fellows at Four Star would also get a laugh or two from it. New paragraph. I'll get the deed transfer stuff to you as soon as I can. My accountants will be in touch. New paragraph. Give my love to Sarah and the kids. Closing. Best and All! Oh, and Maria, get that to me today to sign, OK? Enclose VHS cassette 165. And Maria—send it special delivery."

SIX

Charleston
Tuesday, Dec. 16, 1980

The young woman stood very still, arms extended, both hands wrapped around the butt of the pistol that was aimed at Saul Laski's chest. Saul knew that if he stepped out of the wardrobe she might fire, but no power on earth could have kept him in that dark space with the stink of the Pit in his nostrils. He stumbled out into the gray light of the bedroom.

The woman stepped back and held the pistol level. She did not fire. Saul took deep breaths and noticed that the woman was young and black and that there were drops of moisture on her white raincoat and short Afro hairdo. She might have been attractive, but Saul found it hard to concentrate on anything but the handgun she kept trained on him. It was a small automatic pistol—Saul thought it a .32 caliber—but its smallness did not prevent the dark circle of the muzzle from commanding all of Saul's attention.

"Put your hands up," she said. Her voice was smooth, sensuous, with an educated Southern accent. Saul lifted his hands and locked his fingers behind his neck.

"Who are you?" she asked. She continued to brace the automatic with both hands, but she did not seem confident in the weapon's use. She remained too close to him, within four feet. Saul knew that he would have a better than even chance of deflecting the barrel before she could squeeze the trigger. He made no move to do so. "Who are you?" she repeated.

"My name is Saul Laski."

"What are you doing here?"

"I could ask the same of you."

"Answer the question." She raised the pistol as if that would prompt him. Saul knew now that he was dealing with an amateur with firearms, someone who had been seduced by television into believing that guns were magic wands which could make people do their bidding. He looked at her. She was younger than he had first thought, in her early twenties. She had an attractive, oval face, delicate features, full mouth, and large eyes that appeared all black in the poor light. Her skin was precisely the color of coffee with cream.

"I am looking around," said Saul. His voice was steady, but he was interested to find that his body was reacting much the way it always did to having a firearm pointed at it; his testicles were trying to rise into his body and he had an irresistible urge to hide behind someone, anyone, even himself.

"This house was closed off by the police," she said. Saul noticed that she had said "police" rather than "*po*-lice," the pronunciation he had heard from so many American blacks in New York.

"Yes," he said, "I know they did."

"What are you *doing* here?"

Saul hesitated. He looked at her eyes. There was anxiety there, tension, and great intensity. The human emotions reassured him and convinced him to tell her the truth. "I'm a doctor," he said. "A psychiatrist. I am interested in the murders which occurred here last week."

"A psychiatrist?" The young woman seemed dubious. The pistol did not waver. The house was quite dark now, the only light coming from a gas lamp in the courtyard. "Why did you break in?" she asked.

Saul shrugged. His arms were getting tired. "May I lower my hands?"

"No."

Saul nodded. "I was afraid the authorities would not let me see the house. I had hoped there might be something here to help explain the events. I don't believe there is."

"I should call the police," said the woman.

"By all means," agreed Saul. "I did not see a telephone downstairs, but there must be one somewhere. Let us call the police. Call Sheriff Gentry. I will be charged for breaking and entering. I would think that you will be charged with breaking and entering, deadly menacing, and possession of an illegal weapon. I presume it is *not* registered?"

The woman's head had come up at the mention of Gentry's name. She ignored his question. "What do you know about last Saturday's murders?" Her voice almost broke on the last word.

Saul arched his back to relieve the ache in his neck and arms. "I only know what I have read," he said. "Although I had met one of the women— Nina Drayton. I think that there is more involved here than the police— Sheriff Gentry, the FBI man, Haines—imagine."

"What do you mean?"

"I mean that nine people died in this town last Saturday and no one can explain it," said Saul. "Yet I think there is a common thread which the authorities have missed. My arms ache, Miss. I am going to put them down now, but I will make no other move." He lowered his hands before she could reply. She stepped back a foot. The old house settled around them. Somewhere on the street a car radio blared for a second and was cut off.

"I think you're lying," said the young woman. "You may be a common thief. Or some sort of ghoul hunting for souvenirs. Or you may have had something to do with the killings yourself."

Saul said nothing. He stared at her in the dark. The small automatic was barely visible in her hands. He could feel her indecision. After a moment he spoke. "Preston," he said. "Joseph Preston, the photographer. Wife? No, not his wife. Sheriff Gentry said that Mr. Preston had lived in the area for . . . twenty-six years, I believe. His daughter perhaps. Yes, his daughter."

The woman took another step back.

"Your father was killed on the street," said Saul. "Brutally. Senselessly. The authorities can tell you nothing conclusive and what they do tell you is unsatisfactory. So you wait. You watch. Possibly you have watched this house for days. Then along comes this New York Jew in a tennis hat and climbs the fence. You think, *this will tell me something.* I am right?" The girl remained silent, but the pistol was lowered. Saul could see her shoulders moving slightly and he wondered if she was crying.

"Well," he said and softly touched her arm, "perhaps I *can* help. Perhaps together we can make some sense of this insanity. Come, let us leave this house. It stinks of death."

The rain had stopped. The garden smelled of wet leaves and soil. The girl led Saul to the far side of the carriage house where there was a gap cut between the old iron and the new wire. He squeezed through after her. Saul noticed that she had put the pistol in the pocket of her white raincoat. They walked down the alley, their feet crunching softly on cinders. The night was cool.

"How did you know?" she asked.

"I did not. I guessed."

They reached the street and stood a minute in silence. "My car's around front," the young woman said at last.

"Oh? Then how did you see me?"

"I noticed you when you drove by. You were looking hard and you almost stopped in front of the house. When you turned around the block I came around to check."

"Hmmm," said Saul. "I would make a very poor spy."

"You're really a psychiatrist?"

"Yes."

"Not from here though."

"No. New York. I sometimes work at the clinic at Columbia University."

"You're an American citizen?"

"Yes."

"Your accent. Is it . . . what, German?"

"No, not German," said Saul. "I was born in Poland. What is your name?"

"Natalie," she said. "Natalie Preston. My father was . . . you know all that."

"No," said Saul. "I know very little. At this moment I know only one thing for sure."

"What's that?" The young woman's eyes were very intense.

"I'm starving," said Saul. "I have had nothing since breakfast except terrible coffee at the sheriff's office. If you would join me somewhere for dinner, we could continue our discussion."

"Yes, on two conditions," said Natalie Preston.

"What is that?"

"First, that you tell me anything you know that might help explain my father's murder."

"Yes?"

"And second, that you take that soggy tennis hat off while we eat."

"Agreed," said Saul Laski.

The restaurant was called Henry's and it was only a few blocks away, near the old marketplace. From the outside it did not appear promising. The whitewashed front was windowless and unadorned except for a single illuminated sign over the narrow door. Inside it was old and dark and reminded Saul of an inn near Lodz where his family had eaten occasionally when he was a boy. Tall black men in clean white jackets moved unobtrusively between the tables. The air was thick with the stimulating smell of wine and beer and seafood.

"Excellent," said Saul. "If the food tastes as good as it smells, it will be a wonderful experience." It was. Natalie ordered a shrimp salad. Saul had swordfish served shish kabob with broiled vegetables and small, white potatoes. They both drank cold, white wine and spoke of everything but what they had come to speak of. Natalie ascertained that Saul lived alone although he was plagued by a housekeeper who was part yenta and part therapist. He assured Natalie that he would never need to avail himself of the professional courtesy of colleagues as long as Tema continued to explain his neuroses to him and search for cures.

"You have no family then?" asked Natalie.

"Only a nephew in the States," said Saul and nodded to the waiter as the man cleared away their plates. "I have a cousin in Israel and many distant relatives there."

Saul was able to ascertain that Natalie's mother had died some years before and that Natalie was currently attending graduate school. "You say you're going to university in the North?" he asked.

"Well, not quite the North. St. Louis. Washington University."

"Why did you choose such a distant school? There is the College of Charleston. I had a friend who taught briefly at the University of South Carolina in . . . is it Columbia?"

"Yes."

"And Wofford College. That is in South Carolina, is it not?"

"Sure," said Natalie. "And Bob Jones University is up in Greenville, but my father wanted me to get as far away from what he called the Redneck Belt as I could. Washington University of St. Louis has an excellent graduate school of education . . . one of the best someone with a fine arts major could get into. Or at least get a scholarship for."

"You are an artist?"

"Photographer," said Natalie. "Some filmmaking. A little sketching and oil painting. I had a minor in English. I went to school at Oberlin, in Ohio. Ever hear of it?"

"Yes."

"Anyway, a friend of mine—good watercolorist named Diana Gold— convinced me last year that teaching would be fun. And why am I telling you all this?"

Saul smiled. The waiter came with the check and Saul insisted on paying. He left a generous tip.

"You're not going to tell me anything, are you?" asked Natalie. There was an undertone of pain in her voice.

"On the contrary," said Saul. "I will probably tell you more than I have ever told anyone. The question is . . . why?"

"What do you mean?"

"I mean . . . why are we trusting each other? You see a strange man breaking into a house and two hours later we are chatting here after a fine meal. I meet a young woman who immediately points a pistol at me and within a few hours I am willing to share things which have remained unsaid for many years. Why is this, Ms. Preston?"

"Miss Preston. Natalie. And I can only speak for myself."

"Do so, please."

"You have an honest face, Dr. Laski. Perhaps honest is not the right word. A *caring* face. You've known sadness . . ." Natalie stopped.

"We have all known sadness," Saul said softly.

The black girl nodded. "But some people don't learn from it. I think you have. It's . . . it's in your eyes. I don't know how else to say it."

"So that is what we base our judgment and futures on?" asked Saul. "A person's eyes?"

Natalie looked up at him. "Why not? Do you have a better way?" It was not a challenge but a serious question.

Saul slowly shook his head. "No. There may not be a better way. Not to begin with."

They drove southwest out of Historic Charleston, Saul following the girl's green Nova in his rented Toyota. They crossed the Ashley River on Highway 17 and stopped a few minutes later in an area called St. Andrews. The homes there were white frame, the neighborhood neat but working class. Saul parked in the driveway behind Natalie Preston's car.

Inside, the house was clean and comfortable, a home. A wing chair and heavy sofa took up much of the small living room. The fireplace was ready for a fire; the white mantel was laden with a potted Swedish ivy and numerous family photographs in metal frames. There were more framed photographs on the wall, but these were works of art, not snapshots. Saul moved from picture to picture as Natalie turned on lights and hung up her coat.

"Ansel Adams," said Saul as he stared at a striking black and white photograph of a small, desert village and cemetery glowing in evening light under a pale moon. "I have heard of him." In another print a heavy fog-bank was moving in over a city on a hill.

"Minor White," said Natalie. "Father knew him in the early fifties."

There were prints by Imogen Cunningham, Sebastian Milito, George Tice, André Kertész, and Robert Frank. The Frank picture caused Saul to pause. A man wearing a dark suit and holding a cane was standing on the porch of an ancient house or hotel. A flight of stairs to a second-story porch concealed the man's face. It made Saul want to take two steps to the left to identify the man. Something about the photograph stirred a deep sadness in him. "I'm sorry I do not know these names," said Saul. "Are they very well-known photographers?"

"Some are," said Natalie. "The prints are now worth a hundred times what Father paid for them, but he'll never sell them." The girl paused.

Saul picked up a snapshot of a black family on a picnic. The wife had a warm smile and straight, black hair curled up in the style of the early sixties. "Your mother?"

"Yes," said Natalie. "She died in a freak accident in June of 1968. Two days after Robert Kennedy was killed. I was nine."

The little girl in the photograph was standing on the picnic table, smiling and squinting up at her father. There was another portrait of Natalie's father nearby, a portrait of him as an older man, serious and rather handsome. The thin mustache and luminous eyes made Saul think of Martin Luther King without jowls. "This is a fine portrait," he said.

"Thank you. I took it last summer."

Saul looked around. "There are no framed prints by your father?"

"In here," said Natalie and led the way into the dining room. "Dad wouldn't hang them in the same room as the others." Over a spinet piano on a long wall opposite the dining room table, four black and white photographs were hung. Two were studies of light and shadow on the sides of old brick homes. One was an incredibly lit wide-angle shot of beach and sea stretching away to infinity. The final one was of a forest trail and was a study in planes, shadows, and composition.

"These are wonderful," said Saul, "but there are no people."

Natalie laughed softly. "That's true. Dad did portrait photography for a living and he said that he'd be darned if he'd do it for a hobby. Also, he was a shy person. He never did like shooting candid photos of people . . . and he always insisted that I get a written release if I did. He hated the idea of invading anyone's privacy. Also, Dad was just . . . you know . . . *shy*. If we called for a pizza to be delivered, he'd always ask me to make the phone call." Natalie's voice grew thick and she turned away for a second. "Would you like some coffee?"

"Yes," said Saul. "That would be nice." There was a darkroom off the kitchen. Originally it must have been a pantry or second bathroom. "This is where you and your father did your printing?" asked Saul. Natalie nodded and turned on a safe light. The small room was neatly organized: enlarger, trays, chemical bottles, everything shelved and labeled. Over the sink were eight or ten prints clipped on a nylon line. Saul studied them. They were all of the Fuller house, taken in different light, at different times of day, from different points of view.

"Yours?"

"Yes," said Natalie. "I know it's stupid, but it's better than just sitting in the car all day waiting for something to happen." She shrugged. "I've been to the police or sheriff's office every day and they're no help. Would you like cream or sugar?"

Saul shook his head. They moved into the living room and sat near the fireplace, Natalie in the wing chair, Saul on the sofa. The coffee was in cups of china so thin as to be almost transparent. Natalie poked at the logs and kindling and lit a taper. The fire started readily and burned well. The two sat for several moments watching the flames.

"I was Christmas shopping with friends in Clayton last Saturday," Natalie said at last. "That's a suburb of St. Louis. We went to a movie . . . *Popeye*, with Robin Williams. I got back to my apartment in University City at about eleven thirty that night. As soon as the phone rang I knew something was wrong. I don't know why. I get a lot of late calls from friends. Frederick, he's a very good friend of mine, usually doesn't get out of the computer center 'til after eleven and he often wants to go out for a pizza or something. But this time I knew it was long distance and bad news. It was Mrs. Culver who lives next door here. She and Mother used to be good friends. Anyway, she just kept saying that there's been an accident, that's the word she kept using, 'accident.' It took a minute or two for me to understand that Dad was dead, that he'd been killed.

"I got the earliest flight I could on Sunday. Everything was closed here. I called the mortuary from St. Louis, but when I got here the doors to the mortuary were locked and I had to go all around the place hunting for someone to let me in and they weren't ready for me. Mrs. Culver met me at the airport, but she couldn't stop crying and stayed in the car.

"It didn't look like Dad. Even less so on Tuesday at the funeral, with all the cosmetics. I was pretty confused. No one at the police headquarters on Sunday knew what was going on. They promised that a Detective Holmann would call me back that evening, but he didn't, not until Monday afternoon. Instead, the county sheriff—you said you met him—Mr. Gentry—he came over to the mortuary Sunday. He gave me a ride home later and tried to answer my questions. Everyone else just *asked* questions.

"Anyway, on Monday my Aunt Leah and cousins all arrived and I was too busy to even think until Wednesday. A lot of people came to the funeral. I'd forgotten how well liked Dad had been. A lot of merchants and people from the Old Section were there. Sheriff Gentry came.

"Leah wanted to stay a week or two, but her son, Floyd, had to get back to Montgomery. I told her I'd be all right. I said I might come out there for Christmas." Natalie paused. Saul was leaning forward, hands clasped. She took a breath and made a vague gesture toward the window facing the street. "This is the weekend that Dad and I always put up the tree. It's pretty late, but Dad always said that it was more fun if the tree wasn't around for weeks and weeks. We usually get it at the Dairy Queen lot over on Savannah. You know, I'd just bought him a Pendleton shirt on Saturday, a red plaid. For some reason I brought it with me. I don't know why I did that, I'll just have to take it back now." She stopped and lowered her face. "Excuse me a minute." She went quickly into the kitchen.

Saul sat for several minutes, watching the fire, fingers tightly clasped. Then he went out to join her. She was leaning on the kitchen counter, her arms rigid, a Kleenex grasped tightly in her left hand. Saul stood three feet from her.

"It just makes me so goddamn *mad*," she said, still looking away from Saul.

"Yes."

"I mean, it's like he didn't even *count*. He wasn't important. Do you know what I mean?"

"Yes."

"When I was little I used to watch cowboy shows on television," she said. "And somebody would be killed—not the hero or villain, just some guy—and it'd be like he had never existed, you know? And it bothered me. I was only six or seven, but it bothered me. I always used to think about the person and how he must've had parents and all the years he'd taken to grow up and how he had to have got dressed that morning and then, bang, he doesn't exist anymore because the writer wanted to show how fast the good guy was with a gun or something. Oh, *shit*, I'm not making any sense . . ." Natalie struck the counter with her right hand, palm down.

Saul stepped forward and touched her left arm. "Yes," he said, "you are."

"It just makes me so goddamn *angry*," she said. "My father was *real*. He never hurt anyone. Not *ever*. He was the kindest man I'll ever know and someone *killed* him and no one has any idea why. They just don't *know*. Oh, damn, I'm sorry . . ." Saul took her in his arms and held her as she cried.

Natalie had warmed their coffee. She sat in the wing chair. Saul stood by the fireplace, idly touching the leaves of the Swedish ivy. "There were three of them," he said. "Melanie Fuller, Nina Drayton, and a man called Borden from California. They were killers, all three of them."

"Killers? But the police said that Miz Fuller was an older lady . . . quite old . . . and that Mrs. Drayton was a victim."

"Yes," said Saul, "and all three were killers."

"No one mentioned Borden's name," said Natalie.

"He was there," said Saul. "And he was aboard the plane that blew up Friday night . . . early Saturday morning, actually. Or rather, he was supposed to be aboard."

"I don't understand. That was hours before my father was killed. How could this Borden . . . or any of these other people—have had anything to do with my father's murder?"

"They used people," said Saul. "They . . . *controlled* other people. Each had employees to use. It's hard to explain."

"You mean they were associated with the Mafia or something?"

Saul smiled. "I wish it were that simple."

Natalie shook her head. "I don't understand."

"It's a very long story," said Saul. "Much of it is quite fantastic, beyond belief, actually. It would be better if you did not hear it. You will either think me to be insane or you yourself will become involved in something with terrible implications."

"I'm already involved," Natalie said firmly.

"Yes." Saul hesitated. "But there is no need for further involvement."

"I'm going to *stay* involved, at least until my father's murderer is found. I'll do it with you and your information or I'll do it without you, Dr. Laski. I swear I will."

Saul looked at the young woman for a long moment. Then he sighed. "Yes, I believe you will. Although perhaps you will change your mind when you hear my story. I am afraid that in order to explain at all about the three old people—the three killers who were responsible for your father's death—I will have to tell my own story as well. I have never told it before. It is a very long story."

"Go on," said Natalie Preston. "I have all the time in the world."

"I was born in 1925, in Poland," said Saul, "in the city of Lodz. My family was relatively well-to-do. My father was a doctor. We were Jews but not Orthodox Jews. My mother had considered converting to Catholicism when she was younger. My father considered himself a doctor first, a Pole second, a European citizen third, and a Jew fourth. Perhaps he did not rate his Jewishness even that high.

"When I was a boy, Lodz was as good a place as any for a Jew to be. A third of the six hundred thousand residents were Jews. Many important citizens, businessmen, and artisans were Jews. Several of my mother's friends were active in the arts. Her uncle played in the municipal symphony for years. By the time I was ten years old, much of that had changed. Local political parties had been elected after promising to eliminate Jews from the city. As if possessed of the anti-Semitic contagion raging in our neighbor, Germany, the country was turning against us. My father blamed it on the hard times which we had just come through. He never tired of pointing out that European Jews had become used to waves of pogroms followed by generations of progress. 'We are all human beings,' he used to say, 'despite temporary differences which divide us.' I am sure that my father went to his death believing this."

Saul stopped. He paced back and forth, resting his hands on the back of the sofa when he finally stopped. "You see, Natalie, I am not used to telling this thing. I do not know what is necessary and what is not. Perhaps we should wait for another time."

"No," said Natalie, "now. Take your time. You say that it will help explain why my father died."

"Yes."

"Go on. Tell it all."

Saul nodded and came around to sit on the couch. He rested his elbows on his knees. His hands were large and they made gestures in the air as he spoke. "I was fourteen when the Germans entered our city. It was the September of 1939. At first it was not so bad. They arranged that a Jewish Council be set up to advise in the governing of this new outpost of the Reich. My father explained to me that it showed that anyone could be dealt with through civilized negotiations. He did not believe in devils. Despite my mother's protests, my father offered to serve on the Council. It was not to be. Thirty-one prominent Jews had already been appointed. A month later, in early November, the Germans deported the Council members to a camp and burned our synagogue.

"There was talk then of our family traveling to our Uncle Moshe's farm near Cracow. Already there were severe food shortages in Lodz. We usually spent our summers on the farm and the idea of being there with the rest of our family was an attractive one. Through Uncle Moshe we heard from his daughter Rebecca who had married an American Jew and was planning to go to Palestine to farm. For years she had urged other young members of the family to join her. I, for one, would have gladly gone to the farm. I had already been expelled, as had the other Jews, from my school in Lodz. Uncle Moshe had once taught at Warsaw University and I knew that he would have been happy to tutor me. New laws restricted Father's practice only to Jews—most of whom lived in distant, poorer parts of the city. There were few reasons to stay, many to go.

"But we stayed. It was planned that we would visit Uncle Moshe in June, as we always had, and decide then whether to return to the city. How naive we were.

"In March of 1940 the Gestapo drove us from our homes and created a Jewish ghetto in the city. By my birthday on April 5, the ghetto was completely sealed off. Travel for Jews was absolutely forbidden.

"Again the Germans set up a council—the Judenrat—and this time my father was chosen to serve on it. One of the Elders, Chaim Rumkowski, used to come to our flat—one room in which eight of us slept—and spend the night talking to my father about the administration of the ghetto. Incredibly, in spite of the overcrowding and starvation, order prevailed. I returned to school. When my father was not meeting with the Council, he was working sixteen hours a day at one of the hospitals he and Rumkowski had created from nothing.

"For a year we survived thus. I was small for my age, but I soon learned how to survive in the ghetto, even if it meant stealing, hoarding, or bartering with German soldiers for food and cigarettes. In the autumn of 1941 the Germans began bringing many thousands of western Jews into our ghetto. Some had been shipped from as far away as Luxembourg. Many were German Jews who looked down on the rest of us. I remember a fight I got into with an older boy, a Jew from Frankfurt. He was much taller than I was. I was sixteen by then but could have easily passed for thirteen. But I knocked him down. When he tried to get up, I struck him with a board and opened a large gash on his forehead. He had come in the week before on one of the sealed trains and was still very weak. I forget what the fight was about.

"My sister Stefa died that winter of typhus. So did many thousands of others. We were all grateful to see spring arrive, despite news of renewed German advances on the eastern front. My father saw the imminent fall of Russia as a good sign. He thought the war would end by August. He expected many of the Jews to be relocated in new towns to the east. 'We may have to be farmers to feed their new Reich,' he would say. 'But farming is not a bad life.'

"In May, most of the German and foreign Jews were shipped south to Oswiecim. Auschwitz. Few of us had ever heard of Oswiecim until the transports began rolling out of our ghetto to it.

"Until that spring, our ghetto had been used as a massive holding pen. Now the trains rolled four times a day. As a member of the Judenrat, my father was forced to help supervise the roundup and expulsion of thousands. It was very orderly. My father hated it. He would work around the clock at the hospital as if performing penance.

"Our turn came in late June, about the time we usually would have left for Uncle Moshe's farm. The seven of us were ordered to report to the train station. My mother and my younger brother Josef cried. But we went. I think that my father was relieved.

"We were not sent to Auschwitz. We went north to Chelmno, a village less than seventy kilometers from Lodz. I had once had a playmate, a provincial little fellow named Mordechai, whose family had come from Chelmno. I learned much later that it was at Chelmno that the Germans had carried out their first experiments with gassing . . . just that past winter as poor Stefa had lain dying of typhus.

"Unlike so many of the stories we had heard about the sealed transports, our trip was not unpleasant. We made it in a few hours. We were squeezed tightly into train cars, but they were regular passenger cars. The day was very beautiful. It was June 24. When we arrived it was as if we had traveled to Uncle Moshe's. The Chelmno station was tiny, hardly more than a country depot surrounded by thick, green forest. German soldiers led us to waiting trucks, but the soldiers seemed relaxed, almost jovial. There was none of the pushing and shouting we were used to in Lodz. We were driven several kilometers to a large estate where a camp had been set up. Once there we were registered—I clearly remember the rows of clerks' desks set outside on the gravel and the sound of the birds singing—and then we were segregated by sex for showers and disinfection. I was impatient to catch up to the other men and I never saw my mother and four sisters disappear behind the fence to the women's area.

"We were told to disrobe and stand in line. I was very embarrassed because I had only begun to mature that winter. I do not remember being frightened. The day was warm, we had been promised a meal after we had cleaned up, and the nearby forest and camp noises gave a festive, almost carnival atmosphere to the day. Ahead in a clearing I could see a large van with bright illustrations of animals and trees painted on the sides. Our line had started toward the clearing when an SS man, a young lieutenant with thick glasses and a shy face, came down the line separating the sick, the very young, and the older men from the stronger ones. The lieutenant hesitated when he came to me. I was still small for my age, but I had eaten relatively well that winter and had begun a growth spurt in the spring. He smiled and waved a small baton to send me to the shortened line of able-bodied men. Father was also sent to the line. Josef, who was only eight, was to stay with the children and old men. Josef began to cry and Father refused to leave him. I returned to the line to stand by Father and Josef. The young SS man waved to a guard. Father told me to return with the others. I refused.

"This was to be the only time in my life that Father struck me. He pushed me and said, 'Go!' I shook my head and held my place in line. The guard, a heavyset sergeant, was puffing toward us. Father slapped me once, very hard, and repeated, 'Go!' Shocked, hurt, I stumbled the few paces to the shorter line before the guard arrived. The SS man moved on. I was very angry at Father. I saw no reason why we could not have showered together. He had humiliated me in front of the other men. I watched through tears of anger as he left, his bare back pale in the morning light, carrying Josef who had quit crying and was looking around. Father looked back at me once before he turned out of sight with the line of children and old men.

"The rest of us, about a fifth of the men who had arrived that day, were not disinfected. We were marched directly to barracks and given rough prisoner uniforms.

"Father did not appear that afternoon or evening and as I was going to sleep in the filthy barracks that night I remember crying from loneliness. I was sure that by separating us in line, Father had condemned me to being kept from the part of the camp where families stayed.

"In the morning we were fed cold potato soup and grouped into work details. My group was led to the forest. A pit had been dug there. It was over two hundred feet long, forty feet wide, and it was at least fifteen feet deep. I could tell by the freshly turned soil that other pits had recently been filled in nearby. The smell should have told me everything, but I continued to deny it to myself until the first of the day's vans arrived. They were the same vans I had seen the day before.

"You see, Chelmno had been a test case. From what they had learned, Himmler had ordered gas chambers for prussic acid to be installed there, but that summer they were still using carbon monoxide in sealed chambers and the brightly colored vans.

"Our job was to separate the bodies, actually pry them apart, throw them in the pit, and spread the dirt and lime before the next loads arrived. The gas vans were not efficient. Frequently as many as half the victims survived the exhaust fumes and had to be shot at the edge of the pit by the *Totenkopfverbände*—the Death's Head Troopers—who waited there, smoking and joking with one another between van arrivals. Even then, some of the people survived both the gassing and the shooting and were buried while still stirring.

"I returned to the barracks that evening covered with excrement and blood. That night I considered dying but decided instead that I would live. Live despite all, live in the face of anything, live for no other reason than to live.

"I lied and said that I was a dentist's son and that I had been trained as a dentist myself. The kapos laughed at the idea of such a young apprentice, but within the next week I was put on the tooth detail. Three other Jews and I searched the naked bodies for rings, gold, anything valuable. We probed anuses and vaginas with steel hooks. Then I used a pair of pliers to remove gold teeth and fillings. Often I was sent down into the Pit to work. An SS sergeant named Bauer used to toss clods of dirt on my head and laugh. He had two gold teeth himself.

"After a week or two, Jews on the burial details were routinely shot and new arrivals sent to replace them. Perhaps because I was fast and efficient at my work, I stayed nine weeks at the Pit. Every morning I was sure it would be my turn. Every night in the barracks as the older men were saying Kaddish and I could hear cries of 'Eli, Eli,' being sent up from dark bunks, I made desperate deals with a God I no longer believed in. 'Just one more day,' I would say. 'Just one more day.' But it was *my own* will to survive that I most believed in. Perhaps I was suffering from the solipsism of adolescence, but I was convinced that if I *believed* strongly enough in my own continued existence, then it would be necessarily become to pass.

"In August the camp was enlarged and for some reason I was transferred to the *Waldkommando*, the forest brigade. We cut trees, tore up stumps, and quarried stone to build roads. Every few days an entire line of returning workers would be led off to the vans or straight to the Pit. In that way the brigade was changed. By the first snowfall in November I had been *Waldkommando* longer than anyone except the old kapo, Karski."

"What is a kapo?" asked Natalie.

"A kapo is a Jew with a whip."

"And they helped the Germans?"

"Learned treatises have been written about kapos and their identification with their Nazi masters," said Saul. "Stanley Elkins and others have looked into this kind of concentration camp submission and how it compares to the docility and identification of black American slaves. Just this September I was part of a panel discussing the so-called Stockholm Syndrome, wherein hostages not only identify with their captors but provide active support."

"Oh, like whatshername, Patty Hearst," said Natalie.

"Yes. And this . . . this *dominance* through force of will has been an obsession with me for many years. But we will speak more of this later. For now, let me say only that if there is anything at all to be said in my favor for the time I was in the camps, *I did not become a kapo.*

"In November of 1942, the camp improvement was completed and I was moved from the temporary barracks back to the main compound. I was put on the Pit detail. The ovens had been completed by this time, but they had underestimated the numbers of Jews arriving on the transports so the vans and the Pit were still in use. They no longer required my services as a dentist to the dead. I spread lime, shivered in the early winter cold, and waited. I knew that it had to be just a matter of days until I joined those I was burying each day.

"Then one Thursday night, November 19, 1942, something happened." Saul fell silent. After a few seconds he rose and walked to the fireplace. The fire was almost out. "Natalie, would you have a drink of something stronger than coffee? Sherry, perhaps?"

"Of course," said Natalie. "Would brandy do?"

"Wonderful."

When she returned a moment later with a large brandy snifter almost filled with brandy, Saul had stirred the coals, replenished the wood, and coaxed the fire back to life.

"Thank you, my dear." He swirled the amber liquid and inhaled deeply before drinking. The fire crackled and spit. "On Thursday—I am reasonably sure it was November 19, 1942—five Germans came into our barracks late at night. They had come before. Each time they had removed four men. The men were never seen again. Prisoners in each of the other seven barracks in our compound had told us that the same was true there. We had no idea why the Nazis would choose such a manner of liquidation when thousands went openly to the Pit each day, but there was much we did not understand. There were whispers of medical experiments.

"This night there was a young Oberst, a colonel, with the guards. And this night they chose me.

"I had decided to fight if they came for me at night. I realize that this seems in violation of my decision to live in spite of everything, but there was something about the thought of being taken out into the dark which panicked me, drove all hope from me. I was prepared to fight. When the guards ordered me out of my bunk I knew that I had only seconds to live. I was prepared to try to kill at least one of the swine before they murdered me.

"It did not happen. Instead the Oberst ordered me out *and I obeyed*. Or rather, my body disobeyed me. It was not merely cowardice or submission, the Oberst *entered my mind*. I know of no other way to put it. I felt it, as surely as I was prepared to feel the bullets which never came. I felt *him* move my muscles, shuffle my feet across the floor, and take my body from the barracks. And all the while the SS guards were laughing.

"It is impossible to describe what I felt then. It could only be called a mindrape and even that does not convey the sense of violation. I did not then . . . nor do I now . . . believe in demonic possession or supernatural occurrences. What happened then was the result of some monstrous but very *real* psychic or psychological ability to directly control the minds of other human beings.

"We were loaded aboard a truck. This in itself was incredible. Except for the brief, deceptive ride from Chelmno station, Jews were never allowed to ride in vehicles. Slaves were much cheaper than petrol in Poland that winter.

"They drove us into the forest. There were sixteen of us in the truck, including one young woman from the women's barracks. The mindrape had ended for the time being, but it had left behind a residue more foul and shameful than the excrement I had been smeared with daily while on Pit detail. I could tell from the manner and whispers from the other Jews that they had not yet experienced it. To be honest, I doubted my sanity at that moment.

"The trip took less than an hour. There was one guard in the back of the truck with us. He carried a machine-pistol. Camp guards almost never carried automatic weapons while in the compound because of the danger if they were seized. Had I not been recovering from the terrible experience in the barracks I would have attempted to overpower the German or at least leap from the truck. But the mere unseen presence of the Oberst in the cab of the truck filled me with a terror deeper than any I had known in months.

"It was after midnight when we arrived at an estate larger even than the mansion around which Chelmno had been built. It was deep in the forest. Americans would call the place a castle, but it was more and less than that. It was the kind of ancient Great Hall which one occasionally encounters in the darkest forests of my country: a great heap of stones, old beyond our history, tended and added onto for countless generations by reclusive families which trace their lineage back to pre-Christian times. The two trucks stopped and we were herded into a cellar not far from the main hall. From the sight of the military vehicles parked in what remained of the once-formal gardens and from the raucous noise emanating from the hall, I surmised that the Germans had commandeered the estate as a rest and recreation center for privileged units. Indeed, once inside and locked in a lightless cellar, I heard a Lithuanian Jew from the other truck whisper that he knew the regimental markings of the vehicles. They belonged to *Einsatzgruppe 3*—a Special Action Group—which had liquidated entire villages of Jews near the man's home in Dvensk. The *Einsatzgruppen* were regarded with fear and awe even by the SS *Totenkopfverbände* which carried out the camp exterminations.

"Some time later the guards returned with torches. There were thirty-two of us in the cellar. We were divided into two equal groups and led upstairs to separate rooms. There our group was dressed in rough, red-dyed tunics with white symbols on the front. Guards ordered us into specific uniforms. My symbol—a tower or baroque lamppost—meant nothing to me. The man next to me wore the silhouette of an elephant raising its right front foot.

"We were brought to the Great Hall. There we were greeted with a scene out of the Middle Ages by way of Hieronymous Bosch; hundreds of SS and *Einsatzgruppen* murderers lounged and gambled and whored where they pleased. Polish peasant girls, some only children, were the servants and slaves of the men in gray. Torches had been thrust into brackets on the walls and the tableau was illuminated as in a flickering fever dream of Hell. Scraps of food lay rotting where they had been thrown. Centuries-old tapestries were stained and sooted from the open fires. A once-magnificent banquet table had been almost hacked into pieces where the Germans had carved their names with bayonets. Men lay passed out and snoring on the floor. I watched as two enlisted men urinated on a rug which must have been brought back from the Holy Land in one of the Crusades.

"The hall was huge, but the center of it, an area about eleven meters long by eleven meters wide, was conspicuously empty. The floor was tiled black and white, each tile four feet to a side. At opposite ends of this open square, just below where the balconies began, two heavy chairs had been set on stone slabs. In one of these thrones sat the young Oberst. He was pale, blond, and Aryan. His hands were white and thin. In the other chair sat an old man, as ancient looking as the heap of rocks around us. He was also wearing an SS uniform, that of a general, but the effect was more of a wizened wax dummy dressed in a baggy uniform by malicious children.

"The other truckload of Jews had been led in from a side door. They were dressed in light blue tunics with black symbols similar to ours. I could see that the woman with that group was wearing a light blue gown with the symbol of a crown or coronet on the front. I realized then what was happening. In the state of exhaustion and constant fear I had reached, there was no insanity too bizarre to be believed.

"We were ordered to our squares. I was a pawn, a white king's bishop's pawn. I stood three meters in front of and to the right of the Oberst's throne, facing the frightened-looking Lithuanian Jew who was the black bishop's pawn.

"The shouting and singing was silenced. German troopers gathered around, jostling for a place near the border of the square. Some climbed the stairways or crowded the balconies for a better view. For half a minute there was silence except for the sputtering of the torches and the heavy breathing of the throng. We stood on our appointed squares, thirty-two starved and frightened Jews, white-faced, staring, breathing shallowly, waiting for whatever would come.

"The Old Man leaned forward slightly on his chair and gestured with an open palm toward the Oberst. The younger man smiled slightly and nodded his head. The game began.

"The Oberst nodded again and the pawn to my left, a gaunt, older man with gray stubble on his cheeks, lurched two squares forward. The Old Man responded by advancing his own king's pawn. I could tell by watching the way the poor, confused prisoners moved that they were not in control of their own bodies.

"I had played a little chess with my father and uncle. I knew the standard openings. There were no surprises here. The Oberst glanced to his right and a heavyset Pole wearing the Knight's tunic came forward to stand in front of me. The Old Man sent out the knight on his queen's side. The Oberst brought our bishop, a small man with his left arm bandaged, out from behind me to stand on the fifth rank of the knight's file. The Old Man advanced his queen's pawn one square.

"I wished then that I was wearing any symbol save that of a pawn. The squat form of the peasant in front of me, the knight, offered only the slightest sense of safety. To my right, another pawn turned to look behind him and then grimaced in pain as the Oberst forced him to face forward. I did not turn around. My legs were beginning to shake.

"The Oberst moved our queen's pawn two ranks forward to stand next to the old pawn on the king's file. Our queen's pawn was a boy, barely a teenager, and he glanced furtively to the left and right without turning his head. The peasant knight in front of me was the only protection the boy had from the Old Man's pawn.

"The Old Man made a slight gesture with his left hand and his bishop stepped out in front of the Dutch woman who was his queen. The bishop's face was very pale. The Oberst's fifth move brought out our other knight. I could not see the man's face. The SS men gathered around were beginning to shout and clap after every move as if they were spectators at a football match. I heard snatches of conversation in which the Oberst's opponent was referred to as *Der Alte,* 'The Old One.' The Oberst was being cheered as *Der Meister.*

"The Old Man hunched forward like a pale spider and his king's knight moved out in front of the bishop's pawn. The knight was young and strong, too strong to have been in camp more than a few days. He had an idiot smile on his face as if he were enjoying this nightmare game. As if in response to the boy's smile, the Oberst moved our frail bishop onto the same square. I recognized the bishop now. He was a carpenter from our barracks who had hurt himself two days earlier sawing boards for the guards' sauna. The little man lifted his good arm and tapped the black knight on the shoulder, the way a friend taps another when relieving him on duty.

"I did not see the muzzle flash. The rifle fired from somewhere on the balcony behind me, but the noise was so loud that I jumped and started to turn before the vise of the Oberst's control closed on my neck. The young knight's smile vanished in a red and gray mist and his skull exploded from the bullet's impact. Pawns behind him crouched in terror before being brought upright in pain. The knight's body slid back almost to his starting square. A pool of blood had already formed on the white pawn's square. Two SS men came forward and dragged the corpse away. Splinters of skull and brain matter had spattered several of the adjoining black pieces, but no one else had been injured. The room was loud with cheers.

"The Old Man leaned forward again and his own bishop took a diagonal step to where ours waited. The black bishop lightly touched the carpenter's bandaged arm. There was a pause this time before the rifle spoke. The bullet caught our bishop below the left shoulder blade and the little man staggered forward two steps and then remained standing a second, his right arm coming back as if to scratch an itch, before his knees buckled and he collapsed to the tile. A sergeant came out, placed a Luger to the carpenter's skull, and fired once before dragging the still-twitching corpse off the board. Play resumed.

"The Oberst moved our queen forward two squares. Only one empty square separated the queen from me and I could see where she had bitten her fingernails almost to the quick. This reminded me of my sister, Stefa, and I was amazed to find tears clouding my vision. It was the first time I had cried for Stefa.

"The Old Man made his next move to the roar of the drunken mob. His king's pawn moved quickly to take our queen's pawn. Our pawn was a bearded Pole, obviously an Orthodox Jew. The rifle fired twice in quick succession. The black king's pawn was covered with blood as he took our queen pawn's place on the square.

"No one was in front of me now. I looked across only three empty ranks into the face of the black knight. The torchlight threw long shadows. The SS men screamed advice from the edge of the tile. I did not dare turn to see the Oberst, but I watched as the Old Man stirred on his roost. He must have realized that he was losing control of the center of the board.

He turned his head and his king knight's pawn advanced one square. The Oberst moved our surviving bishop to the next square, blocking the enemy pawn and threatening the Old Man's bishop. The mob cheered.

"The openings completed, the two players proceeded to develop their middle games. Each side castled. Both brought their rooks into play. The Oberst moved our queen to stand in front of me. I stared at her shoulder blades, sharp against the fabric of her gown, and at the tendrils of frizzy hair touching her back. I clenched and unclenched my hands. I had not moved a foot since the game had begun. A terrible headache sent spots dancing before my eyes and I was terrified that I would faint. What would happen then? Would the Oberst allow me to collapse or would my unconscious body be kept upright in its place? I gasped for air and concentrated on watching the torchlight shimmer on a tapestry against the far wall.

"On Black's fourteenth move, the Old Man sent his bishop to where our peasant knight stood in the center of the board. There was no shot this time. The heavy SS sergeant came out onto the board and handed his ceremonial dagger to the black bishop. The room grew silent. Torchlight danced on the sharp steel. The squat peasant knight writhed and squirmed. I could see the muscles in his arms bunch in a vain effort to break free of the Oberst's control. He could not. The bishop slit his throat with a single swing of the blade. The SS sergeant retrieved his knife and gestured for two men to remove the corpse. Play resumed.

"One of our rooks took their intruding bishop. Again the knife was used. I stood behind the young queen and squeezed my eyes shut. I opened them several moves later when the Oberst moved my queen forward a square. I wanted to sob, to cry out, when she left me. The Old Man immediately brought his own queen, a young Dutch girl, down the diagonal to the fifth square on his rook's file. The enemy queen was only one empty square from me on the diagonal. Nothing stood between us. I felt my bowels loosen with fear.

"The Oberst now began his attack. First he advanced his knight's pawn on the left side. The Old Man moved out his rook's pawn, a red-faced man I recognized from the forest brigade, to counter our pawn. The Oberst matched the move with our rook's pawn. It was hard for me to see. Most of the other prisoners were taller than me and I could see backs and shoulders and bald heads and sweating, terrified men rather than chess pieces. I tried to visualize the chessboard in my mind. I knew that only our king and a single rook remained on the rank behind me. The only other piece on the same rank as me was the pawn in front of the king. Ahead and to my left was a cluster of queen, pawn, rook, and bishop. Further left, our surviving knight stood alone. To his left, the two rook pawns were deadlocked. The black queen continued to threaten me from my right.

"Our king, a gaunt Jew in his sixties, moved a diagonal step to his right. The Old Man consolidated his rooks on their king's file. Suddenly my queen moved back to the second square on our own rook's file. I was alone now. I could look straight ahead across four empty squares to where the Lithuanian Jew stared back at me. There was an animal panic in his eyes.

"Suddenly I was moving forward, my feet dragging across the marble tile. There was the terrible, undeniable *presence* in my skull, pushing me, restraining me, clenching my jaws tight against the scream which welled up from the base of my spine. I stopped where our queen had stood earlier, other white pawns on each side of me. The Old Man brought his black knight up to face me across an empty white square. The mob was screaming more loudly now. I heard shouts of *'Meister! Meister!'* building into a chant.

"I stepped forward again—only one square this time. I was now the only white piece beyond the middle of the board. Somewhere behind me and to my right was the black queen. I felt her presence as strongly as I felt the presence of the unseen rifleman on the balcony. Half a meter in front of me were the sweaty face and gaunt eyes of the black knight. Behind him cowered the Lithuanian Jew.

"The black rook passed me on my left. When he entered the white pawn's square the two men grappled. At first I thought this meant a loss of control by the Oberst or the Old Man and then I realized that this was part of the game. The German soldiers screamed their bloodlust. The black rook was stronger, or he was not being restrained, and the white pawn bent under his grip. The rook got both hands on the pawn's throat and squeezed more tightly. There was a long, dry rattling sound and the pawn collapsed.

"They had no sooner removed the body of our pawn when the Oberst moved our surviving knight to the square and the struggle resumed. This time it was the black rook who was dragged away, bare feet scraping on the tile, eyes distended and staring.

"The black knight shuffled past me and again there was a struggle. The two men stumbled against each other, fingers clawing at each other's eyes, knees flailing, until the white knight was forced out of the square onto the empty square behind me. The rifle must have been fired from the balcony directly in front of me. I felt the rush of air as the bullet passed my ear and I heard the impact. The dying knight stumbled against me as he fell. For a second his hand clutched feebly at my ankle as if seeking help. I did not turn around.

"My queen was behind me again. The black pawn on my right moved forward to threaten her. I would have grabbed him then if I had been permitted to do so. I was not. The queen retreated three squares. The Old Man advanced his queen's pawn a square. Our other bishop's pawn was brought up by the Oberst.

"'*Meister! Meister!*' chanted the mob. The Old Man drew his queen back two squares.

"Now I was moved again. I stood face-to-face with the Lithuanian Jew. He stood rigidly, paralyzed with fear. Did he now know that I could not harm him as long as we were on the same file? Perhaps not, but I was acutely aware that the dark queen could remove me at any second. Only the unseen presence of my own queen five squares behind me offered me any security. But what if *Der Alte* was willing to trade queens? Instead, he moved his rook back to the king's original square.

"To my left there was a commotion as the other bishop's pawn removed a black pawn and was removed in turn by the surviving black bishop. For a moment I was alone in enemy territory. Then the Oberst brought the white queen up to stand in the square behind me. Whatever happened next, I would not be alone. I held my breath and waited.

"Nothing happened. Or rather, the Old Man stepped down from his tall chair, made a gesture, and moved away. He had resigned. The drunken mob of *Einsatzgruppen* troopers roared their approval. A contingent of soldiers wearing Death's Head insignia rushed to the Oberst and carried him around the room on their shoulders. I remained standing there, facing the Lithuanian, both of us blinking stupidly. The game was over and I knew that somehow I had been instrumental in winning it for the Oberst, but I was too dull to understand how. All I could see were tired Jews standing in confused relief as the hall resounded to shouts and singing. Six of our men in white had died. Six of the black pieces were missing. The rest of us were able to move, to mill around. I turned to embrace the woman behind me. She was weeping. 'Shalom,' I said and kissed her hands. 'Shalom.' The Lithuanian Jew had collapsed to his knees on his white square. I helped him up.

"A squad of enlisted men with machine-pistols moved us through the mob into an empty foyer. There they had us disrobe and tossed our tunics onto a pile. Then they took us out into the night to shoot us.

"We were ordered to dig our own graves. There were half a dozen shovels lying in a clearing forty meters behind the estate and we used these to excavate a wide, shallow trench while the troopers held torches or stood and smoked cigarettes in the dark. There was snow on the ground. The earth was frozen and as hard as stone. We could dig no deeper than half a meter. Between the dull strokes of the shovels, I could hear renewed laughter from the lodge. Lights burned in high windows and threw yellow rectangles on the slate-tiled gables. Only the exercise and our fear kept us from freezing. My bare feet had turned a terrible white-blue and I could not feel my toes. We were almost finished with the digging and I knew that I had to decide what to do. It was quite dark and I felt that my best bet was to make a break for the forest. It would have been better had we all bolted at once, but several of the older Jews were obviously too cold and exhausted to move and we were not allowed to speak to each other. The two women stood several meters from the trench, vainly trying to cover their nakedness while the guards made crude jokes and held torches near them.

"I could not decide whether to simply run or to use the long-handled shovel in an attempt to club down one of the soldiers and seize a machine-pistol. These were *Einsatzgruppen Totenkopfverbände*, but they were also drunk and in a relaxed mood. I had to decide.

"The shovel. I chose the guard—a short, young man who appeared to be half dozing a few steps from me. I tightened my grip on the long handle.

"'*Halt! Wo ist denn mein Bauer?*' It was the blond Oberst crunching through the snow toward us. He wore a heavy greatcoat and his officer's cap. When he entered the circle of torchlight he looked around. He had asked for his pawn. *Which* pawn?

"'*Du! Komm her!*' He gestured at me. I cringed, expecting the mind-rape again, but it did not come. I jumped out of the shallow pit, handed my shovel to a guard, and stood naked and shivering in front of the Oberst, in front of the one they had called Der Meister.

"'You must finish here,' he said in German to the sergeant in charge. '*Schnell!*'

"The sergeant nodded and moved the Jews together at the edge of the hole. The two women huddled at the far end, their thin arms around one another. The sergeant ordered everyone to lie down in the cold trench. Three men refused and were shot where they stood. One, the man who had been the black king, fell twitching only two meters from me. I looked down at my bloodless feet and tried not to move, but my own shaking intensified. The other Jews were ordered to roll the bodies into the Pit with them. Then there was silence. The pale backs and buttocks of my fellow prisoners glowed in the torchlight. The sergeant gave an order and the shooting began.

"It took less than a minute. The sound of the machine-pistols and light carbines seemed muted, inconsequential, a light *pop* and another naked, white form would twitch and spasm a second in the hole and then be still. The women died in each other's embrace. The Lithuanian Jew cried out in Hebrew and struggled to his knees, arms outflung toward either the guards or the sky—I still do not know which—and then he was cut almost in half by automatic rifle fire.

"Through all of this I stood shaking, staring at my feet, praying that I would become invisible. But even before they were finished the sergeant turned back to me and said, 'This one, *mein Oberst?*'

"'*Mein zuverlässiger Bauer?*' said the Oberst. *My trustworthy pawn?* 'We are to have a hunt,' he said.

"'*Eine Jagd?*' asked the sergeant. '*Heute nacht?*'

"'*Wenn es dämmert.*'

"'*Auch Der Alte?*'

"'*Ja.*'

"'*Jawohl, mein Oberst.*' I could see that the sergeant was disgusted. He would have no time for sleep that night.

"As the guards began shoveling a thin cover of frozen earth over the bodies, I was led back to the lodge and chained up in the same cellar where we had been kept hours earlier. My feet began to tingle and then to burn. It was very painful. In spite of that, I was dozing when the sergeant returned, unlocked my chains, and ordered me into clothes: underwear, blue wool trousers, a shirt and thick sweater, heavy socks, and sturdy boots which were only slightly too small. The honest clothing felt wonderful after months in prison rags.

"The sergeant led me outside to where four SS men stood waiting in the snow. They carried hand torches—flashlights—and heavy rifles. One had a German shepherd on a leash and he let the straining animal sniff at me while we waited. The Great Hall was dark now, the shouting quieted for the night. There was a gray translucence to the night as dawn approached.

"The guards had just turned off their flashlights when the Oberst and the old general emerged. They were not in uniform. They wore heavy, green hunting jackets and capes. Each carried a nonmilitary, large-calibered rifle with a telescopic sight attached. I understood then. I knew exactly what was going to happen next, but I was too exhausted to care.

"The Oberst gestured and the guards walked away from me to stand by the two officers. I stood there for a minute, irresolute, refusing to do what they wanted me to do. The sergeant snarled at me in bad Polish. 'Run! Run, you Jewish vermin. Go!' And still I did not move. The dog flung himself against the leash, snarling and straining. The sergeant raised his rifle and fired a shot which threw snow up between my feet. I did not move. Then I felt the first tentative touches in my mind.

"*Go, kleiner Bauer. Go!* The silky whisper in my mind made me reel with nausea. I turned and ran into the forest.

"I was in no condition to run for very long. Within a few minutes I was panting and stumbling along. My footprints were clearly visible in the snow, but there was nothing I could do about that. The sky grew lighter as I staggered along in what I hoped was a southward direction. I heard frenzied barking behind me and knew that the hunting party had begun to follow my trail.

"I had gone little more than a kilometer when I came to the open area. A strip almost a hundred meters wide had been cleared of trees and undergrowth. Rolls of barbed wire ran down the center of this no-man's land, but it was not the wire which caused me to halt. In the center of the clearing a white sign lettered in German and Polish proclaimed HALT! MINE FIELD!

"The barking grew closer. I turned left and broke into a painful, gasping trot. I knew now that there would be no way out. The mined perimeter would enclose the entire estate—their private hunting preserve. My only hope was to find the road we had come by the night before, an eternity ago. There would almost certainly be gates and guards, but I would try for the road nonetheless. Better that the guards take me down than the obscenities behind me. I resolved that I would run the mine field before allowing the hunting party a clear shot.

"I had just reached a shallow stream when the mindrape began again. I was standing still, staring at the half-frozen stream, when I *felt* him enter me. For a few seconds I fought it, clutching at my temples, falling to my knees in the snow, but then the Oberst was in me, filling my mind in the way water fills the mouth and nostrils and lungs of a drowning man. It was worse than that. It was as if a great tapeworm had entered my skull and bored its way into my brain. I screamed but no sound emerged. I staggered to my feet.

"*Komm her, mein kleiner Bauer!* The Oberst's voice whispered soundlessly to me. His thoughts tumbled into mine, forced my own volition into some dark pit. I glimpsed images of faces, places, uniforms, and rooms. I rode on waves of hate and arrogance. His love of violence filled my mouth with the coppery taste of blood. *Komm!* The mental whisper was seductive, sickening, like a man's tongue entering my mouth.

"I watched myself run into the stream, turning back again to the west, *toward* the hunting party, running hard now, gasping in shallow, painful bursts. The icy water splashed my legs and made the wool trousers heavy. My nose began to hemorrhage and the blood ran freely down my face and neck.

"*Komm her!*

"I left the stream and stumbled through the forest to a pile of boulders. My body twitched and jerked like a marionette as I climbed to wedge myself in a gap between the rocks. I lay there with my cheek against the stone, blood pooling on frozen moss. Voices approached. The hunting party was no more than fifty paces away through the screen of trees. I assumed that they would encircle my pile of rocks and then the Oberst would make me stand so they could have a clean shot. I strained to move my legs, to shift my arm, but it was as if someone had cut the cables connecting my brain to my body. I was pinned there as surely as if the boulders had fallen on me.

"There was the sound of conversation and then, incredibly, the men moved on the way I had gone ten minutes earlier. I could hear the dog barking as it followed my trail. Why was the Oberst playing with me? I strained to make out his thoughts, but my weak probes were brushed away as one would slap away a persistent insect.

"Suddenly I was moving again, running in a crouch past the trees, then crawling on my belly through the snow. I smelled the cigarette smoke before I saw them. The Old Man and the sergeant were in a clearing. The Old Man was sitting on a fallen log. The hunting rifle rested across his knees. The sergeant stood near him with his back to me, his fingers tapping idly at his rifle stock.

"Then I was up and running, moving faster than I had ever moved before. The sergeant wheeled to look just as I jumped and struck him with my shoulder. I was smaller than the sergeant and much lighter, but the speed of the impact knocked him down. I rolled once, screaming silently, wanting only to regain control of my own body and flee into the forest, and then I had grabbed away the Old Man's hunting rifle and was striking the sergeant in the face and neck, using the beautifully carved rifle stock as a club. The sergeant tried to rise and I clubbed him down again. He groped for his own rifle and I smashed his hand under my boot and then drove the heavy stock into his face until bones smashed, until there was no real face left. Then I dropped the rifle and turned to the Old Man.

"He was still sitting on the log, one hand holding a Luger he had removed from his holster, the cigarette still dangled from his thin lips. He looked a thousand years old, but there was a smile on the wrinkled caricature of a face.

" '*Sie!*' he said and I knew he was not speaking to me.

" '*Ja, Alte,*' I said and was amazed to hear the words coming from my own mouth. '*Das Spiel ist beendet.*'

" 'We will see,' said the Old Man and raised the pistol to fire. I jumped then and the bullet passed through my sweater and along my ribs. I grabbed his wrist before he could fire again and we pirouetted there in the snow, the Old Man staggering to his feet to join me in a bizarre dance: the emaciated young Jew with blood streaming from his nose and an ancient old man lost in his wool greatcoat. His Luger fired again, harmlessly into the air, and then I had it and staggered back. I raised the gun.

" '*Nein!*' shouted the Old Man and then I felt *his* presence like a hammer blow to the skull. For a second I was nowhere as those two obscene parasites struggled for the control of my body. Then I seemed to be looking down on the scene from somewhere above myself. I saw the Old Man standing rigid and my own body lurching around as if in the grip of a terrible seizure. My eyes had rolled back in their sockets and my mouth was gaping open like an idiot's. Urine blotted my trousers and steamed in the cold air.

"Then I was watching from my own eyes and the Old Man was no longer in my mind. He took three steps back and sat heavily on the log. 'Willi,' he said. '*Mein Freund . . .*'

"My arm lifted and I shot the Old Man twice in the face and once in the heart. He went over backward and I stood staring at the hobnailed soles of his boots.

"*We are coming, Pawn,* whispered the Oberst. *Wait for us.*

"I stood waiting until I could hear their shouts and the growling of the German shepherd just beyond the trees. The pistol was still in my hand. I tried to relax my body, concentrating all of my will and energy into a single finger of my right hand, not even thinking about what I was going to do. The hunting party was almost in sight when the Oberst's control slipped just enough for me to try. It was the most crucial and difficult struggle of my life. I had only to close one finger a few millimeters, but it took all of the energy and determination left in my body and spirit to do so.

"I succeeded. The Luger fired and the bullet tore a path across my thigh and took off the small toe on my right foot. The pain was like a cleansing fire. It seemed to take the Oberst by surprise and I could feel his presence draw back for a few seconds.

"I turned and ran, leaving bloody footprints in the snow. There were shouts close behind me. An automatic rifle began to chatter and I could hear the steel-jacketed projectiles humming past me like bees. *But the Oberst did not control me.* I reached the mine field and ran into it without pausing. I parted the barbed wire with my bare hands, kicked aside the clinging strands, and ran on. Incredibly, inexplicably, I made it across the clearing. That is when the Oberst reentered my mind.

"*Halt!* I stopped. I turned to see four guards and the Oberst facing me across the strip of death. *Come back, little pawn,* whispered the creature's voice. *The game is over.*

"I tried to lift the Luger to my own temple. I could not. My body began walking toward them, back into the mine field, toward the raised weapons. It was at that second that the German shepherd broke away from the guard holding him and charged at me. The beast had just reached the edge of the strip, not twenty feet from the Oberst, when the mine exploded. It was an antitank mine, very powerful. Earth, metal, and pieces of dog filled the air. I saw all five men go down and then something soft struck my chest and knocked me down.

"I struggled up to see the German shepherd's head lying at my feet. The Oberst and two of the SS men were on their hands and knees, stunned, shaking their heads. The other two did not move. *The Oberst was not with me.* I raised the Luger and emptied the clip at the Oberst. It was too far. I was shaking too badly. None of the slugs hit near the two men. I spent no more time looking but turned and ran.

"I do not know to this day why the Oberst allowed me to escape. Perhaps he had been injured by the explosion. Or perhaps any further demonstration of his control over me would have shown that the death of the Old Man was his doing. I do not know. But to this day I suspect that I escaped that day because it suited the purpose of the Oberst. . . ."

Saul stopped speaking. The fire was out and it was long past midnight. He and Natalie Preston sat in near darkness. Saul's voice had been little more than a hoarse croak for the final half hour of his narrative.

"You're exhausted," said Natalie.

Saul did not deny it. He had not slept for two nights—not since he had seen the photograph of "William Borden" in the newspaper on Sunday morning.

"But there's more to the story, isn't there?" said Natalie. "This all ties in with the people who killed my father, doesn't it?"

Saul nodded.

Natalie left the room and returned a moment later with quilts, sheets, and a thick pillow. She began making the couch into a bed. "Stay here tonight," she said. "You can finish in the morning. I'll make breakfast for us."

"I have a motel room," Saul said hoarsely. The thought of driving that far out Route 52 made him want to close his eyes and go to sleep where he was sitting.

"But I would appreciate it if you would stay," she said. "I want to hear . . . no, I *need* to hear the rest of this story." She paused. "And I don't want to be alone in the house tonight."

Saul nodded.

"Good," said Natalie. "There's a new toothbrush on the counter in the bathroom. I could get a clean pair of Dad's pajamas out if you want . . ."

"No," said Saul. "No need."

"All right, then," said Natalie and stopped at the entrance to the short hallway. "Saul . . ." She paused and rubbed her arms. "This is all . . . it's all true, isn't it?"

"Yes."

"And your Oberst was here in Charleston last week, wasn't he? He was one of those responsible for killing my father."

"I think so."

Natalie nodded, started to speak, bit her lip softly, and said only, "Good night, Saul."

"Good night, Natalie."

Tired as he was, Saul Laski lay awake for some time, watching stray rectangles of reflected car lights move across the photographs on the wall. He tried to think of pleasant things; of golden light touching the limbs of willows by a stream or of a field of white daisies on a farm where he had played as a boy. But when he slept at last, Saul dreamed of a beautiful June day and of his brother Josef following him to a circus in a pleasant meadow where brightly decorated circus wagons led bands of laughing children to a waiting Pit.

SEVEN

Charleston
Wednesday, Dec. 17, 1980

At first, Sheriff Bobby Joe Gentry was delighted to discover that he was being followed. To his knowledge, he had never been tailed before. He had done his own share of following people; just the day before he had followed the psychiatrist, Laski, watched as he broke into the Fuller house, waited patiently in Linda Mae's unmarked Dodge as Laski and the Preston girl had gone out to dinner, and then spent a good part of the night in St. Andrews drinking coffee and watching the front of Natalie Preston's house. It had been a singularly cold and profitless night. This morning he had driven by there early in his own car and the psychiatrist's rented Toyota was still in the driveway. What was their connection? Gentry had a strong hunch about Laski—had felt the twinges of it the first time he had spoken to the psychiatrist on the telephone—and the hunch was fast becoming one of those unscratchable, between-the-shoulder blades itches of intuition that Gentry recognized from experience as being one of the necessary stocks in trade of a good cop. So he had tailed Laski yesterday. And now he—Sheriff Bobby Joe Gentry of Charleston County—was being tailed.

At first he found it hard to believe. This Wednesday morning he had risen at six as usual, tired from too little sleep and too much caffeine the night before, had driven by the Preston home in St. Andrews to verify that Laski had spent the rest of the night there, had stopped for a doughnut at Sarah Dixon's diner on Rivers Avenue, and then had driven to Hampten Park to interview a Mrs. Lewellyn. The lady's husband had left town the same night as the Mansard House murders four days earlier and died in an automobile accident in Atlanta early Sunday morning. When the Georgia state trooper called to inform her that she was a widow, that her husband had driven into an overpass abutment at 85 m.p.h. on the I-285 bypass outside of Atlanta, Mrs. Lewellyn had one question for the officer. "What on earth is Arthur doing in Atlanta? He went out last night to get a cigar and the Sunday paper."

Gentry had thought it a pertinent question. It was still unanswered when he left the Lewellyns' brick home at nine A.M. after a half hour interview with the widow. It was then that Gentry noticed the green Plymouth parked halfway down the block in the shadow of tall trees that overhung the street.

He had first noticed the Plymouth when he pulled out of the diner's

parking lot earlier that morning. He had paid attention to it only because
it was carrying Maryland license plates. It had been Gentry's experience
that cops became obsessed with observing details like that, most of which
were totally useless. As he slid behind the wheel of his cruiser parked in
front of the Lewellyns' house, he adjusted the mirror to take a long look at
the Plymouth parked down the street. It was the same car. He could not
see if it was occupied because of reflections on the car's windshield. Gentry shrugged and pulled away from the curb, turning left at the first stop
sign. The Plymouth began moving just before Gentry's car would have
been lost to sight. He made another left turn and drove south, trying to
decide whether to return to the county building to finish some paperwork
or to drive back to St. Andrews. Behind him he could see the green sedan
staying two cars back.

Gentry drove slowly, tapping the wheel with his large, red hands and
whistling a country-western tune through his teeth. He half listened to the
rasp of his police radio and reviewed all the reasons he could think of for
someone to be following him. There weren't many. Except for a few bel-
ligerents he had jailed in the past couple of years, no one he knew of had a
reason to settle old scores with Bobby Joe Gentry, much less waste time
following him through his daily meanderings. Gentry wondered if he was
starting at shadows. There was more than one green Plymouth in Charleston. *With Maryland plates?* sneered the cop-wise part of his mind. Gentry
decided to take the long way back to the office.

He turned left into busy traffic on Cannon Street. The Plymouth
stayed with him, hanging three cars back. If Gentry hadn't already known
it was there, he would never have spotted it now. Only the emptiness of the
little side street near Hampten Park where Mrs. Lewellyn lived had tipped
the other's hand. Gentry swung the cruiser on a ramp onto Interstate 26,
drove north a little over a mile, and then exited, taking back streets east to
Meeting Street. The Plymouth remained visible in his mirror, shielding
itself behind other vehicles when it could, staying far back when there was
no other traffic.

"Well, well, well," said Sheriff Gentry. He continued north to Charleston
Heights, passing the naval base on his right. Hulking gray ships could be
glimpsed through a latticework of derricks. He turned left onto Dorchester
Road and then reentered I-26, heading south this time. The Plymouth
was no longer in sight. He was almost ready to exit near the downtown
and chalk the whole thing up to watching too many thrillers on cable TV
when a semi-trailer changed lanes half a mile behind him and Gentry
caught a glimpse of the green hood.

Gentry took Exit 221 and was back on the narrow streets near the
County Building. It had begun to drizzle lightly. The driver of the Plymouth had switched his wipers on at the same instant Gentry had. The
sheriff tried to think of any laws that were being broken. Offhand, he
could think of none. All right, thought Gentry, how does one lose a tail?

He thought of all the high-speed chases he had seen in films. No thanks. He tried to remember details of spycraft from the many espionage novels he'd read, but all he could come up with were images of changing trains in the Moscow subway complex. Thanks a lot. It didn't help matters that Gentry was driving his tan cruiser marked with CHARLESTON COUNTY SHERIFF on each side.

Gentry knew that he could get on the police radio, drive around the block a couple of times, and eight county cars and half the Highway Patrol could be waiting for this turkey at the next major intersection. Then what? Gentry saw himself up before Judge Trantor, charged with harassing an out-of-state visitor who was trying to find the ferry to Fort Sumter and who had decided to follow the local constable.

The intelligent thing to do, Gentry knew, was to wait this guy out. Let him follow along as long as he wanted—days, weeks, years—until Gentry could figure out what game was being played. The guy in the Plymouth— if it was a guy—might be a process server or a reporter or a persistent Jehovah's Witness or a member of the Governor's new strike force on police corruption. The intelligent thing to do, Gentry was absolutely positive, was to go back to work at the office, not worry about this, and let things sort themselves out of their own accord.

"Aw, the hell with it," said Gentry. He had never been known for his patience. He whipped the cruiser into a 180-degree skid on the wet pavement, hit the lights and siren, and accelerated back up the narrow, one-way street directly at the oncoming Plymouth. With his right hand he unsnapped the leather strap over his nonregulation pistol. He glanced over to make sure that his nightstick was lying on the seat where he usually left it. Then he was driving hard, honking his horn to add to the commotion.

The grill of the Plymouth looked surprised. Gentry could see that there was only one man in the car. The other vehicle swerved right. Gentry cut left to block it. The Plymouth feinted to far left of the street and then accelerated onto the sidewalk on the right to squeeze past the sheriff's car. Gentry jerked the wheel left, bounced as he went up over the curb, and prepared for a head-on collision.

The Plymouth skidded sideways, took out a row of trash cans with its right rear fender, and broadsided a telephone pole. Gentry slammed the cruiser to a halt in front of the other car's steaming radiator, making sure he was angled in correctly to block it from leaving. Then he was out, slapping away his shoulder harness and lifting the heavy baton in his left hand.

"Could I see your driver's license and registration, sir?" asked Gentry. A pale, thin face stared out at him. The Plymouth had impacted the telephone pole just hard enough to crimp the passenger door shut and to shake up the driver. The man had a receding hairline and very dark hair. Gentry placed him in his mid-forties. He was dressed in a dark suit, white shirt, and thin, dark tie that looked like it belonged in the Kennedy era.

Gentry watched carefully as the man fumbled for his wallet. "Would you please take the license out of the billfold, sir?" The man paused, blinked, and turned away to comply.

Gentry stepped forward quickly and opened the door and with his left hand, letting the baton dangle from its wrist strap. His right hand had gone back to touch the grip of his Ruger Blackhawk. "Sir! Please step out of the . . . shit!"

The driver swung around with the automatic pistol already coming up toward Gentry's face. All of Gentry's 240 pounds went through the open car door as he lunged to seize the man's wrist. The pistol fired twice, one slug passing the sheriff's ear to go through the roof, the other going wider, turning the Plymouth's windshield into a powdery spiderweb. Then Gentry had both hands on the man's wrist and the two of them were sprawled across the front seat like two teenagers at a drive-in. Both men were panting and puffing. Gentry's nightstick was snarled in the ring of the steering wheel and the Plymouth bellowed like a gutshot beast. The driver raised his left hand to claw at the sheriff's face. Gentry lowered his massive head and butted him; once, twice, hearing the air go out of him on the third blow. The automatic tumbled out of the driver's hand, bounced off the steering column and Gentry's leg, and clattered on pavement outside. Having a sportsman's inbred fear of dropped weapons, Gentry half expected it to go off, emptying half the magazine into his back. It did not.

"Fuck this," said Gentry and heaved himself backward, pulling the driver out of the car with him. He had transferred his right hand to the man's collar and after checking that the automatic was nearby, half under the car, he flung the driver to the pavement eight feet away. By the time the other man had scrambled to his feet, Gentry had drawn the heavy Ruger Blackhawk his uncle had given him when he retired. The weapon felt solid in his hand.

"Hold it right there. Don't move a muscle," ordered Gentry. A dozen or so people had emerged from businesses and storefronts to gawk. Gentry made sure that they were out of range and that only a brick wall stood behind the driver. He realized with a sickening lurch that he was preparing to shoot the poor son of a bitch. Gentry had never fired a weapon at a human being before. Instead of leveling the revolver with both hands as he'd been trained, feet braced far apart, Gentry stood upright, elbow cocked, muzzle pointed skyward. The rain was a gentle mist on the sheriff's florid face. "Fight's over," he panted. "Just relax a minute, fella. Let's talk about this."

The driver's hand came out of his pocket with a knife. The blade flicked out with an audible click. The man went into a half crouch, balancing lightly, the fingers of his other hand splayed wide. The sheriff was sorry to see that he held the knife correctly, dangerously, thumb flat over the hilt atop the blade. Already the five-inch steel was swinging in short, fluid arcs. Gentry kicked the automatic pistol farther under the Plymouth and took three steps back.

"Come on now, fella," said Gentry. "Don't do anything stupid. Put it down." He did not underestimate the speed with which the man could cover the fifteen feet separating them. Nor did Gentry doubt that a thrown knife could be as deadly as a bullet at that range. But he also remembered the holes that Blackhawk left in the black target paper at forty paces. He did not want to think about what the .357 slugs would do to human tissue at fifteen feet.

"Put it down," said Gentry. His voice was a smooth monotone, holding no threat, allowing no argument. "Let's just stop a minute and talk about this." The other man had not spoken or made a sound other than grunts since Gentry had approached the Plymouth. Now a strange whistle, like steam from a cooling kettle, came from between his clenched teeth. He began to raise the knife vertically.

"*Freeze!*" Gentry leveled the pistol, one handed, sighting down the barrel at the center of the man's thin tie. If the blade rose to full throwing height, Gentry would have to fire. His finger tension on the trigger was almost strong enough to lift the hammer.

Gentry saw something then that made his thudding heart lock in painful paralysis. The man's face seemed to be quivering, not shaking but *flowing* like an ill-fitted rubber mask sliding over the more solid features beneath it. The eyes had widened, as if in surprise or horror, and now they flicked back and forth like small animals in panic. For just an instant Gentry saw a different personality emerge in that thin face, there was a look of total terror and confusion visible in those captive eyes, and then the muscles of the face and neck went rigid, as if the mask had been pulled down more tightly. The blade continued to rise until it was directly under the man's chin, high enough to be thrown accurately now.

"Hey!" shouted Gentry. He relaxed the tension on the trigger.

The driver inserted the blade into his own throat. He did not stab or lunge or slash, he *inserted* the five inches of steel the way a surgeon would make an initial incision or the way one would carefully pierce a watermelon for carving. Then, with deliberate strength and slowness, he pulled the blade from left to right under the width of his jawline.

"Oh, Jesus," whispered Gentry. Someone in the crowd screamed.

Blood flowed down the man's white shirtfront as if a balloon filled with red paint had burst. The man tugged the knife free and remained standing for an incredible ten or twelve seconds, legs apart, body rigid, expressionless, a cascade of blood drenching his torso and beginning to drip audibly on the wet sidewalk. Then he collapsed on his back, legs spasming.

"Stay the hell back!" Gentry shouted at the bystanders and ran forward. With his heavy boot he pinned the man's right wrist and flicked the knife free with his baton. The driver's head had arched back and the red slash on his throat gaped open like an obscene shark's grin. Gentry could see torn cartilage and the ragged ends of gray fibers before the blood bubbled up and out again. The man's chest began to heave up and down as his lungs filled.

Gentry ran to the cruiser and put in a call for an ambulance. Then he shouted the crowd back again and poked under the Plymouth with his nightstick to retrieve the automatic. It was a 9mm Browning with some sort of double-row clip which made it heavy as hell. He found the safety catch, clicked it up, stuck the gun in his belt, and went to kneel by the dying man.

The driver had rolled on his right side with his knees curled up, arms pulled up tight, fists clenched. The blood filled a four-foot-wide pool now and more pulsed out with each slow heartbeat. Gentry kneeled in the blood and tried to close the wound with his bare hands, but the cut was too wide and ragged. His shirt was soaked in five seconds. The man's eyes had taken on a fixed, glazed look which Gentry had seen on the face of too many corpses.

The ragged breathing and bubbling ceased just as the siren of the approaching ambulance became audible in the distance.

Gentry moved back, dropped to both knees, and wiped his hands against his thighs. Somehow the driver's billfold had been kicked out onto the pavement during the scuffle, and Gentry lifted it away from the advancing rivulet of blood. Ignoring proper procedure, he flipped it open, quickly going through the plastic inserts and compartments. In the wallet were a little over $900 in cash, a small, black and white photograph of Sheriff Bobby Joe Gentry, and nothing else. Nothing. No driver's license, credit cards, family snapshots, social security card, business cards, old receipts—nothing.

"Somebody tell me what's going on here," whispered Gentry. The rain had stopped. The driver's body lay peacefully nearby. The thin face was so white it looked like wax. Gentry shook his head and looked up blindly at the straining crowd and the approaching police and paramedics. "Would somebody tell me *what's going on here*?" he shouted.

No one answered him.

EIGHT

Tony Harod and Maria Chen drove northeast from Munich, past Deggendorf and Regen, deep into the West German forest and mountain country near the Czech border. Harod drove the rented BMW hard, shifting down at high rpm to take the rain-slicked curves in controlled slides, accelerating quickly to one hundred twenty kilometers per hour on the straight stretches. Even this concentration and activity was not enough to drive the tension of the long flight out of his body. He had tried to sleep during the interminable crossing, but he had been aware each second that he was sealed into a fragile, pressurized tube suspended thousands of feet above the cold Atlantic. Harod shivered, turned the BMW's heater up, and passed two more cars. Now there was snow carpeting the fields and lying piled up by the roadside as they climbed into hillier countryside.

Two hours earlier, as they left Munich on the crowded autobahn, Maria had studied her Shell road map and said, "Oh, Dachau is just a few miles from here."

"So?" said Harod.

"So that is where one of those camps was," she said. "Where they sent the Jews during the war."

"So what?" said Harod. "That's fucking ancient history."

"Not so ancient," said Maria Chen.

Harod took an exit marked 92 and traded one overcrowded autobahn for another. He maneuvered the BMW into the left lane and held the speedometer at 100 kph. "When were you born?" he demanded.

"Nineteen-forty-eight," said Maria Chen.

"Anything that happened before you were born isn't worth thinking about," said Harod. "It's ancient fucking history."

Maria Chen fell silent and stared out at the cold ribbon of the Isar River. The late afternoon light was draining out of a gray sky.

Harod glanced at his secretary and remembered the first time he had seen her. It had been four years earlier, in the summer of 1976, and Harod had been in Hong Kong to see the Foy Brothers on business from Willi about bankrolling one of his mindless kung fu movies. Harod had been glad to be out of the States at the height of the Bicentennial hysteria. The younger Foy had taken Harod out for an evening on the town in Kowloon.

It had been some time before Harod had realized that the expensive bar and nightclub they were patronizing on the eighth floor of a Kowloon high-rise was actually a whorehouse, and that the beautiful, sophisticated women whose company they had been enjoying were whores.

Harod had lost interest then and would have left immediately if he had not noticed the beautiful Eurasian woman sitting alone at the bar, her eyes registering a depth of indifference that could not be feigned. When he asked Two-Bite Foy about her, the large Asian grinned and said, "Ah, very interesting. Very sad story. Her mother was an American missionary, her father a teacher on the Mainland. Mother died shortly after they come to Hong Kong. Father dies too. Maria Chen stay here and be very famous model, very high priced."

"A model?" said Harod. "What's she doing here?"

Foy shrugged and grinned, showing his gold tooth. "She make much money, but she need much more. Very expensive tastes. She wants to go to America—she is American citizen—but cannot return because of expensive tastes."

Harod nodded. "Cocaine?"

"Heroin," said Foy and smiled. "You like to meet?"

Harod liked to meet. After the introductions, when they were alone at the bar, Maria Chen said, "I know about you. You make a career out of bad movies and worse manners."

Harod nodded agreement. "And I know about you," he said. "You're a heroin addict and a Hong Kong whore."

He saw the slap coming and reached out with his mind to stop her. And failed. The sound of the blow caused people to stop in mid-conversation and stare. When the background noise rose again, Harod removed his handkerchief and dabbed at his mouth. Her ring had cut his lip.

Harod had encountered Neutrals before—people on whom the Ability had no power whatsoever. But rarely. Very rarely. And never in a situation where he had not known about it in time to avoid pain. "All right," he said, "the introductions are over. Now I have a business proposition for you."

"Nothing you have to offer would be of any interest to me," said Maria Chen. There was no doubt of the sincerity of her statement. But she remained seated at the bar.

Harod nodded. He was thinking rapidly, remembering the concern he had felt for months now. Working with Willi scared him. The old man used his Ability rarely, but when he did there was no doubt that his powers were far greater than Harod's. Even if Harod spent months or years carefully conditioning an assistant, there was little doubt that Willi would be able to turn such a catspaw in a second. Harod had felt a rising anxiety since that goddamned Island Club had induced him to get close to the murderous old man. If Willi found out, he would use whatever instrument there was to . . .

"I'll give you a job in the States," said Harod. "Personal secretary to me and executive secretary in the production company I represent."

Maria Chen looked at him coolly. There was no interest in the beautiful brown eyes.

"Fifty thousand American dollars a year," he said, "plus benefits."

She did not blink. "I make more than that here in Hong Kong," she said. "Why should I trade my modeling career for a lower-paying secretarial job?" The emphasis she put on "secretarial" left no doubt as to the contempt she felt for the offer.

"The benefits," said Harod. When Maria Chen said nothing, Harod went on. "A constant supply of . . . what you require," he said softly. "And you will never need to be involved in the purchasing part of the process again."

Maria Chen blinked then. The self-assurance slipped from her like a torn-away veil. She looked down at her hands.

"Think about it," said Harod. "I'll be at the Victoria and Albert Hotel until Tuesday morning."

She did not look up when Harod left the nightclub. On Tuesday morning he was preparing to leave, the porter had already carried his bags down, and he was taking one last look at himself in the mirror, buttoning the front of his Banana Republic safari travel jacket, when Maria Chen appeared in the doorway.

"What are my duties besides personal secretary?" she said.

Harod turned slowly, resisted the impulse to smile, and shrugged. "Whatever else I specify," he said. He did smile. "But not what you're thinking. I have no use for whores."

"There will be a condition," said Maria Chen.

Harod stared and listened.

"Sometime in the next year I want to . . . stop," she said and sweat appeared on the smooth skin of her forehead. "To go . . . how do you Americans say it? To go cold turkey. And when I specify the time, you will . . . make arrangements."

Harod thought for a minute. He was not sure it would serve his purposes if Maria Chen escaped her addiction, but he doubted if she would ever really ask for that to happen. If she did, he would deal with it then. In the meantime, he would have the services of a beautiful and intelligent assistant whom Willi could not touch. "Agreed," he said. "Let's go see about making arrangements for your visa."

"There is no need," said Maria Chen and stood aside to let him walk ahead of her to the elevator. "All the arrangements have been taken care of."

Thirty kilometers beyond Deggendorf they approached Regen, a medieval city in the shadow of rocky crags. As they wound down a mountain road toward the outskirts, Maria Chen pointed to where the headlights had illuminated an oval board planted upright under the trees near the roadside. "Have you noticed those along the way?" she asked.

"Yeah," said Harod and shifted down to take a hairpin turn.

"The guidebook says that they were used to carry local villagers to funerals," she said. "Each board has the deceased's name on it and a request for prayer."

"Cute," said Harod. The road passed through a town. Harod glimpsed streetlights glowing through the winter gloom, wet cobblestones on side streets, and a dark structure hulking above the town on a forested ridge.

"That castle once belonged to Count Hund," read Maria Chen. "He ordered his wife buried alive after she drowned their baby in the Regen River."

Harod said nothing.

"Isn't that a curious bit of local history?" said Maria Chen.

Harod turned left as he shifted down to follow Highway 11 up into the forested mountain country. Snow was visible in the twin beams of their headlights. Harod reached across to take the guidebook away from Maria Chen and to switch off her map light. "Do me a favor," he said. "Shut the fuck up."

They arrived at their small hotel in Bayerisch-Eisenstein after nine P.M., but their rooms were waiting and dinner was still being served in a dining room barely large enough for five tables. A huge fireplace warmed the room and provided most of the light. They ate in silence.

Bayerisch-Eisenstein had seemed small and empty to Harod from the few glimpses he had caught before they found the hotel. A single road, a few Baravian-looking old buildings huddled in a narrow valley between dark hills; the place reminded him of some lost colony in the Catskills. A sign on the outskirts of town had told them that they were only a few kilometers from the Czech border.

When they returned to their adjoining rooms on the third floor, Harod said, "I'm going to go down and check out the sauna. You get the stuff ready for tomorrow."

The hotel had twenty rooms, most of them taken by cross-country skiers who had come to explore the trails on and near the Grosse Arber, the fourteen-hundred-meter mountain a few miles to the north. Several couples sat in the small common room on the first floor, drinking beer or hot chocolate and laughing in that hearty German tone that always sounded strained to Harod's ear.

The sauna was in the basement and was little more than a white cedar box with ledges. Harod set the temperature up, removed his clothes in the tiny dressing room outside, and stepped into the heated interior, wearing only a towel. He smiled at the small sign in English and German on the door: GUESTS PLEASE BE ADVISED, APPAREL IS OPTIONAL IN SAUNA. Obviously there had been American tourists in the past who had been surprised by the German indifference to nudity in such situations.

He was almost asleep when the two girls entered. They were young—

no more than nineteen—and German, and they giggled as they came in. They did not stop when they saw Harod. *"Guten Abend,"* said the taller of the two blondes. They left their towels wrapped around them. Harod also wore a towel; he did not speak as he peered at the girls from under heavy-lidded eyes.

Harod remembered the month almost three years earlier when Maria Chen had announced that it was time for him to help her go cold turkey.

"Why should I?" he had said.

"Because you promised," she had responded.

Harod had stared at her then and thought of the months of sexual tension, her coolest rejection of his slightest overtures, and of the night he had gone quietly to her room and opened the door. Although it was after two A.M., she had been sitting up in bed reading. As he stood in the doorway, she had calmly set down her book, removed a .38 caliber revolver from her nightstand drawer, rested it comfortably on her lap, and said, "Yes, what is it, Tony?" He had shaken his head and left.

"All right, I promised," Harod said, "what do you want me to do?" Maria Chen told him.

For three weeks she did not leave the locked basement room. At first, she used her long nails to rip at the padding he had helped to set in place on the walls and door. She screamed and pounded, tore at the bar mattress and pillows that were the only furnishings in the small room, and then screamed again. Only Harod, sitting in the media room outside her cell, could hear the screams.

She did not eat the meals he slid through the low slot in the door. After two days she did not rise from the mattress, but lay curled up, sweating and shaking in turns, moaning feebly in one moment and screaming in an inhuman voice the next. In the end, Harod stayed in the room with her for three days and nights, helping her to the adjoining bathroom when she could sit up, cleaning her and caring for her where she lay when she could not. Finally, on the fifteenth day, she slept around the clock, and Harod bathed her and dressed the self-inflicted scratches. As he ran the washcloth across the pale cheeks, the perfect breasts, and the sweat-filmed thighs, he thought about all the times he had watched her silk-clad body in the office and wished that she was not a Neutral.

After bathing and drying her, he had dressed her in soft pajamas, substituted clean sheets and blankets for the soiled rags, and left her alone to sleep.

She had emerged from the room on the third week—her pose and faintly distant manner as intact and flawless as her hair, dress, and makeup. Neither of them had ever spoken of those three weeks.

The younger German girl giggled and raised her arms over her head, saying something to her friend. Harod peered at them through the steam. His black eyes were dark perforations under heavy lids.

The older girl blinked several times and untied her towel. Her breasts were firm and heavy. The younger girl stopped in surprise, her arms still over her head. Harod saw the downy thatches of hair under her arms, wondered why German girls did not shave there. The younger girl started to say something, stopped, and untied her own towel. Her fingers fumbled as if they had been asleep or were unfamiliar with the task. The towel fell just as the older girl raised her hands to her sister's breasts.

Sisters, Harod realized as he squinted better to savor the physical sensations. *Kirsten* and *Gabi*. It was not easy with two. He had to shift back and forth constantly, never letting one slip away while dealing with the other. It was like playing tennis against oneself—not a game one wanted to attempt for long. But, then, it need not be a long game. Harod closed his eyes and smiled.

Maria Chen was standing at the window looking out at a small group of Christmas carolers standing around a horse-drawn sleigh when Harod returned. She turned away just as laughter and a snatch of "Oh Tannenbaum" filled the cold air outside.

"Where is it?" asked Harod. He was dressed in silk pajamas and a gold robe. His hair was wet.

Maria Chen opened her suitcase and removed the .45 caliber automatic. She laid it on the coffee table.

Harod lifted the weapon, dry fired it once, and nodded. "I didn't think they'd bug you at Customs. Where's the clip?"

Maria removed three metal magazines from her suitcase and set them on the table. Harod pushed the unloaded gun across the glass surface until it lay near her hand.

"OK," he said, "let's take a look at this fucking place." He rolled the green and white topographic map out on the table, using the automatic to weight down one end and the ammunition clips to secure the other corners. His short forefinger stopped at a collection of dots on either side of a red line. "Bayerisch-Eisenstein," he said. "Us." The finger stabbed an inch northwest. "Willi's estate is here behind this hill . . ."

"The Grosse Arber," said Maria Chen.

"Whatever. Right here in the middle of the forest . . ."

"The Bayerischer Wald," said Maria Chen.

Harod stared at her a minute and then returned his attention to the map. "Part of a sort of national park . . . but still private property. Makes a fucking lot of sense."

"There are private holdings in American national parks," said Maria Chen. "Besides, the estate is supposed to be empty."

"Yeah," said Harod. He rolled up the map and went into his own room through the connecting door. A minute later he returned carrying a glass of Scotch from a duty-free bottle he had bought at Heathrow. "So," he said, "you understand the drill for tomorrow?"

"Yes," said Maria Chen.

"If he's not there, no sweat," said Harod. "If he is and he's alone and wants to talk, no problem."

"And if there is a problem?"

Harod sat down, set the Scotch on the table, and pushed the ammunition clip in with a click. He held out the pistol and waited until she took it. "Then you shoot him," said Harod. "Shoot him and anyone who is with him. In the head. Twice, if you have time." He went to the door and hesitated. "Any other questions?"

"No," said Maria Chen.

Harod went into his own room and closed the door. Maria Chen heard the lock click. She sat for some time, holding the automatic, listening to occasional sounds of holiday Gemütlichkeit coming from the street, and watching the thin band of yellow light under Tony Harod's door.

NINE

Washington, D.C.
Thursday, Dec. 18, 1980

C. Arnold Barent left the Mayflower Hotel and the president-elect and rode to National Airport by way of the FBI building. His limousine was preceded by a gray Mercedes and followed by a blue Mercedes; both vehicles were leased by one of his companies and the men in them were as well trained as the Secret Service men who had been so visible at the Mayflower.

"I thought the discussion went very well," said Charles Colben, the only other passenger in the limousine.

Barent nodded.

"The president was very open to your suggestions," said Colben. "It sounds like he may even come back to the Island Club retreat this June. That would be interesting. We've never had a president there during his term of office."

"President-elect," said Barent.

"Huh?"

"You said the president was very open," said Barent. "You meant the president-elect. Mr. Carter is our president until January."

Colben made a sound of derision.

"What does your intelligence group say about the hostages?" Barent asked softly.

"What do you mean?"

"Will they be released during the last hours of Carter's term, or during the next administration?"

Colben shrugged. "We're the FBI, not CIA. Our work has to be domestic, not foreign."

Barent nodded, still smiling slightly. "And part of your domestic effort," he said, "is spying on the CIA. So I shall ask again, when will the hostages be coming home?"

Colben frowned and looked out at the bare trees of the mall. "Best we can get is twenty-four hours either side of the inauguration," he said. "But the way the Ayatollah's been shoving it up Carter's ass the last year and a half, I don't see any way he's going to toss him this bone."

"I met him once," said Barent. "Interesting person."

"What? Who?" said Colben, confused. The Carters had been guests at Barent's Palm Springs estate and Thousand Islands castle several times during the past four years.

"The Ayatollah Khomeini," Barent said patiently. "I rode down from Paris to see him shortly after he began his exile. A friend had suggested that I might find the *Imam* amusing."

"Amusing?" said Colben. "That fanatical little fuck?"

Barent frowned slightly at Colben's choice of language. He did not like profanity. He had used the word "bitch" earlier in the week with Tony Harod because he had felt that a vulgar phrase was necessary to drive home a point to a vulgar man. Charles Colben was also a vulgar man. "It was amusing," said Barent, sorry now that he had raised the issue. "We had a fifteen-minute talk with the religious leader—through an interpreter although I was told that the Ayatollah understood French—and you will never guess what the little man did right before our audience was over."

"Ask you to fund his revolution?" said Colben, his tone of voice showing his lack of interest. "I give up."

"He tried to Use me," said Barent, smiling again, truly amused at the recollection. "I could feel him groping at my mind, blindly, instinctively. I received the impression that he thought he was the only one in the world with the Ability. I also received the impression that he thought he was God."

Colben shrugged again. "He would have felt a little less godlike if Carter had had the balls to send in some B-52s the first week they took our people."

Barent changed the subject. "And where is our friend Mr. Harod today?"

Colben took out an inhaler, applied it to each nostril, and grimaced. "He and his secretary—or whatever she is—left for West Germany last night."

"To see if his friend Willi might be alive and well and living in the Vaterland, I presume," said Barent.

"Sure."

"And did you send someone with him?"

Colben shook his head. "No reason. Trask is using some of his Frankfurt and Munich contacts from his days at the Company to check on the castle. Harod's bound to head there. We'll monitor the CIA traffic."

"And will he find anything?"

Charles Colben shrugged.

"You do not believe that our Mr. Borden is still alive, do you?" asked Barent.

"No, I don't see how he could be all that goddamn clever," said Colben. "I mean, it was *our* idea to approach the Drayton woman about eliminating *him*. The vote *was* unanimous that his actions were becoming too public, right?"

"And then we find out about Nina Drayton's little indiscretions," said C. Arnold Barent. "Ah, well, it is a pity."

"What's a pity?"

Barent looked at the bald bureaucrat. "It's a pity that neither of them was a member of the Island Club," he said. "They were distinctive individuals."

"Bullshit," said Colben. "They were fucking lunatics."

The limousine stopped. Locks snapped up on the door next to Colben. Barent looked out at the ugly side entrance to the new FBI building. "Here is your stop," he said, and then as Colben was standing on the curb the chauffeur was ready to close the door, Barent said, "Charles, we simply must do something about your language." He left the balding man standing on the sidewalk, staring as the limousine pulled away.

The ride to National Airport took only a few minutes. Barent's converted 747 sat waiting outside a private hangar; the aircraft's engines were running, the air-conditioning was on, and a glass of iced mineral water sat waiting next to Barent's favorite chair. Don Mitchell, the pilot, came into the aft compartment and touched his hat. "All ready, Mr. Barent," he said. "I need to let the tower know which flight plan is operative. What's our destination, sir?"

"I would like to go to my island," said Barent, sipping the mineral water.

Mitchell smiled slightly. It was an old joke. C. Arnold Barent owned more than four hundred islands around the world and had residences on more than a score of them. "Yessir," said the pilot and waited.

"Inform the tower that Flight Plan E is the pertinent one," said Barent. He rose with the glass still in his hand and went to the door of his bedroom. "I will let you know when I am ready."

"Yessir," said Mitchell. "We have clearance for anytime in the next fifteen minutes."

Barent nodded dismissal and waited for the pilot to leave.

Special Agent Richard Haines was sitting on the queen-size bed as Barent entered. He rose but was waved back to his seat by Barent, who finished his drink and removed his suit coat, tie, and shirt. He tossed the crumpled shirt into a hamper and pulled a fresh one from a drawer built into the aft bulkhead.

"Tell me, Richard," said Barent as he buttoned the shirt, "what is new?"

Haines blinked and began talking. "Supervisor Colben and Mr. Trask met again this morning before your appointment with the president-elect. Trask is on the transition team . . ."

"Yes, yes," said Barent, still standing. "And what about the situation in Charleston?"

"The Bureau is still carrying out surveillance," said Haines. "The crash team is certain that the aircraft was destroyed by a bomb. One of the passengers—listed as George Hummel—used a credit card that was traced back to a theft in Bar Harbor, Maine."

"Maine," said Barent. Nieman Trask was an "aide" to the senior senator from Maine. "Very sloppy."

"Yessir," said Haines. "At any rate, Mr. Colben was very upset at your

directive not to interfere with Sheriff Gentry and the investigation. He
met yesterday with Mr. Trask and Mr. Kepler at the Mayflower and I'm
pretty sure that they dispatched their own party or parties to Charleston
yesterday evening."

"One of Trask's plumbers?"

"Yessir."

"All right, go ahead, Richard."

"At approximately nine-twenty A.M. E.S.T. today, Sheriff Gentry intercepted a man who had been following him in a 1976 Plymouth Volaré.
Gentry attempted to take the man into custody. The man at first resisted
and then cut his own throat with a French-made switchblade knife. He
was pronounced Dead On Arrival at Charleston General Hospital. Neither fingerprint identification nor automobile registration have turned up
anything. Dental records are being checked into, but it will be a few days."

"They won't find anything if it's one of Trask's plumbers," mused Barent. "Was the sheriff hurt?"

"No, sir, not according to our surveillance team."

Barent nodded. He pulled a silk tie from a rack and began knotting it.
He let his mind reach out and touch the consciousness of Special Agent
Richard Haines. He could feel the shield that made Haines a Neutral, a
solid shell surrounding the surge of thoughts, ambitions, and dark urges
that was Richard Haines. Like so many of the others with the Ability, like
Barent himself, Colben had chosen a Neutral as his closest aide. Although
unable to be conditioned, Haines was also free from the threat of being
turned by someone with a stronger Ability. Or so Colben thought.

Barent slid along the surface of the mindshield until he found the inevitable crack, slid deeper through the maze of Haines's pitiful defenses,
ran his own will along the warp and weave of the FBI man's consciousness. He touched Haines's pleasure center and the agent closed his eyes as
if a current were flowing through him.

"Where is the Fuller woman?" asked Barent.

Haines opened his eyes. "Still no word since the screw-up at the Atlanta
airport Monday night."

"Has there been any luck tracing the phone call?"

"No, sir. The airport operator thinks it was a local call."

"Do you think Colben, Kepler, or Trask will have access to any other
information about where she is . . . or Willi?"

Haines hesitated a second. "No, sir," he said at last. "When either one
is found, I think it'll have to come up through the Bureau the usual way.
I'll know about it as soon as Mr. Colben does."

"Before, preferably," said Barent with a smile. "Thank you, Richard.
As always I find your company most stimulating. Lester will be available
at the usual place if you need to contact me. I want to know the instant you
have any information on the whereabouts of either the Fuller woman or
our friend from Germany."

"Yessir." Haines turned to go.

"Oh, Richard." Barent was pulling on a blue cashmere blazer. "Do you still feel that Sheriff Gentry and this psychiatrist . . ."

"Laski," said Haines.

"Yes." Barent smiled. "Do you still think that these gentlemen's contracts should be formally canceled?"

"Yes." Haines frowned and framed his response carefully. "Gentry's just too smart for his own good," he said. "At first I thought he was upset about the Mansard House murders because they made him look bad in his own county, but by the time I left I was convinced that he took them *personally*. Stupid, fat, redneck hick cop."

"But smart," said Barent.

"Yeah." Haines frowned again. "Laski I don't know, but he's too . . . *involved* somehow. He knew Mrs. Drayton and . . ."

"Yes, yes," said Barent. "Well, we may have other plans for Dr. Laski." He stared at the FBI man for a long moment. "Richard?"

"Yes, sir?"

Barent steepled his fingers. "There's something I have been meaning to ask you, Richard. You worked for Mr. Colben for several years before he joined the Club. Isn't that right?"

"Yes, sir."

Barent tapped his lower lip with the tips of his pyramided fingers. "My question, Richard, is . . . ah . . . why?"

Haines frowned his lack of understanding.

"I mean," continued Barent, "why do all of the things Charles asked you to do . . . still asks you to do . . . if you have a choice?"

Haines brightened. His smile showed perfect teeth. "Oh," he said. "Well, I guess I enjoy my work. Will that be all today, Mr. Barent?"

Barent stared at the man a second and then said, "Yes."

Five minutes after Haines had left, Barent used the intercom to call the pilot. "Donald," he said, "please take off now. I would like to go to my island."

TEN

Charleston
Wednesday, Dec. 17, 1980

Saul awoke to the sound of children playing in the street outside and for several seconds he could not place where he was. Not his apartment; he was lying on a hideabed under windows with yellow curtains. For a second the yellow curtains reminded him of his home in Lodz, the children's shouts . . . Stefa and Josef . . .

No, the excited shouts were in English. Charleston. Natalie Preston. He remembered telling the story and felt a rush of embarrassment, as if the young black woman had seen him naked. Why had he told her all of that? After all these years, why . . .

"Good morning." Natalie poked her head in from the kitchen. She was wearing a red sweatshirt and soft-looking jeans.

Saul sat up and rubbed his eyes. His shirt and trousers were neatly draped across the arm of the couch. "Good morning."

"Eggs and bacon and toast all right?" she asked. The air smelled of fresh-roasted coffee.

"It sounds wonderful," said Saul, "except I'll pass on the bacon."

Natalie made a fist and pretended to bop herself on the head. "Of course," she said. "Religious reasons?"

"Cholesterol reasons," said Saul.

They talked about trivial things over breakfast—what it was like to live in New York, to go to school in St. Louis, to have grown up in the South.

"It's hard to explain," said Natalie, "but somehow it's easier being black here than in a northern city. The racism still exists here, but it's . . . I'm not sure how to explain it . . . it's changing. Maybe the fact that people here have dealt with the roles for so long and *have* to change them lets everyone be a little more honest. Up north, things seem raw and mean."

"I don't think of St. Louis as a northern city," said Saul with a smile. He finished the last of his toast and sipped his coffee.

Natalie laughed. "No, and it's not a *southern* city either," she said. "I guess it's just a Midwestern city. I was thinking more of Chicago."

"You've lived in Chicago?"

"Spent time there in the summer," said Natalie. "Dad arranged a photography job for me with an old friend on the *Tribune*." She paused and fell silent, staring at her coffee cup.

Saul said quietly, "It's hard, isn't it? One forgets for a while and then mentions the person's name without thinking and it all comes back . . ."

Natalie nodded.

Saul looked out the kitchen window at the fronds of a palmetto. The window was open a bit and a warm breeze came through the screen. He could barely believe that it was the middle of December.

"You're training to be a teacher," Saul said, "but your first love seems to be photography."

Natalie nodded again and rose to refill both of their coffee cups. "It was an agreement Dad and I had," she said and this time she smiled. "He'd continue helping me with the photography if I agreed to be trained in what he called 'honest work.' "

"Will you teach?"

"Perhaps," said Natalie.

She smiled at him again and Saul noticed how perfect her teeth were. The smile was both warm and shy, a benediction.

Saul helped her wash and dry the few breakfast dishes and they poured fresh cups of coffee and went out onto the small front porch. There was little traffic and the sound of children's laughter was gone. Saul realized that it was a Wednesday; the children would be in school now. They sat on white wicker chairs, facing each other, Natalie with a light sweater over her shoulders and Saul comfortable in the wrinkled corduroy sports coat he had worn the day before.

"You promised the second part of the story," Natalie said quietly.

Saul nodded. "You did not find the first part too fantastic?" he asked. "The ravings of a lunatic?"

"You're a psychiatrist," said Natalie. "You can't be crazy."

Saul laughed loudly. "Ah, there are stories I could tell . . ."

Natalie smiled. "Yes, but first the second part of this story."

Saul fell silent and looked at the black circle of coffee.

"You had escaped from the Oberst," prompted Natalie.

Saul closed his eyes for a minute, opened them, and cleared his throat. When he spoke there was little emotion in his voice—at most a faint hint of sadness.

Natalie closed her own eyes after several minutes as if to picture the scenes that Saul was describing in his soft, strangely pleasant, slightly sad voice.

"There could be no real escape for a Jew in Poland that winter of 1942. For weeks I wandered through the forest to the north and west of Lodz. My foot eventually quit bleeding, but infection seemed inevitable. I swathed it with moss, bandaged it with rags, and staggered on. The long slashes on my side and right thigh throbbed for days but soon were covered with scabs. I stole food from farmhouses, kept away from roads, and avoided the few bands of Polish partisans operating in those forests. The partisans would have shot a Jew as quickly as the Germans would have.

"I do not know how I survived that winter. I remember two farm families—Christians—who allowed me to hide in the straw heaps in their barns and who brought me food when they had almost none themselves.

"In the spring I went south, attempting to reach Uncle Moshe's farm near Cracow. I had no papers, but I was able to join up with a group of workers who were returning from building defenses for the Germans in the east. By the spring of 1943, there was no doubt that the Red Army would soon be on Polish soil.

"I was eight kilometers from Uncle Moshe's farm when one of the workers turned me in. I was arrested by the Polish Blue Police who interrogated me for three days, although I do not think they wanted answers, only an excuse for the beatings. Then they turned me over to the Germans.

"The Gestapo was not interested in me, thinking, perhaps, that I was just one of the many Jews who had run from the cities or escaped from a transport. The German net for Jews had many holes in it. As in so many of the occupied countries, only the willing cooperation of the Poles themselves made it next to impossible for Jews to escape their fate in the camps.

"For some reason I was shipped east. I was not sent to Auschwitz or Chelmno or Belzec or Treblinka, all of which would have been closer, but was sent across the width of Poland. After four days in a sealed boxcar— four days in which a third of the people in the car perished—the doors were slammed back and we staggered out, blinking tears against the unaccustomed light, to find ourselves at Sobibor.

"It was at Sobibor that I again saw the Oberst.

"Sobibor was a death camp. There were no factories there as in Auschwitz or Belsen, no attempt at deception as at Theresenstadt or Chelmno, no ironic slogan of *Arbeit Macht Frei* over the gates as at so many of the Nazi portals to hell. In 1942 and 1943, the Germans were maintaining sixteen huge concentration camps such as Auschwitz, more than fifty smaller ones, hundreds of work camps, but only three *Vernichtungslager* death camps designed only for extermination: Belzec, Treblinka, and Sobibor. In the brief twenty months of their existence, over two million Jews died there.

"Sobibor was a small camp—smaller than Chelmno—and it was situated on the River Bug. This river had been the eastern border of Poland before the war and in the summer of 1943 the Red Army was pushing the Wehrmacht back to it once again. To the west of Sobibor was the wilderness of the Parczew Forest, the Forest of the Owls.

"The entire complex at Sobibor could fit into three or four American football fields. But it was very efficient at its task, which was simply to expedite Himmler's Final Solution.

"I fully expected to die there. We disembarked from the transports and were herded behind a tall hedge down a corridor of wire. They had put thatch in the wire so we could see nothing except one tall guard tower, the tops of trees, and two brick smokestacks directly ahead. There were three signs to the depot pointing the way: CANTEEN→ SHOWERS→ROAD TO HEAVEN→. Someone at Sobibor had expressed the SS sense of humor. We were sent to the showers.

"Jews from the French and Dutch transports walked docilely enough that day, but I remember that the Polish Jews had to be driven on with rifle butts and curses. An old man near me shouted obscenities at every German and shook his fist at the SS men who made us disrobe.

"I cannot tell you exactly what I felt when I entered the shower room. I felt no anger and very little fear. Perhaps the dominant feeling was one of relief. For almost four years I had been driven by a single imperative—*I will live*—and to satisfy that imperative I had watched while my countrymen, my fellow Jews, and my family had been fed into the maw of this obscene German slaughter machine. I had watched. In some ways, I had helped. Now I could rest. I had done the best I could to survive and now it was over. My single regret was that I had not been allowed to kill the Oberst rather than the Old Man. At that moment the Oberst had come to represent everything evil which had brought me to this place. It was the Oberst's face which I had in my mind as they closed the heavy doors to that shower room in June of 1943.

"We were packed in tightly. Men shoved and shouted and moaned. For a minute nothing happened and then the pipes vibrated and rattled. The showers came on and men pushed away from them. I did not. I was standing directly under a showerhead and I raised my face to it. I thought of my family. I wished I had said goodbye to my mother and sisters. It was at that second that the hatred finally came. I concentrated on the Oberst's face as the anger burned in me like an open flame and men cried out and the pipes shook and rattled and spit their contents out at us.

"It was water. Water. The showers—those same showers that claimed so many thousands each day—were also used as showers for a few groups a month. The room was unsealed. We were led outside and deloused. Our heads were shaved. I was given prisoner coveralls. A number was tatooed on my arm. I do not remember any pain.

"At Sobibor, where they were so efficient at processing so many thousands a day, they chose a few prisoners each month to retain for camp maintenance and other work. Our transport had been chosen.

"It was at this moment—still numb, still not believing that I had emerged again into the painful light—that I realized that I had been chosen to fulfill some task. I still refused to believe in God . . . any God who betrayed His People so did not deserve my belief . . . but from that moment on I believed that there was a reason for my continued existence. That reason could be expressed by the single image of the Oberst's face which I had been prepared to die with. The immensity of the evil which had swallowed my people was too great for anyone—let alone a seventeen-year-old boy— to understand. But the obscenity of the Oberst's existence was well within my comprehension. *I would live.* I would live even though I no longer responded to any such imperative toward survival. I would live to fulfill whatever destiny awaited me. I would suffer myself to live and to endure anything in order to one day erase that obscenity.

"For the next three months I lived in Camp I at Sobibor. Camp II was a way station and no one returned from Camp III. I ate what they gave me, slept when they allowed me to, defecated when they ordered me to do so, and carried out my duties as a *Bahnhofkommando*. I wore a blue cap and blue coveralls with a yellow BK emblazoned on them. Several times a day we met the incoming transports. To this day, on nights I cannot sleep, I see the places of origin scrawled in railroad chalk on those sealed cars: Turobin, Gorzkow, Wlodawa, Siedlce, Izbica, Markugzow, Kamorow, Zamosc. We would take the luggage of the dazed Jews and give them baggage checks. Because of the resistance of the Polish Jews—it slowed down the processing—it again became the custom to tell the survivors of the transports that Sobibor was a layover, a rest station before the trip to relocation centers. For a while there were even signs at the depot giving the distances in kilometers to these mythical centers. The Polish Jews rarely believed this, but in the end they shuffled off to the showers with the others. And the trains continued to arrive: Baranow, Ryki, Dubienka, Biala-Polaska, Uchanie, Demblin, Rejowiec. At least once a day we distributed postcards to those on transports from selected ghettos. The messages were pre-written—WE HAVE ARRIVED AT THE RELOCATION CENTERS. THE FARMWORK HERE IS HARD BUT THE SUNLIGHT IS PLEASANT AND THERE IS MUCH GOOD FOOD. WE LOOK FORWARD TO SEEING YOU SOON. The Jews would address and sign these before they were led off to be gassed. Toward the end of the summer, as the ghettos were emptying, this ruse was no longer needed. Konskowola, Jozefow, Michow, Grabowic, Lublin, Lodz. Some transports arrived with no living cargo. Then we *Bahnhofkommando* put aside our baggage check forms and wrestled the naked corpses from the stinking interiors. It was like the gas vans at Chelmno only here the bodies had been locked in their death embrace for days or weeks as the cars sat baking in the summer heat on some rural siding. Once, while tugging at a young woman's corpse which was locked in a final embrace with a child and older woman, I pulled and her arm came off in my hands.

"I cursed God and envisioned the pale, sneering face of the Oberst. I would live.

"In July, Heinrich Himmler visited Sobibor. There were special transports of Western Jews that day so he could see the processing. It took less than two hours from the arrival of the train to the last bit of smoke rising from the six ovens. During that time, every worldly belonging of the Jews was confiscated, sorted, itemized, and stored. Even the women's hair was cut in Camp II and made into felt or woven into slipper linings for U-boat crews.

"I was sorting through luggage at the arrival area when the Kommandant's party led Himmler and his entourage through. I remember little of Himmler—he was a little man with a bureaucrat's mustache and glasses—but behind him walked a young blond officer whom I noticed immediately. It was the Oberst. Twice the Oberst bent to speak softly in Himmler's ear and once the SS Reichsführer threw back his head in a curiously feminine laugh.

"They walked within five meters of me. Bent over my task, I glanced up once to see the Oberst looking directly at me. I do not think he recognized me. It had been only eight months since Chelmno and the estate, but to the Oberst I must have been just another Jew prisoner sorting through the luggage of the dead. I hesitated then. It was my chance and I hesitated and all was lost. I believe I could have reached the Oberst then. I could have had my hands on his throat before the shots rang out. I might even have been able to seize a pistol from one of the officers near Himmler and fire before the Oberst knew there was a threat.

"I have wondered since if something besides surprise and indecision stayed my hand. Certainly I knew no fear at that time. My fear had died with other parts of my spirit weeks before in the sealed shower room. Whatever the reason, I hesitated for several seconds, perhaps a minute, and the time was lost forever. Himmler's party moved on and passed through gates to the Kommandant's Headquarters, an area known as the Merry Flea. As I stared at the gate where they disappeared, Sergeant Wagner began screaming at me to get to work or go to the 'hospital.' No one ever returned from the hospital. I bowed my head and went back to work.

"I watched all the rest of that day, lay awake that night, and waited for a glimpse all the next day, but I did not see the Oberst again. Himmler's group had left during the night.

"On fourteen October, the Jews of Sobibor revolted. I had heard rumors of an uprising, but they had seemed so farfetched that I had taken no interest in them. In the end, their carefully orchestrated plans came down to the murder of a few guards and a mad rush by a thousand or so Jews for the main gate. Most were cut down by machine gun fire in the first minute. Others made it through the wire at the back of the compound during the confusion. My work detail was returning from the depot when the madness erupted. The corporal guarding us was clubbed down by the vanguard of the mob and I had no choice but to run with the others. I was sure that my blue coveralls would draw the fire of the Ukrainians in the tower. But I made the cover of the trees just as two women running with me were cut down by rifle fire. Once there, I changed into the prison-gray tunic of an old man who had reached the safety of the forest only to be struck down by a stray bullet.

"I believe that about two hundred of us made it away from the camp that day. We were alone or in small groups, leaderless for the most part. The group who had planned the escape made no provision for surviving once they were free. Most of the Jews and Russian prisoners were subsequently hunted down by the Germans or discovered and killed by Polish partisans. Many sought shelter at nearby farms and were quickly turned in. A few survived in the forest and a few more made their way across the Bug River to the advancing Red Army. I was lucky. On my third day in the forest I was discovered by members of a Jewish partisan group called *Chil*. They were under the command of a brave and utterly fearless man named Yechiel Greenshpan who accepted me into the band and ordered their surgeon to bring me back to weight and health. For the first time since the previous winter, my foot was properly treated. For five months I traveled with *Chil* in the Forest of the Owls. I was an aide to the surgeon, Dr. Yaczyk, saving lives when possible, even the lives of Germans when I could.

"The Nazis closed down the camp at Sobibor shortly after the escape. They destroyed the barracks, removed the ovens, and planted potatoes in the fields where the Pits had held the thousands not cremated. By the time the partisan band celebrated Hanukkah, most of Poland was in chaos as the Wehrmacht retreated west and south. In March, the Red Army liberated the area in which we were operating and the war was over for me.

"For several months I was detained and interrogated by the Soviets. Some members of *Chil* were sent to Russian camps, but I was released in May and returned to Lodz. There was nothing there for me. The Jewish ghetto had been more than decimated; it had been eliminated. Our old home on the west side of town had been destroyed in the fighting.

"In August of 1945 I traveled to Cracow and then cycled to Uncle Moshe's farm. Another family—a Christian family—occupied it. They had bought it from civil authorities during the war. They said they knew nothing of the whereabouts of the previous owners.

"It was during that same trip that I returned to Chelmno. The Soviets had declared the area off-limits and I was not allowed near the camp. For five days I camped nearby and cycled down every dirt road and path. Eventually I found the remains of the Great Hall. It had been destroyed, either by shelling or by the retreating Germans, and little was left except for tumbled stones, burnt timbers, and the scorched monolith of the central chimney. There was no sign of the tiled floor of the Main Hall.

"In the clearing where the shallow death pit had been, there were signs of recent excavations. The butts of numerous Russian cigarettes littered the area. When I asked at the local inn, the villagers insisted that they knew nothing of mass graves being exhumed. They also insisted—angrily this time—that no one in the area had suspected Chelmno of being anything but what the Germans had said it was: a temporary detention camp for criminals and political prisoners. I was tired of camping and would have stayed the night at the inn before cycling south again, but it was not to be. They did not allow Jews at the inn. The next day I took the train to Cracow to find work.

"The winter of 1945–46 was almost as hard as the winter of 1941–42.

The new government was forming, but the more pressing reality was one of food shortages, lack of fuel, black marketeering, refugees returning by the thousands to pick up the torn strands of their lives, and the Soviet occupation. Especially the occupation. For centuries we had fought the Russians, dominated them, resisted their invasions in return, lived under their threat, and then welcomed them as liberators. Now we awoke from the nightmare of German occupation to the chill morning of Russian liberation. Like Poland, I was exhausted, numbed and somewhat surprised at my own survival, and dedicated only to making it through another winter.

"It was in the spring of 1946 that the letter came from my cousin Rebecca. She and her American husband were living in Tel Aviv. She had spent months corresponding, contacting officials, sending cables to agencies and institutions, all in an effort to find any remaining vestige of her family. She had traced me through friends in the International Red Cross.

"I sent her a letter in response and soon there was a cable arriving which urged me to join her in Palestine. She and David offered to cable the money for the voyage.

"I had never been a Zionist—indeed, our family had never acknowledged the existence of Palestine as a possible Jewish state—but when I stepped off that overcrowded Turkish freighter in June of 1946 and set foot on what would someday be Israel, a heavy yoke seemed to be lifted from my shoulders and for the first time since eight September, 1939, I was able to breathe freely. I confess that I fell to my knees and shed tears that day.

"Perhaps my sense of freedom was premature. A few days after I arrived in Palestine there was an explosion at the King David Hotel in Jerusalem where the British command was housed. As it turned out, both Rebecca and her husband David were active in the Haganah.

"A year and a half later I joined them in the War of Independence, but in spite of my partisan training and experience, I went to war only as a medic. It was not the Arabs that I hated.

"Rebecca insisted that I continue my schooling. David was then the Israeli manager of a very respectable American company and money was not a problem. This was how an indifferent schoolboy from Lodz—a boy whose basic education had been interrupted for five years—returned to the classroom as a man, scarred and cynical, ancient at the age of twenty-three.

"Incredibly, I did well. I entered the university in 1950 and went on to medical school three years later. I studied for two years in Tel Aviv, fifteen months in London, a year in Rome, and one very rainy spring in Zurich. Whenever I could I would return to Israel, work in the kibbutz near the farm where David and Rebecca spent their summers, and renew old friendships. My indebtedness to my cousin and her husband grew beyond repayment, but Rebecca insisted that the only surviving member of the Laski wing of the Eshkol family must amount to something.

"I chose psychiatry. My medical studies never seemed more to me than a necessary prerequisite of studying the body in order to learn about the mind. I soon became obsessed with theories of violence and dominance in human affairs. I was amazed to learn that there was very little actual research in this area. There was ample data to explain the precise mechanisms of dominance hierarchy in a lion pride, there was voluminous research relating to the pecking order in most avian species, more and more information was coming in from primatologists on the role of dominance and aggression in the social groups of our nearest cousins, but almost nothing was known about the mechanism of human violence as it relates to dominance and social order. I soon began developing my own theories and speculations.

"During those years of study I made numerous inquiries after the Oberst. I had a description of him, I knew that he was an officer in *Einsatzgruppe* 3, I had seen him with Himmler, and I remember that *Der Alte's* last words had been 'Willi, my friend.' I contacted the Allies War Crimes Commissions in their various zones of occupation, the Red Cross, the Soviet People's Standing Tribunal on Fascist War Crimes, the Jewish Committee, and countless ministries and bureaucracies. There was nothing. After five years I went to the Mossad, Israel's intelligence agency. They, at least, were most interested in my story, but in those days the Mossad was not the efficient organization it is reputed to be today. Also, they had more famous names such as Eichmann, Murer, and Mengele which were higher on their list of investigations than an unknown Oberst reported by only one survivor of the Holocaust. It was in 1955 that I went to Austria to confer with the Nazi hunter, Simon Wiesenthal.

"Wiesenthal's 'Documentation Center' was one floor of a shabby building in a poor part of Vienna. The building looked as if it had been thrown up as temporary housing during the war. He had three rooms there, two of them crammed with overflowing filing cabinets, and his office had only bare concrete for a floor. Wiesenthal himself was a nervous, intense person with disturbing eyes. There was something familiar about those eyes. At first I thought that he had the eyes of a fanatic, but then I realized where I had seen them before. Simon Wiesenthal's eyes reminded me of the ones I stared into each morning as I shaved.

"I told Wiesenthal an abbreviated version of my story, suggesting only that the Oberst had committed atrocities on Chelmno inmates for the amusement of his soldiers. Wiesenthal became very attentive when I said that I had again seen the Oberst at Sobibor in the company of Heinrich Himmler. 'You are sure?' he asked. 'Positive,' I replied.

"Busy as he was, Wiesenthal spent two days helping me attempt to trace the Oberst. In his cluttered tomb of an office complex, Wiesenthal had hundreds of files, dozens of indexes and cross-indexes, and the names of more than twenty-two thousand SS men. We studied photographs of *Einsatzgruppen* personnel, military academy graduation pictures, newspaper clippings, and photos from the official SS magazine, *The Black Corps*. At the end of the first day, I could no longer focus my eyes. That night I dreamed of photographs of Wehrmacht officers receiving medals from smirking Nazi leaders. There was no sign of the Oberst.

"It was late in the second afternoon when I found it. The news photograph was dated twenty-three November, 1942. The picture was of a Baron von Büler, a Prussian aristocrat and World War One hero, who had returned to active duty as a general. According to the caption under the photograph General von Büler had died in action while leading an heroic counterattack against a Russian armored division on the Eastern Front. I stared a long moment at the lined and craggy face in the fading clipping. It was the Old Man. *Der Alte*. I set it back in the file and went on.

"'If only we had a last name,' said Wiesenthal that evening as we ate in a small restaurant near St. Stephen's Cathedral. 'I feel certain we could track him down if we had his last name. The SS and Gestapo kept complete directories of their officers. If only we had his name.'

"I shrugged and said that I would return to Tel Aviv in the morning. We had all but exhausted Wiesenthal's clippings relating to *Einsatzguppe* and the Eastern Front and my studies would soon be demanding all of my time.

"'But surely no!' Wiesenthal exclaimed. 'You are a survivor of Lodz Ghetto, Chelmno, and Sobibor. You must have much information about the officers, other war criminals. You must spend at least the next week here. I will interview you and have the interviews transcribed for my files. There is not telling what valuable facts you may possess.'

"'No,' I said. 'I am not interested in the others. I am interested only in finding the Oberst.'

"Wiesenthal stared at his coffee and then looked at me again. There was a strange light in his eyes. 'So, you are interested only in revenge.'

"'Yes,' I said. 'Just as you are.'

"Wiesenthal shook his head sadly. 'No,' he said. 'Perhaps we are both obsessed, my friend. But what I seek is justice, not revenge.'

"'Surely in this case they are the same thing,' I said.

"Wiesenthal again shook his head. 'Justice is required,' he said so softly that I could hardly hear him. 'It is demanded by the millions of voices from unmarked graves, from rusting ovens, from empty houses in a thousand cities. But not revenge. Revenge is not worthy.'

"'Worthy of what?' I snapped back, more sharply than I intended.

"'Of us,' said Wiesenthal. 'Of them. Of their death. Of our continued existence.'

"I shook my head in dismissal then, but I have often thought of that conversation.

"Wiesenthal was disappointed, but he agreed to continue his search for any scrap of information which fit my description of the Oberst. Fifteen months later, only a few days after I had received my degree, a letter arrived from Simon Wiesenthal. In it were photostated copies of *Section IV Sonderkommando Sub-section IV-B* pay vouchers for *Einsatzgruppen* 'Special Advisors.' Wiesenthal had circled the name of an Oberst Wilhelm von Borchert, an officer on special assignment to *Einsatzgruppen Drei* from the office of Reinhard Heydrich. Clipped to these photostats was a newspaper clipping Wiesenthal had retrieved from his files. Seven smiling young officers posed for their picture at a special Berlin Philharmonic performance to benefit the Wehrmacht. The clipping was dated twenty-three, six, forty-one. The concert was Wagner. The names of the smiling officers were listed. The fifth from the left, barely visible behind the shoulders of his comrades, his hat pulled low, was the pale countenance of the Oberst. The name in the caption read Oberleutnant Wilhelm von Borchert.

"Two days later I was in Vienna. Wiesenthal had ordered his correspondents to research the background of von Borchert, but the results were disappointing. The von Borcherts were an established family with aristocratic roots in both Prussia and East Bavaria. The family fortune had derived from land, mining interests, and exports of art objects. Wiesenthal's agents could find no record of the birth or christening of a Wilhelm von Borchert in records going back to 1880. They did, however, find a death notice. According to an announcement in the *Regen Zeitung* dated nineteen, seven, forty-five, Oberst Wilhelm von Borchert, only heir to Count Klaus von Borchert, had died in combat while heroically defending Berlin from Soviet invaders. Word had reached the elderly count and his wife while they were staying at their summer residence, Waldheim, in the Bayrische Wald near Bayerisch-Eisenstein. The family was seeking Allied permission to close down the estate and to return to their home near Bremen for memorial services. Wilhelm von Borchert, the article went on to say, had received the coveted Iron Cross for valor and had been recommended for promotion to SS Oberstgruppenführer at the time of his death.

"Wiesenthal had ordered his people to follow any other leads. There were none. Von Borchert's family in 1956 consisted only of an elderly aunt in Bremen and two nephews who had lost most of the family's money in poor postwar investments. The huge estate in East Bavaria had been closed for years and much of the hunting preserve there had been sold to pay taxes. As well as Wiesenthal's limited Eastern Bloc contacts could tell, the Soviets and East Germans had no information on the life or death of Wilhelm von Borchert.

"I flew to Bremen to speak with the Oberst's aunt, but the woman was far gone into senility and could recall no one in her family named Willi. She thought I had been sent by her brother to take her to the Summerfest at Waldheim. One of the nephews refused to see me. The other, a foppish young man I caught up with in Brussels as he was on his way to a spa in France, said that he had met his Uncle Wilhelm only once, in 1937. The nephew had been nine at the time. He remembered only the wonderful silk suit his uncle wore and the straw boater he wore at a jaunty angle. He understood that his uncle had been a war hero and had died fighting Communism. I returned to Tel Aviv.

"For several years I practiced my profession in Israel, learning, as all psychiatrists do, that a degree in psychiatry merely qualifies one to *begin* learning about the intricacies and foibles of the human personality. In 1960 my cousin Rebecca died of cancer. David urged me to go to America to continue my research into the mechanics of human dominance. When I protested that I had access to adequate materials in Tel Aviv, David joked that nowhere would the spectrum of violence be more complete than in the United States. I arrived in New York in January of 1964. The nation was recovering from the loss of a president and preparing to drown its sorrow in adolescent hysteria at the arrival of a British rock group called the Beatles. Columbia University had offered me a one-year visiting professorship. As it worked out, I would stay on there to finish my book on the pathology of violence and eventually to become an American citizen.

"It was in November of 1964 that I decided to stay in the States. I was visiting friends in Princeton, New Jersey, and after dinner they apologetically asked if I would mind watching an hour of television with them. I owned no television of my own and assured them that I would enjoy the diversion. As it turned out, the program was a documentary commemorating the first anniversary of President Kennedy's assassination. I was interested in the program. Even in Israel, obsessed as we had been with our own priorities, the death of the American president had come as a great shock to us all. I had seen photographs of the president's motorcade in Dallas, been touched by the oft-reproduced picture of Kennedy's young son saluting his father's coffin, and had read accounts of Jack Ruby's murder of the probable assassin, but I had never seen the videotape of the actual shooting of Oswald. Now the documentary showed it—the smirking little man in a dark sweater, the Dallas plainclothes officers with their Stetsons and quintessential American faces, the heavyset man lunging out of the crowd, a pistol shoved almost into Oswald's belly, the sharp, flat sound which reminded me of white, naked bodies falling forward into the Pit, Oswald grimacing and clutching his stomach. I watched as police officers grappled with Ruby. In the confusion, the television camera was jostled and swept across the crowd.

"'My God, my God!' I cried out in Polish and leaped to my feet. The Oberst had been in that crowd.

"Unable to explain my agitation to my host and hostess, I left that night and took the train to New York. Early the next morning I was at the Manhattan offices of the network which had aired the documentary. I used my contacts at the university and in publishing to gain access to the network's films, videotapes, and what they called outtakes. Only in the few seconds of tape I had seen in the program did the face in the crowd appear. A graduate student I worked with kindly took still photographs from the network editing monitor and blew them up as large as possible for me.

"Viewed that way, the face was even less recognizable than during the second and a half it was on the screen: a white blur glimpsed between the brims of Texas cowboy hats, a vague impression of a thin smile, eye sockets as dark as openings in a skull. The image would not have served as evidence in any court in the world, but I *knew* it had been the Oberst.

"I flew to Dallas. The authorities there were still sensitive from the criticism of the press and world opinion. Few would speak to me and even fewer would discuss the events in the underground garage. No one recognized the photographs I showed them—either the one taken from the videotape or the old Berlin news photo. I spoke to reporters. I spoke to witnesses. I tried to speak to Jack Ruby, the assassin's assassin, but could not receive permission to do so. The Oberst's trail was a year old and it was as cold as the corpse of Lee Harvey Oswald.

"I returned to New York. I contacted acquaintances in the Israeli Embassy. They denied that Israeli intelligence agencies would ever operate on American soil, but they agreed to make certain inquiries. I hired a private detective in Dallas. His bill ran to seven thousand dollars and his report could have been distilled into a single word: nothing. The embassy charged me nothing for their negative report, but I am sure that my contacts there must have thought me mad to be searching for a war criminal at the site of a presidential assassination. They knew from experience that most ex-Nazis sought only anonymity in their exile.

"I began to doubt my own sanity. The face that had haunted my dreams for so many years had clearly become the central obsession in my life. As a psychiatrist, I could understand the ambiguity of this obsession: burned into my consciousness in a Sobibor death chamber, tempered by the coldest winter of my spirit, my fixation on finding the Oberst had been my *reason to live*; erase one and the other disappears. Acknowledging the Oberst's death would have been tantamount to acknowledging my own.

"As a psychiatrist I understood my obsession. I understood, but I did not believe my own rationale. Even if I had believed it, I would not have worked to 'cure' myself. *The Oberst was real. The chess game had been real.* The Oberst was not a man to die in some makeshift fortification outside Berlin. He was a monster. Monsters do not die. They must be *killed*.

"In the summer of 1965, I finally arranged an interview with Jack Ruby. It was not productive. Ruby was a sad-faced husk of a man. He had lost weight in prison and loose skin hung on his face and arms like folds of dirty cheesecloth. His eyes were vague and absent, his voice hoarse. I tried to draw him out of his mental state that day in November, but he would only shrug and repeat what he had said in interrogations so many times before. No, he did not know that he was going to shoot Oswald until just before the act was performed. It was an accident that he was allowed to enter the garage. Something had come over him when he saw Oswald, an impulse he could not control. This was the man who had killed his beloved president.

"I showed him the photographs of the Oberst. He shook his head tiredly. He had known several of the Dallas detectives and many of the reporters on the scene, but he had never seen this man. Had he felt anything *strange* just before he shot Oswald? When I asked this question, Ruby lifted his tired, basset-hound face for a second and I saw a flicker of confusion in his eyes, but then that faded and he responded in the same monotone as before. No, nothing strange, just fury at the thought that Oswald should still be alive while President Kennedy was dead and poor Mrs. Kennedy and the children were all alone.

"I was not surprised a year later in December of 1966 when Ruby was admitted to Parkland Hospital for treatment of cancer. He had seemed to be a terminally ill man even when I had interviewed him. Few mourned when he died in January of 1967. The nation had expiated its grief and Jack Ruby was only a reminder of a time better forgotten.

"During the late nineteen sixties I became more and more involved with my research and teaching. I tried to convince myself that in my theoretical work I was exorcising the demon which the Oberst's face had symbolized. Inside, I knew better.

"Through the violence of those years, I continued to study violence. Why was it that some people could dominate others so easily? In my research I would bring small groups of men and women together, strangers assembled to complete some irrelevant task, and inevitably a social pecking order would begin to be established within thirty minutes of the group's creation. Frequently the participants were not even aware of the establishment of a hierarchy, but when questioned, almost all could identify the 'most important' member of the group or the 'most dynamic.' My graduate students and I conducted interviews, pored over transcripts, and spent endless hours watching videotapes. We simulated confrontations between subjects and figures of authority—university deans, police officers, teachers, IRS officials, prison officials, and ministers. Always the question of hierarchy and dominance was more complex than mere social position would suggest.

"It was during this time that I began working with the New York police on personality profiles for homicide subjects. The data was fascinating. The interviews were depressing. The results were inconclusive.

"What was the root source of human violence? What role did violence and the threat of violence play in our everyday interactions? By answering these questions, I naïvely hoped to someday explain how a brilliant but deluded psychopath like Adolf Hitler could turn one of the great cultures of the world into a mindless, immoral killing machine. I began with the knowledge that every other complex animal species on earth had some mechanism to establish dominance and social hierarchy. Usually this hierarchy was established without serious injury. Even such fierce predators as wolves and tigers had precise signals of submission which would immediately end the most violent confrontation before death or crippling injury ensued. But what of Man? Were we, as so many assumed, lacking this instinctive submission-recognition signal and therefore doomed to eternal warfare, a type of intraspecies madness predetermined by our genes? I thought not.

"As I spent years compiling data and developing premises, I secretly harbored a theory so bizarre and unscientific that it would have ruined my professional standing if I had so much as whispered it to colleagues. What if mankind had evolved until the establishment of dominance was a psychic—what some of my less rational friends would have called a *parapsychological*—phenomenon? Certainly the pale appeal of some politicians, that thing the media calls *charisma* for want of a better term, was not based upon size, breeding ability, or threat display. What, I surmised, if in some lobe or hemisphere of the brain there were an area devoted to nothing else but projecting this sense of personal domination? I was more than familiar with the neurological studies suggesting that we inherited our hierarchical sense from the most primitive portions of the mind—the so-called reptile brain. But what if there had been evolutionary advances—*mutations*—which endowed some humans with an ability akin to empathy or the concept of telepathy but infinitely more powerful and useful in survival terms? And what if this ability, fueled by its own hunger for dominance, found its ultimate expression in violence? Would the humans who manifested such an ability be truly human?

"In the end, all I could do was theorize endlessly about what I had *felt* when the Oberst's force of will had entered me. As the decades passed, the details of those terrible days faded, but the *pain* of that mind rape, the revulsion and terror of it, still sent me gasping out of sleep. I continued to teach, to research, and to move through the gray realities of day-to-day life. Last spring I awoke one day to realize that I was growing old. It had been almost sixteen years since I had seen the face on videotape. If the Oberst were real, if he were still alive anywhere in the world, he would be a very old man by now. I thought of the toothless, quaking old men who were still being revealed as war criminals. Most probably the Oberst was dead.

"I had forgotten that monsters do not die. They must be killed.

"Less than five months ago I almost walked into the Oberst on a New York street. It was a sweltering July evening. I was near Central Park West, walking, thinking, mentally composing an article on prison reform, when the Oberst emerged from a restaurant not more than fifty feet from me and hailed a cab. There was a woman with him, an older lady but still beautiful, whose white hair flowed down over an expensive silk evening dress. The Oberst himself was dressed in a dark suit. He looked tanned and fit. He had lost much of his hair and what was left had faded from blond to gray, but his face, although heavier and ruddier with age, remained chiseled in the same sharp planes of cruelty and control.

"After several seconds in which I just stood and stared, I ran after the cab. It pulled out into traffic and I dodged vehicles in a frenzied attempt to catch it. The occupants in the back seat never looked back. The cab pulled away in traffic and I staggered to the curb in near collapse.

"The maître d' in the restaurant could not help me. Yes, there had been a distinguished older couple dining there that evening, but he did not know their names. No, they had not had a reservation.

"For weeks I haunted that area of Central Park West, searching the streets, watching for the Oberst's face in every taxi which passed. I hired a young New York detective and again I paid for no results.

"It was at this time that I experienced what I now recognize as a massive nervous breakdown. I did not sleep. I could not work and my classes at the university were canceled or covered by nervous teaching assistants. I wore the same clothes for days on end, returning to my apartment only to eat and pace nervously. At night I walked the streets and was questioned several times by police. Only my position at Columbia and the magical title of 'Doctor' must have saved me from being sent to Bellevue for examination. Then one night I was lying awake on the floor of my apartment when I realized what I had been ignoring. *The woman's face had been familiar.*

"For the better part of that night and the next day I fought to retrieve the memory of where I had seen her before. It had been in a photograph, I was sure of that. Along with her image, I associated vague memories of boredom, uneasiness, and bland music.

"At fifteen minutes after five that afternoon I hailed a cab and rushed uptown to my dentist's office. He had just left for the day, the office was closing, but I prattled some story and bullied the receptionist into allowing me to pour through the stacks of old magazines in the waiting room. There were copies of *Seventeen, GQ, Mademoiselle, U.S. News and World Report, Time, Newsweek, Vogue, Consumer Reports,* and *Tennis World.* The receptionist was becoming truculent and more than a little alarmed by my manic state by the time I began going through the issues a second time. Only the depth of my obsession and the near certainty that no dentist would change his stock of magazines more than four times a year kept me searching while the shrill woman threatened to call the police.

"I found it. Her photograph was a small black and white insert near the front of the thick sheath of glossy ads and breathless adjectives which was *Vogue.* The picture was at the head of a column on purchasing accessories. It had a byline—NINA DRAYTON.

"From there it took only hours to trace Nina Drayton. My New York private detective was pleased to work on something more accessible than my elusive phantom. Harrington reported back in twenty-four hours with a thick dossier on the woman. Most of the information was from public sources.

"Mrs. Nina Drayton was a rich, well-known name in the New York fashion industry, the owner of a chain of boutiques, and a widow. She married Parker Allan Drayton, one of the founders of American Airlines, in August of 1940. He had died ten months after the wedding and his widow had carried on, investing wisely, inserting herself into several boardrooms where no woman had previously been. Mrs. Drayton was no longer active in business other than her boutiques, but she served on the boards of several prestigious charities, had a first-name acquaintance with numerous politicians, artists, and writers, was rumored to have had an affair with a famous New York composer-conductor, and kept up a large sixteenth-floor apartment on Park Avenue as well as several summer and vacation homes.

"It was not too difficult to arrange an introduction. Eventually I thought of going through my patient lists, and I soon found the name of a rich, manic-depressive matron who lived in the same building as Mrs. Drayton and who moved in at least some of the same circles.

"I met Nina Drayton on the second weekend of August at a garden party arranged by my ex-patient. There were few guests. Most people with sense had fled the city for their cottages on the Cape or summer chalets in the Rockies. But Mrs. Drayton was there.

"Even before I shook her hand or stared into those clear blue eyes, I knew beyond a shadow of a doubt that she was one of *them*. She was like the Oberst. Her presence seemed to fill the courtyard, making the Japanese lanterns glow more brightly. I felt the certainty of my knowledge like a cold hand at my throat. Perhaps she sensed my reaction, or perhaps she enjoyed baiting psychiatrists, but Nina Drayton verbally fenced with me that evening with a mixture of amused contempt and mischievous challenge as subtle as a cat's claws sheathed in velvet.

"I invited her to attend a public lecture I was giving that week at Columbia. To my surprise, she appeared, trailing behind her a malevolent-looking little woman named Barrett Kramer. My talk was about the deliberate policies of violence in the Third Reich and how they related to certain Third World regimes of today. I tailored the lecture to suggest a premise contrary to current thinking—that, indeed, the inexplicable brutality of millions of Germans was due, at least in part, to the manipulation of a small and secretive group of powerful personalities. All through the talk I could see Mrs. Drayton smiling at me from the fifth row. It was the type of smile the mouse must see on the face of the cat which is about to devour it.

"After the talk, Mrs. Drayton wished to speak to me privately. She asked if I was still meeting with patients and requested to see me professionally. I hesitated, but each of us knew what my answer would be.

"I saw her twice, both times in September. We went through the motions of initiating therapy. Nina Drayton was convinced that her insomnia was directly related to the death of her father decades ago. She revealed that she had recurrent nightmares wherein she *pushed* her father in front of the Boston trolley which killed him even though she was actually miles away at the time. 'Is it true, Dr. Laski,' she asked at one point in our second session, 'that we always kill the ones we love?' I told her that I suspected that the opposite was true; that we sought, at least in our minds, to kill those we pretended to love but secretly despised. Nina Drayton only smiled at me.

"I had suggested that we use hypnosis during our third session in an attempt to relive her reaction to the news of her father's death. She agreed, but I was not surprised when her secretary called in early October to cancel any further sessions. By this time, I had assigned a private detective to full-time surveillance of Mrs. Drayton.

"When I say private detective, I should clarify the image. Rather than the cynical ex-policeman one would imagine, I had on the advice of friends, hired a twenty-four-year old ex-Princeton dropout who wrote poetry in his spare time. Francis Xavier Harrington had been in the private investigation business for two years, but he had to buy a new suit in order to enter the restaurants where Mrs. Drayton spent her lunch hours. When I authorized twenty-four-hour surveillance, Harrington had to hire two old fraternity friends to round out his agency. But the boy was no fool; he worked quickly and competently and had a written report on my desk every Monday and Friday morning. Some of his accomplishments were not strictly legal, such as his knack of obtaining copies of Nina Drayton's telephone billing statements. She called many, many people. Harrington tracked down the listed numbers on the statement and made a list of the names and addresses. Some were well known. Others were intriguing. None led me to the Oberst.

"Weeks passed. By this time I had used most of my savings to document Nina Drayton's daily doings, her luncheon preferences, her business dealings, and her phone calls. Young Harrington understood that my resources were limited, and he kindly offered to intercept the lady's mail and tap her telephone. I decided against it, at least for a few more weeks. I wanted to do nothing which would tip our hand.

"Then, only two weeks ago, Mrs. Drayton called me. She invited me to a gala Christmas party to be held at her apartment on the seventeenth of December. She was calling personally, she said, so that I would have no excuse for not attending. She wanted me to meet a *dear* friend of hers from Hollywood, a producer who was *so* looking forward to meeting me. She had just sent him a copy of my book, *The Pathology of Violence*, and he had *raved* about it.

"'What is his name?' I asked. 'Never you mind,' she responded. 'You may recognize him when you meet him.'

"I was shaking so badly when I hung up that it took a full minute before I could punch out Harrington's phone number. That evening the three boys and I met to discuss strategy. We went through the phone bills again. This time we called all Los Angeles numbers listed which were not in the city directory. On the sixth call a young man's voice answered, 'Mr. Borden's residence.' 'Is this Thomas Borden's home number?' asked Francis, 'You've got the wrong number,' snapped the voice. 'This is Mr. William Borden's residence.'

"I wrote the names on the chalkboard in my office. Wilhelm von Borchert. William Borden. It was so true to human nature; the adulterer signs a close version of his own name on the hotel register; the wanted felon goes by six aliases, five of which have the same first name as his own. There is something about our names which we have great trouble abandoning completely, no matter how great the justification.

"That Monday, four days before the events here in Charleston transpired, Harrington flew to Los Angeles. I had originally planned to go myself, but Francis pointed out that it would be better if he went ahead to check out this Borden, to photograph him, and to ascertain that it was actually von Borchert. I still wanted to go, but I realized that I had no plan of action. Even after all those years, I had not confronted the details of what I would do once I had found the Oberst.

"That Monday night, Harrington called to report that his in-flight movie had been mediocre, that his hotel was decidedly inferior to the Beverly Wilshire, and that police in Bel Air had the tendency to stop and question you if you drove through the neighborhood twice or had the temerity to park your car on the winding streets to stare at a movie star's home. On Tuesday he called to check on what was new with Mrs. Drayton. I told him that his two friends, Dennis and Selby, were a bit sleepier than him but that Mrs. Drayton was going about business as usual. Francis went on to tell me that he had been to the studio with which Borden had most often been associated—the tour was mediocre—and although Borden had an office there, no one knew when he might be in. The last time anyone had seen him work there was in 1979. Francis had hoped to get a picture of Borden but none were available. He had considered showing the studio secretary the Berlin photograph of von Borchert but decided, in his words, 'That wouldn't have been too cool.' He was planning to take his camera with the long lens out to Borden's Bel Air estate the next day.

"On Wednesday Harrington did not call at the appointed time. I phoned the hotel and they reported that he was still registered but had not picked up his key that evening. On Thursday morning I called the Los Angeles police. They agreed to look into it but, on the limited information I had given them, felt that there was little reason to suspect foul play. 'This is a pretty busy town,' said the sergeant I spoke to. 'A young guy could get involved in a lot of things and forget to call.'

"All that day I attempted to get in touch with Dennis or Selby. I could not. Even the telephone recording device at Francis's agency had been disconnected. I went to Nina Drayton's Park Avenue apartment building. The lobby security man informed me that Mrs. Drayton was on vacation. I was not allowed above the first floor.

"All that day Friday I sat alone in my locked apartment, waiting At eleven-thirty the Los Angeles police called. They had opened Mr. Harrington's room at the Beverly Hills Hotel. His clothes and luggage were gone and there was no sign of foul play. Did I know who would be responsible for the hotel bill of $329.48?

"That night I forced myself to go to a friend's house for dinner as scheduled. The two-block walk from the bus stop to the town house in Greenwich Village seemed interminable. That Saturday evening, the night your father was killed here in Charleston, I was part of a panel on urban violence at the university. There were several political candidates there and over two hundred people attended. All through the discussion, I kept looking out at the audience, expecting to see Nina Drayton's cobra smile or the cold eyes of the Oberst. I felt that I was once again a pawn— but in whose game?

"This past Sunday I read the morning paper. For the first time I heard about the Charleston murders. Elsewhere in the paper, a short column announced that Hollywood producer William D. Borden had been aboard the ill-fated flight which had crashed early Saturday morning in South Carolina. They included a rare photograph of the reclusive producer. The picture was from the nineteen sixties. The Oberst was smiling."

Saul stopped talking. Their coffee cups sat cold and unnoticed on the porch railing. The shadows of the railing slats had crept across Saul's legs as he talked. In the sudden silence, distant street sounds became audible.

"Which one of them killed my father?" asked Natalie. She had pulled her sweater more tightly around her and now she rubbed her arms as if she were cold.

"I don't know," said Saul.

"This Melanie Fuller, she was one of them?"

"Yes, almost certainly."

"And it could've been her?"

"Yes."

"And you're sure this Nina Drayton woman is dead?"

"Yes. I went to the morgue. I saw crime scene photographs. I read the autopsy report."

"But she might have killed my father before she died?"

Saul hesitated. "It is possible," he said.

"And Borden—the Oberst—he's supposed to have died when that plane blew up Friday."

Saul nodded.

"Do you think he's dead?" asked Natalie.

Saul said, "No."

Natalie stood up and paced back and forth on the small porch. "Do you have any proof that he might still be alive?" she asked.

"No."

"But you think he is?"

"Yes."

"And either he or the Fuller woman could have killed my father?"

"Yes."

"And you're still going after him? After Borden . . . von Borchert . . . whatever he's called?"

"Yes."

"Jesus H. Christ." Natalie went into the house and came back out with two glasses of brandy. She gave one to Saul and drank the other in one long gulp. She pulled a pack of cigarettes out of the pocket of her sweater, found matches, and lit a cigarette with shaking hands.

"Those are not good for you," said Saul quietly.

Natalie made a short, sharp sound. "These people are vampires, aren't they?" she said.

"Vampires?" Saul shook his head, not quite understanding.

"They use other people and then throw them away like plastic wrappers or something," she said. "They're like those goddamn corny vampires you see on the late show only these people are *real*."

"Vampires," said Saul and realized that he had spoken in Polish. "Yes," he said in English, "it is not a bad analogy."

"All right," said Natalie, "what do we do now?"

"We?" Saul was startled. He rubbed his hands on his knees.

"We," said Natalie and there was something like anger in her voice. "You and I. Us. You didn't tell me that whole story just to kill time. You need an ally. All right, so what's our next step?"

Saul shook his head and scratched at his beard. "I am not sure why I told you all of this," he said. "But . . ."

"But what?"

"It is very dangerous. Francis, the others . . ."

Natalie crossed the space, crouched, and touched his arm with her right hand. "My father's name was Joseph Leonard Preston," she said softly. "He was forty-eight years old . . . would have been forty-nine next February sixth. He was a good person, a good father, a good photographer, and a very poor businessman. When he laughed . . ." Natalie paused a second. "When he laughed it was very hard not to laugh with him."

For several seconds she crouched there silently, touching his wrist near the faded blue number tatooed there. Then she said, "What do you do next?"

Saul took a breath. "I'm not sure. I need to fly to Washington this Saturday to see someone who might have some information . . . information that might let us know if the Oberst is still alive. It is improbable that my . . . contact will have such information."

"Then what?" pressed Natalie.

"Then we wait," said Saul. "Wait and watch. Search the newspaper."

"The newspapers?" said Natalie. "Search for what?"

"For more murders," said Saul.

Natalie blinked and rocked back on her heels. The cigarette she was holding in her right hand had burned low. She stubbed it out on the wooden floorboards. "You're serious? Surely this Fuller woman and your Oberst would leave the country . . . go into hiding . . . something. Why would they get involved in this sort of thing again so soon?"

Saul shrugged. He suddenly felt very weary. "It is their nature," he said. "Vampires must feed."

Natalie stood and walked to the corner of the porch. "And when you . . . when *we* find them, what do we do?" she asked.

"We will decide then," said Saul. "First we must find them."

"To kill a vampire you have to drive a stake through its heart," said Natalie.

Saul said nothing.

Natalie took out another cigarette but did not light it. "What if you get close to them and they find out you're after them," she said. "What if they come after *you*?"

"That could make it much simpler," said Saul.

Natalie was about to speak when a tan automobile with county markings stopped at the curb. A heavyset man with a florid face under a creased Stetson stepped out of the driver's side. "Sheriff Gentry," said Natalie.

They watched as the overweight officer stood staring at them and then approached slowly, almost hesitantly. Gentry stopped at the porch step and removed his hat. His sunburned face held the expression of a young boy who has seen something terrible.

"Mornin', Ms. Preston, Professor Laski," said Gentry.

"Good morning, Sheriff," said Natalie.

Saul looked at Gentry, so much the caricature of a Southern cop, and sensed there the same keen intelligence and sensitivity he had felt the day before. The man's eyes belied much of the rest of his appearance.

"I need help," said Gentry and there was an edge of pain to his voice.

"What kind of help?" asked Natalie. Saul could hear affection in her voice.

Sheriff Gentry looked down at his hat. He creased the crown with a graceful motion of his chubby, pink hand, and looked up at both of them. "I've got nine citizens dead," he said. "The way they died doesn't make a damn bit of sense no matter which way you put it together. A couple of hours ago I stopped a fellow with nothing in his wallet but a picture of me. Rather'n talk to me, this fellow cuts his own throat." Gentry looked at Natalie and then at Saul. "Now for some reason," he said, "for some reason that doesn't make any more sense than any of the rest of this godawful mess, I have a hunch that you two folks might be able to help."

Saul and Natalie returned his stare in silence.

"Can you?" asked Gentry at last. "*Will* you?"

Natalie looked at Saul. Saul scratched his beard for a second, removed his glasses and put them back on, looked back at Natalie, and nodded slightly.

"Come inside, Sheriff," said Natalie, holding open the front door. "I'll make some lunch. This may take awhile."

ELEVEN

Bayerisch-Eisenstein
Friday, Dec. 19, 1980

Tony Harod and Maria Chen had breakfast in the small hotel dining room. They were downstairs by seven A.M., but the first wave of breakfasters had already eaten and left for the ski trails. There was a fire crackling in the stone fireplace and Harod could see white snow and blue sky through the small, paned window on the south wall.

"Do you think he will be there?" Maria Chen asked softly as they finished their coffee.

Harod shrugged. "How the fuck would I know?" Yesterday he had been sure that Willi would *not* be at the family estate, that the old producer *had* died in the jet crash. He remembered the mention of the family estate from a conversation he and Willi had held five years before. Harod had been quite drunk; Willi had just returned from a three-week trip to Europe and suddenly with tears in his eyes, he said, "Who says you cannot go home again, eh, Tony? Who says?" and then gone on to describe his mother's home in southern Germany. Naming the nearby town had been a slip. Harod had seen the trip as a way to eliminate a disturbing possibility, nothing more. But now, in the sharp morning light, with Maria Chen sitting across from him with the 9mm Browning in her purse, the improbable seemed all too possible.

"What about Tom and Jensen?" asked Maria Chen. She was dressed in stylish blue corduroy knickers, high socks, a pink turtleneck, and a heavy blue and pink ski sweater that had cost six hundred dollars. Her dark hair was tied back into a short ponytail and even with makeup on she looked fresh and well scrubbed. Harod thought she looked like a young Eurasian girl scout out for a day's skiing with her dad's friends.

"If you have to eliminate them, take Tom out first," he told her. "Willi tends to Use Reynolds more easily than he does the nigger. But Luhar is strong . . . *very* strong. Make sure that if he goes down he stays down. But if push comes to shove, it's *Willi* you have to take out first. In the *head*. Eliminate him and Reynolds and Luhar aren't any threat. They're so well conditioned that they can't take a piss without Willi's OK."

Maria Chen blinked and looked around her. The other four tables were filled with laughing, talking German couples. No one appeared to have heard Harod's soft instructions.

Harod gestured the waitress over for more coffee, sipped the black brew, and frowned. He did not know if Maria Chen would carry out his instructions when it came to shooting people. He *assumed* she would—she had never disobeyed an order before—but for a second he wished he had a woman along who was not a Neutral. But if his agent was not Neutral, then there was always the chance that Willi could turn the person for his own Use. Harod had no illusions about the old kraut's Ability—the mere fact that Willi had kept two catspaws around him showed the strength of the bastard's power. Harod had believed that Willi's Ability had indeed faded—dulled by age, drugs, and decades of decadence—but in light of recent events it would be foolish and dangerous to continue to act on that assumption. Harod shook his head. Goddamn it. That fucking Island Club already had him by the balls. Harod had no interest in getting involved with that ancient Charleston broad. Anyone who had played that goddamn game with Willi Borden—von Borchert—whatever the fuck his name was—for fifty years, was not someone Tony Harod wanted to mess with. And what would Barent and his asshole buddies do when they found out that Willi was alive? *If* he was alive. Harod remembered his reaction six days earlier when the call came about Willi's death. First there had come the wave of concern—What about all of the projects Willi was developing? What about the money?—then the rush of relief. The old son of a bitch was dead at last. Harod had spent years containing his secret terror that the old man would find out about the Island Club, about Tony's spying . . .

"*I imagine Paradise as an Island where one can Hunt to his heart's content, eh, Tony?*" Had Willi really said that on the videotape? Harod remembered the sensation of being immersed in ice water that had hit him when Willi's image had spoken those words. But there was no way that Willi could have known. And besides, the videotape had been made before the airline crash. Willi was dead.

And if he wasn't killed then, thought Harod, he soon would be. "Ready?" he said.

Maria Chen dabbed at her lips with a linen napkin and nodded.

"Let's go," said Tony Harod.

"So that's Czechoslovakia?" said Harod. As they drove northwest out of town he caught a glimpse past the train station of a border-crossing barrier, a small white building, and several guards in green uniforms and oddly shaped helmets. A small road sign read *Übergangsstelle*.

"That's it," agreed Maria Chen.

"Big damn deal," said Harod. He drove up the winding valley road, past turn-off signs to the Grosse Arber and the Kleine Arbersee. On a distant hill he could see the white slash of a ski run and the moving dots of a chair lift. Small cars with tire chains and ski racks darted up roads that were little more than corridors of packed ice and snow. Harod shivered as cold air blew in the rear windows of their rented car. The tips of two sets of cross-country skis Maria Chen had rented that morning at the hotel protruded through a gap in the rear window on the passenger's side. "Do you think we'll need those damn things?" he asked, jerking his head toward the backseat.

Maria Chen smiled and raised ten lacquered nails. "Perhaps," she said. She looked at the Shell road map and cross-checked with a topographic map. "Next left," she said. "Then six kilometers to the private access road."

The BMW had to slip and slide the last kilometer and a half up the "access road" that was nothing more than two ruts in the snow between trees. "Someone's been up here recently," said Harod. "How far to the estate?"

"One more kilometer after the bridge," said Maria Chen.

The road took a turn through a thick cluster of bare trees and the bridge came into sight—a small wooden span behind a striped barrier more solid-looking than the roadblock on the Czech border. There was a small, alpine-looking hut twenty yards downstream. Two men emerged and walked slowly toward the car. Harod half expected everyone in these rustic parts to dress in the winter equivalent of lederhosen and felt caps, but these two wore brown wool pants and bright goose-down jackets. Harod thought they looked like father and son, the younger man in his late twenties. The son carried a hunting rifle loosely in the crook of his arm.

"Guten Morgen, haben Sie sich verfahren?" asked the older man with a smile. *"Das hier ist ein Privatgrundstück."*

Maria Chen translated. "They wish us good morning and ask if we're lost. They say this is private property."

Harod smiled at the two. The older man showed gold caps in a return grin; the son showed no expression. "We're not lost," said Harod. "We've come out to see Willi—Herr von Borchert. He invited us. We came all the way from California."

When the older man frowned his incomprehension, Maria Chen translated in rapid-fire German.

"Herr von Borchert lebt hier nicht mehr," said the older man. *"Schon seit vielen Jahren nicht mehr. Das Gut ist schon seit sehr langer Zeit geschlossen. Niemand geht mehr dorthin."*

"He said that Herr von Borchert's no longer living," translated Maria Chen. "Not for many years. The estate is closed. It's been closed for a very long time. No one goes there."

Harod grinned and shook his head. "Then how come you guys are still guarding the place, huh?"

"Warum lassen Sie es noch bewachen?" asked Maria Chen.

The old man smiled. *"Wir werden von der Familie bezahlt, so daß dort kein Vandalismus entsteht,"* said the old man. *"Bald wird all das ein Teil des Nationalwaldes werden. Die alten Häuser werden abgerissen. Bis dahin schickt der Neffe uns Schecks aus Bonn, und wir halten alle Wilddiebe und Unbefugte fern, so wie es mein Vater vor mir getan hatte. Mein Sohn wird sich andere Arbeit suchen müssen."*

"The family pays us to see that no vandalism occurs," translated Maria

Chen. "Uh . . . sometime soon . . . someday soon, this will be part of the National Forest. The old home will be torn down. Until then, the nephew . . . von Borchert's nephew, I guess Tony . . . the nephew sends us checks from Bonn and we keep poachers and trespassers out, just as my father did before me. My son will have to seek work." She added, "They're not going to let us in, Tony."

Harod handed the man a small three-page treatment of Bill Borden's upcoming project *The White Slaver*. A hundred-mark note was just visible between the pages. "Tell him that we came all the way from Hollywood to scout locations," said Harod. "Tell him that the old estate would make a great haunted castle."

Maria Chen did so. The old man looked at the flier and the money, and casually handed both back. *"Ja, es wäre eine wunderbare Kulisse für einen Gruselfilm. Es besteht kein Zweifel, dab es hier spukt. Aber ich glaube, dab es keine weiteren Gespenster braucht. Ich schlage vor, dab Sie umdrehen, so dab Sie hier nicht stecken bleiben. Grüb Gott!"*

"What'd he say?" demanded Harod.

"He agreed that the estate would make an excellent set for a horror movie," said Maria Chen. "He says that it is indeed haunted. He doesn't think it needs more ghosts. He tells us to turn around here so we don't get stuck and wishes us a good day."

"Tell him to go fuck himself," said Harod while smiling at both men.

"Vielen Dank für Ihre Hilfe," said Maria Chen.

"Bitte sehr," said the old man.

"Think nothing of it," said the young man with the rifle.

Harod drove the BMW back down the long lane, turned west on the German equivalent of a country road, and drove half a mile before parking the car in shallow snow fifteen feet from a fence. He took wire cutters out of the trunk and snipped the fence in four places. He used his boots to kick the strands apart. The cut would not be visible from the road because of the trees and there was little traffic. Harod went back to the car, exchanged his mountain boots for cross-country ski boots with funny toes, and let Maria Chen help him into his skis.

Harod had been skiing twice, both times on cross-country tours at Sun Valley, once with Dino de Laurentiis's niece and Ann-Margret, and he had hated the experience.

Maria Chen left her purse in the car, slipped the Browning in the waistband of her knickers under her sweater, put an extra clip in the pocket of a goose-down vest, hung a small pair of binoculars around her neck, and led the way through the cut in the fence. Harod poled clumsily along behind.

He fell down twice in the first mile, both times cursing to himself as he struggled back to his feet while Maria Chen watched with a slight smile. There was no sound except for the soft sloosh of their skis, occasional squirrel chatter, and the ragged bellows of Harod's breathing. When they had gone about two miles, Maria Chen stopped and consulted her compass and the topographic map.

"There's the stream," she said. "We can cross it down at that log. The estate should be in the clearing about another kilometer *that* way." She pointed toward a dense section of forest.

Three football fields more, thought Harod as he fought to catch his breath. He remembered the hunting rifle the young guy had been carrying and realized how useless the Browning would be in a match-up between the two. And for all he knew, Jensen and Luhar and a dozen other of Willi's slaves were waiting in the woods with Uzis and Mac-10s. Harod forced in another breath and noticed the tension in his gut. *Fuck it*, he thought. He'd busted his ass to come this far. He wasn't leaving until he found out if Willi was there.

"Let's do it," he said. Maria Chen nodded, slipped the map in her pocket, and skied gracefully ahead.

There were two corpses in front of the house.

Harod and Maria Chen huddled behind a thin screen of spruce trees and took turns looking through the binoculars at the bodies. From fifty yards away the two dark lumps in the snow could have been anything— bundles of abandoned laundry perhaps—but the binoculars showed the pale curve of a white cheek, the sprawl of limbs twisted at an angle that would have brought excruciating pain to a sleeping person. These two were not sleeping.

Harod peered again. Two men. Dark overcoats. Leather gloves. One had been wearing a brown fedora; it lay six feet away on the snow. The snow itself was spattered with blood around the two bodies. A trail of red joined the footprints to the large french door of the old manor. Another thirty yards to the east, there were deep parallel gouges in the snow, another trail of footsteps to or from the house, and great circular ridges of powdery snow as if a huge fan had been pointed downward. *Helicopter*, thought Harod.

There were no signs of automobiles, snowmobiles, or other ski trails. The lane that connected with the entry road where he and Maria had been stopped earlier was little more than a snowy break between the trees. They could not see the alpine cabin or bridge from here.

The main house itself was something more than a typical mansion, definitely something less than a castle. A huge heap of dark stones and narrow windows, the estate broke off into wings and levels, giving the impression it had started out as an imposing central hall and been added onto over the generations. The color of stone and size of windows changed here and there, but the overall effect remained gloomy: dark stone, little glass, narrow doors, heavy walls painted with the shadow of bare trees. Harod thought that it suited Willi's personality better than the banana republic villa in Bel Air.

"What now?" whispered Maria Chen.

"Shut up," said Harod and lifted the binoculars to look at the two corpses again. They lay not far apart. The face of one was turned away, almost buried in the deep snow so that Harod caught only a glimpse of dark, short-cut hair stirring slightly when the breeze came up, but the other one, the one lying on its back, showed pale cheek and an open, white eye staring toward the line of evergreens as if awaiting Harod's arrival. Harod guessed that they had not been dead long. It did not look like the birds or animals had been at them.

"Let's get out of here, Tony."

"Shut the fuck up." Harod lowered the binoculars and thought. They could not see the other side of the manor from this vantage point. If they were going to approach the house, it made good sense to stay in the woods and ski in a wide circle so they could survey the manor from all directions. Harod squinted out at the large clearing. The trees were scattered in both directions; it would take an hour or more to backtrack into the forest and approach carefully. Clouds had covered the sun and a cold wind had come up. It was beginning to snow lightly. Harod's jeans were soaked through where he had fallen and his legs ached from the exercise. The fading light gave a sense of evening twilight even though it was not yet noon.

"Let's get out of here, Tony." Maria Chen's voice was not pleading or frightened, only calmly insistent.

"Give me the gun," he said. When she pulled it out of her waistband and handed it over, he used it to point toward the gray house and black lumps of bodies. "Go on up there," he said. "On your skis. I'll keep you covered from here. I think the fucking house is empty."

Maria Chen looked at him. There was no question or defiance in her dark eyes, only curiosity, as if she had never seen him before.

"Get *going*," snapped Harod and lowered the automatic, not sure what he would do if she refused.

Maria Chen turned, moved aside the screening spruce limbs with a graceful flick of her ski pole, and skied toward the house. Harod hunched over and moved away from the place where they had been standing, finally stopping behind a broad hardwood tree surrounded by young pines. He raised the binoculars. Maria Chen had reached the bodies. She stopped, dug in both poles, and looked toward the house. Then she glanced back toward where she had left Harod and skied toward the house, pausing by the broad french doors before turning right and skiing the length of the manor. She disappeared around the right side of the building—the corner nearest the access road—and Harod snapped off his skis and crouched in a dry area under the tree.

It seemed an absurdly long time before she appeared at the opposite end of the house, skied back to the central french doors, and waved toward where she thought Harod was waiting.

Harod waited another two minutes, hunched over, and moved toward

the house in a crouching run. He had thought he could maneuver better
without the skis. It was a mistake. The snow only came up to his knees,
but it slowed and tripped him; he would cover ten feet on the frozen crust
and then crash through and have to posthole his way forward. He fell
three times, once dropping the automatic in the snow. He made sure the
barrel was not plugged, brushed powder off the grip, and staggered
ahead.

He paused by the bodies.

Tony Harod had produced twenty-eight movies, all but three with
Willi. All twenty-eight of the movies had held ample elements of sex and
violence, often with the two intertwined. The five *Walpurgis Night* films—
Harod's most successful ventures—had been little more than a succession
of murders, mostly of attractive young people before, after, or during
sexual intercourse. The murders were viewed primarily through subjec-
tive camera simulating the view of the murderer. Harod had dropped in
often during the shooting and had seen people stabbed, shot, impaled,
burned, eviscerated, and decapitated. He had hung around special effects
long enough to learn all of the mysteries of bloodbags, airbags, gouged
eyes, and hydraulics. He had personally written the scene in *Walpurgis
Night V: The Nightmare Continues* where the baby-sitter's head explodes
into a thousand fragments after she swallows the explosive capsule substituted by Golon, the masked murderer.

In spite of all this, Tony Harod had never seen a real murder victim.
The only corpses he had ever come near were his mother and Aunt Mira
in their cosmeticized coffins, surrounded by the buffering distance of funeral home and mourners. His mother's funeral had been when Harod
was nine; Aunt Mira when he was thirteen. No one ever mentioned the
death of Harod's father.

One of the men lying outside Willi Borden's family estate had been shot
five or six times; the other had had his throat ripped out. Both had bled
copiously. The amount of blood present struck Harod as absurd, as if
some overzealous director had poured buckets of red paint on the set.
Even just glancing at the bodies, the blood and the imprints in the snow,
Harod thought he could reconstruct some of the scene. A helicopter had
landed about one hundred feet from the house. These two had emerged,
still in polished black street shoes, and walked to the french doors. They
had begun to fight there on the flagstones. Harod could picture the smaller
of the two, the one lying with his face in the snow, turning suddenly and
jumping at his partner, biting and clawing. The bigger man had backed
away—Harod could see heel prints in the snow—then raised the Luger
and fired repeatedly. The little man had kept coming, perhaps even after
being shot in the face. The smaller corpse had two ragged, bruised holes
in the right cheek. There was also a chunk of muscle and tissue still locked
between the little man's exposed teeth. The larger man had staggered
several yards after the smaller man had gone down; then, as if realizing for

the first time that his throat was half gone, his artery severed and pumping blood into the cold German air, his larynx torn out, he had fallen, rolled over, and died staring at the line of evergreens where Harod and Maria Chen would appear some hours later. The large man's arm was half-raised, locked in the sculpted grip of rigor mortis. Harod knew that rigor mortis began and ended a certain number of hours after death; he could not remember how long. He did not care. He had pictured the two as associates, leaving the helicopter together, dying together. The footprints were not absolute proof of that. Harod did not care. Another trough of footprints from the french doors to the depression that may have been a landing site showed where several people had left the house and departed by helicopter. There was no hint of where the helicopter had come from, who was flying it, who from the house had entered it, or where it was going. Harod did not care.

"Tony?" Maria Chen called softly.

"Just a second," said Harod. He turned, staggered away from the great circle of blood, and vomited in the snow. He bent low, tasted again the coffee and thick German sausage he had had for breakfast. When he was finished he scooped up some clean snow, rinsed his mouth with it, rose and made a wide arc around the corpses to join Maria Chen on the flagstones.

"The door's not locked," she whispered.

Harod could see only curtains through the glass. It was snowing hard now, the heavy flakes obscuring the line of trees two hundred feet away. Harod nodded and took a breath. "Go on out there and get that guy's gun," he said. "And check for I.D."

Maria Chen looked at Harod a second and skied out to the bodies. She had to pry open the taller corpse's hand to free the pistol. The tall man carried his I.D. in his wallet; the other corpse had a billfold and passport in his coat pocket. Maria Chen had to roll both corpses over in the snow before she found what Harod wanted. When she returned to the flagstone, her blue sweater and goose-down vest were liberally spotted with blood. She kicked off her skis and rubbed snow on her arms and vest.

Harod flicked through the billfolds and passport. The taller man was named Frank Lee, international driver's license, temporary Munich address, three-year-old Miami driver's license in the same name. The other man was Ellis Robert Sloan, age thirty-two, resident of New York, visas and passport stamped for West Germany, Belgium, and Austria. Eight hundred dollars American and another six hundred German marks remained in the billfolds. Harod shook his head and dropped the three things to the flagstones. They had revealed nothing important—he knew that he was stalling, delaying the entry into the house.

"Follow me," he said and stepped inside.

The estate was large, cold, dark, and—Harod fervently hoped—empty. He no longer wanted to talk to Willi. He knew that if he saw his old

Hollywood mentor, Harod's first response would be to empty the clip of the Browning into Willi's head. If Willi allowed him to. Tony Harod had no illusions about his own Ability in comparison to Willi's. Harod might tell Barent and the others of Willi's declining powers—and mean some of it—but he knew in his gut that, at his weakest, Willi Borden could mentally overpower Tony Harod in ten seconds. The old bastard was a monster. Harod wished that he had not come to Germany, had never left California, had never allowed Barent and the others to force him into association with Willi. "Be ready," he whispered urgently, idiotically, and led Maria Chen deeper into the dark heap of stones.

In room after room, furniture lay neatly covered with white sheets. As with the bodies outside, Harod had seen this in innumerable films but, encountered in reality, the effect was unnerving. Harod found himself pointing the automatic at every covered chair and lamp, waiting for it to rise up and come stalking toward him like the sheeted figure in Carpenter's first *Halloween*.

The main entrance hall was huge, black-and-white tiled, and empty. Harod and Maria Chen walked lightly, but their footsteps still echoed. Harod felt like a horse's ass walking around in the cross-country ski boots with their square toes. Maria Chen walked calmly behind him, the bloodied Luger held down at her side. Her expression showed no more tension than if she were wandering through Harod's Hollywood home, hunting for a misplaced magazine.

It took fifteen minutes for Harod to be sure that no one was on the first floor or in the echoing, extensive cellar. The huge house had the feel of abandonment to it; if the corpses outside were not there, Harod would have been sure no one had been in the house for years. "Upstairs," he whispered, still holding the automatic high. His knuckles were white.

The west wing was dark, cold, and devoid even of furniture, but when they entered the corridor to the east wing, both Harod and Maria Chen froze. At first, the hallway seemed blocked by some huge pane of rippled ice—Harod thought of the scene where Zhivago and Lara returned to the winter-ravaged country house—but Harod moved forward cautiously and realized that the weak light was reflected off a curtain of thin, translucent plastic hung from a ceiling strip and sealed down one wall. Six feet farther on and another clear curtain slowed them. It was a heat baffle, simple insulation to seal off the east wing. The corridor was dark, but pale light came from several open doors along the fifty feet of hallway. Harod nodded at Maria Chen and moved forward stealthily, both hands on the automatic, legs apart. He swiveled around doorways, ready to fire, alert, poised as a cat. Images of Charles Bronson and Clint Eastwood danced in his head. Maria Chen stood near the plastic curtain and watched him.

"Shit," said Harod after almost ten minutes of this. He acted as if he was disappointed and—in the aftereffects of the flow of adrenaline—*was* a little disappointed.

Unless there were hidden rooms, the house was empty. Four of the rooms along this corridor showed signs of recent habitation—unmade beds, stocked refrigerators, hot plates, desks with papers still strewn across the top. One room in particular, a large study with bookcases, an old horsehair sofa, and a fireplace with ashes still warm to the touch, made Harod think that he had missed Willi by only a few hours. Perhaps the unwelcome visitors in the helicopter had caused the sudden departure. But there were no clothes left, nor other personal belongings; whoever had been staying here had been ready to leave. In the study, near a narrow window, a heavy table held a huge chess set, expensively carved figures deployed in mid-game. Harod walked over to the desk and used the automatic to poke through the few papers still lying there. The adrenaline rush was fading, replaced by a shortness of breath, an increasing shakiness, and a tremendous urge to be elsewhere.

The remaining papers were in German. Even though Harod did not speak the language, he got the sense that they were of trivial matters—property taxes, reports on land use, debits and credits. He swept the desk clean, poked through a few empty drawers, and decided it was time to leave.

"Tony!"

Something in Maria Chen's voice made him whirl with the Browning pointed.

She was standing by the chess table. Harod stepped closer, thinking she had seen something out the high, thin window, but it was the large chess set she was looking at. Harod looked too. After a minute he lowered the automatic, went to one knee, and whispered, "Jesus Fucking Christ."

Harod knew little about chess, had played only a few times when he was a kid, but he recognized that the game being played out on this board was in its early stages. Only a few pieces, two black, one white, had been lost and moved to the side of the board. Harod edged forward, still on one knee, so that his eyes were inches from the nearer pieces.

The chess set had been hand-carved from ivory and some ebony wood. Each piece was five or six inches tall, chiseled in exquisite detail, and must have cost Willi a fortune. Harod knew little about chess, but what he knew suggested that this was a very unorthodox game. The kid who had beaten Harod in his second and final game almost thirty years earlier had laughed when Tony had moved his queen out early in the game. The boy had sneered something about only amateurs using their queens early on. But here both queens obviously had been engaged. The white queen stood in the center of the board, directly in front of a white pawn. The black queen had been removed from the game and stood alone on the sidelines. Harod leaned closer. The ebony face was elegant, aristocratic, still beautiful despite carefully carved lines of age. Harod had seen the face five days earlier in Washington, D.C., when C. Arnold Barent had shown him a photograph of the old lady who had been shot in Charleston and who had been so careless as to leave her macabre scrapbook in her hotel room. Tony Harod was staring at Nina Drayton.

Harod looked urgently from face to face on the chessboard. Most of the faces he did not recognize, but some leaped into clarity like the startling zoom-into-focus that Harod used in some of his movies.

The white king was Willi; there was no doubt, although the face was younger, features sharper, hair fuller, and the uniform was no longer legal in Germany. The black king was C. Arnold Barent, business suit and all. Harod recognized the black bishop as Charles C. Colben. The white bishop was immediately recognizable as the Reverend Jimmy Wayne Sutter. Kepler sat securely in the front row of black pawns, but the black knight had jumped over the row of static pawns to join in battle. Harod turned the piece slightly and recognized the pinched and prissy features of Nieman Trask.

Harod did not recognize the dumpy, old-woman face of the white queen, but he had little trouble guessing her identity. "We will find her," Barent had said. "All we want you to do is kill the meddling bitch." The white queen and two white pawns were far into the black side of the board. Harod did not recognize the pawn that seemed surrounded by threatening black pieces; it looked to be a man in his fifties or early sixties, with beard and glasses. Something about the face made Harod think *Jew*. But the other white pawn, the little one four squares in front of Willi's knight and seemingly exposed to attack from several black pieces at once—this pawn, when slowly turned, was instantly identifiable. Tony Harod was staring at his own face.

"Fuck!" Harod's shout seemed to echo in the huge house. He screamed again and swept the barrel of the Browning across the board once, twice, a third time, scattering ivory and ebony pieces to the floor.

Maria Chen stepped back and turned her gaze to the window. Outside, the last of the day's light seemed to have fled as the clouds came lower, the dark line of trees faded into a gray mist, and the heavy snow gently covered the two corpses lying like fallen chess pieces on the manor lawn.

TWELVE

I t seems as if it should be snowing," said Saul Laski.

The three were sitting in Sheriff Gentry's car: Saul and Gentry in the front seat, Natalie in the back. It was raining softly and the temperature was in the high fifties. Natalie and Gentry wore jackets, Saul had put on a thick blue sweater under an old tweed sports coat. Now he used his index finger to push his glasses up onto the bridge of his nose and squinted out through the rain-streaked windshield. "Six days before Christmas," he said, "and no snow. I don't know how you Southerners get used to it."

"I was seven years old, the first time I saw snow," said Bobby Joe Gentry. "They let school out. Wasn't even an inch on the ground, but all of us ran home like it was the end of the world. I threw a snowball . . . first one I ever made . . . and proceeded to bust ol' Miz McGilvrey's parlor window. It almost *was* the end of the world for me. When my daddy got home I'd been waiting 'nigh onto three hours, missed my supper an' all. I was glad to get the whippin' an' have it over with." Gentry touched a button and the wiper blades beat once, twice, and fell back into place with a clunk. The suddenly cleared arcs of windshield once again began to mottle with rain. "Yessir," said Gentry in that deep, somehow pleasant rumble that Laski was getting to know very well, "I see snow, I always think of getting whipped and trying not to cry. Seems to me that the winters're gettin' colder, the snow comin' more often."

"Is that doctor here yet?" asked Natalie from the backseat.

"Nope. Still three minutes before four," said Gentry. "Calhoun's gettin' old, slowin' down a bit, I hear, but he's as punctual as grandma's old clock. Regular as a cat full of prunes. He says he'll be here at four, he'll be here."

As if to punctuate the comment, a long, dark Cadillac pulled to a stop and began backing into a parking space five cars in front of Gentry's patrol car.

Saul looked up at the building. Several miles from the chic Old Section, the development was attractive, combining the elegance of age with the allure of modern convenience. An old cannery had been turned into an array of town houses and offices—windows and garages added, the brick sandblasted clean, and woodwork added, repaired, or painted. To Saul's eye, it looked as if great care had gone into the restoration and redesign. "Are you sure Alicia's parents are willing to do this?" he asked.

Gentry removed his hat and ran his handkerchief around the leather band inside. "Real willin'," he said. "Mrs. Kaiser's worried sick about the girl. Says Alicia hasn't been eating, wakes up screamin' when she tries to sleep, and just sits and stares a lot of the time."

"It has only been six days since she saw her best friend murdered," said Natalie. "Poor child."

"And her best friend's granddaddy," said Gentry. "And maybe some other folks, for all we know."

"You think she was at the Mansard House?" asked Saul.

"Folks don't remember her being there," said the sheriff, "but that don't mean didley. Unless they're trained otherwise, most folks don't notice most of what's goin' on around them. Course some do—notice *everything*. They're just never the ones who happen to be at the scene of a crime."

"Alicia was found close to the scene, wasn't she?" asked Saul.

"Right between the two biggies," said Gentry. "A neighbor lady saw her standin' on a street corner, cryin' and lookin' sort of dazed, about halfway between the Fuller home and Mansard House."

"Is her arm healing?" asked Natalie.

Gentry turned to look at the woman in the backseat. He smiled and his small, blue eyes seemed brighter than the weak, winter light outside. "Sure is, ma'am. Simple fracture."

"One more ma'am from you, Sheriff," said Natalie, "and I'll break your arm."

"Yes, ma'am," said Gentry with no apparent guile. He looked out the windshield again. "That's ol' Dr. C, all right. He bought that darn black bumbershoot when he went over to England before World War Two. Summer lecture series at London City Hospital, I think. He was part of the prewar disaster planning team. I remember he tol' my Uncle Lee years ago that the British doctors were ready for about a hundred times the weekly casualties than they really got once the Germans started bombin' 'em. I don't mean they were all that *prepared* for more . . . but they expected more."

"Does your Dr. Calhoun have much experience with hypnosis?" asked Saul.

"I'd say so," drawled Gentry. "That's what he went over to advise the Brits about in 1939. Seems some of the experts there thought the bombin'd be so traumatic that all the civilians would go into shock. They thought Jack might help 'em out with his posthypnotic suggestion 'n' all." He started to open the car door. "Comin', Miz Preston?"

"Absolutely," said Natalie and stepped out into the rain.

Gentry stepped out and paused. The soft rain tapped on the brim of his hat. "Sure you don't want to come in, Professor?" he asked.

"No, I do not want to be there," said Saul. "I want there to be no chance of my interference. But I do look forward to hearing what the child has to say."

"Me, too," said Gentry. "I'll try to keep an open mind, no matter what." He closed the door and ran—ran gracefully for so heavy a man—to catch up with Natalie Preston.

An open mind, thought Saul. *Yes, I do believe you will have that. I truly do.*

"I believe you," Sheriff Bobby Joe Gentry had said when Saul finished telling his story the day before.

Saul had condensed the story as much as possible, reducing the narration that had taken much of the morning and previous evening into a forty-five-minute synopsis. Several times Natalie had interrupted to ask him to tell a part that he had skipped over. Gentry asked a few concise questions. They ate lunch while Saul spoke. In an hour the story was finished, the lunch was consumed, and Sheriff Gentry had nodded and said, "I believe you."

Saul had blinked. "Just like that?" he asked.

Gentry nodded. "Yep." The sheriff turned to look at Natalie. "Did you believe him, Miz Preston?"

The young woman hesitated only a second. "Yes, I did." She looked at Saul. "I still do."

Gentry said nothing more.

Saul tugged at his beard, took his glasses off to wipe them, and set them back in place. "Don't you both find what I say as . . . fantastic?"

"I sure enough do," said Gentry, "but I find it pretty fantastic that I got nine people murdered in my hometown here and not a clue as to how their deaths tie together." The sheriff leaned forward. "Haven't you told anyone about it before this? The whole story, I mean."

Saul scratched at his beard. "I told my cousin Rebecca," he said softly. "Not long before she died in 1960."

"Did she believe you?" asked Gentry.

Saul met the sheriff's gaze. "She loved me. She had seen me just after the war, nursed me back to sanity. She believed me. She *said* that she believed me, and I chose to believe her. But why would you accept such a story?"

Natalie said nothing. Gentry sat back in his chair until his back made the wood creak. "Well, speaking for myself, Professor," he said. "I got to confess two weaknesses. One, I tend to judge people by how I *feel* about what they say, how they come across. Take that FBI man you met in my office yesterday—Dickie Haines—I mean, everything he *says* is right an' logical an' up front. He *looks* right. Hell, he *smells* right. But there's somethin' about that guy that makes me trust him 'bout as much as I would a hungry weasel. Our Mr. Haines just isn't fully with us somehow. I mean, his porch light is on an' all, but nobody's home, if you know what I mean. Lot of folks like that. When I meet somebody I believe, I tend to believe 'em, that's all. Gets me into heaps of trouble.

"Second weakness, I tend to read a lot. Not married. No hobbies but my job. Used to think I wanted to be a historian . . . then a popular writer of history like Catton or Tuchman . . . then maybe a novelist. Too lazy to be any of them things, but I still read tons. I like junk. So I make a deal with myself—for every three serious books I read, I indulge in some junk. Well-written junk, y'understand, but junk all the same. So I read mysteries—John D. MacDonald, Parker, Westlake—and I read the suspense stuff—Ludlum and Trevanian and le Carré and Deighton and I read the scary stuff—Stephen King, Steve Rasnic Tem . . . those guys." He smiled at Saul. "Your story's not so strange."

Saul frowned at the sheriff. "Mr. Gentry, you're saying that because you read fantastic fiction, you do not find my fantastic story fantastic?"

Gentry shook his head. "Nossir, I'm saying that what you told me fits the facts and is the first thing I've heard that ties these murders together."

"Haines had a theory about Thorne," said Saul. "The old woman's servant—and the Kramer woman conspiring to steal from their employers."

"Haines is full of shit, pardon the language, ma'am," said Gentry. "And there's no way in the world that little Albert LaFollette, the bellboy who went nuts at the Mansard House, was in cahoots with anybody. I knew Albert's father. That boy was barely bright enough to tie his shoelaces, but he was a nice kid. He didn't go out for football in high school and he told his dad it was because he didn't want to hurt anybody."

"But my story goes beyond logic . . . into the supernatural," said Saul. He felt foolish arguing with the sheriff, but he could not accept the Southerner's immediate acceptance.

Gentry shrugged. "I always hate in those vampire movies where they got corpses stacked up all around 'em, with two little holes in their necks 'n' all, and some of them corpses are comin' back to life 'n' all, and it always takes the good guy ninety minutes of the two-hour movie just to convince the other good guys that the vampires are real."

Saul rubbed his beard.

"Look," Gentry said softly, "for whatever reasons you have, you *did* tell us. So now my choices are—one, you're part of this somehow. I mean, I know you didn't kill any of these folks personally. You were on a panel at Columbia on Saturday afternoon and evening. But you could've been involved. Maybe you hypnotized Mrs. Drayton or something. I know, I know, hypnosis doesn't work like that—but people don't usually take over other folks' minds either.

"Two, you could be crazy as a bedbug. Like one of those yahoos that comes out of the woodwork to confess each time there's a murder.

"Three, you could be telling the truth. I'll go with number three for now. Besides, I got some weirdness of my own goin' on here that fits your story and nothing else."

"What weirdness?" asked Saul.

"Like the guy following me this morning who kills himself rather'n talk to me," said Gentry. "And the old lady's scrapbook."

"Scrapbook?" said Saul.

"What scrapbook?" asked Natalie.

Gentry took his hat off, creased it, and frowned at it. "I was the first law on the scene when Mrs. Drayton got shot," he said. "Paramedics was takin' the body away, city homicide plainclothesmen were still downstairs doing a body count, so I poked around the lady's room for a minute. Shouldn't've done it. Lousy procedure. But what the hell, I'm just a hick cop. So anyway, there was this thick scrapbook in one of her suitcases and I happened to glance through. All these clippings about murders—John Lennon's and a lot of others. Most in New York. Went back to last January. Next day the real police are conducting the investigation, the FBI's all over the place even though it isn't their kind of case, and by the time I get down to the morgue on Sunday evening, no scrapbook, no one's seen it, no crime scene record of it on the city's books, no morgue receipt, nothing."

"Did you ask about it?" asked Saul.

"Sure did," said Gentry. "Everybody from the paramedics to the city homicide boys. Nobody saw it. Everythin' else was taken out at the morgue and listed on Sunday mornin'—the lady's underwear, clothes, blood pressure pills—but no scrapbook with newspaper accounts of twenty or so murders."

"Who did the inventory?" Saul asked.

"City homicide and FBI," said Gentry. "But Tobe Hartner—clerk down at the morgue—says that our Mr. Haines was lookin' at the impounded stuff about an hour before the homicide team arrived. Dickie went straight from the airport to the morgue."

Saul cleared his throat. "You think the FBI is involved in concealing evidence?"

Sheriff Gentry gave a look of wide-eyed innocence. "Now why would the FBI want to go and do something like that?"

The silence stretched. Finally Natalie Preston said, "Sheriff, if one of those . . . those creatures was responsible for the death of my father, what do we do next?"

Gentry folded his hands across his stomach and looked at Saul. The sheriff's eyes were very blue. "That's a real good question, Miz Preston," he said. "What about it, Dr. Laski? Say we caught your Oberst or the Fuller woman, or both of 'em. Don't you think it might be sorta hard to get a grand jury indictment?"

Saul spread his hands. "It sounds insane, I agree. If one believes in this, then no logic seems safe. No convicted murderer stands convicted beyond a shadow of a doubt. No evidence is ample to separate the innocent from the guilty. I understand what you are saying, Sheriff."

"Naw," said Gentry. "It isn't that bad. I mean, *most* cases of murder are still murder, correct? Or do you think that there are hundreds of thousands of these mind vampire people runnin' around?"

Saul closed his eyes at the thought. "I sincerely pray that that is not the case," he said.

Gentry nodded. "So what we have here is sort of a special case, ain't it? Which brings us back to Miz Preston's question. What do we do next?"

Saul took a deep breath. "I need your help in . . . *watching*. There is a chance—a slim chance—that one or the other of the two survivors will return to Charleston. Perhaps Melanie Fuller did not have time to remove things of great importance from her home. Perhaps William Borden . . . if he is alive . . . . will return for *her*."

"And then what?" asked Natalie. "They can't be punished. Not by the courts. What happens if we *do* find them for you? What could *you* do?"

Saul bowed his head, adjusted his glasses, and ran shaking fingers across his brow. "I have thought about that for four decades," he said in a very low voice, "and I still do not know. But I feel that the Oberst and I are destined to meet again."

"They're mortal," said Gentry.

"What?" said Saul. "Yes, of course they're mortal."

"Someone could walk up behind one of them and blow their brains out, right?" said the sheriff. "They don't rise with the next full moon or something."

Saul stared at the lawman. After a minute, he said, "What is your point, Sheriff?"

"My point is . . . accepting your premise that these folks can do what you say they can do . . . then they're the scariest damn critters I've ever heard of. Goin' after one of 'em would be like searchin' around for cottonmouths in the swamps after dark with nothing but your bare hands 'n' a gunnysack. But once they're *identified* they're as much a target as you or me or John F. Kennedy or John Lennon. Anybody with a rifle and a good sight could take one of them out easily enough, correct, Professor?"

Saul returned the sheriff's placid gaze. "I do not own a rifle with a sight," he said.

Gentry nodded. "Did you bring any sort of gun down from New York with you?"

Saul shook his head.

"Do you *own* a gun, Professor?"

"No."

Gentry turned to look at Natalie. "But you do, ma'am. You mentioned that you followed him into the Fuller house yesterday and were prepared to arrest him at gunpoint."

Natalie blushed. Saul was surprised to notice how dark her coffee-colored skin could become when she blushed.

"I don't own it," she said. "It was my father's. He kept it at his photography studio. He had a permit for it. There had been robberies. I stopped by and picked it up on Monday."

"Could I see it?" Gentry asked softly.

Natalie went into the hall closet and removed the weapon from her raincoat pocket. She set it on the table near the sheriff. Gentry used his forefinger to turn the barrel slightly until it aimed away from everyone.

"You know guns, Professor?" asked Gentry.

"Not this one," said Saul.

"How 'bout you, Miz Preston?" said Gentry. "You familiar with firearms?"

Natalie rubbed her arms as if she were cold. "I have a friend in St. Louis who showed me how to shoot," she said. "Aim and squeeze the trigger. It's not too complicated."

"Familiar with this gun?" asked Gentry.

Natalie shook her head. "Daddy bought it after I went off to school. I don't think he ever fired it. I can't imagine he would have been able to shoot at a *person*."

Gentry raised his eyebrows and picked up the automatic, pointing it at the floor and holding it carefully by the trigger guard. "Is it loaded?"

"No," said Natalie. "I took all of the bullets out before I left the house yesterday."

It was Saul's turn to raise his eyebrows.

Gentry nodded and touched a lever to release the magazine from the black plastic grip. He held the clip out to show Saul that it was empty.

"Thirty-two caliber, isn't it?" said Saul.

"Small frame Llama thirty-two automatic," agreed the sheriff. "Real nice little gun. Probably cost Mr. Preston about three hundred dollars new. Miz Preston, nobody likes advice, but I feel like I should give you some, all right?"

Natalie nodded tersely.

"First," said Gentry, "don't point a firearm at somebody unless you're willing to fire it. Second, don't ever point an empty gun. And third, if you're gonna have an empty gun, make sure it's *empty*." Gentry pointed to the weapon. "See that little indicator, ma'am? Where the red's showin' there? That's called a loaded indicator, and the red's tryin' to tell you something." Gentry racked the slide and a round ejected from the chamber and fell to the tabletop with a clatter.

Natalie blanched, her skin going the color of old ashes. "That's impossible," she said in a small voice. "I counted the bullets when I took them out. There were *seven*."

"Your daddy must've jacked one into the chamber an' then lowered the hammer," said Gentry. "Some folks carry 'em that way. That way they can carry eight rounds instead of the usual seven." The sheriff clicked in the empty magazine and squeezed the trigger.

Natalie flinched slightly at the dry *click*. One glance at what Gentry had called "the loaded indicator" told her that the red was no longer showing. She thought of when she had pointed the gun at Saul yesterday . . . of being so sure the weapon was unloaded . . . and she felt a little sick.

"What's your point this time, Sheriff?" Saul asked.

Gentry shrugged and set the small pistol back on the table. "I think that if we're going after these killers, then *somebody'd* better know something about weapons."

"You don't understand," said Saul. "Weapons are useless with these people. They can make you turn the weapon on yourself. They can turn *you* into a weapon. If the three of us went after the Oberst . . . or the Fuller woman . . . as a team, we could never be sure about each other."

"I understand that," said Gentry. "And I also understand that if we find them, then *they* are vulnerable. They're dangerous primarily because no one knows they exist. Now we do."

"But we do *not* know where they are," said Saul. "I thought that I was so close. I *was* so close . . ."

"Borden has a background," said Gentry, "a history, a film production company, associates and friends. That's a place to start."

Saul shook his head. "I thought Francis Harrington would be safe," he said. "A few inquiries. If it *was* the Oberst, he might have recognized me. I thought Francis would be safe and now he's almost certainly dead. No, I want no one else to become directly involved . . ."

"We're *already* involved," snapped Gentry. "We're *in* this thing."

"He's right," said Natalie.

Both men turned toward her. The strength had come back into her voice. "If you're not crazy, Saul," she said, "then these freakish bastards killed my father for no reason at all. With you two or without you, I'm going to find those old murderers and find a way to bring them to justice."

"So let's pretend we're intelligent beings here," said Gentry. "Saul, did Nina Drayton tell you anything in her two sessions with you that can help us out?"

"Not really," said Saul. "She did talk about her father's death. I inferred that she had used her ability to murder him."

"No talk about Borden or Melanie Fuller?"

"Not directly, although she mentioned friends in Vienna in the early thirties. From her description, it could be the Oberst and the Fuller woman."

"Anything useful there?"

"No. Intimations of sexual jealousy and competition."

"Saul, *you* were used by the Oberst," said the sheriff.

"Yes."

"Yet you remember it. Didn't you suggest that Jack Ruby and the others were suffering from something like amnesia after being used?"

"Yes," said Saul. "I think the people that the Oberst and the others used remember their actions—if they remember them at all—as one would remember a dream."

"Isn't that consistent with how psychotics remember violent episodes?"

"Sometimes," said Saul. "At other times, a psychotic's regular life is the dream and he is truly alive *only* when he is inflicting pain or death. But the people the Oberst and the others used are not necessarily psychotics— only victims."

"But *you* remembered exactly what it was like when the Oberst . . . possessed you," said Gentry. "Why?"

Saul took off his glasses and cleaned them. "It was different. It was wartime. I was a Jew from the camp. He knew that I would not survive. There was no need to spend energy erasing my memory. Besides, I escaped of my own volition, shooting myself in the foot, surprising the Oberst . . ."

"I wanted to ask you about that," said Gentry. "You said the pain surprised the Oberst into relinquishing control for a minute or two . . ."

"A few seconds," said Saul.

"OK, a few seconds. But *all* of the people they were using here in Charleston must have been hurting a lot. Haupt . . . Thorne, the ex-thief Melanie Fuller kept around as a servant, lost an eye and kept going. The girl—Kathleen—was beaten to death. Barrett Kramer had fallen down stairs and been shot. Mr. Preston was . . . well, you see what I'm getting at . . ."

"Yes," said Saul, "I have thought a lot about this. Luckily, when the Oberst was . . . in my mind, there is no other way to say it . . . then I caught glimpses of his thoughts . . ."

"Like telepathy?" asked Natalie.

"No," said Saul, "not really. Not as it is generally portrayed in fiction. More like trying to capture the fragments of a dream one sometimes half remembers during waking hours. But I sensed enough of the Oberst's thoughts to understand that his melding with me when he used me to kill *der Alte* . . . the old SS man . . . was unusual. He wanted to experience it totally, to savor every nuance of sense impression. My feeling was that he generally used others with a simple buffer between himself and the pain his victim was feeling."

"Sort of like watching TV with the sound off?" said Gentry.

"Perhaps," said Saul, "but in this case no pertinent information is lost, only the shock of pain. I sensed that the Oberst *enjoyed* not only the vicarious pain of those he murdered, but in those he *used* to commit the murder . . ."

"Do you think memories like that can really be expunged?" asked Gentry.

"In the minds of those he used?" asked Saul. At Gentry's nod he said, "No. Buried perhaps. Much as the victim of some terrible trauma buries the experience deep in the subconscious."

Gentry stood up then, a large grin on his face, and slapped Saul on the shoulder. "Professor," he said, still grinning, "you've just given us the way we can test to see what's true and what isn't, who's crazy and who's sane."

"Really?" asked Saul, beginning to understand even as Sheriff Gentry smiled at Natalie Preston's questioning look.

"Really," said Gentry, "and by tomorrow we can *do* that test and know once and for all."

Saul sat in Sheriff Gentry's car and listened to the rain fall. It had been almost an hour since Gentry and Natalie had gone into the clinic with the old doctor. A few minutes later a blue Toyota had parked across the street and Saul caught a glimpse of a young blond girl, left arm in a sling, eyes dark and fatigued, being herded between a couple dressed in the impeccable but predictable style of young professionals.

Saul waited. It was something he knew how to do well; some skill learned as a teenager in the death camps. For the twentieth time he ran through his rationale to himself for involving Natalie Preston and Sheriff Gentry. The rationale was weak—a sense of arriving at dead ends, a sudden sense of trust toward both of these unlikely allies after years of solitary suspicion, and, finally, a simple need to tell his story.

Saul shook his head. Intellectually he knew it was a mistake, but emotionally the telling and retelling had been incredibly therapeutic. The reassurance of having allies, of others *actively involved*, allowed Saul to sit placidly in Gentry's county automobile and be quite contented to wait.

Saul was tired. He recognized the fatigue as something more than lack of sleep and the aftereffects of too much adrenaline; it was an aching tiredness as painful as a bone bruise and as old as Chelmno. There was a weariness in him that was as permanent as the tattoo on his inner arm. Like the tattoo, he would take the painful weariness to the grave, surrendering to an eternity of it. Saul shook his head again, took off his glasses, and rubbed the bridge of his nose. *Knock it off, Old Man*, he thought. *Weltschmerz is a boring state of mind. More boring to others than to oneself.* He thought of David's farm in Israel, of his own nine acres far removed from the orchards and fields, of a picnic he and David and Rebecca had there shortly before Saul had left for America. Young Aaron and Isaac, David and Rebecca's twins, no more than seven that summer, had played cowboys and Indians among the stones and gullies where Roman legionnaires had once hunted down Israelite partisans.

Aaron, thought Saul. He was still scheduled to meet with the boy on Saturday afternoon, in Washington. Instantly Saul felt his stomach clench at the thought of another unnecessary involvement in the nightmare. Family this time. *How much did he find out?* thought Saul. *How do I keep him uninvolved?*

The couple and the child emerged from the clinic; the doctor followed, shook the man's hand, and the family left. Saul realized that the rain had stopped. Gentry and Natalie Preston stepped out, spoke briefly with the old doctor, and walked briskly to the car.

"Well?" asked Saul after the heavy sheriff slid behind the wheel and the young woman was in the backseat. "What?"

Gentry removed his hat and mopped at his brow with a kerchief. He rolled his window all the way down and Saul caught the scent of moist grass and mimosa on the breeze. Gentry looked back at Natalie. "Why don't you tell him?"

Natalie took a breath and nodded. She looked shaken, upset, but her voice was brisk and firm. "Doctor Calhoun's office has a small observation room off the consulting room," she said. "There is a one-way mirror. Alicia's parents and we were able to observe without interfering. Sheriff Gentry introduced me as his assistant."

"Which, in the context of this investigation, is technically true," said Gentry. "I'm only allowed to deputize folks in the event of a declared emergency in the county, otherwise you'd've been *Deputy Preston*."

Natalie smiled. "Alicia's parents did not object to our presence. Dr. Calhoun used a small device like a metronome with a light to hypnotize the girl . . ."

"Yes, yes," said Saul, fighting to keep his sudden impatience in check, "what did the child *say*?"

Natalie's eyes became slightly unfocused as she recalled the scene. "The doctor had her remember the day . . . last Saturday . . . in detail. Alicia's face had been set, emotionless, almost slack when she had come in, before the hypnosis. Now she lit up, grew animated. She was talking to her friend Kathleen . . . the girl who was killed."

"Yes," said Saul, with no impatience this time.

"She and Kathleen were playing in Mrs. Hodges's living room. Kathleen's sister Debra was in the other room, watching television. Suddenly Kathleen dropped the Barbie doll she was playing with and ran outside . . . across the courtyard to Mrs. Fuller's house. Alicia called after her . . . stood in the courtyard shouting . . ." Natalie shivered. "Then she quit speaking. Her face went slack again. She said she was not allowed to tell any more."

"Was she still under hypnosis?" asked Saul.

Gentry answered. "She was still under hypnosis," he said, "but she was not able to describe what happened next. Dr. Calhoun tried different ways to help her through it. She continued to stare at nothing and reply that she was not allowed to tell any more."

"And that was all?" asked Saul.

"Not quite," said Natalie. She looked outside at the rain-cleansed street and then looked back at Saul. Her full lips were pulled tight with tension.

"Then Dr. Calhoun said, 'You're going into the house across the court-yard now. Tell us *who* you are.' And Alicia did not hesitate a second. She said—in a different voice, old, cracked—'I am Melanie Fuller.'"

Saul sat straight up. His skin tingled as if someone had touched his spine with icy fingers.

"And then Dr. Calhoun asked her if she—Melanie Fuller—could tell us anything," said Natalie. "And little Alicia's face changed—it sort of *rippled*—the flesh showed lines and creases that weren't there a few seconds before . . . and she said, in that same obscene, little old lady's voice, 'I'm coming for you, Nina.' She just kept repeating that phrase, louder each time, 'I'm coming for you, Nina,' until she was screaming it."

"Dear God," said Saul.

"Dr. Calhoun was shaken up," said Natalie. "He calmed the girl down and brought her out, telling her that she would feel happy and refreshed when she woke. She wasn't . . . happy, I mean. When she came out of the trance she began crying and saying that her arm hurt. Her mother said that it was the first time she'd complained about the broken arm since she had been found on the night of the murders."

"What did her parents think of the session with Dr. Calhoun?" asked Saul.

"They were upset," said Natalie. "Alicia's mother started to leave the observation room to be with her when the girl began shouting. But when it was over, they seemed very relieved. Alicia's father told Calhoun that even the girl's discomfort with the arm and the tears were an improvement over the emptiness they'd been seeing all week."

"And Dr. Calhoun?" asked Saul.

Gentry laid his arm on the back of the seat. "Doc said it looks like a case of 'trauma-induced transference,'" he said. "He recommends that they set up visits with a full-time psychiatrist—fellow from Savannah the Doc knows—specializes in children's cases. There was a lot of talk about how much of it the Kaisers' insurance will cover."

Saul nodded and the three sat in silence for a moment. Outside, the evening sunlight broke through the clouds and illuminated trees, grass, and moisture-jeweled greenery. Saul breathed in the scent of new-mown grass and tried to remind himself that it was December. He felt cut loose in space and time, lost on currents that were taking him farther and farther from any recognizable shore.

"I suggest we go out for an early dinner and talk about some of this," Gentry said suddenly. "Professor, you've got an early flight to Washington tomorrow, right?"

"Yes," said Saul.

"Well, let's go then," said Gentry. "Dinner's gonna be on the county."

They ate in an excellent seafood restaurant on Broad Street in the Old Section. There was a line of people waiting, but when the manager saw

Gentry he whisked them into a side room to an empty table that appeared as if by magic. The room was crowded so the three kept their conversation general, discussing New York's weather, Charleston's weather, photography, the Iranian hostage crisis, Charleston county politics, New York politics, and American politics. None of them seemed overjoyed by the outcome of the national election just past. After coffee, they returned to Gentry's car to pick up sweaters and raincoats, and then walked along the Battery wall.

The night was cool and clear. The last of the clouds had dissipated and the winter constellations were visible through the ambient glare of city lights. The streetlights of Mount Pleasant were bright across the harbor to the east. A small boat, navigation lights glowing green and red, moved west past the point, following the buoys of the Intracoastal Waterway. Behind Saul, Natalie, and Gentry, the tall windows of a score of stately homes glowed orange and yellow in the night.

They paused on the Battery wall. Water lapped at the stones ten feet below. Gentry glanced around, saw no one else in sight, and said in a soft voice, "So what next, Professor?"

"Excellent question" said Saul. "Suggestions?"

"Is your meeting in Washington Saturday pertinent to what we're . . . discussing?" asked Natalie.

"Possibly," said Saul. "Probably. I'll know after the meeting. I'm sorry I can't be more specific. It involves . . . family."

"What about this guy who was following me?" said Gentry.

"Yes," said Saul. "Has the FBI been able to give you a name?"

"Nothing," said the sheriff. "The car was reported stolen in Rockville, Maryland, five months ago. But nothing matches on the dead man. Not fingerprints, dental records . . . nothing."

"Isn't that unusual?" asked Natalie.

"Almost unheard of," said Gentry. He picked up a pebble and tossed it into the bay. "In today's society, *everybody* leaves records of some sort."

"Perhaps the FBI is not trying hard enough," said Saul. "Is this your theory?"

Gentry tossed another rock and shrugged. He had been wearing civilian clothes—tan slacks and an old plaid shirt—but before taking the walk along the Battery he had pulled his bulky sheriff's coat and sweat-stained western hat from the trunk of his car and now he was the image of a Southern sheriff again. "I don't think the FBI would use some half-starved jerk off the street like that," he said. "And if the fella isn't working for them, who *would* be using him? And why would he kill himself rather'n be arrested?"

"It would be consistent with the way the Oberst would use someone," said Saul. "Or, most likely, the Fuller woman."

Gentry tossed another pebble and squinted out toward the lights of Fort Sumter two miles away. "Yeah," he said, "but that doesn't make any sense. Your Oberst should have no interest in me . . . hell, I never even heard of him 'til you told me your story, Saul. And if Miz Fuller is worried about who's chasin' after her, she'd do a lot better tailin' the State Highway Patrol, city homicide boys, an' the FBI. This guy had nothing in his wallet but a picture of *me.*"

"Do you have it with you?" asked Saul.

Gentry nodded, removed it from his coat pocket, and handed it to the psychiatrist. Saul walked to a nearby pole lamp to get more light. "Interesting," said Saul. "Is this the front of the City-County Building behind you?"

"Sure is."

"Is there anything in the photograph to suggest when it was taken?"

"Yep," said Gentry. "See that Band-Aid along my jawline, there?"

"Yes."

"I use my daddy's straight razor—use to belong to *his* daddy—but I don't cut myself shavin' too often. But I did last Sunday morning when Lester . . . one of my deputies . . . called me real early. I wore the Band-Aid most of that one day."

"Sunday," said Natalie.

"Yes'm."

"So whoever was interested in following you took this photograph . . . it looks like a thirty-five-millimeter, correct?" said Saul.

"Yep."

"Took a photo of you from across the street on Sunday and then someone began following you on Thursday."

"Yep."

"Could I see the photo, please?" asked Natalie. She studied it under the light for a minute and said, "Whoever took it was using a built-in light meter . . . you see it exposed more for the sunlight on the door here than on your face. Probably had a two-hundred-millimeter lens. That's pretty big. The print was developed in a private darkroom rather than a commercial lab."

"How can you tell that?" asked Gentry.

"See how the paper's been cut? Not exact enough for a commercial job. I don't think they cropped this at all . . . that's why I think it was a long lens . . . but it was printed in a hurry. Private darkrooms that handle color are fairly common these days, but unless your Oberst or Miz Fuller are staying with someone who has a setup like that, *they* didn't process it out of the trunk of their cars. Have you seen anyone recently with an automatic SLR with a long lens, Sheriff?"

Gentry grinned at her. "Dickie Haines had a rig like that," he said. "Little tiny Konika with a big Bushnell lens."

Natalie handed the photograph back and frowned at Saul. "Is it possible that there are . . . others? More of these creatures?"

Saul folded his arms and looked back toward the city. "I don't know," he said. "For years I thought the Oberst was the only one. A terrible freak . . . spawned by the Third Reich, if such a thing is possible. Then our research suggested that the ability to influence other people's actions and reactions was not that uncommon. I read history and wonder if such figures as disparate as Hitler, Rasputin, and Gandhi had this power. Perhaps there is a continuum and the Oberst, the Fuller woman, Nina Drayton, and God knows how many more are at the far end of it . . ."

"So there *could* be others?"

"Yes," said Saul.

"And, for some reason, they're interested in me," said Bobby Joe Gentry.

"Yes."

"Okay, back to square one," said the sheriff.

"Not quite," said Saul. "Tomorrow I will find out what I can in Washington. Perhaps, Sheriff, you can continue to look into the whereabouts of Mrs. Fuller and the current status of the investigation into the airline explosion."

"What about me?" asked Natalie.

Saul hesitated. "It might be wise if you returned to St. Louis and . . ."

"Not if I can be of help here," insisted the young woman. "What can I do?"

"I have some ideas," said Gentry. "We can talk about 'em tomorrow when we take the professor to the airport."

"All right, then," said Natalie. "I'll stay here at least through the first of the year."

"I will give you both my home and office numbers in New York," said Saul. "We should talk by telephone every other day at least. And, Sheriff, even if all of our inquiries turn up negative, there is a way in which we can search for them through the news media . . ."

"Oh yeah? What's that?"

"Miss Preston's metaphor of them being vampires is not so far from the mark," said Saul. "And like vampires, they are driven by their own dark needs. These needs do not go unnoticed when they are satisfied."

"You mean reports of more murders?" said Gentry.

"Precisely."

"But this country has more murders per day than England has in a year," said Gentry.

"Yes, but the Oberst and the others have a penchant for . . . bizarreness," Saul said softly. "I doubt if they can alter their habits so completely that some flavor of their particular sickness does not come through."

"All right," said Gentry. "If worse comes to worst, we wait 'til these . . . these *vampires* begin killing again and track them down that way. We find them. *Then* what?"

Saul removed a handkerchief from his pants pocket, took his glasses off, and squinted out at the harbor lights as he cleaned the lenses. The lights were unfocused prisms to him, the night diffused and encroaching. "We find them and we follow them and we catch them," he said. "And then we do what should be done to all vampires." He put his glasses back on and gave Natalie and the sheriff a thin, cold smile. "We drive a stake through their hearts," he said. "Drive stakes through their hearts, cut off their heads, and stuff garlic in their mouths. And if that does not work . . ." Saul's thin smile became something infinitely colder, ". . . we will think of something that will."

THIRTEEN

Charleston
Wednesday, Dec. 24, 1980

It was the loneliest Christmas Eve Natalie Preston had ever experienced and she decided to do something about it. She took her purse and her Nikon with the 135mm portrait lens, left the house, and drove slowly into the Old Section of Charleston. It was not quite four P.M., but already the evening light was fading.

As she drove past the old homes and posh shops, she listened to Christmas music on the radio and let her mind wander.

She missed her father. Even though she had seen less and less of him the past few years, the thought of his not being there—not being *somewhere*—not thinking about her, not waiting for her—made her feel as if something were collapsing inside her, folding inward and pulling at the very fabric of her being. She wanted to cry.

She had not cried when she had heard the news on the telephone. Had not cried when Fred drove her to the St. Louis airport—he insisting on accompanying her, she insisting he not, he allowing her to convince him. She had not cried at the funeral or during the hours and days of confusion with friends and relatives that followed. It was not until five days after her father's murder, four days after her return to Charleston, that she had been hunting for a book one night when she was unable to sleep and—finding a new Dell paperback of Jean Shepherd's humor—the book had fallen open and there, in the margins, in her father's looping, generous handwriting—*Share with Nat this Xmas*. And she had read the page describing a boy's hysterically funny and terrifying visit to a department store Santa—so reminiscent of when Natalie's own parents brought her downtown when she was four and waited in line for an hour only to have their daughter flee in panic at the crucial moment—and when she was finished reading, Natalie had laughed until the laughter turned to tears and then the tears to sobs; she had cried much of that night, sleeping only an hour or so before dawn, but rising with the winter sunrise and feeling empty, drained, but better the way a nausea victim feels after the first spasm of being ill. The worst was behind her.

Natalie turned left and drove past the stucco town houses of Rainbow Row, colorful facades muted now as the gas lamps were coming on, and she wondered.

It had been a mistake to stay in Charleston. Mrs. Culver came over from next door almost hourly, but Natalie found the conversations with the older widow strained and painful. She began to suspect that Mrs. Culver had had hopes of being the second Mrs. Preston, and the thought made Natalie want to go in the bedroom and hide when she heard the familiar, timid knock at the door.

Frederick called from St. Louis every evening, precisely at eight, and Natalie could imagine the stern expression on her friend and one-time lover's dark face as he would be saying, "Babe, get *back* here. You're not doing any good hanging around your father's house. I miss you, babe. C'mon home to Frederick." But home to her little apartment in University City no longer seemed like home to her . . . and Frederick's cluttered room on Alamo Street was little more than a sleeping place for him between fourteen-hour stints at the computer center as he wrestled with the mathematics of the distribution of mass in galactic clusters. Frederick, the smart but poorly educated boy she had heard about from mutual friends who had come back from two tours in Vietnam with a murderous temper, a renewed ferocity in defense of dignity, and revolutionary spirit that had been channeled into becoming the extraordinary research mathematician whom Natalie knew and . . . at least for much of the previous year . . . had loved. Had thought she loved. "Come on home here, babe," came the voice every evening and Natalie—lonely, aching from the bruises of loss still inside of her—would say, "A few more days, Frederick. A few more days."

A few more days for what? she thought. The big old houses along South Battery were bright with window lights illuminating tiers of porches, palmettos, cupolas, and balustrades. She had always loved this part of the city. She and her father had come up here to walk along the Battery when she was a girl. She had been twelve before she realized that no black people lived there—that all of the fine old homes and fine old shops held only whites. Years later she marveled that such a revelation could come so late to a black girl growing up in the South in the sixties. So many things came naturally, so many of the old ways had to be *resisted* daily, that she could not believe that she had never noticed that the avenues of her evening walks—the big old homes of her dreams as a child—were as off-limits to her and her kind as some of the swimming pools, movie theaters, and churches that she would have never considered entering. By the time Natalie was old enough to travel the streets of Charleston by herself, the blatant signs had been removed, the public fountains were truly public, but habit persisted, boundaries set by two centuries of tradition still remained, and Natalie found it incredible that she could still remember the day—a damp, chill November day in 1972—when she had stood in shock not far from this place on old South Battery and stared at the big homes and *realized* that no one in her family had ever lived there, *would* ever live there. But the second thought had been banished as quickly as it had appeared. Natalie had inherited her mother's eyes and her father's pride. Joseph Preston had been the first black businessman to own and run a shop in the prestigious bayfront area. She was Joseph Preston's daughter.

Natalie drove down Dock Street, past the renovated Dock Street The-
atre with its wrought-iron tracery clinging to the second-floor balcony like
a riot of metal ivy.

Ten days she had been home and everything that had come before
seemed like a different life. Gentry should be off duty by now, bidding
good evening and Merry Christmas to his deputies and secretaries and
the other whites that inhabited the old hulk of the City-County Building.
He would be calling her about now.

She parked the car near St. Michael's Episcopal Church and thought
about Gentry. About Robert Joseph Gentry.

After seeing Saul Laski off at the airport the previous Friday, they had
spent most of that day together. And the next. Much of the first day's discussion had been about Laski's story—about the entire idea of people who
could mentally use others. "If the Professor is crazy, it probably isn't going
to hurt anybody," Gentry had said. "If he's not crazy, it explains why a lot
of people got hurt."

Natalie had told the sheriff about peeking out from her room when the
exhausted New York psychiatrist had been returning from the bathroom
to the hide-a-bed in her living room. He had been barefoot, wearing only
trousers and what she thought of as "an old man's undershirt." She had
looked at his right foot. The little toe was missing, old scar tissue visible
like white veins on pale skin.

"That doesn't prove anything," Gentry had reminded her.

Sunday they had talked of other things. Gentry made dinner for the
two of them at his home. Natalie had loved his house—an aging Victorian
structure about ten minutes from the Old Section. The neighborhood was
in transition; some homes fading into disrepair, others being renovated to
full beauty. Gentry's block was populated with young couples—black and
white—with tricycles on front walks, jump ropes lying on the small front
lawns, and the sounds of laughter from backyards.

Three rooms on the first floor had been filled with books: lovely built-
in bookshelves in the library/study off the entrance hall, handmade
wooden shelves on either side of the bay windows in the dining room, and
inexpensive metal shelves along a blank, brick wall of the kitchen. While
Gentry had been preparing the salad, Natalie had, with the sheriff's blessing, wandered from room to room, admiring the aged, leather-bound
volumes, noticing the shelves of hardback books dealing with history, so-
ciology, psychology, and a dozen other topics, and smiling at the row upon
row of espionage, mystery, and suspense paperbacks. Gentry's study made
her want to curl up with a book immediately. She compared the huge roll-
top desk littered with papers and documents, the overstuffed leather club
chair and couch, and the walls with built-in and overflowing bookshelves to
her spartan workroom back in St. Louis. Sheriff Bobby Joe Gentry's study
had the lived-in, center-of-everything feel to it that her father's darkroom
had always imparted to her.

The salad tossed, the lasagna cooking, she and Gentry had sat in the study, enjoyed a premium unblended Scotch whiskey, and talked again—their conversation circling back to Saul Laski's reliability and their own reaction to his story.

"The whole thing has the classic feel of paranoia to it," Gentry had said, "but, then, if a European Jew had predicted the details of the Holocaust a decade before it was set in motion, any good psychiatrist—even a Jewish one—would have diagnosed him as a probable paranoid schizophrenic."

They had watched the last light fade out the bay windows as they ate a leisurely dinner. Gentry had rummaged around in a basement well stocked with wine bottles and had almost blushed with embarrassment at her suggestion that he owned a wine cellar before coming up with two bottles of excellent BV Cabernet Sauvignon to go with dinner. She had thought the dinner excellent, had complimented him on being a gourmet chef. He had riposted with the comment that women who could cook were known as good cooks, old bachelors who could get by in the kitchen had to be gourmet cooks. She had laughed and promised to cross that particular stereotype off her list.

Stereotypes. Alone on Christmas Eve, sitting in a rapidly chilling car near St. Michael's Episcopal, Natalie thought about stereotypes.

Saul Laski had seemed a wonderful example of a stereotype to Natalie: a New York Polish Jew complete with a beard, sad, Semitic eyes that seemed to stare out at her from some European darkness that Natalie could not even *conceive* of, much less understand. A professor . . . a psychiatrist . . . with a soft, foreign accent that might as well be Freud's Viennese dialect for all Natalie's untrained ear could detect. The man wore glasses held together by *adhesive tape*, for heaven's sake, like Natalie's Aunt Ellen who had suffered from senility—Alzheimer's they called it now—for eleven years, most of Natalie's life at the time, until she finally died.

Saul Laski looked different, sounded different, acted different, *was* different from most of the people—black or white—whom Natalie had ever known. Even though Natalie's stereotype of Jews was sketchy—dark clothes, strange customs, an ethnic look, a closeness to money and power at the expense of her own people's proximity to money and power—there should be no problem letting Saul Laski's basic strangeness fall into those stereotypes.

But it did not. Natalie did not delude herself into thinking that she was too intelligent to reduce people to stereotypes; she was only twenty-one years old, but she had seen intelligent people such as her father and Frederick—intelligent people—simply *shift* the stereotypes they chose to apply to people. Her father—as sensitive and generous as he had been, as ferociously proud of race and heritage as he was—had seen the rise of the so-called New South as a dangerous experiment, a manipulation by radicals of both colors to change a system that had finally changed enough in its own framework to allow some success and dignity for hardworking men of color such as himself.

Frederick saw people as dupes of the system, managers of the system, or victims of the system. The system was very clear to Frederick; it was the political structure that had made the Vietnam war inevitable, the power structure that had maintained it, and the social structure that had fed him into that waiting maw. Frederick's response had been twofold: to step *outside* of the system into something as irrelevant and invisible as research mathematics, and to make himself so good at it that he would have the power to stay there and elude the system for the rest of his life. In the meantime, Frederick lived for the hours he spent interfaced with his computers, avoided human complications, made love to Natalie as fiercely and competently as he fought anyone who gave the appearance of offense, and taught Natalie how to fire the .38 revolver he kept in his cluttered apartment.

Natalie shivered and turned on the engine so the heater would work. She drove past St. Michael's, noticed the people arriving for some sort of early Christmas Eve service, and turned toward Broad Street. She thought of the Christmas morning church services she had attended with her father for so many years at the Baptist church three blocks from home. She had resolved not to accompany him this Christmas, not to be hypocritical about it all. She had know that her refusal would hurt him, anger him, but she had been prepared to insist on her point of view. Natalie felt the emptiness in her seem to grow in a lurch of sorrow that was physically painful. She would give anything at this moment to lose the argument and attend church tomorrow morning with her father.

Her mother had died in an accident during the summer when Natalie was nine years old. It was a freak accident, her father told her that evening, kneeling next to the couch, holding Natalie's hands in both of his; her mother had been walking home from work, crossing through a small park, a hundred feet from the street, when a convertible filled with five white college boys, all drunk, had cut across the lawn on a lark. They swerved around a fountain, lost traction in the loose sod of the park lawn, and struck the thirty-two-year-old woman walking home to join husband and daughter for a Friday afternoon picnic, not seeing the vehicle until the last second according to witnesses, looking up at the onrushing car with an expression that one bystander described as containing only surprise, no shock or horror.

On the first day of fourth grade, Natalie's teacher had had them write an essay on what had happened during their summer vacation. Natalie had looked at the blue-lined paper for ten minutes and then written, very carefully, using her best handwriting and her new fountain pen purchased the day before at Keener's Drugs: *This summer I went to my mother's funeral. My mother was very sweet and kind. She loved me very much. She was too young to die this summer. Some people who should not have been driving a*

car ran over her and killed her. They did not go to jail or anything. After my
mother's funeral, my father and I went to see my Aunt Leah for three days. But
then we came back. I miss my mother very much.

After finishing the essay, Natalie had requested permission to go to the bathroom, walked quickly down the familiar-strange halls, and had quietly and repeatedly thrown up in the third stall of the girls' rest room.

Stereotypes. Natalie turned off Broad Street toward Melanie Fuller's home. She drove by it every day, feeling the familiar pain and anger, knowing that it was the same instinct that sent one's tongue searching out the painful tooth, but driving by all the same. Each day she looked at the house—as dark as its neighbor now that the woman next door, Mrs. Hodges, had moved away—and thought of last Tuesday when she had followed the man with the beard into that house.

Saul Laski. He should be easy to stereotype, but he was not. Natalie thought of his sad eyes and soft voice and wondered where Saul was. What was going on? He had agreed to call every other day, but neither she nor Gentry had heard from Saul since they had seen him off at the Charleston airport on Friday. Yesterday, Tuesday, Gentry had called Saul's home and university numbers. No one answered at home and a secretary in Columbia's psychology department said that Dr. Laski was on vacation until January 6. No, Dr. Laski had not been in touch with his office since he left for Charleston on December 16, but he would definitely be back by January 6. His classes resumed at that time.

On Sunday, as she and Gentry had sat in his study talking, Natalie had shown the sheriff a news story from Washington, D.C., about an explosion in a senator's office the night before. Four people had been killed. Could it have anything to do with Saul's mysterious meeting on the same day?

Gentry had smiled and reminded her that an Executive Office Building guard had been killed in the same incident, that both Washington police and the FBI were sure that it had been an isolated terrorist incident, that none of the four confirmed dead had been identified as Saul Laski, and that *some* of the world's mindless violence was separate from the nightmare Saul had described.

Natalie had smiled in agreement and sipped her Scotch. Three days later there was still no word from Saul.

On Monday morning, Gentry had called her from work. "Would you like to help us out in the official investigation into the Mansard House murders?" he had asked.

"Of course," said Natalie. "How can I do that?"

"Well, it's a matter of trying to find a photograph of Miz Melanie Fuller," said Gentry. "According to the city homicide fellas and the local branch of the FBI, no pictures of the lady exist. They couldn't find any relatives, the neighbors said they didn't have any pictures of her, and a search of her house didn't turn up any. The bulletin they sent out just carried a description of her. But I think it might be sort of useful to have a picture, don't you think?"

"How can I help?" asked Natalie.

"Meet me in front of the Fuller house in fifteen minutes," said Gentry. "You'll know me 'cause I'll be the one wearin' a rose in my lapel."

Gentry arrived wearing a rose tucked into the buttonhole of his uniform shirt. He offered it to her with a flourish as they approached the locked courtyard gate in front of the Fuller house.

"How do I deserve this?" asked Natalie, sniffing the pale pink flower.

"It may be the only payment you'll receive for a long, frustrating, and probably fruitless search," said Gentry. He pulled out a huge ring of keys, found a heavy old-fashioned one, and unlocked the gate.

"Are we going to search the Fuller house again?" asked Natalie. She felt a strong reluctance to enter that place another time. She remembered following Saul into the house five days earlier. Natalie shivered in spite of the day's warmth.

"Nope," said Gentry, and led her across the small space to the other old brick home that shared the courtyard. He looked on the ring for another key and unlocked the carved wooden door. "After her husband and granddaughter were killed, Ruth Hodges went to stay with her daughter out in the Sherwood Forest development on the west end of town. Got her permission to pick up this stuff."

The interior was dark—oiled wood and old furniture—but it did not have the musty, unlived-in feel to it that Natalie had sensed in the Fuller house. On the second floor, Gentry turned on a table lamp in a small room with a worktable, couch, and large, framed prints of racehorses on the wall. "This was George Hodges's den," said Gentry. The sheriff touched a book holding a stamp collection, gently turned the stiff pages, and lifted a magnifying glass. "Poor old guy never hurt anybody. Thirty years clerking in the post office and the last nine years as a night watchman down at the marina. Then this stuff comes along . . ." Gentry shook his head. "Anyway, Mrs. Hodges says that until about three years ago, George had a camera and used to use it on a regular basis. She was sure that Miz Fuller never let him take her picture . . . said the old lady absolutely refused to be in photographs . . . but George took a lot of slides and Mrs. Hodges couldn't swear that there might not be a snap of Melanie Fuller somewhere . . ."

"So you want me to look through the slides and see if she's there," said Natalie. "Sure. But I've never seen Melanie Fuller."

"Yeah," said Gentry, "but I'll give you a copy of the description we sent out. Basically, pull any photos of ladies in their seventies or thereabouts." He paused. "Did you or your daddy have a light board or some sort of slide sorter?"

"Down at the studio," said Natalie. "A big light table, about five feet long. But couldn't I just use a projector?"

"Might be faster with the light table," said Gentry, and opened the closet door.

"Good heavens," said Natalie.

The closet was large and layered with handmade shelves. The shelves on the left side held books and boxes labeled *stamps*, but the rear and right side from floor to ceiling were lined with long, open boxes filled with yellow Kodak slide containers. Natalie did a slow double take and looked at Gentry. "There are *thousands* here," she said. "Maybe tens of thousands."

Gentry raised his hands, palms upward, and gave her his widest, most boyish grin. "I said it was a job for volunteers," he said. "I'd put a deputy on it, but the only deputy I got with free time is Lester and he's sort of a nitwit . . . real nice fella, but about as sharp as the blunt end of a hog . . . and I'm afraid he wouldn't hold his concentration."

"Hmm," said Natalie. "Strong recommendation of Charleston's Finest."

Gentry continued to grin at her.

"What the hell," said Natalie. "I'm not doing anything else, and the studio's free until Lorne Jessup . . . my father's lawyer . . . either finalizes the sale of the whole thing to the Shutterbug Shops franchise people or sells the building. OK, let's get started."

"I'll help you carry these boxes out to your car," said Gentry.

"Thanks heaps," said Natalie. She sniffed at the rose and sighed.

There were thousands of slides and every single one of them was on the level of amateur snapshot or below. Natalie knew how hard it was to take a really good photograph—she had spent years trying to please her father after he had given her her first camera, an inexpensive, manual Yashica, on her ninth birthday—but, good heavens, anyone who shot *thousands* of photographs over what looked to be two or three *decades, must* have produced one or two interesting slides.

George Hodges had not. There were family pictures, vacation pictures, vacationing family pictures, pictures of houses and boats, pictures of houseboats, special event pictures, holiday pictures—Natalie eventually saw every Hodges' Christmas tree from 1948 to 1977—and everyday pictures, but every single one of them was of snapshot quality or less. In eighteen years of picture-taking, George Hodges had never learned not to shoot into the sun, not to have his subjects squint into the sun, not to place his subjects in front of trees, poles, and other objects that seemed to grow out of ears and obsolete haircuts and perms, not to let the horizon tilt, not to stiffly pose his human subjects nor to photograph his inanimate objects from what seemed like miles away, not to depend on his flash for objects or people very close or very far from the lens, and not to include *all* of the person in his portraits.

It was this final amateur habit that led to Natalie's discovery of Melanie Fuller.

It was past seven P.M., Gentry had come by the studio with Chinese carry-out the two had eaten while standing by the light table, and Natalie showed him her small stack of possibles. "I don't think she's any of those elderly ladies," she said. "They're all posing voluntarily and most seem too young or too old. At least Mr. Hodges marked the boxes by year."

"Yeah," said Gentry, holding the slides over the table for a quick scan. "None of these quite fit the description. Hair's not right. Mrs. Hodges said Miz Fuller's had that same hairstyle since the late sixties, at least. Sort of short and curled up and blue. Kind of the way you look like you feel right now."

"Thanks," said Natalie but smiled as she set down the white carton of sweet and sour pork and took the rubber band off yet another yellow box. She began setting the slides out in order. "The hard part is not just sweeping each batch onto the floor when you're through looking," she said. "Do you think Mrs. Hodges will go through these someday?"

"Probably not," said Gentry. "She said one of the reasons George finally gave up photography was that she was never interested in looking at his slides."

"I don't know why not," said Natalie and set out the three-hundredth set of photographs of son Lawrence and daughter-in-law Nadine—most of the slides were labeled—standing in the courtyard, squinting into bright sunlight, holding up a squinting baby Laurel while three-year-old Kathleen tugged at her mother's too-short skirt and also squinted. Lawrence was wearing white socks with his black shoes. "Wait just a minute," said Natalie.

Reacting to the sudden excitement in her voice, Gentry set down the other slides and leaned forward. "What?"

Natalie stabbed a finger at the tenth slide in the series. "There. See that? Two of them. The tall man with no hair, wouldn't that be . . . what was his name?"

"Mr. Thorne," said Gentry, "a.k.a. Oscar Felix Haupt. Yes, yes, yes. And this lady with the dumpy dress and short blue curls . . . Well, hello, Miz Fuller." They both leaned closer and used a large magnifying lens to study the image.

"She didn't notice the group was being photographed," Natalie said softly.

"Uh-uh," agreed Gentry. "I wonder why not."

"Based on the number of slides of this particular family tableau," said Natalie, "I would estimate that Mr. Hodges had them standing out there about two hundred days of each year. Miss Fuller probably thought they were statuary for the courtyard."

"Yeah," said Gentry with a huge grin. "Hey, will these print up OK? Just her, I mean."

"It should," said Natalie in a much different tone. "It looks like he was using Kodachrome sixty-four daylight and it can take a lot of enlargement before the grain gets too bad. Get an internegative cut for the best quality print. Crop right here and here and here and you've got a good three-quarters profile."

"Great!" said Gentry. "You did a wonderful job. "We're going to . . . hey, what's wrong?"

Natalie looked up at him and gripped her upper arms more tightly to stop the shivering. It would not stop. "She doesn't look old enough to be seventy or eighty," she said.

Gentry looked back at the slide. "It was taken . . . let's see . . . about five years ago, but no, you're right. She looks . . . maybe sixty or so. But the courthouse has records of her ownin' the house back in the late twenties. But that's not what's botherin' you, is it?"

"No," said Natalie. "I've seen so many pictures of little Kathleen. I keep forgetting that the child is dead. *And* her grandfather . . . who took the photos . . . he's dead."

Gentry nodded. He looked at Natalie as she stared down at the slide. His left hand rose, moved toward her shoulder, and then dropped. Natalie did not notice. She leaned even closer to the slide.

"And this is the monster that probably killed them," she said. "This harmless little old lady. Harmless like a big, black widow spider that kills anything that enters its lair. And when it comes out, other people die. Including my father." Natalie turned off the light table, handed the slide to Gentry, and said, "Here, I'll go through the remaining slides in the morning to see if there's another one. In the meantime, get that printed and put it out on your warrants or memos or all-points-bulletins or whatever the hell you call them."

Gentry had nodded and held the slide gingerly, at arm's length, as if it were a spider, and still alive, and still very, very deadly.

Natalie parked the car across from the Fuller house, glanced at the old building as part of her ritual, shifted into gear to drive somewhere to call Gentry about dinner that night, and then suddenly froze. She put the car in park and turned off the engine. With shaking hands she lifted the Nikon and looked through the viewfinder, propping the 135mm lens against the partially opened window on the driver's side to steady it.

There was a light on in the Fuller house. On the second floor. Not in one of the rooms facing the street, but close enough to let light leak into the second-floor hall and through the shutters there. Natalie had driven by on each of the past three evenings after dark. There had been no light.

She lowered the camera and took a deep breath. Her heart was pounding at a ridiculous rate. There *had* to be a rational explanation. The old woman could not just have come home and set up housekeeping again in her old house when the police in a dozen states and the FBI were searching everywhere for her.

Why not?

No, thought Natalie, there's an explanation. Perhaps Gentry or some of the other investigators were there today. It could have been the city people; Gentry had told her that they were considering storing the old lady's goods until the hearings and inquiries were completed. It could have a hundred rational explanations.

The light went out.

Natalie jumped as if someone had touched her on the back of the neck. She fumbled for the camera, raised it. The second-story window filled the viewfinder. The light was gone from between the pale shutters.

Natalie set the camera carefully on the passenger seat and sat back, took a few calming breaths, and pulled her purse from the center console and set it on her lap. Without taking her eyes off the dark front of the house, she felt in the purse, removed the .32 Llama automatic, and set the purse back. She sat there with the barrel of the small gun resting on the lower curve of the steering wheel. The pressure of her hand automatically released the grip safety. There was still the second safety, but it would take less than a second to slide it off. On Tuesday evening, Gentry had taken her to a private firing range and shown her how to load, handle, and fire the weapon. It was loaded now with all seven shells tight as metal eggs in their spring-loaded nest. The loaded indicator showed red as blood.

Natalie's thoughts scurried like laboratory mice searching for the maze entrance. What the hell to do? Why do anything? There had been prowlers before . . . Saul had been a prowler . . . Where the hell *was* Saul? Could it be him again? Natalie rejected that as absurd even before the thought was fully formed. Who then? Natalie had an image of Melanie Fuller and her Mr. Thorne from the slide. No, Thorne is dead. Melanie Fuller might well be dead also. *Who then?*

Natalie clenched the grip of the gun, careful to keep her finger away from the trigger, and looked at the dark house. Her breathing was rapid but controlled.

Get away. Call Gentry.

Where? At his office or home? Either. Talk to a deputy if you have to. Seven o'clock on a Christmas Eve. How fast would the sheriff's office or the city police respond? And where was the nearest phone? Natalie tried to visualize one and came up only with the darkened shops and restaurants which she had been driving past.

So drive to the City-County Building or Gentry's home. It's only ten minutes away. *Whoever is in the house will be gone in ten minutes.* Good.

One thing that Natalie knew she would *not* do is go into the house herself. The first time had been stupid, but she had been driven by anger, grief, and a bravado born of ignorance. Going in there tonight would be criminally stupid. Gun or no gun.

When Natalie was a little girl, she had loved to stay up late on Friday or Saturday nights to watch the Creature Feature. Her father would let her roll out the hide-a-bed so she could go to sleep right after the show was over . . . or, more often, while the image was still flickering. Sometimes he would join her—he in his blue and white striped pajamas, she in her flannel Pjs—and they would recline and eat popcorn and comment on the improbable gore and action. One thing they agreed upon wholeheartedly: Never pity the heroine who acted stupidly. The young woman in the lacy nightgown would be warned repeatedly DO NOT OPEN THE LOCKED DOOR AT THE END OF THE DARK HALLWAY. And what would she do as soon as everyone was out of sight? As soon as their Friday night heroine unlocked the locked door, Natalie and her father would begin rooting for whatever monster lay in wait. Natalie's father had a saying for that behavior—Stupidity has a price and it always gets paid.

Natalie opened the car door and stepped out into the street. The automatic pistol was a strange weight in her right hand. She stood there a second, gazing at the two dark houses and adjoining courtyard. A streetlight thirty feet away illuminated brick and tree shadow. *Just to the gate*, thought Natalie. If someone came out, she could always run. The gate would be locked anyway.

She crossed the quiet street and approached the gate. It was unlocked, slightly open. She touched the cool metal with her left hand and stared at the dark windows of the house. Adrenaline had her heart pounding at her ribs but also made her feel strong, light, quick. It was a real pistol in her hand. She clicked off the safety the way Gentry had shown her. She would shoot only if attacked . . . attacked in any way . . . but shoot she would.

She knew it was time to go back to the car, drive away, call Gentry. She pushed the gate open and stepped into the courtyard.

The large old fountain threw a deep shadow that sheltered her for a long minute. Natalie stood there and watched the windows and front door of the Fuller house. She felt like a ten-year-old who had been dared to touch the front door of the local haunted house. *There had been a light.*

If someone had been in there, they could have gone out the back, the way she and Saul had come and gone. They would not come out the front door in plain sight of the sidewalk. In any case, she had come far enough. Time to get in the goddamn car and drive the hell away from there.

Natalie walked slowly to the small stoop, lifting the pistol slightly. Standing there, she could see what the shadows from the small porch roof had concealed; the front door was partially opened. Natalie was panting, almost gasping, but still could not get enough air in her lungs. She took three deep breaths and held the third one. Her breathing and pulse steadied. She reached out with the automatic and gave the door a gentle push. It swung inward noiselessly, as if on frictionless hinges, revealing the wood of the entrance hall and a glimpse of the lower steps of the staircase. Natalie imagined that she could see the stains where Kathleen Hodges and the Kramer woman had died. Someone descending the staircase now would come into view as two feet, then dark legs . . .

Fuck this, thought Natalie and turned and ran. The heel of her shoe caught on a loose cobblestone and she almost stumbled just before reaching the gate. She caught her balance, threw a frightened glance over her shoulder at the open door, dark fountain, shadows on brick, glass, and stone, and then was out the gate and across the street, fumbling at the latch on her car door, opening it, and in.

She slammed the door latch down, had the presence of mind to set the safety on the pistol before dropping it onto the passenger seat, and reached for the key, praying that she had left it in the ignition. She had. The engine started immediately.

Natalie reached for the stick shift just as two arms came over and around from the backseat, one hand closing over her mouth as the other clamped on her throat with expert force. She screamed and then screamed again as the fierce pressure of the hand on her mouth stifled the sound and forced the burst of breath back into her constricted throat. Both of her hands were free and she clawed at a thick coat, heavy gloves against her face and throat. She pushed up high in the driver's seat in a desperate attempt to relieve the pressure, to reach her assailant with hands and nails.

The gun. Natalie thrust out with her right hand but could not reach the passenger seat. She batted at the stick shift for a second, then clawed behind her again. Her body was rigid now, pulled half out of her seat, her knees above the bottom of the steering wheel. Someone's face was heavy and damp against her neck and right cheek. The fingers of her left hand clawed at some sort of heavy cap. The hand on her mouth released its pressure, caught her throat. Her assailant's long right arm shot out toward the passenger seat and Natalie heard the pistol thud to the rubber floor mat. She clawed at heavy gloves as the hand returned to her throat. She tried to rip at the face against her neck, but her attacker easily slapped her arm away. Her mouth was free now, but she had no air left with which to scream. Bright dots leaped in the corners of her vision and there was a roaring of blood in her ears.

This is what it's like to be strangled, she thought even as she clawed at fabric, kicked at the dash, and tried to raise her knees high enough to strike the horn ring on the steering wheel. She caught a glimpse in the rearview mirror of blood-red eyes against her neck, a red slab of cheek, and then realized that her own skin was red, the light was red, as red dots filled her vision.

Flesh scraped against her cheek, breath was hot against her face, a thick voice whispered in her ear, "You want to find the woman? Look in Germantown."

Natalie arched high and snapped her head back and to the side as fast as she could, feeling the satisfying pain of her skull butting flesh and bone.

The pressure released for a split second, Natalie collapsed forward, forced a painful breath into her aching throat and lungs, took another, and leaned right, falling forward now, fumbling past the stick shift and seat for the automatic pistol.

The fingers closed on her throat, more painfully this time, feeling for some crucial spot. She was dragged upright again.

There was a flash of red spots, a searing pain in her neck.

Then there was nothing at all.

BOOK TWO
Middle Game

*"O the mind, mind has mountains; cliffs of fall
Frightful, sheer, no-man-fathomed . . ."*

—GERARD MANLEY HOPKINS

FOURTEEN

Melanie

*T*ime is all a jumble to me now. I remember those final hours in Charleston so clearly and the days and weeks which followed so poorly. Other memories push to the forefront. I remember the glass eyes and missing tufts of hair on the life-size boy in the haunted nursery in Grumblethorpe. Odd that I should recall that; I spent so little time in there. I remember the children playing and the young girl's singing in the winter twilight on that hillside above the forest on the morning the helicopter struck the bridge. I remember the white bed, of course, that strange, imprisoning landscape which held the actual prison of my body. I remember Nina awakening from her death-sleep, blue lips pulled back from yellow teeth, blue eyes floating up into their sockets on a rising crest of maggots, the blood flowing once again from the dime-size hole in her pale forehead. But that is not a true memory. I do not think it is.

When I attempt to recall those hours and days immediately following that final Reunion in Charleston, I think first of a sense of exhilaration, of buoyance, of youth restored. I thought then that the worst was over.

How foolish I was.

I was free!

Free of Willi, free of Nina, free of the Game and all of its accompanying nightmares.

I left the noise and confusion of the Mansard House and walked slowly through the silence of the night. In spite of the aches and pains suffered that day, I felt younger than I had in many, many years. Free! I stepped lightly, savoring the darkness and the cool night air. Somewhere sirens were screaming their mournful tune, but I paid no attention to them. I was free!

I paused at the crosswalk of a busy intersection. The light turned red and a long, blue car—a Chrysler, I believe—pulled to a stop. I stepped off the curb and tapped at the window on the passenger's side. The driver, a heavyset, middle-aged man with only a fringe of hair, leaned over to peer suspiciously at me. Then he smiled and touched a button to lower the window. "Yes, ma'am, something wrong?"

I nodded and let myself in. The cushions were of some artificial velvet and very soft. "Drive," I said.

A few minutes later we were on the Interstate and leaving town. I spoke only to give directions. As exhausted as I was, it took almost no effort to maintain control. With my buoyant sense of regained youth had come a

sure strength of power I had not known in years. I settled back in the
cushions and watched the lights of Charleston pass by and recede. We
were miles from town when I realized that the driver was smoking a cigar.
I loathed cigars. He rolled down the window and threw it out. I had him
adjust the heater a bit and then we continued on in silence, driving northwest.

Sometime before midnight we passed the dark stretch of swamp where
Willi's aircraft had gone down. I closed my eyes and called back memories of those early days in Vienna: the gaiety of the *biergartens* lit with
strings of yellow bulbs, the late-night walks along the Danube, the excitement the three of us shared in each other's company, the thrill of those
first conscious Feedings. In those first few summers we had met Willi in
various capitals and spas, I had thought that perhaps I was falling in love
with him. Only my dedication to the memory of my dear Charles had
kept me from considering any feelings for our dashing young fellow traveler in the night. I opened my eyes to peer out at the dark wall of trees
and undergrowth to the right of the road. I thought of Willi's mutilated
body lying out there somewhere amid the mud and insects and reptiles. I
felt nothing.

We stopped to fill the gas tank in Columbia and drove on. After the
driver had paid, I took his billfold and went through it. He had only thirty
dollars left along with the usual clutter of cards and photographs. His
name was unimportant, so I glanced over the driver's license but did not
bother remembering it.

Driving is almost a reflex action. It took very little concentration for me
to keep him on task. I actually dozed briefly as we continued along I-20
past Augusta into Georgia. He was stirring when I awoke, beginning to
mumble and shake his head in confusion, but I tightened my hold and he
returned his gaze to the road. Filtered images of headlights and reflectors
came to me as I closed my eyes once again.

We arrived in Atlanta at a little after three in the morning. I had never
liked Atlanta. It lacked all of the grace and charm which typified Tidewa-
ter culture and, as if to show its continued disregard for Southern style, it
sprawled now in all directions, an endless series of industrial parks and
formless housing developments. We exited the Interstate near a large stadium. The downtown streets were deserted. I had my driver take me by
the bank which was my destination, but its dark, glass front only intensified my frustration. It had seemed like a good idea to keep the documents
of my new identity in a safe-deposit box; how could I have known that I
would need them at 3:30 on a Sunday morning?

I wished that I had not lost my purse to the day's violence. The pockets
of my tan raincoat were bulging with all of the things I had transferred
from my ruined coat. I looked in my billfold to make sure the safe-deposit
key and my bank card were still there. They were. I had my driver circle
the downtown area several times, but it seemed a useless act. Amber lights

were blinking at most intersections and an occasional police car moved past slowly, exhaust curling up like steam in the cool air.

There were several decent hotels downtown, near my bank, but my disheveled appearance and lack of luggage eliminated these as possible havens for the night. I ordered my driver, without verbalizing this time, to take us out another expressway toward the suburbs. It took another forty minutes before we found a motel with a vacancy sign still lit. We exited after a green sign which said Sandy Springs, and approached one of those dreary establishments with a name like Super 8 or Motel 6 or somesuch nonsense as if people were too cretinous to remember the name without a number attached. I debated sending my driver in to register, but it would have been difficult; there might have been conversation and I was too tired to Use him that smoothly. I was sorry that I had not had the time to condition him properly, but such was the case. In the end I brushed my hair as well as I could while peering in the rearview mirror and then went in and registered us myself. The clerk was a sleepy-eyed woman in shorts and a stained Mercer U T-shirt. I invented our names, address, and license number, but the woman made no effort to even glance outside at the idling Chrysler. As was usually the case with such puerile establishments, she asked for payment in advance.

"One night?" she asked.

"Two," I said. "My husband will be out all day tomorrow. He's a salesman for Coca-Cola and will be visiting the plant. I plan to . . ."

"Sixty-three dollars an' eighty-five cents," she said.

There was a time when my family could have stayed at a fine hotel in Maine for an entire week for that amount. I paid the woman.

She handed me a key attached to a plastic pine tree. "Twenty-one sixteen. Drive allaway aroun' and park near the Dumpsters."

We drove all of the way around and parked near the Dumpsters. The parking lot was absurdly filled; there were even several semitrailers parked near the rear fence. I unlocked the room and returned to the car.

The driver was hunched over the wheel and shaking. Sweat covered his forehead and his jowls quivered as he struggled to escape the small space in which I had left his will. I was very tired, but my control remained firm. I missed Mr. Thorne. For years I had not needed to speak my wishes aloud for them to be realized. Using this heavy little man was most frustrating, like dealing with dross when one was used to shaping the finest metals. I hesitated. There were advantages to keeping him with me until Monday, not the least of which was the automobile. But the risks outweighed the advantages. His absence might already have been noted. The police might already have been alerted to watch for his car. All this was relevant, but what finally decided me was the terrible fatigue which had taken the place of my earlier exhilaration. I had to sleep, to recover from the injuries and tensions of that nightmarish day. Without proper conditioning, the driver could not be trusted to remain passive while I slept.

I leaned close to him and touched his neck lightly with my hand. "You will return to the Interstate," I whispered. "Circle the city. Each time you pass an exit, increase your speed by ten miles per hour. When you pass the fourth exit, close your eyes and do not open them again until I tell you to do so. Nod if you understand."

The man nodded. His eyes were glazed and staring. It would not have been a proper Feeding with this one, even if I had wished it.

"Go," I said.

I watched the Chrysler leave the parking lot and turn left toward the expressway. By closing my eyes I could see the long hood, the glare of on-coming lights, and the reflectors passing as the car accelerated to highway speed. I could feel the hum of the heater and the scratch of a wool sweater against his bare forearms. There was the stale taste of cigar in my mouth. I shuddered and withdrew my awareness somewhat. The driver smoothly increased his speed to 65 m.p.h. as he passed the first exit. He was several miles away now and my perceptions were growing fainter, mixing with the sounds of the parking lot and the breeze against my face. I only dimly sensed the moment when the car reached 95 m.p.h. and the driver closed his eyes.

The motel room was as drearily utilitarian as I had imagined. It did not matter. I took off my raincoat and torn print dress. The cut on my left side was the thinnest of scratches, but my dress and slip were ruined. The cut on my little finger throbbed much more painfully than my side. I held sleep off long enough to take a hot bath and to wash my hair. Afterward, I sat wrapped in two towels and sobbed. I did not have even a nightgown or change of underwear. I did not have a *toothbrush*. The bank would not open until Monday morning, more than twenty-four hours away. I sat and wept, feeling old and forgotten and forlorn. I wanted to go home and sleep in my own bed and have Mr. Thorne bring me my coffee and croissant in the morning, as always. But there was no going back. My sobs were more like those of an abandoned child than of a woman my age.

After awhile, still wrapped in towels, I lay on my side, pulled the sheet and coverlet up, and slept.

I awakened briefly around noon when a maid attempted to enter the room. I went to the bathroom to get a drink of water, carefully avoiding the re-flection in the mirror, and then returned to bed. The room was dark be-hind thick drapes, the ventilator was purring softly, and I returned to sleep the way a wounded animal returns to the dark protection of its den. I do not remember any dreams.

That evening I arose, still groggy and aching more than the previous day, and attempted to improve my appearance. There was little I could do. The print dress was ruined, I would have to leave the raincoat on when-ever possible. I was in desperate need of a hairdresser. Despite all this, there was a certain glow to my skin, a previously unnoticed firmness of flesh under my chin, and a smoothness where wrinkles had earlier carved Time's claim. I felt younger. In spite of the horror of the previous day, the Feeding had served me well.

There was a restaurant across the endless expanse of parking lot. It was an inhuman place—lights bright enough for an operating room, red-checked plastic tablecloths still damp from their last wipe with the bus-boy's filthy sponge, and huge, plastic menus with color photographs of the establishment's "special platters." I assumed the photographs were pro-vided for illiterate clientele who could not decode the inflated prose tout-ing "delectable, crispy-brown home fries" and "those all-time Southern favorites, delicious hominy and grits just like Grandma used to make!!" The menu was dense with asides and breathless exclamations. A sidebar explained what these strange Southern delicacies were and urged the Yan-kee tourists to be daring. I thought of how strange it was that the tiresome subsistence diet of a people too poor or too ignorant to eat well inevitably becomes the traditional "soul food" of the next generation. I ordered tea and an English muffin and waited half an hour for it to arrive, all the while suffering the bickering and feeding noises of a huge family of Northern boors at the next table. I speculated, not for the first time, that the sanity of the nation would be much improved if children and adults were re-quired by law to eat in separate public establishments.

It was dark when I returned to the motel. For want of anything better to do, I turned on the television. It had been over a decade since I had watched TV but little had changed. The mindless collisions of football occupied one channel. The "educational" channel offered to tell me more than I wanted to know about the aesthetics of Sumo wrestling. My third try brought me a frequently interrupted made-for-TV movie about a teen-age prostitute ring and a young, male social worker who dedicated his life to saving the heroine from such a life of degradation. The idiotic program reminded me of the scandalous pulp "detective gazettes" popular when I was young; in decrying the outrages of taboo behavior—then it was *free love*, now what I believe the media call "kiddie-porn"—they allow us to wallow in the titillating details.

The local news was on the last channel.

The young, colored, female newscaster was smiling the entire time she spent reading the report on what they called the Charleston Murders. Police were hunting for suspects and motives. Witnesses had described the carnage in a well-known Charleston hotel. State police and the FBI were interested in the whereabouts of a Mrs. Fuller, a longtime Charles-ton resident and employer of one of the victims. There were no photo-graphs of the lady. The entire report lasted less than forty-five seconds.

I turned off the television, switched off the lights, and lay shivering in the dark. Within forty-eight hours, I told myself, I would be safe and warm at my villa in the south of France. I closed my eyes and tried to picture the small, white flowers which grew up between the flagstones leading to the well. For a second I could almost smell the salt-sea freshness which came in with the summer storms blowing up from the south. I thought of the tiled roofs of the nearby village, red and orange trapezoids visible above the green rectangles of the orchards which filled the valley. These pleasant images were suddenly superimposed over my last view of Nina, her blue eyes wide with disbelief, her mouth slightly open, the hole in her forehead no more terrifying than a temporary smudge which she would soon brush away with a pass of her long, perfectly manicured fingers. Then, in my presleep dreaming, the blood welled up and began to flow, not only from the wound but also from Nina's mouth and nose and wide, accusing eyes.

I pulled the covers up tightly under my chin and concentrated on thinking of nothing.

I simply had to have a purse. However, if I was to pay for a taxi to take me downtown to the bank, I would not have enough money left to buy a purse. But I could not *go* to the bank *without* a purse. I again counted the cash in my billfold, but even taking change into account, I would not have enough. As I stood there in the motel room, the taxi I had summoned began honking impatiently from the parking lot.

I solved the problem by having the driver stop at a discount drugstore on the way into town. I purchased a perfectly atrocious straw "tote bag" for seven dollars. The cab ride, including the metered time while I had shopped for my treasure, cost just over thirteen dollars. I tipped the driver a dollar and kept the remaining dollar as mad money.

I must have been a sight as I stood on the sidewalk waiting for the bank to open. My hairdo was beyond repair. I was wearing no makeup. My tan raincoat, still smelling slightly of gunpowder, was buttoned tightly to my throat. In my right hand I clutched my stiff new straw bag. Only the tennis shoes were lacking in order to complete the image of what I believe people now refer to as a "shopping bag lady." Then I realized that I was still wearing the low-heeled deck shoes which did somewhat resemble sneakers.

Incredibly, the assistant manager recognized me and seemed delighted to see me. "Ah, Mrs. Straughn," he said as I diffidently approached his desk, "a pleasure to see you again!"

I was astounded. It had been almost two years since my last visit to this bank. My savings account was not so large that I should earn such courtesy from an assistant manager. For a few panicked seconds I was sure that the police had already been there and that it was a trap. I was glancing at the customers and clerks, trying to decide which were the plainclothes officers, when I took notice of the assistant manager's relaxed manner and satisfied grin. I let out a long breath. I was dealing with a man who took pride in remembering his customers' names, nothing more.

"It's been a long time," he said affably and glanced quickly at my ensemble.

"Two years," I said.

"Is your husband well?"

My husband? I desperately tried to recall what story I had given in previous visits. I had not mentioned . . . with a start I realized that he was speaking of the tall, bald gentleman who had stood silently by my side each time I had come. "Ah," I said, "you mean Mr. Thorne, my secretary. I am afraid that Mr. Thorne is no longer in my employ. As for Mr. Straughn, he died of cancer in 1956."

"Oh," said the assistant manager, his florid face becoming even more flushed, "I'm sorry."

I nodded and we both observed a few seconds of silence for the mythical Mr. Straughn.

"Well, how can we help you today, Mrs. Straughn? A deposit, I hope."

"A withdrawal, I fear," I said. "But first I would like to see my safe-deposit box."

I presented the proper card, being careful not to confuse it with the half dozen other bank identification cards I had carried for so long in my billfold. We went through the solemn ritual of the double keys. Then I was alone in a small confessional of a space and lifting the lid to my new life.

The passport was four years old but still valid. It was a Bicentennial passport—the one with the red and blue background to the paper—and the gentleman at the Atlanta post office had told me that those would be worth something someday. The cash, twelve thousand dollars of it in various denominations, was also still valid. And heavy. I stuffed the sheaths of bills into my bulging tote bag and prayed that the cheap straw would not give way. The stocks and bonds made out to Mrs. Straughn were not relevant to my present purposes, but they fit nicely over the heavy lump of bills. I ignored the keys to the Ford Granada. I had no wish to go through the effort of getting the automobile out of storage and there would be questions if it were discovered at the airport parking lot. The final thing in the box was the tiny Beretta pistol, meant for Mr. Thorne's use if events had called for it, but I would not need it where I was going.

Where I thought I was going.

After returning the box with the same funereal solemnity as in the earlier ritual, I stood in line for the teller.

"You-all want all ten thousand out today?" asked the gum-chewing girl behind the bars.

"Yes, as it says on the slip."

"This means you'll be closing out your account with us then?"

"Yes, it does." It was amazing how years of training could produce such paragons of efficiency. The girl glanced over to where the assistant manager was standing with his fingers folded across his stomach like a paid mourner. He nodded curtly and the girl popped her gum in a faster rhythm. "Yes, ma'am. How do you-all want it?"

In Peruvian nickels, I was tempted to say. "Traveler's checks, please." I smiled. "A thousand dollars in fifties. A thousand in hundreds. The rest in five hundreds."

"There's a charge for those," said the girl with a slight frown, as if the prospect would make me change my mind.

"That's fine, dear," I said. The day was still young, *I* felt young. It would be cool in southern France, but the light would be as rich as melted butter. "Take your time, dear. There's no rush."

The Atlanta Sheraton was two blocks from the bank. I took a room there. They asked for an imprint of my credit card. Instead, I paid with a five-hundred-dollar traveler's check and put the change in my billfold. The room was a bit less plebeian than the one at the motel with the number, but no less sterile. I used the room phone to contact a downtown travel agency. After several moments of consulting with their resident computer, the young lady gave me a choice of leaving Atlanta at six that same day on a TWA flight which had a forty minute layover at Heathrow before going on to Paris, or a ten P.M. Pan Am flight direct to Paris. In each case I would catch the same late afternoon flight from Paris to Marseilles. She recommended the later flight because it was slightly cheaper. I chose to go first class on the earlier one.

There were three respectable department stores within a short cab ride of the hotel. I called all three and found the one least shocked by the idea of actually *delivering* items to their customer's hotel. Then I called a cab and went shopping.

I purchased eight dresses with a label by Albert Nipon, four skirts—one a delightful green wool design by Cardin—a complete set of tan Gucci luggage, two Evan-Picone suits, including one which, a few days earlier, I would have thought appropriate for a much younger woman, adequate amounts of underwear, two handbags, three nightgowns, a comfortable blue robe, five pairs of shoes including a pair of high-heeled black pumps by Bally, a half dozen wool sweaters, two hats—one a wide-brimmed straw hat which went rather well with my seven-dollar tote bag—a dozen blouses, toiletries, a bottle of Jean Paton perfume which claimed to be "the most expensive perfume in the world" and well could have been, a digital alarm clock and calculator for only nineteen dollars, makeup, nylons (neither support hose nor those awkward "panty hose" but actual nylon stockings), half a dozen paperback bestsellers from the book department, a Michelin tour guide of France, a larger billfold, a variety of chocolates and English biscuits, and a small metal trunk. Then, while the clerk hunted for an employee to deliver the goods to my hotel, I went next door to an Elizabeth Arden Salon for a complete makeover.

Later, refreshed, relaxed, my skin and scalp still tingling, dressed in a comfortable skirt and white blouse, I returned to the Sheraton. I ordered lunch—coffee, a cold roast beef sandwich with Dijon mustard, potato salad, vanilla ice cream—and tipped the young bellboy five dollars when he brought it. There was a noon television news program, but it did not mention Saturday's events in Charleston. I went in and took a long, hot bath.

For traveling I laid out the dark blue suit. Then, still in my slip, I set about packing. I put a change of clothes, a nightgown, toiletries, snacks, two paperbacks, and most of my cash in the small carry-on bag. I had to send down to room service again for a scissors to snip off tags and strings. By two o'clock I was finished—although the small trunk was only half filled and had to be packed down with a blanket I found in the closet to keep things from shifting—and I lay down to take a nap before the 4:15 limousine would take me to the airport. I found it pleasing to watch the black digits shift fluidly on the gray display surface of my new travel alarm. I had no idea how the gadget worked. There was much about this last quarter of the twentieth century that I did not understand, but it did not matter. I fell asleep with a smile on my lips.

The Atlanta airport was like every other major airport I had ever been in and I have been in most of them. I missed the great train stations of decades ago: the marbled, sun-shafted dignity of Grand Central in its prime, the open-air majesty of Berlin's prewar terminal, even the architectural overkill and peasant chaos of Bombay's Victoria Station. Atlanta's airport was the epitome of classless travel: endless tile concourses, molded-plastic seating, and banks of video monitors mutely announcing arrivals and departures. The corridors were filled with scurrying businessmen and loud, sweating families in pastel rags. It did not matter. In twenty minutes I would be free.

I had checked my luggage through except for my carry-on bag and purse. An airline employee took me the length of the concourse on a small electric cart. In truth, my arthritis *was* troubling me and my legs were aching abominably from Saturday's exertions. I checked in again at the departure area, confirmed that there would be no smoking in my section of first class, and sat to wait out the final minutes until boarding.

"Ms. Fuller. Melanie Fuller. Please pick up the nearest white paging phone."

I sat rigid, listening. The public address system had been babbling incessantly since my arrival, paging people, threatening that cars left in the loading zone would be ticketed and towed away, disavowing responsibility for the religious fanatics who roamed the terminal like packs of pamphleted jackals. Surely it was a mistake! If my name had actually been called I would have heard it earlier. I sat upright, scarcely breathing, listening as the sexless voice ran through its litany of paged names. I relaxed somewhat when I heard a Miss Reneé Fowler paged. It was a natural enough mistake. My nerves had been on edge for days, weeks. The Reunion had been on my mind since early autumn.

"Ms. Fuller. Melanie Fuller. Please pick up the nearest white paging phone."

My heart stopped for a second. I could feel the pain in my chest as muscles constricted. *It's some mistake. A common enough name. I'm sure I misheard what was announced* . . .

"Mrs. Straughn. Beatrice Straughn. Please pick up the nearest white paging phone. Mr. Bergstrom. Harold Bergstrom. . . ."

There was a moment when I was sure—sickeningly sure—that I was about to faint right there in the Overseas Departure Lounge of Trans World Airlines. I lowered my head as the red and blue room swam out of focus and a myriad of small dots danced in the periphery of my vision. Then I was up and moving, purse, tote bag, and carry-on bag clutched to me. A man with a blue blazer and plastic nametag went by and I seized him by the arm. "Where *is* it?"

He stared at me.

"The white telephone," I hissed. "Where *is* it?"

He pointed to a nearby wall. I approached the instrument as if it were a viper. For a minute—an eternity—I could not reach for it. Then I set down my carry-on bag, lifted the receiver, and whispered my new name into it. A strange voice said, "Mrs. Straughn? One moment, please. There is a call for you."

I stood motionless while hollow sounds signified connections being made. When the voice came it was also hollow, empty, echoing, as if emanating from a tunnel or bare room. Or from a tomb. I knew the voice very well.

"Melanie? Melanie, darling, this is Nina . . . Melanie? Darling, this is Nina . . ."

I dropped the receiver and backed away. The noise and bustle all around receded until it was a distant, unrelated buzz. I seemed to be staring down a long tunnel at tiny figures flitting to and fro. I turned in a spasm of panic and fled down the concourse, forgetting my carry-on suitcase, forgetting the money in it, forgetting my flight, forgetting everything except the dead voice which rang in my ears like a scream in the night.

As I approached the terminal doorway a redcap hurried toward me. I did not think. I glanced at the hurrying Negro and the man collapsed to the floor. I do not believe that I had ever Used anyone that brutally or quickly before. The man writhed in the grip of a massive seizure, striking his face repeatedly against the tile. I slipped through the automatically opening doors as people rushed toward the spasming redcap.

I stood on the curb and unsuccessfully tried to fight down the whirlwind of panic and confusion which whipped at me. Each approaching face threatened to resolve itself into the pale and smiling death mask I half expected to see. I spun around clutching my purse and tote bag to my chest, a pathetic old woman on the verge of hysteria. *Melanie? Darling, this is Nina.* . . .

"Cab, lady?"

I whirled to look at the source of the question. The green and white cab had pulled up next to me without my noticing. More waited behind it in a special lane for taxis. The driver was white, in his thirties, clean-shaven but with the type of translucent skin that showed the darkness of the next day's beard.

"You wanta cab?"

I nodded and struggled with the door. The driver leaned back and unlocked it for me. The interior smelled of stale cigarette smoke, sweat, and vinyl. I swiveled to look out the rear window as we swept down the curved drive. Green rectangles of light washed across the window and rear deck of the cab. I could not tell if any of the other automobiles were following us. There was an insane amount of traffic.

"I said, where to?" shouted the driver.

I blinked. My mind was blank.

"Downtown?" he said. "Hotel?"

"Yes." It was as if I did not speak his language.

"Which one?"

A great pain blossomed behind my left eye. I felt it flow down from my skull to my neck and then fill my body like a liquid flame. For a second I could not breathe. I sat there, clutching my purse and tote bag, waiting for the pain to fade.

". . . or what?" asked the driver.

"Pardon me?" My voice was the rasp of dead corn stalks in a dry wind.

"Should I get on the expressway or what?"

"Sheraton." The word was a nonsense syllable to me. The pain began to recede, leaving an echo of nausea.

"Downtown or airport?"

"Downtown," I said, having no idea what we were negotiating.

"Got it."

I sat back in the cold vinyl. Strips of light moved through the fetid interior of the cab with hypnotic regularity and I concentrated on slowing my breathing. The sound of tires on wet pavement slowly penetrated the buzzing which had filled my ears. *Melanie, darling. . . .*

"Your name?" I whispered.

"Huh?"

"Your name?" I demanded.

"Steve Lenton. It's on the card there. Why?"

"Where do you live?"

"Why?"

I had had enough of this one. I pushed. Even through the headache, even through the swirl of nausea, I pushed. The impact was strong enough to make him double over the wheel for a few seconds, and then I allowed him to straighten up and return his attention to the road.

"Where do you live?"

Pictures, images, a woman with stringy, blond hair in front of a garage. *Verbalize.*

"Beulah Heights." The driver's voice was flat.

"Is it far from here?"

"Fifteen minutes."

"Do you live alone?"

Sadness. Loss. Jealousy. A pain-filled image of the blonde with a runny-nosed child in her arms, voices raised in anger, a red dress retreating down the walk. The last sight of her station wagon. Self-pity. Words from a country-western song ringing with truth.

"We will go there," I said. I believe I said it. I closed my eyes and listened to the sound of tires on wet pavement.

The driver's house was dark. It was a duplicate of all the other shabby little homes we had passed in this development—stucco walls, a single "picture window" looking out onto a tiny rectangle of yard, a garage as big as all the rest of the house combined. No one was watching as we drove up. The driver opened the garage door and drove the cab in. There was a new-model Buick there, dark blue or black, I could not tell in the poor light. I had him back the Buick out onto the driveway and then return. We left the cab's engine running. The driver pulled down the garage door.

"Show me the house," I said softly. It was as predictable as it was depressing. Dishes were stacked up in the sink, socks and underwear littered the floor of the bedroom, newspapers were everywhere, and cheap paintings of doe-eyed children stared down at the mess.

"Where is your gun?" I asked. I did not have to probe to find out if he owned a firearm. This was the South, after all. The driver blinked and led me downstairs to a poorly lit workshop. Old calendars with photographs of naked women hung on the cinderblock walls. The driver nodded to a cheap metal cabinet where a shotgun, a hunting rifle, and two pistols were stored. The pistols were wrapped in oily rags. One was some sort of long-barreled target pistol, single-shot, low-caliber. The other was a more familiar revolver, .38 caliber, six-inch barrel, somewhat reminiscent of Charles's heirloom. I put three boxes of cartridges in my tote bag with the revolver and we went back upstairs to the kitchen.

He brought me the keys to the Buick and the two of us sat down at the kitchen table while I composed the note for him to write. It was not very original. Loneliness. Remorse. Inability to continue. Authorities might notice the missing firearm and would certainly search for the automobile, but the authenticity of the note and the choice of method would allay most suspicions of foul play. Or so I hoped.

The driver returned to the cab. Even in the few seconds the kitchen door was open to the garage, the fumes caused my eyes to water. The cab's engine seemed absurdly loud to me. My last glimpse of my driver was of him sitting upright, hands firm on the steering wheel, gaze set ahead on the horizon of some unseen highway. I closed the door.

I should have left immediately, but I had to sit down. My hands were shaking and a tremor pulsed in my right leg, sending stabs of arthritic pain into my hip. I clutched the Formica tabletop and closed my eyes. *Melanie?*

Darling, this in Nina . . . There had been no mistaking that voice. Either Nina was still pursuing me or I had lost my mind. *The hole in her forehead had been dime-sized and perfectly round. There had been no blood.*

I searched the cupboards for wine or brandy. There was only a half bottle of Jack Daniels whiskey. I found a clean jelly glass and drank. The whiskey burned my throat and stomach, but my hands were steadier as I carefully washed the glass and set it back in the cupboard.

For a second I considered returning to the airport but quickly rejected the idea. My luggage would be on its way to Paris by now. I could catch up to it by taking the later Pan American flight, but even the thought of boarding an aircraft made me shudder. *Willi relaxing, turning to speak to one of his companions. Then the explosion, the screams, the long, dark fall into oblivion.* No, I would not be flying for some time to come.

The sound of the taxi's motor came through the door to the garage; a dull, persistent throbbing. It had been more than half an hour. It was time for me to leave.

I made sure that no one was around and closed the front door behind me. There was the sound of finality to the click of the lock. I could barely hear the taxi's engine through the broad garage door as I slipped behind the wheel of the Buick. For a panicked few seconds I could make none of the keys fit the ignition, but then I tried again, took my time, and the engine promptly started. It took another minute to adjust the seat forward, position the rearview mirror, and to find the light switch. I had not driven a car—directly driven it—for many years. I backed out the driveway and drove slowly through the winding residential streets. It occurred to me that I had no destination, no alternative plans. I had been fixated on the villa near Toulon and the identity awaiting me there. The persona of Beatrice Straughn had been a temporary thing, a traveling name. With a lurch I realized that the twelve thousand dollars in cash was in the carry-on bag which I had left by the telephone at the airport. I still had more than nine thousand dollars in traveler's checks in my purse and tote bag along with my passport and other identification, but the blue suit I was wearing constituted all of the clothing I now owned. My throat tightened as I thought of the lovely purchases I had made that morning. I felt the sting of tears, but I shook my head and drove on as a light changed and some cretin behind me honked impatiently.

Somehow I managed to find the Interstate loop and drove north. I hesitated when I saw the green sign for the airport exit. My carry-on bag might still be sitting near the phone. It would be easy to arrange an alternate flight. I drove on. Nothing in the world could have made me set foot in that well-lit mausoleum where Nina's voice awaited me. I shuddered again as an image formed, unbidden, of the TWA departure lounge where I had been two hours, an eternity, ago, Nina was there, sitting primly, still in the soft pink dress in which I had last seen her, hands folded atop the purse on her lap, eyes blue, her forehead marked with the dime-size hole and a spreading bruise, her smile wide and white. Her teeth had been filed to points. She was going to board the aircraft. She was waiting for me.

Glancing frequently in my mirror, I changed lanes, altered my speed, and exited twice only to go back down the opposite ramp to return to the freeway. It was impossible to tell for certain if anyone was following me, but I thought not. Headlights burned my eyes. My hands began to shake again. I put the window down a crack and let the cold night air sting my cheek. I wished that I had brought the bottle of whiskey.

The sign read I-85 NORTH, CHARLOTTE, N.C. North. I hated the North, the Yankee terseness, the gray cities, the deep cold and sunless days. Anyone who knew me also knew that I detested the northern states, especially in winter, and that I would avoid them if at all possible.

I followed the traffic onto the curve of the exit cloverleaf. Reflecting letters on an over-hanging sign read CHARLOTTE, N.C. 240 Mi., DURHAM, N.C., 337 Mi., RICHMOND, VA 540 Mi., WASHINGTON, D.C. 650 Mi.

Gripping the steering wheel with all of my strength, trying to keep up with the insane speed of the traffic, I drove north into the night.

"Hey, lady!"

I snapped awake and stared at the apparition inches from my face. Bright sunlight illuminated long, stringy hair half covering a rodent's features; tiny, shifty eyes, long nose, dirty skin, and thin, chapped lips. The apparition forced a smile and I saw a brief flash of sharp, yellowed teeth. The front tooth was broken. The boy could not have been more than seventeen years old. "Hey, lady, you goin' my way?"

I sat up and shook my head. The late morning sunlight was warm in the closed car. I looked around the interior of the Buick and for a second I could not remember why I was sleeping in a car rather than my bed at home. Then I recalled the interminable night of driving and the terrible weight of fatigue which had finally forced me into an empty rest area. How far had I driven? I vaguely remembered passing an exit sign for Greensboro, North Carolina, just before I stopped.

"Lady?" The creature tapped at the window with a knuckle creased with dirt.

I pressed the button to lower the window, but nothing happened. Claustrophobia threatened me for a second before I thought to turn on the ignition. Everything in this absurd vehicle was electrically powered. I noticed that the fuel indicator read almost full. I remembered stopping in the night, leaving several stations before I found a place which was not all self-service. Come what may, I was not about to descend to the level of pumping my own gasoline. The window slid down with a hum.

"You takin' riders, lady?" The boy's voice, a nasal whine, was as repulsive as his appearance. He wore a soiled military jacket and carried only a small pack and bedroll as luggage. Behind him, cars moved by on the Interstate with sunlight flashing on their windshields. I had the sudden, liberating sense of playing hookey on a school day. Outside, the boy sniffled and wiped at his nose with a sleeve.

"How far are you going?" I asked.

"North," said the boy with a shrug. It constantly amazes me that we have somehow contrived to raise an entire generation which cannot answer a simple question.

"Do your parents know that you're hitchhiking?"

Again he offered the shrug, a half shrug really, with only one shoulder rising as if the complete gesture would require too much energy. I knew immediately that this boy was almost certainly a runaway, probably a thief, and quite possibly a danger to anyone foolish enough to pick him up.

"Get in," I said and touched a button to unlock the door on the passenger's side.

We stopped in Durham to have breakfast. The boy frowned at the pictures on the plastic menu and then squinted at me. "Uh, I can't. I mean I don't have no money for this. You know, like I got enough to get my uncle's an' all, but . . ."

"That's all right," I said. "This is my treat." We were both supposed to believe that he was traveling to his uncle's home in Washington. When I had again asked him how far he was going, he had squinted one of his ferrety glances at me and said, "How far *you* goin'?" When I suggested Washington as my destination he had graced me with another glimpse of nicotine-stained teeth and said, "*Awright*, that's where my uncle lives. That's where I'm goin', my uncle's. In Washington. *Awright*." Now the boy mumbled his order to the waitress and hunched over to play with his fork. As was the case with so many young people I encountered these days, I could not tell if the boy was truly retarded or just pitifully ill educated. Most of the population under thirty appears to fall into one or the other category.

I sipped my coffee and asked, "You say that your name is Vincent?"

"Yeah." The boy lowered his face to his cup like a horse at a trough. The noises were not dissimilar.

"That's a pleasant name. Vincent what?"

"Huh?"

"What is your last name, Vincent?"

The boy lowered his mouth to the cup once again to gain time to think. He darted his rodent glance at me. "Uh . . . Vincent Pierce."

I nodded. The boy had almost said Vincent Price. I had met Price once in an art auction in Madrid in the late 1960s. He was a most gentle man, truly refined, with large, soft hands which were never still. We had discussed art, cooking, and Spanish culture. At that time Price was buying original art on behalf of some monstrous American company. I thought him a delightful person. It was years later that I found out about his roles

in all of those dreadful horror films. Perhaps he and Willi had worked together at some time.

"And you are hitchhiking to your uncle's home in Washington?"

"Yeah."

"Christmas vacation, no doubt," I said. "School must be out."

"Yeah."

"In what part of Washington does your uncle live?"

Vincent hunched over his cup again. His hair hung down like a tangle
of greasy vines. Every few seconds he would lift a languid hand and flip a
strand out of his eyes. The gesture was as constant and maddening as a
tic. I had known this vagabond for less than an hour and already his man-
nerisms were driving me crazy.

"A suburb, perhaps?" I prompted.

"Yeah."

"Which one, Vincent? There are quite a few suburbs around Washington. Perhaps we'll pass through it and I can drop you. Is it one of the more
expensive areas?"

"Yeah. My uncle, he's gotta lotta money. My whole family's like rich,
you know?"

I could not help but glance at his filthy army jacket, opened now to reveal a ragged black sweatshirt. His stained jeans were worn through in
several places. I realized, of course, that dress signifies nothing these days.
Vincent could be the grandson of J. Paul Getty and sport such a wardrobe. I remembered the crisp, silk suits which my Charles had worn. I remembered Roger Harrison's elaborate costuming for every occasion;
traveling cape and suit for the briefest excursions, riding breeches, the
dark tie and tails for evening events. America has certainly reached its
egalitarian summit as far as dress goes. We have reduced the sartorial options of an entire people to the tattered, filthy rags of the society's least
common denominator.

"Chevy Chase?" I said.

"Huh?" Vincent squinted at me.

"The suburb. Perhaps it is Chevy Chase?"

He shook his head.

"Bethesda? Silver Spring? Takoma Park?"

Vincent furrowed his brow as if considering these. He was about to
speak when I interrupted. "Oh, I know," I said. "If your uncle is rich, he
probably lives in Bel Air. Isn't that right?"

"Yeah, that's it," agreed Vincent, relieved. "That's the place."

I nodded. My toast and tea arrived. Vincent's eggs and sausage and
hash browns and ham and waffles were set in front of him. We ate in silence broken only by his feeding noises.

Past Durham, I-85 turned due north again. We crossed into Virginia a
little over an hour after we finished breakfast. When I was a girl my family

often had traveled to Virginia to visit friends and relatives. Usually we had taken the train, but my favorite method of travel had been the small but comfortable overnight packet ship which had docked at Newport News. Now I found myself driving an oversized and underpowered Buick north on a four-lane highway, listening to gospel music on the FM radio and leaving my window down a crack to dispel the sweat and dried-urine smell emanating from my sleeping passenger.

We had passed Richmond and it was late afternoon when Vincent awoke. I asked him if he would like to drive for a spell. My arms and legs ached from the strain of keeping up with the traffic. No one obeyed the 55 m.p.h. speed limit. My eyes were also tired.

"Hey, yeah. I mean, you sure?" asked Vincent.

"Yes," I said. "You will drive carefully, I presume."

"Yeah, sure."

I found a rest area where we could exchange places. Vincent drove at a steady 68 m.p.h. with only his wrist on the wheel, his eyes so heavy-lidded that for a moment I feared that he had fallen asleep. I reassured myself by remembering that modern automobiles are simple enough to be driven by chimpanzees. I adjusted my seat as far back into a reclining position as it would go and closed my eyes. "Wake me when we arrive at Arlington, would you please, Vincent?"

He grunted. I had set my purse between the two front seats and I knew that Vincent was glancing at it. He had not been able to hood his eyes quickly enough when I had removed the thick pile of cash to pay for breakfast. I was taking a chance by napping, but I was very tired. A Washington FM station was playing a Bach concerto. The hum of tires and gentle swish of traffic lulled me to sleep in less than a minute.

The absence of motion woke me. I came awake instantly, totally, alertly—the way a predator awakes at the approach of its prey.

We were parked in an unfinished rest stop. The evening slant of winter sunlight suggested that I had been asleep for about an hour. The heavy traffic suggested that we were close to Washington. The switchblade knife in Vincent's hand suggested darker things. He looked up from counting my traveler's checks. I impassively returned his stare.

"You gotta sign these," he whispered.

I stared at him.

"You gotta sign these fuckin' things over to me," hissed my hitchhiker. His hair fell in his eyes and he flipped it out. "You gotta sign 'em *now*."

"No."

Vincent's eyes widened with surprise. Spittle wet his thin lips. He would have killed me then, I believe, in broad daylight, with heavy traffic passing twenty yards away, and with nowhere to put an old lady's corpse except the Potomac, but—and even dear, dull Vincent was capable of comprehending this—he needed my signature on the checks.

"Listen, you old cunt," he said and seized the front of my dress, "you sign these fucking checks or I'll cut your fucking nose off your fucking face. You unnerstand me, *cunt?*" He brought the steel blade to a stop inches in front of my eyes.

I glanced down at the grimy hand holding my dress front and I sighed. For the briefest of seconds I recalled entering my hotel suite three decades earlier, in a different country, in a different world, and finding a bald but handsome gentleman in evening dress going through my jewel case. *That* thief had smiled ironically and given a short bow when discovered. I would miss that grace, the ease of Use, the quiet efficiency which no amount of conditioning could impart.

"Come *on*," hissed the filthy youth holding me. He moved the blade toward my cheek. "You're fucking asking for this," said Vincent. There was a gleam in his eyes that had nothing to do with the money.

"Yes," I said. His arm stopped in mid-motion. For several seconds he strained until the veins stood out on his forehead. He grimaced and his eyes widened as his hand tilted, turned, and moved the stiletto blade back toward his own face.

"Time to start," I said softly.

The razor-sharp blade turned until it was vertical. It slid between the thin lips, between the stained and broken front teeth.

"Time to teach," I said softly.

The blade slid in, slicing gums and tongue. His lips curled back and then closed on steel. The blade grew moist with blood as the tip touched soft palate.

"Time to learn." I smiled and we began the first lesson.

FIFTEEN

Washington, D.C.
Saturday, Dec. 20, 1980

Saul Laski stood motionless for twenty minutes looking at the girl. She stared back, unblinking, equally motionless, frozen in time. She wore a straw hat, tilted back slightly on her head, and a gray apron over a simple white shift. Her hair was blond, and her eyes blue. Her hands were folded in front of her, arms stretched in the awkward grace of childhood.

Someone stepped between him and the painting and Saul stepped back, moved sideways to get a better view. The girl in the straw hat continued to stare at the empty space he had vacated. Saul did not know why the painting moved him so; most of Marie Cassat's work struck him as too sentimental, a soft-edged blur of pastels, but this piece had moved him to tears the first time he had visited the National Gallery almost two decades ago and now no trip to Washington was complete without a pilgrimage to the "Girl With the Straw Hat." He thought that perhaps somehow the pudgy face and wistful stare brought back the presence of his sister Stefa— dead of typhus during the war—although Stefa's hair had been much darker and her eyes far from blue.

Saul turned away from the painting. Each time he visited the museum he promised himself that he would see new sections, spend more time with the modern work, and each time he spent too much time here with the girl. Next time, he thought.

It was after one P.M. and the crowd in the gallery restaurant was thinning out by the time Saul reached the entrance and stood there scanning the tables. He saw Aaron immediately, seated at a small table near the corner, his back to a tall potted plant. Saul waved, and joined the young man.

"Hello, Uncle Saul."

"Hello, Aaron."

His nephew rose and gave Saul a hug. Saul grinned, gripped the boy by the arms, and looked at him. No boy now. Aaron would be twenty-six in March. No longer a boy perhaps, but still thin, and Saul saw David's smile, the upward curve of muscle at each corner of the mouth, but Rebecca's dark curls and large eyes looked out from behind the glasses. But something about the darker skin and high cheeks were David's alone, as if an additional inheritance for being sabra, a native-born Israeli. Aaron and his twin had been thirteen, small for their age, when the Six Day War had erupted. Saul had flown into Tel Aviv five hours too late to join the fighting even as a medic, but not too late to hear young Aaron and Isaac tell and retell the secondhand exploits of their older brother, Avner, a captain in the air force. And Saul had listened to additional details of Aaron and Isaac's cousin Chaim's bravery in leading his battalion on the Golan Heights. Two years later young Avner was dead, shot down by an Egyptian SAM during the War of Attrition, and the following August it was Chaim's turn to die, a victim of a misplaced Israeli mine field during the Yom Kippur War. Aaron had been eighteen that summer, frail from the asthma that had afflicted him from infancy. David, his father, foiled every scheme Aaron came up with to enter the fray.

Aaron had his heart set on being a commando or paratrooper like his brother Isaac. When all of the services rejected him because of his asthma and poor vision, the boy finished college and then played his final card. Aaron approached his father and asked David . . . pleaded with David . . . to use his old contacts in the nation's intelligence service to find him a position. Aaron entered the Mossad in June of 1974.

He was not trained as a field agent; Israel had too many ex-commandos and other heroes serving in the Mossad to need to put this slight, cerebral young man always hovering on the edge of ill health, in such a demanding role. Aaron did receive the standard training in self-defense and weapons' handling, even becoming minimally proficient in using the little .22 Berettas favored by the Mossad at the time, but his real skill had been at cryptography. After three years working at communications in Tel Aviv and another year in the field somewhere in the Sinai, Aaron had come to Washington to work with a task force at the Israeli Embassy. The fact that he was David Eshkol's son had not hurt the chances for such a choice appointment.

"How are you, Uncle Saul?" Aaron asked in Hebrew.

"Well," said Saul. "Speak English please."

"All right." There was no hint of accent.

"How are your father and brother?"

"Better even than the last time we spoke," said Aaron. "The doctors think that Father will be able to spend some time at the farm this summer. Isaac has been promoted to colonel."

"Good, good," said Saul. He glanced down at the three dossiers his nephew had set out on the table. He was trying to think of a way to reverse events so that he had never involved the boy, while still getting whatever information Aaron had been able to obtain.

As if reading his mind, Aaron leaned forward and said in an urgent whisper, "Uncle Saul, *what* are you involved in here?"

Saul blinked. Six days ago he had called Aaron and asked him if he could get any information on William Borden or the whereabouts of Francis Harrington. It had been a stupid thing to do; for many years Saul had avoided going to family or the family's connections, but he had been distraught at the thought of young Harrington's disappearance and desperate that if he went to Charleston, he would miss some crucial bit of information about Borden—about the Oberst. Aaron had called him back on a secure telephone and said, "Uncle Saul, this is about your German colonel, isn't it?" Saul had not denied it. Everyone in the family had known of Uncle Saul's obsession with an elusive Nazi encountered in the camps during the war. "You know the Mossad would never operate in the United States, don't you?" Aaron had added. Saul had said nothing to that and his silence had said everything. He had worked with Aaron's father when the Irgun Zvai Leumi and Haganah were illegal and active, buying American armaments and armaments *factories* to be shipped piece by piece to Palestine, to be reassembled and ready when the Arab armies inevitably rolled across the borders of the newborn Zionist state. "All right," Aaron had responded to the silence, "I will do what I can."

Saul blinked again and took off his glasses to wipe them with a napkin. "*Nu*, what do you mean?" he said. "I was curious about the man Borden. Francis was once a student of mine. He went to Los Angeles to find something out about this man. Probably divorce work, who knows? When Francis did not return on time and Mr. Borden is said to have died, I was asked by a friend, could I help? I thought of you, Aaron."

"Uh-huh," said Aaron. He stared steadily at his uncle, shook his head at last, and sighed. He looked to make sure that no one was in earshot or close enough to see past Saul's back. Then he opened the first dossier. "I flew out to Los Angeles on Monday," Aaron said.

"You did!" Saul was startled. He had meant for his nephew to make a few phone calls in Washington, to use whatever sophisticated computers the Israeli Embassy had these days—especially the office that housed the six Mossad agents—and perhaps even to look into Israeli or American classified files. He did *not* expect the boy to fly off to the West Coast the next day.

Aaron made a gesture with his hand. "It was no trouble," he said. "I had weeks of leave accumulated. Since when have you ever asked anything of us, Uncle Saul? Always it had been give and give and give from you, since I was a child. The money from New York put me through the university at Haifa even though we could have afforded it. So when you ask one little thing, I shouldn't do it?"

Saul rubbed his forehead. "You're no James Bond, Moddy," he said, using Aaron's childhood nickname. "Besides, the Mossad does not operate in the States."

Aaron did not react. "It was a vacation, Uncle Saul," he said. "So do you want to hear what I did on my vacation or not?"

Saul nodded.

"This is where your Mr. Harrington was staying," said Aaron, sliding across a black and white photograph of a hotel in Beverly Hills. Saul left the picture flat on the table as he looked at it and slid it back.

"I learned very little," said Aaron. "Mr. Harrington checked in on December eighth. A waitress remembered that a red-haired young man fitting

Harrington's description had breakfast in the hotel coffee shop the morning of the ninth. A porter *thinks* he remembers seeing a man driving the
yellow Datsun like the one Harrington rented leave the hotel parking lot
at about three P.M. that Tuesday. He couldn't be sure." Aaron slipped
across two more sheets of paper. "Here are photocopies of the newspaper
article . . . one paragraph . . . and the police report. The yellow Datsun
was found parked near the airport Hertz office on Wednesday, the tenth.
The Hertz people eventually billed Harrington's mother. An anonymous
money order for the $329.48 hotel bill arrived in the mail on Monday, the
fifteenth. Same day I got there. The envelope was postmarked New York.
Would you know anything about that, Uncle Saul?"

Saul looked at him.

"I didn't think so," said Aaron. He closed the dossier. "What makes
this really strange is that Mr. Harrington's two part-time assistants in his
amateur detective agency—Dennis Leland and Selby White—were killed
in an automobile accident that same week. Friday, December twelfth.
They were driving from New York to Boston after receiving a long distance call. . . . What's the matter, Uncle Saul?"

"Nothing."

"You looked sort of sick there for a second. Did you know these two
guys? White had gone to Princeton with Harrington . . . he's from the
Hyannis Port Whites."

"I met them once," said Saul. "Go on."

Aaron squinted slightly at his uncle. Saul remembered the same expression on a small boy's face when the child was not certain about the
veracity of his uncle's fantastic bedtime stories. "So whatever happened, it
sounds very professional," said Aaron. "Something the American crime
families—the new Mafia—would carry out. Three hits. Very clean. Two
of the bodies in an automobile accident; the truck that ran them off the
road still unaccounted for. The third body gone for good. But the question is, what was Francis Harrington working on in California that would
so upset the professionals—if it was the Mafia—that they would go back
to their old style of doing things? And why all three? Leland and White
had real jobs, their involvement with Harrington's half-assed detective
agency was an occasional weekend lark. Harrington had about three cases
last year, and two of them were divorce things for friends. The third was a
waste of time where he tried to track down some poor old schmuck's biological parents forty-eight years after they deserted him."

"Where did you learn all this?" Saul asked softly.

"I talked to Francis's part-time secretary after I got back on Wednesday
and visited the office one evening."

"I take it back, Moddy. You do have a streak of James Bond in you."

"Uh-huh," said Aaron. He looked around. The restaurant was no longer serving lunch and the tables were thinning out as people left. Enough
slow eaters were left so as not to make Saul and Aaron conspicuous, yet no

one sat within fifteen feet of them. Somewhere in the basement hallway outside the restaurant a child began to cry with a voice like a klaxon. "You ain't heard nothing yet, Uncle Saul," Aaron said in his best cowboy drawl.

"Go on."

"The secretary said Harrington had been getting a lot of phone calls from a man who never identified himself," said Aaron. "The police wanted to know who this guy was. She told them she didn't know . . . and Harrington had kept no records of the case except for travel expenses and so forth. Whatever it was, this new client got Francis busy enough that he got his old college buddies to help him out."

"Uh-huh," said Saul.

Aaron sipped from his coffee cup. "You said Harrington was an old student of yours, Uncle Saul. He didn't have any transcripts in the Columbia record office."

"He audited two courses," said Saul. "*War and Human Behavior* and the *Psychology of Aggression*. Francis did not fail at Princeton because he was slow . . . he was brilliant and bored. My classes did not bore him. Now go on, Moddy."

Aaron's mouth was set in a determined way that reminded Saul of David Eshkol's most stubborn expression when the two would argue the morality of guerrilla warfare late into the pale night on the farm outside of Tel Aviv. "The secretary told the police that Harrington's client sounded like a Jew," said Aaron. "She told me she could always tell a Jew by the way they spoke. This one sounded foreign. German or Hungarian maybe."

"*Nu?*"

"Are you going to tell me what's going on, Uncle Saul?"

"Not right now, Moddy. I do not know for sure myself."

Aaron's mouth remained set. He tapped the other two dossiers. They were thicker than the first one. "I've got some other stuff here that is a lot wilder than the dead end with Harrington," he said. "It seems to me that it would be a fair trade."

Saul raised his eyebrows slightly. "So now it is a transaction, not a favor?"

Aaron sighed and opened the second folder. "Borden, William D. Supposedly born August 8, 1906, in Hubbard, Ohio, but no documentation between birth certificate in 1906 and a sudden rush of social security cards, driver's licenses, and so forth, in 1946. It's the kind of thing the FBI computers usually pay attention to, but no one seems to have given a damn in this case. My guess is that if we visited cemeteries around Hubbard, Ohio . . . wherever the hell that is . . . we'd find a little gravestone for Baby Billy Borden, may angels fly him to his rest, et cetera, et cetera. Meanwhile, our grown-up Mr. Borden seems to have popped into existence in Newark, New Jersey, in early 'forty-six. Moved to New York City the next year. Whoever he was, he had money. He was one of those invisible backers of Broadway plays during the 'forty-eight and 'forty-nine seasons. Bought in with the big boys but didn't wine and dine with them it seems . . . at least I can't find any gossip about it in the old columns and none of the old crones who work for some of the old-line producers and agents remember him.

"Anyway, Borden went out to Los Angeles in 1950, bankrolled his first picture that same year, and has been a fixture ever since. He became more visible in the sixties. Hollywood insiders knew him as The Kraut or Big Bill Borden. Threw occasional parties, but never a loud enough one to get the cops involved. The man was a saint . . . no traffic violations, no tickets for jaywalking . . . nothing. Either that or he had enough clout to get anything naughty taken off the record. What do you think, Uncle Saul?"

"What else do you have?"

"Nothing," said Aaron. "Nothing except some studio flack stuff, a photo of Herr Borden's front gate in Bel Air . . . you can't see the house . . . and the *L.A. Times* and *Variety* clippings about his death in that airline crash last Saturday."

"Could I see those, please?" asked Saul.

When Saul had finished reading, Aaron said quietly, "Was he your German, Uncle Saul? Your Oberst?"

"Probably," said Saul. "I wanted to know."

"And you sent Francis Harrington out to find out the same week that Borden dies in an airline bombing."

"Yes."

"And your ex-student and both of his associates die during the same three-day period."

"I did not know about Dennis and Selby until you told me," said Saul. "I had no real idea that they could be in danger."

"In danger from *whom*?" pressed Aaron.

"I honestly do not know at this point," said Saul.

"Tell me what you do know, Uncle Saul. Perhaps we can help."

"We?"

"Levi. Dan. Jack Cohen and Mr. Bergman."

"Embassy people?"

"Jack is my supervisor but also a friend," said Aaron. "Tell us what's going on and we'll help."

"No," said Saul.

"No you can't tell me or no you won't?"

Saul looked back over his shoulder. "The restaurant will be closing up in a few minutes," he said. "Should we go elsewhere?"

The muscles at the corners of Aaron's mouth tightened. "Three of those people . . . that couple near the entrance and the young guy nearest you . . . are our people. They will stay as long as we need others here."

"So you've told them already?"

"No, only Levi. He did the camera work anyway."

"What camera work?"

Aaron slid a photograph out of the third and fattest dossier. It showed a small man with dark hair, on open-collared shirt and leather coat, dark, hooded eyes, and a cruel mouth. He was crossing a narrow street, his coat open and flying back. "Who is he?" asked Saul.

"Harod," said Aaron. "Tony Harod."

"William Borden's associate," said Saul. "His name was in the *Variety* article."

Aaron slid two more photographs out of the dossier. Harod was standing in front of a garage door, holding a credit card, apparently ready to insert it in a small device set into the brick wall. Saul had seen such security locks before. "Where was this taken?" he asked.

"Georgetown, four days ago."

"*This* Georgetown?" asked Saul. "What was he doing in Washington? What were you doing photographing him?"

"Levi photographed him," said Aaron with a smile. "I attended Mr. Borden's memorial service at Forest Lawn on Monday. Tony Harod gave the eulogy. What small background check I had time for suggested that Mr. Harod was very close to your Mr. Borden. When Harod flew to Washington on Tuesday, I followed him. It was time to come home anyway."

Saul shook his head. "So you followed him to Georgetown."

"I didn't have to, Uncle Saul. I'd phoned Levi and he followed him from the airport. I joined him later. That's when we got the photos. I wanted to talk to you before we showed the photographs to Dan or Mr. Bergman."

Saul frowned at the two photographs. "I don't see any special significance to these," he said. "Is the address important?"

"No," said Aaron. "It's a town house leased to Bechtronics, a subsidiary of HRL Industries."

Saul shrugged. "Is that important?"

"No," said Aaron, "these are." He moved five more photographs across the tabletop. "Levi had his Bell Telephone van," said Aaron with a tone of some satisfaction. "He was thirty feet up on a utility pole when he got these pictures of them leaving by the alley. The alley is perfectly shielded otherwise. These guys go down the covered back sidewalk here, open the gate, and step right into the limousine and go. Neighbors couldn't see them. Wouldn't be visible from the end of the alley. Perfect."

The black and white photographs had caught each man in the same instant of stepping between gate and limousine; the prints were grainy from being greatly enlarged. Saul studied each one carefully and said, "They mean nothing to me, Moddy."

Aaron cradled his head in his hands. "How long have you lived in this country, Uncle Saul?" When Saul said nothing, Aaron stabbed a finger at the photo of a man with small eyes, generous jowls, and a full head of wavy, white hair. "This is James Wayne Sutter, better known to the faithful as the Reverend Jimmy Wayne. Ring any bells?"

"No," said Saul.

"TV evangelist," said Aaron. "Started with a drive-in movie church in Dothan, Alabama, in 1964, and now has his own satellite and cable channels and tax-free corporate income profits of about seventy-eight million dollars a year. His politics are a little to the right of Attila the Hun. If Reverend Jimmy Wayne announces that the Soviet Union is Satan's instrument—which he does every day on the tube—about twelve million people say 'Hallelujah.' Even Prime Minister Begin makes overtures to the schmuck. Some of their love donations end up coming to Israel in the form of weapons purchases. Anything to save the Holy Land."

"It's no news that Israel has made contacts with these fundamentalist right-wingers," said. Saul. "So this was what worked you and your friend Levi up? Maybe Mr. Harod is a believer."

Aaron was agitated. He set the photos of Harod and Sutter back in the folder and smiled at the waitress as she came over to refill his coffee cup. The restaurant was almost empty now. When she moved away, Aaron said with some excitement, "Jimmy Wayne Sutter is the least of our worries here, Uncle Saul. Do you recognize this man?" He touched the photograph of a thin-faced man with dark hair and deep-set eyes.

"No."

"Nieman Trask," said Aaron. "Close adviser to Senator Kellog from Maine. Remember? Kellog almost got the nod for the vice-presidential slot on the party ticket last summer."

"Really?" said Saul. "Which party?"

Aaron shook his head. "Uncle Saul, what do you *do* if you don't pay any attention to things going on around you?"

Saul smiled. "Not much," he said. "I teach three undergraduate courses each week. Still serve as faculty adviser even though I don't have to. Have a full research schedule at the clinic. My second book is due at the publishers on January sixth . . ."

"All right . . ." said Aaron.

"I still contribute at least twelve hours of direct counseling at the clinic each week. I traveled to four seminars in December, two of them in Europe, delivered papers at all four . . ."

"OK," said Aaron.

"Last week was unusual because I only hosted the one university panel," said Saul. "Usually the Major's Commission and the State Advisory Council take up at least two evenings. Now, Moddy, why is Mr. Trask so important? Because he is one of Senator Kellog's advisers?"

"Not *one*," said Aaron, "*the* adviser. The word is that Kellog doesn't go to the bathroom without checking with Nieman Trask. Also, Trask was the big fund-raiser for the party during the last campaign. The saying is that wherever he goes, money flows."

"Cute," said Saul. "What about this gentleman?" He tapped the forehead of a man who bore a slight resemblance to the actor Charlton Heston.

"Joseph Phillip Kepler," said Aaron. "Ex-number three man in Lyndon Johnson's CIA, ex-State Department troubleshooter, and currently a media consultant and commentator on PBS."

"Yes," said Saul, "he did look familiar. He has a Sunday evening program?"

"*Rapid Fire*," said Aaron. "Invites government bureaucrats on to embarrass them. This one"—Aaron tapped the photograph of a short bald man with a scowl—"is Charles C. Colben, Special Assistant to the Deputy Director of the Federal Bureau of Investigation."

"Interesting title," said Saul. "It could mean nothing or everything."

"It means a hell of a lot in this case," said Aaron. "Colben is about the only one of the middle-level Watergate suspects that didn't serve time. He was the White House contact in the FBI. Some say he was the brains behind Gordon Liddy's antics. Instead of being indicted, he became even more important after all the other heads rolled."

"What does all this mean, Moddy?"

"Just a minute, Uncle Saul, we've saved the best for last." Aaron put away all the photographs except for that of a thin, exquisitely tailored man in his early or mid-sixties. The gray hair was distinguished, its styling impeccable. Even in the grainy black and white print, Saul could see the combination of tan and clothes and subliminal sense of command that only great wealth could bring.

"C. Arnold Barent," said Aaron, paused for a second, and went on, "the 'friend of presidents.' Every First Family since Eisenhower's has spent at least one vacation at one of Barent's hideaways. Barent's father was in steel and railroads . . . a mere millionaire . . . poverty-stricken compared to Barent Jr. and his billions. Fly over any section of Manhattan and pick a skyscraper, any skyscraper, and odds are better than even that one of the corporations on the top floor is owned by a parent company that is a subsidiary of a conglomerate that is managed by a consortium that is principally owned by C. Arnold Barent. Media, microchips, movie studios, oil, art, or baby food Barent has a part of it."

"What does the 'C' stand for?" asked Saul.

"No one has the foggiest idea," said Aaron. "C. Arnold, Sr., never revealed it and the son isn't talking. Anyway, the Secret Service loves it when the president and his family visit. Barent's homes are usually on islands . . . he owns islands all over the world, Uncle Saul . . . and the layout, security, helipad facilities, satellite links, and so forth are better than the White House's.

"Once a year—usually in June—Barent's Heritage West Foundation runs its 'summer camp'—a week-long bash for some of the biggest little boys in the Western Hemisphere. The thing is by invitation only and to be invited you have to be at least cabinet level and up-and-coming . . . or over the hill and a legend in your own time. The rumors that've come out the past few years tell of German ex-chancellors dancing around the campfires singing bawdy songs with old American secretaries of state and

an ex-president or two. It's supposed to be a place where the leaders can
let everything hang out . . . is that the American phrase, Uncle Saul?"

"Yes," said Saul. He watched as Aaron put the last photograph away.
"So tell me what it means, Aaron. Why did Tony Harod from Hollywood
go to a clandestine meeting with these five people whom I should—God
knows—have known, and didn't?"

Aaron put the dossiers in his briefcase and folded his hands. The
corners of his mouth pulled tight. "*You* tell *me*, Uncle Saul. An ex-Nazi
producer, you think he is your ex-Nazi, is killed in an airline crash that
probably was the result of a bomb. You send a rich college boy playing
detective to Hollywood to look into the producer's history and your
friend is abducted . . . almost certainly killed . . . as are his two amateur colleagues. A week later your Nazi-producer's associate . . . a man
who, by all accounts, combines all the charm of a charlatan and a child
molester . . . flies to Washington and meets with the strangest assortment
of insiders and shady powerbrokers since Yassir Arafat's first Executive
Council meeting. What's going *on*, Uncle Saul?"

Saul took his glasses off and cleaned the lenses. He did not speak for a
full minute. Aaron waited. "Moddy," Saul said at last, "I do not know what
is going on. I was interested only in the Oberst . . . in the man I believe to
have been William D. Borden. I have never heard of *any* of these people
before today. I had no idea who Borden was until I saw his photograph in
the Sunday *New York Times* and felt sure that he was Oberst Wilhelm von
Borchert, Waffen SS . . ." Saul stopped, put his glasses on, and touched his
forehead with shaking fingers. He knew that he must look to his nephew
like a shaken, confused old man. At that moment it was not an act.

"Uncle Saul, you can tell me what is wrong," Aaron said in Hebrew.
"Let me help."

Saul nodded. He felt tears come to his eyes and he looked away quickly.

"If it could possibly have any importance to Israel," pressed Aaron, "be
any threat . . . we need to work together, Uncle Saul."

Saul sat straight up. *Be any threat.* He suddenly could see his father
carrying little Josef in that line of pale, naked men and boys at Chelmno,
feel the sting of the slap and humiliation on his own cheek again, and
knew precisely . . . as his father had known precisely . . . that saving family sometimes *had* to be the first priority, the only priority. He took Aaron's
hand in both of his. "Moddy . . . you must trust me in this. I think many
things are happening here that have nothing to do with one another. The
man I thought was the Oberst I had known in the camps probably was not.
Francis Harrington was brilliant but unstable . . . he dropped out of every
responsibility the way he dropped out of Princeton three years ago. I gave
him an embarrassingly large advance on expenses so that he could look
into William Borden's background. I am sure that Francis's mother . . . or
secretary . . . or girlfriend will get a postcard from him, postmarked Bora
Bora or somesuch place, any day now . . ."

"Uncle Saul . . ."

"Please, Moddy, listen. Francis's friends . . . they died in an accident. You've never known anyone who died in an accident? Your cousin Chaim, maybe, driving his Jeep down from the Golan to see a girl little better than a *nafkeh* . . ."

"Uncle Saul . . ."

"*Listen*, Moddy. You're playing James Bond again the way you used to play Superman. You remember? The summer I visited . . . you were nine . . . too old to be leaping from the terrace with a towel around your neck. The whole summer you couldn't play with your favorite uncle because of the cast on your left leg."

Aaron blushed and looked down at his hands.

"Your pictures are interesting, Moddy. But what do they suggest? A conspiracy against Jerusalem? A cell of Arafat's Fatah ready to ship bombs to the border? *Moddy*, you saw rich, powerful people meeting with a pornographer in a rich, powerful city. Do you think that was a *secret* meeting? You said yourself, C. Arnold Barent owns islands and homes where even the president is safer than in his own home. This was just not a *public* meeting. Who knows what dirty little movie deals these people put money into or what dirty little movies your Born-Again Reverend Wayne Jim bankrolls."

"Jimmy Wayne," said Aaron.

"Whatever," said Saul. "Do you really think we should bother your superiors at the embassy and get *real* agents involved and perhaps even let all this come to the attention of David, sick as he is, for some *meshuggener* meeting to discuss some dirty movie or something?"

Aaron's thin face was beet red. For a second Saul thought the young man was going to cry. "All right, Uncle Saul, you *won't* tell me anything?"

Saul touched his nephew's hand again. "I swear to you on your mother's grave, Moddy, I've told you everything that makes sense to me. I'll be in Washington another day or two. Perhaps I could come over and see you and Deborah again and we could talk. Across the river, isn't it?"

"Alexandria," said Aaron. "Yes. What about tonight?"

"I have a meeting," said Saul. "But tomorrow . . . I would love a home-cooked meal." Saul looked over his shoulder at the three Israelis who now made up the rest of the restaurant's clientele. "What do we tell them?"

Aaron adjusted his own glasses. "Only Levi knows why we're here. We were all going out to lunch anyway . . ." Aaron looked fiercely into Saul's eyes. "Do you know what you're doing, Uncle Saul?"

"Yes," said Saul, "I do. And right now I want to do as little as possible, relax a bit over the rest of the vacation, and prepare for January's classes. Moddy, you wouldn't have one of them"—Saul cocked his head—"follow me or anything, would you? It might be embarrassing to a certain . . . ah, female colleague I hope to have dinner with tonight."

Aaron grinned. "We couldn't spare the manpower anyway," he said.

"Only Levi there has any field status. Harry and Barbara work with me in ciphers." Both men stood. "Tomorrow, Uncle Saul? Shall I come in to pick you up?"

"No, I have a rental car," said Saul. "About six?"

"Earlier if you can," said Aaron. "You'll have time to play with the twins before dinner."

"Four-thirty then," said Saul.

"And we will talk?"

"I promise," said Saul.

The two men walked up the stairs to the area under the dome, hugged, and went their separate ways. Saul stood just inside the gift shop until he saw Harry, Barbara, and the swarthy man named Levi depart together. Then he went slowly upstairs to the Impressionist section.

The girl in the straw hat was still waiting, looking up and out with the slightly startled, slightly puzzled, slightly hurt expression that moved something within Saul. He stood there a long time, thinking about family and about vengeance and about fear. He found himself wondering about his own morality—if not about his sanity—at involving two goyim in what could never be their struggle.

He decided that he would go back to the hotel, take a very long and very hot shower, and read a bit of the Mortimer Adler book. Then, when the rates went down, he would call Charleston, talk to both Natalie and the sheriff if possible. He would tell them that his meeting had gone well; that he knew now that the producer who had died on the flight from Charleston had not been the German colonel who haunted his nightmares. He would admit that he had been under stress recently and let them draw their own conclusions about his analysis of Nina Drayton and the events in Charleston.

Saul was still in front of the painting of the girl in the straw hat and was lost deep in thought when the low voice behind him said, "It's a very pretty picture, is it not? It seems so sad that the girl who posed for it must be dead and rotted away by now."

Saul spun around. Francis Harrington stood there, eyes gleaming strangely, freckled face as pale as a death mask. The slack lips jerked upward as if pulled by hooks and strings until a rictal grimace showed a wide expanse of teeth in a terrible simulation of a smile. The arms and hands moved upward as if to embrace or engulf Saul.

"*Guten Tag, mein alte Freund,*" said the thing that had been Francis Harrington. "*Wie geht's, mein kleiner Bauer?* . . . My favorite little pawn?"

SIXTEEN

Charleston
Thursday, Dec. 25, 1980

The lobby of the hospital held a three-foot silver Christmas tree set in the center of the waiting area. Five empty but brightly wrapped presents were scattered around its base and children had made paper ornaments to hang from the branches. Sunlight painted white and yellow rectangles on the tile floor.

Sheriff Bobby Joe Gentry nodded at the receptionist as he crossed the lobby and headed for the elevators. "Mornin' and Merry Christmas, Miz Howells," he called. Gentry punched the elevator button and stood waiting with a large white paper sack in his arms.

"Merry Christmas, Sheriff!" called the seventy-year-old volunteer. "Oh, Sheriff, could I bother you for a second?"

"No bother, ma'am." Gentry ignored the opening elevator doors and walked over to the woman's desk. She wore a pastel-green smock that clashed with the darker green of plastic pine boughs on the Formica counter in front of her. Two Silhouette romance novels lay read and discarded near her rolodex. "How can I help you, Miz Howell?" asked Gentry.

The old woman leaned forward and lowered her bifocals so that they hung by their beaded chain. "It's about that colored woman on four they brought in last night," she began in an excited whisper that fell just short of sounding conspiratorial.

"Yes'm?"

"Nurse Oleander says that you were sitting up there all night . . . sort of like a guard . . . and that you had a deputy there outside the room this morning when you had to leave . . ."

"That's Lester," said Gentry. He shifted the weight of the sack against his shirt. "Lester and I are the only one's in the sheriff's office that aren't married 'n' all. We tend to hold down the holiday duty."

"Well, yes," said Mrs. Howell, thrown off the track a bit, "but we were wondering, Nurse Oleander and I, it being Christmas Eve and morning and everything, well . . . what was this colored girl *charged* with? I mean, I know it may be official business and everything, but it is true that this girl is a suspect in the Mansard House murders and had to be brought in by force?"

Gentry smiled and leaned forward. "Miz Howell, can you keep a secret?"

The receptionist set her thick glasses back in place, pursed her lips, sat very erect, and nodded. "Certainly, Sheriff," she said. "Whatever you tell me won't go any further than this desk."

Gentry nodded and leaned over farther to whisper close to her ear. "Ms. Preston is my fiancée. She doesn't like the idea much so I've been keeping her locked up down in my cellar. She tried to up and get away last night while we was out wassailing so I had to whup her one. Lester's up there holdin' a gun on her now 'til I get back."

Gentry looked back once to wink before entering the elevator. Ms. Howell's posture was as perfect as before, but her glasses had slipped down to the tip of her nose and her mouth hung slightly open.

Natalie looked up as Gentry entered the double room she had all to herself.

"Good mornin' and Merry Christmas!" he called. He pulled her wheeled tray over and plunked the white sack onto it. "Ho, ho, ho."

"Merry Christmas," said Natalie. Her voice was strained and husky. She winced and raised her left hand to her throat.

"Seen the bruises there yet?" asked Gentry, leaning forward to inspect them again himself.

"Yes," whispered Natalie.

"Whoever did that had fingers like Van Cliburn," said Gentry. "How's your head?"

Natalie touched the large bandage on the left side of her head. "What happened?" she asked huskily. "I mean, I remember being choked but not hitting my head . . ."

Gentry began removing white Styrofoam food cartons from the sack. "Doctor been in yet?"

"Not since I've been awake."

"Doc thinks you banged it against the door frame of the car when you were strugglin' with the fella," said Gentry. He took the lid off of large Styrofoam cups of steaming coffee and plastic glasses of orange juice. "Just a bruise that bled a little. It was the chokin' that knocked you out."

Natalie touched her throat and winced at the memory. "Now I know what it's like to be strangled," she whispered with a weak smile.

Gentry shook his head. "Nope. He knocked you out with a choke hold, but it was by shuttin' blood off to the brain, not by shutting air off. Knew what he was doing. Bit more and there'd've been brain damage at the very least. You want an English muffin with your scrambled eggs?"

Natalie stared at the huge breakfast set out before her: coffee, toasted muffins, eggs, bacon, sausage, orange juice, and fruit. "Where on earth did you get all this?" she asked incredulously. "They already brought a breakfast I couldn't eat . . . a rubber poached egg and weak tea. What restaurant is open on Christmas morning?"

Gentry took his hat off, held it over his heart, and looked hurt. "Restaurant? *Restaurant*? Why, ma'am, this is a Christian God-fearin' city.

There's no restaurant open this mornin' . . .'cept maybe Tom Delphin's diner out to the Interstate. Tom's an agnostic. No, Ma'am, this grub comes from yours truly's kitchen. Now eat up before it all gets cold."

"Thank you . . . Sheriff," said Natalie. "But I can't eat all this . . ."

"Not supposed to," said Gentry. "This is my breakfast too. Here's the pepper."

"But my throat . . ."

"Doc says it'll be sore for a while, but it'll work OK for eating. Eat up."

Natalie opened her mouth, said nothing, and picked up her fork instead.

Gentry removed a small transistor radio from the sack and set it on the table. Most of the FM stations carried Christmas music. He found a classical station playing Handel's *Messiah* and let the music soar.

Natalie appeared to be enjoying her scrambled egg. She took a sip of hot coffee and said, "This is excellent, Sheriff. What about Lester?"

"He's not always best described as excellent," said Gentry.

"No, I mean is he still here?"

"Nope," said Gentry. "He's back at the station 'til noon. Then Stewart comes in to relieve him. Don't worry, Lester has had breakfast already."

"Good coffee," said Natalie. She looked at Gentry over the clutter of Styrofoam containers. "Lester said that you spent the night here."

Gentry managed to combine a gesture in which he removed his hat and shrugged at the same time. "Darn eggs get cold even when I pack 'em in these stupid Styrofoam things," he said.

"Did you think he . . . whoever it was . . . would come back?" asked Natalie.

"Not especially," said Gentry, "but we didn't have too much time to talk before they gave you the shot last night. I figured it wouldn't hurt to have somebody here to chat with you when you woke up."

"So you spent Christmas Eve in a hospital chair," said Natalie.

Gentry grinned at her. "What the heck. It's more fun than watching Mr. Magoo as Scrooge for the twentieth year."

"How did you find me so fast last night?" asked Natalie, her voice still husky but not as strained as before.

"Well, we'd agreed to get together, after all," said Gentry. "When you weren't home and my answerin' machine didn't have a message on it, I just sort of drove by the Fuller place on the way home. I knew you had a habit of checking it out."

"But you didn't see my assailant?"

"Nope. Just you in the front seat, sort of hunkered over holding a bloodied camera."

Natalie shook her head. "I still don't remember hitting him with the camera," she said. "I was trying to reach Dad's gun."

"Mmmm, that reminds me," said Gentry. He walked over to the green sheriff's jacket he had hung on a chair and removed the .32 automatic from a pocket and set it on the far end of the tray table near Natalie's orange juice. "I put the safety back on," he said. "It's still loaded."

Natalie lifted a wedge of toast but did not bite into it. "Who *was* it?"

Gentry shook his head. "You say he was white?"

"Yes. I only saw his nose . . . a bit of cheek . . . and his eyes, but I'm sure he was white . . ."

"Age?"

"I'm not sure. I had the sense he was about your age . . . early thirties maybe."

"Do you remember anything you didn't tell me last night?" asked Gentry.

"No, I don't think so," said Natalie. "He was in the car when I ran back to it. He must have been on the floor in the back . . ." Natalie put down the toast and shivered.

"He broke the overhead light in your car," said Gentry, finishing the last of his scrambled eggs. "That's why it didn't come on when you opened the door on the driver's side. You say you saw a light on the second floor of the Fuller house?"

"Yes. Not the hall light or in her bedroom. Perhaps from the guest room up there. I could see it through the gaps in the shutters."

"Here, finish up," said Gentry, pushing the small plate of bacon toward her. "Did you know that the electricity was turned off in the Fuller house?"

Natalie's eyebrows went up. "No," she said.

"Probably was a flashlight," said Gentry, "Maybe one of those big electric lanterns."

"Then you believe me?"

Gentry was closing up his Styrofoam containers and tossing them in the wastebasket nearby. He paused to stare at her. "Why wouldn't I believe you? You didn't put those marks on your throat all by yourself."

"But why would anyone try to kill me?" asked Natalie in a voice smaller than her sore throat demanded.

Gentry packed up the dishes and containers in front of her. "Uh-uh," he said. "Whoever this guy was, he wasn't tryin' to kill you. He wanted to *hurt* you . . ."

"He succeeded there," said Natalie, gingerly touching her throat and bandaged head.

". . . and to *scare* you."

"Ditto there," said Natalie. She looked around. "God, I hate hospitals."

"And there was what he said," said Gentry. "Tell me again."

Natalie closed her eyes. "You want to find the woman? Look in Germantown."

"Say it again," urged Gentry. "Try to put it in the same tone, the same phrasing as you heard it."

Natalie repeated it in a flat, emotionless tone.

"That's it?" said Gentry. "No accent or dialect?"

"Not really," said Natalie. "Very flat. Rather like a radio announcer giving the weather on an FM station."

"Not a local sound," said Gentry.

"No."

"A Yankee dialect maybe?" asked Gentry. He repeated the phrase with a New York accent so pronounced and accurate that Natalie laughed out loud in spite of her sore throat.

"No," she said.

"New England? German? New Jersey—Jewish-American?" asked Gentry and performed flawlessly in all three dialects.

"No," laughed Natalie. "You're good," she said. "No, it was just . . . flat."

"How about tone and pitch?"

"Deep, but not nearly as deep as yours" said Natalie. "Sort of a soft baritone."

"Could it have been a woman?" asked Gentry.

Natalie blinked. She thought of the glimpse in the mirror, red already clotting her vision—the thin face, slash of cheek, slate eyes. She thought of the strength of the arms and hands. *It could have been a woman*, she thought. *A very powerful woman.* "No," she said aloud. "It's just a feeling, but it *felt* like a man's attack, if you know what I mean. Not that I've been attacked by men before. And it wasn't sexual or anything . . ." She stopped, flustered.

"I know what you mean," said Gentry. "Anyway, that's another clue that whoever he was, he wasn't trying to kill you. People usually don't give messages to someone they're in the act of murdering."

"Message to whom?" said Natalie.

"Maybe 'warning' is a better word," suggested Gentry. "Anyway the attack went into the log as a random assault and possible attempted rape. I could hardly label it a robbery attempt since he didn't take your purse or anything." He cleared away everything except their coffee cups and pulled a short thermos out of the depleted white sack. "Feel up to a little more coffee?"

Natalie hesitated. "Sure," she finally said and pushed her cup toward him. "This stuff usually makes me very jittery, but it seems to be counteracting the effects of that shot they gave me last night."

"Besides," said Gentry, pouring coffee for both of them, "it's Christmas." They sat awhile listening to the triumphant conclusion of *Messiah*.

When it was finished and the announcer was discussing the program, Natalie said, "I didn't really have to stay here last night, did I?"

"You had a pretty bad trauma," said Gentry. "You'd been unconscious for at least ten minutes. Your scalp took eight stitches from where you hit the shoulder harness clip."

"But I could have gone home, right?"

"Probably," said Gentry. "But I didn't want you to. It wouldn't have been a good idea for you to stay alone, you weren't in any shape to deal with a suggestion to come to my place, and I didn't want to spend Christmas Eve sitting in my unmarked car outside your house. Besides, you *should* have stayed overnight for observation. Even the doc said so."

"I would have come to your place," Natalie said softly. There was no hint of coquettishness in her voice. "I'm scared," she said simply.

Gentry nodded. "Yeah." He finished his coffee. "I am too. I'm not even sure why, but I've got a feeling we're neck deep in something we don't understand."

"So you still believe Saul's story?"

"I'd feel better if we'd heard from him since he left six days ago," said Gentry. "But we don't have to buy every part of his story to know that something's going on around us."

"Do you think you'll catch whoever attacked me last night?" asked Natalie. Suddenly tired, she lay back on the pillows and adjusted the bed to a more upright position.

"Not if we depend on fingerprints or forensic stuff," said Gentry. "We're checkin' into the blood on the Nikon, but that won't tell us much. The only way we're going to find out is by continuing some sort of investigation."

"Or waiting for the guy to come after me again," said Natalie.

"Uh-uh," said Gentry. "I don't think so. I think they delivered their message."

" 'You want to find the woman? Look in Germantown,' " intoned Natalie. "The woman would be Melanie Fuller?"

"Can you think of anyone else?"

"No. Where is Germantown? Is it a real place? Do you think it relates to Saul's Oberst in some way . . . like a code?"

"I know of a couple of Germantowns," said Gentry. "Parts of cities in the north. Philadelphia has an historic section with that name, I think. But there may be a hundred towns around the country actually named that. My little atlas didn't show them, but I'll get to a library to check better references. It doesn't sound like a code . . . just a place name."

"But why would somebody tell us where she is?" asked Natalie. "And who would know? And why tell us?"

"Great questions," said Gentry. "I don't have any answers yet. If Saul's story is true, then there seems to be a lot more to this than even he understood."

"Could that guy last night have been . . . like an agent for Mrs. Fuller herself? Somebody she used the way Saul said the Oberst used him? Could she still be in Charleston, trying to throw us off the track?"

"Sure," said Gentry, "but every scenario like that *I* come up with is full of holes. If Melanie Fuller is alive and in Charleston, why tip her hand to us in any way? Who the hell are *we*? They've got two city agencies, three state law enforcement divisions, and the damned FBI lookin' into this. All three TV networks did stories last week, there were fifty reporters at the D.A.'s press conference a week ago Monday, and a few of them are still sniffin' around . . . though they don't pay too much attention to our office anymore. Another reason I didn't specify in the log that you were parked right across from the Fuller house last night. I can see the *National Perspirer* headlines: KILLER CHARLESTON HOUSE ALMOST CLAIMS ANOTHER VICTIM."

"So which scenario makes the most sense to you?" asked Natalie.

Gentry finished tidying up the room, moved the tray table aside, and sat on the edge of her bed. For a big man, he gave a strange sense of lightness and grace, as if there were a honed athlete beneath the pink skin and fat. "Let's say Saul's story was true," Gentry said softly. "Then we've got the situation where we had several of these mind vampires turnin' on one another. Nina Drayton's dead. I saw the body before and after the trip to the morgue. Whatever else she was, she's a memory now . . . ashes . . . folks who claimed her body had her cremated."

"Who claimed the body?" asked Natalie.

"Not family," said Gentry. "Nor friends, really. A New York lawyer who was executor of her estate and two members of a corporation that she served on the Board of Directors of."

"So Nina Drayton is gone," said Natalie. "Who does that leave?"

Gentry held up three fingers. "Melanie Fuller, William Borden . . . Saul's Oberst . . ."

"That's two," said Natalie, staring at the remaining finger. "Who's left?"

"A set of millions of unknowns," said Gentry and waggled all ten fingers. "Hey, I've got a Christmas present for you." He went over to his jacket and returned with an envelope. Inside were a Christmas card and airline tickets.

"A flight back to St. Louis," said Natalie. "For tomorrow."

"Yep. There weren't any available for today."

"Are you running me out of town, Sheriff?"

"You could say that." Gentry grinned at her. "I know it's taking liberties, Miz Preston, but I'd feel a hell of a lot better if you were out and away from here until all this nonsense is over."

"I don't know how I feel about this," said Natalie. "Why am I safer back in St. Louis? If someone's after me, why couldn't they just follow me there?"

Gentry folded his arms. "That's a good point, but I don't think someone's *after* you, do you?" When she did not answer he went on, "Anyway, you told me the other day that you had friends there . . . Frederick could stay with you . . ."

"I don't need a bodyguard or baby-sitter," said Natalie in a cold voice.

"No," said Gentry, "but back there you'd be busy and surrounded by friends. And you'd be out of whatever is going on here."

"What about finding my father's killer?" said Natalie. "What about watching the Fuller house until Saul gets in touch?"

"I'm going to have a deputy keep a watch on the Fuller house," said Gentry. "I OK'd it with Mrs. Hodges to have someone stay in her house . . . upstairs in Mr. Hodges's den. It looks down on the courtyard."

"And what will you be doing?"

Gentry lifted his hat off the bed, creased the crown, and put it on. "I sorta thought I'd take a vacation," he said.

"A vacation!" Natalie was startled. "In the middle of all of this? With everything going on?"

Gentry smiled. "That's almost exactly what they said downtown. Thing is though, I haven't gone on vacation for the last two years and the county owes me at least five weeks. Guess I can take a week or two off if I want to."

"When do you start?" asked Natalie.

"Tomorrow."

"And where will you be going?" There was more than curiosity in Natalie's voice.

Gentry rubbed his cheek. "Well, I thought I might mosey up north and visit New York for a few days. Been a long time since I've been there. Then I thought I'd spend a day or two in Washington."

"Looking for Saul," said Natalie.

"I may look him up," drawled Gentry. He glanced at his watch. "Hey, it's getting late. Doc should drop by about nine. You can probably leave right after that." He paused. "Let's back the conversation up to where you said you would have come to my place to be a houseguest . . ."

Natalie propped herself up on the pillows. "Is that an invitation?" she asked.

"Yes'm," said Gentry. "I'd feel better if you didn't spend much time at your place before you leave. Course you could get a hotel room somewhere tonight and I could ask Lester or Stewart to work shifts waiting with me on the . . ."

"Sheriff," she said, "before I say yes there's one thing we have to settle."

Gentry looked serious. "Go ahead, ma'am."

"I'm tired of calling you Sheriff and even more tired of being called ma'am," said Natalie. "It's going to be first names or nothing."

"That suits me," said Gentry with a grin, "ma'am."

"There's only one problem" said Natalie. "I can't bring myself to call you Bobby Joe."

"Neither could my folks," said Gentry. "The Bobby Joe didn't catch on until fellows called me that when I was a deputy here in Charleston. I sort of kept it when I ran for office."

"What did the other kids and your folks call you?" asked Natalie.

"The other kids tended to call me Tubby," said Gentry with a smile. "My mother called me Rob."

"Yes," said Natalie. "Thank you for the invitation, Rob. I accept."

They stopped by Natalie's home long enough for her to pack and to call her father's lawyer and a few friends. The settling of the estate and dealings for the sale of the studio would take at least a month. There was no reason for Natalie to stay.

Christmas Day was warm and sunny. Gentry drove slowly and took the long way back to the city, taking Cosgrove Avenue across the Ashley River and coming down Meeting Street. It was a Thursday, but it felt like a Sunday.

They had an early dinner: Gentry prepared baked ham, mashed potatoes, broccoli with cheese sauce, and a chocolate mousse. The round dining room table was set near the large bay windows and the two sipped their coffee and watched the early twilight seep color out of the houses and trees of the neighborhood. Afterward they put on jackets and took a long walk as the first stars came out. Children were being called in from playing with their new toys. Darkened rooms flickered to the colored lights of television.

"Do you think Saul's all right?" asked Natalie. It was the first time since morning that they had discussed serious things.

Gentry stuck his hands deep in his jacket pockets. "I'm not sure," he said. "But I have a feeling that something happened."

"I don't feel right about hiding out in St. Louis," said Natalie. "Whatever's going on, I feel I owe it to my father to follow through on it."

Gentry did not argue. "I'll tell you what," he said. "Let me check out where the professor's got to and then we'll get back in touch and plan our next step. I think it'd be easier for one person to take care of this part."

"But Melanie Fuller might be right here in Charleston," said Natalie. "We don't even know what that guy meant last night."

"I don't think the old lady is here," said Gentry. He told her about Arthur Lewellyn's short drive to the cigar store on the night of the murders—a drive that had ended up with a ninety-seven-mile-per-hour impact with a bridge abutment on the outskirts of Atlanta. "Mr. Lewellyn's cigar store wasn't far from the Mansard House," said Gentry.

"So if Melanie Fuller is capable of what Saul was talking about . . ."

"Yeah," said Gentry. "It's absolutely nuts, but it makes sense."

"So you think she is hiding in Atlanta?"

"I wouldn't think so," said Gentry. "Too close. My guess is she would've flown or driven out of there as soon as possible. So I've been on the phone all week. There was a ruckus out at Hartsfield International Airport a week ago Monday—two days after the murders here. A woman left twelve thousand dollars in cash in a bag there . . . no one could describe her. A redcap there . . . a forty-year-old man with an almost perfect health record . . . died after having a grand mal seizure. I checked into all the deaths that same night. A family of six killed in an accident on I-285 when their station wagon was rear-ended by a semi; the truck driver had fallen asleep. A man in Rockdale Park shot his brother-in-law in a dispute over who owned a boat that had been in the family for years. They found the corpse of a derelict near Atlanta Stadium . . . Sheriff's office said the body had been there almost a week. And a cabdriver named Steven Lenton committed suicide at his home. Police said his friends reported he'd been depressed since his wife left him."

"How can any of that relate to Melanie Fuller?" asked Natalie.

"That's the fun part," said Gentry. "Speculatin'." They came to a small park. Natalie sat on a swing and moved easily back and forth. Gentry held on to the chain of the next swing. "The funny thing about Mr. Lenton's suicide is that it was while he was on duty. Most folks don't take time out from their jobs to kill themselves. You'll never guess where he was when he called in his last fare . . ."

Natalie stopped swinging. "I don't . . . Oh! The airport?"

"Yup."

She shook her head. "That doesn't make any sense. If Melanie Fuller was flying somewhere from the Atlanta airport, why would she leave money behind or bother to kill a redcap or cabdriver?"

"Let's just imagine that something alarmed her," said Gentry. "Maybe she changed her mind in a hurry. The cabdriver's personal car was missing—his ex-wife had been bugging the police about it for almost a week before it finally turned up."

"Where?" asked Natalie.

"Washington, D.C.," said Gentry. "Right downtown."

"None of this makes sense," said Natalie. "Isn't it more likely that the man simply committed suicide and someone stole his car and abandoned it in Washington?"

"Sure," said Gentry. "But the nice thing about Saul Laski's story is that it replaces a long column of coincidences with a single explanation. I've always been a big fan of Occam's Razor."

Natalie smiled and swung high again. "As long as you handle it carefully," she said. "If it gets dull you can cut your own throat."

"Mmmm," said Gentry. He felt very good. The evening air, the rusty, childhood sound of the swing, and Natalie's presence all conspired to make him happy.

Natalie stopped again. "I still want to be involved in this," she said. "Maybe I could go to Atlanta and look into that stuff while you're in Washington."

"Just a few days," said Gentry. "You touch base in St. Louis and I'll be in contact soon."

"That's what Saul Laski said."

"Look," said Gentry, "I have one of those phone-answering devices. I've got an instrument that lets me play back the message over the phone when I can't get home. I always lose things, so I have two of the tone things. You take one. I'll call my own number every day at eleven A.M. and eleven P.M. If you have anything to tell me, just leave it on the recorder. You can check the same way."

Natalie blinked. "Wouldn't it be easier for you just to call me?"

"Yeah, but if you needed to get in touch with me it might be difficult."

"But . . . all your private phone messages . . ."

Gentry grinned at her in the dark. "I have no secrets from you, ma'am," he said. "Or rather, I won't after I give you the electronic thingamawhat-sis."

"I can hardly wait," said Natalie.

Someone was waiting for them when they returned to Gentry's house. From deep within the shadows on the long porch a cigarette glowed. Gentry and Natalie stopped on the stone walk and as the sheriff slowly unzipped his jacket Natalie caught sight of the handle of a revolver tucked in his waistband. "Who's there?" Gentry asked softly.

The cigarette glowed more brightly and then disappeared as a dark shape rose to its feet. Natalie gripped Gentry's left arm as the tall shadow moved toward them, pausing by the front steps of the porch. "Hey there, Rob," came a rich, raspy voice, "good night to be flying. Just came by to see if you wanted to go for a ride up the coast."

"Howdy, Daryl," said Gentry and Natalie could feel the big man relax.

Natalie's eyes had adjusted to the dark and now she could make out a tall, thin man with long hair going to gray on the sides. He was dressed in cut-off jeans, thongs, and a sweatshirt bearing the legend CLEMSON UNIVERSITY in faded letters. His face had a craggy-reflective quality which Natalie found reminiscent of a younger Morris Udall.

"Natalie," said Gentry, "this here is Daryl Meeks. Daryl's got himself a charter flyin' service across the harbor. Spends part of the year travelin' with a rock and roll band, flyin' them places and playin' drums too. He thinks he's part Chuck Yeager and part Frank Zappa. Daryl and I went to school together. Daryl, this here's Miz Natalie Preston."

"Pleased to meet you," said Meeks.

The man's handshake was firm and friendly and Natalie liked it.

"Pull up some chairs," said Gentry. "I'll get us some beers."

Meeks stubbed the cigarette out on the railing and tossed it into the bushes while Natalie turned a wicker chair around to face the porch swing. Meeks sat on the swing and crossed his bony legs, allowing one thong to dangle from its strap.

"Which school did you two go to?" asked Natalie. She thought that Meeks looked older than Rob.

"Northwestern," said Meeks in his friendly rasp, "but Rob graduated with honors while I flunked out and got drafted. We were roommates for a couple of years. Just two scared Southern boys in the big city."

"Uh-huh, sure," said Gentry, returning with three cold cans of Michelob. "Daryl grew up in the South all right—the south side of Chicago. He was never south of the Mason-Dixon line except for one summer vacation he spent with me down here. He showed his good taste by moving down here after he got back from Vietnam. And he didn't flunk out, either. He quit school to enlist even though he'd been a marine *before* he went to college and was an antiwar activist while he was *in* college."

Meeks drank deeply, stared at the beer can in the dim light, and made a face. "Jesus, Rob, you still drinking this dishwater? Pabst is the good stuff. How many times do I have to tell you?"

"So you were in Vietnam?" asked Natalie. She thought of Frederick and his refusal to talk about his year there, his fury at the simple mention of the country's name.

Meeks smiled and nodded. "Yes'm. I was an FAC—forward air controller—for two years there. I just flew around in my little Piper Cub and told the fast movers, the real pilots in their jets, where to drop their ordnance. I never fired a shot in anger the whole time I was there. It was the cushiest job I could find."

"Daryl was shot down twice," said Gentry. "He's the only forty-year-old hippie I know who has a drawer full of medals."

"Bought them all at the PX," said Meeks. He finished the last of his beer, burped, and said, "I guess tonight wouldn't be the best time for a plane ride, eh, Rob?"

"Next time, amigo," said Gentry.

Meeks nodded, rose, and bowed toward Natalie. "It was a pleasure, ma'am. If you ever need crops dusted or a charter trip or a good drummer, just look me up out at the Mt. Pleasant airport."

"I'll do that," said Natalie with a smile.

Meeks clapped Gentry on the shoulder and bounced down the steps into the dark, whistling the theme to *The High and the Mighty* as he left.

Through the evening they listened to music, discussed their childhoods, played chess, talked about growing up in the South and going to school in the North, washed the dishes, and had a late brandy. Natalie realized that there was almost no tension between them, that she felt that she had known Rob Gentry for years.

Natalie had been surprised and delighted by the beautiful guest room Gentry kept dusted and ready. The bare wood and simple string bed complemented a room as clean as a Shaker's, but the effect was saved from Spartan grimness by colorful quilts on the bed and by a subtle stenciling of a pineapple motif on the walls.

Gentry showed Natalie clean towels in the hall bathroom, wished her good night, made a final check of the door locks and yard lights, and went to his own bedroom. He changed into a comfortable set of clean sweatpants and T-shirt. Over the previous eight years Gentry had been hospitalized with four kidney stones. Each time the attacks had occurred at night. They were calcium stones—not preventable although he usually followed a low-calcium diet—and invariably the incredible pain at the onset of an attack left him capable of no action except dialing for an ambulance to transport him to the emergency room. It bothered Gentry that anything could make him so helpless and that no amount of foresight or preparation could prevent that helplessness, but he had long ago traded pajamas for sweatpants and T-shirt so that on that average of one night every two years that he would be hospitalized, he would not arrive in his pajamas.

Gentry hung his holster with the .357 Ruger Blackhawk on the chair by his bed. It was always there; he could find it with a single sweep of his hand on the darkest night.

Gentry did not go to sleep right away. He was aware of the attractive young woman two rooms away down the hall and he was also aware that he would not make the trip down the hall to her room this night. He sensed the quality of the pleasant tension between them, was capable of separating the amount of attraction she held for him and—by a simple subtraction of that attraction from the general sexual tension between them—arrive at a rough estimate of how much that attraction was reciprocated. Gentry watched reflections of car lights march across the ceiling and frowned slightly. Not tonight. Whatever possibilities the relationship might hold, this was not the time. Every instinct in the sheriff's mind and body screamed at him to get Natalie Preston out of Charleston, out of whatever insanity was being played out around them. Gentry's instincts always had been excellent; they had saved his life more than once. He trusted them now.

He was taking a great risk letting her stay at his house, but he knew no other way to watch over her until he could get her on a plane in the morning. Someone was following him . . . no, not someone, *several* someones. He had not been sure until yesterday—Wednesday, Christmas Eve. In the morning he had driven around for more than ninety minutes, confirming the fact, identifying the vehicles. It was not as crude as the week before; actually the job of trailing was so smooth and professional that only Gentry's heightened level of paranoia tipped him off.

There were at least five cars involved; one of them a cab, the other four as nondescript as Detroit could make them. But three of them were the same ones that he had played cat and mouse with the day before. One vehicle would follow—staying far back, never closing—until he made a sharp change in direction, at which time another would pick him up. It took Gentry two days to realize that sometimes the contact vehicle would be *ahead* of him. To set up a tail that elaborate, he knew, it would take at least half a dozen vehicles, probably twice that many personnel, and a radio linkup. Gentry considered the possibility of Charleston P.D. Internal Affairs being involved but quickly rejected it; one, there was nothing on his record, life-style, or current caseload that would warrant it. Two, the Charleston police budget would not support it. Three, the cops he knew couldn't tail a suspect that well if their lives depended on it.

Whom did that leave? FBI? Gentry did not like or trust Richard Haines, but he knew no reason for the FBI to suspect a Charleston sheriff in either the airline explosion or the Mansard House murders. CIA? Gentry shook his head and stared at the ceiling.

He had just gotten to sleep, was dozing lightly—dreaming that he was back in Chicago, trying to find a class at the university—when Natalie screamed.

Gentry grabbed the Ruger and was padding down the hall before he was fully awake. There was a second, somewhat muffled cry, and then a sob. Gentry dropped to one knee beside the door, tried the knob—it was not locked—and flung the door open while leaning back, out of sight. Four seconds later he went in low, crouching, the Ruger extended and swiveling.

Natalie was alone, sitting up in bed, sobbing, her face in her hands. Gentry scanned the room, checked to make sure that the window was locked, set the Ruger quietly on the nightstand, and sat on the edge of the bed next to her.

"I . . . I . . . I'm sorry," she stammered through tears. There was no affectation in her voice, only fright and embarrassment. "Ev . . . every . . . every time I st . . . start to go to sleep, that man's ar . . . arms come over the car seat at me . . ." She forced herself to quit sobbing, hicupped, and felt around for the box of Kleenex on the nightstand.

Gentry put his left arm around her. She remained rigid a second and then collapsed softly against him, her hair just touching his cheek and chin. For several minutes her body continued to shake with small aftershocks of the tremor of fright that had brought her awake. "It's OK," Gentry murmured as he stroked her back. "Everything's all right." Calming her was as smooth and soothing as stroking a kitten.

It was sometime later, Gentry was almost asleep, sure that she was asleep, when Natalie slowly raised her head, lifted her arms around his neck, and kissed him. The kiss was very long, very soft, and made them both dizzy. Her breasts were soft and full against him.

Later still, Gentry looked up at her as she straddled him, her long neck and oval face thrown back in silent passion, their fingers tightly interlocked, and he felt again the tremors pass through her, through him inside her, but not tremors of fear this time, no, not fear . . .

Natalie's flight for St. Louis departed two hours before Gentry's plane for New York. She kissed him good-bye. Each of them, Southern born, raised, and conditioned, was aware that a black woman and a white man kissing in a public place, even in the South of 1980, would raise eyebrows, bring silent rebukes. Neither of them gave the slightest goddamn.

"Goin' away presents," said Gentry and gave her a *Newsweek*, a morning paper, and the other tone transmitter for his answering machine. "I'll check tonight," he said.

Natalie nodded, decided to say nothing, and turned quickly down the jetport ramp.

An hour later, somewhere over Kentucky, she set the *Newsweek* down, picked up the paper, and found the article that would change her life forever. It was on the third page.

PHILADELPHIA (AP)

Philadelphia police still have no solid leads or suspects in the Christmas Eve slaying of four young Germantown gang members in a crime that homicide detective Lieutenant Leo Hartwell described as "one of the grisliest things that I've seen in my ten years on the force."

Four members of the juvenile "Soul Brickyard" street gang were found murdered on Christmas morning in the Market Square area of Germantown. While the names of the victims and the specific details of the multiple murders have not been released, it is known that all four of the victims were between 14 and 17 years old and that their bodies were mutilated. Lieutenant Hartwell, officer in charge of the investigation, will neither confirm nor deny crime-scene witness reports that all four of the boys had been decapitated.

"We have launched a thorough and ongoing investigation," said Captain Thomas Morano, chief of Germantown's homicide division. "We are following up all leads."

The Germantown area of Philadelphia has a history of gang violence, with two prior deaths in 1980 and six murders in 1979 attributed to gang warfare. "The Christmas Eve murders are surprising," said Rev. William Woods, director of the Community Settlement House in Germantown. "Gang violence has been on the wane during the past ten months and I am not aware of any current disputes or vendettas."

The Soul Brickyard gang is one of dozens of youth gangs in the Germantown area and is said to be comprised of about forty full-time members with twice as many auxiliaries. As is true of most Philadelphia street gangs, it has a long history of conflict with local law enforcement authorities, although in recent years there have been attempts to improve the image of such gangs through city-sponsored outreach programs such as Covenant House and Community Access. All four of the murdered youths were members of the Soul Brickyard Gang.

Natalie knew immediately, instinctively, and without doubt that this had something to do with Melanie Fuller. She had no idea how the old woman from Charleston could be involved in gang warfare in Philadelphia, but she once again felt the hands on her neck and heard the warm, sibilant whisper in her right ear, "You want to find the woman? Look in Germantown."

At St. Louis International Airport—what the locals still called Lambert Field—Natalie decided and acted upon her decision before she became too afraid to follow through. She knew that once she phoned Frederick, saw her friends, she would never leave again. Natalie closed her eyes and remembered the image of her father, lying alone, face not yet cosmeticized, in the empty funeral home, the irritated mortician saying over and over, "We did not expect family until tomorrow."

Natalie used her credit card to buy a ticket on the next TWA flight to Philadelphia. She checked her billfold; she still had two hundred dollars in cash and six hundred and fifty in traveler's checks. She made sure that she still had her press credentials from her summer job with the *Chicago Sun-Times* and then called Ben Yates, the photo editor there.

"Nat!" his voice came over the rasp of static and the babble of airport noise. "I thought you were in school until May."

"I am, Ben," said Natalie, "but I'm going to be in Philadelphia for the next few days and I wondered if you wanted pictures on that gang slaying story."

"Sure," said Yates hesitantly. "What gang slaying?"

Natalie told him.

"Hell," said Yates, "that thing's not going to yield any pictures. And if it does, they'll come over the wire."

"But if I do get something interesting, do you want them, Ben?"

"Yeah, sure," said the photo editor. "What's going on, Nat? Are you and Joe all right?"

Natalie felt as if someone had punched her in the stomach. Somehow Ben had not yet heard about the death of her father. She waited until she could breathe and said, "I'll tell you all about it later, Ben. For now, if the Philadelphia police or someone calls, can you confirm that I'm freelancing for the *Sun-Times*?"

The silence lasted only a few seconds. "Yeah, sure, Nat. I can do that. But let me know what's going on, will you?"

"Sure, Ben. First chance I get. Honest."

Before leaving, Natalie called the university's computer center and left word for Frederick that she would be calling soon. Then she called Gentry's number in Charleston, listened to his voice on the answering machine's tape, and said after the beep, "Rob, this is Natalie." She told him about her change of plans and the reasons. She hesitated. "Be careful, Rob."

The direct flight to Philadelphia was crowded. The man next to her was black, extremely well dressed, and handsome in a thick-necked, lantern-jawed way. He was busy reading his *Wall Street Journal* and Natalie looked out the window awhile and then napped. When she awoke forty-five minutes later she felt groggy, vaguely displaced, sorry that she had set out on what was almost certainly a wild-goose chase. She pulled the Charleston paper out of her camera bag and read the article for the tenth time. It seemed like days to her since she had been in Charleston . . . with Rob Gentry.

"I see you're reading about the trouble in my backyard there."

Natalie turned. The well-dressed man next to her had put down his *Wall Street Journal.* He smiled at her over a glass of Scotch. "You were asleep when the stewardess took orders," he said. "Would you like me to call her back?"

"No, thanks," said Natalie. She was vaguely put off by something in the man's manner, although everything about him—his grin, soft voice, easy posture—suggested open amiability. "What do you mean 'trouble in your backyard'?" she asked.

He moved his Scotch glass toward her paper. "The gang stuff," he said. "I live in Germantown. That garbage goes on all the time."

"Can you tell me about it?" asked Natalie. "About the gangs . . . about the murders?"

"The gangs, yes," he said in a voice that reminded Natalie of the actor James Earl Jones's bass rumble, "the murders, no. I've been out of town the last few days." He grinned more widely at her. "Besides, miss, I come from a slightly more upwardly mobile section of town than those poor chaps. Are you going to be visiting Germantown when you're in Philadelphia?"

"I don't know," said Natalie. "Why?"

The big man's smile became even broader, although his brown eyes were hard to read. "Just hoping you would," he said easily. "Germantown's an historic, interesting place to visit. It has beauty and wealth as well as its slums and gangs. I'd like you to know about both sides if you're just visiting Philadelphia. Or maybe you live there. I shouldn't jump to conclusions."

Natalie forced herself to relax. She could not spend all of her time in a state of paranoid anxiety. "No, I'm just visiting," she said. "And I'd like to hear all about Germantown . . . the good and the bad."

"Fair enough," said her fellow traveler. "I'm going to order another drink." He waved the stewardess over. "Sure you wouldn't like something?"

"I think I would like a Coke," said Natalie.

He ordered the two drinks and turned back to her with a grin. "All right," he said, "If I'm going to be your official Philadelphia tour guide, I suppose we should at least exchange introductions . . ."

"I'm Natalie Preston," said Natalie.

"Pleased to meet you, Miss Preston," said her seatmate with a courtly nod. "My name is Jensen Luhar. At your service."

The Boeing 727 continued eastward, effortlessly sliding toward the fast-approaching winter night.

SEVENTEEN

Alexandria, Virginia
Thursday, Dec. 25, 1980

They came for Aaron Eshkol and his family just after two A.M. on Christmas morning.

Aaron had been sleeping fitfully. Sometime after midnight he had risen and gone downstairs to eat a couple of the holiday cookies their neighbors the Wentworths had given them. The evening had been pleasant; the third year in a row that they had joined the Wentworths and Don and Tina Seagram for Christmas Eve dinner. Aaron's wife Deborah was a Jew, but neither of them took their religion seriously; Deborah was uncomfortable with the way Aaron still considered himself a Zionist. She fit in well in America, Aaron often thought to himself. *She sees every side of every issue. She sees sides that aren't even there.* Aaron was always uncomfortable at embassy parties when Deborah would defend the PLO's point of view. No, not the PLO, Aaron corrected himself as he finished his third and final cookie—the Palestinians'. *Just for argument's sake,* she would say, but she was good at argument . . . better than Aaron, who sometimes thought that he was good at little except codes and ciphers. Uncle Saul always enjoyed debating with Deborah.

Uncle Saul. For four days he had debated whether to bring up his uncle's apparent disappearance with Jack Cohen, his supervisor and the Mossad station head at the Washington embassy. Jack was a short, quiet man who gave off a sense of slightly awkward amiability. He had also been a captain in the paratroops when he had taken part in the Entebbe raid four years earlier and he was reputed to have been the mastermind behind the capture of an entire Egyptian SAM missile during the Yom Kippur War. Jack would know if Saul's disappearance was serious or not. But Levi urged caution. Aaron's friend in ciphers, Levi Cole, had taken the photographs and helped Aaron with the identification. Levi was enthusiastic— he was sure that Aaron's uncle had stumbled upon something big—but he did not want to approach Jack Cohen or Mr. Bergman, the ambassador's attaché, without more detailed information. It was Levi who had quietly helped Aaron check the local hotels the previous Sunday in a fruitless search for Saul Laski.

At one-ten A.M. Aaron switched off the kitchen lights, checked the security panel in the downstairs hall, and went up to lie in bed and stare at the ceiling.

The twins were very disappointed; Aaron had told Beck and Reah that

Uncle Saul would be there Saturday evening. Saul did not come down from New York more than three or four times a year, but Aaron's twin four-year-old girls loved it when he did. Aaron could understand it; he remembered looking forward to Saul's visits when he was a boy in Tel Aviv. Every family should have an uncle who did not cater to the children but who *paid attention* when they said something important, who always brought the right present—not large, necessarily, but reflecting the child's true and deep interests—and who told jokes and stories in that dry, quiet tone that was so much more enjoyable than the forced gaiety of so many adults. It was not like Saul to miss an opportunity like that.

Levi suggested that Saul had been involved in the bombing of Senator Kellog's office that same Saturday. The connection with Nieman Trask was too obvious to discount, but Aaron knew that his uncle would never be party to a bombing—Saul had had his chance in the 1940s when everyone from Aaron's father to Menachim Begin was involved in the kind of Haganah activities that those same ex-guerrillas now condemned as terrorism. Aaron knew that Saul had gone to the front in three wars, but always as a medic, not a combatant. He remembered falling asleep in the apartment in Tel Aviv and on summer nights at the farm to the voices of his father and Uncle Saul arguing the morality of bombing—Saul pointing out loudly that reprisal raids with A-4 Skyhawks killed babies just as dead as did PLO guerrillas with Kalashnikovs.

Four days of investigation into the Senate Office Building explosion had brought Levi and Aaron no nearer to the truth. Levi's usual sources in the U.S. Justice Department and FBI either knew nothing or would not talk in this case. Aaron's calls to New York had not turned up any sign of Saul.

He's all right, thought Aaron, and added in Uncle Saul's voice, *Don't play James Bond, Moddy.*

Aaron was just dozing off, weaving a dream that held the images of the twins playing near the Wentworths' Christmas tree, when he heard a noise in the hall.

Aaron came fully awake in an instant. He threw off the covers, retrieved his glasses from the top of the nightstand, and lifted the loaded .22 Beretta from the drawer.

"Wha . . ." asked Deborah sleepily.

"Shut up," he hissed.

There should have been no way someone could have entered the house without warning. In years past, the embassy had used the Alexandria house as a safe house. It was on a quiet cul-de-sac, set back from the road. The yard was floodlit, the gates and walls laced with electronic sensors that would set off alarms on the security panels in the master bedroom and downstairs hall. The house itself was protected by steel-reinforced doors and a lock system that would turn away the most professional burglar; sensors in doors and windows were also tied into the security system.

Deborah had been irritated by the numerous false alarms set off by the perimeter alarms and actually had disconnected part of the system shortly after they moved in. It was one of the few times in their marriage that Aaron had screamed at her. Now Deborah accepted the security arrangements as a price to pay for living so far out in the suburbs. Aaron hated living so far from his job, so far from the other embassy employees, but accepted the situation because the twins liked the country and the situation made Deborah happy. He did not think it possible for an intruder to penetrate both levels of the security system without triggering an alarm.

There was another sound in the hallway, from the direction of the back stairway and the twins' room. Aaron thought he could hear a low whisper.

Aaron waved for Deborah to get on the floor on the far side of the bed. She did so, pulling the princess telephone out of sight with her. Aaron took three steps to the open bedroom door. He breathed deeply, pushed his glasses up with his left hand, lifted the Beretta high with his right hand, chambered the first round into the breech, and stepped out into the hall.

There were three men, perhaps more, no more than five meters away down the dark hallway. They wore heavy fatigue jackets, gloves, and ski masks. The two in front held long-barreled handguns against the heads of Rebecca and Reah; the twins' eyes were wide above the muffling hands over their mouths, their pajamaed legs were pale as they dangled in front of the dark jackets.

Without thinking, Aaron went into the wide-legged, two-handed firing stance he had been drilled in. He could hear Eliahu's voice, and perfectly remember the old instructor's slow but stern words: "If they are not ready, *fire*. If they are ready, *fire*. If they have hostages, *fire*. If there is more than one target, *fire*. Two shots each, *two*. Do not think—*fire*."

But these were not hostages; these were his *daughters*—Rebeccah and Reah. Aaron could see the Mickey Mouse print on their pajamas. He aimed the small Beretta at the first ski mask. On the firing range, even in bad light, he would have wagered any amount that he could have put two shots into any target the size of the man's head, swiveled, arms still straight, entire body turning, and drilled two more into the second face. At fifteen feet Aaron had been able to put his entire clip of ten .22 rounds into a circle the size of his fist.

But these were his *daughters*.

"Drop the gun." The man's flat voice was muffled by the ski mask. His pistol—a long-barreled Luger with a black tube of silencer—was not even aimed exactly at Becky's head. Aaron was sure that he could shoot both men before they could fire. He felt the soles of his bare feet against the wood floor. Two seconds had elapsed since he had stepped into the hall. *Never surrender your weapon*, Eliahu had drilled them that hot summer in Tel Aviv. *Never. Always shoot to kill. Better you or the hostage should be wounded or die and the enemy be killed than to surrender your weapon.*

"Drop it."

Still crouching, Aaron laid the Beretta on the floor and stretched his hands wide. "Please. Please don't hurt my girls."

There were eight of them. They secured Aaron's hands behind him with surgical tape from a roll, pulled Deborah from behind the bed, and brought all four downstairs to the living room. Two of the masked men went into the kitchen.

"Moddy, the line was dead," gasped Deborah before the man tugging her along put tape across her mouth.

Aaron nodded. He did not trust himself to speak.

The leader had Aaron sit on the piano stool. Deborah and the girls were on the floor, backs to the white wall. They had not taped the children's wrists or mouths and both girls were sobbing and hugging their mother. A man in fatigue jacket, jeans, and ski mask crouched on either side of the two. At a nod from their leader, all six pulled off their masks.

Oh, God, they're going to kill us, thought Aaron. He would, at that second, have given anything he had ever owned or hoped to own just to back up time three minutes. He would have fired twice, swiveled, fired twice, swiveled . . .

All six of the men visible were white, tanned, well groomed. They did not look like Palestinian agents or Bader-Meinhof commandos. They looked like men Aaron passed on the street every day in Washington. The one standing in front of him leaned over so their faces were inches apart. The man's eyes were blue, his teeth perfect. He had a light Midwestern American accent. "We want to talk to you, Aaron."

Aaron nodded. His hands were taped so tightly behind him that the circulation was being cut off. If he fell backward on the stool he might get one good kick in at the handsome man leaning over him. The other five were armed and too far away to reach under any circumstances. Aaron tasted bile and willed his heart to stop racing.

"Where are the photographs?" asked the handsome man next to him.

"What photographs?" Aaron could not believe that his voice had worked, much less come out so firm and emotionless.

"Aw, Moddy, don't play games with us," said the man and nodded at a thin man near the wall. Without changing expression, the man slapped four-year-old Becky across the face.

The child wailed. Deborah struggled against her bonds, cried out behind the tape. Aaron rose off the stool. "You son of a bitch!" he cried in Hebrew. The handsome man kicked Aaron's legs out from under him. Aaron landed hard on his right shoulder, banging his nose and cheekbone against the polished floor. Both children were screaming now. Aaron heard tape being torn off a roll and the screams were cut off. The thin man stepped over and pulled Aaron to his feet, slammed him back onto the piano stool.

"Are they in the house?" the handsome man asked softly.

"No," said Aaron. Blood ran from his nose onto his upper lip. He tilted his head back and could feel the bruise already starting on his cheek. His right arm was numb. "They're in the safe at the embassy," he said and licked away some of the trickle of blood.

The handsome man nodded and smiled slightly. "Who else has seen them besides your Uncle Saul?"

"Levi Cole," said Aaron.

"Head of communications," the man said softly, encouragingly.

"Acting head," said Aaron. Perhaps there was a chance after all. His heart began racing again. "Uri Davidi is on leave."

"Who else has seen them?"

"No one," managed Aaron.

The handsome man shook his head as if disappointed in Aaron. He nodded at a third man. Deborah screamed as the heavy boot thudded into her side.

"*No one!*" screamed Aaron. "I *swear* it! Levi didn't want to talk to Jack Cohen until we had more information. I swear it. I can get you the photographs. Levi has the negatives in the safe. You can have all of the . . ."

"Hush, hush," said the handsome man. He turned as the two came in from the kitchen. They nodded. The man next to Aaron said, "Upstairs." Four departed.

Aaron suddenly smelled gas. *They've turned the oven gas on*, he thought. *Opened the valves.* Oh God, why?

The remaining three taped the children's arms and legs, Deborah's legs. Aaron tried desperately to think of anything he had to bargain with. "I'll take you there now," he said. "The place is almost empty. Someone could come in with me. I'll get the photographs . . . whatever documents you want. Tell me what you want and I'll ride in with you and I swear . . ."

"Shhh," said the man. "Has Hany Adam seen them?"

"No," gasped Aaron. They were laying Deb and the twins on the floor, carefully, making sure their heads did not bump against the wood. Deborah looked very white, eyes rolled up. Aaron wondered if she had fainted.

"Barbara Green?"

"No."

"Moshe Herzog?"

"No."

"Paul Ben-Brindsi?"

"No."

"Chaim Tsolkov?"

"No?"

"Zvi Hofi?"

"No."

The litany continued through every level of the embassy to the ambassador's staff. It was, Aaron realized from the start, a game . . . a harmless way to kill time while the search went on upstairs and in the den. Aaron would play any game, reveal any secret, if it meant another few minutes free of pain for Deborah and the twins. One of the girls moaned and tried to roll over. The thin man patted her small shoulder.

The four returned. The tallest shook his head.

The handsome man sighed and said, "All right, let's do it."

One of the men who had been upstairs was carrying a white sheet from one of the twins' beds. Using surgical tape, he hung it against the wall. They propped Deborah and the children up in front of it.

"Wake her up."

The thin man brought a capsule of smelling salts from his pocket and broke it under Deborah's nose. She returned to full consciousness with a snap of her head. Two men grabbed Aaron by the hair and shoulders and dragged him to the wall, pushed him to his knees.

The thin man stepped back, unfolded a small Polaroid camera, and took three pictures. He waited for them to develop and showed the handsome man. Another man produced a small Sony tape recorder and held the microphone near Aaron's face.

"Please read this," said the handsome man, uncreasing a double-spaced sheet of typing. He held it ten inches in front of Aaron's eyes.

"No," said Aaron, and braced for the blow. If he could change their agenda—gain time in any way.

The handsome man nodded thoughtfully and turned away. "Kill one of the children," he said softly. "Either one."

"No, wait, stop, please! I'll do it!" Aaron was screaming. The thin man had set the silencer against Rebecca's temple and had cocked the hammer of the automatic. He did not pause or look up at Aaron's cries.

"Just a second, please, Donald," said the handsome man. He held the paper in front of Aaron's face again and clicked on the recorder.

"Uncle Saul, Deb and the kids and I are fine, but please do what they say . . ." began Aaron. He read the few paragraphs. It took less than a minute.

"Very good, Aaron," said the handsome man. Two men grabbed Aaron's hair again and bent his head far back. Aaron gasped for breath against a tight throat and strained to see out of the corners of his eyes.

The sheet was removed and carried out of sight. A man pulled a black plastic tarp out of his jacket pocket and unrolled it on the floor in front of Deborah. It was no larger than three by four feet and smelled like a cheap shower curtain.

"Bring him over here," said the handsome man and Aaron was dragged back to the piano stool. The second they released his hair, Aaron moved— his legs uncoiling like a spring, the top of his head striking the handsome man in the chin, turning, butting another in the belly, pulling away from the six hands grabbing at him, kicking at someone's crotch, missing, and then going down, one man under him, two on top, hitting his right cheek again, hard, and not caring . . .

"Let us start again," said the handsome man quietly. He was fingering a cut on his chin and yawning, stretching the jaw muscles. Most of the bruise probably would be under the chin.

"Who are you?" gasped Aaron as they dragged him upright and set him on the piano stool. Someone taped his ankles together.

No one answered. The thin man moved Deborah forward until she was kneeling on the black plastic. Two men held six-inch lengths of thin wire, sharpened on one end, embedded in a taped wooden grip at the other. The room reeked of gas. The smell made Aaron want to vomit.

"What are you going to do?" Aaron's throat was so dry that the words were little better than clicks. Even as the handsome man answered, Aaron felt his mind skid like an automobile on black ice, felt his point of view shift so that he was looking down at all this, not accepting what would happen next but *knowing* what would happen, feeling—in his total inability to change one second of the past or future—the incredible, total unrelenting wave of *helplessness* that a hundred generations of Jews had felt before him, felt at the lip of the oven, felt at the door to the showers, felt while watching the flames rise from the old cities and while listening to the shouts of the goyim rise in ferocity and nearness. *Uncle Saul knew*, thought Aaron as he squeezed his eyes shut and willed his mind not to understand the words.

"There will be a gas explosion," said the handsome man. He had a patient voice—a teacher's voice. "A fire. The bodies will be found in bed. Very badly burned. A very good coroner or medical examiner could tell that the persons had died shortly before the fire charred the bodies, but that will not be discovered. The wire goes in at the corner of the eye . . . directly into the brain. It leaves a very tiny hole, even on a body that has not been burned." He spoke to the others. "I think we will have Mrs. Eshkol found in the upstairs hall . . . a child in each arm . . . almost successful in escaping the flames. Do the woman first. Then the twins."

Aaron struggled, cried out, kicked. Hands and arms held him in place. "Who are you?" he screamed.

Surprisingly, the handsome man responded. "Who are we?" he said. "Why we're no one. No one at all." He moved out of the way so Aaron could have a better view of what the others were doing.

Aaron made no protest when they finally came to him with the wire.

EIGHTEEN

Melanie

Riding north on the bus, through the endless row house slums of Baltimore and the industrial cloaca of Wilmington, I was reminded of a line from the writings of St. Augustine: "The Devil hath established his cities in the North."

I had always hated the large northern cities: their reek of impersonal madness, their coal smoke gloom and grit, and the sense of hopelessness that seems to coat the filthy streets and the equally unclean inhabitants. I had always thought that the most visible aspect of Nina's long betrayal had been her abandonment of the South for the cold canyons of New York. I had no intention of going as far north as New York.

A sudden, brief flurry of snowflakes cut off the depressing view, and I returned my attention to the interior of the bus. The woman across the aisle from me glanced up from her book and gave me a sly smile, the third since we had left the Washington suburbs. I nodded and continued with my knitting. Already I suspected that the timid lady across from me—a woman who was probably in her early fifties but who generated an impression of spinsterish decrepitude twenty years beyond that—might well be part of the solution to my problem.

To one of my problems.

I was glad to be out of Washington. In my youth I had rather enjoyed that sleepy, southern-feeling city; even until the Second World War it had retained an air of relaxed confusion. But now that marble hive of a city made me think of a pretentious mausoleum filled with bustling, power-hungry insects.

I glanced out at the snow flurries and for a second could not think of what day or month it was. The day came first—Thursday. We had spent Tuesday and Wednesday nights in a dreary motel some miles from the center of Washington. On Wednesday I had Vincent drive the Buick to the vicinity of the Capitol, abandon it, and walk back to the motel. The walk had taken him three hours, but Vincent did not complain. He would not be complaining in the future. On Tuesday night I had had him take care of necessary personal details, using simple sewing thread and a needle I had heated over a candle flame.

The purchases I had made in a shopping mall that Wednesday morning—a few dresses, robe, underwear—were all the more depressing in contrast to the fine things that I had lost in Atlanta. I still had almost nine thousand dollars in my absurd straw tote bag. There was, of course, much more money available in safe-deposit boxes and savings accounts in Charleston, Minneapolis, New Delhi, and Toulon, but I had no intention of trying to retrieve those funds at this time. If Nina had known about my Atlanta account, she must know about the others.

Nina is dead, I thought.

But her Ability had been the strongest of us all. She had Used one of Willi's cat's-paws to destroy his plane even as she sat chatting with me. Her Ability was incredible, frightening. It might reach me even from the grave, grow in power even as Nina Drayton's body rotted in its coffin. My heart began to race and I glanced over my shoulder at the faces visible in the dim rows of bus seats . . .

Nina is dead.

It was a Thursday, exactly one week before Christmas. That made it December 18. The Reunion had been on December 12. Eons separated those two dates. For the past two decades my life had suffered few outward changes beyond the necessary indulgences I had allowed myself. Now everything had changed.

"Excuse me," said the woman across the aisle from me, "but I can't help but admire what you are knitting there. Is it going to be a sweater for a grandchild?"

I turned and gave the little woman the full radiance of my smile. When I was very young, before I discovered that there were many things that a young lady simply did not do, I used to go fishing with my father. It was that first nibble on the line, those first tentative tugs and tremors of the bobber that I found most exciting. It was at that instant, when the hook had not yet slammed home, that all the fisherman's skills had to be brought to play.

"Why, yes, it is," I said. The thought of having a mewling grandchild somewhere actually nauseated me, but I had long since discovered both the therapeutic effects of knitting and the psychological camouflage it offered in public.

"A grandson?"

"Granddaughter," I said and slipped into this woman's mind. It was like stepping through an open door. There was no resistance. I was as careful and subtle as possible, sliding along mental corridors and passageways and through more open doors, never intrusive, until I found the pleasure center of her brain. Holding the image of petting a Persian cat, although I loathed cats, I stroked her, feeling the onrush of pleasure flow through her, and out of her like an unexpected gush of warm urine.

"Oh," she said, blushed, then blushed again at not knowing why she blushed. "A granddaughter, how wonderful."

I moderated the stroking, modulated it, coordinated it with each shy glance she gave me, increased it when she heard my voice. Some people strike us with this force naturally when we meet them. With young people it is called falling in love. With politicians it is called generating charisma.

When it is handled by a master speaker who has a touch of the Ability, we tend to call the results mob hysteria. One of the frequently mentioned but rarely noted facts alluded to by contemporaries and associates of Adolf Hitler is that *people felt good* in his presence. A few weeks of the conditioning level I had just initiated with this woman would create an addiction much more potent than that caused by heroin. We love being in love because it is as close as humans can come to feeling this psychic addiction.

After a moment or two of idle conversation, this lonely woman, who looked as much older than her true age as I look younger than mine, patted the seat next to her and said, blushing once again, "There is plenty of room over here. Would you care to join me so that we can continue our discussion without speaking so loudly?"

"I would love to," I said, and stuffed the yarn and needles into my tote bag. The knitting had served its purpose.

Her name was Anne Bishop and she was returning to her home in Philadelphia after a lengthy and unsatisfactory visit in Washington with her younger sister's family. Ten minutes of conversation told me everything I needed to know. The mental stroking would not have been necessary; this woman was dying to talk to someone.

Anne had come from a well-thought-of and well-to-do Philadelphia family. A trust fund set up by her father remained her major source of income. She had never married. For thirty-two years this faded shade of a woman had looked after her brother Paul, a paraplegic slowly transforming into a quadriplegic through a progressive nerve disease. This past May, Paul had died, and Anne Bishop had not yet become attuned to a world in which she was not responsible for him. Her visit with her sister Elaine—the first such reunion in eight years—had been a sad affair; Anne impatient with Elaine's loutish husband and ill-mannered children—the family obviously put off by the spinsterish habits of Auntie Anne.

I knew Anne Bishop's type well—I had even masqueraded as this sort of defeated female during my long hibernation from life. She was a satellite in search of a world around which to orbit. Any world would do as long as it did not require the cold, solitary ellipse of independence. Paraplegic brothers were a gift from God for such women; endless and single-minded devotion to a husband or child would have been an alternative, but caring for a failing brother offered so many more excuses for avoiding the other commitments and tangles and bothersome details of living. In their unflagging service and selflessness, these women are invariably selfish monsters. In her modest, self-effacing, and loving comments about her dear departed brother, I sensed the perverse fetish of the bedpan and wheelchair, the sick self-indulgence of denying all else for thirty years in a sacrifice of young womanhood, adulthood, and parenthood to serve the odorous needs of a semi-ambulatory corpse. I knew Anne Bishop well: a practitioner of a sort of slow and masturbatory suicide. The thought makes me ashamed to be the same sex. Frequently when encountering these poor slugs, I am tempted to help them stick their hands and arms down their own throats until they choke on their own vomit and have done with it.

"There, there. I understand," I said and patted her arm as she shed tears over the telling of her travails. "I understand just how it is."

"You *do* understand," said Anne. "It is so rare that one meets someone who can comprehend another's grief. I feel we have much in common."

I nodded and looked at Anne Bishop. Fifty-two years old, she easily could have passed for seventy. She dressed well, but she was the type of hunched-over wallflower that could make any suit or gown wear like a frumpy housedress and sweater. Her hair was a faded brown, with a center part she had plowed in the same row for forty-five years, and her bangs hung in limp defeat. Her eyes were circled and darkened, made for weeping. Her mouth was thin and prim, not quite assertive enough to be called censorius but obviously rarely given to laughter. Her wrinkles all flowed downward; gravity's verdict was etched deeply. Her mind had the skittish, hungry shallowness of a frightened squirrel.

She was perfect.

I told her my tale, using the name Beatrice Straughn since I still carried that identification. My husband had been a successful Savannah banker. His passing eight years earlier had left an estate to be mismanaged by my sister's son . . . Todd . . . who, it seems, was able to lose all of my money as well as his before he and his graceless wife killed themselves this past autumn in a dramatic automobile accident, leaving me with funeral expenses, bad debts to pay off, and their son Vincent to take care of. My own son and his pregnant wife were in Okinawa, teaching in a mission school. Now I had sold the Savannah house, paid the last of Todd's debts, and was venturing north to find a new life for my grandnephew and myself.

The story was nonsense, but I helped Anne Bishop believe it with subtle strokes of pleasure punctuating each revelation.

"Your nephew is very handsome," said Anne.

I smiled and glanced across the aisle to where Vincent was sitting. He wore the cheap white shirt, dark tie, blue windbreaker, creased slacks, and black shoes we had purchased at a Washington K-Mart. I had trimmed his hair a bit, but then decided on a whim to leave it long; now it was clean and neatly tied back in a pony tail. He stared without expression at the snow flurries and passing scenery. There was no way to change his chinless ferret's face or the pustules of acne there. "Thank you," I said. "He takes after his mother . . . God rest her soul."

"He is very quiet," said Anne.

I nodded and allowed tears to come to my eyes. "The accident . . ." I began and had to pause before I could go on. "The poor darling lost much of his tongue in the automobile accident. They tell me that he will never be able to speak again."

"My dear, my dear," clucked Anne. "God's Will is not for us to understand, only to bear."

We consoled each other as the bus hissed along on a stretch of elevated highway above the endless slums of South Philadelphia.

Anne Bishop was pleased that we accepted her invitation to spend a few days with her.

Downtown Philadelphia was crowded, noisy, and filthy. With Vincent carrying our bags, we walked to a subterranean train station and Anne purchased tickets on the Chestnut Hill local to Chelten Avenue. During the bus ride she had told me about her lovely home in Germantown. Even though she had mentioned that the city had deteriorated in recent decades with the introduction of "undesirable elements," I still had pictured the Germantown as a separate entity from the brick and iron sprawl of Philadelphia. It was not. The weak afternoon light out the train window illuminated rowhouses, crumbling brick factories, sagging landings, narrow streets littered with the metal corpses of abandoned automobiles, empty lots, and Negroes. Except for some of the train passengers and glimpses of white faces in the automobiles on the expressway that paralleled the tracks, the city seemed to be inhabited solely by Negroes. I sat exhausted and dispirited, staring out the greasy train window at Negro children running through empty lots, small black faces emerging from grimy parkas; Negro men ambling in their dull and threatening way down cold streets, broad Negro women pushing purloined shopping carts, glimpses of Negro faces through dark panes . . .

I set my head against the cold window and resisted the urge to cry. My father had been right, in those last sunlit days before the Great War, when he prophesied that the country would rot away when the colored began to vote. They had reshaped a once great nation into the littered ruins of their own lazy despair.

Nina would never find me here. My movements over the past few days had been random. Spending a week, or several weeks, with Anne—even if it meant descending into this pit of unemployed colored people—would add another element of randomness to an already random pattern.

We disembarked at an urban station marked Chelten Avenue. The tracks ran between sheer concrete walls, the city loomed above. Suddenly frightened, too tired to climb the stairs to street level, I had us sit and rest several minutes on an uncomfortable bench the color of bile. A train roared past us, headed back to the center city. A group of colored teenagers bounded up the stairs, shouting obscenities and shoving each other and anyone who got in their way. I could hear street sounds in the distance. The wind was terribly cold. Snow flurries appeared from nowhere and pelted our cement waiting area. Vincent did not flinch or close his windbreaker.

"We will get a cab," said Anne.

I nodded but did not rise until I noticed two rats the size of small cats emerge from a crack in the concrete cliff across the tracks and begin to forage in the refuse and dried-out gutters there.

The cabdriver was colored and sullen. He overcharged us for the eight-block ride. Germantown was a mixture of stone and brick and neon and billboard. Chelten Avenue and Germantown Avenue were crowded with cars, lined with cheap stores, pockmarked with bars, and populated with the human refuse common to any northern city. But real trolleys rumbled along Germantown Avenue, and squeezed in between the banks and bars and junk shops were line old stone homes, or a brick shop from a previous century, or a small apron of park with iron fences and green statuary. Two centuries ago this must have been a tiny hamlet graced with fine homes and genteel citizen-farmers or merchants who chose to live six to ten miles from Philadelphia. One hundred years ago it would have been a quiet town a few minutes' train ride from Philadelphia—still a place of charm and large homes set down leafy lanes with an occasional inn along the highway. Today Philadelphia had engulfed Germantown the way some huge, bottom-eating carp would swallow an immeasurably more beautiful but tinier fish, leaving only the perfect white bones of its past to mix with the raw garbage in the terrible digestive juices of progress.

Anne was so proud of her little house that she kept blushing as she showed it to us. It was an anachronism: a pleasant white frame home—it might once have been a farmhouse—set a few dozen yards from German-town Avenue on a narrow street called Queen Lane. It had a high wooden fence, badly scarred and graffitied in front despite obvious efforts to keep it clean, a postage stamp of a yard smaller than the courtyard at my Charleston house, a minuscule front porch, two dormer windows pro-claiming a second floor, and a single stunted peach tree that looked as if it would never bloom again. The house itself was sandwiched between a dry cleaning establishment that seemed to be advertising dead flies in the front window and a three-story apartment building that appeared to have been abandoned for decades except for the evidence of dark faces peering out of windows. Across the street was an assortment of small warehouses, sagging brick buildings turned into duplexes, and the beginning of the ubiquitous rowhouses half a block to the south.

"It isn't much, but it's home," said Anne, waiting for me to contradict the first part of her statement. I contradicted her.

Anne's large bedroom and a smaller guest room were on the second floor. A tiny bedroom off the kitchen had been her brother's, and the room still smelled of medicine and cigars. Anne obviously had planned to offer the lower room to Vincent and the small guest room to me. I helped her offer us the two upstairs rooms while she took the downstairs room. I looked at the rest of the house while she moved her clothes and personal items.

There was a small dining room, too formal for its size, a tiny living room with too much furniture and too many prints on the wall, a kitchen as prim and unpleasant in appearance as Anne herself, the brother's room, a bathroom, and a small back porch that looked out on a backyard no larger than a dog run.

I opened the backdoor to let a bit of air into the stuffy house and a fat, gray cat brushed past my legs. "Oh, that's Fluff," said Anne as she carried an armload of clothes into the small bedroom. "He's my widdle baby. Mrs. Pagnelli has been watching after him, but he knew that Mommy was coming home. Didn't ooow?" She was addressing the cat.

I smiled and stepped back. Women my age are supposed to love cats, fill their homes with them at every opportunity, and generally act like idiots around the arrogant, treacherous creatures. When I was a child—no older than six or seven—my aunt brought her fat Siamese with her each summer she visited. I was always afraid the beast would lie on my face in the night and smother me. I remember stuffing that cat in a burlap sack one afternoon when the grown-ups were having lemonade in the backyard. I drowned it in a water trough behind the neighbor's carriage house and left the damp corpse behind a barn where a pack of yellow dogs often congregated. After Anne's conditioning was completed, I would not be at all surprised if her "widdle baby" was fated to have a similar accident.

If one has the Ability, it is relatively easy to Use someone, much harder to successfully condition them. When Nina, Willi, and I began the Game in Vienna almost half a century ago, we amused ourselves by Using others, strangers usually, and there was little thought given to the necessity of always having to discard these human instruments. Later, as we grew older and more mature in our exercise of the Ability, each of us found need for a companion—part servant, part bodyguard—who would be so attuned to our needs that it took almost no effort to Use them. Before I discovered Mr. Thorne in Switzerland some twenty-five years ago, I traveled with Madame Tremont, and before her, a young man I had named—with youthful, shallow sentimentality—Charles, after my last beau. Nina and Willi had their long succession of catspaws, culminating in the disastrous presence of Willi's final two companions and Nina's loathsome Miss Barrett Kramer. Such conditioning takes some time, although it is the first few days that are critical. The trick is to leave at least a hollow core of the personality without leaving any possibility of independent action. And although the action must not be independent, it must be *autonomous* in the sense that simple duties and daily routines can be initiated and carried out without any direct Using. If one is to travel in public with these conditioned assistants, there must also be at least a simulacrum of the original persona left in place.

The benefits of such conditioning are obvious. While it is difficult—almost impossible, although Nina may have been capable of it—to Use two people at the same time, there is little difficulty in directing the actions of two conditioned catspaws. Willi never traveled with fewer than two of his "boyfriends," and before her feminist phase, Nina was known to travel with five or six young, single, handsome bodies.

Anne Bishop was easily conditioned, eager for a subjugation of self. In the three days I rested in her home, she was thoroughly brought into line. Vincent was another case entirely. While my initial "teaching" had destroyed all higher order volition, his subconscious remained a riotous and largely unrestrained tangle of surging hatreds, fears, prejudices, desires, and dark urges. I did not wish to eradicate these, for here were the sources of energy I would tap at a later date. For those three long days on the weekend before Christmas 1980, I rested in Anne's slightly sour-smelling home and explored the emotional jungle of Vincent's dark undermind, leaving trails and leverages there for future use.

On Sunday, December 21, I was eating a late breakfast that Anne had prepared and asking her about her friends, her income, and her life. It turned out that she had no friends and very little life. Mrs. Pagnelli, a neighbor down the alley, occasionally came to visit and sometimes watched over Fluff. At the mention of the missing feline, Anne's eyes filled with tears and I could feel her thoughts sheer sideways like an automobile on black ice. I tightened my mental grip and brought her back to her new and central passion—pleasing me.

Anne had over seventy-three thousand dollars in savings. Like many selfish old women approaching a boring end to a boring life, she had lived on the edges of poverty for decades while storing away money, stocks, and bonds like a compulsive squirrel hoarding acorns it would never eat. I suggested that she might consider converting the various commodities to cash during the coming week. Anne thought this was an excellent idea.

We were discussing her sources of income when she mentioned Grumblethorpe. "The Society pays me a small stipend for watching over it, leading occasional private tours, and checking it when it is closed for long periods, as it is now."

"What Society?" I asked.

"The Philadelphia Society for the Preservation of Landmarks," said Anne.

"And what kind of landmark is this Grumblethorpe?" I asked.

"I would love to show it to you," Anne said eagerly. "It is less than a block from here."

I was bored after three days of resting and conditioning these two in the confines of Anne's little house. I nodded. "After breakfast," I said. "If I feel up to the walk."

It is hard for me, even now, to convey the charm and incongruity of Grumblethorpe. It sits directly on the deteriorating brick thoroughfare of Germantown Avenue. The few fine old buildings there are flanked by bars and junk shops, delicatessens and five-and-dime stores. The narrow streets that lead off this section of the main avenue soon turn into true slums, rowhouses, and empty lots. But there at 5267 Germantown Avenue, behind a picket line of parking meters and two soot-blackened, knife-gashed oaks, not ten feet from the traffic and trolleys and endless parade of colored pedestrians, sits the stone-walled, shuttered, and shingled perfection of Grumblethorpe.

There were two front doors. Anne brought out a cluttered key ring and let us in the eastern entrance. The interior was dark, the windows shielded by heavy drapes and tightly closed blinds. The house smelled of age and centuries-old wood and furniture polish. It smelled like home to me.

"The home was built in 1744 by John Wister," said Anne, her voice growing stronger and taking on a tour-guide's tone. "He was a Philadelphia merchant who used this as a summer home. Later, it became the family's year-round residence."

We stepped from the small entrance hall into the parlor. The broad floorboards were highly polished, the elegantly simple ceiling molding was in the "Wedding Band" style, and there was one wing-backed chair next to the small fireplace. A period chairside table held a single candle. There were no electric lights or outlets.

"During the Battle of Germantown," said Anne, "the British General James Agnew died in this room. His bloodstains are still visible." She gestured toward the floor.

I glanced at the faint discoloration of the wood. "There are no signs outside," I said.

"There used to be a small card in the window," said Anne. "The house was open to the public on Tuesday and Thursday afternoons between two o'clock and five o'clock. The Society arranged private tours for those interested in the history of the area. It is closed now—and will be for at least another month—until funds become available to complete some restoration begun in the kitchen."

"Who lives here now?" I asked.

Anne laughed—a small, mousy squeak. "No one *lives* here," she said. "There is no electricity, no heating except for the fireplaces, and no plumbing whatsoever. I check on the place regularly and once every six to eight weeks, Mrs. Waverly from the Society makes an inspection tour."

I nodded. "There is a Courting Door here," I said.

"Ah yes," said Anne. "You know the custom. It was also used for funerals."

"Show me the rest of the house," I commanded.

The dining room held a rustic table and chairs harking back to the simpler beauty of early Colonial design. There was an incredible journeyman's bench there that combined all of the skills of a cabinetmaker. Anne pointed out a chair crafted by Soloman Fussel, who had made the chairs for Independence Hall.

The kitchen looked out into the backyard and despite the brown, frozen soil and traces of snow, I could make out the plan for the beautiful old garden that must bloom there in the summer. The kitchen floors were of stone and the fireplace was large enough to walk into without stooping. There was an odd assortment of old tools and utensils pegged to one wall—antique shears, a six-foot scythe, a hoe, an ancient rake, iron tongs, other things—while a large pedal-driven whetstone sat nearby. Anne pointed to a large section of the corner that had been torn up, stone stacked, and an ugly piece of black plastic covering an excavation. "There were loose stones here," said Anne. "During some maintenance in November, the workers discovered a rotted wooden door under the floor and a partially collapsed tunnel."

"An escape tunnel?"

"Probably," said Anne. "There was still some Indian activity when the house was built."

"Where does it go?"

"They found what must be the stone exit point just beyond that neighboring garage," said Anne, gesturing through ice-rimmed panes. "But the Society did not have enough funds to continue excavating until a grant from the Philadelphia Historical Commission comes through in early February."

"Vincent would like to look into the tunnel," I said.

"Oh," said Anne and seemed to waver, running a hand across her forehead, "I am not sure if it would be proper . . ."

"Vincent will take a look," I said.

"Of course," agreed Anne.

There was a candle in the parlor, but I had to send the boy back to Anne's house to get matches. When he removed the plastic tarp and descended the short ladder to the tunnel, I closed my eyes to get a better view.

Dirt, rock, the smell of dampness and the grave. The tunnel had been excavated barely a dozen feet out under the backyard. Fresh timber shored up the ceiling of the partially reopened tunnel. I brought Vincent back up and opened my eyes.

"Would you like to see the upstairs?" asked Anne.

I assented without speaking or gesturing.

The nursery whispered to me as soon as I entered it.

"The legend is that this room is haunted," said Anne. "Mrs. Waverly's dogs will not enter it."

I assumed that Anne heard the whispers, but when I touched her mind there was no awareness of them, only the growing eagerness to please me.

I stepped deeper into the room. The window facing the street allowed almost no light through the wooden blinds. In the gloom I could make out a low metal crib that was ugly and out of era—a tarnished cage for an evil infant. There were two small string beds and a child's chair, but the items that commanded attention were the toys and dolls and life-size mannequin. A large dollhouse sat in one corner. The thing was also from the wrong time period—it must have been constructed at least a century after the real house—but the striking thing about it was that it had rotted away and partially collapsed much like a real abandoned home. I half expected to see tiny rats scurrying through the miniature halls. Near the dollhouse, half a dozen dolls lay tossed on a low string bed. Only one looked old enough to date back to the eighteenth century, but several looked real enough to be the mildewing corpses of actual children.

But it was the mannequin that dominated. It was the size of a living seven- or eight-year-old boy. The clothes were old reconstructions of a Revolutionary War-era boy's outfit, but the cloth had faded over the past decades, seams had parted, and a scent of rotting wool filled the room. The hands and neck and face had lost their pink surface in many spots, showing the dark porcelain beneath. Real human hair had once made up a lustrous wig, but only scabrous patches remained and the scalp was mottled with cracks. The eyes seemed absolutely real and I realized that they were human prostheses. The glass eyes alone had retained their luster and luminous quality as the mannequin decayed: a boy's eager eyes in a standing corpse's body.

For some reason I assumed that the whispering emanated from the mannequin, but when I approached it the vague susurrations grew fainter rather than louder. It was the walls that were speaking. As Anne and Vincent watched passively, I leaned against the plaster walls and listened. The whispers were audible, but just below the level where individual words could be distinguished. It sounded like more than one voice, but I had the distinct impression that I was hearing sentences directed at me rather than eavesdropping on a conversation.

"Do you hear anything?" I asked Anne.

She frowned, trying to discern the response that would most please me. "Only the traffic," she said at last. "Some boys shouting down the street."

I shook my head and set my ear to the wall again. The whispers continued, neither urgent nor threatening. I thought that I could make out the syllables of my name in the soft flow of sound.

I do not believe in ghosts. I do not believe in the supernatural. But as I grow older, I am coming to believe that just as radio waves continue to travel outward long after the transmitter is shut off, so do the transmissions of some individuals' force of will continue to be broadcast after they are gone. Nina once told me that an archaeologist had discovered the voice of a potter, dead thousands of years, recorded in the grooves of his pot, the iron in his clay and the vibrations of his fingertips acting like record disk and stylus. I do not know if this was true, but it is the same concept that I have come to believe in. People—especially we few with the

Ability—might be able to impress our force of will on objects just as we do on people.

I thought of Nina again and quickly stepped away from the wall. The whispers died. "No," I said aloud, "this has nothing to do with Nina. These are friendly voices."

My two companions looked on silently; Anne not knowing what to say and Vincent unable to say anything. I smiled at them and Anne smiled back.

"Come," I said. "We will have lunch and return here later. I am very pleased with Grumblethorpe, Anne. You did well to bring me here."

Anne Bishop beamed at me.

By Monday noon, Anne and Vincent had brought a roll-away bed and new mattress to Grumblethorpe, purchased additional candles and three kerosene space heaters, half filled the kitchen shelves with cans and nonperishable foods, set the small butane stove in place on the massive kitchen table, and cleaned and dusted each room. I had the bed set up in the nursery. Anne brought clean sheets, blankets, and her favorite Amish quilt. Vincent set out his array of new shovels and buckets against one of the kitchen walls. There was nothing I could do about the absence of plumbing at present— besides which, I still planned to stay at Anne's most of the time. I was merely making Grumblethorpe more comfortable for my inevitable visits.

On Monday afternoon Anne withdrew all the money from her savings and checking accounts—almost forty-two thousand dollars—and began the process of translating stocks, bonds, and securities to cash. In some cases she had to pay a penalty, but neither of us minded. I put the money in my luggage.

By four P.M.—the last bit of winter light outside—Grumblethorpe glowed brightly in each room from dozens of candles, the parlor, kitchen, and nursery had been nicely warmed by the glowing kerosene heaters, and Vincent had been working for three hours digging out the tunnel and transporting the dirt to a far corner of the backyard under a massive ginkgo tree. It was dirty, difficult, and possibly dangerous work, but it was good for Vincent to work on such a task. Some of his pent-up fury found release in these labors. I had known that Vincent was very strong—much stronger than his lean body and slumped posture would ever suggest—but now I discovered the true extent of his wiry strength and almost demonic energy. He almost doubled the length of the tunnel in that first afternoon of digging.

I did not sleep at Grumblethorpe, not that first night, but as we were snuffling the candles and shutting off the heaters in preparation to leave, I went alone to the nursery and stood there with only a single candle burning, the flame reflected in the button eyes of the rag dolls and the glass eyes of the life-size boy.

The whispers were louder now. I could sense the gratitude in the tone if not the actual words. They were wishing me goodwill—and bidding me to return.

Vincent removed half a ton of dirt on Tuesday, the day before Christmas Eve. After clearing another twelve feet of passage we found that much of the remaining tunnel was intact except for small amounts of loose rock and dirt that had collapsed over the past two centuries. On Wednesday morning he unblocked most of the exit just short of the alley that bordered the yards and the backs of rowhouses on the block behind us. He set boards over the exit and returned to Grumblethorpe. Vincent was a sight; filthy, the old clothes he had worn for the work torn and muddy, his long hair untied and hanging in filthy strands over a streaked face and staring eyes. I had only one large thermos of water with me that day at Grumblethorpe; I had Vincent strip and sit near the heater in the kitchen while I walked back to Anne's house to clean his clothes in her washer and dryer.

Anne had been working all afternoon on a special Christmas Eve meal. The streets were dark and almost empty. A single trolley rumbled past, its yellow interior lights glowing warmly. It was beginning to snow.

Thus it was that I found myself walking alone, undefended. Normally I would never have walked even a single city block without the company of a well-conditioned companion, but the day's work at Grumblethorpe and a strange tone of warning in the nursery's whispers had preoccupied me, made me careless. Also, I was thinking about Christmas.

Christmas always had been important for me. I remembered the large tree and even larger dinner we would have when I was a child. My father would carve the turkey; it had been my job to hand out small presents to the servants. I remember planning for weeks ahead of time the exact wording of the brief sentences of appreciation to the staff of mostly older colored men and women. I would praise most of them, gently chastise a few for lack of diligence through a careful omission of key phrases. The finest presents and warmest words were invariably saved for Auntie Harriet, the aging, bosomy old woman who had nursed me and raised me. Harriet had been born a slave.

It was interesting how, years later in Vienna, Nina, Willi, and I could each trace such common elements of our childhood as kindness to servants. Even in Vienna, Christmas had been an important time for us. I remember the winter of 1928, sleigh rides along the Danube and a huge banquet at Willi's rented villa south of the city. It is only in recent years that I have not celebrated Christmas as thoroughly as I would like. Nina and I had been discussing the sad secularization of the Christmas spirit just two weeks earlier at our last Reunion. People do not know what Christianity means anymore.

There were eight boys, all colored. I do not know how old they were. They were all taller than me; three or four of them had black fuzz above their large upper lips. They seemed to be all noise and elbows and knees and raucous obscenities as they came around the corner of Bringhurst Street onto Germantown Avenue and directly into my path. One of them carried a large radio that blared toneless noise.

I looked up, startled, still distracted by my thoughts about Christmas and absent friends. Still not thinking, I paused, waiting for them to step off the curb, out of my way. Perhaps it was something in my face or proud posture, something too unlike the cringing deference whites habitually assume in Negro sections of northern cities, that caused one to notice me.

"What the fuck you lookin' at, lady?" asked a tall boy with a red cap. His face held all of the gap-toothed denseness and contempt bred into his race by centuries of tribal ignorance.

"I am waiting for you boys to move aside and let a lady pass," I said. I spoke softly, politely. Normally I would have said nothing, but I had been thinking of other things.

"Boys!" said the one in the red cap. "Who the fuck you calling boys?" The others gathered around me in a half circle. I stared at a point above their heads.

"Hey, who the fuck you think you are?" asked a fat one in a grimy gray parka.

I said nothing.

"Come on," said a shorter but less crude-looking boy. He had blue eyes. "Let's go, man."

They started to turn away, but the Negro in the red cap had to make a final point. "Watch who you be tellin' to get out your way, old broad," he said and made as if to prod me on the chest or shoulder.

I stepped back quickly to avoid being touched. My heel caught in a crack in the sidewalk and I lost my balance, flailed my arms, and sat down heavily in the area of snow and dog excrement between sidewalk and street. Most of the Negroes roared in laughter.

The shorter boy with blue eyes hushed them with a wave of his hand and stepped forward. "You OK, lady?" He held out his hand as if to help me up.

I stared, ignoring his hand. After a second he shrugged and led the others off down the street. Their vile music echoed off storefronts and silent shops.

I remained sitting there until the eight of them were out of sight and then I tried to stand, gave it up, and turned to crawl on my hands and knees until I reached a parking meter that I could use to pull myself to my feet. For some time I stood there leaning on the meter and shaking. Occasionally a car would pass—perhaps someone hurrying home on Christmas Eve—and tires would throw slush at me. Once two heavy young Negro women hurried by, chattering to each other in plantation voices. No one stopped to help me.

I was still shaking by the time I arrived at Anne's house. Later I realized that I could easily have had her come out to help me, but at the time I was not thinking clearly. The cold wind had caused tears to form, fall, and freeze on my cheeks.

Anne immediately drew a hot bath for me, helped me out of my sodden dress, and laid out a dry change of clothes while I bathed.

It was nine P.M. by the time I ate—alone while Anne sat in the next room—and by the time I had finished the dessert, cherry pie, I knew precisely what must be done.

I brought my nightgown and necessary things. I had Anne bring a bedroll for herself, a change of clothing for Vincent, some extra food and drink, and the pistol I had borrowed from the Atlanta cabdriver.

The walk back to Grumblethorpe was brief and uneventful. It was snowing heavily now. I looked away from the place where I had fallen.

Vincent was sitting where I had left him. He dressed and ate ravenously. I was not worried about Vincent missing a few meals, but he had been burning thousands of calories over the past two days of digging and I wanted him to replenish his energy. He ate like an animal. Vincent's hands, arms, face, and hair were still filthy, caked and streaked with red mud, and the visual and auditory effect of his feeding was truly animal-like.

After eating, Vincent set to work with the whetstone, sharpening both the scythe and one of the spades Anne had bought at a hardware store on Chelten Avenue two days before.

It was almost midnight when I went upstairs to bed in the nursery. I closed the door and changed into my nightgown. The dusty, bright glass eyes of the boy-mannequin watched me in the flickering candlelight. Anne sat downstairs in the parlor, watching the front door, content, smiling slightly, the loaded .38 caliber pistol comfortable in her aproned lap.

Vincent left through the tunnel. Mud and moisture further streaked his face and hair as he dragged the scythe and spade through the black passage. I closed my eyes and saw clearly the snow falling past a dim alley light as he emerged near the garage, dragged the long implements out, and scuttled off down the alley.

The air smelled clean and cold. I could feel Vincent's heart pounding strong and sure, feel the jungle inside his mind whip and ripple as if to a strong wind as the adrenaline surged through his system. I felt the muscles around my own mouth move in sympathetic response as I realized that Vincent was grinning widely, very widely, in a feral snarl.

We moved quickly down an alley, paused at the entrance to a slum street of blackened rowhouses, and ran along the south side where the deepest shadows lay. We paused and I had Vincent raise his head in the direction the eight had disappeared. I could feel Vincent's nostrils flare as he sniffed the night air for the scent of Negroes.

It was snowing very hard now. The night was still except for the distant peal of churchbells announcing the birth of our Savior. Vincent lowered his head, raised spade and scythe to his shoulder, and scuttled off into the blackness of an alley.

Upstairs in Grumblethorpe I smiled, turned my face to the nursery wall, and was vaguely aware of the sibilant rush of whispers rising around me like the sound of an inrushing sea.

NINETEEN

Washington, D.C.
Saturday, Dec. 20, 1980

Y ou know nothing about the true nature of violence," the thing that once had been Francis Harrington said to Saul Laski.

They were walking east along the mall, toward the Capitol. Cold shafts of evening sunlight illuminated white granite buildings and white wisps of vapor from bus and car exhausts. A few pigeons hopped gingerly near empty benches.

Saul felt tremors in his stomach muscles and upper thighs and he knew it was not just reaction to the cold. A great excitement had seized him as they had left the National Art Gallery. *After all these years.*

"You fashion yourself an expert on violence," said Harrington in German, a language Saul had never heard the boy speak, "but you know nothing of it."

"What do you mean?" asked Saul in English. He thrust his hands in the pockets of his topcoat. His head was constantly moving, looking at a man coming out of the East Building of the National Gallery, squinting at a lone figure on a distant park bench, trying to see through the polarized windshield of a slowly moving limousine. *Where are you, Oberst?* The thought that the Nazi colonel might be nearby made the muscles in Saul's diaphragm constrict.

"You treat violence as an aberration," Harrington continued in flawless German, "when in truth it is the norm. It is the very essence of the human condition."

Saul forced himself to pay attention to the conversation. He must draw the Oberst out . . . find some way to free Francis from the old man's control . . . find the Oberst himself. "That's nonsense," said Saul. "It's a common failing, but it is no more the essence of the human condition than is disease. We are eradicating diseases like polio and smallpox. We can eradicate violence in human affairs." Saul had slipped into his professional tone. *Where are you, Oberst?*

Harrington laughed. It was an old man's laugh, jerky, full of phlegm. Saul started at the young man next to him and shivered. He had the terrible thought that Francis's face—short reddish hair, freckles on high cheekbones—looked like a mask of flesh drawn down across another man's skull. Harrington's body under the long raincoat looked strangely blocky, as if the boy had put on rolls of fat or was wearing multiple layers of sweaters.

"You can no more eradicate violence than you could eradicate love or hate or laughter," said Willi von Borchert's voice from Francis Harrington's mouth. "The love of violence is an aspect of our humanity. Even the weak wish to be strong primarily so they can wield the whip."

"Nonsense," said Saul.

"Nonsense?" repeated Harrington. They had crossed Madison Drive onto the mall below the Capitol Reflecting Pool. Now Harrington sat down on a park bench facing Third Street. Saul did also, turning to scan every face in sight. There were not many. None looked like the Oberst.

"My dear Jew," said Harrington, "look at Israel."

"What?" Saul swiveled to look at Francis. It was not the same man he had known. "What do you mean?"

"Your dear, adopted country is famed for its prowess at delivering violence to its enemies," said Harrington. "Its philosophy is 'An eye for an eye,' its policy one of sure retribution, its pride is at the efficiency of its army and air force."

"Israel defends itself," said Saul. The surreal quality of this discussion made his head spin. Above them, the dome of the Capitol caught the last rays of light.

Harrington laughed again. "Ah yes, my faithful pawn. Violence in the name of defense is always more palatable. Thus the Wehrmacht." He stressed the *Wehr*—defense. "Israel has enemies, *nicht wahr*? But so did the Third Reich. And not the least of those enemies were the very vermin that postured as helpless victims when they strove to destroy the Reich and now posture as heroes as they wreak violence on the Palestinians."

Saul did not respond to this. The Oberst's anti-Semitism was a childish provocation. "What do you want?" Saul asked quietly.

Harrington raised his eyebrows. "What is wrong with looking up an old acquaintance to have an interesting conversation?" he said in English.

"How did you find me?"

Harrington shrugged. "I would say that *you found me*," he said in a strange, throaty rumble that was not Francis Harrington's voice. "Imagine my surprise when my dear pawn arrives in Charleston. My young Wandering Jew is very far from Chelmno."

Saul began to ask, *How did you know me?* but stopped. Those hours almost forty years ago when the two of them had shared Saul's body had created a foul intimacy more long-lasting than words could convey. Saul knew that he would recognize the Oberst at once—had recognized him—in spite of the erosion of time. Instead, Saul asked, "You followed me from Charleston?"

Harrington smiled. "It would have given me great pleasure to hear one of your lectures at Columbia. Perhaps we could have debated the ethics of the Third Reich."

"Perhaps," said Saul. "And perhaps we could debate the relative sanity of a rabid dog. Still, there is only one solution to such an illness. Shoot the dog."

"Ah yesss," hissed Harrington. "The final solution in yet another form. You Jews were never a subtle race."

Saul shivered. Behind the calm voice and the human puppet was a man who had directly murdered scores—perhaps thousands—of human beings. The only possible reason Saul could think of that the Oberst would have sought him out, followed him from Charleston, was to kill him. Oberst Wilhelm von Borchert, a.k.a. William Borden, had gone to great efforts to convince the world that he was dead. There was no reason to reveal himself to perhaps the only person in the world who knew his identity unless it was the final play of a cat and mouse game. Saul felt deeper in his pocket and closed his hand around a roll of quarters he kept there. It was the only weapon he had carried since the Forest of the Owls in Poland, thirty-six years ago.

If he did manage to knock Francis out—a much harder feat than suggested by television and the movies, Saul knew—what to do then? Run. But what would keep the Oberst from entering *his* mind? Saul shuddered at the thought of experiencing that mindrape again. He would not have to be the victim of an assault, merely another statistic, an absentminded professor who had wandered into busy Washington traffic just after dusk . . .

He would not leave Francis behind. Saul closed his fist around the quarters, began slowly withdrawing his hand. He did not know if the boy could be brought back—one look at the mask of a face in front of him made Saul think he could not—but he knew he must try. How does one transport an unconscious body along the mall for a block and a half to one's rented car? Knowing Washington, Saul suspected that it had been done at one time or another. He decided that he would leave the boy on the bench, make a dash for the car, and drive quickly to Third Street, stop at the curb, and throw the tall young man's body in the backseat.

Saul could think of nothing he could do to protect himself from being taken over by the Oberst. It did not matter. He casually removed the fist with the roll of quarters from his pocket, blocking the sight of it by the position of his body.

"I want you to meet someone," said Harrington.

"What?" Saul's heart was pounding so fiercely that he could barely speak.

"I have someone I want you to meet," repeated the Oberst, having Harrington stand up. "I think you will be interested in meeting him."

Saul sat where he was. His arm vibrated with the tension of his clenched fist.

"Are you coming, Jew?" The German words and tone were almost identical to those the Oberst had used in the Chelmno barracks thirty-eight years before.

"Yes," said Saul and rose, put his hands in his coat pockets, and followed Francis Harrington into the sudden winter darkness.

It was the shortest day of the year. A few hardy tourists waited for buses or hurried for their cars. They walked down Constitution Avenue past the Capitol and stood by the exit to the parking garage to the Senate Office Building. After a few minutes, automatic doors opened and a limousine glided out. Harrington hurried down the ramp and Saul followed, ducking as the metal door slid down. Two guards stood staring at them. One, a red-faced, overweight man, marched their way. "Goddammit, you're not allowed in here," he shouted. "Turn around and get out of here before you get your asses arrested."

"Hey, sorry!" called Harrington, his voice sounding like Francis Harrington's. "The thing is, you know, we've got passes to see Senator Kellog, but the door he said to use is locked and nobody answered when we knocked . . ."

"Main door," said the guard, still flapping his hands. The other guard stood by an enclosed area. His right hand was on his revolver and he watched Saul and Harrington very carefully. "No visitors after five though. Now get the hell out of here or get arrested. *Move.*"

"Sure," said Harrington amiably and drew an automatic pistol from his coat. He shot the heavy guard through the right eye. The other guard stood transfixed. Saul had flinched away at the first shot and now he noticed that the guard's immobility was not a natural reaction of fear. The man was straining with all of his might to move his right arm, but his hand merely vibrated as if palsied. Sweat broke out on the guard's forehead and upper lip and his eyes protruded.

"Too late," said Harrington and shot the man four times in the chest and neck.

Saul heard the pfft-pfft-pfft-pfft and realized that part of the long barrel was a silencer. He started to move and then froze as Harrington swung the weapon in his direction. "Drag them inside." Saul did so, his breath fogging in the cold air as he dragged the heavy man across the exit ramp and into the booth.

Harrington ejected a clip and slid another one home with a slap of his palm. He crouched to pick up five shell casings. "Let us go upstairs," he said.

"They have video cameras," gasped Saul.

"Yes, in the building itself," said Harrington, speaking in German once more. "Only a telephone to the basement."

"They will miss the guards," said Saul in a firmer voice.

"Undoubtedly," said Harrington. "I suggest you go up these stairs more quickly."

They emerged on the first floor and walked down a hall. A security man reading a newspaper looked up in surprise. "I'm sorry, sir, but this wing is closed after . . ." Harrington shot him twice in the chest and dragged his body to the stairwell. Saul sagged against a wooden doorway. His legs felt like liquid and he wondered if he was going to be ill. He considered running, considered screaming, and did nothing but clutch at the oak doorway for support.

"The elevator," said Harrington.

The third floor hall was empty, although Saul heard conversation and laughter from around a corner. Harrington opened the fourth door on the right.

A young woman was in the act of putting a dust cover on an IBM typewriter. "I'm sorry," she said, "but it's past . . ."

Harrington swung the pistol in an arc that caught her solidly on the left temple. She crumpled to the floor with almost no noise. Harrington lifted the plastic dust cover from where she had dropped it and slid it over the typewriter. Then he caught Saul's coat and pulled him through an empty anteroom and a large, darkened office. Saul caught a glimpse of the lighted Capitol dome between dark drapes.

Harrington opened another door and stepped through. "Hello, Trask," he said in English.

The thin man behind the desk looked up in mild surprise and in the same instant a stocky man in a brown suit exploded off a leather couch at them. Harrington shot the bodyguard twice, went over to look at the small automatic the man had dropped, and then shot him a third time behind the left ear. The thick body spasmed, kicked once on the thick carpet, and was still.

Nieman Trask had not moved. He still held a three-ring notebook in his left hand and a gold Cross pen in his right.

"Sit down," said Harrington and gestured Saul to the leather couch.

"Who are you?" Trask asked Harrington. His tone held what sounded like mild curiosity.

"Questions and answers later," said Harrington. "First, please understand that my friend here"—he gestured at Saul—"is to be left alone. If he stirs from that couch, I will open my left hand."

"Open your hand?" said Trask.

Harrington's left hand had been empty when he had entered the room; now it held a palm-size plastic ring with a small bulb in the center. An insulated wire ran up the sleeve of his raincoat. His thumb depressed the center of the bulb.

"Oh, I see," Trask said tiredly and set down the three-ring binder. He held the gold pen in both hands. "Explosives?"

"C-4," said Harrington and used the hand holding the pistol to unbutton his raincoat. He was wearing a baggy fishing vest underneath and every pocket bulged to capacity. Saul could see small loops of wire. "Twelve pounds of plastic explosive," added Harrington.

Trask nodded. He looked composed, but the tips of his fingers were white on the pen. "More than enough," he said. "What would you like?"

"I would like to talk," said Harrington, taking a seat in the chair three feet in front of Trask's desk.

"By all means," said Trask and leaned back in his chair. His gaze flicked to Saul and back. "Please start."

"Get Mr. Colben and Mr. Barent on the conference line," said Harrington.

"I'm sorry," said Trask and set down his pen. He spread his fingers. "Colben's on his way to Chevy Chase by now and I believe Mr. Barent is out of the country."

Harrington nodded. "I will count to six," he said. "If you've not made the call, I will release my thumb. One . . . two . . ."

Trask had picked up the phone by the count of four, but it was another several minutes before all of the connections were made. He caught Colben in his limousine on the Rock Creek Expressway and Barent somewhere over Maine.

"Put it on the speaker," said Harrington.

"What is it, Nieman?" came a smooth voice with a trace of Cambridge accent. "Richard, are you there also?"

"Yeah," came Colben's rumble. "I don't know what the fuck this is about. What's going on, Trask? You've had me on hold for two fucking minutes."

"I have a slight problem here," said Trask.

"Nieman, this is not a secure line," came the soft voice Saul guessed to be Barent's. "Are you alone?"

Trask hesitated and looked at Harrington. When Francis did nothing but smile, Trask said, "Ah, no, sir. There are two gentlemen here in Senator Kellog's office with me."

Colben's voice crackled on the speaker phone. "What the fuck's going on there, Trask? What's this all about?"

"Calmly, Richard," came Barent's voice. "Go ahead, Nieman."

Trask raised his hand, palm up, toward Harrington in an "after you" gesture.

"Mr. Barent, we would like to apply for membership in one of your clubs," said Harrington.

"I'm sorry, you have the advantage of me, sir," Barent said.

"My name is Francis Harrington," said Harrington. "My employer here is Dr. Saul Laski of Columbia University."

"Trask!" came Colben's voice. "What's happening?"

"Hush," said Barent. "Mr. Harrington, Dr. Laski, pleased to make your acquaintance. How can I be of help?"

On the couch, Saul Laski let out a tired sigh. Until the Oberst had given his name, he had held out some hope of emerging alive from this nightmare. Now, although he had no idea what game the Oberst was playing or who these people were in relation to the trio of Willi, Nina, and the Fuller woman, he doubted if the Oberst would name him if he were not willing to sacrifice him.

"You mentioned a club," prompted Barent's voice. "Can you be more specific?"

Harrington grinned horribly. His left arm remained raised, his thumb on the detonator trigger. "I would like to join *your* club," he said.

Barent's voice sounded amused. "I belong to many clubs, Mr. Harrington. Can you be even more specific?"

"I am only interested in the most select club possible," said Harrington. "And I have always had a weakness for islands."

The speaker phone chuckled. "As have I, Mr. Harrington, but although Mr. Trask is an excellent sponsor, I am afraid that most of the clubs to which I belong require additional references. You mention that your employer Dr. Laski is there. Do you also wish an application, Doctor?"

Saul could think of nothing that would improve his situation. He remained silent.

"Perhaps you . . . ah . . . represent someone else as well," said Barent.

Harrington only chuckled.

"He has twelve pounds of plastic explosive hooked to a dead man's switch," Trask said without emotion. "I find that an impressive reference. Why don't we all agree to meet somewhere else and talk about this?"

"I have men on the way," came Colben's clipped voice. "Hang tight, Trask."

Nieman Trask sighed, rubbed his brow, and leaned closer to the speaker phone. "Colben, you miserable fuck, if you put anyone within ten blocks of this building, I'll personally rip your goddamn heart out. Now stay the fuck *out* of this. Barent, are you there?"

C. Arnold Barent spoke as if he had heard none of the preceding dialogue. "I'm terribly sorry, Mr. Harrington, but I make it a personal policy never to be on the selection committees of any of the clubs I happen to frequent. I do enjoy sponsoring the occasional new member, however. Perhaps you would be so kind as to see if you could give me the forwarding address of some prospective members I had hoped to contact."

"Shoot," said Harrington.

It was at that moment that Saul Laski felt Trask slip into his mind. It was exquisitely painful—as if someone had slid a long, sharp wire into his left ear. He shuddered once but was not allowed to cry out. His eyes moved to the automatic still on the carpet a foot beyond the dead bodyguard's outstretched hand. He sensed Trask's cold calculations of timing and effort: two seconds to spring, a second to rise and fire into Harrington's brain while simultaneously grabbing his fist, holding the trigger down like the spoon of a grenade. Saul felt his hands clench and unclench as if of their own volition, watched his legs stir slightly, stretching like a runner before a race. Pushed farther and farther into the helpless attic of his own mind, Saul wanted to scream but had no voice. Is this what Francis had been experiencing for weeks?

"William Borden," said Barent.

Saul had all but forgotten what the discussion was about. Trask moved Saul's right leg a bit, changed his center of gravity, tensed his right arm.

"Don't know the gentleman," Harrington said lightly. "Next?"

Saul felt every muscle in his body tense as Trask prepared him. He sensed the slight change of plan. Trask would have him hit Harrington on the run, push him backward, hold the left hand clenched until he had shoved Francis into the senator's main office, then block the forward force of the explosion with his body while Trask dropped under the massive oak desk. Saul wanted to scream a warning at the Oberst.

"Miss Melanie Fuller," said Barent.

"Oh yes," said Harrington. "I believe she can be reached in Germantown."

"Which Germantown is that?" asked Trask even as he readied Saul for the attack. Ignore the gun. Grab the hand. Force him back, away. Keep your body between Harrington and Trask's desk.

"The suburb of Philadelphia," Harrington said amiably. "I can't recall the precise address, but if you check the listings along Queen Lane you should be able to contact the lady."

"Very good," said Barent. "One more thing. If you could . . ."

"Excuse me a second," said Harrington. He laughed an old man's laugh again. "Good God, Trask," he said. "Do you think I can't feel that? You could not commandeer this shell in a month . . . *Mein Gott*, man, you sneak and grope around like a teenager trying to cop a feel . . . is that the expression? . . . in the balcony of a movie house. And release my poor Jewish friend while you are at it. The instant he moves, I trigger this. That desk will become a thousand flying splinters. Ah, that is better . . ."

Saul collapsed onto the couch. His muscles spasmed in sudden release from the tight vise of control.

"Now, where were we, Mr. Barent?" said Harrington.

There was static for several seconds before Barent's calm voice came back on the speakerphone. "I'm sorry, Mr. Harrington, I'm talking to you from my private aircraft and I am afraid I have to go now. I appreciate your call and look forward to speaking to you again soon."

"Barent!" yelled Trask. "Goddamn you, stay on the . . ."

"Good-bye," said Barent. There was a click. The open line spat static.

"Colben!" screamed Trask. "Say something."

The heavy voice came on the line. "Sure. Get fucked, Nieman old pal." Another click and a hum.

Trask looked up with the expression of a cornered animal.

"It's all right," soothed Harrington. "I can leave my message with you. We can still do business, Mr. Trask. But I'd prefer that it be private. Dr. Laski, do you mind?"

Saul adjusted his glasses and blinked. He stood up. Trask glared at him. Harrington smiled. Saul turned, walked quickly through the senator's office, and was running by the time he got to the first waiting room. He was out of the office and running down the hall before he remembered the secretary. He hesitated, then began running again.

Ahead of him, four men came around the corner. Saul turned, saw five men in dark suits run from the other direction, two veering toward Trask's office.

He looked around in time to see three of the men at the end of the hall raise their revolvers in almost a single motion, hands together, arms extended, black circles of muzzles seeming very large even from a distance. Suddenly Saul was elsewhere.

Francis Harrington screamed in the silence of his own mind. Dimly he sensed Saul's sudden presence there in the darkness with him. Together they watched through Harrington's eyes as Nieman Trask shouted something, half rose from his chair, raised both hands in supplication.

"Auf Wiedersehen," the Oberst said with Francis Harrington's voice and released the trigger.

The south doors and wall to the corridor exploded outward in a ball of orange flame. Saul was suddenly flying through the air toward the three men in dark suits. Their raised arms flew back, one of the guns discharged— silently in the overwhelming rage of noise filling the corridor—and then they were also flying, tumbling backward, and striking the wall at the end of the corridor a scant second before Saul did.

After the impact, even as the crest of darkness broke over him, Saul heard the echo—not of the explosion, but of the old man's voice saying *Auf Wiedersehen.*

TWENTY

New York
Friday, Dec. 26, 1980

Sheriff Gentry enjoyed air travel but cared very little for his destination. He liked to fly because he found the phenomenon of being wedged into a coach seat of a pressurized tube suspended thousands of feet above the clouds a definite incentive to meditation. His destination, New York City, always struck him as a temptation toward other types of mindlessness: hive-think, street violence, paranoia, information overload, or gibbering insanity. Gentry had decided long ago that he was not a big-city person.

Gentry knew his way around Manhattan. When he had been in college a dozen years earlier, during the height of the Vietnam era, he and friends had spent more than a few weekends in the city—once renting a car in Chicago where his girlfriend worked at a Hertz outlet near the university, postdating the mileage 2,000 miles and driving straight through. After four days without sleep, six of them had ended up driving around the Chicago suburbs for two hours in the wee hours of the morning to bring the actual mileage up to and beyond what had been recorded as the starting mileage on the form.

Gentry took a shuttle bus into the Port Authority. There he hailed a cab to the Adison Hotel just off Times Square. The place was old and sliding into disrepute, its patrons mostly hookers and tourists from the sticks, but it retained a somewhat matronly air of pride about it. The Puerto Rican cook in the coffee shop was loud, profane, and skilled at his craft, and the room cost a third of what most Manhattan hotels charged. The last time he had been to New York, to transport an extradited eighteen-year-old who had murdered four convenience store clerks in Charleston, the county had been picking up Gentry's tab and had booked his room.

Gentry showered some of the travel fatigue away and changed into comfortable blue corduroy slacks, an old turtleneck, his tan corduroy sports coat, a soft cap, and a topcoat that worked fine in Charleston but barely served to take the edge off New York's winter wind. He hesitated and then removed the .357 Ruger from the suitcase and slipped it into the pocket of his overcoat. No, too bulky and obvious. He slid it into the waistband of his slacks. Definitely not. He had no clip-on holster for the Ruger; he always wore the belt and holster with his uniform and carried the department's .38 Police Special when he was off duty. Why the hell had he brought the Ruger instead of the smaller gun? He finally ended up slipping the revolver into his sports coat pocket. He would have to leave his topcoat unbuttoned to the weather outside and leave it on inside to conceal the lump of the weapon. *What the hell*, thought Gentry. *We can't all be Steve McQueen.*

Before leaving the hotel he called his home in Charleston and triggered his answering machine. He did not expect a message from Natalie, but he had been thinking about her through the entire flight and looked forward to the chance of hearing her voice. Hers was the first message. "Rob, this is Natalie. It's about two P.M. St. Louis time. I just got into St. Louis, but I'm leaving on the next flight to Philadelphia. I think I've got a lead on where we can find Melanie Fuller. Check page three of today's Charleston paper . . . or one of the New York papers will probably have it. Gang murders in Germantown. Yeah, I don't know *why* the old woman would be involved with a street gang, but it's in *Germantown*. Saul said that our best bet in finding these people was to follow a trail of senseless violence like this. I promise I'll keep a low profile . . . I'll just look around and see if there's anything promising for us to follow up on later. I'll leave a message tonight when I know where I'll be staying. Gotta run. Be *careful*, Rob."

"Shit," Gentry said softly when he hung up the phone. He dialed his number again, let out a breath as his own voice told him to leave a message, and said after the beep, "Natalie, goddammit, do *not* stay in Philadelphia or Germantown or wherever you are. Someone *saw* you on Christmas Eve. Goddammit, if you're not going to stay in St. Louis, join me here in New York. It's *stupid* for us to be running around separately playing Joe Hardy and Nancy Drew. Call me here as soon as you get this message." He gave his hotel phone and room numbers, paused, and hung up. "Damn," he said. He brought his fist down hard enough to make the cheap desk wobble.

Gentry took the subway down to the Village and got off near St. Vincent's. He flipped through his small notebook during the ride, reviewing all the notes he had taken: Saul's address, Natalie's comment that Saul had mentioned a housekeeper named Tema, his extension at Columbia, the dean's number that Gentry had called almost two weeks ago, the late Nina Drayton's number. Not much, he thought. He called Columbia and confirmed that no one would be in the psychology department offices until next Monday.

Saul's neighborhood did not fit Gentry's preconceptions about the lifestyle of a New York psychiatrist. The sheriff reminded himself that Saul was more of a professor than a psychiatrist and then the neighborhood seemed more appropriate. The buildings were mostly four-and five-story tenements, restaurants and delis were to be found on most corners, and there was a sense of small town in the compactness of it all. A few couples hurried by—one of them a pair of males holding hands—but Gentry knew that most of the local inhabitants were uptown, ensconced in publishing houses, brokerages, bookstores, agencies, and other steel and glass cages, each floating somewhere between secretary and vice-president, earning the necessary thousands to lease their two or three rooms in the Village and waiting for the big move, the breakthrough, the inevitable rise to the higher floor, the bigger office, the corner windows, and the short cab ride home to the Central Park West brownstone. The wind gusted. Gentry clutched his topcoat tighter and hurried on.

Dr. Saul Laski was not home. Gentry was not surprised. He knocked again and stood awhile on the narrow landing, listening to the muted garble of televisions and children's wails, smelling the corned beef and cabbage echo of decades gone by. Then he removed a credit card from his wallet and slipped the lock. Gentry shook his head; Saul Laski was a nationally recognized expert on violence, a survivor of the death camp, but his home security left a lot to be desired.

It was a large apartment by Village standards—a comfortable living room, small kitchen, smaller bedroom, and a large study. Every room—even the bathroom—had books in it. The study was laden with notebooks, files, shelves of carefully labeled abstracts, and hundreds of books—many in German or Polish. Gentry checked each room, paused a minute to glance through a manuscript stacked near the IBM typewriter, and prepared to leave. He felt like an intruder. The apartment smelled as if it had not been lived in for a week or two, the kitchen was spotless, the refrigerator almost empty, but there was no dust, no stack of accumulated mail, nor other outward signs of absence. Gentry made sure there were no messages near the phone, walked through each room quickly to make sure that he had missed no clues to Saul's whereabouts, and quietly let himself out.

He had gone down a flight when he passed an old woman, graying hair done up in a bun. Gentry stopped after she passed and then tipped his cloth cap and said, "Excuse me, ma'am. Might you be Tema?"

The woman stopped and squinted suspiciously at him. Her voice held a thick accent of Eastern Europe. "I don't know you."

"No, ma'am," said Gentry and removed his cap. "And I'm sorry for using your first name, but Saul didn't mention your last name."

"Mrs. Walisjezlski," said the old woman. "Who are you?"

"I'm Sheriff Bobby Gentry," he said. "I'm a friend of Saul's and I'm trying to find him."

"Dr. Laski never mentioned any Sheriff Gentry." She gave his name a hard G.

"No, ma'am, I don't suppose he did. We just met a couple of weeks ago when he came down to Charleston. That's South Carolina. Maybe he mentioned that he was comin' down there for a visit?"

"Dr. Laski just said he had business," snapped the woman. She snorted. "As if the plane tickets weren't right there for a blind person to see! Two days, he said. Maybe three. Mrs. W, he says, if you will be so kind as to

HAZEL M. LEWIS LIBRARY
POWERS, OREGON 97466

water the plants. Ten days later, his plants would be dead if I did not faithfully come."

"Mrs. Walisjezlski, have you seen Dr. Laski in the past week?" asked Gentry.

The woman tugged her sweater tighter and said nothing.

"We had an appointment," said Gentry. "Saul said that he'd call when he got back . . . probably last Saturday. But I haven't heard from him."

"He has no sense of time," said the woman. "His own nephew calls me from Washington last week. 'Is Uncle Saul all right?' he says. 'He was supposed to come to dinner Saturday,' he says. Knowing Dr. Laski, he just forgot . . . went off to a seminar somewhere. Am I to tell his nephew that? His only family in America?"

"Is that the nephew that works in Washington?" said Gentry.

"Which one else?"

Gentry nodded, noticed from the woman's posture and tone that she was uneasy talking, ready to move on. "Saul said I could contact him at his nephew's, but I lost the number. It's right in Washington, isn't it?"

"No, no," said Mrs. Walisjezlski. "That is the embassy. Dr. Laski says they live way out in the country now."

"Could Saul be at the Polish Embassy?"

She squinted at him. "Why would Dr. Laski be at the Polish Embassy? Aaron works at the Israeli Embassy, but he does not *live* there. You say you are a *sheriff*? What business does the doctor have with a sheriff?"

"I'm an admirer of his book," said Gentry. He clicked a ballpoint pen and scribbled on the back of one of his poorly printed business cards. "Here is where I'm staying tonight. The other number is my home phone in Charleston. As *soon* as Saul gets back, have him call me. It is very important." He started down the stairs. "Oh, by the way," he called up to her, "when I call the embassy, does Saul's nephew spell his last name with one 'e' in it or two?"

"How could there be two e's in Eshkol?" clucked Mrs. Walisjezlski.

"How indeed?" said Gentry and clumped downstairs.

Natalie did not call. Gentry waited until after ten, called Charleston, and was rewarded by nothing but her original message and his own tirade. At ten after eleven he phoned again. Still nothing new. At one-fifteen A.M. he gave it up and tried to sleep. The noise through the thin wall sounded like half a dozen Iranians arguing. At three A.M. Gentry called Charleston again. Still nothing new. He left another message apologizing for his cursing and emphasizing the importance of her not wandering around Philadelphia alone.

Early the next morning, Gentry tried his answering machine again, left the name of the Washington hotel where he had booked a room, and caught the 8:15 shuttle. The flight was too brief for him to do any serious

HAZEL M. LEWIS LIBRARY
POWERS OREGON 97465

thinking, but he removed his notebook and a file from his briefcase and studied them.

Natalie had read about the December 20 bombing at the Senate Office Building and had been concerned that Saul might have been involved. Gentry had pointed out that not *every* murder, accident, and terrorist attack in America could be traced back to Laski's aging Oberst. He reminded her that the television news had suggested that Puerto Rican nationalists had been behind the explosion that had killed six people. He pointed out that the attack on the Senate Office Building had occurred only a few hours after Saul would have arrived in the city, that his name had not been listed among the dead—although the terrorist himself had not been identified, and that she was getting paranoid. Natalie had been reassured. Gentry still had his doubts.

It was after eleven by the time Gentry arrived at the FBI building. He had no idea if anyone would be working on a Saturday. A receptionist confirmed that Special Agent Richard Haines was in and then kept Gentry waiting several minutes before buzzing the busy man. She announced that Special Agent Haines would see him. Gentry contained his glee. A young man with an expensive suit and an unsuccessful mustache, a sort of Jimmy Olsen version of a Junior G-man, led Gentry to a security area where they took his photograph, recorded pertinent data, passed him through a metal detector, and gave him a laminated visitor's pass. Gentry was glad that he had left the Ruger in the suitcase at the hotel. The young man wordlessly led Gentry down corridors, into an elevator, through an area of three-sided cubicles, down another corridor, and then knocked on a door clearly marked Special Agent Richard Haines. When Haines's voice called "Come on in," the youth nodded and turned on his heel. Gentry stifled the urge to call him back to give him a tip.

Richard Haines's office was as large and tastefully decorated as Gentry's was small and cluttered. Photographs hung on the walls. Gentry caught a glimpse of a joweled and pig-eyed man who might have been the late J. Edgar Hoover shaking hands with a somewhat less gray-haired Richard Haines, and then he was being waved to his seat. Haines did not stand up or offer to shake hands.

"What brings you up to Washington, Sheriff Gentry?" Haines asked in his smooth baritone.

Gentry shifted his bulk in the small chair to get more comfortable, decided that the thing had been designed to keep people from getting comfortable, and cleared his throat. "Just on vacation, Dick, an' thought I'd drop in to say hello."

Haines raised an eyebrow. He did not stop shuffling papers. "That's nice of you, Sheriff, but it's sort of hectic around here this weekend. If it's about the Mansard House murders, I don't have anything new that I haven't sent to you through Terry and the Atlanta office."

Gentry crossed his legs and shrugged. "I was just in the neighborhood and thought I'd drop in. Real impressive setup you boys got here, Dick."

Haines grunted.

"Hey," said Gentry, "what happened to your chin? Looks like someone clipped you a good one there. Have trouble makin' an arrest?"

Haines touched his chin where the butterfly bandage was visible against a broad, yellowish bruise. Flesh-colored makeup failed to conceal it. He smiled ruefully. "No purple heart for this one, Sheriff. I slipped getting out of the tub on Christmas Day and slammed my chin against a towel rack. Lucky I didn't kill myself."

"Yeah, they say most accidents happen in the home," drawled Gentry.

Haines nodded and glanced at his wristwatch.

"Say," said Gentry, "did you get the picture we sent you?"

"Picture?" said Haines. "Oh, the one of the missing woman. Mrs. Fuller. Yes, thanks, Sheriff. It's gone out to all of our agents in the field."

"Good, good," said Gentry. "Haven't heard anymore about where she might be, have you?"

"The Fuller woman? No. I still think she's dead. My guess is that we'll never find the body."

"Probably right," agreed Gentry. "Say, Dick, I passed the Capitol on the bus comin' over here, and right catty-corner across the street was this big building with some police barricades outside and a second-story window being worked on. Is that the whatchamacallit . . ."

"Senate Office Building," said Haines.

"Yeah, isn't that where the terrorists blew up the senator about a week ago?"

"Terrorist," said Haines. "Just one. And the senator from Maine wasn't even in town when it happened. His political adviser—fairly important guy in the G.O.P. by the name of Trask—was killed. Nobody else who was important."

"I imagine you're involved in that case, huh?"

Haines sighed and put down his papers. "It's a pretty large office here, Sheriff. Quite a few agents."

"Yeah," said Gentry. "Sure are. They say that the terrorist was a Puerto Rican fellow. That right?"

"Sorry, Sheriff. We can't comment on ongoing investigations."

"Sure," said Gentry. "Say, remember that New York psychiatrist, Dr. Laski?"

"Saul Laski," said Haines. "Teaches at Columbia. Yes, we checked on his whereabouts during the weekend of the thirteenth. He was on that panel, just as your sources suggested. He probably came down to Charleston to get some publicity for his next book."

"Could be," said Gentry. "Thing is, though, he was gonna send me some information on this mass murder stuff and now I can't get hold of him anywhere. You haven't kept track of him, have you?"

"No," said Haines and glanced at his watch again. "Why should we have?"

"No reason. But I think Laski was coming here to Washington. Last Saturday, I think it was. Same day you had that terrorist thing over to the Senate Office Building."

"So?" said Haines.

Gentry shrugged. "Just had a feeling this fella was trying to solve things on his own. Thought he might've showed up here."

"He didn't," said Haines. "Sheriff, I'd like to chat with you, but I've got another appointment in a couple of minutes."

"Sure, sure," said Gentry, rising and tugging on his cap. "You ought to have somebody see to that."

"What's that?" asked Haines.

"Your chin," said Gentry. "That's a real nasty bruise."

Gentry wandered down Ninth Street toward the mall, crossing Pennsylvania Avenue and passing the Department of Justice. He went right on Constitution, up Tenth past the I.R.S. building, left on Pennsylvania again, and jogged up to the steps of the Old Post Office. No one seemed to be following him. He continued on up Pennsylvania Avenue to Pershing Park and peered across the street at the roof of the White House. He wondered if Jimmy Carter was in there now, brooding about the hostages and blaming the Iranians for his defeat.

Gentry sat on a park bench and took his notebook out of his pocket. He flipped through the pages with their tightly scrawled script, closed the notebook, and sighed.

Dead end.

What if Saul was a fraud? A paranoid nutso?

No.

Why not?

Just no.

Okay, then where the hell is he? Walk over to the Congressional library and check the last week's papers, death notices, accident reports. Call the hospitals.

And what if he's in the morgue under a Puerto Rican John Doe?

Doesn't make sense. What does the Oberst have to do with a senator's adviser?

What did he have to do with Kennedy and Ruby?

Gentry rubbed his eyes. The thing had almost made sense back in Charleston when he was sitting at Natalie Preston's kitchen table listening to Saul's story. Things had clicked into place; the apparently random murders becoming a series of feints and thrusts from two or three old opponents with truly incredible powers. But now nothing made any sense. Unless . . .

Unless there were more of them.

Gentry sat straight up. Saul had to talk to someone here in Washington. Despite all of the recently shared confidences, he would not reveal

who he was meeting. *Family.* For what reason? Gentry remembered the
pain with which Saul had discussed the disappearance of his hired
detective—Francis Harrington. So maybe Saul had asked for help. From
a nephew in the Israeli Embassy? But maybe someone else also got involved. *Who?* The government? Saul could think of no reason the federal
government would be in the business of protecting an aging ex-Nazi. But
what if there were more like the Oberst, Fuller, and Drayton?

The sheriff shivered and pulled his coat tighter. It was a clear, bright
day. The temperature was in the thirties. Weak winter light added a
golden tint to the brown and brittle grass in the park.

He found a pay phone on the corner near the Washington Hotel and
used his credit card to call Charleston. There still was no message from
Natalie. Gentry found the number he had copied from his hotel room directory and called the Israeli Embassy. He wondered if anyone would be
there on their Sabbath day.

A woman answered.

"Hello," said Gentry, stifling the sudden urge to say "Shalom." "Could
I speak to Aaron Eshkol."

There was a brief hesitation and the woman said, "Who is calling,
please?"

"This is Sheriff Robert Gentry."

"One second please."

The second was more like two minutes. Gentry stood cradling the
phone and stared at the Treasury building across the street.

If there were more people . . . mind vampires . . . like the Oberst, it
might explain a lot. Such as why the Oberst felt it necessary to fake his
own death. And why the Charleston County Sheriff had been followed for
a week and a half. And why everything a certain FBI agent said made
Gentry want to smash his teeth in. And what happened to a certain scrapbook of grisly newspaper clippings last seen at the scene of a murder . . .

"Hello."

"Oh, hi, Mr. Eshkol, this is Sheriff Bobby Gentry . . ."

"No, this is Jack Cohen speaking."

"Oh. Well, Mr. Cohen, I'm calling for Aaron Eshkol."

"I am the supervisor of Mr. Eshkol's department. Please tell me your
business, Sheriff."

"Actually, Mr. Cohen, this is sort of a personal call."

"Are you a friend of Aaron's, Sheriff Gentry?"

Gentry knew something was wrong, but could not put his finger on
what it was. "No, sir," he said. "I'm more a friend of Aaron's uncle, Saul
Laski. I need to speak to Aaron."

There was a brief silence. "It would be best if you were to come here in
person, Sheriff."

Gentry glanced at his watch. "I'm not sure if I'll have time, Mr. Cohen.
If you could put me in touch with Aaron, I'll see if it's necessary."

"Very well. Where are you calling from, Sheriff? Here in Washington?"

"Yeah," said Gentry. "A pay phone."

"Are you in the city itself? Someone can give you directions to the embassy."

Gentry tried to control his rising anger. "I'm right near the Washington Hotel," he said. "Just put Aaron Eshkol on or give me his home phone number. If I need to see him at the embassy, I'll grab a cab."

"Very well, Sheriff. Please call back in ten minutes." Cohen hung up before Gentry could protest.

He paced back and forth in front of the hotel, irritated, tempted to pick up his stuff at the hotel and fly straight to Philadelphia. This was ridiculous. He knew how hard it was to find a missing person in Charleston, where he had six deputies and ten times that many contacts. This was absurd.

He called back two minutes before the ten minutes were up. The woman answered again. "Yes, Sheriff. One second please."

Gentry sighed and leaned against the metal frame of the telephone stand. Something sharp poked him in the side. Gentry turned, saw the two men standing close, too close, saw the taller of the two smiling broadly at him. Then Gentry looked down and saw the barrel of the small-caliber automatic touching his side.

"We're going to walk to that car and get in," said the big man with a hearty grin. He clapped Gentry on the back as if they were two old friends meeting after a long absence. The barrel dug deeper.

The tall man was too close, Gentry thought. There was a better than even chance that he could slap away the weapon before the man could fire. But his partner had stepped back five feet, his right hand in his raincoat pocket, and no matter what Gentry might do, the second man would have a clear field of fire.

"Walk now," said the tall man.

Gentry walked.

It was not a bad tour. They drove around the Ellipse, west to the Lincoln Memorial, around the Tidal Basin, then up Jefferson Drive to the Capitol, past Union Station, and back around again. No one called out the sights. The limousine was plush, wide, and soundless. The windows were opaque from the outside, the doors locked automatically from the driver's seat, there was a Plexiglas partition behind the driver, and the two men from the corner sat on either side of Gentry. Across from him sprawled on a jump seat sat a man with poorly cut white hair, sad eyes, and a lumpy, pockmarked face that somehow managed to be handsome.

"I'll let you guys in on something," said Gentry. "Kidnapping's against the law in this country."

The white-haired man said softly, "Could I see some identification, Mr. Gentry?"

Gentry considered several self-righteous and indignant protests. He shrugged and handed over his wallet. No one jumped when he reached for it; the two men had frisked him as he entered the car. "You sound like Jack Cohen," said Gentry.

"I am Jack Cohen," said the other, rifling through Gentry's wallet, "and you have all the proper identification, credit cards, and miscellania of a Southern sheriff named Robert Joseph Gentry."

"Bobby Joe to my friends and constituents," said Gentry.

"There is no place in the world where I.D. means less than in America," said Cohen.

Gentry shrugged. His instinct was to explain to them precisely how little he cared and to suggest certain airborne carnal acts that they could perform on themselves. He said, "Can I see your identification?"

"I am Jack Cohen."

"Uh-huh. And are you really Aaron Eshkol's boss?"

"I am head of the Communications and Interpretations section of the embassy," said Cohen.

"Is that Aaron's department?"

"Yes," said Cohen. "Is this news to you?"

"As far as I know, one of you three is Aaron Eshkol," said Gentry. "I've never met the man. And from the sound of things, I'm not going to."

"Why do you say that, Mr. Gentry?" Cohen's voice was as flat and cold as a killing blade.

"Call it a guess," said Gentry. "I phone asking for Aaron and the entire embassy puts me on hold while you guys leap into the nearest limousine and burn rubber to take me on a tour by gunpoint. Now if you *are* who you say you are . . . and who the hell knows at this point . . . you're acting a little out of character for ambassadors of our loyal and dependent ally in the Middle East. My guess is that Aaron Eshkol is dead or missing and you're a bit upset . . . even to the point of sticking guns in the ribs of duly elected law enforcement officers."

"Go on," said Cohen.

"Get fucked," said Gentry. "I've said my say. Tell me what's going on and I'll tell you why I called Aaron Eshkol."

"We could invite your participation in this discussion by . . . ah . . . other means," said Cohen. The absence of threat in his tone served as a threat.

"I doubt it," said Gentry. "Unless you're not who you say you are. Either way, I'm saying nothing else until *you* tell *me* something worth learning."

Cohen glanced out at the passing marble scenery and looked back at Gentry. "Aaron Eshkol is dead," he said. "Murdered. Him, his wife, and two daughters."

"When?" said Gentry.

"Two days ago."

"Christmas Day," muttered Gentry. "This has been a hell of a holiday season. How were they killed?"

"Someone pushed a wire into their brains," said Cohen. From the tone of his voice, he might have been describing a new way to fix an auto engine.

"Ah, Jesus," breathed Gentry. "Why didn't I read about this?"

"There was an explosion and fire," said Cohen. "The Virginia coroner ruled accidental death . . . a gas leak. Aaron's association with the embassy has not been picked up by the news services."

"Your own doctors found the true cause of death?"

"Yes," said Cohen. "Yesterday."

"But why go apeshit when I call?" asked Gentry. "Aaron must have had . . . no, wait. I mentioned Saul Laski. You think Saul is connected to Aaron's death in some way."

"Yes," said Cohen.

"All right," breathed Gentry. "Who killed Aaron Eshkol?"

Cohen shook his head. "Your turn, Sheriff Gentry."

Gentry paused to gather his thoughts.

"You should realize," continued Cohen, "that it would indeed be disastrous for Israel to offend American taxpayers at this sensitive period in our countries' histories. We are willing to risk the embarrassment when you convince us of your innocence and we release you. If you fail to convince us, it would be much easier for everyone involved if you just disappear."

"Shut up," said Gentry. "I'm thinking." They passed the Jefferson Memorial for the third time and crossed a bridge. The Washington Monument loomed ahead of them. "Saul Laski came to Charleston ten days ago to inquire about the Mansard House murders . . . CBS called the mess the Charleston Massacre . . . you heard about our little trouble?"

"Yes," said Cohen. "Several old people murdered for their money and some innocent witnesses eliminated, no?"

"Close enough," said Gentry. "One of the old people that was involved was an ex-Nazi living under the name of William D. Borden."

"A film producer," said the tall, frizzy-haired Israeli on Gentry's left.

Gentry jumped. He had almost forgotten that the bodyguards could speak. "Yeah," he said. "And Saul Laski had been hunting for this particular Nazi for forty years—ever since Chelmno and Sobibor."

"What are they?" asked the young man to Gentry's right.

Gentry stared. Cohen snapped something in Hebrew and the young agent blushed. "The German . . . Borden . . . died, did he not?" said Cohen.

"In an air crash," said Gentry. "Supposedly. But Saul didn't think so."

"So Dr. Laski assumed his old tormenter was still alive," mused Cohen. "But what did Borden have to do with the murders in Charleston?"

Gentry removed his cloth cap and poked at the crown. "Settling old scores," said Gentry. "Saul didn't know for sure. He just felt that the Oberst . . . that's what he called Borden . . . was involved somehow."

"Why did Laski meet with Aaron?"

Gentry shook his head. "I didn't know they had met. I didn't even know Aaron Eshkol existed until yesterday. Saul flew from Charleston to be in Washington on December twentieth to interview somebody . . . he wouldn't say who. He was going to stay in touch with me, but I haven't heard from him since he left Charleston. Yesterday I visited Saul's apartment building in New York and talked to his housekeeper . . ."

"Tema," said the tall man and silenced himself after a harsh glance from Cohen.

"Yeah," said Gentry. "She mentioned Aaron. Here I am."

"What did Dr. Laski want to talk to Aaron about?" asked Cohen.

Gentry set his cap on his knee and opened his hands. "Damned if I know. I had the impression that Saul was expecting to get more information about Borden's life out in California. Could Aaron have helped him there?"

Cohen bit his lip for some time before responding. "Aaron took four days of personal leave before meeting with his uncle," he said. "He spent part of that time in California."

"What did he learn there?" asked Gentry.

"We don't know."

"How did you know about his meeting with Saul? Did Saul come to your embassy?"

The tall man said something in Hebrew that sounded like a warning. Cohen overrode him. "No," he said. "Dr. Laski met with Aaron a week ago today at the National Gallery. Aaron and Levi Cole, a coworker in communications, thought the meeting was important. According to friends in the department, Aaron and Levi kept some files that they thought were of great importance in the cryptography safe that week."

"What was in them?" asked Gentry, not really believing he would get an answer.

"We don't know," said Cohen. "A few hours after Aaron's family was murdered, Levi Cole logged into the embassy and removed the files. He has not been seen since." Cohen rubbed the bridge of his nose. "And none of it makes sense. Levi is the bachelor. No family here in the States, none left in Isreal. He is an ardent Zionist, ex-commando. I cannot imagine what hold they could have used on him. Logic dictates that it was him they should have eliminated, Aaron Eshkol they should have blackmailed. Only the question is, of course, who are *they*?"

Gentry said nothing.

"All right, Sheriff," said Cohen. "Please tell us anything else that might be of help."

"That's about it," said Gentry. "Unless you want to hear Saul Laski's story." *How do I tell it without getting into the Oberst's powers, the old ladies' abilities?* thought Gentry. *They won't believe me and if they don't believe me I'm dead.*

"We want everything," said Cohen. "From the beginning."

The limousine glided past the Lincoln Memorial and headed for the Tidal Basin.

TWENTY-ONE

Germantown
Saturday, Dec. 27, 1980

Natalie Preston used her Nikon with the 135mm lens to record the decaying contradictions of the dying city: stone homes, brick row houses, a bank designed to blend in with eighteenth-century buildings on either side, antique stores filled with broken junk, Salvation Army outlets filled with junk, empty lots filled with junk, narrow streets and alleys filled with junk. Natalie had loaded the Nikon with black and white Plus-X, not worried about the graininess, taking long, slow exposures that should bring out every chip and crack in every wall. There was no sign of Melanie Fuller.

After she had loaded the film, she had worked her courage up and loaded the .32 Llama automatic. It now lay at the bottom of her big purse, under the clutter and lens caps and cardboard false bottom.

The city was not so frightening in the daylight. The previous evening, landing after dark, feeling displaced and disoriented, she had allowed the man who sat next to her on the plane—Jensen Luhar—to drive her to Germantown. He said it was on his way. His gray Mercedes was parked in the long-term lot. At first she was glad she had accepted; the ride was long—down a busy expressway, across a two-level bridge, into the core of Philadelphia, out another winding, hectic freeway, across the river again—or perhaps it was another river—and then onto Germantown Avenue, a broad, brick thoroughfare wandering past dark slums and empty shops. By the time they were approaching the heart of Germantown, nearing the hotel he had suggested she stay at, she was sure the proposition was coming: "How about if I come up for a minute?" or "I'd love to show you my place—it's just a little farther." Probably the first; he wore no wedding ring, but that meant nothing. The only thing that Natalie was sure of was that there would be the inevitable proposition and then her clumsy rejection.

She was wrong. He parked in front of the old hotel, helped her in with her bags, wished her luck, and drove off. She wondered if he was gay.

Natalie had called Charleston before eleven and left her hotel phone and room number on Rob's answering machine. She had expected him to call right after eleven, probably suggesting that she go back to St. Louis, but he did not. Disappointed, feeling strangely hurt, fighting sleep, she called Charleston again at 11:30 and used the device Rob had loaned her. There was no message from him, only her two calls on the tape. She had gone to sleep puzzled and a little frightened.

It was better in the daylight. Although there still was no message from Gentry, she called the *Philadelphia Inquirer* and by invoking her Chicago editor's name she was able to get a little information out of the city editor. The details of the crime were still largely unknown, but it was certain that some or all of the four gang members had been decapitated. The Soul Brickyard Gang had their headquarters in a city-funded settlement house off Bringhurst Street, only a mile or so from Natalie's Chelten Avenue hotel. Natalie looked up the settlement house's phone number, called, and identified herself as a *Sun Times* reporter. A minister named Bill Woods gave her fifteen minutes at three o'clock.

Natalie spent the day exploring Germantown, wandering farther and farther down depressing side streets, and shooting photographs. The place had a strange charm. North and west of Chelten Avenue, large old homes held their ground in a reduced role of duplexes while black and white families carried on a semblance of middleclass life, while east to Bringhurst Street, the neighborhood decayed into burned-out rowhouses, abandoned cars, and the sightless stare of the hopeless.

The sun was out, however, and for a while children followed her in a giggling pack, beseeching her to take their picture. Natalie did so. A train roared by overhead, a woman's voice bellowed from a doorway half a block away, and the entire pack scattered like leaves in a wind.

There was no message from Rob at ten, twelve, or two. She would wait until eleven P.M. *Damn.*

At three she knocked at the door of a large 1920s-style home set in the midst of rubble, burned-out apartment buildings, and factory yards. Part of the railing along the wraparound porch had been knocked out. Windows on the third floor had been boarded over, but someone had added a thin coat of cheap yellow paint during the past year. The house looked jaundiced.

The Reverend Bill Woods was white and lumpy. He sat with her in a cluttered office on the first floor and complained about the lack of city funding, the bureaucratic nightmare of administering a community action project such as Community House, and the lack of cooperation from the youth groups and community in general. He refused to use the word "gang." Natalie caught glimpses of young black men coming and going in the halls and heard shouts and laughter from the basement and second floor.

"Can I speak to someone in the Soul Brickyard . . . group?" she asked.

"Oh, no," cried Woods. "The boys do not wish to speak to anyone except the television people. They enjoy being on camera."

"Do they *live* here?" asked Natalie.

"Oh, heavens no. They simply congregate here frequently for fellowship and recreation."

"I need to talk to them," said Natalie and rose from her seat.

"I'm afraid that won't be . . . hey, wait a minute!"

Natalie strode down the hall, opened a door, and went up a narrow flight of stairs. On the second floor a dozen black males huddled around a pool table or sprawled on mattresses scattered on the plaster-strewn floor. There were steel shutters on the windows and Natalie counted four pump shotguns propped near them.

Everyone froze when she entered. A tall, incredibly lean man in his early twenties leaned on his pool cue and snapped, "What you want, bitch?"

"I want to talk to you."

"Shee-it," said a bearded youth lying on one of the mattresses. "Listen that. 'Ah want tuh talk to yoah.' Where the fuck you from, woman? Some cracker state down south somewhere?"

"I want to do an interview," said Natalie, marveling that her voice or knees had not yet betrayed her. "About the murders."

Silence stretched until it grew mean. The tall youth who had spoken first raised the pool cue and walked slowly toward her. Four feet away he stopped, extended the cue, and ran the chalky tip between the open flaps of her goose-down jacket, down her blouse, to hook on the belt of her jeans. "I be givin' you a interview, bitch. A real in-depth interview, you get what I mean."

Natalie forced herself not to flinch. She shifted her Nikon to one side, reached into her coat pocket, and held out a color print of Mr. Hodges's slide. "Have any of you seen this woman?"

The man with the cue looked at it and waved over a boy who could not have been more than fourteen. The boy stared, nodded, and went back to his place by the window.

"Get Marvin up here," snapped the one with the pool cue. "Move your ass."

Marvin Gayle was nineteen, was strikingly handsome with pale blue eyes, long lashes, skin the exact color of Natalie's, and was a born leader. Natalie knew that the instant he entered the room. Somehow the focus in the room *shifted*, the posture of the others changed ever so slightly, and Marvin was the *center*. For ten minutes Marvin demanded to know who the white woman was. For ten minutes, Natalie offered to tell them *after* they told her about the murders.

Finally Marvin showed beautiful teeth in a broad smile. "You sure you want to know, babe?"

"Yes," said Natalie. Frederick called her babe. It disconcerted her to hear it here.

Marvin clapped his hands together. "Leroy, Calvin, Monk, Louis, George," he said. "The rest of you stay here."

There was a chorus of protests.

"Shut the fuck *up*," snapped Marvin. "We still at war, you know? Somebody still out there waitin' to *do* us. We find out who this honky old bitch is, what she do with this, we know *who* to get. Got it? *Get* it. Now shut the fuck up."

They went back to their mattresses and pool table.

It was four o'clock and getting dark out. Natalie zipped her coat tight and blamed her sudden attack of shivers on the wind. They went north on Bringhurst, under the train tracks, and west on a street Natalie had thought was an alley. There were no streetlights. It was trying to snow. The night air smelled of sewage and soot.

They stopped at an entrance to a real alley. Marvin pointed at the fourteen-year-old. "Monk, tell what happened, man."

The boy put his hands in his pockets and spat into the frozen weeds and tumbled bricks of a vacant lot. "Muhammed, he and the three others, they got to right here, you know? I come after them but wasn't there yet, you know? It was, like, Christmas at the Pit, and Muhammed and Toby was doing a little coke, you know? They left without me to make another score at Zig's brother's place, you know? In Pulaski Town, right? But, like, I was so fucking stoned I didn't see 'em leave and come running after them, you know?"

"Tell about the white dude," said Marvin.

"Fucking white dude, he come out of the fucking alley here, give Muhammed the fucking finger. Right here, about. I be half a block down the fuckin' street, hear old Muhammed say, Shit, you believe this shit? Little fucking white dude right there, flipping off Muhammed and three brothers."

"What did he look like?" asked Natalie.

"Shut up," snapped Marvin. "I ask the questions. Tell her what he look like."

"He look like *shit*," said Monk and spat again. Hands still in his pockets, he wiped his chin on his shoulder. "Little honky motherfucker look like he been dipped in shit, you know? Like he been eatin' garbage for about a year, man. You know? Stringy hair, like. Sort of like dirty vines hangin' down over his face, you know? All streaked, all over, like he be all bloody or something. Shit." Monk shivered.

"Are you sure he was white?" asked Natalie.

Marvin glared, but Monk laughed loudly and said. "Oh yeah, he *white*. He one white honky motherfucking monster. That no lie."

"Tell her about the sickle," said Marvin.

Monk nodded rapidly. "Yeah, so this white dude, he run down this alley. Muhammed, Toby, and them, they stand there like they don't get it, you know? Then Muhammed he say, get him, and they all run in there, you know? Not packing anything. Just their knives, you know? Don't matter. They gonna cut that little motherfucker up good."

"Tell her about the sickle."

"Yeah." Monk's eyes seemed to glaze over. "I hear the noise and come up here and look in. Don't run or nothing, you know? I figure, shit, on probation with that King Liquor thing, don't need no murder shit, you know? So I just look in to watch the shit go down. But this white dude, he ain't the one bleeding, dig? He got this big sickle thing . . . like in the cartoons?"

"Which cartoons?" asked Natalie.

"Shit, you know, old dude with the skull and stick with a sickle on it. Like a hourglass too, you know? Comes to get dead folks in the cartoon. Shit."

"A scythe?" said Natalie. "Like they used to cut wheat with?"

"Yeah, shit," said Monk and pointed at her. "Only this honky monster motherfucker, he be cuttin' down Muhammed and the bros. He *fast*. Oh, shit, he fast. I see enough, I hide right there . . ." He pointed at a large Dumpster. "I wait 'til he *done*, you know? And then wait 'til he gone a long time. I don't *need* that shit, man. Then, when it get light, I go tell Marvin, you know?"

Marvin crossed his arms and looked at her. "Got enough, babe?"

It was very dark now. Far down the alley, Natalie saw the lights and traffic of what had to be Germantown Avenue. "Almost," she said. "Did he . . . did the white dude kill all of them?"

Monk hugged his arms and laughed. "You fucking *know* it. Took his fucking time, too. He *like* it."

"Were they decapitated?"

"Huh?"

"She means did he cut their heads off," said Marvin. "Tell her, Monk."

"Fuck yes they capitated. He fuckin' *sawed* they fucking heads off with that sickle and shovel. Stuck the heads on the parking meters out on the avenue, you know?"

"Dear God," said Natalie. Snowflakes pelted her face and froze on her cheeks and lashes.

"Wasn't all," said Monk. His laughter was so ragged that it verged on being sobs. "He cut their fucking hearts out, man. I think he ate them."

Natalie backed away from the alley. She turned to run, saw nothing but bricks and darkness everywhere, and stood stock-still.

Marvin took her by the arm. "Come on, babe. You coming back with us. Time to tell us. Time to talk."

TWENTY-TWO

Beverly Hills
Saturday, Dec. 27, 1980

Tony Harod was deep in an aging starlet when the call came from Washington.

Tari Easten was forty-two, at least twenty years too old for the part she wanted in *The White Slaver*, but her breasts were the right age and shape for the part. Looking at them from beneath as she labored over him, Harod thought he could see the faint pink lines, where her breasts met her rib cage, showing where the silicone gel had been injected. The breasts were so artificially firm that they barely wobbled as Tari worked up and down, throwing her head back in an excellent simulation of passion, mouth open, shoulders thrust back. Harod was not Using her, just using her.

"Come on, baby, give it to me. Come on. Give it to me," panted the aging ingenue whom a 1963 *Variety* had called "the next Elizabeth Taylor." Instead, she had been the next Stella Stevens.

"Give it to me," she breathed. "Shoot it in me, baby. Come on, come on."

Tony Harod was trying. Sometime in the past fifteen minutes their passion had descended through mere friction to real work. Tari knew all of the right moves; she performed as well as any porno starlet that Harod had ever directed. She was a perfect fantasy, anticipating his every wish, giving pure pleasure with every touch, centering the entire act around the self-centered penis worship she had learned long ago resided in every male. She was perfect. Harod thought that he might as well have been screwing a knothole for all the involvement and excitement he felt.

"Come on, baby. Give it to me now," she panted, still in character, bobbing up and down like one of those cowgirls on the mechanical bull at Gilleys.

"Shut up," said Harod and concentrated on reaching an orgasm. He closed his eyes and remembered the stewardess on the flight from Washington two weeks earlier. Had that been the last one? The two German girls playing with each other in the sauna . . . no, he didn't want to think about Germany.

The harder they both worked, the less erect Harod became. Sweat dripped from Tari's breasts onto his chest. Harod remembered Maria Chen going cold turkey, three years past, the sweat on her brown, nude body, the small nipples erect from the cold water Harod sponged on her, droplets beading in the black triangle of her pubic hair.

293

"Come on, baby," whispered Tari, sensing triumph, perking up like a trail-savvy pony seeing the stable ahead. "Give it to me, baby."

Harod did. Tari moaned, thrashed, let her whole body go rigid in simulated ecstasy that would have guaranteed a Lifetime Achievement Award if they gave Oscars for orgasms.

"Oh, baby, baby, you're so good," she crooned, hands in his hair, face against his shoulder, breasts brushing back and forth against him.

Harod opened his eyes and saw the phone light blinking. "Get off," he said.

She nestled against him as he told Maria Chen that he would take the call.

"Harod, this is Charles Colben," growled the familiar bully's voice.

"Yeah?"

"You're flying out to Philadelphia tonight. We'll meet you at the airport."

Harod pushed Tari's hand away from his groin. He stared at the ceiling. "Harod, you there?"

"Yeah. Why Philadelphia?"

"Just be there."

"What if I don't want to?"

It was Colben's turn to be silent.

"I told you guys last week, I'm out of this," said Harod. He glanced at Tari Easten. She was smoking a mentholated cigarette. Her eyes were as blue and empty as the water in Harod's swimming pool.

"You're out of nothing," said Colben. "You know what happened to Trask."

"Yeah."

"That means there's a vacancy in the Island Club steering committee."

"I'm not sure I'm interested anymore."

Colben laughed. "Harod, you poor dumb fuck, you just better hope to hell that *we* don't lose interest in *you*. The second we do, your fucking Hollywood friends are going to be trooping out to Forest Lawn for another memorial service. Be on the two A.M. United flight."

Harod carefully set the receiver down, rolled out of bed, and pulled on his monogrammed orange robe.

Tari stubbed out the cigarette and looked up at him through her lashes. Her sprawled posture reminded Harod of a low-budget Italian nudie flick that Jayne Mansfield did not long before she'd lost her head in an auto accident. "Baby," she breathed, obviously almost overwhelmed with satisfaction, "you want to talk about it?"

"About what?"

"About the *project*, of course, silly," she giggled.

"Sure," said Harod, standing at the bar and pouring himself a tall glass of orange juice. "It's called *The White Slaver*, based on that paperback that was near all the checkout counters last fall. Schu Williams is directing.

We're budgeted at twelve million, but Alan expects us to run over, a million up front plus a straight cut."

Harod knew Tari was close to an unsimulated orgasm now.

"Ronny says I'm perfect for the part," she whispered.

"That's what you pay him for," said Harod and took a long gulp of orange juice. Ronny Bruce was her agent and pet poodle.

"Ronny said *you* said I'd be perfect." There was a hint of a pout in her voice.

"I did," said Harod. "You are." He smiled his crocodile smile. "Not for the lead, of course. You're twenty-five years too old, you've got cellulite on your ass, and your tits look like they each swallowed a softball."

Tari let out a sound as if someone had hit her in the stomach. Her mouth moved, but no words came out.

Harod finished his drink. His eyelids were very heavy. "Thing is, we've got a bit part for the girl's middle-aged aunt who's out searching for her. Not much in the way of dialogue, but she's got a good scene where some Arabs rape her in a bazaar in Marrakesh."

The words began to come. "Why you cocksucking little dwarf-bastard . . ."

Harod grinned. "I'll take that as a maybe. Think about it, baby. Have Ronny give me a call and we'll do lunch." He put down his glass and padded off to the Jacuzzi.

"Why a flight in the middle of the night?" asked Maria Chen when they were somewhere over Kansas.

Harod looked out at darkness. "I suspect they're just pulling my strings." He leaned back and looked at Maria Chen. Something had changed between them since Germany. He closed his eyes, thought of his own face carved on an ivory chess piece, opened them again.

"What is in Philadelphia?" asked Maria Chen.

Harod framed a wise-ass comment about W. C. Fields, then decided he was too tired to be flippant. "I dunno," he said. "Either Willi or the Fuller woman."

"What do you do if it's Willi?"

"Run like hell," said Harod. "I expect you to help." He glanced around. "Did you pack the Browning the way I said?"

"Yes." She put away the calculator she had been using to figure a wardrobe budget. "What if it is the Fuller woman?"

No one was sitting within three rows of them. The few others in the first-class section were asleep. "If it's just her," said Harod, "I'll kill her."

"You will or we will?" asked Maria Chen.

"*I* will," snapped Harod.

"Are you sure you can?"

Harod glared at her and had the distinct tactile image of his fist slamming into those perfect teeth. It would be almost worth it, arrest, exposure, everything, just to break through that fucking Oriental composure. Just once. Slug her and fuck her, right here in United first class, LAX to O'Hare to Philly. "I'm sure," he said. "She's a goddamn old lady."

"Willi was . . . is an old man."

"You saw what Willi can do. He must've flown straight from Munich to Washington to waste Trask like that. He's fucking crazy."

"You don't know about the Fuller woman."

Harod shook his head. "She's a woman," he said. "There's no woman in the world as mean as Willi Borden."

Their connecting flight arrived in Philadelphia half an hour before dawn. Harod had not been able to sleep, the first-class section had been freezing all the way from Chicago, and the inside of Harod's eyelids felt as if they had been coated with gravel and glue. It made his mood even more murderous to note that Maria Chen looked fresh and alert.

They were met by three disgustingly clean-cut FBI types. The leader— a handsome man with a butterfly bandage and fading bruise on his chin— said, "Mr. Harod? We will take you to Mr. Colben."

Harod handed his carry-on bag to the handsome agent. "Yeah, well get a move on. I want to get to a bed."

The agent handed the bag to one of the others and led them down escalators, through doors marked NO ACCESS, and out onto the tarmac between the main terminal and a private hangar complex. A smeary streak of red and yellow in the cloudy east promised sunrise, but field lights still glared.

"Oh fuck," said Harod with feeling. It was an expensive six-passenger helicopter, streamlined and striped orange and white, rotors turning slowly, navigation lights blinking. One agent held the door open while the other stowed Harod's and Maria Chen's luggage. Charles Colben was visible through the open door. "Fuck," repeated Harod to Maria Chen. She nodded. Harod hated to fly in anything, but he hated helicopters the most. At a time when every fifth-rate director in Hollywood spent a third of his budget leasing the dangerous, insane machines, buzzing, swooping, and hovering over every shot like demented buzzards with Jehovah complexes, Tony Harod refused to fly in them.

"Isn't there any goddamn, fucking, son-of-a-bitching ground transport?" he screamed over the slow whoop-whoop of the rotors.

"Get in!" called Colben.

Harod made a few final comments and followed Maria Chen into the thing. He *knew* the rotors had at least eight feet ground clearance, but there was no way a sane person walked under those invisible blades without adopting a low, crablike walk.

They were still fumbling with seat belts on the cushioned rear bench when Colben swiveled his chair and gave a thumbs-up signal to the pilot. Harod thought the man at the stick was straight out of central casting—

worn leather jacket, thin, craggy face under a red cap, eyes that looked like they had seen combat and were bored by anything less. The pilot spoke into his headset mike, pushed forward on a stick with his left hand, pulled backward on a stick with his right hand, and the chopper roared, rose, pitched nose down, and taxied forward a steady six feet above the ground. "Aw, shit," muttered Harod. It felt like they were riding a board atop a thousand ball bearings.

They reached a zone clear of the hangar and terminal, exchanged babble with the tower, and shot forward and up. Harod glimpsed oil refineries, a river, and the incredible bulk of an oil tanker beneath them before he closed his eyes.

"The old woman's here in town," said Colben.

"Melanie Fuller?" said Harod.

"Who the fuck you think I mean?" snapped Colben. "Helen Hayes?"

"Where is she?"

"You'll see."

"How did you find her?"

"That's our business."

"What happens next?"

"We'll tell you when it's time."

Harod opened his eyes. "I like talking to you, Chuck. It's sort of like talking to your own fucking armpits."

The bald man squinted at Harod and then smiled. "Tony, baby, I happen to think that you're a piece of dogshit, but for some reason Mr. Barent thinks that you might belong in the Club. This is your big chance, punk. Don't blow it."

Harod laughed and closed his eyes.

Maria Chen watched as they flew along a winding, gray river. The tall buildings of downtown Philadelphia receded to their right. Rowhouses and the brick-brown grid of the city, stitched with expressways, spread out to their right while a seemingly endless expanse of park, low hills stubbled with bare trees and pockets of snow, paralleled the river to the left. The sun rose, a golden searchlight wedged between horizon and low clouds, and hundreds of windows on high-rises and hillside homes threw back the light. Colben put his hand on Maria's knee. "My pilot's a Vietnam vet," he said. "He's like you."

"I've never been to Vietnam," Maria Chen said softly.

"No," said Colben and slipped his hand up toward her thigh. Harod seemed to be asleep. "I mean he's a Neutral. Nobody messes with him."

Maria Chen tightened her legs, blocked the FBI man's advancing hand with her own. The other three agents in the cabin watched, the man with the bruised chin smiling slightly.

"Chuck," said Harod, eyes still closed, "you left-handed or right-handed?"

Colben scowled. "Why?"

"I was just curious if you were going to be able to keep pulling your pud after I break your right hand," said Harod. He opened his eyes. The two men stared at each other. The three agents unbuttoned their coats in a movement that seemed to have been choreographed.

"Coming in," said the pilot.

Colben removed his hand and swiveled forward. "Put us down near the communications center," he said. It was an unnecessary command. A small city block in the middle of a run-down neighborhood, all rowhouses and abandoned factories, had been enclosed by a high wooden construction fence. Four mobile homes had been connected to each other near the center of the lot and a scattering of cars and vans were parked on the south side of them. One of the vans and two of the mobile home units had microwave antennas on the roof. There was a landing site already marked with orange plastic panels.

Everyone except Maria Chen duck-walked out of the range of the rotor blades. Harod's assistant walked upright, carefully setting her high heels between puddles and patches of mud, her posture giving no hint of tension. The pilot stayed with the machine and the rotors kept turning.

"Brief stop," said Colben as he led the procession into a certain trailer. "Then you've got work to do."

"Only work I'm doing this morning is to find a bed," said Harod.

The two center trailers ran north and south and were connected by a wide common door at their ends. The west wall was a mass of television monitors and communication consoles. Eight men in white shirts and dark ties sat viewing the monitors and occasionally whispering into microphones.

"It looks like fucking mission control," said Harod.

Colben nodded. "This is our communications and control center," he said with a faint pull of pride in his voice. The man at the first panel looked up and Colben said, "Larry, this is Mr. Harod and Ms. Chen. The Director asked them to fly out and take a look at our operation." Larry nodded at the supposed VIPs and Harod got the message that these were regular FBI men, almost certainly ignorant of their real mission.

"What are we looking at?" asked Harod.

Colben touched the first monitor. "This is the house on Queen Lane where the suspect and an unidentified young male Caucasian are staying with a certain Anne Marie Bishop, fifty-three, unmarried, living alone since her brother died in May of this year. Alpha team established the surveillance base on the second floor of a warehouse across the street. Number two shows the back of the same house—shot from the empty third floor of a rowhouse across the alley. Number three, the alley from a mobile van, Bell Telephone markings."

"She there now?" asked Harod, nodding toward the black and white image of the small, white house.

Colben shook his head and led them down the row to a monitor that showed an old stone home. The camera evidently was looking across a busy street from a ground-floor location and traffic occasionally obscured the view. "She is currently in Grumblethorpe," said Colben.

"In what?"

"Grumblethorpe." Colben pointed to two enlarged photocopied sets of architectural drawings taped to the wall above the monitor. "It's an historic landmark. Closed to the public most of the time. She spends a lot of time there."

"Let me get this straight," said Harod. "The lady we've been talking about is hiding out in a national landmark?"

"Not a national landmark," snapped Colben, "just a local site of historic interest. But yes, she does spend most of her time there. In the morning . . . at least the two mornings we've been watching, she and the other old lady and the kid walk over to the Queen Lane house, presumably for showers and hot meals."

"Jesus," said Harod. He looked around at the men and equipment. "How many men you got on this little job, Chuck?"

"Sixty-four," said Colben. "The local authorities know we're here, but they have orders to keep out of it. We may need some traffic control help when it finally goes down."

Harod grinned and looked at Maria Chen. "Sixty-four G-men, a goddamned helicopter, a million dollars of Star Wars shit, all to nail an eighty-year-old broad." Larry and a couple of the other agents looked up with quizzical expressions. "Keep up the good work, men," Harod said in his best VIP voice, "your nation's proud of you."

"Let's go into my office," Colben, said coldly.

Offices took up all of the trailer that ran east and west on the south end of the complex. Colben's office was something more than a cubicle, something less than a room.

"What's on the other end of this setup?" asked Harod when he and Maria Chen and the FBI assistant director settled around an undersized desk.

Colben hesitated. "Detention and interrogation facilities," he said at last.

"You plan to interrogate the Fuller woman?"

"No," said Colben. "She's too dangerous. We plan to kill her."

"You detaining and interrogating anybody now?"

"Perhaps," said Colben. "No need for you to know."

Harod sighed. "OK, Chuck, what is there a need for me to know?"

Colben glanced at Maria Chen. "This is confidential. Can you function without Connie Chung here, Tony?"

"No," said Harod. "And if you put your mouth or hand on her again. Chucky babe, Barent'll have another Island Club seat to fill."

Colben smiled thinly. "This is something that we will definitely have to settle. Later. Meanwhile, we have a mission to complete and you—for a change—have work to do." He slid a photograph across the desktop.

Harod studied it: Polaroid snapshot, color, in outdoor light, of an attractive young black woman—twenty-two or twenty-three—standing on a street corner waiting for a light to change. She had a full head of curly hair just too short to be called an Afro, rich eyes, delicate oval face, and full lips. Harod's eyes wandered to her breasts, but the camel coat she wore was too bulky to give him a reading. "Decent-looking chick," he said. "Not star status, but I could probably get her a screen test or a bit part. Who the fuck is she?"

"Natalie Preston," said Colben.

Harod stared his lack of recognition.

"Her daddy got in the way of the Nina Drayton-Melanie Fuller spat in Charleston a few weeks ago."

"So?"

"So he's dead and suddenly the young Miss Preston is here in Philly."

"Now?"

"Yes."

"Think she's after the Fuller broad?"

"No, Tony, we think that the bereaved daughter left her daddy's corpse, dropped her graduate work in St. Louis, and flew to Germantown, PA, out of sudden interest in early American history. *Of course*, she's on the old lady's trail, you dumb fuck."

"How'd she find her?" asked Harod. He was staring at the photograph.

"The gang members," said Colben. At Harod's blank stare, he said, "Jesus Christ, don't they have papers and TV out in Hollywood?"

"I've been busy setting up a twelve-million-dollar movie project," said Harod. "What murders?"

Colben told him about the Christmas Eve killings. "And two more since," he said. "Grisly stuff."

"Why would this luscious piece of chocolate relate some spades killing each other in Philadelphia to Melanie Fuller?" said Harod. "And how'd you get on to both her and the old lady being here?"

"We had our own sources," said Colben. "As for this black bitch, we were tapping her phone and the phone of a cracker sheriff she's been shacking up with. They leave cute little messages on his answering machine. We sent a guy in to leave the messages we want left, erase the rest."

Harod shook his head. "I don't get it. What do I have to do with this shit?"

Colben picked up a letter opener and played with it. "Mr. Barent has decided that this is right up your line, Tony."

"What is?" Harod handed the photograph to Maria Chen.

"Taking care of Miss Preston."

"Uh-uh," said Harod. "Our deal was for the Fuller woman. Just her."

Colben raised an eyebrow. "What's the matter, Tony? This kid scare you the way flying does? What else scares you, hotshot?"

Harod rubbed his eyes and yawned.

"Take care of this detail," said Colben, "and it's possible you won't have to concern yourself with Melanie Fuller."

"Who says?"

"Mr. Barent says. Christ, Harod, this is a free ride into the most select club in history. I know you're a schmuck, but this is stupid even for you."

Harod yawned again. "Has it occurred to any of you intellectual quadriplegics that you don't need me to do your dirty work?" he said. "You've got the old lady in your camera lens several times a day, you said so yourself. Substitute a telescopic sight on a thirty-aught-six and problem's solved. And what's the big deal with little Natalie Whatshername? She have the Ability or something?"

"No," said Colben. "Natalie Preston has a B.A. from Oberlin and two-thirds of a teaching certificate. Very nonviolent young lady."

"Then why me?"

"Dues," said Colben. "We all pay our dues."

Harod took the photograph back from Maria Chen. "What do you want done? Detained and interrogated?"

"No need," said Colben. "We have all the information she might give us from . . . ah . . . another source. We just want her taken out of the game."

"Permanently?"

Colben chuckled. "What else do you have in mind, Mr. Harod?"

"I though perhaps she might like a little involuntary vacation to Beverly Hills," said Harod. His eyes were very heavy. He moistened his lips with a quick movement of tongue.

Colben chuckled again. "Whatever," he said. "But eventually the solution has to be permanent with regards to this . . . how'd you put it? This luscious piece of chocolate. What you do with her before that is up to you, Tony baby. Just no chance of a slip-up."

"There won't be," said Harod. He glanced at Maria Chen and then looked back to the photograph. "You know where she is right now?"

"Yes," said Colben. He picked up a clipboard and glanced at a computer printout on it. "She's still at the Chelten Arms. Little hotel about twelve blocks from here. Haines can drive you over now."

"Uh-uh," said Harod. "First I want a hotel room for each of us . . . a *good* one, suite if possible. And then seven or eight hours' sleep."

"But Mr. Barent . . ."

"Screw C. Arnold Barent," said Harod with a smile. "Let him come to get this chick himself if he's not satisfied. Now get Haines or whoever to drive us to a good hotel."

"What about Natalie Preston?"

Harod stopped by the door. "I assume the lady is also under surveillance?"

"Of course."

"Well, tell your boys to try to hang on to her for eight or nine more hours, Chuck." He turned toward the door but then paused again, staring at Colben. "You never answered my question. You've been on top of Melanie Fuller for the past few days at least. Why drag this shit out? Why don't you terminate her and get out of here?"

Colben picked up the letter opener. "Why, we're waiting to see if there's any connection between little Miz Melanie and your old boss, Mr. Borden. We're waiting for Willi to make a mistake, show his hand."

"And if he does?"

Colben smiled and drew the dull blade of the letter opener across his throat. "If he does . . . *when* he does, then your friend Willi is going to wish he'd been in that room with Trask when the bomb went off."

Harod and Maria got rooms at the Chestnut Hill Inn, an upscale motel seven miles out of Germantown Avenue, beyond the slums and city, in an area of tree-lined lanes and secluded office parks. Colben was also registered there. The agent with the bruised chin assigned a blond FBI man to remain there with a car. Harod slept six hours and awoke disoriented and wearier than when he arrived. Maria Chen poured him a vodka and orange juice and sat on the edge of the bed while Harod drank it.

"What are you going to do about the girl?" she asked.

Harod put down the glass and rubbed his face. "What does it matter to you?"

"It doesn't."

"Then you don't have to know anything about it."

"Do you want me along?"

Harod thought about it. He did not feel comfortable without someone watching his back, but in this case it might not be necessary. The more he thought about it, the less necessary it seemed. "No," he said. "You stay here and work on the Paramount correspondence. It won't take long."

Maria Chen left the room without a word.

Harod showered and dressed in a silk turtleneck, expensive wool slacks, and a black bomber jacket with fleece lining. He called the number Colben had given him.

"Natalie Whatshername still around?" Harod asked.

"She's been walking around the slums, but she's back at the hotel for dinner," said Colben. "She spends a lot of time with that nigger gang."

"The one that's been losing members?"

Colben laughed heartily.

"What's so fucking funny?" said Harod.

"Your choice of words," laughed Colben. "Losing members. That's exactly what's been happening. The last two got chopped to bits and had their cocks cut off."

"Jesus," said Harod. "And you think Melanie Fuller's doing it?"

"We don't know," replied Colben. "We haven't seen that kid with her leave Grumblethorpe when the murders went down, but she could be Using someone else."

"What kind of surveillance do you have on Grumblethorpe?"

"It could be better," said Colben. "We can't park a telephone truck in every alley, even an old lady might get suspicious. But we have good coverage in the front, a camera covering the backyard, and agents all around the block. If the old bitch pokes her head out, we've got her."

"Good for you," said Harod. "Look, if I take care of this other detail tonight, then I want to be out of here in the morning."

"We'll have to check with Barent."

"Fuck that," said Harod. "I'm not waiting around here for Willi Borden to show up. That would be a long wait. Willi's dead."

"It won't be that long," said Colben. "We got the go-ahead to take care of the old lady."

"Today?"

"No, but soon enough."

"When?"

"We'll tell you if you need to know."

"Nice talking to you, armpit," said Harod and hung up.

A young blond agent drove Harod into town. He pointed out the Chelten Arms and found a parking space half a block away. Harod tipped him a quarter.

It was an old hotel, fighting to retain its dignity in reduced circumstances. The lobby was threadbare, but the bar/dining room was pleasantly dark and recently renovated. Harod thought that the place probably got most of the lunch trade from the few remaining white businessmen in the area. The black girl was easy to spot—sitting alone in a corner, eating a salad and reading a paperback. She was as attractive as the Polaroid snap had promised—more so, Harod realized, as he saw the full breasts filling her tan blouse. Harod spent a minute at the bar, trying to pick out the FBI tails. The young guy alone at the bar—overpriced three-piece suit and hearing aid—was a sure bet. Harod took a little longer spotting the overweight black man eating clam chowder and looking over at Natalie every few minutes. *Do they hire nigger FBI men these days?* wondered Harod. *Probably have a quota.* He guessed there would be at least one more agent in the lobby, probably reading a newspaper. He picked up his vodka and tonic and walked over to Natalie Preston's table. "Hi, do you mind if I join you for a minute?"

The young woman looked up from her book. Harod read the title: *Teaching As a Conserving Activity.* "Yes," she said, "I do mind."

"That's OK," said Harod and draped his jacket over the back of a chair. "I don't mind." He sat down.

Natalie Preston opened her mouth to speak and Harod reached out with his mind and *squeezed* . . . lightly, lightly. No words came out. She tried to stand and froze in mid-movement. Her eyes grew very large.

Harod smiled at her and slumped back in his chair. No one was sitting within hearing range. He folded his hands over his stomach. "Your name is Natalie," he said. "Mine's Tony. What would you say to a little fun?" He relaxed his grip enough to let her whisper but not to shout or scream. She lowered her head and gasped for breath.

Harod shook his head. "You're not playing the game right, Natalie baby. I said, what would you say to a little fun?"

Natalie Preston looked up, still panting as if she had been jogging. Her brown eyes glinted. She cleared her throat, found that her voice worked and whispered, "You go to hell . . . you son of a bitch . . ."

Harod sat straight up. "Uh-uh," he said, "*wrong* answer."

He watched as Natalie bent over with the sudden pain in her skull. Harod had suffered terrible migraines as a child. He knew how to share. A passing waiter stopped and said, "Are you all right, miss?"

Natalie straightened up slowly, like a mechanical doll unwinding. Her voice was husky. "Yes," she said, "I'm fine. Just menstrual cramps."

The waiter moved away, embarrassed. Harod had to grin. *Jesus*, he thought, *what a ventriloquist I could have made.* He leaned forward and stroked her hand. She tried to pull away. It took a fair amount of Harod's concentration to keep her from succeeding. Her eyes began to take on the trapped-animal look that he enjoyed.

"Let's start again," whispered Harod. "What would you like to do this evening, Natalie?"

"I'd . . . like . . . to . . . suck . . . your . . . cock." Each syllable was dragged out of her, but that was all right with Harod. Natalie's large brown eyes filled with tears.

"What else?" crooned Harod. He was frowning with the concentrated effort of control. This particular piece of chocolate took more work than he was used to. "What else?"

"I . . . want you . . . to . . . fuck . . . me."

"Sure, kid, I don't have anything better to do in the next couple of hours. Let's go up to your room."

They rose together. "Better leave some money," whispered Harod. Natalie dropped a ten-dollar bill on the table.

Harod winked at the two agents in the bar as they left. Another man in a dark suit lowered his newspaper and peered at them as they waited for the elevator. Harod smiled, made a circle with his left index finger and thumb, and ran his right middle finger through it six times in rapid succession. The agent blushed and raised his paper. No one followed them into the elevator or down the third-floor hall.

Harod took the keys from her and opened the door. He left her standing there, staring vacantly, while he checked out the room. Clean but small, bed, bureau, black and white TV on a swivel stand, open suitcase on a low rack. Harod picked up a pair of her underwear, ran it across his face, peered in the bathroom and out the window at fire escape, alley, the low rooftops beyond.

"OK!" he said merrily, tossing her underwear aside and pulling a low green chair away from the wall. He sat down. "Show time, kiddo." She stood between him and the bed. Her arms were down at her sides, her expression slack, but Harod could see the effort she was expending to break free as tiny shudders passed through her. Harod smiled and tightened his grip. "A little striptease before bed is always fun, don't you think?" he said.

Natalie Preston continued to stare straight ahead as her hands came up and slowly unbuttoned her blouse. She tugged it off and dropped it on the floor. Her large breasts in the old-fashioned white bra reminded Harod of someone . . . who? He suddenly remembered the airline stewardess two weeks earlier. Her skin had been as pale as this chick's was dark. Why do they wear those plain, unexciting bras?

Harod nodded and Natalie reached behind her to unsnap the hooks. The bra slipped forward, down, and off. Harod stared at the brown areolae and licked his lips. She should play awhile before she began on him. "OK," he said softly, "I think it's time to . . ."

There was an explosion of noise and Harod swiveled in time to see the door crash inward, a large bulk of a body obscure the light from the hallway in time to realize that he had left the Browning in Maria Chen's luggage.

Harod had started to rise, started to raise his arms, when something the size and weight of an anvil landed on top of his head and drove him down, into the chair, through the cushions, through the soft substance of a floor suddenly taking on the texture of tapioca, down into the warm waiting darkness beneath.

TWENTY-THREE
Melanie

Vincent was a hard boy to keep clean. He was one of those children who seems to exude dirt from every pore. His nails were rimmed with black an hour after I had him clean them. It was a constant struggle to keep him in clean clothes.

On Christmas Day we rested. Anne made meals, put holiday records on the Victrola, and did several loads of wash while I read passages from the Scripture and contemplated them. It was a quiet day. Occasionally Anne would make as if to turn on the television—she had watched six to eight hours a day before I met her—but then the conditioning would take over and she would find something else to do. I indulged in a few mindless hours of TV viewing myself the first week we were at Anne's, but one night while watching the eleven o'clock news there was a thirty-second update on what they were calling the Charleston Murders. "State police are still searching for the missing woman," read the young woman. I decided then that there would be no more television viewing at Anne Bishop's house.

On Saturday, two days after Christmas, Anne and I went out shopping. She had a 1953 DeSoto stored in her garage; it was an ugly green vehicle with a grill that made me think of a frightened fish. Anne drove so hesitantly and cautiously that before we were out of Germantown I had her pull over and let Vincent take the wheel. She directed us away from Philadelphia, out to an expensive shopping mall in an area called King of Prussia—possibly the most absurd name I had ever heard of for a suburb. We shopped for four hours and I made several nice purchases, though none so nice, I fear, as the clothes I had left in the Atlanta airport. I did find a pleasant three-hundred-dollar coat—deep blue with ivory buttons—that I thought might help ward off the bone-chilling cold of the Yankee winter. Anne enjoyed buying me these few things and I did not want to stand in the way of her happiness.

That night I returned to Grumblethorpe. It was so pleasant in the candlelight, moving from room to room with nothing but the shadows and the faint whispers to keep me company. That afternoon Anne had purchased two shotguns at a sporting goods store in the mall. The young salesman with greasy blond hair and dirty sneakers had been amused at the naïveté of this older woman buying a gun for her grown son. The man had recommended two expensive pump shotguns—either the 12-gauge or the 16-gauge, depending upon the type of hunting Anne's son was interested in. Anne bought them both, as well as six boxes of shells for each. Now, as I carried the candle holder from room to room at Grumblethorpe, Vincent oiled and caressed the weapons in the stony shadows of the kitchen.

I had never Used anyone quite like Vincent before. Earlier, I had compared his mind to a jungle and now I found the metaphor even more apt. The images that flitted across what remained of his consciousness were almost invariably ones of violence, death, and destruction. I caught glimpses of murders of family members—mother in the kitchen, father sleeping, an older sister on the tile floor of a laundry room—but I do not know if they were reality or fantasy. I doubt if Vincent knew. I never asked him and he could not have answered if I had.

Using Vincent was rather like riding a high-spirited horse; one had only to release the reins to get the beast to do what one wished. He was incredibly strong for his size and frame, almost inexplicably so. It was as if great surges of adrenaline filled Vincent's system at the most mundane of times, and when he was truly excited his strength became almost superhuman. I found it exhilarating to share this, even in a somewhat passive way. Each day I felt younger. I knew that by the time I reached my home in southern France, possibly in the next month, I would be so rejuvenated that even Nina would not recognize me.

Only bad dreams about Nina spoiled those days after Christmas Eve. The dreams were always the same: Nina's eyes opening, Nina's face a white mask with a dime-size hole in the forehead, Nina sitting up in her coffin, teeth yellowed and sharpened, blue eyes rising in their empty sockets on a tide of maggots.

I did not like these dreams.

On Saturday night I left Anne on the first floor of Grumblethorpe, watching the door, while I curled up on the roll-away in the nursery and let the whispers carry me into a half-sleep.

Vincent went out through the tunnel. It suggested images of birth: the long narrow tunnel, rough walls pressing in, the sweet, sharp smell of soil not unlike the coppery scent of blood, the narrow aperture at the end, the quiet night air seeming like an explosion of light and sound.

Vincent glided across the dark alley, over a fence, through a vacant lot, and into the shadows of the next street. The shotguns remained behind in Grumblethorpe's kitchen; he carried only the scythe—its long wooden handle shortened by fourteen inches—and his knife.

I had no doubt that in summer these streets would be teeming with Negroes—fat women sitting on stoops and chattering back and forth like baboons or staring dully while ragged children played everywhere and loose-boned males with no work, no aspirations, and no visible means of support ambled off to bars and street corners. But tonight, deep in the belly of a harsh winter, the streets were dark and quiet, shades pulled on the narrow windows of the narrow houses and doors closed in the flat fronts of rowhouses. Vincent did not move like a silent shadow, he *became* one—sliding from alley to street, street to empty lot, empty lot to yard with no more disruption to the stillness than a dark wind would bring.

Two nights before he had tracked the members of the gang to a large old home bound around by empty lots, a long stone's throw from the elevated train whose embankment cut through this part of the ghetto like some overgrown Great Wall, a futile attempt by some more civilized group to wall *in* the barbarians. Vincent nested in the frozen weeds by an abandoned car and watched.

Black shapes moved in front of lighted windows like caricatures of darkies in a magic lantern minstrel show. Eventually five of them emerged. I did not recognize them in the dim light, but that did not matter. Vincent waited until they were almost out of sight down the narrow alley by the railway embankment and then he slipped along behind. It was exhilarating to share that silent stalking, that almost effortless glide through the darkness. Vincent's eyes worked almost as well in near total darkness as most people's do in daylight. It was like sharing the mind and senses of a strong, sleek hunting cat. A hungry cat.

There were two colored girls in the group. Vincent paused when the group paused. He sniffed the air, actually picking up the strong, animal-like scent of the bucks. It is no longer polite in the South to use that word, but few words apply as well. It is a simple fact that a Negro male is quick to excite and as thoughtless of his surroundings as a stallion or a male dog near a bitch in heat. These two colored girls must have been in heat; Vincent watched as they copulated there on the shadowy embankment, the third boy also watching until his turn came, the girls' bare, black legs opening and closing against the bobbing haunches of the thrusting males. Vincent's entire body surged with the need to act *then*, but I made him look away, wait until the boys were finished with their lust, the girls gone calling and laughing—as guiltless and guileless as sated alley cats—toward their own homes. Then I unleashed Vincent.

He was waiting when the three turned a corner at the base of Bringhurst Street near the abandoned shoe factory. The scythe took the first boy in the stomach, passed through his body, and caught on the spine coming out. Vincent left it there and went for the second one with his knife. The third one ran.

Back when I used to go to the motion picture theater, before World War Two, before films deteriorated into the obscene, mindless claptrap I read about today, I would always enjoy the scenes of frightened colored servants. I remember seeing *Birth of a Nation* as a child and laughing when the colored children were terrified by the sight of someone in a sheet. I recall sitting in a five-pfennig theater in Vienna with Nina and Willi, watching an old Harold Lloyd film that needed no subtitles, and roaring with the crowd at the dull-witted fright of Stepin Fetchit. I remember watching an old Bob Hope movie on television—before the vulgarity of the 1960s made me give up television forever—and laughing out loud at the white-faced fear of Bob Hope's colored assistant in some haunted house farce. The second of Vincent's victims looked like one of these film comedians—huge, white, staring eyes, one hand raised to his open mouth, knees together, feet splayed. Back in Grumblethorpe I laughed aloud in the silence of the nursery even as Vincent used his knife to do what had to be done.

The third boy escaped. Vincent wanted to go after him, *strained* to go after him like a dog pulling hard at a leash, but I held him back. The Negro knew the streets better and Vincent's effectiveness lay in concealment and surprise. I knew how risky this game was, and I had no intention of squandering Vincent after all the work I had put in on him. Before bringing Vincent back, however, I let him have his way with the two he had already accounted for. His little games did not take long and they satisfied something that still lurked in the deepest part of the jungle inside his skull.

It was after he removed the jacket of the second boy that the photograph fell out. Vincent was too busy to notice, but I had him set down his scythe and pick up the photograph. It was a picture of Mr. Thorne and me.

I sat straight up in bed in the Grumblethorpe nursery.

Vincent returned immediately. I met him in the kitchen and took the photograph from his stained and grimy fingers. There was no doubt—the image was fuzzy, obviously a section enlarged from a larger photograph—but I was quite visible and Mr. Thorne was unmistakable. I knew at once that it had to be Mr. Hodges's doing. For years I had watched that miserable little man and his miserable little camera taking snapshots of his miserable little family. I had thought that I took the necessary precautions to avoid being in his pictures, but obviously this had not been the case.

I sat by candlelight in the chill of Grumblethorpe's stone and brick kitchen and shook my head. How had this come into the possession of the young Negro? Obviously someone was searching for me, but who? The police? How could they have any inkling that I was in Philadelphia? Nina? Nothing I could think of made any sense at all.

I had Vincent bathe in a large galvanized tub that Anne had bought. She brought in a kerosene heater, but it was a cold night and the steam rose from Vincent's white flesh as he bathed. After awhile I went over and helped to wash his hair. What a picture the three of us must have made— two dignified aunts bathing the gallant young man just home from the wars, flesh steaming in the cold air while candlelight threw our shadows ten feet tall on the rough-hewn wall.

"Vincent, my dear," I whispered as I rubbed the shampoo into his long hair, "we must find out where the photograph came from. Not tonight, my dear, the streets will be far too busy tonight when your handiwork is discovered. But soon. And when you find who gave the colored boy that picture, you will bring that person here . . . to me."

TWENTY-FOUR

Washington, D.C.
Saturday, Dec. 27, 1980

Saul Laski lay in his steel tomb and thought about life. He shivered in the chill from the air-conditioning, raised his knees toward his chest, and tried to remember details of a spring morning on his uncle's farm. He thought about golden light touching the heavy limbs of willows and about a field of white daisies beyond the stone fortress of his uncle's barn.

Saul hurt; his left shoulder and arm hurt constantly, his head throbbed, his fingers tingled with pain, and the inside of his right arm pulsed with the pain of all the injections they had given him. Saul welcomed the pain, encouraged it. The pain was the only dependable beacon he had in a thick fog of medication and disorientation.

Saul had become somewhat unhinged in time. He was sometimes aware of this but could do nothing about it. The details were there—at least up to the second of the explosion in the Senate Office Building—but he could not set them in sequence. One minute he would be lying on his narrow bunk in the chilly stainless steel cell—inset bunk, air conditioner grill, stainless steel bench and toilet, metal door that slid up into the wall—and the next minute he would try to burrow into cold straw, would feel the cold Polish night air coming through the cracked window, and would know that the Oberst and German guards could be coming for him soon.

Pain was a beacon. The few minutes of clarity in those first days after the explosion had been forged by pain. The intense pain after they set his broken collarbone; green surgical gowns in an antiseptic environment that might have been any surgery, any recovery room, but then the cold shock of white corridors and the steel cell, men in suits, colorful ID badges clipped to pockets and lapels, the pain of an injection followed by dreams and discontinuities.

The first interrogations had offered pain. The two men—one bald and short, another with a blond crew cut. The bald man had rapped Saul's shoulder with a metal baton. Saul had screamed, wept with the sudden pain of it, but welcomed it—welcomed the clearing of fogs and vapors.

"Do you know my name?" asked the bald man.

"No."

"What did your nephew tell you?"

"Nothing."

"Who else have you told about William Borden and the others?"

"No one."

Later—or earlier, Saul was not sure—the pain gone, in the pleasant haze after injections:

"Do you know my name?"

"Charles C. Colben, special deputy assistant to the deputy director of the FBI."

"Who told you that?"

"Aaron."

"What else did Aaron tell you?"

Saul repeated the conversation as completely as he could recall it.

"Who else knows about Willi Borden?"

"The sheriff. The girl." Saul explained about Gentry and Natalie.

"Tell me everything you know."

Saul told him everything he knew.

The fog and dreams came and went. The steel room was frequently there when Saul opened his eyes. The cot was built into the walls. The toilet was too small and had no flush lever: it flushed automatically at irregular intervals. Meals, on steel trays, appeared when Saul slept. He ate the meals on the metal bench, left the tray. It was gone when he awoke from his next nap. Occasionally men in the white attendants' uniforms came through the metal doorway to give him shots or to take him down white hallways to small rooms with mirrors on the wall he was facing. Colben or someone else in a gray suit would ask questions. If he refused to answer there were more shots, urgent dreams in which he desperately wanted to be friends with these people, and told them whatever they wished to hear. Several times he felt someone—Colben?—slide into his mind, the old memory of a similar rape rising from forty years before. These times were rare. The shots were frequent.

Saul slid backward and forward in time; calling to his sister Stefa on his Uncle Moshe's farm, running to keep up with his father in the Lodz ghetto, shoveling lime onto bodies in the Pit, drinking lemonade and talking to Gentry and Natalie, playing with a ten-year-old Aaron and Isaac at David and Rebecca's farm near Tel Aviv.

Now the drug-induced discontinuities were fading. Time stitched itself together. Saul lay curled on the bare mattress—there was no blanket, the air through the steel grill was too cold—and thought about himself and his lies. He had lied to himself for years. His search for the Oberst had been a lie—an excuse not to act. His life as a psychiatrist had been a lie, a way to remove his obsessions to a safe, academic distance. His service as a medic in three of Israel's wars had been a lie, a way to avoid direct action.

Saul lay in the gray hinterland between drug-induced nirvana and painful reality and saw the truth of his years of lies. He had lied to himself about his rationale for telling the Charleston sheriff and the Preston girl about Nina and Willi. He had secretly hoped that *they* would act— removing the burden of responsibility for revenge from *him*. Saul had asked Aaron to look for Francis Harrington *not* because he was too busy, but because he secretly wanted Aaron and the Mossad to do what had to be done. He knew now that part of his motive for telling Rebecca about the Oberst twenty years ago had been the secret and self-denied hope that she would tell David, that David would handle things in his strong, capable American-Israeli way—

Saul shivered, raised his knees to his chest, and stared at the lies that were his life.

Except for rare minutes such as when he had resolved in the Chelmno camp to kill rather than be taken into the night, his entire life had been a paean to inaction and compromise. Those in power seemed to sense this. He understood now that his assignment to the Pit detail in Chelmno and the rail yards at Sobibor had been more than chance or good luck; the bastards with power over him had sensed that Saul Laski was a born *kapo*, a collaborator, someone safe to *use*. There would be no violence from this one, no revolt, no sacrifice of his life for the others—not even to save his own dignity. Even his escape from Sobibor and from the Oberst's hunting preserve before that, largely had been due to accident, allowing events to sweep him along and away.

Saul rolled out of bed and stood swaying in the center of the small, steel cell. He was wearing gray coveralls. They had taken his glasses and the metal surfaces only a few feet away seemed blurred and faintly insubstantial. His left arm had been in a sling, but now it hung loose. He moved it tentatively and the pain shot up through shoulder and neck—a searing, cauterizing, brain-clearing pain. He moved it again. Again.

Saul staggered to the steel bench and sat down heavily.

Gentry, Natalie, Aaron and his family—all were in danger. From whom?

Saul lowered his head to his knees as dizziness washed over him. Why had he been so stupid as to assume that Willi and the old ladies were the only ones with such a terrible power? How many others shared the Oberst's abilities and addiction? Saul laughed raggedly. He had enlisted Gentry, Natalie, and Aaron without even considering a serious plan of dealing even with just the Oberst. He had vaguely imagined some entrapment— the Oberst unaware, Saul's friends safe in their anonymity. And then what? The sound of the Mossad's little .22 caliber Berettas?

Saul leaned back against the cold metal wall, set his cheek against the steel. How many people had he sacrificed because of his cowardice and inaction? Stefa. Josef. His parents. Now, almost certainly, the sheriff and Natalie. Francis Harrington. Saul let out a low moan as he remembered the guttural *Auf Wiedersehen* in Trask's office and the following explosion. For a second before that, the Oberst had somehow given him a glimpse through Francis's eyes and Saul had sensed the terrified presence of the boy's consciousness, prisoner in his own body, waiting for the inevitable sacrifice. Saul had sent the boy to California. His friends, Selby White and Dennis Leland. Two more victims on the altar of Saul Laski's timidity.

Saul did not know why they were allowing the drugs to wear off this time. Perhaps they were finished with him; the next visit could be to take him out for execution. He did not care. Rage coursed through his bruised body like an electric current. He would *act* before the inevitable, long-delayed bullet slammed into his skull. He would hurt *someone* in retaliation. At that second, Saul Laski would gladly have given his life to warn Aaron or the other two but he would have given *all* of their lives to strike back at the Oberst, at any of the arrogant bastards who ran the world and sneered at the pain of human beings they used as pawns.

The door slammed up. Three large men in white coveralls entered. Saul stood up, staggered toward them, swung a heavy fist at the first one's face.

"Hey," laughed the big man as he easily caught Saul's arm and pinned it behind him, "this old Jew wants to play games."

Saul struggled, but the big man held him as if he were a child. Saul tried not to weep as the second man rolled up his sleeve.

"You're going bye-bye," said the third man as he stabbed the needle of the syringe into Saul's thin, bruised arm. "Enjoy your trip, old man."

They waited thirty seconds, released him, and turned to go. Saul staggered after them, fists clenched. He was unconscious before the door slammed down.

He dreamed of walking, being led. There was the sound of jet engines and the smell of stale cigar smoke. He walked again, strong hands on his upper arms. Lights were very bright. When he closed his eyes he could hear the click-click-click of metal wheels on rails as the train carried them all to Chelmno.

Saul came to in the comfortable seat of some sort of conveyance. He could hear a steady, rhythmic *thwop*, but it took him several minutes to place it as the sound of a helicopter. His eyes were closed. A pillow was under his head, but his face touched glass or Plexiglas. He could feel that he was dressed and wearing glasses once again. Men were speaking softly and occasionally there came the rasp of radio communications. Saul kept his eyes closed, gathered his thoughts, and hoped that his captors would not notice that the drugs were wearing off.

"We know you're awake," said a man from very close by. The voice was strangely familiar.

Saul opened his eyes, moved his neck painfully, adjusted his glasses. It was night. He and three other men rode in the passenger seats of a well-appointed helicopter. A pilot and copilot sat bathed in red light from the instruments. Saul could see nothing out the window to his right. In the seat to his left, Special Agent Richard Haines sat with his briefcase on his lap, reading papers by the light of a tiny overhead spot. Saul cleared his throat and licked dry lips, but before he could speak Haines said, "We'll be landing in a minute. Get ready." The FBI man had the remnant of a bruise under his chin.

Saul thought of pertinent questions, discarded them. He looked down and realized for the first time that his left wrist was handcuffed to Haines's right wrist. "What time is it?" he asked, his voice little better than a croak.

"About ten."

Saul glanced back at the darkness and assumed it was night. "What day?"

"Saturday," grunted Haines with a slight smile.

"Date?"

The FBI man hesitated, shrugged slightly. "The twenty-seventh, December."

Saul closed his eyes at a sudden dizziness. He had lost a week. It seemed much longer. His left arm and shoulder ached abominably. He looked down and realized that he was dressed in a dark suit and tie, white shirt. Not his own. He removed his glasses. The prescription was correct, but the frame was new. He looked carefully at the five men. He recognized only Haines. "You work for Colben," Saul said. When the agent did not respond, Saul said, "You went down to Charleston to make sure the local police didn't find out what really happened. You took Nina Drayton's scrapbook from the morgue."

"Tighten your seat belt," said Haines. "We're going to land."

It was one of the most beautiful sights Saul had ever seen. At first he thought it was a commercial ocean liner, ablaze with lights, white against the night, leaving a phosphorescent wake in black-green waters, but as the helicopter descended toward the illuminated orange cross on the aft deck, Saul realized that it was a privately owned ship, a yacht, sleek and white and as long as an American football field. Crewmen with hand-held, glowing batons waved them down and the helicopter touched the deck gently in the glare of spotlights. The four of them were out and moving away from the helicopter before the rotors began to slow.

Several crewmen in white joined them. When they could stand upright, Haines unlocked the handcuffs and dropped them in his coat pocket. Saul rubbed at his wrist just below where the blue numbers were tattooed.

"This way." The procession went up stairways, forward along wide walkways. Saul's legs were unsteady even though there was no motion to the ship. Twice Haines reached out to steady him. Saul breathed in warm, moist, tropical air—rich with the distant scent of vegetation—and stared through open doors at the sleek opulence of the cabins, staterooms, and bars they passed. Everything was teaked and carpeted, interior-designed and plated with brass or gold. The ship was a floating five-star hotel. They passed near the bridge and Saul caught a glimpse of uniformed men on watch, the green glow of electronic equipment. An elevator took them to a private stateroom with a balcony—perhaps flying bridge was the proper term here. A man in an expensive white jacket sat there with a tall drink. Saul stared beyond him at an island perhaps a mile away across dark waters. Palm trees and a riot of tropical vegetation were festooned with hundreds of Japanese lanterns, walkways were outlined by white lights, a long beach lay illuminated by a score of torches, while rising above everything else, ablaze in the beams of vertical searchlights that reminded Saul of films of Nuremburg rallies in the thirties, a wooden-walled and red-tiled castle seemed to float above a cliff of white stone.

"Do you know me?" asked the man in the canvas chair.

Saul squinted at him. "Is this a credit card commercial?"

Haines kicked Saul behind the knees, dropping him to the deck.

"You can leave us, Richard."

Haines and the others left. Saul rose painfully to his feet.

"Do you know who I am?"

"You're C. Arnold Barent," said Saul. He had bitten the inside of his cheek. The taste of his own blood mingled with the scent of tropical vegetation in Saul's mind. "No one seems to know what the C stands for."

"Christian," said Barent. "My father was a very devout man. Also something of an ironist." He gestured toward a nearby deck chair. "Please sit down, Dr. Laski."

"No." Saul moved to the railing of the balcony, bridge, whatever the hell it was. Water moved by in a white bow wake thirty feet below. Saul grasped the railing tightly and looked back at Barent. "Aren't you taking a risk being alone with me?"

"No, Dr. Laski, I am not," said Barent. "I do not take risks."

Saul nodded toward the distant castle blazing in the night. "Yours?"

"The Foundation's," said Barent. He took a long sip of his cold drink. "Do you know why you are here, Dr. Laski?"

Saul adjusted his glasses. "Mr. Barent, I don't even know where 'here' is. Or why I am still alive."

Barent nodded. "Your second statement is the more pertinent," he said. "I presume the . . . ah . . . medication is out of your system sufficiently for you to think through to some conclusions on that."

Saul chewed at his lower lip. He realized how shaky he actually was . . . half starved, partially dehydrated. It would probably take weeks to get the drugs completely out of his system. "I imagine you think that I'm your avenue to the Oberst," he said.

Barent laughed. "The Oberst. How quaint. I imagine that would be the way you think of him, given your . . . ah . . . unusual relationship. Tell me, Dr. Laski, were the camps as bad as the media portrays them? I have always suspected that there has been some attempt—perhaps subliminal— to overstate the case a trifle. Expiate subconscious guilt by exaggeration perhaps?"

Saul stared at the man. He took in every detail of the flawless tan, the silk sports coat, soft Gucci loafers, the amethyst ring on Barent's little finger. He said nothing.

"It does not matter," said Barent. "You're right, of course. You are still alive because you are Mr. Borden's messenger and we want very much to talk to the gentleman."

"I am not his messenger," Saul said dully.

Barent moved a manicured hand. "His message then," he said. "There is little difference."

A series of chimes sounded and the yacht picked up speed, turned to port as if it planned to circle the island. Saul saw a long dock lit with mercury vapor lamps.

"We would like you to convey a message to Mr. Borden," continued Barent.

"There isn't much chance of that while you keep me doped up in a steel cell," said Saul. He felt a stirring of hope for the first time since the explosion.

"This is very true," said Barent. "We will see to it that you have the best possible opportunity to meet him again . . . ah . . . at a place of his own choosing."

"You know where the Oberst is?"

"We know where . . . ah . . . he has chosen to operate."

"If I see him," said Saul, "I will kill him."

Barent laughed gently. He had perfect teeth. "This is very unlikely, Dr. Laski. We would, nonetheless, appreciate it if you would convey our message to him."

Saul took a deep breath of sea air. He could think of no reason why Barent and his group would require him to carry messages, could see no reason for him to be allowed to use his own free will to do so, and could imagine no way that it would profit them to keep him alive once he had done what they required. He felt dizzy and slightly drunk. "What's your message?"

"You will tell Willi Borden that the club would be most pleased if he would agree to fill the vacancy on the steering committee."

"That's all?"

"Yes," said Barent. "Would you like something to eat or drink before you leave?"

Saul closed his eyes a minute. He could feel the surge of the ship up his legs, through his pelvis. He gripped the railing very tightly and opened his eyes. "You're no different than they were," he said to Barent.

"Who is that?"

"The bureaucrats," said Saul, "the commandants, the civil servants turned *Einsatzgruppen* commandos, the railway engineers, the I. G. Farben industrialists, and the fat, beer-breathed sergeants dangling their fat legs in the Pit."

Barent mused a moment. "No," he said at last, "I suppose none of us is different in the end. Richard! See Dr. Laski to his destination, will you please?"

They flew by helicopter to the large island's airstrip, then north and west by private jet as the sky paled behind them. Saul dozed for an hour before they landed. It was his first undrugged sleep in a week. Haines shook him awake. "Look at this," he said.

Saul stared at the photograph. Aaron, Deborah, and the children were bound tightly but obviously alive. The white background gave no clue to their location. The flash caught the children's wide eyes and panicked expressions. Haines lifted a small cassette recorder. "Uncle Saul," came Aaron's voice, "please do what they ask. They will not harm us if you do what they ask. Carry out their instructions and we will be freed. Please, Uncle Saul . . ." The recording ended abruptly.

"If you try to contact them or the embassy, we will kill them," Haines whispered. Two of the agents were asleep. "Do what you are told and they'll be all right. Do you understand?"

"I understand," said Saul. He set his face against the cool plastic of the window. They were descending over the downtown of a major American city. By the glow of streetlights, Saul glimpsed brick buildings and white spires between office towers. He knew at that second that there was no hope for any of them.

TWENTY-FIVE

Washington, D.C.
Sunday, Dec. 28, 1980

Sheriff Bobby Joe Gentry was angry. The rented Ford Pinto had an automatic transmission, but Gentry slammed the shift selector from second to third gear as if he were driving a sportscar with a six-speed transmission. As soon as he exited the Beltway to I-95 he kicked the protesting Pinto up to seventy-two, defying the green Chrysler that was following him to keep up and daring the Maryland Highway Patrol to pull him over. Gentry tugged his suitcase into the front seat, fumbled in the outer pocket a minute, set the loaded Ruger in the center console, and tossed the suitcase into the backseat. Gentry was angry.

The Israelis had kept him until dawn, interrogating him first in their damned limousine, then in a safe house somewhere near Rockville, then in the damned car again. He had stayed with his original story—Saul Laski hunting for a Nazi war criminal to settle an old score, Gentry trying to tie it all into the Charleston Murders. The Israelis never resorted to violence—or, after Cohen's first remarks—the threat of violence, but they worked in teams to wear him down through sheer repetition. If they *were* Israelis. Gentry *felt* that they were . . . believed Jack Cohen to be exactly who he said he was . . . accepted the fact that Aaron Eshkol and his entire family had been murdered, but Gentry *knew* nothing for sure anymore. He knew only that a huge and dangerous game was being played by people who must view him as little more than a minor nuisance. Gentry whipped the Pinto up to seventy-five, glanced at the Ruger, and slowed to a steady sixty-two. The green Chrysler stayed two cars behind.

After the long night, Gentry had wanted to crawl into the huge bed in his hotel room and sleep until New Year's Eve. Instead he used a lobby pay phone to call Charleston. Nothing on the tape. He called his own office. Lester told him that there had been no messages and how was his vacation? Gentry said great, seeing all the sights. He called Natalie's St. Louis number. A man answered. Gentry asked for Natalie.

"Who the hell is this?" rasped an angry voice.

"Sheriff Gentry. Who is this?"

"Goddammit, Nat told me about you last week. Sounds like your basic Southern asshole cop to me. What the fuck do you want with Natalie?"

"I want to talk to her. Is she there?"

"No, goddammit, she's not here. And I don't have time to waste on you, Cracker Cop."

"Frederick," said Gentry.

"What?"

"You're Frederick. Natalie told me about you."

"Cut the crap, man."

"You didn't wear a tie for two years after you got back from Nam," said Gentry. "You think mathematics is the closest thing to eternal truth there is. You work in the computer center from eight P.M. to three A.M. every night but Saturday."

There was a silence on the line.

"Where's Natalie?" pressed Gentry. "This is police business. It concerns the murder of her father. Her own safety may be in jeopardy."

"What the hell do you mean her . . ."

"Where *is* she?" snapped Gentry.

"Germantown," came the angry voice. "Pennsylvania."

"Has she called you since she arrived there?"

"Yeah. Friday night. I wasn't home, but Stan took the message. Said she was staying at a place called the Chelten Arms. I've called six times, but she's never in. She hasn't returned my calls yet."

"Give me the number." Gentry wrote it in the little notebook he always carried.

"What kind of trouble is Nat in?"

"Look, Mr. Noble," said Gentry, "Miss Preston is searching for the person or persons who killed her father. I don't want her to find those people or those people to find her. When she comes back to St. Louis, you need to make sure that—a) she doesn't leave again and b) she isn't left alone for the next couple of weeks. Clear?"

"Yeah." Gentry heard enough solid anger in the voice to know that he never wanted to be on the receiving end of it.

He had wanted to go up to bed then, get a fresh start that evening. Instead he had called the Chelten Arms, left his own message for the absent Miss Preston, arranged for a rental car—no easy trick early on a Sunday morning—paid his bill, packed his bag, and driven north.

The green Chrysler stayed two cars back for forty miles. Just out of Baltimore he exited onto the Snowden River Parkway, took it a mile to Highway I, and stopped at the first diner he saw.

The Chrysler parked across the highway at the far end of a large lot. Gentry ordered coffee and a doughnut and stopped a busboy as the youngster walked by with a tray of dirty dishes. "Son, how would you like to earn twenty dollars?" The boy squinted suspiciously at him. "There's a car out there I'd like to know more about," said Gentry, pointing out the Chrysler. "If you'd get a chance to take a stroll that way, I'd like to know what the license number is and anything else you could notice."

The boy was back before Gentry finished his coffee. He reported breathlessly, finished with, "Geez, I don't think they noticed me. I mean,

I was just takin' out the garbage to the Dumpster like Nick usually has me do at noon. Geez, who are they, anyway?" Gentry paid the boy, went to the rest room, and used the pay phone in the back hallway to call the Baltimore Harbor Tunnel Authority. The main offices were closed on Sunday morning, but a tape recording gave a number for emergencies. A woman with a tired voice answered.

"Shit, I shouldn't be callin' ya, 'cause they'd kill me if they knew," started Gentry, "but Nick, Louis, and Delbert just left here to start the revolution by blowin' up the Harbor Tunnel."

The woman's voice no longer sounded tired as she demanded his name. Gentry heard a background beep as a tape recorder started.

"No time for that, no time for that!" he said excitedly. "Delbert, he got the guns and Louis got thirty-six sticks of dynamite from the construction site an' they got it stuck in the hidden compartment in the trunk. Nick says the revolution starts today. He got 'em the phony IDs an' everything."

The woman squawked a question and Gentry interrupted her. "I gotta get out of here. They'll kill me if they find out I tol'. They're in Delbert's car . . . a green 'seventy-six LeBaron. Maryland license DB7269. Delbert's drivin'. He's the one with the mustache, wearing a blue suit. Oh, Jesus, they all got guns and the whole damn car's wired to go up." Gentry broke the connection, ordered a coffee to go, paid his bill, and sauntered back to the Pinto.

He was only a few miles from the tunnel and in no particular hurry to get there so he drove up to the University of Maryland campus, let the Pinto wander through the Louden Park Cemetery, and drove down along the waterfront. The Chrysler had to stay far back because of the sparse Sunday traffic, but the driver was good, neither completely losing sight of Gentry's car nor becoming too obvious.

Gentry followed signs to the Harbor Tunnel Thruway, paid his toll, and watched in the rearview mirror as he pulled slowly into the lighted tunnel. The Chrysler never got to the toll booth. Three highway patrol vehicles, a black van with no markings, and a blue station wagon boxed it in fifty yards from the tunnel entrance. Four other police cruisers stopped traffic behind them. Gentry caught a glimpse of men leaning across hoods with shotguns and pistols leveled, saw the three men in the Chrysler waving arms out windows, and then he was busy driving as fast as he could to get out of the tunnel. If it was the FBI behind him, they could probably extricate themselves in a few minutes. God help them if they were Israelis and armed.

Gentry got off the Thruway as soon as he was out of the tunnel, got lost for a few minutes near the downtown, oriented himself when he saw Johns Hopkins, and took Highway I out of town. Traffic was light. He noticed an exit to Germantown, Maryland, a few miles out of town, and had to smile to himself. How many Germantowns were there in the United States? He hoped that Natalie had chosen the wrong one.

Gentry reached the southwest environs of Philadelphia by 10:30 and was in Germantown by 11:00. There had been no sign of the Chrysler and if someone else had picked up the surveillance, they were too smooth for Gentry to pick out of the traffic. The Chelten Arms looked as if it had seen better days on the Avenue but would not last long enough to see them return. Gentry parked the Pinto half a block away, slipped the Ruger into his sports coat pocket, and walked back. He counted five winos—three black, two white—huddled in doorways.

Miz Preston did not answer a call from the front desk. The clerk was an officious little white man, mostly nose, who combed his three remaining strands of hair from just above his left ear to just above his right ear. He clucked and shook his head when Gentry asked for a passkey. Gentry showed his badge. The clerk clucked again. "*Charleston?* Friend, you're going to have to do a lot better than some dime store badge. A Georgia policeman wouldn't have any jurisdiction here."

Gentry nodded, sighed, looked around at the empty lobby, and turned back around to grasp the clerk's greasy tie four inches below the knot. He jerked only once, but it was sufficient to bring the man's chin and nose to within eight inches of the countertop. "Listen, *friend*," Gentry said softly, "I'm here working liaison through Chief of Detectives Captain Donald Romano, Franklin Street Precinct, Homicide. That woman may have information leading to the apprehension of a man who murdered six people in cold blood. And I've been awake for forty-eight hours getting here. Now do I call Captain Romano *after* I bounce your goddamn face off the wood a few times just for the hell of it, or do we do it the simple way?"

The clerk fumbled behind himself and produced a passkey. Gentry released him and he bounced up like a jack-in-the-box, rubbing his Adam's apple and swallowing tentatively.

Gentry took three steps toward the elevator, wheeled, took two long strides back to the counter, and got a second grip on the clerk's tie before the red-faced man could back away. Gentry pulled him close, smiled at him, and said, "And son, Charleston County is in South Carolina, not Georgia. Remember that. There'll be a quiz later."

There was no corpse in Natalie's room. No bloodstains other than a few remnants of squashed bugs near the ceiling. No ransom notes. Her suitcase lay open on the fold-out rack, clothes neatly packed, a pair of dress shoes on the floor. The dress she had worn to the Charleston airport two days earlier was hanging in the open closet. There were no toiletries set out in the bathroom; the shower was dry although one bar of soap had been unwrapped and used. Her camera bag and cameras were not there. The bed either had been made already or not slept in the previous night.

Guessing at the efficiency of the Chelten Arms, Gentry thought that it had not been slept in.

He sat down on the edge of the bed and rubbed his face. He could think of nothing clever to do. The only path that made much sense was to start walking through Germantown, hoping for a chance encounter, checking back at the hotel every hour and hoping that the clerk or manager would not call the Philly police. Well, a few hours of walking in the brisk weather wouldn't hurt him.

Gentry took off his coat and sports coat, lay back on the bed, set the Ruger next to his right hand, and was asleep in two minutes.

He awoke in a dark room, disoriented, feeling that something was terribly wrong. His Rolex, a gift from his father, read 4:35. There was a dim, gray light outside, but the room had become dark. Gentry went into the bathroom to wash his face and then called down to the front desk. Miss Preston had not come in or called for her messages.

Gentry walked the half block to his car, transferred his suitcase to the trunk, and went for a walk. He went southeast on Germantown Avenue for a couple of blocks, past a small, fenced park. He would have loved to stop somewhere for a beer, but the bars were closed. It did not feel like a Sunday to Gentry, but he could not decide what day of the week it *did* feel like. It was snowing lightly as he stopped to get his suitcase and walked back to the hotel. A much younger and more polite clerk was on duty. Gentry checked in, paid thirty-two dollars in advance, and was ready to follow a porter to his room when he thought to ask about Natalie. Gentry still had the passkey in his pocket; perhaps potato-nose had gone off duty without mentioning it to anyone.

"Yes, sir," said the young clerk. "Miss Preston picked up her messages about fifteen minutes ago."

Gentry blinked. "Is she still here?"

"She went up to her room for a few minutes, sir, but I believe I just saw the lady go into the dining room."

Gentry thanked him, tipped the bellhop three dollars to carry his bag up, and walked over to the entrance of the small dining room bar.

He felt his heart leap as he saw Natalie sitting at a small table across the room. He started toward her and then stopped. A short man with dark hair and an expensive leather jacket was standing by her table, talking to her. Natalie stared up at the man with a strange look on her face.

Gentry hesitated only a second, then got in line for the salad bar. He did not look in Natalie's direction again until he was seated. A waitress bustled over and took his order for coffee. He began eating slowly, never looking directly at Natalie's table.

Something was very wrong. Gentry had known Natalie Preston for less than two weeks, but he knew how animated she was. He was just beginning to learn the nuances of expression that were so much a part of her personality. He saw neither animation nor nuance now. Natalie stared at the man across from her as if she had been drugged or lobotomized. Occasionally she spoke and the rigid movements of her mouth reminded Gentry of his mother's last year, after her stroke.

Gentry wished he could see more of the man's face, something other than the black hair, jacket, and pale hands folded on the tabletop. When he did turn around, Gentry caught a glimpse of hooded eyes, sallow complexion, and a small, thin-lipped mouth. Who was he looking for? Gentry picked up a newspaper from a nearby table and spent several minutes becoming a lonely, overweight salesman eating his salad. When he looked over toward Natalie again he was sure that the man with her was the focus of attention of at least two others in the room. Cops? FBI men? Israelis? Gentry finished the last of his salad, speared a runaway cherry tomato, and wondered for the thousandth time that day what he and Natalie had blundered into.

What next? Worst-case scenario: the man with the lizard eyes was one of *them*, one of Saul's mind-monsters, and his intentions toward Natalie were not friendly. The stakeout in the restaurant was a backup for whatever move this guy made. Probably more in the lobby. If they left and Gentry followed, he would be immediately visible. He had to precede them to follow them—but which way?

Gentry paid his bill and returned for his topcoat just as Natalie and the man rose from their seats. She looked straight at Gentry from twenty feet away, but there was no recognition in her eyes; there was *nothing* there. Gentry moved quickly through the lobby and paused by the front door to make a show of tugging on his coat.

The man led Natalie to the elevator, pausing to make an obscene gesture at another man seated on a worn couch. Gentry took a chance. Natalie was in Room 312. Gentry had asked for Room 310. The hotel had only three floors of guest rooms. If the man with the dead eyes was taking her anywhere but her room, Gentry would lose them.

He crossed quickly to the stairway, took the stairs two and three at a time, stood panting for ten seconds on the top landing, and opened the door in time to see the man follow Natalie into 312. He stood there for almost a minute, waiting to see if any of the others from the lobby were following. When no one appeared he moved lightly down the hall to pause with three fingers touching the door to Natalie's room. He found the grip of the Ruger and then decided against it. If this man was like Saul's Oberst, he could make Gentry use the revolver on himself. If he wasn't like the Oberst, Gentry did not think he would need the weapon.

Jesus, thought Gentry, what if I break in and this is some good friend of Natalie's who she's inviting up? He remembered the expression on her face and silently slid the passkey into the lock.

Gentry went in fast, filling the short interior hallway, seeing the man seated, turning, opening his mouth to speak. Gentry took half a second to notice Natalie's semi-nakedness and the terror visible on her face and then he swung his arm up and then down, bringing his fist down on the top of the man's head as if he was driving a huge nail with the base of his hand. The man had been rising; now he went deep into the sagging cushion, bounced twice, and sprawled unconscious across the left arm of the chair.

Gentry made sure the man was out of action and then he turned to Natalie. Her blouse was unbuttoned, bra undone, but she made no move to cover herself. Her entire body began shaking as if she were in the beginning of a seizure. Gentry pulled off his coat and draped it around her just as she collapsed forward into his arms, her head snapping from side to side in silent negation. When she tried to speak, her teeth were chattering so hard that Gentry could hardly understand her. "Oh . . . R-Rob . . . hu . . . hu . . . he tried t . . . to . . . I . . . c-c-couldn't d-d-do any—y-thing."

Gentry held her, supported her, and stroked her hair. He was wondering feverishly what the next move should be.

"Oh, G-g-god, I'm . . . g-going . . . to . . . b-be sick." Natalie rushed into the bathroom.

Gentry could hear retching sounds from behind the closed door as he bent over the unconscious man, lowered him to the floor, frisked him quickly and efficiently, and lifted his billfold. Anthony Harod, Beverly Hills. Mr. Harod had about thirty credit cards, a Playboy Key Card, a card identifying him as a member in good standing of the Writers Guild of America, and other plastic and paper tying him to Hollywood. There was a key to a Chestnut Hills Hotel in his jacket pocket. Harod was beginning to stir very slightly when Natalie came out of the bathroom, her clothing set right, her face still damp from washing. Anthony Harod moaned and rolled over on his side.

"God*damn* you," Natalie said with feeling and unleashed a kick at the fallen man's groin. She was wearing solid, low-heel loafers and the energy behind the kick would have served well in a forty-yard field goal attempt. She aimed for Harod's testicles, but Harod was rolling over and the blow took him just inside the hip, flipping him over twice and bringing his head hard up against the wooden leg of the bed.

"Easy, easy," said Gentry and knelt to check the man's pulse and breathing. Anthony Harod of Beverly Hills, California, was still alive, but was quite unconscious. Gentry moved to the door. The room had no bolt and chain; the other lock was on. He came back and put his arm around Natalie.

"Rob," she gasped, "he was *in* my m-m-mind. He m-made me do things, made me say things . . ."

"It's all right," said Gentry. "We're going to get out of here right now." He gathered up her extra shoes, snapped her suitcase shut, helped her into her coat, and threw her camera bag over his own shoulder. "There's a fire escape going down to that alley. Do you think you can get down there with me all right?"

"Yes, but why do we have to . . ."

"We'll talk when we're out of here. My car's just down the block. Come on."

It was dark out. The fire escape was sagging and slippery and Gentry expected half the hotel staff to come rushing out when he dropped the screeching, rusted ladder the last eight feet. No one appeared at the backdoor.

He helped Natalie down the last few rungs and they moved quickly down the dark alley. Gentry smelled snow and rotting garbage. They emerged on Germantown Avenue, went west thirty yards, and came around the corner ten yards from Gentry's Pinto. No one was in sight; no one emerged from the dark storefronts or distant hotel as Gentry turned on the ignition, shifted gear, and swung onto Chelten Avenue.

"Where are we going?" asked Natalie.

"I don't know. We'll just get the hell out of this place and talk it over."

"All right."

Gentry turned east onto Germantown Avenue and had to slow for a trolley going the same direction. "Hell," he said.

"What?"

"Oh, nothing. I just left my suitcase in a room at your hotel."

"Anything important in it?"

Gentry thought of the changes in shirt and slacks and chuckled. "Nope. And I'm sure'n hell not going back."

"Rob, what's going *on*?"

Gentry shook his head. "I thought maybe you could tell me."

Natalie shivered. "I never felt . . . felt anything like that before. I couldn't do anything. It was like my body wasn't my own anymore."

"So we know they're real," said Gentry.

Natalie laughed a little too loudly. "Rob, the old lady . . . Melanie Fuller . . . she's *here*. Somewhere in Germantown. Marvin and the others have seen her. And she killed two more of the gang members last night. I was with . . ."

"Wait a minute," said Gentry, passing the trolley and a city bus marked SEPTA. The brick street lay straight and empty ahead. "Who's Marvin?"

"Marvin's the leader of the Soul Brickyard Gang," said Natalie. "He . . ."

Something hit the Pinto hard from behind. Natalie bounced forward, using her hands to keep from hitting her head against the windshield. Gentry cursed and swiveled to look behind him. The huge grill of the city bus filled the Pinto's rear window as it accelerated to hit them again. "Hang on!" shouted Gentry and floored the accelerator. The bus came on fast, tapping the Pinto's rear end again before the little car began moving ahead.

Gentry got the Pinto up to fifty-five, shaking and bouncing over the irregular brick surface and the ruts of trolley tracks. Even through the closed windows he could hear the roar of the bus's diesel as the huge vehicle accelerated through half a dozen gears to catch up. "Oh, damn," said Gentry. A block ahead, a semitrailer was backing into a loading space, temporarily obstructing the avenue. Gentry considered going up onto the sidewalk on the right, saw an old man rummaging through a trash container, and took a hard left into a narrow street, the rear end of the Pinto bouncing off the curb in a controlled slide. From the sound of it, Gentry guessed that the rear bumper had been torn loose during the first collision and was dragging behind them. Rowhouses flashed by on either side. Junkers, new model cars, and wheel-less derelicts lined the right curb.

"It's still coming!" cried Natalie.

Gentry checked the rearview mirror in time to see the huge bus take the turn by bouncing up onto the sidewalk, taking out two no-parking signs and a mailbox, then accelerating down the hill after them in a cloud of diesel fumes. Gentry saw the small dent in the wide front bumper from the first tap. "I really don't believe this," said Gentry.

The street came to a T-intersection at the bottom of the hill, a snowy railroad embankment ahead of them, vacant lots and warehouses to the east and west. Gentry took a hard left, heard the rear bumper tear loose, listened to the little four-cylinder engine revving its heart out.

"Can they catch us?" breathed Natalie as the bus crashed around the corner behind them and roared partway up the embankment before bounding back onto the pavement. Gentry caught a glimpse of a driver in khaki, straight-arming the large steering wheel, dark figures lurching in the aisle behind him.

"It can't catch us unless we do something stupid," said Gentry. The narrow street cut sharply to the right in front of an abandoned factory, ran fifty yards downhill between empty tenements and brick-strewn lots, and dead-ended at the railway embankment. There had been no dead-end sign.

"Like this?" said Natalie.

"Yeah." Gentry skidded the Pinto to a stop in the narrow turnaround.

Gentry knew that there was no way the Pinto was going to climb thirty feet of junk-strewn hillside. To their left, an empty brick building offered a high gate and twenty feet of chain link fence separating a muddy parking lot from the street. Gentry thought that it was possible that the Pinto could crash through the gate, but he doubted that the lot would be an improvement over their present position. To their right, a row of empty two-story buildings showed boarded-up windows and doors covered with graffiti. A narrow alley ran east from the street.

Behind them, the bus made the right turn and started down the hill. It growled like some gut-shot beast as the driver shifted down two gears.

"Out!" shouted Gentry. He had time to grab Natalie's suitcase, she took the camera bag. They ran for the alley on their right.

· The bus was moving fast when it struck the Pinto a glancing shot on the left rear fender. The smaller vehicle spun completely around, metal flying, rear window popping out, as the bus bounced left, almost tipping over as the right wheels gouged up the embankment, brake lights flashing as it crashed through the chain link fence and came to a stop in the frozen mud of the parking lot. Gears ground and the bus backed over the flattened fence, caught the Pinto squarely in the passenger-side door, and shoved the rental car backward until it caught on the curb not twenty feet from the alley where Gentry and Natalie watched. The Pinto struck a fire hydrant and flipped over with a great tearing of metal. No water came from the fractured hydrant, but the stink of gasoline filled the night air.

"This is a nightmare," said Natalie.

Gentry realized that he had pulled the Ruger free and was holding it in his right hand. He shook his head and dropped it into the pocket of his topcoat.

The bus shifted gears and pulled into the center of the street, dragging tatters of chrome and engulfing them in diesel fumes. Gentry pulled Natalie a few feet deeper into the four-foot wide alley.

"Who's doing this?" whispered Natalie.

"I don't know." For the first time, Gentry believed, in his gut rather than just in his consciousness, that human beings were capable of doing what Saul and Natalie had actually experienced. He remembered reading *The Exorcist* years before and understanding the agnostic priest's glee at witnessing a power that could only be demonic in nature. The existence of demons suggested, if not proved, the existence of a God the priest had doubted. But what did this incredible series of events prove? Human perversity? The perfection of some parapsychological power that had always been part of being human?

"It's stopping," said Natalie. The bus had backed to the embankment and turned left sharply enough to be facing back up the hilly street.

"Perhaps it's over," said Gentry. He put his arm around the shivering young woman next to him. "Whatever happens, the damn bus can't get at us here."

The doors of the bus were on the opposite side of the vehicle, but both of them heard the compressed-air hiss. Gentry could see silhouettes against the pale glow of the interior lights as the passengers moved forward or to the rear. What must they be thinking as they were released after such an insane ride? What was the driver doing now? Gentry could make out only a tall shadow hunched over the wheel. Then he saw the seven passengers moving hesitantly, three around the front of the bus, four around the back. They walked like polio victims with steel braces, like awkwardly handled marionettes. The rest would pause as one shuffled forward, then another. An old man in the lead dropped to all fours and scuttled toward the alley, seeming to sniff the pavement as he came.

"Oh, dear God," breathed Natalie.

They ran up the narrow alley, jumping over debris, scraping their arms and shoulders against brick. Gentry realized that he was still carrying Natalie's suitcase in his left hand while he gripped her hand with his right. The end of the alley had rusted wire mesh across it. Behind them, Gentry heard a heavy, animallike panting as someone entered the narrow passage. He let go of Natalie's hand, used the suitcase and his body as a battering ram, and tore the wire loose.

They emerged on a street that dead-ended to their right, but to their left it ran downhill under a dark railway overpass, and continued north past lighted rowhouses. Gentry turned left and ran, Natalie passing him before they reached the broken sidewalk. Someone clawed through the wire behind them. Gentry looked over his shoulder and saw a man with white hair and a business suit scramble over tilted slabs of concrete like a frenzied Doberman. Gentry pulled the Ruger out and ran.

There was ice in the darkness under the railroad bridge. Natalie reached it first. Gentry saw her feet fly out from under her and heard her hit hard in the blackness. He had time to slow but still spun and went to one knee.

"Natalie!"

"I'm all right."

He felt toward her voice and helped her up. "I'm going to leave your suitcase here," he said.

Natalie barked a laugh. "Let's go." They came up out of the darkness into a street made narrower by parked cars, most of them derelicts. Burned-out buildings mixed with rowhouses with lights on in the windows. There were no streetlights. Gentry could hear footsteps clapping down the hill, echoing under the railroad bridge. There were no shouts or curses when the figure fell heavily, only scrabbling sounds on ice and brick.

"Over there," called Gentry and half pushed Natalie uphill toward the first lighted house a hundred feet away.

He was panting, half staggering by the time they reached the three-step concrete stoop. He turned and stood guard as Natalie pounded on the door and called for help. A dark silhouette pulled a torn shade aside for a second, but no one appeared at the door. "Please!" screamed Natalie.

"Natalie," called Gentry. The man in the torn and soiled business suit was rushing the final thirty feet at them. In the light from the single window, Gentry could see the wide, white eyes and the mouth agape, saliva streaming down over chin and collar. Gentry aimed the Ruger and applied enough pressure to pull the hammer back. Then he lowered the hammer and the gun. "To hell with it," he said and lowered his shoulder to meet the man's charge.

The attacker hit Gentry's shoulder at full speed and flipped into the air, landing on his back on the sidewalk and lowest step. There was a sickening sound as the man's head bounced, Gentry leaned toward him, and the older man was on his feet at once, blood streaming from his disarrayed hair, his dentures clacking as he went for Gentry's throat. The sheriff picked him up by the lapels and swung him out over the street; let him fall. The man hit, rolled, let out an inhuman snarl that was part laugh, and immediately was on his feet, lunging. Gentry clubbed him down with the barrel of the Ruger. The body lay on its face, twitching.

Gentry sat on the lowest step and lowered his head between his knees. Natalie kicked and pounded at the door. "Please let us in!"

"I'm a police officer!" yelled Gentry with the last of his breath. "Let us in." The door remained locked.

More footsteps echoed from under the bridge. "God," gasped Gentry, "I thought . . . Saul said . . . the Oberst could . . . control only one . . . at a time."

The figure of a tall woman emerged from the shadows under the bridge. She was running in her stocking feet and held something sharp in her right hand.

"Come on," said Gentry. They had run thirty feet uphill when they heard the roar of the city bus around the bend in the street. Headlights flashed off brick rowhouses across the street to their left.

Gentry looked for an alley, a vacant lot, anything, but there was only the solid facade of uninterrupted rowhouses for the 120 feet back down to the railroad bridge. "Back down there!" he shouted. "Up the embankment to the tracks." He turned just as the tall blond woman silently covered the last ten feet on stocking feet and crashed into him. They both went over, rolling onto the wet street, Gentry dropping the Ruger in an attempt to hold her head and snapping teeth away from his throat, trying to get a choke hold on her. The woman was very strong. She swiveled her head and bit deeply into his left hand. Gentry made a fist, struck at her jaw, but she was able to get her head down in time for her skull to take most of the impact. Gentry pushed her away, trying to decide how to knock her out without permanently injuring her, just as her right hand came around and under his arm. He felt a cold shock and did nothing but watch as the scissors slashed in a second time. She pulled back her arm to strike a third time and Gentry swung a roundhouse that would have taken her head off if it had connected. It did not connect.

The blond woman danced back two paces and raised the scissors to eye level just as Natalie brought her loaded camera bag down full force on the woman's head. She crumpled bonelessly to the street just as Gentry was able to get to one knee. His left side and left hand were on fire. There was a rising roar and the headlights of the oncoming bus froze them in their glare. Gentry felt around for the Ruger, knew it must be there somewhere. The bus was fifty feet from them and accelerating downhill.

Natalie had the gun. She had dropped the camera bag and now she took a wide stance, cradled the weapon with both hands, and fired four times the way Gentry had taught her.

"No!" shouted Gentry even as the first bullet struck, taking out a headlight. The second one starred the broad windshield just to the left of the driver's position. Recoil made the other two go high.

Gentry grabbed the camera bag and pulled Natalie toward the curb and a rowhouse stoop even as the bus swerved left toward them. It caromed off the stoop, sparks flying, the right wheels rolling over the unconscious blond woman without a noticeable bounce. Natalie and Gentry pulled each other up as the bus hit ice, spun ninety degrees to the left, and went under the railroad bridge broadside. There was a scream of metal on wood.

"Now!" gasped Gentry and they ran for the embankment. Gentry ran in a half-crouch, holding his left arm against his side.

A diesel engine roared, gears screamed, and a single, skewed headlight beam lanced out of the far side of the underpass as the rear wheels of the bus spun, found purchase, spun again. A wooden timber gave way with a shriek and the rear end of the bus emerged just as Gentry and Natalie reached the embankment and began to scramble up the littered, frozen slope. A rusted loop of wire caught Gentry around the ankle and brought him down heavily. For a second he was in the full beam of the crazy headlight and he looked down to see his coat slashed to tatters and hanging open, blood dripping down his arm onto his chewed hand. He looked over his shoulder as Natalie grasped his right arm and helped him up. "Give me the Ruger," he said.

The bus was backing up the hill, getting a run at the slope.

"The *gun.*"

Natalie handed him the pistol just as the driver slammed the big vehicle into first gear. Both of the bodies on the street looked flattened now. "Go!" Gentry commanded. Natalie turned and began climbing, using her hands. Gentry followed. They were less than halfway up the slope when they came to the fence.

The bus picked up speed quickly, shifting gears, the noise echoing off brick buildings, the single headlight cocked upward at such an angle that it illuminated Gentry and Natalie on the slope.

The fence had been invisible from below. It had sagged and rolled until it resembled concertina wire. Natalie was snagged on the second tier of ripped metal. Gentry pulled wire loose from Natalie's pant leg, heard cloth rip, and pushed her uphill. She took four steps and stopped, snagged again. Gentry turned, braced his feet on the slope, and raised the Ruger. The city bus was almost as long as the embankment was high. Gentry's coat hindered him. He took it off and turned sideways, raising the Ruger, feeling the weakness in his arm.

The bus rolled over the bodies, shifted gear, bounced enough on an unseen curb to avoid burying its nose in the cold ground, and began climbing the hill.

Gentry lowered his aim to compensate for the tendency to shoot high when firing downhill. The light reflected from the snowy hillside clearly illuminated the driver. It was a woman in khaki, eyes very wide.

They . . . he . . . won't let her live anyway, thought Gentry and fired the last two rounds. Two stars appeared directly in front of the driver, the entire windshield went white and collapsed into powder, and Gentry turned and ran hard. He was ten feet from Natalie when the bus caught him, the grill hitting him hard, sending him flying out and upward like an infant carelessly tossed skyward. He hit hard on his left side, felt Natalie next to him, leaned across a cold rail, and watched.

The bus came to within five feet of the top of the embankment, lost traction, and went slewing back down with its headlight swinging like a frenzied searchlight. The right rear fender caught the pavement with a solid, final sound and the long bus tried to stand on its end, the nose hitting and bouncing thirty degrees off the slope before it rolled slowly to its right, went almost over on its back, and settled on its side with wheels spinning.

"Don't move," whispered Natalie, but Gentry fought his way to his feet. He looked down and almost laughed aloud to see the Ruger still clenched in his cold hand. He went to put it in his coat pocket, found that he was no longer wearing topcoat or sports coat, and tucked it in his waistband.

Natalie held him up. "What do we do?" she said very softly.

Gentry tried to clear his head. "Wait for the cops, the fire department. Ambulances," he said. He knew something was wrong with the idea, but he was too tired to think through it.

Lights had gone on in more rowhouse windows, but no one had emerged. Gentry stood leaning on Natalie for several long, cold minutes. It began to snow. There was no sign of ambulances.

Below them, there was the hollow sound of pounding and a window on the side of the toppled bus popped out and fell to the ground. At least three dark forms emerged, scurrying like huge, dark spiders across the metal carcass of the bus.

Without saying anything, Gentry and Natalie turned and began hobbling quickly down the rail bed. Once he fell against the rail and felt a solid persistent humming. Natalie pulled him up and urged him into a run. He could hear distant footsteps on the cinders behind them.

"There!" Natalie suddenly gasped. "There. I know where we are."

Gentry opened his eyes to see an old three-story home sandwiched between empty lots. Lights burned from a dozen windows.

He stumbled and fell down the steep hillside. Something sharp tore at his right leg. He staggered to his feet and helped Natalie up as a commuter train roared by above them.

There were people on the porch. Black-sounding voices shouted challenges. Gentry saw two young men with shotguns. He fumbled for the Ruger, but his fingers failed to close on the grip.

Natalie's voice came from very far away, urgent, insistent. Gentry decided to close his eyes for a second or two just long enough to get his strength back.

Strong hands closed on him as he collapsed.

TWENTY-SIX

Germantown
Monday, Dec. 29, 1980

Natalie looked in on Rob throughout the day Monday. He was feverish, vague about his whereabouts, and occasionally he would talk in his sleep. She had lain next to him during the night, being careful not to brush against his taped ribs or bandaged left hand. Once in his sleep he had put out his right hand and gently stroked her hair.

Marvin Gayle had not looked overjoyed when she and Gentry had staggered up to the front door of Community House on Sunday night.

"Who your fat friend, babe?" Marvin had called from the top step. He was flanked by Leroy and Calvin carrying sawed-off shotguns.

"It's Sheriff Rob Gentry," said Natalie, regretting at once that she had identified him as a lawman. "He's hurt."

"I see that, babe. Why don't you take him out to the white folks' hospital?"

"Someone's after us, Marvin. Let us in." Natalie knew that if she could get through to the charismatic young gang leader, he would listen. Natalie had spent most of the weekend at Community House. She had been there on Saturday night when word came that Monk and Lionel had been killed. At Marvin's request she had gone with them and photographed the dismembered bodies. Then she had staggered around a corner to be quietly sick in the dark. Only later did Marvin tell her that Monk had been carrying a print of the Melanie Fuller photograph, showing it to inactive members in the neighborhood, trying to track down the old lady. The photograph was not on Monk's body. Natalie's skin had gone absolutely icy when she heard that.

Incredibly, neither the police nor the news media responded to the murders. There had been no witnesses other than George, the terrified fifteen-year-old who had escaped, and George had told no one except Soul Brickyard. The gang kept it that way. The two mutilated bodies were wrapped in shower curtains and stored in a freezer in Louis Taylor's tenement basement. Monk had lived alone in a condemned building off Pastorius Street. Lionel lived with his mother on Bringhurst, but the old woman was in an alcoholic stupor much of the time and would not miss him for days.

"First we fix the honky motherfucker that did this, then we tell the cops and TV people," Marvin said late that Saturday night. "We tell them now, they won't be enough room to *move* around here." The gang had followed orders. Natalie had stayed with them through Sunday afternoon, repeating her edited description of Melanie Fuller's powers again and again, then listening to their war plans. The plans were simple: They were going to find the Fuller woman and the "honky monster" with her and kill them both.

On Sunday night, the snow falling heavily, she stood on the sidewalk while trying to support the semiconscious bulk of Rob Gentry, and pleaded, "There are people after us."

Marvin made a motion with his left hand. Louis, Leroy, and a gang member Natalie did not recognize jumped from the porch and faded into the night. "Who's after you, babe?"

"I don't know. People."

"They be voodooed like the honky monster?"

"Yes."

"Same old woman be the one doing it?"

"Maybe. I don't *know*. But Rob is hurt. There're people out there after us. Let us *in*. Please."

Marvin had stared at her with those cold, beautiful blue eyes and then stepped aside and motioned them in. Gentry had to be carried to a mattress in the basement. Natalie had insisted on calling a doctor, or ambulance, but Marvin had shaken his head. "Uh-uh, babe. We got two dead we ain't telling nobody about until we find the Voodoo Lady. No way we bringing the Man down on us for your hurt cracker boyfriend. We'll get Jackson."

Jackson was George's thirty-year-old half brother, a quiet, balding, competent man who had been a medic in Vietnam and who had finished two and a half years of medical school before dropping out. He arrived with a blue rucksack filled with bandages, syringes, and drugs. "Two ribs broken," he said softly after inspecting Gentry. "Deep cut there, but that's not what broke his ribs. Half inch lower, inch and a half deeper, and he would have been dead from the puncture wound. Somebody's been chewing on his hand for sure. Probable concussion. Can't tell how bad without some X-rays. Look out, please, so I can work on the man." He had proceeded to staunch the bleeding, clean and dress the deeper cuts and lacerations, tape the broken ribs, and give Gentry a shot for the bite that had almost chewed through the webbing on his left hand. Then he broke a capsule under Gentry's nose, bringing the sheriff awake almost instantly. "How many fingers?"

"Three," said Gentry. "Where the hell am I?"

They had spoken several minutes, long enough for Jackson to decide it was not a severe concussion, and then he had given Gentry another shot and allowed him to float back into sleep. "He'll be all right. I'll check with you tomorrow."

"Why didn't you finish med school?" Natalie asked, blushing at her own inquisitiveness.

Jackson shrugged. "Too much bullshit. Came back here instead. Keep waking him up every couple of hours."

She had wakened Gentry briefly every ninety minutes in the curtained corner of the basement where Marvin let them sleep. Natalie's watch read 4:38 when she shook him awake for the last time and he gently touched her hair.

"Bunch a strange dudes around this neighborhood," said Leroy.

A dozen of the gang members sat around the kitchen table, dangled legs from the counter, or leaned against cabinets and walls. Gentry had slept until two P.M. and awakened ravenous. By four the war council was convened, and Gentry was still eating, nibbling on Chinese food he had paid one of the young members to bring back. Natalie was the only female in the room except for Marvin's silent girlfriend, Kara.

"What kind of strange dudes?" asked Gentry around a mouthful of Moo Shu pork.

Leroy looked at Marvin, received a nod, and said, "Strange white *police* dudes. Pigs. Like you, man."

"In uniform?" asked Gentry. He stood at a counter, his taped ribs and bandaged side making him look bulkier than he was.

"Sheet no," said Leroy. "They in *plainclothes*. Real subtle motherfuckers. Black pants, windbreakers, them little pointy Florsheim shoes. Fuckers *blendin' in* with the neighborhood. Hah."

"Where are they?"

Marvin answered. "Man, they're all over the place. Couple unmarked vans each end of Bringhurst. Got a phony telephone truck been in the alley off Greene and Queen for two days now. Got twelve dudes in four unmarked cars between Church and here. Whole mess of them hangin' around on second floor of some buildings on Queen and Germantown."

"How many all told?" asked Gentry.

"Figure forty. Maybe fifty."

"Working eight-hour shifts?"

"Yeah. Dudes think they invisible, sittin' out there near the laundromat on Ashmead. Only honkys on the fucking block. Punching in and out like they work for fucking Bethlehem Steel, man. One dude does nothing but run and get doughnuts for them."

"Philadelphia police?"

The tall, thin one named Calvin laughed. "Shit, no, man. Local pigs wear that Banlon suit, white socks, *orthopedic* shoes . . . all that shit when they on a stakeout."

"Besides," said Marvin, "they're too many of them. All of vice and homicide and local narcs with the kiddy cops thrown in don't put fifty of them on the street. Got to be like the federal narcs or something."

"Or FBI," said Gentry. He rubbed absently at his left temple. Natalie noticed the slight wince of pain.

"Yeah." Marvin's eyes lost their intense focus for a few minutes as he pursued a thought. "Could be. I don't understand it, man. Why so many? I thought, like, maybe they were after Zig and Muhammed's and everybody's killers, but no, they don't give a shit who offed some niggers. Unless they already after the Voodoo Lady and the honky monster. That it, babe?"

"That could be it," said Natalie. "Only it's more complicated . . ."

"How come?"

Gentry moved up to the table, his upper body stiff. He laid his bandaged left hand on the table. "There are others with the . . . voodoo power," he said. "There's a man who is probably hiding somewhere here in the city. Others in positions of authority have the same power. There's a sort of war going on."

"Man, I love the way you talk," snorted Leroy and imitated Gentry's slow, soft tones. "Theah's a saht of wah goin' ohn."

"I find your patois equally agreeable," drawled Gentry.

Leroy half rose, scowling fiercely. "What the fuck you say, man?"

"He say you shut the fuck up, Leroy," Marvin said softly. "*Do* it." He shifted to look at Gentry. "OK, Mr. Sheriff, tell me this . . . that man who's hiding, he white?"

"Yep."

"The dudes after him, they white?"

"Yep."

"Other dudes might be in this. They white?"

"Uh-huh."

"They all as rat's-ass mean as this Voodoo Lady and her honky monster?"

"Yes."

Marvin sighed. "It figures." He reached into the loose pocket of his fatigue jacket, extracted Gentry's Ruger, and laid it on the table with a solid *thunk*. "Fuckin' big piece of iron you carry, Mr. Sheriff. Ever think of putting bullets in it?"

Gentry did not reach for the weapon. "I have extra cartridges in my suitcase."

"Where you suitcase, man? It in the squashed Pinto, it *gone*."

"Marvin went back to get my bag from the alley," said Natalie. "It was gone. So was the wreck of your rental car. So was the bus."

"The bus?" Gentry's eyebrows show up so high that he winced and held his head. "The *bus* was gone? How soon after we got here did you go back?"

"Six hours," said Leroy.

"We gotta take babe's word for it that you was chased by a big, bad city bus," said Marvin. "She says you had to shoot and kill it. Maybe it crawled off into the bushes to die, Mr. Sheriff."

"Six hours," said Gentry. He leaned against the refrigerator for support. "The news? It must be on the national networks by now."

"No news," said Natalie. "No TV coverage. Not even a sidebar inside the *Philadelphia Inquirer.*"

"Jesus Christ," said Gentry. "They must have incredible connections to clean it up and cover it up so fast. There must have been . . . at least four people killed."

"Yeah, man and SEPTA be pissed," said Calvin, referring to the transit authority. "I don't recommend you take any mass transit while you here. Killin' their buses really piss off ol' SEPTA." Calvin laughed so hard that he almost fell off his chair.

"So where's your suitcase, man?" said Marvin.

Gentry shook himself out of reverie. "I left it at the Chelten Arms. Room 310. But I only paid for one night. They would have picked it up by now."

Marvin swiveled in his chair. "Taylor, you work in the old Chicken Arms. You get into their storage room, man?"

"Sure, man." Taylor was a seventeen- or eighteen-year-old with dark scars of acne on a gaunt face.

"It may be dangerous," said Gentry. "It may not be there at all, and if it is, it's probably watched."

"By some of the voodoo pigs?" asked Marvin.

"Among others."

"Taylor," said Marvin. It was a command. The boy grinned, lowered himself from the counter, and was gone.

"We got other business to discuss," said Marvin. "White folk can adjourn themselves."

Natalie and Gentry stood on the small back porch of Community House and watched as the last of the gray winter light faded to night. The view was of a long lot filled with mounds of broken, snow-covered bricks and the backs of two condemned apartment buildings. The glow of kerosene lamps through several begrimed windows showed that the condemned building was still occupied. It was very cold. Occasional flurries of snow were visible around the solitary undamaged streetlight half a block away.

"We're staying here then?" asked Natalie.

Gentry looked at her. Only his head was visible outside of the army blanket he had thrown over his shoulders in lieu of a jacket. "It makes as much sense as anything for tonight," he said. "We may not be among friends, but we have a common enemy."

"Marvin Gayle is smart," said Natalie.

"As a whip," agreed Gentry.

"Why do you think he's wasting his life with a gang?"

Gentry squinted at the dirty twilight. "When I was in school in Chicago I got to do some work with city gangs there. A few of their leaders were jerks—one of them was a psychopath—but most were pretty smart individuals. Put an alpha personality in a closed system and he or she'll rise to the top of whatever represents the most competitive power ladder. In a place like this, that's the local gang."

"What's an alpha personality?"

Gentry laughed but stopped abruptly and touched his ribs. "Students of animal behavior look at pecking order, group dominance, and call the top ram or sparrow or wolf or whatever the alpha male. Didn't want to be sexist so I think of it in terms of personality. Sometimes I think discrimination and other stupid social roadblocks breed an inordinate number of alpha personalities. Maybe it's a sort of natural selection process by which ethnic and cultural groups affirm their fair places in unfair societies."

Natalie reached out and touched his arm through the blanket. "You know, Rob, for a good-old-boy sheriff, you have some interesting thoughts."

Gentry looked down. "Not terribly original thoughts. Saul Laski discussed something similar in his book, *The Pathology of Violence.* He was talking about how downtrodden and often unlikely societies tend to produce incredible warriors when national or cultural survival depends upon it . . . sort of specialized alpha personalities. Even Hitler fit that description in a sick, perverted way."

A snowflake landed on Natalie's eyelid. She blinked it away. "Do you think Saul's still alive?"

"Logic suggests that he shouldn't be," said Gentry. He had told Natalie about his last few days during a long talk after he awoke that afternoon. Now he tugged the blanket tighter around him and rested his bandaged hand on the splintered porch rail. "But still," he said, "something makes me think he *is* still alive. Somewhere."

"And somebody has him?"

"Yeah. Unless he was able to drop out of sight completely. But he would have warned us."

"How?" said Natalie. "You and I left messages on your phone machine that somebody erased. How could Saul get through if we couldn't? Especially if he's on the run?"

"Good point," said Gentry. Natalie shivered. Gentry moved closer and enclosed her in the blanket. "Thinking about yesterday?" he asked.

She nodded. Every time she began to feel in the least bit secure, some part of her remembered the sensation of Anthony Harod's consciousness in her mind and her entire body shuddered as if recalling a brutal rape. It *had been* a brutal rape.

"It's over," he said. "They won't get at you again."

"But they're still *out* there," whispered Natalie.

"Yes. Which is another reason we probably shouldn't try to get out of Philadelphia tonight."

"And you still don't think it was . . . Harod . . . who made the bus . . . who set them after us?"

"I don't see how it could be," said Gentry. "The man was truly and sincerely unconscious when we left. He may have come to ten minutes later, but he would've been in no shape to do mental gymnastics. Besides, didn't you say that you got the impression that he used his . . . voodoo power . . . only on women?"

"Yes, but that's just a *feeling* I had when he . . . when he was . . ."

"Trust the feeling," said Gentry. "Whoever was siccing those folks on us last night used men too."

"If it wasn't this Anthony Harod, who *was* it?" It was dark now. Somewhere in the city a siren howled. The streetlight, the dimly lit windows, the low-cloud reflection of the city's countless mercury vapor lamps, all seemed unreal to Natalie, as if light had no place in the canyons of dirty brick, rusted metal, and darkness.

"I don't know," said Gentry. "But I know that our job right now is to hunker down and survive. The one good thing about yesterday is that now that I've thought about it, I'm almost certain that whoever was after us wanted to *keep* us here but didn't want to kill us . . . or at least not kill *you.*"

Natalie's mouth opened in surprise. "How can you say that? Look at what they did! The bus . . . those people . . . look at what they did to you."

"Yep," said Gentry, "but think of how they could've handled it in a much simpler way."

"How?" Even as Natalie spoke she realized what Rob was going to say.

"If they could see us to chase us," said Gentry, "they could see us to physically control us. I had a gun the entire time. They could have made me use it on you and then turn it on myself."

Natalie shivered under the blanket. Gentry put his right arm around her. She said. "So you think they weren't really trying to kill us?"

"That's one possibility," said Gentry and stopped abruptly.

Natalie sensed that he did not want to complete the thought. "What is the other possibility?" she pressed.

Gentry pursed his lips and then smiled weakly. "The other possibility— and this fits the evidence too—is that they're so sure we can't get away that they're having a little fun and playing with us."

Natalie jumped as the door crashed open behind her. It was Leroy. "Hey, Marvin say you two get in here. Taylor's back and he got your bag, man. Louis back and he got some good news. He and George and them, they found where the Voodoo Lady live and track her down, wait 'til she asleep and get her, man. Honky monster, too."

Natalie's heart pounded against her ribs. "What do you mean they got them?"

Leroy grinned at them. "They *killed* them, woman. Louis cut the old Voodoo Lady's throat while she asleep. George and Setch, they got the honky monster with their knives. Ten, twelve times, man. Cut him to shit, man. That fucker not gonna cut on Soul Brickyard people no more."

Natalie and Gentry looked at each other and followed Leroy into a house filled with the sounds of celebration.

Louis Solarz was heavyset and light skinned with large, expressive eyes. He sat at the head of the kitchen table while Kara and another young woman worked to clean and bandage his throat. The front of the young man's yellow shirt was dappled with blood.

"What happened to your throat, man?" asked Marvin. The gang leader had just come downstairs. "I thought you say you cut *her* throat."

Louis nodded excitedly, tried to speak, managed only a croak, and started again in a hoarse whisper. "Yeah. I did. Honky monster cut me before we did him." Kara slapped Louis's hands away from the cut and set a dressing in place.

Marvin leaned on the table. "I don't get it, man. You say you get the Voodoo Lady while she asleep, but the honky motherfucker had time to cut you. Where the fuck is George and Setch?"

"They still there, man."

"They OK?"

"Yeah, they OK. George want to cut the honky monster's head off, but Setch say wait."

"Wait for what?" said Marvin.

"Wait for *you*, man."

Natalie and Gentry stood near the rear of the crowd. She looked at Rob with a questioning look. He shrugged under the blanket.

Marvin crossed his arms and sighed. "OK, tell it again, Louis. Whole thing."

Louis touched his bandaged throat. "This *hurts*."

"Tell it," snapped Marvin.

"OK. OK. George, Setch, and me, we out talking to people just like you say, and we thought we had enough, like nobody seen nothing, you know? Then we on Germantown when she come out of that store on corner of Wister."

"Sam's Deli?" said Calvin.

"Yeah, that the one," said Louis and grinned. "It be the Voodoo Lady herself."

"You recognized her from my photo?" asked Natalie. Everyone turned to look at her and Louis gave her a long, strange look. Natalie wondered if women were supposed to keep their mouths shut in a war council. She cleared her throat and said again, "Did my photo help?"

"Yeah, that it," Louis whispered huskily. "But the honky monster with her too."

"You sure it was *him*?" snapped Leroy.

"Yeah, I sure," said Louis. "And George seen him before, remember. Skinny dude. Long, greasy hair. Weird eyes. How many dudes like that walking around with old lady not be Voodoo Lady and honky mofo?"

There was a loud laughter from the twenty-five people in the room. Natalie thought it sounded like the laughter of anxiety release.

"Go on," said Marvin.

"We followed 'em, man. They go to an old house. We follow them, man. Setch say, get you, but I say let's see what's going down. George he go up a tree on the side and see the Voodoo Lady sleeping. I say, let's *do* it. Setch say OK, he get the lock open, we go in."

"Where the house?" asked Marvin.

"I show you, man."

"*Tell* me," snapped Marvin and grabbed Louis by the collar.

The heavier boy whimpered and held his throat. "It be on Queen Lane, man. Not far from the Avenue. I show you, man. Setch and George be waiting."

"Finish the story," Marvin said softly.

"We go in quiet," said Louis. "It only four o'clock, you know? But the Voodoo Lady, she be asleep upstairs in a room full of dolls . . ."

"Dolls?"

"Yeah, like a kid's room, you know? Only she not exactly asleep, more like she do too much dope, you know?"

"In a trance," said Natalie.

Louis looked at her. "Yeah. Like that."

"Then what?" said Gentry.

Louis grinned at everyone. "Then I cut her throat, man."

"She's dead?" said Leroy.

Louis's grin got wider. "Oh yes. She *dead*."

"What about the honky monster?" asked Marvin.

"Setch, George, and me, we find him in the kitchen. He be sharpening that big curve blade of his."

"The scythe?" said Natalie.

"Yeah," said Louis. "And he had a knife, you know? That what cut me, when we took it away. Then Setch and George cut him. Got him good. Cut his fucking throat, man."

"He dead?"

"Yeah."

"You sure?"

"Fuck yes we sure. You think we don't know when somebody dead, man?"

Marvin stared at Louis. There was a strange gleam to the gang leader's startling blue eyes. "This honky motherfucker killed five good brothers, Louis. Muhammed, be six-two, mean dude. How come you an' Setch an' little George take this motherfucker so easy?"

Louis shrugged. "I don't know, man. When the Voodoo Lady dead, the honky no monster. Just a skinny little white kid. He crying when Setch cut his throat."

Marvin shook his head. "I don't know, man. Sounds too easy. What about the pigs?"

Louis stared. "Hey, man," he said at last. "Setch say bring you right away. You want to see them or not?"

"Yeah," said Marvin. "Yeah."

"You're not going," said Gentry.

"What do you mean I'm not going?" said Natalie. "Marvin wants photographs taken."

"I don't give a damn what Marvin wants," said Gentry. "You're staying here."

They were on the second floor in the curtained alcove. All the gang members were downstairs. Gentry had carried his suitcase up and was changing to corduroy slacks and a sweater. Natalie saw where blood had soaked through the bandages above his ribs. "You're hurt," she said. "You shouldn't be going either."

"I have to see if the Fuller woman is dead."

"I want to see too . . ."

"No." Gentry pulled a goose-down vest over the sweater and turned to her. "Natalie . . ." He raised one huge hand and touched her cheek gently. "Please. You . . . you're important to me."

Natalie moved gently against him, careful not to brush against his side. She raised her face to kiss him. Afterward, nestling her face against wool, she whispered. "You're important to me, too, Rob."

"All right. I'll be back as soon as we see what's going on."

"But the pictures . . ."

"I'll use your Nikon, OK?"

"All right, but I don't feel right about . . ."

"Look," said Gentry and shifted into his thickest drawl, "this here Marvin fella ain't no fool. He isn't going to take no chances."

"Don't *you* take chances."

"No, ma'am. I gotta go." He pulled her to him for a long, full kiss that made her forget about his ribs as she put her arms around him and held on tightly.

Natalie watched from the second-story window as the group set out. With Louis went Marvin, Leroy, the tall youth named Calvin, a sullen-faced, older gang member called Trout, twin boys Natalie did not know, and Jackson. The ex-medic had shown up just as the expedition was departing. Everyone was armed except Louis, Gentry, and Jackson. Calvin and Leroy carried sawed-off shotguns under their loose coats, Trout carried a long-barreled .22, and the twins had small, cheap-looking pistols that Rob had called Saturday Night Specials. Gentry had asked Marvin for the Ruger, but the gang leader had laughed, finished loading the heavy weapon, and slid it into the pocket of his own army jacket. Gentry looked up and waved the Nikon at her when they left.

Natalie sat on the mattress in the corner and fought the urge to cry. She went through all of the possibilities and permutations in her mind.

If Melanie Fuller was dead, they might be able to leave. *Might*. But what about the authorities Rob had talked about? And the Oberst?

And what about Anthony Harod? Natalie tasted bile when she thought about that lizard-eyed little son of a bitch. The memory of the fear and hatred of women she had sensed during those few minutes under his control made her gorge rise. She wished that she had kicked his ugly face in when she had had the chance.

A noise on the stairs made her stand up.

Someone was emerging into the dim light at the head of the stairs. The second floor was empty except for her. Taylor had been left in charge, some of the gang members had gone off to alert others, and Natalie heard laughter from the first floor. The person at the top of the stairs moved hesitantly toward the light and Natalie caught a glimpse of a white hand, pale face.

She looked around quickly. No weapons had been left upstairs. She ran to the pool table, brilliantly lit under the single, hanging lamp, and lifted a pool cue, swinging it slightly to find the balance of it. She held it in both hands and said, "Who is it?"

"Only me." Bill Woods, the minister who supposedly ran Community House, stepped into the light. "I'm sorry if I scared you."

Natalie relaxed her posture but did not put down the pool cue. "I thought you were gone."

The frail-looking man leaned over the table to play with the white cue ball. "Oh, I've been in and out all afternoon. Do you know where Marvin and the other boys have gone?"

"No."

Woods shook his head and adjusted thick glasses. "It's terrible the discrimination and exploitation these children suffer. Did you know that unemployment among black teenagers in this area is over ninety percent?"

"No," said Natalie. She had moved around the table from this thin, intense man, but she sensed nothing in him but a burning desire to communicate.

"Oh yes," said Woods. "The shops and stores along the Avenue are owned almost exclusively by whites. Mostly Jews. They no longer live around here, but they continue to control what business remains. Nothing new there."

"What do you mean?" said Natalie. She wondered if Rob and the group were there yet. If the dead woman was *not* Melanie Fuller, what would Rob do?

"The Jews, I mean," said Woods. He perched on the edge of the pool table and tugged his pant leg down. He touched his little mustache, a fuzzy black line that looked like a nervous caterpillar on his upper lip. "There is a long history of the Jews exploiting the underprivileged in America's cities. You are black, Miss Preston. You must understand this implicitly."

"I don't know what the hell you're talking about," said Natalie just as an explosion rocked the front of the home.

"Good heavens!" cried Woods as Natalie ran to one of the windows.

Two abandoned automobiles along the curb were burning fiercely. Flames leaped thirty feet into the air and illuminated empty lots, abandoned row houses across the way, and the railroad embankment to the north. A dozen gang members ran into the front sidewalk, shouting and brandishing shotguns and other weapons.

"I had better get back to the Youth Center and call the fire department," said Woods. "The phone here was not working earlier when . . ."

Natalie turned to see why the minister had stopped talking. Woods was staring at someone standing at the head of the stairs, just at the edge of the circle of light.

He was young and thin, almost cadaverous, dressed in a torn and stained army jacket. His gaunt cheeks glowed whitely and long, tangled hair hung down over eyes set so deeply that they seemed to burn out of pits in a fleshy skull. The mouth was wide and open and Natalie could see the stub of a tongue moving like a small, pink, mutilated creature in a dark hole. He held a scythe taller than himself and when he stepped forward his shadow leaped ten feet high onto the patched and plastered wall.

"You don't belong here," began the Reverend Bill Woods. The scythe actually whistled as it completed its arc. Woods's head was not completely severed. Rags of tissue and a shred of spinal cord connected it loosely as the body slowly toppled over onto it. There was a soft thump and blood pumped across the green felt top of the pool table, pooling in the nearest pocket. The silent, long-haired figure jerked the scythe blade from the body and turned toward Natalie.

Even as Woods had said his last, absurd words, Natalie was using the pool cue to shatter the window. There were metal bars on all of the windows. She screamed as loudly as she could, the hysteria she heard there surprising her, bringing her back to herself. The flames and shouts outside masked her screams. No one looked up.

Natalie flipped the pool cue so the heavy side was farthest from her and she ran toward the table. The thing with the scythe edged to its right; Natalie edged to her right, keeping the table between them, glancing toward the stairway. There was no way she could reach the stairs in time. Her legs went weak, threatening to drop her to the floor. Natalie screamed, yelled for help, swung the heavy cue, feeling the adrenaline beginning to pump inside her. The longhaired nightmare shuffled quickly to its right. Natalie shifted, keeping the table between them, moving ever so slightly closer to the stairs. The thing lifted the scythe, breaking the glass shade on the hanging lamp and setting it swinging.

There was the sound of water lapping. Natalie looked down and realized that it was blood still pumping from the neck of the corpse on the table. Even as she watched, it stopped. The swinging light threw incredible shadows on the wall and changed the color of the blood and baize from red and green to black and gray with every swing. Natalie screamed just as the thing across the table leaped, seemed to fly over the top of the pool table, and brought the scythe down in a wide arc.

She jumped in under the blade and staff, flipping the pool cue and bringing it up like a spear, feeling the point bury itself in the thing's jacket even as he crashed down on her. The base of the pool cue hit the floor as she went to one knee and the stick acted like a lever, vaulting the figure over her.

He landed on his back with a thump and swung the scythe at her legs as he lay there, the blade rattling along the boards. Natalie jumped high, clearing the blade by two feet, and ran for the stairs even as the jacketed shadow rolled to his feet.

She threw the pool cue at him, heard it hit, and did not wait to see the result. Natalie went down the stairs three at a time. Heavy footsteps clattered behind her.

She crashed into the hallway, bounced off Kara at the entrance to the kitchen, and kept running.

"Where the hell are you going, girl?" called Kara.

"Run!"

The staff of the scythe came through the kitchen doorway and caught Kara solidly between the eyes. The beautiful young woman went down without a sound, her head striking the base of the stove. Natalie slammed through the backdoor, vaulted the railing, landed and rolled on the frozen ground four feet below, and was up and running before the door crashed open behind her.

Natalie ran through the cold night air, across the tumbled wasteland behind Community House, down a pitch black alley, across a street, and down another alley. Behind her the footsteps grew heavier and closer. She heard heavy breathing, an animal's raspy panting.

Natalie put her head down and ran.

TWENTY-SEVEN

Germantown
Sunday, Dec. 28, 1980

Tony Harod was only half aware of what Colben and Kepler were talking about as they drove him back to the Chestnut Hills Inn on Sunday evening. Harod was half reclining in the backseat of the car, holding an ice pack in place. His attention seemed to slip in and out of focus with the tides of pain that ebbed and flowed through his head and neck. He was not sure why Joseph Kepler was there or where he had come from.

"Pretty damn sloppy if you ask me," said Kepler.

"Yeah," said Colben, "but tell me you didn't enjoy it. Did you see the look on the passengers' faces when that bus driver floored it?" Colben barked a peculiarly childish laugh.

"Now you have three dead civilians, five injured, and a crashed bus to explain."

"Haines is handling it," said Colben. "No sweat. We have backing all the way to the top on this one, remember?"

"I can't imagine Barent is going to enjoy hearing about it."

"Barent can go fuck himself."

Harod moaned and opened his eyes. It was dark, the streets almost empty. Every bounce on the bricks or trolley tracks sent spasms of pain up through the base of his skull. He started to speak but discovered that his tongue seemed too thick and too clumsy to function. He decided to close his eyes.

". . . important part was keeping them in the secure area," Colben was saying.

"And what if we hadn't been there as backup?"

"We *were* there. Do you think I'm going to leave anything important to that *putz* in the backseat?"

Harod kept his eyes closed and wondered who they were talking about.

Kepler's voice came again. "You're sure those two are being used by the old man?"

"By Willi Borden?" said Colben. "No, but we're sure the Jew was. And we're sure that these two were involved with the Jew. Barent thinks the kraut's up to something bigger than settling Trask's hash."

"Why would Borden go after Trask in the first place?"

Colben barked his laugh again. "Old Nieman baby sent a few of his plumbers to Germany to terminate Borden. They ended up in body bags and you saw what happened to Trask."

"And why is Borden here? To get the old woman?"

"Who the hell knows? All those old farts were crazy as cockroaches."

"Do you know where Borden is?"

"Do you think we'd be dicking around like this if we did? Barent says the Fuller broad is the best bait we have, but I'm getting goddamned tired of the waiting. It takes a hell of a lot of effort to keep the local cops and city authorities out of all this."

"Especially when you use city buses the way you do," said Kepler.

"They way *we* do," said Colben and both men laughed.

Maria Chen looked up in surprise as Colben and a man she did not know half carried Tony Harod into the sitting room of the motel suite. "Your boss bit off more than he could chew tonight," said Colben, dropping Harod's arm and letting him drop to a sofa.

Harod tried to sit upright on the edge of the couch, swayed, and fell back into the cushions.

"What happened?" asked Maria Chen.

"Tony baby got caught in a lady's bedroom by a jealous boyfriend," laughed Colben.

"We had the doctor at operation headquarters look at him," said the other man, the one who looked a little bit like Charlton Heston. "He thinks it may be a mild concussion, nothing more serious."

"We have to get back," said Colben. "Now that your Mr. Harod has fucked up this part of the operation, all hell is ready to break loose in spade city." He pointed at Maria Chen. "See to it that he's down at the command trailer by ten o'clock in the morning. Got that?"

Maria Chen said nothing, showed nothing by her expression. Colben grunted as if satisfied and the two men left.

Harod was fully aware of only parts of that evening; he distinctly remembered throwing up repeatedly in the small, tiled bathroom, he recalled Maria Chen tenderly undressing him, and he remembered the cool slide of sheets against his skin. Someone applied cold cloths to his forehead during the night. He awakened once to find Maria Chen in bed next to him, her skin brown in white bra and panties. He reached for her, felt vertigo rise in him, and closed his eyes for a few more seconds.

Harod awoke at seven A.M. with one of the worst hangovers of his life. He felt for Maria Chen, found no one there, and sat up with a groan. He was sitting on the edge of the bed and wondering what Sunset Strip motel he was in when he remembered what had happened. "Oh, Christ," said Harod.

It took him forty-five minutes to shower and shave. He was reasonably certain that any sudden movement would send his head falling to the floor, and he had no interest in crawling around on all fours in the headless dark to find it.

Maria Chen entered loudly just as Harod shuffled out to the sitting room in his orange robe.

"Good morning," she said.

"Bullshit."

"It's a beautiful morning."

"Screw it."

"I brought some breakfast from the coffee shop. Why don't we have something to eat."

"Why don't you shut the fuck up?"

Maria Chen smiled and set the white carry-out sacks on the counter at the far end of the room. She reached into her purse and pulled out the Browning automatic. "Tony, listen. I'm going to suggest once more that we have breakfast together. If I get another obscenity from you . . . or the slightest hint of a sullen response . . . I'm going to fire this entire pistol-load of bullets into that refrigerator. I would guess that the noise would not be helpful to your precarious state of health at this moment."

Harod stared at her. "You wouldn't dare."

Maria Chen pulled back the slide, aimed the cocked weapon at the refrigerator, and looked away with eyes half shut.

"Wait!" said Harod.

"Would you care to have breakfast with me?"

Harod brought both hands to his temples and rubbed. "I'd be delighted," he said at last.

Maria had brought four covered Styrofoam cups and after they finished the eggs, bacon, and cold hash browns they each had a second cup of coffee.

"I'd pay ten thousand dollars to know who hit me," said Harod.

Maria Chen produced Harod's checkbook and the Cross pen he used for initialing contracts. "His name is Sheriff Bobby Joe Gentry. He comes from Charleston. Barent thinks that he's here after the girl, the girl is here after Melanie Fuller, and they've all got something to do with Willi."

Harod set the cup down and mopped at spilled coffee with the flap of his robe. "How in hell do you know *that*?"

"Joseph told me."

"Who the *fuck* is Joseph?"

"Ah, ah," said Maria Chen and pointed a finger at the refrigerator.

"Who is Joseph?"

"Joseph Kepler."

"Kepler. I thought I'd dreamed that he was here. What the goddamn hell is Kepler doing here?"

"Mr. Barent sent him down yesterday," said Maria Chen. "He and Mr. Colben were outside the hotel yesterday when Haines's men radioed about the sheriff and the girl getting away. Mr. Barent did not want the two to leave. It was Mr. Colben who first Used the bus."

"The what?"

Maria Chen explained.

"Fan-fucking-tastic," said Harod. He closed his eyes and slowly massaged his scalp. "That goddamn cracker cop gave me a goose egg the size of Warren Beatty's ego. What the fuck did he hit me with?"

"His fist."

"No shit?"

"No shit," said Maria Chen.

Harod opened his eyes. "And you heard all this from that inflammable hemorrhoid J. P. Kepler. Did you spend the night with him?"

"Joseph and I went jogging together this morning."

"He's staying here?"

"Room 1010. Next to Haines and Mr. Colben."

Harod stood up, caught his balance, and lurched toward the bathroom.

Maria Chen said, "Mr. Colben requested that you be at the command trailer at ten A.M."

Harod smiled, returned to pick up the automatic, and said, "Tell him to stuff it up his ass."

The ringing began at 10:13. At 10:15:30, Tony Harod sat up and groped for the phone. "Yeah?"

"Harod, get the hell down here."

"Chuck, that you?"

"Yeah."

"Stuff it up your ass, Chuck."

Maria Chen answered the second call that evening. Harod had just finished dressing to go out to dinner.

"I believe you'll want to take it, Tony," she said.

Harod grabbed the phone. "Yeah, what is it?"

"I think you'll want to see this," said Kepler.

"What?"

"The sheriff you went waltzing with yesterday is out and moving."

"Yeah, where?"

"Come down to the command trailer and we'll show you."

"Can you send a goddamn car?"

"One of the agents at your motel will drive you down."

"Yeah," said Harod. "Look, don't let that shithead get away. I have a score to settle with him."

"You'd better hurry then," said Kepler.

It was dark and snow was coming down heavily by the time Harod stepped into the cramped control room. Kepler looked up from where he leaned over one of the video screens. "Good evening, Tony, Ms. Chen."

"Where the fuck is this cracker cop?" said Harod.

Kepler pointed to a monitor showing Anne Bishop's home and an empty street. "They went up Queen Lane past the Blue Team observation post about twenty minutes ago."

"Where is he now?"

"We don't know. Colben's men were unable to follow."

"Unable to follow?" said Harod. "Jesus Christ. Colben must have thirty or forty agents in the area . . ."

"Almost a hundred," interrupted Kepler. "Washington sent reinforcements in this morning."

"A hundred fucking G-men, and they can't follow a fat, white cop in a ghetto full of jigaboos?"

Several of the men at consoles looked up disapprovingly and Kepler motioned Harod and Maria Chen into Colben's office. When the door was closed, Kepler said, "Gold Team was ordered to follow the sheriff and the young blacks who were with him. But Gold Team was unable to carry out orders because their surveillance vehicle was temporarily disabled."

"What the hell does that mean?"

"Someone had slashed the tires on the fake AT&T truck they were in," said Kepler.

Harod laughed. "Why didn't they follow on foot?"

Kepler sat back in Colben's chair and folded his hands across his flat stomach. "First, because everyone on Gold Team was white that shift and they thought they would be too conspicuous. Second, they had standing orders not to leave the truck."

"Why's that?"

Kepler smiled ever so slightly. "It's a bad neighborhood. Colben and the others were afraid that it might be stripped."

Harod roared. Finally he said, "Where the hell is Chucky baby, anyway?"

Kepler nodded toward a radio receiver on the console along the north wall of the office. Static and radio babble muttered from it. "He's up in his helicopter."

"Figures," said Harod. He folded his arms and scowled. "I want to see what this damn sheriff looks like."

Kepler keyed the intercom and spoke softly. Thirty seconds later a video monitor on the console lit and showed a tape of Gentry and the others passing. A light-enhancement lens spotlighted the scene in a green-white haze, but Harod could make out the heavyset man among the young blacks. Pale numerals, codes, and a digital time record were superimposed along the bottom of the screen.

"I am going to see *him* again soon," whispered Harod.

"We have another team out on foot, looking," said Kepler. "And we're fairly certain the whole group will be going back to that community center where the gang's been congregating."

Suddenly the radio band-monitor began squawking and Kepler turned it up. Charles Colben's voice was almost quaking with excitement. "Red

Leader to Castle. Red Leader to Castle. We have a fire on the street near CH-1. Repeat, we have a . . . negative, make that *two* fires . . . on the street near CH-1."

"What's CH-1?" asked Maria Chen.

"Community House," said Kepler, switching channels on the monitor. "The big old house I just mentioned where the gang's headquartered. Charles calls it Coon Hole 1." The monitor showed the flames from half a block away. The camera seemed to be in some vehicle parked along the curb. The light-enhancement equipment turned the two burning cars into pyres of light that blobbed out the entire image until someone changed the lens. Then there was still enough light to see dark figures scurrying from the house, and brandishing weapons. Kepler switched on the audio. ". . . ah . . . negative, Red Leader. This is Green Team near CH-1. No sight of the intruder."

"Well, goddammit," came Colben's voice, "get Yellow and Gray to cover the area. Purple, you have anybody coming from the north?"

"Negative, Red Leader."

"Castle, you copying this?"

"Affirmative, Red Leader," came the bored tones from the agent in the control room of the trailer.

"Get the E-M Van we used yesterday over there to douse that fire before the city gets involved."

"Affirmative, Red Leader."

"What's the E-M Van?" Harod asked Kepler.

"The Emergency-Medical Van. Colben brought it down from New York. It's one reason this operation is costing two hundred thousand dollars a day."

Harod shook his head. "A hundred federal cops. Helicopter. Emergency vans. To corner two old people who don't even have their own teeth anymore."

"Maybe not," said Kepler as he put his feet up on Colben's desk and made himself comfortable, "but at least one of them can still bite."

Harod and Maria Chen turned their chairs and sat back to watch the show.

On Tuesday morning Colben called a conference to be held at nine A.M. at five thousand feet. Harod showed his disgust but boarded the helicopter. Kepler and Maria Chen smiled at each other, both still slightly flushed from their six-mile run through Chestnut Hill. Richard Haines sat in the copilot's seat while Colben's Neutral pilot remained expressionless behind his aviator glasses. Colben swiveled his jump seat around and faced the three on the rear bench as the helicopter followed a pattern south to the river and Fairmont Park, east to the expressway, and then north and west to Germantown again.

"We still don't know what that little gang fight was about last night," said Colben, "with the coons shooting each other up. Maybe it's something Willi or the old broad is involved in. But the mounting casualty rate around here must have helped Barent decide. He's given us the go-ahead. The operation's on."

"Great," said Harod, "because I'm getting the fuck out of here by tonight."

"Negative," said Colben. "We have forty-eight hours to flush your friend Willi out. Then we move on the Fuller bitch."

"You don't even know Willi's here," said Harod. "I still think he's dead."

Colben shook his head and leveled a finger at Harod. "No you don't. You know as well as we do that that old son of a bitch is around here and up to something. We don't know if the Fuller woman is working *with* him or not, but by Thursday morning it won't matter."

"Why wait so long?" asked Kepler. "Harod's here. Your people are in place."

Colben shrugged. "Barent wants to use the Jew. If Willi rises to the bait, we'll move immediately. If not, we'll terminate the Jew, finish the old woman, and see what develops."

"What Jew?" asked Tony Harod.

"One of your friend Willi's old catspaws," said Colben. "Barent did one of his $29.95 conditioning jobs on him and wants to turn him loose on the old kraut."

"Quit calling him 'my friend,'" snapped Harod.

"Sure," said Colben. "Does 'your boss' sound better?"

"You two knock it off," Kepler said emotionlessly. "Tell Harod what the plan is."

Colben leaned over and said something to the pilot. They hovered motionless five thousand feet above the gray-brown geometries of Germantown. "Thursday morning we'll seal the entire area," said Colben. "Nobody in, nobody out. We'll have the Fuller woman located precisely. Most of the time she spends the night in that Grumblethorpe shack on Germantown Avenue. Haines will lead a tactical team in a forced entry. Agents will take care of the Bishop woman and the kid she's been Using. That leaves Melanie Fuller. She's all yours, Tony."

Harod folded his arms and looked down at the empty streets. "Then what?"

"Then you terminate her."

"Just like that?"

"Just like that, Harod. Barent says that you can Use anybody you want. But *you* have to be the one to do it."

"Why me?"

"Dues, Harod. Dues."

"I would think you'd want to interrogate her."

Kepler spoke. "We considered it, but Mr. Barent decided that it was more important to neutralize her. Our real goal is to bring the old man out of hiding."

Harod chewed on his thumbnail and looked down at rooftops. "And what if I don't succeed in . . . terminating her?"

Colben smiled. "Then we take her out and the Club still has a vacant seat. It's not going to break anybody's heart, Harod."

"But we still have the Jew to try," said Kepler. "We don't know what results that may bring."

"When does that go down?" asked Harod.

Colben looked at his watch. "It's already started," he said. He motioned to the pilot to go lower. "Want to see what happens?"

TWENTY-EIGHT

Melanie

W^e had a quiet weekend.
On Sunday, Anne made a pleasant dinner for the three of us. The stuffed pork chops were quite good, but I felt that she had a tendency to overcook the vegetables. Vincent cleared the table while Anne and I sipped tea from her best china cups. I thought of my own Wedgwood gathering dust in Charleston and felt a twinge of loss and homesickness.

I was too tired to send Vincent out that evening despite my curiosity about the photograph. Everything could wait. More important were the voices in the nursery. Every evening they became clearer, bordering on the understandable now. The previous night, after bathing Vincent and before going to sleep, I had been able to separate the whispers into discreet voices. There were at least three—a boy and two girls. It did not seem unlikely that children's voices were to be heard in the two-century-old nursery.

Late Sunday night, after nine, Anne and Vincent returned to Grumblethorpe with me. Sirens wailed nearby. After securing the doors and shutters, I left Anne in the parlor and Vincent in the kitchen and went upstairs. It was a cold night. I crawled under the covers and watched the heater filaments glow in the shadowy room. The eyes of the life-size boy reflected the light and his few remaining tufts of hair glowed orange.

The voices were very clear.

On Monday I sent Vincent out.

I did not like to let him go out in the daytime; it was a bad neighborhood. But I needed to know about the photograph.

Vincent carried his knife and the revolver I had borrowed from the Atlanta cabdriver. He squatted in the torn-out backseat of an abandoned car for several hours, watching colored teenagers pass. Once a stubble-cheeked drunk thrust his face in the rear window and yelled something, but Vincent opened his mouth and hissed and the drunk quickly disappeared.

Finally Vincent saw someone we recognized. It was the third boy, the young one who had run away on Saturday night. He was walking with a heavyset teenager and an older boy. Vincent let them get a block ahead and followed.

They passed by Anne's house and continued south to where the commuter train line created an artificial canyon. A narrow street ran east and west and the three boys entered an abandoned apartment building there. The structure was a strange caricature of an antebellum mansion; four disproportionate columns falling from a flat overhang, tall windows with rotting lintels, and the remnants of a wrought-iron fence demarcating a plot of frozen weeds and rusted tin cans. The windows on the ground floor were boarded up and the main door chained, but the boys went to a basement window where bars had been bent, the pane broken out, and slipped in there.

Vincent jogged the four blocks back to Anne's house. I had him take the large feather pillow on Anne's bed, stuff it in his oversize rucksack, and jog back to the apartment building. It was a gray, tired day. Snow fell in desultory flurries from a low sky. The air smelled of exhaust fumes and old cigars. There was little traffic. A train roared by as Vincent stuffed the backpack in ahead of himself and slipped through the shattered window.

The boys were on the third floor, crouched in a tight circle among shards of fallen plaster and pools of icy water. Windows had been broken and there were glimpses of gray sky through the rotted ceiling. Graffiti covered every inch of the walls. All three of the boys were on their knees, as if worshiping the white powder that bubbled in spoons held over a single can of sterno. Their left arms were bare; rubber cords were bound tightly around their biceps. Syringes were set out on dirty rags before them. I looked through Vincent's eyes and realized that this *was* a sacrament—the holiest sacrament in the urban Negro's modern Church of Despair.

Two of the boys looked up and saw Vincent just as he stepped out of hiding, holding the pillow in front of him like a shield. The young boy— the one we had let get away on Saturday night—started to shout something just as Vincent shot him through his open mouth. Feathers fluttered like snow and there was the smell of the scorched pillowcase. The older boy pivoted and tried to run away on his knees, scrabbling over chunks of plaster. Vincent fired twice more, the first shot slapping the youth onto his stomach, the second one missing. The boy rolled over, clutching his stomach and writhing like some sea creature thrown up on an inhospitable shore. Vincent set the pillow firmly over the Negro's terrified face, pressed the pistol deep, and fired again. The writhing ceased after one more violent kick.

Vincent lifted the revolver and turned to the third boy. It was the heavyset one. He continued to kneel where he had been, syringe still poised above his left arm, eyes wide. There was a look approaching religious awe and reverence on his fat, black face.

Vincent dropped the pistol into his jacket pocket and flipped open his long knife. The boy began to move—slowly—every movement as exaggerated as if he were underwater. Vincent kicked him in the forehead, toppling him over backward and kneeling on his chest. The syringe spun away on the filthy floor. Vince inserted the point of the blade under the skin of the boy's throat, just to the right of the Adam's apple.

It was here that I realized I had a problem. Much of my energy at that moment went toward restraining Vincent. I needed this boy to tell me about the photograph; who brought it to Philadelphia, how this colored riffraff received it, and what they were using it for. But Vincent could not ask the questions. I had vaguely considered Using the boy directly, but this now seemed unlikely. It is possible to Use someone you have not seen firsthand—difficult, but possible. I have done it on several occasions where I have used a conditioned catspaw as the instrument of making contact. The difficulty here was twofold: first, it would be extremely difficult if not impossible to interrogate someone while Using them. Although there is a glimmer of the surface of their thoughts, especially at the second of contact, the very act of suppressing their will so necessary to Using them also has the effect of inhibiting or eliminating rational thought processes in the subject. I could no more read the subtleties of this fat Negro's mind than he could read mine. Using him would be like sitting in a repugnant but necessary vehicle for a short drive; it would take me to my destination but could not answer my questions. Second, if I shifted my focus sufficiently to Use the boy—perhaps to return him to Anne's house—I was not sure that my conditioning of Vincent was sufficient to keep him from following his own impulses and cutting the Negro's throat.

A dilemma.

In the end, I had Vincent keep the boy there while I sent Anne to join them. I was not comfortable with staying alone—even in Grumblethorpe— but I had little choice. I did not want to bring the boy back to either house while there was a chance of him or Vincent being seen.

Anne drove the DeSoto and parked it down the street, taking care to lock the car. It was difficult for her to go through the basement window so I had Vincent drag the heavyset boy downstairs and the two broke the lock on a side door. It was quite dark in the first-floor room when Anne began asking questions.

"Where did the photograph come from?"

The boy's eyes widened further and he licked his lips. "Wha' photograph?"

Vincent struck the boy, low, very hard. The Negro gasped, struggled. Vincent brought the blade up against a raw throat.

"The photograph of the elderly woman. It was on one of the boys who died Saturday," Anne said softly. Because of the conditioning, it was not difficult to Use her while restraining Vincent.

"You mean the Voodoo Lady," gasped the boy. "But you ain't her!"

Anne smiled when I did. "Who is the Voodoo Lady?"

The boy tried to swallow. His expression was comical. "She be the lady

who make the honky mo . . . who make this dude do what he does. That is
what the woman say."

"What woman is that?"

"The one that talks funny."

"How is it that she speaks funny?"

"You know," the boy was panting as if he had run a race, "like the fat
honky pig. Like they from down south somewhere."

"And she brought the photograph? Or did the . . . overweight police
officer?"

"She did. Day before yesterday. She be lookin' for the Voodoo Lady.
Marvin saw the picture, he remember right away. Now we all looking."

"For the woman in the photograph. The . . . Voodoo Lady."

"Yeah." The boy began to twist away. Vincent struck him on the side of
the head with the heel of his hand, rolled him over, slammed him against
the wall twice, and lifted him by his torn shirtfront. The knife blade was
an inch from the Negro's eye.

"We're going to talk again," Anne said softly. "You're going to tell me
everything I would like to know."

The boy did as he was told.

In the end I sent Vincent out of the room before Using the boy. There was
no difficulty. I could not approximate the youth's loose-jointed, exaggerated style of walking, but there was no reason to do that. Of more concern
were his speech patterns—tone, vocabulary, syntax. I had him speak to
Anne for over an hour before I began to Use him directly. There was no
real resistance. At first the voice and phrasing came only with difficulty,
but by relaxing, allowing some of the boy's subconscious flair for dialect to
come through, I was able to speak through him in a way I hoped would be
believable.

Anne drove the two back to the vicinity of Grumblethorpe where she
dropped Vincent and the boy, Louis, off on the corner. Vincent disappeared for a few minutes and then returned with cartridges for the revolver. I sent Louis back to their Community House while Vincent came
in through the tunnel and Anne returned the car to the garage behind her
house on Queen Lane.

The charade with the gang members went very well. Once or twice I
felt my control slipping for a split second but concealed it by having Louis
simulate problems with his throat. I recognized the gang leader—
Marvin—at once. It had been his blue eyes that stared at me so pitilessly
on Christmas Eve as I lay in the dog feces. I looked forward to settling accounts with this boy.

In the middle of the discussion, just when I was beginning to feel secure, a young black woman in the back of the crowd said, "You recognized
her from my photo?" and I almost lost control of Louis. Her voice was free
of the flat, ugly northern dialect. It reminded me of home. Next to her,

wrapped in an absurd blanket, was a white man whose face seemed very familiar to me. It took me a minute to realize that he also must be from Charleston. It seemed to me that I had seen his photograph in one of Mrs. Hodges's evening papers, years before . . . Something about an election.

". . . Sounds too easy," Marvin was saying. "What about the pigs?"

He meant police. I knew from interrogating Louis that there were plainclothes officers in the neighborhood. He had no more idea why they were there than I did, although I assumed that the elimination of five people, even worthless gang members, would bring *some* official reaction. But his use of the ugly vernacular *pigs* for police sparked the connection. The red-faced white man was a Charleston police officer—the sheriff if I remembered correctly. I had read an article about him some years ago. "Hey, man," I had Louis say to Marvin, "Setch say bring you right away. You want to see them or not?"

Although the presence of these two Charleston people and the knowledge that there were numerous plainclothes police in the area created deep anxiety in me, the rush of concern was counterbalanced by a thrill approaching true exhilaration. This was *exciting*. I felt younger each hour this game was played.

The timing was very tricky. Vincent set off the gasoline bombs in the abandoned vehicles just when Louis led the gang leader, the sheriff whose name I could not remember, and six others onto the street near the apartment building. I stayed with Vincent then as he ran around behind the Community House, eliminated the single gang member remaining on the back porch, and went upstairs with his awkward scythe.

I had hoped the girl would go with Louis and the others. It would have been helpful, but I learned long ago to deal with reality as it was, not as I wished it to be. But I wanted the girl *alive*.

There was a brief scuffle on the second floor of the Community House. Just when Louis needed my attention, I found myself working to restrain Vincent from being too rough. Because of that temporary awkwardness, the girl escaped into the streets behind the house. I let Vincent follow in pursuit and returned my attention to where Louis stood swaying on the curb near the apartment building.

"What the fuck the matter, man?" The gang leader's name was Marvin something.

"Nothing, man," I had Louis say. "Throat hurts."

"You sure they in there?" the one called Leroy said. "I don't hear nothing."

"They in back," I had Louis say. The white sheriff stood nearby in the light from the only working street lamp on the block. As far as I could tell, he was unarmed except for a camera much like the one Mr. Hodges used to drag out at every opportunity. Two trains roared by, out of sight in their cement canyon.

"The side door's open," Louis said. "Come on, I'll show you." He had unzipped his jacket moments earlier. Under the sweater and rough wool shirt, I could distantly feel the cold steel of the cabdriver's revolver. Vincent had reloaded it in the dark alley earlier.

Marvin hesitated. "No," he said. "Leroy and Jackson and him and me will go." He jerked a thumb at the sheriff. "Louis, you stay here with Cal and Trout and G. R. and G. B."

I had Louis shrug. The sheriff gave me a long look before he turned and followed Marvin and the other two around to the side door. "They on the third floor, man!" I had Louis call after them. "In the back!"

They disappeared into the snowy darkness. I did not have much time. Part of my consciousness was aware of the warm glow of the heater and the staring eyes of the mannequin in the nursery, part of me ran with Vincent through the darkened alleys, heard the labored panting of our tired quarry ahead, while part of my attention had to be with Louis as the one called Calvin shifted from foot to foot and said, "*Shit*, it's cold. You got something to smoke, man?"

"Yeah," I had Louis say, "I got something good here." He reached under his shirt, pulled the pistol free, and shot Calvin in the stomach from two feet away. The tall boy did not go down. He staggered backward, put his hand to the hole in his coat front, and said, "*Fuck*, man." The twins took one look and ran back toward Queen Lane. The twenty-year-old named Trout tugged a long-barreled revolver from under his coat. Louis swiveled, leveled the pistol, and shot Trout in the left eye. There was no way to muffle the noise.

Calvin had gone down to his knees in the street, holding his stomach with both hands and looking irritated. He grabbed at Louis's leg when I tried to walk by. "Hey, Jesus fuck, man, why'd you do that?"

There were three sharp, flat sounds from the direction the twins had run toward parked cars on Queen Lane and something hit Louis in the upper part of his left arm. I blocked the pain for both of us, but felt the numbness there. He raised the pistol and emptied it in the direction from which the shots had come. Someone screamed and there was another shot, but no impact.

I had Louis drop the revolver and rip open Calvin's coat, pulling the shotgun free. He stepped over and pried the pistol out of Trout's clenched hand. Three more shots slapped from the direction of Queen Lane and something struck Calvin with the sound of a hammer hitting a side of beef. Incredibly, the tall boy still clung to Louis's leg. "Oh, fuck, why, man?" he kept repeating softly. Louis shoved him away, slid the target pistol in his coat pocket, hefted the shortened shotgun, and ran for the side of the apartment building. There were no more shots from the direction of Queen Lane.

Vincent had cornered the girl in a burned-out row house not far from

Germantown Avenue. He stood just inside the doorway and listened to her stumble around amid the charred timbers and tumbled stairways in the rear of the structure. The windows were boarded. As far as we knew, there was no exit except for the single doorway. I used the full force of my will to make Vincent move just inside the door and to squat in the darkness there, listening, sniffing the air, smelling the faint, sweet scent of the woman's fear and moving the scythe blade gently back and forth.

Louis stepped through the side door of the apartment building, moving quickly so as not to silhouette himself against the lighter doorway. Those inside must have heard the shots. Or found the bodies on the third floor.

There were no shots as Louis moved quickly down the hall. He stopped outside the first room and peered in. There was no light. Something moved down the hall in the direction of the main stairway and Louis fired the shotgun, the recoil flinging his right arm up. He braced the short stock against his thigh to pump another shell into the chamber and then squatted, watching for shadows.

For a second I had the sense-impression overlay of the two young men, Vincent and Louis, more than a mile apart, squatting in almost identical positions, ears straining to hear the slightest sound. Then there was a flash and an echoing roar, plaster pelted Louis's cheeks, and Vincent and I flinched reflexively even as I had Louis up and running toward the flash, firing, pausing to pump in another shell, running again.

There was the sound of footsteps on the littered stairs. Someone shouted from the second floor.

Louis squatted at the base of the stairs while I thought it out. Louis was eminently expendable. Already his reflexes had been dulled by the shock of the small bullet in his left upper arm. I would love to Use one of the others in the building, but that was too much to ask; already I was straining to keep Anne alert on the first floor of Grumblethorpe, hold Vincent in check in the burned-out row house, and keep Louis functioning. I wanted the blue-eyed Negro. I wanted him very badly. I also wanted to see the sheriff again, to get as close as possible. I had questions to ask of him, and possible uses for him after I received the answers.

A large handgun flashed from the next landing and a piece of banister splintered away. Louis crouched lower. There were four of them. Marvin, who had loaded a heavy revolver and laughed when the sheriff had asked for it back in the Community House. Leroy, the bearded one, who had been carrying a shortened shotgun identical to the one Louis now held. The sheriff, who had no weapon visible. And Jackson, the older Negro, who had been carrying a blue backpack. Also, G. B. and G. R., the young twins, might at that minute be returning with their cheap little pistols.

Louis ran up the stairs, stumbling once, missed a step and fell forward onto the second-floor landing. A shotgun blasted from fifteen feet away.

Something ripped at Louis's scalp and the side of his face. I blocked the pain but used the back of his hand to touch his cheek and left ear. The left ear was gone. Louis extended the shotgun straight-armed and fired in the direction of the flash.

"God *damn* it," shouted a black voice I thought was Leroy's.

A handgun roared from the opposite direction and a bullet pierced Louis's calf and struck a railing slat. I had him run in the direction of the handgun flash, pumping the shotgun by bracing it against his chest. Someone ran down the dark hallway ahead of him and then created a racket slipping and falling. Louis stopped, found a lighter shadow against the dark background, raised the shotgun. The figure rolled into a black rectangle of a doorway just as Louis fired. The muzzle flash showed the one named Marvin rolling out of sight even as the doorway splintered.

Louis pumped, extended the shotgun around the corner, and squeezed the trigger. Nothing. He pumped and fired again. Nothing. I had him throw the useless weapon even as the handgun flashed again and something struck Louis hard on the left collarbone, spinning him around. He struck a wall and slid to the floor, pulling out the long-barreled pistol as he fell. There was another shot, high, striking the wall three feet above Louis's head. I helped him aim carefully, very carefully, precisely where the muzzle flash had been.

The pistol did not fire. Louis fumbled for a safety catch, found a lever, pushed it down. He fired twice toward the corner and then rolled to his left over his dead arm, struggling to his feet.

Louis ran into someone, felt the breath go out of himself and heard it go out of the other man even as the two crashed into the corner. I knew from the size of the figure that it was the sheriff. I raised the pistol until it touched his chest.

Light exploded into our eyes. Louis backed away and I had the frozen image of the sheriff standing there, triggering the electronic flash on the camera at his side. There was a second flash, a third; Louis tried to blink away blue retinal echoes, and I turned him toward the real threat, pistol extended, but too late; even as we turned and squinted through blue haze the gang leader was crouching with the heavy revolver braced in both hands, squeezing, squeezing.

I felt no pain but sensed the impact as the first bullet caught Louis in the groin and the second one struck his chest with the sound of splintering ribs. I would have Used him still if the third bullet had not struck him in the face.

There was a loud rushing noise and I lost the contact. As many times as I have experienced the death of someone I was Using, it remains an unsettling experience, like being cut off in mid-conversation on the telephone.

I rested a moment, sensing only the hiss of the heater, the scabbed face of the life-size doll, and the now-audible whispering of the nursery walls. *"Melanie,"* they called. *"Melanie, there is danger. Listen to us."*

I listened even as I returned my attention to Vincent.

The noises in the back of the charcoal-smelling row house had all but stopped. The girl had nowhere to go.

I felt the adrenaline surge through Vincent's powerful body as he stood, hefted the balanced deadliness of the scythe, and moved surely and silently toward her through the darkness.

TWENTY-NINE

Germantown
Monday, Dec. 29, 1980

They operated on Saul Laski on Monday afternoon. He was unconscious about twenty minutes and woozy for another hour. When he was aware of his surroundings—the same small cell he had been in since Sunday morning—he peeled back the dressings and inspected the incision.

They had cut into the fleshy part of the inside of his lower left arm, about three inches above the faded tattoo of his camp number. The surgery had been competently carried out, the stitches carefully done. Despite the postoperative soreness and swelling, Saul could make out a lump that had not been there before. They had inserted something about the size of a thick quarter beneath the large muscle of his forearm. Saul replaced the dressings and lay back to think.

He had had much time to think. It had been a surprise when they had not released him or used him for some purpose on Sunday morning. He was certain that they had brought him to Philadelphia for a reason.

The helicopter had landed at a remote section of a large airport, and Saul had been blindfolded and transferred to a limousine. From the stops and starts and muffled street sounds, he was sure that they had driven through busy parts of the city. Once he heard the hum of bridge metal under tires.

They had bumped across a rough area before stopping. If it had not been for city sounds—a distant siren, shouts, the rush of a commuter train moving up to speed—Saul would have thought they were out in the country. Not the country then, but an open, muddy, rutted area in the middle of a city. An empty lot? Construction site? Park land? He had gone up three steps before being led through a door, right down a narrow corridor, right again. He had bumped the wall twice and something about the feel of it and the echoes in the narrow room made him believe he was in a trailer or mobile home.

The cell was less sturdy and impressive than the one in Washington. There was a cot, a chemical toilet, a small ventilator grill through which came muted voices, occasional laughter. Saul would have killed for a book. It was odd how the human organism adapted to almost any condition, but he could never get used to going entire days without reading. He remembered as a boy in the Lodz ghetto how his father had taken it upon

himself to list available books and set up a sort of lending library. Sometimes those who were being shipped to the camps brought the books
with them and Saul's father scratched the title off the list with a sigh, but
usually the tired men and sad-eyed women returned them religiously,
sometimes with a bookmark still in place. "You will finish it when you return," Saul's father would say and the people would nod.

Two or three times Colben came in to carry on a halfhearted interrogation, but Saul felt the man's lack of interest. Like Saul, Colben was waiting.
Everyone in the complex of trailers was waiting. Saul could feel it. Waiting
for what?

Saul used the time to think. He thought about the Oberst, Melanie
Fuller, Colben, Barent, and the unknown others. For years he had labored
under a basic and fatal misperception. He had thought that if he could
understand the psychology of such evil that he could cure it. He realized that
he had been searching for the Oberst not only for his own clouded personal reasons, but also with the same eager scientific curiosity that an im-
munologist at the Centers for Disease Control would try to track down
and isolate a new and lethal virus. It was interesting. Intellectually stimulating. Find it, understand it, cure it.

But there would be no antibodies for this plague bacillus.

For years Saul had been aware of the research and theories of Lawrence Kohlberg. Kohlberg had devoted his life to studying ethical and
moral development. For a psychiatrist steeped in postwar psychotherapy
theory, Kohlberg's musings seemed simplistic to the point of childishness,
but lying in his cell listening to the whisper of ventilation, Saul realized
how much sense Kohlberg's theory of moral development made in this
situation.

Kohlberg had discovered seven levels of moral development—supposedly
consistent through disparate cultures, times, and places. A Level One was
the essential infant—no sense of good or bad, all actions regulated by
needs and wants, actions inhibited only by negative stimuli. The classic
pleasure-pain basis for ethical judgments. By Level Two, humans responded to "right and wrong" by accepting the authority of power. The
big people know best. A Level Three person was fixated on rules. "I followed orders." Level Four ethics were dictated by the majority. A Level
Five person devoted his or her life to creating and defending laws that best
served the widest common good, while defending the legal rights even of
those whose views the Level Five person could not accept. Level Five
people made wonderful A.C.L.U. lawyers. Saul had known his share of
Level Fives in New York. Level Sixes were able to transcend the legalistic
fixation of Level Fives, focusing on the common good and higher ethical
realities across national, cultural, and societal boundaries. Level Sevens
responded *only* to universal principles. Level Sevens appeared to be represented by the occasional Jesuses, Gandhis, and Buddhas.

Kohlberg was not an ideologue—Saul had met him several times and enjoyed his boyish sense of humor—and the researcher enjoyed pointing out simple paradoxes arising from his own hierarchy of moral development. America, Kohlberg had said at one cocktail party at Hunter College, was a Level Five nation, established and founded by the most incredible assortment of practical Level Sixes in any nation's history, and was populated primarily by Level Fours and Threes. Kohlberg stressed that in day-to-day decisions we often ranged *below* our highest level of moral development, but we *never* went higher than our developmental level. Kohlberg would sadly cite the inevitable destruction of all Level Sevens' teachings. Christ handing his legacy to the Level Three Paul, the Buddha being represented by generations of priests never capable of rising above Level Six and rarely reaching that.

But the one thing Kohlberg never joked about was his later research. He found—to his early amazement and disbelief, fading to acceptance and shock—that there was a Level Zero. There were human beings beyond the fetal stage who had no moral bearings whatsoever; not even pleasure/pain stimulus was a reliable guide to these people—if "people" was what they were.

A Level Zero could walk up to a fellow citizen on the street, kill that person on a whim, and walk away without the slightest trace of guilt or afterthought. Level Zeroes did not want to be caught and punished, but did not base their actions upon avoidance of punishment. Nor was it a simple case of the pleasure of the forbidden criminal act outweighing fear of punishment. Level Zeroes could not differentiate criminal acts from everyday functions; they were morally blind. Hundreds of researchers were testing Kohlberg's hypotheses, but the data seemed solid, the conclusions convincing. At any given time, in any given culture, *one or two* percent of the population was at a Level Zero stage of human moral development.

They came for Saul on Monday afternoon. Colben and Haines held him while a third man injected him. He was unconscious in three minutes. When he awoke later with a headache and sore left arm, someone had inserted something in his flesh.

Saul inspected the incision, shrugged, and rolled over to think.

It was sometime Tuesday, he did not know when, that they released him. Haines blindfolded him while Colben spoke. "We're going to let you go. You're not to go six blocks in any direction beyond the place where we release you. You're not to use the telephone. Someone will be in touch later to tell you what to do next. Talk to no one who does not speak to you first. If you break any of these rules, it will go hard on your nephew Aaron, Deborah, and the children. Do you understand this perfectly?"

"Yes."

They led him to the limousine. The ride lasted less than five minutes. Colben pulled the blindfold off and pushed Saul out the open door.

Saul stood on a curb and blinked stupidly in the dim afternoon light. He looked too late to make out the license plate on the retreating limousine. Saul stepped back, bumped into a black woman carrying a shopping bag, apologized, and could not stop grinning. He walked along the narrow sidewalk, taking in every detail of the brick city street, worn shops, gray clouds . . . a paper blowing against a copper-green lamppost. Saul walked quickly, ignoring the pain in his left arm, crossing against the light, waving inanely to a cursing trolley driver. He was FREE.

Saul knew it was an illusion. Undoubtedly some of the people he was walking past on the street were watching *him*, following him. Some of the passing cars and vans almost certainly carried humorless men in dark suits, whispering into their radios. The bump on his arm probably contained a radio transmitter or explosive device or both. It simply did not matter.

Saul's pockets were empty so he walked up to the first man he saw—a huge, black man in a worn red macinaw—and asked for a quarter. The black man stared at the strange bearded apparition, raised a massive hand as if to swat Saul away, and then shook his head and handed Saul a five-dollar bill. "Get help, brother," growled the giant.

Saul went into a corner coffee shop, changed the five for quarters, and used the pay phone in the foyer to call the Israeli Embassy in Washington. They could not connect him with Aaron Eshkol or Levi Cole. Saul gave his name. The receptionist did not audibly gasp, but her voice tone shifted as she said, "Yes, Dr. Laski. If you can hold one minute I am sure that Mr. Cohen would like to speak to you."

"I'm calling from a pay phone in Philadelphia, Pennsylvania," said Saul. He gave the number. "I'm out of quarters, can you call me back so we can keep this line open?"

"Of course," said the Israeli Embassy receptionist.

Saul hung up. The phone rang, the receiver buzzed once when he lifted it, and the line went dead. He moved to a second phone, tried to make a collect call to the Embassy, and listened to the second line go dead.

He stepped out onto the sidewalk, walking aimlessly. Moddy and his family were dead. Saul had known it in his heart, but now he *knew* it. They could do little else to him now. Saul stopped, looked around, tried to spot the agents following him. There were few white men visible, but that meant nothing; the FBI had black agents.

A handsome black man in an expensive camel coat crossed the street and approached Saul. The man had strong, broad features, a wide smile, and large mirrored sunglasses. He carried an expensive leather briefcase. The man grinned as if he knew Saul, stopped, and removed a deerskin glove before offering his hand. Saul took it.

"Welcome, my little pawn," the man said in perfect Polish. "It is time you joined our game."

"You're the Oberst." Saul felt a strange rippling, shifting sensation deep inside himself. He shook his head and the feeling faded somewhat.

The black man smiled and spoke in German. "Oberst. An honorable title and one I have not heard in too long a time." He stopped in front of a Horn and Hardart restaurant and gestured. "You hungry?"

"You killed Francis."

The man idly rubbed his cheek. "Francis? I'm afraid I do not . . . oh yes. The young detective. Well . . ." He smiled and shook his head. "Come, I will treat us to a late lunch."

"You know they are watching us," said Saul.

"Of course. And we are watching them. Not the most productive of activities at the best of times." He opened the door for Saul. "After you," he said in English.

"My name is Jensen Luhar," said the black man as they sat at a table in the almost empty restaurant. Luhar had ordered a cheeseburger, onion rings, and a vanilla malt. Saul stared at a cup of coffee.

"Your name is Wilhelm von Borchert," said Saul. "If there ever was a Jensen Luhar, he is long since destroyed."

Jensen Luhar made a curt motion with his hand and removed his sunglasses. "A matter of semantics at this point. Are you enjoying the game?"

"No. Is Aaron Eshkol dead?"

"Your nephew? Yes, I am afraid he is."

"Aaron's family?"

"Also deceased."

Saul took a deep breath. "How?"

"As far as I can tell, your Mr. Colben sent his pet Haines and some others to your nephew's home. There was a fire, but I feel sure that the unfortunate family was dead before the first flames were lit."

"Haines!"

Jensen Luhar sipped from his long straw. He took a large bite of cheeseburger, delicately dabbed at his mouth, and smiled. "You play chess, Doctor." It was not a question. Luhar offered Saul an onion ring. Saul stared at him. Luhar swallowed it and said, "If you have any feel for the game, Doctor, you must appreciate what is going on at this moment."

"Is that what this is for you? A game?"

"Of course. To view it as anything more would be to take life and oneself far too seriously."

"I'm going to find you and kill you," Saul said softly.

Jensen Luhar nodded and took another bite of his cheeseburger. "Were we to meet in person, you would certainly try. You have no choice in the matter now."

"What do you mean?"

"I mean that the esteemed president of what is euphemistically known as the Island Club, a certain Mr. C. Arnold Barent, has conditioned you to fill that single purpose—killing a film producer whom the world thinks already dead."

Saul sipped cold coffee to hide his confusion. "Barent did no such thing."

"Of course he did," said Luhar. "He would have had no other reason for seeing you in person. How long do you think your interview with him lasted?"

"A few minutes," said Saul.

"A few hours is more likely. The conditioning would have had two purposes: to kill me on sight and to make certain that you would never be a threat to Mr. Barent."

"What do you mean?"

Luhar finished the last of his onion rings. "Play a simple game. Visualize Mr. Barent and then visualize yourself attacking him."

Saul frowned but did so. It was very difficult. When he recalled Barent as he last saw him—relaxed, tanned, sitting on the ship's balcony overlooking the sea—he was amazed to find a blend of friendship, pleasure, and loyalty stirring in him. He forced himself to imagine hurting Barent, swinging a fist toward those smooth, handsome features . . .

Saul doubled over with the sudden pain and sickness. He gasped on the verge of vomiting. Cold sweat erupted on his brow and cheeks. Saul fumbled for a glass of water and swallowed convulsively, thinking of other things, slowly untwisting the knot of pain in his belly.

"Interesting, *ja*?" said Luhar. "It is Mr. Barent's single greatest strength. No one who spends time with him could ever wish to do him harm. Serving Mr. Barent is a source of pleasure to a great many people."

Saul finished the water and used a napkin to wipe the sweat off his brow. "Why are you fighting him?"

"*Fighting* him? No, no, my dear pawn. I am not fighting him, I am *playing* him." Luhar looked around. "As of yet they have no microphones close enough to pick up our conversation, but in a minute a van will park outside and our privacy will disappear. It is time for us to take a walk."

"And if I don't go?"

Jensen Luhar shrugged. "Within a few hours the game will grow very interesting indeed. There is a part for you in it. If you wish to do anything about the people who terminated your nephew and his family, it would serve your purposes to accompany me. I offer you freedom . . . at least from them."

"But not from you?"

"Nor from yourself, dear pawn. Come, come, it is time to decide."

"I will kill you someday," said Saul.

Luhar grinned and pulled on his gloves and sunglasses. "*Ja, ja.* Are you coming?"

Saul stood up and looked out of the window. A green van had pulled to the curb. Saul followed Jensen Luhar outside.

The streets off Germantown Avenue were narrow and contradictory. At one time the tall skinny buildings might have been pleasant houses—some reminded Saul of the narrow houses of Amsterdam. Now they were overcrowded slum dwellings. The small shops and businesses might once have been the nucleus of a true community—small delicatessens, tiny grocery stores, family shoe stores, small businesses. Now they advertised dead flies in the windows. Some had been turned into low-rent apartments; a grimy three-year-old stood in a display window and pressed her cheek and smudgy fingers against the glass.

"What did you mean when you said you were 'playing' Barent?" asked Saul. He looked over his shoulder but caught no sight of the green van. It did not matter; Saul was sure that they were still under surveillance. It was the Oberst he wanted to find.

"We play chess," said Luhar. The big man turned his face and Saul could see his own reflection in the dark glasses.

"And the stakes are our lives," said Saul. He desperately tried to think of a way to cause the Oberst to reveal his location.

Luhar laughed, showing broad, white teeth. "No, no, my little pawn," he said in German. "Your lives mean nothing. The stakes are nothing less than who makes the rules of the game."

"The game?" echoed Saul. They had turned onto another side street. No one was visible except a pair of heavy black women coming out of a laundromat at the end of the street.

"Surely you are aware of the Island Club and its annual games?" said the Oberst. "Herr Barent and the rest of those cowards have been afraid to let me play. They know that I would demand a wider scope to the play. Something that would befit a race of *Übermenschen.*"

"Didn't you get enough of that in the war?"

Luhar grinned again. "You seek to provoke me," he said softly. "A foolish goal." They had stopped in front of a nondescript cinderblock building next to the laundromat. "The answer is 'no,'" he said. "I did not get enough of it in the war. The Island Club thinks that it has some claim to power merely because it *influences* . . . leaders, nations, economies. *Influences.*" Luhar spat on the sidewalk. "When I set the rules to the game, they will see what real power can do. The world is a piece of rotted, wormridden old meat, pawn. We will cleanse it with fire. I will show them what it is to play with *armies* rather than their pitiful little surrogates. I will show them what it is like to see cities die at the loss of a piece, entire races captured and utilized for projects at the whim of the User. And I will show them what it means to play this game on a global scale. We all die, pawn, but what Herr Barent fails to see is that there is no reason for the world to survive us."

Saul stood on the sidewalk and stared. The cold wind tugged at his coat and made his skin crawl with gooseflesh.

"Here we are," said Luhar and produced a ring of keys to open the door of the featureless building in front of them. He stepped into the darkness and gestured to Saul. "Are you coming, pawn?"

Saul swallowed. "You're more insane than I had dreamed," he whispered.

Luhar nodded. "Perhaps," he said softly. "But if you come with me you will have a chance to continue in the game. Not the larger game, regretfully. You will have no place in that. But your inevitable sacrifice will allow that game to be played. If you come with me now . . . of your own free will . . . we will remove those impediments which Herr Barent has shackled you with so that you might continue to serve me as a loyal pawn."

Saul stood in the cold, clenching his fist and feeling the pain in his left arm where the surgical implant throbbed. He stepped into the darkness.

Luhar grinned and bolted the door behind them. Saul blinked in the dim light. The first floor was empty except for sawdust and stacks of loading skids on a wide expanse of warehouse floor. A wooden staircase led to a loft. Luhar pointed and Saul went up the stairs.

"Good God," said Saul. In the loft a single table and four chairs were visible in the dim light filtering through a begrimed skylight. Two naked corpses occupied two of the chairs.

Saul stepped closer and inspected the bodies. They were cold and locked in the vise of rigor mortis. One was a black man, about Luhar's height and weight. His eyes were opened and filmed with death. The other corpse was a white man a few years older than Saul, bearded and balding. His mouth hung open. Saul could see the exploded capillaries of cheeks and nose that suggested advanced alcoholism.

He watched as Luhar took off his expensive camel's hair coat. "Our doppelgängers?" said Saul.

"Of course," said the Oberst through Luhar. "I have already removed all or most of the compulsion which Herr Barent has set in place in your mind. Are you ready to continue, pawn?"

"Yes," said Saul. *To continue to seek to find a way to kill you,* he thought.

"Very good," said Luhar. He glanced at his watch. "We have about thirty minutes before Mr. Colben decides that he should join our party. It should be enough time." He set his briefcase on the table near the black corpse's left arm. When he snapped it open, Saul saw that it was filled with the same type of plastic explosive that Harrington had worn.

"Should be enough time for what?" said Saul.

"Preparations. This building has an unmarked crawlspace that connects to the basement next door. The basement next door has an access to a short segment of the city's old storm sewer system. It will take us only a block, but it should be outside of the immediate circle of vigilance. A car will be waiting for me. You are welcome to go wherever you wish."

"You're so damned clever it makes me want to vomit," said Saul. "It won't work."

"Oh?" Luhar raised heavy eyebrows.

Saul took off his coat and rolled up his shirtsleeve. The bandages had a slight yellow stain from ointment they had used. "They inserted something yesterday. I'd guess it's a radio transmitter."

"Of course it is," said Luhar. From the briefcase he removed a bundle wrapped in green cloth and unrolled it. A bottle of iodine and surgical instruments gleamed in the dim light from above. "The procedure should not take more than twenty minutes, should it?"

Saul picked up a scalpel in its sterilpac. "And you will do the honors, I presume?"

"If you insist," said Luhar, "but I should point out that I have never had medical training."

"So I have the pleasure," said Saul. He looked in the briefcase and glanced up. "No syringes? No local anesthetic?"

Jensen Luhar's mirrored sunglasses reflected the room. There was no expression on the heavy face. "Unfortunately, no. How much do you value your freedom, Dr. Laski?"

"You are insane, Herr Oberst," said Saul. He sat at the table, laid out the instruments, and pulled the bottle of iodine closer.

Luhar pulled a gym bag out from under the table. "First we change clothes," he said. "In case you do not feel like it later."

When the corpses were dressed in their clothes and Saul was wearing slightly baggy jeans, a black turtleneck sweater, and heavy shoes a half size too small, Luhar said, "About eighteen minutes remaining, Doctor."

"Sit down," said Saul. "I'm going to explain precisely what to do if I pass out." He pulled packaged gauze and dressings from a clear bag. "You're going to have to close it up."

"Whatever you say, Doctor."

Saul shook his head, raised his eyes to the skylight for a moment, and then looked down and, with a single, sure move of the scalpel, made the initial incision.

Saul did not pass out. He did scream twice and just after the transmitter filaments were separated from muscle fibers he leaned over and vomited. Luhar closed the wound with rough stitches and butterfly bandages, wrapped gauze and tape around it, and tugged a bulky coat on the semi-conscious psychiatrist. "We are five minutes over schedule," hissed Luhar. "Hurry."

The seemingly solid concrete floor had a trapdoor under wooden skids in a far corner. As Luhar pulled the door down, Saul could hear the roar of a helicopter and distant pounding. "Move!" hissed the big man in the cramped darkness. Saul tried to crawl, cried out as his arm burned with pain, and fell forward. A tremendous explosion from above shook the earth and sent powder and spiderwebs dropping into Saul's face and hair. "Move!" hissed Luhar and shoved Saul ahead of him.

Loose cement blocks. Luhar kicked them out of the way, pulled Saul to his feet in a dark basement smelling of mildew and old newspapers, kept him moving. They squeezed between a grate and bricks and then they were crawling again, Saul's hands and knees submerged in icy water, touching slick, slimy things in the dark. Saul tried to cradle his left arm to him and crawl on three limbs. Twice he slipped and banged his left shoulder, soaking his jacket. Luhar laughed and shoved from behind. Saul closed his eyes and thought of Sobibor, the shouting masses, the quiet of the Forest of the Owls.

Finally they could stand. Luhar led a hundred paces, turned right down a narrower conduit, and paused under a grill. His strong arms strained to move the iron lattice. Saul squinted in the gray light, concentrated on keeping the vertigo at bay, and slipped his hand in his coat pocket to feel the cold handle of the scalpel he had palmed while Luhar was making final adjustments to the timing device in the briefcase.

"Ahh, *there*," panted Luhar and shoved the grate aside. Both arms were still raised. The big man's jacket hung open, exposing belly and chest under thin cloth. Saul braced himself and lunged with the scalpel, imagining a target for the blade somewhere beyond the man's spine.

Jensen Luhar's left arm came down in a blur, a massive hand closed on Saul's forearm, and the blade halted three inches above the black man's sternum. "Tsk, tsk," said Luhar. With his right hand he chopped at Saul's bleeding left arm. Saul gasped and dropped to his knees while red circles swam in his narrowing field of vision. Luhar gently lifted the scalpel out of his limp right hand. "Naughty, naughty, *mein kleine Jude*," he whispered. *"Auf wiedersehen."*

The light was blocked for a second and Luhar was gone. Saul knelt in the darkness, lowering his forehead to the water and cold stone for several minutes, fighting to stay conscious. *Why?* he thought. *Why stay awake? Sleep awhile.*

Shut up, he snarled at himself.

After an eternity he stood up, raised his good arm to the grate above, and tried to pull himself up and out. It took five tries and his jeans were soaked from falling, but eventually he clawed his way into sunlight.

The storm drain was behind a metal Dumpster a dozen feet into a narrow alley. He did not recognize the street he staggered onto. Rowhouses stretched up a long hill.

Saul made half a block before dizziness claimed him. He stopped and held his left arm. The wound had opened. The bleeding had soaked through the thick jacket, dripped down his arm, and stained the entire left side of his coat. He looked back from where he had come and laughed to see a distinct trail of crimson spatters. He squeezed the arm and staggered against the plate glass window of an abandoned store. The sidewalk was rising and falling like the deck of a small ship on a rough sea.

It was getting dark. Snow flurries glowed like fireflies in front of a distant streetlight. A large, dark figure was walking downhill on Saul's side of the street. Saul staggered backward into the doorway of the shop, slid down the rough wall, pulled his knees up, and tried hard to be as invisible as any wino who had ever sought such shelter.

Just as the man walked slowly past, Saul felt something else tear in the muscles of his left arm. He clutched at it and gritted his teeth until their grinding was audible. The man walked past, carrying something heavy and metallic in his right hand.

Saul felt the blackness winning even as the heavy footsteps stopped a few yards down the hill and then slowly returned. Saul rolled to his left, only distantly feeling his head strike the door. His left arm was on fire and he felt the blood soaking his wrist and hand.

A flashlight beam stabbed into his eyes. The big man leaned over him, blotting out the street, the world. Saul clenched his right fist and fought to stay above the whirling vortex of unconsciousness. A heavy hand closed on his right shoulder.

"Sweet Christ," said a slow, familiar voice. "Saul, is that you?"

Saul nodded and felt his head continue forward, his chin on his chest, his eyes closing, even as the soft voice continued saying things he did not understand and the strong arms of Sheriff Bobby Joe Gentry lifted him and cradled him as easily as one would carry a sleeping child.

THIRTY

Germantown
Tuesday, Dec. 30, 1980

G entry wondered if he was going insane. As he rushed back to Community House, he wished Saul was conscious so they could talk about it. It seemed to Gentry that the world had become a paranoid nightmare where cause-effect chains had broken down completely.

The twin called G. B. stopped Gentry half a block from the house. The sheriff stared at the muzzle opening of the crude pistol and snapped, "Let me through. Marvin knows I'm coming back."

"Yeah, but he don't know you bringing some dead honky dude back with you."

"He's not dead and he may be able to help us. If he *does* die, I'll make sure that Marvin holds you responsible. Now let me through."

G. B. hesitated. "Fuck you, pig," he said at last, but stood aside.

Gentry had to pass three more sentries before getting to the house. Marvin had extended their defensive perimeter a hundred yards in each direction. Any unknown vehicle on the block was to be fire-bombed if it did not get moved. A green van with two whites in front and God knows how many in back had spent thirty seconds considering Leroy's ultimatum before moving out at high speed. Perhaps it was the liter bottle of Shell unleaded in Leroy's right hand that convinced them.

Monday night had been entry into nightmare.

Marvin and the others had returned to Community House through alleys and backyards, Leroy bleeding from a dozen shotgun pellet wounds, all of them except Marvin semi-hysterical in the aftermath of the gun battle in the dark apartment building. They had dragged Calvin's and Trout's bodies into the building and Marvin had planned to send Jackson or Taylor back with Jim Woods's panel truck, but the confusion they returned to sidelined that for hours. By the time they did send a truck shortly before sunrise, the five bodies were gone and only anonymous pools of blood remained on the second and third floors. No authorities were on the scene.

The Community House was bedlam when they returned. Shots were being fired at every shadow. Someone had put out the fires in the derelict autos, but smoke still hung over the block like a cloud of death.

"He was here, man, the honky monster, man, *here*, like in the house, he got, like, the wimp Woods and hit Kara real hard, man, and Raji like saw him chasing the camera chick across the yard, man, and . . ." babbled Taylor when they arrived.

"*Where* is Kara!" roared Marvin. It was the first time Gentry had heard the young man shout.

Kara was upstairs, said Taylor, on the mattress behind the curtain, hurt real bad. Gentry followed them upstairs. Most of the gang members there were staring at Woods's headless body on the pool table, but Marvin and Jackson went straight to where Kara lay unconscious, being tended to by four other girls.

"Doesn't look good," said Jackson. The girl's beautiful face was almost unrecognizable, the forehead swollen grotesquely, eyes darkened with draining blood. "Should be in the hospital. Pulse and blood pressure way down."

"Hey, man," protested Leroy, showing a right arm and leg peppered with bloody circles, "I hurt. Lemme go with you and get fixed up and . . ."

"Stay *here*," snapped Marvin. "Get these assholes together. Nobody gets within half a block of here, dig? Tell Sherman and Eduardo to get their asses over to Dogtown and give Mannie the word. We want the troops he promised us last winter when we helped them out in the Pastorius thing. We want them *now*. Tell Squeeze that we want all the midgets and auxiliaries on the street *now*. I want to know where that fucking Voodoo Lady is."

As he continued to snap orders and while Jackson tenderly carried Kara downstairs, Gentry pulled Taylor to one side. "Where's Natalie?"

The youth shook his head and then let out a gasp as Gentry closed his grip on an upper bicep. "Shit, man. Honky monster after her. Raji seen them going across that yard, between the buildings, man. It was *dark*. We went after him, couldn't see nothing."

"How long ago?" Gentry squeezed harder.

"Hey, *shit*. Twenty minutes. Maybe twenty-five."

Gentry went quickly downstairs and caught Marvin before he left. "I want my gun."

The gang leader stared with pale blue eyes that were as cold as sea ice.

"That son of a bitch is after Natalie and I'm going after him. Give me the Ruger." He held out his hand.

Leroy let his shotgun slide into his right hand. The barrel moved toward Gentry and he looked to Marvin for the word.

Marvin tugged out the heavy Ruger and handed it to Gentry. "Kill him, man."

"Yeah." Gentry went upstairs, dug out the extra box of cartridges, and reloaded. The heavy Magnum bullets slid in smooth and heavy to Gentry's touch. He realized that his hand was shaking. He leaned over and took deep breaths until the shaking stopped, went downstairs to find a flashlight, and went out into the night.

Saul Laski regained consciousness just as Jackson inspected the wound. "Somebody been working on you with a can opener it looks like," said the ex-medic. "Give me your other arm. I'm going to give you an ampule morphine while I work on this."

Saul put his head back against the mattress. His face and lips were white behind dark whiskers. "Thanks."

"Thanks, nothing. You going to get my bill. There are brothers here that would kill for this morphine." He injected Saul with a swift, sure motion. "You white boys don't know how to take care of your bodies."

Gentry talked quickly before the morphine put the psychiatrist out of touch. "What the hell are you doing here, Saul?"

The older man shook his head. "Long story. There are more people involved in this than I ever imagined, Sheriff . . ."

"We're finding that out," said Gentry. "Do you know where your Oberst is?"

Jackson finished cleaning the wound and began restitching it. Saul took one glance and then looked away. "No, not exactly. But he is here somewhere. Close by. I just met a black man named Jensen Luhar who has been one of the Oberst's agents for years. The others . . . Colben, Haines . . . let me loose in the chance I could lead them to the Oberst."

"Haines!" said Gentry. "Damn, I knew I didn't like that sonofabitch."

Saul licked his lips. His voice was growing thick and dreamy. "Natalie? She is here?"

Gentry looked away, glowered at shadows. "She was. Someone got her . . . took her away . . . twenty-four hours ago."

Saul tried to sit up. Jackson cursed and pushed him back. "Alive?" managed Saul.

"I don't know. I've been searching the streets for the past twenty-four hours," said Gentry. He rubbed his eyes. He had not slept for over forty-eight hours. "There's no reason to think that Melanie Fuller would keep Natalie alive when she's murdered so many others," he said. "But something keeps me looking. I just have this *feeling*. If you can tell me everything you know, then maybe together we can . . ." Gentry stopped. Jackson was almost finished. Saul Laski was fast asleep.

"How's Kara?" asked Gentry as he came into the kitchen.

Marvin looked up from the table. A cheap city map lay spread out there, anchored by beer cans and bags of potato chips. Leroy sat near him, white bandages showing through torn clothing. Various lieutenants came and went, but the house had a quiet, purposeful atmosphere far different from the chaos of the day before. "She's not good," said Marvin. "The doctor says she's hurt bad. Cassandra and Shelli over there now. They'll send someone over if anything changes."

Gentry nodded and sat down. He could feel the fatigue toxins working at him, putting a sheen of dull light on every surface he looked at. He rubbed his face.

"Dude upstairs going to help you find your woman?"

Gentry blinked. "I don't know."

"Can he help us find the Voodoo Lady?"

"Maybe," he said. "Jackson says he'll be able to talk to us in a couple of hours. Any of your people have anything?"

"Just a matter of time, man," said Marvin. "Just a matter of time. We got the girls, the auxiliaries, all going door to door. No way white old woman like that be here and *no one* know it. Soon as we find her, we're ready."

Gentry tried to focus on what he wanted to say. Words were becoming hard to manipulate. "You know about the others . . . the federal cops."

Marvin laughed. It was a thin, cold sound. "Yeah, sure, they're all over the fucking place. But they're keeping the local pigs and TV people out of this, right?"

"Must be," said Gentry. "But my point is that they're as dangerous as the Voodoo Lady. Some of them have the same . . . the same powers as she does. And they're hunting for a man who's even more dangerous."

"You think they done any of the stuff to Soul Brickyard, man?" asked Marvin.

"No."

"They have anything to do with the honky monster?"

"No."

"Then we let them wait awhile. They get in our way, we'll do them too."

"You're talking about forty or fifty plainclothes federal officers," said Gentry. "They're usually armed to the teeth."

Marvin shrugged. Someone rushed in and spoke softly to him. The gang leader gave quick, sure orders in a calm voice. The other man went out.

Gentry lifted a can, found there was some warm beer left, and took a drink. "Have you considered just walking away while you can?" he said. "I mean, just getting everyone under cover and letting all these vampires fight it out?"

Marvin looked straight at Gentry. "Man," he said in a voice not much louder than a whisper, "you don't understand much. White folks, government, the pigs, the greasy white politicians around here—they all be fucking us over for a long time. Nothing new about what the honky monster's doing to black people, but he doing it to *us* on our turf, man. You and Natalie say the Voodoo Lady really doing it, and I think that's right. It *feels* right. But not just the Voodoo Lady, either. Behind her, be others ready to shit on us. Be doing it a long, long time. But this is Soul Brickyard. The people they kill here—Muhammed, George, Calvin . . . maybe Kara . . . they're *ours*, man. We're going to kill that honky monster and the white bitch for that. We don't expect no one to help us. But if you want to be with us, you can be, man."

"I want to be with you," said Gentry. His own voice sounded slowed down, a 45 r.p.m. record played at 331/3.

Marvin nodded and stood up. His hand was very strong on Gentry's arm as he pulled the lawman to his feet, moved him toward the stairway. "What you got to do now, my man, is to go sleep. We call you when something goes down."

Jackson woke him at 5:30 the next morning. "Your friend's awake," said the ex-medic.

Gentry thanked him and sat on the edge of his mattress for several minutes, holding his head and trying to get his mind to work. Before seeing Saul he clumped downstairs, made coffee in an ancient percolator, and came back up with two steaming, chipped cups. A dozen or so gang members snored on mattresses in various rooms. There was no sight of Marvin or Leroy.

Saul took the coffee cup with a heartfelt thanks. "I woke up and thought I'd dreamed everything," he said. "I expected to find myself in my apartment with a class to teach at the university. Then I felt this." He held up his bandaged left arm.

"How did that happen?" asked Gentry.

Saul sipped coffee and said, "I'll tell you what, Sheriff. We will do a deal. I will start with the most important information and talk awhile. Then you will do the same. If our stories connect in any way, we will pursue the connections. Agreed?"

"Agreed," said Gentry.

They talked for an hour and a half and then questioned each other for another half hour. When they stopped, Gentry helped the older man up and they walked to a barred window and looked out at the first grayings of dawn.

"It's New Year's Eve day," said Gentry.

Saul reached to adjust his glasses, realized that he did not have them on. "It is all too incredible, is it not?"

"Yes," said Gentry. "But Natalie Preston is out there somewhere and I'm not leaving this city until I find her." They went back to the alcove to pick up Saul's glasses and then went downstairs together to see if they could find anything to eat.

Marvin and Leroy were back by ten A.M., talking earnestly with two tall Hispanics. Three low-slung automobiles idled at the curb, each filled with Chicano youths eyeing the blacks on Community House porch. The black gang members glowered back.

The kitchen had become a command center, entered by invitation only, and twenty minutes after the Hispanics left, Saul and Gentry were summoned. Marvin, Leroy, one of the twins, and half a dozen others stared at them in silence.

"How is Kara?" asked Gentry.

"She died," said Marvin. He looked at Saul. "You told Jackson you wanted to talk to me."

"Yes," said Saul. "I think you can help me find the place where I was held prisoner. It can't be very far from here."

"Why should we do that?"

"The place is a control center for the police that have the area staked out."

"So? Fuck them."

Saul tugged at his beard. "I think that the police . . . the federal people . . . know where Melanie Fuller is."

Marvin's head came up. "Are you sure?"

"No," said Saul, "but based on what I saw and overheard, it makes sense. I think the Oberst tipped them to her whereabouts for his own reasons."

"This Oberst be your Voodoo Man?"

"Yes."

"A lot of the government pigs are on the street. Would one of them know about the Voodoo Lady?"

"Perhaps," said Saul, "but if we could get at the control center, ah . . . talk to someone there . . . I think we would have a better chance to find out."

"Talk to me, man," said Marvin.

"It's in an open area about eight minutes' drive from here," began Saul. "I think a helicopter has been landing and taking off from there regularly. The structures are temporary . . . possibly mobile homes or the kind of trailers you find on construction sites."

Saul wore a balaclava and gloves when he left the house with Gentry and five of the gang members. If Colben and Haines believed he was dead, Gentry had suggested they not disabuse them of the notion. They took Woods's panel truck for the short drive west on Germantown Avenue, south on Chelten, and then west on an unnamed street into a warehouse district.

"Blue Ford following us," said Leroy at the wheel.

"Do it," said Marvin.

The panel truck bounced across a littered parking lot and down an alley, pausing by a sagging, corrugated tin shed only long enough for Marvin, Saul, Gentry, and one of the G. twins to jump out and hide in the shadows of the open doorway. The truck quickly accelerated down the alley and spun east onto the narrow street. Twenty seconds later a blue Ford with three white men in it roared past.

"This way," said Marvin and led them across a wasteland of oil drums and metal tailings to a small junkyard where flattened automobiles had been stacked thirty feet high. Marvin and the younger boy clambered up the stack in seconds; Gentry and Saul took quite a bit longer.

"That it, man?" asked Marvin as Saul crawled the last six feet, finally resting on the precarious, rusted summit and leaning against the panting sheriff for support. Marvin handed a small pair of binoculars to the psychiatrist.

Saul cradled his left arm in his open jacket and peered through the lenses. A high, wooden fence enclosed half a city block. To the south, a foundation had been excavated and concrete poured. Two bulldozers, a backhoe, and smaller equipment sat idle. In the center of the remaining space, three mobile home units formed an E with the middle segment missing. Seven government-issue cars and a Bell Telephone van were parked nearby. Microwave antennae bristled from the center trailer segment. In the open field, a circle of red lights had been set in the ground and a small windsock hung limply from a metal pole.

"Has to be," said Saul Laski.

As they watched, a man in shirtsleeves came out of the center trailer and briskly walked the twenty yards to one of three port-a-toilets set up near where the cars were parked.

"One of those dudes be the one you like to talk to?" asked Marvin.

"Probably," said Saul. They were almost certainly invisible amid the piles of rusted metal, but Gentry and the others found themselves crouching behind axles, wheels, and flattened hardtops.

Marvin looked at his watch. "About five hours before it gets dark." he said. "Then we do it."

"God*damn*it," snarled Gentry. "Do we have to wait that long?"

As if in answer, a sleek helicopter came in from the north, circled the field once, and settled in the circle of lights. A man in a thick goose-down parka jumped out and ran to the command trailer. Saul took the binoculars back from Marvin and caught a glimpse of Charles Colben's round face. "That is a man you do *not* want to encounter," he said. "Wait until he is gone."

Marvin shrugged.

"Let's get out of here," said Gentry. "I'm going to look for Natalie by myself."

"No," said Saul, his voice muffled by the balaclava. "I will go too."

"Are you looking for her body?" Saul Laski asked as the two poked through the rubble of yet another half-demolished rowhouse.

Gentry sat down on a three-foot-high wall of bricks. The last of the day's cloudy light was visible through gaps in the ceiling above them and holes in the roof above that. "Yes," said Gentry, "I suppose I am."

"You think Melanie Fuller's agent killed her and left her body in some place like this?"

Gentry looked down and pulled out the Ruger. It was fully loaded. The safety was off. The action worked smoothly, oiled and reoiled by Gentry that morning. He sighed. "At least that would be a confirmation. Why would the old woman keep her alive, Saul?"

Saul found a block of masonry to sit on. "One of the problems with working with psychotics is that their thought processes are not easily accessible. That is good, I suspect. If everyone understood the working of a psychopath's mind, we undoubtedly would be closer to insanity ourselves."

"Are you sure that the Fuller woman is psychotic?"

Saul spread the fingers of his right hand. He had pulled the balaclava up until it made a lumpy stocking cap. "By every definition we have now, she is certifiable. The problem is not that she has retreated into a psychotic's warped and twisted view of reality, but that her power allows her to confirm and maintain that world." Saul adjusted his glasses. "Essentially that was the problem with Nazi Germany. A psychosis is like a virus. It can multiply and spread almost at will when it is accepted by the host organism and transmitted freely."

"Are you saying that Nazi Germany did what it did because of people like your Oberst and Melanie Fuller?"

"Not at all," said Saul and his voice was as firm as Gentry had ever heard it. "I am not even sure if those people are fully human. I regard them as faulty mutations—victims of an evolution that includes almost a million years of breeding for interpersonal dominance along with other traits. It is not the Obersts or Melanie Fullers or even the Barents or Colbens who create violence-oriented fascist societies."

"What is it then?"

Saul gestured toward the street visible through shattered windowpanes. "The gang members think there are dozens of federal agents involved in this operation. I would guess that Colben is the only one among them who has even a touch of this bizarre mutant ability. The others allow the virus of violence to grow because they are 'only following orders,' or are part of a social machine. The Germans were experts at designing and building machines. The death camps were part of a larger death machine. It has not been destroyed, only rebuilt in a different form."

Gentry stood up and walked toward a hole in the rear wall. "Let's go. We can do the rest of this block before it gets dark."

They found the scrap of material amid the ashes and charred rafters of two rowhouses that had burned but were never torn down. "I'm sure it's from the shirt she was wearing Monday," said Gentry. He fingered the piece of cloth and used his flashlight to study the carpet of ashes. "Lots of footprints here. It looks like they struggled there, in the corner. This nail could have torn the sleeve of her shirt if she had been thrown up against the wall here."

"Or if she was being carried over someone's shoulder," said Saul. The psychiatrist cradled his left arm with his right hand. His face was very pale.

"Yeah. Let's look for signs of blood or . . . anything." The two men searched for twenty minutes in the failing light, but there was nothing else. They were outside, speculating on which way Natalie's abductor might have gone in the maze of alleys and empty buildings, when the youth named Taylor came running down the street waving at them. Gentry held the Ruger loosely at his side and waited. The boy stopped ten feet from them. "Hey, Marvin wants you two back at the house now. Leroy got one of the dudes from the trailer. He told Marvin where to find the Voodoo Lady."

"Grumblethorpe," said Marvin. "She's in Grumblethorpe."

"What on earth is a Grumblethorpe?" asked Saul.

Gentry and the psychiatrist stood crowded into the kitchen with thirty other people. More gang members filled the halls and downstairs rooms. Marvin sat at the head of the kitchen table and laughed. "Yeah, that's what I say—What's a Grumblethorpe? Then this dude, he tells me where the fuck it is and I say, yeah, I know that place."

"It's an old house on the Avenue," said Leroy. "Real old. It was built when the honkys wore them funny three-sided hats."

"Whom did you interrogate?" asked Saul.

"Huh?" said Leroy.

"Which of the guys did you grab?" interpreted Gentry.

Marvin grinned. "Leroy, G. B., and me, we went back when it was getting dark. The chopper was gone, man. So we wait by those toilets 'til dude comes out. He got his piece in this little bitty clip holster on his pants. G. B. and me, we let the dude drop his pants before we say hi. Leroy brought the truck up the side. We let the dude finish his business before we take him with us."

"Where is he now?" asked Gentry.

"Still in Rev Woods's truck. Why?"

"I want to talk to him."

"Uh-uh," said Marvin. "He sleeping now. Dude says he a special agent, video technician. Say he didn't know nothing about anything. Says he won't talk to us and we in deep shit, assaulting federal pig an' all. Leroy and D. B. help him talk. Jackson say dude be all right, but he's asleep now."

"And the Fuller woman is in a place called Grumblethorpe on Germantown Avenue," said Gentry. "The agent was sure?"

"Yeah," said Marvin. "Old Voodoo Lady been staying with another white broad on Queen Lane. Should've thought've that. Old white broads stick together."

"What's she doing at this Grumblethorpe place then?"

Marvin shrugged. "Federal pig said she had been staying there more and more this week. We figure that's where the honky monster coming from."

Gentry shouldered his way through the crowd until he stood next to Marvin. "All right. We know where she is. Let's go."

"Not yet," said Marvin. He turned to say something to Leroy, but Gentry grabbed his shoulder and turned him around.

"To hell with this 'not yet' stuff," said Gentry. "Natalie Preston may still be alive there. Let's *go*."

Marvin looked up with cold, blue eyes. "Back off, man. When we do this, we're going to do it right. Taylor out talking to Eduardo and his boys. G. R. and G. B. over at the Grumblethorpe place checking it out. Leila and the girls, they're making sure where all the federal pigs at."

"I'll go by myself," said Gentry and turned away.

"No," said Marvin. "You get close to that place, all the federal pigs recognize you and our surprise be shot to shit. You wait 'til we ready or we leave you here, man."

Gentry turned back. Marvin stood as the big, white southern sheriff loomed over him. "You'd have to kill me to keep me from going," said Gentry.

"Yeah," said Marvin, "that right."

The tension in the room was palpable. Someone turned on a radio somewhere in the house and in the few seconds before it was cut off, the sound of Motown filled the air.

"Few hours, man," said Marvin. "I know where you're coming from. Few hours. We do it together, man."

Gentry's huge form relaxed slowly. He held up his right hand and Marvin gripped it, fingers interlaced. "A few hours," said Gentry.

"Right on, bro," said Marvin and smiled.

Gentry sat alone on the mattress on the empty second floor, cleaning and oiling the Ruger for the third time that day. The only light came from the hanging lamp with the damaged tiffany shade. Dark stains mottled the surface of the pool table.

Saul Laski came into the circle of light, looked around hesitantly, and came over to where Gentry was sitting.

"Howdy, Saul," Gentry said without looking up.

"Good evening, Sheriff."

"Seeing as how we've been through more than a little bit together, Saul, I'd appreciate it if you'd call me Rob."

"Done, Rob."

Gentry snapped the cylinder back in place on the Ruger and spun it. Carefully, with full concentration, he inserted the cartridges one by one.

Saul said, "Marvin is sending the early teams out already. In twos and threes."

"Good."

"I've decided to go with Taylor's group . . . the command center," said Saul. "I suggested it. A distraction."

Gentry looked up briefly. "All right."

"It's not that I don't want to be there when they get the Fuller woman,"

Saul said, "but I don't think they understand how dangerous Colben can be . . ."

"I understand," said Gentry. "Did they say how soon it will be?"

"Not long after midnight," said Saul.

Gentry set the gun aside and pulled the mattress up against the wall like a pillow. He laced his hands behind his head and lay back. "It's New Year's Eve," he said. "Happy New Year."

Saul took his glasses off and wiped them with a Kleenex. "You got to know Natalie Preston very well, did you not?"

"She was in Charleston for just a few days after you left," said Gentry. "But yes, I was beginning to get to know her."

"A remarkable young woman," said Saul. "She makes one feel as if one has known her for years. A very intelligent and perceptive young person."

"Yep," said Gentry.

"There is a chance she is alive," said Saul.

Gentry looked at the ceiling. The shadows there reminded him of the stains on the pool table. "Saul," he said, "if she's alive, I'm going to get her out of this nightmare."

"Yes," said Saul, "I believe you will. You must excuse me, I am going to get an hour or two of sleep before the revels commence." He went off to a mattress near the window.

Gentry lay looking at the ceiling for some time. Later, when they came upstairs looking for him, he was ready and waiting.

THIRTY-ONE

Germantown
Wednesday, Dec. 31, 1980

The room was windowless and very cold. It was more of a closet than a room, six feet long, four feet wide, with three stone walls and a thick wooden door. Natalie had slammed and kicked at the door until her fists and feet were bruised, but it had not budged. She knew the thick oak must have massive hinges and bolts on the outside.

The cold had brought her awake. At first the panic had risen in her like vomit, more urgent and painful than the cuts and bruises on her forehead. She immediately remembered crouching behind charred timbers, the world smelling of ashes and fear while the hulking shadow with the scythe shuffled toward her through the darkness. She remembered jumping, throwing the brick she had been clutching, trying to run past the swiftly turning shadow. Hands had closed on her upper arms; she had screamed, kicked wildly. Then the heavy blow to her head, and another blow cutting across her temple and brow, blood flowing into her left eye and the sensation of being lifted, carried. A glimpse of sky, snow, a tilting streetlight, then blackness.

She had awakened to the cold and darkness severe enough to make her wonder for several minutes if she had been blinded. She crawled from a nest of blankets on the stone floor and felt the roughhewn confines of her stone and wood cell. The ceiling was too high to touch. There were cold metal brackets on one wall, as if shelves had once rested there. After several minutes, Natalie was able to make out small bands of lesser darkness at the top and base of the door, not light as such, but an external darkness relieved by at least the hint of reflected light.

Natalie had felt around for the two blankets and crouched shivering in a corner. Her head hurt abysmally and nausea combined with fear to keep her on the verge of being violently sick. All of her life Natalie had admired courage and calmness in emergencies, had aspired to be like her father— quietly competent in situations that would have others babbling uselessly— and instead she crouched hopelessly in a corner, shaking violently and praying to no deity in particular that the honky monster would not return.

The room was cold but not with the sub-freezing chill of the out-of-doors; it had the cold, steady clamminess of a cave. Natalie had no idea where she could be. Hours had passed and she was close to dozing, still shivering, when light flickered under the doorway, there came the sound of multiple bolts slamming back, and Melanie Fuller stepped into the room.

Natalie was sure it was Melanie Fuller, although the dancing light from the single candle the old lady held illuminated her face from below and showed a bizarre caricature of humanity: cheeks and eyes gullied with wrinkles, corded neck a mass of wattles, eyes like marbles staring from dark pits, the left eyelid drooping, thinning blue-white hair flying out from a mottled scalp like a nimbus of static electricity. Behind this apparition, Natalie could make out the lean form of the honky monster, hair hanging over a face streaked with dirt and blood. His broken teeth glinted yellowly in the light from the old woman's candle. His hands were empty and the long white fingers twitched randomly, as if surges of current were passing through his body.

"Good evening, my dear," said Melanie Fuller. She wore a long night-gown and a thick, cheap robe. Her feet were lost in pink fluffy slippers.

Natalie pulled the blanket tighter around her and said nothing.

"Is it chilly in here, dear?" asked the old woman. "I am sorry. If it is any consolation, the entire house is rather cold. I don't know how people lived in the North before central heating." She smiled and candlelight gleamed off slick, perfect dentures. "Would you speak with me a minute, dear?"

Natalie considered attacking the woman while she was free to do so, then pushing past her into the dark room beyond. She caught a glimpse of a long, wooden table—certainly an antique—and stone walls beyond that. But between her and the room stood the boy with the demon eyes.

"You brought a picture of me all the way from Charleston to this city, didn't you, dear?"

Natalie stared.

Melanie Fuller shook her head sadly. "I have no wish to harm you, dear, but if you will not speak to me willingly, I will have to ask Vincent to remonstrate with you."

Natalie's heart pounded as she watched the honky monster take a step forward and stop.

"Where did you get the photograph, dear?"

Natalie tried to find enough moisture in her mouth to allow her to speak. "Mr. Hodges."

"Mr. Hodges gave it to you?" Melanie Fuller's tone was skeptical.

"No. Mrs. Hodges let us go through his slides."

"Who is us, dear?" The old woman smiled slightly. Candlelight illuminated cheekbones pressing against skin like knife blades under parchment.

Natalie said nothing.

"I presume then that 'us' includes you and the sheriff," Melanie Fuller said softly. "Now why on earth would you and a Charleston policeman come all this way to harass an old woman who has done you no harm?"

Natalie felt the anger burning up through her, igniting her limbs with strength, banishing the weakness of terror. "You killed my father!" she screamed. Her back scraped against rough stone as she tried to rise.

The old woman looked puzzled. "Your father? There must be some mistake, dear."

Natalie shook her head, fighting back the hot tears. "You used your goddamn servant to kill him. For no reason."

"My servant? Mr. Thorne? I am afraid you are confused, dear."

Natalie would have spit at the blue-haired monster then, but her mouth held no saliva.

"Who else is searching for me?" asked the old woman. "Are you and the sheriff alone? How did you follow me here?"

Natalie forced a laugh; it sounded like seeds rattling in an empty tin. "*Everyone* knows you're here. We know all about you and the old Nazi and your other friend. You can't kill people anymore. No matter what you do to me, you're finished . . ." She stopped because her heart was beating hard enough to hurt her breast.

The old woman looked alarmed for the first time. "Nina?" she said. "Did Nina send you?"

For a second the name meant nothing to Natalie, and then she remembered the third member of the trio Saul Laski had described. She remembered Rob's description of the murders in the Mansard House. Natalie looked into Melanie Fuller's wildly dilated eyes and saw madness there. "Yes," said Natalie firmly, knowing that she might be dooming herself but wanting to strike out at any cost, "Nina sent me. Nina knows where you are."

The old woman staggered back as if she had been struck in the face. Her mouth sagged in fear. She grasped the doorway for support, looked at the thing she had called Vincent, found no help there, and gasped, "I am tired. We will talk later. Later." The door crashed shut, bolts slid into place.

Natalie crouched in the darkness and shivered.

Daylight came as thin bands of gray above and below the thick door. Natalie dozed, feverish, her head aching. She awoke with a sense of urgency. She had to relieve herself and there was no place to do, not even a pot. She pounded on the door and shouted until she was hoarse, but there was no response. Finally she found a loose stone in the far corner, clawed at it until it tilted out of the dirt, and used the small niche as a latrine. Finished, she pulled her blankets closer to the door and lay there sobbing.

It was dark again when she awoke with a start. The bolts slammed back and the thick door squeaked open. Vincent stood there alone.

Natalie scrambled backward, feeling for the loose stone to use as a weapon, but the youth was on her in a second, grabbing her hair and tugging her upright. His left arm went around her throat, cutting off her wind and will. Natalie closed her eyes.

The honky monster roughly pulled her out of her cell and half dragged, half pushed her to a steep, narrow stairway. Natalie had time to catch a glimpse of a dark kitchen out of colonial times and a small parlor with a kerosene heater glowing in a tiny fireplace before she was stumbling up the stairway. There was a short, dark hall at the top, and then Vincent shoved her into a room aglow with candlelight.

Natalie stood in shock, staring. Melanie Fuller lay curled in a fetal position amid a tangle of quilts and blankets on a low rollaway. The room had high ceilings, a single shuttered and draped window, and was lit by at least three dozen candles set on floor, tables, moldings, windowsills, mantel, and in a square around the old lady's bed. Here and there were the rotting mementos of children long since dead—a broken dollhouse, a crib with metal bars making it look like the case for some small beast, ancient rag dolls, and a disturbing four-foot-tall mannequin of a boy looking as if it had suffered prolonged exposure to radiation: patches of hair missing and molted, peeling paint on the face looking like pools of subcutaneous blood.

Melanie Fuller rolled over and looked at her. "Do you hear them?" she whispered.

Natalie turned her head. There was no sound but Vincent's heavy breathing and the pounding of her own heart. She said nothing.

"They say it is almost time," the old woman hissed. "I sent Anne home in case we need the car."

Natalie glanced toward the stairway. Vincent blocked her escape. Her eyes moved around the room, searching for a possible weapon. The metal crib was too bulky. The mannequin almost certainly too awkward. If she had a knife, anything sharp, she could go for the old woman's throat. What would the honky monster do if the Voodoo Lady died? Melanie Fuller looked dead; her skin seemed as blue as her hair in the pulsing light and the old lady's left eyelid drooped almost shut.

"Tell me what Nina wants," whispered Melanie Fuller. Her eyes shifted back and forth, seeking Natalie's gaze. "Nina, tell me what you want. I did not mean to kill you, my darling. Can you hear the voices, dear? They have told me you were coming. They tell me about the fire and the river. I should get dressed, dear, but my clean clothes are at Anne's and it is far too far to go. I have to rest awhile. Anne will bring them when she comes. You will like Anne, Nina. If you want her, you can have her."

Natalie stood, panting slightly, with a strange visceral terror rising within her. It might be her last chance. Should she make an effort to brush past Vincent, get down the stairs and find an exit? Or go for the old woman? She looked at Melanie Fuller. The woman smelled of age and baby powder and old sweat. At that second Natalie knew without a doubt that this was the thing responsible for her father's death. She remembered the last time she had seen her father—hugging a good-bye at the airport two days after Thanksgiving, the soap and tobacco smell of him, his sad eyes and kind smell.

Natalie decided that Melanie Fuller had to die. She tensed her muscles to jump.

"I'm tired of your impertinence, girl!" screamed the old woman. "What are you doing up here? Get back to your duties. You know what Papa does to bad niggers!" The old woman in the bed closed her eyes.

Natalie felt something cleave her skull like an ax. Her mind was on fire. She pivoted, fell forward, tried to regain her balance. Synapses misfired as she staggered around in a palsied dance. She struck the wall, struck it again, and fell back against Vincent. The boy put streaked, filthy hands on her breasts. His breath smelled like carrion. He ripped Natalie's shirt down the front.

"No, no," said the old woman from the bed. "Do it downstairs. Take the body back to the house when you are done." The hag sat up on her elbow and looked at Natalie with one eye open, the other showing only white under a heavy lid. "You lied to me, dear. You don't have a message from Nina after all."

Natalie opened her mouth to say something, to scream, but Vincent grabbed her by the hair and clamped a powerful hand over her face. She was dragged from the room, shoved down the steep stairs. Stunned, she tried to crawl away, her hands scrabbling on rough boards. Vincent did not hurry. He took his time coming down the stairs, caught her as she got to her knees, and kicked her brutally in the side.

Natalie rolled against the wall, tried to huddle into a tight, invisible ball. Vincent grabbed her by the hair with both hands and pulled hard.

She rose, screaming, and kicked as hard as she could at his testicles. He easily caught her foot and twisted sharply. Natalie spun but not fast enough; she heard her ankle snap like a dry twig and she fell hard on her hands and left shoulder. Pain surged up her right leg like blue flame.

Natalie looked back just as Vincent pulled the knife from his army jacket and flipped open the long blade. She tried to crawl away, but he reached down, half lifted her by the shirt. The fabric tore again and Vincent ripped at the rest of the material. Natalie kept crawling down the dark hallway, feeling ahead of her for some kind of weapon. There was nothing but cold floorboards.

She rolled onto her back as Vincent stepped forward with a crash of heavy boots, stood straddling her. Natalie turned and bit through filthy denim, feeling her teeth sink deep into his calf muscle. He did not flinch or make a noise. The blade moved in a blur past her ear, cutting her bra strap and leaving a long line of pain down her back.

Natalie let out a gasp, rolled on her back again, and raised her hands in a futile effort to stop the blade's return.

Outside, the explosions started.

THIRTY-TWO

Germantown
Wednesday, Dec. 31, 1980

The problem is," said Tony Harod, "I've never killed anyone."
"No one?" asked Maria Chen.
"No one," said Harod. "Never."
Maria Chen nodded and poured more champagne into each of their glasses. They lay naked, facing each other in the long bathtub in Room 2010 of the Chestnut Hills Inn. Mirrors reflected the light of a single scented candle. Harod lay back and looked at Maria Chen through heavy-lidded eyes; her brown legs rose between the sharp white boundaries of his knees, her thighs were parted, her ankles touched his ribs in the soapy water. Bubbles hid all but the top curve of her right breast, but he could see the other nipple, as sweet and heavy as a strawberry in the dark water. He admired the curve of her throat and heavy weight of her black hair as she threw back her head to drink from the overflowing champagne glass.

"It's midnight," said Maria Chen, glancing at his gold Rolex on the counter. "Happy New Year."

"Happy New Year," said Harod. They clinked glasses. They had been drinking since nine P.M. It was Maria Chen's idea to take a bath. "Never killed anyone," muttered Harod. "Never had to."

"It looks like you will have to now," said Maria Chen. "When Joseph left today, he reiterated Mr. Barent's insistence that you be the one to . . ."

"Yeah." Harod stood up and set his glass on the counter. He toweled off and held out his hand. Maria Chen took it and rose slowly from the bubbles. Harod used the towel gently, dabbing her dry, running both arms around her from behind to draw the thick terry cloth across her breasts. She shifted her weight to one foot and moved her thighs apart slightly as he dried between her legs. Harod dropped the towel, lifted Maria Chen in both arms, and carried her into the bedroom.

It was like the first time for Harod. He had not had a woman on her terms since he was fifteen years old. Maria Chen's skin tasted of soap and cinnamon. She gasped when he entered her and they rolled across a wide expanse of soft sheets; Maria Chen lying atop him when they stopped, still joined, still moving, their hands and mouths sliding against one another. Maria Chen's orgasm was sudden and powerful, her moans soft. Harod came seconds later, closing his eyes and clinging to her as a falling man clings to the last thing that might break his fall.

The phone rang. Continued to ring.

Harod shook his head. Maria Chen kissed his hand, slid across the sheets to answer it. She handed the receiver to him.

"Harod, you've got to get down here now," came Colben's excited voice. "All hell's breaking loose!"

Colben went back into the control room. Men sat at monitors, scribbled notes, whispered into headset microphones. "Where the hell is Gallagher?" bellowed Colben.

"Still no word, sir," answered the technician at Console Two.

"Fuck it then," said Colben. "Tell Green Team to quit looking for him. Assign them to back up Blue Two near Market."

"Yes, sir."

Colben strode down the narrow corridor to stand behind the last console. "The spooks still at Home Castle?"

"Yes, sir," said the young woman in front of the monitor. She threw a switch and the view shifted from the front of Anne Bishop's house to the alley behind it. Even with the light-intensifying lenses, the figures near the garage fifty meters down the alley were mere shadows.

Colben counted twelve shadows. "Get me Gold One," he snapped.

"Yes, sir." The technician handed him an extra headset.

"Peterson, I see a dozen of them now. What the fuck is going on there?"

"Don't know, sir. You want us to move in?"

"Negative on that," said Colben. "Stand by."

"Eight more unknowns on Ashmead," said the agent at Console Five. "Just passed White Team."

Colben pulled his headset off. "Where the hell is Haines?"

"Just picked up Harod and his secretary," called the man at Console One. "ETA in five minutes."

Colben lit a cigarette and tapped the female technician on the shoulder. "Get Hajek and the chopper over here right away."

"Yes, sir."

Agent James Leonard stepped out of Colben's office and beckoned him over. "Mr. Barent on line three."

Colben closed the door. "Colben here."

"Happy New Year, Charles," came Barent's voice. From the static and hollow tone, it sounded like a satellite call to Colben.

"Yeah," said Colben. "What's up?"

"I was talking to Joseph earlier," said Barent. "He has some concerns about the way the operation is going."

"So what's new?" said Colben. "Kepler is always bitching about something. Why didn't he stay here if he was so fucking concerned?"

"Joseph said that he had other things to take care of in New York," said Barent. There was a pause. "Is there any sign of our friends?"

"You mean the old kraut," said Colben. "No. Not since the explosion in the warehouse yesterday."

"Do you have any idea why Willi would sacrifice one of his own operatives to terminate Dr. Laski? And why such overkill? Joseph said the city fire department had to be called in."

"How the hell should I know?" snapped Colben. "Look, we're not even sure that was Luhar and the Jew in there."

"I thought your forensics people were working on it, Charles."

"They are. But it's a federal holiday tomorrow. Besides, as close as we can tell, Luhar and Laski were sitting on top of thirty pounds of C-4. There wasn't much left for forensics to look at."

"I understand, Charles."

"Look," said Colben, "I'm going to have to go. We have a situation developing here."

"What kind of situation?" asked Barent through the static.

"Nothing serious. Some of those goddamn kids from the gang are farting around in the secured zone."

"This will not complicate the morning's business, will it?" asked Barent.

"Negative," snapped Colben. "I've got Harod on the way over here now. If need be, we can seal off the area in ten minutes and take care of the Fuller woman ahead of schedule."

"Do you think Mr. Harod is up to the task, Charles?"

Colben stubbed out his cigarette and lit another one. "I don't think Harod's up to the task of wiping his own ass," he said. "The question is, what do we do when he screws up?"

"I presume you have considered the options," said Barent.

"Yeah. Haines is ready to step in to take care of the old woman. Once Harod fucks up, I'd like to deal with that Hollywood phony myself."

"I presume you would recommend termination."

"I recommend that I stick a Police Special in that punk's mouth and blow his fucking brains all over West Philly," said Colben.

There was a brief silence broken only by static. "Whatever you feel is necessary," Barent said at last.

"Oh," said Colben, "his chink secretary will have to disappear too."

"Of course," said Barent. "Charles, just one other thing . . ."

Agent Leonard stuck his head in the office and said, "Haines just got here with Mr. Harod and the girl. They're all aboard the chopper."

Colben nodded. "Yeah, what's that?" he said to Barent.

"Tomorrow is very important to us all," said Barent. "But please remember that once the old woman is removed from the board, Mr. Borden remains our chief interest. You will contact him to negotiate if possible, but terminate him if the situation dictates. The Island Club is putting much trust in your judgment, Charles."

"Yeah," said Colben. "I'll remember. I'll talk to you later, all right?"

"Good luck, Charles," said Barent. The line hissed and went dead.

Colben hung up, pulled on a flak vest and baseball cap, and slipped his .38 and clip-on holster into the front pocket of his arctic parka.

The rotor blades began turning faster even as he ran crouching toward the open door of the helicopter.

Saul Laski, Taylor, Jackson, and six younger members of Soul Brickyard watched the helicopter rise and depart to the northeast. The panel truck had stopped along the high wooden fence half a block from the entrance gate to the FBI control compound.

"What do you think?" Taylor asked Saul. "There go your voodoo man?"

"Perhaps," said Saul. "Are we near the construction end of the lot here?"

"Near's I can tell," said Taylor.

"Are you sure you can get the equipment started without keys?"

Jackson spoke. "Shoot, man. Three months in the motor pool of a construction battalion in Nam before I ended up out in the boonies. I could hot-wire your mama."

"The bulldozers will suffice," said Saul, knowing, as Jackson knew, that a bulldozer required more than a simple hot-wiring to start it.

"Hey," said Jackson, "I get 'em started, are you going to be able to handle yours?"

"Four years building and maintaining a kibbutz," said Saul. "I could bulldoze your mama."

"Careful, man," said Jackson, grinning broadly. "Don't start playing no dozens with me, babe. White boys just don't have the knack for good insults."

"In my cultural group," said Saul, "we make a habit of trading insults with God. What better practice could one have for playing the dozens?"

Jackson laughed and slapped Saul on the shoulder.

"You two cut the shit," said Taylor. "We two minutes behind."

"You're sure your watch is correct?" said Saul.

Taylor looked indignant. He held out his wrist to show an elegant Lady Elgin complete with 24-karat gold trim and inlaid diamond chips. "This don't lose five seconds a year," he said. "We got to *move*."

"Fine," said Saul. "How do we get in?"

"Catfish!" Taylor called and one of the boys in back pushed open the rear door, swung himself onto the roof of the van, jumped to the top of the ten-foot-high wooden fence, and dropped out of sight on the other side. The other five in the rear followed. They carried heavy backpacks in which bottles clinked.

Saul looked at his taped left arm.

"Come on," hissed Taylor, pulling himself out of the cab.

"That arm's going to hurt," said Jackson. "You want a shot of something?"

"No," said Saul. He followed the others up and over.

"This can't be legal," said Tony Harod. He was watching streetlights, high-rises, and expressways pass under them as they roared along at only three hundred feet of altitude.

"Police helicopter," said Colben. "Special clearance."

Colben had his jumpseat swiveled so that he could almost lean out a window panel that had been opened on the starboard side. Cold air roared in and sliced at Harod and Maria Chen like invisible blades. Colben held a Colt .30 caliber military sniper's rifle cradled in a special mount in the open window. The weapon looked clumsy with its bulky nightscope, a laser sighting device, and an oversize magazine clip. Colben grinned and whispered into the headset mike just visible under his parka hood. The pilot banked hard right, circling above Germantown Avenue.

Harod held on to the padded bench with both hands and closed his eyes. He was sure that only his seat belt kept him from tumbling out the open window and falling thirty stories to the brick street below.

"Red Leader to Control," Colben called, "status report."

"Control here," came Agent Leonard's voice. "Blue Team Two reports incursion of four automobiles carrying Hispanic males into secured area at Chelten and Market. More unidentified groups in alley behind Castle One and Castle Two. Group of fifteen unidentified black males just passed White Team One on Ashmead. Over."

Colben turned and grinned at Harod. "I think it's just a fucking *rumble*. Spades versus greasers on New Year's Eve."

"It's past midnight," said Maria Chen. "It is New Year's Day."

"Whatever," said Colben. "Well, what the fuck. Let them fight as long as they don't interrupt our Sunrise Operation. Right, Harod?"

Tony Harod held on and said nothing.

Sheriff Gentry was panting heavily as he ran to keep up with the leaders. Marvin and Leroy led a loose line of ten gang members through a dark maze of alleys, backyards, junk-strewn empty lots, and abandoned buildings. They reached the entrance to an alley and Marvin waved everyone down. Gentry could see a van parked sixty yards away, past Dumpsters and sagging garages.

"Federal pigs," whispered Leroy. The bearded youth glanced at his watch and grinned. "We a minute early."

Gentry rested his arms on his knees and panted. His ribs hurt. He was cold. He wished he were home in Charleston, listening to the Dave Brubeck Quartet on the stereo and reading Bruce Catton. Gentry rested his head against cold brick and thought of something that had happened when they were leaving Community House, something that had changed the way he looked at Germantown and Soul Brickyard.

A young boy—no older than seven or eight—had come running in just as the last team was ready to leave. The youngster had run straight to Marvin. "Stevie," the gang leader said, "I told you not to come down here." The little boy had been crying, brushing away tears with his arm. "Mama say you should come straight home, Marvin. Mama say she and Marita need you at home and you should come now." Marvin had taken the child into another room, his arm around him. Gentry had heard ". . . you tell Mama I'll be home first thing in the morning. Marita, she stays there and takes care of things. You tell them that, OK, Stevie?"

It had disturbed Gentry. So far the gang had been part of a five-day nightmare he had been living. Germantown and its inhabitants had been perfectly consistent with the nightmarish sequence of pain, darkness, and seemingly unrelated events going on around Gentry. He had known that the gang members were young—Jackson was an exception, but he was a lost soul, a visitor, an alumnus returned to his old haunts because life had left him nowhere else to go. Gentry had seen few other adults on the cold streets; those he had seen had been silent, bruised-looking women on hurried errands, old men walking nowhere, peering out from tavern doors, the inevitable winos lying in littered storefronts. He had known that this was not the true community, that in summer the streets and stoops would be filled with families, children jumping double dutch, teenagers shooting baskets, young men laughing, leaning against polished automobiles. He had known that the nightmarish emptiness was a result of cold, and new violence on the streets, and the presence of an invading army that thought itself invisible, but with Stevie's arrival the knowledge had become reality. Gentry felt himself lost in a strange, cold place, fighting in the company of children against adult opponents who held all the power.

"They're here, man," whispered Leroy.

Three loud automobiles, slung low, roared to a stop on the street at the opposite end of the alley. Young men poured out, laughing, singing, shouting in Spanish. Several of them went over to the van and began beating on its side with baseball bats and pipes. The vehicle's lights came on. Someone inside shouted. Three men jumped out the side door of the van; one fired a shotgun into the air.

"Come on," hissed Marvin.

The line of gang members silently sprinted twenty yards down the alley, staying close to the sides of garages and fences. They paused in an empty area behind a shed, most leaning against a low metal fence. More shots rang out from the direction of the van. Gentry heard the low riders accelerate away toward Germantown Avenue.

"Grumblethorpe," Leroy said, and Gentry peered through the fence to see a small backyard, large, bare tree, and the rear of a stone house.

Marvin crawled near. "They got bars on the first-floor windows. One door in back. Two in front. We're going in both ways. Come on." Marvin, Leroy, G. B., G. R., and two others flowed over the fence like shadows. Gentry tried to follow, got hung up on torn wire, and landed heavily on one knee in frozen soil. He pulled the Ruger free of his pocket and ran to catch up.

Marvin and G. B. beckoned him to the side of the house. Both carried pump shotguns and Marvin had tied a red kerchief around his forehead and Afro. "We gonna do the street doors."

There was a four-foot-high wooden fence between the stone house and the delicatessen next door. The three of them waited for an empty trolley to rumble past and then Leroy kicked open the gate and he and G. B. stepped out boldly, nonchalantly walking past shuttered windows to the two doors. Low railings stood on either side of each door like entrance stiles. There was a padlocked cellar door slanting almost to the sidewalk. Gentry stepped back and looked up at the front of the old house. No light was visible in any of the nine windows. Germantown Avenue was empty except for the receding trolley two blocks to the west. Bright, "anticrime" streetlights threw a yellow glare on storefronts and brick. The night had a late, cold smell to it.

"Do it," said Marvin. G. B. stepped to the west door and kicked hard. The stout oak did not budge. Marvin nodded and the two of them pumped their shotguns, stepped back, and fired at the locks. Splinters flew and Gentry spun away, instinctively covering his eyes. The two fired again and Gentry looked back in time to see the west door sag open. G. B. grinned at Marvin and held up his fist in a victory salute just as a single small red dot appeared on his chest and moved upward to the side of his head. G. B. looked up, touched his forehead so that the circle of light appeared on the back of his hand, and glanced over at Marvin with a look of amused surprise. The sound of the shot was small and distant. G. B.'s body was driven into the wooden door and then back onto the sidewalk.

Gentry had time to notice that most of the youth's forehead was missing, and then he was running, falling on all fours, scrambling for the gate to the side yard. He was barely aware that Marvin had jumped the low railings and had dived for the open west door. Small red dots danced on the stone above Gentry, two shots kicked stone dust in his face, and he was through the gate, rolling to his right and coming up hard against something even as several shots tore through the fence and slammed into frozen ground to his left. Gentry crawled blindly toward the rear of the yard. More shots came from the direction of the avenue, but nothing hit near him.

Leroy ran up, panting, and dropped to one knee. "What the fuck?"

"Shots from across the street," gasped Gentry, amazed to find that he was still holding the Ruger. "Second floor or rooftop. They're using some sort of laser sighting device."

"Marvin?"

"Inside, I think. G. B.'s dead."

Leroy stood up, motioned with his arm, and was gone. Half a dozen shadows ran by toward the front of the house.

Gentry ran to the side of the stone building and peered into the backyard. The backdoor gaped open and a faint light was visible from inside. Then a van slid to a stop in the alley; a door opened, the interior light briefly silhouetting a man stepping down from the driver's seat, and half a dozen shots rang out from dark areas near the shed. The man fell into the interior and the door was pulled shut. Someone shouted from the direction of the shed and Gentry saw shadows running quickly toward the large tree. From overhead there came the roar of a helicopter and, without warning, a brilliant searchlight stabbed down to illuminate most of the backyard in white glare. A boy Gentry did not know by name froze like a deer in a headlight and squinted up into the beam. Gentry saw a red dot dance on the boy's chest for a split second before his rib cage exploded. Gentry heard no shot.

Gentry braced the Ruger with both hands and fired three times in the direction of the searchlight. The beam stayed on but pivoted wildly, illuminating branches, rooftops, and the van as the helicopter spun away higher into the night.

There was a riot of shots from the front of the house. Gentry heard someone screaming in a high, thin voice. There were more explosions and muzzle flashes from the direction of the van in the alley and Gentry heard other cars nearby. He glanced at the Ruger, decided there was no time to reload, and ran for the open rear door of Grumblethorpe.

Saul Laski had not driven a bulldozer in years, but as soon as Jackson had replaced a magneto to get the thing roaring to life, Saul was in the padded seat and working to remember skills he had not used since he had helped to clear a kibbutz almost two decades earlier. Luckily, this was an American Caterpillar D-7, direct descendent of his kibbutzim machines: Saul disengaged the flywheel clutch lever, set the speed selector level to neutral, pushed the governor control to the firewall, stood on the right steering brake and locked it in position with a clamp, checked to make sure that important gears were in neutral, and then started searching for the starter engine controls.

"Ahhh," he whispered when he found them. He set the transmission and compression levers to their proper settings—he hoped—pushed the starting engine clutch in, opened a fuel valve, set the choke, dropped the idling latch, and clicked on the ignition switch. Nothing happened.

"Hey!" shouted the skinny youth named Catfish who was crouching next to the seat. "You know what the fuck you doing, old man?"

"Absolutely!" Saul shouted back. He reached for a lever, decided it was the clutch, grasped a different one, and pulled it back. The electric starter whined and the engine roared to life. He found the throttle, let the clutch out, gave too much traction to the right tread, and almost ran over Jackson as the man crouched to start the second bulldozer on Saul's left. Saul got the machine straightened out, almost stalled it, and managed to get it lined up with the trailer complex sixty yards away. Diesel exhaust and black smoke blew back into their faces. Saul glanced to his right and saw three of the gang members sprinting across the broken ground alongside the machine.

"Can't this thing go any faster?" screamed Catfish.

Saul heard a loud scraping noise and realized that he had not yet elevated the blade. He did so and the machine moved forward with much more enthusiasm. There was a roar behind them as Jackson's bulldozer moved out of the construction area.

"What you going to do when we get there?" shouted Catfish.

"Just watch!" called Saul and adjusted his glasses. He had not the slightest idea what he was going to do. He knew that any second now the FBI agents could come outside, step to either side, and open fire. The slow-moving bulldozers would be easy targets. Their chances of making it all the way to the trailers seemed incredibly remote. Saul had not felt so good in decades.

Malcolm Dupris led eight members of Soul Brickyard into Anne Bishop's house. Marvin had been reasonably certain that the Voodoo Lady was in the other place—the old house on the Avenue—but Malcolm's team had been assigned to check out the house on Queen Lane. They had no radios; Marvin had arranged for each group to have at least two midgets—members of the auxiliary gang in the eight-to-eleven-year-old range—to act as runners. There had been no word from Marvin's group, but as soon as Malcolm heard the rattle of gunfire from the direction of the avenue he took half his group out of the alley and into Anne Bishop's backyard. The other six stayed behind to watch the telephone van that sat dark and silent at the end of the alley.

Malcolm, Donnie Cowles, and fat little Jamie—Louis Solarz's younger brother—went in first, kicking open the kitchen door and moving fast. Malcolm swung the oiled and shiny 9mm automatic pistol that he had bought from Muhammed for seventy-five dollars. It carried a staggered box magazine with fourteen rounds in it. Donnie held a crude little zip gun with a single .22 caliber cartridge chambered in the makeshift barrel. Jamie had brought only his knife.

The old woman who lived there was not home and there was no sign of the Voodoo Lady or the honky monster. They took three minutes to search the little house and then Malcolm was back in the kitchen while Donnie checked the front yard.

"Bunch of shit on the bed upstairs," said Jamie, "like somebody packing in a hurry."

"Yeah," said Malcolm. He waved at the group in the backyard and Jefferson, their ten-year-old midget runner, hurried up. "Get over to the old house on the Avenue and see what Marvin's going to . . ."

There was the sound of garage doors scraping open and a car engine idling. Malcolm waved to the others, slammed through the back gate, and skidded into the alley just as a funny old car with a weird grill pulled out of the garage. The car had no headlights on and the old lady in the driver's seat clutched the wheel with the desperate grip of a timorous driver. Malcolm recognized the white woman as Miss Bishop; he had seen her around the neighborhood his entire life, had even cut her tiny yard for her when he was a little kid.

Five of the gang members blocked the car's path while Malcolm stepped up to the driver's side. The frightened-looking woman looked around and then rolled down her window. Her voice had a strange, sleep-walking quality to it. "You boys will have to move. I must get by."

Malcolm glanced into the car to make sure no one else was in it; there was only Miss Bishop. He lowered his automatic and leaned closer. "Sorry, but you can't go nowhere until . . ."

Anne Bishop's hands shot straight out, fingers hooked into claws. Malcolm would have lost both eyes if he had not instinctively thrown his head back. As it was, the white woman's long nails left eight bloody streaks on his cheeks and eyelids. Malcolm screamed and the old car leaped ahead with a roar, knocking little Jefferson into the air and crushing Jamie under the left wheel.

Malcolm cursed, felt around in the cinders for his pistol, dropped to one knee when he found it, and squeezed off three rounds at the disappearing car before someone shouted at him to look out. Malcolm whirled, still on one knee. The telephone van that had been parked at the end of the alley was roaring directly at him. Malcolm brought the pistol around and realized that in so doing he had wasted his few seconds on the wrong motion. He opened his mouth to scream.

The FBI van was doing at least sixty miles per hour when the front bumper caught Malcolm in the face.

"Let's get the hell *out* of here!" shouted Tony Harod as something struck the left skid of the helicopter with a thunk and a flash of sparks. They had been hovering sixty feet over a flat-roofed building while Colben blazed away with his Star Wars rifle, all the while keeping a huge, stupid grin on his face. Hajek, the pilot, obviously agreed with Harod since he had the chopper banking right and clawing for altitude before Colben turned away from the window to give a command. Richard Haines sat stoically in the copilot's left seat, watching out his window as if they were on a nocturnal sight-seeing tour. Maria Chen sat on Harod's right with her eyes tightly closed.

"Red Leader to Control," called Colben. Harod and Maria Chen were wearing earphones and microphones for internal communication amid the roar of wind, engine, and rotors. "Red Leader to Control!"

"Control here," came a woman's voice. "Go ahead, Red Leader."

"What the hell's going on? We have spooks all over Castle Two."

"That's affirmative, Red Leader. Green Team confirms contact with an unknown number of armed blacks attempting a B and E at Castle Two. Gold Team is in pursuit of Target Two in a 1953 DeSoto, heading north parallel to Queen Lane. Teams White, Blue, Gray, Silver, and Yellow all report contact with hostile unknowns. The mayor has called twice. Over."

"The *mayor*," said Colben. "Jesus Christ. Where's Leonard for Chrissakes? Over."

"Agent Leonard is outside investigating a disturbance at the construction site. I'll have him get back to you as soon as he comes in, Red Leader. Over."

"Goddamnit," said Colben. "OK, listen. I'm going to put Haines on the ground to supervise things at Castle Two. Get Teams Blue and White to seal off the area from Market to Ashmead. Tell Green and Yellow that *no one* is to get in or out of Castle Two. Got that?"

"Affirmative, Red Leader. We have a . . ." There was a loud scraping noise and the contact was broken.

"Shit," said Colben. "Control? Control? Haines, switch to Tactical Two-Five. Gold Team? Gold Team, this is Red Leader. Peterson, do you copy?"

"Affirmative, Red Leader," came a man's voice under stress.

"Where the hell are you? Over."

"Going west on Germantown in pursuit of Target Two, Red Leader. Over."

"The Bishop woman? Where is she . . ."

"Ah . . . we need assistance, Red Leader," broke in the same voice. "Two vehicles, Hispanic males, ah . . . We'll get back to you, Red Leader. Over."

Colben leaned forward and shouted at the pilot. "Put it down."

The cool man in the baseball cap was chewing gum. "No place open, sir. I'm holding it at one triple zero."

"Fuck that," said Colben. "Put it down on Germantown Avenue if you have to. *Now*."

The pilot glanced to his right, rotated the helicopter, and nodded.

Tony Harod almost screamed as the machine dropped like a cableless elevator. Streetlights seemed to rush up at them, there was a glimpse of something burning a block to their left, and the helicopter flared out and settled gently onto brick and asphalt in the center of the street. Haines was out immediately, running toward the sidewalk in a graceful crouch.

"Up!" shouted Colben and jerked his thumb at the pilot.

"No!" shouted Harod. He nodded to Maria Chen and both of them fumbled at their lap straps. "We're getting out too."

"The hell you are," said Colben over the intercom.

Harod pulled his headset off just as Maria Chen brought the Browning out of her purse and leveled it at Colben's chest. "We're getting out now," shouted Harod.

"You're a dead man, Harod," Colben said softly.

Tony Harod shook his head. "Can't hear you, Chuck," he shouted. *"Ciao!"* Harod jumped out the left door and ran for an alley in a direction opposite of that Haines had gone. Maria Chen waited another thirty seconds and then slid toward the door.

"You're both dead," said Colben and smiled. He glanced at the rifle set in clips on the starboard bulkhead and then relaxed.

Maria Chen nodded, jumped out, and ran.

"A hundred feet," Colben said into the microphone.

The helicopter cleared the wires and rooftops, rotated left, and hovered ten stories above the Avenue. Colben slid the .30 caliber Colt rifle into the firing brace and swept the alleys with the nightscope. Nothing moved. "Too many fucking overhangs," muttered Colben. The tactical channel filled his earphones with urgent chatter. He heard Haines's voice demanding a response from the sniper team at Green One.

Colben shook his head. "Back to Castle Two," he snapped. "We'll deal with this shithead later."

The helicopter spun and pitched forward as it gained altitude and headed east.

THIRTY-THREE

Germantown
Thursday, Jan. 1, 1981

Natalie Preston lay on her back, hands raised against Vincent's knife, when something exploded against Grumblethorpe's front door six feet down the hallway. Splinters flew into the confined corridor. There was a second explosion and Natalie looked left, through the doorway to the small parlor, to see a street door shatter and fly open.

In the sudden silence, Vincent's head went up and back, swiveling like a poorly programmed robot's. The knife glinted in his right hand. Natalie did not move or speak or breathe.

There was a second series of explosions, more distant this time. Suddenly a dark figure came hurtling into the parlor, rolling once into the wing chair by the fireplace. A shotgun skittered across bare boards and clattered against the legs of a table.

Vincent stepped over her and strode into the parlor. Natalie caught a glimpse of Marvin Gayle's wide, blue eyes as Vincent lifted him, and then she was scrabbling on her knees toward the rear of the house. She almost screamed at the pain in her ankle, but she bit her lip until she tasted blood and stayed quiet. There were more shots from outside the front of the house, and she heard crashes from the parlor as Marvin and the honky monster struggled. Natalie pulled herself up to stand on her left leg at the entrance to what must be the kitchen. The long room had shuttered windows, a huge fireplace, two candles burning on a long table, and a heavy bolted door. There was a pump shotgun leaning against the wall by the door.

Natalie let out a soft noise and hopped toward the weapon. She was almost to it when three blasts in rapid succession slammed into the door from the outside. The fourth and fifth explosions shattered the iron lock and wooden bolt, sending splinters into her left leg and arm. Natalie jumped aside, put her weight down on her right foot, and tumbled into the table, pulling it over and hitting the stone floor hard. Two more blasts hit the door, knocking it visibly inward. Six feet in front of Natalie, the door to the pantry where she had been imprisoned gaped open, offering some concealment. She scrabbled forward, tumbling into the darkness just as someone kicked the kitchen door in from the outside.

A boy whom Natalie recognized as one of the twins in Marvin's gang came in fast, followed by another youth. Both carried shotguns. Both jumped behind the overturned table.

"Don't shoot!" screamed Natalie. "It's me!"

"Who's that?" shouted the twin. He rose swinging the shotgun in short arcs.

Natalie slid back into the pantry just as Marvin Gayle staggered into the kitchen. His arms and chest were streaked with blood and he dragged the stock of his shotgun along the floor as if he was too tired to lift it.

"Marvin! Fuck, man, how'd you get in here?" The twin stood up and lowered his weapon. The other boy raised his head from behind the table.

Marvin swung the shotgun up and fired twice. The twin was knocked backward into the cold fireplace. The second boy rolled into the corner, shouted something, tried to rise. Marvin swiveled and fired from the hip. The boy struck the wall, tumbled forward, and simply disappeared into a hole that had been invisible in the shadows.

Natalie realized that she was crouching, still holding her torn bra in place. She peered through the crack in the pantry door and saw Marvin walking woodenly to the fireplace to inspect the twin's body. He turned and strode over to stare down into the entrance to the tunnel. Then he lowered his shotgun into the hole and fired again.

Natalie hopped quickly down the hallway, letting the bra fall and feeling the goose bumps break out all over her upper body. There was a tremendous sound of firing from outside.

This is all a bad dream, thought Natalie. *I will make myself wake up.* The intense pain from her broken ankle told her otherwise.

Vincent stepped into the hallway, legs apart, the long knife held loosely in his right hand.

Natalie stopped, holding on to the wainscoting for support. The steep stairway to the second floor rose to her left.

Vincent took a step toward her.

Natalie jumped to the left, screamed as her ankle struck a step. Sobbing, she pulled her way up the stairs even as she heard Rob Gentry's voice calling from the kitchen.

Saul Laski had proposed the idea of the strike at the control center as a harassing raid, hit fast, cause as much confusion as possible, and get out. Ideally there would be no casualties, preferably no shots fired. Privately, he hoped to find Colben or Haines there. Now, as the bulldozer covered the last twenty yards to the trailer, he wondered if his theory made any sense.

There was a sudden concussion to his left and flowers of flame blossomed twenty feet into the air as Taylor and the others tossed their Molotov cocktails into the parked cars. The field was briefly illuminated by the flames as a man in a white shirt and dark tie stepped out of the door of the main trailer. He stared at the flames and then at the two advancing bulldozers, yelled something inaudible, and pulled a pistol from a small holster on his belt.

Saul was ten yards from the trailer. He elevated the blade as a shield and realized that it effectively blocked his view. He did not hear the shots over the engine noise and the sudden krup of another Molotov cocktail, but something dinged against the blade twice and a louder thump came from the grill. The bulldozer did not falter. Saul raised the blade a foot and peered through the crack in time to see the man dodge back into the trailer.

"Here where I get off!" called Catfish and jumped over the right tread, rolling away in the darkness.

Saul considered jumping, shrugged, and grabbed metal to brace himself. He pulled the blade up another foot.

The last ten feet to the trailer were slightly uphill and the bulldozer blade went into the trailer about eight feet above the ground, just to the right of the doorway. The wooden entrance platform splintered and twisted aside as Saul bounced forward, bit his tongue, and settled back in the thick seat as the treads dug in to the real business of toppling the long mobile home.

The entire complex shuddered and then shuddered again as Jackson's bulldozer made contact about twenty feet to the left of the door. The thin aluminum twisted and tore away in strips. An entire window assembly popped out and was ground under the tread of Saul's machine. For several seconds, Saul was sure that the blades were going to plow straight through the trailer, but then the steel blade contacted solid metal, both bulldozers strained, and the center trailer separated itself from the other two with a great screeching of flanges as the long box began to tip backward.

The main door opened a few feet from Saul's left shoulder and a man's upper torso emerged, a revolver swung searching for a target, and then the trailer found its center of gravity and went over. The arm stuck straight up, fired two shots into the air, and fell out of sight.

Saul put the bulldozer in neutral and jumped down. Jackson was walking away from his machine and the two looked at each other in tired silence as they crouched behind the fender of one of the FBI vehicles.

"What now?" asked Jackson after a minute.

Men were crawling out of the tumbled wreckage of the torn trailer. Saul saw a woman being helped through a rip in the roof. Most of them acted dazed, sitting on the cold ground or moving directionlessly like victims in the aftermath of an auto accident, but a few had drawn pistols. Saul knew it would be foolish to remain where he was. Taylor and the others were not to be seen and Saul assumed they had returned to the truck. "I'm hunting for someone," said Saul.

Saul waited until the last of the agents crawled from the trailer like ants boiling from an overturned anthill. There was no sign of either Charles

Colben or Richard Haines. Saul tasted the disappointment like bile in his mouth.

"We better move," whispered Jackson. "They're beginning to get it together."

Saul nodded and followed the bigger man into the shadows.

Leroy saw G. B.'s body lying on the curb and caught a glimpse of muzzle flashes from the third floor across the street before he had to drop and roll right toward the gate. High velocity bullets tore through the fence to his left. It sounded to him like some of the brothers were returning fire from the west side of the house and from down the avenue, but he knew that their assortment of handguns and few shotguns would be no match for the rifles that the federal pigs were using. Leroy pressed his face to the cold ground as more shots tore through the fence. "Fucking wild, man," he whispered.

There was a body lying next to the stone wall ten inches from Leroy's right arm. He rolled the heavy form over, hearing bottles clinking in the cheap thrift store rucksack. There was a sharp smell of gasoline.

It was Deeter Coleman, a junior at Germantown High and a new member of Soul Brickyard. Deeter had dated Leroy's sister a couple of times. Leroy knew the boy had been more interested in the school drama club and computer lab than in the street, but he had begged Marvin for years to get a chance at joining the gang. The gang leader had given him a chance only a week earlier. The high velocity bullet had removed most of the boy's throat.

Leroy pulled the corpse back over and tugged at the backpack straps, all the while muttering to himself. "You're just fucking dumb, Leroy babe. Stupid shit, man. Always doing the dumb stuff."

He pulled the straps tight, felt the gasoline from the broken bottle already soaking his back, and shook his head. He tucked the useless little .25 caliber pistol in his belt, and without giving himself time to think about, swung the gate open and ran hard.

Two shots rang out and something tugged at the heel of his sneaker, but Leroy did not pause. He crashed through a row of garbage cans at the entrance to the alley and then was jumping for the fire escape ladder. "Goddamn stupid idea to start with," he muttered as he clambered up the fire escape.

There were no windows on the alley side of the third floor, only a locked metal door without an outside handle. "Stupid, stupid," whispered Leroy and crouched to the right of the door. He patted his pant and coat pockets. He had no matches, no lighter, nothing. He was laughing out loud when the three shadows ran into the alley from the rear of the building. From his vantage point thirty feet above them, Leroy could see their white faces and hands as they looked up at him, weapons raised. "Nowhere to go, man," he muttered.

He pressed his face and stomach tight against the brick wall as the first bullet screeched through the grating with a flash of sparks. The second one tore through the sole of his right sneaker, kicking his leg a foot into the air. Leroy felt the sudden numbness and stared at the black exit hole in the top of his white sneaker. "You shitting me?" he whispered.

The steel door opened and a man in a dark suit stepped out onto the fire escape. He was carrying a weird-looking rifle. Leroy took the rifle away from him and hit him in the throat with it, bending him backward over the railing, using his numb right leg to keep the door from swinging shut. There were no shots from below, but Leroy could see white faces moving to get an angle of fire. The man squirmed and sputtered under him, one hand clawing at Leroy's face, the other pulling at the rifle breech embedded in his throat.

Leroy got his weight and shoulder into it, pushing the man farther over the railing. "Got a match, man?" he whispered. There were footsteps in the room behind them. Leroy got his left hand in the agent's suit coat pocket and came away with a gold cigarette lighter. "Thank you, Jesus," Leroy said aloud and let the man drop, rifle and all, to the alley thirty feet below. He stepped into the room just as the shooting from below started up again.

"Did you get . . ." began another honky with a drawn pistol. Three others stood by the window where fancy rifles and telescopes were mounted on heavy tripods. Leroy caught a glimpse of folding chairs, card tables with food and pop cans, and a bunch of radios against the wall.

"Freeze!" screamed the honky and leveled the pistol at Leroy's chest.

Leroy's hands were already rising. His thumb sparked the flint; he felt the heat from the tiny flame near his right ear. "My luck. Lights the first fucking time," said Leroy and dropped the lighter into his open pack of gasoline-soaked bottles of Shell unleaded premium.

Anne Bishop was half a block from Grumblethorpe when the explosion occurred. She continued driving at a steady fifteen miles per hour, hands clenching on the wheel of the DeSoto, eyes straight ahead and unblinking. Every window on the third floor of the building across from Grumblethorpe flew outward in a thousand pieces. Glass glittered and shimmered as it fell like snow across Germantown Avenue. Thirty seconds later, the flames appeared. Anne Bishop pulled to the curb in front of Grumblethorpe and shifted the transmission lever to park. Working from reflexes a third of a century old, she carefully set the parking brake on.

The flames from the burning building were much brighter now, casting an orange glow on Grumblethorpe and this entire section of the avenue. There came a scattered rattle of gunshots. Fifty yards down the block, half a dozen long-legged figures sprinted across the street. Just beyond the right wheel of the DeSoto, a boy lay facedown near the curb. A small, black pool had appeared under his shattered head and run down into the gutter.

The burning building across the street made a loud crackling noise, as if hundreds of heavy twigs were being snapped. Occasionally ammunition would go off, sounding amazingly like popcorn being popped. Someone screamed in the distance. There came the wail of sirens. Anne Bishop sat in her 1953 DeSoto with her eyes straight ahead, hands on the wheel, waiting.

Gentry had come through the open rear door quickly, Ruger ahead of him. An overturned table offered shelter and he took it, dropping heavily to one knee and looking around.

The old kitchen was illuminated by a candle on a countertop and another burning on its side on the floor. The twin named G. R. lay dead in a huge fireplace six feet behind Gentry, his goose-down coat shredded from throat to crotch. Feathers covered the face, torso, and legs of the corpse. The rest of the kitchen was empty. A narrow door to the pantry or small room hung open near the entrance to a hallway, obscuring the view.

Gentry aimed the Ruger at the pantry door, hearing noises in the hall beyond it. He realized that he was breathing through his mouth, too rapidly, coming close to hyperventilating. He held his breath for ten seconds. There was a pause in the rattle of gunfire outside, and in the momentary silence Gentry heard a gentle scraping in the shadowy corner behind him. He swiveled on his knee and watched as Marvin Gayle seemed to rise out of the stone floor, pulling himself up like a man coming out of a swimming pool. Even in the faint light, Gentry could see that the gang leader's face was absolutely expressionless, the eyes little more than white slits with only a hint of iris.

"Marvin?" Gentry said aloud at the same instant the boy raised a shotgun from whatever hole he was standing in, aimed it at Gentry's head and squeezed the trigger.

There was a click as the firing pin struck.

Gentry brought the Ruger to bear even as Marvin pumped the shotgun and fired again. Again the shotgun's hammer fell on emptiness.

Gentry had squeezed the trigger hard enough to raise the Ruger's hammer; now he caught it with his thumb and lowered it. "Shit," he said softly and jumped forward even as the parody of Marvin Gayle dropped the shotgun and scrambled out of the tunnel entrance.

The boy was shorter and lighter than Rob Gentry, but he was also younger, and faster and powered by a demon's energy. Gentry did not know what it would take to beat him in what might be called a fair fight; he did not wait to find out. He got to the corner while Marvin was still scrambling to his feet and swung the Ruger in a vicious arc, clipping the youth on the temple with the long barrel. Marvin went down, rolled once, and was still.

Gentry crouched next to him, found a pulse, and looked up in time to see the honky monster standing at the pantry door. Gentry fired twice; the first shot striking stone where the apparition had been standing a second before, the second punching through the pantry door. There were heavy footsteps in the hallway. From outside came the muffled concussion of an explosion.

"Natalie!" yelled Gentry. He waited a second, yelled again.

"Here, Rob! Be careful, he's . . ." Natalie's voice was cut off. It sounded like she was just down the hall.

Gentry stood, shoved the table aside, and ran in the direction of her voice.

Natalie had crawled as high as she could on the stairway, hoping to be able to kick at Vincent's face if nothing else, when she realized she was not alone. She forced herself to quit peering back over her shoulder and to look up.

Melanie Fuller stood at the top of the stairs, three feet from Natalie's head. She was wearing a long flannel nightgown, a cheap pink robe, and fuzzy pink slippers. Candlelight from the nursery illuminated a face beyond years, wrinkles blending into folds eroding to tendons, a skull straining to escape a mask of dead skin. Her spiky nimbus of blue hair seemed far too sparse, her mottled scalp showing in patches, as if chemotherapy or some drug had caused much of her hair to come out in ragged clumps. Melanie Fuller's left eye was closed and grotesquely swollen, her right eye showed only as a yellow orb. She smiled, and Natalie saw that the woman's upper denture hung loose from her gums. Her tongue appeared black as dried blood in the candlelight.

"Shame on you, dear," said Melanie Fuller. "Cover your nakedness."

Natalie shivered and clutched the rags of her blouse to her breasts. The old woman's voice was a sibilant death rattle; her breath fouled the stairway with the scent of decay. Natalie tried to crawl toward her, to get her hands on that corded neck.

"Natalie!" Rob's voice.

She clutched at the torn wooden steps and called back to him. *Where was Vincent?* She was trying to warn Rob when Melanie Fuller came down three steps and touched her shoulder with a pink slipper. "Hush, dear."

Gentry came down the hall with a pistol raised. He looked up at Natalie and his eyes grew wide. "Natalie. Dear God."

"Rob!" she cried, using every second her mind remained free. "Be careful! The honky monster is right there . . ."

"Shhh, dear," said Melanie Fuller. The old woman cocked her head to one side and looked at Gentry with the intense scrutiny of the insane. "I know who you are," she whispered, the loose dentures causing saliva to spray with each word. "But I did not vote for you."

Gentry glanced behind him down the hall, toward the parlor and front room. He stepped onto the staircase, pressed his back against the wall, and raised the revolver until it aimed at Melanie Fuller's chest.

The old woman shook her head slowly.

The revolver dropped lower as if pulled by some powerful magnetic force, wavered, steadied, remained aimed directly at Natalie Preston's face.

"Yesss, now," whispered Melanie Fuller.

Gentry's body spasmed, his eyes widened, and his face grew more and more red. His arm shook violently as if every nerve in his body were fighting the commands of his brain. His hand clenched on the pistol, his finger tightened on the trigger.

"Yesss," hissed Melanie Fuller. Her voice was impatient.

Sweat broke out on Gentry's face and soaked the shirt visible through the open jacket. Tendons stood out in his neck and veins bulged on his temples. His face was drawn into the mask of effort and agony visited only on those engaged in some supreme effort, an impossible task of muscle, mind, and will. His finger tightened on the trigger, loosened, tightened until the revolver's hammer rose, fell back.

Natalie could not move. She stared at that mask of agony and saw the blue eyes of Rob Gentry, nothing else.

"Thisss takesss too long," whispered Melanie Fuller. She brushed at her forehead as if tired.

Gentry flew backward as if he had been engaged in a tug of war with titans and his opponents had released their end of the rope. He stumbled backward across the hall and slid down the wall, dropped the revolver on the floor as he gasped for breath. Natalie saw the elation in Rob's face for the split second their eyes met.

Vincent stepped out from the parlor and swung the knife twice in a waist-level blur. Gentry gasped and raised his hands to his throat as if he could seal the gaping wound with pressure. For three seconds it seemed to work and then blood flowed between his fingers, poured in unimaginable quantities down over his hands and chest and torso. Gentry slid sideways down the wall until his head and left shoulder gently touched the floor. His gaze never left Natalie's face until his eyes slowly closed, a young boy sleepily closing his eyes for an afternoon nap. Gentry's body spasmed once and relaxed in death.

"No!" Natalie screamed and jumped at the same instant. She had come up eight steps and now she went down those headfirst, striking the lowest step so hard with her left arm that she felt something break in her shoulder. She ignored it, ignored the pain, ignored the feeling of fingers pawing at her mind like moths against a windowpane, ignored the second impact as she rolled across the hard wood, Rob's legs, the back of Vincent's legs.

Natalie did not think. She let her body do what it had to do, what she had ordered it to do eons ago before she had leaped.

Vincent teetered above her, waving his arms to keep his balance in the aftermath of her collision with him. He had to swivel his upper body around to bring the knife toward her.

Natalie did not pause to think as she rolled on her back, let her right hand fall back to find the heavy revolver where she knew it had to be, brought it up and forward. She shot Vincent through his open mouth.

The recoil knocked her arm back to the floor and the impact of the bullet lifted Vincent completely into the air. He struck the wall seven feet above the floor and left a broad smear sliding down it.

Melanie Fuller slowly shuffled down the stairs, her slippers making a soft scraping sound on the wood.

Natalie tried to use her left arm to pull herself up, but fell sideways onto Rob's legs. She lowered the gun and levered herself to a sitting position. She had to brush away tears to aim the pistol at Melanie Fuller.

The old woman was five feet away, two steps above her. Natalie expected the fingers in her mind to seize her, stop her, but there was nothing. She squeezed the trigger once, twice, a third time.

"One must always count the cartridges, dear," whispered the old woman. She descended the stairs, stepped over Natalie's legs, and shuffled toward the door. She paused once and looked back. "Goodbye, Nina. We shall meet again."

Melanie Fuller took a last look around the hallway and the house, unbolted the splintered front door, stepped into a street lighted with flames, and was gone.

Natalie dropped the pistol and sobbed. She crawled to Rob, pulled him by the shoulders until he was free of Vincent's sprawled body, and propped his head on her leg. Blood soaked her pant leg, the floorboards, everything. She tried to use the rags from her torn shirt to mop at his coat and shirtfront but gave it up.

When Saul Laski and Jackson entered five minutes later, hurried by the flames, sirens, and renewed shots outside, they found her with Rob's head still resting on her lap, singing softly to him, and stroking his forehead with gentle fingers.

THIRTY-FOUR

Melanie

I hated to leave Grumblethorpe, but there was little choice at the time. The neighborhood simply had become too unruly; the coloreds had chosen New Year's Eve to stage one of the senseless riots I had read about for so long. These things never happened before the so-called civil rights agitations of the past two or three decades. Father used to say that if you give Negroes an inch, they will ask for a yard and take a mile.

Nina's messenger—a colored girl who would have been attractive had it not been for the nappy hair that made her look like a pickaninny—had almost convinced me that Nina had not sent her before I saw through her ruse. The voices told me. They were very loud that last day and night in Grumblethorpe. I confess I had difficulty concentrating on less important things as I strained to understand what the voices—unmistakably a young boy's and girl's, with quaint, almost-British accents—were telling me.

Some of it made little sense. They warned me about the fire, the bridge, the river, and the chessboard. I wondered if these were actually events in their own lives—perhaps the final disasters that claimed their young lives. But the warnings about Nina were clear enough.

In the end, Nina's two emissaries—brought all the way from Charleston—were little more than nuisances. I was sorry to lose Vincent but, if the truth be told, he had served his purpose. I do not clearly remember all of those last moments at Grumblethorpe. I do remember that I had a terrible headache on the right side of my head. When Anne had been packing, prior to picking me up, I had her bring along a bottle of Dristan. It was little wonder that my sinuses were acting up in such a cold, damp, inhospitable northern climate.

Anne slid across the front seat and opened the car door for me when I left Grumblethorpe. The building across the street was burning, undoubtedly the handiwork of Negro looters. When Mrs. Hodges used to visit and cluck about the most recent atrocities in the North, she rarely failed to point out that the supposedly poor, underfed, discriminated-against minorities invariably stole expensive television sets and fancy clothes at the first opportunity. It was her feeling that the coloreds had stolen whites blind when they were servants and they continued to do so now that they were welfare dependents. It was one of the few opinions I shared with that nosy old woman.

There were three suitcases in the backseat of Anne's DeSoto. One of the large ones held my clothes, the other contained the cash and remaining stocks Anne had accumulated, and the smaller one held some clothes and personal things of Anne's. My straw tote bag was also there. On the floor by the rear seat lay the 12-gauge shotgun Anne had been keeping at her house.

"Let us go, dear," I said and leaned back in the car seat.

Anne Bishop drove like an old woman. We left Grumblethorpe and the burning building and drove slowly northwest along Germantown Avenue. I looked behind us and noticed that there had been some sort of collision or altercation near where Queen Lane comes into the Avenue. A van and two low-slung, unattractive automobiles were tangled in the intersection. There was no sign of the police.

We passed Penn Street and Coulter and were approaching Church Street when two commercial-looking vans pulled out across the street, blocking our way. I had Anne drive up onto the sidewalk on the left side and scrape by. Men jumped out of the truck and were brandishing weapons, but they were quickly distracted when the man I was watching turned his revolver in their direction and started firing at his colleagues.

It was all nonsense. If they were there to arrest colored looters they should have done so and left two white ladies alone.

We came to Market Street and even in the darkness I could make out the bronze Yankee soldier standing atop his monument. Anne had told me on our first outing that the granite was from Gettysburg. I thought of General Lee retreating in the rain, beaten that day but not defeated, carrying all the pride of the Confederacy away intact from that terrible carnage, and I felt better about my own temporary withdrawal from the field.

Flashing lights of fire trucks, police cars, and other emergency vehicles rushed at us down Germantown Avenue. Behind us, one of the vans and a dark sedan were accelerating our way. I heard a strange noise and looked up to see flashing red and green lights above the rooftops.

"Turn left," I said. As we did so, I was close enough to see the face of the helmeted driver of the fire engine. I closed my eyes and pushed. The long fire truck cut abruptly across the middle of the Avenue, bounced over trolley tracks, and struck the van near the passenger door. The van rolled over several times and came to rest upside down in the center of Market Square. I caught a glimpse of the dark sedan skidding to avoid the red wall of the fire truck that now blocked the street, and then we were moving down School House Lane and away from the commotion.

Of all the things I had helped Anne to do, getting her to drive over thirty miles per hour was the hardest. I had to concentrate all of my will to have her operate the motorcar the way I wanted. Eventually it was through her senses that I saw the streets flash by, heard the sound of rotors still overhead, and watched what little traffic was left on the streets scurry to get out of our way.

School House Lane was a pleasant street but had not been designed to accommodate a 1953 DeSoto traveling at 85 m.p.h. A green car skidded into the street to follow us. Occasionally I caught a glimpse of the helicopter roaring over rooftops parallel to us on our left or right. I had Anne brake to slide through a curve, then accelerate, and suddenly the right rear window starred and exploded glass inward. I looked back and saw two holes the size of my fist.

A black man with no coat on stood weaving by the side of the road as we approached Ridge Avenue. He ran out as the green car approached and threw himself in front of the vehicle. I watched in the mirror as the green car swerved right, struck the curb at over 70 m.p.h., and did a complete spiral in the air before rolling through the glass front of a Gino's hamburger stand.

I fumbled in the glove compartment for a street map of Philadelphia while simultaneously keeping control of the car through Anne. I wanted an expressway out of this nightmarish city, and although there was a plethora of green signs, arrows, and overpasses approaching, I did not know which road to take.

There was an incredible noise through the broken window and the large helicopter roared by thirty feet to our right. In the flash of passing streetlights, I could see the pilot on the far side and a man wearing a baseball cap leaning toward us in the back. The man had a maniacal grin and something cradled in his arms.

I had Anne turn right onto an entrance ramp. The DeSoto's left rear wheel slid onto a soft shoulder and for a second I was fully involved with her steering, counter-steering, tapping the accelerator, trying to keep us from crashing.

The helicopter roared to our left as we curved around the endless cloverleaf. A red dot danced for the briefest second on Anne's window and left cheek. Instantly, I had her floor the accelerator, the old car leaped ahead, the dot disappeared, and something struck the rear left fender of the car with a solid thunk.

We were suddenly on a bridge high over a river. I did not want to be on a bridge; I wanted an expressway.

The helicopter was to our right now, at the same level as us. A red light shone in my eyes for a second and then I had Anne swerve left and pull up next to a Volkswagen microbus, using it as a shield between the flying machine and ourselves. The driver of the Volkswagen suddenly slumped forward and the car swerved right into the railing. The helicopter drifted closer, somehow managing to fly sideways at 80 m.p.h.

We were off the bridge. Anne cut hard left and we bounced across a median, barely missed a semi-trailer truck that blasted its air horn at us, and exited at a large sign that said Presidential Apartments. Four empty lanes curved ahead of us, mercury vapor lamps creating an artificial daylight. There was a flash of red and green lights as the helicopter roared no more than fifteen feet over our heads, circled, and hovered broadside a hundred yards ahead of us.

It was too bright, too bare, too easy. It was a long shooting gallery and we were the little metal ducks.

I had Anne turn sharp left. The DeSoto's tires made a terrible noise on the asphalt and then found traction, catapulting us onto a narrow, unmarked access road not much wider than a driveway.

The road ran southeast under an elevated section of what the map said was the Schuylkill Expressway. "Road" was too generous a term. It was little more than a rutted, graveled lane. Concrete pillars and supports flashed in our headlights and snapped by the windows. Anne's dress and sweater were soaked with sweat and her face was very strange to look at. The helicopter appeared to our left, flying low above a railroad line paralleling the expressway. Pillars flashed between us and it, enhancing the sense of speed. Our old speedometer read 100 m.p.h.

Ahead of us, the gravel road ended, as a maze of cloverleafs above generated hundreds of pillars, abutments, and cross-braces. It was a forest of steel and concrete.

I was careful not to have Anne lock up the brakes, but we must have skidded half the length of a football field, throwing up a cloud of dust that covered us and showed our headlight beams as two skewed shafts of yellow light. The dust passed. We had stopped less than a yard from an abutment the size of a small house.

The DeSoto crept around it, rolled slowly between pylons, and moved cautiously out from under one roadway into the concealment of another. There must have been at least fifteen lanes of traffic on the cloverleafs above us, many curling toward a bridge that added more trunks to the stone and steel forest of supports.

We rumbled another fifty yards into the maze and I had Anne pull next to a concrete island, cut the engine, and turn out the lights.

I opened my eyes. We were like mice trespassing in a bizarre cathedral. Huge pillars lifted fifty feet to a roadbed here, eighty feet there, and even higher to the bases of three bridges rising across the dark Schuylkill River. There was silence except for the distant hum of traffic far overhead and the even more distant call of a train. I counted to three hundred before daring to hope that the helicopter had lost us and flown on.

The roar, when it came, was terrifying.

The infernal machine hovered thirty feet under the highest roadbed, the sound of its engine and rotors racketing off every surface, a searchlight stabbing ahead of it. The helicopter moved slowly, rotors never approaching pylon or embankment, the fuselage pivoting like the head of a watchful cat.

The searchlight found us eventually, and pinned us there in its relentless glare. I had Anne outside by that time. She held the shotgun awkwardly, bracing it on the roof of the DeSoto.

I knew as soon as I had her fire that it was too soon, that the helicopter was too far away. The blast of the shotgun added to the already intolerable noise but achieved nothing else.

The recoil pushed her back two steps. The impact of a high velocity bullet sent the shotgun flying and knocked her down. I was on the floor-boards when the second shot shattered the windshield and scattered pow-dered glass onto the front seat.

Anne was able to stand, stagger back to the car, and turn the ignition key with her left hand. Her right arm hung useless, almost separated at the shoulder. Bare bone gleamed through torn cloth and wool.

We drove directly under the helicopter—the desperate mouse scurry-ing beneath the legs of the startled cat—and then we were roaring up a gravel road, temporarily headed away from the river, curving up a wooded bluff toward a dark bridge.

The helicopter hurtled after us, but the bare trees on either side of the graveled lanes overhung enough to shield us as long as we kept moving. We emerged on a wooded ridge line, the lanes of the south-curving ex-pressway to our right, the rail line and river to our left. I saw that our road hooked left to the southernmost of two dark bridges. We had no choice; the helicopter was behind us again, the trees were too sparse for cover here, and there was no way the DeSoto could get down the steep and wooded embankment to the expressway hundreds of yards below.

We turned left and accelerated onto the dark bridge. And stopped.

It was a railroad bridge, a very old one. Low stone and iron railings bordered each side. Rusting rails, wooden ties, and a narrow cinder road-way stretched ahead into darkness a sheer eighty feet above the river.

Thirty feet out, a thick barricade blocked our way. It would not have helped had we broken through the barricade; the roadbed was too narrow, too exposed, too slow with its obstacle course of ties.

We did not pause more than twenty seconds, but that was too long. There came the roar, a rising cloud of dust and twigs enveloped us, and I ducked as a heavy mass occluded the sky. Five holes appeared in the wind-shield, the steering wheel and dash shattered, and Anne Bishop thrashed as bullets struck her in the stomach, chest, and cheek.

I opened the car door and ran. One of my slippers tumbled down the embankment into the brush. My robe and nightgown billowed in the hur-ricane gale from rotors. The helicopter hurtled by, skids five feet above my head, and disappeared beyond the ridge line.

I staggered along the wooden ties, away from the bridge. Beyond the ridge and the reflected light haze of the expressway, I could see the relative darkness of Fairmount Park. Anne had told me that it was the largest city-owned park in the world, more than four thousand acres of forest along the river. If I could get there . . .

The helicopter rose above the tree line like a spider climbing its web. It slid sideways toward me. From the side window I could see a thin, red beam slicing through the dusty air.

I turned and staggered back onto the bridge, toward the parked DeSoto. That was exactly what they wanted me to do.

A steep trail cut through brush to the right down the embankment. I slid down it, slipped, lost my other slipper, and sat down heavily on the cold, damp ground. The helicopter roared overhead, hovered fifty feet over the river and set its searchlight stabbing along the bank. I stumbled along the trail, slid twenty feet down the steep hillside, feeling brushes and branches tearing at my skin. The searchlight pinned me again. I stood up, shielded my eyes, and squinted into the glare. If I could Use the pilot . . .

A bullet tugged at the hem of my robe.

I fell to all fours and clawed my way along the slope forty feet under the bridge. The helicopter dipped lower and followed.

It was not Nina in the helicopter. Then who? I crawled behind a rotting log and sobbed. Two bullets struck the wood. I tried to curl into myself. I had a terrible headache. My robe and nightgown were soiled.

The helicopter hovered almost level with me, thirty or forty feet out, not quite under the bridge. It pivoted on its own axis, playing with me, a hungry predator, almost ready to end the game.

I raised my head, focused all of my attention on the machine and its passengers. Through the agony of my headache I extended my will farther and harder and with more finality than ever before.

Nothing.

There were two men in the machine. The pilot was a Neutral . . . a hole in the fabric of thought. The other man was a User . . . not Willi . . . but as willful and intent on blood as Willi ever was. Without knowing him, seeing him, confronting him, I could never override his Ability sufficiently to Use him.

But *he* could kill *me*.

I tried to crawl forward, toward a stone archway support twenty feet away. The bullet slammed into the earth ten inches from my hand.

I tried to back up the narrow trail toward a thick bush. The bullet almost grazed the sole of my foot.

I pressed my cheeks against the ground and my back against the rotted log and closed my eyes. A bullet tore through pulped wood inches from my spine. Another thudded into the dirt between my legs.

Anne had been struck by four bullets. One had passed through her stomach and just missed her spine. One had struck her third rib, ricocheted out her chest wall, and shattered her left arm. The third one had passed through her right lung and lodged in her right shoulder blade. The final bullet had struck her left cheek, removed her tongue and most of her teeth, and exited through her right jawbone.

To Use her I had to experience all of the pain she was feeling as she died. Any buffer at all would have been enough to allow her to slip away from me, from everything. I could not allow her to die yet. I had a final use for her.

The ignition was on. The automatic transmission was set in park. To shift into drive, Anne had to lower her face through the broken steering wheel and wedge the metal lever with what remained of her front teeth. She had set the parking brake out of decades of habit. We used her knee to pull back and trip the brake release.

Her vision grayed and faded to nothing. I forced it back through the strength of my will. Bone fragments from her jaw clouded her right eye. It did not matter. She levered her shattered arms onto the metal horn ring, and hooked her clenched right hand onto the broken plastic of the wheel.

I opened my own eyes. A red dot danced on the dead grass near me, found my arm, traveled to my face. The rotted log had been shot away to nothing.

I tried to blink away the red beam.

The sounds of the DeSoto accelerating and crashing through the railing high above was audible even over the rotor noise. I looked up in time to see the twin headlights stabbing out and then down. There was a glimpse of dark transmission and oil pan as the 1953 DeSoto fell almost vertically.

The pilot was very, very good. He must have glimpsed something above him in his peripheral vision and reacted almost instantaneously. The helicopter's engine screamed and the fuselage pitched forward steeply even as it turned toward the open river. Only the tip of one rotor contacted the falling car.

It was enough.

The red beam was gone from my eye. There was an almost human scream of tortured metal. The helicopter seemed to transfer all of its rotational energy from the rotors to the fuselage as the sleek cabin whipped around counterclockwise once, three, five times, before slamming into the stone arch of the railroad bridge.

There was no fire. No explosion. The shattered mass of steel, Plexiglas, and aluminum fell a silent sixty feet to splash in the water not ten feet from where the DeSoto had disappeared not three seconds earlier.

The current was very strong. For several bizarre seconds the helicopter's searchlight remained on, showing the dead machine sliding deeper underwater and farther downstream than one could imagine in so short a time. Then the light went out and the dark waters closed over everything like a muddy shroud.

It was a minute before I sat up, half an hour before I tried to stand.

There was no sound except the soft lapping of the river and the distant, unchanging susurration of the unseen expressway.

After awhile I brushed the twigs and dust off my nightgown, tightened the belt of my robe, and began walking slowly up the trail.

THIRTY-FIVE

Philadelphia
Thursday, Jan. 1, 1981

The children had been allowed to leave the house to play for an hour before breakfast. The morning was cold but very clear, the rising sun a distinct orange sphere struggling to separate itself from the innumerable bare branches of the forest. The three children laughed, played, and tumbled on the long slope that led to the woods and to the river beyond that. Tara, the oldest, had turned eight just three weeks earlier. Allison was six. Justin, the redhead, would be five in April.

Their laughs and shouts echoed on the forested hillside. All three looked up as an elderly lady emerged from the trees and walked slowly toward them.

"Why are you still in your bathrobe?" asked Allison.

The woman stopped five feet from them and smiled. Her voice sounded strange. "Oh, it was such a sunny morning, I didn't feel like getting dressed before I took a walk."

The children nodded their understanding. They often wanted to play outside in their pajamas.

"Why don't you have any teeth?" asked Justin.

"Hush," said Tara quickly. Justin looked down and fidgeted.

"Where do you live?" asked the lady.

"We live in the castle," said Allison. She pointed up the hill toward a tall old building made of gray stone. It sat alone amid hundreds of acres of parkland. A narrow ribbon of asphalt wound along the ridge into the forest.

"My daddy is assistant grounds superintendent," intoned Tara.

"Really?" said the lady. "Are your parents there now?"

"Daddy's still asleep," said Allison. "He and Mommy were up late at the New Year's Eve party last night. Mommy's awake, but she has a headache and she's resting before breakfast."

"We're going to have french toast," said Justin.

"And watch the Rose Parade," added Tara.

The lady smiled and looked up at the house. Her gums were pale pink.

"You want to see me do a tumblesalt?" asked Justin, tugging at her hand.

"A tumblesalt?" said the lady. "Why yes, I do."

Justin unzipped his jacket, squatted on his knees, and rolled awkwardly forward, landing on his back with a thud of sneakers slapping the ground. "See?"

"Bravo!" cried the lady and applauded. She looked back at the house.

"I'm Tara," said Tara. "This is Allison. Justin's just a baby."

"Am not!" said Justin.

"Yes you are," Tara said primly. "You are the youngest so you are the baby of the family. Mom says so."

Justin frowned fiercely and went over to take the elderly woman's hand. "You're a nice lady," he said.

She idly stroked his head with her free hand. "Do you have a car?" asked the lady.

"Sure," said Allison. "We have the Bronco and the Blue Oval."

"Blue Oval?"

"She means the blue Volvo," said Tara, shaking her head. "Justin calls it that and now Mommy and Daddy do too. They think it's *cute*." She made a face.

"Is anyone else in the house this morning?" asked the lady.

"Uh-uh," said Justin. "Aunt Carol was coming, but she went to somewhere else instead. Daddy says it's just as well 'cause Aunt Carol's a pain in the ass."

"*Hush!*" snapped Tara and aimed a slap at Justin's arm. The boy hid behind the lady.

"I bet you get lonely in the castle," said the lady. "Are you ever afraid of robbers or bad people?"

"Naw," said Allison. She threw a rock toward the distant line of trees. "Daddy says the park is the safest, best place in the city for us kids."

Justin peeked around the bathrobe, looking up at the lady's face. "Hey," he said, "what's wrong with your eye?"

"I have a bit of a headache, dear," said the lady and brushed at her forehead with shaking fingers.

"Just like Mommy," said Tara. "Did you go out to a New Year's Eve party last night too?"

The lady showed her gums and looked up at the house. "Assistant grounds superintendent sounds very important," she said.

"It is," agreed Tara. The other two had lost interest in the conversation and were playing tag.

"Does your father have to keep something to protect the park from bad people?" asked the lady. "Something like a pistol?"

"Oh yeah, he has one of those," Tara said brightly. "But we aren't allowed to play with it. He keeps it on the shelf in his closet. He has more bullets in the blue and yellow box in his desk."

The lady smiled and nodded.

"Do you want to hear me sing?" asked Allison, pausing in her hectic game of tag with Justin.

"Of course, dear."

The children sat cross-legged on the grass. The lady remained standing. Behind them, the orange sun fought free of morning haze and bare branches and floated into a cold, azure sky.

Allison sat upright, folded her hands, and sang the Beatles' "Hey, Jude," acapella, three verses, each note and syllable as clear and sharp as the frost crystals on grass that caught the rich morning light. When she finished, she smiled and the children sat in silence.

Tears filled the lady's eyes. "I believe I would like to meet your father and mother now," she said softly.

Allison took the lady's left hand, Justin took her right, and Tara led the way. Just as they reached the flagstone walk to the kitchen door, the lady put her hand to her temple and turned away.

"Aren't you coming in?" asked Tara.

"Perhaps later," said the lady in a queer voice. "I suddenly have a terrible headache. Perhaps tomorrow."

The children watched as the lady took several hesitant steps away from the house, let out a small cry, and fell into the rose bed. They ran to her and Justin tugged at her shoulder. The old woman's face was gray and distorted in a terrible grimace. Her left eye was completely closed, the other showed only white. The lady's mouth gaped open, showing blood-red gums and a white tongue curled back like a mole burrowing toward her throat. Saliva hung from her chin in a long, beaded string.

"Is she dead?" gasped Justin.

Tara had her knuckles in her mouth. "No. I don't think so. I don't know. I'll go and get Daddy." She turned and ran for the house. Allison hesitated a second and then turned and followed her older sister.

Justin knelt in the rose bed and pulled the unconscious lady's head onto his knees. He lifted her hand. It was cold as ice.

When the others emerged from the house, they found Justin kneeling there, patting her hand gently and saying over and over, "Don't die, nice lady, OK? Please don't die, nice lady. OK?"

BOOK THREE

End Game

"I wake and feel the fell of dark, not day."

—GERARD MANLEY HOPKINS

THIRTY-SIX

Dothan, Alabama
Wednesday, April 1, 1981

The World Bible Outreach Center, five miles south of Dothan, Alabama, consisted of twenty-three glaringly white buildings spread over 160 acres. The center of the complex was the huge granite and glass Palace of Worship, a carpeted and curtained amphitheater that could seat six thousand of the faithful in air-conditioned comfort. Along the half mile curve of the Boulevard of Faith, each gold brick represented a five-thousand-dollar pledge, each silver brick a one-thousand-dollar pledge, and each white brick a five-hundred-dollar pledge. Coming in from the air, perhaps in one of the Center's three Lear executive jets, visitors often looked down at the Boulevard of Faith and thought of a huge white grin emphasized by several gold teeth and a row of silver fillings. Each year the grin grew wider and more golden.

Across the Boulevard of Faith from the Palace of Worship, the long, low Bible Outreach Communications Center might have been mistaken for a large computer factory or research facility except for the presence of six huge GTE satellite broadcast dishes on the roof. The Center claimed that its twenty-four-hour television broadcasting, relayed through one or more of three communications satellites to cable companies, television stations, and church-owned earth stations, reached more than ninety countries and a hundred million viewers. The Communications Center also contained a computerized printing plant, the press for records, recording studio, and four mainframe computers hooked into the Worldwide Evangelist Information Network.

Just where the white, gold, and silver grin ended, where the Boulevard of Faith passed out of the high security area and became County Road 251, were the Jimmy Wayne Sutter Bible College and the Sutter School of Christian Business. Eight hundred students attended the two nonaccredited institutions, 650 of them living on campus in rigidly segregated dormitories such as Roy Rogers West, Dale Evans East, and Adam Smith South.

Other buildings, concrete-columned, granite-facaded, looking like a cross between modern Baptist churches and mausoleums with windows, provided office space for the legions of workers carrying out duties of administration, security, transportation, communications, and finances. The World Bible Outreach Center kept its specific income and expenses secret, but it was public knowledge that the Center complex, completed in 1978, had cost more than forty-five million dollars and it was rumored that current donations brought in around a million and a half dollars a week.

In anticipation of rapid financial growth in the 1980s, the World Bible Outreach Center was preparing to diversify into the Dothan Christian Shopping Mall, a chain of Christian Rest motels, and the 165-million-dollar Bible World amusement park under construction in Georgia.

The World Bible Outreach Center was a nonprofit religious organization. Faith Enterprises was the taxable corporate entity created to handle future commercial expansion and to coordinate franchising. The Reverend Jimmy Wayne Sutter was the president of the Outreach Center and currently the chairman and sole member of the board of directors for Faith Enterprises.

The Reverend Jimmy Wayne Sutter put on his gold-rimmed bifocals and smiled into camera three. "I'm just a country preacher," he said, "all this highfalutin financial and legal stuff just passes me by . . ."

"Jimmy," said his second banana, an overweight man with horn-rimmed glasses and jowls that quivered when he got excited as he was now, "the whole thing . . . the IRS investigation, the FCC persecution . . . is just so *transparently* the work of the Enemy . . ."

". . . but I know *persecution* when I see it," continued Sutter, his voice rising, smiling ever so slightly as he noticed that the camera had stayed on him. He saw the lens extend as three moved in for an E.C.U. The director up in the booth, Tim McIntosh, knew Sutter well after eight years and more than ten thousand shows. "And I know the stench of *the Devil* when I smell it. And this *stinks* of the Devil's work. The Devil would like nothing *better* than to block the Word of God . . . the Devil would like nothing *better* than to use Big Gov'ment to keep the Word of *Jesus* from reaching those who cry out for His help, for His forgiveness, and for His salvation . . ."

"And this . . . this *persecution* is so obviously the work of . . ." began the second banana.

"But Jesus does not abandon His People in time of need!" shouted Jimmy Wayne Sutter. He was standing and moving now, whipping the traveling mike cord behind him as if he were tweaking Satan's tail. "Jesus is on the *home team* . . . Jesus is calling our plays and *confounding* the Enemy and the Enemy's players . . ."

"Amen!" cried the overweight ex-TV actress in the interview chair. Jesus had cured her of breast cancer during a live television crusade broadcast from Houston a year earlier.

"Praise Jesus!" said the mustached man on the couch. In the past sixteen years he had written nine books about the imminent end of the world.

"*Jesus* takes no more notice of these . . . Big Gov'ment bureaucrats . . ." Sutter almost spit the phrase, "than a noble lion notices the bite of an itty bitty flea!"

"Yes, Jesus!" sighed the male singing star who had not had a hit record since 1957. The three guests appeared to use the same brand hair spray and to shop in the same section of Sears for double-knit bargains.

Sutter stopped, tugged on the microphone cord, and swiveled to stare at the audience. The set was huge by television standards—larger than most Broadway stages—three levels, carpeted in red and blue, picked up here and there by arrays of fresh, white flowers. The upper level, used primarily for song numbers, resembled a carpeted terrace backed by three cathedral-style windows through which an eternal sunset—or sunrise— glowed. The middle level held a crackling fireplace—crackling even on days where the temperature in Dothan was 100 degrees in the shade—and was centered around a conversation/interview area with imitation-antique, gold-filigreed couch and chairs, as well as a Louis XIV writing table behind which the Reverend Jimmy Wayne Sutter usually sat in an orna- mented, high-backed chair only slightly more imposing than the throne of a Borgia pope.

Now the Reverend Sutter hopped down to the lowest set level, a series of carpeted ramps and semicircular extensions of the main set that al- lowed the director to use angles from the recessed camera positions to show Sutter in the same shot as the six hundred members of the audience. This studio was used for the daily "Bible Breakfast Hour Show" as well as the longer "Bible Outreach Program with Jimmy Wayne Sutter" now be- ing taped. Shows requiring the larger cast or bigger audience were taped in the Palace of Worship or on location.

"I'm only a modest, backwoods preacher," Sutter said in a sudden shift to a conversational tone, "but with *God's* help and *your* help, we'll put these trials and tribulations behind us. With *God's* help and *your* help, we will pass through these times of persecution so that God's Word will come through LOUDER and STRONGER and CLEARER than ever before."

Sutter mopped his sweaty brow with a silk handkerchief. "But if we are to stay on the air, dear friends . . . if we are to continue bringing *you* the Lord's message through *His* gospels . . . we need *your* help. We need your prayers, we need your defiant letters to those Big Gov'ment bureaucrats who hound us, and we need your love offerings . . . we need whatever you can give in Christ's name to help us keep the Word of God coming to *you*. We *know* that *you* will not let us down. And while you are calling in those pledges—addressing those love-offering envelopes that Kris and Kay and brother Lyle have sent to you this month—let's hear Gail and the Gospel Guitars along with our own Bible Outreach Singers reminding you that— 'You Don't Need To Understand, You Just Need To Hold His Hand.' "

The floor director gave Sutter a four-fingered countdown and cued him with a flick of his baton when it was time to come back from the pledge break. The Reverend was seated at his writing table; the chair next to it was empty. The couch was beginning to look crowded.

Sutter, looking relaxed and somewhat buoyant, smiled into the lens of camera two. "Friends, speaking of the power of God's love, speaking of the power of eternal salvation, speaking of the gift of being born again in Jesus' name . . . it gives me very great pleasure to introduce our next guest. For years our next guest was lost in that west coast web of sin we have all heard about . . . for years this good soul wandered far from Christ's light into the dark forest of fear and fornication that lies in wait for those who fail to heed God's Word . . . but here tonight to witness to Jesus' infinite mercy and power, His infinite love that allows no one wishing to be found to remain lost . . . here is the famed filmmaker, Hollywood director and producer . . . *Anthony Harod!*"

Harod crossed the wide set to the sound of enthusiastic applause from six hundred Christians who had not the faintest idea of who he was. He held out his hand, but Jimmy Wayne Sutter jumped to his feet, embraced Harod, and waved him to the guest's chair. Harod sat down and crossed his legs nervously. The singer grinned at him from his place on the couch, the apocalyptic writer looked coolly at him, and the overweight actress made a cute face and blew him a kiss. Harod was wearing jeans, his favorite snakeskin cowboy boots, an open red silk shirt, and his R2-D2 belt buckle.

Jimmy Wayne Sutter leaned closer and folded his hands. "Well, Anthony, Anthony, Anthony."

Harod smiled uncertainly and squinted out toward the audience. Because of the bright television lights, only an occasional glint of glasses was visible.

"Anthony, you have been a fixture on the tinsel town scene for . . . how many years now?"

"Ah . . . sixteen years," said Harod and cleared his throat. "I started there in 1964 . . . uh . . . I was nineteen. Started as a screenwriter."

"And Anthony . . ." Sutter leaned forward, his voice managing to be both jovial and conspiratorial, "is it true what we hear . . . about the sinfulness of Hollywood . . . not all of Hollywood, mind you, not everyone there . . . Kay and I have several good Christian friends there, yourself included, Anthony . . . but generally speaking, is it as sinful as they say?"

"It's pretty sinful," said Harod and uncrossed his legs. "It's . . . ah . . . it's pretty bad."

"Divorce?" said Sutter.

"Everywhere."

"Drugs?"

"Everyone does them."

"Hard stuff?"

"Oh yes."

"Cocaine?"

"Common as candy."

"Heroin?"

"Even the stars have track marks, Jimmy."

"People taking the name of the Lord God in vain?"

"Constantly."

"Blaspheming?"

"It's the in thing to do."

"Satan worship?"

"So the rumors say."

"Worship of the Almighty Dollar?"

"No doubt of that."

"And what about the Seventh Commandment, Anthony?"

"Uh . . ."

"Thou shalt not commit adultery?"

"Ah . . . ignored completely, I'd say . . ."

"You've seen those wild Hollywood parties, Anthony?"

"I've gone to my share . . ."

"Drug abuse, fornication, blatant adultery, pursuit of the Almighty Dollar, worship of the Evil One, defiance of God's Laws . . ."

"Yeah," said Harod, "and that's at just one of the duller parties." The audience emitted a sound that was somewhere between a cough and a stifled gasp.

The Reverend Jimmy Wayne Sutter steepled his fingers. "And Anthony, tell us your story, your history, your descent and ultimate elevation from this . . . this . . . mink-lined *pit*."

Harod smiled slightly, the corners of his mouth flicking up. "Well, Jimmy, I was young . . . impressionable . . . willing to be led. I confess that the lure of that life-style led me down the dark path for some time. Years."

"And there were worldly compensations . . ." prompted Sutter.

Harod nodded and found the camera with the red light on. He gave the lens a look both sincere and slightly sad. "As you've said here, Jimmy, the Devil has his levers. Money . . . more money than I knew what to do with, Jimmy. Fast cars. Big houses. Women . . . beautiful women . . . famous stars with famous faces and beautiful bodies . . . all I had to do was pick up the telephone, Jimmy. There was a sense of false power. There was the false sense of status. There was the drinking and drugs. The road to hell can run straight through a hot tub, Jimmy."

"Amen!" cried the overweight TV actress.

Sutter nodded, looked earnest and concerned. "But, Anthony, the really *frightening* part . . . the fact we have most to *fear* . . . is that these are the people who are producing films, movies, so-called *entertainments* for our *children*. Isn't that right?"

"Exactly right, Jimmy. And the movies they make are ruled by only one consideration . . . profit."

Sutter looked into camera one as it zoomed in for a close-up. There was no levity in his face now; the strong jaw, dark brows, and long, wavy white hair might have been that of an Old Testament prophet. "And what our

HAZEL M. LEWIS LIBRARY
POWERS, OREGON 97466

children get, dear friends, is *dirt*. Dirt and garbage. When I was a boy . . .
when most of us were children . . . we saved up our quarters and went to
the moving picture show . . . if we were allowed to go to the moving picture
show . . . and we went to the Saturday matinee and we saw a cartoon . . .
Whatever happened to cartoons, Anthony? And after the cartoon we saw a
Western . . . remember Hoot Gibson? Remember Hopalong Cassidy? Remember Roy Rogers? God bless him . . . Roy was on our show last
week . . . a fine man . . . a generous man . . . and then perhaps a John
Wayne movie. And we would go home and know that the good guys win
and that America was a special place . . . a blessed country. Remember
John Wayne in *The Fighting Seabees*? And we would go home to our families . . . remember Mickey Rooney in *Andy Hardy*? Go home to our families and know that the family was important . . . that our country was
important . . . that goodness and respect and authority and loving one
another was important . . . that restraint and discipline and self-control
was important . . . that GOD WAS IMPORTANT!"

Sutter took off his bifocals. His forehead and upper lip were sheened
with sweat. "And what do our children see NOW?! They see pornography
and godlessness and filth and garbage and dirt. You go to a movie now . . .
a PG movie mind you, I am not even talking about the filthy R-rated and
X-rated movies that are everywhere, spreading like cancers, any child can
get in, there is no age limit anymore, though that too is hypocrisy . . . filth
is filth . . . what is not good for our sixteen-year-olds is not good for
grownup, God-fearing citizens . . . but the children go, oh, how they go!
And they see PG movies that show them nakedness and profanity . . . one
curse word after the other, one profanity after the other . . . and the movies tear down the family, *tear* it down, and tear down the country, *tear* it
down, and tear down the Laws of God and laugh at the Word of God and
give them sex and violence and filth and excitation. And you say, what can
I do? What can *we* do? And I say this: Get close to God, get full of the
Word, get so full of Jesus Christ that this garbage, this trash holds no attraction . . . and get your CHILDREN to accept Jesus, accept Jesus into
their HEARTS, accept Jesus as their SAVIOR, their PERSONAL Savior,
and then the movie filth will have no attraction, this Hollywood version of
Gomorrah will have no appeal . . . 'The Father hath committed all judgment unto the Son . . . the Father hath given him authority to execute
judgment . . . the hour is coming . . . all that are in the graves shall hear
His voice, and shall come forth; they that have done good unto the resur-
rection of life; and they that have done evil . . . *they that have done evil* . . .
will rise to hear their doom' John 5:22–26–28."

The crowd shouted hallelujahs. "Praise Jesus!" cried the singer. The
apocalyptic writer closed his eyes and nodded. The overweight actress
sobbed.

"Anthony," Sutter said in a low voice that drew attention back to him,
"you have accepted the Lord?"

"I have, Jimmy. I found the Lord . . ."

"And accepted him as your personal Savior?"

"Yes, Jimmy. I took Jesus Christ into my life . . ."

"And allowed him to lead you out of the forest of fear and fornication . . . out of the false glare of Hollywood's sickness into the healing light of God's Word . . ."

"I have, Jimmy. Christ has renewed the joy in my life, given me purpose to continue living and working in His name . . ."

"God's name be praised," breathed Sutter and smiled beatifically. He shook his head as if overcome and turned toward camera three. The floor director was rolling his fingers in an urgent circle. "And our good news . . . in the near future, the very near future, I hope . . . Anthony will be bringing his skills and talents and expertise to a *very special* Bible Outreach project . . . we can't say too much about it now, but be assured that we will be using all of the wonderful skills of Hollywood to bring *God's Word* to millions of the good Christians who hunger for solid family entertainment."

The audience and other guests responded with enthusiastic applause. Sutter leaned toward the microphone and spoke over the noise. "Tomorrow, a special Bible Outreach service of Sacred Music . . . our special guests, Pat Boone, Patsy Dillon, the Good News Singers, and our own Gail and the Gospel Guitars . . ."

The applause grew louder as electronic prompters flashed. Camera three came in for an extreme close-up of Sutter. The reverend smiled. "Until next time, remember John 3:16—'God so loved the world that he gave his only begotten Son, whosoever believeth in Him shall have everlasting life.' Good-bye! God bless you all!"

Sutter and Harod left the set as soon as the red On-the-Air lights went off, before the applause had ended, and walked quickly through carpeted and air-conditioned corridors. Maria Chen and the Reverend's wife, Kay, were waiting in Sutter's outer office. "What do you think, dear?" asked Sutter.

Kay Ellen Sutter was tall and thin, weighted down with layers of makeup and a hairdo that looked as if it had been sculpted and left in place for years. "Wonderful, dear. Excellent."

"We'll have to get rid of that blame fool singer's monologue when he started raving on about Jews in the record business," said Sutter. "Oh, well, we've got to cut about twenty minutes before it's ready to broadcast anyway." He put on his bifocals and peered at his wife. "Where you two ladies headed?"

"I thought I would show Maria the day-care and nursery over at married student housing," said Kay Sutter.

"Great, great!" said the Reverend. "Anthony and I've got one more brief meeting and then it'll be time to get you good folks out to the airstrip for the hop up to Atlanta."

Maria Chen gave Harod a look. Harod shrugged. The two women left with Kay Ellen Sutter talking at a brisk pace.

The Reverend Jimmy Wayne Sutter's office was huge, thickly carpeted, and decorated in subtle beiges and earth tones in great contrast to the red, white, and blue decor prevailing elsewhere in the complex. One long wall was a curved window looking out on pastureland and a small patch of woodland preserved by the developers. Behind Sutter's broad desk, thirty feet of teak wall space was literally covered with signed photographs of the famed and powerful, certificates of merit, service awards, plaques, and other documentation of the status and lasting power of Jimmy Wayne Sutter.

Harod sprawled in a chair and straightened his legs. "Whew!"

Sutter pulled off his suit jacket, draped it over the back of his leather executive's chair, and sat down, rolling up his sleeves and clasping his hands behind his head. "Well, Anthony, was it the lark you expected it to be?"

Harod ran his hands through his permed hair. "I just hope to hell that none of my backers saw that."

Sutter smiled. "Why is that, Anthony? Does associating with the godly cause one to lose points in the film community?"

"Looking like an asshole does," said Harod. He glanced toward a kitchen area at the far end of the room. "Can I get a drink?"

"Certainly," said Sutter. "Do you mind making it yourself? You know the way."

Harod had already crossed the room. He filled a glass with Smirnoff's and ice and pulled another bottle from the concealed cupboard. "Bourbon?"

"Please," said Sutter. When Harod handed him his drink, the Reverend said, "Are you glad you accepted my little invitation to come visit for a few days, Anthony?"

Harod sipped at his vodka. "Do you think it was smart to tip our hand by having me on the show?"

"They knew you were here," said Sutter. "Kepler is keeping track of you and both he and Brother C. are watching over me. Maybe your witnessing will serve to confuse them a might."

"It sure as hell served to confuse me," Harod said and went to refill his drink.

Sutter chuckled and sorted through papers on his desk. "Anthony, please do not get the idea that I am cynical about my ministry."

Harod paused in the act of dropping ice chips into his glass and stared at Sutter. "You have to be shitting me," he said. "This setup is the most cynical rube trap I've ever seen."

"Not at all," Sutter said softly. "My ministry is real. My care for the people is real. My gratitude for the Ability God has granted me is real."

Harod shook his head. "Jimmy Wayne, for two days you've been showing me around this fundamentalist Disneyland and every goddamn thing

I've seen is designed to separate some provincial moron's money from his genuine K-Mart imitation cowhide wallet. You've got machines sorting the letters with checks from the empty ones, you've got computers scanning the letters and writing their own replies, you've got computerized phone banks, direct mail campaigns that'd make Dick Viggerie want to cream his pants, and televised church services that make Mr. Ed reruns look like highbrow programming . . ."

"Anthony, Anthony," said Sutter and shook his head, "you must look beyond the superficial at the deeper truths. The faithful in my electronic congregation are . . . for the most part . . . simpletons, hicks, and the born again brain dead. But this does not make my ministry a sham, Anthony."

"It doesn't?"

"Not at all. I *love* these people!" Sutter pounded the desk with his huge fist. "Fifty years ago when I was a young evangelist . . . seven years old and filled with the Word . . . going from tent revival to tent revival with my daddy and Aunt El, I knew then that Jesus had given me the Ability for a reason . . . and not just to make money." Sutter picked up a slip of paper and peered at it through his bifocals. "Anthony, tell me who you think wrote this:

> Preachers . . . 'dread the advance of science as witches do the approach of daylight and scowl on the fatal harbinger announcing the subversion of the duperies on which they live.' "

Sutter looked over the top of his bifocals at Harod. "Tell me who you think wrote that, Anthony."

Harod shrugged. "H. L. Mencken? Madalyn Murray O'Hair?"

Sutter shook his head. "Jefferson, Anthony. *Thomas* Jefferson."

"So?"

Sutter pointed a large, blunt finger at Harod. "Don't you see, Anthony? For all the evangelicals' talk about this nation being founded on religious principles . . . this being a Christian nation and all . . . most of the Founding Fathers were like Jefferson . . . atheists, pointy-headed intellectuals, *Unitarians* . . ."

"So?"

"So the country was founded by a flock of fuzzy-minded secular 'humanists, Anthony. That's why we can't have God in our schools anymore. That's why they're killing a million unborn babies a day. That's why the Communists are growin' stronger while we're talking arms reduction. God gave *me* the Ability to stir the hearts and souls of common people so that we can *make* this country a Christian nation, Anthony."

"And that's why you want my help in exchange for your support and protection from the Island Club," said Harod.

"You scratch my back, boy," said Sutter with a smile, "I'll keep 'em off'n yours."

"It sounds like you want to be president someday," said Harod. "I thought that yesterday we were just talking about rearranging the pecking order in the Island Club a little bit."

Sutter opened his hands, palms up. "What's wrong with thinking big, Anthony? Brother C., Kepler, Trask, and Colben've all been foolin' around with politics for decades. I *met* Brother C. forty years ago at a political rally of conservative preachers at Baton Rouge. There's nothing wrong with the idea of putting a good Christian in the White House for a change."

"I thought Jimmy Carter was supposed to have been a good Christian," said Harod.

"Jimmy Carter was a born-again wimp," said Sutter. "A real Christian would have known just what to do with the Ayatollah when that pagan put his hands on American citizens. The Bible says . . . 'An eye for an eye, a tooth for a tooth.' We should've left those Moslem Shee-ite bastards toothless."

"To hear NCPAC tell it, it's the Christians who just put Reagan in," said Harod. He got up to pour more vodka. Political discussions always bored him.

"Bull-hockey," said Jimmy Wayne Sutter. "Brother C., Kepler, and that donkey's behind Trask, put our friend Ronald where he is. Dolan and the NCPAC nitwits are premature. The country is taking a turn to the right, but there will be temporary reversals. By 1988 or '92, however, the way will be prepared for a *real* Christian candidate."

"You?" said Harod. "Aren't there others in line before you?"

Sutter scowled. "Who, for instance?"

"Whatshisname," said Harod, "the Moral Majority guy. Falwell."

Sutter laughed. "Jerry was *created* by our right-wing friends in Washington. He's a golem. When his financing dries up, everybody may notice that he's a man-shaped heap of mud. And not very smart mud at that."

"What about some of those older guys," said Harod, trying to remember the names of the faith healers and snake charmers he had flipped by on L.A. cable. "Rex Hobart . . ."

"*Humbard*," corrected Sutter, "and Oral Roberts, I suppose. Are you out of your mind, Anthony?"

"What do you mean?"

Sutter extracted a Havana cigar from a humidor and lit it. "We're talking about people here with cowflop still sticking to their boots," said the Reverend Jimmy Wayne Sutter. "We're talking about good old boys who go on TV and say, 'Put your sick or ailing body part against the television screen, friends, and I will *heal* it!' Can you image, Anthony, all the hemorrhoids and boils and sores and yeast infections . . . and the man who *blesses* all that biology meeting foreign dignitaries, sleeping in Lincoln's bedroom?"

"It boggles the mind," said Harod, starting on his fourth vodka. "What about some of the others. You know, your competitors?"

The Reverend Sutter linked his hands behind his head again and smiled. "Well, there's Jim and Tammy, but they're up shit creek half the time with the FCC . . . makes my troubles look pretty piddlin'. Besides they take turns having nervous breakdowns. I don't blame Jim. With a wife like that, I would too. Then there's Swaggart over in Louisiana. He's a smart 'un, Anthony. But I think he really wants to be a rock 'n' roll star like his cousin . . ."

"His cousin?" said Harod.

"Jerry Lee Lewis," said Sutter. "So who else is there? Pat Robertson, of course. My guess is that Pat will run in '84 or '88. He's formidable. His network makes my little Outreach project look like a tin can and a bunch of strings going nowhere. But Pat has liabilities. Folks sometimes forget that he's supposed to be a minister and so does Pat . . ."

"This is all very interesting," said Harod, "but we're getting away from the reason I came down here."

Sutter took off his glasses, removed the cigar from his mouth, and stared. "You came down here, Anthony, because your useless ass is in a sling and unless you get some help on your side, the Club is going to end up using you for one of its after-dinner amusements on the Island . . ."

"Hey," said Harod, "I'm a full-fledged member of the Steering Committee now."

"Yes," said Sutter. "And Trask is dead. Colben is dead. Kepler is lying low, and Brother C. was embarrassed by the fiasco in Philadelphia."

"Which I had nothing to do with," said Harod.

"Which you managed to extricate yourself from," said Sutter. "Dear God, what a mess. Five FBI agents and six of Colben's special people dead. A dozen local blacks killed. A local minister murdered. Fires, destruction of private and public property . . ."

"The media still buys the gang warfare story," said Harod. "The FBI was supposed to be there because of the black militant group of terrorists . . ."

"Yes, and the repercussions are reaching all the way to the mayor's office and beyond . . . to Washington even. Did you know that Richard Haines is now working privately—and discreetly—for Brother C.?"

"Who gives a shit?" said Harod.

"Precisely." Jimmy Wayne Sutter smiled. "But you see why your addition to the Steering Committee comes at a . . . sensitive time."

"You're sure they want to use me to get to Willi," said Harod.

"Absolutely," said Sutter.

"And then they'll dump me?"

"Literally," said Sutter.

"Why?" asked Harod. "Why would they take a murderous old psychopath like Willi?"

"There's an old desert saying that was never included in Scripture but was old enough to have been recorded in the Old Testament," said Sutter.

"What's that?"

" 'It's better to have a camel inside the tent pissing out than outside pissing in,' " intoned Sutter.

"Thank you, Reverend," said Harod.

"You're welcome, Anthony." Sutter glanced at his watch. "You'd better hurry if we're going to get you to Atlanta in time for your flight."

Harod sobered up quickly. "Do you know why Barent called this meeting for Saturday?"

Sutter made a vague gesture. "I presume Brother C. called it because of this Monday's events."

"Reagan's shooting . . ."

"Yes," said Sutter, "but did you know who was with the president . . . three steps behind him . . . when the shots rang out?"

Harod raised his eyebrows.

"Yes, Brother C. himself," said Sutter. "I imagine we will have lots to talk about."

"Jesus" said Harod.

Jimmy Wayne Sutter scowled. "You will *not* take the name of the Lord God in vain in this room," he snapped. "Nor would I advise that you do it in the presence of Brother C."

Harod walked to the door, paused. "One thing, Jimmy, why do you call Barent 'Brother C.'?"

"Because C. Arnold does not care for it when I call him by his Christian name," said Sutter.

Harod looked amazed. "You *know* it?"

"Of course," said Sutter. "I have known Brother C. since the nineteen thirties when both of us were little more than children."

"What is it?"

"C. Arnold's Christian name is Christian," said Sutter with a smile.

"Huh?"

"Christian," repeated Sutter. "Christian Arnold Barent. His daddy believed even if Brother C. does not."

"Well I'll be goddamned," said Harod and hurried out of the room before Sutter could say a word.

THIRTY-SEVEN

Caesarea, Israel
Tuesday, April 2, 1981

Natalie Preston landed at the David Ben-Gurion Airport near Lod on the El Al flight from Vienna at 10:30 A.M. local time. Israeli Customs was calm and efficient if not overly courteous. "Welcome back to Israel, Miss Hapshaw," said the man behind the counter as he checked her two bags. It was her third entry into the country on the false passport and her heart still pounded as she waited. It was only slightly reassuring that the Mossad, Israel's own intelligence agency, had forged the documents in the first place.

Once through Customs she took the El Al bus to Tel Aviv and walked from the bus station on Jaffa Road to the ITS/Avis outlet on Hamasger Street. She paid the weekly rate and left a four-hundred-dollar deposit for a green 1975 Opel with brakes that pulled to the left every time she stopped.

It was early afternoon by the time Natalie left the ugly suburbs of Tel Aviv and drove north along the coast on the Haifa Road. It was a sunny day, the temperature was in the high 50s, and Natalie pulled on her sunglasses as midday glare reflected off the highway and the Mediterranean. About twenty miles from Tel Aviv she passed through Netanya, a cluttered little resort town set on cliffs above the beach. Some miles beyond that she saw the sign for Or Akiva and left the four-lane highway for a narrower asphalt road that wound through sand dunes toward the beach. She caught a glimpse of the Roman aqueduct and the massive ramparts of the Crusader City, and then she was following the old coastal road past the Dan Caesarea Hotel with its eighteen-hole golf course secured behind a perimeter of high fence and concertina barbed wire.

She turned east onto a gravel road and followed a sign for Kibbutz Ma'agan Mikhael until another, narrower lane intersected it. The Opel bounced its way a quarter of a mile uphill through stands of carob trees, around thick clusters of pistachio bushes, and past an occasional pine tree before stopping at a padlocked gate. Natalie got out of the car, stretched her legs, and waved at the white house on the hilltop.

Saul Laski came down the lane to let her in. He had lost weight and shaved his beard. His thin legs protruding from baggy khaki shorts and his narrow chest under a white T-shirt should have made him look like a parody of a prisoner from *The Bridge on the River Kwai*, but the effect was more of deeply tanned skin over lean muscle. His bald spot was more pronounced because of sunburn, but the rest of his hair had bleached grayer and grown longer, curling down over his ears and the back of his neck. He had traded his broken horn-rimmed glasses for a pair of silver aviator-style glasses that darkened in the bright sun. The scar on his left arm was still a raw red.

He unlocked the gate and they hugged each other briefly.

"Did it go well?" he asked.

"Very well," said Natalie. "Simon Wiesenthal says to say hello."

"He is in good health?"

"Very good health for a man his age."

"And was he able to direct you to the right sources?"

"Better than that," said Natalie, "he did the searching himself. What he didn't have in that strange little office of his, he had his researchers bring from the various Vienna libraries and registries and such."

"Excellent," said Saul. "And the other things?"

Natalie gestured toward her large suitcase in the backseat. "Filled with photocopies. It's terrible stuff, Saul. Are you still going to Yad Vashem twice a week?"

"No," said Saul. "There is a place not far from here, Lohame HaGeta'ot, built by Poles."

"And it's like Yad Vashem?"

"On a smaller scale," said Saul. "It will suffice if I have the names and case histories. Come drive through, and I will lock the gate and ride up with you."

There was a very large white house on the summit of the hill. Natalie followed the road past it, down the south side of the hill, to where a small whitewashed bungalow sat at the edge of an orange grove. The view was incredible. To the west, beyond the groves and cultivated fields, lay sand dunes and ruins and the serried breakers of the blue Mediterranean. To the south, shimmering in the heat daze of distance, rose the forested cliffs of Netanya. East lay a series of hills and the orange-scented Sharon Valley. North, beyond Templars' castles, fortresses old in Solomon's time, and the green ridge of Mount Carmel, lay Haifa with its narrow streets of rain-washed stone. Natalie was glad to be back.

Saul held the door open for her as she carried her bag in. The cottage was just as she had left it eight days earlier; small kitchen and dining room combined in a long room with fireplace: simple wooden table with three chairs, another chair by the fireplace, small windows spilling rich sunlight onto whitewashed walls, and two bedrooms. Natalie carried her bags into her room and tossed them on the big bed. Saul had set fresh flowers in the white vase on her nightstand.

He was brewing coffee when she came out to the main room. "Good trip?" he asked. "No problems?"

"No problems," said Natalie. She laid out some dossiers on the rough wood of the table. "Sarah Hapshaw is getting to see all the places Natalie Preston never saw."

Saul nodded and set a white mug of rich, black coffee in front of her.

"Any problems here?" she asked.

"None," said Saul. "None were expected."

She added sugar from a blue bowl and stirred. She realized that she was very tired. Saul sat down across from her and patted her hand. Even though his thin face was etched with planes and lines, she thought that he looked younger than when he had worn a beard. Three months ago. Centuries ago.

"More news from Jack," he said. "Would you like to take a walk?"

She glanced at her coffee.

"Take it with you," said Saul. "We'll walk toward the hippodrome." He stood up and went into his bedroom for a second. When he returned, he was wearing a loose khaki shirt with the shirttails out. It did not quite hide the bulge of the .45 automatic in the waistband of his shorts.

They strolled west, downhill, past the fences and orange groves to where sand dunes crept toward the cultivated fields and green private grounds of villas. Saul walked out from the top of a dune onto the surface of an aqueduct that rose twenty-five feet above the sand and stretched for miles toward the cluster of ruins and new buildings near the sea. A young man in a white shirt ran toward them, shouting and waving his arms, but Saul spoke to him quietly in Hebrew and the man nodded and turned away. Saul and Natalie walked along the rough top of the aqueduct.

"What did you say to him?" asked Natalie.

"I mentioned that I knew the trinity of Frova, Avi-Yonah, and Negev," said Saul. "Those three have been excavating the sites here since the nineteen fifties."

"Is that all?"

"Yes," said Saul. He stopped and looked around. The Mediterranean lay to their right; a riot of low new buildings caught afternoon sunlight a mile ahead.

"When you told me about your place here, I imagined a shack in the desert," said Natalie.

"That is what it was when I came here right after the war," said Saul. "First we built and enlarged Kibbutzum Gaash, Kfar Vitkin, and Ma'agan Mikhael. After the War of Independence, David and Rebecca built their farm here . . ."

"It's an estate!" said Natalie.

Saul smiled and sipped at the last of his coffee. "The Baron Rothschild's place is an estate. That is now the five-star Dan Caesarea Hotel down there."

"I love the ruins," said Natalie. "The aqueduct, the theater, the Crusader City, it's all so . . . *old*."

Saul nodded. "I missed that sense of overlay of ages when I was in America."

Natalie removed the red shoulder bag she had been carrying and set their empty coffee cups in it, wrapping them carefully in a towel. "I miss America," she said. She hugged her knees and looked out over the expanse of sand that lapped against the yellow stone aqueduct like a tan and frozen sea. "I *think* I miss America," she said. "Those last days were so nightmarish . . ."

Saul said nothing and the two sat in silence for several unstrained minutes.

Natalie spoke first. "I wonder who went to Rob's funeral."

Saul glanced at her, his polarized glasses reflecting the light. "Jack Cohen wrote that Sheriff Gentry was buried in a Charleston cemetery with members of several local agencies and police forces attending."

"Yes," said Natalie, "but I mean who was *close* to him. Were there any family members there? His friend Daryl Meeks? Anyone who had . . . had loved him?" Natalie stopped.

Saul handed her his handkerchief. "It would have been madness for you to go," he said softly. "*They* would have recognized you. Besides, you were in no condition. The doctors in Jerusalem Hospital said that your ankle had a very bad break." Saul smiled at her and accepted his handkerchief back. "I noticed almost no limp today."

"No," said Natalie, "it's much better." She returned Saul's smile. "OK," she said, "who goes first?"

"You, I think," said Saul. "Jack had some very interesting news, but I want to hear about Vienna."

Natalie nodded. "Hotel registries confirmed that they were there . . . Miss Melanie Fuller and Nina Hawkins . . . that was the Drayton woman's maiden name . . . the Hotel Imperial . . . 1925, '26, and '27. The Hotel Metropole in '33, '34, and '35. They could have been there other years, in other hotels that lost their records because of the war or some other reason. Mr. Wiesenthal is still checking."

"And von Borchert?" said Saul.

"No hotel registration," said Natalie, "but Wiesenthal confirmed that Wilhelm von Borchert rented a small villa in Perchtoldsdorf just outside of the city from 1922 until 1939. It was torn down after the war."

"What about . . . the others?" asked Saul. "Crimes."

"Murders," said Natalie. "The usual assortment of street crime, political killings . . . crimes of passion and so forth. Then, in the summer of 1925, three bizarre, inexplicable murders. Two important men and a woman—a prominent Vienna socialite—murdered by acquaintances. In each case, the murderers had no motives, no alibis, no excuses. The papers called it 'summer insanity' because each of the killers swore they had no memory of their deeds. All three were found guilty. One man was executed, one committed suicide, and the third . . . a woman . . . was sent to an asylum where she drowned in a fish pond a week after she was institutionalized."

"Sounds like our young mind vampires were beginning their game," said Saul. "Getting a taste for blood."

"Mr. Wiesenthal couldn't understand the connections," said Natalie, "but he kept researching for us. Seven unexplained murders in the summer of 1926. Eleven between June and August of 1927 . . . but that was the summer of an abortive *Putsch* . . . there were eighty workers killed in a demonstration that got out of hand . . . Vienna authorities had more to worry about than the deaths of some lower-class citizens."

"So our trio changed their targets," said Saul. "Perhaps the deaths of members of their own social circle put too much pressure on them."

"We couldn't find any crime reports that fit in the winter or summer of 1928," said Natalie, "but in 1929, there were seven mysterious disappearances in the Austrian resort town of Bad Ischl. Vienna press talked about the 'Zauner Werewolf' because all of the people who disappeared—several of them very important figures in Vienna or Berlin—had last been seen in the chic Café Zauner on the Esplanade."

"But no confirmation that our young German and his two American ladies were there?" asked Saul.

"Not yet," said Natalie. "But Mr. Wiesenthal points out that there were scores of private villas and hotels in the area that no longer exist."

Saul nodded in satisfaction. Both of them looked up as a formation of five Israeli F-16s roared low over the Mediterranean, headed south. "It's a beginning," said Saul. "We will need more detail, much more detail, but it is a beginning." They sat in silence for several minutes. The sun was getting lower in the southwest, throwing the intricate shadows of their aqueduct farther across the dunes. The world seemed wrapped in a red and golden glow. Finally, Saul said, "Herod the Great, a fawning sycophant, started this city in 22 B.C., dedicating it to Caesar Augustus. It was a center of power by 6 A.D., the theater, hippodrome, and aqueducts all gleaming white. For a decade, Pontius Pilate was prefect here."

Natalie frowned at him. "You told me most of this when we first came here in February," she said.

"Yes," said Saul. "Look." He pointed to the dunes lapping high on the stone arches. "Most of this has been buried for the last fifteen hundred years. The aqueduct we're sitting on was not excavated until the early sixties."

"So?" asked Natalie.

"So what of Caesar's power?" asked Saul. "What of Herod's ingratiating schemes? What of the apostle Paul's fears and apprehensions when he was imprisoned here?" Saul waited several seconds. "All dead," he said. "Dead and covered with the sands of time. Power gone, the artifacts of power toppled and buried. Nothing left but stone and memories."

"What are you saying, Saul?" asked Natalie.

"The Oberst and the Fuller woman must be at least in their seventies by now," said Saul. "The photograph Aaron showed me was of a man in his sixties. As Rob Gentry once said, they are mortal. They will not rise with the next full moon."

"So we just stay here?" snapped Natalie, her voice rising in anger. "We just hunker down here until these . . . these *monsters* die of old age or kill each other off?"

"Here or somewhere else safe," said Saul. "You know what the alternative is. We, too, must take life."

Natalie stood up and paced back and forth on the narrow stone wall. "You forget, Saul, I've already taken life. I shot that awful boy—Vincent—the one whom the old lady was using."

"He was a thing by that time," said Saul. "You did not take his life, Melanie Fuller did that. You released his body from her control."

"They're *all* things as far as I'm concerned," said Natalie. "We *have* to go back."

"Yes, but . . ." began Saul.

"I can't believe you're serious about not going after them," said Natalie. "All the risk that Jack Cohen has taken for us in Washington, using his computers to dig up all this information. My weeks of research in Toronto and France and Vienna. The hundreds of hours you've spent on Yad Vashem . . ."

Saul stood up. "It was just a suggestion," he said. "At the very least, it might not be necessary for both of us to . . ."

"Ah, so *that's* it," said Natalie. "Well, forget it, Saul. They killed my father. They killed Rob. One of them touched me with his filthy mind. There are only the two of us and I still don't know what we can do, but I *am* going back. With you or without you, Saul, I'm going back."

"All right," said Saul Laski. He handed her the shoulder bag and their hands touched. "I just had to be sure."

"*I'm* sure," said Natalie. "Tell me about the new stuff from Cohen."

"Later," said Saul, "after dinner." Touching her lightly on the arm, they turned back for the long walk along the aqueduct, their shadows mingling, bending, and twisting along the high banks of encroaching sand.

Saul prepared an excellent dinner of salad with fresh fruit, homebaked bread he called *bagele* which looked and tasted nothing like a bagel, mutton cooked in the Oriental style, and sweet Turkish coffee. It was dark when they went into his room to work and turned up the hissing Coleman lantern.

The long table was covered with folders, stacks of photocopied documents, piles of photographs—the top ones showing concentration camp victims staring passively out—and dozens of yellow pads filled with Saul's tight scribble. Sheets of white paper covered with names, date, and maps of concentration camps were taped to the rough white walls. Natalie noticed the aging photocopy of the young Oberst and several SS officers smiling from their newspaper photograph next to an 8×10 color print of Melanie Fuller and her manservant crossing the courtyard of their Charleston house.

They sat at heavy, comfortable chairs and Saul pulled over a thick dossier. "Jack thinks that they've located Melanie Fuller," he said.

Natalie sat straight up. "Where?"

"Charleston," said Saul. "Her old house."

Natalie slowly shook her head. "Impossible. She couldn't be that stupid."

Saul opened the file and looked at the sheets typed on Israeli Embassy stationery. "The Fuller house had been closed pending final legal determination of the status of Melanie Fuller. It would have taken some time for the courts to declare her legally dead, much longer for the estate to be worked out. There seemed to be no surviving relations. In the meantime, a certain Howard Warden appeared claiming to be Melanie Fuller's grandnephew. He showed letters and documents—including a last will and testament dated January 8, 1978—deeding the house and its possessions to him as of that date . . . *not* in the case of her death . . . and giving him full power of attorney. Warden explained that the old lady had been concerned about failing health and the onset of senility. He said that it had been a technicality, that he fully expected his great aunt to live out her life in the house, but with her disappearance and presumed death, he felt it was important that someone maintain the place. He is currently living there with his family."

"Could he really be a long-lost relative?" asked Natalie.

"It seems unlikely," said Saul. "Jack managed to get some information about Warden. He grew up in Ohio and moved to Philadelphia about fourteen years ago. He had been assistant grounds superintendent for the city park for the last four years, actually living in Fairmount Park the last three . . ."

"Fairmount Park!" gasped Natalie. "That's near where Melanie Fuller disappeared."

"Exactly," said Saul. "According to sources in Philadelphia, Warden—who's thirty-seven—had a wife and three children, two girls and a boy. In Charleston, his wife fits the same description, but they have only one child . . . a five-year-old boy named Justin."

"But . . ." began Natalie.

"Wait, there's more," said Saul. "The Hodges place next door was also sold in March. It was purchased by an M.D. named Stephen Hartman. Dr. Hartman lives there with his wife and their twenty-three-year-old daughter."

"What's wrong with that?" asked Natalie. "I can understand why Mrs. Hodges wouldn't want to return to that house."

"Yes," said Saul and pushed his aviator's glasses higher on his nose, "but it seems that Dr. Hartman is also from Philadelphia . . . a very successful neurologist . . . who suddenly quit his practice, got married, and left the city in March. The same week that Howard Warden and family felt a need to move south. Dr. Hartman's new wife—his third—and friends were amazed that he married again—is Susan Oldsmith, the former head nurse in the intensive care wing of Philadelphia General Hospital . . ."

"There's nothing terribly unusual about a doctor marrying a nurse, is there?" asked Natalie.

"No," said Saul, "but according to Jack Cohen's inquiries, Dr. Hartman's relationship with Nurse Oldsmith might have been described as coolly professional up to the week they both resigned and were married. Perhaps more interestingly, neither of the happy newlyweds had a twenty-three-year-old daughter . . ."

"Then who . . . ?"

"The young lady whom Charleston now knows as Constance Hartman bears a strong resemblance to a certain Connie Sewell, a nurse in intensive care at Philadelphia General who resigned the same week as Nurse Oldsmith. Jack hasn't been able to make a certain match, but Ms. Sewell left her apartment and friends with no word of where she was going."

Natalie stood up and paced back and forth in the small room, ignoring the hiss of the lantern and the dramatic shadows she threw on the wall. "So we assume that Melanie Fuller was hurt or injured in the craziness in Philadelphia. Those newspaper stories talked about a car and body being found in the Schuylkill River near where the FBI helicopter crashed. It wasn't her. I *knew* she was alive somewhere. I could *feel* it. Okay, so she's hurt somehow. She gets this park guy to take her to a local hospital. Did Cohen check the hospital records?"

"Of course," said Saul. "He found that the FBI—or someone posing as the FBI—had been there before him. No record of a Melanie Fuller. Lots of old ladies in the hospitals, but none who fit the profile of Ms. Fuller."

"That doesn't matter," said Natalie. "The old monster covered her tracks somehow. We know what she can do." Natalie shivered and rubbed her arms. "So when it came time to convalesce, Melanie Fuller had her group of conditioned zombies bring her home to Charleston. Let me guess . . . Mr. and Mrs. Warden have an invalid grandmother with them . . ."

"Mrs. Warden's mother," said Saul with a slight smile. "Neighbors haven't seen her, but some commented to Jack about all the sickroom equipment that had been carried in. It's doubly strange because Jack's inquiries in Philadelphia showed that Nancy Warden's mother had died in 1969."

Natalie paced back and forth excitedly. "And Dr. Whatshisname . . ."

"Hartman."

"Yeah . . . he and Nurse Oldsmith are there to keep up the first-class health service." Natalie stopped and stared. "But, my God, Saul, it's so *risky*! What if the authorities . . ." She stopped.

"Precisely," said Saul. "Which authorities? The Charleston police are not about to suspect that Mr. Warden's invalid mother is the missing Melanie Fuller. Sheriff Gentry may have become suspicious . . . Rob had an incredible mind . . . but he is dead."

Natalie looked down quickly and took a deep breath. "What about Barent's group?" she said. "What about the FBI and the others?"

"Perhaps a truce has been called," said Saul. "Possibly Mr. Barent and his surviving friends can tolerate no more publicity of the kind they received in December. If you were Melanie Fuller, Natalie, fleeing from fellow creatures of the night who wanted no more notice of their bloody doings, where would *you* go?"

Natalie slowly nodded. "To a house that's received national attention because of a series of bizarre murders. *Incredible.*"

"Yes," said Saul, "Incredible and incredibly good luck for us. Jack Cohen has done all he can do without eliciting the wrath of his superiors. I've sent him a coded message thanking him and asking him to hold further investigations pending word from us."

"If only the *others* had believed us!" cried Natalie.

Saul shook his head. "Even Jack Cohen knows and believes only part of the story. What he knows for sure is that someone murdered Aaron Eshkol and his entire family, and that I was telling the truth when I said that the Oberst and U.S. authorities were involved in ways that I did not understand."

Natalie sat down. "My God, Saul, what happened to Warden's other two children? The two girls Jack Cohen mentioned?"

Saul closed the dossier and shook his head. "Jack couldn't find anything," he said. "No signs of mourning. No death notices in Philadelphia or Charleston. It's possible that they were sent off to close relatives, but Jack could find no way to check that without making himself visible to everyone. If they are all serving Melanie Fuller, it seems possible that the old lady simply grew tired of having so many children around."

Natalie's lips grew pale. "That bitch has to die," she whispered.

"Yes," said Saul. "But I think that we have to stick with our plan. Especially now that we have located her."

"I guess so," said Natalie, "but the thought of her not being stopped . . ."

"They will be stopped," said Saul, "all of them. But if we are to have a chance, we have to have a plan. It was *my* fault that Rob Gentry died. *My* fault that Aaron and his family died. I thought that there would be little danger if we could approach these people unobserved. But Gentry was right when he said that it would be like trying to catch poisonous snakes with one's eyes closed." He pulled another dossier closer and ran his fingers over the cover. "If we are to reenter the swamp, Natalie, we have to become the hunters, and not merely wait for these lethal monsters to strike."

"You didn't see her," whispered Natalie. "She's . . . not human. And I had my chance, Saul. She was distracted. For a few seconds I had the loaded pistol in my hands . . . but I shot the wrong *thing*. Vincent hadn't killed Rob, *she* had. I didn't think fast enough."

Saul firmly gripped her upper arm. "Stop it. Now. Melanie Fuller is just one viper in the nest. If you had eliminated her at that second, the others would have remained free. Their numbers would even have remained the same if we assume that it was the Fuller woman who killed Charles Colben."

"But if I had . . ."

"No more," insisted Saul. He patted her hair and touched her cheek. "You're very tired, my friend. Tomorrow, if you like, you can ride with me to Lohame HaGeta'ot."

"Yes," said Natalie, "I would like that." She bowed as Saul kissed her on the top of her head.

Later, when Natalie had gone to bed, Saul opened the thin folder labeled HAROD, TONY and read for some time. Eventually he put that aside and went to the front door, unlocking it. The moon was out, bathing the hillside and distant dunes in silver. David Eshkol's large home lay dark and quiet on the hilltop. The scent of oranges and the sea came from the west.

After several minutes, Saul locked and bolted the door, checked the shutters, and went into his room. He opened the first file that Wiesenthal had sent him. Atop the stack of banal forms in Polish civil service double-talk and terse Wehrmacht shorthand was clipped a photograph of a Jewish girl of eighteen or nineteen, small mouth, wan cheeks, dark hair hidden under a cotton scarf, and huge, dark eyes. Saul gazed at the photograph for several minutes, wondering what had been in the young woman's mind as she stared into the official camera lens, wondering how and when she died, wondering who had mourned her and if any of the answers might be in the dossier; at least the bare facts of when she was arrested for the capital crime of being a Jew, when she was transported, and perhaps . . . just perhaps . . . when her file was closed as all the hopes, thoughts, loves, and potentials that had been her short life were scattered like a handful of ashes in a cold wind.

Saul sighed and began reading.

They rose early the next day and Saul fixed one of the huge breakfasts that he insisted was an Israeli tradition. The sun was barely over the hills in the east when they tossed a backpack in the rear of his venerable Landrover and drove north along the coastal highway. Forty minutes later they reached the port city of Haifa spread out at the base of Mount Carmel. "Your head crowns you like Carmel, and your flowing locks are like purple," said Saul over the rush of wind.

"Nice," said Natalie. "Song of Solomon?"

"Song of Songs," said Saul.

Nearing the northern sweep of Haifa Bay, signs announced Akko and translated it as both Acre and Saint John of Acre. Natalie looked west at the white, walled city gleaming in the rich morning light. It was going to be a warm day.

A narrow road led off the Akko-Nahariyya Highway to a kibbutz where a sleepy security guard waved Saul through. They passed verdant fields and the kibbutz complex to stop at a large blocky building with a sign outside announcing in Hebrew and English: LOHAME HAGETA'OT, GHETTO FIGHTER'S HOUSE and giving the times it was open. A short man with three fingers missing on his right hand came out and chatted with Saul in Hebrew. Saul pressed some money into the man's hand and he led the way in, smiling and repeatedly saying *Shalom* to Natalie.

"*Toda raba*," said Natalie as they entered the dim central room. "*Boker tov.*"

"*Shalom.*" The little man smiled. "*L'hitra'ot.*"

Natalie watched him leave and then wandered past glass cases with journals, manuscripts, and relics of the hopeless Warsaw ghetto resistance. Blown-up photographs on the walls depicted life in the ghetto and the Nazi atrocities that had destroyed that life. "It's different from Yad Vashem," she said. "It doesn't have the same sense of oppression. Maybe because the ceiling is higher."

Saul had pulled over a low bench and now sat cross-legged on it. He set a stack of dossiers on his left and a small, battery-powered stroboscope on his right. "Lohame HaGeta'ot is dedicated more to the idea of *resistance* than to the memory of the Holocaust," he said.

Natalie stood gazing at the photograph of a family disembarking from a cattle car, their possessions lying in a heap on the ground near them. She turned quickly. "Could you hypnotize *me*, Saul?"

Saul adjusted his glasses. "I could. It would take much longer. Why?"

Natalie shrugged. "I guess I'm curious to find out what it feels like. You seem to do it so . . . easily."

"Years of experience," said Saul. "For years I used a form of autohypnosis to fight migraine headaches."

Natalie picked up a folder and looked at the photograph of the young woman inside it. "Can you really make all this part of your subconscious?"

Saul rubbed his cheek. "There are levels of consciousness," he said. "On some levels, I'm simply trying to recover memories that are already there by trying to . . . block out the blocks, I guess you'd say. In another sense, I'm trying to lose myself to some extent by empathizing with others who shared a common experience."

Natalie looked around. "And all this helps?"

"It does. Especially in subliminally absorbing some of the biographical data."

"How much time do you have?" she asked.

Saul glanced at his watch. "About two hours, but Shmuelik promised that he would turn tourists away until I was done."

Natalie tugged at her heavy shoulder bag. "I'll take a walk and start collating and memorizing some of this Vienna stuff."

"Shalom," said Saul. When he was alone he read the first three dossiers through carefully. Then he turned sideways and switched on the small strobe, setting the timer. A metronome ticked in beat with the pulsing light. Saul relaxed completely, emptied his mind of everything except the regular throb of light, and opened himself to another time and another place.

On the walls around him, pale faces stared down through smoke and flames and years.

Natalie stood outside the square building and watched the young kibbutzniks going about their business, a final truckload of workers heading out to the fields. Saul had told her that this kibbutz had been settled by survivors of the Warsaw Ghetto and concentration camps set in Poland, but most of the workers Natalie saw were Sabra—native-born Israelis—as lean and tan as young Arabs.

She walked slowly to the edge of the field and sat in the shade of a single eucalyptus tree as a tall sprinkler pulsed water toward the crops with a beat as hypnotic as Saul's metronome. Natalie pulled a bottle of Maccabee beer from the bottom of her shoulder bag and used the can opener on her new Swiss Army knife to pop the lid. It was warm already but tasted very good, blending nicely with the unseasonable warmth of the day, the sound of sprinklers, and the smell of wet earth and growing plants.

The thought of returning to the United States made her stomach constrict and her pulse race. Natalie had only the haziest of memories of those hours and days after the death of Rob Gentry. She recalled flames and darkness and flashing lights and sirens as if from a dream. She remembered cursing Saul and striking him for leaving Rob's body behind in that cursed house, remembered Saul carrying her through the darkness, the pain in her leg making her shift in and out of consciousness like a swimmer rising and falling beneath the surface of a rough sea. She remembered—she thought she remembered—the older man named Jackson running beside them with the limp body of Marvin Gayle strung over his shoulder in a fireman's carry. Saul had later told her that Marvin was unconscious but alive when the two pairs of survivors parted company in that night of dark alleys and screaming sirens.

She recalled lying on a park bench while Saul made a phone call from an open booth and then it was daylight—almost daylight, a cold, gray twilight—and she was lying in the back of a station wagon filled with strange men, Saul in the front seat with someone she later learned was Jack Cohen, Mossad station chief at Israel's embassy in Washington.

Natalie could not sort out the forty-eight hours that followed. A motel room. Shots of painkiller for her fractured ankle. A doctor setting it with a strange inflatable cast. Sobbing for Rob, calling his name in her sleep. Screaming as she remembered the sound the bullet made striking the roof of the honky monster Vincent's mouth, the gray and red smear of brains on the wall. The old woman's mad eyes burning into Natalie's soul. "Good-bye, Nina. We shall meet again."

Saul said later that he had never worked harder in his life than during those first forty-eight hours of talking with Jack Cohen. The scarred, white-haired agent could never have accepted the whole truth yet had to be convinced of the essence of that truth through lies. In the end, the Israeli believed that Saul and Natalie and Aaron Eshkol and the missing cipher chief named Levi Cole had become enmeshed in something large and lethal, something involving high figures in Washington and an elusive ex-Nazi colonel. Cohen had received little support from his embassy or his superiors in Tel Aviv, but early on Sunday, January 4, the station wagon with Saul, Natalie, and two American-born Israeli agents passed over the Peace Bridge from Niagara Falls, New York, to Niagara Falls, Canada. Five days later they flew from Toronto to Tel Aviv with their new identities.

The following two weeks held few referents for Natalie. Her ankle grew inexplicably worse her second day in Israel, fever flared, and she was only semi-aware of the short flight by private plane to Jerusalem where Saul called in favors from old medical acquaintances to find her a private room in the Hadassah-Hebrew Medical Center. Saul himself underwent surgery on his arm during that week. She was there five days and during the last three days she used crutches at dawn and dusk to visit the synagogue and to stare at the stained glass windows created by Marc Chagall. Natalie felt numbed, as if her entire body had been given a massive dose of Novacaine. Each night she closed her eyes and saw Rob Gentry staring back at her. His blue eyes were filled with that terrible second of temporary triumph before the blade appeared and slashed sideways . . .

Natalie finished the beer and set the bottle back in her handbag, feeling vaguely guilty about drinking so early while others worked. She drew out the first stack of folders: clusters of photocopied pictures and written information about Vienna in the twenties and thirties, police reports translated by Wiesenthal's assistants, a thin biography of Nina Drayton, typed by the late Francis Harrington and added to in Saul's wild, hard-to-read script.

Natalie sighed and began to work.

They drove south in the early afternoon and stopped in Haifa for a late lunch before everything closed down for the sabbath. They picked up falafels at a stand on HaNevi'im Street and munched them as they walked down to the busy port. Several black market entrepreneurs hovered close, trying to sell toothpaste, blue jeans, and Rolexes, but Saul snapped something in Hebrew and they backed away. Natalie leaned on a railing and watched a large freighter moving out to sea.

She said, "How long until we go back to America, Saul?"

"I will be ready in three weeks. Perhaps sooner. When do you think you will be prepared?"

"Never," said Natalie.

Saul nodded. "But when will you be willing to return?"

"Any time," said Natalie. "The sooner the better, actually." She let out a breath. "Jesus, the thought of going back makes my legs go weak."

"Yes," agreed Saul, "The feeling is mutual. Let us review our facts and assumptions to see if there is a weak point in our plan."

"*I'm* the weak point," Natalie said softly.

"No," said Saul. He squinted out at the water. "All right, we assume that Aaron's information was accurate and that there were—at a minimum—five of them in the central cabal: Barent, Trask, Colben, Kepler, and the evangelist named Sutter. I watched Trask die at the Oberst's hands. We will assume that Mr. Colben perished as a result of Melanie Fuller's actions. That leaves three in that group."

"Four if you count Harod," said Natalie.

"Yes," said Saul, "we know that he appeared to be acting in concert with Colben's people. That is four of them. Perhaps Agent Haines, but I suspect that he is an instrument rather than initiator. Question: Why did the Oberst kill Trask?"

"Revenge?" said Natalie.

"Perhaps, but I got the impression that there was a power play under way. Let us assume for the time that the entire charade in Philadelphia was aimed toward finding the Oberst rather than the Fuller woman. Barent allowed me to live only because I was to be another weapon aimed at the Oberst. But why did the *Oberst* allow me to live . . . and introduce you and Rob into the equation?"

"To confuse the issue? A diversion?"

"Possibly," said Saul, "but let us return to a former assumption and say that he was indirectly using us as instruments. There is no doubt that Jensen Luhar was William Borden's assistant in Hollywood. Jack Cohen has confirmed Harrington's notes on that. Luhar identified himself to you on the plane. There was no need for that unless the Oberst wanted both of us to know that he is manipulating us. And the Oberst went to great lengths to convince Barent's and Colben's surrogates that I had died in the explosion and fire in Philadelphia. Why?"

"He has further use for you," said Natalie.

"Exactly. But why did he not use each of us directly?"

"Perhaps it was too difficult for him," said Natalie. "Proximity seems to be important for these mind vampires. Maybe he was never in Philadelphia at all."

"Only his conditioned proxies," agreed Saul. "Luhar, poor Francis, and his white assistant, Tom Reynolds. It was Reynolds who attacked you outside the Fuller home on Christmas Eve."

Natalie gasped. She had not heard this assumption before. "Why do you say that?"

Saul took his glasses off and wiped them on his shirttail. "What reason did the assault have except to set you and Rob back on the right track? The Oberst wanted both of you on the scene in Philadelphia when the final showdown with Colben's people occurred."

"I don't understand," said Natalie. She shook her head. "Where does Melanie Fuller come in?"

"Let us continue with the assumption that Miss Fuller is in collaboration with neither the Oberst nor his enemies," said Saul. "Did you get the impression that she was aware of either group?"

"No," said Natalie. "She mentioned only Nina . . . Nina Drayton, I assumed."

"Yes. 'Good-bye, Nina. We shall meet again.' Yet, if we are to follow Rob's logic . . . and I see no reason not to . . . it was Melanie Fuller who shot and killed Nina Drayton in Charleston. Why would Fuller think you were the agent of a dead woman, Natalie?"

"Because she's as crazy as a goddamned bedbug," said Natalie. "You should have seen her, Saul. Her eyes were . . . sick."

"We hope this is the case," said Saul. "Even though Melanie Fuller may be the most deadly viper of all, her insanity might yet serve us. And what of our Mr. Harod?"

"I wish he was dead," said Natalie, remembering his clammy, insistent presence in her mind.

Saul nodded and put his glasses on. "But Harod's control was interrupted—much as the Oberst's was with me four decades ago. As a result, each of us has some memory of the experience and an impression of the other's . . . what, thoughts?"

"Not quite," said Natalie. "Feelings. *Persona*."

"Yes," said Saul, "but whatever the transfer consists of, you came away with a clear sense that Tony Harod had an aversion to using his Ability with males?"

"I was sure of it," said Natalie. "His feeling toward women was so *sick*, but I sensed that it was only women he . . . assaulted. It was like I was his mother and he had to have intercourse with me to prove something . . ."

"Conveniently Freudian," said Saul, "but we will take a leap and accept your feeling that Harod has the ability to influence only women. If this is true, then this particular nest of monsters has at least two weak points—a powerful female who is not part of the group and who is as crazy as a goddamned bedbug and a male figure who may or may not be part of their group but who is unable or unwilling to use his Ability on men."

"Great," said Natalie. "Assuming all this is true, where does it leave us?"

"With the same plan we first discussed in February," said Saul.

"Which will get us killed," said Natalie.

"Quite possibly," said Saul. "But if we are going to remain in the swamp with these poisonous creatures, do you want to spend the rest of your life waiting for them to bite you or risk being bitten while hunting *them*?"

Natalie laughed. "A hell of a choice, Saul."

"It remains the only one we have."

"Well, let's go get the gunny sack and practice catching snakes," said Natalie. She gazed up at the gold dome of the Baha'i shrine gleaming on Mount Carmel and looked back at the freighter disappearing out at sea. "You know," she said, "it doesn't make any sense, but I have a feeling that Rob would have loved this part. The planning. The tension. Even if it is all nuts and doomed, he would have seen the humor in it."

Saul touched her shoulder. "Then let's get on with our crazy planning," he said, "and not let Rob down."

Together they walked up toward the Jaffa Road and the waiting Landrover.

THIRTY-EIGHT

Melanie

It was so nice to come home.

I had grown tired of the hospital, even with the private room, the wing closed off for my convenience, and the entire staff there to serve me. In the end, there is no place like home to raise one's spirits and aid in the healing process.

Years ago I had read about so-called out-of-body events supposedly experienced by dying patients, hapless individuals clinically dead on the operating table before resuscitation, and so forth, and I had put no stock in such stories—more absurd sensational journalism so common these days. But that is precisely the sensation I experienced upon regaining consciousness in the hospital. For a time I seemed to be hovering near the ceiling of my room, seeing nothing but sensing everything. I was aware of the shrunken, curled body on the bed, and of the sensors and tubes and needles and catheters attached to it. I was aware of the hustle and bustle of nurses, doctors, orderlies, and others as they worked to keep that body alive. When I finally reentered the world of sight and sound, I realized that I was doing so through the eyes and ears of these people. And so many at once! It had never been possible for me—or for Willi or Nina, I knew—so totally to Use someone that clear sensory data came from more than one person at a time. While it was possible, with experience, to Use a stranger while keeping control of a conditioned cat's-paw, or, with even more effort and experience, to Use two strangers by alternating control quickly back and forth, access to such clear sight, sound, touch, and ease of control as I was now experiencing was simply unheard of. More than that, our Use of others invariably involved awareness of our presence by those Used, resulting in either destruction of the instrument or the blocking of all memories afterward—a simple enough process but one which left an inexplicable gap in the subject's memory. Now I watched from half a dozen viewpoints and knew that the observers had absolutely no awareness of my presence.

But could I Use them? Carefully I experimented with subtle exercises of control, having a nurse lift a glass here, an orderly close a door there, helping a doctor say a few words he would otherwise not have uttered. Never did I interfere so completely that their medical expertise was compromised. Never was my presence in their minds sensed by any of them.

Days passed. I found that while my body lay in an apparent coma, kept alive by machines and constant vigilance, apparently confined to the

smallest space imaginable, in reality I roamed and explored with an ease
never before approached or dreamed of. I would leave the room behind
the eyes of a young nurse, feeling the animal strength and vitality in her,
tasting the spearmint gum she was chewing, and at the end of the corridor I would transfer an additional tendril of awareness—never losing
contact with my young nurse!—to the mind of the Chief of Surgery, ride
down an elevator with him, start his Lincoln Continental, and drive six
miles toward suburb and waiting wife . . . all the while still in intimate
contact with my nurse, the candy-striper in the hallway, the intern looking
at X rays on the floor below me, and the second doctor now standing in
my room looking down at my comatose body. Distance had ceased to be a
barrier to my Ability. For decades Nina and I had marveled at Willi's
power to Use his subjects over greater distances than we could, but now I
was by far the more powerful.

And each day my powers grew.

On the second day, just as I was testing my new perceptions and abilities,
the family returned. I did not recognize the tall, redheaded man or his thin,
blond wife, but I looked out at the lobby through the receptionist's eyes and
saw the three children and knew them at once: the children in the park.

The redheaded man looked alarmed at my appearance. I was in the
intensive care unit, a web of pie-shaped cubicles radiating from a central
nurse's station. Within that web I was tied into an even tighter web of intravenous tubes and sensor wires. The doctor moved the redheaded man
away from the clear partition looking into what my nurse called I.C.

"Are you a member of the family?" asked the doctor. He was a skillful,
precise man with a mane of graying hair. His name was Dr. Hartman and
I felt the nurses' pleasure, anxiety, and respect when they were in his presence.

"Uh, no," said the large redhead. "My name is Howard Warden. We
found her . . . that is, my kids found her yesterday morning, wandering in
our . . . uh . . . our yard. She collapsed when . . ."

"Yes, yes," said Dr. Hartman, "I read the report you gave the E.R.
nurse. You have no idea who the lady is?"

"No, she only had on the bathrobe and a nightgown. My kids said they
saw her walking out of the woods when they . . ."

"And no real idea of where she came from?"

"Uh-uh," said Warden. "I was . . . well, I didn't call the police. I guess
I should have. Nancy and I waited around here for several hours and when
it was obvious that she . . . the old lady . . . wasn't going to . . . I mean,
that she was stable . . . we went home. It was my day off. I was going to
call the police this morning, but I thought we would see how she's doing
first . . ."

"We have already informed the police," lied Dr. Hartman. It was the
first time I had Used him. It was as easy as pulling on an old and favorite

coat. "They came and took a report. They seemed to have no idea where Mrs. Doe came from. No one has reported a missing relative."

"Mrs. Doe?" said Howard Warden. "Oh, like Jane Doe. Right. Well, it's a mystery to us, Doctor. We live about two miles into the Park and from what the kids say, she wasn't even walking along the access drive." He glanced back toward the intensive care unit. "How is she, Doctor? She looks . . . well . . . terrible."

"The lady has suffered a massive stroke," said Dr. Hartman. "Perhaps a series of them." At Howard's blank look, the doctor went on, "She's had what we call a CVA, a cerebrovascular accident, what used to be called a cerebral hemorrhage. There has been a temporary cutoff of oxygen to the brain. As far as we can tell, the incident seems to have been located in the right hemisphere of this patient's brain, resulting in disruption of cerebral and neurological function. Most of the effects are to be seen on her left side—drooping eyelid, limb paralysis—but in a sense this may be a welcome sign since aphasia . . . speech problems . . . generally are associated with accidents in the left hemisphere. We've run both an EEG and a CAT scan, and, to be honest, the results are somewhat confusing. While the CAT scan has confirmed infarction and probable obstruction of the middle cerebral artery, the EEG readings are not at all what we would expect following an episode of this nature . . ."

I lost interest in the medical double-talk and returned my primary awareness to the middle-aged receptionist in the lobby. I had her rise and walk over to the three children. "Hello," I had her say, "I bet I know who you're here to visit."

"We can't visit," said the six-year-old one, the girl who had sung "Hey, Jude" as the sun rose. "We're too young."

"But I bet I know who you would *like* to see," the receptionist said with a smile.

"I wanna see the nice lady," said the little boy. There were tears in his eyes.

"I don't," the oldest girl said adamantly.

"I don't either," said her six-year-old sister.

"Why not?" I asked. I was hurt.

"'Cause she's *weird*," said the oldest girl. "I thought I liked her, but when I touched her hand yesterday, it was all funny."

"What do you mean, funny?" I asked. The receptionist wore thick glasses and I found the view distorted. I had never needed glasses for anything besides reading.

"Funny," said the girl. "Weird. Like a snake's skin or something. I let go real fast, even before she got sick, but it was like I knew she was real mean."

"Yeah," said her sister.

"Shut up, Allie," said the oldest girl, obviously sorry she had spoken to me.

"I *liked* the nice lady," said the five-year-old boy. It looked as if he had been crying before he came to the hospital.

I beckoned the two girls away from the boy, toward the reception desk. "Come here, girls. I have something for you." I rummaged through the drawer and came up with two wrapped spheres of peppermint candy. When the oldest girl reached for one, I grasped her firmly by the wrist. "First let me tell your fortune," I had the receptionist whisper.

"Leggo," the girl whispered back.

"Shut up," I hissed. "Your name is Tara Warden. Your sister's name is Allison. Both of you live in a big stone house on the hill, in the park, and you call it the castle. And some night soon a huge, green boogeyman with sharp yellow teeth is going to come into your room when it is dark and he is going to *chop you up into little pieces*—both of you—*and eat the pieces.*"

The girls staggered backward, their faces pasty white and their eyes huge as saucers. Their mouths hung slack with fear and shock.

"And if you tell anyone . . . your father, mother, *anyone,*" I had the receptionist hiss after them, "the boogeyman is going to come for you *tonight!*"

The girls staggered back to their seats, staring at the woman as if she were a snake. A minute later an elderly couple arrived asking directions to a room and I let the receptionist return to being her sweet, simple, slightly officious self.

Upstairs, Dr. Hartman had finished explaining my medical condition to Howard Warden. Down the hall, Head Nurse Oldsmith checked medication for the patients, taking great care in double-checking anything labeled for Mrs. Doe. In my room, the young nurse named Sewell was gently bathing me with cold compresses, massaging my skin almost reverently. The sensation was only a distant one at best, but I felt better knowing that all possible attention was being given to me. It was good to be back among family.

On the third day, the third night actually, I was resting . . . I never really slept anymore, merely allowed my consciousness to float, moving from recipient to recipient in a random, dreamlike way . . . when suddenly I became aware of a physical excitement I had not known for years, the presence of a man, his arms around me, loins thrusting against me. I felt my heart pounding, as the fullness of my young breasts pressed against him, my nipples erect. His tongue was in my mouth. I felt his hands fumbling at the buttons of my nurse's uniform even as my own hands undid the clasp of his belt, tugged at his zipper, and grasped at his erect male member.

It was disgusting. It was obscene. It was Nurse Connie Sewell in a supply closet with some intern.

Since I could not sleep anyway, I allowed my consciousness to return to

Nurse Sewell. I consoled myself with the thought that I was not *initiating*, merely *participating*. The night passed quickly.

I am not sure when I had the idea of returning home. The hospital had been necessary for those first few weeks, that first month, but by mid-February my thoughts turned more and more to Charleston and my home. It was only mildly difficult to stay in the hospital without drawing attention to myself; by the third week Dr. Hartman had moved me to a large private room on the seventh floor and most of the staff was under the impression that I was a very wealthy patient deserving special care. This was true.

There was a certain administrator, a Dr. Markham, who continued to ask questions about my case. He returned to the seventh floor daily, sniffing around like a hound on a scent. I had Dr. Hartman reassure him. I had Head Nurse Oldsmith explain things to him. Finally I entered the little man's mind and reassured him my own way. But he was insistent. Four days later he was back, questioning nurses about the extra service and care I was receiving, demanding to know who was paying for the additional medicines, tests, CAT scans, and specialist consultations. Markham pointed out that the business office had no records of my admission, no 26479B15-C sheets, no computer printouts of itemized costs, and no information on how payment would be met. Nurse Oldsmith and Dr. Hartman agreed to be present at a meeting the next morning with our inquisitor, the head of the Hospital board, the chief of the business office, and three other supernumeries.

That evening I joined Markham as he drove home. The Schuylkill Expressway was crowded and it brought back bad memories of New Year's Eve. Just before we reached the junction with the Roosevelt Expressway I had our friend pull his car into the narrow shoulder, turn on the blinking emergency lights, and step out to stand in front of the Chrysler. I helped him remain standing there for over a minute, scratching his balding head and wondering what was wrong with his car. When the time came, it was obvious: All five lanes filled with traffic moving at speed. A large truck on the inner lane.

Our administrator friend jumped quickly in three long strides. There was time for me to record the roar of the air horns, to see the shocked expression on the truck driver's rapidly approaching face, and to sense the disbelieving scurry of Markham's thoughts before the impact sent me sliding back to other viewpoints. I sought out Nurse Sewell and shared her eagerness for the shift change and the arrival of her young intern.

Time meant very little to me during this period. I would shift backward and forward in time as easily as I slipped from one viewpoint to the next. I especially enjoyed reliving those summers in Europe with Nina and our new friend Wilhelm.

I remember the cool summer evenings, the three of us walking along the stylish Ringstrasse where everyone who was anyone in Vienna could be found parading in their finest livery. Willi had loved going to the Colosseum Cinema on Nussdorferstrasse, but the films there were invariably those boring German propaganda things, and Nina and I usually prevailed in coaxing our young guide to the Krüger-Kino where the new American gangster films were common. I remembered laughing until I cried one evening at the spectacle of Jimmy Cagney spitting words in ugly Austrian-German in the first dubbed talkie I had ever seen.

Afterward we frequently would have drinks in the Reiss-Barr off Kärntnerstrasse, greeting other groups of young merrymakers and relaxing in the chic comfort of the real leather chairs while enjoying the play of light off mahogany, glass, chromium, and the gilt and marble tables. Sometimes a few of the more stylish prostitutes from the nearby Kruggerstrasse would come in with their dates and add a daring, illicit feel to the evening.

Often we would end our nights out on the town with a visit to Simpl, the finest cabaret in Vienna. The establishment's full name was Simplicissimus and I can clearly recall that it was run by two Jews—Karl Frakas and Fritz Grunbaum. Even later, when the Brownshirts and storm troopers were raising havoc on the streets of the old city, these two comics would have the patrons pealing with laughter at their satirical sketches of Nazi stereotypes blundering their way through a social encounter or arguing fine points of fascist doctrine while Sieg Heiling dogs, cats, and passersby. I remember Willi roaring with laughter until tears ran down his red cheeks. Once he laughed so hard that he choked until Nina and I patted him resoundingly on the back and offered our glasses of champagne to him. Some years after the war, Willi idly mentioned during one of our Reunions that either Frakas or Grunbaum—I cannot remember which one—died in one of the camps Willi had administered briefly before his transfer to the Eastern Front.

Nina was very beautiful in those days. Her blond hair had been cut and curled in the most current fashion and because of her inheritance she could afford the finest silk dresses from Paris. I especially remember one green gown, cut very low in front, the soft material clinging to her small breasts, and how magnificently the green brought out the delicate blush of her peaches and cream complexion while oddly complementing the blue of her eyes.

I do not remember who formally proposed that we play the Game that first summer, but I remember our excitement and the thrill of the vicarious chase. We took turns Using different catspaws—acquaintances of ours, friends of our intended targets—a mistake that we did not make again. The next summer we played the Game even more earnestly, sitting together in our hotel rooms on Josefstadterstrasse and Using the same instrument—a dull-witted and thick-necked working-class peasant who was never caught but who Willi disposed of later—and the act of the three of us present in that same mind, and sharing the same sharp experiences was somehow more intimate and thrilling than any sexual ménage we might have experimented with.

I remember the summer we spent at Bad Ischl, Nina made a joke about the station where we had our single train change from Vienna . . . a small village named Attnang-Puchheim. Repeated at a quickening rate, Attnang-Puchheim soon became the sound of the train itself. We laughed until we could laugh no more and then would begin again. I remember the scolding glances of an old dowager across the aisle from us.

It was in Bad Ischl that I found myself alone in the Cafe Zauner one early afternoon. I had gone off for my voice lessons as always, but the instructor was ill and when I returned to the café where Willi and Nina always waited for me, our usual table was empty.

I returned to the hotel where Nina and I were staying on the Esplanade. I remember being slightly curious as to what impromptu excursion my friends had embarked on and why they had not waited for me. I had unlocked the door and walked halfway through the sitting room before I heard the sounds from Nina's bedroom. At first I took them for noises of distress, and I ran toward her room with some naive notion of offering assistance to the chambermaid or whoever was in trouble.

It was Nina and Willi, of course. They were not in trouble. I remember how pale Nina's thighs and Willi's thrusting flanks were in the dim light filtering through the maroon drapes. I stood there for a full minute, watching, before turning and silently leaving the suite. During that long minute, Willi's face remained turned away, hidden in Nina's shoulder and the eiderdown pillow, but Nina turned her face and clear blue eyes toward me almost at once. I am sure she saw me. She did not stop, however, nor did she cease the rhythmic grunt of animal sounds that came from her open, pink, and perfect mouth.

By mid-March I decided that it was time to leave the hospital and Philadelphia and go home.

I had Howard Warden take care of the details of moving. Even with his savings, however, Howard could scrape together only about $2,500. The man would never have amounted to anything. Nancy, on the other hand, closed out the savings account started from her mother's estate and it came to a comfortable $48,000. It had been put aside for the children's college expenses, but that was no longer a concern now.

I had had Dr. Hartman visit the castle. Howard and Nancy waited in their rooms while the doctor visited the girls' bedroom with his two syringes. Afterward, the doctor took care of the details. I had remembered a pleasant little clearing in the forest of Fairmont Park a mile toward the railroad bridge. In the morning, Howard and Nancy fed five-year-old Justin and—due to the strength of my conditioning—noticed nothing unusual except for an occasional flash of recognition not too dissimilar from those dreams where one suddenly realizes that he or she has forgotten to dress and is sitting naked in school or some other public place.

These passed. Howard and Nancy adjusted nicely to having only one child and I was pleased that I had decided not to Use Howard in the necessary actions. Conditioning is always easier and more successful if there is no vestigial trauma or resentment.

The wedding of Dr. Hartman and Head Nurse Oldsmith was a small affair, officiated by a Philadelphia justice of the peace and witnessed only by Nurse Sewell, Howard, Nancy, and Justin. I thought that they were a good-looking couple, although some say that Nurse Oldsmith has a harsh and humorless face.

When the move was set, Dr. Hartman contributed to the collective fund. It took him awhile to sell certain stocks and real estate interests, as well as to get rid of that absurd new Porsche he so prized, but when trusts were set aside to continue alimony to his two ex-wives, he was still able to bring $185,600 to our venture. Considering that Dr. Hartman would, in effect, be entering early retirement, it was enough for basic expenses during the immediate future.

It did not, however, offer enough to settle the problem of purchasing either my old home or the Hodges' place. I no longer had any interest in allowing strangers to live across the courtyard from me. Foolishly, the Wardens had taken out no life insurance on their children. Howard retained a $10,000 policy on his own life, but this was laughable in light of real estate prices in Charleston.

In the end it was Dr. Hartman's mother, eighty-two, in perfect health, and living in Palm Springs, whose estate offered the best solution. It was on Ash Wednesday the doctor was in surgery when the word came about his mother's sudden embolism. He flew to the West Coast that same afternoon. The funeral was on Saturday, March 7, and because there were several legal details to settle, he did not fly home until Wednesday, the eleventh. I saw no reason why Howard should not return on the same flight. The initial cash settlement of the estate came to a little over $400,000. We moved south a week later, on St. Patrick's Day.

There were a few final details to take care of before we left the north. I was comfortable with my little family—Howard, Nancy, and young Justin, as well as with our future neighbors, Dr. Hartman, Nurse Oldsmith, and Miss Sewell, but I felt that a certain security aspect was missing. The doctor was a small man, five feet five and thin, and while Howard was substantial in height and girth, he was as slow moving as he had been slow thinking and much of his weight had gone to fat. We needed one or two more members of our group to help me feel more secure.

Howard brought Culley into the hospital on the weekend before we left. He was a giant of a man, at least six-feet-five, weighing at least 280 pounds, all of it that was visible compacted into slabs of muscle. Culley was dim-witted, almost unable to speak coherently, but as quick and nimble on his feet as a jungle cat. Howard explained that Culley had been an assistant foreman in Park Grounds Maintenance before being sent away for manslaughter seven years earlier. He had returned the year before to work on the lowest, toughest level of Maintenance—clearing stumps, tearing down old structures, paving asphalt trails and lanes, clearing snow. Culley had worked without complaint and was no longer on parole.

Culley's head tapered from its broadest point at juncture of jaw and neck to its narrowest at the crest of an almost pointed skull stubbled with a crew cut so short and rough it looked as if it had been administered by a blind sadist of a barber.

Howard had told Culley that there was a unique employment opportunity open to him, although he had used simpler words. Bringing him to the hospital had been my idea.

"This will be your boss," Howard said, gesturing to the bed that held my husk of a body. "You will serve her, protect her, give your life for her if you must."

Culley made a sound like a cat clearing its throat. "That old bag still alive?" he said. "She looks dead to me."

I entered him then. There was little in that pinched skull except basic motivations—hunger, thirst, fear, pride, hate, and an urge to please based on a vague sense of wanting to belong, to be loved. It was that final need that I enlarged upon, built upon. Culley sat in my room for eighteen consecutive hours. When he left to help Howard with the packing and other trip preparations, there was nothing of the original Culley left except his size, strength, quickness, and need to please. To please me.

I never found out whether Culley was his first or last name.

When I was young I had a weakness whenever I traveled; I could not resist picking up souvenirs. Even in Vienna with Willi and Nina, my compulsive souvenir shopping soon became a source of humor for my companions. Now it had been some years since I had traveled, but my weakness for souvenirs had not totally disappeared.

On the evening of March 16, I had Howard and Culley drive to Germantown. Those sad streets were like the landscape of a half-remembered dream to me. I believe Howard would have been nervous in that Negro section—in spite of his conditioning—if it had not been for the reassuring presence of Culley.

I knew what I wanted; I remembered his first name and description but nothing else. The first four youngsters Howard approached either refused to respond or did so in colorful epithets, but the fifth one, a scruffy ten-year-old wearing only a ragged sweatshirt despite the freezing weather, said, "Yeah, man, you talking about Marvin *Gayle*. He just got out of *jail*, man, for citin' riot or some shit. What you want with Marvin?"

Howard and Culley elicited directions to his house without answering that question. Marvin Gayle lived on the second floor of a rotting, shingled town house shoe-horned in between two overhanging tenements. A little boy opened the door and Culley and Howard stepped into a living room with a sagging couch covered with a pink spread, an ancient television where a green-skinned game show host blared enthusiasm, peeling walls with a few religious prints and a photograph of Robert Kennedy, and a teenage girl lying on her stomach staring up vacuously at the visitors.

A large black woman came in from the kitchen, drying her hands on a checked apron. "What do you two want?"

"We'd like to talk to your son, ma'am," said Howard.

"What about?" demanded the woman. "You're not the police. Marvin hasn't done anything. You leave my boy alone."

"No, ma'am," said Howard unctuously, "it's nothing like that. We just want to offer Marvin a job."

"A job?" The woman looked suspiciously at Culley and then back to Howard. "What kind of *job*?"

"It's all right, Ma." Marvin Gayle stood in the door to the inside hallway, dressed in nothing but an old pair of shorts and an oversize T-shirt. His face was slack and his eyes were vague, as if he had just awakened.

"Marvin, you don't have to talk to these people if . . ."

"It's all right, Ma." He stared at her with that dead face until she looked down and then he turned the gaze on Howard. "What you want, man?"

"Can we talk outside?" asked Howard.

Marvin shrugged and followed us outside despite the darkness and freezing wind. The door closed on the mother's protests. He stared up at Culley and then stepped closer to Howard. There was the slightest flicker of animation in his eyes, as if he knew what was coming and almost welcomed it.

"We're offering you a new life," whispered Howard. "A whole new life . . ."

Marvin Gayle started to speak then, but from ten miles away I *pushed* and the colored boy's mouth fell slack and he did not finish the first word. Technically speaking, I had Used this boy before, briefly, in those last, mad minutes before I bid adieu to Grumblethorpe, and that might have made the feat the slightest bit easier. But that did not really matter. I *never* would have been able to do what I did that evening before my illness. Working through the filter of Howard Warden's perceptions, while simultaneously controlling Culley, my doctor, and half a dozen other conditioned catspaws in as many differing locations, I was still able to project my force of will so powerfully that the colored boy gasped, staggered backward, stared blankly, and awaited my first command. His eyes no longer looked drugged and defeated; they now reflected the bright, transparent stare of the terminally brain damaged.

Whatever had been the sad total of Marvin Gayle's life, thoughts, memories, and pitiful aspirations was gone forever. I had never done this type of total conditioning in a single blow before, and for a long minute my almost forgotten body twitched in the vice of total paralysis on the hospital bed while Nurse Sewell massaged me.

The receptacle that had been Marvin Gayle waited quietly in the freezing wind and darkness.

I finally spoke through Culley, not needing the verbal command but wanting to hear it through Howard's awareness. "Go get dressed," he said, "give your mother this. Tell her it is an advance on salary." Culley handed the young Negro a hundred dollar bill.

Marvin disappeared into the house and came out three minutes later. He was wearing only jeans, a sweater, sneakers, and a black leather jacket. He brought no luggage. That is as I wished; we would prepare an appropriate wardrobe for him when we moved.

In all my years of growing up, I do not remember a time when we did not have colored servants. It seemed appropriate upon my return to Charleston that this again be the case.

I could not leave Philadelphia without bringing home a souvenir.

The convoy of trucks, two sedans, and the rented van with my bed and medical apparatus made the drive down in three days. Howard had gone ahead in the family Volvo, which Justin called the "Blue Oval," to make final arrangements, air the house out, and prepare the way for my homecoming.

We arrived long after dark. Culley carried me upstairs, with Dr. Hartman attending and Nurse Oldsmith walking alongside with the intravenous bottle.

My bedroom glowed in the lamplight, the comforter was turned down, the sheets were clean and fresh, the dark wood of the bed, bureau, and wardrobe smelled of lemon polish, and my hairbrushes lay in a perfect row on my dressing table.

We all wept. Tears coursed down Culley's cheeks as he set me tenderly, almost reverently in the long bed. The smell of palmetto fronds and mimosa came through the slightly opened window.

Equipment was brought in and set up. It was odd to see the green glow of an oscilloscope in my familiar bedroom. For a minute everyone was there—Dr. Hartman and his new wife, Nurse Oldsmith, performing their final medical tasks, Howard and Nancy with little Justin between them as if they were posing for a family photograph, young Nurse Sewell smiling at me from near the window, and near the door, Culley standing there filling the doorway, looking no less massive for his white orderly's uniform, and just visible in the hallway, Marvin dressed in formal tails and tie, white gloves on his well-scrubbed hands.

There was a small problem that Howard had encountered with Mrs. Hodges; she was willing to rent the house next door, but she did not want to sell. That was unacceptable to me.

But I would deal with that in the morning. For the time being I was home—home—and surrounded by my loving family. For the first time in weeks I would really sleep. There were bound to be small problems—Mrs. Hodges was one—but I would deal with those tomorrow. Tomorrow was another day.

THIRTY-NINE

35,000 feet over Nevada
Sunday, April 4, 1981

P lay it again, Richard," said C. Arnold Barent.
The cabin of the customized Boeing 747 grew dark and once again the images danced on the large video screen: The president turned toward a shouted question, raised his left hand to wave, and grimaced. There were shouts, confusion. A Secret Service agent leaped forward and seemed to be lifted onto his toes by an invisible wire. The shots sounded small and insubstantial. An Uzi submachine gun appeared in another agent's hand as if by magic. Several men scuffled a young man to the ground. The camera shifted, and swung to a fallen man with blood on his bald head. A policeman lay facedown. The agent with the Uzi crouched and snapped orders like a traffic cop while others struggled with the suspect. The president had been pushed forward into his limousine by a surge of agents and now the long black car accelerated away from the curb, leaving confusion and crowd noise behind.

"All right, freeze it there, Richard," said Barent. The image of the receding limousine stayed on the screen while the cabin lights came back up. "Gentlemen?" said Barent.

Tony Harod blinked and looked around. C. Arnold Barent sat on the edge of his large curved desk. Telephone and computer extensions gleamed behind him. It was dark outside the cabin windows and the noise of the jet engines was muffled by the teak finish of the cabin's interior. Joseph Kepler sat across the circle from Barent. Kepler's gray suit looked freshly pressed, his black shoes gleamed. Harod looked at the craggy-handsome face and decided that Kepler looked a lot like Charlton Heston and that they were both assholes. Slumped in a chair near Barent, the Reverend Jimmy Wayne Sutter folded his hands across his ample stomach. His long, white hair gleamed in the glow of the overhead recessed lights. The only other person in the room was Barent's new assistant, Richard Haines. Maria Chen and the others sat waiting in the forward cabin.

"It looks to me." said Jimmy Wayne Sutter, his pulpit-trained voice rolling and rising, "that someone tried to kill our beloved president."

Barent's mouth twitched. "That much is obvious. But why would Willi Borden take that risk? And was Reagan the target, or was I?"

"I didn't see you in the clip," said Harod.

Barent glanced toward the producer. "I was fifteen feet behind the president, Tony. I had just come out the side door of the Hilton when we

Dan Simmons

heard the shots. Richard and my other security people quickly moved me back into the building."

"I still can't believe that Willi Borden had anything to do with this," said Kepler. "We know more now than we did last week. The Hinckley kid had a long record of mental problems. He kept a journal. The whole thing hinged on an obsession he's had with Jodie Foster, for Christ's sake. It just doesn't fit the profile at all. The old man could have used one of Reagan's own Secret Service agents or a Washington cop like the one who got shot. Also, the kraut's an old Wehrmacht officer, right? He would have known enough to use something more solid than a .22 caliber popgun!"

"Loaded with explosive bullets," Barent reminded him. "It's only an accident that they did not explode."

"It's only an accident that the one bullet ricocheted off the car door and got Reagan," said Kepler. "If Willi had been involved, he could have waited until you and the president were comfortably seated and then had the agent with the Uzi or the Mac-10 or whatever it was hose you down with no risk of failure."

"A comforting thought," Barent said dryly. "Jimmy, what do you think?"

Sutter mopped his brow with a silk handkerchief and shrugged. "Joseph has a point, Brother C. The boy is a certified loonie-tunes. It seems like an absurd amount of effort to create that much of a background story and then miss."

"He didn't miss," Barent said softly. "The president was shot in the left lung."

"I mean miss *you*," said Sutter with a wide smile. "After all, what's our producer friend got against poor old Ronnie? They're both products of Hollywood."

Harod wondered if Barent would ask his opinion. It was, after all, his first appearance as a member of the Island Club Steering Committee.

"Tony?" said Barent.

"I don't know," said Harod. "I just don't know."

Barent nodded at Richard Haines. "Perhaps this will help us in our deliberations," said Barent. The lights went down and the screen showed leader and jerky, grainy eight-millimeter film that had been transferred to videotape. There were random crowd scenes. Several police cars and a cavalcade of limousines and Secret Service vehicles swept by. Harod realized that he was watching the arrival of the president at the Washington Hilton.

"We found and confiscated as much private still and home movie film as we could," said Barent.

"Who is 'we'?" asked Kepler.

Barent raised one eyebrow. "Even though Charles's untimely death was a great loss, Joseph, we still have some contacts within certain agencies. Here, this is the part."

The film had been showing mostly the empty street and backs of heads.

Harod guessed that it had been taken from thirty or forty yards from the shooting, on the wrong side of the street, by a blind person with cerebral palsy. There was almost no attempt to steady the camera. There was no sound. When the shootings took place they were obvious only by increased commotion in the small crowd; the photographer had not been aiming at the president at the time.

"Here!" said Barent.

The film stopped with a single freeze-frame on the large video screen. The angle was bizarre, but an old man's face was visible between the shoulders of two other spectators. The man, who appeared to be in his early seventies, had white hair emerging from under a plaid sportscar cap and was intently watching the scene across the street. His eyes were small and cold.

"Is that him?" asked Sutter. "Can you be sure?"

"It doesn't look like the photographs of him I've seen," said Kepler.

"Tony?" said Barent.

Harod felt beads of perspiration break out on his upper lip and forehead. The frozen image was grainy, distorted by the poor lens, odd angle, and cheap film. There was an octagon of light glare on the lower right third of the frame. Harod realized that he could say that the picture was too fuzzy, that he did not really know. He could stay the fuck *out* of it. "Yeah," said Harod, "that's Willi all right."

Barent nodded and Haines killed the video image, brought the lights back up, and departed. For several seconds there was only the reassuring drone of the jet engines. "Just a coincidence, perhaps, Joseph?" said C. Arnold Barent. He walked around and sat behind his low, curved desk.

"No," said Kepler, "but it still doesn't make any sense. What's he trying to prove?"

"That he's still out there, maybe," said Jimmy Wayne Sutter. "That he's waiting. That he can get to us, any of us, whenever he wants to." Sutter lowered his chin so that his jowls and chins furrowed and he smiled at Barent over his bifocals. "I presume that you will not be making anymore personal appearances for a while, Brother C.," he said.

Barent steepled his fingers. "This will be our last meeting before the Island Club summer camp in June. I will be out of the country . . . on business . . . until then. I urge all of you to take appropriate precautions."

"Precautions from what?" demanded Kepler. "What does he *want*? We've offered him membership in the Club through every channel we can think of. We even sent that Jew psychiatrist out with a message and we're sure he was in touch with Luhar before the explosion killed them both . . ."

"The identification was incomplete," said Barent. "Dr. Laski's dental records were missing from his dentist's office in New York."

"Yeah," said Kepler, "but so what? The message almost certainly got through. What does Willi *want*?"

"Tony?" said Barent. All three men were staring at Harod.

"How the hell should I know what he wants?"

"Tony, Tony," said Barent, "you were the gentleman's colleague for years. You ate with him, spoke with him, joked with him . . . what does he *want*?"

"The game."

"What?" said Sutter.

"What game?" asked Kepler, leaning forward. "He wants to play the game on the Island after summer camp?"

Harod shook his head. "Uh-uh," he said. "He knows about your island games, but *this* is the game he likes. It's like the old days—in Germany, I guess—when he and the two old broads were young. It's like chess. Willi's fucking crazy about chess. He told me once he dreams about it. He thinks we're all in a fucking chess game."

"Chess," muttered Barent and tapped his fingertips together.

"Yeah," said Harod. "Trask made a bad move, sent a couple of pawns too deep into Willi's territory. Bam. Trask gets removed from the board. Same with Colben. Nothing personal just . . . chess."

"And the old woman," said Barent, "was she a willing queen or just another of Willi's many pawns?"

"How the fuck should I know?" snapped Harod. He stood up and paced, his boots making no noise in the thick carpeting. "Knowing Willi," he said, "he wouldn't trust anybody as an ally in this sort of thing. Maybe he was afraid of her. One thing's for sure, he led us to her because he knew we'd underestimate her."

"We did that," said Barent. "The woman had an extraordinary Ability."

"Had?" asked Sutter.

"We have no proof that she is alive," said Joseph Kepler.

"What about the watch on her house in Charleston?" asked the reverend. "Did someone pick that up from Nieman and Charles's group?"

"My people are there," said Kepler. "Nothing to report."

"How about the airlines and such?" pressed Sutter. "Colben was sure she was trying to leave the country before something spooked her in Atlanta."

"The issue is not Melanie Fuller," interrupted Barent. "As Tony has so correctly pointed out, she was a diversion, a false track. If she is alive we can ignore her and otherwise it is irrelevant what her role was. The question now before us is how do we respond to this most recent . . . gambit . . . by our German friend?"

"I suggest we ignore it," said Kepler. "The incident on Monday was just the old man's way of showing us that he still has teeth. We've all agreed that if he'd meant to get to Mr. Barent, he could have done so. Let the old fart have his fun. When he's done, we'll talk to him. If he understands the rules, he can have the fifth seat in the Club. If not . . . I mean, *goddamn*, gentlemen, between the three of us . . . excuse me, Tony, the *four* of us . . . we have hundreds of paid security people at our disposal. How many does Willi have, Tony?"

"Two when he left L.A.," said Harod. "Jensen Luhar and Tom Reynolds. They weren't paid, though, they were his personal pets."

"See?" said Kepler. "We wait until he gets tired of playing this one-sided game and then we negotiate. If he doesn't negotiate, we send Haines and some of your people out, or some of my plumbers."

"No!" roared Jimmy Wayne Sutter. "We have turned the other cheek too many times. 'The Lord avengeth and is full of wrath . . . Who can stand before His indignation? And who can abide by the fierceness of His anger? His fury is poured out like fire, and the rocks are broken asunder by Him . . . He will pursue His enemies into darkness!' Nahum 1:2"

Joseph Kepler stifled a yawn. "Who's talking about the Lord, Jimmy? We're talking about how to deal with a senile Nazi with a chess hangup."

Sutter's face grew red and he leveled a blunt finger at Kepler. The large ruby in his ring caught the light. "Do not mock me," he warned in a bass growl. "The Lord has spoken to me and through me and He will not be denied." Sutter looked around. "'If any of you lacks wisdom, let him ask of God who gives to all men generously and without reproaching, and it will be given him,'" he rumbled. "James 1:5."

"And what does God say on this issue?" Barent asked quietly.

"This man may well be the Antichrist," said Sutter, his voice drowning out the faint hum of the jet engines. "God says we must find him and root him out. We must smite him hip and thigh. We must find him and find his minions . . . 'the same shall drink the wine of the wrath of God; and he shall be tormented with fire and brimstone in the presence of the holy angels, and in the presence of the Lamb; and the smoke of their torments ascendeth up for ever and ever.'"

Barent smiled slightly. "Jimmy, I presume from what you say that you are not in favor of negotiating with Willi and offering him a membership in the Club?"

The Reverend Jimmy Wayne Sutter took a long sip of his bourbon and branch water. "No," he said so quietly that Harod had to lean forward to hear him, "I think we should kill him."

Barent nodded and swiveled his large leather chair. "Tie vote," he said. "Tony, your thoughts?"

"I pass," said Harod, "but I think deciding is one thing, actually tracking Willi down and dealing with him will be another. Look at the mess we made with Melanie Fuller."

"Charles made that mistake and Charles paid for it," Barent said. He looked at the other two men. "Well, since Tony abstains on this matter, it looks as if I have the honor of casting the deciding vote."

Kepler opened his mouth as if to speak and then thought better of it. Sutter drank his bourbon in silence.

"Whatever our friend Willi was up to in Washington," said Barent, "I did not appreciate it. However, we will interpret it as an act of pique and let it go for now. Perhaps Tony's insight on Willi's obsession with chess is

the best guide we have in this matter. We have two months before summer camp on Dolmann Island and our . . . ah . . . ensuing activities
there. We must keep our priorities clear. If Willi abstains from further
harassment, we will consider negotiation at a later date. If he continues to
be troublesome . . . so much as a single incident . . . we will use every resource, public and private, to find him and destroy him in a method
not . . . ah . . . inconsistent with Jimmy's advice from Revelation. It was
Revelation, was it not, Brother J?"

"Just so, Brother C."

"Fine," said Barent. "I think I will go forward and get some sleep. I
have a meeting in London tomorrow. All of you will find your sleeping
compartments made up and ready for you. Where would you like to be
dropped off?"

"L.A.," said Harod.

"New Orleans," said Sutter.

"New York," said Kepler.

"Done," said Barent. "Donald informed me a few minutes ago that we
were then somewhere over Nevada so we'll drop Tony first. I'm sorry you
won't be able to enjoy the accommodations overnight, Tony, but you
might want to catch forty winks before we land."

"Yeah," said Harod.

Barent rose and Haines appeared, holding the door to the forward corridor open. "Until we meet again at the Island Club Summer Camp, gentlemen," said Barent. "*Ciao*, and good fortune to each of you."

A servant in a blue blazer showed Harod and Maria Chen forward to their
stateroom. The rear part of the 747 had been turned into Barent's large
office, a lounge, and the billionaire's bedroom. Forward of the office, to
the left of a corridor that reminded Harod of all the European trains he
had ever traveled on, were the large staterooms, decorated in subtle shades
of green and coral, consisting of a private bath, sleeping area with a
queen-size bed, and couch and color TV. "Where's the fireplace?" Harod
muttered to the servant in the blazer.

"I believe that is Sheik Muzad's aircraft that has a working fireplace,"
answered the handsome young man with no trace of a smile.

Harod had poured another vodka on ice and joined Maria Chen on the
couch when there was a soft knock at the door. A young woman in a blazer
identical to the male aide's said, "Mr. Barent wondered if you and Ms.
Chen would care to join him in the Orion Lounge."

"The Orion Lounge?" said Harod. "Sure, what the hell." They followed the young woman down the corridor and through a security-card
locked door to a spiral staircase. On a commercial 747, Harod knew, the
staircase would lead up to the first-class lounge. As they stepped off the
dark staircase at the top, both Harod and Maria Chen stopped in awe.

The woman went back down the stairs, securing the door at the bottom and shutting off the last gleam of reflected light from below.

The room was the same size as a normal 747 lounge, but it was as if someone had removed the top of the aircraft, leaving a platform open to the skies at 35,000 feet. Thousands of stars blazed overhead, seeming not to twinkle at all at this altitude, and Harod could look left and right at the dark wedge of wings, the blinking red and green navigation lights, and a carpet of starlit cloud tops a mile or more below them. There was absolutely no sound and no sense of separation between where they stood and an infinite expanse of night sky. Only low silhouettes suggested the presence of shadowy furniture and a single, seated person in the lounge itself. Behind and below them receded the long metallic bulk of the airliner, the top of its fuselage glowing slightly in the starlight, a single, bright beacon flashing on the tall tail.

"Jesus Christ," whispered Harod. He heard Maria Chen's sudden intake of breath as she remembered to breathe.

"I'm glad you like it," came Barent's voice from the darkness. "Come and sit down."

Harod and Maria Chen walked carefully to a cluster of low chairs around a circular table, their eyes adjusting to the starlight. Behind them, the entrance to the spiral staircase had a single warning strip of red light on the top step and the bulkhead to the crew compartment was a black hemisphere against the western starfield. They collapsed on soft cushions and continued to stare at the sky.

"It's a translucent plastic compound," said Barent. "More than thirty layers, actually, but almost perfectly transparent and much stronger than Plexiglas. There are scores of support ribs, but they are fiber thin and do not interfere with the view at night. The outer surface polarizes in the daylight and looks like a glossy black paint job from the outside. It took my engineers a year to develop it and then it took me two years to convince the CAB that it was airworthy. If it was left to the engineers, aircraft would have no windows for passengers at all."

"It is beautiful," said Maria Chen. Harod could see starlight reflected in her dark eyes.

"Tony, I asked both of you here because this concerns both of you," said Barent.

"What does?"

"The . . . ah . . . dynamics of our group. You may have noticed a little tension in the air."

"I noticed that everyone's on the verge of losing their fucking minds."

"Just so," said Barent. "The events of the past few months have been . . . ah . . . troublesome."

"I don't see why," said Harod. "Most people don't get worked up when their colleagues are blown to shit or dropped into the Schuylkill River."

"The truth is," said C. Arnold Barent, "that we had grown far too complacent. We have had our Club and our way for too many years . . . decades actually . . . and it may be that Willi's little vendettas have offered a necessary . . . ah . . . pruning."

"As long as none of us are next in line to be pruned," said Harod.

"Precisely." Barent poured wine into a crystal goblet and set it in front of Maria Chen. Harod's eyes had adapted so that he could see the others clearly now, but it only made the stars brighter, the cloud tops more milkily iridescent. "In the meantime," said Barent, "there are bound to be certain imbalances in a group dynamic that had been so precariously established under circumstances no longer operative."

"What do you mean?" said Harod.

"I mean that there is a power vacuum," said Barent and his voice was as cold as the starlight that bathed them. "Or more precisely, the *perception* of a power vacuum. Willi Borden has made it possible for little people to think they can be giants. And for that he will have to die."

"Willi will?" said Harod. "So all that talk about possible negotiations and Willi joining the Club was bullshit?"

"Yes," said Barent. "If necessary, I will run the Club by myself, but under *no* circumstances will that ex-Nazi ever sit at our table."

"Then why . . ." Harod paused and thought a minute. "You think Kepler and Sutter are ready to make their move?"

Barent smiled. "I have known Jimmy for many years. The first time I saw him preach was in a tent revival in Texas four decades ago. His Ability was unfocused but irresistible; he could make a tent full of sweating agnostics do whatever he wanted them to and do it happily in the name of God. But Jimmy is getting old and he uses his real persuasive powers less and less while relying upon the apparatus of persuasion he's built. I know he had you out at his little fundamentalist magic kingdom last week . . ." Barent held up his hand to cut off Harod's explanation. "That's all right, Jimmy must have told you that I would know . . . and understand. I don't believe that Jimmy wants to upset the applecart, but he senses a possible shift in power and wants to be on the correct side when the shifting subsides. Willi's meddling has appeared—on the surface—to have changed a very delicate equation."

"But not in reality?" said Harod.

"No," said Barent and the softly spoken syllable was as final as a rifle shot. "They forgot essential facts." Barent reached into a drawer of the low table in front of them and withdrew a double-action semiautomatic pistol. "Pick it up, Tony."

"Why?" asked Harod, his skin bristling.

"The weapon is real and it is loaded," said Barent. "Pick it up, please."

Harod lifted the weapon and held it loosely in both hands. "OK, so what's the deal?"

"Aim it at me, Tony."

Harod blinked. Whatever demonstration Barent had in mind, he wanted no part of it. He knew that Haines and a dozen other security people were within a critical distance. "I don't want to aim it at you," said Harod. "I don't like these fucking games."

"Aim the gun at me, Tony."

"Screw you," said Harod and stood up to leave. He made a dismissive motion with his hand and walked to where the red light showed the top step of the staircase.

"*Tony,*" came Barent's voice, "*come here.*"

Harod felt as if he had walked into one of the plastic walls. His muscles cramped into tight knots and sweat broke out all over his body. He tried to surge forward, away from Barent, but only succeeded in dropping to his knees.

Once, four or five years before, he and Willi had had a session where the old man had tried to exert power over him. It had been a friendly exercise, in answer to some question Harod had asked about the Vienna Game Willi had been rambling on about. Instead of feeling the warm wave of domination that Harod knew he used on women, Willi's onslaught had been like a vague but terrible pressure in Harod's skull, white noise and a claustrophobic closeness all at once. But no loss of self-control on Harod's part. He had recognized immediately that Willi's Ability was much stronger than his own—more *brutal* was the phrase that had come to mind— but although Harod had doubted if he could have Used someone else during Willi's assault, there was no sense that Willi could have Used *him*. "*Ja,*" Willi had said, "it is always like that. We can turn on one another, but those that Use cannot be Used, *nicht wahr*? We test our strength through third parties, eh? A pity really. But a king cannot take a king, Tony. Remember that."

Harod had remembered that. Until now.

"Come here," said Barent. His voice was still soft, well modulated, but it seemed to reverberate until it filled Harod's skull, filled the room, filled the universe so that the stars shook to the echo of it. "*Come here, Tony.*"

Harod, on his knees, arms, neck, and body straining, was jerked onto his back like some stuntman being pulled off his horse by an invisible wire. Harod's body spasmed and his booted feet beat on the carpet. His jaws clenched and his eyes bulged in their sockets. Harod felt the scream build in his throat and knew that it could never be released, that it would grow there until it exploded, throwing shards of his flesh across the room. On his back, legs stiff and spasming, Harod felt the muscles of his arms contract and expand, contract and expand, his elbows digging into the carpet, fingers hooked into claws, as he slid backward toward the seated shadow. "*Come here, Tony.*" Like a palsied ten-month-old learning to crawl on its back, Tony Harod obeyed.

When his head touched the low coffee table, Harod felt the vise of control release him. His body spasmed in such release that he almost urinated.

He rolled over and got to his knees, his forearms on the black glass of the tabletop.

"Aim the gun at me, Tony," Barent said in the same conversational tone as before.

Harod felt a killing rage surge through him. His hands shook wildly as he felt for the gun, found the grip, raised it . . .

The barrel had not been leveled when the sickness struck. Years ago, his first year in Hollywood, Harod had suffered a kidney stone. The pain had been incredible, unbelievable. A friend later told Harod that he imagined it was like being knifed in the back. Harod knew otherwise; he had been knifed in the back while running with a Chicago gang as a kid. The kidney stone hurt more. It was like being knifed from the inside out, like someone dragging razor blades through your entrails and veins. And along with the incredible pain of the stone itself had come instant nausea, vomiting, cramps, and fever.

This was worse. Far worse.

Before the barrel came level, Harod was curled on the floor, vomiting on his silk shirt and trying to wrap himself in a knot. Along with the pain and sickness and humiliation there was the overwhelming knowledge that *he had tried to hurt Mr. Barent.* The idea was insupportable. It was the saddest thought Tony had ever suffered. He wept as he vomited and groaned with pain. The pistol had fallen out of his limp fingers onto the black glass tabletop.

"Oh, you don't feel well," Barent said softly. "Perhaps Ms. Chen should aim the weapon at me."

"No," gasped Harod, curling into a tighter ball.

"Yes," said Barent. "I want her to. *Tell her to aim the gun at me, Tony.*"

"Aim the gun!" gasped Harod. "Aim it at him!"

Maria Chen moved slowly, as if underwater. She lifted the revolver, steadied it in her small hands, and aimed it at Tony Harod's head.

"No! At him!" Harod doubled over as the cramps struck him again. "At him!"

Barent smiled. "She does not have to hear my orders to obey them, Tony."

Maria Chen pulled the hammer back with her thumb. The black opening was aimed directly at Harod's face. Harod could see the terror and sorrow building behind her brown eyes. Maria Chen had never been Used before.

"Impossible," gasped Harod, feeling the pain and illness recede and knowing that he might have only seconds to live. He staggered to his knees and held his hand up as a useless shield against the bullet. "Impossible . . . she's a *Neutral!*" He almost screamed it.

"What is a Neutral?" inquired C. Arnold Barent. "I have never encountered one, Tony." He turned his head. "Pull the trigger, please, Maria."

The hammer fell. Harod heard the solid click. Maria Chen squeezed the trigger again. Again.

"How careless," said Barent. "We forgot to load it. Maria, could you help Tony to his seat, please?"

Harod sat shaking, sweat and vomit plastering his shirt to his stomach, his head bowed, forearms on his knees.

"Debra will take you below and help you clean up, Tony," said Barent, "and Richard and Gordon will clean up in here. If you would like to come up later and have a drink in the Orion Lounge before we land, do feel free. It is a unique place, Tony. But please remember what I said about the temptation others will have to . . . ah . . . rearrange the natural order of things. It is at least partially my fault, Tony. It has been too many years since most of them have experienced a . . . ah . . . demonstration. Memory fades, even when it is in the best interest of the individual for it not to." Barent leaned forward. "When Joseph Kepler comes to you with an offer, you will agree to it. Is that understood, Tony?"

Harod nodded. Sweat fell onto his stained slacks.

"Say yes, Tony."

"Yes."

"And you will contact me immediately?"

"Yes."

"Good boy," said C. Arnold Barent and patted Harod's cheek. He turned his tall chair so that only the back of it was visible, a black obelisk against the star field. When it swiveled back, Barent was gone.

Men came in to clean and disinfect the carpet. A minute later the young woman came with a flashlight and took Harod's elbow. He thrust her hand away. Maria Chen tried to touch him on the shoulder, but he turned his back on her and staggered down the stairs.

Twenty minutes later they landed at LAX. A driver and limousine met the plane. Tony Harod did not look back to watch the ebony 747 taxi and take off.

FORTY

Tijuana, Mexico
Monday, April 20, 1981

Shortly before sundown, Saul and Natalie drove the rented Volkswagen northeast out of Tijuana. It was very hot. Once off Highway 2 the suburbs turned into a maze of dirt roads through villages of tin shacks and lean-tos sprawled between abandoned factories and small ranches. Natalie read from Jack Cohen's hand-drawn map while Saul drove. They parked the VW near a small tavern and walked north through a cloud of dust and small children. Fires were burning on the hillside as the last of the blood-red twilight faded. Natalie checked the map and pointed to a path down a hillside littered with junk and small groups of men and women sitting by open fires or squatting in the dark under low trees. Half a mile north across the valley a tall fence glowed white against a black hillside.

"Let's stay here until it's really dark," said Saul. He set down his suitcase and lowered a heavy knapsack to the ground. "There are supposed to be bandits working both sides of the border these days. It would be ironic to come this far and be killed by a border bandit."

"It suits me to sit awhile," said Natalie. They had walked less than a mile, but her blue cotton shirt was plastered to her skin and her sneakers were caked with dust. Mosquitoes whined past her ears. A single electric light glowing by a bar on the hill behind them had attracted so many moths that snow appeared to be falling in front of it.

They sat in exhausted silence for half an hour, worn out by thirty-six hours of flying by jet and commuter airline and by the constant tension of traveling under false passports. Heathrow Airport had been the worst—three hours' layover under the gaze of security people.

Natalie was dozing despite the heat, insects, and her uncomfortable position squatting next to a large rock when Saul awoke her with a gentle hand on her shoulder. "They're moving," he whispered. "Let's go."

At least a hundred illegals were heading toward the distant fence in small shuffling groups. More bonfires had appeared on the hillside behind them. Far to the northwest were the twinkling lights of an American town; ahead lay only dark canyons and hillsides. A single pair of headlights disappeared to the east on some unseen access road on the American side of the fence.

"Border patrol," said Saul and led the way down the steep trail and then up another hill. They were both panting audibly within minutes, sweating under their rucksacks and struggling with their large suitcases weighted with papers. Although they tried to remain separated from the others, they soon had to join a long line of sweating men and women, some speaking softly or swearing in Spanish, others plodding along in stolid silence. Ahead of Saul, a tall, thin man carried a seven- or eight-year-old boy on his back while a heavier woman carried a large cardboard suitcase.

The queue came to a stop in a dry riverbed twenty yards from a culvert that ran under the border fence and the gravel road beyond. Groups of three or four would spring across the streambed and disappear into the black circle of the culvert. There were occasional shouts from the other side and once Natalie heard a scream that must have come from just beyond the road. Natalie realized that her heart had been pounding for minutes and her skin was clammy with sweat. She took a grip on her suitcase and forced herself to relax.

The entire line of fifty or sixty people hid behind the rocks, bushes, and each other when a second border patrol vehicle came by and stopped. A bright spotlight swept across the arroyo and passed within ten feet of the pitiful thorn tree Natalie and Saul were trying to use for cover. Shouts and the slap of a gunshot from the northeast sent the car away at high speed, radio blaring in police English, and the line of illegals began its steady progress into the culvert once again.

Within minutes Natalie found herself crawling on all fours behind Saul, shoving the heavy suitcase ahead of her while her backpack banged against the corrugated roof of the tunnel. It was pitch black. The culvert smelled of urine and excrement and her hands and knees encountered moist softness interspersed with broken glass and bits of metal. Somewhere behind her in the stifling dark a woman or child began to cry until a man's sharp voice bullied them into silence. Natalie was sure that the culvert led nowhere and that it would grow narrower and narrower, the rough ceiling coming down to crush them into the mud and excrement, the water rising over their faces . . .

"Almost there," whispered Saul. "I see moonlight."

Natalie realized that her ribs hurt from the panicked pounding of her heart and because she had been holding her breath. She exhaled just as Saul tumbled forward two feet to a rocky streambed and helped her out of the stinking pipe.

"Welcome back to America," he whispered as they gathered their bags and ran for the darkened safety of an arroyo where murderers and thieves undoubtedly lay in wait for some of the night's hopeful immigrants.

"Thanks," Natalie whispered back between gasps for air. "Next time, I'm going direct even if it means flying People's Express."

Jack Cohen was waiting for them at the top of the third hill. Once every two minutes he had blinked the headlights of the old blue van he had parked there and that had been the beacon that brought Natalie and Saul in. Cohen shook hands with Saul and then Natalie and said, "Come, we must hurry. This is not a good place to park. I brought the things you asked for in your letter and I have no wish to explain them to the Border Patrol or the San Diego police. Hurry."

The rear of the van was half filled with boxes. They threw their luggage in back, Natalie took the passenger's seat, Saul sat in a low crate behind and between the two front seats, and Jack Cohen drove. They bounced along dirt ruts for half a mile, turned east onto a gravel road, and found an asphalt county road headed north. Ten minutes later they were descending an access ramp to an Interstate highway and Natalie felt displaced and disoriented, as if the United States had changed in various and subtle ways during the three months of her absence. *No, it was more like I've never lived here at all*, she thought as she watched suburbs and small shopping malls pass her window. She stared at the streetlights and cars and wondered at the incredible fact that thousands of people here were going about their evening business just as if nothing was happening—as if men and women and children were not crawling through shit-filled culverts ten miles from these comfortable middle-class homes, as if sharp-eyed young Sabras were not right at that minute riding armed guard on the boundaries of their kibbutzim while masked PLO killers—boys themselves—oiled their Kalashnikovs and waited for dark, as if Rob Gentry was not dead, murdered, dead and buried, as finally unreachable as her father who used to come in every evening to tuck her in bed and tell her stories about Max, the inquisitive Dachshund who was always . . .

"Did you get the gun in Mexico City where I told you to?" asked Cohen.

Natalie startled awake. She had been dozing with her eyes open. She felt the novacaine high of total fatigue. There was the muted roar of jet engines in her ears. She concentrated on listening to the two men.

"Yes," said Saul. "No problem, although I was worried about what would happen if the *federales* found it on me."

Natalie worked to focus her eyes to better see the Mossad agent. Jack Cohen was in his early fifties but seemed older, older even than Saul, especially now that Saul had shaved his beard and let his hair grow. Cohen's face was thin and pockmarked, set off by large eyes and a nose that obviously had been broken more than once. He had thin white hair that looked as if he had tried to trim it himself and given up before the job was done. Cohen's English was fluent and idiomatically correct but overlaid with an accent that Natalie could not place—it was as if a West German had been taught his English from a Welshman who had learned his from a Brooklyn scholar. Natalie liked Jack Cohen's voice. She liked Jack Cohen.

"Let me see the gun," said Cohen.

Saul pulled a small pistol from his waistband. Natalie had had no idea that Saul had a weapon. It looked like a cheap cap pistol.

They were alone in the left lane of a bridge. No one was behind them for at least a mile. Cohen took the pistol and threw it out the window, over the railing toward the dark ravine below. "It would probably have exploded the first time you tried to use it," said Cohen. "I was sorry I suggested it, but it was too late to wire you. You're right about the *federales*—papers or no papers, if they found that gun on you they would have hung you up by the *cojones* and checked in every second or third year to make sure you were still moaning. Not pleasant people, Saul. It was the damn money that made me think it was worth the risk. How much money did you end up bringing in?"

"About thirty thousand," said Saul. "Another sixty is being wired to a bank in Los Angeles by David's attorney."

"Is it yours or David's?" asked Cohen.

"Mine," said Saul. "I sold a nine-acre farm I've had near Netanya since before the War of Independence. I figured that it would be foolish to try to get to my New York savings account."

"You figured correctly," said Cohen. They were in a city now. Mercury vapor lamps passed lighted rectangles over the windshield and made Cohen's ugly-handsome face look yellow. "My God, Saul," he said, "do you know how hard it was to get some of those things on your shopping list? One hundred *pounds* of C-4 *plastique*! Compressed air gun. Tranquilizer darts! Good God, man, do you know that there are only six suppliers in the entire United States that sell tranquilizer darts and that you have to be a certified zoologist to have the *foggiest* idea of where to find these places?"

Saul grinned. "Sorry, but you can't complain, Jack. You see you're our resident deus ex machina."

Cohen smiled ruefully. "I don't know about deus," he said, "but I've certainly been run through the machina. Do you know that I've used up two and a half years of accumulated leave in running your little errands?"

"I'll try to make it up to you someday," said Saul. "Have you had further problems with the director?"

"No. The call from David Eshkol's office settled most of that. I hope that twenty years after my retirement that I have pull like that. Is he well?"

"David? No, he's not well after two heart attacks, but he is busy. Natalie and I saw him in Jerusalem five days ago. He told us to give you his best."

"I only worked with him once," said Cohen. "Fourteen years ago. He came out of retirement then to direct the operation where we snatched an entire Russian SAM site right out from under the Egyptians' noses. It saved a lot of lives during the Six Day War. David Eshkol was a brilliant tactician."

They were in San Diego now and Natalie watched with a strange sense of detachment as they turned onto Interstate Five and drove north.

"What are your plans for the next few days?" asked Saul.

"Get you installed," said Cohen. "I should be back in Washington by Wednesday."

"No problem," said Saul. "Will you be available to give advice?"

"At any time," said Cohen, "providing you answer one question."

"What is that?"

"What's really going on here, Saul? What is the bottom line connection between your old Nazi, this group in Washington, and the old woman in Charleston? No matter which way I put it together, it makes no sense. Why would the U.S. government harbor this war criminal?"

"They're not," said Saul. "Groups in the government are trying to find him as hard as we are, but for their own purposes. Believe me, Jack, I could tell you more, but it would do little to enlighten you. Much of this affair goes beyond logic."

"Wonderful," Cohen said sarcastically. "If you can't tell me more, there is no hope of my getting the agency involved, no matter how much everyone respects David Eshkol."

"That is probably for the best," said Saul. "You saw what happened when Aaron and your friend Levi Cole became involved. I have finally realized that there will be no trumpet blast and charge of cavalry over the hill in the nick of time. In a real sense, I have deferred action for decades while waiting for the cavalry to arrive. Now I realize that this is something I must do . . . and Natalie feels the same."

"Bullshit," said Cohen.

"Yes," agreed Saul, "but all of our lives are governed by a certain degree of faith in bullshit. Zionism was blatant bullshit a century ago, but today our border—Israel's border—is the only purely political boundary that is visible from orbit. Where the trees end and the desert begins, there ends Israel."

"You're changing the subject," Cohen said flatly. "I've done these things because I liked your nephew and loved Levi Cole like a son and I believe you're after who killed them. This is true?"

"Yes."

"And the woman you think has returned to Charleston, she is part of it, not a victim?"

"Part of it, yes," said Saul.

"And your Oberst is still killing Jews?"

Saul hesitated. "He is still killing innocent people, yes."

"And this *putz* in Los Angeles is involved?"

"Yes."

"All right," said Cohen, "you will continue to have my help, but some day there will be an accounting."

"If it helps," said Saul, "Natalie and I have left a sealed letter with David Eshkol. Even David does not know the details of this nightmare. If Natalie and I die or disappear, David or his executors will open the letter. They are directed to share the contents with you."

"Wonderful," Cohen said again. "I can hardly wait until you are both dead or missing."

They drove in silence toward Los Angeles. Natalie dreamed that she and Rob and her father were walking through the Old Section of Charleston. It was a beautiful spring evening. The stars burned behind palmettos and new buds; the air smelled of mimosa and hyacinth. Suddenly a dog with a light-colored head on a dark body came from out of the darkness and growled at them. Natalie was afraid, but her father told her that the dog only wanted to make friends. He knelt and extended his right hand for the dog to smell it, but the dog bit it, bit and kept chewing, growling and swallowing until the hand was gone, his arm was gone, and then her father was gone. The dog had changed then, become much larger, while Natalie realized that she had grown smaller, become a little girl. The dog turned on her then, its incongruously white head glowing in the starlight, and she was too terrified to turn or run or scream. Rob touched her cheek and stepped in front of her just as the dog leaped. It struck him in the chest and knocked him down. As they struggled Natalie noticed that the dog's strange head was growing smaller, disappearing. Then she realized that the dog had chewed and burrowed its way through Rob's chest. She could hear the noise of its eating.

Natalie sat down heavily on the sidewalk. She was wearing skates and the blue dress she had received from her favorite aunt on her sixth birthday. Rob's back was in front of her, a large gray wall. She looked at the pistol on the holster at his hip, but it was secured by a flap of leather and a snap and she could not bring herself to reach for it. His body shook with the violence of the animal's movements and she could hear the chewing, snapping sounds very clearly.

She tried to rise, but each time she got her feet under her the skates would fly out and she would sprawl on her behind again. One of the skates had come loose now and hung by a green strap. She rolled to her knees and was only inches from Rob's impossibly tall, gray back when the dog's head burst through. Fibers of flesh and shirt clung to the thing's cheeks and teeth. It thrashed to widen the hole; its eyes gleaming madly, its powerful jaws working like a shark's.

Natalie crawled backward two feet, but could move no further. Her attention was riveted on the dog as it growled and snapped and burrowed to get at her. Its neck and shoulders were through the opening now. Saliva and blood splattered her. She could see the dark, matted fur of the thing's shoulders and forelegs as it fought to free itself of its fleshy burrow. It was like watching some terrible, nightmarish birth, all the while knowing that its birth meant one's own death.

But it was the face that riveted Natalie, froze her into immobility and made the weakness of terror rise in her throat like vomit. For above the dark fur of the powerful, thrusting shoulders and scrabbling paws, above where the blood-streaked fur paled to blue-gray, there began the whiteness—the

Dan Simmons

deathmask whiteness of Melanie Fuller's face distorted by its insane grin and the poor fit of the gigantic, oversize dentures that came to gleaming white points inches from Natalie's eyes.

The dog-thing let out a howl, convulsed its entire body in a feral, bloody thrust of effort, and was born.

Natalie snapped awake, gulping air. She extended her hand to the van's dash and steadied herself. The wind blowing through the open window carried the scent of sewage and diesel fumes. Headlights flared at them across the median of the interstate.

Saul was saying in a low voice, "Perhaps the advice I need is how to kill someone."

Cohen gave him a sideways glance. "I am not a killer, Saul."

"No. Nor am I. But between us we have seen a lot of killing. I have seen it cold and efficient in the camps, fast and fleeting in the forests, hot and patriotic in the desert, and random and mean in the streets. Perhaps it is time I learned how it is done professionally."

"You want a seminar on killing?" asked Cohen.

"Yes."

Cohen nodded, fumbled a cigarette out of a pack in his shirt pocket, and used the van lighter on it. "These things will kill," he said, exhaling smoke. A semitrailer going 75 m.p.h. passed in a rush of wind.

"I was thinking of something faster and less injurious to innocent people in the vicinity," said Saul.

Cohen smiled and talked with the cigarette still in his mouth. "The most efficient way to kill someone is to hire someone who is good at killing." He glanced at Saul. "I'm serious. Everyone does it—KGB, CIA, all the little fish in between. Americans were upset a few years ago to discover that the CIA was hiring Mafia hit men to take out Castro. When you think about it, it makes sense. Would it have been more moral to train people in an agency of a democratic government to go out and gun people down? The James Bond stuff is sheer crap. Professional killers are controlled psychopaths, about as sympathetic as Charles Manson, but in tighter control. Using Mafia people might just have got the job done and also kept those particular psychopaths from killing other Americans for a few weeks."

Cohen drove in silence for a moment, his cigarette glowing each time he inhaled. Finally he tapped the ash out the window and said, "We all use mercenaries when it comes to premeditated killing. One of my jobs when I worked in-country was to turn young PLO recruits to carry out executions of other Palestinian leaders. I would guess that a third of the internecine hits within the terrorist community are a result of our operations. Sometimes all we have to do to eliminate A is to take a wild potshot at D, then get the word to D that C was paid by B to eliminate D on the orders of A, and sit back and wait for the fireworks."

"Assume that hiring someone is out of the question," said Saul.

Natalie realized that from their quiet tones that they thought she was asleep. She realized that her eyes had almost closed again, the headlights and occasional overhead lights filtering through her eyelashes. She remembered dozing in the backseat of the car as a child, listening to the soft monotone of her parents' conversation. But their conversation had never sounded like this.

"All right," said Cohen, "assume that you cannot hire someone for political, practical, or personal reasons. Then things get complicated. The first thing one must decide is whether or not you are willing to trade your own life for your target's. If you are, then you have a great advantage. Traditional methods of security are essentially useless. Most of the great assassins of history have been willing to give up their own lives . . . or at least to be apprehended immediately . . . in order to carry out their sacred missions."

"Assume in this case that the . . . killer . . . prefers to stay at large after the deed is performed," said Saul.

"Then the difficult becomes more difficult," said Cohen. "Choices: Military action . . . our F-16 strikes into Lebanon are nothing but indiscriminate attempts at assassination, selective use of explosives, rifles at a distance, handguns close in with an avenue of escape prepared, poison, knives, or hand-to-hand combat." Cohen tossed out the stub of the first cigarette and lit another. "Explosives are in vogue at present, but they are very tricky, Saul."

"How so?"

"Take the C-4 that you have ten years' supply of in the back right now. Safe as silly putty. You can bounce it, mold it, submerge it, sit on it, shoot it, or use it as caulking compound and it will not ignite. What ignites it is nitric acid, the explosive in the deadly little detonators packed away very, very carefully in a special box set in plastic noodles in another box back there. Have you ever used *plastique*, Saul?"

"No."

"God help us," said Cohen. "All right, tomorrow at the safe house we will have a *plastique* seminar. But say you have the explosive set in place, how will you detonate it?"

"What do you mean?"

"I mean the choices are infinite—mechanical, electrical, chemical, electronic—but none are safe. Most explosive *experts* die preparing their little bombs. It is the single greatest killer of terrorists next to other terrorists. But let us say that you manage to plant your plastic explosive, attach the detonator, rig an electrical trigger to your detonator—to be activated by a radio signal from a transmitter—and everything is ready. You are in a car a safe distance behind the target's vehicle. You will wait until his vehicle is in the country, away from witnesses and innocent bystanders. Instead, with your transmitter off, his car blows up while passing a school bus full of handicapped children."

"Why?"

Natalie could hear the fatigue in Saul's voice and she realized that he must be as bone tired as she was.

"Garage door openers, aircraft transmissions, children's walkie-talkies, citizen-band radios," intoned Cohen. "Even a television remote control device could set off such a trigger. So you work with a minimum of two switches on your *plastique*, a manual one to arm it and a line-of-sight electronic one to trigger it. The chances of failure are still great."

"Other ways," said Saul.

"The rifle," said Cohen. The second cigarette was almost gone. "It grants the safety of distance, allows time for retreat, is selective, and almost always efficient when used correctly. The weapon of choice. Endorsed by Lee Harvey Oswald and James Earl Ray and countless unsung others. A few problems, though."

"What?"

"First of all, forget all that television crap about the sniper bringing his weapon somewhere in an attaché case and snapping it together while the target obligingly gets into position. A rifle and scope have to be sighted in, adjusted for distance and angle and wind velocity and the vagaries of the weapon itself. The marksman needs to have experience with that weapon and with distance and velocity ratios. A military sniper works at distances where the target has time to walk three paces between the shot and the impact. Have you had experience with rifles, Saul?"

"Not since the war . . . the European war," said Saul. "And then never to kill a man."

"That is all they are good for," said Cohen. "I have things on your list back there . . . eighteen thousand dollars of your money invested in the damndest selection of things I've ever had to track down . . . but no rifle."

"What about security?" said Saul.

"Yours or theirs?"

"Theirs."

"What about it?"

"How does one deal with it?"

Cohen held his cigarette European-style and squinted at the tunnel of light the headlights burrowed through the night. "Security is . . . at best . . . a doomed attempt to postpone the inevitable if someone is intent on killing you. If the target has a public life—commitments—the best security can only make it difficult for the successful assassin to escape. You saw the result last month when an untrained punk decided he wanted to shoot the American president with a .22 caliber popgun . . ."

"Aaron told me that you train your agents to use .22 Berettas," said Saul.

"We have in recent years," said Cohen, "but they used them close in, where knives might be expected, in situations that call for lack of noise or quick handling rather than firepower. If we sent a team in to kill someone, it would be a *team* . . . after weeks of following the target, rehearsing the operation, and testing the escape route. This boy who shot your president last month did so with no more preparation than you or I would use to go down to the corner to buy a newspaper."

"So what does that prove?"

"It proves that there is no such thing as security when one's movements are predictable," said Cohen "A good security chief will allow his client to abide by no timetables, follow no routines, and make no engagements that might become public knowledge. Unpredictability saved Hitler's life half a dozen times. It is the only reason we have not terminated the top three or four Palestinians on our official shit list. Whose security are we talking about in this hypothetical discussion?"

"Hypothetically?" said Saul. "Let us hypothetically discuss the security of Mr. C. Arnold Barent."

Cohen's head snapped around. He flicked his cigarette out the window and did not light another one. "This is why you asked for the files on Barent's Summer Camp?"

"We are speaking hypothetically," said Saul.

Cohen ran his hand through his hair. "Good God, man, you are insane."

"You said that security is a hopeless attempt to forestall the inevitable," said Saul. "Is Mr. Barent an exception?"

"Listen," said Jack Cohen, "when the president of the United States travels anywhere . . . *anywhere*, even to visit leaders of other countries in secluded security zones . . . the Secret Service shits bricks. If it was up to them, the president would never leave the sub-basement of the White House and they're not very pleased with that location. The one place . . . the *one* place where the Secret Service breathes a sigh of relief, is when a president spends time with C. Arnold Barent . . . which presidents have been doing for thirty-some years now. In June, Barent's Heritage West Foundation throws its annual summer camp and forty or fifty of the most powerful men in the world will be kicking off their shoes and letting their proverbial hair down on his island. Now does *that* tell you anything about the man's security?"

"Good?"

"The best in the world," said Cohen. "If Tel Aviv sent the word tomorrow that the future of the state of Israel depended upon C. Arnold Barent's sudden death, I would call in the best men we have from Israel, alert the commando teams that made Entebbe look easy, pull our revenge squads in from Europe, and *still* not give us a one-in-ten chance of coming close."

"How would you try?" asked Saul.

Cohen drove in silence for several minutes. "Hypothetically," he said at last, "I would wait until he was dependent upon someone else's security . . . like the president's . . . and try then. My God, Saul, all this talk of killing Barent. Where were you last March thirtieth?"

"In Caesarea," said Saul. "In full view of witnesses. What else would you try?"

Cohen chewed his lip. "Barent flies constantly. Whenever there are aircraft involved there is vulnerability. The security on the ground would almost certainly preclude smuggling explosives aboard, but that would leave interception or ground-to-air missiles. *If* you knew where the aircraft was going to be ahead of time, when it was taking off, and how to identify it once airborne."

"Could you do that?" asked Saul.

"Yes," said Cohen, "if we had all of the resources of the Israeli Air Force tied in with electronic intelligence services *and* the help of American satellite and NDA intelligence *and* if Mr. Barent obliged us by flying over the Mediterranean or extreme southern Europe with a flight plan filed weeks ahead of time."

"He has a boat," said Saul.

"No," said Cohen, "he has a two-hundred-sixteen-foot yacht, the *Antoinette*, that cost sixty-nine million dollars twelve years ago when it was sold to him by a certain late unnamed Greek shipping magnate best known as the second husband of an American widow whose first husband got too close to a rifle that had been well sighted in by an ex-marine marksman." Cohen took a breath. "Barent's 'boat' has as much security aboard and around it as one of his residential islands. No one knows where it is bound or when the man will be aboard. It has landing pads for two helicopters and speedboats that serve as outriders whenever there is traffic near. A torpedo or Exocet missile *might* sink it, but I doubt it. It has better radar, maneuverability, and damage control systems than most modern destroyers."

"End of hypothetical discussion," said Saul and Natalie guessed from his tone of voice that he had known everything Cohen had told him.

"This is where we get off," said Cohen and headed up an exit ramp. The sign had said San Juan Capistrano. They stopped at an all-night gas station and Cohen paid with his credit card. Natalie got out and stretched her legs, still fighting sleep. The air was cool now and she thought she could smell the sea. Cohen was getting a cup of coffee from a machine as she walked up to the station.

"You're awake," he said. "Welcome back."

"I was awake in the car . . . most of the time," said Natalie.

Cohen sipped his coffee and made a face. "A bizarre conversation. Have you discussed Saul's plans?"

"Yes, we worked on them together."

"And you know the kinds of things that are in the back of the van?"

"If they're what were on our list, yes," said Natalie.

Cohen began walking toward the vehicle with her. "Well, I hope you both know what you're doing."

"We don't," said Natalie and smiled at him, "but we *do* appreciate your help, Jack."

"Uh-huh," he said and opened the door for her, "as long as my help doesn't end up letting you kill yourselves faster."

They drove eight miles up Highway 74, away from the sea, and turned north through scrub forest before stopping at the farmhouse. The building was dark, set a quarter of a mile down a narrow lane.

"It used to be used by our West Coast people as a safe house,' said Cohen. "No one's had a reason to use it for the last year or so, but somebody keeps it up, mows the yard. Locals think it's a summer house owned by a couple of Anaheim Hills young professional types."

There were two floors, with too many cheap beds in the upstairs bedrooms. A dozen people could sleep in the three bedrooms. Downstairs, in an addition on the back of the old frame building, a one-way mirror looked into a small room with couches and a low coffee table. "This was put on for one long summer of interrogation of a member of Black September who thought he had turned himself over to the CIA. We helped keep him away from the big, bad Mossad until he'd told us everything he had. I thought this room fit your specifications rather nicely."

"Perfectly," said Saul. "It saves us weeks of preparation."

"I wish I was going to be here for the fun," said Cohen.

"If it's fun," said Saul, stifling a huge yawn, "we'll sit down and tell you all about it someday."

"That's a deal," said Jack Cohen. "What do you say we each choose a room and get some sleep? I have an eleven-thirty A.M. flight out of L.A. tomorrow."

Shortly after eight A.M., Natalie awoke to the sound of an explosion. She looked around, not registering where she was for a few seconds, and then found her jeans and pulled them on. She called Saul's name, but there was no answer from the room next door. Jack Cohen was not in his room.

Natalie went downstairs and out the front door, marveling at the blue sky and warm air. Some sort of low crop stretched away toward the road they had come in on. She went around behind the house and found Saul and Cohen crouching over an old door that had been propped sideways against a fence. A ten-inch hole had been blown in the center panel of the door.

"*Plastique* seminar," Cohen said to her as she came up. He turned to Saul. "That was less than half an ounce. You can guess what your forty pounds would do." He got up and brushed his pant legs off. "Breakfast."

The refrigerator had been empty and turned off, but Cohen carried in a large cooler from the van and for twenty minutes all three were busy digging out pans and coffeepots, taking turns at the stove, and generally getting in each other's way. When order returned, the kitchen smelled of coffee and eggs and the three of them sat at the table by the large bay window in the dining room. In the middle of the idle breakfast conversation, Natalie felt a deep and sudden twinge of sadness and realized that the room had reminded her of Rob's house. Charleston seemed ten thousand miles and twice as many years away from her at that minute.

After breakfast they emptied the van. It took all three of them to carry in the large crate with the electroencephalograph in it. The electronic equipment also went into the room on the observer's side of the one-way mirror. They set the boxes of C-4 and the larger crate of detonators in the basement.

When they were finished, Cohen set two small boxes on the dining room table. "This is a gift from me," he said. Inside were two semiautomatic pistols. The markings on blue steel read: COLT MK IV SERIES GOVERNMENT MODEL 380 AUTO. "I would have preferred giving you the forty-five-caliber version I carry," said the Israeli. "Something with real stopping power. But each of these is almost a pound lighter than a forty-five Government Model, the barrel's almost two inches shorter, it holds seven rounds rather than six, it's got lower recoil for beginners, and it should be easier to conceal. And, used close in, it should still get the job done." He laid three boxes of shells on the table. "The hardware can't be traced," he said. "It was part of an intercepted I.R.A. shipment that got lost in the shuffle somehow." He lifted a larger box onto the table and removed a long, heavy weapon that looked like a toymaker's caricature of a gun. The grip was dwarfed by the long, metal rectangular prism of the barrel. It might have been some sort of prototype of a submachine gun except for the tiny muzzle opening and lack of an ammunition clip. "I almost had to call Martin Perkins before I could find one of these with a range over ten feet," said Cohen. "Most of the game people use specially made rifles." He broke the weapon and lifted a dart from the box, inserted it in the single-shot breech. "CO_2 cartridge is good for about twenty shots," said Cohen. "Want to see it in operation?"

Natalie stepped off the front porch, looked at the van, and started laughing. The lettering was yellow on blue.

JACK & NAT'S POOLS
INSTALLATION AND REPAIR
HOT TUBS AND SPAS OUR SPECIALTY

"Did it come this way or did you have it decorated?" Natalie asked Cohen.

"I did."

"Won't it be a bit conspicuous?"

"Perhaps, but I hope it will serve the opposite purpose."

"How so?"

"You're going into a definite high-rent neighborhood," said Cohen. "It has one of the most security-conscious local police forces in the country. Plus the community is paranoid. If you're parked somewhere for half an hour, people will notice. This might help."

Natalie chuckled and followed them around to the barn. A small pig trotted toward them in the pen. "I thought the farm wasn't used anymore," said Natalie.

"It's not," said Cohen. "I picked this fellow up yesterday morning. It was Saul's idea."

Natalie looked at Saul.

"He weighs about a hundred forty pounds," said Saul. "You remember the problems Itzak discussed at the Tel Aviv Zoo."

"Oh," said Natalie.

Cohen lifted the air pistol. "It's awkward, but you aim it about the same as any pistol. Just pretend the barrel is your forefinger, aim, and shoot." Cohen lifted the bulky pistol and there was a loud *pffft*. The small dart with its blue-feathered tail appeared in the center of the barn door fifteen feet away. Cohen broke the pistol and opened the box of darts. "The blue row on top here are the empty ones. Mix up your own solution. The red row are the fifty cc syringes, the green row are forty cc, the yellow thirty cc, and the orange twenty cc. Saul has the extra vials if you want to mix your own." He lifted a red dart and inserted it in the breech. "Natalie, you want to try?"

"Sure." She closed the air gun and aimed it at the barn door.

"Uh-uh," said Saul. "Let's try it on our friend here."

Natalie turned and looked dubiously at the pig. Its snout flared at her as he snuffled the air.

"The compound is based on curare," said Cohen. "Very expensive and nowhere near as safe as the wildlife specials suggest. You have to have the right amount for body weight. It doesn't really knock them all the way out . . . it's not a tranquilizer, really . . . it's more like a specific nerve toxin that paralyzes the nervous system. Too little and the target feels a sort of novocaine numbness but can hop away. Too much and it inhibits breathing and heart rate as well as the voluntary functions."

"Is this the right amount?" asked Natalie, looking at the dart gun.

"One way to find out," said Cohen. "Porker here is the weight Saul specified and the fifty cc dart was recommended for animals that size. Give it a try."

Natalie walked around the pen to get a clear shot. The pig poked its head through the slats as if expecting a treat from Saul and Jack Cohen. "Any special spot?" asked Natalie.

"Try to avoid the face and eyes," said Cohen. "The neck can give problems. Anywhere on the torso is fine."

Natalie lifted the air pistol and shot the pig in the rump from twelve feet away. The pig jumped, squealed once, and gave Natalie a reproachful look. Eight seconds later its hind legs gave way, it made a half circle with its front legs, and it fell over, sides heaving.

All three got in the pen with it. Saul laid his palm on the pig's side. "Its heart is going crazy. This amount may be a bit too concentrated."

"You wanted it fast acting," said Cohen. "This is as fast as it gets without killing the animal you're capturing."

Saul looked into the pig's open eyes. "Can it see us?"

"Yes," said Cohen. "The animal may fade in and out, but most of the time the senses are working. He can't move or make noise, but old Porker's taking down your names for future reference."

Natalie patted the paralyzed pig's flank. "His name isn't Porker," she said.

"Oh?" Cohen looked at her with a smile. "What is it?"

"Harod," said Natalie. "Anthony Harod."

FORTY-ONE

Washington, D.C.
Tuesday, April 21, 1981

Jack Cohen thought about Saul and Natalie during his entire flight east. He worried about them, unsure of what they were planning or of their ability to carry it out. In his thirty years of experience in intelligence, he knew it was invariably the amateurs who ended upon the casualty list at the end of an operation. He reminded himself that this was not an operation. *What was it?* he wondered.

Saul had been concerned—overly concerned, Cohen thought—about the agent's efforts to elicit information about Barent and the others. Had Cohen taken every precaution not to be discovered during his computer searches? Had he been cautious enough during his trips to Charleston and Los Angeles? Cohen finally had to remind the psychiatrist that he had been carrying out this kind of work since the 1940s.

As the plane approached Washington, Cohen realized that he was feeling the rising anxiety and vague guilt that he associated with running an operation where civilians were being used. He reminded himself for the fiftieth time that he was not using them. *Are they using me?*

Cohen was certain that a rogue element in Colben's wing of the FBI counterintelligence team had killed Saul Laski's nephew and Levi Cole. The murder of Aaron Eshkol's entire family, however, was incredible and inexplicable. Cohen knew that the CIA might blunder into a situation like that through losing control of its contract people—Cohen himself had watched an operation in Jordan go sour at the expense of the lives of three civilians—but he had never heard of the FBI acting so blatantly. Once pointed out by Laski, however, the ties between Charles Colben and the billionaire, Barent, quickly had become visible. Cohen was committed to tracking down the last bit of evidence relating to the murder of Levi Cole. Levi had been Cohen's protégé, a brilliant young operative, temporarily placed in communications and ciphers to get the necessary experience but destined for big things. Levi had possessed the necessary qualities of that rarest of species—a successful field agent. Levi was instinctively cautious but responded to the lure of the pure game, the intricate and often boring matching of wits between adversaries who would never meet and probably never know the other's true name or position.

Cohen looked down and saw afternoon sunlight on new buds and blossoms. He had his own theory as to why the FBI might have gone mean so quickly. Cohen thought it was possible that Aaron and Levi's unintentional fumblings had tipped Colben to Operation Jonah, a seven-year infiltration of American counterintelligence agencies. In the arrogance of the months following the Six Day War, a plan was proposed in Tel Aviv to tap into the main channels of U.S. intelligence by placing moles and paid informants in key positions. Infiltration of the CIA and other agencies was not necessary; the Mossad had analyzed where to tap into the FBI and other domestic agencies sources of information on the competing groups. Besides giving access to sources of electronic intelligence far beyond the Mossad's capability, the argument had gone, placing key sources in the FBI would offer avenues of domestic American information—specifically dossiers on key political figures that the Bureau had been collecting in its own interest since the early days of J. Edgar Hoover—that would provide incalculable leverage when American congressional or executive support was needed in future crises.

The operation had been considered too risky—as insane as Gordon Liddy's Gemstone plan—until the terrifying surprise of the Yom Kippur War had shown the old men in Tel Aviv that nothing less than the survival of Israel depended upon access to such improved and extensive intelligence as only the Americans could provide. Operation Jonah was begun the same month Jack Cohen had become Head of Station in Washington in 1974. Now Jonah had become the whale that had swallowed the Mossad. A disproportionate amount of time and money had been put into the project—first to expand it, then to cover it up. Politicians in Tel Aviv lived in constant fear that the Americans would discover Jonah at a crucial moment when U.S. support was critical. Much of the information that flowed from Washington could not be used because it might expose the existence of the penetration itself. Cohen thought that the Mossad had begun acting like the classic adulterer—dreading the day his affair would be exposed but feeling so guilty and tired of feeling guilty that he half welcomed the exposure.

Cohen considered his options. He could continue his liaison with Saul and Natalie, keeping a formal distance between the Mossad and their puzzling amateur endeavors, and see what resulted. Or he could intervene now. Have at least the West Coast station take a more active role. He had not told Saul that the safe house was bugged. Cohen could have three people take the Los Angeles communications van out to the woods a mile from the safe house and set up a real-time link over secure lines. It would mean active involvement by at least half a dozen Mossad personnel, but Cohen saw no alternative.

Saul Laski had talked about no longer waiting for the cavalry to come chasing over the hill, but in this case, thought Cohen, the cavalry was coming whether the wagon train wanted it or not. Cohen could see no connection between Operation Jonah and the Barent-Colben contacts, nor between Laski's absent and possibly mythical Nazi and the rest of the insanity occurring in Washington and Philadelphia, but *something* was going on.

Cohen would find out what it was and if the director objected, so be it.

Cohen had brought a single, small bag but had not carried it on because it held his .45 automatic. Airline security was, Cohen decided as he waited at Dulles baggage claim carousel, a pain in the ass.

He felt good about his decision as he carried his bag out to the long-term lot where he had left his old blue Chevrolet. He would call John or Ephraim in Los Angeles that afternoon, alert them to the use of the safe house, and have them begin surveillance. If nothing else, Saul and Natalie would have a backup team in whatever they were doing.

Cohen squeezed between his car and the one next to him, unlocked the door, and tossed his bag onto the passenger's seat. He looked back in irritation as someone stepped into the narrow space with him. They would have to wait until he backed out. . . .

It took Jack Cohen a second before old instincts took over, another second before he made out the man's face in the dim light. It was Levi Cole.

Cohen's hand still went into his sports coat before he remembered the .45 was packed away under his socks and shorts. He brought his hands out in a defensive position, but the fact that it was Levi Cole confused him. "Levi?"

"Jack!" It was a cry for help. The young agent looked thin and pale, as if he had spent weeks in a locked room. His eyes seemed shocked, almost blank. He raised empty hands as if to hug Cohen.

Cohen stepped out of his defensive stance but stopped the young man with palm on his chest. "What is going on, Levi?" he asked in Hebrew. "Where have you been?"

Levi Cole was left-handed. Cohen had forgotten. The spring-loaded scabbard slipped the short-bladed knife into Levi's palm without a sound. Levi's arm and hand came up so quickly that the movement was almost spasmodic, followed two seconds later by Cohen's own involuntary spasm as the blade passed up under his rib and into his heart.

Levi eased the body into the front seat and looked around. A limousine pulled up to idle behind the Chevrolet, blocking the view from the rear. Levi removed Cohen's wallet, took the money and credit cards, searched the dead man's sports coat pockets and the suitcase, tossing clothing into the backseat. He came away with the .45, Cohen's airline tickets, money, credit cards, and an envelope of receipts. Levi rolled the body to the floor, locked the Chevrolet's door, and walked to the waiting limousine.

They left the parking garage and drove toward Arlington on the expressway.

"Not much here," Richard Haines said into the radio telephone. "Two receipts for gas at the San Juan Capistrano Shell station. Hotel receipts, Long Beach. Mean anything?"

"Put your people on it," came Barent's voice. "Start with the hotel and gas station. Is it time for the swallows to return to Capistrano?"

"I think we missed that," Haines said on the secured line. He glanced at Levi Cole sitting next to him, staring straight ahead. "What do we do with your friend here?"

"I am finished with him," said Barent.

"For today or for good?"

"Completely finished, I believe."

"Okay," said Haines. "We'll take care of it."

"Richard?"

"Yes?"

"Do begin your inquiries at once, please. Whatever attracted the curious Mr. Cohen's interest out there has certainly captured mine. I expect a report by Friday at the latest."

"You'll have it," said Richard Haines. He placed the phone in its cradle and watched the Virginia countryside pass by. A large jet flashed overhead, gaining altitude, and Haines wondered if it was Mr. Barent's aircraft on its way somewhere. Through the heavily tinted glass, the clear sky appeared to be the color of brandy, shedding a sick copper light that made one think that a terrible storm was brewing.

FORTY-TWO

Near Meriden, Wyoming
Wednesday, April 22, 1981

The area northeast of Cheyenne, Wyoming, was the type of western landscape that made some people rhapsodic and gave others instant agoraphobia. Once the state road left sight of the interstate, forty miles of driving afforded views of endless grasslands, windblown snow fences looking dwarfed and forgotten against great expanses of prairie, occasional ranches set back miles from the road, buttes to the north and east rising like massive keeps, an occasional stream huddled about with cottonwood and brush, hesitant clusters of antelope, and small groups of cattle looking unworthy of their millions of acres of grazing land.

And the missile silos.

The silos were as unprepossessing as any man-made thing could be against that expansive landscape; small, square, hurricane-fenced plots of gravel, usually set fifty to a hundred yards from the state road. The only visible indications that the fenced squares were anything but a natural gas pumping station or empty lot were the metal weather vane, the four pipes with reflecting mirrors, and the low, massive concrete roof set on rusting rails. The last details could be seen only if the viewer approached on the gravel ruts close enough to see the signs that read NO TRESPASSING— U.S. GOVERNMENT PROPERTY—*use of deadly force authorized beyond this point.* There was nothing else to see. There was no sound except the wind across the prairie and the occasional lowing of cattle in the fields beyond.

The blue air force van left Warren Air Force Base at 6:05 A.M., returning with the last of its squadron personnel at 8:27 A.M., in the interim dropping members of the next shift at their appointed command stations. In the van that morning were six young lieutenants, two for the SAC missile wing control HQ eight miles southeast of Meriden, and four for the bunker thirty-eight miles farther toward Chugwater.

The two lieutenants in the backseat watched the passing landscape with eyes dulled by routine. They had seen satellite photographs showing the six thousand-square-mile area the way the Soviets saw it—ten rings of silos, circles with an eight-mile diameter, each of the sixteen silos in each circle loaded with an MRVed Minuteman III missile. In recent months there had been talk of the vulnerability of these aging silos, discussions of the Soviet "pin-down strategy" that could keep a nuclear warhead exploding above these grasslands once a minute for hours, and whispers of hardening the silos or filling them with newer weapons. But these were policy issues of little direct interest to Lieutenant Daniel Beale or Lieutenant Tom Walters; they were simply two young men commuting to work on a chilly spring morning.

"Tom, you with it today?" asked Beale.

"Yeah," said Walters. His gaze did not shift from the distant horizon.

"Out partying with those tourists 'til late last night, man?"

"Uh-uh," said Walters. "In by eight."

Beale adjusted his sunglasses and grinned. "Yeah, I bet."

The air force van slowed and turned left onto two gravel ruts rising above the highway up a gradual slope to the northwest. They passed three signs demanding that unauthorized personnel stop, turn around, and leave. A quarter mile from the control station, they stopped for the first gate and sentry. Each man showed his ID tag while the sentry radioed ahead. The process was repeated at the entrance to the main complex. Lieutenants Beale and Walters walked along the fenced corridor to the vertical access building while the van turned around and parked facing downhill. Its exhaust floated upward in the cold morning air.

"So did you get in Smitty's pool?" asked Lieutenant Beale as they waited for the elevator cage. A bored security man with an M-16 stifled a yawn.

"No," said Lieutenant Walters.

"No kidding? I thought you were eager to get your money in."

Lieutenant Walters shook his head and they stepped into the smaller cage and descended three stories to the launch command center. They passed through two clearance checkpoints before saluting the duty officer in the anteroom outside the missile control room. It was 0700 hours.

"Lieutenant Beale reporting for duty, *sir.*"

"Lieutenant Walters reporting for duty, *sir.*"

"Your identification, gentlemen," said Captain Peter Henshaw. He carefully compared the photographs on their identification tags to the two men even though he had known them for over a year. Captain Henshaw nodded and the sergeant slipped a coded security card into the lock box and the outer door hissed open. Twenty seconds later the inner door cycled and two air force lieutenants stepped out. The four men saluted each other and grinned.

"Sergeant, log it in that Lieutenants Beale and Walters relieved Lieutenants Lopez and Miller at . . . 0701.30 hours," said Captain Henshaw.

"Yes, *sir.*"

The two tired men handed over their bolstered sidearms and two thick three-ring binders.

"Anything?" asked Beale.

"Communications check showed some trouble with the land lines at 0350," said Lieutenant Lopez. "Gus is on it. We had a standup at 0420 and a full run at 0510. Terry had a wire alert on Six South at 0535. Checked it out."

"Rabbits again?" asked Beale.

"Faulty pressure sensor. That's about it. You awake, Tom?"

"Yes," said Walters and flashed a grin.

"Don't take any wooden PC-380s," said Lieutenant Lopez and the two men left.

Beale and Walters closed both airlock doors behind them as they entered the long, narrow missile control room. Each man strapped into one of the blue, heavily cushioned chairs that ran on rails along the control boards on the north and west walls. Working efficiently, occasionally talking to men in other parts of the command center through headset microphones, they ran through their first five checklists. At 0743 there was an Omaha command link check through Warren and Lieutenant Beale handled the twelve-channel acknowledgments. When the phone was set back in its blue box, he looked over at Lieutenant Walters. "You sure you feel OK, Tom?"

"Headache," said Walters.

"Got some aspirin over here in the kit."

"Later," said Walters.

At 1156 hours, just as Beale was breaking out the thermoses and brown bags, a full stand-up order came through Warren Air Force Base. At 1158 hours, Beale and Walters unlocked the red safe below console two, took out their keys, and activated missile launch sequences. At 1210:30, missile launch sequences were completed except for the actual arming and launch of the sixteen missiles and their 120 warheads. They received a "well done" from Warren and Beale was beginning the two-minute stand-down sequence when Walters undid his shoulder harness and began walking away from his console.

"Tom, what are you doing? We've got to get this back to El Con Two before we eat," said Beale.

"Headache," said Walters. His face was a sick white, his eyes glazed.

Beale reached for the medkit on the shelf that held his Thermos. "I think there's some extra-strength Anacin in here . . ."

Lieutenant Walters removed his .45 automatic and shot Lieutenant Beale in the back of the head, making sure that the trajectory was down and to the side so an exiting bullet would not strike the console. The bullet did not exit. Beale spasmed once and slumped forward against his harness. Hydrostatic pressures caused blood to pour from his eyes, ears, nose, and mouth. Within seconds of the shot, two yellow intercom lights began blinking and a telltale showed that the outer airlock door was cycling open.

Walters walked unhurriedly to the inner door and fired two bullets into the electronic lockbox. He walked back to Beale's console and threw the switch that put the self-contained missile control room on one hundred percent reserve oxygen. Then Walters returned to his own chair and studied the manual for several minutes.

Frenzied pounding was just barely audible through the thick steel door as Walters stood up, took seven paces to Beale's seat, took the long ignition switch key from the dead man's pocket, and inserted it in the proper panel. He threw the five switches to arm the missiles, did the same at his own console, and inserted his own key.

Lieutenant Walters flicked the intercom switch on.

". . . the hell are you doing, Lieutenant?" It was the voice of Colonel Anderson from the command center at Warren. "You know it takes two men on the key. Now open that door *immediately*!"

Walters turned off the intercom and watched the digital clock back through ninety seconds and continue to drop. According to the operations manual, the huge concrete silo cover explosives would be arming at this time, preparing to blow the 110-ton silo doors a quarter mile across the grasslands and expose the slick steel pits and nose cones of the inert Minutemen. At ignition minus sixty seconds, air horns would blast at each site, ostensibly to warn any repair or inspection crews at the location. In reality the shrieks would alarm only rabbits, nearby cattle, and the occasional rancher passing by in his pickup. The Minuteman missiles were solid-fueled, awaiting only the electronic match to light them. Targeting instructions, guidance programming, gyroscopes, and the electronic accessories to launch had been powered up during the drill segment of the launch sequence. At ignition minus thirty seconds the computers would halt the sequence and wait for the twin-key launch activation signal. Without the turn of those two keys, the hold would be indefinite.

Walters looked over at Beale's console. The two keys were sixteen feet apart. They had to be turned within one second of each other. The air force had gone to great lengths to insure that it would be impossible for one man to activate his own key and then race to the other within the necessary time interval.

The corners of Tom Walters's mouth twitched up. He walked over to Beale's console, slid the seat and corpse out of the way along the rail, and withdrew a spoon and two lengths of string from his pocket. The spoon was a regular dinner spoon, filched from the officer's mess at Warren. Walters tied the bowl of the spoon to the flange of the key, bringing the handle down at right angles, and knotted the longer string to the end of the handle. He walked over to his own panel, pulled the string taut, waited until the clock reached 30, turned his own key and tugged hard at the string. The spoon provided enough leverage to turn Beale's key.

The computer acknowledged launch-activation signal, verified the launch code he and Beale had programmed in during the drill, and proceeded with the final thirty seconds of the launch sequence.

Walters pulled a memo pad over and wrote a brief note. He looked at the door. A section of steel near the lock handle glowed cherry red from the acetylene torch they were wielding in the airlock. The metal would take at least two more minutes to burn through.

Lieutenant Tom Walters smiled, strapped himself into his chair, set the muzzle of the .45 in his mouth so the sight touched his palate, and pulled the trigger with his thumb.

Three hours later, General Verne Ketchum, USAF, and his aide Colonel Stephen Anderson, walked away from the control center complex to get a breath of fresh air and to view the chaos. Almost a dozen military vehicles and three ambulances filled the parking area and spilled down the hill beyond the inner security zone. Five helicopters were parked in the field beyond the west perimeter and Ketchum could see and hear two more throbbing in from the southwest.

Colonel Anderson looked at the cloudless sky. "Wonder what the Russians think is going on."

"Fuck the Russians," said Ketchum. "Today I've had my ass chewed by everybody up to the vice-president. When I go back in, he'll be on the line. Every one of them demands to know how it happened. What do I tell 'em, Steve?"

"We've had a few problems before," said Anderson. "Nothing like this. You saw Walters's last psych report. Just two months ago. The man was moderately intelligent, unmarried, reacted well to stress, was ambitious only within the service, obeyed orders to the letter, was on the winning team last fall in the Vanderburg launch competitions, and he had all the imagination of that piece of sagebrush over there. Perfect profile for a missile jock."

Ketchum lit a cigar and glowered through the smoke. "So what the fuck *happened?*"

Anderson shook his head and watched the chopper coming in. "It doesn't make any sense. Walters knew that the final missile activate sequence had to be done in tandem with two other keys in a separate control center. He knew that the computers would hold at the T-5 second mark unless there was that verification. He killed himself and Beale for nothing."

"You have that note?" growled Ketchum around the cigar.

"Yessir."

"Give it to me."

Walters's last note had been wrapped in plastic although Ketchum could not see the sense of that. They sure as hell did not have to dust it for fingerprints. The writing was clear enough through the plastic:

> WvB to CAB
> King's pawn to QB6. Check
> Your move, Christian.

"Some kind of goddam code, Steve?" asked Ketchum. "Does this chess shit mean anything to you?"

"No, sir."

"You think the CAB is the Civil Aeronautics Board?"

"It doesn't make much sense, sir."

"And what's this Christian crap? Was Walters born again or something like that?"

"No, sir. According to the base chaplain, the lieutenant was a Unitarian but never attended services."

"The W and B could be Walters and Beale," mused Ketchum, "but what's the v in between?"

Anderson shook his head. "No idea, sir. Maybe Intelligence or the FBI people can figure it out. I think that green chopper's bringing in the FBI guy from Denver."

"I wish to hell they didn't have to be brought in," grumbled Ketchum. He removed the cigar and spat.

"It's the law, sir," said Anderson. "They have to be."

General Ketchum turned and gave the colonel a look that made the younger man look down and become suddenly interested in the crease in his trousers. "All right," Ketchum said at last, flicking the cigar toward the perimeter, "let's go talk to these civilian hotshots. What the hell, the day isn't going to get any worse." Ketchum swiveled on his heel and strode toward the distant delegation.

Colonel Anderson ran over to where the general had thrown his cigar, made sure the stogie was out, and then hurried to catch up.

FORTY-THREE
Melanie

Somehow the world seemed safer.
The light came softly through my drapes and shutters, illuminating familiar surfaces; the dark wood of the baseboard of my bed, the tall wardrobe my parents had ordered built the year of the centennial, my hairbrushes lined up on the dressing table just as they had always been, and my grandmother's quilt laid across the foot of my bed.

It was pleasant simply being there and listening to the purposeful bustle of people in the house. Howard and Nancy occupied the guest room next to my bedroom, the room that had once been Mother's and Father's. Nurse Oldsmith slept on a roll-away near the door inside my room. Miss Sewell spent much of her time in the kitchen, preparing meals for everyone. Dr. Hartman ostensibly lived across the courtyard, but he, like the others, spent most of his time in the house, looking after my needs. Culley slept in the small room off the kitchen that had been Mr. Thorne's. He did not sleep much. At night he sat in the chair in the hall by the front door. The Negro boy slept on a cot we fixed for him on the back porch. It was still chilly out there at night, but he did not mind.

The boy, Justin, spent much time with me, brushing my hair, looking at books which I would read, and being there when I needed someone to run an errand. Sometimes I would simply send him to my sewing room to sit there on the wicker chaise longue, enjoying the sunlight and glimpses of sky beyond the garden and the scent of the new plants Culley had purchased and repotted. My Hummels and other porcelain figurines were on display in the glass case I'd had the Negro boy repair.

It was pleasant and somewhat disconcerting to spend much time seeing the world through Justin's eyes. His senses and perceptions were so acute, so unbuffered by interference from the conscious self, that they were almost painful. They were certainly addicting. It made it all the more difficult to return my attention to the limits of my own body.

Nurse Oldsmith and Miss Sewell were optimistic about my recovery and persistent in their attempts at therapy. I allowed them—even encouraged them—to continue with this attitude because I did want to walk and speak and reenter the world again, but I was also ambiguous about the progress they professed to see because I was certain that it entailed a lessening of my heightened Ability.

Each day Dr. Hartman tested me, examined me, and talked encouragingly to me. The nurses bathed me, turned me every two hours, and moved my limbs to keep muscles and joints loose. Soon after our return to Charleston, they began therapy that demanded active participation on my part. I was *able* to move my left arm and leg, but when I did so control of my little family became quite difficult, almost impossible, so it soon became our custom during those two half hours of therapy each day for everyone except the nurses and me to be seated or in bed, quiescent, requiring no more direct attention or control than would horses in their stalls.

By late April, the vision had returned to my left eye and I was able to move my limbs, after a fashion. Sensation on my entire left side was very strange—as if I had been given shots of novacaine in jaw, arm, side, hip, and leg. It was not unpleasant.

Dr. Hartman was quite proud of me. He said that I was quite unusual in that while I had undergone major sense deprivation in those first weeks following my cerebrovascular accident and while there was obvious left hemiparesis, there was no sign of paroxia or visual perception. I did not make paraphasic errors or perserverate.

The fact that I had not spoken at all for three months did not mean the doctor was in error in deciding that I was free of the speech dysfunctions that so frequently afflict stroke victims. I spoke every day through Howard or Nancy or Miss Sewell or one of the others. After listening to Dr. Hartman for some time, I drew my own conclusions as to why this faculty had not been impaired.

The fact that the stroke was an ischemic infarction restricted primarily to the right hemisphere of the brain was certainly a major reason, since, like most right-handed people, the language centers of my brain were located in the left—and unaffected—hemisphere. Nonetheless, Dr. Hartman pointed out that victims of such massive CVAs as I had frequently have some speech and perceptual problems until functions are transferred to new, undamaged areas of the brain. I realized that such transfers occur constantly with me because of my Ability—and now, with my magnified Ability, I was confident that I could have retained all language, speech, and personality functions even if both hemispheres of my brain had been affected. I had an unlimited supply of healthy brain tissue to use! Every person I came in contact with became a donor of neurons, synapses, language associations, and memory storage.

In a real sense I had become immortal.

This was the point in time where I began to understand both the addictive qualities and health benefits of our Game. Using our Abilities, especially in the ultimate Using required by the Game, *had* made us younger. Just as patients' lives were now being renewed by organ and tissue transplants, so were *our* lives renewed through the Use of other minds, the transplantation of energy, the borrowed use of RNA and neurons and all the other esoteric compounds to which modern science has reduced the mind.

When I looked at Melanie Fuller through Justin's clear eyes, I saw an old woman sleeping in a fetal position, intravenous solutions trickling into an emaciated arm, skin pale and pulled tight over bone, but I knew now that this was completely misleading—that I was younger now than ever before, absorbing the energy of those around me the way a sunflower stores light. Soon I would be ready to rise from my sickbed, resurrected by the renewal of radiant energy I could feel flowing into me, day by day, week by week.

My eyes snapped open in the middle of the night. *Dear God, perhaps this is how Nina has survived death.*

If my Ability could grow in strength and range and scope through the oxygen-death of one small part of my brain, what could Nina's much greater Ability have managed in that microsecond after I shot her? What was the bullet I had fired into her brain from Charles's Colt Peacemaker except a larger, more dramatic version of my own cerebrovascular accident?

Nina's control and consciousness could have leapt to a hundred subservient minds in the hours and days after our confrontation. I had read enough in recent years to know that people were now being kept alive by machines that replaced, stimulated, or simulated functions of heart, kidneys, and God knows what other organs. I saw no contradiction in the concept of Nina's pure and forceful consciousness keeping its hold on life through others' minds.

Nina rotting in her coffin while her Ability allowed her mind to stalk the night like a formless, malevolent ghost.

Nina's blue eyes rising in their sockets on a tide of maggots while her ruined brain repaired itself even as it rotted away.

The energy from all those she Used flowing back to her until Nina rose in the same radiant burst of youth I felt flowing into me—only Nina a corpse moving through the darkness.

Would she come here?

All my family stayed awake that night, some with me, some between me and the darkness, but still I did not sleep.

Mrs. Hodges would not sell her house until Dr. Hartman offered—and paid—an outrageous sum. I could have interfered in the negotiations but after seeing Mrs. Hodges, I decided not to.

It had been less than five months since George, her husband, had suffered his unfortunate accident, but the old woman had aged twenty years. She had always taken care to tint her hair a fake and obvious brown, but now it hung in limp, white strands. Her eyes were listless. She had always been unattractive, but now she took no pains to hide the wrinkles, warts, and wattles behind a mask of makeup.

We paid her outrageous price. Money would soon be no problem, and, besides, as soon as I saw Mrs. Hodges again I thought of other uses she might serve in days or weeks to come.

Spring came gracefully as it always does in my beloved South. Sometimes I allowed Culley to carry me to the sewing room and once—just once—outside to recline in the chaise longue while the Negro boy worked to prepare the garden. Culley, Howard, and Dr. Hartman had erected tall fences around the entire compound, ten-foot privacy fences in back, so peering eyes were not a problem. I just did not like being directly in the sunlight. It was far more enjoyable to me when I shared Justin's perceptions as he sat in the grass or joined Miss Sewell as she sunbathed naked on the patio.

The days grew longer and warmer. Soft air came through my open windows. Occasionally I thought I heard the squeals and laughter of Mrs. Hodges's granddaughter and her friend coming from the courtyard, but then I realized it must be other children from down the block.

The days smelled of new-mown grass and the nights of honeysuckle. I felt safe.

FORTY-FOUR

Beverly Hills
Thursday, April 23, 1981

Early on a Thursday afternoon, Tony Harod lay on a queen-size bed in the Beverly Hilton Hotel and thought about love. He had never had much interest in the topic. For Harod, love was the farce that had launched a thousand banalities; it was the excuse for all of the lies, self-deceits, and hypocrisies that made up relations between the sexes. Tony Harod took pride in the fact that he had screwed hundreds of women, perhaps thousands, and had never pretended to be in love with any of them, even though he had thought that in those final seconds of their submission, in his moment of orgasm, he had felt something approaching love.

Now Tony Harod was in love.

He found himself thinking constantly of Maria Chen. His palm and fingers could recall the precise texture of her skin. He dreamed her sweet scent. Her dark hair, dark eyes, and soft smile hovered at the edge of his consciousness like an image at the periphery of vision—elusive, vanishing at the turn of a head. Even saying her name made him feel strange inside.

Harod put his hands behind his head and stared at the ceiling. The tangled sheets still held the seashore scent of sex. In the bathroom, the shower pounded on.

Harod and Maria Chen carried out their daily lives as always. She brought the mail to him in the Jacuzzi each morning, handled phone calls, took dictation, then went with him to the studio to watch some of the shooting of *The White Slaver* and to review the previous day's footage. The studio segments had been moved from Pinehurst to Paramount because of British union problems and Harod welcomed the chance to keep watch over the production without spending weeks away from home. The day before, Harod had been watching rushes of Janet Delacourte—the twenty-eight-year-old cow that had filled the role written for a nubile seventeen-year-old—and he suddenly imagined Maria Chen in the lead role, Maria Chen's subtle expressions rather than Delacourte's gross emotings, Maria Chen's alluring and sensuous nudity rather than the pale, white starlet's heavy nakedness.

Harod and Maria Chen had made love only three times since Philadelphia—a restraint that Harod did not understand but which inflamed him with a desire for her that spread from the physical to the psychological; she was in his thoughts most of the day. The simple act of watching her walk across the room gave Tony Harod pleasure.

The shower went off and Harod heard the muffled sounds of toweling and the roar of a hair dryer.

Harod tried to imagine a life with Maria Chen. Between them, they had enough money that they could pick up and leave without being uncomfortable for two or three years. They could go anywhere. Harod had always wanted to chuck it all, find a small island in the Bahamas or somewhere and see if he could write anything besides formula slice-and-dice flicks. He imagined leaving a fuck-you note for Barent and Kepler and just getting the hell away from it all; Maria Chen coming back from the beach in her blue bathing suit, the two of them talking over croissants and fresh-ground coffee as the sun rose over the lagoon. Tony Harod enjoyed being in love.

Janet Delacourte came naked out of the bathroom and shook her long blond hair out over his shoulders. "Tony, baby doll, do you have a cigarette?"

"No." Harod opened his eyes to look at her. Janet had a face of a hardened fifteen-year-old and breasts to fill a Russ Meyer wet dream. After three films her acting ability remained mercifully undiscovered. She had married a sixty-three-year-old Texas millionaire who had bought her her own thoroughbred, bought her the role of diva for an evening of opera that had been the laugh of Houston for months, and now was in the process of buying Hollywood for her. Schu Williams, the director of *The White Slaver*, had suggested to Harod over drinks the week before that Delacourte couldn't emote falling if someone shoved her off a fucking cliff. Harod had reminded Williams where three mill of the nine-million-dollar budget was coming from and suggested that they do a fifth rewrite to get rid of the scenes where Janet had to do something beyond her range—such as talk—and add a couple of more bathtub and harem scenes.

"That's OK, I've got one here in my purse." She rummaged through a canvas handbag larger than Harod's usual carry-on luggage.

"Don't you have a second call today?" asked Harod. "Another try at that seraglio scene with Dirk?"

"Uh-uh." She was chewing gum as she smoked, somehow managing to do both things with her mouth open. "Schuey says that the take we did Tuesday's about the best we're going to get." She sprawled across the bed on her stomach, elbow propped, huge breasts on top of Harod's shins like pale casaba melons on a grocer's discount shelf.

Harod closed his eyes.

"Tony, baby doll, is it true you've got the original of that tape?"

"What tape?"

"You know. The one where little old Shayla Barrington's tugging some dude's dork."

"Oh, that one."

"Jeez, I must've seen that ten-minute video at at least about sixty parties the last few months. You think people'd get tired of watching her. She's hardly got any tits at all, has she?"

"Mmmm," said Harod.

"I was at that benefit thing she was at. You know, the one for the spazzy kids with whatchamacallit? She was up at the table with Dreyfus and Clint and Meryl. I think Shayla's so stuck up she thinks her doo-doo doesn't smell, you know what I mean? It sort of serves her right, everybody laughing at her and looking at her funny and all."

"Were they doing that?"

"Oh yeah. Don's so funny. He's giving this real funny talk, you know, sort of shooting down everybody at this front table like? And he gets to Shayla and he says something like 'And we're graced with the presence of one of the prettiest young mermaids since Esther Williams traded in her bathing cap' or something like that, you know, only funnier. So do you have it?"

"Have what?"

"You know, the original tape?"

"What does it matter who has the original if copies are all over town?"

"Tony, baby doll, I'm just *curious*, is all. I mean, I think it'd be sort of a stitch if you'd made that tape after Shayla babe turned you down for the White Slobber and all."

"The White Slobber?"

"Oh, that's what Schuey calls the project. Sort of like Chris Plummer always calling *The Sound of Music* the *Sound of Mucus*, you know? We all call it that on the set."

"Cute," said Harod. "Who said Barrington was ever offered the part?"

"Oh, baby doll, *everybody* knows she was first pick. It would've got the twenty mill behind it if little Miss Sunshine had signed up, I guess." Janet Delacourte stubbed out her cigarette and laughed. "Course now she can't get *anything*. I hear the Disney people canceled that big musical thing they had planned for her and Donny and Marie booted her off that special they were doing in Hawaii. Her little Old Mormon Mama shit a couple of bricks and had a coronary or something. *Too bad*." She played with Harod's toes and wiggled her breasts back and forth over his legs.

Tony Harod pulled his legs away and sat on the edge of the bed. "I'm going to take a shower. You going to be here when I come out?"

Janet Delacourte popped her gum, rolled on her back, and gave him an upside down smile. "You want me to be, baby doll?"

"Not particularly," said Harod.

She rolled onto her stomach. "Well then fuck you," she said with no animosity in her voice. "I'm going shopping."

Forty minutes later Harod came out under the Beverly Hilton awning and handed his keys to the boy in the red vest and white slacks.

"Which one today, Mr. Harod?" asked the boy. "The Mercedes or the Ferrari?"

"I'm in the gray kraut cart today, Johnny," said Harod.

"Yessir."

Harod squinted through his mirrored glasses at the palms and blue sky while he waited. He decided that Los Angeles probably had the most boring climate in the goddamned world. Except maybe the south side of Chicago where he had grown up.

The Mercedes pulled up, Harod walked around, started to extend his hand with the five-dollar bill in it, and looked down into the smiling face of Joseph Kepler.

"Get in, Tony," said Kepler. "We've got some talking to do."

Kepler drove toward Coldwater Canyon. Harod stared at him through his mirrored glasses. "The Hilton's security is really getting shitty," said Harod. "They let all sorts of street flotsam into your car these days."

Kepler twitched his Charlton Heston grin. "Johnny knows me," he said. "I told him it was a practical joke."

"Ha ha," said Harod.

"We have some talking to do, Tony."

"You said that already."

"You're quite the wiseass, aren't you, Tony?"

"Cut the crap," said Harod. "If you have something to tell me, tell me."

Kepler was driving the Mercedes too fast up the winding canyon drive. He drove arrogantly, with only his right arm involved, wrist propped on the top of the wheel. "Your friend Willi has made his next move," he said.

"Ground rule," said Harod. "We'll have our nice little talk here, but if you refer to him as 'your friend Willi' one more time I'll be obliged to knock your capped teeth down your fucking throat. All right, Joseph old pal?"

Kepler glanced at Harod. "Willi's made his next move and there's going to have to be some response."

"What'd he do this time? Bugger the president's wife or something?"

"A little more dramatic and difficult than that."

"Are you playing twenty questions?"

"It doesn't matter what he did," said Kepler, "and you won't be reading about it in the paper, but it was something Barent can't ignore. It means that your . . . that Willi is prepared to play for high stakes and we'll have to respond in some way."

"So now we go to the scorched earth policy, huh?" said Harod. "Kill every German-American over fifty-five."

"No, Mr. Barent's going to negotiate."

"How do you do that if you can't even find the old bastard?" Harod looked out at the arid hillside flashing by. "Or do you guys still think I'm in touch with him?"

"No," said Kepler, "but I am."

Harod sat up. "With Willi?"

"Who else are we talking about?"

"Where . . . how did you find him?"

"I didn't find him," said Kepler. "I wrote to him. He wrote back. We're maintaining a very pleasant correspondence."

"Where did you write, for Chrissake?"

"I sent a registered letter to his little house in the woods in Bavaria."

"Waldheim? The old estate near the Czech border? No one's there. Barent's had people watching it since I was there in December."

"True," said Kepler, "but the family retainers still guard the place. German father and son named Meyer. My letter never came back and a few weeks later I heard from Willi. Postmarked in France. Second letter from New York."

"What does he say?" asked Harod. He was angered that his heart was pounding at twice its normal speed.

"Willi says that all he wants is to join the Club and have a relaxing time on the island this summer."

"Huh!" said Harod.

"I believe him," said Kepler. "I think that the old gentleman was hurt that we did not think to invite him sooner."

"And he may be a trifle put out that you tried to blow him up in midair and set his old girlfriend Nina against him?"

"That, too, perhaps," said Kepler. "But I think he's willing to let bygones be bygones."

"What does Barent say?"

"Mr. Barent doesn't know that I've been in touch with Willi."

"Jesus," said Harod, "aren't you taking one big fucking chance?"

Kepler grinned. "He really worked you over with that conditioning session the other day, didn't he, Tony? No, it's not too much of a chance. Barent isn't going to do anything too brash even if he finds out. With Charles and Nieman gone, C. Arnold's coalition is getting a bit shaky. I don't think Barent wants to have his island sport all to himself."

"Are you going to tell him?"

"Yes," said Kepler. "After yesterday I think Barent will be grateful that I found a way to contact Willi. Barent'll agree to the old man's inclusion in the summer camp follies if he's sure it will be safe."

"How could it be safe?" asked Harod. "Don't you *see* what Willi can do? That old sonofabitch won't stop at anything."

"Precisely," said Kepler, "but I think that I've convinced our fearless leader that it's safer having Willi with us, where we can keep an eye on him, than out in the shadows playing Spider King and picking us off one by one. Besides, Barent still has faith that anyone he comes into . . . ah . . . *personal* contact with will never be a threat again."

"Do you think he can neutralize Willi?"

"Don't you?" Kepler sounded sincerely curious.

"I don't know," Harod said at last. "Barent's Ability seems unique, but Willi . . . well, I'm not sure Willi is completely human."

"It really doesn't matter, Tony."

"What do you mean?"

"I mean that it's quite probable that the Island Club is overdue for a change of executive leadership."

"You mean dump Barent? How do we do that?"

"We don't have to, Tony. All we have to do is stay in contact with our pen pal Wilhelm and assure him that we'll stay neutral in case of any . . . unpleasantness on the island."

"Willi's coming in during Summer Camp?"

"On the last night of the public segment," said Kepler. "Then he'll join us during the hunt through the next week."

"I can't believe Willi would put himself in Barent's power like that," said Harod. "Barent must have . . . what . . . a hundred security people around?"

"More like two hundred," said Kepler.

"Yeah, so Willi's Ability isn't worth shit against an army like that. Why would he do it?"

"Barent will be giving his word of honor that Willi will have safe passage," said Kepler.

Harod laughed. "Oh, right, I guess it's OK then. Willi should put his head on the block if Barent gives his fucking *word*."

Kepler had been coming down Mulholland Drive. They could see the freeway below them. "But you see the possibilities here, Tony. If Barent eliminates the old gentleman, we simply go back to business as usual with you as a full member. If Willi has some surprise up his sleeve, we welcome him aboard with open arms."

"You think you could coexist with Willi?" asked Harod.

Kepler turned into a parking area near the Hollywood Bowl. A gray limousine with blackened glass sat waiting. "When you've lain down with snakes as long as I have, Tony," he said, "it doesn't especially matter what variety of poison the new one carries as long as it doesn't bite its bedfellows."

"What about Sutter?"

Kepler turned off the Mercedes' ignition. "I just came from a long conversation with the Reverend. While he places much sentimental value in his long relationship with his friend Christian, he also is willing to render into Caesar what is Caesar's."

"Meaning?"

"Meaning that Willi can be assured that Jimmy Wayne Sutter will bear no grudges if Mr. Barent's portfolio changes hands."

"You know something, Kepler?" said Tony Harod. "You couldn't frame a simple declarative sentence if your fucking life depended on it."

Kepler smiled and opened the door. Over the noise of the warning buzzer he said, "Are you with us or not, Harod?"

"If being with you is keeping my head down and staying out of this shit, I'm with you," said Harod.

"Simple declarative sentence," snapped Kepler. "*Your friend* Willi needs to know where you stand. With us or not?"

Harod glanced out at the bright expanse of parking lot. He looked back at Kepler and his voice was tired. "I'm with you," he said.

It was almost eleven P.M. when Harod decided that he wanted two hot dogs with mustard and onion. He set down the script revisions he'd been working on and walked to the west wing where Maria Chen's light still shone under the door. He rapped twice. "I'm going to Pinks. Want to come?"

Her voice was muffled, as if she were calling from the bathroom. "No thank you."

"Sure?"

"Yes. Thank you anyway."

Harod pulled on his leather flight jacket and got the Ferrari out of the garage. He enjoyed the drive, shifting hard through the gears, shaving the yellow lights, and blowing off two low riders that made the mistake of challenging him for three blocks on the Boulevard.

Pinks was crowded. Pinks was always crowded. Harod ate his two hot dogs at the counter and took a third one out to the parking lot. Two teenage boys were standing between a dark van and his car, one of them actually leaning against the Ferrari as he talked to two girls. Harod walked up to him and thrust his face within inches of the other's. "Move it off or kiss it good-bye, kid," he said.

The boy was six inches taller than Harod, but he jerked away from the side of the sports car as if it were a hot stove. The four of them moved away slowly, glancing back at Harod, waiting to get the proper distance away before shouting snide remarks. Harod studied the two girls. The shorter one looked like an upscale Chicano, black hair and brown skin, the whole package wrapped in expensive shorts and a halter top that looked like it was under too much stress. Harod imagined how surprised the two beach boys would be if that particular piece of chocolate came over to join him in the Ferrari and decided to take some of the stress off the elastic. *To hell with it*, thought Harod. *I'm too tired.*

He finished off the third dog sitting behind the wheel, washed it down with the last of his Tab, and had switched on the ignition when a soft voice said, "Mr. Harod."

The van door had opened four feet from him. A black chick was sitting sideways in the passenger seat. There was something familiar about her and Harod had given her an automatic smile before he registered where he had seen her before. She was holding something in her lap, bracing it.

Harod kicked the clutch in and was reaching for the gear shift when there was a soft noise like the silencers made in his spy movies and a wasp stung him high on the left shoulder. "Shit!" cried Harod, raised his right hand to brush the insect away, had time to realize that it was not a wasp, and then the interior of the car lurched sideways and the console and passenger seat came up sharply to strike him in the face.

Harod never totally lost consciousness, but the effect was the same. It was as if someone had banished him to the storm cellar of his own body. Sights and sounds came through—vaguely—but it was like watching a distant UHF station on a cheap black and white TV while a radio in another room provided garbled sound. Then someone put a hood over his face. It made little difference. From time to time he would become aware that he was rolling slightly, as if he was on the deck of a small boat, but the tactile sensations were fleeting and false and far too much trouble to sort out.

People were carrying him. He thought they did. Perhaps those were his own hands on his arms and legs. No, his own hands were behind him somewhere, welded together by a band of skin and cartilage that seemed to have grown from nowhere.

For an indefinite period of time Harod was nowhere—neither conscious nor unconscious—floating somewhere inside himself in a pleasant primordial soup of false sensations and confused memories. He was distantly aware of two voices, one of them his own, but the conversation—if that is what it was—bored him and he soon returned to the inner darkness the way a skin diver allows his weights and a gentle current to carry him deeper into purple depths.

Tony Harod knew that something was definitely wrong, but he just did not give a damn.

The light woke him. The light and the pain in his wrists. The light, the pain in his wrists, and a pain that made him think of Ridley Scott's *Alien* where the thing comes busting out of that poor sonofabitch's chest. Who was that actor? John Hurt. Why the hell was the light in his eyes and why did his wrists hurt and what had he been drinking to turn his skull inside out like this?

Harod sat up . . . tried to sit up. He tried again and shouted with the pain. The shout seemed to clear some last film between himself and the world and he lay there and paid attention to things that had not seemed important before.

He was handcuffed. Lying in a bed, handcuffed. His right arm was on the pillow next to him, the manacle around the right wrist connected to the heavy white metal of the headboard. His left arm was down at his side, but the handcuffs there were connected to something solid below the side of the mattress. Harod tried to lift his left arm; metal rattled on metal.

The side of the bed then. Or a pipe. Or something. He wasn't ready to move his head yet to check. Maybe later.

Who the hell was I with last night? Harod knew a few female friends who were heavily into bondage, light S & M, but he had never allowed himself to be on the receiving end. *Too much to drink? Vita finally got me in her chamber of pleasures?* He opened his eyes again and held them open against the pain of light striking his optic nerves.

A white room. White bed—sheets, brass painted white—white walls, small mirror in the opposite wall with white painted frame, a door. A white door with a white knob. Single, naked light bulb—about ten million watts, Harod judged from the glare—hanging from a white cord. Harod was wearing a white hospital gown. He could feel the slit up the back and that he was naked underneath.

OK, not Vita. Her pleasure chamber ran to velvet and stone. Who did he know that had a hospital hang-up? No one.

Harod rattled the cuffs and felt the raw skin where he had already chafed his wrists. He leaned left and looked down. White floor. Left wrist cuffed to white metal bed frame. No need to move again for a while unless he had the urge to throw up all over the nice white floor. Let's think about this.

Harod went away for a little while. When he realized where he was sometime later—the light the same, the white room the same, the headache a little better—he thought about mental hospitals. Had someone committed him when he wasn't looking?

They don't handcuff people in mental hospitals. *Do they?*

A stab of fear struck through him hard enough to set him struggling and kicking, rattling metal against metal until he fell back panting. Barent. Kepler. Sutter. Those lowlife sons of bitches had put him away somewhere safe where he could spend the rest of his life staring at white walls and peeing in his sheets.

No, that group would just kill him and have done with it.

Then Harod remembered Pinks, the kids, the van, the black chick. She'd been the one. What had Colben said about her in Philadelphia? They thought Willi had been Using her and that sheriff. But the sheriff was dead . . . Harod had still been there when Kepler and Haines arranged to have the body discovered in a Baltimore bus station so there would be no connection with the Philadelphia fiasco.

Who was Using her now? Willi? Possibly. Perhaps he hadn't been satisfied with the message relayed through Kepler. But why all this?

Harod decided to quit thinking for a while. It hurt too much. He would wait for a visitor. If the black chick came in and Willi or whoever didn't have a *very* tight grip on her, someone would be in for a surprise.

Harod was feeling the definite need to urinate and had tried some serious shouting when the door finally opened.

It was a man. He was wearing a green surgical outfit and a black bala-
clava with mirrored sunglasses in the place of eyes. Harod thought of
Kepler's sunglasses, then about the serial killer in Willi and his *Walpurgis
Night* movies. He almost urinated then and there.

It was not Willi. Harod could tell that at once. Nor was he the right size
or apparent age for Tom Reynolds, Willi's queer cat's-paw with the strangler's fingers. It didn't matter. Willi had had time to recruit legions of new
nobodies.

Harod *tried* to go for the man. He did try. But at the last second the old
revulsion washed over him—stronger than the earlier nausea and
headache—and he pulled away before his will touched the other's mind. It
would have been easier and less intimate for Harod to have licked another
man's anus or taken another man's penis in his mouth. The idea alone
made him shudder and break out in a cold sweat.

"Who are you? Where am I?" Harod's words were almost unintelligible,
falling from a tongue carved from cheap wood.

The man walked to the bedside and looked down at Harod. Then he
reached under his surgical blouse and pulled out an automatic pistol. He
aimed it at Harod's forehead, "Tony," he said in a soft accent, "I'm going
to count to five and fire. If you're going to do something, you had better do
it now."

Harod pulled at the cuffs hard enough to move the bed.

"One . . . two . . . three . . ."

Harod's mind leaped, but thirty years of self-conditioning prevented
him from completing the contact.

". . . four . . ."

Harod closed his eyes.

". . . five." The hammer fell and went *click*.

When Harod opened his eyes the man was standing by the door and
the gun was out of sight. "Do you need anything?" came the soft, accented syllables.

"Bedpan," whispered Harod.

The balaclava nodded. "The nurse will bring it."

Harod waited until the door was closed and then squeezed his eyes shut
in concentration. *The nurse*, he thought. *Dear God, let it be the old-fashioned
tits on top, slit between the legs kind of nurse.*

He waited.

The nurse was the black woman. The one from Philadelphia. The one
who had shot him and brought him here.

He remembered her name. Natalie. He owed her a lot.

She wore no balaclava but appeared to have white patches on her temples, wires in her hair. She carried a bedpan and set it in place professionally. Stood back to wait.

Harod brushed over her mind lightly as he relieved himself. No one was Using her. He could not believe that they had been so stupid—whoever *they* were. Maybe it was just this stupid black bitch and an accomplice. Colben had said something about the two of them being after Melanie Fuller. Obviously they did not know what *he* could do.

Harod waited until she had retrieved the bedpan and walked to the door. He had to make sure the door was unlocked. It would be just Willi's kind of joke to have them both locked in—to give Harod someone to Use and no way to Use her. What the hell were those little wires in her hair? Harod saw them in hospital movies, but on *patients*, not nurses. Some sort of sensors.

She opened the door.

He hit her so fast and so hard that she dropped the bedpan, spilling urine down the front of her white skirt. *Tough titty*, thought Harod and took her out through the door, seeing through her eyes. *Get the keys*, he ordered. *Kill that other cocksucker any way you can, get the keys, and get me out of here.*

There were six feet of corridor and another door. This one was locked. He threw Natalie against it until he felt her shoulder twist, had her claw at the wood. It did not budge. *Fuck this.* He brought her back into the room. Nothing that could be used as a weapon. She walked over to the bed, tugged at the cuffs. If she could dismantle the bed for him, tear the frame apart. But there was no way to do that quickly while Harod was cuffed to frame and headboard both. He looked at himself through her eyes and saw black stubble on his white cheeks, eyes wide and staring, curling hair matted.

The mirror. Harod looked at it and knew that it had to be one of those one-way things. He'd have Natalie break it with her bare hands if need be. If there was no way out through it, he'd have her use shards of glass for a weapon when the fucker in the balaclava came in. If the mirror wouldn't break, he'd assume it was one-way and just have her bash her pretty little face against it until it was just bones sticking out of black mush. Give whoever was on the other side a good show. Then, when they came in, she could tear their throats out with her nails and remaining teeth, get the gun, get the keys . . .

The door opened and the man in the balaclava came in. Natalie whirled, crouched to leap. Her snarl was something seen in a zoo when feeding time was long delayed.

The man in the balaclava shot her in the hip with the dart gun in his hand. She leaped, claws extended. The man caught her and lowered her to the floor. He knelt beside her for a minute, taking her pulse, lifting an eyelid to check her pupil. Then he got up and walked over to Harod's bed. His voice was shaking. "You son of a bitch," he said. He turned and walked out of the room.

When he returned he was filling a syringe from an upended bottle. He squirted a few drops and turned to Harod. "This is going to hurt a little bit, Mr. Harod," he said in a small, tight voice.

Harod tried to jerk his left arm away, but the man stabbed the syringe through the gown, directly into his hip. For a second there was numbness and then it felt to Tony Harod as if someone had poured Scotch directly into his veins. Flame moved from his abdomen to his chest. He gasped as the warmth moved through his heart. "What . . . is it?" he whispered, knowing that the man in the balaclava had killed him. A lethal injection, the tabloids called it. Harod had always been in favor of capital punishment. "What *is* it?"

"Shut up," said the man and turned his back even as the blackness swirled and whirled and tumbled Tony Harod away like a chip on a hurricane sea.

FORTY-FIVE

Near San Juan Capistrano
Friday, April 24, 1981

Natalie came up out of the fog of anesthesia to the sight and soft touch of Saul cleansing her forehead with a wet cloth. She looked down, saw the straps around her arms and legs, and began to cry.

"There, there," said Saul. He bent close and kissed her hair gently. "It's all right."

"How . . ." Natalie paused and licked her lips. They felt remote and rubbery. "How long?"

"About thirty minutes," said Saul. "We may have been too conservative with the mixture."

Natalie shook her head. She remembered the horror of watching herself, *feeling* herself preparing to leap at Saul. She knew she would have killed him with her bare hands. "Had to be . . . fast," she whispered "Harod?" She could barely bring herself to say his name.

Saul nodded. "The first interrogation went very well. The EEG recordings are extraordinary. He should be coming out of it very soon. That's why the . . ." He gestured at the straps.

"I know," said Natalie. She had helped set up the bed with its canvas restraints. Her pulse was still racing from the incredible adrenaline flow during Harod's possession of her and from her fear prior to going in the room. Entering that room had been the hardest thing she had ever done.

"I think it looks very good," said Saul. "According to the EEGs there was no attempt to use his powers on either you or me while he was under Sodium Pentothal. He's been coming out of it for about fifteen minutes now . . . his readings are almost back to the base we established this morning . . . and he's not tried to reestablish contact with you. I feel reasonably certain that it's a line of sight process for either initial contact or once after contact is broken. Certainly it would be different for subjects he has conditioned, but I don't think he can reestablish contact with you now without seeing you."

Natalie tried hard not to cry. The straps were not uncomfortable, but they gave her an overwhelming sense of claustrophobia. Wires ran from the electrodes on her scalp to the small telemetry pack taped to her waist. Saul had known about the equipment from colleagues doing dream studies and had been able to tell Cohen exactly where to purchase it. "We just don't *know*," she said.

"We know a lot more than we did twenty-four hours ago," said Saul. He held up two long strips of paper from the EEG readout. The computer stylus had traced a mad scribble of peaks and valleys. "Look at this. First what appears to be this random misfiring in his hippocampus. Harod's alpha waves peak, drop to almost nothing, and then go into what appears to be REM state. Three point two seconds later . . . look . . ." Saul showed her a second strip where the peaks and valleys perfectly matched the first. "Perfect sympathy. You lost all higher order functions, no control of voluntary reflexes, even your autonomous nervous system had become slaved to his. Less than four seconds to join him in this altered REM state or whatever it is.

"And perhaps the most interesting anomaly, here Harod generates a theta rhythm. It is unmistakable. Here your hippocampus responded with an identical theta rhythm while the neocortical EEG flattened. Natalie, this theta rhythm phenomenon is well documented in rabbits, rats, and so forth during species-specific activities—such as aggression and dominance displays—but never in a primate!"

"Are you saying I had the brain of a rat?" said Natalie. It was a weak joke and did not stop her from wanting to cry.

"Somehow Harod . . . and presumably the others . . . generates this exceptional theta rhythm activity in both his own hippocampus and that of his victim," Saul said half to himself. He had not noticed Natalie's attempt at humor. "The sympathetic effect on your brain was to flatten neocortical activity while generating an artificial REM state. You received sensory input but could not act on it. Harod could. *Incredible.* This . . ." He pointed to a sudden flattening of the squiggles on her chart ". . . is precisely where the nerve toxins in the tranquilizer dart take effect. Notice the lack of reciprocity on his chart. Whatever he willed evidently could be transmitted to neurochemical commands in your body, but what you experienced was only vicariously transmitted to Harod. He felt no more of your pain or paralysis than one would feel in a dream. Here, forty-eight seconds later, is when I injected him with the Amatyl-Pentothal mixture." Saul showed her where the various lines of brain wave functions fell out of their frenzied state. "God, what I would give to have him somewhere for a month with CAT-scan equipment."

"Saul, what if I . . . what if he does reestablish control over me?"

Saul adjusted his glasses. "I'll know it at once, even if I'm not watching the readouts. I've reprogrammed the computer alarm to go off at first sign of that erratic activity of his hippocampus, the sudden drop in either of your alpha wave patterns, or at the appearance of the theta rhythm."

"Yes," said Natalie and took a breath, "but what will you *do* then?"

"We'll run the time-distance studies as planned," said Saul. "All of the data channels should be clear at twenty-five miles if we use the transmitter Jack bought."

"But what if he can do it at a hundred miles, a thousand?" Natalie strained to keep her voice calm. She wanted to scream, *what if he never lets me go?* She felt as if he had agreed to a medical experiment where some loathsome parasite had been allowed to grow inside her body.

Saul took her hand. "Twenty-five miles is all we need to know at this time. If it comes to that, we'll just return and I'll put him under again. We know that he cannot control you when he is unconscious."

"He never could again if he was dead," said Natalie.

Saul nodded and squeezed her hand. "He's awake now. We'll wait forty-five minutes and if he makes no attempt at seizing you, you can get up. I personally do not believe our Mr. Harod can do it. Whatever the source of our monsters' powers, all preliminary indications suggest that Anthony Harod is a very minor monster indeed." He went to the sink, brought back a cup of water, and held Natalie's head up while she drank it.

"Saul . . . after you release me, you're still going to have the computer alarm hooked up and you'll keep the dart gun, won't you?"

"Yes," said Saul. "As long as we have this viper in the house, we will keep him in his cage."

"Second interrogation of Anthony Harod. Friday, April twenty-fourth, 1981 . . . seven twenty-three P.M. Subject currently injected with Sodium Pentothal and Meliritin-C. Data also available on videotape, EEG read-out, polygraph, and bio-sensor channels.

"Tony, can you hear me?"

"Yeah."

"How do you feel?"

"OK Funny."

"Tony, when were you born?"

"Huh?"

"When were you born?"

"October seventeenth."

"What year, Tony?"

"Uh . . . 1944."

"And how old are you now?"

"Thirty-six."

"Where did you grow up, Tony?"

"Chicago."

"When was the first time you knew you had the power, Tony?"

"What power?"

"Your ability to control people's actions."

"Oh."

"When was the first time, Tony?"

"Uh . . . when my aunt told me I had to go to bed. I didn't want to. I made her say it was all right for me to stay up."

"How old were you?"

"I don't know."

"How old do you think you were, Tony?"

"Six."

"Where were your parents?"

"My daddy was dead. He killed himself when I was four."

"Where was your mother?"

"She didn't want me. She was mad at me. She gave me to Auntie."

"Why didn't she want you?"

"She said it was my fault."

"What was your fault?"

"Daddy dying."

"Why did she think that?"

"Because Daddy hit me . . . he hurt me . . . he hurt me right before he jumped."

"Jumped? From a window?"

"Yeah. We lived way high up on the third floor. Daddy hit one of those fences with the spikes on it."

"Did your father hit you often, Tony?"

"Yeah."

"Do you remember it?"

"Now I do."

"Do you remember why he hit you on the night he killed himself?"

"Yeah."

"Tell me about it, Tony."

"I got scared. I was sleeping in the front room where the big closet was and the closet was dark. I woke up and I was scared. I went into Mommy's room like I always did, only Daddy was there. He wasn't usually there because he sold things and had to be gone all the time. Only he was there this time and he was hurting Mommy."

"How was he hurting her?"

"He was on top of her and he didn't have any clothes on and he was hurting her."

"And what did you do, Tony?"

"I cried and yelled at him to stop."

"Did you do anything else?"

"Uh-uh."

"What happened next, Tony?"

"Daddy . . . stopped. He looked funny. He took me in the living room and hit me with his belt. He hit me real hard. Mommy told him to stop but he kept hitting me. It hurt bad."

"And did you make him stop?"

"No!"

"What happened next, Tony?"

"Daddy quit hitting me all of a sudden. He held his head and sort of walked funny. He looked at Mommy. She wasn't crying anymore. She was wearing Daddy's flannel robe. She used to wear that when he was gone because it was warmer than hers. Then Daddy went to the window and fell through it."

"The window was closed?"

"Yeah. It was real cold out. The fence was new. The landlord had just put it up right before Thanksgiving."

"And how soon after that did you go to live with your aunt, Tony?"

"Two weeks."

"And why did you think your mother was angry at you?"

"She told me."

"That she was angry?"

"That I'd hurt Daddy."

"By making him jump?"

"Yeah."

"Did you make him jump, Tony?"

"No!"

"Are you sure?"

"Yes!"

"Then how did your mother know you could make people do things?"

"I don't know!"

"Yes, you do, Tony. Think back. Are you sure the time you made your aunt let you stay up late was the first time you ever controlled someone?"

"Yes!"

"Are you certain, Tony?"

"Yes!"

"Then why did your mother think you could do such a thing, Tony?"

"Because *she* could!"

"Your mother could control people?"

"Mommy did. She always did. She made me sit on the potty when I was too little. She made me not cry when I wanted to. She made Daddy do things for her when he was there so he kept going away. She did it!"

"She made him jump that night?"

"No. She made *me* make him jump."

"Third interrogation of Anthony Harod. Eight-oh-seven P.M., Friday, April twenty-fourth. Tony, who killed Aaron Eshkol and his family?"

"Who?"

"The Israeli."

"Israeli?"

"Mr. Colben must have told you about it."

"Colben? Oh, no, Kepler told me about it. That's right. The kid from the embassy."

"Yes, the kid from the embassy. Who killed him?"

"Haines had a team go talk to him."

"Richard Haines?"

"Yeah."

"The FBI agent Haines?"
"Uh-huh."
"Did Haines personally kill the Eshkol family?"
"I guess so. Kepler said he led the team."
"Who authorized this operation?"
"Uh . . . Colben . . . Barent."
"Which one, Tony?"
"Doesn't matter. Colben was just Barent's finger puppet. Can I close my eyes? I'm very tired."
"Yes, Tony. Close your eyes. Sleep until we talk again."

"Fourth interrogation of Anthony Harod. Friday, April twenty-fourth, 1981. Ten-sixteen P.M. Sodium Pentothal intravenously administered. Amobarbital sodium reintroduced at ten-oh-four P.M. Data available on videotape, polygraph, EEG, and bio-sensor.
"Tony?"
"Yes."
"Do you know where the Oberst is?"
"Who?"
"William Borden."
"Oh, Willi."
"Where is he?"
"I don't know."
"Do you have any idea where he is?"
"No."
"Is there any way you can find out where he is?"
"Uh-uh. Maybe. I don't know."
"Why don't you know? Is there someone else who knows where he is?"
"Kepler. Maybe."
"Joseph Kepler?"
"Yeah."
"Kepler knows where Willi Borden is?"
"Kepler says he's gotten letters from Willi."
"How recent were these letters?"
"I don't know. Last few weeks."
"Do you believe Kepler?"
"Yeah."
"Where do the letters come from?"
"France. New York. Kepler didn't tell me everything."
"Did Willi initiate the correspondence?"
"I don't get what you mean."
"Who wrote first—Willi or Kepler?"
"Kepler did."
"How did he get in touch with Willi?"
"Mailed it to the guys who guard his house in Germany."

"Waldheim?"

"Yeah."

"Kepler sent a letter to Willi care of the caretakers at Waldheim and Willi has written back?"

"Yes."

"Why did Kepler write him and what did Willi say in return?"

"Kepler's playing both ends against the middle. He wants to get on Willi's good side if Willi steps into the Island Club."

"The Island Club."

"Yeah. What's left of it. Trask is dead. Colben's dead. I guess Kepler figures Barent'll have to negotiate if Willi keeps the pressure on."

"Tell me about the Island Club, Tony . . ."

It was after two A.M. when Saul joined Natalie in the kitchen. The psychiatrist looked tired and very pale. Natalie poured a fresh cup of coffee for him and they sat looking at a large road atlas. "This is the best I could do," said Natalie. "I found it at an all-night truck stop on I-5."

"We need a real atlas or some sort of satellite data. Perhaps Jack Cohen can help us." Saul ran his finger down the South Carolina coast. "It's not even on here."

"No," said Natalie, "but if it's twenty-three miles off the coast the way Harod says, it probably wouldn't be on this map. I figure it to be here, east of Cedar and Murphy Islands . . . no farther south than Cape Romain."

Saul removed his glasses and rubbed the bridge of his nose. "This isn't some low tide key or sandbar," he said. "According to Harod, Dolmann Island is almost seven miles long and three miles across at its widest. You lived in Charleston most of your life, wouldn't you have heard of it?"

"I didn't," said Natalie. "Are you sure he's asleep?"

"Oh yes," said Saul. "I couldn't wake him for another six hours if I tried." Saul took out the map he had drawn from Harod's instructions and compared it to the map from Cohen's dossier on Barent. "You awake enough to review this?"

"Try me," said Natalie.

"All right. Barent and his group . . . the surviving members . . . will be meeting for their Dolmann Island Summer Camp during the week of June seventh. That's the public part. The people Harod said will be there match the caliber of notables that Jack Cohen told us about. All men. No women allowed. Even Margaret Thatcher couldn't get in if she wanted to. All the support personnel are male. According to Jack, there will be scores of security men. The public fun ends Saturday, June thirteenth. On Sunday, June fourteenth, according to Harod, the Oberst will arrive and join the four Island Club members—including Harod—for five days of sport."

"Sport!" breathed Natalie. "I would hardly call it that."

"Blood sport," amended Saul. "It does make sense. These people possess the same power that the Oberst, Melanie Fuller, and the Drayton

woman have. The taste of violence is as addictive to them, but they are
public figures. It is more difficult for them to be even tangentially involved
in the types of vicarious street violence our three old people appeared to
have begun in Vienna."

"So they save it up for one terrible week a year," said Natalie.

"Yes. And it also serves as a painless way . . . painless for *them* . . . to reestablish their pecking order each year. The island is incredibly private. Technically it is not even under U.S. jurisdiction. When Barent is there, he and
his guests stay in this area . . . the southern tip. His estate is there as well as
the so-called summer camp facilities. The other three miles of jungle trails
and mangrove swamps are separated by security zones, fences, and mine
fields. It is there that they play their own version of the Oberst's old game."

"No wonder he's gone to such great lengths to be invited," said Natalie.
"How many innocent people are sacrificed during this week of madness?"

"Harod says that each Island Club member receives five surrogates,"
said Saul. "That would be one a day for each of the five days."

"Where on earth would they find these people?"

"According to Harod, Charles Colben used to provide the bulk of
them," said Saul. "The idea is that they draw their . . . what would you
call them? Their playing pieces. They draw them at random each morning
for the day's fun. The evening's fun, actually. Harod says the play does
not begin until almost nightfall. The idea is for them to test their Ability
with some element of chance involved. They did not want to lose . . .
pieces . . . that they had conditioned over long periods."

"Where are they getting their victims this year?" asked Natalie. She
went to the cupboard and returned with a bottle of Jack Daniels. She
added a healthy share to her coffee.

Saul smiled at her. "Exactly. As junior partner or apprentice vampire or
whatever our Mr. Harod is, he was charged with the task of providing fifteen of the surrogates. They have to be people in reasonably good physical
condition but people who will not be missed."

"That's absurd," said Natalie. "Almost anyone would be missed."

"Not really," sighed Saul. "There are tens of thousands of teenage runaways in this country each year. Most never return home. Every major city
has mental wings of hospitals half filled with people with no backgrounds,
no family searching them out. Police are besieged with reports of missing
husbands and wayward wives."

"So they just grab a couple of dozen people, ship them out to this goddamn island, and make them kill each other?" Natalie's voice was thick
with fatigue.

"Yes."

"You believe Harod?"

"He may have been relaying faulty information, but the drugs left him
in no condition to construct lies."

"You're going to let him stay alive, aren't you, Saul?"

"Yes. Our best chance to find the Oberst is if this group goes ahead with their island madness. Eliminating Harod . . . or even keeping him in captivity much longer . . . would probably spoil the entire thing."

"You think that it won't be spoiled when this . . . this *pig* runs to Barent and the others and tells them all about us?"

"I think it is probable that he will not do that."

"Dear Christ, Saul, how can you be sure?"

"I am not, but I *am* sure that Harod is very confused. One minute he is convinced that you and I are agents of the Oberst. The next he believes that we were sent by Kepler or Barent. He simply cannot believe that we are independent actors in this melodrama . . ."

"Melodrama is right," said Natalie. "Dad used to let me stay up to watch this kind of crap on the Friday night Creature Feature. *The Most Dangerous Game.* This is bullshit, Saul."

Saul Laski slammed the kitchen table with his palm so hard that the noise echoed in the tiled kitchen like a rifle shot. Natalie's coffee cup jumped and spilled its contents on the wooden tabletop. "Don't tell *me* it's bullshit!" shouted Saul. It was the first time in five months that Natalie had heard him raise his voice. "Don't tell *me* that this is all bad melodrama. Tell your father and Rob Gentry with their throats cut! Tell my nephew Aaron and his wife and children! Tell all of them . . . tell the thousands that the Oberst led to the ovens! Tell my father and brother Josef . . ."

Saul stood so quickly that his chair went over backward. He leaned over the table and Natalie noticed the muscles under the tanned flesh of his forearms, the terrible scar on his left arm, the faded tattoo. His voice was lower when he spoke again, but not calmer; the ferocity was simply under control now. "Natalie, this entire century has been a miserable melodrama written by third-rate minds at the expense of other people's souls and lives. We can't stop it. Even if we put an end to these . . . these aberrations, it will only shift the spotlight to some other carrion-eating actor in this violent farce. These things are done every day by people with no shred of this absurd psychic ability . . . people exercising power in the form of violence by right of their place, position, by bullet or ballot or the point of their knife blade . . . but *by God* these sons of bitches hurt *our* family, *our* friends, and we're going to stop them." Saul stopped, leaned on his hands, and lowered his head. Sweat dripped to the table.

Natalie touched his hand. "Saul," she said softly, "I know. I'm sorry. We're very tired. We need sleep."

He nodded, patted her hand, and rubbed his cheeks. "You get a few hours' sleep. I'm going to bed down on the roll-away in the observation room. I have the sensors programmed to set off the alarm when Harod wakes. With luck, both of us can get seven hours' sleep."

Natalie flicked off the light and walked with him to the bottom of the stairs. As she started up she paused and said, "This means that we definitely have to go ahead with the next part, don't we? Charleston?"

Saul nodded tiredly. "I think so. I see no other way. I am sorry."

"That's all right," said Natalie although her skin tightened with fear at the thought of what lay ahead. "I knew it would come to that."

Saul looked up at her. "It doesn't have to."

"Yes," said Natalie. She started slowly up the stairs, whispering the next sentence only to herself, "Yes, it does have to."

FORTY-SIX

Los Angeles
Friday, April 24, 1981

Special Agent Richard Haines used a Bureau scrambler phone to contact Mr. Barent's communications center in Palm Springs. He had no idea where Barent was when the billionaire answered the phone.

"Richard, what do you have to report?"

"Not much, sir," said Haines. "The Bureau here has been keeping track of the local Israeli consulate—that's standard procedure—but they don't have any record of Cohen visiting either the consulate or the import office that is the Los Angeles front for in-county Mossad operatives. We've got a man in their operations here, and he swears that Cohen wasn't here on business."

"That's all you have?"

"Not quite. We checked out the Long Beach motel and confirmed that Cohen was there. The day clerk said that he'd been driving a rental car the morning he checked in—Thursday the sixteenth—but that he'd had a van, the clerk was pretty sure that it was a Ford Econoline, when he checked out on Monday morning. One of the maids remembered that there were several large boxes—almost crate-size, she said—stored in his room on Saturday and Sunday. She said that one of them was labeled Hitachi."

"Electronics?" said Barent. "Surveillance equipment?"

"Possibly," said Haines, "but the Mossad usually provides that kind of equipment without buying it over the counter."

"What if Cohen was working alone . . . or for someone else?"

"We're going under that assumption right now," said Haines.

"Have you been able to ascertain whether Willi Borden was in the area?"

"No, sir. We staked out his house again . . . it hasn't been sold yet . . . but there's no sign of him or Reynolds or Luhar."

"What about Harod?"

"Well, we haven't been able to get in touch with him."

"What does that mean, Richard?"

"Well, sir, we haven't had any surveillance on Harod for several weeks and when we've tried to call yesterday and today, his secretary tells us that he's out and she doesn't know where he is. We have people over there today, but so far he hasn't left his house or shown up on the Paramount set."

"I am somewhat disappointed, Richard."

Haines began to shake slightly down the length of his body. He propped his elbows on the desk and gripped the receiver tightly in both hands. "I'm sorry, sir. It's been difficult handling the Wyoming investigation while supervising the special team here in California."

"What else has come of the Wyoming search?"

"Ah . . . nothing concrete, sir. We're sure that Walters, the affected air force officer who . . ."

"Yes, yes."

"Well, Walters was in a Cheyenne bar on Tuesday evening. The bartender is pretty sure he remembers a group of men who included someone who fit Willi's description . . ."

"Pretty sure?"

"It was very crowded, Mr. Barent. We're assuming it *was* Willi. We've checked all of the hotels and motels in an expanding radius that's reached Denver, but no one remembers seeing him or his two companions."

"This is becoming a litany of futile actions, Richard. Have you had *any* leads in discovering Willi's current location?"

"Well, sir, we have all airline. Amtrak, and bus line scheduling computers on alert should any of Willi's entourage use a credit card or fly under their own names. We've expanded that alert to include the Jew psychiatrist who probably died in Philly, and the Preston girl. We have Customs covered; it's an A-1 priority on the Bureau's weekly list. And there are alerts to each of our regional offices and their local liaisons . . ."

"I *know* all of this, Richard," Barent said softly. "I asked if there were any new leads."

"Not since we got the trace on Jack Cohen's computer incursions last Tuesday."

"You still believe that Cohen was being Used by Willi?"

"I don't know anyone else who would be exploring connections between Reverend Sutter, Mr. Kepler, and yourself, sir."

"Perhaps we were premature in . . . ah . . . greeting Mr. Cohen the way we did upon his return."

Haines said nothing. The visible shaking had stopped, but a slick sheen of sweat stood out on his forehead and upper lip.

"What about the gas station receipt, Richard?"

"Ah . . . yes, sir. We checked that out. The owner says that it's very busy, he can't remember everyone who stops there. We confirmed through his credit card carbons that it was Cohen. The boy who filled out the credit card form has a week off and is backpacking in the Santa Ana Mountains somewhere. It's a long shot anyway . . ."

"It seems to me, Richard, that it is time you began following up on the long shots. I want Willi Borden found and I want the Cohen connection nailed down. Is that clear?"

"Yes, sir."

"I would hate to become so disappointed that I had to call you back here for disciplinary action, Richard."

Haines used the sleeve of his Joseph Banks poplin sports coat to wipe the sweat from his face. "Yes, sir."

"Now did you not mention that you considered it a possibility that the Israelis had a safe house . . . or more than one . . . near Los Angeles. Ones that your Bureau would not have yet discovered?"

"Uh . . . I said it was possible, Mr. Barent. It doesn't seem very likely."

"But it is possible?"

"Yessir. You see, a couple of years ago there was this middle-level Al Fatah Palestinian who'd been the accountant for Black September. He agreed to defect to the U.S.A., but the CIA agents he'd thought he was dealing with were actually Cohen's Mossad. So they brought this man to the States, let him see that he was in L.A., and then spirited him away somewhere where neither the CIA nor the Bureau could find them to . . ."

"Richard, this is irrelevant. You have reason to believe that there might be another safe house somewhere near Los Angeles?"

"Yessir."

"And it might be near the San Juan Capistrano gas station."

"Yessir, but it might be anywhere."

"All right, Richard. Here is what you will do. First, you will immediately go to Mr. Harod's house and conduct a thorough interrogation . . . I emphasize *thorough*, Richard . . . of Miss Chen. If Harod is there, interrogate him. If he is not there, find him. Second, you will utilize the full resources of your Los Angeles Bureau station and whatever other local resources are necessary to find that backpacking gas station attendant and any other witnesses you may want to question. I want to know precisely what vehicle Mr. Cohen was driving, who was with him, and what direction they went from this particular gas station. Third, begin a survey of electronics supply stores in the Long Beach and surrounding areas. Find out if Jack Cohen or Willi purchased anything there. Fourth, re-interrogate the maids and clerks at the Long Beach motel to discover the smallest bits of additional information. You may use whatever form of persuasion you deem necessary.

"Finally, I will offer some help from this end. A dozen of Joseph's plumbers will be sent out this afternoon to aid you in your . . . ah . . . confidential investigations. Also, we will find out about that additional safe house. I will have that information to you within twenty-four hours.

Haines rubbed his eyebrows. "But how . . ." He shut up.

C. Arnold Barent's chuckle sounded static-filled over the scrambled circuit. "Richard, you certainly don't believe that you and Charles were my only sources of information? If all else fails, I will telephone certain . . . ah . . . contacts I have within the Israeli government. Because of the time difference, it may be tomorrow morning before I have a specific address for you. Do not wait that long. Begin a search of the area around San Juan Capistrano this afternoon. Check land sales records, homes that are unattended much of the year . . . simply drive around and look for a dark

Econoline van if nothing else occurs to you. Remember, you are looking for a private dwelling in a secure area, most probably away from residential areas."

"Yessir," said Haines.

"I will be back to you as soon as possible," said C. Arnold Barent. "And Richard?"

"Yessir?"

"Do not disappoint me again."

"No, *sir*," said Richard Haines.

FORTY-SEVEN

Los Angeles
Saturday, April 25, 1981

H arod was blindfolded and drugged when they dropped him off a
block from Disneyland. When he returned to full consciousness
he was sitting behind the wheel of his Ferrari, fully clothed, his
hands untied, his eyes covered with a simple black sleep mask. The car
was parked behind a discount rug store, between a garbage Dumpster and
a brick wall.

Harod got out of the car and leaned on the hood until most of the nausea and dizziness was gone. It was thirty minutes before he felt well enough
to drive.

Avoiding the freeways, heading west through Saturday traffic and then
north on Long Beach Boulevard, Harod tried to sort things out. Much of
the previous forty hours was blurred or dreamlike—long conversations he
could recall only fragments of—but the intravenous bruises and vestigial
tingling from the final tranquilizer dart left no doubt that he had been
drugged, dragged off, and put through hell.

It had to be Willi. The last conversation—the only one he could remember completely—left no doubt of that.

The man in the balaclava had come in and sat on the bed. Harod wanted
to see the man's eyes, but there were only the mirrored lenses reflecting his
own pale and stubbled face.

"Tony," the man said softly in that irritatingly familiar accent, "we are
going to let you go."

At that second Harod was sure that he was going to die.

"I have a question for you before you leave, Tony," the man said. His
mouth was the only human part of his head. "How is it that you're going
to provide most of the human surrogates for the island Club's five-day
competition this year?"

Harod tried to lick his lips, but there was no saliva to wet his tongue. "I
don't know anything about that."

The black balaclava went back and forth, mirrored lenses reflecting
white and white. "Oh, Tony, too late for that. We know you're providing
the bodies, but how are you going to do that? With your preferences for
using women? Are they really willing to carry on the games with just
women this year?"

Harod shook his head.

"I need to understand this before we say good-bye, Tony."

"Willi?" croaked Harod. "For Chrissakes, Willi, you don't have to do all this to me. TALK to me!"

The twin mirrors steadied on Harod's face. "Willi? I don't think we know anyone named Willi, do we? Now, how is it that you are supplying both sexes when we both know you can't?"

Harod had strained against the handcuffs, arching his back to kick the man's balaclavaed head off his fucking shoulders. Without hurry, the man stood up and moved to the head of the bed, out of range of Harod's feet or hands. He gently grasped Harod's hair and lifted his head free of the pillow. "Tony, we will get the answer from you. That much must be obvious. Perhaps we already have. What we need now is for you to confirm it while you are conscious. If we have to sedate you again, it will necessarily delay your release time."

Delay your release time sounded like a euphemism to Harod for "put off the time until we kill you" and that was fine with him. If silence—even silence under pain and duress—could postpone the inevitable bullet in the brain, Harod was willing to be as silent as the fucking Sphinx.

Except that he did not believe it. He knew from fragments of memories that he had done all the talking anyone could want; he had spilled his guts while under whatever chemical stimulus they had given him. If it *was* Willi, which seemed probable, then he would find out. It might even be in Harod's interest that Willi found out. Harod still held out hope that Willi had further use for him. He remembered the pawn's face on the chessboard at Waldheim. If these two were being run by Barent or Kepler or Sutter or a coalition of these three, then they wanted confirmation of things they either knew or could easily find out. Either way, what Harod needed now was a *dialogue*.

"I'm paying Haines to find bodies for me," he said. "Runaways, ex-cons, former informers with new identities. He'll set it up. *They'll* be working for pay, thinking they're involved in some sort of government scam. By the time they realize that the only pay they'll get is a shallow grave, they'll be on the island and in one of the holding pens."

The man in the balaclava chuckled. "*Paying* Agent Haines. How does his real master feel about that?"

Harod tried to shrug, realized that it was impossible in his handcuffed position, and shook his head. "I don't really give a damn and I don't think Barent does either. It was Kepler's idea to give this shitty assignment to me. It's basically an IQ test, not a test of my Ability . . ."

The mirrored lenses went up and down. "Tell me more about the island, Tony. The layout. The holding pens. The camp area. The security. Everything. Then we have a favor to ask."

That was the instant that Harod had been certain that he was dealing with Willi. So he had talked for an hour. And he had lived.

By the time Harod reached Beverly Hills, he had decided to tell Barent and Kepler about it. He couldn't keep straddling the fence forever—if it was Willi behind the abduction, the old man might even expect him to go to Barent. Knowing Willi, it probably was part of the master plan. But if it was a test of loyalty set up by Barent and Kepler, failure to report it might have fatal consequences.

When Harod had finished telling what he knew about Dolmann Island and the Club's sport there, the man in the balaclava had said, "All right, Tony. Your help has been appreciated. There is only one favor we have to ask as a condition of your release."

"What?"

"You say that you are to pick up the . . . volunteers . . . from Richard Haines on Saturday, the thirteenth of June. We will contact you on Friday the twelfth. There will be one or more people we will be substituting for some of Haines's volunteers."

Of course, Harod had thought. *Willi's trying to mark the deck somehow.* Then the impact of that fact really hit him. *Willi's really coming to the island!*

"Is that agreed?" asked the man behind the mirrored lenses.

"Yeah, right." Harod still could not believe they were going to let him go. He could agree to anything and then do whatever he damned pleased.

"And you'll keep the substitution to yourself?"

"Yeah."

"You realize that your life depends on doing this? Depends on it now and in the future. There is no statute of limitations on betrayal, Tony."

"Yeah, I understand." Harod wondered how stupid Willi thought he was. And how stupid had Willi become? The "volunteers" as this guy called them were numbered and kept waiting naked in a pen until a random drawing determined who would fight and when. Harod could see no way that Willi could rig that, and if he hoped to bring weapons in that way through Barent's security screen, Willi had become the senile old fart Harod had earlier mistaken him for. "Yeah," repeated Harod, "I understand. I agree."

"*Sehr güt*," the man in the balaclava had said.

And they let him go.

Harod decided to call Barent as soon as he got a bath and a drink and had discussed the whole mess with Maria Chen. He wondered if she had missed him, worried about him. He grinned as he imagined her calling the police to report him missing. How many times over the years had he disappeared for days—even weeks—without letting her know where he was going? Harod's grin faded as he realized just how vulnerable that sort of life-style had left him to precisely what had just happened to him.

He slid the Ferrari to a stop under the baleful gaze of his faithful satyr and plodded toward the house. Perhaps he would call Barent after a bath, a drink, a massage, and . . .

The front door was open . . .

Harod froze in his tracks for several interminable seconds before lurching through the open door, feeling the drug-induced dizziness rise up as he careened off walls and furniture, calling Maria Chen's name, barely noticing the toppled furniture until he tried to jump an overturned chair and fell heavily to the carpet. He jumped to his feet and resumed his shouting and searching.

He found her in her office, curled on the floor behind her desk. Her black hair was matted with blood in front and her face was swollen almost beyond recognition. The grimace on her face showed purpled lips pulled back and at least one broken tooth in front.

Harod vaulted over the desk, went to one knee, and cradled her head on his other knee. She moaned when he moved her. "Tony."

Tony Harod found that in the pure white heat of the profoundest fury he had ever felt, no obscenities came to mind. No shouts formed themselves. His voice, when he could speak, was little more than a murmur. "Who did this to you? When?"

Maria Chen started to speak, but her damaged mouth made her stop and fight back tears. Harod leaned closer so he could hear the whispers when she tried again. "Last night. Three men. Looking for you. Didn't say who sent them. But I saw Richard Haines . . . in car . . . before they rang bell."

Harod hushed her with a gesture and lifted her in his arms with infinite care. As he carried her toward his room, realizing with growing wonder that it had been only a severe beating and that she would survive and be well, he found to his total amazement that tears were coursing down his cheeks.

If Barent's men had been here last night looking for him, he realized, then it left no doubt that it had been Willi who had kidnapped him.

He wished that he could lift a phone and call Willi at that moment. He would like to tell him that there was no more reason for the elaborate game, the absurd precautions.

Whatever Willi wanted to do to Barent, Harod was more than ready to help.

FORTY-EIGHT

Near San Juan Capistrano
Saturday, April 25, 1981

Saul and Natalie drove back to the safe house early on Saturday after-noon. Natalie's relief was obvious, but Saul had ambiguous feelings. "The research potential was awesome," he said. "If I had been able to study Harod for a week, there's no end to the data I could have accumulated."

"Yes," said Natalie, "and odds are that he would have found a way to get to us."

"I think not," said Saul. "Just the use of the barbiturates appeared to have inhibited his ability to generate the rhythms necessary to contact and control other neural systems."

"But if we'd kept him a week, people *would* have been looking for him," said Natalie. "No matter how much you learned, you wouldn't have been able to go on to the next part of the plan."

"Yes, there's that," agreed Saul, but there was regret in his voice.

"Do you really believe that Harod will live up to his part of the bargain about getting someone onto the island?" asked Natalie.

"There's a chance he will," said Saul. "Right now Mr. Harod appears to be operating under a policy of damage limitation. There are certain incentives urging him to go along with the plan. If he does not cooperate, we are no worse off than we were."

"What if he cooperates to the point of taking one of us to the island and then handing us over to Barent and the others as a prize catch? That's what I would do if I were him."

Saul shivered. "In that case, we would be worse off than we had been. But there are other things to take care of before we face that possibility."

The farmhouse was as they had left it. Natalie watched as Saul replayed segments of the videotapes. Even the sight of Tony Harod on tape made her a little sick. "What next?" she asked.

Saul looked around. "Well, there are a few things to do. Transcribe and evaluate the interrogations. Go through and relabel the EEG and med-sensor tapes. Begin the computer analysis and integration of all that data. Then we can begin the biofeedback experiments using the information we've gained. You need to practice the hypnosis techniques we started and to study your files on the Vienna years and Nina Drayton. We both need to take a critical look at our plans now in light of the Dolmann Island data, possibly reassess the role Jack Cohen should play in them."

Natalie sighed, "Great. What do you want me to start on first?"

"Nothing." Saul grinned. "In case you didn't notice during your stay in Israel, today is my people's Sabbath. Today we rest. You go on upstairs while I get ready to prepare a real welcome-back-to-America meal: steak, baked potatoes, apple pie, and Budweiser beer."

"Saul, we don't have any of that. Jack stocked up with canned goods and freeze-dried stuff."

"I know that. That is why, while you take a nap, I will be shopping in that little store down the canyon."

"But . . ."

"But nothing, my dear." Saul turned her around and gave her a pat on the small of the back. "I'll call you when the steaks are cooking and we can have a celebration drink of that Jack Daniels you've been hoarding."

"I want to help make the pie." Natalie said sleepily.

"Deal," said Saul. "We will drink Jack Daniels and bake an apple pie."

Saul took his time shopping, pushing the cart down brightly lighted aisles, listening to featureless music, and thinking about theta rhythms and aggression. He had long ago discovered that American supermarkets offered one of the easiest possible avenues to successful self-hypnosis. He also had long had the habit of shifting into a light hypnotic trance to deal with complex problems.

Saul realized as he moved from aisle to aisle that he had spent the last twenty-five years following the wrong paths in trying to find the mechanism of dominance in humans. As with most researchers, Saul had postulated a complicated interaction of social cues, physiological subtleties, and higher-order behaviors. Even with his knowledge of the primitive nature of the Oberst's possession of him, Saul had searched for the trigger in the unmapped convolutions of the cerebral cortex, descending occasionally to the cerebellum. Now the EEG data suggested that the ability originated in the primitive brainstem and was somehow broadcast by the hippocampus in conjunction with the hypothalamus. Saul had long thought of the Oberst and his ilk as some form of mutation, an evolutionary experiment or statistical quirk illustrating normal human powers in diseased excess. The forty hours with Harod had changed that forever. If the source of this inexplicable ability was the brainstem and early mammalian limbic system, Saul realized, then the mind vampire's ability must predate Homo sapiens. Harod and the others were sports, random throwbacks to an earlier evolutionary stage.

Saul was still thinking about theta rhythms and REM status when he realized he had paid for the groceries and was being presented with two overflowing sacks. On a whim he asked for four dollars in quarters. Carrying the groceries to the van, Saul considered whether to call Jack Cohen or not.

Logic argued against it. Saul was still resolved not to involve the Israeli more than was absolutely necessary, so he could share none of the details of the past few days. And he had no other requests of the agent. Not yet. Calling Jack would be sheer self-indulgence.

Saul stowed the groceries in the van and trotted over to a stand of pay phones near the supermarket entrance. Perhaps it was time for a little self-indulgence. Saul was in a triumphant mood and wanted to share his good feelings with someone. He would be circumspect, but Jack would get the message that his time and effort had paid off for them.

Saul dialed the number he had memorized for Jack's home phone. No one was home. He retrieved his change and direct dialed the Israeli Embassy, asking the receptionist for Jack's extension. When another secretary asked who was calling, Saul gave the name Sam Turner as Cohen had suggested. He was to have left word that Sam Turner had immediate priority.

There was a delay of almost a minute. Saul fought the sick feeling of déjà vu rising in him. A man came on the line and said, "Hello, who is this please?"

"Sam Turner," said Saul, feeling the nausea grow. He knew he should hang up.

"And who are you calling for, please?"

"Jack Cohen."

"Could you please tell me the nature of your business with Mr. Cohen?"

"Personal."

"Are you a relative or personal friend of Mr. Cohen's?"

Saul hung up. He knew that it was more difficult to trace a telephone call than the movies and television suggested, but he had been on the line long enough. He called information, received the number of the *Los Angeles Times*, and used the last of his change to dial directly.

"*Los Angeles Times.*"

"Yes," said Saul, "my name is Chaim Herzog and I am adjutant information officer for the Israeli consulate office here in town, and I am calling to check on an error in an article you carried this week."

"Yes, Mr. Herzog. You want Files and Records. Just a second and I'll connect you."

Saul stared at the long shadows on the hillside across the highway and when the woman said "Morgue," he jumped. He repeated his cover story to her.

"Which day did this article run, sir?"

"I'm sorry," said Saul, "I do not have the clipping here and I forgot which day."

"And what was the name of the gentleman you mentioned?"

"Cohen," said Saul, "Jack Cohen." He leaned against the telephone and watched large blackbirds work at something lying in the bushes just off the highway. Overhead, a helicopter roared west at five hundred feet. He imagined the woman in Files and Records tapping at her computer keys.

"Here it is," she said. "Wednesday's paper, April twenty-second, fourth page. 'Israeli Embassy Official Killed in Airport Mugging.' Is that the article to which you are referring, sir?"

"Yes."

"That was an Associated Press story, Mr. Herzog. Any error would have originated with the wire service office in Washington."

"Could you read it to me, please?" asked Saul. "Just so I can see if the mistake was actually there?"

"Certainly." The woman read the four-paragraph article, starting with—"The body of Jack Cohen, fifty-eight, senior agriculture attaché at the Israeli Embassy, was discovered in the Dulles International Airport parking lot this afternoon, an apparent victim of robbery and assault" and ending with—"Although there are no leads at this time, police are continuing their investigation."

"Thank you," said Saul and hung up. Across the road, the blackbirds abandoned their unseen meal and flapped skyward in a widening spiral.

Saul drove up the canyon at 70 m.p.h., straining the van to its limit of power and maneuverability. He had spent at least a full minute standing by the phone, trying to construct a logical, reassuring argument that Jack Cohen's death could, indeed, have been a mugging gone wrong. Such coincidences occurred all the time in real life. Even if not, part of his mind argued, it had been four days. If the murderers had been able to tie Cohen to the safe house, they would have arrived by now.

Saul did not buy it. He turned onto the farm lane in a cloud of dust and accelerated past trees and fences. He had not brought the Colt automatic with him. It was in his bedroom, upstairs next to Natalie's room.

There were no cars in front of the house. The front door was locked. Saul opened it and stepped in. "Natalie!" There was no answer from upstairs.

Saul looked around, saw nothing out of place, walked quickly through the dining room and kitchen to the observation room, and found the dart gun where he had left it. He checked to make sure there was a red dart in the chamber and took the box of darts with him as he ran back to the living room. "Natalie."

He had gone up three of the steps, dart gun half raised, when Natalie came to the head of the stairs. "What is it?" She rubbed sleep out of her eyes.

"Get packed. Grab everything and just throw it in. We have to get out of here now."

She asked no questions as she turned and headed for her room. Saul went to his, lifted the pistol from where it lay atop his suitcase, checked the clip, and pulled back the action to put a round into the chamber. He made sure the selector was on safe and dropped the pistol in the pocket of his sports coat.

Natalie had her suitcase in the back of the van by the time Saul brought his own backpack and bag out. "What shall I do?" she said. Her own Colt was visible as a lump in the large pocket of her peasant skirt.

"Remember those two jerry cans of gasoline Jack and I found in the barn? Bring them to the porch and then stay out here and watch for a car turning into the lane. Or for a helicopter approaching. Wait, here's the van key. Keep it in the ignition. Right?"

"Right."

Saul trotted inside and began detaching wires from the electronic equipment, pulling adapters, and tossing equipment into boxes with no regard to what belonged where. He could leave the video recorder and camera, but he would need the EEG, telemetry packs, tapes, the computer, printer, paper, and radio transmitters. Saul carried boxes out to the van. It had taken Saul and Natalie two days to set up and calibrate the equipment, and prepare the interrogation room. It took him less than ten minutes to tear it down and get everything in the back of the van. "Anything?"

"Nothing yet," called Natalie.

Saul debated only a second and then carried the cans of gasoline into the back of the house and began dousing the interrogation room, the observation room, kitchen, and living room. It struck him as a barbaric and ungrateful act somehow, but he had no idea what Haines's or Barent's people could surmise from what was left behind. He tossed the empty cans outside, checked to make sure the rooms on the second floor were empty, and loaded the last of the things from the kitchen. He took his lighter out and paused on the porch. "Am I forgetting anything, Natalie?"

"The plastic explosive and detonators in the basement!"

"Good God," said Saul and ran to the stairway. Natalie had made a nest in the center of the boxes in the back of the van for the cushioned crate of detonators, and when Saul returned she set it in.

He made a final tour of the house, pulled the bottle of Jack Daniels from a cupboard shelf, and ignited the gasoline trails. The effect was immediate and dramatic. Saul shielded his face from the heat and thought, *I'm sorry, Jack.*

Natalie was behind the wheel when he came out and she did not wait for him to pull his door shut before the van was moving toward the lane, throwing gravel high into the weeds. "Which way?" she asked when they reached the road.

"East."

Natalie turned east.

FORTY-NINE

Near San Juan Capistrano
Saturday, April 25, 1981

Richard Haines arrived in time to see smoke just beginning to rise from the Israeli safe house. He turned left onto the farm lane and led the caravan of three cars toward the house at high speed.

Flames were visible in first-floor windows as Haines skidded the government Pontiac to a stop and ran to the front porch. He shielded his face with his forearm, peered into the living room, tried to go in, but was driven back by the heat. "Shit!" He directed three men around back and four others to search the barn and other outbuildings.

The house was fully engaged as Haines stepped back off the porch and walked thirty paces to the car.

"Shall I call it in?" asked the agent holding the radio.

"Yes, you might as well," said Haines. "But by the time anyone gets here, this place will be gone." Haines walked to one side and watched the flames appear in the second-floor windows.

An agent in a dark summer suit came running up, pistol in his hand. He was panting slightly. "Nothing in the barn or shed or chicken coop, sir. Just one pig wandering around in the backyard."

"In the backyard?" said Haines. "You mean in a pen?"

"No, sir. He's just sort of walking around free. The gate to the pen was wide open."

Haines nodded and watched as the fire began to work at the roof of the house. The three cars in front had backed up farther from the flames and men milled around with their hands on their hips. Haines went to the first car and spoke to the man sitting by the radio. "Peter, what's the name of that county mountie who's heading up the search for the gas station kid?"

"Nesbitt, sir. Sheriff Nesbitt out of El Toro."

"They're up east of here, aren't they?"

"Yes, sir. They think the kid and his friend went backpacking up Travuco Canyon. They've got the Forest Service people out hunting and . . ."

"Are they still using that helicopter?"

"Yes, sir. I heard it check in awhile ago. It's not just doing the search, though. There's a fire up in the Cleveland National Forest and . . ."

"Find the right frequency and get Nesbitt for me," ordered Haines. "Then patch me into wherever the closest CHP headquarters is."

The first fire engine was arriving when the agent handed Haines the radio microphone. "Sheriff Nesbitt?" said Haines.

"Affirmative. Who's this?"

"This is Special Agent Richard Haines, Federal Bureau of Investigation. I'm the one who authorized the search you're conducting for the Gomez boy. Something more important has come up and we need your help. Over."

"Go ahead. I'm listening. Over."

"I'm putting an all points bulletin out on a dark, 1976 to '78 Ford Econoline van," said Haines. "Occupant or occupants are wanted for arson and murder. They may have just left this location at . . . ah . . . twelve point two miles up San Juan Canyon. We don't know if they went east or west, but our guess is east. Can you set up roadblocks on Highway seventy-four east of our location? Over."

"Who's picking up the tab on all of this? Over."

Haines gripped the microphone hard. Behind him, parts of the farmhouse roof fell in and flames licked at the sky. Another fire engine roared to a stop and men began uncoiling heavy hoses. "This is a matter of national security and great urgency," he shouted. "The Federal Bureau of Investigation formally requests local assistance in this matter. Now can you set up roadblocks? Over."

There was a long pause as static rasped. Then Nesbitt's voice came through. "Agent Haines? I've got two deputy cars east of you on seventy-four. We were checking out the Blue Jay Campground and some trailheads up there. I'll have Deputy Byers establish a roadblock on the main road up there right at the county line west of Lake Elsinore. Over."

"Good," said Haines. "Are there any other roads branching off before there? Over."

"Negative," said Nesbitt. "Just national forest access roads. I'll have Dusty take the second unit and block those where they intersect. We'll need a better description of the vehicle's occupants unless you just want us to arrest the Econoline. Over."

Haines squinted toward the flames as the front of the farmhouse fell inward. The thin streams of water from the four hoses were making no difference. Haines thumbed the microphone. "We're not sure of the number or description of suspects," said Haines. "Possibly a Caucasian male, seventy years old, German accent, white hair . . . accompanied by a Negro male, thirty-two, six feet one inch tall, two hundred pounds, and/or a white male, twenty-eight, blond hair, five feet eleven inches tall. These men are armed and extremely dangerous. However, the van may be driven by others at this time. Locate and stop the *van*. Take great caution in approaching any of the vehicle's occupants. Over."

"You copy that, Byers?"

"Roger."

"Dusty?"

"Affirmative, Carl."

"Okay, Special Agent Haines. You got your roadblocks. Anything else? Over."

"Yes, Sheriff. Is your search helicopter still airborne? Over."

"Ah . . . yeah, Steve's just finishing his search up around Santiago Peak. Steve, you hearing this? Over."

"Yes, Carl, I've been listening. Over."

"Haines, you want our chopper, too? He's on special contract to the Forest Service and us right now. Over."

"Steve," said Haines, "as of this moment you are under contract to the United States government on a matter of national security. Do you copy? Over."

"Yeah," came the laconic reply, "thought the Forest Service *was* U.S. government. Where do you want me? I just fueled up, so I have about three hours of flying time at this altitude. Over."

"What is your present location? Over."

"Ah . . . moving south between Santiago and Trabuci Peaks. About eight miles from your position. Do you want map coordinates? Over."

"Negative," said Haines. "I want you to pick me up here. Farmhouse on the north side of San Juan Canyon, about five miles above Mission Viejo. Can you find the place? Over."

"Are you kidding?" said the helicopter pilot. "I can see the smoke from here. Hell of an LZ you feds prepare. Be there in two minutes. NL 167-B. Out."

Haines unlocked the trunk of the Pontiac. A passing fireman looked at the clutter of M-16s, shotguns, sniper rifles, flack vests, and ammo clips and whistled. "Holy shit," he said to no one in particular.

Haines extracted an M-16, tapped a magazine against the rim of the trunk to settle the loads, and slapped the clip in. He took off his suit coat, folded it carefully, set it in the trunk, and pulled on a flak vest, loading the oversize pockets with extra clips. He pulled a blue baseball cap from atop the spare tire and tugged it on. The agent at the radio called to him. "I have the CHP commander on line, sir."

"Give him the same information for the APB," said Haines. "See if he can extend it from Orange County to all the highway cops."

"Roadblocks, sir?"

Haines stared at the young agent. "On Interstate five, Tyler? Are you as stupid as that remark suggests, or just prone to lapses? Tell him we want the bulletin put out on that Econoline. Officers should get tag numbers, carry out surveillance, and get in touch with me through the Bureau's L.A. communications center."

Agent Barry Metcalfe of the L.A. branch came up to Haines. "Dick, I confess I don't understand any of this. What're a bunch of Libyan terror-ists doing using an Israeli safe house and why did they torch it?"

"Who said they were Libyan terrorists, Barry?"

"Well . . . you said in the briefing that they were Mideast terrorists . . ."

"Haven't you ever heard of Israeli terrorists?"

Metcalfe blinked and said nothing. Behind him, the front of the farm-house collapsed inward, sending sparks flying. The firefighters contented themselves with pouring water onto the nearby outbuildings. A small, Plexiglas-bubbled Bell helicopter throbbed in from the northeast, circled once, and set down in the field south of the house. Metcalfe said, "Want me to come with you?"

Haines gestured at the helicopter. "Looks like there's just room for one passenger in that old thing, Barry."

"Yeah, it does look like something out of *M*A*S*H*."

"Hold down the fort here. When they get the fire out, we're going to have to sift through the ashes with a fine-tooth comb. There may even be bodies in there."

"Oh, boy," Metcalfe said without enthusiasm and walked toward his men.

As Haines jogged toward the helicopter, the man known as Swanson approached. He was the oldest of the six Kepler's Plumbers Haines had brought along. He gave the FBI man a quizzical look.

"It's all a long shot," Haines shouted over the noise of the rotors, "but I have a hunch that this is Willi's operation. Probably not the old man him-self but maybe Luhar or Reynolds. If I can flush them, kill them."

"What about the paperwork?" said Swanson, nodding toward Metcalfe and his group.

"I'll take care of it," said Haines. "Just do the job."

Swanson's head went slowly up and down.

Haines was barely airborne, the small chopper spiraling upward through the smoke from the burning house, when the first radio report came in.

"Ah, this is Deputy Byers in Unit Three at the seventy-four east road-block to Agent Haines. Over."

"Go ahead, Byers." The mountainous countryside was rising under the helicopter, the canyon road winding through it like a pale gray ribbon. Traffic was light.

"Ah, Mr. Haines, this may not be anything, but I think a few minutes ago I saw a dark van . . . may have been a Ford . . . make a U-turn about two hundred yards from my position. Over."

"Which way is it headed now? Over."

"Coming your way, sir, back down seventy-four. Unless it takes one of the forest roads. Over."

"Could it get around you on those roads? Over."

"Negative, Mr. Haines. They all either dead end or turn into goat trails except for the Forest Service fire road that Dusty's on. Over."

Haines turned to the pilot, a short, heavyset man in an L.A. Dodgers windbreaker and Cleveland Indians baseball cap. "Steve, can you get Dusty on here?"

"He fades in and out," the pilot said over the intercom. "Depends on which side of the hill he's on."

"I want him on the line," Haines said and watched the countryside flash by three hundred feet below. Scrub brush and piñon pines flickered past in a blur of light and shadow. Larger pines and cottonwood trees lined the dried creek beds and lower areas. Haines estimated that there was an hour and a half of daylight remaining.

They reached the summit of the pass and the helicopter gained altitude and circled. Haines could see the blue haze of the Pacific to the west and the orange-brown haze of the smog above Los Angeles to the northwest. "Roadblock's just over the hill here," said the pilot. "I didn't see any dark van on the highway. Want to go south toward Dusty's area?"

"Yes," said Haines. "Have you got him yet?"

"He hasn't been answering his . . . oops, here he is." He threw a switch on the console. "On two-five, Mr. Haines."

"Deputy? This is Special Agent Haines. Do you copy? Over."

"Ah . . . yes, sir. Read you five-by. Uh . . . I've got something you might want to look at here, Mr. Haines. Over."

"What's that, Deputy?"

"Ah . . . dark blue 1978 Ford van . . . Uh . . . I was driving up to get closer to the hard road and found it abandoned here. Over."

Haines touched his headphone mike and grinned. "Anyone in it? Over."

"Ah . . . negative. Bunch of stuff in the back though. Over."

"Goddamn it, Deputy, be specific. What kind of stuff?"

"Electronic stuff, sir. Not sure. You better come and take a look yourself. Uh . . . I'm going to check out the woods . . ."

"Negative, Deputy," snapped Haines. "Secure the van and sit tight. What are your coordinates? Over."

"Coordinates? Uh . . . tell Steve that I'm half a mile down the main fire road from Coot Lake. Over."

Haines looked at the pilot. Steve nodded. "Roger," said Haines. "Just stay there, Deputy. Keep your revolver ready and stay alert. These are international terrorists we're dealing with." The helicopter banked steeply to the right and dropped toward wooded hillsides. "Taylor, Metcalfe, you getting this?"

"Roger, Dick," came Metcalfe's voice. "We're ready to roll."

"Negative that," said Haines. "Stay at the farmhouse. Repeat, stay at the farmhouse. I want Swanson and his men to meet me at the van. Got that?"

"Swanson?" Metcalfe's voice sounded puzzled. "Dick, this is our juris-diction . . ."

"I want *Swanson*," snapped Haines. "Don't make me repeat myself. Over."

"Richard, we copy that and we're on our way," came Swanson's voice.

Haines leaned out the open door as they flew six hundred feet above Coot Lake and dropped into a small valley. He cradled the M-16 and smiled. He was pleased that he was going to make Mr. Barent happy, and he was looking forward to the next few minutes. He knew now that it almost certainly was not Willi himself . . . the old man would have Used the deputy and gone past the roadblock rather than abandon the van . . . but whoever it was, they had lost the ballgame. There were many hundreds of square miles of national forest up here, but once Willi's people had to set out on foot, it was all over but the shouting. Haines had almost unlimited resources at his disposal and the "forest" was mostly shrub.

But Haines did not want to use unlimited resources or to wait for morning to conduct a search. He wanted to end this part of the game before it got dark.

It might not be Luhar or Reynolds, thought Haines. Probably isn't. It could be the black woman Willi had used in Germantown. She'd dropped from sight completely. It might even be Tony Harod.

Haines remembered the questioning of Maria Chen the previous evening and he smiled. The more he thought about it, the more sense it made that it could be Harod. Well, it was past time that they quit humoring that little Hollywood twerp.

Richard Haines had worked for Charles Colben and C. Arnold Barent for more than a third of his life. As a Neutral he could not be conditioned by Colben, but he had been well rewarded with money and power. Richard Haines found the work itself rewarding. He liked his job.

The helicopter came in over the clearing two hundred feet high at 70 m.p.h. The black van was parked in the open, its rear doors open. Near it, a heavy four-wheel-drive sheriff's vehicle sat empty. "Where the hell is the deputy?" snapped Haines.

The pilot shook his head and tried to raise Dusty on the radio. There was no answer. They circled the clearing in a widening spiral. Haines raised the M-16 and watched between the trees for a sign of movement or color. Nothing. "Take it around again," ordered Haines.

"Look, Captain," said the pilot, "I'm not a police officer or federal agent or a hero and I've served my time in Nam. This machine's my livelihood, friend. If there's a chance of it or us sprouting bullet holes, you're going to have to rent a different whirlybird and driver."

"Shut up and take it around again," said Haines. "This is a matter of national security."

"Yeah," said the pilot, "and so was Watergate. I didn't care much for it neither."

Haines swiveled so the rifle rested across his knees with the muzzle toward the pilot. "Steve, I'll ask one more time. Take it around again. If we don't see anything, you're going to put it down on the south side of the clearing. *Comprende?*"

"Yeah," said the pilot, "*yo comprendo*. But not because you've got that fucking M-16 looking this way. Even federal assholes don't shoot pilots unless they can fly the machine themselves and are damn sure somebody's not going to fall on the controls."

"Land it," said Haines. They had circled the clearing four times and he could see no sign of the deputy or anyone else.

The pilot brought the small craft in low and fast, actually having to lift it over the tree line before flaring out and setting it solidly on it skids precisely where Haines had designated.

"Out," said the FBI agent and gestured with the rifle.

"You have to be fucking kidding," said Steve.

"If we have to leave in a hurry, I want to make sure we leave together," said Haines. "Now *out* before I put a hole or two in your livelihood."

"You *are* fucking crazy," said the pilot. He pushed his cap back on his head. "I'm going to raise a stink that'll have J. Edgar Hoover crawling out of his grave to get at your ass."

"*Out*," said Haines. He took the safety off and set the weapon on full automatic.

The pilot made adjustments on the center console, the rotors slowed, and he unbuckled himself and stepped down. Haines waited until the pilot was thirty feet from the aircraft, standing near the edge of the woods, and then he undid his own straps and ran toward the sheriff's Bronco, moving in a crouching, weaving jog, weapon half raised. He crouched behind the Bronco's left rear quarter panel, scanning the hillsides for a flicker of movement or a glint of sunlight on metal or glass. There was nothing.

Haines carefully raised his head. He checked out the backseat, and then slid along the driver's side until he could see that the front seat was empty. There were brackets for two rifles on the metal screen between front and back seats. Both racks were empty. Haines tried the front door. It was locked. He dropped to one knee and inspected the hillsides in the 120 degrees of arc he could see.

If the stupid deputy had gone traipsing into the woods, against orders, it made sense he would take the rifle and lock the doors behind him. If. If there had been only one rifle racked. If there had been any rifle. If the deputy was still alive.

Haines peered around the front of the Bronco at the van twenty feet away and suddenly wished he had stayed airborne until Swanson and his team had arrived. How long until they should be here? Ten minutes? Fifteen? Probably less, unless the lake was farther from the highway than it had seemed from the air.

Haines had a sudden literal image of Tony Harod's head on a platter. He smiled and ran the twenty feet to the side of the van.

The back doors were wide open. Haines slid along the hot metal of the van's side until he could peer in. He knew he was a perfect target to anybody with a rifle in the hills on the south side of the clearing, but there was little he could do about that. He had chosen to come from that direction because with the exception of the fringe of woods where the pilot still stood, the hillside was mostly grass and small rocks with little opportunity for concealment. Haines had seen nothing in the trees during their four passes. He held the M-16 at his hip and stepped around behind the van.

Boxes, a litter of cables and electronic equipment. Haines recognized a radio transmitter and an Epson computer. There was no place large enough for a man to hide. Haines stepped into the interior of the van, and poked through the equipment and boxes. The box in the center held what appeared to be sixty or seventy pounds of gray modeling clay, carefully wrapped in separate plastic packets. "Oh, shit," whispered Haines.

He no longer wanted to be in the truck.

"Hey, Captain, can we get going now?" called the pilot from thirty yards away.

"Yeah, warm it up!" shouted Haines. He let the pilot walk back toward the machine before he began his crouching, dodging run to the open door on the right side of the Plexiglas bubble.

He was halfway there when a voice too loud to be human bellowed, "HAINES!" from the north slope. The first shots came a second later.

FIFTY

S aul and Natalie had not driven fifteen minutes when they saw the first roadblock. It was a single police car pulled broadside across the highway with flares marking narrow lanes on either side. Four cars were stopped on the eastbound lane, three in the westbound lane facing Saul and Natalie.

Natalie pulled the van to the shoulder at the top of a hill a quarter of a mile from the tie-up. "Accident?" she said.

"I don't think so," said Saul. "Turn around. Quickly."

They drove back over the summit of the pass they had just traversed. "Back down the canyon the way we came?" said Natalie.

"No. There was a gravel road about two miles back this way."

"Where the campground sign was?"

"No, a mile or so past that on the south side of the road. We may be able to bypass the roadblock to the south."

"Do you think that policeman saw us?"

"I don't know," said Saul. He pulled a cardboard box out from behind the passenger's seat, extracted the Colt automatic pistol, and made sure it was loaded.

Natalie found the gravel road and they turned left, passing through thick pine forests and a few grassy meadows. Once they had to pull to one side to let a pickup pulling a small trailer pass. Several side roads left the main track, but they appeared too narrow and unused to go anywhere, and Natalie kept the van on the fire road as it degraded from gravel to dirt and wound south and then east and then south again.

They saw the police vehicle parked in the clearing two hundred yards below them as they descended a wooded hill on a series of steep switchbacks. Natalie stopped the van as soon as she was sure they were out of sight. "Damn!" she said.

"He didn't see us," said Saul. "I caught a glimpse of the sheriff or whatever he was, out of the vehicle, looking the other way through binoculars."

"He'll see us when we cross that open space going back up," said Natalie. "It's so narrow here that I'll have to back up the hill until we get to that wide area two turns back. Damn!"

Saul thought a minute. "Don't back up," he said. "Go on down and see if he stops you."

"But he'll *arrest* us," said Natalie.

Saul rummaged around in the back until he came up with the balaclava and dart gun they had used with Harod. "I won't be in the truck," he said. "If they're not hunting for us, I'll rejoin you on the other side of the clearing where the road turns east to go over that saddle."

"And what if they are looking for us?"

"Then I'll rejoin you sooner. I'm pretty sure this guy is all alone down there. Maybe we can find out what is going on."

"Saul, what if he wants to search the truck?"

"Let him. I'll get as close as I can, but keep him occupied so I can get across that last bit of clearing. I'll come from the south side, behind the van on the passenger's side if I can."

"Saul, he can't be one of *them*, can he?"

"I don't see how he could be. They must have the local authorities involved."

"So he's just . . . sort of an innocent bystander."

Saul nodded. "So we have to make sure that he doesn't get hurt. And that *we* don't get hurt." He looked down the wooded slope. "Give me about five minutes to get in position."

Natalie touched his hand. "Be careful, Saul. We only have each other now."

He patted her cool, thin fingers, nodded, took his gear, and moved quietly into the trees.

Natalie waited six minutes, started the van, and drove slowly downhill. The man leaning against the Bronco with county markings seemed startled when she pulled into the clearing. He pulled his pistol from its holster and braced it by laying his right arm across the hood. When she was twenty feet away, he called to her through an electric bullhorn he held in his left hand. "STOP RIGHT THERE!"

Natalie shifted into park and left her hands in clear view on the top of the steering wheel.

"SHUT IT OFF. GET OUT OF THE VEHICLE. KEEP YOUR HANDS IN THE AIR."

She could feel her pulse in her throat as she killed the engine and opened the van door. The sheriff or deputy or whatever he was seemed very nervous. As she stood by the van with her hands up, he glanced into his Bronco as if he wanted to use the radio but did not want to relinquish either gun or bullhorn. "What's going on, Sheriff?" she called. It felt funny to use the word sheriff again. This man looked nothing like Rob; he was tall, thin, in his early fifties perhaps, with a face etched in wrinkles and lines as if he had spent his life squinting into the sun. "QUIET! MOVE AWAY FROM THE VEHICLE. THAT'S IT. KEEP YOUR HANDS BEHIND YOUR HEAD. NOW LIE DOWN. ALL THE WAY DOWN ON YOUR STOMACH."

Lying in the brown grass, Natalie called out, "What's the matter? What did I do?"

"SHUT UP. YOU IN THE VAN—OUT! NOW!"

Natalie tried to smile. "There's no one but me. Look, this is some mistake, Officer. I've never even gotten a parking . . ."

"QUIET!" The law officer hesitated a second and then set the bullhorn down on the hood. Natalie thought that he seemed a little sheepish. He glanced toward his radio again, seemed to make up his mind, and came quickly around the Bronco, keeping his revolver trained on Natalie while he nervously watched the van. "Don't move a muscle," he shouted at her as he stood behind the open driver's door. "If anybody's in there, you'd better tell 'em to get the hell out now."

"I'm all alone," said Natalie. "What's going on? I haven't done anything . . ."

"Shut up," said the deputy. In a sudden and awkward movement, he lunged into the driver's seat, swept his pistol toward the interior of the van, and visibly relaxed. Still half in the vehicle, he aimed his gun at Natalie again. "You make one move, missy, and I'll blow you in half."

Natalie lay uncomfortably with her elbows in the dust, hands behind her neck, trying to look over her shoulder at the rangy deputy. The pistol he was pointing at her seemed impossibly large. A place on her back between her shoulders physically ached with the tension and the thought of a bullet striking her there. What if he *was* one of them?

"Hands behind your back. *Now!*"

As soon as Natalie's hands touched above the small of her back, he loped over and slapped handcuffs on her. Natalie's cheek went into the dust and she tasted dirt. "Aren't you going to read me my rights?" she said, feeling adrenaline and anger beginning to burn away the semi-paralysis of fear.

"To hell with your rights, missy," said the deputy as he straightened up with an obvious release of tension. He holstered the long-barreled pistol. "Get up. We're going to get the FBI up here and see just what the hell's going on."

"Good idea," said a muffled voice behind them.

Natalie twisted sideways to see Saul in the balaclava and reflecting glasses coming around the front of the van. The Colt automatic was extended in his right hand and the blocky-looking dart gun hung at his left side.

"Don't even think about it!" snapped Saul and the deputy froze in midmotion. Natalie looked at the pointed weapon, the black mask, and the silver, reflecting glasses and felt fear herself. "On your face in the dirt. *Now!*" commanded Saul.

The deputy seemed to hesitate and Natalie knew that his pride was warring with his sense of self-preservation. Saul racked the slide of the automatic back, cocking it with an audible click. The deputy got to his knees and dropped to his stomach.

Natalie rolled away and watched. It was a tricky moment. The deputy's pistol was still in his holster. Saul should have had him throw it away before having him lie down. Now Saul would have to get within grabbing distance to remove it. *We're amateurs at all this,* she thought. She wished Saul would just shoot the deputy in the butt with a tranquilizer dart and be done with it.

Instead, Saul moved quickly forward and dropped onto the thin man's back with one knee, forcing the wind out of him and pressing his face forward with the muzzle of the Colt. Saul tossed the deputy's pistol ten feet away and then threw a ring of keys to Natalie. "One of them will undo those handcuffs," he called to her.

"Thanks a lot," said Natalie as she struggled to get her hands under her behind and to pull her legs through one at a time.

"Time to talk," Saul said to the deputy and pressed harder with the pistol. "Who organized these roadblocks?"

"Go to hell," said the deputy.

Saul stood up quickly, took four steps backward, and fired the automatic into the dirt four inches from the man's face. The noise made Natalie drop the keys.

"Wrong answer," said Saul. "I'm not asking you to reveal state secrets, I'm asking who authorized these roadblocks. If I don't get an answer in five seconds, I'm going to put a bullet in your left foot and start working my way up your left leg until I hear what I want to hear. One . . . Two . . ."

"You sonofabitch," said the deputy.

"Three . . . Four . . ."

"The FBI!" said the deputy.

"Who in the FBI?"

"I don't know!"

"One . . . Two . . . Three . . ."

"Haines!" shouted the deputy. "Some agent named Haines out of Washington. He came on the radio about twenty minutes ago."

"Where is Haines now?"

"I don't know . . . I swear."

The second shot kicked up dust between the deputy's long legs. Natalie got the smallest key in and the cuffs fell away. She chafed her wrists and scrambled to retrieve the deputy's gun from the dust where it lay.

"He's in Steve Gorman's helicopter, flyin' along the highway," said the deputy.

"Did Haines put out descriptions of people or just the van?" snapped Saul.

The deputy raised his head and squinted at them. "People," he said. "Black girl, in her twenties, accompanied by male Caucasian."

"You're lying," said Saul. "You would never have approached that van if you knew there were two people wanted. What did Haines say we did?"

The deputy mumbled something.

"Louder!" snapped Saul.

"Terrorists," repeated the deputy in a surly tone. "International terrorists."

Saul laughed behind the black cloth of the balaclava. "How right he is. Put your hands behind you, Deputy." The mirror lenses turned toward Natalie. "Handcuff him. Give me the other gun. Stay to one side. If he makes any move toward you at all, I'm going to have to kill him."

Natalie snapped the handcuffs on and backed away. Saul handed her the long gun. "Deputy," he said, "we're going over to the radio and make a call. I'll tell you what to say. You have a choice right now of dying or calling in the cavalry and getting a chance to be rescued."

After the charade on the radio, Natalie and Saul led the deputy up the hill and handcuffed him with his arms around the bole of a small, fallen pine sixty yards up the south-facing slope. Two trees had tumbled together, the trunk of the larger one falling onto the top of a four-foot-high boulder. The proliferation of branches concealed the rock and made for excellent cover and a good view of the clearing below.

"Stay here," said Saul. "I'm going back down to the van and get syringes and the pentobarbital. Then I'll get his rifle out of the Bronco."

"But Saul, they're *coming*!" said Natalie. "Haines is coming. Use the tranquilizer dart!"

"I'm not pleased with that drug," said Saul. "Your pulse was way too high when we had to use it. If this fellow has a heart condition, he might not be able to handle it. Stay here. I'll be right back."

Natalie crouched behind the boulder while Saul ran to the Bronco and then disappeared into the van.

"Missy," hissed the deputy, "you're in a shitload of trouble. Undo these cuffs and give me my gun and there's a chance you'll get out of this alive."

"Shut up!" whispered Natalie. Saul was running up the slope carrying the deputy's rifle and the small blue knapsack. She could hear the sound of a helicopter in the distance, growing closer. She was not afraid, only terribly excited. Natalie set the deputy's pistol on the ground and thumbed off the safety on the Colt automatic Saul had handed her. She practiced bracing her hands on the flat rock in front of her and aiming at the van, its back doors open now, even though she knew it was too far away for a pistol shot.

Saul burst through the screen of branches and dead needles just as the helicopter roared over the ridge behind them. He crouched, panting, filling a syringe from an upended bottle. The deputy cursed and protested as he was injected, struggled for a moment, and slumped into sleep. Saul pulled his balaclava and glasses off. The helicopter circled again, lower this time, and Saul and Natalie huddled together under the roof of branches.

Saul dumped the contents of the backpack out, setting aside a red and white box of copper-jacketed shells and feeding them into the deputy's rifle one by one. "Natalie, I am sorry I didn't confer with you before doing this. I could not pass up the opportunity—Haines is so close."

"Hey, it's OK," said Natalie. She was too excited to stay still, moving from one knee to a squatting position and then back to her knees. She licked her lips. "Saul, this is *fun*."

Saul looked at her.

"I mean, I know it's scary and all, but it's *exciting*. We're going to get this guy and get out of here and . . . *ouch*."

Saul had grasped her shoulder and squeezed very hard. He set the rifle against the rock and put his right hand on her other shoulder. "Natalie," he said, "at this moment our systems are full of adrenaline. It *seems* very exciting. But this is not television. The actors will not stand up and go out for coffee after the shooting is over. Someone will be hurt in the next few minutes and it will be no more exciting than the aftermath of an automobile accident. *Concentrate*. Let the accident occur to someone else."

Natalie nodded.

The helicopter circled a final time, disappeared briefly over the ridge to the south, and came back to land in a cloud of dust and pine needles. Natalie lay on her stomach and pressed her shoulder against the rock as Saul lay prone with the rifle against his shoulder.

Saul breathed in the scent of sun-baked soil and pine needles and thought of another time and place. After his escape from Sobibor in October of 1944, he had run with a Jewish partisan group called *Chil* in the Forest of the Owls. In December, before he began working as an aide and orderly for the group's surgeon, Saul was given a rifle and put on sentry duty.

It had been a cold, clear night—the snow blued by light from the full moon—when the German soldier staggered into the clearing where Saul lay in ambush. The soldier was little more than a boy and carried neither helmet nor rifle. His hands and ears were wrapped about with rags, his cheeks white from frostbite. Saul knew instantly from his regiment insignia that the youth was a deserter. The Red Army had launched a major offensive in the area the week before, and although it would be ten more weeks before the Wehrmacht was to be totally beaten, this youth had joined hundreds of others in headlong retreat.

Yechiel Greenshpan, *Chil*'s leader, had given explicit instructions on what to do with solo German deserters. They were to be shot, their bodies thrown in the river or left to rot. No effort at interrogation was to be expended. The only exception to this execution order was if the noise of the shot would reveal the partisan band to the infrequent German patrols. Then the sentries were to use knives or let the deserter pass.

Saul had called out a challenge. He could have fired. The band he was
with lay concealed in a cave hundreds of meters away. There was no German activity in the area. But he had challenged the German instead of
firing immediately.

The boy had dropped to his knees in the snow and begun weeping,
imploring Saul in German. Saul had worked around behind the boy so
that the muzzle of the ancient Mauser was less than three feet from the
back of the blond head. Saul had thought of the Pit then—of the white
bodies tumbling forward and of the sticking plaster on the Wehrmacht
sergeant's cheek as he took a cigarette break with his legs dangling above
the horror.

The boy wept. Ice glinted on his long lashes. Saul had raised the
Mauser. And then he had stepped back and said "Go" in Polish, watching
as the young German stared over his shoulder in disbelief and then crawled
and stumbled from the clearing.

The next day, as the group moved south, they had found the boy's frozen body lying facedown in an open spot in a stream. That was the same
day that Saul had gone to Greenshpan and asked to be made an aide to
Dr. Yaczyk. The *Chil* leader had stared at Saul for some time before saying
anything. The group had no time for Jews who would not or could not kill
Germans, but Greenshpan knew that Saul was a survivor of Chelmno and
Sobibor. He agreed.

Saul had gone to war again in 1948 and in 1956 and in 1967 and, for
only a few hours, in 1973. Each time he had gone as a medical officer. Except for those terrible hours under the Oberst's control when he had
stalked *Der Alte*, Saul had never killed a human being.

Saul lay on his stomach in the soft bed of sun-warmed pine needles and
glanced at his watch as the helicopter landed. It was in a bad place, on the
far side of the clearing, partially obscured by the deputy's Bronco. The
deputy's rifle was old—wooden stock, bolt action, with only a notched
sight. Saul adjusted his glasses and wished it had a telescopic sight. Everything about this was wrong according to Jack Cohen's advice—a strange
weapon that he had never fired, a cluttered field of fire, and no avenue of
retreat.

Saul thought of Aaron and Deborah and the twins and used the bolt to
slide a round into the chamber.

The pilot got out first and moved slowly away from the helicopter. This
surprised and bothered Saul. The man waiting in the right side of the
bubble was armed with an automatic rifle and wore dark glasses, a long-
billed cap, and a massive vest of some sort. At sixty yards, with the glare of
the setting sun on the Plexiglas, Saul could not be sure that the man was
Richard Haines. Saul held his fire. He felt a sudden nausea rise in him
along with a certainty that this was the wrong thing to do. He had heard
Haines's call to Swanson on the deputy's radio when he was retrieving the

rifle. This *had* to be Haines. But all the FBI man had to do was sit and wait for the others to arrive. Saul set the deputy's bullhorn next to his left hand and sighted down the barrel again. The man in the flak jacket moved then, running in a combat crouch to the cover of the Bronco. Saul did not get a clear shot, but he did see the strong jaw and carefully trimmed hair under the cap. He was looking at Richard Haines.

"Where is he?" whispered Natalie.

"Shhh," whispered Saul. "Behind the van now. He has a rifle. Stay low." He set the bullhorn on the ground in front of his face, made sure it was on, and braced the rifle with both hands.

The pilot called something and the agent behind the van shouted back. The pilot moved slowly toward the helicopter and five seconds later the other figure appeared, moving swiftly.

"Haines!" shouted Saul and the amplified boom made Natalie jump and came echoing back from the opposite hillside. The pilot ran for the trees as the flak-jacketed figure swiveled, dropped to his right knee, and began raking the hillside with automatic fire. Saul thought the popping sound tiny and toylike. Something whined through the branches eight or nine feet above them. Saul squeezed the oiled stock against his cheek, took aim, and fired. The recoil slammed the butt against his shoulder with surprising strength. Haines was still up and firing, sweeping the M-16 in small, deadly arcs. Two bullets struck the boulder in front of Saul and another buried itself in the fallen log above him with the sound of an ax splitting wood. Saul wished he had handcuffed the deputy deeper under the woodpile.

Saul had seen the pine needles jump ahead and to the left of Haines. He raised his sights up and to the right and was vaguely aware in the periphery of his vision that the pilot had turned and run for the trees. Saul could see the muzzle flashes from the M-16 as Haines blazed away. A final rattle of bullets struck the boulder where Natalie was curled in a fetal position, the firing stopped abruptly, the kneeling figure threw a rectangular clip away while pulling another from his vest pocket, and Saul took careful aim and shot Haines.

The special agent seemed to be pulled backward by the tug of an invisible cable. His sunglasses and cap flew off and he landed on his back, legs spraddled, the rifle six feet beyond his head.

The sudden silence was deafening.

Natalie was up on her knees, peeking around the side of the boulder and breathing heavily through her mouth. "Oh, Jesus," she whispered.

"Are you all right?" asked Saul.

"Yeah."

"Stay here."

"Forget that," she said and stood with him as he got up to descend the hillside.

They were forty feet down the slope when Haines rolled over, scrabbled onto his knees, retrieved the rifle, and bolted for the opposite tree line. Saul dropped to one knee, fired, and missed. "Damn! This way." He pulled Natalie to their left, through thick brush.

"The others will be coming," panted Natalie.

"Yes," said Saul. "No noise." They continued moving left, from tree to tree. Across the clearing, the hillside was too bare for Haines to move clockwise ahead of them. He would have had to stay where he was or be moving toward them. Saul wondered whether the pilot was armed.

Saul and Natalie moved as quickly as possible while staying behind trees and keeping back from the edge of the clearing. When they were approaching the point where Haines had entered the trees, Saul waved Natalie to a stop in a thick copse of second growth while he moved forward in a crouch, looking to the left and right after each step. Extra cartridges jingled in the pockets of his sports coat. It was getting dark under the trees. Mosquitoes were coming out, buzzing by Saul's sweaty face. He felt like hours had elapsed since the helicopter had landed. A glance at his watch told him that it had been six minutes.

A horizontal band of light on the forest floor caught something bright against dark needles. Saul dropped to his stomach and wiggled forward on his elbows. He stopped, gripped the rifle in his left hand, and extended his right hand to touch the blood that had splattered needles and dirt. Other spatters were visible to the left, disappearing where the trees grew thicker.

Saul was edging backward when the roar of automatic fire began to his left and behind him, anything but toylike now, loud and frenzied. He pressed his cheek to the soil and tried to will his body and backbone into the dirt with him as bullets ripped branches, stitched tree trunks, and whined into the clearing. He heard at least two strike metal there, but he did not raise his head to see which vehicle was hit.

There was a terrible scream not forty feet from Saul and then a moan that started low and seemed to ascend into the ultrasonic. He jumped up and ran to his left, catching his glasses as a branch batted them off, almost falling over Natalie where she crouched behind a rotten stump. He threw himself down next to her and whispered, "You all right?"

"Yes." She gestured with her pistol toward a thick growth of young pines and spruce where the hill bent toward a ravine to their left. "The noise came from over there. He wasn't firing at us."

"No." Saul looked at his glasses. The frames were bent. He tapped at his sports coat pockets. Cartridges clinked. The pistol was still in his left pocket. His elbows were a muddy mess. "Let's go."

They crawled forward, Natalie three yards to Saul's right. As they approached a small stream running out of the ravine the undergrowth grew thicker, sporting tender young spruce and fir, stands of low birch, and clusters of ferns. Natalie found the pilot. She almost set her forearm on his chest as she moved around a thick juniper bush. He had been cut almost in half by rapid fire from the M-16. His abdominal wall hung in loose flaps of red striated muscle, and his fingers were clenched around the white and gray ropes of intestines as if he had tried to tuck himself back in. The small man's head was thrown far back and his mouth was wide open in an unfinished scream, the clouded eyes fixed on a small patch of blue sky between branches far above.

Natalie turned and vomited silently into ferns.

"Come on," whispered Saul. The noise of the stream was loud enough to cover soft sounds.

There were tiny asterisks of blood on a fallen log behind a wall of spruce saplings. Haines must have crouched there minutes before until he heard the sound of the pilot moving through the bushes seeking his own shelter.

Saul peered through the spruce. Which way had Haines gone? To the left, across twenty-five feet of open space, the mature forest began again, filling the valley and rising over the low saddle to the southeast. To the right, the ravine was filled with young trees, narrowing forty yards above to a narrow gap filled with three-foot-high juniper.

Saul had to decide. A movement either way would expose him to view to someone who had gone the other way. It was the psychological barrier of the clearing to the left that made him decide that Haines had gone to the right. Saul slid backward and handed the rifle to Natalie, putting his mouth almost against her ear as he whispered to her. "Going up there. Tuck in right under the log. Give me exactly four minutes then fire the rifle into the air. Stay low. If you don't hear anything, wait one more minute and fire another round. If I'm not back in ten minutes, get back into the van and get the hell out of here. He can't see the road from up here. Do you understand?"

"Yes."

"You still have the passport," whispered Saul. "If things go bad, use it to get to Israel."

Natalie said nothing. She was very tense, but the line of her lips was thin and firm.

Saul nodded at her and crawled through the barrier of soft firs, staying close to the stream as he moved uphill.

He could smell the blood. There was more of it now as he crawled through tunnels of low juniper. He was moving too slowly; three minutes had passed and he was not far enough up the ravine. His right hand was sweaty around the grip of the Colt and his glasses kept slipping down his nose. His elbows and knees were very sore and his breath rattled in his chest. Flies buzzed up from another bright spattering of blood and batted against his face.

Half a minute left. Haines could not have gone much farther unless he had been running. He could have run. Ten yards would make all the difference. The M-16 had twenty times the range of Saul's pistol, including the extra bullet he had loaded after racking a round into the chamber. Saul had eight shots. His pockets were filled with the heavy cartridges for the deputy's rifle, but he had left the three extra magazines for the pistol neatly arrayed back where the deputy was handcuffed.

It didn't matter. Twenty seconds until Natalie fired. Nothing would matter unless he got close enough. Saul lunged forward on his elbows and knees, panting audibly now, knowing he was making too much noise. He fell forward under an overhanging branch of juniper and gasped through his open mouth, trying to regulate his breathing.

Natalie's shot echoed up the ravine.

Saul rolled onto his back, holding his forearm to his mouth so the sound of his panting would be muffled. Nothing. No answering shots or movement from above.

Saul lay on his back, pistol alongside his face, knowing that he should move forward, get farther uphill. He did not move. The sky was darkening. A ripple of cirrus caught the last pink light of evening and a single star gleamed near the edge of the ravine. Saul raised his left wrist and looked at his watch. Twelve minutes had passed since the helicopter had landed.

Saul breathed in the cooling air. He smelled blood.

Too much time had passed since Natalie's first shot. Saul had raised his wrist again to check the time when Natalie's second shot rang out, closer this time, the ricochet tearing at rock thirty feet up the side of the ravine.

Richard Haines rose out of the shrubbery not eight feet from Saul and poured automatic fire down the ravine. Saul could see the muzzle flashes above him and smell the cordite. Bullets ripped apart the shrubbery he had just crawled through. Young trees two inches thick were sliced off as if harvested by an invisible scythe. Bullets struck rock on the east side of the ravine, screamed again on the west side, and kicked up dirt far below on the east wall. The air filled with the scent of sap and cordite. The firing seemed to go on and on and on. When it paused Saul was too numbed to move for two or three seconds. He heard the metal click of one clip being ejected from the M-16 and the tap of another one going in. Twigs snapped as Haines rose to his feet again. Then Saul rose, saw Haines standing less than ten feet away, extended his right arm, and fired six times.

The agent dropped the rifle and sat down with a grunt. He stared curiously at Saul as if they had been two children playing a game and Saul had cheated. Haines's hair was sweaty and disarrayed, the flak vest hung loose at one side, and his face was streaked with dirt. His left pants leg was soaked with blood. Three of Saul's shots must have struck the vest and driven him backward, but Haines's left arm was shattered at the shoulder and at least one bullet had gone in where the vest hung loose at the throat. Saul saw white splinters of collarbone protruding from flesh as he stepped

forward through the low juniper bush and crouched three feet from Haines. Saul moved the M-16 to one side with his left hand.

Haines sat with his legs out, black shoes pointed skyward. His mangled left arm hung at a sickening angle, but his right hand lay limply on his knee in a relaxed, almost casual manner. The handsome man's mouth opened and closed several times and Saul saw bright blood on his tongue.

"It hurts," Richard Haines said in a small voice.

Saul nodded. He squatted and stared at the man, assessing the wounds out of professional instinct and old habit. Haines would almost certainly lose the left arm, but with immediate attention, ample plasma, and an airlift in the next twenty or thirty minutes, his life could be saved. Saul thought of the last time he had seen Aaron, Deborah, and the twins. Yom Kippur. The children had fallen asleep on the couch between them as he and Aaron had talked.

"Help me," whispered Haines. "Please."

"No, I think not," said Saul and shot him twice in the head.

Natalie was working her way uphill with the rifle when Saul descended the ravine. She looked at the M-16 in his hands and the extra clips in his pockets and raised her eyebrows.

"Dead," said Saul. "We have to hurry."

Seventeen minutes had elapsed from the time the helicopter landed when Natalie started the van again.

"Wait," said Saul. "Did you check the deputy after the first shooting?"

"Yes," said Natalie. "He was asleep but okay."

"Just a minute," said Saul. He jumped out of the van with the M-16 and looked at the helicopter forty feet away. Two teardrop gas tanks were visible behind the bubble. Saul set the selector on single shot and fired the rifle. There came a sound like a crowbar striking a boiler, but no explosion. He fired again. The air suddenly filled with the strong reek of aviation fuel. The third shot started a fire that engulfed the engine and bloomed skyward.

"Go," said Saul as he jumped in the van. They bounced forward past the Bronco. They had just reached the trees on the southeast side of the clearing when the second fuel tank exploded, throwing the bubble cockpit cover into the trees and scorching the left side of the Bronco.

Two dark cars flashed through the open switchback on the hill a quarter of a mile behind them.

"Quickly," said Saul as they drove into the darkness of the forest.

"There's not much chance for us, is there?" said Natalie.

"No," said Saul. "They'll have every cop in Orange and Riverside counties after us. They'll seal off the highway between here and the other side, close all routes to I-fifteen, and send helicopters and four-wheel-drive vehicles into the hills even before first light."

They rocketed across a stream and roared over the saddle at 70 m.p.h. in a shower of gravel. Natalie slid the van around a corner, counter-steered perfectly, and said "Was it worth it, Saul?"

He looked up from trying to adjust his bent glasses. "Yes," he said. "It was."

Natalie nodded and drove down a long slope toward an even darker stretch of forest ahead.

FIFTY-ONE

Dothan, Alabama
Sunday, April 26, 1981

On Sunday morning, before a live in-person audience of eight thousand and a live television audience of perhaps two and a half million, the Reverend Jimmy Wayne Sutter preached a fire and brimstone sermon so bone-rattling that members of the audience in the Palace of Worship were on their feet and speaking in tongues while those at home were on their phones and giving their Visa and Master Charge numbers to waiting pledge takers. The televised worship service lasted ninety minutes and seventy-two minutes of it consisted of the Reverend Sutter's sermon. Jimmy Wayne read excerpts from the Letters to the Corinthians to the faithful, and then followed that with a much longer segment where he imagined Paul writing updated letters to the Corinthians in which he reported on the moral tone and prospects in the United States. To hear the Reverend Jimmy Wayne put words in Paul's mouth, the current climate in the U.S. was one of prayerlessness, pornography, creeping secular humanism inculcating defenseless youth in the secret rites of sinful socialism, permissiveness, promiscuity, demonic possession advanced by rock videos and by Dungeons and Dragons games, and a general and pervasive rottenness manifested most visibly by the sinfuls' refusal to accept Christ as their personal Savior while giving generously to such urgent Christian causes as Bible Outreach, 1-800-555-6444.

When the Outreach Gospel Choir had sung their final triumphant chord and the red lights were out on the nine massive cameras, the Reverend Jimmy Wayne swept through the private corridors to his office, accompanied only by his three bodyguards, his accountant, and his media consultant. Sutter left all five in his outer office and shed clothes as he moved across the carpeted expanse of his sanctum sanctorum, leaving a trail of sweat-soaked garments on the floor until he stood naked by the bar. As he poured himself a tall bourbon, the high-backed leather chair behind his desk swiveled around and an old man with a flushed face and pale eyes said, "A very stimulating sermon, James."

Sutter jumped, spilling bourbon on his wrist and arm.

"Goshdarnit, Willi, I thought you were coming this afternoon."

"*Ja,* but I decided to arrive early," said Wilhelm von Borchert. He steepled his fingers and smiled at Sutter's nakedness.

"You come in the private way?"

"Of course," said Willi. "Would you prefer that I came in with the tourists and said good morning to Barent's and Kepler's men?"

Jimmy Wayne Sutter grunted, finished his drink, and went into his private bathroom to turn on the shower. He called over the running water, "I got a call from Brother Christian about you this morning."

"Oh, really?" said Willi, still smiling slightly. "What did our old dear friend want?"

"Just letting me know that you'd been busy," called Sutter.

"*Ja?* How so?"

"Haines," said Sutter. His voice echoed on the tile walls as he stepped into the shower.

Willi walked to the bathroom door. He was wearing a white linen suit with a lavender shirt, open at the neck. "Haines the FBI person?" he said. "What about him?"

"As if you didn't know," said Sutter, scrubbing his broad stomach and soaping his genitals. His body was very pink and devoid of hair, somewhat like a huge, newborn rat.

"Pretend I do not know and tell me," said Willi. He took his coat off and hung it on a hook.

"Barent's been following up on the Israeli connection after Trask's death," said Sutter, spluttering as he dunked his head under the stream of water. "They found that someone in the Israeli Embassy's been doing computer searches through limited access files. Searches on Brother C. and the rest of us. But this isn't news, is it?"

"Go on," said Willi. He pulled off his shirt and set it on the hook with the sports coat. He slipped off his three-hundred-dollar Italian loafers.

"So Barent eliminates the meddler and Haines traces the connections out to the West Coast where you were playing whatever game you were playing. Last night Haines almost catches your people but has an accident himself. Someone lured him to the forest and shot him. Who were you Using? Luhar?"

"Did they not catch the perpetrators?" asked Willi. He carefully folded his slacks across the back of the commode. He was wearing pressed, blue boxer shorts.

"Nope," said the Reverend Jimmy Wayne. "They got about a million police in those woods but haven't found 'em yet. How'd you get them out?"

"Trade secret," said Willi. "Tell me, James, would you believe me if I told you I was not involved in this?"

Sutter laughed. "Sure! Just as much as you'd believe me when I tell you that all of our donations go toward buying new Bibles."

Will took off his gold wristwatch. "Will this have an adverse effect on our timetable or plans, James?"

"I don't see why it should," said Sutter, rinsing the shampoo out of his long, silver hair. "Brother Christian'll be even more eager to get you on the island where he can deal with you." Sutter opened the sliding door and looked at Willi standing there naked. The German had a massive erection. The head of his glans was almost purple.

"We will not falter, will we, James?" said Willi, stepping into the shower next to the evangelist.

"No," said Jimmy Wayne Sutter.

"How do we know what we must do?" asked Willi, his voice taking on the lilt of litany.

"The Book of Revelation," said Sutter and groaned as Willi gently cupped his testicles.

"And what is our goal, *mein Liebchen*?" whispered Willi, stroking the heavier man's penis.

"The Second Coming," moaned Sutter, his eyes closed.

"And whose Will do we fulfill?" whispered Willi, kissing Sutter's cheek.

"God's Will," answered the Reverend Jimmy Wayne, loins moving in response to the rise and fall of Willi's hand.

"And what is our divine instrument?" Willi whispered into Sutter's ear.

"Armageddon," Sutter said loudly. "Armageddon!"

"His Will be done!" cried Willi, pumping Sutter's penis with strong, rapid strokes.

"Amen!" cried Sutter. "Amen!" He opened his mouth to Willi's questing tongue just as he climaxed, the thin white ribbons of semen swirling on the floor of the shower stall for several seconds before disappearing forever down the drain.

FIFTY-TWO

Melanie

I had been having romantic thoughts about Willi. Perhaps it was the influence of Miss Sewell; she was a vital and sensuous young woman with definite needs and the capacity to enjoy fulfilling them. Now and then, when these urges distracted her from completely serving me, I allowed her a few minutes with Culley. Sometimes I eavesdropped on these brief, violent interludes of the flesh from her point of view. Sometimes from Culley's. Once I indulged myself by experiencing it through both of them. But always it was Willi I thought of when the tides of passion flowed through them to me.

Willi was so handsome in those halcyon days before the war—the second war. His thin, aristocrat's face and pale blond hair proclaimed his Aryan heritage to all who saw him. Nina and I enjoyed being seen with him and I believe he took pride in sharing the company of these two attractive and playful American women—the stunning blonde with the cornflower blue eyes and the shyer, quieter, yet somehow beguiling young belle with brown curls and long lashes.

I remember a walk in Bad Ischl—before the bad times began—when Willi had made some joke and as I laughed had taken my hand in his. The effect was immediate and electric. My laughter had stopped at once. We leaned closer, his beautiful blue eyes so aware of me, our faces close enough to reflect the other's heat. But we did not kiss. Not then. Denial was part of the dance of courtship in those days, a sort of fasting before the gourmet meal so as to sharpen the appetite. Today's young gluttons know nothing of such subtleties and restraint; any appetite to them is something to sate at once. No wonder that all pleasures hold the flat taste of long-opened champagne to them, all conquests the hollow core of disappointment.

I think now that Willi would have fallen in love with me that summer if it had not been for Nina's crass seduction. After that terrible day in Bad Ischl I refused to play our Vienna Game for more than a year, refusing even to meet them in Europe the following summer, and when I did resume social intercourse with both of them it was in our new and more formal relationship. I realize now that Willi's brief affair with Nina was long over by that point. Nina's flame burned brightly but briefly.

During our final summers in Vienna, Willi was all but consumed by his obsession for his Party and his Führer. I remember he wore his brown shirt and ugly armband to the premiere of *Das Lied von der Erde* when

Bruno Walter conducted it in 1934. That was the terribly hot summer that we stayed with Willi in a gloomy old house he had rented on the Hohe Warte near where that stuck-up Alma Mahler lived. The pretentious woman never invited us to any of her parties and we reciprocated. More than once I was tempted to focus my attention on her during the Game, but we did very little playing in those days because of Willi's silly political preoccupations.

Now, as I lay recuperating in my own bed in my own home in Charleston, I frequently recalled those days and thoughts of Willi and wondered how things might have turned out differently if, by the smallest sigh or smile or glance, I had encouraged him earlier and helped him to avoid Nina's destructive advances.

Perhaps these thoughts were subconscious preparation for the events soon to come. During my illness, time had come to mean less and less to me, so that perhaps by this point I had become able to roam forward through the corridor of events as easily as I had gone backward. It is hard to say.

By May I had grown so accustomed to the ministerings of Dr. Hartman and Nurse Oldsmith, the gentle therapies of Miss Sewell, the services of Howard and Nancy and Culley and the Negro boy, and the constant and tender care of young Justin, that I might have stayed in that comfortable status quo for more months or years if someone had not come knocking at the iron front gate one warm spring evening.

It was the messenger I had met before. The one named Natalie.

Nina had sent her.

FIFTY-THREE

Charleston
Monday, May 4, 1981

L ater, Natalie would remember it as the three-thousand-mile dream.
It began with the miracle of the truck.
All night they had driven through the blackness of the Cleveland National Forest, backtracking and getting off the main fire road after they had seen lights ahead from a hilltop bend in the road, creeping southward along lanes little better than trails. Then the trails had given out and only the openness of that particular stretch of wooded valley had allowed them to continue onward, first following a dry streambed for four miles, the van bouncing and clattering with only its parking lights showing the way, then up and across another low ridge, striking hidden logs and rocks in the concealing grass. Hours passed. Inevitably it happened. Saul was driving by then, Natalie half asleep despite the lurching, bouncing, grinding washboard ride. The final unseen boulder was halfway up a steep slope the van was clawing at in second gear. Somehow the front axle had bounced over it, but the jagged rock tore out the oil pan, ripped loose part of the drive shaft, and left them teetering on what was left of the rear axle.

Saul crawled under the vehicle with a flashlight and wiggled out in thirty seconds. "That's it," he said. "We walk."

Natalie was too tired to cry, too tired even to feel like crying. "What do we bring?" she asked.

Saul played the light over the interior. "The money," he said. "In the backpack. The map. Some of the food. The pistols, I guess." He looked at the two rifles. "Is there any reason to bring these?"

"Are we going to shoot at innocent police officers?" asked Natalie.

"No."

"Then let's leave the pistols, too." She looked around at the starlit night and dark wall of hill and trees above them. "Do you know where we are, Saul?"

"We were headed toward Murrietta," he said, "but we've taken so many zigs and zags that I don't have the foggiest idea anymore."

"Will they be able to follow us?"

"Not in the dark," said Saul. He glanced at his watch. It was four A.M. "When it's light, they'll find the trail we left. They'll search the forest roads first. Sooner or later an aircraft will spot the van."

"Is there any use trying to camouflage it?"

Saul looked up the hill. It was another hundred yards to the nearest trees. It would take the rest of the night to break enough pine boughs to cover the truck and to shuttle back and forth with them. "No," he said, "let's just get the stuff packed and go."

Twenty minutes later they were puffing and panting their way to the top of the hill, Natalie with the backpack and Saul carrying the heavy suitcase full of money and the dossiers he refused to leave behind. When they reached the trees, Natalie said, "Stop a minute."

"Why?"

"Because I have to go to the bathroom, that's why." She dug through the pack for Kleenex, took the flashlight, and moved off through the trees.

Saul sighed and sat on the suitcase. He found that if he closed his eyes for even a few seconds he would begin to doze, and each time he dozed the same image would float to the surface of his mind—Richard Haines, white face and surprised eyes, mouth moving and the sound coming later, as in a poorly dubbed film. "Help me. Please."

"Saul!"

He lunged awake, pulled out the Colt automatic he had brought along and ran into the screen of trees. Natalie was thirty feet in, playing her flashlight over a shiny, red Toyota four-wheel-drive vehicle built to look like a British Landrover.

"Am I dreaming?" she asked.

"If you are, we're having the same dream," he said. The car was so new that it seemed to belong on a showroom floor. Saul played his light on the ground; there was no road, but he could see where the vehicle had been driven in under the trees. He tried the doors and the rear hatch: all locked.

"Look," said Natalie, "there's something under the wiper blade." She pulled a scrap of paper loose and held it under her flashlight beam. "It's a note," she said. "'Dear Alan and Suzanne: No problems getting in. Packing two point five miles down the Little Margarita. Bring the beer. Love, Heather and Carl.'" She shone her flashlight through the rear window. There was a case of Coors beer on the cargo deck. "Great!" said Natalie. "Shall we hot-wire it and get out of here?"

"Do you know how to hot-wire a car?" asked Saul, sitting on his suitcase again.

"No, but it always looks so simple on TV."

"Everything is simple on TV," said Saul. "Before we go fooling around with the ignition system—which is probably electronic and probably beyond my crude ability to outsmart—let us think a moment. How are Alan and Suzanne supposed to retrieve the beer? The doors are locked."

"Second set of keys?" said Natalie.

"Perhaps," said Saul, "or perhaps a prearranged hiding place for the first set?"

They were in the second place Natalie looked—the tailpipe. The key ring was as new as the car and carried the name of the San Diego Toyota dealership. When they unlocked the door, the fresh upholstery and new-car smell brought tears to Natalie's eyes.

"I'm going to see if I can safely get it downhill," said Saul.

"Why?"

"I'm going to transfer the things we need—the C-4 and detonators, the EEG equipment."

"You think we'll need that again?"

"I need it for the biofeedback work," said Saul. He opened the door for her, but she stepped back. "Something wrong?" he said.

"No, pick me up when you come back up the hill."

"Did you forget something?" asked Saul.

Natalie squirmed. "Sort of. I forgot to go to the bathroom."

They encountered one roadblock. The Toyota rode smoothly even across open ground in four-wheel drive and within a mile and a half they found a crude set of ruts that became a forest road that led to a gravel county road. Sometime before dawn they realized that they had been paralleling a high wire fence for some time, and Natalie called out for Saul to stop while she looked at a sign set six feet up on the wire. "U.S. Government Property—No Trespassing—by Order of the Commandant, Camp Pendleton, USMC."

"We were more lost than we realized," said Saul.

"Amen," said Natalie. "Want another beer?"

"Not yet," said Saul.

They ran into the roadblock a mile onto the asphalt road just short of a small community of Fallbrook. As soon as they hit the paved road, Natalie had curled into the space between the seats and the rear deck, pulling a navy blanket over herself and trying to get comfortable on the transmission hump. "It shouldn't be for long," said Saul, arranging gear and the case of beer over her breathing space. "They're looking for a young black woman and an unidentified male accomplice in a dark van. I hope that a good old boy alone in his new Toyota will throw them off. What do you think?"

Natalie's snore answered him.

He woke her five minutes later when the police roadblock came into sight. A single highway patrol car sat astride the road, two sleepy-looking officers drinking coffee out of a metal Thermos as they stood near the rear of their vehicle. Saul pulled the Toyota into the narrow lane and stopped.

One officer stayed behind the police car while the other shifted his cup to his left hand and walked slowly over to the car. "Good morning."

Saul nodded. "Good morning, Officer. What's up?"

The patrolman leaned over to look in the window. He peered at the stack of gear in back. "You coming out the National Forest?"

"Yep," said Saul. The tendency of the guilty, he knew, was to babble, to offer too many explanations for everything. When Saul had worked briefly with the NYPD as a consultant on the Son of Sam killings, a police lieutenant who was an expert on interrogations had told him that he always caught on to the smart guilty ones because they were too quick with the fluent, plausible stories. Innocent people tended toward guilty incoherence, the lieutenant had said.

"Up there just one night?" asked the officer, moving back a bit to peer in the space where Natalie lay under a blanket, backpack, and stack of beer cans.

"Two," said Saul. He looked at the other policeman as he moved around behind his partner. "What's going on?"

"Camping?" asked the first officer. He took a sip of coffee.

"Yes," said Saul, "and trying out the new four-wheel drive."

"It's a beauty," said the state trooper. "Brand new?"

Saul nodded.

"Where'd you buy it?"

Saul gave the name of the dealership embossed on the key ring.

"Where do you live?" asked the officer.

Saul hesitated a second. The false passport and driver's license Jack Cohen had made up for him gave a New York address. "San Diego," said Saul. "Moved there two months ago."

"Whereabouts in San Diego?" The officer was all amiable chattiness, but Saul noticed that his right hand rested on the wooden grip of his pistol and that the leather safety strap had been unstrapped.

Saul had been in San Diego only once, six days earlier, when Jack Cohen had driven them through on the Interstate. His tension and travel fatigue had been so great that every sight and sound had made a profound impression on him that night. He could recall at least three exit signs. "Sherwood Estates," he said. "1990 Spruce Drive, just off Linda Vista Road."

"Oh yeah," said the officer. "My brother-in-law used to have his dentist's office on Linda Vista. You near the university?"

"Not too near," said Saul. "I take it you aren't going to tell me what's going on."

The patrolman looked in the back of the Toyota as if trying to decipher what was in the boxes there. "Some trouble up toward Lake Elsinore," he said. "Where'd you say you were camping?"

"I didn't say," said Saul, "but I was on the Little Margarita. And if I don't get home soon, my wife's going to miss church and I'm going to be in big trouble."

The officer nodded. "You didn't happen to see a blue or black van up that way, did you?"

"Nope."

"Didn't think so. Aren't any connecting roads between here and the Coot Lake area. How 'bout folks on foot? Black woman? In her twenties? Older guy, maybe a Palestinian?"

"A Palestinian?" said Saul. "No, I didn't see anybody but a young white couple named Heather and Carl. They're up there on their honeymoon. I tried to stay out of their way. Is there some sort of Mideast terrorist stuff going on?"

"Might be," said the trooper. "Looking for a black girl and a Palestinian, both of them carrying a real arsenal. I can't help but notice your accent, Mr. . . ."

"Grotzman," said Saul. "Sol Grotzman."

"Hungarian?"

"Polish," said Saul. "But I've been an American citizen since just after the war."

"Yessir. Do those numbers mean what I think they mean?"

Saul glanced down to where his arm rested on the window, sleeve rolled up. "It's a Nazi concentration camp tattoo," he said.

The patrolman nodded slowly. "Never saw one of those. Mr. Grotzman, I'm real sorry to delay you, but I've got just one more important question."

"Yes?"

The patrolman stepped back, set his hand back on his revolver, and looked at the back of the Toyota. "How much does one of these Jap jeeps set a fellow back, anyway?"

Saul laughed. "According to my wife, too much, Officer. Way too much," He nodded at both men and drove on.

They drove through San Diego, went east on I-8, to Yuma where they parked the Toyota on a side street, and had lunch at a McDonald's.

"Time to get a new car," said Saul as he sipped at his milkshake. He sometimes wondered what his kosher grandmother would say if she was watching him.

"So soon?" said Natalie. "Is this where we learn how to hot-wire?"

"You can if you wish," said Saul. "But I was thinking of an easier way." He nodded at a used car lot across the street. "We can spare some of the thirty-thousand dollars that is burning a hole in my suitcase."

"All right," said Natalie, "but let's get something with air-conditioning. We have a lot of desert to cross in the next day or two."

They left Yuma in a three-year-old Chevrolet station wagon with air-conditioning, power steering, power brakes, and power windows. Saul disconcerted the salesman twice—first when he inquired whether it had power ashtrays and second when he paid the asking price with no haggling. It was good they did not spend time bargaining. When they returned to the side street where they had left the Toyota, a group of brown-skinned preteens were in the process of breaking the side window with a rock. They ran away laughing and giving the finger to Saul and Natalie.

"That would have been cute," said Saul. "I wonder what they would have done with the plastic explosive and the M-16."

Natalie gave him a look. "You didn't tell me you brought the M-16 along."

Saul adjusted his glasses and looked around. "We need a little more lead time than this neighborhood will give us. Follow me."

They drove to the nearest shopping mall where Saul transferred all of the gear and left the keys in the car with the windows rolled down. "I don't want it vandalized," he explained, "just stolen."

After the first day they traveled at night, and Natalie, who had always wanted to tour the southwestern United States, retained the images only of bright star fields above the sameness of Interstate highways, incredible desert sunrises bleeding pinks and oranges and indigos into a gray world, and the thump and throb of laboring air conditioners in the small motel rooms that smelled of old cigar smoke and disinfectant.

Saul retreated farther into himself, allowing Natalie to do most of the driving, stopping earlier each morning so that he could spend time with his dossiers and machines. By the time they reached East Texas, Saul spent the night in the back of the station wagon, sitting cross-legged in front of the computer monitor and EEG machine connected to the battery pack he had purchased at a Radio Shack in Fort Worth. Natalie could not even play the car radio for fear of disturbing him.

"You see, the theta rhythm is the key," he would say during the few times he spoke to her about it. "It's the perfect signal, an infallible indicator. I cannot generate it myself, but I can play it back through the biofeedback loop so I *know* the indications. By training myself to react to that initial alpha peak, I can condition my own triggering mechanism for the posthypnotic suggestions."

"Is that a way to counteract their . . . powers?" asked Natalie.

Saul adjusted his glasses and frowned. "No, not really. I doubt if there is any way to really counteract such an ability unless one had it himself. It would be interesting to test a variety of individuals in a controlled . . ."

"Then what *good* is it?" cried Natalie, exasperated.

"It offers a chance . . . a *chance*," said Saul, "to create a sort of distant early warning system in the cerebral cortex. With the proper conditioning and biofeedback work, I think that I can use the theta rhythm phenomenon to trigger the posthypnotic suggestions to recall the data I've been memorizing."

"Data?" said Natalie, "you mean all those hours at Yad Vashem and the Ghetto Fighters' House . . ."

"Lohame HaGeta'ot," said Saul. "Yes. Reading the dossiers Wiesenthal sent you, memorizing the photographs and biographies and tapes while doing auto-recall in a light, self-induced trance . . ."

"But what good will sharing all those other people's pain do if it is no defense against these mind vampires?" asked Natalie.

"Imagine a carousel slide projector," said Saul. "The Oberst and the others have the ability to advance that neurological carousel at will and insert their own slides, intrude their own organizing will and superego on that bundle of memories, fears, and predilections that we call a personality. I am merely trying to insert more slides in the tray."

"But you don't know if it will work?"

"No."

"And you don't think it would work with me?"

Saul removed his glasses and rubbed the bridge of his nose. "*Something* comparable might be possible with you, Natalie, but it would have to be uniquely suited to your own background, traumatic experiences, and empathic pathways. *I* could not create the hypnotic induction sessions to produce the necessary . . . ah . . . slides."

"But if this stuff *does* work for you, it wouldn't work on any of the mind vampires except your Oberst."

"I would think not. Only he would share the common background necessary to flesh out the personae that I am creating . . . endeavoring to create . . . in these empathy sessions."

"And it can't really stop him? Only confuse him for a few seconds if all these months of work and EEG thingamagigs worked at all?"

"Correct."

Natalie shook her head and stared at the twin cones of headlights illuminating the endless strip of asphalt ahead of them. "Then how can it be worth all of your time, Saul?"

Saul opened the dossier he had been studying of a young girl, white face, frightened eyes, dark coat and kerchief. The black pants and high boots of a Waffen SS man were just visible in the upper left of the photograph. The girl was turning toward the camera quickly enough so that her face was little more than a blur. In her right arm she carried a small valise, but her left arm clutched a worn, homemade doll to her chest. Half a page of typed German on Simon Wiesenthal's thin stationery was all that accompanied the photograph.

"Even if it all fails, it was worth the time," Saul Laski said softly. "The powerful have received their share of the world's attention even when their power has been shown as sheer evil. The victims remain the faceless masses. Numbers. Mass graves. These monsters have fertilized our century with the mass graves of their victims and it is time that the powerless had names and faces—and *voices*." Saul turned off the flashlight and sat back. "I am sorry," he said, "my obsession may well be clouding my reasoning."

"I'm beginning to understand obsessions," said Natalie.

Saul looked at her in the soft light from the instrument panel. "And you're still willing to act on yours?"

Natalie gave a nervous laugh. "I can't think of any other way, can you? But every mile closer we get, the more frightened I become."

"We don't have to get any closer," said Saul. "We can go to the airport in Shreveport and fly to Israel or South America."

"No, we can't," said Natalie.

After a minute Saul said, "No, you are right."

They changed places and Saul drove for several hours. Natalie dozed. She dreamed of Rob Gentry's eyes and his look of shock and disbelief when the blade slashed across his throat. She dreamed that her father called her in St. Louis and told her that it was all a mistake, that everyone was all right, that even her mother was home and safe and well, but when she arrived home the house was dark and the rooms were filled with sticky spiderwebs and the sink was filled with a dark congealing liquid. Natalie, suddenly a little girl again, ran crying to her parents' room. But her father was not there, and her mother, when her mother rose from the web-shrouded sheets, was not her mother at all. She was a moldering corpse with a face little more than a flesh-crusted skull carrying Melanie Fuller's eyes. And the corpse was laughing.

Natalie jerked awake, her heart pounding. They were on the Interstate. It seemed light outside. "Is it dawn yet?" she asked.

"No," said Saul and his voice was very tired. "Not yet."

Into the Old South and the cities were constellations of suburbs along the Interstate bypasses: Jackson, Meridian, Birmingham, Atlanta. They left the Interstate system at Augusta and took Highway 78 across the south third of South Carolina. Even at night the landscape became recognizable to Natalie—St. George where she had gone to summer camp when she was nine, that endless, lonely summer after her mother had died, Dorchester where her father's sister had lived before she died of cancer in 1976, Summerville where she used to drive out on Sunday afternoons to take photographs of some of the old estates—Charleston.

Charleston.

They came into the city on the fourth night of their travels, shortly before four A.M., in that breathless hour of the night when the spirit does indeed seem weakest. For Natalie, the familiar scenes of her childhood appeared tilted and distorted, the poor, neat neighborhoods of St. Andrews somehow as insubstantial as poorly projected images on a dull screen. Her home was dark. There was no For Sale sign in front, no strange car in the drive. Natalie did not have the foggiest notion of who had handled the disposition of property and possessions after her sudden disappearance. She looked at the strange-familiar house with its small porch where she and Saul and Rob had sat and discussed the silly myth of mind vampires over lemonade five months earlier, and she did not have the slightest urge to go in. She wondered who had inherited her father's

photographs—the Minor White and Cunningham and Milito and her father's own modest prints—and she was amazed to feel sudden tears scald
her eyes. She drove down the street without slowing.

"We don't have to go into the Old Section tonight," said Saul.

"Yes, we do," said Natalie and headed east, across the bridge, into the
old city.

There was a single light on in Melanie Fuller's house. In what had been
her room, second floor front. It was not an electric light, nor even the soft
glow of candle, but a sick pulse of weak green like the corrupt phosphores-
cence of rotting wood deep in swamp darkness.

Natalie gripped the steering wheel tightly to stop her shivering.

"The fence in front has been replaced with that high wall and double
gate," said Saul. "The place is a fortress."

Natalie watched the pale green glow ebb and flow between shutters and
shades.

"We don't know it's her," said Saul. "Jack's information was circum-
stantial and several weeks old."

"It's her," said Natalie.

"Let's go," said Saul. "We're tired. We'll find a place to sleep today and
get some place tomorrow where we can leave our stuff set up without a
chance of it being disturbed."

Natalie put the station wagon in gear and moved slowly away down the
dark street.

They found a cheap motel on the north end of town and slept like the dead
for seven hours. Natalie woke at noon, feeling disoriented and vulnerable,
fleeing from complex and urgent dreams in which hands grasped at her
through broken windowpanes.

Both of them tired and irritable, barely speaking, they bought fast food
chicken and ate in a North Charleston park near the river. The day was
hot, in the eighties, and the quality of sunlight was as unrelenting as overhead lights in an operating room.

"I suppose you shouldn't go out in the daylight," said Saul. "Someone
might recognize you."

Natalie shrugged. "They're the vampires and we end up the night
dwellers," she said. "Doesn't seem fair."

Saul squinted out against the sun glare across the water. "I've been
thinking a lot about that deputy and the pilot."

"What about them?"

"If I hadn't made the deputy put in that call to Haines, the pilot would
still be alive," said Saul.

Natalie sipped her coffee. "So would Haines."

"Yes, but I realized at the time that if I had had to sacrifice *both* the pilot *and* the deputy, I would have done it. Just to get at one man."

"He killed your family," said Natalie. "Tried to kill you."

Saul shook his head. "But these were noncombatants," he said. "Don't you see where this leads? For twenty-five years I've despised the Palestinian terrorists in their checkered *kefiyas*, striking out blindly at innocents because they are too weak to stand up and fight openly. Now we have adopted the same tactics because we are too weak to face these monsters."

"Nonsense," said Natalie. She watched a family of five picnicking near the water. The mother was warning the preschooler to stay away from the riverbank. "You're not dynamiting air craft or machine-gunning buses," said Natalie. "We didn't kill that pilot, Haines did."

"We caused him to die," said Saul. "Think a minute, Natalie. Assume that all of them—Barent, Harod, the Fuller woman, the Oberst—all of them—were aboard the same commercial airliner with a hundred uninvolved civilians. Would you be tempted to end it with a single bomb?"

"No," said Natalie.

"Think," said Saul. "These monsters have been responsible for hundreds—thousands—of deaths. The death of another hundred innocents brings it all to a close. Forever. Would it not be worth it?"

"No," Natalie said firmly. "It doesn't work like that."

Saul nodded. "You're right, it does not work like that. In thinking that way, we would become one of them. But in expending the life of the pilot, we have started down that road."

Natalie stood up angrily. "What are you trying to do, Saul? We talked about this in Tel Aviv, Jerusalem, and Caesarea. We knew the risks. Look, my *father* was an innocent bystander. So was Rob—and Aaron and Deborah and the twins—and Jack—and . . ." She stopped, folded her arms, and looked out at the water. "What are you trying to do?"

Saul stood up. "I've decided that you're not going to go ahead with the next part."

Natalie whirled and stared at him. "You're crazy! It's our only chance at the rest of them!"

"Nonsense," said Saul. "We simply haven't come up with a better way yet. We will. We are in too much of a rush."

"Too much of a rush!" shouted Natalie. The family near the water turned to look at her. She lowered her voice but spoke in an urgent whisper. "Too much of a rush? We have the FBI and half the country's cops looking for us. We know one time—*one time*—when all of these sons of bitches are going to be together. Every day they get stronger and more cautious and we get weaker and more frightened. There's just the two of us now and I'm scared so shitless that in another week I won't be able to function at all . . . and you say we're in too much of a goddamn rush!" She was shouting again by the time she finished.

"All right," he said, "but I've decided that it does not have to be you."

"What are you talking about? Of course it has to be me. We decided that on David's farm."

"We were wrong," said Saul.

"She'll *remember* me!"

"So? We will convince her that a second emissary has been sent."

"You, huh?"

"It makes sense," said Saul.

"No it doesn't," snapped Natalie. "What about all those stacks of facts and figures, dates and deaths and places I've been memorizing since Valentine's Day?"

"They're not that important," said Saul. "If she is as insane as we suspect, logic will have little impact. If she is coldly rational, our facts are too few, our story too flimsy."

"Oh, *great*, goddamn it," said Natalie. "I've been screwing my courage to the sticking point for five months to be able to do this, and now you tell me it's not necessary and wouldn't work anyway."

"I'm not saying that," soothed Saul. "I'm simply saying that we should take some time to look at alternatives and that I don't believe you are the right person to do it in any case."

Natalie sighed. "All right. What do you say we don't talk about it until tomorrow? We're tired from the trip. I need a good night's sleep."

"Agreed," said Saul. He took her arm and squeezed it lightly as they walked back to the car.

They decided to pay two weeks' rent on the cabin with adjoining rooms at the motel. Saul carried his biofeedback equipment in and worked until nine when Natalie made him stop for some dinner she had made.

"Is it working?" she asked.

Saul shook his head. "Biofeedback is not always successful in the easiest of cases. This is not easy. I am convinced that the things I have committed to memory are ready to be recalled by posthypnotic suggestion, but I have not been able to set up the trigger mechanism. The theta rhythm is flatly impossible to replicate and I've not been able to stimulate the alpha peak."

"So all of your work's been for nothing," said Natalie.

"So far, yes," agreed Saul.

"Are you going to get some sleep?" she asked.

"Later," said Saul. "I'm going to work on this for a few more hours."

"All right," said Natalie. "I'll make us some coffee before I go back to my room."

"Fine."

Natalie went to the small kitchen area, boiled water on a hot plate, poured an extra half spoonful in each cup of coffee to make it extra-strong, and carefully mixed in the precise amount of phenthiazine Saul had shown her in California in case she had had to sedate Tony Harod.

Saul grimaced a bit when he first tasted it.

"How is it?" asked Natalie, sipping at her own cup.

"Nice and strong," said Saul. "Just the way I like it. You'd best go to bed. I may be up late with this."

"All right," said Natalie. She gave him a kiss on the cheek and went through the door to her adjoining room.

Thirty minutes later she came back in quietly, dressed in a long skirt, dark blouse, and light sweater. Saul was asleep in the green vinyl chair, the computer and EEG still on and a stack of dossiers on his lap. Natalie switched off the equipment, set the folders on the table with her brief note on top, removed Saul's glasses and covered him with a light blanket. She gently touched his shoulder for a few seconds before she left.

Natalie made sure nothing of value was in the station wagon. The C-4 had been stored in the closet of her room, the detonators in Saul's. She remembered the motel key and carried it into her room. She carried neither purse nor passport, nothing that might reveal any additional information.

Natalie drove carefully to the Old Section, obeying traffic lights and speed limits. She parked the station wagon near Henry's Restaurant, right where she had told Saul in the note that it would be, and walked the few blocks to Melanie Fuller's home. The night was dark and humid, the heavy foliage seeming to come together overhead to shut off starlight and soak up oxygen.

When she arrived at the Fuller house, Natalie did not hesitate. The tall gate was locked, but it had an ornamental knocker. Natalie banged metal against metal and waited in the darkness.

No lights were on in either building except for the green glow from Melanie Fuller's room. No lights came on, but after a minute two men approached in the darkness. The taller of the two shuffled forward, a hairless mountain of flesh with the small eyes, unfocused gaze, and microcephalic skull of the terminally retarded. "What do you want?" he mumbled, each word enunciated as if it had been formed by a faulty speech synthesizer.

"I want to talk to Melanie," Natalie said loudly. "Tell her that Nina is here."

Neither man moved a muscle for over a minute. Insects made noises in the undergrowth and a night bird flapped its way out of a tall palmetto near the second-story bay window of the old house. Somewhere several blocks away a siren screamed a single, sustained note of pain and was cut off. Natalie concentrated on standing upright on legs gone weak with fear.

Finally the huge man spoke. "Come." He opened the gate with a turn of a key and a jerk, pulled Natalie inside the courtyard, and locked the gate behind her.

Someone opened the front door from the inside. Natalie saw only darkness there. Walking quickly between the two men, her right arm still in the giant's grip, she entered the house.

FIFTY-FOUR

Melanie

She said she was from Nina.

For a minute I was so frightened that I escaped into myself, tried to crawl from my bed, my right arm and leg flailing, dragging the dead side of my body along like so much wasted meat. Tubes pulled out of my arms, stands toppled. For a second I lost control of all of them—Howard, Nancy, Culley, the doctor and nurses, the Negro boy still standing in the darkness of the side yard with the butcher knife—and then I relaxed, let my body slide into curled stillness, and I was in control again.

My first thought was to let Culley, Howard, and the colored boy finish her in the courtyard. They could use water from the fountain to wash away any stains on the courtyard bricks. Howard would take her around to the garage, wrap the remains in a shower curtain to keep the interior of Dr. Hartman's Cadillac clean, and Culley would be down the alley and off to the dump in five minutes.

But I did not know enough. Not yet. If she was from Nina, I had to learn more. If she was not from Nina, I wanted to find out who had sent her before we did anything.

Culley and Howard led her into the house. Dr. Hartman, Nurse Old-smith, Nancy, and Miss Sewell gathered around while Marvin stood guard outside. Justin kept me company upstairs.

The Negro girl who said she was from Nina looked around my parlor at my family. "It's dark," she said in a strange, small voice.

I rarely use the lights anymore. I know the house so well that I could make my way through it blindfolded and the family members have no real use for electric lights except when they are tending me, and up here the soft, pleasant glow from the medical monitors is usually adequate.

If this colored girl was speaking for Nina, I found it odd that Nina was not used to the dark yet. Her coffin certainly must be dark enough. If the girl was lying, she would be familiar with the dark soon enough.

Dr. Hartman spoke for me. "What do you want, girl?"

The Negress licked her lips. Culley had helped her into her seat on the divan. My family members were all standing. Faint lines of light fell across a white face or arm here or there, but the rest of us must have looked like dark masses to her as she stared up at us. "I've come to talk to you, Melanie," said the girl. Her voice held a soft quaver unlike anything I had ever heard in Nina's speech.

"There's no one here by that name," said Dr. Hartman in the darkness.

The Negro girl laughed. Had there been a hint of Nina's husky laugh in that sound? The thought of it chilled me. "I know you're here," she said. "Just like I knew where to find you in Philadelphia."

How had she found me? I had Culley's huge hands rise to the top of the divan behind the girl.

"We don't know what you're talking about, miss," said Howard.

The girl shook her head. *Why would Nina Use a Negro?* I wondered. "Melanie," she said, "I know you're here. I know you're not feeling well. I've come to warn you."

To warn me of what? The whispers had warned me in Grumblethorpe, but she had not been part of the whispers. She had come later, when things went bad. Wait, she had not found me—I found her! Vincent had fetched her and brought her back to me.

And she had killed Vincent.

If this girl were truly an emissary from Nina, it might still be best to kill her. That way Nina would understand that I was not to be trifled with, that I would not allow her to eliminate my cat's-paws without some retribution.

Marvin still waited in the darkness outside with a long knife Miss Sewell had left lying on the butcher block. It would be better outside. I would not have to worry about stains on the carpet and hardwood floors.

"Young lady," I had Dr. Hartman say, "I'm afraid that none of us know what you are talking about. There's no one here named Melanie. Culley will see you outside."

"Wait!" cried the woman as Culley lifted her by the arm. He turned her toward the door. "Wait a minute!" she said in a voice not even remotely like Nina's unhurried drawl.

"Good-bye," the five of us said in unison.

The colored boy waited just beyond the fountain. It had been weeks since I had Fed.

The girl twisted in Culley's grasp just as she reached the door. "Willi isn't dead!" she cried.

I had Culley stop. None of us moved. After a moment I had Dr. Hartman say, "What was that?"

The Negro girl looked at us with an insolent defiance. "Willi is not dead," she said calmly.

"Explain yourself," said Howard.

The girl shook her head. "Melanie, I will speak to *you*. Only to you. If you kill this messenger, then I will not try to contact you again. The people who tried to kill Willi and who are planning to kill you can have their way." She turned and stared into the corner, disinterested, paying no attention to Culley's huge hand where it was clasped tightly on her arm. The girl looked like a machine that someone had switched off.

Upstairs, alone except for the silent company of little Justin, I writhed in indecision. My head hurt. It was all like a bad dream. I wanted this woman just to go away and leave me alone. Nina was dead. Willi was dead.

Culley brought her back across the room and sat her on the divan.

All of us watched her.

I considered Using the girl. Sometimes—frequently—during the transition to another's mind, during the second of dominance, there is a shared flow of surface thoughts accompanying the sensory impressions. If Nina was Using this one, I might not be able to break the conditioning, but I might be able to sense Nina herself. If it was not Nina, I might catch a glimpse of her true motivations.

Howard said, "Melanie will be right down," and in that second of reaction—whether fright or satisfaction I do not know—I slipped into the girl's mind.

There was no opposition. I had been braced to try to wrest control from Nina, and the lack of opposing force caused me to mentally stumble forward like a person in the dark leaning his weight on a chair or dresser that was not there. Contact was brief. I caught the fear-scent of panic, the sense of *not again* common to people who had been Used before but not conditioned in the interval, and a scurry of thoughts like a stampede of small animals in the dark. But no coherent thoughts. There was a fragment of image—an old stone bridge of sun-warmed stone crossing a strange sea of sand dunes and shadows. It meant nothing to me. I could not associate it with any of Nina's memories, although there were too many years after the war where I had not been with her for me to be sure.

I withdrew.

The girl convulsed, sat upright, swept her stare around the dark room. Nina regaining control or an impostor flailing for composure?

"Do *not* do that again, Melanie," said the Negress and in her imperial tone I heard the first convincing echo of Nina Drayton.

Justin entered the room carrying a candle. The flame illuminated his six-year-old face from below and by a trick of light caused his eyes to look ancient. And mad.

The Negro girl watched him, watched me, as a skittish horse would watch the approach of a snake.

I set the candle on the Georgian tea table and looked at the Negro girl. "Hello, Nina," I said.

The girl blinked once, slowly. "Hello, Melanie. Aren't you going to say hello in person?"

"I am somewhat indisposed at the moment," I said. "Perhaps I will come down when you choose to come in person."

The black girl showed a hint of a smile. "That would be difficult for me to do."

The world spun before my eyes and for several seconds it was all I could do to keep control of my people. *What if Nina had not died?* What if she had been injured but not mortally?

I saw the hole in her forehead. Her blue eyes rolling up in her head.

The cartridges were old. What if the bullet had struck the skull, even entered it, but done no more damage to her brain than my cerebral-vascular-incident had done to me?

The news had announced that she had died. I had heard and read her name among the victims.

As was my name.

Next to my bed, one of the medical monitors began beeping a shrill alarm. I forced my breathing and heart rate to calm. The beeping ceased.

From my other viewpoints I could see that Justin's expression had not changed in the few seconds that had passed. His six-year-old's face was still distorted by the leaping candle flame into the mask of a young demon. His small saddle shoes pointed straight up on the cushion of the uphol-stered leather chair that had always been Father's favorite.

"Tell me about Willi," I said through Justin.

"He is alive," said the girl.

"Impossible. His plane was destroyed with all aboard."

"All except Willi and his two henchmen," said the Negress. "They got off before it departed."

"Then why did you turn on *me* if you knew that you had not succeeded with Willi?" I snapped.

The girl hesitated a second. "I did not destroy the plane," she said.

Upstairs, my heart pounded and an oscilloscope showed green peaks that caused the green light in the room to pulse along with my heartbeat. "Who did?" I asked.

"The others," she said flatly.

"What others?"

The girl took a deep breath. "There is a group of others with our power. A secret group of . . ."

"Our power?" I interrupted. "Do you mean the Ability?"

"Yes," she said.

"Nonsense. We have never encountered anyone with more than a shade of our Ability." I had Culley raise his hands in the darkness. Her neck rose thin and straight from her dark sweater. It would snap like a dry twig.

"These others have it," the colored girl said in a strong voice. "They tried to kill Willi. They tried to kill *you.* Didn't you wonder who it was in Germantown? The shooting? The helicopter that crashed into the river?"

How could Nina know about that? How could anyone know?

"You could be one of *them,*" I said craftily.

The girl nodded calmly. "Yes, but if I were, would I come to you to warn you? I tried to warn you in Germantown, but you would not listen."

I tried to remember. Had the Negro girl warned me of anything? The whispers had been so loud then; it had been hard to concentrate. "You and the sheriff came to kill me," I said.

"No." The girl's head moved slowly, a rusty metal marionette. Nina's

Barret Kramer had moved like that. "The sheriff was sent by Willi. He also came to warn you."

"Who are these others?" I asked.

"Famous people," she said, "Powerful people. People with names such as Barent, Kepler, Sutter, and Harod."

"Those names mean nothing to me," I said. Suddenly I was shouting in Justin's shrill, six-year-old voice. "You're lying! You're not Nina! You're dead! How would you know about these people?"

The girl hesitated as if debating whether to speak. "I knew some of them in New York," she said at last. "They talked me into doing . . . what I did."

There was a silence so still and so prolonged that through all eight of my sources I could hear doves roosting on the ledge outside the bay window on the second floor. I had the boy outside shift the knife from his cramped right hand to his left. Miss Sewell had backed softly into the kitchen and returned now to stand in the shadows of the doorway with the meat cleaver held behind her beige skirt. Culley stirred and in his hungry impatience I caught an echo of Vincent's sharp-edged eagerness.

"They urged you to kill me," I said, "and promised to eliminate Willi while you dealt with me."

"Yes," she said.

"But they failed and so did you."

"Yes."

"Why are you telling me this, Nina?" I said. "It only makes me hate you more."

"They betrayed me," she said. "They left me alone when you came for me. I want you to finish *them* before they return for you."

I had Justin lean forward. "Talk to me, Nina," I whispered. "Tell me about old times."

She shook her head. "There is no time for this, Melanie."

I smiled, feeling the saliva moistening Justin's baby teeth. "Where did we meet, Nina? Whose ball were we at when we first compared dance cards?"

The Negro girl trembled slightly and raised a dark hand to her forehead. "Melanie, my memory . . . there are gaps . . . my injury."

"It did not seem to bother you a moment ago," I snapped. "Who went with us to Daniel Island on our picnics, Nina, dear? You do remember him, do you not? Who were our beaus that long-ago summer?"

The girl swayed, her hand still at her temple. "Melanie, please, I remember and then I forget . . . the pain . . ."

Miss Sewell approached the girl from behind. Her thick-soled nurse's shoes made no sound on the rug.

"Who was the first one claimed in our Game that summer at Bad Ischl?" I asked just to allow Miss Sewell time to take the last two silent steps. I knew this colored impostor could not answer. We would see if she could imitate Nina when her body remained sitting on the divan while her head rolled across the floor. Perhaps Justin would like something new to play with.

The Negro girl said, "The first one was that dancer from Berlin— Meier I think her name was—I do not remember all the details, but we spotted her from the Cafe Zauner as always."

Everything stopped.

"What?" I said.

"The next day . . . no, it was two days later, a Wednesday . . . there was that ridiculous little iceman. We left his body in the ice house . . . hanging from that iron hook . . . Melanie, it *hurts*. I remember and then I don't!" The girl began to cry.

Justin scrunched to the edge of the cushion, dropped to the floor, and went around the tea table to pat her on the shoulder. "Nina," I said, "I am sorry. I am so sorry."

Miss Sewell made tea and served it in my best Wedgwood china. Culley brought in more candles. Dr. Hartman and Nurse Oldsmith came upstairs to check on me while Howard, Nancy, and the others found seats in the parlor. The little black boy stayed in the bushes outside.

"Where is Willi?" I asked through Justin. "How is he?"

"He is well," said Nina, "but I am not sure where because he must remain in hiding."

"From those same people you mentioned?" I asked.

"Yes."

"Why do they wish us harm, Nina, dear?"

"They fear us, Melanie."

"Why would they fear us? We've done them no harm."

"They fear our . . . our Ability. And they were frightened that they would be exposed because of Willi's . . . excesses."

Little Justin nodded. "Did Willi also know about the others?"

"I think so," said Nina. "At first he wanted to join their . . . their club. Now he simply wants to survive."

"Their club?" I said.

"They have a secret organization," said Nina. "A place where they meet each year to hunt preselected victims . . ."

"I see why Willi would want to join them," I said. "Can we trust him now?"

The girl paused. "I think so," said Nina. "But if nothing else, the three of us need to band together for protection until this threat has passed."

"Tell me more about these people," I said.

"I will," said Nina, "but later. Another time. I . . . tire easily . . ."

Justin put on his most angelic smile. "Nina, darling, tell me where you are right now. Let me come to you, help you."

The girl smiled and said nothing.

"Very well," I said. "Will I see Willi?"

"Perhaps," said Nina, "but if not we will have to work in concert with him until the appointed time."

"The appointed time?"

"A month from now. On the island." The girl brushed her hand across her forehead again and from her trembling I could see the exhaustion there. It must have taken all of Nina's energy just to make the girl move and talk. I had a sudden image of Nina's corpse moldering in the darkness of the grave and Justin shivered.

"Tell me," I said.

"Later," said Nina. "We will meet again and speak of what has to be done . . . how you can help. Now I must go."

"Very well," I said and my child's voice could not hide the childish disappointment I felt.

Nina—the Negress—stood, walked slowly to Justin's chair, and kissed him—kissed me—gently on the cheek. How many times had Nina given me just this Judas kiss before one of her betrayals? I thought of our last Reunion.

"Good-bye, Melanie," she whispered.

"Good-bye for now, Nina, dear," I replied.

She walked to the door, glancing to either side as if Culley or Miss Sewell would stop her at any moment. We all sat smiling in the candlelight, our teacups on knees and laps.

"Nina," I said as she reached the door.

She turned slowly and I was reminded of Anne Bishop's cat when Vincent finally cornered it in the upstairs bedroom. "Yes, dear?"

"Why did you send this nigger girl tonight, dear?"

The girl smiled enigmatically. "Why, Melanie, didn't you ever send a colored servant on an errand?"

I nodded. The girl left.

Outside, the colored boy with the butcher knife drew deeper into the bushes and watched her pass. Culley had to come out to unlock the gate for her.

She turned left and walked slowly up the dark street.

I had the colored boy slide along in the shadows behind her. A minute later Culley opened the gate and followed.

FIFTY-FIVE

Charleston
Tuesday, May 5, 1981

N atalie forced herself to walk the first block. As she turned the corner and stepped out of sight of the Fuller house, she knew that she faced the choice of letting her knees buckle and collapsing to the sidewalk or running.

Natalie ran. She covered the first block in a wind sprint, paused at the corner to look back, and caught a glimpse of a dark form crossing a yard as headlights from a turning car swept across him. The young man looked vaguely familiar, but from that distance she could not see details of the face or features. But she could see the knife in his hand. Another, larger figure, came into sight around the corner. Natalie ran south for a block and turned east again, panting now, fire burning at her ribs as she tired, but paying no attention to the pain.

There were brighter streetlights on the block where she had left the station wagon, but the shops and restaurants were closed, the sidewalks empty. Natalie skidded to a stop, pulled open the door on the driver's side, and threw herself into the front seat. For a second a deeper, more mindless panic seized her as she found no keys in the ignition and realized that she had no purse or pockets. Almost at once she remembered that she had left them under the seat where Saul could find them when he came to get the car. As she bent over to reach for them, the door on the passenger's side opened and a man stepped into the car.

Natalie forced herself not to scream as she straightened up and raised her fists in a reflexive response.

"It's me," said Saul. He straightened his glasses. "Are you all right?"

"Oh, Jesus," breathed Natalie. She felt around, found the keys, and started the car with a roar.

A shadow separated itself from the shrubbery and ran into the street fifty feet away. "Hang on!" cried Natalie. She slammed the car into gear and pulled into the street, accelerating to fifty miles per hour by the time they reached the end of the block. The headlights illuminated the young man for two seconds before he leaped to one side.

"My God," said Natalie, "did you see who that was?"

"Marvin Gayle," said Saul and braced himself against the dash, "turn right up here."

"What could he be doing here?" cried Natalie.

"I don't know," said Saul. "You'd better slow down. No one is following us."

Natalie slowed to fifty miles per hour and got on the highway heading north. She found that she was alternating laughter and tears. She shook her head, laughed again, and tried to modulate her voice. "My God, it worked, Saul. It worked. And I was never even in a school play. It worked. I don't believe it!" She decided to give in to the laughter and found that tears came instead. Saul squeezed her shoulder and she looked at him for the first time. For a single, terrible second then she knew that Melanie Fuller had outsmarted her, that somehow the old monster had discovered them and known about their plans and managed to take over Saul . . .

Natalie cringed from his touch.

Saul looked puzzled for a second and then shook his head. "No, it's all right, Natalie. I awoke and found your note and took a cab to within a block of Henry's . . ."

"The phenothiazine," whispered Natalie, barely able to watch the traffic and Saul at the same time.

"I didn't drink all of the coffee," said Saul. "Too bitter. Besides, you mixed it in the proportions for Anthony Harod. He is a smaller man."

Natalie watched him. Part of her mind wondered if she was going mad.

Saul adjusted his glasses. "All right," he said. "We had decided that these . . . things . . . had no access to memories. I was supposed to quiz you, but we can start with me. Shall I describe David's farm at Caesarea? The restaurants we patronized in Jerusalem? Jack Cohen's directions from Tijuana?"

"No," said Natalie. "It's all right."

"Are *you* all right?"

Natalie brushed away the tears with her wrist and laughed. "Oh, Christ, Saul, it was *awful*. The place was all dark and this retarded giant and this other zombie brought me into the living room or parlor or whatever the hell you call it and there were half a dozen of them standing around in the *dark*. Jesus, they were like corpses that had been propped up there—this one woman had buttoned her white dress all wrong and her mouth hung open the entire time—and I just couldn't *think*, and every second I was sure I wouldn't be able to *talk* anymore, my voice just wouldn't work right, and when this little . . . little . . . *thing* came in with a candle it was worse than Grumblethorpe, worse than I'd imagined, and his eyes looked—they were her eyes, Saul, mad, staring—oh, God, I never believed in demons or Satan or hell, but this little *thing* was straight out of Dante or some Hieronymous Bosch *nightmare*, and she kept asking me questions through him and I couldn't answer any of them and I knew this nurse, this creature dressed like a nurse who was *behind* me was going to do something, but then Melanie, actually the little boy-demon, but it was *really* Melanie, mentioned Bad Ischl and my mind just clicked, Saul, it just *clicked*, all those hours reading and memorizing those files Wiesenthal had put together and I remembered the dancer, the one from Berlin, Berta Meier, and then it was easy, but I was terrified that she was going to ask about their early years again, but she didn't, Saul, I think we *have* her, I think she's hooked, but I was so *scared* . . ." Natalie stopped, gasping slightly.

"Pull over here," Saul said, pointing to an empty parking lot near a Kentucky Fried Chicken outlet.

Natalie stopped the car and set it in park, fighting to regulate her breathing. Saul leaned over, took her face in his hands, and kissed her first on her left cheek and then on her right cheek. "You are the most courageous person I have ever known, my dear. If I had had a daughter, I would have been proud if she was like you."

Natalie brushed away the last of her tears. "Saul, we have to hurry back to the motel, hook up the EEG thing like we planned. You have to ask me questions. She *touched* me . . . I felt it . . . it was worse than the time Harod . . . it was *cold*, Saul, as cold and slimy as . . . I don't know . . . as something from the grave."

Saul nodded. "She thinks *you* are someone from the grave. We can only hope that she fears another contest with Nina enough that she won't try to take you away from her supposed nemesis. If she was going to use her power on you, it seems logical that she would have done it while you were in contact."

"Ability," said Natalie, "she called it 'our Ability,' and I could hear the capital A." She looked around with fright in her eyes. "We need to get back, Saul, and do the twenty-four-hour quarantine just as we planned. You've got to ask me questions, make sure I . . . *remember* things."

Saul laughed softly. "Natalie, we'll hook up the EEG telemetry pack while you sleep, and you *will* sleep, but we have no need for the questions and answers. Your little monologue here in the car convinces me that you are who you have always been . . . and that is a very brave and beautiful young lady. Scoot over here, I'm going to come around and drive."

Natalie put her head back against the headrest as Saul drove the last few miles to the motel. She was thinking of her father—remembering quiet times in the darkroom or at dinner with him—remembering the time she had sliced her knee on a shard of rusted metal behind Tom Piper's house—she must have been five or six, her mother was still alive—and running home, her father coming to her across the yard, leaving the lawn mower running where it was and coming to her, staring in shock at her leg and white ankle socks stained red with blood, but she had not cried, and he had lifted her and carried her through the screen door, all the while calling her "my brave little girl, my brave little girl."

And she was. Natalie closed her eyes. She was.

"It's the beginning," Saul was saying. "It's definitely the beginning. And it's the beginning of the end for them."

Her eyes still closed, her heart rate slowing at last, Natalie nodded and thought of her father.

FIFTY-SIX

Melanie

In the daylight it was harder to believe that Nina had contacted me. My first response was one of anxiety and a sense of vulnerability at being discovered. But this soon faded, to be replaced by a sense of resolve and renewed energy. Whoever this girl represented, she had stimulated me to think about my future once again.

That Wednesday, I believe it was the fifth of May, the Negress did not return so I took some action of my own. Dr. Hartman went from hospital to hospital, ostensibly considering a new residency but actually checking to see if there were any long-term patients there who might fit Nina's medical description. Remembering my own stay at the Philadelphia hospital, Dr. Hartman did not inquire of medical personnel or hospital administrators but gained access to the hospital computers and reviewed medication lists, surgical histories, and material requirements under the guise of inspecting the hospital's facilities. The hunt continued until Friday and still there was no sign of the Negro girl or word from Nina. By the weekend, Dr. Hartman had inspected all hospitals, nursing homes, and medical centers with provisions for such long-term care. He also had checked with the county morgue—which insisted that Ms. Drayton's body had been claimed and cremated by executors of her estate—but that only confirmed the possibility that she might be alive . . . or her body secreted away . . . because when I slipped quickly into each of the morgue attendants' minds, I found one—a dull-witted, middle-aged man named Tobe—who had the unmistakable mental imprints of someone who had been Used and ordered to forget that Use.

Culley began visiting the Charleston cemeteries that week, searching for any grave less than a year old that might hold Nina's corpse. Nina's family had come from Boston, so when the search of Charleston-area cemeteries yielded nothing, I sent Nancy north—I did not want Culley to be gone during this time—and she found the Hawkins family crypt in a small, private cemetery in old North Boston. She entered the crypt that Friday night, after midnight, and with a crowbar and pickax purchased at a K-Mart in Cambridge she carried out a thorough search. There were Hawkinses galore, eleven in all, nine adults, but none of them looked to have been lying there for less than half a century. I stared through Miss Sewell's eyes at the crushed skull of what had to be Nina's father—I could see the gold tooth we had made jokes about—and I wondered, not for the first time, if she had forced him under the wheels of that trolley in 1921 because of her pique at not being allowed to purchase the blue coupé she had set her heart on that summer.

The Hawkinses on display that night were all bones and dust and long-rotted remnants of burial finery, but to be absolutely sure, I had Miss Sewell crack open each skull and peer inside. We found nothing but gray dust and insects. Nina was not hiding there.

As disappointing as these searches were, I was pleased that I was thinking so clearly. My months of convalescence had confused me somewhat, slowed my usually acute perceptions of things, but now I could feel the old intellectual rigor returning.

I should have guessed that Nina would not choose to be buried with her family. She had hated her parents and loathed her only sister, who had died young. No, if Nina were indeed a corpse, I imagined that I would find her lying in state in some newly purchased mansion, perhaps right there in Charleston, prettily dressed and daily cosmeticized, reclining in cushioned luxury in a bowered bier amid a veritable necropolis of servants of the dead. I confess that I had Nurse Oldsmith dress in her finest silk and walk to Mansard House for lunch in their Plantation Room, but there was no hint of Nina's presence there and although her sense of irony had been almost as keen as mine, she would not have been so foolish as to return there.

I do not want to give the impression that my week was occupied with fruitless searches for a possibly nonexistent Nina. I took practical precautions. Howard flew to France on Wednesday and began preparations for my future sojourn there. The farmhouse was as I had left it eighteen years earlier. The safe-deposit box in Toulon held my French passport, updated and delivered by Mr. Thorne only three years ago.

It was a sign of my immeasurably enhanced Ability that I was able to perceive impressions received by Howard even when he was more than two thousand miles away. In the past, only such superbly conditioned catspaws as Mr. Thorne could travel so far, and then acting only in a pre-programmed sort of way that denied me any direct control.

Through Howard's eyes I stared at the wooded hills of southern France, the orchards and orange rectangles of rooftops in the village in the valley near my farm, and wondered that escape from America seemed so difficult.

Howard had returned by Saturday evening. Everything had been expedited for Howard, Nancy, Justin, and Nancy's "invalid mother" to leave the country on an hour's notice. Culley and the others would follow later unless a rearguard action was called for. I had no intention of losing my personal medical staff, but if it came to that, there were excellent doctors and nurses in France.

Now that an avenue of retreat had been insured, I was not sure that I wanted to retreat. The thought of a final Reunion with Nina and Willi was not unpleasant. These months of wandering, pain, and solitude had been additionally disturbing because of the sense of unfinished business hanging over it all. Nina's phone call at the Atlanta airport six months earlier had sent me fleeing in headlong panic, but the actual arrival of Nina's representative—if that is what she was—was not nearly so disturbing.

One way or the other I thought, I will find the truth of things.

On Thursday, Nurse Oldsmith went to the public library and searched out all references to the names the Negress had mentioned. There were several magazine articles and a recent book on the elusive billionaire C. Arnold Barent, mentionings of a Charles Colben in several books on Washington politics, several books about an astronomer named Kepler—but an unlikely choice since he had been dead for centuries—but no mention anywhere of the other names she had given. The books and articles convinced me of nothing. If the girl had not been sent by Nina, she was almost certainly lying. If she *had* been sent by Nina, I felt it was equally possible that she was lying. It would not have taken the provocation of a cabal of others with the Ability to incite Nina to turn on me.

Was it possible, I wondered, *that death has driven Nina insane?*

On Saturday I took care of a final detail. Dr. Hartman had dealt with Mrs. Hodges and her son-in-law about the purchase of the house across the courtyard. I knew where she lived. I also knew that she drove alone to the old city marketplace every Saturday morning to shop for the fresh vegetables that were such a fetish with her.

Culley parked next to Mrs. Hodges's daughter's car and waited for the old lady to come out of the city market. When she did, with both arms full of groceries, he approached her and said, "Here, let me help you."

"Oh," said Mrs. Hodges, "no, I can . . ." Culley took one bag of groceries, squeezed her left arm tightly, and led her to Dr. Hartman's Cadillac, thrusting her in the front seat the way an exasperated adult would seat a balky two-year-old. She was fumbling at the locked door, trying to get out, when Culley slid behind the steering wheel, reached out a hand as large as the silly old woman's head, and squeezed once. She slumped heavily against the door. Culley checked to make sure that she was breathing and then drove home, playing Mozart on the car's stereo tape deck and foolishly trying to hum along with the music.

On Sunday, May 10, Nina's Negro messenger knocked at the gate shortly after noon.

I sent Howard and Culley out to let her in. This time I was ready for her.

FIFTY-SEVEN

Dolmann Island
Saturday, May 9, 1981

N atalie and Saul left Charleston by plane shortly after 7:30 A.M. It was the first time in four days that Natalie had not worn the EEG telemetry pack and she felt strangely naked—and free—as if truly released from a quarantine.

The little Cessna 180 took off from the airport across the harbor from Charleston, turned toward the morning sun, and then banked right again as they crossed over the green and blue waters where the bay became ocean. Folly Island appeared below their right wing. Natalie could see the Intracoastal Waterway slicing south through a mad web of inlets, bays, estuaries, and coastal marshes.

"How long do you think?" Saul called to the pilot. Saul sat in the right front seat, Natalie behind him. The large, plastic-wrapped bag lay at her feet.

Daryl Meeks glanced at Saul and then looked back over his shoulder at Natalie. "About an hour and a half," he called. "A little more if the winds kick up out of the southeast."

The charter pilot looked much as he had seven months earlier when Natalie had met him on Rob Gentry's front porch; he wore cheap plastic sunglasses, boat shoes, cutoff jeans, and a sweatshirt with faded letters which read WABASH COLLEGE. Natalie still thought that Meeks looked like a somewhat younger, long-haired version of Morris Udall.

Natalie had remembered Meeks's name and the fact that Rob Gentry's old friend was a charter pilot, and it had taken only a check through the yellow pages to find his office at a small airport north of Mt. Pleasant, across the river from Charleston. Meeks had remembered her and after a few minutes of chatting, mostly anecdotes of mutual remembrance of Rob, he had agreed to take Saul and her on a fly-by of Dolmann Island. Apparently Meeks had accepted their explanation that Natalie and Saul were doing a story on the reclusive billionaire C. Arnold Barent and Natalie was sure that the pilot was charging them less than his going rate.

The day was warm and cloudless. Natalie could see where the lighter coastal waters bled into the blue-purple depths of the true Atlantic along a hundred miles of serrated coast, the green and brown of South Carolina receding toward the heat-hazed horizon to the southwest. They spoke very little as they flew, Saul and Natalie lost in their own thoughts and Meeks busy with occasional radio calls to controllers and evidently content just to be airborne on such a beautiful day. He did point out two distant smudges to the west as their flight path took them farther out to sea. "The big island's Hilton Head," he said laconically. "Favorite hangout for the upper classes. I've never been there. The other bump is Parris Island, marine camp. They gave me an all-expense paid vacation there a few police actions ago. They knew then how to turn boys into men and men into robots there in less'n ten weeks. Still do, from what I hear."

South of Savannah they angled in toward the coast again, gaining sight of long stretches of sand and greenery that Meeks identified as St. Catherines, Blackbeard, and then Sapelo Islands. He banked left, steadied on a heading of 112 degrees, and pointed out another smudge a dozen miles farther out to sea. "Thar be Dolmann Isle," said Meeks in a mock-pirate growl.

Natalie readied her camera, a new Nikon with a 300mm lens, and braced it against the side window, using a monopod to steady it. She was using very fast film. Saul set his sketchbook and clipboard on his lap and thumbed through maps and diagrams he had taken from Jack Cohen's dossier.

"We'll come in north of it," shouted Meeks. "Come down the seaward side, like I said, then circle around to get a look at the old Manse."

Saul nodded. "How close in can you get us?"

Meeks grinned. "They're real picky out here. Technically the north part of the island's a big wildlife refuge, major coastal flyway and all that, so airspace is restricted. The fact of it is that big Heritage West Foundation owns the whole thing and guards it like it was a Russian missile base. One flyover and when you land anywhere near the coast you get your ass chewed and your license pulled by the CAB as soon as they verify your registration numbers."

"Did you do what we discussed?" called Saul.

"Yep," said Meeks. "Don't know if you noticed, but a lot of them numerals is made of red tape. Tape comes off, we have us a different registration. OK, look there." He pointed to a tall-masted gray boat moving slowly northward a mile east of the island. "That's one of their picket boats. Radar. They got fast patrol boats scooting up and down and if any poor fool thinks he's going to put into Dolmann for a picnic and some bird-watching, he's got a big shock waitin' for him."

"What about in June when the camp thing is going on?" asked Saul.

Meeks laughed. "Coast Guard and navy gets into the act then," he said. "*Nothing* gets close to Dolmann by sea, unless it's got an invite. Rumor has it that the company's got armed jet turbine helicopters flying off the airstrip I'll show you on the southwest side. Friends tell me they'd force down any light aircraft tryin' to get within three miles. OK, there's the north beach. That's the only stretch of sand except for the swimmin' beach around by the Manse and the summer camp." Meeks swiveled to look at Natalie. "Hope you're ready, ma'am. This is going to be a one-time excursion 'long this side."

"Ready!" called Natalie. She began snapping pictures as they flew in at four hundred feet, a quarter of a mile off the beach. She was grateful for the autowind and oversize filmpack, although normally she would have had little use for them.

Both she and Saul had studied Cohen's maps of the island, but the reality was more interesting, even if it did flash by in a blur of palmettos, shoals, and half-glimpsed details.

Dolmann Island was typical of the barrier and sea islands more commonly found closer to the coast; a crudely penned L extending almost perfectly north and south, the island ran 6.8 miles lengthwise and was 2.7 miles wide at its base, narrowing to less than a half mile just above where the land curved northward from the base of the L.

Beyond the long white beach on the north tip of the island, its eastern coast showed glimpses of the sea marshes, swamps, and wild subtropical forests that filled the northern third of it. A frenzied flash of white wings rising from palmetto and cypress confirmed that egrets were bountiful in the ostensible wildlife refuge. Natalie shot film as fast as the autowind would advance it, catching a glimpse of burned stone ruins in the underbrush just south of a rocky point.

"That's what's left of the old slave hospital," shouted Saul, making a mark on his map. "Forest swallowed the Dubose Plantation behind it. There's a slave cemetery somewhere . . . look there's the security zone!"

Natalie raised her eye from the viewfinder. The land had risen as they approached the base of the L, the forest still so thick as to look impenetrable but given over now to live oak, cypress, and sea pine as much as palmetto and tropical growth. Ahead there was a glimpse of low, half-buried concrete buildings looking like pillboxes along the Normandy coast, an asphalt road running black and smooth between palm trees, and then an area a hundred yards wide between tall fences, a slash totally devoid of any sort of vegetation, cutting full across the island. It looked as if the ground was paved with sharp-edged shells. Natalie swung the long lens and took photographs.

Meeks pulled off his earphones. "Jeez, you should hear the things that radar picket boat guy is shouting. Too bad my radio's busted." He grinned at Saul.

They were approaching the east-west segment of the island and Meeks banked hard to avoid flying directly over it.

"Higher!" called Saul.

As they gained altitude, Natalie had a better view. She switched cameras, lifting the Ricoh fitted with the wide-angle lens and shooting manually, advancing film as quickly as she could, lunging to the left window to get a few shots of the long coast extending back the way they had come.

The north side of the base of the L looked like a different island: oak and pine forests south of the security zone, the land rising gently to wooded hills two hundred feet above sea level on the distant south side, and signs of careful construction. The asphalt road continued along the coast, just back from the beach, a perfectly smooth ribbon of asphalt shaded by palm trees and ancient live oaks. There were glimpses of green rooftops among the trees and a circle of benches in a grassy clearing near the center of the island became visible as they leveled off at five hundred feet.

"Summer camp dorms and the amphitheater," called Saul.

"Hang on," said Meeks and they banked hard left again, out over what looked like a purple scythe of reef, in order to avoid flying directly over the artificial harbor and long concrete dock at the southeast corner of the island. "I don't think they'd shoot at us," said Meeks with a grin, "but what the hell."

Beyond the harbor they banked steeply to the right, following the high, rocky eastern coast. Meeks nodded toward a rooftop farther south just visible above a canopy of ancient oak and colorful magnolias at the highest point of the island. "That's the Manse," he said. "Used to be the Vanderhoof Plantation. Old minister married into money. Built around 1770 outta cypress weatherboarding. There's twenty-one dormers up there above the third floor . . . suppose ta be more'n a hundred twenty rooms. Thing's survived four hurricanes, an earthquake, and the Civil War. Heliport this side of the trees . . . there, in the clearing."

The Cessna banked right again and lost enough altitude to be roaring along parallel to the tops of white cliffs that fell two hundred feet to a rough surf. Natalie shot five pictures with the long lens and got two with the wide angle. The Manse was visible down a long green corridor of oaks; a huge, weathered building with a quarter mile of manicured lawn leading to the vertical drop of the cliffs.

Saul checked his map and squinted at the rooftops of the Manse as they disappeared behind the tall oaks. "There's supposed to be a road . . . or avenue coming to the Manse from the north . . ."

"Live Oak Lane," said Meeks. "Over a mile, straight from the harbor to the base of the hill on the other side of the Manse, where the gardens are. But no road. It's a grassy lane, thirty yards wide, between live oaks a hundred feet tall and two hundred years old. They got soft lights like Japanese lanterns up in the trees . . . seen 'em at night from ten miles out . . . they drive the VIPs up Live Oak Lane to the Manse at night when they arrive. There's the airstrip!"

They had flown two miles west along the base of the L and the cliffs had dropped to a low, rocky shoreline and then to a broad white beach when the airstrip came into sight: a long, dark slash heading northeast into the forest.

"They come in by plane, still get the Live Oak Lane tour," said Meeks. "Just not as much of it. Thing can handle private stuff up to the executive jet level. Probably land a seven-two-seven in a pinch. Hang on."

They pitched steeply to the right as they came around the southwest corner of the island, the swimming beach disappearing behind them.

Ahead, the straight line of the L was ruined by a jagged inlet with the fenced security zone extending inland across the isthmus. The hundred yards of nothingness looked shocking amid the tropical lushness: the Berlin Wall transposed to paradise. North of the security zone along the west side of the island there was no sign of any man-made objects, not even ruins, and the profusion of palmetto, sea pine, and magnolia ran all the way to the water's edge.

"How do they explain the security zone?" asked Saul.

Meeks shrugged. "S'posed to separate the wildlife refuge from the private land," he said. "Truth of it is, it's all private. During their summer camp—stupid name, isn't it?—they got prime ministers and ex-presidents up here by the bushel. They keep the important folks south of the line to make their security jobs easier. Not that the whole island isn't secure. That's the western picket boat out there." He nodded to his left. "Three more weeks an' there'll be a dozen more ships, coast guard cutters, the whole mess. Even if you got onto the island you wouldn't get far. There'd be Secret Service an' private security forces about everywhere. If you're doin' a piece on C. Arnold Barent, you must know already that this man likes his privacy."

They were approaching the northern end of the island. Saul pointed to it and said, "I'd like to land there."

Meeks turned his sunglasses toward him. "Look, friend," he said, "we can get around filin' a false flight plan. We might not even get caught cutting the corners on Barent's airspace. But if I set a wheel down on that airstrip, I'll never see my plane again."

"I'm not talking about the airstrip," said Saul. "The beach on the north end is straight and hard-packed and looks long enough to land on."

"You're crazy," said Meeks. He frowned and adjusted something on the controls. Ocean was visible beyond the north end of the island.

Saul removed four five-hundred-dollar bills from his shirt pocket and set them on the instrument console.

Meeks shook his head. "That won't come close to buying a new plane or paying hospital expenses if we hit a rock or some soft sand."

Natalie leaned forward and grasped the pilot by his shoulder. "Please, Mr. Meeks," she said over the engine noise, "it's *very* important to us."

Meeks shifted so he could look at Natalie. "This isn't just a magazine article, is it?"

Natalie glanced at Saul and then looked back to Meeks as she shook her head. "No, it's not."

"Does it have something to do with Rob's death?" asked Meeks.

"Yes," said Natalie.

"I thought so." Meeks nodded. "I was never satisfied with any of the goddamned explanations about what Rob was doin' in Philadelphia and what the hell the FBI had to do with it all. Is this billionaire Barent involved somehow?"

"We think so," said Natalie. "We need to get more information."

Meeks pointed toward the beach passing under them. "And landing there for a few minutes'll help you figure somethin' out?"

"Maybe," said Saul.

"Well, shit," murmured Meeks. "I suppose you're both terrorists or something, but terrorists've never done me any harm and bastards like Barent've been screwin' me over for years. Hang on." The Cessna banked hard right until they came around again to pass over the north beach at two hundred feet of altitude. The strip of sand was only ten yards across at its widest and heavy vegetation came right to its edge. Several streams and inlets cut deep swaths through the northwest end of the beach. "Can't be more than a hundred an' twenty yards," called Meeks. "Have to set it down right at the edge of the surf and pray that we don't find a hole or rock or something." He checked the instruments and looked down at the white lines of surf and the swaying tops of trees. "Wind's out of the west," he said. "Hang on."

The Cessna banked hard right once more and they came around over the sea, losing altitude. Saul tightened his seat belt and braced himself against the console. In the backseat, Natalie secured her camera gear, tucked the Colt automatic under her loose blouse, checked her own seat belt, and braced herself.

Meeks throttled back so that the Cessna dropped in so slowly that it seemed to hang over the waves east of the island for a full minute. Saul saw that their trajectory would take them into the surf rather than onto the sand, but at the last second Meeks gave the Cessna a burst of throttle, sideslipped over a cluster of rocks that grew alarmingly to the size of boulders as they dropped toward them, and set the light aircraft down firmly on wet sand ten feet beyond.

The nose came down fast, saltwater whipped across the windscreen, Saul felt the left wheel slew to one side, and then Meeks was very busy as he seemed to work throttle, rudder, brakes, and ailerons all at the same time. The tail came down and the plane was slowing but not quickly enough as the tidal inlets that had seemed so far away on the northwest corner of the beach rushed at them through the blurred disk of the slowing propeller. Five seconds before they tumbled over the banks of the ravine, Meeks brought the right wheel down low enough to throw spray onto Saul's window, burped the throttle and brakes to bring the tail up and around as they skidded in a broad, sweeping turn that lifted the left wheel off the ground and brought the right wheel within inches of inlet and dunes before the aircraft stopped, prop turning idly, windscreen looking due east back along a strip of wet beach sand marked with three parallel lines that were not straight at all.

"Three minutes," said Meeks, already pulling back the throttle. "I'll be at the east end of the beach and if the wind dies or I see their boat comin' around Slave Point, adios. Lady stays in the plane to help me lift the tail at the turnaround."

Saul nodded, clicked off his belt, and was out the flimsy door, his long hair blowing in the wind and propeller blast. Natalie shoved out the long, heavy bag, wrapped in plastic tarp with leather handles protruding.

"Hey!" yelled Meeks. "You didn't say anything about . . ."

"Go!" yelled Saul and ran for the edge of the forest near where the tidal inlet disappeared under thick palm fronds and tropical blossoms.

It was a swamp. Saul was up to his knees within ten yards of the beach, the fringe of magnolias and palmettos giving way to ancient cypress and gnarled oak draped with Spanish moss. An osprey exploded from a large nest six feet from Saul's head and something swam away ten feet to his right, leaving a large V in its wake and making Saul remember what Gentry had said about catching snakes in the dark.

Saul's three minutes were almost up when he took his compass reading and decided that he was far enough in. He was carrying the heavy bag on his right shoulder and now he looked around and saw an ancient cypress scarred by fire or lightning, its two lower branches extending over the brackish water like the charred arms of a screaming man. He waded toward it and was up to his waist before he reached the massive trunk. The lightning strike had ripped open a jagged cleft on this side, exposing the rotted interior.

Mud and currents tugged at Saul's left pant leg under the water as he jammed the long bag into the cleft, pushing it up and out of sight, wedging it securely with pressure and a cross brace made from short, dead limbs snapped from the gray trunk. He waded back ten paces, satisfied himself that the heavy bag was invisible, and began memorizing the shape and location of the old tree in relation to the inlet, other trees, and a patch of sky visible above between hanging moss and contorted limbs. Then Saul turned and tried to hurry toward the beach.

The mud held him, tried to pull him down, and threatened to pull his boots off or snap his ankles. A layer of brackish scum coated his shirt, the dead water smelling of sea and corruption. Fronds and ferns batted at his head while a swarm of stinging insects hovered in a thick cloud around his sweaty face and shoulders. The vegetation seemed immeasurably thicker going out, the struggle endless. Then he was through the last barrier of branches and stumbling across the sandy, shallow inlet, struggling up the deep ravine onto the beach and realizing that even with the compass he had come out thirty yards farther west than he had entered.

The Cessna was gone.

Saul stopped in a second of throat-filling disbelief and then ran forward fifty feet, seeing the glint of sunlight on metal and glass where it sat a seemingly impossible distance away around a curve of low dunes. He could hear the engine pitch rising even as he sprinted toward it down the wet sand, noticing with an almost detached sense of detail that the tide seemed to be coming in; it already covered the seaward wheel track and was quickly narrowing the usable expanse of sun-baked beach. Two-thirds of the way there he was panting so loudly that he did not hear the higher drone of a speedboat before he saw it, white spray flashing, arcing around the northeast point of the island. At least five dark figures with rifles were visible. Saul ran faster, his boots kicking up water as he sprinted to the edge of the surf directly in front of the Cessna. If the aircraft started its takeoff run now, Saul would have the choice of diving into the water or being cut in half by the propeller.

He was ten yards from the plane when three small plumes of sand leaped up under the left wing; a strange sight, as if some burrowing creature or giant sand flea was stitching its way toward him. He heard the sharp *crack-crack-crack* of shots a second later. The speedboat was two hundred yards out, well within rifle range. Saul assumed that only the rough chop of the surf and the boat's speed had ruined the marksman's aim.

The left door opened as Saul sprinted the last twenty feet, jumped from the strut to the passenger seat, and collapsed, soaked with sweat. The aircraft leaped forward even as he came through the opening, pitching and slewing its way down the narrowing strip of wet beach while Natalie struggled to secure the banging door. There was a heavy thunk of a bullet striking metal behind them and Meek cursed, did something with an overhead control, pulled the throttle full back, and wrestled with the vibrating control yoke.

Saul sat up and looked through the windscreen just as the Cessna reached the end of the beach, still not airborne, and roared off the sandy ramp over the saltwater inlet and narrow streams. Sharp rocks and low foliage faced them on the western side.

The three feet of air under them made the difference. The right wheel splashed spray once and they were airborne, clearing the rocks by less than a foot, banking right over the waves as they climbed to twenty feet, then thirty. Saul looked right and saw the speedboat still coming, bouncing wildly. Muzzle flashes flared directly at Saul's eyes.

Meeks kicked hard at the pedals and pulled the yoke back and then forward, sending the Cessna into a strange, skidding arc and left bank that left them five feet above the waves and accelerating, lunging to put the wall of the western point and its screen of trees between them and the patrol boat.

Still not strapped in, Saul struck his head against the roof, ricocheted off the unlatched door and grabbed the seat and console to keep himself from falling against the pilot and control yoke.

Meeks looked at him sourly. Saul strapped in and looked around. Trees flashed by to their left. A half mile ahead, three speedboats were headed directly toward them, their bows lifted completely out of the water.

Meeks sighed and banked right so steeply that Saul could make out the dark shape of a manta ten feet under the water, directly below him. He could have spanned the distance between wingtip and wave with his forearm.

They leveled off and flew west, leaving the island and boats behind but staying low enough that their sense of speed was tangible as they accelerated through 150 m.p.h. Saul wished the Cessna had retractable landing gear and found himself resisting the urge to lift his feet off the floor. Meeks braced the yoke with his knees while he removed a red kerchief from his pocket and loudly blew his nose.

"We're going to have to fly all the way up to my friend Terence's private field at Monck's Corner and call Albert and have him file that alternate flight plan," said Meeks, "in case they're checkin' the coastal airports that far north. What a damned mess." He shook his head but ruined the effect by grinning.

"I know we said three hundred dollars," said Saul, "but I don't think that's the price for this junket anymore."

"No?" said Meeks.

"No," said Saul. He nodded at Natalie and she fumbled in her camera bag for the four thousand dollars bundled in fifties and twenties. Saul set it on the edge of the pilot's seat.

Meeks set the bundle on his lap and thumbed through it. "Look," he said, "If any of this's helped you get any information on who killed Rob Gentry, then that's worth it to me without this bonus."

Natalie leaned forward. "It's helped," she said. "But keep the bonus."

"Are you two going to tell me anything about how that bastard Barent had anything to do with Rob?"

"When we know more," said Natalie. "And we may need your help again."

Meeks scratched at his sweatshirt and grinned. "You bet, ma'am. Just don't let the revolution start without me, all right?"

Meeks turned on a transistor radio hanging by a strap from a knob on the dash. They flew toward the mainland to the beat of steel bands and Spanish song lyrics.

FIFTY-EIGHT

Melanie

Nina's catspaw took Justin for a drive on Sunday. She knocked at the gate shortly before eleven A.M., when decent people would be in church. She declined Culley's invitation to enter and asked that Justin—she said "the boy"—come out for a ride.

I considered for a moment. The thought of having Justin leave the compound was disturbing—of all of my family he was my favorite—but not allowing the colored girl into the house had its advantages. Also, there was the chance that the excursion might shed some light on the mystery of Nina's whereabouts. In the end, the girl waited by the fountain until Nurse Oldsmith had dressed Justin in his cutest outfit—blue shorts and a sailor's shirt—and he joined the young Negress for the ride.

Her car told me nothing; it was an almost-new Datsun with the look and smell of a rental vehicle. The colored girl was dressed in a tan skirt, high boots, and beige blouse—no purse or sign of a billfold that might carry identification. Of course, if she were Nina's conditioned instrument, she would no longer have an identity.

We drove slowly up East Bay Drive and then north along the highway to Charleston Heights. There, at a small park that looked down on the navy yards, the girl parked, took a pair of binoculars from the otherwise empty rear seat, and led Justin to a black iron fence. She studied the thicket of dark gantries and gray ships across the water and turned to me.

"Melanie, are you willing to help save Willi's life as well as protect your own?" she asked.

"Of course," I said in my childish contralto. I was not concentrating on what she said but on the station wagon that had pulled into the parking lot and stopped at the far end. There was one man in it, his face concealed by shadows, dark glasses, and distance. I was sure that I had seen that vehicle behind us on East Bay Drive shortly after we had turned left from Calhoun Street. It had been easy to conceal Justin's covert glances behind the facade of childish wiggles.

"Good," said the Negro girl and repeated the farfetched story of others with the Ability staging a bizarre version of our Game on an island somewhere.

"How can I help?" I asked, contorting Justin's face in what I was sure was an expression of interested concern. It is hard to distrust a child. While the Negro girl told me how I could help, I thought about my options.

Previously it would have benefited me little to Use the girl. My experimental probe had shown that either—a) Nina was Using her but showed absolutely no willingness to fight to keep her should I attempt to usurp control b) the girl was a superbly conditioned cat's-paw, demanding no supervision from Nina or whoever *had* conditioned her or c) she was not being Used at all.

Now things had changed. If the man in the station wagon was connected with the colored girl in some way, Using her might be an excellent way to gain information.

"Here, look through the binoculars," she said and held them out to Justin. "It's the third ship from the right."

I took the glasses and slid into her mind. I sensed her shock and the image of a strange pattern on a machine called an oscilloscope—familiar to me only from the equipment Dr. Hartman had arrayed in my bedroom—and then I had her. The transition was as effortless as I had come to expect with my enhanced Ability. The Negro girl was young and strong; I could feel the vitality in her. I thought that such strength might be useful in the minutes to come.

I left Justin there, still holding the absurd binoculars, and walked quickly back toward the station wagon, wishing that the colored girl had brought something that might be used as a weapon. The vehicle was at the far end of the parking lot and because of the sun glare on the windshield I was halfway to it before I realized that it was empty, the driver's door open.

I had the girl pause a moment and look around. There were several people in the park: A colored couple strolled near the fence; a young woman in jogging attire reclined shamelessly under a tree, her nipples clearly visible through thin fabric; two businessmen were talking earnestly near a drinking fountain; an older man with a short beard stood watching me from his place near another car; and an entire family sat at a nearby picnic table.

For a second I felt something like the old panic well in me as I searched the area for Nina's face. It was noon on a bright, spring Sunday and I felt that at any second I would see a rotting corpse sitting on a park bench or staring at me from the front seat of a car, blue eyes rising into place on a tide of maggots . . .

Justin picked up a fallen branch in the carefree manner of a playful child, and swinging it in front of him, came near the colored girl, staying close behind her as I had her approach the station wagon. Peering in the window on the driver's side, I could see the profusion of electronic instruments and cables snaking over the seat into the back of the vehicle. Justin turned to keep watch on the people in the park.

I had the colored girl move to look in the backseat. There was a sudden, slight impression of pain which I quickly damped, and I felt myself losing control of her. For a second I was sure that Nina was attempting to seize her, but then I realized that the girl was collapsing onto the pavement. I shifted full awareness to Justin in time to see the girl fall heavily, her head sliding against the metal of the car door. She had been shot.

I backed away on Justin's short legs, still holding the branch that originally had seemed so formidable from Justin's point of view, but which I now realized was an absurd little twig. The binoculars still hung around my neck. I backed toward an empty picnic table, swiveling my head, not knowing who my enemy was or from which direction he might come. No one seemed to have noticed the colored girl's fall or to see her body where it lay between the station wagon and a blue sports car. I had no idea who had killed her or what method they had used. Justin had caught a glimpse of a spot of red on the back of her beige shirt, but it had not seemed large enough for a bullet hole. I thought of silencers and other exotic devices in the movies I had watched on late shows before I had Mr. Thorne get rid of the television set forever.

It had not been a good idea to Use the colored girl. Now she was dead— or so I assumed, I had no interest in having Justin approach her body—and Justin was trapped in this park miles from home. I backed farther away from the parking lot, moving toward the fence. One of the men dressed in a business suit turned and began walking in my direction and I swiveled toward him, raising the branch and snarling like a feral creature. The man merely glanced at me and continued on his way toward the picnic pavilion where the rest rooms were. I had Justin turn and run toward the fence, stopping at the far corner of the park, his back against cold iron.

The colored girl's body was not visible from this angle. Two men stepped off large motorcycles at my end of the parking lot and walked toward me.

Culley and Howard ran to the garage to get the Cadillac. Howard had to get back out of the vehicle to open the garage door. It was dark in there.

Nurse Oldsmith gave me a shot to slow the mad beating of my heart. The light was strange, falling across Mother's quilt at the foot of my bed, reflecting off the water on Cooper River into Justin's eyes, through the grimed window of the garage as Howard fumbled for the latch.

Miss Sewell stumbled on the stairs, the colored boy in the kitchen moaned and held his head for no reason, Justin's vision blurred, cleared again, there were more men on the grass . . . it was *hard* to control so many at once, my head hurt, I sat up in bed, watching myself from Nurse Oldsmith's eyes . . . *where* was Dr. Hartman?

Damn Nina!

I closed my eyes. All of my eyes except Justin's. There was no reason to panic. Justin was too short to drive the car, even if he found the keys, but through him I could Use anyone he could see to have them drive him home. But I was so tired. My head hurt.

Culley backed the Cadillac through the closed garage doors, almost striking Howard, driving off down the alley without him, fragments of rotted wood on the trunk and rear window.

I am coming, Justin. There is nothing to worry about. And even if they take you, there are others to stay here with me.

What if it is all a diversion? Culley gone. Howard crawling in the garage, trying to get to his feet. What if Nina's agents were approaching through the front gate at that moment? Crawling over the fence?

I concentrated on sending the colored boy named Marvin out front with an ax from the back porch. He struggled to resist. It lasted only a second, less than a second, *but he struggled*. My conditioning had been too lax. Too much of him remained.

I forced the colored boy into the courtyard, past the fountain. No one was there. Miss Sewell joined them and they kept watch. I awoke Dr. Hartman from his nap in the Hodgeses' parlor and brought him to me on the run. Nurse Oldsmith fetched a shotgun from the closet and pulled the chair close to the bed. Culley was on Meeting Street, approaching the Spruil Avenue exit near the navy yards. Howard stood guard in the backyard.

I felt better. Control returned. It had been only that old panic that only Nina could cause. It was over now. If anyone threatened Justin, I would have that person impale him or herself on the iron fence. I would happily help him rip his own eyes out and . . .

Justin was gone.

While my attention had been diverted I had left him to his own conditioning. Left him standing with his back to the fence and river, a six-year-old boy holding the world at bay with his stick.

He was gone. There was no sensory input at all. I had felt no impact, sensed neither bullet nor knife. Perhaps it had been clouded by Howard's pain or the struggle with the flicker of consciousness in the colored boy or Miss Sewell's awkwardness. I did not know.

Justin was gone. Who would comb my hair at night?

Perhaps Nina had not killed him, only taken him. For what purpose? As a trade because I had caused the death of her silly little pickaninny messenger? Could Nina be so petty?

Yes, she could.

Culley arrived at the park and lumbered around until people stared at him. Stared at me.

The rental car was still there and empty. The station wagon was gone. The colored girl's body was gone. Justin was gone.

I leaned Culley's massive forearms against the metal railing and stared down at the river forty feet below. Gray currents rippled and swirled.

Culley wept. I wept. We all wept.

Damn you, Nina.

It was late that night as I hung in the half sleep the drugs provided that there came an angry banging at the front gate. Groggily I had Culley, Howard, and the colored boy go outside. I saw who was there and froze.

It was Nina's colored girl, face ashen, clothing soiled and rent, eyes staring. She held Justin's limp body in her arms. Nurse Oldsmith parted the drapes and peered through the shutters to give me another angle of view.

The colored girl raised a long finger and pointed directly at my room, directly at *me*.

"You, *Melanie!*" she shouted so loudly that I was sure it would awake everyone in the Old Section. "Melanie, open this gate *immediately*. I want to talk to *you*."

Her finger remained raised and pointing. It seemed that a very long time elapsed. The green spikes of the monitor near the bed pulsed wildly. All of us closed our eyes and then looked again. The colored girl was still there, still pointing, still staring imperiously with an arrogance I had not seen since the last time I had foiled one of Nina Drayton's plans.

Slowly, hesitantly, I sent Culley forward to unlock the gate and step back quickly before the thing Nina had sent could touch him. She entered briskly, striding toward and through the open front door.

The rest of us made way and drew back as she entered the parlor. She laid Justin's body on the divan.

I was unsure of what to do. We waited.

FIFTY-NINE

Charleston
Sunday, May 10, 1981

S aul was watching Natalie and Justin in the park and listening to their conversation via the microphone she had clipped to the collar of her blouse when the computer gave its shrill alarm. His eyes flashed to the screen of the portable computer on the passenger seat of the station wagon, thinking for a second that it must be a failure of the telemetry pack, sensors, or the battery pack in the backseat rather than the event both of them dreaded. One glance told him that it was not equipment failure. The theta rhythm pattern was unmistakable, the alpha pattern already showing the peaks and valleys of rapid eye movement. At that second he found the answer to a problem he had been wrestling with for months and at the same instant he realized that his life was in imminent danger.

Saul looked out and saw Natalie turning in his direction even as he grabbed the dart gun and rolled out his door, scuttling away from the station wagon, trying to keep it and the other vehicles between Natalie, the boy, and himself. *No, it's not Natalie,* he thought and slid to a stop behind the last car in the lot, twenty-five feet from the station wagon.

Why had the old lady decided to Use Natalie now? Saul wondered if he had done a poor job of following them. He had been forced to stay close—the microphone and transmitter they had added to Natalie's belt of devices had a range of less than half a mile—and the traffic had been light. They had grown overconfident as a result of last week's successes and their expedition to the island the previous day. Saul cursed softly and crouched to peer through the window of a white Ford Fairmont as Natalie strode toward the station wagon.

The boy advanced fifteen paces behind Natalie, carrying a branch he had picked off the grass. In that second Saul felt an overwhelming urge to kill the child, to empty the entire magazine of the Colt automatic in his jacket pocket into that small body, to drive the demons out by death. Saul took a deep breath. He had lectured at Columbia and other universities on the peculiar and perverse strain of modern violence in such books and movies as *The Exorcist, The Omen,* and innumerable imitations, going back to *Rosemary's Baby.* Saul had seen the rash of demonic-children entertainments as a symptom of deeper underlying fears and hatreds; the "me-generation's" inability to shift into the role of responsible parenthood at the cost of losing their own interminable childhood, the transference of guilt from divorce—the child is not really a child, but an older, evil thing, capable of *deserving* any abuse resulting from the adult's selfish actions— and the anger of an entire society revolting after two decades of a culture dominated by and devoted to youthful looks, youth-oriented music, juvenile movies, and the television and movie myth of the adult-child inevitably wiser, calmer, and more "with-it" than the childish adults in the household. So Saul had lectured that the child-fear and child-hatred becoming visible in popular shows and books had its irrational roots in common guilts, shared anxieties, and the universal angst of the age. He had warned that the national wave of abuse, neglect, and callousness toward children had its historical antecedents and that it would run its course, but that everything possible must be done to avoid and eliminate that brand of violence before it poisoned America.

Saul crouched, peered through the rear window at the loathsome sight of the small thing that had been little Justin Warden, and decided not to shoot him. Not yet. Besides, gunning down a six-year-old in a park on a Sunday afternoon was not the best way to assure their continued anonymity in Charleston.

Natalie walked around the station wagon and peered in, bending slightly to look in the rear seat, her back to Saul. At that second the boy turned to watch people at a nearby table. Saul rose, braced the dart gun on the roof, fired, and dropped out of sight.

For several seconds he was sure that he had missed, that the distance had been too great for the tiny gas-propelled dart, but then he caught a glimpse of the red tail feathers on the back of Natalie's blouse an instant before she fell. He wanted to run to her then to check that she had not been injured by the drug or the drop to the pavement, but Justin looked back his way and Saul dropped to all fours behind the Ford, fumbling out the small box of anesthetic darts and breaking the pistol open to load a second one.

Two short, bare legs came to a running stop six feet from Saul's face. He jerked his head up in time to see a boy of about eight or nine retrieving a blue kickball. The boy stared at Saul and the air pistol. "Hey, mister," he said, "you gonna shoot somebody?"

"Go away," hissed Saul.

"You a cop or something?" asked the boy, his face interested.

Saul shook his head.

"That an Uzi pistol or somethin'?" asked the boy, tucking the ball under his arm. "It sorta looks like an Uzi with a silencer on it."

"Piss off," whispered Saul, using the favorite phrase of the British soldiers in occupied Palestine when they were confronted with street urchins.

The boy shrugged and ran back to his game. Saul lifted his head in time to see Justin also running, his back to the parking lot, stick waving in his right hand.

Saul made a quick decision and walked quickly toward the picnic area, away from the cars. He could see the tan fabric of Natalie's skirt where she lay on the pavement. He walked quickly, keeping the trees between himself and Justin. No one in the park seemed to have noticed Natalie yet. Two motorcycles pulled into the parking lot with an explosion of noise.

Saul walked briskly, getting forty feet closer to where Justin stood with his back against the fence above the river. The boy had a fixed, unfocused stare. His mouth hung open and there was a trickle of saliva running to his chin. Saul leaned his back against a tree, took a breath, and checked the CO_2 charge in the handle of the weapon.

"Hey," called a nearby man in a gray Brooks Brothers summer suit, "that's pretty neat. You have to have a license to carry one of those?"

"No," said Saul, glancing around the tree to confirm that Justin was still staring sightlessly. The boy was fifty or sixty feet away. Too far.

"Neat," said the young man in the gray suit. "It fires .22s or pellets or what?"

Graysuit's partner in conversation, a young blond man with a mustache, blow-dried hair, and a blue summer suit said, "Where can you buy one of those, fella? K-Mart have them?"

"Excuse me," said Saul and stepped around the tree and walked in plain sight to the fence. Justin's head did not turn toward him. The boy's blank gaze was fixed on some spot above the roof of the cars in the lot. Saul kept the pistol behind him as he walked along the fence toward the frozen figure of the six-year-old. Twenty paces away he paused. Justin did not stir. Feeling like a cat stalking a toy mouse, Saul covered the last fifteen paces, brought the pistol around, and shot the boy on his bare right leg with a blue-tipped dart. When Justin fell forward, still rigid, Saul was there to catch him. No one appeared to have noticed.

He restrained himself from running back to the parking lot but still moved at something better than a brisk walk. The two longhaired men who had come in on motorcycles were on the sidewalk staring down at Natalie's limp form. Neither had made a move to help her.

"Excuse me, please," said Saul, squeezing past, stepping over Natalie, tugging the left rear door of the station wagon open, and gently setting Justin next to the battery packs and radio receiver.

"Hey, man," said the fatter of the two bikers, "she dead or what?"

"Oh, no," said Saul with a forced chuckle, grunting with the effort of lifting her onto the front seat and shoving her as far to the right as he could. Her left shoe slid off and fell to the pavement with a soft sound. He picked it up, smiling at the staring bikers. "I'm a doctor. She just has a little problem with *petit mal* seizures induced by neurologically deficient cardiopulmonary edema." He got into the station wagon, dropped the dart gun on the seat, and continued smiling at the bikers. "So does the boy," he said. "It . . . ah . . . runs in the family." Saul shifted into gear and backed out, half expecting a car filled with Melanie Fuller's zombies to intercept him before he made it to the street. No car appeared.

Saul drove around until he was sure that they were not being followed and then returned to the motel. Their cabin unit was almost out of sight of the road, but he made sure there was no traffic before he carried them in, first Natalie and then the boy.

Natalie's EEG sensors were still in place, hidden in her hair but functional. The microphone and telemetry pack were still working. Saul paused a minute before disconnecting the computer and carrying it in. The theta rhythm was gone, the REM peaks absent. The EEG readout was consistent with a deep, dreamless, drug-induced sleep.

After carrying in the equipment, Saul made Natalie and Justin comfortable and checked their vital signs. He activated the second telemetry pack, attached electrodes to the boy's skull, and keyed in a code to initiate a program that would display both sets of EEG data on the computer screen at once. Natalie's continued to show a normal deep sleep pattern. The child's showed the traditional flat lines of clinical brain death.

Saul checked the boy's pulse, heartbeat, and retinal response, took his blood pressure, and tried sound, scent, and pain stimuli. The computer continued to indicate no higher neurological functions whatsoever. Saul switched telemetry packs and sensors, checked the transmitter's power cells, reverted to a single-display mode, and used more electrolytic paste and two additional electrodes. The readings were identical with the first. Six-year-old Justin Warden was legally brain dead, literally nothing more than a primitive brain-stem that kept the heart pumping, the kidneys filtering, and the lungs moving air through a husk of mindless meat.

Saul lowered his head to his hands and stayed in that position for a very long time.

"What do we do?" asked Natalie. She was on her second cup of coffee. The tranquilizer had kept her out for just under an hour, but it took her another fifteen minutes before she could think clearly.

"We keep him sedated, I guess," he said. "If we let him come out of deep sleep, Melanie Fuller may regain control. The little boy who was Justin Warden—memories, loves, fears, everything that is human—is gone forever."

"Can you be sure about that?" asked Natalie, her voice thick.

Saul sighed, set down his own cup of coffee, and added a small measure of whiskey. "No," he admitted, "not without better equipment, more complicated tests, and observation of the boy under a much wider range of conditions. But with indications that flat, I would say that the odds are overwhelmingly against him recovering anything close to human consciousness, much less memory or personality." He took a long drink.

"All those dreams of releasing them . . ." began Natalie.

"Yes." Saul slapped down the empty cup. "It makes sense, when you think about it. The more conditioning the old lady has carried out, the less chance of a personality surviving. I suspect that the adults function with a residue of their identities . . . personalities . . . certainly it would do no good for her to have kidnapped medical personnel the way she did if they had no access to their former skills. But even there, extended mental control . . . this mind vampirism . . . must kill the original personality after awhile. It is like a disease, a brain cancer, that grows over time, bad cells killing good ones."

Natalie rubbed her aching head. "Is it possible that some of her . . . her people . . . have been controlled less than others? Are less infected?"

Saul opened the fingers of one hand in a quizzical gesture. "Possible? Yes, I suppose. But if they are conditioned—tampered with—enough for her to trust them as servants, I fear that their personalities and higher-order functions have been seriously damaged."

"But the Oberst Used you," said Natalie without any emotional overtones. "And I've been leeched onto twice by Harod and at least as many times by this old witch."

"Yes?" said Saul, removing his glasses and rubbing the bridge of his nose.

"Well, have they harmed us? Is the cancer growing inside us right now? Are we different, Saul? *Are we?*"

"I don't know," said Saul. He sat motionless until Natalie looked away.

"I'm sorry," she said. "It's just so . . . awful . . . having that scaly old witch in my mind. It's the most helpless feeling I've ever had . . . it must be worse than being raped. At least when someone violates your body, your mind is still your own. And the worst part . . . the worst part is . . . after it's happened once or twice . . . you . . ." Natalie could not go on.

"I know," said Saul, holding her hand. "A part of you wants to experience it again. Like a terrible drug with painful side effects, but as equally addictive. I know."

"You never talked about . . ."

"It is not something one wishes to discuss."

"No." Natalie shuddered.

"But that is not the cancer we were discussing," said Saul. "I feel certain that addiction comes with the intense conditioning these things carry out with their chosen few. Which leads us to another moral dilemma."

"What?"

"If we follow our plan, it will require weeks of conditioning for at least one person—perhaps more—an innocent."

"It wouldn't be the *same* . . . it would be temporary, for a specific function."

"For *our* purposes it would be temporary," said Saul. "As we now know, the effects can be permanent."

"Goddamnit!" snapped Natalie. "It doesn't *matter*. That's our plan. Can you think of another?"

"No."

"Then we go ahead," Natalie said firmly. "We go ahead even if it costs us our minds and our souls. We go ahead even if other innocents have to suffer. We go ahead because we have to, because we owe it to our dead. Our families and the people we love have paid the price and now we go ahead . . . make their killers pay . . . there can't be any justice if we stop now. No matter what the price we have to go on."

Saul nodded. "You are right, of course," he said sadly. "But that is precisely the same imperative that compels the angry young Palestinian to set the bomb aboard the bus, the Basque separatist to fire into a crowd. They have no other choice. Is that so different from the Eichmanns following orders? Responding to the imperatives of no personal responsibility?"

"Yes," said Natalie, "it is different. And right now I'm too goddamned frustrated to give a damn about your ethical niceties. I just want to see what to do and go *do* it."

Saul stood up. "Eric Hoffer says that to the frustrated, freedom from responsibility is more attractive than freedom from restraint."

Natalie shook her head vehemently. Saul could see the fine black filaments from the EEG sensors running into the collar of her blouse. "I'm not hunting for freedom *from* responsibility," she said. "I'm *taking* the responsibility. Right now I'm trying to decide whether to return that boy to Melanie Fuller."

Saul's surprise showed on his face. "Return him? How can we do that? He . . ."

"He's brain dead," interrupted Natalie. "She's already murdered him as surely as she did his sisters. I have a use for him when I go back tonight."

"You can't go there again today," said Saul, staring at her as if he did not know her. "It's too soon. She's too unstable . . ."

"That's why I need to go *now*," Natalie said firmly. "While she's reeling, unsure. The old lady has half her bolts loose, but she's not stupid, Saul. We need to know that she's convinced. And we can't equivocate any longer. I have to quit farting around about who *I* am . . . a messenger . . . an ambiguous somebody . . . and *become* Nina Drayton for this old monster."

Saul shook his head. "We're working on shaky premises, based on inadequate information."

"And that's all we have," said Natalie. "We're going with it. We're committed—there's no sense failing with half measures. We need to talk, you and I, until I find something that *only* Nina Drayton would have known, something that even Melanie Fuller will be surprised at."

"Wiesenthal's dossiers," said Saul, absently rubbing his brow.

"No," said Natalie, "something more powerful. Something that came out of your two sessions with Nina Drayton when she came to you in New

York. She was playing with you, but you were still functioning as a therapist. People open up more than they know."

Saul steepled his fingers and looked at nothing for a moment. "Yes," he said, "there is something." His sad eyes focused on Natalie. "It is a terrible risk for you."

Natalie nodded. "So that we can get to the next phase where you take a risk that makes me sick just to think about," she said. "Let's get on with it."

They talked for five hours, going over details that they had discussed innumerable times before but which now had to be sharpened like a sword for battle. They were finished by eight P.M., but Saul suggested that they wait a few hours more.

"You think she sleeps?" asked Natalie.

"Perhaps not, but even a fiend must be subject to fatigue toxins. At least her pawns will be. Besides, we're dealing with a truly paranoid personality here and the invasion of her personal space—her territory—and there's every evidence that these mind vampires are as territorial as their primitive use of the hypothalamus suggests. If so, then the invasion at night will be more effective. The Gestapo made it standard practice to come at night."

Natalie looked at the sheaf of notes she had taken. "So it's the paranoia we work at? Assuming that she follows the classic symptomology of paranoid schizophrenic?"

"Not just that," said Saul. "We have to remember that we're dealing with a Kohlberg Level Zero here. Melanie Fuller has not gone beyond the infantile stage of development in a number of areas. Perhaps none of them have. Their parapsychic ability is a curse, not allowing them to move beyond the level of demanding and expecting immediate gratification. Anything that thwarts their will is unacceptable, thus the inevitable paranoia and addiction to violence. Tony Harod may be more advanced than most—perhaps his psychic ability developed later and less successfully—but his use of that limited power merely serves to gratify the masturbatory fantasies of early adolescence, at best. Combined with Melanie Fuller's infantile ego and advanced paranoia, we have the caldron of schoolgirl jealousies and unrecognized homosexual attractions inherent in her long competition with Nina."

"Great," said Natalie, "in evolutionary terms they're supermen. In psychological development, they're retarded. In moral terms, they're subhuman."

"Not subhuman," said Saul. "Merely nonexistent."

They sat in silence for a long interval. Neither had eaten since breakfast twelve hours earlier. The oscilloscope pattern on the computer screen showed the active peaks and valleys of Natalie's scurrying thoughts.

Saul shook himself. "I've solved the posthypnotic trigger stimulus problem," he said.

Natalie sat up. "How, Saul?"

"My mistake was in trying to condition a response to the theta rhythm or the artificial alpha peak. I cannot create the former and the latter is too unreliable. It is the waking REM state that has to be the trigger."

"Can you duplicate that while you're awake?" asked Natalie.

"Perhaps," said Saul. "But not reliably so. Instead, I will develop an interim stimulus—perhaps a soft bell—and use the natural REM state to trigger it."

"Dreams," mused Natalie. "Will there be time?"

"Almost a month," said Saul. "If we can cause Melanie to condition the people we need, I can prevail upon my own mind to condition itself."

"But all those dreams you'll have," said Natalie. "The people dying . . . the hopelessness of the death camps . . ."

Saul smiled wanly. "I have those dreams anyway," he said.

It was after midnight when Saul drove her to the Old Section and parked half a block from the Fuller house. There was no equipment in the station wagon; Natalie wore neither microphone nor sensors.

The street and sidewalk were empty. Natalie lifted Justin out of the backseat, tenderly brushed back a strand of hair that had fallen over his forehead, and said to Saul through his open window, "If I don't come out, go ahead with the plan."

Saul nodded toward the backseat where twenty pounds of remaining C-4 plastic explosives had been parceled into packets and clipped onto a web belt. "If you don't come out," he said, "I'm coming in to get you. If she's hurt you, I'll kill all of them and carry on with the plan as best I can."

Natalie hesitated and then said, "Good." She turned and carried Justin toward the house that was illuminated only by a green glow from the second floor.

Natalie set the unconscious boy on the ancient couch. The house smelled of mildew and dust. Melanie Fuller's "family" had gathered around like so many ambulatory corpses—the huge, retarded-looking one the old woman called Culley, a shorter, darker man whom Natalie imagined to be Justin's father even though he had not so much as glanced at the boy, the two women in dirty nurse's outfits, one of whom wore thick makeup so poorly applied that she looked like a blind clown, another woman in a torn, striped blouse and mismatched print skirt. The only light was the glow from a single, sputtering candle that Marvin had carried in. The ex-gang leader held a long knife in his right hand.

Natalie Preston did not care. Her body was so full of adrenaline, her heart pounding so fiercely, her mind so filled with the persona she had poured into it during the preceding weeks and months, that she just wanted something to *start*. Anything was better than waiting, fearing, fleeing . . . "Melanie," she snapped in her best southern belle honky drawl, "here's your little toy. Don't *ever* do that again."

The mass of white flesh called Culley ambled forward and peered at Justin. "Is he dead?"

"*Is he dead?*" mimicked Natalie. "No, my dear, he is not dead. But he could be and possibly should be and so might you. What on earth were you thinking of?"

Culley mumbled something about not knowing if the colored girl was really from Nina.

Natalie laughed. "Are you bothered that I Use this black? Or are you jealous, dear? You never cared for Barrett Kramer either as I remember. How many of my assistants *have* you liked over the years, my dear?"

The nurse with the clown's makeup spoke. "Prove yourself!"

Natalie wheeled on her. "*Damn you, Melanie!*" she shouted. The nurse took a step backward. "Choose which mouth you're going to speak out of and stay with it. I'm *tired* of this. You've lost all sense of hospitality. If you try to seize my messenger again, I will kill whomever you send out and then come for you. My power has grown immensely since you shot me, my dear. You were never my equal in the Ability and now you have no chance at all of competing with me. *Do you understand?*" Natalie screamed this last at the nurse with the lipstick carefully smeared across her cheek. The nurse took another step backward.

Natalie turned, looked at each waxlike face, and sat down on the chair closest to the tea table. "Melanie, Melanie, why does it have to be like this? My darling, I've forgiven you for killing me. Do you have any idea how painful it is to die? Do you have any concept of how hard it is to concentrate with that lump of lead from your stupid, ancient pistol lodged in my brain? If I can forgive you for that, how can you be so *stupid* as to endanger Willi and yourself—*all of us*—because of old grudges. Let bygones be bygones, my dear, or *by God I'll burn this rat trap of a house to the ground and carry on without you.*"

There were five of Melanie's people in the room, not counting Justin. Natalie suspected that there were more upstairs with the old lady, perhaps even more in the Hodgeses' house. When Natalie paused in her shouting, all five flinched backward perceptibly. Marvin bumped into a tall wood and crystal cupboard. Plates and delicate, fussy figurines vibrated on the shelves.

Natalie took three steps forward and peered into the clown-nurse's face. "Melanie," she said, "look at me." It was a flat command. "Do you recognize me?"

The nurse's smeared mouth moved. "I . . . I am not . . . it is hard to . . ."

Natalie nodded slowly. "After all these years is it still difficult for you to

know me? Are you so far gone into yourself, Melanie, that you do not realize that no one else could know about you . . . about us . . . or if they *did*
know, would simply eliminate you as a danger to themselves?"

"Willi . . ." managed the clown-nurse.

"Ah, Willi," said Natalie. "Our dear friend Wilhelm. Do you think
Willi is clever enough for this, Melanie? Or this subtle? Or would Willi
have settled things with you the way he did with that artist in the Imperial
Hotel in Vienna?"

The nurse shook her head. Her eyes dripped mascara; eye shadow was
laid on so heavily that her face gave the appearance of a skull in the candlelight.

Natalie leaned closer, whispering next to the woman's rouged cheek.
"Melanie, if I murdered my own father, do you think I will hesitate to kill
you if you get in my way again?"

Time seemed to stop in the dark house. Natalie might have been in a
room with carelessly dressed, damaged mannequins. The clown-nurse
blinked, false eyelashes askew, eyelids moving in slow motion. "Nina, you
never told me that . . ."

Natalie stepped backward, amazed to feel real tears wetting her cheeks.
"I've never told anyone, my dear," she whispered, knowing that her life
was forfeit if Nina Drayton had told her friend Melanie what she had con-
fided to Dr. Saul Laski. "I was angry with him. He was waiting for the
trolley. I *pushed* . . ." She looked up quickly, locking her gaze with the
blind stare of the nurse. "Melanie, I want to see *you*."

The painted face moved back and forth. "Impossible, Nina, I do not
feel well. I . . ."

"*Not* impossible," snapped Natalie. "If we are to continue this effort together . . . to reestablish trust . . . I have to know that you are here, alive."

Everyone in the room except Natalie and the unconscious boy was
shaking his or her head in unison. "No . . . not possible . . . I am not
well . . ." came from five mouths.

"Good-bye, Melanie," said Natalie and turned to stalk out.

The nurse rushed to take her arm before she reached the courtyard.
"Nina . . . darling . . . please don't go. I am so lonely here. There's no one
to play with."

Natalie stood still, her flesh crawling.

"All right," said the nurse with the skull face, "this way. But first . . .
no weapons . . . nothing." Culley stepped closer and searched Natalie, his
huge hands compressing her breasts, sliding up her legs, touching everywhere, searching, probing. Natalie did not look at him. She closed her
teeth on her tongue as the hysterical scream tried to break free from her.

"Come," said the nurse, and with Culley carrying the candle they
made a solemn procession of candles, from the parlor to the entrance
foyer, from the foyer up the wide staircase, from the staircase to the landing where shadows leaped on a twelve-foot-high wall and where the hall-

way was as black as any tunnel. The door to Melanie Fuller's bedroom was closed.

Natalie remembered entering that room six months earlier, her father's pistol in her coat pocket, hearing the faint stirrings in the tall wardrobe and finding Saul Laski. There were no monsters then.

Dr. Hartman opened the door. The sudden draft blew the candle out, leaving only the soft green glow from medical monitors on either side of the high canopied bed. Fine lace curtains hung from the canopy like rotted cheesecloth, like the thick webbing of a black widow spider's lair.

Natalie took three steps forward and was stopped just inside the room by a quick motion of the doctor's grimy hand.

It was close enough.

The thing in the bed had once been a woman. Her hair had fallen out in large clumps, but what remained had been carefully combed out so it lay on the huge pillow like a corona of sick blue flame. The face was ancient, wizened, mottled by sores and etched with cruel lines, the left side sagging like a wax deathmask brought too close to the flames. The toothless mouth opened and closed like the maw of a centuries-old snapping turtle. The thing's right eye moved restlessly and aimlessly, shifting now toward the ceiling and a second later sliding upward until nothing but the white showed, an egg embedded in a skull, covered by a loose flap of browning parchment.

Behind the gray lace, the face turned Natalie's way, the snapping-turtle mouth making wet, smacking noises.

The clown-nurse behind Natalie whispered, "I am growing younger, am I not, Nina?"

"Yes," said Natalie.

"Soon I will be as young as when we all went out to Simpls before the war. Do you remember that, Nina?"

"Simpls," said Natalie. "Yes. Vienna."

The doctor moved them all back, closed the door. The five of them stood on the landing. Culley suddenly reached out and gently held Natalie's small hand in his huge fist. "Nina, darling," he said in a girlish, almost coquettish falsetto. "Whatever you wish me to do shall be done. Tell me what to do next."

Natalie shook herself, looked at her hand in Culley's. She squeezed his palm, patting his arm with her free hand. "Tomorrow, Melanie, I will pick you up for another ride. Justin will be awake and alert in the morning if you wish to Use him."

"Where are we going, Nina, dear?"

"To begin preparing," said Natalie. She squeezed the giant's callused hand a final time and forced herself to walk rather than run down the infinitely long staircase. Marvin stood by the door, no recognition in his dulled eyes, a long knife in his hand. When Natalie reached the foyer, he opened the door for her. She stopped, used the last of her willpower to look up the staircase at the insane tableau arrayed there in the dark, smiled, and said, "Adieu until tomorrow, Melanie. Do not disappoint me again."

"No," said the five in unison. "Good night, Nina."

Natalie turned and left, allowing Marvin to unlock the outer gate for her, not turning or looking back even when she passed Saul in the parked station wagon, taking deeper and deeper breaths as she walked, keeping them from becoming sobs by sheer force of will.

SIXTY

Dolmann Island
Saturday, June 13, 1981

B y the end of the week Tony Harod was sick and tired of mingling
with the rich and powerful. It was his measured decision that the
rich and powerful had a pronounced tendency toward assholism.

He and Maria Chen had arrived by private plane in Meridian, Georgia,
the sweatiest seventh circle of desolation Harod had ever encountered,
early on the previous Sunday evening only to be told that a *different* private
aircraft could take them to the island. Unless they wanted to take a boat.
It had been no decision for Harod.

The fifty-five-minute boat ride had been rough, but even hanging over
the railing waiting to lose his vodka and tonic and airline snacks, Harod
had preferred bouncing from whitecap to whitecap to suffering the eight-
minute flight. Barent's boathouse, marina, whatever it was, had to be the
most impressive shed Harod had ever seen. Three stories tall, the walls of
gray weathered cypress, the interior as open and majestic as a cathedral
with stained glass windows reaffirming that image and casting shafts of
colored light on water and rows of gleaming brass and wood speedboats
with crisp pennants furled at the bow, the place was perhaps the most os-
tentatious obscure structure he had ever passed through.

Women were not allowed on Dolmann Island during Summer Camp
week. Harod had known that, but it was still a pain in the ass for him to go
fifteen minutes out of their way to drop Maria Chen off at Barent's yacht, a
gleaming, white thing the length of a football field, all streamlined super-
structure and white-domed bulges and arrays housing radar and Barent's
ubiquitous communications equipment. Harod realized for the thousandth
time that C. Arnold Barent was not a man who liked to be out of touch
with things. A streamlined helicopter looking as if it had been designed for
the mid-twenty-first century sat on the fantail, rotor idle but not tied down,
obviously ready to rush islandward at a whistle from its master.

The water was full of boats: sleek speedboats carrying security men
with M-16s, the bulky radar picket boats with antennae turning, various
private yachts flanked by security vessels from half a dozen countries, and,
becoming visible as they came around the corner of the island toward the
harbor, a U.S. naval destroyer a mile out. The thing was impressive, slate
gray and shark sleek, slicing through the water toward them at high speed,
radar dishes turning and flags whipping, giving the impression of a hungry greyhound closing on a hapless rabbit.

"What the fuck's that?" Harod shouted to the man driving their speedboat.

The man in the striped shirt grinned, showing white teeth against tanned skin, and said, "That's the U.S.S. *Richard S. Edwards*, sir. Forrest Sherman class destroyer. It's on picket duty here every year during Heritage West's Summer Camp as a service to our foreign guests and domestic dignitaries."

"The same boat is?" said Harod.

"The same *ship*, yes, sir," said the driver. "Technically, it's conducting blockade and interdiction maneuvers here each summer."

The destroyer had come around so that Harod could see the white numerals 950 on its bow. "What's that box thing back there?" asked Harod. "Near the rear gun or whatever that is."

"ASROC, sir," said the driver, swinging their speedboat to port and toward the harbor, "modified for ASW by taking out their five-inch MK 42 and a couple of three-inch MK 33s."

"Oh," said Harod, clinging tightly to the railing, spray mixing with sweat on his pale face. "Are we almost there?"

A souped-up golf cart with a driver in a blue blazer and gray slacks drove Harod from the dock to the Manse. Live Oak Lane was a broad avenue of grass clipped as close as a putting green between two lines of massive oaks stretching off to where they seemed to meet in the distance, huge limbs crisscrossing a hundred feet overhead to create a shifting canopy of leaves and light through which glimpses of evening sky and clouds offered a pastel counterpoint to green foliage. As they glided silently down the long tunnel created by trees older than the United States, photoelectric cells sensed the twilight and switched on an array of subtle floodlights and softly glowing Japanese lanterns hidden among the high limbs, hanging ivy, and massive roots, creating an illusion of a magical forest, a fantasy of a wyrwood alive with light and music as hidden speakers lifted the clear sound of classical flute sonatas into the evening air. Elsewhere in the oak forest, hundreds of tiny wind chimes added elfin notes to the music as a breeze from the ocean rustled the foliage.

"Big fucking trees," said Harod as they glided through the last quarter mile of oak lane toward the extensive, terraced garden at the northern base of the south-facing Manse.

"Yes, sir," said the driver and drove on.

C. Arnold Barent was not there to meet Harod, but the Reverend Jimmy Wayne Sutter was, a tall glass of bourbon in his hand, his face flushed. The evangelist crossed an expanse of black and white tile in an empty main hall that reminded Harod of Chartres Cathedral even though he had never been there.

"Anthony, m'boy," boomed Sutter, "welcome to Summer Camp." His voice echoed for seconds.

Harod leaned back and gawked like a tourist, looking up at an immensity of space bounded by mezzanines and balconies, lofts and half-glimpsed corridors, the open space rising to an arched roof five and a half stories above that was braced by exquisitely carved rafters and a maze of gleaming buttresses. The roof itself was a parquetry of cypress and mahogany set off by a stained glass skylight, darkening now so the reds struck dark wood with the deepening hues of drying blood, by dormers, and by a massive chain supporting a central chandelier so solid that a regiment of "Phantoms of the Opera" could have swung on it to no effect.

"Fan-fucking-tastic," said Harod. "If this is the servants' entrance, show me to the front door."

Sutter frowned at Harod's language while a servant in a blue blazer and gray slacks clicked across an acre of tile to lift Harod's battered carry-on bag and to stand at attention.

"Would you prefer to stay here or in one of the bungalows?" asked Sutter.

"Bungalows?" said Harod. "You mean like cabins?"

"Yes," said Sutter, "if you consider a cottage with five-star accommodations, catered by Maxim's, a cabin. A majority of the guests opt for the bungalows. It is, after all, Summer Camp week."

"Yeah," said Harod, "forget that. I'll take the cushiest room they have here. I've served my time as a Boy Scout."

Sutter nodded at the servant and said, "The Buchanan Suite, Maxwell. Anthony, I'll show you the way in a minute. Come over to the bar."

They walked to a small, mahogany-paneled room off the main hall while the butler took an elevator to the upper levels. Harod poured himself a tall vodka. "Don't tell me this place was built in the seventeen hundreds," he said. "Too damn big."

"Pastor Vanderhoof's original structure was impressive for its time," said Sutter. "Subsequent owners have enlarged the Manse a bit."

"So where is everybody?" asked Harod.

"The less-important guests are arriving now," said Sutter. "The princes, potentates, ex-prime ministers, and oil sheiks will be arriving for the customary Opening Brunch tomorrow at eleven in the morning. We get our first glimpse of an ex-president on Wednesday."

"Whoopee," said Harod. "Where's Barent and Kepler?"

"Joseph will be joining us later this evening," said the evangelist. "Our host will arrive tomorrow."

Harod thought of his last sight of Maria Chen at the railing of the yacht. Kepler had told him earlier that all female aides, adjutants, executive secretaries, mistresses, and a few wives who could not be jettisoned earlier were welcome aboard the *Antoinette* while their masters let their hair down on Dolmann Island. "Is Barent aboard his boat?" he asked Sutter.

The airwaves minister spread his hands. "Only the Lord and Christian's pilots know where he is on a day-to-day basis. The next twelve days are the only ones on our host's yearly calendar where a friend—or adversary—would know where to find him."

Harod made a rude sound and took a drink. "Not that it'd help an adversary," he said. "You see the goddamn destroyer on the way in?"

"Anthony," warned Sutter, "I've told you before about taking the Lord's name in vain."

"What are they guarding against?" said Harod. "A landing by Russian marines?"

Sutter replenished his bourbon. "Not too far from the mark, Anthony. A few years ago there was a Russian trawler prowling around a mile off the beach. It had come up from its usual station off Cape Canaveral. I don't have to tell you that, like most Russian trawlers near American shores, this was an intelligence craft loaded down with more sneaky listenin' devices that you could shake a Communist stick at."

"So what the hell could they hear from a mile out at sea?" said Harod.

Sutter chuckled. "I imagine that that shall remain between the Russians and their Antichrist," he said, "but it discomfited our guests and concerned Brother Christian, thus the big mean dog you saw patrolling nearby."

"Some dog," said Harod. "Does all of this security hang around for the second week?"

"Oh, no," said Sutter, "what transpires during the Hunt segment of the summer's entertainment is strictly for our eyes only."

Harod stared hard at the red-cheeked minister. "Jimmy, do you think Willi's going to show next weekend?"

The Reverend Jimmy Wayne Sutter looked up quickly with a flash of his tiny, lively eyes. "Oh yes, Anthony. I have no doubt that Mr. Borden will be here at the prearranged time."

"How do you know that?"

Sutter smiled beatifically, raised his bourbon, and said softly, "It is written in Revelation, Anthony. It has all been prophesied millennia ago. There is nothing we do that has not been carved long ago in the corridors of time by a Sculptor who sees the grain in the stone much more clearly than we ever could."

"Is that so?" said Harod.

"Yes, Anthony, that is so," said Sutter. "You can bet your heathen ass on it."

Harod's thin lips twitched in a smile. "I think I'm already doing that, Jimmy," he said. "I'm not sure I'm ready for this week."

"This week is nothing," said Sutter, closing his eyes and holding the cold glass of bourbon to his cheek. "It is mere prelude, Anthony. Mere prelude."

The week of prelude seemed endless to Harod. He mingled with men whose pictures he had seen in *Time* and *Newsweek* all of his life and found that—except for the aura of power that rose from them like the omnipresent scent of sweat from a world-class jock—they were visibly human, frequently fallible, and all-too-often asinine in their frenzied attempt to escape the boardrooms and situation rooms and conference halls and briefing sessions that served as the iron bars and cages of their rich and powerful lives.

On Wednesday night, June 10, Harod found himself lounging in the fifth tier of the Campfire Ampitheatre, watching a vice-president of the World Bank, a crown prince of the third richest oil-exporting country on the planet, a former U.S. president, and his ex-secretary of state do a hoola dance with mops for hair, halved coconut shells for breasts, and grass skirts made from hastily gathered palm fronds, while eighty-five of the most powerful men in the western hemisphere whistled, shouted, and generally acted like college freshmen on their first public drunk. Harod stared at the bonfire and thought of the rough cut of *The White Slaver*, still on the editing reels at his workshop, now three weeks overdue for the laying down of a soundtrack. The composer-conductor was getting his three thousand a day for doing nothing but cooling his heels at the Beverly Hilton and waiting to lead a full orchestra in a score that was guaranteed to sound just like the score he had done for his past six movies—all romantic woodwinds and heroic brasses made even more indistinguishable by Dolby.

On Tuesday and Thursday, Harod had taken a launch out to the *Antoinette* to see Maria Chen, making love to her in the silk and paneled silences of her stateroom. Then talking with her before heading back to the evening's Summer Camp festivities.

"What do you do out here?" he asked.

"Read," she said. "Work on the Orion treatment. Catch up on the correspondence. Lie in the sun."

"Ever see Barent?"

"Never," said Maria Chen. "Isn't he ashore with you?"

"Yeah, I see him around. He's got the whole west wing of the Manse—him and whoever the top guy is that day. I just wondered if he ever comes out here."

"Worried?" asked Maria Chen. She rolled on her back and brushed dark hair away from her cheek. "Or jealous?"

"Fuck that," said Harod and got out of bed, walking naked to the liquor cabinet. "It'd be better if he was screwing you. Then we might be able to get an angle on what the hell's going on."

Maria Chen slipped from the bed, walked to where Harod stood with his back to her, and slipped her arms around him. Her small, perfect breasts flattened against his back. "Tony," she said, "you are a liar."

Harod turned angrily. She slipped more tightly against him, her left hand cupping him gently.

"You want no one with me," she whispered. "Ever."

"That's bullshit," said Harod. "Pure bullshit."

"No," whispered Maria Chen, moving her lips along his neck between whispers. "It is love. You love me as I love you."

"Nobody loves me," said Harod. He had meant to say it with a laugh, but it came out a choked whisper.

"I love you," said Maria Chen. "and you love me, Tony."

He pushed her to arm's length and glowered at her. "How can you say that?"

"Because it is true."

"Why?"

"Why is it true?"

"No," managed Harod, "why do we love each other?"

"Because we have to," said Maria Chen and led him to the wide, soft bed.

Later, listening to the lap of water and host of subtle boat sounds that he couldn't put a name to, Harod lay with his arm around her, his hand idle on her right breast, his eyes closed, and was afraid, perhaps for the first time since he was old enough to think, of absolutely nothing at all.

The ex-president left on Saturday after the midday luau and by seven P.M. the only guests left were middle- and low-level hangers on, lean and hungry Cassiuses and Iagos in sharkskin suits and Ralph Lauren denim. Harod thought it was a good time to go back to the mainland.

"The Hunt starts tomorrow," said Sutter. "You don't want to miss the festivities."

"I don't want to miss Willi's arrival," said Harod. "Is Barent sure that he's still coming?"

"Before sunset," said Sutter. "That was the final word. Joseph is being coy about his lines of communication to Mr. Borden. Perhaps too coy. I believe Brother Christian is growing annoyed."

"That's Kepler's problem," said Harod. He stepped from the dock onto the deck of the long cabin cruiser.

"Are you sure you need to pick up these extra surrogates?" asked the Reverend Sutter. "We have plenty in the common pool. All young, strong, healthy. Most came from my rehabilitation center for runaways. There are even enough women for you to choose from, Anthony."

"I want a couple of my own," said Harod. "I'll be back late tonight. Early morning at the latest."

"Good," said Sutter and there was a strange glint in his eye. "I wouldn't want you to miss anything. This may prove to be an exceptional year."

Harod nodded good-bye and the launch roared to life and left the harbor slowly, building to speed once beyond the breakwater. Barent's yacht was the last large ship left except for the picket ships and departing destroyer. As always, a speedboat with armed guards approached, visually confirmed Harod's identity, and followed them as they covered the last few hundred yards to the yacht. Maria Chen was waiting by the stern staircase, overnight bag in hand.

The night crossing to the coast was much smoother than the trip out. Harod had requested a car and a small Mercedes was waiting behind Barent's boathouse, courtesy of the Heritage West Foundation.

Harod drove, taking Highway 17 to South Newport and taking I-95 the last thirty miles into Savannah.

"Why Savannah?" asked Maria Chen.

"They didn't say. The guy on the phone just told me where to park—near a canal on the outskirts of town."

"And you think it was the same man who kidnapped you?"

"Yeah," said Harod. "I'm sure of it. Same accent."

"Do you still think it's Willi's doing?" asked Maria Chen.

Harod drove a minute in silence. "Yeah," he said at last, "that's the only thing that makes sense. Barent and the others already have the means to get preconditioned people into the surrogate pool if that's what they want. Willi needs an edge."

"And you're willing to go along with it? You still feel loyalty toward Willi Borden?"

"Fuck loyalty," said Harod. "Barent sent Haines into my house . . . beating you up . . . just to pull my chain tighter. Nobody treats me that way. If this is Willi's long shot, then what the fuck. Let him go for it."

"Couldn't it be dangerous?"

"The surrogates you mean?" said Harod. "I don't see how. We'll make sure they're not armed and once they get on the island there's not a chance in hell they could create a problem. Even the winner of that fucking five-day splatter Olympics ends up six feet under mangrove roots in an old slave cemetery up the island somewhere."

"So what is Willi trying to do?" she asked.

"Beats the shit out of me," said Harod, exiting at the I-16 interchange. "All we have to do is watch and stay alive. Which reminds me—you bring the Browning?"

Maria Chen removed the automatic from her purse and handed it to him. Driving with one hand, Harod slid the ammunition clip from the handle, checked it, and pressed it back in against his thigh. He tucked it into his waistband, pulling his loose Hawaiian shirt over it.

"I hate guns," Maria Chen stated flatly.

"I do too," said Harod. "But there are people I hate more, and one of them's that bastard with the ski mask and the Polack accent. If he's the surrogate Willi's going to send with me to the island, it'll be everything I can do to keep from blowing his brains out before we start."

"Willi would not be pleased," said Maria Chen.

Harod nodded, turning off the side road that had led from the highway to an abandoned boat launch area along an overgrown section of the Savannah & Ogeechee Canal. A car was waiting, a station wagon. Harod parked sixty feet away as prearranged and blinked his headlights. A man and a woman got out of the car and walked slowly toward them.

"I'm tired of worrying about what'll please Willi or please Barent or please fucking anybody," Harod said through gritted teeth. He stepped out of the car and pulled the automatic loose. Maria Chen opened her overnight bag and removed the chains and padlocks. When the man and woman were twenty feet away, hands still empty, Harod leaned toward Maria Chen and grinned. "It's time they all began worrying about how to please Tony Harod," he said and raised the pistol, aiming it steadily and precisely at the head of the man with the short beard and long graying hair over the ears. The man stopped, stared at the muzzle of Harod's pistol, and adjusted his glasses with his index finger.

SIXTY-ONE

Dolmann Island
Sunday, June 14, 1981

S aul Laski felt as if he had been through it all before.

It was after midnight when the boat bumped against the concrete dock and Tony Harod herded both Saul and Miss Sewell off. They stood on the dock, Harod no longer showing the weapon since these were two catspaws he was supposed to be controlling. Two electric golf carts glided up and Harod said to a man in a blazer and slacks, "Take these two to the surrogate pens."

Saul and Miss Sewell sat passively in the middle seat of the cart as a man with an automatic rifle stood behind them. Saul glanced at the woman next to him; her face showed no emotion or interest. She wore no makeup, her hair was clipped back, and her inexpensive print dress hung loosely on her. As they stopped at a checkpoint on the south end of the security zone and then rolled forward through a no-man's-land paved with crushed shells, Saul wondered what, if anything, was being relayed to Natalie via Melanie Fuller's six-year-old familiar.

The concrete installation beyond the north fence of the security zone was awash with bright lights. Ten other surrogates had just arrived and Saul and Miss Sewell joined them in a concrete courtyard the size of a basketball court surrounded by high barbed wire fences.

There were no blue blazers and gray slacks on this side of the security zone. Men in green coveralls and black nylon baseball caps stood cradling automatic weapons. From Cohen's notes, Saul was sure that these were members of Barent's private security force, and from interrogating Harod two months earlier, he was equally sure that every one of them had been conditioned to some extent by their master.

A tall man with a holstered sidearm stepped forward and said, "Awright, people, *strip!*"

The dozen prisoners, mostly young men although Saul could see two women—little more than girls—near the forefront, looked at each other dully. All of them seemed drugged or in shock. Saul knew the look. He had seen it approaching the Pit at Chelmno and leaving the trains at Sobibor. He and Miss Sewell began discarding their clothing while most of the others stood where they were and did nothing.

"I said *strip!*" shouted the man with the sidearm and another guard with a rifle stepped forward and clubbed the nearest prisoner, a boy of eighteen or nineteen with thick glasses and an overbite. The boy pitched forward without a word, his face striking the concrete. Saul could clearly hear his teeth breaking. The nine other young people began taking off their clothes.

Miss Sewell finished first. Saul noticed that her body looked younger and smoother than her face except for a livid appendectomy scar.

They put the prisoners into lines without segregating men from women and marched them down a long concrete ramp into the earth. Out of the corner of his eye, Saul caught glimpses of doors leading to tiled corridors running off from this central subterranean avenue. Security men in coveralls came to doorways to watch as the surrogates were marched by and once the two lines had to press against the walls as a convoy of four Jeeps came by, filling the tunnel with noise and carbon monoxide fumes. Saul wondered if the entire island was honeycombed with security tunnels.

They were marched into a bare, brightly lighted room where men in white coats and surgical gloves looked in mouths, anuses, and the women's vaginas. One of the young women began sobbing until she was slapped into silence by a guard.

Saul felt strangely calm even as he wondered where these other surrogates had come from, if they had been Used yet, and how his own behavior might visibly differ from theirs. From the examination room they were led down a long, narrow hall seemingly cut from the stone of the island itself. The dripping walls were painted white and small, hemispherical niches in the rock held naked, silent forms.

As the line stopped for Miss Sewell to enter her hole in the rock, Saul realized that full-size cells were not required because no one would be kept on the island longer than a week. Then it was Saul's turn.

The niches were staggered at different heights, tiers of crescent-shaped cracks with steel bars set in white stone, and Saul's niche was four feet above the ground. He rolled into it. The stone was cool against his flesh, the ledge just long enough to lie full length. A gutter and foul-smelling hole carved into the rear of the shelf showed him where he would relieve himself. The bars slid hydraulically from the roof of the niche into deep holes in the shelf, with the exception of a slit that left a two-inch gap where food trays must be inserted.

Saul lay on his back and stared at the stone fifteen inches from his face. Somewhere down the corridor a man began to cry out in a ragged voice. There were footsteps and the sounds of blows on metal and flesh, and silence returned. Saul felt calm. He was committed. In a strangely intimate way, he felt closer to his family—his parents, Josef, Stefa—than he had for decades.

Saul felt his eyes closing and he forced them open, rubbed them, and set his glasses back in place. Strange they let him keep his glasses. Saul tried to remember if they had let the naked prisoners wear their glasses to the Pit at Chelmno. No. He remembered being part of a detail that shoveled hundreds of glasses, thousands of glasses, great heaps of glasses, from a room onto a crude conveyor belt where other prisoners separated the glass from the metal, the precious metals from steel. Nothing was wasted in the Reich. Only people.

He forced his eyes open, pinched his cheeks. The stone was hard, but he knew he could slide into sleep with little trouble. Slide into dreams. He had not truly slept for three weeks as each night the onset of dream state, rapid eye movement, triggered the posthypnotic suggestions which now formed his dreams. He had not needed the stimulus of the bell for eight nights now. REM alone triggered the dreams.

Were they dreams or memories? Saul no longer knew. The dream-memories had become reality. His days with Natalie, preparing, planning, and plotting were dreams. That is why he felt so calm. The dark, the cold corridor, the naked prisoners, the cell—all this was much closer to his dream-reality, the unrelenting, self-induced memories of the camps, than were the hot summer days in Charleston watching Natalie and the child Justin. Natalie and the dead thing that looked like a child . . .

Saul tried to think of Natalie. He squeezed his eyes shut tightly until they filled with tears, opened them wide, and thought of Natalie.

It was two days earlier, three now, a Thursday, when Natalie had come up with the solution. "Saul," she cried, setting down the maps and turning toward him as they sat at the small table in the motel kitchenette, "we *don't* have to do this alone. We *can* have somebody at the extraction while someone else watches in Charleston!" Behind her, blown-up photographs of Dolmann Island covered one wall of the kitchen in a grainy mosaic.

Saul had shaken his head, too stupid with fatigue to respond to her enthusiasm. "How? They're all gone, Natalie. All dead. Rob, Aaron, Cohen. Meeks will be flying the plane."

"No—someone!" she said and slapped her forehead with the heel of her hand. "All these weeks I've been thinking there's *someone*—someone with a vested interest. And I can get them tomorrow. I won't be seeing Melanie until our Saturday morning session at the park."

She told him then, and eighteen hours later he watched as she disembarked from the flight from Philadelphia, a black man on either side of her. Jackson looked older than he had just six months earlier, his balding head gleaming under the bright terminal lights, his face set in lines that declared a final, tacit state of neutrality with the world. The youth to Natalie's right might have been an antimatter opposite of Jackson's: tall, skinny, loose limbed, with a face so fluid that expressions and reactions flowed across it like light on a mercurial surface. The young man's high, loud laughter echoed in the terminal corridor and caused heads to turn. Saul remembered that the man's nickname was Catfish.

Later, during the drive into Charleston, Jackson said, "Laski you sure this's Marvin we talking about?"

"It's Marvin," said Saul. "But he's . . . different."

"Voodoo Lady got him good?" asked Catfish. He was fiddling with the car radio, trying to find a good station.

"Yes," said Saul, still not believing that he was talking to anyone besides Natalie about this. "But there may be a chance we can recover him . . . rescue him."

"Yeah, man, we going to do that," said Catfish. "One word to our main men and Soul Brickyard'll be all over this cracker city like a rubber on a trick's dick, you know?"

"No," said Saul, "that won't work. Natalie must have told you why."

"She told us," said Jackson. "But what do you say, Laski? How long do we wait?"

"Two weeks," said Saul. "One way or the other it'll be all over in two weeks."

"Two weeks you got," said Jackson. "Then we'll do whatever we have to do to get Marvin back, whether your part is finished or not."

"It will be finished," said Saul. He looked at the big man sitting in the backseat. "Jackson, I don't know whether that's your first or last name."

"Last," said Jackson. "I gave up my first name when I came back from Nam. Didn't have any use for it anymore."

"My name ain't really Catfish, neither, Laski," said Catfish. "It Clarence Arthur Theodore Varsh." He shook Saul's preferred hand. "But, hey, man," he said with a grin, "being 'cause you be a friend of Natalie and all, you can call me Mr. Varsh."

The last day before leaving had been the worst. Saul had been sure that nothing would work—the old lady would not come through with her part of the bargain or had not been capable of the conditioning she said she had been carrying out for three weeks in May as Justin and Natalie had stared across the river through binoculars. Or Cohen had been mistaken in his information—or had been correct, but the plans had been changed in the intervening months. Or Tony Harod would not respond to the phone call in early June—or would tell the others once on the island—or would not tell them, but would kill Saul and whomever Melanie Fuller sent as soon as they were out of sight of land. Or he would deliver Saul to the island and then Melanie Fuller would choose that time to turn on Natalie, slaughtering her while Saul was locked away, awaiting his own death.

Then Saturday afternoon arrived and they were driving south to Savannah, getting set in the parking area near the canal even before twilight had faded. Natalie and Jackson hid themselves in underbrush sixty yards to the north, Natalie with the rifle they had pulled from the deputy's vehicle in California and kept separate when they packed away the M-16 and most of the C-4 explosive.

Catfish, Saul, and the thing Justin had referred to as Miss Sewell waited, the two men occasionally drinking coffee from a metal Thermos.

Once the woman's head had swiveled like the head of a ventriloquist's dummy, she stared straight at Saul, and said, "I don't know you."

Saul said nothing, staring back impassively, trying to imagine the mind behind so many years of mindless violence. Miss Sewell had closed her eyes with the mechanical abruptness of a clockwork owl. No one had spoken again until Tony Harod arrived shortly before midnight.

Saul had thought for a second that the diminutive producer was going to shoot during the long seconds he stood aiming the pistol at Saul's face. Tendons had stood out on Harod's throat and Saul could see the trigger finger growing white from tension. Saul had been frightened then, but it was a clean, controllable fear—nothing like the anxiety of the past week or the raging, debilitating fear of the Pit and the hopelessness of his nightly dreams. Whatever happened next, Saul had *chosen* to be there.

In the end, Harod had contented himself with cursing Saul and striking him twice across the face, the second backhanded blow laying open a shallow cut on Saul's right cheek. Saul had not spoken or resisted and Miss Sewell remained equally impassive. Natalie had orders to fire from ambush only if Harod actually shot Saul or Used another to assault him with intent to kill.

Saul and Miss Sewell were put in the backseat of the Mercedes, thin chains wrapped repeatedly around their legs and wrists. Harod's Eurasian secretary—Saul knew from Harrington's and Cohen's reports that her name was Maria Chen—was efficient but careful not to shut off circulation as she pulled the chains tight and set the small locks in place. Saul looked at her quizzically, wondering what had brought her here, what motivated her. He suspected that this had always been the downfall of his people, the eternal Jewish quest for understanding, motivation, and the *reasons* for things, endless Talmudic debates over nuance even as their shallow and efficient enemies chained them securely and carried them off to the ovens; their murderers never worried about the questions of means versus ends or morality as long as the trains ran on time and the paperwork was properly done.

Saul Laski jerked awake just before his slide into the REM state triggered his dreams. He had entered a hundred of the biographies Simon Wiesenthal had provided into the catalog of hypnotically induced personas, but only a dozen kept recurring in the dreams he had conditioned himself to have. He did not dream their faces—despite his hours staring at photographs in Yad Veshem and Lohame HaGeta'ot—because he was looking through their eyes, but the landscapes of their lives, dormitories and workhouses, barbed wire and staring faces, had again become the true landscape of Saul Laski's existence. He realized, as he lay in the stone niche under the rock of Dolmann Island, that he had never really left the landscape of the death camp. In truth, it was the only country of which he was a true citizen.

He knew then, as he teetered on the brink of sleep, whose dreams would claim him that night: Shalom Krzaczek, a man whose face and life he had memorized but which were lost to him now that the details had become induced reality, data lost in the haze of true memories. Saul had never been to the Warsaw Ghetto, but he remembered it nightly now—the line of refugees fleeing the fires through the sewers, excrement tumbling onto them as they crawled through black and narrowing pipes, one at a time, cursing and praying that no one ahead of them would die and block their way as scores of panicked men and women scraped and crawled and forced their way into the Aryan sewers, beyond the wall and the wire and lines of Panzers; Krzaczek leading his nine-year-old grandson Leon through the Aryan sewers where Aryan excrement rained down on them and floated around them as the water rose, choking them, drowning them, then light ahead, and Krzaczek was leading no one, crawling alone into the Aryan sunlight, but turning then, turning, forcing his body back into that narrow, stinking hole after fourteen days in the dark sewers. Going back to find Leon.

Knowing that this would be the first of his dreams that were not dreams, Saul accepted it. And slept.

SIXTY-TWO

Dolmann Island
Sunday, June 14, 1981

Tony Harod watched Willi arrive an hour before sunset on Sunday, the twin-engined executive jet setting down on a smooth runway painted with the shadows of tall oaks. Barent, Sutter, and Kepler joined Harod in the small, air-conditioned terminal at the end of the taxi apron. Harod was so sure that Willi would not be on the plane that when the familiar faces of Tom Reynolds, Jensen Luhar, and then Willi Borden himself appeared, Harod almost gasped in surprise.

No one else seemed shocked. Joseph Kepler made the introductions as if he were an old friend of Willi's. Jimmy Wayne Sutter bowed and smiled enigmatically as he shook Willi's hand. Harod could only stare as they shook hands and Willi said, "You see, my friend Tony, paradise *is* an island." Barent was more than gracious as he pumped Willi's hand in welcome, grasping the producer's elbow in a politician's grip. Willi was dressed in evening clothes: black tie and tails.

"This is a long overdue pleasure." Barent grinned, not releasing Willi's hand.

"*Ja*," said Willi, smiling, "it is."

The entourage moved to the Manse in a convoy of golf carts, picking up aides and bodyguards as they went. Maria Chen greeted Willi in the Great Hall, kissing him on each cheek and beaming at him. "Bill, we're so glad that you're back. We missed you terribly."

Willi nodded. "I have missed your beauty and your wit, my dear," he said and kissed her hand. "Should you ever get tired of Tony's poor manners, please consider my employ." His pale eyes sparkled.

Maria Chen laughed and squeezed his hand. "I hope we all will be working together soon," she said.

"*Ja*, perhaps very soon," said Willi and took her arm as they followed Barent and the others into the dining room.

Dinner was a banquet that lasted until well after nine. There were more than twenty people at the dinner table—only Tony Harod had brought a single aide—but afterward, when Barent led the way to the Game Room in the empty west wing, there were just the five of them.

"We don't start right away, do we?" asked Harod with some alarm. He had no idea whether he could Use the woman he'd brought from Savannah and he had not even seen the other surrogates.

631

"No, not yet," said Barent. "It is customary to conduct Island Club business in the Game Room before choosing the surrogates for tonight's game."

Harod looked around. The room was impressive: part library, part Victorian English club, and part executive boardroom: two walls of books with balconies and ladders, leather chairs with softly glowing lamps, separate snooker and pool tables, and—near the far wall—a massive circular, green-baized table illuminated by a single hanging lamp. Five leather wingback chairs sat in the shadows around the circumference of the table.

Barent touched a button on a recessed panel and heavy curtains silently drew back to reveal thirty feet of window looking down on floodlit gardens and the long tunnel of Live Oak Lane. Harod was sure that the faintly polarized glass was opaque from the outside and quite bulletproof.

Barent held his hand out palm up, as if presenting the room and the view to Willi Borden. Willi nodded and sat in the nearest leather chair. The overhead lighting transformed his face into a lined mask and set his eyes in pools of darkness. "*Ja*, very nice," he said. "Whose chair is this?"

"It was . . . ah . . . Mr. Trask's" said Barent. "It seems fitting that it is now yours."

The others sat, Sutter pointing Harod to the proper chair. Harod sank into the aged, luxurious leather, folded his hands on the baize tabletop, and thought of Charles Colben's body feeding fish for the three days until they had found it in the dark waters of the Schuylkill River. "Not a bad clubhouse," he said. "What do we do now—learn the secret oath and sing songs?"

Barent chuckled indulgently and looked around the circle. "The twenty-seventh annual session of the Island Club is now convened," he said. "Is there any old business?" Silence. "New business that needs to be dealt with tonight?"

"Will there be other plenary sessions when new business can be discussed?" asked Willi.

"Of course," said Kepler. "Anyone can call a session at any time this week except when the games are actually in progress."

Willi nodded. "In that case I will save my new business until a future session." He smiled at Barent, his teeth glowing yellowly in the harsh light from above. "I must remember my place as a new member and act accordingly, *nicht wahr*?"

"Not at all," said Barent. "We are all equal around this table . . . peers and friends." Barent looked directly at Harod for the first time. "There being no new business tonight, is everyone ready to tour the surrogate pens and make their choices for tonight?"

Harod nodded, but Willi spoke up. "I would like to use one of my own people."

Kepler frowned slightly. "Bill, I don't know if . . . I mean, you can if you wish, but we try to avoid using our . . . uh . . . permanent people. The chance of winning all five nights is . . . ah . . . quite low, really, and we want to avoid offending anyone or having him depart with bad feelings because of . . . uh . . . losing a valuable resource."

"*Ja*, I understand," said Willi, "but I still would prefer to use one of my own. It is allowed, yes?"

"Yep," said Jimmy Wayne Sutter, "but you have to have him inspected and kept in the surrogate pens just like the others if he survives tonight."

"Agreed," said Willi. He smiled again, increasing Harod's impression that he was listening to an eyeless skull speak. "It is nice of you to humor an old man. Shall we see the pens and choose the pieces for tonight's game?"

It was the first time Harod had been north of the security zone. The underground complex surprised him even though he had known there must be a security headquarters somewhere on the island. Although twenty-five or thirty men in coveralls were visible at guard posts and monitoring rooms, the security seemed almost nonexistent compared to the crush of bodyguards during Summer Camp week. Harod realized that the bulk of Barent's security force must be at sea—billeted on the yacht or the picket ships—concentrating on keeping people *away* from the island. He wondered what these guards thought of the surrogate pens and the games. Harod had worked in Hollywood for two decades; he knew that there was nothing people would not do to other people if the price was right. Sometimes they would line up to do it for free. Harod doubted that Barent would have had trouble finding people for this kind of work even without his unique Ability.

The pens were strange, carved into native rock in a corridor much older and narrower than the rest of the complex. He followed the others past the shelves holding curled, naked forms, and thought for the twentieth time that this was real B-movie stuff. If a writer had presented Harod with a treatment like this he would have strangled the dumb bastard and then had him posthumously kicked out of the Guild.

"These holding pens predate the original Vanderhoof plantation and even the older Dubose place." Barent was saying. "An archaeologist-historian I employed theorized that these particular cells were used by the Spanish to house rebellious elements of the island Indian population, although the Spanish rarely established bases this far north. The cells, at any rate, were carved out prior to 1600 A.D. It is interesting to contemplate the fact that Christopher Columbus was the first slave-master of this hemisphere. He shipped several thousand Indians to Europe and enslaved or killed many thousands more on the islands themselves. He might have wiped out the entire indigenous population if the Pope had not intervened with threats of excommunication."

"The Pope probably stopped it because he wasn't getting a big enough share of the action," said the Reverend Jimmy Wayne Sutter. "Can we pick from any of these?"

"Any except the two Mr. Harod brought in last night," said Barent. "I presume they are for your personal use, Tony?"

"Yeah," said Harod.

Kepler came closer and jostled Harod's elbow. "Jimmy tells me one of them is a man, Tony. Are you changing your preferences or is this a special friend of yours?"

Harod looked at Joseph Kepler's perfectly trimmed hair, perfect teeth, and perfectly tanned skin, and seriously considered reducing the arrangement to something less than perfection. He said nothing.

Willi raised an eyebrow. "A male surrogate, Tony? I leave for only a few weeks and you surprise me. Where is this man you will use?"

Harod stared at the old producer but could detect no message in Willi's countenance. "Down there somewhere," he said, gesturing vaguely down the full length of the corridor.

The group spread out, inspecting bodies like judges at a dog show. Either someone had warned the prisoners to stay quiet or the mere presence of the five quelled any noise immediately, for the only sounds were the echoes of footsteps and a slight trickle of water from the darkest, unused section of the ancient tunnel.

Harod was nervous, going from niche to niche in search of the two he had brought from Savannah. Was Willi playing with him again, Harod wondered, or had he been off on his assessment about what was going on? No, goddammit, it made no sense for any of the others to have him smuggle specially conditioned surrogates onto the island. Unless Kepler or Sutter were up to something. Or Barent was playing an especially cute game. Or unless it was simply a trap to discredit him.

Harod felt sick. He hurried down the corridor, peering through bars at white, frightened faces, wondering if his own looked as terrified.

"Tony," said Willi from twenty paces down the tunnel. There was the snap of command in his voice. "Is *this* your male surrogate?"

Harod hurried over and stared at the man lying on the chest-high ledge. The shadows were deep, gray stubble outlined the man's gaunt cheeks, but Harod was sure it was the man he had brought from Savannah. What the hell was Willi up to?

Willi leaned closer to the bars. The man stared back, eyes red from being awakened. Something beyond recognition seemed to pass between the two. "*Wilkommen in der Hölle, mein Bauer*," Willi said to the man.

"*Geh zum Teufel*, Oberst," said the prisoner through gritted teeth.

Willi laughed, the noise echoing in the narrow corridor, and Harod knew that he had royally fucked up.

Unless Willi was jerking him around.

Barent came up to them, his blow-dried gray hair glowing softly in the light from a bare 60-watt bulb. "Is there something funny, gentlemen?"

Willi clapped Tony oh the shoulder and smiled at Barent. "A little joke that my protégé was telling me, C. Arnold. Nothing more."

Barent looked at both of them, nodded, and moved away down the narrow corridor.

Still holding Harod's shoulder, Willi squeezed until Harod grimaced with the pain. "I hope you know what you are doing, Tony," Willi hissed, his face red. "We will talk later." Willi turned and followed Barent and the others toward the security complex.

Shaken, Harod looked at the man he had been sure was Willi's pawn. Naked, his pale face almost swallowed by shadows, curled on cold stone behind steel bars, the man seemed old, frail, and all but worn away by age and hard times. A livid scar ran the length of his left forearm and his ribs were clearly visible. To Harod, the old man seemed harmless enough; the only possible sense of threat coming from the visible glare of defiance smoldering in the large, sad eyes.

"Tony," called the Reverend Jimmy Wayne Sutter, "hurry and choose your surrogates. We want to return to the Manse and begin our play."

Harod nodded, took a last look at the man behind bars, and moved away, peering intently at faces, trying to find a woman young enough and strong enough, yet easy to dominate for the night's activities.

SIXTY-THREE

Melanie

*W*illi was alive!

Staring through Miss Sewell's eyes, I looked up through the bars of the cage and recognized him at once, even with the light bulb behind his head throwing a halo of harsh light around his remaining white wisps of weasel-fur hair.

Willi alive. Nina had not been lying to me about that at least. I understood almost none of this: Nina and I bringing our sacrificial victims to this vicious feast while Willi—whose life Nina claimed was in imminent danger—laughed and moved freely among his nominal captors.

Willi looked almost the same—perhaps a bit more marked by his self-indulgences than he had been six months earlier. When his face first became clear in the stark light and deep shadow of the corridor, I had Miss Sewell turn away, pulling back into the shadows of her cell before I realized how silly that was. Willi spoke in German to the man Nina's Negress had called Saul, welcoming him to hell. The man had told Willi to go to the devil, Willi had laughed and said something to a younger man with reptilian eyes, and then a very handsome gentleman came up. Willi addressed him as C. Arnold, and I knew that this must be the legendary Mr. Barent that Miss Sewell had done research on. Even in the harsh light and the squalid surroundings of this tunnel, I could tell at once that here was a man of noble bearing and refinement. His voice held the educated Cambridge accent of my beloved Charles, his dark blazer was exquisitely tailored, and if Miss Sewell's research was correct, he was one of the eight richest men in the world. I suspected that this was a man who could appreciate my own maturity and genteel upbringing, someone who would understand me. I had Miss Sewell move closer to the bars, look up, and half close her eyes with a provocative lowering of lashes. Mr. Barent did not seem to notice. He walked away even before Willi and his young friend left.

"What's going on?" asked Nina's Negress, the one who had called herself Natalie.

I had Justin turn toward her in anger. "See for yourself."

"I can't right now," said the colored girl. "As I explained before, at this distance the contact is imperfect." The girl's eyes were luminous in the candlelight as we sat in the parlor. I could see no trace of Nina's cornsilk blue in those muddy brown irises.

"Then how can you keep control, my dear?" I asked, Justin's slight lisp making my voice even sweeter than I had intended.

"Conditioning," said Nina's catspaw. "What is going on?"

I sighed. "We are still in the little cells, Willi was just here . . ."

"Willi!" cried the girl.

"Why so surprised, Nina? You yourself told me that Willi had been ordered to be there. Were you lying when you said that you have been in touch with him?"

"Of course not," snapped the girl, recovering her composure in that quick, sure way that did remind me of Nina. "But I've not seen him in some time. Does he look well?"

"No," I snapped. I hesitated, decided to test her. "Mr. Barent was there," I said.

"Oh?"

"He is very . . . impressive."

"Yes, he is, isn't he?"

Was there a hint of coyness there? "I see why you allowed him to talk to you into betraying me, Nina, dear," I said. "Did you . . . sleep with him?" I hated the absurd aphorism, but I could think of no less crude way to confront her with the question.

The colored girl merely stared at me and for the hundredth time I silently cursed Nina for Using this . . . *servant* . . . in place of a person I could treat as an equal. Even the loathsome Miss Barrett Kramer would have been preferable as an interlocutor.

We sat in silence for some time, the Negress lost in whatever reverie Nina placed in her head and my own attention divided among my new family, Miss Sewell's limited sensory impressions of cold stone and the empty corridor, Justin's careful monitoring of Nina's catspaw, and the final, most tenuous of touches in the mind of our new friend at sea. This final contact was by far the hardest to maintain—not merely because of distance, for distance had ceased to be much of an obstacle since my illness—but because the connection had to remain subtle to the point of invisibility until that moment when Nina decreed otherwise.

Or so she thought. I had accepted the challenge because of my need to play along with Nina at the time and because of her somewhat childish taunt that it would not be possible for me to establish and maintain such a contact with someone I had seen only through binoculars. But now that I had proven my point, I had little need to follow the rest of Nina's plan. This was especially true now that I better understood the severe limitations that death had placed on Nina's Ability. I doubt if she could have Used someone at a distance of almost two hundred miles *before* our disagreement six months earlier in Charleston, but I was sure that she would *not* have revealed her weakness or placed herself in a situation where she was in any way dependent upon me.

As she was dependent now. The Negress sat in my parlor, wearing a loose and strangely lumpy sweater over her drab dress, and to all intents and purposes Nina was blind and deaf. Whatever happened on the island would be known to her now—I was increasingly convinced—only if I told her. I did not believe her for a second when she said that she had intermittent control over the catspaw called Saul. I had touched his mind for the merest fraction of a second during the boat trip out, and although I glimpsed the resonances of someone who had been Used—massively Used at some time in the past—and also sensed something else, something layered and latent and potentially dangerous, as if Nina had booby-trapped his mind in some inexplicable manner, I also sensed that this was a person not under her present control. I knew how limited the Use of even the most adequately conditioned catspaw was when conditions changed or unexpected contingencies arose. Of all of our merry trio through years past, I had held the honor of having the strongest Ability when it came to conditioning my people. Nina had teased me that it was because I was afraid to move on to new conquests; Willi had been contemptuous of any sort of long-term relationship, moving from catspaw to catspaw with the same shallow alacrity he moved from one bed partner to the next.

No, Nina was doomed to disappointment if she hoped to be effective on the island only through a conditioned instrument. And at this point I felt the balance shift between us—after all these years!—so that the next move would be mine to make at my own choosing of time and place and circumstance.

But I did so want to know where Nina was.

The Negress in my parlor—in the parlor! Father would have died!—sipped her tea in the mindless ignorance of the fact that as soon as I had an alternate route of tracing Nina's whereabouts, this particular colored instrument of my embarrassment would be eliminated in such a way that even Nina would be impressed with my originality.

I could wait. Every hour improved the strength of my position and weakened Nina's.

The grandfather clock in the hall had just struck eleven, Justin was on the verge of dozing, when the jailers in their drab overalls crashed open the ancient iron door at the end of the corridor and hydraulically raised the bars on five cages. Miss Sewell's cell was not one opened, nor was Nina's catspaw's on the niche above.

I watched the four men and one woman walk by, obviously already being Used, and I realized with a strong shock of recognition that the tall, heavily muscled Negro was the one Willi had shown difficulty handling at our last Reunion—Jensen something.

I was curious. Using every last shred of my enhanced Ability, dimming my awareness of Justin, the family, the man asleep in his small, softly pitching wardroom, *everyone*—even myself—I was able to project myself to one of the guards with enough control to receive at least dim sensory impressions, somewhat like watching a dull reflection of a poorly tuned television, while the group walked the length of the corridor, passed the iron doors and ancient portcullis, passed down the same subterranean avenue we had entered by, and climbed the long, dark ramp toward the smell of rotting vegetation and the tropical night.

SIXTY-FOUR

Dolmann Island
Monday, June 15, 1981

On the second night, Harod had no choice but to try to Use the man he had brought from Savannah.

The first night had been a nightmare for him. It had been very difficult to control the woman he had chosen—a tall, solid, strong-jawed Amazon with small breasts and hair chopped off in an unappealing manner, one of Sutter's born-again street people that he kept isolated and well fed each year at the Bible Outreach Institute until the Island Club needed a surrogate. But she was a poor surrogate; Harod had to use every ounce of his Ability just to get her to walk with the four male surrogates to the clearing fifty yards beyond the north fence of the security zone. A large pentagram had been burned into the soil there with a chalked circle at each point of the star. The other four took their places—Jensen Luhar walking to his circle with strong, sure strides—and waited while Harod's female staggered drunkenly to her place. Harod knew there were many excuses: he was used to controlling women at closer, more intimate distances, this one was far too masculine for his tastes, and—not the least of factors—he was terrified.

The other men at the great, round table in the Game Room sat comfortably in their chairs as Harod fidgeted and squirmed, fighting to keep contact with the woman and move her to the right place. When he did have her standing still in the approximate center of her circle, he returned his attention to the room and nodded, wiping sweat from his cheek and brow.

"Very well," said C. Arnold Barent with more than a hint of condescension in his voice, "we appear to be ready. You all know the rules. If anyone survives until sunrise but fails to make a kill, fifteen points will be awarded but the surrogate will be terminated. If your surrogate amasses one hundred points by eliminating the others *before* sunrise, he . . . or she . . . may be used in tomorrow night's game if you so choose. Is this clear to our new players?"

Willi smiled. Harod nodded tersely.

"Just a reminder," said Kepler, resting his forearm on the deep baize and turning toward Harod, "if your surrogate is removed early, you may watch the rest of the game from the monitor room next door. There are more than seventy cameras on the northern part of the island. The coverage is quite good."

"Not as good as remaining in the game though," said Sutter. A film of perspiration beaded the minister's forehead and upper lip.

"Gentlemen," said Barent, "if we are quite ready. The starshell will be fired in thirty seconds. At its signal, we will commence."

The first night was a nightmare for Harod. The others had closed their eyes and taken immediate control while he had struggled just to reestablish full contact during most of the thirty-second preparatory period.

Then he was in her mind, feeling the jungle breeze on her bare skin, sensing as her small nipples rose in the cool night air, and becoming vaguely aware that Jensen Luhar was leaning from his circle ten feet away, pointing at her—at Harod—and saying with that peculiar leering smile of Willi's, "You will be last, Tony. I will save you for last."

Then the red flare exploded three hundred feet above the canopy of palmetto fronds, the four men moved, and Harod turned his surrogate and had her flee headfirst into the jungle to the north.

Hours passed in a fever dream of branches and insects and the adrenaline rush of fear—his and his surrogate's—and an endless, headlong, stumbling rush through jungle and swamp. Several times he had been sure that he was almost to the north end of the island only to emerge from trees to find the line of the security zone fence ahead of him.

He tried to develop a strategy, create some enthusiasm for a course of action, but all he could do as the hours eroded toward morning was block his reception of pain from his surrogate's bleeding feet and skin lacerated from a thousand branches and have her flee, a heavy stick held uselessly in her hands.

The game was not thirty minutes old when Harod heard the first scream in the night, not fifty feet from where he had hidden her in a small canebrake. When he had his surrogate emerge ten minutes later, crawling on all fours, he saw the corpse of the heavyset blond man Sutter had been Using, the handsome face staring into the dirt on a neck twisted 180 degrees from the front of the body.

Hours later, shortly after he emerged from a swamp infested with snakes, Harod's surrogate screamed as Kepler's tall, thin Puerto Rican leaped from cover and struck her repeatedly with a heavy branch. Harod felt her go down and rolled her to one side, but not in time as a second blow landed across her back, Harod blocked the pain but felt the stunning numbness spread through her as the Puerto Rican, laughing insanely, raised the blunt limb for a final blow.

The javelin—a peeled and sharpened sapling—flew out of the darkness to pierce the Puerto Rican's throat, fourteen inches of bloodied spear-point protruding where the man's Adam's apple had been a second before. Kepler's surrogate clutched at his neck, went to his knees, fell sideways into a thick nest of ferns, kicked twice, and died. Harod forced his woman to all fours, then to one knee, as Jensen Luhar walked into the clearing, pulled the crude spear from the corpse's neck, and lifted the dripping point to within inches of her eyes. "One more, Tony," said the huge black with a smile that gleamed in the starlight, "then it is your turn. Enjoy the hunt, *mein Freund*." Luhar tapped Harod's surrogate once on the shoulder and was gone, blending into the night.

Harod had her run along the narrow beach, heedless of the threat of being seen, stumbling over rocks and roots in the narrow strip of dirt, falling into the surf where there was no beach, always moving farther away from where he thought Luhar might be—where Willi might be.

He had not seen Barent's man with the crew cut and wrestler's physique since the beginning of the game but knew instinctively that the surrogate would have no chance against Luhar. Harod found a perfect place to hide deep in the vine-filled ruins of the old slave plantation. He made his surrogate wedge her bruised and torn body deep in the web of leaves, trailers, ferns, and old beams along a burned-out wall in the deepest corner of the ruins. He would not receive any points for a kill, but the fifteen points for surviving until sunrise would put him on the board, and he would not have to be with his surrogate when Barent's security patrol terminated her.

It was almost dawn and Harod and his surrogate were on the verge of dozing, staring dazedly up through a hole in the foliage at a small patch of sky in which clouds and dimming stars exchanged places, when Jensen Luhar's face appeared there, the grin grown wide and cannibalistic. Harod screamed as the huge hand descended, dragging her up by her hair, throwing her into the sharp-edged pile of rubble at the far end of the slave house.

"Game is over, Tony," said Luhar/Willi, his black body, oiled in sweat and blood, blocking out the stars as he leaned over Harod.

Harod's surrogate was beaten and raped before Luhar grabbed her face and the back of her head and snapped her neck with a single, sharp twist. Only the kill added points to Willi's score; the rape was permitted but irrelevant. The game clock showed that Harod's surrogate died two minutes and ten seconds before sunrise, thus denying him his fifteen points.

The players slept late on Monday. Harod awoke last, showering and shaving in a daze and going down to an elaborate buffet brunch shortly before noon. There was laughter and story-telling among the other four players, everyone congratulating Willi—Kepler laughingly vowing revenge in that night's play, Sutter talking about beginner's luck, and Barent being his sincere, smiling self while telling Willi how good it was to have him aboard. Harod took two Bloody Marys from the man at the bar and sat in a remote corner to brood.

Jimmy Wayne Sutter talked to him first, approaching across an expanse of black and white tile while Harod was working on his third Bloody Mary. "Anthony, my boy," said Sutter as they stood alone by the broad doors to the terrace that looked down a long swale to the sea cliffs, "you'll have to do better tonight. Brother Christian and the others are looking for style and enthusiasm, not necessarily points. Use the man tonight, Anthony, and show them that they made the right decision letting you into the club." Harod had stared and said nothing.

Kepler approached him while they were all touring the Summer Camp facilities for Willi's edification. Kepler bounded up the last ten steps of the ampitheater and gave Harod his Charlton Heston grin. "Not bad, Harod," he said, "almost made it to sunup. But let me give you a little advice, OK, kid? Mr. Barent and the others want to see a little initiative. You brought your own male surrogate along. Use him tonight . . . if you can."

Barent had Harod ride with him in his electric cart as they returned to the Manse. "Tony," said the billionaire, smiling softly at Harod's sullen silence, "we're very pleased you've joined us this year. I think it might sit well with the other players if you worked with a male surrogate as soon as possible. But only if you want to, of course. There's no hurry." They rode in silence to the estate.

Willi came last, confronting Harod as he left the Manse to join Maria Chen on the beach in the hour before the evening meal. Harod had slipped out a side door and was finding his way through winding garden paths recessed below ground level, the maze further complicated by high banks of ferns and flowers, when he crossed a small, ornamental bridge, turned left through a miniature Zen garden, and came across Willi sitting on a long white bench, looking like a pale spider in an iron web. Tom Reynolds stood behind the bench, his dull eyes, lank blond hair, and long fingers making Harod think—not for the first time—that Willi's second favorite catspaw looked like a rock star turned executioner.

"Tony," murmured Willi in his husky, accented tones, "it is time we talked."

"Not now," said Harod and started to pass. Reynolds slid sideways to block his path.

"Do you know what you are doing, Tony?" Willi asked softly.

"Do you?" snapped Harod, knowing instantly how feeble it sounded, wanting only to be away from there.

"*Ja*," murmured Willi, "I do. And if you tamper with things now, you will be destroying years of effort and planning."

Harod looked around, realizing that they were out of sight of the Manse and of the security cameras in this flowered cul-de-sac. He would not retrace his steps to the estate and Reynolds still blocked the way out. "Look," Harod said, hearing his voice rise with tension, "I don't give a fuck about any of this and I don't have the least fucking idea what you're talking about and I just *don't fucking want to be involved*, okay?"

Willi smiled. His eyes did not seem human. "*Ja*, that is very well, Tony. But we are in the final moves here and I will not be interfered with. Is that clear?"

Something in his former partner's voice made Harod more afraid than he had ever been in his life. He could not speak for a moment.

Willi's tone changed, becoming almost conversational. "I presume you found my Jew when I was finished with him in Philadelphia," he said. "Either you or Barent. It does not matter, even if they ordered you to play this gambit for them."

Harod started to speak, but Willi held up his hand and silenced him. "Play the Jew tonight, Tony. I have no further use for him and I *do* have a place for you in my plans after this week . . . *if* you offer no complications beyond this point. *Klar?* Is this clear, Tony?" The slate-colored, executioner's eyes bored into Harod's brain.

"It's clear," managed Harod. In a second's vivid, hallucinatory vision, Harod realized that Willi Borden, Wilhelm von Borchert, *was* dead, that Harod was staring at a corpse, and that it was not just a skull smiling at him like something sculpted from sharp-edged bone, but a skull that was a repository of millions of other skulls with a shark-toothed maw that breathed out the stink of the charnel house and the mass grave.

"*Sehr gut*," said Willi. "I will see you later, Tony, in the Game Room."

Reynolds moved aside with the same simulacrum of Willi's smile that Harod had seen on Jensen Luhar's face the night before, seconds before the black snapped the neck of Harod's surrogate.

Harod went down to the beach and joined Maria Chen. He could not stop shivering, even on the hot sand in the glare of the hot sun.

Maria Chen touched his arm. "Tony?"

"Fuck it," he said, his teeth chattering violently. "Fuck it. They can have the Jew. Whoever's behind it, whatever they're doing, they can have him tonight. Fuck it. Fuck them. Fuck them all."

The banquet on the second night was subdued, as if each of them was contemplating the hours ahead. All but Harod and Willi had visited the surrogate pens earlier in the day, choosing their favorites with the care usually given to inspecting thoroughbred race horses. Barent let it be known at dinner that he would be using a Jamaican deaf mute that he had brought and submitted for inspection—a man who had fled his home islands after murdering four men in a family feud. Kepler took some time in choosing his second surrogate, giving special attention to the younger men, twice passing Saul's cage without looking carefully. In the end he chose one of Sutter's born-again street orphans, a tall, lean boy with strong legs and shoulder-length hair. "A greyhound," Kepler said at dinner. "A greyhound with teeth." Sutter also relied on a conditioned catspaw this second night, announcing that he would be using a man named Amos who had served him as a personal bodyguard at the Bible Outreach Center for two years. Amos was a short, powerful-looking man with a bandit's mustache and a linebacker's neck and shoulders.

Willi appeared to be content to use Jensen Luhar a second night. Harod said only that he would be using a man—the Jew—and took part in none of the rest of the conversation that evening.

Barent and Kepler had made bets of more than ten thousand dollars on the outcome of the previous night's game and they doubled it this night. All agreed that the stakes had grown unusually high, the competition unusually fierce, for only the second night of the tournament.

The sunset Monday night was obscured by clouds and Barent announced that the barometer was dropping rapidly as a storm approached from the southeast. At 10:30 P.M. they adjourned from the dinner table, left bodyguards and aides behind, and took the teak-lined private elevator to the Game Room.

Behind locked doors, the single hanging light shone on the great green table and turned the five faces to shadowed masks. Through the long window, lightning was visible as it rippled along the horizon. Barent had ordered the compound and garden floodlights switched off so as not to compete with the storm's splendor, and now all eyes were on the lightning in the lull before Barent said, "The starshell will be fired in thirty seconds. At its signal we will commence."

Four of them closed their eyes, faces tense with expectation. Harod turned to watch the white flashes to the southeast show silhouettes of trees along Live Oak Lane and illuminate the interiors of the blue-black storm clouds themselves.

He had no idea what would happen when they removed the bars holding the Jew named Saul. Harod had no intention of touching the man's mind and without a surrogate he would be out of touch with the night's events. It suited Harod perfectly. Whatever was going on, whoever was stacking the proverbial deck by bringing in the Jew, however they planned to use their advantage, it meant very little to Tony Harod. He knew that he would have nothing to do with the events of the next six hours, that this was one game he would sit out completely. Of that he was sure.

Harod never had been so wrong.

SIXTY-FIVE

Dolmann Island
Monday, June 15, 1981

S aul had been imprisoned in the tiny cell for more than twenty-four hours when a mechanism in the stone walls whined and the steel bars slid up. For a second he did not know what to do.

He had been strangely at ease with his imprisonment, almost content, as if forty superfluous years had slipped away, returning him to the essential moments of his life. For twenty hours he lay in the cold, stone niche and thought about life, remembering in complete detail the evening walks with Natalie near the farm at Caesarea, the sunlight on the sand and bricks and the lazy green swells from the Mediterranean. He remembered conversations and laughter, confidences and tears, and when he slept the dreams took him immediately, carrying him to other affirmations of life in the face of brutal abnegations.

Guards slipped food through the slot twice a day and Saul ate it. The low plastic trays were filled with dehydrated freeze-dried stews, meat, and noodles. Astronaut food. Saul did not wonder at the irony of the space shuttle meals in a seventeenth-century slave pen; he ate everything, drank the water, and continued with his exercises to keep his muscles from cramping, his body from growing too chilled.

His one great concern was for Natalie. Each had known for months what they would have to do and how alone they would have to be to do it, but the actual parting had held the flavor of finality. Saul thought of the sunlight on his father's back, Josef's arm over his father's shoulder.

Saul lay in the darkness that smelled of four centuries of fear and he thought about courage. He thought about the Africans and American natives that had lain in these very stone cages, smelling—as he was smelling— the scent of human hopelessness, not knowing that they would prevail, their descendents demanding the light and freedom and dignity denied those who awaited death or chains there. He closed his eyes and immediately saw the cattle cars rolling into Sobibor, the emaciated bodies intertwined, cold corpses huddling for a warmth that could not be found, but even through that image of frozen flesh and accusing eyes he also saw the young Sabra of the kibbutzim going out for morning work in the orchards or arming themselves for evening perimeter patrol, their eyes stern and confident, too confident perhaps, but alive, so very alive: their very existence an answer to the questioning eyes of the cattle car corpses being pried from one another on a frost-lined siding in 1944.

Saul worried about Natalie and was afraid for himself, terribly afraid, with the testes-raising fear of blades approaching the eyes and cold steel in the mouth, but he recognized the fear and welcomed it back—knowing very well that it had never left—and let it flow through him and past him rather than over him. A thousand times he rehearsed what he wanted to do and what might stop him. He reviewed his options. He considered courses of action should Natalie keep the old woman on track precisely as planned and other actions in the more probable event that Melanie Fuller would act as unpredictably as her madness predicted. If Natalie died, he would go ahead. If nothing went as planned, he would go ahead. If there was no hope at all, he would go ahead.

Saul lay in the dark crack in cold stone and thought about life and contemplated death, his own and others'. He reviewed every possible contingency and then invented more.

And even then, when the bars slid up and out of sight and the four others stirred and slid from their recesses and walked toward the distant opening, Saul Laski, for an eternal minute, did not know what to do.

Then he slid from his own niche and stood. The stone floor was cold under his bare feet. The thing that had been Constance Sewell stared up at him through steel bars and a veil of tangled hair.

Saul hurried to follow the others toward the doorway into darkness.

Tony Harod sat in the Game Room and stared from under lowered lids at the faces of the four men awaiting the beginning of the night's competition. Barent's face was calm and composed, his fingers steepled beneath his lower lip, a slight smile moving the muscles at the corners of his mouth. Kepler's head tilted back as he frowned with the effort of concentration. Jimmy Wayne Sutter sat forward, arms on the green baize of the table, sweat on his furrowed forehead and long upper lip. Willi sat back so deeply in his chair that the light touched only brow, sharp cheeks, and the blade of his nose. Still, Harod had the strong impression that Willi's eyes were open, staring at him.

Harod himself felt panic rise in him as he realized the absurdity of his position; there was no way he could know what was going on. He did not wish to even try to touch the Jew-surrogate's consciousness and knew that even if he did try, whoever was controlling the Jew would not allow him access. Harod scanned the faces a final time. Who could be handling two surrogates at once? Logic dictated that it had to be Willi—both motive and the extent of the old man's ability suggested it—but then why the ruse in the garden? Harod was confused and frightened. It was little consolation at that moment that Maria Chen was waiting downstairs or that she had smuggled her gun onto the boat waiting at the island's dock should there be need for a sudden departure.

"What the goddamn hell!" shouted Joseph Kepler. All four men had opened their eyes and were staring at Harod.

Willi leaned forward into the light, his face a reddened mask of fury.

"What are you doing, Tony?" The cold glare swept over the other men. "Or *is* it Tony? Is this the way you play your games of honor?"

"Wait! Wait!" cried Sutter, his eyes closed again. "Look. He's running. We can . . . all of us together . . ."

Barent's eyes had snapped open like a predator waking for the night's stalk. "Of course," he said softly, fingers still steepled. "Laski, the psychiatrist. I should have noticed earlier. The lack of a beard fooled me. Whoever thought of this has a very poor sense of what constitutes a prank."

"Prank my ass," said Kepler, his eyes tightly shut again. "Get him."

Barent shook his head. "No, gentlemen, because of the irregularities here, tonight's competition is canceled. The security forces will bring Laski in."

"*Nein!*" snapped Willi. "He is *mine.*"

Barent was still smiling as he swiveled to face Willi. "Yes, he may well be yours. We shall see. In the meantime, I have already pressed the button that notifies Security. They monitor the opening of the game and will know whom to seek. You may aid in the capture if you wish, Herr Borden, but see to it that the psychiatrist does not die before interrogation."

Willi made a sound amazingly like a snarl and closed his eyes. Barent turned his deadly placid gaze toward Harod.

Saul had followed the other four surrogates up the ramp and outside into a tropical night thick with humidity and the oppressive threat of a storm. No stars were visible but lightning flashes showed trees and a cleared area north of the Security Zone. He stumbled once, falling to his knees, but rising quickly and moving forward. There was a huge pentagram emblazoned there and the other surrogates already had taken their places at the points of the star.

Saul debated making a break for it then, but two guards with M-16s and nightscopes were visible across the Security Zone each time the lightning flashed. He would wait. Saul had to take the empty circle between Jensen Luhar and a tall, thin young man with long hair. Somehow it seemed appropriate that all of them were naked. Saul was the only one of the five who was not in superb physical condition.

Jensen Luhar's head swiveled as if it was on a turntable. "If you can hear me, my little pawn," it said in German, "I will say goodbye. I do not kill you in anger. It will be quick." Luhar's head turned back to the sky, watching—as were the others—for some sort of signal. The flashes of lightning etched the black man's powerful profile in liquid silver.

Saul pivoted, cocked his arm, and hurled the palm-size stone he had picked up when he had deliberately fallen to his knees a minute before. The rock caught Luhar just behind his left ear and the big man went down at once. Saul turned and ran. He was through the bushes and into the tropical forest before the other three surrogates had done anything but turn to watch him go. There were no shots.

His first five minutes of running were sheer, mindless flight, with pine needles and fallen palmetto fronds pricking his bare feet, branches and undergrowth raking at his ribs, and his breath rasping in his throat. Then he controlled himself to the point of pausing, crouching at the fringes of a small canebrake and listening. To his left he could hear the lap of waves and a more distant sound of powerful outboard motors. A strange rasping could have been the sound of electric bullhorns bleating across the water, but the words were indistinct.

Saul closed his eyes and tried to picture the maps and photo montage of the island, remembering the many hours in the motel kitchenette with Natalie. It was more than four miles—almost five—to the northern tip of the island. He knew that the forest he was in would soon condense to real jungle, opening slightly to saltwater marshes a mile below the northern end but closing in again to swamp and jungle before the beach could be reached. The only structures along the way would be the ruins of the slave hospital, the overgrown foundations of the Dubose Plantation near the rocky point along the eastern coast, and the tumbled headstones of the old slave cemetery.

Saul glanced at the canebrake during the white flash from the approaching storm and felt an overwhelming urge to hide in there, simply to crawl in and crouch and curl in a fetal position and become invisible. He knew that he would only die sooner if he did so. The monsters in the Manse—three of them at least—had spent years stalking each other through these few miles of jungle. Under interrogation at the safe house, Harod had told Saul about the "Easter egg hunt" on the last night when the Island Club released all of the unused surrogates—a dozen or more naked and helpless men and women—and then used their own favorite surrogates to hunt them with knives and handguns. Barent, Kepler, and Sutter would know every hiding place, and Saul could not get over the feeling that Willi could sense his whereabouts. He expected the old man's foul touch in his mind at any moment, knowing that such a seizure at these distances would mean total failure of all of his plans, months of wasted work, a lifetime of his own dreams sacrificed for nothing.

Saul knew that his only chance was in flight to the north. He moved from the canebrake and ran as the approaching storm flashed and crashed behind him.

"There," said Barent, pointing to the pale, naked figure stumbling past the panning range of a screen in the fifth row of monitors. "There's no doubt it is the psychiatrist, Laski."

Sutter sipped at a tall bourbon and crossed his legs in the cushioned comfort of one of the Monitor Room's deep couches. "There never was any doubt," he said. "The question is—who introduced him into the game and why?"

The other three stared at Willi, but the old man was watching a monitor in the first row where security guards were carrying away the

still-unconscious form of Jensen Luhar. The three surrogates had been
sent into the jungle after Laski. Willi turned toward them with a thin smile.
"It would have been stupid for me to have inserted the Jew," he said. "I do
not do stupid things."

C. Arnold Barent stepped away from the monitors and folded his arms.
"Why stupid, William?"

Willi scratched at his cheek. "You all associate the Jew with me even
though it was *you*, Herr Barent, who most recently conditioned him and,
alone among us, have nothing to fear from him."

Barent blinked but said nothing.

"If I were to bring a—how do you say it?—a ringer into your games,
why would I not have brought one unknown to you all? And one in much
better physical condition?" Willi smiled and shook his head. "No, you
need only to think a minute to realize how absurd it would be for me to do
this. I do not do stupid things and you would be stupid to think I would."

Barent looked at Harod. "Tony, do you still want to hold to your story
of an abduction and blackmail?"

Harod slumped in the low couch and chewed on his knuckle. He had
told the truth because he suspected that they were ready to turn on him
and he wanted to divert their suspicions. Now they thought he was a liar
and he had succeeded only in relieving some of their natural fear of Willi's
involvement. "I don't *know* who's fucking responsible," snapped Harod,
"but somebody here's playing with this shit. What would I have to gain
doing it?"

"What indeed?" said Barent in a conversational tone.

"I think it's a diversion of some sort," gritted Kepler, glancing toward
Willi with obvious tension.

It was the Reverend Jimmy Wayne Sutter who laughed. "A diversion
from what?" he asked, chuckling. "The island is sealed from the outside
world. No one is allowed on this end of the island except Brother C's personal security force, and they are all Neutrals. I have no doubt that at the
first sign of irregularity in the game, all of our aides were . . . ah . . .
escorted to their rooms."

Harod looked up in alarm, but Barent only continued smiling. Harod
realized how foolish it had been of him to hope that Maria Chen might be
able to help in a crisis.

"Diversion from what?" continued Sutter. "It would seem to this poor
old backwoods minister to be a poor excuse for a diversion."

"Well, *somebody's* controlling him," snapped Kepler.

"Perhaps not," Willi said softly.

All heads turned toward him. "My little Jew has been amazingly persistent over the years," said Willi. "Imagine my surprise when I discovered
him in Charleston seven months ago."

Barent's smile had disappeared. "Wilhelm, you are contending that
this . . . man . . . came here of his own free will?"

"*Ja.*" Willi smiled. "My pawn from the old days still follows me."

Kepler was livid. "So you admit that you're the reason he's here, even if he came on his own to find you."

"Not at all," Willi said affably. "It was your genius that had the Jew's family killed in Virginia."

Barent tapped his lower lip with a crooked finger. "Assuming he knew who was responsible, how did he find out the details of the Island Club?" Even before he had finished the question, Barent had turned to look at Harod.

"How could I have known he was acting *alone*?" Harod asked plaintively. "They shot me full of fucking *drugs*."

Jimmy Wayne Sutter stood and approached a monitor where light-enhancement lenses showed a pale, naked figure struggling through vines and tumbled tombstones. "Then who is working with him now?" Sutter asked so softly that he seemed to be speaking to himself.

"*Die Negerin,*" said Willi. "The black girl. The one with the sheriff in Germantown." He laughed, throwing his head back so that fillings were visible in molars worn down by age. "*Die Untermenschen* are rising up just as the Führer feared."

Sutter turned away from the screen just as Barent's Jamaican surrogate appeared on it, moving quickly and surely through the vine-covered cemetery where Laski had stumbled out of sight a moment before. "Where is the girl then?" asked Sutter.

Willi shrugged. "It does not matter. Were there any black bitches in your surrogate pens?"

"No," said Barent.

"Then she is elsewhere," said Willi. "Perhaps dreaming of her revenge on the cabal that killed her father."

"We did not kill her father," said Barent, obviously deep in thought. "Melanie Fuller or Nina Drayton did."

"Exactly." Willi laughed. "Another small irony. But the Jew is here, and it seems almost certain that *die Negerin* helped him get here."

They all looked at the monitors, but the only surrogate visible was Sutter's man Amos, looking like a diminutive Sumo wrestler as he thrashed his way through high grass just south of the old DeBose plantation. Sutter's eyes were closed with the concentration of controlling the man.

"We need to question Laski," said Kepler. "Find out where the girl is."

"*Nein,*" said Willi, staring intently at Barent. "We need to kill the Jew as quickly as possible. Even if he is insane, he might have some way to strike at us."

Barent unfolded his arms and smiled again. "Worried, William?"

Willi shrugged again. "It only makes sense. If we all cooperate in killing the Jew, it eliminates any possible chance that he was brought here by one of us to gain some advantage. The girl will be easy enough to find, *ja?* My guess is that she is in Charleston again."

"Guesses aren't good enough," snapped Kepler. "I say we interrogate him."

"James?" said Barent.

Sutter opened his eyes. "Kill him and get back to the game," he said and closed his eyes.

"Tony?"

Harod looked up with a start. "You mean I get a fucking vote?"

"We will deal with the other issues later," said Barent. "Right now you are a member of the Island Club and have voting privileges."

Harod showed his small, sharp teeth. "Then I abstain," he said. "Just leave me the hell alone and do whatever you want with that guy."

Barent tapped his lip and watched an empty monitor. A lightning flash overloaded the sensitive lens for a second and filled the screen with white light. "William," said Barent, "I fail to see how this man could be a threat, but I agree with your logic that he would be less a threat if he were dead. We will find the girl and any other would-be avengers without much problem."

Willi leaned forward. "Can you wait until Jensen—my surrogate—is recovered?"

Barent shook his head. "It would only delay the game," he said and raised a microphone from the console. "Mr. Swanson?" he said and listened on a small headphone set for a response. "Are you tracking the surrogate who ran north? Good. Yes, I also show him in Sector two-seven-bravo-six. Yes, it is time we terminated this particular intruder with extreme prejudice. Have the shore patrol units close in now and release helicopter number three from sentry duty. Yes, use the infrared if possible and relay the ground sensor data directly to the search teams. Yes, I'm sure you will, but quickly, please. Thank you. Barent out."

Natalie Preston sat in Melanie Fuller's dark house in Old Charleston and thought about Rob Gentry. She had thought about him often in the past months, almost every evening as she drifted off to sleep, but in the two months since leaving Israel she had tried to push her grief and regret farther back to make room for the grim determination she felt must fill her mind. It had not worked. Since arriving in Charleston she had contrived to drive by Rob's house daily, usually in the evening. She had spent her few hours away from Saul taking walks in the quiet streets where she and Rob had walked, remembering not just the trivial details of their conversations but the deeper feelings that had been growing between them, deepening and opening in spite of their mutual understanding of how complicated and poorly timed a love affair between them would be. She had visited Rob's grave three times, each time being overcome with a sense of loss that she knew no amount of revenge could overcome or compensate for, and each time vowing that she would not return.

As Natalie began the second endless night in Melanie Fuller's house of horrors, she knew beyond any shade of doubt that if she was to survive the next few hours and days it would be through the recall of love rather than a determination to gain revenge.

It had been a little more than twenty-four hours that Natalie had been alone with Melanie Fuller's brain-dead menagerie. It had been an eternity.

Sunday night had been very bad. Natalie had stayed in the Fuller house until four o'clock Monday morning, leaving only when it seemed certain that Saul was safe until the next evening's slaughter. If he *was* still alive. Natalie knew only what the Melanie monster told her through the mouth of the brain-dead child who had once been Justin Warden. The cover story that Nina could not control Saul at such a distance—that Nina required Melanie's help if they were to save Willi and themselves from the Island Club's wrath—seemed less and less satisfactory as the hours crawled by.

For long periods during the first night Justin would sit silent and sightless, the other members of Melanie's "family" also as lifeless as mannequins. Natalie assumed that the old woman was busy controlling Miss Sewell or the man they had watched through binoculars for weeks as she and Justin stood in the park overlooking the river. No, it was too early for that. Justin had said that Melanie had watched the first night's slaughter on the island through the eyes of one of the security guards. Natalie had summoned her strongest Nina persona to warn Melanie not to meddle too soon and give away her presence. Justin had glared and said nothing for an hour, leaving Natalie helpless, waiting for information. Waiting for the old woman to slip into her mind and kill her. Kill them both.

Natalie sat in the house that smelled of garbage and rotting food and tried to think about Rob, what Rob would say in such a situation, what joke he might make. Sometime after midnight, Natalie used Nina's arrogant tones to demand that a light be turned on. The giant called Culley had shuffled over to switch on a single 40-watt bulb in a lamp whose shade had been torn half off. The flat, naked glare was worse than the darkness. The parlor was filled with dust, pieces of forgotten clothing, cobwebs, and a mad litter of rotting food. A browning, half-chewed ear of corn was visible under the sagging sofa. Orange rinds were scattered under the Georgian tea table. Someone, perhaps Justin, had heedlessly smeared raspberry or strawberry jam on the arms of the chair and sofa, leaving caked handprints that made Natalie think of drying blood. She heard rats scurrying in the walls, perhaps in the hallways themselves; entrance would have been easy enough from the palmetto trees through the cracked window panes Natalie could see from the courtyard each time she approached the house. Sometimes there were stirrings from the second floor, but these were much too loud to be made by rats. Natalie thought of the dying thing she had glimpsed upstairs, the old woman as wrinkled and twisted as some ancient tortoise ripped from its shell, kept alive by intravenous saline solutions and merciless machines, and sometimes—when long periods passed with none of the obscene "family" moving or even appearing to breathe—Natalie wondered if perhaps Melanie Fuller had died and these flesh and blood automatons simply continued to act out the last fetid fantasies in a decaying brain, marionettes dancing to the puppet master's death spasms.

"They have your Jew," lisped Justin late on the second night. It was after midnight.

Natalie startled from her half doze. Culley stood behind the child's chair, his bloated face lit from below by the single bulb. Marvin, Howard, and the Nurse Oldsmith were somewhere in the shadows behind Natalie. "Who took him?" she gasped.

The child's face looked phony in the cold light, a doll's visage molded in flaking rubber. Natalie remembered her glimpse of the life-size doll in Grumblethorpe and realized with a cold internal twist that Melanie had somehow transformed this child into an imitation of that decaying thing. "No one took him," snapped Justin. "They opened the bars an hour ago and let him out for the evening's fun. Have you *no* contact, Nina?"

Natalie chewed her lip and looked around her. Jackson was in the car a block away, Catfish watching the house from an alley across the street. They might as well have been on a different planet. "Melanie, it's too soon," she snapped. "Tell me what's going on."

Justin showed his baby teeth. "I think not, Nina, darling," he hissed. "It is time to tell me where *you* are." Culley stepped around the chair. Marvin came in from the kitchen. He was carrying a long knife that caught the light from the 40-watt bulb. Nurse Oldsmith made a noise behind Natalie.

"Stop," whispered Natalie. Her throat had constricted at the last second so that what should have been Nina's authoritative command emerged as a choked entreaty.

"No, no, no," hissed Justin and slid from his chair. He moved toward her in a half crouch, fingers touching the grimed Oriental carpet as if he were climbing a wall like a fly. "Time to tell us all, Nina, or lose this colored one. Show me, Nina. Show me what Ability you have left. If you *are* Nina." The child's face was contorted into a feral mask, as if the rubber doll's head were melting in unseen flames.

"No," said Natalie, standing. Culley blocked her way to the door. Marvin moved around the edge of the sofa. He ran his cupped hand up the length of the knife, and the blade came away slickened with his blood.

"Time to tell all, Nina," whispered Justin. There was a thrashing, sliding sound from the second floor. "Or time for this one to die."

The wind struck before the rain, whipping the palm trees back and forth in a frenzy, blowing fronds and branches through the air in a shower of sharp-edged debris. Saul stumbled to his knees and covered his head with his arms as the foliage thrashed at him with a thousand small claws. Lightning froze the wind-tossed chaos in a series of stroboscopic images as thunderclaps overlapped to provide a solid wall of noise.

Saul was lost. He curled under a massive fern as the storm front struck and tried to sort some sense of direction out of the night's confusion. He had reached the salt marshes, but then became disoriented, emerging into what should have been the final stretch of jungle only to find himself back at the slave cemetery an hour later. A helicopter roared overhead, its searchlight probing with a shaft of white light no less intense than the lightning behind it.

Saul crawled deeper under the fern, not knowing which side of the salt marsh he was now on. Just after he had reached the slave cemetery again, hours before, the tall, lanky surrogate with long hair had exploded from the shadows behind a fallen wall and had gone for Saul with teeth and fingernails. Exhausted, dazed with fatigue and fear, Saul had grasped at the nearest object—a rusted iron rod that might once have been a support for a grave marker—and tried to fend off the boy. The rod had struck the youth on the side of the head and opened a long gash. The boy fell unconscious. Saul kneeled at his side, found a pulse, and ran on into the jungle.

The helicopter came over again just as Saul reached the cover of cypress trees beyond the salt marsh. The wind roar drowned any noise of the rotors even though the machine was only twenty feet above the trees as it slid past, fighting the gusts. Saul felt little fear of the helicopter; it was too unstable to be used as a gun platform in the storm and he doubted if they could see him unless they caught him in the open.

Saul wondered why the sun had not risen. He was sure that more than enough hours had passed since his torment had begun for a dozen nights to have burned themselves out. He had been running forever. Crouching near the base of the cypress, Saul gasped, drawing in deep breaths, and stared at his legs and feet. They looked as if someone had drawn racks of razor blades across them. For a second he entertained the illusion that he was wearing red and white striped socks and crimson slippers.

The wind dropped and in the momentary lull before the rain began, Saul lifted his face to the sky and cried in Hebrew. "Hoy! What other jokes do you have in store?"

A bright beam stabbed horizontally at him from beyond the cypress. For a second Saul thought it was lightning and then wondered how the helicopter had managed to land, but in a second he realized it was neither. Beyond the screen of cypress was a narrow beach and beyond that the ocean. The guard boats were probing the shore with their searchlights.

Heedless of the light, Saul crawled toward the sand. The only beach this side of the Security Zone was at the northern tip of the island. He had made it. How many times, he wondered, had he come within yards of the beach only to be disoriented and turned back by swamp and jungle?

The beach was narrow here, no more than ten or twelve feet across, and tall waves crashed against rocks just beyond. Until the lull in the storm, wind and thunder had masked the sound of the breakers. Saul stumbled to his knees in the sand and looked out to sea.

There were at least two small boats out there beyond the line of surf, their powerful searchlights raking the beach with pitching shafts of white light. Lightning silhouetted both craft for a second, and Saul could see that they were less than a hundred meters out. The dark forms of men with rifles were clearly visible.

One of the searchlights slid along the beach and wall of foliage toward Saul and he ran toward the jungle, throwing himself into the ferns and tall sea grass an instant before the light struck. Crouching on all fours behind a low dune, he thought about his position. The helicopter and patrol boats showed that Barent and the others had abandoned their game with surrogates and almost certainly knew who they were chasing. Saul could hope that his presence had spread confusion if not actual dissension in their ranks, but he was not counting on it. Underestimating the intelligence or tenacity of one's enemies was never profitable. Saul had flown home during the most panicky hours of the Yom Kippur War and knew quite well how complacency often could prove fatal.

Saul plunged ahead, paralleling the beach, thrashing through thick undergrowth and tripping over mangrove roots, unsure even if he was headed in the right direction. Every minute or two he would throw himself flat as the searchlights flashed past or the helicopter roared along the beach. Somehow, he knew, they had narrowed his whereabouts to this tip of the island. He had seen no cameras or sensors during his hours of stumbling flight, but he had no doubt that Barent and the others used every piece of technology available to record their sick games and to reduce the chance that a clever surrogate might hide out for weeks or months on the island.

Saul tripped over an invisible root and sprawled forward, his head striking a thick branch before his face landed in six inches of brackish swamp water. He was just conscious enough to roll to one side, grabbing at sharp-edged grass to pull himself toward the beach. Blood ran down his cheek and into his open mouth; it tasted much like the salty swamp water.

The beach was wider here, although not as wide as the strip where the Cessna had landed. Saul realized that he would never find the tidal inlet and streams if he stayed in the trees. He might already have passed them without noticing it in the nightmare jungle of swamp and branches. If it was any real distance away it would take hours to traverse at this rate. His only hope lay on the beach.

More boats were closing in on the area. Saul could see four from where he lay under the low branches of a cypress and one was moving closer, less than thirty meters out, tossed high by each storm-driven wave. It was beginning to rain now, and Saul prayed for a tropical downpour, a deluge that reduced visibility to zero and drowned his enemies like the Pharaoh's soldiers. But the rain held steady in a light drizzle that might be only the prelude to the real storm or might pass completely, eventually opening the skies to a tropical sunrise that would seal Saul's fate.

He waited five minutes under the limbs, crouching behind sea grass and a fallen log when the boats came close with their lights or the helicopter passed over. He felt like laughing, like standing up and throwing stones and curses at them for the few blessed seconds before the bullets struck. Saul crouched and waited, peering out as yet another patrol boat roared by in the rain, its rooster tail adding to the curtain of salt spray already blowing in to the beach.

Explosions ripped through the jungle behind him. For a second Saul thought that the lightning strikes had come closer, but then he heard the whap-whap of rotors and realized that the searchers must be dropping explosive charges from the helicopter. The discharges were too powerful to be grenades; Saul could feel the vibration of each explosion through the deep sand and the quivering branches of the cypress. The tremors grew stronger as the explosions grew louder. Saul guessed that they were walking the charges up the beach, perhaps twenty or thirty meters into the jungle, at sixty- or eighty-meter intervals. Despite the drizzle, the smell of smoke drifted to him from down the beach to his right. If the storm was still coming in from the southeast, Saul realized, the direction of the smoke confirmed that he was near the northern tip of the island but still around the northeast point, not yet to the Cessna's take-off point and more than a quarter of a mile from the tidal inlet.

It would take hours to hack his way through the beach-edge jungle to the inlet and any shortcut through the swamps all but assured his becoming lost again.

An explosion ripped the night not two hundred meters south of him. There came an incredible screeching as a flight of herons broke cover and disappeared into the dark sky, and then a more prolonged and terrible scream as a human being cried out in pain. Saul wondered if a surrogate would do that. Either that or there were ground patrols moving in behind him and someone had been caught in the blast from the helicopter's bombing.

Saul could hear rotor blades more clearly now, high and to the south but coming closer. There was the rattle of automatic weapons as someone in a boat moving along the surf line fired randomly into the wall of jungle.

Saul wished he were not naked. Cold rain dripped on him through the leaves, his legs and ankles were in agony, and every time he glanced down the storm light showed him his wrinkled, emaciated belly, bony white legs, and genitals contracted with fear and cold. The sight did not fill him with confidence and make him want to rush out and do battle. Mostly, it made him want to take a hot bath, dress himself in several layers of warm clothes, and find a quiet place to sleep. His body had been tugged by the tidal pull of adrenaline rushes for hours now and was suffering from the ebb tide of aftereffects. He felt cold, lost, and terrified, a husk of humanity devoid of almost all emotion except for fear, and of all motivation except an obsolescent, atavistic urge to survive for reasons he had forgotten. In short, Saul Laski had become exactly the person he had been as he worked in the Pit forty years earlier, except now the stamina and hopefulness of youth were gone.

But that was not the only difference, Saul realized as he raised his face to the increasingly violent storm. "I *choose* to be here!" he shouted in Polish toward the skies, not caring if his pursuers heard him. He raised a fist but did not shake it, merely clenched it on high, whether as a sign of affirmation, triumph, defiance, or resignation, even he did not know.

Saul ran through the screen of cypress, turned left past the last of the sea grass, and sprinted onto the open beach.

"Harod, come in here," said Jimmy Wayne Sutter.

"Just a minute," said Harod. He was the only one left in the monitor room. While the ground-based cameras no longer showed anything important, there was a black and white camera on one of the patrol boats off the north point and a color one aboard the chopper that had been dropping shaped charges and napalm canisters into the trees. Harod thought that the camera work was shitty—they needed a Steadicam for the aerial shots and all the pitching and yawing on both monitors was making him nauseated—but he had to admit that the pyrotechnics out-budgeted anything he and Willi had ever done and were getting close to Coppola's orgasm-by-fire at the end of *Apocalypse Now*. Harod had always thought Coppola was nuts to have cut the napalm scenes out of the next-to-final version, and he had not been mollified much to see them slipped under the credits in the final cut. Harod wished he had a couple of Steadicams and a dolly-mounted Panavision unit preset for this night's work—he'd use the footage for *something* even if he had to write the fucking film around the fireworks.

"Come on, Tony, we're waiting," said Sutter.

"In a minute," said Harod, tossing another handful of peanuts into his mouth and taking a sip of vodka. "According to the radio chatter, they've got this poor schmuck cornered at the north end and they're burning the fucking jungle down to . . ."

"*Now*," snapped Sutter.

Harod looked at the evangelist. The other four had been in the Game Room for the better part of an hour, talking, and from the look on Sutter's face, something was very wrong. "Yeah," said Harod. "I'm coming." He looked over his shoulder as he left the room in time to see a naked man running along the beach in clear view of both cameras.

The atmosphere in the Game Room conveyed as much tension as had the carnage on the television monitors. Willi was seated directly opposite Barent, and Sutter moved to stand next to the old German. Barent's arms were folded and he looked very displeased. Joseph Kepler was pacing back and forth in front of the long window The row of drapes was pulled back, rain streaked the glass, and Harod caught glimpses of Live Oak Lane when the lightning rippled. Thunder was audible even through the multi-layered glass and thick walls. Harod glanced at his watch; it was 12:45 A.M. He wondered tiredly if Maria Chen was still in custody or if the aides had been released. He wished to hell that he had never left Beverly Hills.

"We have a problem, Tony," said C. Arnold Barent. "Sit down."

Harod sat. He expected Barent, or more likely Kepler, to announce that his membership had been terminated and that he would be too. Harod knew that he had no chance at a test of Ability with Barent, or Kepler, or Sutter. He did not expect Willi to lift a finger to help him. Maybe, Harod thought with the sudden epiphany granted to the condemned man, maybe Willi *had* planted the Jew on him so he would be discredited and removed. *Why?* wondered Harod. *How was I a threat to Willi? How does my removal benefit him?* Except for Maria Chen, there was not a woman on the island he might use. The thirty or so security men Barent allowed south of the Security Zone were all highly paid Neutrals securely in the billionaire's employ. Barent would not have to use his Ability to eliminate Tony Harod, merely push a button. "Yeah," said Harod tiredly, "what is it?"

"Your old friend Herr Borden has come up with a surprise for the evening," Barent said coolly.

Harod blinked and looked at Willi. He thought that the "surprise" would be at his expense but was not sure how Willi figured in it.

"We have merely suggested an amendment to the Island Club agenda," said Willi. "C. Arnold and Mr. Kepler do not agree with our suggestion."

"It's goddamned insane," snapped Kepler from his place by the window.

"Silence!" commanded Willi. Kepler silenced himself.

"We?" Harod said stupidly. "Who's we?"

"The Reverend Sutter and myself," said Willi.

"It turns out that my old friend James has been a friend of Herr Borden's for some years," said Barent. "An interesting turn of events."

Harod shook his head. "Do you guys know what's going on up on the north end of your fucking island?"

"Yes," said Barent. He removed from his ear a flesh-colored earphone smaller than a hearing aid and tapped the bead microphone attached to it by a fine filament of wire. "I do. It is of little import compared to this discussion. Absurd as it appears, in your first week on the Steering Committee you seem to have the deciding vote in your hands."

"I don't even know what the fuck you're talking about," said Harod.

Willi said, "We are talking about an amendment to widen the Island Club's hunting activities to . . . ah . . . a more appropriate scale, Tony."

"The world," said Sutter. The evangelist's face was flushed and filmed with sweat.

"The world?"

Barent showed a sardonic smile. "They wish to use surrogate nations instead of surrogate players," he said.

"Nations?" repeated Harod. A bolt of lightning struck somewhere beyond Live Oak Lane, darkening the polarized window.

"Goddammit, Harod," yelled Kepler, "can't you do anything but stand there and repeat things? These two idiots want to blow it all away. They're demanding we play with missiles and submarines rather than individuals. Whole countries burned up for points."

Harod leaned on the table and stared at Willi and Sutter. He could not speak.

"Tony," said Barent, "is this the first you have heard of this proposal?"

Harod nodded.

"Mr. Borden never raised the issue with you?"

Harod shook his head.

"You see the importance of your vote," Barent said quietly. "This would change the tenor of our annual entertainment to a significant measure."

Kepler laughed a strange, broken laugh. "It'd blow up the entire goddamn son-of-a-bitching world," he said.

"*Ja*," said Willi. "Perhaps. And perhaps not. But the experience would be fascinating."

Harod sat down. "You're shitting me," he managed to say in a cracked voice he had not used since puberty.

"Not at all," Willi said smoothly. "I have already demonstrated the ease with which even the highest levels of military security can be circumvented. Mr. Barent and the others have known for decades how simple it is to influence national leaders. We need only to remove the restraints of time and scale to make these competitions infinitely more fascinating. It would mean some travel and a safe place to convene once the competition gets . . . ah . . . heated, but we are sure that C. Arnold can provide these details. *Nicht wahr*, Herr Barent?"

Barent rubbed his cheek. "Undoubtedly. The objection is not resources—nor even the inordinate amount of time such an expanded competition would consume—but the waste of resources, human and otherwise, accumulated over such a lengthy period of time."

Jimmy Wayne Sutter gave the rich, deep laugh that was familiar to millions who watched him on television. "Brother Christian, you don't think you can take all this with you now, do you?"

"No," said Barent softly, "but I see no reason to destroy it all simply because I will not be here to enjoy it."

"*Ja*, but I do," Willi said flatly. "You entertained new business. The motion is on the floor. Jimmy Wayne and I vote yes. You and that coward Kepler vote no. Tony, vote now."

Harod jumped. Willi's voice was not to be resisted. "I abstain," he said. "Fuck you all."

Willi slammed his fist into the table. "Harod, goddamn you, you Jew-loving piece of shit. *Vote!*"

A great vise seemed to clamp on Harod's head, sinking steel clamps into his skull. He clutched his temples and opened his mouth in a silent scream.

"Stop!" snapped Barent and the vise was ripped away. Harod almost screamed again in relief. "He has voted," said Barent. "He has the right to abstain in any vote. Without a majority, the motion is defeated."

"*Nein,*" said Willi and a blue flame seemed to have ignited behind his cold gray eyes, "without a majority we are in stalemate." He swiveled toward Sutter. "What do you say, Jimmy Wayne, can we leave this issue in stalemate?"

Sutter's face was slick with sweat. He stared at a spot above and to the right of Barent's head as he said, "Now the seven angels who had the seven trumpets made ready to blow them. The first angel blew his trumpet, and there followed hail and fire, mixed with blood which fell on the earth; and a third of the earth was burned up . . .

"The second angel blew his trumpet, and something like a great mountain, burning with fire, was thrown into the sea; and a third of the sea became blood . . .

"The third angel blew his trumpet and a great star fell from heaven, blazing like a torch, and it fell on a third of the rivers and on the fountains of water . . .

"The fourth angel blew his trumpet and a third of the sun was struck, and a third of the moon, and a third of the stars . . .

"Then I looked and I heard an eagle crying with a loud voice, as it flew in mid-heaven, 'Woe, woe, woe to those who dwell on the earth, at the blasts of the other trumpets which the three angels are about to blow!'

"And the fifth angel blew his trumpet, and I saw a star fallen from heaven to earth, and he was given the key of the shaft of the bottomless pit . . ." Sutter stopped, drained the last of his bourbon, and sat in silence.

Barent asked, "And what does that mean, James?"

Sutter seemed to snap out of his reverie. He mopped his face with a lavender silk handkerchief from the breast pocket of his white suit coat. "It means that there can be no stalemates," he said in a hoarse whisper. "The Antichrist is here. His hour has come 'round at last. All we can do is carry out what is written and witness as best we can as the tribulations descend upon us. We have no choice."

Barent crossed his arms and smiled. "And which of us is your Antichrist, James?"

Sutter looked from Willi to Barent with wild eyes. "God help me," he said. "I don't know. I have surrendered my soul to serve him and *I do not know.*"

Tony Harod pushed back from the table. "This is too fucking weird," he said. "I'm out of here."

"Stay where you are," snapped Kepler. "No one's leaving this room until we get this settled."

Willi sat back and clasped his fingers across his stomach. "I have a suggestion," he murmured.

"Go ahead," said Barent.

"I suggest that we complete our chess game, Herr Barent," said Willi.

Kepler stopped pacing and stared first at Willi and then at Barent. "Chess game," he said. "What chess game?"

"Yeah," said Tony Harod. "What chess game?" He rubbed his hand across his closed eyes and saw the image of his own face carved in ivory.

Barent smiled. "Mr. Borden and I have been playing a game of chess through the mails for some months now," he said. "A harmless diversion."

Kepler sagged against the window. "Oh, Jesus Christ God Almighty," he said.

"Amen," said Sutter, his eyes unfocused once again.

"Months," repeated Harod. "Months. You mean all of this shit's been going down . . . Trask, Haines, Colben . . . and you two've been playing *fucking chess* the whole time?"

Jimmy Wayne Sutter made a sound somewhere between a belch and a laugh. "If any man worship the beast and his image, and receive his mark in his forehead, or in his hand, the same shall drink the wine of the wrath of God," he muttered. "And he shall be tormented with fire and brimstone in the presence of the holy angels, and in the presence of the Lamb; and the smoke of their torments ascendeth up for ever and ever." Sutter made the sound again. "And he causes all, small and great, rich and poor, free and bond, to receive a MARK in their right hand, or in their foreheads . . . and his number is six hundred, threescore and six."

"Shut up," Willi said amiably. "Herr Barent, do you agree? The game is nearly done, we need only to play it out. If I win, we enlarge the . . . competition . . . to a larger scale. If you win, I will content myself with the current arrangement."

"We were adjourned in the thirty-fifth move," said Barent. "Your position was not . . . ah . . . enviable."

"*Ja*." Willi grinned. "But I will play it. I do not demand a new game."

"And if this game ends in stalemate?" asked Barent.

Willi shrugged. "You win if it is a stalemate," he said. "I win only with a clear victory."

Barent looked out at the lightning.

"Don't pay attention to that bullshit," cried Kepler. "He's totally mad."

"Shut up, Joseph," said Barent. He turned toward Willi. "All right. We will finish the game. Do we play with the pieces available?"

"That is more than agreeable," said Willi with a broad smile that showed perfect dentures. "Shall we adjourn to the first floor?"

"Yes," said Barent. "Just a second, please." He picked up his headset and listened for a moment. "Barent here," he said into the bead microphone. "Put one team ashore and terminate the Jew immediately. Is that understood? Good." He set the headset on the table. "All ready."

Harod followed them to the elevator. Sutter, walking ahead of him, suddenly stumbled, turned, and grasped Harod's arm. "An in those days, men will seek death and will not find it," he urgently whispered in Harod's face. "They will long to die and death will fly from them."

"Fuck off," said Harod and pulled his arm free.

Together the five descended in silence.

SIXTY-SIX

Melanie

I remember the picnics we used to have in the hills outside Vienna: the pine-scented hills, meadows of wildflowers, and Willi's open Peugeot parked near some stream or scenic overlook. When Willi was not dressed in his ridiculous brown shirt and armband, he was the picture of sartorial splendor with his silk summer suits and a broad-brimmed, rakish white hat given to him by one of the cabaret performers. Before Bad Ischl, before Nina's betrayal, I took pleasure in simply being with two such beautiful people. Nina was never lovelier than during those final summers of our contentment, and although both of us were entering the years where we were no longer girls—nor even young ladies by yesterday's standards—merely watching Nina in her blond, blue-eyed enthusiasm kept me feeling and acting young.

I know now that it was their betrayal at Bad Ischl, even more than Nina's initial betrayal with my Charles years earlier, that marked the point where I began to grow old while Nina did not. In a sense, Nina and Willi have been Feeding on me all these years.

It was time for this to stop.

On the second night of my strange vigil with Nina's Negress, I decided to end the waiting. Some demonstration was due. I was sure that even with the colored girl removed from the scene, Willi would be able to tell me of Nina's true whereabouts.

I confess that my attention was divided. For days as I had felt the youth and vitality returning to by body, as the paralysis slowly yielded its twisted grip on my left arm and leg, I felt a commensurate slackening of control in dealing with my family and other contacts. Sometime after Miss Sewell watched Jensen Luhar, the one called Saul, and the other three depart the cell area, I said to the colored girl, "They have your Jew."

I sensed Nina's own lack of control in the confusion of her catspaw's response. I brought my people into tight focus and demanded that Nina tell me where she was. She refused, moving her pathetic little servant girl toward the door. I felt sure that Nina had lost all contact with her person on the island and therefore was also out of touch with Willi. The girl was literally at my mercy.

I moved Culley where he could reach the Negress in two steps and brought the Negro boy from Philadelphia into the room. He carried a knife. "Time to tell all," I teased Nina, "or time for this one to die."

I guessed that Nina would sacrifice the girl. No cat's-paw—no matter how well conditioned—would be worth Nina revealing her hiding place. I prepared Culley for the two steps and swift movement of arms and hands that would leave the girl lifeless on the carpet with her head turned at an impossible angle like the chickens Mammy Booth used to kill out back behind the house before dinner. Mother would choose; Mammy Booth would grab and twist and fling the feathered corpse onto the porch before the bird knew it had been killed.

The girl did a surprising thing. I had expected Nina to have her flee or fight, or at the very least for there to be a mental struggle as Nina attempted to seize control of one of my people, but the colored girl stood where she was, opened her oversize sweater, and exposed an absurd belt—a sort of Mexican bandit's *bandilero*—filled with what looked like cellophane-wrapped modeling clay. Wires ran from a gadget that looked like a transistor radio to the packets of clay. "Melanie, stop!" she shouted.

I did so. Culley's hands froze in the act of rising toward the Negress's skinny throat. I felt no concern at this point, only a mild curiosity at this manifestation of Nina's madness.

"These are explosives," panted the girl. Her hand went to a switch on the transistor radio. "If you touch me, I'll trigger them. If you touch my mind, the monitor here will trigger them automatically. The explosion will flatten this smelly mausoleum of a house."

"Nina, Nina," I had Justin say, "you're overwrought. Sit down a minute. I'll have Mr. Thorne bring us some tea."

It was a perfectly natural mistake, but the Negro girl showed her teeth in something not even close to a smile. "Mr. Thorne's not here, Melanie. Your mind is turning to sludge. Mr. Thorne . . . whatever his real name was . . . killed my father and then one of your stinking friends killed *him*. But it was always you, you ancient bag of pus. You've been the spider at the center of every . . . *don't try it!*"

Culley had barely moved. I had him lower his hands, slowly, and step back. I considered seizing the girl's voluntary nervous system. It would take only seconds—just long enough for one of my people to get to her before she could push that little red button. Not that I believed for a second that there was anything to her silly threats. "What kind of explosive did you say that was, dear?" I asked through Justin.

"It's called C-4," said the girl. Her voice was steady and calm, but I could hear the rapid rise and fall of her breathing. "It's a military thing . . . plastic explosive . . . and there are twelve pounds here, more than enough to blow you and this house to hell and destroy half of the Hodges place too."

It did not sound like Nina speaking. Upstairs, Dr. Hartman clumsily removed an IV from my arm and began to turn me onto my right side. I shoved him away with my good arm. "How could you detonate this explosive if I took your little pickaninny away from you?" I had Justin ask. Howard lifted the heavy .45 pistol from my night table, removed his shoes, and moved silently down the stairs. I still had the faintest of contacts, through Miss Sewell, of a security guard's perceptions as they carried the unconscious form of Jensen Luhar back to the security tunnel while others continued to chase after the one the Negress had called Saul. There were alarms audible even to Miss Sewell in the surrogate holding area. The storm was approaching the island; a deck officer reported waves of six feet and rising.

The colored girl took a step closer to Justin. "See these wires?" she asked, leaning forward. Thin filaments ran down from her scalp into the collar of her blouse. "These sensors carry the electrical signals of my brain waves to this monitor. Can you understand that?"

"Yes," lisped Justin. I had no idea what she was talking about.

"Brain waves have certain patterns," said the girl. "These patterns are as characteristic as fingerprints. As soon as you touch my mind with that filthy, rotten, diseased brain of yours, you'll create a thing called a theta rhythm—it's found in rats, lizards, and lower life forms like you—and the little computer in this monitor will sense it and ignite the C-4. In less than a second, Melanie."

"You're lying," I said.

"Try me," said the girl. She took another step forward and shoved Justin very hard, propelling the poor child backward until he collided with Father's favorite chair and sat down with a rattle of small heels. "Try me," she repeated, voice rising with anger, "just try me, you desiccated old bitch, and I'll see you in hell."

"Who are you?" I asked.

"No one," said the girl. "Just someone whose father you murdered. Nothing important enough for you to remember."

"You're not Nina?" I asked. Howard had reached the bottom of the stairs. He raised the pistol in readiness to swing around the edge of the doorway and fire.

The girl glanced around at Culley and the foyer. The green glow from the second-floor landing threw the vaguest of shadows where Howard stood. "If you kill me," the girl said, "the monitor will sense the cessation of brain waves and detonate instantly. It will kill everyone in this house." I sensed no fear in her voice, only something approaching elation.

The girl was lying, of course. Rather, it was Nina who was lying. There was no way that some colored girl off the street could have learned those things about Nina's life, about the death of Nina's father, about the details of the Vienna Game. But this girl *had* mentioned something about me murdering her father that first time we met in Grumblethorpe. Or had she? Things were becoming very confused. Perhaps death had indeed driven Nina insane and now she had confused things to the point that she thought *I* had pushed her father in front of that Boston trolley. Perhaps in her last seconds of life, Nina's consciousness had sought refuge in the inferior brain of this girl—could she have been a maid at Mansard House?—and now Nina's memories were confused and intertwined with the mundane memories of a colored domestic. I almost had Justin laugh aloud at that thought. What an irony that would have been!

Whatever the truth of it, I had no fear of her imaginary explosive. I had heard the term "plastic explosive," but I was sure that such a device did not resemble these lumps of clay. They did not even look like plastic. Besides, I remember when Father had to dynamite a beaver dam on our Georgia property before the War, just he and the foreman were allowed to ride out to the lake with the treacherous dynamite and elaborate care was taken with the blasting caps. Explosives would be much too unreliable to carry around on a silly belt. The rest of the girl's story—brainwaves and computers—simply made no sense at all. Such ideas belonged in the realm of the science fiction Willi used to read in those lurid, penny-dreadful German magazines. Even if such an idea were possible—which I was confident this was not—it would not lie in the realm of understanding of a Negro. *I* had difficulty comprehending the concept.

Still, it made little sense to push Nina further. There was always the remote chance that something in her catspaw's apparatus might include real dynamite. I saw no reason not to humor Nina a few minutes longer. The fact that she was as mad as a proverbial hatter made her no less dangerous. "What do you want?" I asked.

The girl licked her thick lips and glanced around her. "Get all of your people out of here. Except Justin. He stays in the chair."

"Of course," I purred. The black boy, Nurse Oldsmith, and Culley left by separate doors. Howard stepped back as Culley passed, but he did not lower the pistol.

"Tell me what is happening," snapped the Negress. She remained standing with her finger near the red button of the device on her belt.

"What do you mean, dear?"

"On the island," demanded the girl. "What's happened to Saul?"

I had Justin shrug. "I've lost interest in that," I said.

The girl took three steps forward and I thought she was going to strike the helpless child. "God*damn* you," she said. "Tell me what I want to know or I'll trigger this right now. It'd be worth it just to know that you're dead . . . frying in your bed like some hairless old queen rat held over the flames. Make up your mind, you bitch."

I have always despised profanity. My repugnance at such vulgarity was not lessened by the images she conjured. My mother was unduly afraid of floods and rising water. Fire has always been my bête noire. "Your Jewish person threw a rock at Willi's man and ran into the forest before the game was to begin," I said. "Several of the others followed. Two security guards carried the one called Jensen Luhar into the infirmary area of this absurd little tunnel complex of theirs. He has been unconscious for hours."

"Where's Saul?"

Justin made a face. His voice conveyed more of a whine than I had intended. "How should *I* know? I can't be everywhere." I saw no reason to tell her that at that moment the guard I had made contact with via Miss Sewell had glanced into the infirmary in time to see Willi's Negro rise from the table and strangle both the guards who had carried him there. The sight caused me a strange sense of déjà vu until I remembered going to the Kruger-Kino in Vienna with Willi and Nina to see the motion picture *Frankenstein* in the summer of 1932. I remember screaming when the monster's hand had twitched on the table and then risen to choke the life out of the unsuspecting doctor bending over it. I had no urge to scream now. I had my security guard move on, passing the room where other guards watched banks of television sets, bringing him to a halt near the administrative offices. I saw no reason to tell Nina's Negress about these developments.

"Which way did Saul go?" asked the girl.

Justin crossed his arms. "Why don't *you* tell *me* if you're so smart?" I said.

"All right," said the Negress. She lowered her eyelids until only a hint of white showed. Howard waited in the shadows of the foyer. "He's running north," said the girl, "through heavy jungle. There's a . . . some sort of ruined building. Headstones. It's a cemetery." She opened her eyes.

Upstairs, I moaned and thrashed in my bed. I had been so *sure* that Nina was unable to contact her catspaw. But I had seen that very image on the security guards' television less than a minute before. I had lost track of Willi's Negro in the maze of tunnels. Was it possible that Willi was Using this girl? He seemed to enjoy Using colored and other less-developed races. If it was Willi, then where was Nina? I could feel a headache coming on.

"What do you want?" I said again.

"You're going ahead with the plan," said the girl, still standing near Justin. "Just the way we discussed it." She glanced at her wristwatch. Her hand was no longer next to the red button, but there was still the matter of brainwaves and computers.

"It seems to make little sense to continue with all this," I suggested. "Your Jew's bad sportsmanship has ruined the evening's program and I doubt if the rest of them will be . . ."

"Shut up," snapped the girl, and although the language was vulgar, the tone was Nina's. "You're going to go ahead as planned. If you don't, we'll see if the C-4 can level this entire house at once."

"You never liked my house," I said. Justin extended his lower lip.

"*Do it, Melanie,*" ordered the girl. "If you don't, I'll know it. If not at once, very soon. And I'll give *you* no warning when I detonate this stuff. *Move.*"

I came very close to having Howard shoot her at that instant. No one speaks to me that way in my own home, certainly not a colored wench who should not even be in my parlor. But I restrained myself, made Howard gently lower the pistol. There were other things to consider here.

It would be just like Nina—or Willi for that matter—to provoke me in just such a manner. If I killed her now, there would be the mess in the parlor to clean up and I would be no nearer to ferreting out Nina's hiding place. And there was always the possibility that some part of her previous story was true. Certainly the bizarre Island Club she had described to me was real enough, although Mr. Barent was much more of a gentleman than she had let on. There did seem ample evidence that the group was a threat to me, although I failed to see where Willi was in danger. If I let this opportunity pass, I would not only lose Miss Sewell but would have to live with the anxiety and uncertainty of what this group might decide to do about me in the months and years to come.

So despite the melodrama of the previous half hour, I had come full circle to the position of uneasy alliance with Nina's Negress—the same place I had been for the past several weeks.

"Very well," I sighed.

"*Now,*" said the girl.

"Yes, yes, yes," I muttered. Justin slumped into immobility. My family froze into statues. My gums rubbed against one another as I clenched my jaws, eyes closed, my body straining with the effort.

Miss Sewell looked up when the heavy door at the end of the corridor slammed open. The security guard sitting on a stool in the booth there jumped to his feet just as Willi's Negro entered. The guard raised his machine pistol. The Negro took it away from him and slammed his open palm into the man's face, flattening the guard's nose and sending slivers of bone into his brain.

The Negro reached into the booth and threw a switch. The bars slid up into the wall and while the other prisoners cowered in their niches, Miss Sewell stepped out, stretched to improve circulation, and turned to face the colored man.

"Hello, Melanie," he said.

"Good evening, Willi," I said.

"I knew it was you," he said softly. "It is incredible how we recognize each other through all of our disguises, even after all of these years. *Nicht wahr?*"

"Yes," I said. "Would you get this one something to wear? It is not right that she is naked here."

Willi's Negro grinned but nodded, reached over, and ripped the shirt off the dead guard. He draped it over Miss Sewell's shoulders. I concentrated on manipulating the two remaining buttons. "Are you going to take me up to the big house?" I asked.

"Yes."

"Is Nina there, Willi?"

The Negro's brow furrowed and one eyebrow lifted. "Do you expect her to be there?" he asked.

"No."

"Others will be there," he said and again showed the colored man's teeth.

"Mr. Barent," I said. "Sutter . . . and the others in the Island Club."

Willi's cat's-paw laughed heartily. "Melanie, my love," he said, "you never fail to amaze me. You know nothing, but you always succeed in knowing everything."

I showed my slight pout on Miss Sewell's features. "Do not be unkind, Willi," I said. "It does not become you."

He laughed again. "Yes, yes," he boomed. "No unkindness tonight. It is our last Reunion, *Liebchen*. Come, the others await."

I followed him down corridors and up and out into the night. We saw no other security people although I retained my slight contact with the guard still standing near the administrative office.

We passed a tall fence where the body of a guard still sizzled and smoked, spread-eagled against the electrified wire. I saw pale forms moving through darkness as the other naked prisoners fled into the night. Overhead, the clouds raced. The storm was coming. "The people who hurt me are going to pay for that tonight, aren't they, Willi?" I said.

"Oh yes," he growled through white teeth. "Oh yes, indeed, Melanie, my love."

We walked toward the large house bathed in white light. I had Justin point his finger at Nina's Negress. "You wanted this!" I screamed at her in a six-year-old's shrill voice. "You wanted this. Now just you *watch*!"

SIXTY-SEVEN

Dolmann Island
Tuesday, June 16, 1981

S aul had never been in a rain like this one. As he sprinted along the beach, the downpour filled the air with a weight of water that threatened to crush him to the sand like a massive curtain smashing some hapless actor who had missed his mark. Searchlights stabbing in from the boats beyond the surf or downward from the helicopter served only to illuminate sheets of the torrent gleaming like lines of tracer shells in the night. Saul ran, bare feet sliding on sand turned to the consistency of mud in the downpour, and concentrated on not slipping and falling, sure in some strange way that if he went down he would not rise again.

As suddenly as the deluge worsened, it quickly let up. One second the rain battered at his head and bare shoulders as the thunder and pounding of water on thick foliage drowned out all other sound, and the next instant the pressure lightened, he could see more than ten meters through blowing curtains of mist, and men were shouting at him. The sand leaped up in small spurts ahead of him and for a mad second Saul wondered if it was some reaction of buried clams or crabs to the storm before he realized that people were shooting at him. Overhead, the roar of rotors overcame storm sounds and a huge shape flashed by, white light slashing across the beach at him. The helicopter banked hard and skidded through thick air ahead of him, slewing sideways only twenty feet above sand and surf. Outboard motors screamed as two boats cut in through the white line of the outer breakers.

Saul stumbled, caught himself before he went to his knees, and ran on. He did not know where he was. He distinctly remembered the north beach being shorter than this, the jungle set farther back. For a second, as the searchlights swept across him and the helicopter completed its turn, Saul was sure he had run past his inlet in the downpour. Things had been changed by the night and storm and tide and he had run right past. He went on, his breath a ragged, hot wire in his throat and chest, hearing the shots now and watching as the sand leaped ahead and to either side of him.

The helicopter roared back up the beach with its skids flashing toward him at head height. Saul threw himself forward, scraping his chest and belly and genitals against sand as harsh as sandpaper. The blast from the rotor blades pressed his face deeper into the sand as the helicopter passed over. Whether automatic weapons fire meant for him found the machine or something mechanical found its own breaking point, Saul did not know, but there came a sudden sound like a wrench dropped into a rolling steel barrel and the helicopter surged and shuddered even as it passed over Saul's prone form. Fifty yards down the beach it tried to climb for altitude but succeeded only in slewing left over the surf and then banking too steeply to the right as the rotor assembly and tail boom tried to counter-rotate with a will of their own. The helicopter flew directly into the line of trees.

For a few seconds it appeared that the rising craft would use its own rotors to hack a path through the top thirty feet of vegetation—palm fronds and leafy debris were flying above the tree line like ditchdiggers leaping out of the way of a runaway motorcycle in a Mack Sennet comedy—but seconds later the helicopter itself appeared above the forest's edge, completing an impossible loop, the cabin's Plexiglas gleaming in rain and reflected glare from its own spotlight which now stabbed skyward from its inverted belly. Saul threw himself down again as bits and pieces of the helicopter began crashing down across a fifty-meter segment of beach.

The cabin hit the edge of the beach, bounced once, skipped across the first three white lines of surf like a hard-flung stone, and disappeared in ten feet of water. A second later something triggered the explosive charges still in the cabin, the sea glowed like an open flame seen through thick green glass, and a geyser of white spray rose twenty feet into the air and blew in toward Saul. Small bits of wreckage continued to patter onto the sand for half a minute.

Saul stood, brushed sand from his skin, and stared stupidly. He had just realized that he was standing in a small stream set in a broad depression on the beach when the first bullet struck him. There was a stinging on his left thigh and he spun around just in time for a second, more solid blow near his right shoulder blade to send him sprawling in the muddy stream.

Two speedboats were coming in on the surf while a third circled a hundred feet out. Saul moaned and rolled to one side to look at his left thigh. The bullet had drawn a bloody groove just below his hip bone on the outside of his leg. He fumbled with his left hand to find the wound on his back, but whatever had hit him there had left his shoulder blade numb. His hand came away bloody, but that told him little. He raised his right arm and wiggled his fingers. At least his arm still functioned.

To hell with it, Saul thought in English and crawled toward the jungle. Twenty yards down the beach, the bow of the first boat touched sand and four men waded ashore, rifles held high.

Still crawling, Saul looked straight up and saw the ragged edge of clouds pass over. Stars became visible even as lightning continued to illuminate the world to the north and west. Then the last of the clouds passed over like some vast curtain pulling back for a third and final act.

Tony Harod realized that he was scared shitless. The five of them had descended to the main hall where Barent's people had already set out two huge chairs facing each other across an expanse of tiled floor. Barent's Neutrals stood guard at each door and window, automatic weapons looking incongruous with their blue blazers and gray slacks. A small cluster of them stood around Maria Chen, including a man named Tyler who was Kepler's aide, and Willi's other catspaw, Tom Reynolds. Harod could see out the broad french doors to where Barent's executive helicopter sat idling thirty yards down the swale toward the sea cliffs, a squad of Neutrals surrounding it and squinting into the glare of floodlights.

Barent and Willi seemed to be the only ones who really understood what was going on. Kepler continued pacing and wringing his hands like a condemned man while Jimmy Wayne Sutter had the glazed, smiling, slightly stunned look of someone deep in a peyote dream. Harod said, "So where's the fucking chessboard?"

Barent smiled and walked to a long, Louis XIV table covered with bottles, glasses, and a breakfast buffet. Another table held an array of electronic equipment and the mustached FBI man named Swanson stood nearby with earphones and a microphone. "One does not need a chessboard to play, Tony," said Barent. "It is, after all, primarily an exercise of the mind."

"And you two've been playing through the mails for months, you say?" asked Joseph Kepler. His voice was strained. "Since just after we turned Nina Drayton loose in Charleston last December?"

"No," said Barent. He nodded and a servant in a blue blazer poured him a glass of champagne. He sipped and nodded. "Actually, Mr. Borden contacted me with the opening move a few weeks before Charleston."

Kepler laughed harshly. "So you let me think I'd been the only one to make contact with him when you and Sutter've been in touch all along."

Barent glanced toward Sutter. The minister was staring blankly out the french doors. "Reverend Sutter's contact with Mr. Borden goes back much farther," said Barent.

Kepler walked to the table and poured a tall glass of whiskey. "You used me just like you did Colben and Trask." He downed most of the drink in one gulp. "Just like Colben and Trask."

"Joseph," soothed Barent, "Charles and Nieman were in the wrong place at the wrong time."

Kepler laughed again and poured another drink. "Captured pieces," he said. "Taken off the board."

"*Ja,*" Willi heartily agreed, "but I have lost some of my own pieces." He salted a hard-boiled egg and took a large bite of it. "Herr Barent and I were much too careless with our queens early in the game."

Harod had moved close to Maria Chen and now took her hand in his. Her fingers were cool. Barent's guards were several yards away. She leaned close to Harod and whispered. "They searched me, Tony. They knew all about the gun in the boat. There's no way off the island now."

Harod nodded.

"Tony," she whispered, squeezing his hand, "I'm frightened."

Harod looked around the large room. Barent's people had rigged small spotlights to illuminate only a portion of the black-and-white tiled Grand Hall. Each tile looked to be about four feet square. Harod counted eight rows of illuminated squares, each row having eight squares across. He realized that he was looking at a giant chessboard. "Don't worry," he whispered to Maria Chen, "I'll get you out of here, I swear it."

"I love you, Tony," whispered the beautiful Eurasian.

Harod looked at her for a minute, squeezed her hand, and walked back to the buffet table.

"Something I don't understand, Herr Borden," Barent was saying, "is how you deterred the Fuller woman from leaving the country. Richard Haines's people never found out what happened at the Atlanta airport."

Willi laughed and picked small, white flecks of egg from his lips. "A phone call," he said. "A simple phone call. I had prudently tape-recorded certain telephone conversations between my dear friend Nina and Melanie years before and had done some editing." Willi's voice shifted to a falsetto. "Melanie, darling, is that you, Melanie? This is Nina, Melanie." Willi laughed and helped himself to a second hard-boiled egg.

"And had you already chosen Philadelphia as the playing area for our middle game?" asked Barent.

"*Nein*," said Willi. "I was prepared to play wherever Melanie Fuller went to ground. Philadelphia was quite acceptable, however, since it allowed my associate Jensen Luhar to move freely among the other blacks."

Barent shook his head ruefully. "Some very costly exchanges there. Some very careless moves on both our parts."

"*Ja*, my queen for a knight and a few pawns," said Willi and frowned. "It was necessary to avoid an early draw, but not up to my usual tournament play."

The FBI man, Swanson, came up and whispered to Barent. "Excuse me a second, please," said the billionaire and went over to the communications table. When he returned he glowered at Willi. "What are you up to, Mr. Borden?"

Willi licked his fingers and stared at Barent in wide-eyed innocence.

"What is it?" snapped Kepler. "What's going on?"

"Several of the surrogates are out of their pens," said Barent. "At least two of the security people are dead north of the security zone. My own security people have just detected Mr. Borden's black colleague and a woman . . . the female surrogate Mr. Harod brought onto the island . . . not a quarter of a mile from here on Live Oak Lane. What do you have in mind, sir?"

Willi opened his palms. "Jensen is an old and valued associate. I was only bringing him back here for the end game, Herr Barent."

"And the woman?"

"I confess that I planned to utilize her as well." Willi shrugged. The old man looked around the grand hall at two dozen of Barent's Neutrals armed with automatic rifles and Uzis. More security people were visible only as shadows on the balconies above. "Surely two naked surrogates do not pose a threat to anyone," he said and chuckled.

The Reverend Jimmy Wayne Sutter turned away from the windows. "But if the Lord creates something new," he said, "and the ground opens its mouth and swallows them up, with all that belongs to them, and they go down alive into Sheol, then you shall know that these men have despised the Lord." He looked back out into the night. "Numbers sixteen," he said.

"Hey, thanks a whole fucking shitload of a lot," said Harod. He removed the cap on a quart of expensive vodka and drank straight from the bottle.

"Quiet, Tony," snapped Willi. "Well, Herr Barent, will you bring my poor pawns in so we can resume the game?"

Kepler's eyes were wide with rage or fear as he tugged at C. Arnold Barent's sleeve. "Kill them," he insisted. He thrust a finger at Willi. "Kill *him*. He's insane. He wants to destroy the whole goddamned world just because *he's* going to die soon. Kill him before he can . . ."

"Shut up, Joseph," said Barent. He nodded at Swanson. "Bring them in and we will begin."

"Wait," said Willi. He closed his eyes for half a minute. "There is another." Willi opened his eyes. His smile grew very, very wide. "Another piece has arrived. This game will be more satisfying than even I had anticipated, Herr Barent."

Saul Laski had been shot by the Wehrmacht SS sergeant with the piece of sticking plaster on his chin and had been dumped into the Pit to lie with the hundreds of other dead and naked Jews. But Saul was not dead. In the sudden darkness he crawled across the wet sand of the Pit and the smooth, cooling flesh of corpses that had been men, women, and children from Lodz and a hundred other Polish towns and cities. The numbness in his right shoulder and left leg were turning into searing cords of pain. He had been shot twice and dumped into the Pit—at last—but he was still alive. Alive. And angry. The fury flowing through him was stronger than the pain, stronger than fatigue or fear or shock. Saul crawled across naked bodies and the wet bottom of the Pit and let the anger fuel his absolute determination to stay alive. He crawled forward in the darkness.

Saul was vaguely aware that he was experiencing a waking hallucination and the professional part of his mind was fascinated, wondering if the shock of being shot had triggered it, marveling at the verisimilitude of the sudden overlay of realities separated by forty years of time. But another part of his consciousness accepted the experience as reality itself, a resolution of the most unresolved part of his life—a guilt and obsession that had left him *without* much of a life for four decades, a fixation that had denied him marriage, family, or thought of the future in forty years of reliving his own inexplicable failure to die. Failure to join the others in the Pit.

And now he had.

The four men who had come ashore shouted to each other and fanned out behind him to cover thirty yards of beach. Small arms fire rattled into the jungle. Saul concentrated on crawling forward in the almost total darkness, feeling ahead with his hands as beach sand and loam gave way to more fallen logs and deeper swamp. He lowered his face into the water and raised it with a gasp, shaking droplets and twigs out of his hair. He had lost his glasses somewhere, but it did not seem to make a difference in the darkness; he might be ten feet or ten miles from the tree he was searching for and it would never matter in such blackness. Starlight did not penetrate the heavy foliage overhead and only a faint gleam of his own white fingers inches from his face convinced Saul that the impact of the bullet in his right shoulder had not blinded him somehow.

As a doctor, Saul wondered how badly he was bleeding, where the bullet was lodged—he had not succeeded in finding an exit wound—and how soon he would need medical treatment to have a chance of survival. It seemed an academic question as a second round of rifle fire ripped through foliage two feet above Saul's head. Branches and twigs dropped into the swamp with soft, plopping sounds. Thirty feet behind him, a man's voice shouted, "This way! He went in here! Kelty, Suggs, come with me. Overholt, move down the beach and make sure he don't come out that way!"

Saul crawled forward, getting to his feet as the water deepened to waist height. Powerful flashlight beams illuminated the jungle behind him in sudden strobes of yellow light. Saul staggered ahead for ten or fifteen feet and suddenly stumbled over a submerged log, scraping his thighs across it as he fell forward, breathing in scummed water as his face went under.

As he fought his way to his knees and brought his head up, a flashlight beam shone straight in his eyes.

"There he is!" The beam slid away for a second and Saul pressed his face against the rotting log as bullets struck all around him. One tore through the soft wood not ten inches from his cheek and went skittering across the surface of the swamp with a sound like a maddened insect. Saul instinctively turned his face away and at that second one of the three flashlight beams probing the area for him flashed across the trunk of a dead tree scarred and scoured by a deep slash of lightning.

"Back to the left!" screamed a man. The roar of the automatic rifles was incredible, the rooftop of thick foliage making it seem as if the three men were firing in a large, enclosed room.

Before the flashlight beams returned, Saul stood up and stumbled toward the tree twenty feet away. One beam of light swung back his way, caught him, and lost him again as the security man raised his weapon. Saul noted that bullets made a sound rather like furious bees as they hummed past one's ears. Water splashed him as a line of slugs stitched its way across the swamp and drummed hollowly into the tree itself.

The flashlights found him just as he reached the tree and stuck his arm up into the scar.

The bag he had wedged there was gone.

Saul threw himself underwater as bullets tore into the tree at the level his head and shoulders had been a second before. More bullets striking the water made an eerie, singing sound as he pulled his way across the bottom, filling his hands with roots, strands of aquatic plants, and whatever else he could grasp. He popped up behind the tree, gasping for air, praying for a stick, a rock, anything substantial to have in his hands as he rushed them in his last, futile seconds of life. His anger was a transcendent thing now, banishing the pain of his wounds. Saul imagined it shining out of him like the horns of light with which Moses reputedly returned from the mountain or like the narrow shafts of light now shining through the hollow tree where the bullets had punched through.

In the glare of those thin strands of light, Saul saw something gleaming in the shattered tree right at the waterline.

"Come on!" screamed the man who had shouted earlier, and the firing stopped as he and another man began splashing across the swamp, moving to their right to get a clear shot. The third man moved to his left, holding his flashlight steady.

Saul made a fist and struck the thick wood where light made the bark translucent. Once. Twice. His hand went through on the third blow and his fingers closed on wet plastic where the bag had fallen.

"See him?" screamed a man to his left. The flashlight beams were partly obscured by dangling webs of Spanish moss from low branches.

"Shit, get closer!" called the man to his right. He was almost visible around the curve of the trunk.

Saul clutched at the slippery plastic and tried to pull it through the small cleft he had made. The bag was too large to fit through. He released it and tore at bark with both hands, clawing an opening with his nails. The charred and rotted wood came away in strips and chunks, but segments of the trunk were as hard as steel.

"I see him!" screamed a second man to his left and a burst of fire made Saul duck into the water, still clawing, as splashes erupted all around.

The noise stopped after two or three seconds and Saul came up gasping and shaking water out of his eyes.

". . . Barry, you motherfucking idiot!" one of the men was screaming not twenty-five feet to Saul's left. "I'm right in your fucking line of fire, you stupid son of a bitch."

Saul reached inside the trunk and found only water. The bag had slipped lower. He stepped sideways and thrust his left arm as far as he could through the ragged hole. His fingers closed around a handle on the top of a long bundle.

"I see him!" screamed the man on his right.

Saul moved backward, feeling the presence of the two men behind him as a tensing in his aching shoulder blade, and pulled with all of his might. The bag came up and wedged tightly, still far too large for the opening.

The man on Saul's right steadied his flashlight and fired a single shot. A shaft of light angled up through the new hole in the trunk inches above Saul's head. Saul half crouched, shifted hands, and tugged again. The bag did not move. The second bullet threw a shaft of light between his right arm and his ribs. Saul realized that the men behind him were not firing only because their comrade was directly opposite them now, wading closer for his third shot, never letting the flashlight waver.

Saul grabbed the plastic strip with both hands, crouched, and threw himself backward with all of the force he could muster. He expected the handle to tear free and it did, but not before the bulky bag ripped through the opening in a shower of bark and water. Saul clutched at the wet bag, almost dropped it, and hugged it to his chest as he turned and ran.

The man to his right fired once and then switched to full automatic as Saul ran out of his flashlight beam. Another shaft of light from Saul's left found him but dropped away suddenly as the man screamed in pain and began shouting curses. A second weapon opened up fifteen feet from where it had fired earlier. Saul ran and wished he'd not lost his glasses.

The water was only knee-deep when he tripped over a fallen log and rolled onto a low island of shrubbery and swamp debris. He could hear at least two men splashing toward him as he flipped the heavy bag over, found the zipper, opened it, and unsealed the waterproof inner bag.

"He's got something!" one man shouted to another. "Hurry!" They splashed closer across the strip of shallow swamp.

Saul tugged out the web belt of C-4, tossed it aside, and pulled out the M-16 he had taken from Haines. It was not loaded. Taking care not to drop the bag in the water, Saul fumbled for one of the six ammunition clips, pulled one out, identified by feel that it was upside down, and slapped it into the magazine slit. During the scores of hours he had practiced breaking down, loading, and firing the weapon during those weeks in Charleston, he had never considered the *reason* behind Cohen's advice months earlier that anyone using a rifle should know how to assemble it while blindfolded.

The flashlight beams raked across the log Saul crouched behind and from the sounds of splashing Saul knew that the lead man was no more than ten feet away and closing quickly. Saul rolled over, clicked the selector from SAFE to SEMI with a movement born of habit, shouldered the plastic grip, and put a burst of copper-jacketed bullets into the man's chest and belly at a distance of less than six feet. The man jackknifed forward and seemed to rise backward into the air as his flashlight dropped into the swamp. The second man stopped twenty feet to Saul's right and shouted something unintelligible. Saul fired right down the beam of the flashlight. Glass and steel shattered, there was a single scream, and then darkness descended.

Saul blinked, made out a ghostly green glow only feet from him, and realized that the flashlight belonging to the first man he had killed was still glowing under twenty inches of water.

"Barry?" called a low voice forty feet from Saul's left, back where the two men had first tried to flank him. "Kip? What the fuck's going on? I'm hurt. Quit screwing around."

Saul pulled another clip from the bag, dropped the C-4 belt back in, and moved quickly to his left, trying to stay in the shallows.

"Barry!" came the voice again, twenty feet away now. "I'm getting out of here. I'm hurt. You shot me in the fucking leg, you asshole."

Saul slipped forward, moving when the man made noise.

"Hey! Who's that?" cried the man in the darkness. From fifteen feet away Saul clearly heard the sound of a safety being clicked off.

Saul put his back against a tree and whispered, "It's me. Overholt. Give us a light."

The man said, "*Shit*," and turned on his flashlight. Saul peered around the tree and saw a man with a gray security uniform bloodied at the left leg. He was cradling an Uzi submachine gun and fumbling with the flashlight. Saul killed him with a single bullet to the head.

The security uniform was a single-piece coverall with a zipper down the front. Saul switched off the flashlight, tugged the uniform off the corpse, and pulled it on in the dark. There were distant shouts from the beach. The coverall was too big, the boots too small even without socks, but Saul Laski·had never appreciated clothing so much in his life. He felt around in three inches of water for the long-billed cap the man had been wearing, found it, and tugged it on.

Cradling the M-16, the Uzi in his right hand and three extra clips for it in the deep pocket of his coverall, the flashlight clipped on his belt loop, Saul waded back to where he had left his bag. The web belts of C-4, extra magazines for the rifle, and the Colt automatic were dry and accounted for. He dropped the Uzi in, sealed and shouldered the bag, and walked out of the swamp.

A second boat had landed twenty yards down the beach and the fourth man had walked down to join the five new arrivals. He swiveled as Saul emerged west of the inlet and strolled across the beach.

"Kip, that you?" shouted the man over wind and surf sounds.

Saul shook his head. "Barry," he called, hand cupped half over his mouth.

"What the hell's all the shooting? Did you get him?"

"East!" Saul shouted cryptically and waved his hand down the beach beyond the men. Three of the guards raised weapons and jogged that way. The man who had shouted raised a hand radio and talked quickly. Two of the boats patrolling beyond the breakers swung east and began playing their searchlights along the tree line.

Saul waded to the first beached boat, lifted the small anchor out of the sand and dropped it in the back, and climbed in, dropping his bag onto the passenger seat. Blood from his back had soaked the long carrying strap. There were two huge outboard motors mounted, but the boat had an electronic ignition and required a key. The key was in the dash-mounted ignition switch.

Saul started the motors, backed away from the beach in a snarl of foam and sand, swung it into the breakers, and pounded through to open sea. Two hundred yards out he swung the boat east and opened the throttles to full speed. The bow raised and he came around the northeast edge of the island and roared south at forty-five knots. Saul felt the crashing of the bow and keel against the waves as a pounding through his very bones. The radio rasped and he turned it off. A boat heading north blinked at him, but he ignored it.

Saul slid the M-16 lower so the salt spray could not get at it. The water beaded on his stubbled cheeks and refreshed him as a cold shower might. He knew he had lost blood and was losing more—his leg continued to bleed and he could feel the stickiness against his back—but even in the post-adrenaline letdown, determination burned in him like a blue flame. He felt strong and very, very angry.

A mile ahead a green light blinked at the end of the long dock that led to Live Oak Lane and to the Manse and to Oberst Wilhelm von Borchert.

SIXTY-EIGHT

Charleston
Tuesday, June 16, 1981

It was after midnight and Natalie Preston felt trapped in a nightmare she had suffered as a child. An event that occurred the evening of her mother's funeral had brought her awake screaming for her father at least once a week for months that long-ago summer and fall.

The funeral had been an old-fashioned one with hours of visitation in the old mortuary. Friends and relatives had arrived and filed by the open coffin for what seemed like days to Natalie as she sat in sad silence next to her father. She had cried for the past two days and had been empty of tears as she sat holding her father's hand, but at some point she had felt the pressing need to go to the bathroom and whispered the fact to her father. He rose to lead her to the rest room, but another contingent of older relatives had come up to him just then and an elderly aunt had offered to take her. The old lady had taken her hand and led her down hallways, through several doorways, and up a flight of stairs before pointing to a white door.

When Natalie emerged, pressing down the skirt of her stiff, dark blue dress, the elderly aunt was gone. Natalie confidently turned left instead of right, went through doors, down halls and stairways, and was lost within a minute. It did not frighten her. She knew the chapel and receiving rooms must take up most of the first floor and if she opened enough doors she would find her father. What she did not know was that the rear staircase descended directly to the basement.

Natalie had looked through two doors opening into bare, empty rooms when she swung open a door and let the corridor light illuminate steel tables, racks of huge bottles holding dark fluid, and long, hollow steel needles attached to thin rubber hoses. She had covered her mouth with her hands and backed down the corridor, turning to run through broad double doors. She was halfway across a large, box-filled room before her eyes adjusted to the weak light filtering through the small curtained windows.

Natalie stopped in the middle of the room. No sounds disturbed the heavy air. The objects around her were not boxes; they were coffins. The heavy, dark wood of their surfaces seemed to absorb the diffused light. Several of the caskets had their hinged lids open at the top, just as her mother's did. Not five feet away from Natalie was a small, white box—just her size—with a crucifix on top. Years later, Natalie realized that she had stumbled into a casket storeroom or showroom, but at the time she was sure that she stood alone in the dim light in the middle of a dozen filled coffins. She expected white-faced corpses to sit up at any second, jack-knifing rigidly into a sitting position, heads turning and eyes opening to-ward her just like they did on the Friday Creature Feature vampire movies she and her dad watched.

There had been another door, but it seemed miles away and to get to it Natalie would have had to walk within clutching distance of four or five dark caskets. She did so, looking ahead only at the door and walking slowly, waiting for the pale arms and hands to lunge at her but refusing to run or scream. It was too important a day; it was her mother's funeral and she loved her mother.

Natalie had gone through the door, climbed a lighted stairway, and emerged in the hall near the front door. "There you are, dear!" exclaimed the elderly aunt and had brought her back to her father in the next room with whispered admonitions not to go wandering off to play again.

She had not thought of her old nightmare in a dozen years, but as she sat in Melanie Fuller's parlor with Justin sitting across from her, staring at her with his mad, old-woman eyes set in that pale, pudgy face, Natalie's reaction was the same as it had been in her dream when the coffin lids *had* been pushed back, when a dozen corpses *had* sat up stiffly in their boxes, and when two dozen hands *had* clutched at her and dragged her—resisting but still not screaming—toward the small white coffin that lay empty and waiting for *her*.

"A penny for your thoughts, dear," came the old woman's voice from the mouth of the child across from her.

Natalie jerked fully awake. It was the first time either of them had spo-ken since the senseless pointing and shouting the child had gone through twenty minutes earlier. "What's happening?" asked Natalie.

Justin shrugged, but his smile was very wide. His baby teeth looked as if they had been sharpened to points.

"Where is Saul?" demanded Natalie. Her fingers went to the monitor pack on her belt. "Tell me!" she snapped. Saul had designed the telemetry pack hookup to the explosives, but had balked at her actually using it when she was with Melanie. They had compromised with a monitor that trans-mitted a warning to the second receiver in the car with Jackson rather than triggering the C-4. It had been Natalie who reattached the wires to the C-4 on her web belt after Saul left for the island. During the last twenty-seven hours she had found herself half hoping that the old monster would try to seize her mind and that the thing would trigger the explosive. Natalie was exhausted and drained by fear and at times it seemed preferable just to have it *over* with. She did not know if the C-4 was certain to kill the old woman from this distance, but she *was* certain that Melanie's zombies would not let her get any closer to the creature upstairs.

"Where's Saul?" repeated Natalie.

"Oh, they have him," the boy said casually.

Natalie stood up. There were stirrings in the shadows of adjoining rooms. "You're lying," she snapped.

"Am I?" Justin smiled. "Now why would I do that?"

"What happened?"

Justin shrugged again and stifled a yawn. "It's after my bedtime, Nina. Why don't we continue this conversation in the morning?"

"*Tell me!*" shouted Natalie. Her finger found the override button on the monitor.

"Oh, all right," pouted the boy. "Your Hebrew friend got away from the guards, but Willi's man caught him and took him back to the Manse."

"The Manse," breathed Natalie.

"Yes, yes," snapped the boy. He kicked his heels against the leg of the chair. "Willi and Mr. Barent want to talk to him. They're playing a game."

Natalie looked around her. Something moved in the foyer. "Is Saul hurt?"

Justin shrugged.

"Is he still *alive?*" demanded Natalie.

The boy made a face. "I *said* they wanted to talk to him, Nina. They can't talk to a dead person, now can they?"

Natalie lifted her free hand and chewed at a nail. "It's time to do what we planned," she said.

"It's *not*," whined the six-year-old. "It's not at all the situation you told me to wait for. They're just playing."

"You're lying," said Natalie. "They can't be playing the game if Willi's man is out and Saul's at the Manse."

"Not *that* game," said the boy, shaking his head at her stupidity. It was difficult for Natalie to remember that he was only a flesh and blood marionette being manipulated by the ancient crone upstairs. "They're playing *chess*," said the boy.

"Chess," said Natalie.

"Yes. The winner gets to decide on the next game. Willi wants to play for bigger stakes." Justin shook his head in an old woman's gesture. "Willi always had a Wagnerian preoccupation with Ragnarok and Armageddon. It comes with German blood, I'm sure."

"Saul is hurt and captured at the Manse where they're playing chess," said Natalie in a monotone. She remembered the afternoon seven months earlier when she and Rob had listened to Saul Laski retell his story of the camps and the run-down castle keep in the Polish forest where the young Oberst had challenged *Der Alte* in a final game.

"Yes, yes," Justin said happily. "Miss Sewell will also get to play. On Mr. Barent's team. He's very handsome."

Natalie stepped back. Saul and she had discussed what she should do if the plan fell apart. He recommended that Natalie throw the satchel charges with the forty-second timer and run, even though it meant letting Barent and the others escape. The second possibility was to continue the bluff, force Melanie's hand, in the hopes of still getting Barent and possibly other members of the Island Club.

Now Natalie saw a third possibility. At least six hours of darkness remained. She realized that while the demand for justice and revenge for her father's murder was still strong in her, that her love for Saul was stronger. She also knew that Saul's discussion with her of exit plans had been only talk; that he had made no escape plans.

Natalie knew that justice demanded that she stay and follow the plan through, but justice was second in her heart at that moment to the rising urge to save Saul if there was any chance at all.

"I'm leaving for a few minutes," she said firmly. "If Barent tries to leave or the other conditions apply, do precisely what we planned. I *mean it*, Melanie. I will brook no failure here. Your own life depends on this. If you fail, the Island Club will surely plan to kill you, but they will be too late because *I* will kill you. Do you understand, Melanie?"

Justin stared at her, a slight smile on his round face.

Natalie whirled and walked toward the foyer. Someone moved quickly in the darkness ahead of her, going through the door to the dining room. Justin followed her. Someone moved on the landing at the head of the stairs and there were sounds in the kitchen. Natalie stopped in the foyer, her finger still on the red button. Her scalp itched under the round tape of the electrodes. "I will be back before sunrise," she said.

Justin smiled up at her, his face glowing slightly in the faint green glow from the second floor.

Catfish had been watching for more than six hours when Natalie emerged from the Fuller house. That wasn't on the night's flight plan. He squeezed the transmitter button on the cheap CB twice—what Jackson had called "breaking squelch"—and crouched in the bushes to see what was going on. He had yet to see Marvin, but when he did he was going to make his move to save his old gang leader from the Voodoo Lady, no matter what else was going down.

Natalie was moving fast when she crossed the courtyard. She waited while some dude Catfish couldn't see unlocked the gate for her.

She crossed the street without looking back and turned right past Catfish's alley rather than turning left toward where Jackson was parked down the street. That was the prearranged signal that she might be followed. Catfish broke squelch three times letting Jax know to head around the block for the pickup point and then he crouched lower and waited.

A man moved out of the shadows of the Fuller courtyard and jogged across the street in a half crouch the minute Natalie was out of sight. Catfish caught a glimpse of reflected light from the streetlight on the blue steel of the barrel of a handgun. Big automatic from the looks of it. "Shit," whispered Catfish, waited a minute to make sure no one else was following, and slipped along in the shadow of parked cars on the east side of the street.

The guy with the gun was a dude Catfish didn't recognize—too small to be the Culley monster he'd glimpsed in the courtyard, too white to be Marvin.

Catfish moved silently to the corner and crawled through some screening shrubbery to poke his head out. Natalie was halfway down the block, ready to cross to the other side. White dude with the gun was moving real slow in the shadow on this side. Catfish broke squelch four times and followed, his black pants and windbreaker making him invisible.

He hoped Natalie'd unplugged all that C-4 shit. High explosives made Catfish nervous. He'd seen the bits and pieces that were all that was left of his best friend Leroy after the crazy dude'd set off that dynamite he was carrying. Catfish didn't mind dying—he'd never expected to see thirty—but he wanted his smiling self to be laid out in one big gorgeous piece, wrapped in his best seven-hundred-dollar suit, for Marcie, Sheila, and Belinda to weep over.

Warned by the four-squelch signal, Jackson accelerated down the street and swung to the left side of the street to shield Natalie as he picked her up. The dude with the gun braced it with both hands on the roof of a parked Volvo and took aim at the reflection of a streetlight on the windshield right in front of Jackson's face.

Wasn't all tea and crumpets with the Voodoo Lady tonight, thought Catfish. *Old broad must be pissed off.* He moved forward, running silently on fifty-dollar Adidases, and kicked the white dude's legs out from under him. The man's chin hit the rooftop and Catfish banged the dude's face against the passenger side window for good measure, getting his hand on the gun and the web between his thumb and forefinger on the hammer just in case. Movies, they toss guns around like toys, but Catfish had seen brothers shot by weapons barely dropped. *People don't kill people,* he thought as he laid the white dude on the shadowed sidewalk, *fuckin' guns do.*

Jackson broke squelch twice as he drove away with Natalie. Catfish looked around, checked to see that the white dude was out but still breathing, and triggered the transmit button. "Hey, bro," he said, "what's happenin'?"

Jackson's voice was distorted by the cheap speaker and low volume. "Lady all right, man. What's with you?"

"Dude with a big service four-five, he don't like your face, man. He asleep now."

"How asleep?" rasped Jax's voice.

"Just dozin', man. What you want done with it?" Catfish had his knife, but they had decided that bodies being discovered in such an uptight whitey neighborhood might not be good for business.

"Put it someplace quiet," said Jackson.

"Yeah, great," said Catfish. He dragged the unconscious honky into shrubbery under a willow tree. Brushing his clothes off, he keyed the transmit button. "You two comin' back or you going to elope or something?"

Jackson's voice was faded by distance. Catfish wondered where the hell they were headed. "Later, man," said Jax. "Be cool. We'll be back. Lay low."

"Shit," said Catfish over the CB, "you get to take the fox for rides and I get to sit in ofay's alleys."

"Seniority, man," called Jackson, his voice barely audible. "I was Soul Brickyard when you was just a bulge in your daddy's britches. Stay low, bro."

"Fuck you, too, Stu," said Catfish, but there was no reply and he guessed they were out of range. He pocketed the CB and moved quickly and quietly back to his alley, checking every shadow to make sure the Voodoo Lady hadn't sent out any other troops.

He had been sitting in his hidey-hole between a garbage can and an old fence less than ten minutes and was fast-forwarding and freeze-framing one of his favorite memories of Belinda in bed at the Chelten Arms, when there was the merest whisper of sound in the alley behind him.

Catfish came up fast, flicking his stiletto open even as he rose. The man behind him was too big and too bald to be real.

Culley slapped the knife out of Catfish's hand with a sweep of his massive palm. With his right hand he seized the thin black by the throat and lifted him off the ground.

Catfish felt his air cut off and his vision fading, but even as the massive vise of flesh lifted him off the ground he kicked the man-mountain twice in the balls and slapped his hands over the bald dude's ears hard enough to burst eardrums. The monster did not even blink. Catfish's fingers were going for the dude's eyes when the hand on his throat squeezed harder, impossibly hard, and there was a loud snap as Catfish's larynx broke.

Culley dropped the thrashing, gasping black man onto the cinders of the alley and watched impassively. It took him almost three minutes to die, the broken larynx swelling to stop any air from passing. In the end, Culley had to hold the thrashing, bucking body down with his massive, booted foot. When he was finished, Culley retrieved the knife and performed a few experiments to make sure the colored man was dead. Then he went around the corner, picked up Howard's unconscious form, and effortlessly carried both bodies across the street and into the house where the only light was the green glow from the second floor.

The rain began again before they were halfway to Mt. Pleasant. Jackson tried raising Catfish on the CB, but the storm and ten miles of distance appeared to be defeating the small radios.

"Do you think he'll be all right?" asked Natalie. She had discarded the web belt of C-4 as soon as she had entered the car, but retained the EEG monitor. If a theta rhythm appeared, an alarm would sound. The fact did not reassure Natalie much. Her main hope lay in Melanie's reluctance to this point at challenging Nina's control. Natalie wondered if she had signed her own death warrant by telling the old monster that she was not Nina's cat's-paw.

"Catfish?" said Jackson. "Yeah, he's been through a lot. Man's no fool. Besides, somebody got to stay behind to make sure the Voodoo Lady doesn't go away." He glanced at Natalie. The wipers beat monotonously at the rain-streaked windshield. "We got a change in plans here, Nat?"

Natalie nodded.

Jackson shifted a toothpick from the left to the right side of his mouth. "You're going to the island, aren't you?"

Natalie let out a breath. "How'd you know?"

"Pilot lives out this way. That who you called this afternoon and say hang around, maybe you have some business for him?"

"Yes," said Natalie, "but I was thinking of tomorrow after all this is over."

Jackson moved the toothpick. "Is this all going to be over tomorrow, Natalie?"

Natalie stared straight ahead through a window made opaque by the downpour. "Yes," she said firmly, "it is."

Daryl Meeks stood in the kitchen of his trailer, his thin form wrapped in a ratty blue bathrobe, and squinted at his two dripping guests. "How do I know you're not two black revolutionaries trying to get me involved in some crazy plot?" he said.

"You don't know," said Natalie. "You just have to take my word for it. It's Barent and his group who are the bastards. They have my friend Saul and I want to get him out of there."

Meeks scratched at gray stubble. "On your way in, did either of you two notice that it was pouring rain with Force Two gale conditions?"

"Yeah," said Jackson, "we noticed."

"You still want to buy a plane ride, huh?"

"Yes," said Natalie.

"I'm not sure what the going rate for this kind of excursion is," said Meeks, pulling the tab on a Pabst.

Natalie pulled a heavy envelope out of her sweater and laid it on the kitchen table. Meeks opened it, nodded, and sipped his beer.

"Twenty-one thousand, three hundred seventy-five dollars and nineteen cents," said Natalie.

Meeks scratched his head. "Dumped the whole PLO piggy bank out for this one, huh?" He took a long swallow of beer. "What the hell," he said, "it's a nice night for a flight. You two wait here 'til I get changed. Help yourself to a beer if it isn't against KGB rules."

Natalie watched the rain move across the yard and field in curtains that obscured the small hangar under spotlights forty yards away.

"I'm going too," said Jackson.

She looked around and said in a preoccupied tone, "No."

"*Bullshit*," growled Jackson. He lifted the heavy black bag he had brought in from the car. "I got plasma, morphine, battle dressings . . . the whole fucking kit. What happens if you pull off this freakin' dust-off and the man needs a medic? You think of that, Nat? Say you get him out and he bleeds to death on the trip back—you want that?"

"All right," said Natalie.

"Ready!" called Meeks from the hallway. He was wearing a blue baseball cap with the legend YOKOHAMA TAIYO WHALES in white stitching, an ancient leather flight jacket, jeans, green sneakers, and a gun belt with a pearl-handled, long-barreled Smith & Wesson .38 protruding from the holster. "Only two rules," he said. "One, I say we can't land, it means we *can't land*. I still keep a third of the money. Two, don't pull that goddamned Colt out again in the backseat unless you plan to use it, and you damn better not think of settling any arguments with me that way, or you'll swim the whole way back."

"Agreed," said Natalie.

Natalie had been on a roller coaster once, with her father, and had been smart enough never to go on another one. This ride was a thousand times worse.

The cockpit of the Cessna was small and steamy, the windscreen was a wall of water, and Natalie was not even able to tell when exactly they had left the ground except for the fact that the bumps, bounces, slews, and sideslips grew wider. Lighted from below by the red glow of the instruments, Meek's face looked both demonic and moronic. Natalie was sure that her own appearance was equally moronic with the added element of pure terror. Every once in a while Jackson would bounce around the backseat and say, "Shit, man," and then there would be silence except for the rain, the wind, assorted tortured mechanical sounds, thunder, and the pitifully inadequate tiny noise of the engine.

"So far, so good," said Meeks. "We're not going to be able to get above this crap, but we'll get past it before we get to Sapelo. So far everything's copacetic." He turned to Jackson and said, "Nam?"

"Yeah."

"Grunt?"

"Medic, one hundred first."

"When'd you DEROS?"

"Didn't. Me and two bros got fucked up on an LRRP when some little

ARVN Kit Carson dude tripped his own claymore while we were in our NDP."

"Other two make it?"

"Uh-uh. Sent 'em home in zip-locks. They gave me another ribbon and didi-maud me Stateside just in time to vote for Nixon."

"Did you?"

"Shee-it," said Jackson.

"Yeah," said Meeks. "I can't remember the last time any politician did me a favor neither."

Natalie stared at the two of them.

The Cessna was suddenly illuminated by a bolt of lightning that appeared to pass through their starboard wing. At the same instant a gust of wind tried to toss them upside down while the bottom seemed to disappear as they dropped two hundred feet like a cableless elevator. Meeks adjusted something above him, tapped at an instrument that showed a black and white ball rolling drunkenly, and yawned, " 'Bout another hour and twenty minutes," he said, stifling another yawn. "Mr. Jackson, there's a big Thermos back there somewhere by your feet. Some Twinkies and stuff, too, I think. Why don't you have some coffee and pass some up? I'll take a Hostess Ding-Dong. Miz Preston, you want something? First-class fare entitles you to an in-flight snack."

Natalie turned her face to the window. "No thanks," she said. Lightning rippled through a thunderhead a thousand feet *below* her, showing fragments of black clouds racing by like tatters of some witch's gown. "Nothing just yet," she said. She tried closing her eyes.

SIXTY-NINE

Dolmann Island
Tuesday, June 26, 1981

Saul throttled back and let the speedboat slide in to touch the dock. The green light at the end of the pier blinked on, sending its unheeded signal to the empty Atlantic. Saul tied up, tossed his plastic bag to the dock, and stepped up, dropping to one knee on the pier, keeping the M-16 ready. The dock and surrounding area were empty. Untended golf carts sat waiting where the asphalt road ran south along the shoreline. There were no other boats tied up.

Saul slung the duffel bag over his shoulder and moved cautiously toward the trees. Even if most of the security people had gone north to search for him, Saul could not believe that Barent would leave the northern approach to the Manse unguarded. He trotted into the darkness under the trees, his body tensed against the half-expected impact of bullets. There was no movement except for the slight shift of leaves in the lessening sea breeze. The lights of the Manse were just visible to the south. Saul's only objective at this point was to get into the Manse alive.

There were no lights along Live Oak Lane. Saul remembered the pilot, Meeks, talking about how the way would be lighted for visiting dignitaries and VIPs, but the grassy walkway was forest-dark this night. Moving from tree to tree, shrub to shrub, took time. Thirty minutes passed, he had covered half the distance to the Manse, and still there was no sign of Barent's security people. Saul had a sudden thought that froze him with a fear colder and deeper than his dread of death; what if Barent and Willi had left already?

It was possible. Barent was not a man who would expose himself to danger. Saul had been counting on using the billionaire's overconfidence as a weapon—everyone who spent time with the man, including Saul, had been conditioned to be incapable of hurting him—but perhaps Willi's intervention in Philadelphia or the incongruity of Saul's escape had changed that. Heedless of danger, Saul gripped the rifle at port arms and ran along the grassy lane between the oaks, his duffel bag banging against his injured shoulder.

He had run only two hundred yards and was panting painfully when he slid to a stop, dropped to one knee, and raised the rifle. He squinted and wished he had his glasses. A naked body lay facedown in the shadow of a small oak. Saul glanced left and right, lowered the duffel bag, and moved forward in a sprint.

The woman was not quite naked. A torn and bloodied shirt covered one arm and part of her back. The woman lay on her stomach, her face turned away and hidden by her hair, arms thrown out, fingers clenching the earth, and her right leg bent as if she had been running hard when her assailant had run her to the ground. Peering around suspiciously, M-16 at the ready, Saul touched her neck to feel for a pulse.

The woman's head snapped around and Saul caught a glimpse of Miss Sewell's wide, mad eyes and her open mouth before her teeth clamped hard on his left hand. She made a noise that was not human. Saul grimaced and raised the butt of the M-16 to smash into her face just as Jensen Luhar dropped from the branches of the oak tree and slammed a heavy forearm into Saul's throat.

Saul yelled and fired the M-16 on full automatic, trying to angle the fire back into Luhar but succeeding only in ripping branches and leaves above him. Luhar laughed and jerked the rifle out of Saul's hand, flinging it twenty feet into the darkness. Saul struggled, forcing his chin down against Luhar's powerful forearm to keep from being strangled and trying to wrench his left hand free from the woman's bulldog grip. His right hand clawed over his shoulder, trying to find the black man's face and eyes.

Luhar laughed again and lifted Saul in a half nelson. Saul felt the flesh in the web of his left hand rip away and then Luhar pivoted and threw him seven or eight feet through the air. Saul hit hard on his wounded left leg, rolled on a shoulder turned to fire, and scrabbled on hands and knees toward the duffel bag where he had left the Colt and Uzi. A glance over his shoulder showed Jensen Luhar poised in a wrestler's crouch, his naked body glistening with sweat and Saul's blood. Miss Sewell was on all fours, tensed as if ready to spring, her wild hair over her eyes. Blood ran onto her chin as she spit out a chunk of Saul's hand.

He made it to within three feet of the bag before Luhar sprinted forward, fast and silent on bare feet, and kicked him solidly in the ribs. Saul rolled over four times, feeling the air and energy go out of him in a rush, trying to get his knees under him again even as his vision dimmed and narrowed to a long, dark tunnel with Luhar's advancing face in the center.

Luhar kicked Saul once more, threw the duffel bag far away into the darkness, and grabbed the psychiatrist by his fringe of hair. He pulled Saul's face up to his own and shook him. "Wake up, little pawn," he said in German. "Time to play."

The spotlights in the Great Hall illuminated eight rows of squares. Each square was a white or black tile four feet on a side. Tony Harod was looking at a chessboard that stretched thirty-two feet in each direction. Barent's security people made soft noises in the shadows and there were muted electronic sounds from the table holding the electronic gear, but only the Island Club members and their aides stood in the light.

"It has been an interesting game to this point," said Barent. "Although there have been several times when I was certain that it could only lead to a draw."

"*Ja*," said Willi, stepping from the shadows into the light. He wore a white silk turtleneck under a white suit, giving him the appearance of a negative-image priest. The overhead spots made his thinning white hair gleam and emphasized the ruddiness on the ridges of his cheeks and jowls. "I have always preferred the Tarrasch Defense. It has gone out of style since it was popular in my youth, but I still consider it sound when used with the proper variations."

"It was a positional game until move twenty-nine," said Barent. "Mr. Borden offered me his king rook pawn and I took it."

"A poisoned pawn," said Willi, frowning at the board.

Barent smiled. "Fatal for a lesser player, perhaps. But when the exchanges were finished, I retained five pawns to Mr. Borden's three."

"And a bishop," said Willi, looking to where Jimmy Wayne Sutter stood near the bar.

"And a bishop," agreed Barent. "But two pawns frequently defeat a lone bishop in an end game."

"Who's winning?" demanded Kepler. The man was drunk.

Barent rubbed his cheek. "It is not that simple, Joseph. At this moment, black—that is my color—holds a distinct advantage. But things change quickly in an end game."

Willi walked out onto the chessboard. "Do you want to change sides, Herr Barent?"

The billionaire laughed softly. "*Nein, mein Herr.*"

"Then let's get on with it," said Willi. He looked around at the people standing at the edge of shadow.

The FBI man Swanson whispered in Barent's ear. "Just a second," said their host. He turned to Willi. "What the hell are you up to now, old man?"

"Let them in," said Willi.

"Why should I," snapped Barent. "They're your people."

"Exactly," said Willi. "It is obvious that my black is unarmed and I've brought my Jew pawn back to serve in the way he was destined to."

"An hour ago you said we should kill him," said Barent.

Willi shrugged. "You still can if you wish, Herr Barent. The Jew is almost dead as it is. But it suits my sense of irony that he has come so far to serve me again."

"You still contend that he came to the island on his own?" sneered Kepler.

"I contend nothing," said Willi. "I request permission to use him in the game. It pleases me." Willi leered at his host. "Besides, Herr Barent, you must be sure that the Jew was well conditioned by you. You would have nothing to fear from him even if he arrived armed."

"Then why is he here?" asked Barent.

Willi laughed. "To kill me," he said. "Come. Make up your mind. I want to play."

"What about the woman?" said Barent.

"She has been my queen's pawn," said Willi. "I give her to you."

"Your *queen's* pawn," repeated Barent. "And does your queen still rule her?"

"My queen has been removed from the board," said Willi. "But you can ask the pawn when she arrives."

Barent snapped his fingers and half a dozen men with weapons stepped forward. "Bring them in," he said. "If they make any suspicious moves, kill them. Tell Donald that I may be flying out to the *Antoinette* earlier than we had anticipated. Recall the patrols and double the security south of the zone."

Tony Harod did not at all care for the smell of recent events. As far as he could tell, he had no way off the fucking island. Barent had his helicopter waiting just beyond the french doors, Willi had his Lear jet at the landing strip, even Sutter had a plane waiting; but as far as Harod could make out, he and Maria Chen were stranded. Now a new phalanx of security people had entered, herding Jensen Luhar and the two surrogates Harod had picked up in Savannah. Luhar was naked, all muscled black flesh. The woman wore only a torn and bloodied shirt that looked as if it came from one of the security zone guards. Her face was smeared and smudged with dirt and blood, but it was her eyes that bothered Harod the most; they were almost comically wide, staring roundly from behind dangling strands of hair, their irises completely surrounded by white. If the woman looked bad, the man named Saul whom Harod had brought onto the island looked terrible. Luhar appeared to be holding the Jew upright as they stood ten paces in front of Barent, and Harod's former surrogate was a mess: blood dripping from his face and soaking through his shirt and left pant leg. The man's left hand looked as if it had been run through a mangle with metal teeth. Blood fell from the dangling hand onto a white-tiled square. But something about his gaze suggested alertness and defiance.

Harod could figure out none of this. It was immediately obvious that Willi knew both the man and the woman—even admitting that the Jew had been a surrogate of his once—but Barent seemed to be going along with a proposition that both of these wretched prisoners had come to the island of their own choice. Willi had said earlier that *Barent* had been the one who had conditioned the Jew, but the billionaire had not brought him to the island. He seemed to be treating him as a free agent. The dialogue with the woman was even more bizarre. Harod was confused.

"Good evening, Dr. Laski," Barent had said to the bleeding man. "I'm sorry I did not recognize you sooner."

Laski said nothing. His gaze shifted to where Willi sat in one of the high-backed chairs and did not change even when Jensen Luhar jerked his head around to face Mr. Barent.

"It was your airplane that landed on the north beach some weeks ago," said Barent.

"Yes," said Laski, his eyes never leaving Willi.

"A clever arrangement," said Barent. "A pity it did not succeed. Do you admit that you came here to kill us?"

"Not all of you," said Laski, "only him." He did not point at Willi, but he did not have to.

"Yes," said Barent. He rubbed his cheek and glanced at Willi. "Well, Dr. Laski, do you still plan to kill our guest?"

"Yes."

"Are you worried, Herr Borden?" asked Barent.

Willi smiled.

Barent then did an incredible thing. Leaving the chair he had been sitting in since just before the three surrogates' arrival, he walked to the woman, lifted her filthy right hand, and kissed it gently. "Herr Borden informs me that I have the honor of addressing Miz Fuller," he said in a voice smoother than melted margarine. "Is this correct?"

The wild-eyed woman smiled and simpered. "You do," she said in a thick Southern drawl. There was dried blood on her teeth.

"This is indeed a pleasure, Miz Fuller," said Barent, still holding the woman's hand. "It has been a source of great disappointment to me that we have not met before this. May I ask what has brought you to our little island?"

"Mere curiosity, sir," said the wild-eyed apparition. When she moved slightly, Harod could see the thick V of her pubic hair through the opening of her shirt.

Barent stood straight-backed and smiling, still fondling the woman's grimy hand. "I see," he said. "There was no need to arrive incognito, Miz Fuller. You would be most welcome in person on the island—at any time—and I am sure that you would find our . . . ah . . . accommodations more comfortable in the guest wing of the Manse."

"Thank you, sir." The surrogate smiled. "I am currently indisposed, but when my health improves, I shall avail myself of your generous invitation."

"Excellent," said Barent. He released her hand and walked back to his chair. His security people relaxed a bit and lowered their Uzis. "We were just about to finish a game of chess," he said. "Our new guests must join us. Miz Fuller, would you honor me by allowing your surrogate to play on our side? I assure you that I shall not allow any threat of capture to spoil her participation."

The woman smoothed down the rags of her shirt and fluttered her hands at the tangle of hair, moving some from in front of her eyes. "The honor would be all mine, sir," she said.

"Wonderful," said Barent. "Herr Borden, I presume you wish to use your two pieces?"

"*Ja*," said Willi. "My old pawn will bring me luck."

"Fine," said Barent, "shall we pick up on the thirty-sixth move?"

Willi nodded. "I had taken your bishop on the previous move," he said. "Then you moved toward centering your king with a response of K-Q3."

"Ah," said Barent, "my strategies are far too transparent for a master."

"*Ja*," agreed Willi. "They are. Let us play."

Natalie breathed a deep sign of relief when they broke out of the storm clouds somewhere east of Sapelo Island. The wind still battered at the Cessna and the starlight illuminated a whitecapped ocean far below, but at least the roller coaster ride had flattened out. "About forty-five minutes out now," said Meeks. He rubbed his face with his left hand. "Head winds are addin' about a half hour to the flight."

Jackson leaned forward and said softly next to Natalie's ear, "Do you really think they're going to let us land?"

Natalie set her cheek against the window. "If the old woman does what she said she would. Maybe."

Jackson snorted a laugh. "You think she will?"

"I don't know," said Natalie. "I just think it's more important that we get Saul out. I think we did everything we could to show Melanie that it was in her self-interest to act."

"Yeah, but she's crazy," said Jackson. "Crazy folks don't always act in their own self-interest, kid."

Natalie smiled. "I guess that explains why we're here, huh?"

Jackson touched her shoulder. "Have you thought about what you're going to do if Saul's dead?" he asked softly.

Natalie's head moved up and down an inch. "We get him out," she said. "Then I go back and kill the thing in Charleston."

Jackson sat back, curled up in the backseat, and was breathing loudly in his sleep a minute later. Natalie watched the ocean until her eyes hurt and then turned toward the pilot. Meeks was looking at her strangely. Confronted with her stare, he touched his baseball cap and turned his attention back to the glow of the instruments.

Wounded, bleeding, fighting just to stay standing and conscious, Saul was pleased to be precisely where he was. His gaze never left the Oberst for more than a few seconds. After almost forty years of searching, he—Saul Laski—was in the same room as Oberst Wilhelm von Borchert.

It was not the best of situations. Saul had gambled everything, even allowing Luhar to overpower him when he *could* have gotten to his weapons in time, on the slim hope of being brought into the Oberst's presence. It was the scenario he had shared with Natalie months earlier as they sat drinking coffee in the orange-scented Israeli dusk, but these were not optimum conditions. He would have a chance of confronting the Nazi murderer only if Willi were the one to use his psychic abilities on Saul. Now all of the mutant throwbacks were there—Barent, Sutter, the one named Kepler, even Harod and Melanie Fuller's surrogate—and Saul was terrified that one of *them* would attempt to seize his mind, squandering the single, slim chance he might have to surprise the Oberst. Then there was the fact that in his scenario to Natalie, Saul had always painted the picture of a one-to-one confrontation with the old man, with Saul being the physically stronger of the two. Now Saul was using most of his strength of will and body just to remain standing, his left hand hung bleeding and useless, and there was a bullet lodged somewhere near his collarbone, while the Oberst sat looking fit and rested, thirty pounds heavier in muscle than Saul and surrounded by at least two superbly conditioned cat's-paws with at least half a dozen other people nearby whom he could use at will. Nor did Saul believe that Barent's security people would allow him to take more than three unauthorized strides before they gunned him down in cold blood.

But Saul was happy. There was no place else in the world he would rather be.

He shook his head to focus his attention on what was happening. Barent and the Oberst were seated while Barent set the human chess pieces in place. For the second time in that endless day, Saul had a waking hallucination as the Grand Hall shimmered like a reflection on a wind-rippled pond and suddenly he saw the wood and stones of a Polish keep, with gray-garbed *Sonderkommandos* taking their pleasure under centuries-old tapestries while the aging *Alte* sat huddled in his general's uniform like some wizened mummy wrapped in baggy rags. Torches sent shadows dancing across stone and tile and the shaven skulls of the thirty-two Jewish prisoners standing at tired attention between the two German officers. The young Oberst brushed his blond hair off his forehead, propped his elbow on his knee, and smiled at Saul.

The Oberst smiled at Saul. "*Willkommen, Jude*," he said.

"Come, come," Barent was saying, "we shall all play. Joseph, you come here to king's bishop three."

Kepler stepped back with an expression of horror on his face. "You have to be fucking kidding," he said. He backed into the bar table hard enough to topple several bottles.

"Oh, no," said Barent, "I am not kidding. Hurry, please, Joseph. Herr Borden and I wish to settle this before it gets too late."

"Go to *hell*!" screamed Kepler. He clenched his fists as cords stood out in his neck. "I'm not going to be used like some fucking surrogate while you . . ." Kepler's voice cut off as if a needle had been pulled from a faulty record. The man's mouth worked a second, but not the faintest hint of sound emerged. Kepler's face grew red, then purple, and then darkened toward black in the seconds before he pitched forward onto the tiles. Kepler's arms seemed to be jerked behind him by brutal, invisible hands, his ankles bound by invisible cords, as he propelled himself forward by a spastic, humping, flopping action—a disturbed child's idea of a worm's locomotion—his chest and chin slamming onto the tile with each absurd spasm. In this way, Joseph Kepler inched his way on his face and belly and thighs across twenty-five feet of open floor, leaving streaks of blood from his torn chin on the white tiles, until he arrived at the king-bishop-three square. When Barent relaxed his control, Kepler's muscles visibly twitched and spasmed in relief, and there was a soft sound as urine soaked the man's pant leg and flowed onto the dark tile.

"Stand up, please, Joseph," Barent said softly. "We want to start the game."

Kepler pushed himself to his knees, stared in shock at the billionaire for a moment, and silently stood on shaky legs. Blood and urine stained the front of his expensive Italian slacks.

"Are you going to Use all of us like that, Brother Christian?" asked Jimmy Wayne Sutter. The evangelist was standing at the edge of the improvised chessboard, the light from the overhead spots gleaming on his thick, white hair.

Barent smiled. "I see no reason to Use anyone, James," he said. "Provided they do not become an obstacle to the completion of this game. Do you, Herr Borden?"

"No," said Willi. "Come here, Sutter. As my bishop, you are the only surviving piece other than kings and pawns. Come, take your place here next to the queen's empty square."

Sutter raised his head. Sweat had soaked through his silk sports coat. "Do I have a choice?" he whispered. His theater-trained voice was raw and ragged.

"*Nein,*" said Willi. "You must play. Come."

Sutter turned his face toward Barent. "I mean a choice in which side I serve," he said.

Barent raised an eyebrow. "You have served Herr Borden well and long," he said. "Would you change sides now, James?"

"'I find no pleasure in the death of the wicked,'" said Sutter. "'Believe in the Lord Jesus Christ and ye shall be saved.' John 3:16, 17."

Barent chuckled and rubbed his chin. "Herr Borden, it seems that your bishop wishes to defect. Do you have any objections to his ending the game on the black side?"

The Oberst's face bore the petulant expression of a child. "Take him and be damned," he said. "I don't need the fat faggot."

"Come," Barent said to the sweating evangelist, "you shall be at the king's left hand, James." He pointed to a white tile one space advanced from where the black king's pawn would have begun the game.

Sutter took his place on the board next to Kepler.

Saul allowed himself a glimmer of hope at the thought that the game might proceed without the mind vampires using their power on their pawns. Anything to defer the moment when the Oberst would touch his mind.

Leaning forward in his massive chair, the Oberst laughed softly. "If I am to be denied my fundamentalist ally," he said, "then it amuses me to promote my old pawn to the rank of bishop. *Bauer, verstehts Du?* Come, Jew, and accept your miter and crook."

Quickly, before he could be prompted, Saul moved across the lighted expanse of tile to the black square in the first rank. He was less than eight feet from the Oberst, but Luhar and Reynolds stood between them while a score of Barent's security people scrutinized every step he took. Saul was in great pain from his wound now—his left leg was stiff and aching, his shoulder a mass of flame—but he tried to show none of this as he strode forward.

"Like old times, eh, pawn?" the Oberst said in German. "Excuse me," he added. "I mean, Herr *Bishop*." The Oberst grinned. "Quickly, now, I have three pawns remaining. Jensen, to K1, *bitte*. Tony, to QR3. Tom will serve as pawn in QN5."

Saul watched as Luhar and Reynolds took their places. Harod stood where he was. "I don't know where the fuck QR3 is," he said.

The Oberst beckoned impatiently. "The second square in front of my queen rook's tile," he snapped. "*Schnell.*"

Harod blinked and lurched toward the black square on the left side of the board.

"Fill your last three pawn spaces," the Oberst said to Barent.

The billionaire nodded. "Mr. Swanson, if you don't mind. Next to Mr. Kepler, please." The mustached security man looked around, set down his automatic weapon, and walked to the black square to the left and rear of Kepler. Saul realized that he was a king knight's pawn who had not yet moved from his original square.

"Ms. Fuller," said Barent, "if you would allow your delightful surrogate to proceed to the queen rook's pawn original position. Yes, that is correct." The woman who had once been Constance Sewell stepped gingerly forward on bare feet to stand four squares in front of Harod. "Ms. Chen," continued Barent, "next to Miz Sewell, please."

"No!" cried Harod as Maria Chen stepped forward. "She doesn't play!"

"*Ja* she does," said the Oberst. "She brings a certain beauty to the game, *nicht wahr?*"

"No!" Harod screamed again and pivoted toward the Oberst. "She's not part of this."

Willi smiled and inclined his head toward Barent. "How touching. I suggest that we allow Tony to trade places with his secretary if her pawn position becomes . . . ah . . . threatened. Is that agreeable to you, Herr Barent?"

"Yes, yes, yes," said Barent. "They can exchange places when and if Harod wishes, as long as it does not disrupt the flow of the game. Let's get on with it. We still need to set our kings in place." Barent looked at the remaining clusters of aides and security people.

"*Nein*," called the Oberst, standing and walking onto the board. "*We* are the kings, Herr Barent."

"What are you talking about, Willi?" the billionaire asked tiredly.

The Oberst opened his hands and smiled. "It is an important game," he said. "We must show our friends and colleagues that we support their efforts." He took his place two squares to the right of Jensen Luhar. "Besides, Herr Barent," he added, "the king cannot be captured."

Barent shook his head but stood and walked to the Q3 position next to the Reverend Jimmy Wayne Sutter.

Sutter turned vacant eyes toward Barent and said loudly, " 'And God said unto Noah, The end of all flesh is come before me; for the earth is filled with violence through them; and, behold, I will destroy them with the earth . . .' "

"Oh, shut the fuck up, you old queer," called Tony Harod.

"Silence!" bellowed Barent.

In the brief absence of noise that followed, Saul tried to visualize the board as it stood at the end of Move 35:

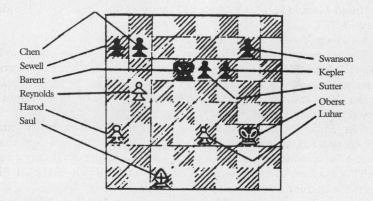

The direction of the end game was too complicated to predict with Saul's modest chess ability—he knew that he was about to witness a contest between masters—but he could sense that Barent had gained a strong advantage in recent moves and seemed confident of a win. Saul failed to see how the Oberst's white could achieve much more than a draw with even the best of play, but he had heard the Oberst say that a draw would constitute a victory for Barent.

One thing Saul did know: as the sole surviving important piece in a field of three pawns, the bishop would be used extensively, even if at great risk. Saul closed his eyes and attempted to withstand the sudden, resurgent waves of pain and weakness.

"All right, Herr Borden," Barent said to the Oberst. "It is your move."

SEVENTY

Melanie

Willi and I consummated our love that mad evening. After all those years.

It was through our catspaws, of course, prior to our arrival at the Manse. Had he suggested such a thing, or even hinted at it before acting, I would have slapped his face, but his agent in the form of the giant Negro offered no preliminaries. Jensen Luhar grasped Miss Sewell by the shoulders, pushed her forward to the soft grass in the darkness under the oaks, and brutally had his way with her. With us. With me.

Even while the Negro's heavy weight still lay atop Miss Sewell, I could not help but recall those whispered conversations between Nina and me during our teenage slumber parties, when the worldly-wise Nina would tell me breathless and obviously overheard stories about the supposed exaggerated anatomy and prowess of colored men. Seduced by Willi, still pinned facedown to the cold ground by Jensen Luhar's weight, I returned my awareness from Miss Sewell to Justin before remembering, in my dazed state, that Nina's colored girl had said that she was not from Nina at all. It was good that I knew the girl had been lying. I wanted to tell Nina that she had been right . . .

I do not relate this casually. Except for my unexpected and dreamlike interludes via Miss Sewell in the Philadelphia hospital, this was my first such experience with the physical side of courtship. However, I would hardly call the rough exuberance of Willi's man an extension of courtship. It was more like the frenzied spasms of my aunt's male Siamese when it seized a hapless female who was in heat through no fault of her own. And I confess that Miss Sewell seemed to be in constant heat since she responded to the Negro's rough and almost nonexistent overtures with an instant lubricity that no young lady of my generation would have allowed.

At any rate, any reflection or response to this experience was further cut short by Willi's man suddenly pushing himself upright, his head swiveling in the night, his broad nostrils flaring. "My pawn approaches," he whispered in German, He pressed my face back to the ground. "Do not move." And with that, Willi's surrogate had scrambled into the lower branches of the oak tree like some great, black ape.

The absurd confrontation that followed was of little importance, resulting in Willi's man carrying Nina's supposed surrogate, the one called Saul, back to the Manse with us. There was one magical moment when, seconds after Nina's poor wretch was subdued and before the security people surrounded us, all of the external spotlights and floodlights and softly glowing electric lanterns in the trees were switched on and it was as if he had entered a fairy kingdom or were approaching Disneyland via some secret, enchanted entrance.

The departure of Nina's Negress from my home in Charleston and the nonsense that followed distracted me for a few minutes, but by the time Culley had carried in Howard's unconscious form and the body of the colored interloper, I was ready to return my full attention to my meeting with C. Arnold Barent.

Mr. Barent was every inch a gentleman and greeted Miss Sewell with the deference she deserved as my representative. I sensed immediately that he saw through my catspaw's sallow veil to the face of mature beauty beneath. As I lay on my bed in Charleston, bathed in the green glare of Dr. Hartman's machines, I knew that the feminine glow that I was feeling somehow had been accurately transmitted through the rough dross of Miss Sewell to the refined sensibilities of C. Arnold Barent.

He invited me to play chess and I accepted. I confess that until that moment, I had never held the slightest interest in the game. I had always found chess to be pretentious and boring to watch—my Charles and Roger Harrison used to play regularly—and I had never bothered to learn the names of the pieces or how they moved. More to my liking had been the spirited games of checkers contested between Mammy Booth and myself during the rainy days of my childhood.

Some time passed between the beginning of their silly game and the point of my disillusionment with Mr. C. Arnold Barent. Much of the time my attention was divided as I sent Culley and the others upstairs to make preparations for the possible return of Nina's Negress. Despite the inconvenience, it seemed the appropriate time for me to set into motion the plan I had conceived some weeks earlier. During the same period, I continued to maintain contact with the one I had watched for so many weeks during Justin's outings along the river with Nina's girl. At this point I had abandoned plans to use him as directed, but maintaining the charade of consciousness with him had become an ongoing challenge because of the visibility of his position and the complexities of the technical vocabulary at his command.

Later, I would be more than a little pleased that I had taken the effort to maintain this contact, but at the time it was merely another annoyance.

In the meantime, the silly chess game between Willi and his host progressed like some surreal scene expurgated from the original *Alice in Wonderland*. Willi shuffled back and forth like a well-dressed Mad Hatter as I allowed Miss Sewell to stand and be moved occasionally—always trusting in Mr. Barent's promise that she would not be placed in harm's way—while the other pitiful pawns and players marched to and fro, captured others, were captured in return, died their unimportant little deaths, and were removed from the board.

Until the instant Mr. Barent disappointed me, I paid little attention and had little involvement in their boys' game. Nina and I had our own contest to complete. I knew that her Negress would be back before sunrise. As tired as I was, I hurried to make things ready for her return.

SEVENTY-ONE

Dolmann Island
Tuesday, June 16, 1981

Harod desperately wanted to find an angle. Bad situations were bad enough by themselves; they made him feel goddamned stupid if he didn't have an angle. So far Harod had not found an angle.

As far as he could tell, Willi and Barent were completely serious about playing the chess game for high stakes. If Willi won—and Harod had rarely seen the old bastard lose—he and Barent would be continuing their competition on a level that included nuking cities and frying whole countries. If Barent won, the idea was to maintain the status quo, but that concept didn't impress Harod much because he'd just watched Barent dump the status quo of the entire Island Club just to set up the fucking game. Harod stood on his black tile two squares removed from the rear of the board, three tiles away from the crazy Sewell broad, and tried to think of an angle.

He would have been content to stand there until he figured something out, but Willi had the first move and said, "P to R-4, *bitte*."

Harod stared. The others stared back. It was fucking eerie the way there were twenty or thirty of the security goons in the shadows, but no one made a damned sound.

"That refers to you, Tony," Barent said softly. The billionaire in his black suit stood ten feet away across the diagonals of two tiles.

Harod's heart began to beat at his ribs. He was terrified that Willi or Barent would Use *him* again. "Hey!" he shouted. "I don't understand this shit! Just tell me where to go, for Chrissakes."

Willi folded his arms. "I did," he said disgustedly. "P to R-4 means pawn to rook four. You are on rook three, Tony. Move one forward."

Harod quickly stepped onto the white tile in front of him. Now he was one diagonal step away from the blond zombie Tom Reynolds and only two empty squares away from the Sewell woman. Maria Chen stood silently on the white square next to Melanie Fuller's surrogate. "Look, you've got three pawns," he called. "How the fuck am I supposed to know you mean *me*?" Harod had to peer around the dark bulk of Jensen Luhar to see Willi.

"How many pawns do I have on the rook's file, Tony?" Willi asked rhetorically. "Now shut up, before I move you."

Harod turned and spat into the shadows, trying to quell the sudden shaking of his right leg.

Barent spoke quickly, ruining Harod's image of chess players pondering for long periods between moves. "King to queen four," he said with an ironic smile as he took a step forward.

It seemed like a stupid move to Harod. Now the billionaire was ahead of all his other pieces, only a move forward and a step sideways away from Jensen Luhar. Harod had to stifle an hysterical giggle as he remembered that the huge black man was supposed to be a white pawn. Harod bit the inside of his cheek and wished he were home in his Jacuzzi.

Willi nodded as if he had expected the move—Harod remembered him saying something earlier about Barent centering his king—and waved his hand impatiently at the bleeding Jew. "Bishop to rook three."

He watched the ex-surrogate named Saul limp the three black diagonal tiles to the square Harod had been standing in a moment earlier. Close up, the man looked worse than he had from a distance. The baggy coveralls were soaked through with blood and sweat. The Jew peered at him with the pained, vaguely defensive squint of the terminally nearsighted. Harod was sure that it was the same son of a bitch who had drugged him and interrogated him in California. He didn't give a good goddamn what happened to the Jew, but he hoped that the guy would take out a few of the white pieces before he got sacrificed. *Jesus fucking Christ*, thought Harod. *This is weird.*

Barent put his hands in his pockets and took a diagonal step to stop on the white square directly in front of Luhar. "King to king five," he said.

Harod couldn't figure the damn game out. The few times he had played as a kid—just enough to learn how the pieces moved and to know he didn't like the game—he and his hotshot opponents wiped out all their pawns first and then started trading bigger pieces. They *never* moved their kings unless they were going to castle, a trick Harod had forgotten how to do, or unless someone was chasing them. Now here were these two world chess biggies who had almost nothing *but* pawns left and were letting their kings hang out like some perverts' dicks. *Screw it*, thought Harod and quit trying to figure out the game.

Willi and Barent were only six feet apart. Willi frowned, tapped his lower lip, and said "*Bauer . . . entschutdigen . . . Bischric zum Bischof funf.*" Willi looked at Jimmy Wayne Sutter across ten feet of tile and translated, "Bishop to bishop five."

The skinny Jewish guy behind Harod had rubbed his face and limped along the black tiles to stand to the right of Reynolds. Harod counted from the back of the board and confirmed that it was the fifth square in the bishop's row or rank or whatever the fuck it was called. It took him several more seconds to realize that the Jew now protected Luhar's pawn position while threatening the Sewell woman along the black diagonal. Not that the woman seemed to know she was in danger. Harod had seen corpses that were more animated. He looked at her again, trying to catch a glimpse of her muff under the tattered shirt. Now that some of the basics of chess were coming back to him, Harod felt more relaxed. He couldn't see any way that he could get hurt as long as Willi left him where he was. Pawns couldn't take pawns in a head-on collision and Reynolds was one step ahead of him to his right, facing Maria Chen, guarding Harod's forward flank, so to speak. Harod stared at the Sewell woman and guessed that she wouldn't look so bad if someone gave her a bath.

"Pawn to rook three," said Barent and gestured politely.

For a panicked second Harod thought that _he_ had to move again, but then he remembered that Barent was the black king. Miss Sewell caught the billionaire's gesture and took a dainty step forward onto a white tile.

"Thank you, my dear," said Barent.

Harod felt his heart rate kicking into high gear again. The Jew-bishop no longer threatened the Sewell-pawn. _She_ was a diagonal step away from Tom Reynolds. If Willi didn't have Reynolds capture her, she could take out Reynolds on the next move. And then she'd be a diagonal step away from Tony Harod. _Shit,_ thought Harod.

"Pawn to knight six," snapped Willi with no delay. Harod swiveled his head, trying to figure out how he could get there from here, but it was Reynolds who was moving even before Willi had spoken. The blond catspaw stepped forward into the black square even with Miss Sewell and facing Maria Chen.

Harod licked his suddenly dry lips. Maria Chen was in no immediate danger. Reynolds couldn't capture her straight on. _Jesus,_ thought Harod. _What happens to us pawns if we get captured?_

"Pawn to bishop four," Barent said dispassionately. Swanson gave Kepler a polite shove and the Island Club member blinked and stepped forward one square. Barent suddenly looked much less alone than did Willi.

"The fortieth move, I believe?" said Willi and stepped diagonally forward to a black square. "King to rook four, _Mein Herr._"

"Pawn to bishop five," said Barent and motioned Kepler forward another square.

The man in the soiled suit stepped forward gingerly, sliding his foot onto the black tile as if the square alongside Barent held a trapdoor. When he was fully on the tile he remained in the rear of it, staring at the naked black man six feet away on the adjoining black diagonal. Luhar stared forward at Barent.

"Pawn takes pawn," murmured Willi.

Luhar took a step forward and to his right and Joseph Kepler screamed and turned to run.

"No, no, no," said Barent with a frown.

Kepler froze in mid-leap, his muscles going rigid, his legs straightening. He swiveled to stand motionless in front of the advancing black man. Luhar paused on the same black square. Only Kepler's straining eyes showed his terror.

"Thank you, Joseph," said Barent. "You have served well." He nodded to Willi.

Jensen Luhar took Kepler's craggy face in both hands, squeezed, and twisted savagely. The snapping of Kepler's neck echoed in the Grand Hall. He kicked once and died, soiling himself again as he fell. At a gesture from Barent, security men jogged forward and dragged the body away, the head swinging loosely.

Luhar stood alone in the black square now, staring ahead at nothing. Barent pivoted to face him.

Harod couldn't believe that Willi was going to let Barent take Luhar. The black man had been a favorite of the old producer's for at least four years, sharing his bed at least twice a week. Evidently Barent had the same doubts; he raised a finger and half a dozen security men stepped out of the shadows with their Uzis trained on Willi and his catspaw.

"Herr Borden?" said Barent, raising an eyebrow. "We can call it a draw and continue with the regular competition. Next year . . . who knows?"

Willi's face was a passionless mask of flesh above his white silk turtleneck and white suit jacket. "My name is Herr General Wilhelm von Borchert," he said tonelessly. *"Play."*

Barent paused and then nodded to his security people. Harod expected a fusillade of gunfire, but they merely made sure they had clear fields of fire and stood in readiness. "So be it," said Barent and set his pale hand on Luhar's shoulder.

Harod thought later that he might have tried to simulate on the screen what came next if he had an unlimited budget, Albert Whitlock, and a dozen other hydraulic and blood bag technicians, but he *never* would have gotten the sound right, or the looks on the other extras' faces.

Barent set his palm gently on the black man's shoulder and within a second Luhar's flesh began to writhe and contort, his pectorals expanding until his chest threatened to explode, the muscled ridges of his flat belly writhing like a tent flap caught in a rising wind. Luhar's head seemed to be rising on a hidden steel periscope, the cords in his neck straining, flexing, and finally snapping with an audible ripping sound. The cat's-paw's body was oscillating in the grip of a terrible spasm now—Harod had the image of a sculptor's clay sketch being squeezed and smashed in a fit of artist's pique—but it was the eyes that were the worst. Luhar's eyes had rolled back into his head and now the whites seemed to expand until they were the size of golf balls, then baseballs, then white balloons straining to explode. Luhar opened his mouth, but instead of the expected scream a torrent of blood exploded out over his chin and chest. Harod heard sounds coming from inside Luhar as if muscles in the man's body were tearing loose like piano wires stretched beyond their limits.

Barent stepped back to keep his dark suit, white shirt, and polished pumps from being spattered. "King takes pawn," he said and adjusted his silk tie.

Security men came out and removed Luhar's body. Only a single empty white square separated Barent and Willi now. The rules of chess prevented either from moving into it. Kings were not allowed to move into check.

"I believe it is my move," said Willi.

"Yes, Herr Bor . . . Herr General von Borchert," said Barent.

Willi nodded, clicked his heels, and announced his next move.

"Shouldn't we be there already?" asked Natalie Preston. She leaned forward to peer through the streaked windscreen.

Daryl Meeks had been chewing on an unlit cigar and now he shifted it from one side of his mouth to the other. "Head winds're worse than I thought," he said. "Relax. We'll be there soon enough. Watch for party lights off the right side there."

Natalie sat back and resisted the urge to reach in her purse to feel the Colt for the thirtieth time.

Jackson slid forward and leaned on the back of her seat. "I still don't understand what a kid like you's doing in a place like this," he said.

He had meant it as a cliché, a joke, but Natalie rounded on him and snapped, "Look, I know what *I'm* doing here. What are *you* doing here, smartass?"

As if noticing her tension, Jackson only grinned slowly and said in a calm voice, "Soul Brickyard doesn't take kindly to these folks coming in and messing over brothers and sisters on our own turf, babe. Got to be an accounting sometime."

Natalie made a fist. "This isn't just anyone," she said. "These people are mean."

Jackson closed his hand around her fist and squeezed softly. "Listen, babe, only three types of people in this world: mean motherfuckers, mean black motherfuckers, and mean white motherfuckers. Mean white motherfuckers're the worst because they've been at it the longest." He looked at the pilot, "No offense meant, man."

"No offense taken," said Meeks. He shifted the cigar and stabbed at the windscreen with a blunt finger. "That could be one of our lights on the horizon there."

Meeks checked his airspeed indicator. "Twenty minutes," he said. "Maybe twenty-five."

Natalie freed her hand and felt in her purse to find the .32 Colt. It seemed smaller and less substantial each time she touched it.

Meeks adjusted the throttle and the Cessna gradually began to lose altitude.

Saul forced himself to pay attention to the game through a haze of pain and fatigue. He was most afraid that he would fall unconscious or—through his inattention—force Willi to use his powers on him prematurely. Either event would trigger Saul's dream state, and the rapid eye movement would trigger much more.

More than anything else at that moment, Saul wanted to lie down and sleep a long, dreamless sleep. For almost six months he had not slept without dreaming the same recurrent, preprogrammed dreams, and it seemed to Saul that if death were only dreamless sleep it might be welcomed as a friend.

But not quite yet.

After the death of Luhar and the loss of the only friendly piece within five squares, the Oberst—Saul refused to grant him a promotion in his mind—had taken advantage of his forty-second move to step forward another tile, moving the white king to rook five. The Oberst looked very calm for being the only white piece on the right side of the board; two squares from Swanson, three from Sutter, and two from Barent himself.

Saul was the only white piece who might come to the old German's aid and he forced himself to concentrate. If Barent's next move set up the sacrifice of the Oberst's bishop, Saul, he would rush the Nazi now. It was almost twenty feet to the Oberst. Saul's only hope would be if Barent's presence blocked the line of fire for some of the security people. There still remained the problem of Tom Reynolds, ostensibly a white pawn, standing on the black square three feet from Saul. Even if none of Barent's people reacted, the Oberst would use Reynolds to run him down.

Barent's forty-second moved him to his king bishop's four, still one empty tile away from the Oberst and adjoining Sutter's square.

"Bishop to king three," announced the Oberst and Saul shook himself out of his fugue state and moved quickly, before the Oberst prompted him.

Even after he had moved it was hard for him to fully visualize the clusters of tired bodies in a strategic sense. He closed his eyes and imagined the chessboard as Barent moved to K5 and stepped into the square next to him:

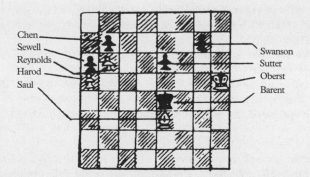

If the Oberst did not order Saul to move immediately, Barent would take him on the next move. Saul kept his eyes closed, forcing himself not to run, remembering the night in Chelmno barracks when he had been ready to fight and die rather than be taken into the darkness.

"Bishop to bishop two," commanded the Oberst.

Saul stepped back and to his right, a tile and a diagonal step away from Barent.

The billionaire paused to consider his move. He glanced at the Oberst and smiled. "Is it true, Herr General," he asked, "that you were with Hitler at the end?"

Saul stared. It was an incredible breach of chess etiquette to speak to one's opponent in the middle of a game.

The Oberst did not seem to mind. "*Ja*, I was in the *Führerbunker* during those last days, Herr Barent. What of it?"

"Nothing," mused Barent. "I was just wondering if your flair for *Götterdämmerung* stemmed from those formative years."

The Oberst chuckled. "The Führer was a cheap *poseur*," he said. "On April twenty-second . . . I remember it was two days after his birthday . . . the Führer decided to leave for the south to take command of Schoerner and Kesselring's army groups before Berlin fell. I persuaded him to stay. The next day I flew out of the city in a light plane, using as a runway an avenue that ran through the shattered Tiergarten. Move, Herr Barent."

Barent waited another forty-five seconds and stepped back diagonally to his own bishop's fourth square. Once again he stood near Sutter. "King to bishop four."

"Bishop to rook four," snapped the Oberst.

Saul walked diagonally across two black squares to stand behind the Oberst. The wound on Saul's leg opened up as he limped the short distance and he stood pressing the fabric of the coverall against the gash when he stopped. He was so close to the Oberst that he could smell him, a mixture of age, cologne, and halitosis as sweet and acrid as he imagined the first and final scent of Zyklon-B.

"James?" said Barent, and Jimmy Wayne Sutter came out of his reverie and stepped forward one square to stand next to Barent in the fourth file of the king's rank.

The Oberst glanced at Saul and motioned abruptly toward the empty square between Barent and himself. Saul stepped into it.

"Bishop to knight five," the Oberst announced to the silent house.

Saul faced forward, looking at the impassive face of the agent named Swanson two squares ahead, but feeling the presence of Barent two feet to his left and of the Oberst an equal distance to his right. Saul imagined that one would feel like this if he was thrust into a small hole between two angry cobras.

The proximity to the Oberst urged Saul to act *now*. All he had to do was turn and . . .

No. The time was not right.

Saul sneaked a glance to his left. Barent seemed almost disinterested, staring toward the cluster of four forgotten pawns at the far left of the board. He patted Sutter on his broad back and murmured. "Pawn to king five." The airwaves minister stepped forward into the white space.

Saul immediately saw the threat that Sutter posed to the Oberst. A "passed pawn" allowed to advance to the eighth rank could assume the powers of any piece.

But Sutter was only on the fifth rank. As a bishop, Saul controlled the diagonal which included the sixth rank square. It seemed probable at that moment that he—Saul—would be called upon to "capture" Sutter. As much as Saul detested the loathsome hypocrite, he resolved at that instant that he would never allow himself to be used by the Oberst in that way again. A command to kill Sutter would mean that Saul had to turn on the Oberst whether there was a chance at success or not.

Saul closed his eyes and almost slipped into dream sleep. He slammed awake, squeezing his injured left hand to let the pain revive him. His right arm tingled from the shoulder down, the fingers of his right hand barely responding when he tried to move them.

Saul wondered where Natalie was. Why the hell hadn't she forced the old woman to act? Miss Sewell stood far away in the third row of the queen rook's rank, an abandoned statuette, gaze lost in the shadowed rafters of the Grand Hall.

"Bishop to king three," said the Oberst.

Forcing air into his lungs, Saul staggered back to his earlier position and blocked Sutter's advance. He could not harm the man as long as the black pawn stayed on a white tile. Sutter could not hurt him as long as they faced each other this way.

"King moves to bishop three," said Barent, stepping backward one square. Swanson stood behind him to his left.

"White king to knight four," intoned the Oberst. He moved a step closer to Sutter and Saul.

"And the black king does not flinch," Barent called almost playfully. "King to K-4." He stepped ahead and diagonally to stand just behind Sutter. The pieces were closing to do battle.

From two feet away, Saul stared directly into the Reverend Jimmy Wayne Sutter's green eyes. There was no panic there, only a great questioning, an overwhelming desire to understand what was going on.

Saul sensed that the game was entering its final moments.

"King to knight five," the Oberst announced, moving to the black square on the same row as Barent.

Barent paused, looked around, and stepped a tile to his right, away from the Oberst. "Herr General, would you like to break for refreshments? It is after two-thirty in the morning. We could resume in thirty minutes, after we have a bite to eat."

"No!" snapped the Oberst. "It is, I believe, the fiftieth move." He took a step toward Barent and moved into the white square touching Sutter's.

The minister did not turn or look over his left shoulder. "King to bishop five," said the Oberst.

Barent swiveled away from the Oberst's glare. "Pawn to rook four, please," he called. "Miz Fuller, do you mind?"

A shudder ran through the woman in the distant rook's rank and her head swiveled like a rusty weathervane. "Yes?"

"Move forward a square, please," said Barent. There was a faint edge of anxiety in his voice.

"Of course, sir," said Miss Sewell and started to step forward. She paused. "Mr. Barent, this does not pose a risk to my young lady, does it, sir?"

"Of course not, ma'am." Barent smiled.

Miss Sewell walked forward in her bare feet and stopped a foot from Tony Harod.

"Thank you, Miz Fuller," called Barent.

The Oberst folded his arms. "Bishop to bishop two."

Saul moved back and to his right a square. He did not understand the move.

Barent smiled broadly. "Pawn to knight four," he said immediately.

The agent named Swanson blinked and moved forward briskly two squares—it was his first move, the only time a pawn could move two squares forward—to stand in the same rank as the Oberst.

The Oberst sighed and turned to meet the diversion. "You are growing desperate, Herr Barent," he said and stared at Swanson. The agent made no move to flee or respond. Someone's mental grip—Barent's or the Oberst's—allowed him not the slightest flicker of volition. Nor was the Oberst's capture as dramatic as Barent's had been; one second Swanson was standing at parade rest, and the next he was dead, sprawled across the line where black and white square joined. "King takes pawn," said the Oberst.

Barent moved a step closer to Harod. "Black king to bishop five," he said.

"Yes," said the Oberst. He stepped onto the black square adjoining Jimmy Wayne Sutter's box. "White king to white bishop five." Saul realized that the Oberst was closing in on Sutter while Barent sealed Harod's fate.

"King to knight five," said Barent and stepped into the square next to Harod.

Saul watched as Tony Harod realized that he was Barent's next victim. The sallow-faced producer licked his lips and glanced over his shoulder as if he might sprint into the shadows. Barent's security men moved closer.

Saul returned his attention to Jimmy Wayne Sutter. The evangelist had only seconds to live; it was inconceivable that the Oberst's next move was anything but a capture of the hapless pawn.

"King takes pawn," confirmed Willi von Borchert, stepping forward into Sutter's white square.

"One second!" cried Sutter. "Just one. I have something to tell the Jew!"

Willi shook his head in disgust, but Barent said, "Give him a second, Herr General."

"Quickly," snapped the Oberst, obviously eager to end the game.

Sutter reached for his pocket handkerchief, could not find it, and wiped the sweat from his upper lip with the back of his hand. He looked directly at Saul and his voice was low and firm rather than the modulated roar he used for television audiences.

"From the Book of Wisdom," he said. "Third Chapter:

'But the souls of the virtuous are in the hands of God,
no torment shall ever touch them.
In the eyes of the unwise they did appear to die,
their going looked like a disaster,
their leaving us, like annihilation;
but they are in peace.
If they experience punishment as men see it,
their hope was rich with immortality;
slight was their affliction, great will their blessing be.
God has put them to the test
and proved them worthy to be with Him;
He has tested them like gold in a furnace,
and accepted them as a holocaust.
When the time comes for His visitation they will shine out;
as sparks run through the stubble so will they.
They who trust in Him will understand the truth,
those who are faithful will live with Him in love;
for grace and mercy await those He has chosen.'"

"Is that all, Brother James?" asked the Oberst in a slightly amused voice.

"Yes," said Sutter.

"King takes pawn," repeated the Oberst. "Herr Barent, I am tired. Have your people take care of this."

At Barent's nod, a security guard came out of the shadows, set an Uzi to the base of Sutter's skull, and shot him once in the head.

"Your move," the Oberst said to Barent as they removed the corpse.

Saul and the Oberst stood alone on the right center of the board Barent waited in his cluster of pawns, stared at Tony Harod, looked back at the Oberst, and asked, "Would you accept a draw if it is only a draw? I will negotiate an expanded competition with you."

"*Nein,*" said Willi. "Play."

C. Arnold Barent took a step and reached a hand toward Tony Harod's shoulder.

"No! Wait just a minute, just a fucking second?" screamed Harod. He had backed away as far as he could without leaving the white square. Two security guards moved to either side to have a clear line of fire.

"It's late, Tony," said Barent. "Be a good boy."

"*Auf Wiedersehen*, Tony," said Willi.

"Wait!" cried Harod. "You said I could trade. You *promised*!" Harod's voice had risen to a petulant whine.

"What are you talking about?" said Barent, annoyed.

Harod's mouth hung open as he gasped for air. He pointed at Willi. "*You* promised. You said I could trade places with *her* . . ." Harod jerked his head in the direction of Maria Chen without taking his eyes off Barent's extended hand. "Mr. Barent *heard* you. He said it was all right."

Willi's expression changed from one of irritation to mild amusement. "He is right, Herr Barent. We agreed that he could trade."

Barent was angry. "Nonsense. He was talking about trading with the girl if *she* were threatened. This is absurd."

"You *said*!" whined Harod. He rubbed his hands together and extended them toward the Oberst as if praying for intercession. "Willi, tell him. You both promised I could switch if I wanted to. Tell him, Willi. Please. Tell him."

The Oberst shrugged. "It is up to you, Herr Barent."

Barent sighed and glanced at his watch. "We will let the lady decide. Ms. Chen?"

Maria Chen was looking intently at Tony Harod. Saul could not read the expression in her dark eyes.

Harod fidgeted, looked in her direction, jerked his head away.

"Ms. Chen?" said Barent.

"Yes," whispered Maria Chen.

"What? I couldn't hear you."

"Yes," said Maria Chen.

Harod sagged.

"It seems a waste," mused the Oberst. "Your position is safe, fräulein. However the game ends, your pawn is secure. It seems a shame to exchange places with this worthless piece of dogshit."

Maria Chen did not answer. Head high, not looking at Harod as they exchanged places, she walked to his dark square. Her high heels echoed on the tile. When she turned, Maria Chen smiled at Miss Sewell and turned her face toward Harod. "I am ready," she said. Harod did not look at her.

C. Arnold Barent sighed and stroked her raven hair with a light touch of his fingers. "You are very beautiful," he said. He stepped onto her square. "King takes pawn."

Maria Chen's neck arched back and her mouth opened impossibly wide. Dry, rattling sounds emerged as she tried unsuccessfully to draw a breath. She fell backward, fingers raking at the flesh of her own throat. The terrible sounds and thrashing continued for almost a full minute.

As they removed the body, Saul tried to analyze what Barent and the Oberst were doing. He decided that they were not manifesting some new dimension of their ability, but merely using their existing power in a brutal demonstration of force as they seized control of the person's voluntary and autonomous nervous systems and overrode basic biological programming. It was visibly tiring for the two of them, but the process must be the same: sudden appearance of the theta rhythm in the victim followed by onset of artificial REM state and loss of control. Saul was willing to bet his life on it.

"King to queen five," said the Oberst and advanced toward Barent.

"King to knight four," replied Barent, moving diagonally one black tile.

Saul tried to see a way Barent could salvage the situation. He could see none. Miss Sewell—Barent's black pawn on the rook's file—could be advanced but had no chance of being passed to the eighth rank as long as the Oberst controlled a bishop. Harod's pawn was blocked by Tom Reynolds and was useless.

Saul peered nearsightedly at Harod twenty feet away. He was looking at the floor, apparently oblivious to the game rapidly drawing to a close around him.

The Oberst had full use of Saul—his bishop—and could close in on the black king at will. Saul could see no way out for Barent.

"King to queen six," said the Oberst, stepping onto a black square in the same rank as Reynolds. One black tile separated Willi and Barent on the diagonal. The Oberst was playing with the billionaire.

Barent grinned and lifted three fingers in a mock salute. "I resign, Herr General."

"*Ich bin Der Meister,*" said the Oberst.

"Sure," said Barent. "Why not?" He crossed the six-foot gap of tile and shook hands with the Oberst. Barent looked around the Grand Hall. "It's late," he said. "I've lost interest in the party. I will contact you tomorrow regarding the details of our next competition."

"I will fly home tonight," said the Oberst.

"Yes."

"You remember," said the Oberst, "that I have left letters and instructions with certain friends in Europe concerning your worldwide enterprises. Safeguards, as it were, for my safe return to Munich."

"Yes, yes," said Barent. "I have not forgotten. Your aircraft is cleared for takeoff and I will be in touch via our usual channels."

"*Sehr gut,*" said the Oberst.

Barent looked around at the almost empty board. "It was as you predicted months ago," he said. "A very stimulating evening."

"*Ja.*"

Barent's footfalls echoed as he walked briskly to the french doors. A phalanx of security people surrounded him while others moved outside. "Do you want me to take care of Dr. Laski?" asked Barent.

The Oberst swiveled and looked Saul's way as if he had forgotten. "Leave him," he said at last.

"What about our hero of the evening?" asked Barent, gesturing toward Harod. The producer had sat down in his white square and was cradling his head in his hands.

"I will deal with Tony," said the Oberst.

"The woman?" said Barent, nodding toward Miss Sewell.

The Oberst cleared his throat. "Dealing with my dear friend Melanie Fuller must be first on our agenda when we speak tomorrow," he said. "We must show the proper respect." He rubbed his nose. "Kill this one now."

Barent nodded and an agent stepped forward and unleashed a burst from his Uzi submachine gun. The impact caught Miss Sewell in the chest and stomach and flung her backward as if a giant hand had slapped her off the board. She slid across the slippery floor and came to a stop with her legs flung wide and her only garment torn from her body.

"*Danke,*" said the Oberst.

"*Bitte sehr,*" said Barent. "*Gute Nacht, Meister.*"

The Oberst nodded. Barent and his entourage left. A moment later the helicopter lifted off and arced out to sea toward the waiting yacht.

The Grand Hall was empty except for Reynolds, the slumped form of Tony Harod, bodies of the recent dead, the Oberst, and Saul.

"So," said the Oberst, putting his hands in his pockets and looking almost mournfully at Saul from fifteen feet away. "It is time to say good night, my little pawn."

SEVENTY-TWO

Melanie

I t was obvious that C. Arnold Barent was not the gentleman I had assumed him to be.

I had been busy with other things in Charleston and when Mr. Barent murdered poor Miss Sewell it was a shock, to say the least. It is never pleasant to have bullets striking one's flesh, no matter how vicarious the experience, and because of my temporary distraction the sensation was doubly surprising and disagreeable. Miss Sewell had been common and rather vulgar before coming into my service and her responses were never quite freed from these base beginnings, but she had been a loyal and useful member of my new family and deserved a more dignified departure.

Miss Sewell ceased to function seconds after she was shot by Barent's man—at Willi's suggestion, I was sorry to note—but those few seconds allowed me time to transfer conscious control to the security man I had left near the administrative offices of the underground complex.

The guard carried some complicated machine pistol. I had no idea how to operate the absurd weapon, but he did. I allowed his reflexes to function while he carried out my commands.

Five off-duty security people were sitting around a long table, drinking coffee. My guard fired in short bursts, knocking three from their chairs and wounding the fourth as he leaped toward his own weapon lying on a nearby counter. The fifth man escaped. My guard went around the table, stepped over bodies to get to the wounded man who was vainly trying to crawl into a corner, and shot him twice. Somewhere an alarm set up a banshee wailing that filled the maze of tunnels.

My guard walked toward the main exit, turned a corner, and was immediately shot by a bearded Mexican-looking security man. I jumped control to the Mexican and had him run up the concrete ramp. A Jeep with three men in it pulled up, the officer in back shouting questions at my Mexican. I shot the officer in the left eye, jumped to the corporal behind the wheel, and watched from the Mexican's point of view as the Jeep accelerated into the electrified security fence. The two men in the front seats were thrown over the hood of the vehicle into the live wire as the Jeep rolled over twice in a shower of sparks and triggered a land mine in the security zone.

As my Mexican walked slowly down the paved path across the zone, I jumped to a young lieutenant rushing up with his nine men. Both of my new catspaws laughed at the sight of the guards' faces as the lieutenant turned his weapon on them.

Another group was returning from the north with the last of the surrogates who had been rounded up after Jensen Luhar's escape. I had the Mexican throw a phosphorous grenade in their direction. Nude figures were silhouetted by fire and ran screaming into the darkness. Gunshots rattled all around as small groups of panicked men opened fire on one another. Two patrol boats pulled in closer to the shore to see what was going on and I had the young lieutenant run down to the beach to greet them.

I would have preferred watching the events then transpiring at the Manse, but Miss Sewell had been my only contact there. Barent's Neutrals were beyond my reach, and the only player left alive in the Grand Hall whom I might have Used was the Hebrew man, and I sensed something not *right* about him. He was Nina's and I wanted nothing to do with her at that moment.

The one contact I did renew at that moment was not on the island. It was a near thing. During the previous busy hours in Charleston I had all but lost touch with this one. Only the many hours of conditioning at a distance allowed me to reestablish the link at all.

I had thought Nina truly mad when her Negress had dragged Justin to that park overlooking the river and the navy yards, as day after day we stared through silly binoculars to catch a glimpse of the man. As it was, it took four observations before I made the first, tentative contacts. It was Nina's Negress who had urged me to exercise more subtlety than ever before . . . as if Nina could teach me anything about subtlety!

It had been a source of some pride to me that I had maintained the contact for so many weeks without the subject having the faintest understanding of what was happening to him, or his colleagues perceiving a change. It is incredible what one can learn—the technicalities and jargon one can absorb—when passively watching through another's eyes.

Until the moment Miss Sewell was cut down, I had not planned to use this resource in spite of Nina's entreaties and machinations.

That had all changed now.

I awoke the man named Mallory, had him rise from his bunk, and walked him down the short corridor and up a ladder into a room lighted by red lamps.

"Sir," said the one named Leland. I remembered that Leland was called an XO. I remembered the lonely tic-tac-toe games I had played with myself as a child, moving the X's and O's around.

"Very good, Mr. Leland," I had Mallory say crisply. "You keep it. I'll be in CIC."

I had Mallory out the door and down the ladder before any of the men there could see his expression change. I was glad that no one was in the red-lit corridor to see Mallory's face as he passed. It would have been odd, even unnerving, for someone to have seen an anticipatory grin so wide that it pulled the man's lips back from even the rearmost of his teeth.

SEVENTY-THREE

Dolmann Island
Tuesday, June 16, 1981

H ang on," said Meeks. "This is the fun part."
A small box of the Cessna's console had beeped and Meeks
immediately had put the plane into a steep dive, leveling off five
feet above wind-tossed waves. Natalie gripped the edges of the seat as the
aircraft raced toward the dark bulk of the island six miles ahead.

"What's that?" asked Jackson, gesturing toward the black box that had
stopped buzzing and beeping.

"Fuzzbuster," said Meeks. "Radar'd started tracking us. Either we're
too low now or I managed to get the island between us."

"But they know we're coming?" said Natalie. She found it difficult to
keep her voice calm as the vaguely phosphorescent water whipped by at a
hundred miles per hour. She knew that the slightest miscalculation by
Meeks would put the landing gear into the wave tops that appeared to be
only inches away. Natalie fought the urge to lift her feet into the air.

"They must know we're out here," said Meeks. "But I had us set pretty
much on a due easterly course that had us plotted to miss the island to the
north by five or six miles. As far as they're concerned, we just dropped off
their scope. Right now we're comin' in from the northeast, since I'd guess
they keep a better perimeter on the western approaches."

"Look!" cried Natalie. The green light of the dock was visible and beyond it a fire burned. She swiveled toward Jackson. "Maybe it's Melanie,"
she said excitedly. "Maybe she's started!"

Meeks glanced at them. "I hear they have bonfires in a big amphitheater there," he said. "Probably some sort of show going on."

Natalie looked at her watch. "At three o'clock in the morning?" she
asked.

Meeks shrugged.

"Can we go in over the island?" pressed Natalie. "I want to see the
Manse before we land."

"Uh-uh," said Meeks. "Too risky. I'll take her around the east side and
come back in along the south shore like the first time."

Natalie nodded. The fire was no longer visible, the dock was out of
sight, and the island might have been uninhabited for all they could see as
they flew down the east shore of it. Meeks moved another hundred yards
out to sea and gained altitude as they came around the cliffs of the southeast point.

CARRION COMFORT

721

"Jesus Christ!" shouted Meeks and all three of them leaned to the left to get a better view even as Meeks banked the Cessna steeply to the right and dove for the relative safety of the sea.

To the south, the ocean was ablaze with light as an expanding mushroom of flame billowed skyward while arcing lines of yellow and green licked toward the Cessna itself. As they leveled off six feet above the surf, Natalie watched two bright flares ignite on the ship silhouetted against the flames to the south and grow brighter as they leaped toward their aircraft. One struck the sea and was extinguished, but the second raced past and struck the cliff face a hundred yards behind them. The explosion lifted the Cessna sixty feet, the way a good wave lifts a surfboard, and brought it hurtling back down toward the black surface of the water. Meeks fought the controls, pulled the throttle full out, and let go with something that sounded like a rebel yell.

Natalie pressed her cheek to the window to see the ball of flame behind them tumbling into a hundred smaller fires as part of the cliff face collapsed into the sea. She snapped her head to the left in time to see three more flashes of light on the silhouetted ship as more missiles leaped their way.

"Holy shit," breathed Jackson.

"Hang on, kids!" shouted Meeks and banked the aircraft so steeply to the right that she watched palm fronds pass twenty feet directly below her window.

Natalie hung on.

C. Arnold Barent had been relieved to get away from the Manse and into the air. The jet turbine of the Bell executive 'copter roared, the rotors changed pitch, and Donald, his pilot, lifted them above the tree line and glare of floodlights on the lawn. To their left, a larger, older Bell UH-1 Iroquois "Huey" chopper shuttled the nine men of Barent's Special Security Detail—minus Swanson—and to their left rose the sleek and deadly shape of the only privately owned Cobra attack helicopter in the world. The heavily armed Cobra provided their air cover and would stay on station until his yacht, the Antoinette, was well out to sea.

Barent sat back in the deep leather seat and let out a breath. The showdown with Willi had seemed a safe enough proposition, with his Neutral sharpshooters on the balcony and in the shadows, but Barent was relieved to be away from it. He started to straighten his tie and was amazed to notice that his hand was shaking.

"Coming in, sir," said Donald. They had circled the Antoinette once and were settling gently toward the raised helipad on the fantail. Barent was pleased to see that the sea was calming, the three-foot waves posing no problem for the yacht's efficient stabilizers.

Barent had considered not letting Willi leave the island, but the inconveniences promised by the old man's European contacts had proved too great. In a way Barent was glad that the preliminary game was over—old impediments removed—and despite himself he was looking forward to the expanded competition the old Nazi had proposed months earlier. Barent was sure that he could negotiate the old man into something very satisfying but not quite so extreme: the Middle East, perhaps, or something in Africa. It would not be the first time the games had been played on an international scale.

But the old woman in Charleston was not something that could be negotiated away. Barent made a mental note to have Swanson arrange for her termination in the morning and then he smiled at his own forgetfulness. He was tired. Well, if not Swanson, then the new assistant director, DePriest, and if not him then an infinite set of others.

"Down, sir," said the pilot.

"Thank you, Donald. Please radio Captain Shires and let him know that I will be dropping by the bridge before turning in. We may get under way as soon as the aircraft is secured."

Barent made the two-hundred-foot walk to the bridge with four members of his Special Security Detail in the usual formation, the other helicopter having dropped them off first. Second to his custom 747, the *Antoinette* was Barent's most secure environment. Manned by a select crew of only twenty-three superbly conditioned Neutrals and his security detail, the yacht was even better than an island—swift, secretly armed, surrounded by fast perimeter patrol boats when close to land as it was tonight, and private.

The captain and two officers on the bridge nodded respectfully when Barent entered. "Course set for Bermuda, sir," reported Captain Shires. "We'll be under way as soon as we recover the Cobra and get it under the hard tarp."

"Very good," said Barent. "Has island security reported the take-off of Mr. Borden's aircraft yet?"

"No, sir."

"Please let me know as soon as his jet is airborne, would you, Jordan?"

"Yes, sir."

The second officer cleared his throat and addressed the captain. "Sir, radar reports a large ship rounding the southeast point. Bearing one-six-nine, sir. Distance four miles and closing."

"Closing?" said Captain Shires. "What does Picket One say?"

"Picket One does not respond to calls, sir. Stanley reports the contact is now three-point-five miles out and doing twenty-five knots."

"Twenty-five knots?" said the captain. He took a large pair of night vision binoculars and joined the first mate at the starboard windows. The soft, red glow of instrument lights on the computerized, automated bridge did not impair night vision.

"Identify it at once," snapped Barent.

"I have it, sir," said Shires. "It's the *Edwards*." There was relief in his voice. The *Richard S. Edwards* was the *Forrest Sherman*-class destroyer that had been assigned to picket duty around Dolmann Island during Summer Camp Week. Lyndon Baines Johnson had been the first president to "loan" the *Edwards* and each president since had followed the custom.

"What's the *Edwards* doing back?" demanded Barent. He was not relieved at all. "It was supposed to have left these waters two days ago. Get its captain on the radio immediately."

"Range two-point-six miles," said the second officer. "Radar profile confirms it's the *Edwards*. No response to radio queries, sir. Shall we go to semaphore?"

Barent walked to the window as if in a dream. He could see nothing but night outside the glass.

"Coming off his sprint at two miles, Captain," said the second officer. "Swinging broadside to us. Still no response to our calls."

"Perhaps Captain Mallory thought there was a problem," said Captain Shires.

Barent snapped out of his dream-walking state. "Get us *out* of here!" he screamed. "Tell the Cobra to attack it! No, wait! Tell Donald to get the Bell ready, I'm going aft. Hurry, goddamn you, Shires!"

While the three officers stared, Barent ran through the door, scattering his waiting security detail, and clattered down the bridge staircase to the main deck. He lost a polished loafer on the steps but did not pause to retrieve it. Approaching the lighted helipad, Barent tripped over a coiled line and tore his blazer as he rolled on the deck. He was up and running again before his panting security people could catch up.

"Donald, *goddamn* you!" screamed Barent. The pilot and two crewmen had torn off the skid lines they had just attached and were wrestling with the rotor tie-downs.

The Cobra gunship, armed with mini-guns and two heat-seeking missiles, roared by thirty feet above the *Antoinette*, putting itself between the yacht and its erstwhile protector. The sea was temporarily illuminated by flashes that reminded Barent giddily of fireflies along the forest's edge in his Connecticut childhood. He saw the outline of the destroyer for the first time, and the Cobra exploded in midair. One of its missiles ignited and scrawled an aimless scribble of smoke across the night sky before splashing harmlessly into the ocean.

Barent turned away from the helicopter and staggered to the starboard railing. He saw the flash of the forward five-inch-gun a fraction of a second before he heard the report and the freight train rush of the incoming shell.

The first shot missed the *Antoinette* by ten yards, rocking the ship with its shock wave and throwing enough water on the fantail to knock Donald and three of the security men off their feet. The flash of the second shot came even before the water of the first one quit falling.

Barent braced his legs wide and gripped the railing until the steel wire cut into his palms. "Goddamn you, Willi," he said through gritted teeth.

The second shell, radar-corrected and radar-guided, struck the *Antoinette*'s fantail twenty feet from where Barent stood, penetrated two decks, and exploded the aft engine compartment and both main tanks of diesel fuel.

The original fireball consumed half the *Antoinette* and climbed eight hundred feet before curling into itself and beginning to fade.

"Target destroyed, sir," came Executive Officer Leland's voice from the bridge.

In the Combat Information Center of the *Richard S. Edwards*, Captain James J. Mallory, U.S.N., lifted a growler phone. "All right, XO," he said, "bring it around so the SPS-10 can acquire our shore targets."

The antisubmarine warfare and gunnery officers stared at their captain. They had been at general quarters for four hours, battle stations for forty-five minutes. The captain had said it was a national emergency, top secret. The men had only to stare at the skipper's pale, lifeless face to know that *something* terrible was happening. They knew one thing for sure; if tonight's work was a mistake, the Old Man's career was definitely in jeopardy.

"Stop and search for survivors, sir?" came the XO's voice.

"Negative that," said Mallory. "We will acquire targets B three and B four and commence firing."

"Sir!" cried the air defense officer as he hunched over his SPS-40 air-search radar screen. "Aircraft just appeared. Distance: two-point-seven miles. Parallel track, sir. Speed: eighty knots."

"Stand by the Terriers, Skip," said Mallory. Normally the *Edwards* carried only 20-millimeter Phalanx guns for air-defense, but for this summer's picket operations it had been configured with four Terrier/Standard-ER surface-to-air missiles aft of the bulky ASROC launchers. The men had griped for five weeks because the Terriers had usurped the only space large enough and flat enough for their Frisbee tournaments. One of the Terriers had been used to destroy the attacking helicopter three minutes earlier.

"It's a civilian aircraft, sir," said the radar officer. "Single engine. Probably a Cessna."

"Fire Terriers," ordered Captain Mallory.

From the cramped CIC, the officers could hear two missiles launch, the reloader clunk, another missile launch, and the reloader cough on empty.

"Shit," said the fire control officer. "Excuse me, Captain. Target dropped below the cliff's edge and Bird One lost it. Bird Two impacted on the cliff face. Bird Three hit *something*, sir."

"Is the target on the screen?" asked Mallory. His eyes were those of a blind man.

"No, sir."

"Very good," said the captain. "Gunnery?"

"Yes, sir?"

"Commence fire with both turrets when the airfield acquisition is confirmed. After five salvos, direct fire on the structure called the Manse."

"Aye, aye, sir."

"I'll be in my cabin," said Mallory.

All of the officers stared at the empty door when the captain exited. Then the fire-control officer announced, "Target B-3 acquired."

The men put aside their questions and did their jobs. Ten minutes later, just as Executive Officer Leland was ready to rap on his door, there came the sound of a single gunshot from the captain's quarters.

Natalie had never flown *between* trees before. The fact that it was a moonless night did not make the experience more enjoyable. Black masses of foliage would rush at them and then fall below as Meeks jerked the Cessna over another line of trees and dove for another clear area. Even in the dark, Natalie could make out cabins, pathways, a swimming pool, and an empty ampitheater as they hurtled beneath and beside the plane.

Whatever mental radar Meeks was using evidently was superior to the merely mechanical sensors in the third missile; it struck an oak tree and exploded in an incredible shower of bark and branches.

Meeks swung right above the bare strip of the security zone. There were fires below, at least two vehicles smoldering, and muzzle flashes winking in the forest. A mile to the south, shells began falling on the single landing strip. "Wow," breathed Jackson as the fuel tanks near the hangar went up.

They flew over the north dock and headed out to sea.

"We have to go back," said Natalie. Her hand was in her straw bag, finger touching the trigger guard of the Colt.

"Give me one good reason," said Meeks, lifting the plane to a safe fifteen feet above the ocean.

Natalie took her empty hand out of the bag. "*Please*," she said.

Meeks looked at her and cocked an eyebrow at Jackson. "What the hell," he said. The Cessna banked steeply to the right and came around in a graceful turn until the blinking green light of the dock lay dead ahead.

SEVENTY-FOUR

Dolmann Island
Tuesday, June 16, 1981

In the silence that followed the departure of Barent's helicopter, the Oberst remained standing with his hands in his pockets. "So," he said to Saul. "It is time to say good night, my little pawn."

"I thought that I was a bishop now," said Saul.

The Oberst chuckled and walked to the high-backed chair Barent had sat in earlier. "Once a pawn, always a pawn." said the Oberst, seating himself with the grace of a king assuming his throne. He glanced at Reynolds and the tall man came over to stand next to the Oberst's chair.

Saul did not look away from the Oberst, but out of the corner of his eye he saw Tony Harod crawl into the shadows and lift the head of his dead secretary onto his lap. Harod made sick, mewling sounds.

"So, a productive day, *nein*?" said the Oberst.

Saul said nothing.

"Herr Barent said that you killed at least three of his people tonight," said the Oberst, smiling slightly. "How does it feel to be a killer, *Jude*?"

Saul measured the distance between them. Six squares and another six feet or so. About thirty feet. A dozen paces.

"They were innocent men," said the Oberst. "Paid security people. Undoubtedly they left wives and families. Does this bother you, Jew?"

"No," said Saul.

The Oberst raised an eyebrow. "So? You understand the necessity of taking innocent lives when it is required? *Sehr gut*. I feared that you would go to your grave filled with the same sickening sentimentality I sensed when we first met, pawn. This is an improvement. Like your mongrel nation, Israel, you have learned the necessity of slaughtering innocents when your survival depends upon it. Imagine how this necessity has weighed on me, my little pawn. People born with my Ability are rare, perhaps no more than one in several hundred million, a few dozen each human generation. Throughout history my race has been feared and hunted. At the first sign of our superiority we are branded as witches or demons and destroyed by the mindless mobs. We cut our teeth while learning to hide the brilliant flame of our difference. If we survive the fearful cattle, we fall prey to the few others with our power. The problem of being born a shark amidst schools of tuna is that when we encounter other sharks we have no choice but to defend our feeding grounds, eh? I am, as you are, first and last a survivor. You and I are more alike than we care to admit, eh, pawn?"

"No," said Saul.

"No?"

"No," said Saul. "I am a civilized human being and you *are* a shark—a mindless, moral-less, garbage-eating killing machine, an evolutionary obscenity fit only to chew and swallow."

"You seek to provoke me," sneered the Oberst. "You are afraid that I will draw out your end. Do not fear, pawn. It will be quick. And soon."

Saul took a deep breath, trying to fight off the physical weakness that threatened to drop him to his knees. His wounds were still bleeding, but the pain had faded to an encroaching numbness that he found a thousand times more ominous. Saul knew that he had only minutes left in which to act.

The Oberst was not finished with his tirade. "Like Israel, you prattle about morality while you behave like the Gestapo. All violence flows from the same source, pawn. The need for power. Power is the only true morality, Jew, the only deathless god, and the appetite for violence is its only commandment."

"No," said Saul. "You are a hopeless and pathetic creature who will never understand human morality and the need for love that is behind it. But know this, Oberst. Like Israel, I have come to know that there is a morality that demands a sacrifice and imperative above all others—and that is never again to allow ourselves to be victims of your kind and of those who serve your kind. A hundred generations of victims demand this. There is no choice."

The Oberst shook his head. "You have learned nothing," he spat. "You are as stupidly sentimental as your idiot relatives who went passively to the ovens, grinning and tugging at their sidelocks and beckoning at their idiot children to follow. You are a hopeless, filthy race and the Führer's only crime was in not achieving his goal of eliminating all of you. Still, when I terminate you, pawn, it will not be a personal thing. You served well, but you are too unpredictable. That unpredictability no longer serves my purposes."

"When I kill you," said Saul, "it will be totally personal." He took a step toward the Oberst.

The Oberst sighed tiredly. "You will die now," he said. "Goodbye, Jew."

Saul felt the full force of the Oberst's power hit him like a massive blow to the brain and to the base of his spine, as intrusive and irresistible as being impaled on a sharpened steel spit. In an instant, Saul felt his own consciousness being stripped away like flimsy clothing being ripped from a rape victim as somewhere near the base of his brain a theta rhythm leaped to life and triggered a waking REM state in his cerebellum, leaving Saul as unable to control his actions as a sleepwalker, a walking corpse, a Müsselman.

But even as Saul's consciousness was flung to the darkened attic of his own mind, he was aware of the Oberst's presence in his brain, a fetid stench as sharp and painful as the first scalding lungful of poison gas. And while sharing that consciousness in that first second, Saul was aware of the Oberst's surprise when the rapid onset of REM state triggered the flow of memories and impressions hypnotically buried in Saul's subconscious like land mines in a field of winter wheat.

Having thrown aside Saul Laski's consciousness, the Oberst was suddenly confronted with a second persona—flimsy, to be sure, hypnotically induced and wrapped around the delicate neurological control centers like a pathetic suit of tin pretending to be true armor. The Oberst had encountered this kind of thing only once before, in 1941, while with the *Einsatzgrüppen* during the termination of several hundred patients at a Lithuanian mental hospital. Out of sheer boredom, the Oberst had slipped into the mind of a hopeless schizophrenic seconds before the SS guard's bullet shattered the man's brain and sent him tumbling into the cold pit. The second personality embedded there had surprised the Oberst then too, but it had been no more difficult to overcome than the first one. This artificially created second personality would pose no greater problem. The Oberst smiled at the pathetic futility of the Jew's little surprise and took a few seconds to savor Saul's hopeless handiwork before shattering it.

Mala Kagan, twenty-three years old, carrying her four-month-old daughter, Edek, toward the Auschwitz crematoria, keeps her right fist closed around the razor blade she had hidden all these months. An SS officer shoves his way through the crowd of naked, slowly moving women. "What do you have there, Jewish whore? Give it to me." Thrusting the baby into her sister's arms, Mala turns toward the SS man and opens her hand. "Take it!" she cries, slashing at his face. The officer shrieks and staggers backward, blood spurting from between his raised fingers. A dozen SS men raise their weapons as Mala advances on them, the small blade clenched between her finger and thumb. "Life!" she screams as all the machine guns fire at once.

Saul felt the Oberst's sneer and the unspoken question. *You try to frighten me with ghosts, pawn?*

It had taken Saul thirty hours of self-induced hypnotic effort to recreate that final minute of Mala Kagan's existence. The Oberst knocked the persona away in a second, as effortlessly as a man slapping away cobwebs in a darkened room.

Saul took a step forward.

Relentlessly, the Oberst reentered Saul's brain and reached for the centers of control, easily triggering the required REM state.

Sixty-two-year-old Shalom Krzaczek crawls on his hands and knees through the underground sewers of Warsaw. It is pitch black and excrement tumbles on the silent line of survivors as the "Aryan toilets" flush above them. Shalom had entered the tunnels fourteen days earlier, on April 25, 1943, after six days of hopeless fighting against thousands of crack Nazi troops. Shalom has brought his nine-year-old grandson Leon with him. The boy is the last living member of Shalom's extended family. For two weeks the ever-dwindling line of Jews has crawled through the reeking maze of narrow sewers as the Germans poured bullets, fire from flamethrowers, and canisters of poison gas into every ghetto manhole and latrine. Shalom had brought along six pieces of bread and these he has shared with Leon as they crouch in the darkness and excrement. For fourteen days they have hidden and crawled, trying to get outside the walls of the ghetto, drinking from dripping effluents they hope are storm sewers; surviving. Now a lid of a sewer opening slides back overhead and the rough face of a Polish resistance fighter stares down. "Come!" he says. "Come out. You are safe here." With the last of his strength, blinded by the sunlight, Shalom crawls out and lies on the cobblestone surface of the street. Four others emerge. Leon is not among them. Tears running down his face, Shalom tries to remember when he had last spoken to the boy in the darkness. An hour? A day? Weakly thrusting away the hands of his would-be rescuers, Shalom descends into the dark pipe and begins crawling back the way he had come, calling Leon's name.

The Oberst destroyed the thick protective membrane that was Shalom Krzaczek.

Saul took a step forward.

The Oberst shifted in his chair and struck with a mental force of a dull ax piercing Saul's skull.

Seventeen-year-old Peter Gine sits in Auschwitz drawing as the long line of boys files past him toward the showers. For the past two years in Terezin, Peter and his friends have produced a newsletter, Vedem—*"We're Leading"—which he and other young artists have filled with their poetry and drawings. Peter's last act before being transported had been to give all 800 pages to young Zdenek Taussig to hide in the old forge behind Magdeburg Barracks. Peter has not seen Zdenek since the boys arrived at Auschwitz. Now Peter uses his last sheet of paper and stub of charcoal to sketch the endless line of naked boys passing him in the frigid November air. With bold, sure strokes, Peter catches the protruding ribs and staring eyes, the shaking, fleshless legs and hands held shyly over fear-contracted genitals. A kapo with warm clothing and a wooden club strides up. "What is that?" he demands. "Get with the others." Peter does not look up from his drawing. "Just a minute," he says. "I'm almost finished." Furious, the kapo strikes Peter in the face with the club and grinds the boy's hand under his heel, breaking three fingers. He grabs Peter by the hair, pulls him to his feet, and shoves the boy into the slowly advancing line. As Peter cradles his hand, he looks back over his shoulder to see his sketch being lifted by the brisk November breeze, catching briefly on the upper strand of barbed wire on the high fence, and then blowing free, tumbling and skipping toward the line of trees to the west.*

The Oberst swept aside the persona.

Saul took two steps forward. The pain of the Oberst's continued mind-rape seared him like steel spikes behind the eyes.

In the dark holding cells of Birkenau, on the night before they are to be gassed, the poet Yitzhak Katznelson recites his poem to his eighteen-year-old son and a dozen other huddled forms. Before the war, Yitzhak had been known

*throughout Poland for his humorous verses and songs for children, each celebrat-
ing the joys of youth. Yitzhak's own youngest children, Benjamin and Bension,
had been murdered with their mother at Treblinka eighteen months earlier. Now
he recites in Hebrew, a tongue none of the listening Jews except his son understands, and then translates in Polish:*

I had a dream
A dream so terrible:
My people were no more,
No more!

I wake up with a cry.
What I dreamed was true:
It had happened indeed,
It had happened to me.

*In the silence that followed the poem, Yitzhak's son slides closer in the cold
straw. "When I get older," whispers the boy, "I also will write great poems."
Yitzhak sets his arm around his son's thin shoulders. "So you shall," he says and
begins singing a slow, sweet Polish lullaby. The other men pick it up and soon the
entire barracks is filled with the gentle sound of their singing.*

The Oberst destroyed Yitzhak Katznelson with a flick of his iron will.
Saul took a step forward.

To Tony Harod's stunned, staring eyes, it was as if Saul Laski was moving
toward Willi the way a man would wade upstream against a terrible current or walk into a raging windstorm. The battle between the two was
soundless and invisible, but as tangible as an electrical storm; and at the
end of each silent surge of conflict, the Jew would raise a leg, move it forward, and set a foot down like a paraplegic learning to walk. In this way
the torn and bleeding man had crossed six squares and reached the last
row of the chessboard when Willi seemed to shake himself out of his waking dream and glance toward Tom Reynolds. The blond killer leaped toward the Jew with his long, powerful fingers extended.

Three miles away, the *Antoinette* exploded with a force powerful enough
to shatter several panes of glass in the french doors. Neither Willi nor
Laski took notice. Harod watched the three men come together, watched
Reynolds strangling Laski, and listened to more explosions begin in the
direction of the airport. Gently, ever so gently, Harod lowered Maria
Chen's head to the cold tile, smoothed her hair, and stood up to walk
slowly past the struggling forms.

Saul was eight feet from the Oberst when the mindrape stopped. It was
as if someone had shut off an incredible, nerve-deadening noise that had
filled the world. Saul stumbled and almost fell. He retook control of his
own body the way someone returns to the home of his early childhood;

tentatively, almost sadly, aware of the light years of time and distance separating oneself from the once-familiar surroundings.

For several minutes—eons—Saul and the Oberst had been almost one person. In the terrible clash of mental energy, he had been in the Oberst's mind as surely as the Oberst had been in his. Saul had felt the monster's overwhelming arrogance shift to uncertainty and the uncertainty to fear as the Oberst realized that he faced not just a few adversaries but armies, legions of the dead rising from the mass graves he had helped dig, screaming their defiance one last time.

And Saul himself had been amazed and almost frightened by the shades that walked with him, rising to defend him before being slapped back into darkness. Some of them he could not even remember constructing— from a photograph here, a dossier there, a scrap of fabric in Yad Vashem— the way he had the others: the young Hungarian cantor, Warsaw's last rabbi, the teenage girl from Transylvania committing suicide on the Day of Atonement, the daughter of Theodor Herzl starving to death in Theresienstadt, the six-year-old girl killed by wives of the SS guards in Ravensbruck—*where had they come from?* For a terrifying second, locked in the helpless recesses of his own mind, Saul wondered if he had tapped into some impossible racial memory that had nothing to do with his hundreds of hours of careful hypnosis and months of self-directed nightmares.

The last persona the Oberst slapped aside was the fourteen-year-old Saul Laski himself, standing helplessly in Chelmno watching the departing backs of his father and brother Josef as they were marched toward the showers. Only this time, in the seconds before the Oberst banished them, Saul remembered what his mind had not allowed him to recall before—his father turning, Josef held securely in the crook of his arm—and calling in Hebrew, "Hear! O Israel! My eldest son survives!" And Saul, who for forty years had sought forgiveness for that single most unpardonable of sins, now saw that forgiveness on the face of the only person who *could* give such dispensation—the fourteen-year-old Saul Laski.

Saul staggered, caught himself, and ran toward the Oberst.

Tom Reynolds rushed to intervene, strong hands rising toward Saul's throat.

Saul ignored him, pushed him aside with the strength of all those who had joined him, and closed the last five feet separating him from the Oberst.

Saul had a second's impression of the Oberst's shocked face, pale eyes widening in disbelief, and then Saul was on him, his fingers finding the old man's corded throat, the chair tumbling over backward with Saul and the clinging Reynolds going over with it on top of the Oberst.

Herr General Wilhelm von Borchert was an old man, but his forearms were powerful as they pounded at Saul, pressed against Saul's face and chest, pummeled him in a desperate attempt to break free. Saul ignored the blows, ignored the old man's knees crashing into his groin, ignored the smashing fists of Tom Reynolds as the catspaw pounded him on his back and head, Saul let their combined weight add gravity's force to the power of his straightened arms as his fingers found the Oberst's throat, closed on it, and met around it. He knew that he would never release that grip as long as the Oberst was alive.

The Oberst pounded, writhed, clawed at Saul's fingers and then at his eyes. Spittle flew from the man's gaping mouth onto Saul's cheeks. The Oberst's ruddy face grew blood red and shifted into darker colors as his chest heaved. Saul felt supernatural strength flow through his arms as his hands sank deeper into the Oberst's throat. The old man's heels clattered and rattled on the horizontal legs of the massive chair.

Saul did not notice as another explosion blew in the french doors and forty feet of windows, showering glass over all of them. He did not notice as a second shell struck the upper regions of the Manse and instantly filled the Grand Hall with smoke as the aged cypress rafters burst into flame. He did not notice Reynolds doubling and tripling his efforts, clawing, thrashing, slashing and pounding at Saul like some maddened, over-wound clockwork toy. He did not notice when Tony Harod crunched his way through the broken glass, carrying two heavy bottles of Dom Perignon '71 from the bar table, and struck Reynolds in the back of the head with one. The cat's-paw rolled off Saul, unconscious but still twisting and vibrating from random nerve impulses generated by the Oberst's commands. Harod sat down on a black tile, opened the second bottle, and drank deeply. Saul did not notice. He had his hands around the Oberst's neck and he closed them tighter, oblivious even of the blood flying from his own lacerated face and throat as it spattered on the Oberst's darkening face and bulging eyes.

A period unmeasurable by time passed before Saul realized that the Oberst was dead. Saul's fingers had sunk so deeply into the monster's throat that even after Saul forced his hands to unclench, deep grooves remained in the flesh like a sculptor's handprints in soft clay. Willi's head was arched back, his larynx crushed like brittle plastic, his eyes bulging sightlessly from a bloated, black face. Tom Reynolds lay dead on an adjoining square with his face a contorted caricature of his dead master's death agonies.

Saul felt the last of his own strength run out of him like water out of a punctured vessel. He knew that Harod was somewhere in the room and had to be dealt with, but not just yet. Perhaps never.

With the return of consciousness came a return of pain. Saul's right shoulder was broken and bleeding, feeling as if shards of ragged bone there were rubbing against one another. The Oberst's chest and neck were covered with Saul's blood, painting a pale outline on the old man's throat where Saul's hands had been.

Two more explosions rocked the Manse. Smoke billowed in the Grand

Hall and ten thousand shards of glass reflected flames from somewhere
behind Saul. He felt heat against his back and knew that he should rise,
see what the source was, and leave. But not just yet.

Saul lowered his cheek to the Oberst's chest and let gravity pull him
down. There was another loud noise from just outside the shattered french
doors, but Saul paid no attention to it. Content just to rest a moment,
needing only a short nap before he went on, Saul closed his eyes and let
the warm darkness claim him.

SEVENTY-FIVE

Dolmann Island
Tuesday, June 16, 1981

W ell, that's that," said the pilot.
As soon as the shelling had stopped, Meeks had brought the Cessna in lower over the landing strip. The shelling itself had dug only a few craters that might have been avoidable with good piloting and even better luck, but two trees had toppled across the tarmac near the south end of the field and the north end was ablaze from burning aviation fuel. An executive jet was burning on the main taxi apron and several other smoldering airframes littered the tie-down area and the heap of ashes and girders that had been the hangar.

"That's all she wrote," said Meeks. "We gave it the old college try. Fuel gauge says it's time to head home. We're going to be getting back on fumes as it is."

"I have an idea," said Natalie. "We can land somewhere else."

"Uh-uh," said Meeks, shaking his head. The bill of the blue baseball cap moved slowly back and forth. "You saw the beach on the north end when we came around a few minutes ago," he said. "Tide's in and the storm tossed it all to hell. No chance."

"He's right, Nat," Jackson said tiredly. "There's nothing else we can do here."

"The destroyer . . ." began Meeks.

"You said yourself that it's five miles east of the southeast point by now," snapped Natalie.

"It has long teeth," said Meeks. "Just what the hell do you have in mind, kid?"

They were approaching the south end of the landing strip on their third fly-by. "Turn left," said Natalie. "I'll show you."

"You have to be kidding," said Meeks as they circled a few hundred yards out from the cliffs.

"I think it's perfect," said Natalie. "Let's do it before the boat comes back."

"Ship," Meeks corrected automatically. "And you're crazy."

Shrubbery still burned on the cliff face where the missile had self-destructed twenty minutes earlier. The sky to the west was lit by the airfield fires. Three miles behind them, bits and pieces of the *Antoinette* still smoldered like embers on a black cloth. After the destroyer had finished

734

with the landing strip it had come back east along the coast and put at least half a dozen explosive rounds in or near the Manse. The roof of the huge structure was ablaze, the east wing had been destroyed, smoke billowed in the surviving floodlights, and it looked as if one shell had landed near the patio on the south side, blowing in the windows and riddling the side facing the long lawn that ran to the sea cliffs.

The lawn itself looked undamaged, although parts of it were dark where floodlights were missing. The fire on the cliffs revealed low shrubs and dwarf trees at the cliff's edge that would have been invisible if not for the nearby flames. The last, lighted twenty yards or so of lawn looked smooth enough except for the shell crater and its detritus near the shattered patio.

"It's perfect," said Natalie.

"It's nuts," said Meeks. "It must slope on an angle of thirty degrees by the time it gets to the Manse."

"Perfect for a landing," said Natalie. "You'll need less runway. Don't British aircraft carriers have pitched decks for just that reason?"

"She's got you there, man," said Jackson.

"Phooey," said Meeks, "*Thirty degrees?* Besides, even if we *could* come to a stop before we ran into that burning building, the dark spots on that lawn . . . and *most* of it is dark . . . could hold limbs, pits, and ornamental rock gardens. It's nuts."

"I vote aye," said Natalie. "We've *got* to try to find Saul."

"Aye," said Jackson.

"What's this *voting* shit?" Meeks said incredulously. "Since when does an aircraft become a democracy?" He tugged at his baseball cap and looked at the destroyer retreating to the east. "Tell me the truth," he said. "This is just the beginning of the revolution, isn't it?"

Natalie glanced at Jackson and took a chance. "Yes," she said. "It is."

"Uh-*huh*," said Meeks, "I knew it. Well, I'll tell you, boys and girls, you're flying with the only dues-paid socialist in Dorchester County." He took the cold cigar out of his shirt pocket and chewed on it for a moment. "Oh, what the hell," he said at last, "we'll probably run out of fuel before we make it back anyway."

With the engine throttled down, the plane seemed to be stalling as it slideslipped its way toward the cliff face glowing white in the starlight. Natalie had never been so excited. With her broad lap belt cinched so tight she couldn't breathe, she leaned forward and gripped the console as the cliffs rushed at them with throat-closing suddenness. A hundred feet out, Natalie realized that they were too low—the Cessna was going to crash directly into the rocks.

"Crosswind's a big, goddamn help," grumbled Meeks. He tweeked the throttle and pulled the wheel back gently. They cleared the cliff edge and shrubs by ten feet and entered the darkness in the lane between tall trees. "Mr. Jackson, you let me know if that ship's comin' back."

Jackson made a noise from the backseat.

It was thirty yards to the first floodlit strip and Meeks put the gear of the Cessna down precisely on the beginning of the white strip of light. It was rougher than Natalie had dreamed. She tasted blood and realized that she had bitten her tongue. Within seconds they had rolled into darkness between the strips of light. Natalie thought of fallen tree limbs and ornamental rock gardens.

"So far so good," said Meeks. The aircraft bounced through the penultimate strip of light and plunged back into darkness. It seemed to Natalie that they were climbing a vertical wall of cobblestones. Something banged and tugged at the right wheel, the Cessna slewed and threatened to tip over at fifty miles an hour, and Meeks played the throttle, brakes, and rudder pedals like a demented organist. The aircraft settled back and rolled through the last floodlit strip, the light starring the windscreen and blinding them. The south wall of the burning Manse was moving toward them much too quickly.

They rolled through loose clods of dirt and made a bouncing turn that swung the starboard wing over the edge of the shell crater. The patio was fifteen feet away. A tattered table's shade umbrella blew away in the wake of their prop-wash.

Meeks slammed the machine to a stop facing downhill. Natalie was sure that she had been to the summit of blue diamond ski slopes that were less steep. Their pilot removed his cigar and stared at it as if just discovering it was unlit. "All out for a rest stop," he said. "Anyone not back in five minutes or at the first sight of hostiles walks home." He removed the pearl-handled .38 from the holster lying between the seats and tapped the barrel against his temple in a rough salute. "*Viva la revolución!*"

"Come on," said Natalie, struggling to get the door open and her lap belt unhooked. She all but fell out of the aircraft, dropping her purse and almost twisting her ankle. She pulled the .32 Colt out, let the rest lie, and stepped aside as Jackson jumped down. He carried only his black medical bag and a flashlight, but he had tied a red bandanna around his head.

"Where to?" he shouted over the noise of the still-turning propeller. "People likely to have noticed us arriving. Better hurry."

Natalie nodded toward the Grand Hall. The electric lights were out in this part of the Manse, but the orange glow of a fire outlined vague shapes in the smoky vastness visible through the shattered french doors. Jackson picked his way across tilted patio stones, kicked open the sprung main door, and flicked on his heavy-duty flashlight. The beam stabbed through thick smoke to illuminate a huge, tiled area littered with broken glass and bits and pieces of masonry. Natalie stepped ahead of Jackson and kept the Colt held high. She lifted a handkerchief to her mouth and nose to breathe more easily in all the smoke. Far to the left, beyond a cleared area of the huge hall, two tables held food, drink, and a tumbled clutter of electronic equipment. Between the door and the tables, the floor was littered with what Natalie thought for a second were limp bundles of laundry before she realized that they were bodies. Jackson held the light study and moved cautiously toward the first one. The flashlight beam showed the dead face of the beautiful Eurasian woman who had been in the car with Tony Harod when Saul had rendezvoused with him in Savannah three days before.

"Don't shine that light in her eyes," came a familiar voice from the darkness to her left. Natalie crouched and swung the gun as Jackson swept the flashlight beam toward the sound. Harod sat cross-legged on the floor next to an overturned chair with more bodies near it. There was a half-empty bottle of wine in his lap.

Natalie moved to Jackson's side, gestured for the flashlight, and made him take the Colt. "He Uses women," she said, pointing at Harod. "If he moves or I act weird, kill him."

Harod shook his head morosely and took a long swallow of wine. "That's all over with," he slurred. "All done."

Natalie looked up. She could see stars through the shattered roof three stories up. From the sound of it, an automatic sprinkler system was working somewhere, but the fire appeared to have a good hold on the second and third floors. In the distance she could hear the rattle of small arms fire.

"Look!" called Jackson. The flashlight illuminated the three bodies near the massive chair.

"Saul!" cried Natalie rushing forward. "Oh, God. Jackson! Is he dead? Oh, God, Saul." She rolled him off the other body, prying Saul's hands loose from the man's shirt. She knew at once that the dead man must be the Oberst—Saul had shown her newspaper photographs of "William Borden" from his files—but the contorted, blackened face and bulging eyes, the liver-spotted hands frozen into claws, did not look human, much less recognizable. It was as if Saul had been lying on the corpse of some twisted, mummified *thing*.

Jackson knelt next to Saul and felt for a pulse, lifted an eyelid and held the flashlight close. All Natalie could see was blood; blood covering Saul's face and shoulders and arms and throat and clothes. It was obvious to her that he was dead.

"He's alive," said Jackson. "Got a pulse. Weak but still there." He ripped open Saul's coverall and gently turned the psychiatrist over, running the light down the length of his body. Jackson opened his bag, prepared a syringe, stabbed it into Saul's left arm, swabbed his back, and began applying a dressing. "Jesus," he said. "He's been shot twice. Leg isn't anything, but we've got to stop the bleeding on this shoulder. Somebody sure as hell worked over his hand and throat." He glanced up at the fire. "We've got to get out of here, Nat. I'll get the plasma going in the plane. Give me a hand, will you?"

Saul moaned as they got him upright. Jackson got under his left arm and lifted him clumsily.

"Hey," said Harod from the darkness. "Can I come?"

Natalie almost dropped the flashlight as she hurriedly stopped to pick up the Colt from where Jackson had left it on the floor. She thrust the gun into Jackson's left hand and held Saul up so Jackson could free his arm. "He's going to *Use* me, Jax," she said. "Shoot him."

"No." It was Saul who spoke. His eyelids fluttered. Even his lips were bruised and swollen. He licked them before trying to speak again. "Helped me," he croaked and jerked his head in Harod's direction. One eye was sealed shut with dried blood, but the other one opened and focused on Natalie's face. "Hey," he said softly. "What kept you?" His attempt at a smile made Natalie give way to tears. She started to hug him but released the embrace when she saw him wince at the pressure on his ribs.

"Let's go," said Jackson. The rattle of gunfire was coming closer.

Natalie nodded and swept the flashlight beam around the Grand Hall a final time. The flames were closer now as the fire took hold in the adjoining corridors of the second floor, and the brightening red glow made the scene into something out of Hieronymous Bosch's details of hell with broken glass gleaming like the eyes of an untold number of demons in the darkness. She looked one last time at the corpse of the Oberst, shrunken to nothingness by death. "Let's go," she agreed.

All of the three remaining floodlights had gone out on the hillside. Natalie moved ahead with the flashlight and Colt while Jackson supported Saul. The psychiatrist had slid into unconsciousness again even before they were through the french doors. The Cessna was still there, the prop was still turning, but the pilot was gone.

"Oh, Jesus," breathed Natalie, playing the light in the backseat and on the ground near the plane.

"Can you fly this thing?" asked Jackson, getting Saul onto the padded back bench and crouching next to him. He was already ripping open sterile dressings and preparing the plasma.

"No," said Natalie. She looked downhill. What had been a rough approximation of a landing field now was total darkness. Dazzled by the flashlight, her eyes could not make out even where the tree lines began.

There came a huffing, panting sound from down the hill and Natalie leveled the flashlight with her left hand while steadying the Colt on the strut with her right. Daryl Meeks raised his hand to block the light and bent over to wheeze and gasp.

"Where were you?" demanded Natalie, lowering the flashlight.

Meeks started to speak, spat, wheezed a second, and said, "Lights went off."

"We know that. Where . . ."

"Get in," said Meeks, mopping his face with the YOKAHAMA TAIYO WHALES baseball cap.

Natalie nodded and jogged around behind the plane to get in her side rather than crawl past the controls and risk knocking off the emergency brake or something. Tony Harod was waiting under the wing on the other side.

"Please," he whined. "You have to take me with you. I really did save his life, honest. Please."

Natalie felt the faintest hint of something sliding into her consciousness, like a furtive hand in the dark, but she had not waited for that. She had moved in closer as soon as Harod began to speak and now she kicked him in the testicles with as much swing as she could get into the kick, glad that she had worn solid hiking shoes rather than sneakers. Harod dropped the bottle he was still carrying and folded up on the grass with both hands between his legs.

Natalie stepped onto the strut and fumbled the door open. She didn't know how much concentration a mind vampire required to do his trick, but she assumed it was more than Tony Harod could muster at the moment. "Go!" she cried, but it was redundant; Meeks had the aircraft rolling even before her door was closed.

She fumbled for her seat belt, could not find it, and settled for hanging on to the console with both hands, the Colt getting in the way. If the uphill landing had been exciting, the trip back down was Space Mountain, the Matterhorn Ride, and her dad's favorite—the Wildcat Rollercoaster—all in one. Natalie saw at once what Meeks had been up to. Two railroad flares sputtered redly thirty feet apart at the end of the long corridor of darkness.

"Gotta know where the ground ends and the drop starts!" Meeks shouted over the rising roar of the engine and bouncing landing gear. "Used to work pretty well when Pop and I played horseshoes in the dark. Put our cigarettes on the stakes."

There was no more time for talk. The bouncing got worse, the flares rushed toward them and were suddenly *past*, and Natalie realized the worst fear of a rollercoaster phobia—what if you came rushing over the top of one of those hills and the rails just *stopped* and the car kept *going*?

Natalie had estimated—at a calmer time when the information had seemed mildly interesting—that the sea cliffs below the Manse were about two hundred feet high. The Cessna had fallen half that distance and showed no signs of a miraculous recovery when Meeks did an interesting thing; he put the nose of the aircraft *down* and revved the throttle to push them faster toward the white lines of surf which filled the windscreen. Natalie later had no memory of screaming or of inadvertently pulling the trigger on the Colt, but Jackson later assured her that the scream was impressive, and the bullet hole in the roof of the Cessna spoke for itself.

Meeks was surly about that for much of the ride back. As soon as they had pulled out of the dive that gave them sufficient airspeed and had begun to climb west to cruising altitude, Natalie turned her mind to other things. "How's Saul?" she asked, swiveling in her seat.

"Out," said Jackson. He was still kneeling in the cramped space. He had worked on Saul right through the E-ticket takeoff.

"Will he live?" asked Natalie.

Jackson looked at her, his eyes just visible in the dim instrument glow. "If I can get him stable," he said. "Probably. I can't tell about other things—internal stuff, concussion. The bullet in his shoulder's not as bad as I thought. It looks like the slug came a long way or ricocheted before it got him. I can feel it about two inches under, right up by the bone here. Saul must've been bending over when it caught him. If he'd been straight up and down, it would've taken his right lung out when it exited. He bled a lot, but I'm pumping him full of plasma. Got plenty of that left. Know something, Nat?"

"What?"

"Black man invented plasma. Fellow named Charles Drew. I read somewhere that he bled to death after a car accident in the nineteen fifties because some cracker North Carolina hospital didn't have any 'Negro blood' in the fridge and refused to give him 'white blood.'"

"That hardly seems relevant right now," snapped Natalie.

Jackson shrugged. "Saul would've liked it. The man has a better sense of irony than you do, Nat. Comes from being a shrink probably."

Meeks removed his cigar. "I hate to break up this romantic chatter," he said, "but does your friend need to get to the nearest hospital?"

"You mean like somewhere other than Charleston?" asked Jackson.

"Yeah," said Meeks. "Savannah's an hour closer than Charleston 'n Brunswick or Meridian or one of those places is a lot closer than either. Make me feel easier about the gas problem, too."

Jackson glanced at Natalie. "Give me ten minutes with him," he said to Meeks. "Let me get some blood into him and check his signs and we'll see."

"If we can get back to Charleston without putting Saul at risk, I want to," said Natalie, surprising even herself. "I need to."

"It's your outing." Meeks shrugged. "I can head straight in rather than hug the coast, but it makes for a real wet landing if I misjudge the fuel situation."

"Don't misjudge it," said Natalie.

"Yeah," said Meeks. "You got some gum or something?"

"Sorry," said Natalie.

"Well then, stick your finger in the hole you put in my roof," said Meeks. "That whistling noise gets on my nerves."

In the end, it was Saul who decided that they would return to Charleston. After three pints of plasma his signs were stable, his pulse strong, and he ended any further argument by fluttering his good eye open and saying, "Where're we?"

"Heading home," said Natalie, kneeling next to him. She and Jackson had exchanged places after the medic had checked Saul's vital signs and

announced that both of *his* legs had fallen asleep. Meeks had not appreciated the exchange and suggested that people who stood up in canoes and
airplanes were crazy.

"You're going to be okay," Natalie added, stroking Saul's forehead.

Saul nodded. "Feel a little funny," he said.

"That's the morphine," said Jackson, leaning back and taking Saul's
pulse.

"Feels sort of good," said Saul and seemed ready to drift away again.
Suddenly he forced both eyes open and his voice was stronger. "The Oberst.
He's really dead?"

"Yes," said Natalie. "I saw him."

Saul took a ragged breath. "Barent?"

"If he was on his yacht, he's gone," said Natalie.

"The way we planned?"

"Sort of," said Natalie. "Nothing worked right, but Melanie came
through in the end. I have no idea why. If she wasn't lying, the last I heard
she and the Oberst and Mr. Barent were getting along swimmingly."

Saul moved his swollen lips in a painful smile. "Barent eliminated Miss
Sewell," he said. "It may have irritated Melanie." He moved his head to
frown directly at Natalie. "What are you two doing here? We never discussed your coming to the island."

Natalie shrugged. "Shall we take you back to the island and start over?"

Saul closed his eyes and said something in Polish. "It's hard to concentrate," he added in slurred English. "Natalie, can we leave the last part of
it? Deal with her later? She's the worst of all of them, the most powerful. I
think even Barent was afraid of her at the end. You can't do it alone, Natalie." His voice was trailing off into sleep. "It's over, Natalie," he mumbled.
"We've won."

Natalie held his hand. When she felt him slide into sleep, she said
softly, "No, it's not over yet. Not quite."

They flew northwest toward the uncertain coast.

SEVENTY-SIX

Charleston
Tuesday, June 16, 1981

With perfect navigation and a strong tailwind, they landed at Meek's small airstrip north of Charleston forty-five minutes before sunrise. The reserve tank had registered empty for the last ten miles when they floated down for a perfect touchdown between the rows of marker lights.

Saul did not awaken when they transferred him to a canvas stretcher Meeks had stored in the hangar. "We need a second vehicle," said Natalie as the two men carried the sleeping psychiatrist from the plane. "Is that for sale?" she asked, nodding toward a twelve-year-old VW Microbus parked near Meeks's new souped-up pickup.

"My Electric Kool-Aid Express?" said Meeks. "I suppose so."

"How much?" asked Natalie. The ancient vehicle had sixties psychedelic designs showing through a faded green paint job, but it was the curtains on the windows and the fact that the rear seats were wide and long enough for the stretcher that she found most useful.

"Five hundred?"

"Sold," said Natalie. While the men secured the stretcher on the long bench behind the driver's seat, Natalie dug through the suitcases in the back of the station wagon and came out with the nine hundred dollars in twenties that had been hidden in Saul's extra loafers. It was the last of their money. She transferred the suitcases and extra bags to the microbus.

Jackson looked up from taking Saul's blood pressure. "Why two cars?"

"I want to get him to medical facilities as soon as possible," she said. "Will it be too risky to drive him to Washington?"

"Why Washington?"

Natalie removed a manila folder from Saul's briefcase. "There's a letter here from . . . a relative of Saul's. It explains enough to get him help at the Israeli Embassy. It's been our emergency exit, so to speak. If we take him to a Charleston doctor or hospital, the gunshot wounds will get the police involved. We can't risk it if we don't have to."

Jackson crouched on his toes and nodded. He took Saul's pulse. "Yeah, I think Washington'll be all right if they can get him to good medical facilities quickly."

"They'll take care of him at the embassy."

"He'll need *surgery*, Nat."

"They have an operating room right there in the embassy."

"Yeah? That's weird." He made a gesture with both palms up. "Okay, so why don't you come too?"

"I want to pick up Catfish," said Natalie.

"We can swing by before leaving town to do that," said Jackson.

"I need to get rid of the C-four and electronic junk too," she said. "You get going, Jackson, and I'll join you at the embassy by this evening."

Jackson looked at her a long minute and nodded. They stepped out of the van and Meeks came up to join them. "No news about the revolution on the radio," he said. "Isn't this stuff timed to all start at once?"

"Keep listening," said Natalie.

Meeks nodded and took the five hundred dollars from her. "The revolution keeps going this way, I may make a profit yet."

"Thanks for the ride," said Natalie. They shook hands.

"You three should go into a different line of business if you want to enjoy life after the revolution," said Meeks. "Stay cool." Whistling an indecipherable tune, he went into his trailer.

"See you in Washington," said Natalie, pausing by the door of the station wagon to shake hands with Jackson.

He took her by the shoulders, pulled her close, and kissed her firmly on the lips. "You be careful, babe. There's nothing you have to do tonight that the three of us can't do when Saul's taken care of."

Natalie nodded but did not trust herself to speak. She drove quickly away from the airstrip and found the main road to Charleston.

There were too many things to do while driving a car at high speed. On the front seat she arrayed the web belt with the C-4, the EEG monitor and electrodes, the hand radio, the Colt and two extra clips, and the tranquilizer gun with a box of darts. In the backseat were the extra electronic equipment and a blanket covering an ax they had bought the previous Friday. Natalie wondered what a traffic cop would make of all this if she got stopped for speeding.

The night was fading into the dim, gray glow that her father had called a false dawn, but another thick cloud bank to the east kept it dark enough to keep all of the streetlights on. Natalie drove slowly through the streets of the Old Section, her heart pounding much too hard. She stopped half a block from the Fuller house and broke squelch on the radio, receiving no reply. Finally she triggered the transmit button and said, "Catfish? Are you there?" Nothing. After several minutes of this, she drove by the house but could see nothing in the alley across the street where Catfish was supposed to be waiting. She set the radio aside and hoped that he was asleep somewhere, or had gone hunting for them, or even had been arrested for loitering.

The Fuller house and courtyard were dark under tall trees still dripping from the night's storm. Except for a faint green glow through the shutters of the upstairs room.

Natalie drove around the block slowly. Her heart was racing so quickly that it was physically painful. Her palms were sweaty and her hands felt too weak to make a fist. She was giddy from lack of sleep.

It made no sense to go on alone. She should wait for Saul to get better, wait for Catfish and Jackson to help her come up with a plan. It made so much sense just to turn the station wagon around and to head for Washington . . . away from that dark house hulking there a hundred yards ahead with its faint green glow like phosphorescent fungus burning there in the dim reaches of some forest.

Natalie let the car idle while she tried to slow her panicked breathing. She lowered her forehead to the cool steering wheel and forced her tired mind to think.

She missed Rob Gentry. Rob would know what to do next.

She thought that it was a sign of her fatigue that the tears flowed so easily. She sat up abruptly and wiped her runny nose with the back of her hand.

So far, she thought, everyone had gone the extra mile in this nightmare except for Little Miss Natalie. Rob had done his part and was dead for his efforts. Saul had gone to the island alone . . . *alone*. . . . knowing there were five of the creatures there. Jack Cohen had died trying to help. Even Meeks and Jackson and Catfish ended up doing most of the work when Little Miss Natalie wanted it done.

Somehow, deep in her heart, Natalie *knew* that Melanie Fuller would not be there if they delayed even a few hours. She might already be gone.

Natalie gripped the steering wheel so tightly that her knuckles paled. She forced her tired mind over hurdles to analyze her motivations. Natalie knew that her own hunger for revenge had been blunted by time and events and the insanity of the past seven months. She was not the same woman who had stood helpless and lost outside a locked mortuary on a distant December Sunday, knowing her father's body was inside and vowing revenge on his unknown murderer. Unlike Saul, she was no longer driven by a quest for unlikely justice.

Natalie looked at the Fuller house half a block away and realized that the force that drove her now was closer to the imperative that had moved her to train to be a teacher. Leaving Melanie Fuller alive in the world was like running from a school building while a deadly snake was loose among unsuspecting children.

Natalie's hands shook badly as she clipped on the clumsy web belt and attached the heavy C-4. The EEG monitor needed batteries replaced and she had a terrible minute when she remembered that she had left the replacements in one of the bags in the microbus. With clumsy fingers she broke open the CB radio and transferred its batteries to the EEG monitor.

Two of the electrode tapes on the sensor filaments failed to stick and she let them dangle, clipping the trigger lead to the C-4 detonator. The prime detonator was electrical, but there was a mechanical timer backup and even a coiled fuse she and Saul had clipped to a thirty-second length. Tasting the bile of panic again, she patted her pockets, but the lighter she had carried around for so long must have been left on the island with the rest of the contents of her bag. Natalie rummaged in the glove compartment. Stuck between state maps was a single book of matches from a restaurant they had stopped at in Tulsa. None had been used. She stuck them in her pocket.

Natalie glanced at the things on the seat beside her and shifted the wagon into gear while keeping her foot on the brake. Once, when she was about seven, a friend had double dared her to go off the high diving board while they were swimming at the new Municipal Pool. The springboard the friend had pointed to was the highest of six, ten feet above the next highest, on a tower reserved for adults who were serious divers. Natalie could barely swim. Nonetheless, she had immediately pulled herself out of the shallow end, walked confidently past a lifeguard who was too busy chatting with a teenage girl to take notice of a seven-year-old, climbed the seemingly endless ladder, walked out to the tip of the narrow board, and jumped toward a pool so far below her that it seemed to be shrunken by distance.

Natalie had known then as she knew now that to *think* about it was to stop oneself, that the only way to carry through was to make one's mind a careful blank with no thought of the next action until it was initiated. But as she shifted into gear and accelerated down the quiet street, she shared the same splinter of thought now as she had that instant she had stepped off the diving board and known there was no going back—*Am I really doing this?*

The Fuller compound had added a six-foot brick wall in front since the old lady's return, with four feet of black iron railing on top of the brick. But the original ornamental gate had been preserved with three feet of iron latticework on each side. The gate was padlocked but not set deeply into cement. Natalie's station wagon was doing 33 m.p.h. when she cut sharply to the right, bounced over the curb with a tooth-rattling jolt, and crashed through the black iron.

The top of the gate crashed down to turn the windshield into a web of white fractures, the right fender struck the ornamental fountain and ripped free, and the vehicle skidded across the courtyard and through shrubs and dwarf trees to smash into the front of the house.

Natalie had forgotten to put on her seat belt. She bounced forward, banged her forehead against the windshield, and crashed back into her seat, seeing stars and feeling like she was going to vomit. For the second time in three hours she had bitten her tongue hard enough to taste blood. The weapons that had been so carefully laid out on the seat were scattered over the floorboards.

Great start, thought Natalie groggily. She leaned over to retrieve the

Colt and the dart gun. The box of darts had bounced under the seat somewhere, as had the extra clips for the automatic. To hell with it; both were loaded.

She kicked open the door and stepped out into the predawn darkness. The only sounds were of water pouring out of the fractured fountain and dribbling from the car's smashed radiator, but she was sure that her entrance must have been noisy enough to awaken half the block. She had only minutes now in which to do what had to be done.

The idea had been to knock on the front door of the house with three thousand pounds of automobile, but Natalie had missed by two feet. The .32 pistol in her belt, the dart gun in her right hand, she tried the door. Maybe Melanie would make it easy.

The door was locked. Natalie remembered seeing an array of locks and chains on the inside.

Setting the dart gun on the roof of the station wagon, she pulled the ax from the backseat and went to work on the hinge side of the door. Six heavy blows and sweat mixed with blood from her bounce off the windshield was dripping into Natalie's eyes. Eight blows and the wood around the lower hinge splintered. Ten blows and the heavy door ripped away and sagged open, still attached on the left side by bolts and chains.

Natalie panted, resisted the renewed urge to vomit, and tossed the ax into the bushes. Still no sound of sirens nor any movement from the house. The green glow from the second floor bled its sick light into the courtyard.

Natalie tugged the Colt out and cocked a bullet into the chamber, remembering that there were seven bullets left out of the original eight because of the accidental discharge in the Cessna. She retrieved the dart pistol and paused for a second with a weapon in each hand, feeling absurd. Her father would have said she looked like his favorite cowboy, Hoot Gibson. Natalie had never *seen* a Hoot Gibson movie, but to this day he was also *her* favorite cowboy.

She kicked the sagging door farther inward and stepped into the dark hallway, not thinking about the next step or the next one after that. She was amazed that a human heart could beat so wildly without tearing itself free from the person's chest.

Catfish sat straddling a chair six feet from the door. His dead eyes stared at and through Natalie and the string to a crude sign was looped over the teeth of his gaping lower jaw. In the dim light from the courtyard she could read the rough lettering Magic-Markered onto the placard: GO AWAY.

Maybe she's gone, maybe she's gone, thought Natalie, stepping around Catfish to move toward the stairway.

Marvin burst through the door to the dining room on her right a split second before Culley filled the doorway of the parlor on her left.

Natalie shot Marvin in the chest with a tranquilizer dart and dropped the now useless dart gun. Her left hand then shot up quickly to grasp Marvin's right wrist as he swung the butcher knife downward in a deadly arc. She slowed its descent, but the tip of the blade sunk a half inch into her left shoulder as she strained to hold his arm back, swinging the boy around in a clumsy dance step as Culley threw his huge arms around both of them in a bare-armed hug. Feeling his hands clasping behind her back, knowing that it would take the giant two seconds to snap her spine, she thrust the Colt under Marvin's left arm, buried the muzzle in Culley's soft belly, and fired twice. The noise was obscenely muffled.

Culley's bland face briefly took on the expression of a disappointed child, his fingers unclasped behind her, and he staggered back, clutching at the frame of the parlor doorway as if the floor had suddenly become vertical. With a pressure that knotted his huge biceps and splintered wood, he resisted the invisible force that had been pulling him back into the parlor and began climbing that imaginary wall, taking a heavy step in Natalie's direction, his right arm extended as if seeking a handhold on her body.

Natalie braced her arm on Marvin's suddenly sagging shoulder and fired twice more; the first bullet going through Culley's palm into his belly, the second plucking off the lobe of his left ear as smoothly as if in a magic trick.

Natalie realized that she was sobbing and screaming, "Fall down! Fall down!" He did not fall but grasped the door frame again and slowly lowered himself to a sitting position, his descent perfectly choreographed with Marvin's slow-motion slump. The knife clattered to the floor. Natalie caught the young black man's head before his face struck polished wood; laid him near Catfish's feet, and whirled upright, swinging the pistol in short arcs to cover the dining room door and the short hall to the kitchen door.

Nothing.

Still sobbing, gulping for air, Natalie started up the long staircase. She slapped at a light switch. The crystal chandelier overhanging the hall stayed dark and the landing at the head of the stairs remained a mass of shadows. Five steps up and she could make out the green glow oozing from under the door to Melanie Fuller's bedroom.

Natalie realized that her sobs had turned into small whimpering noises. She silenced them. Three steps from the top, she paused and unhooked her web belt, slinging the pouches of C-4 over her left arm with the mechanical timer face up, its dial set to thirty seconds. A flick of the arming lever would activate it. She glanced at her EEG-monitor. The green active light still blinked; the trigger jack was still connected to the C-4 detonator. She paused another twenty seconds to let the old woman make her move if she was going to.

Silence.

Natalie peered at the landing. A single cane-seated Bentwood chair was placed to the left of the door to Melanie's bedroom. Natalie knew immediately and with irrational certainty that this is where Mr. Thorne had sat guard through long years of nightly vigils. She could not see around the corner down the dark hall that led left off the landing to the back of the house.

Natalie heard a noise below and jerked around, seeing only the three bodies on the floor. Culley had slumped forward, his forehead making a soft noise as it contacted the polished wood.

Natalie swung back, raised the Colt, and stepped onto the landing.

She expected the rush from the dark hallway, was braced for it, and almost fired the pistol into the deeper darkness there even when none came.

The hallway was empty; the doors closed.

Natalie turned back to Melanie's bedroom door, finger taut on the trigger, left arm half extended with the heavy belt of C-4. Somewhere downstairs a clock ticked.

Perhaps it was a noise that alerted her, perhaps a slight current of air against her cheek, but some subliminal clue caused her to look upward at that instant, upward toward the ten-foot-high ceiling lost in shadows and to the darker square there—a small trapdoor to the attic—open, framing the tensed, poised body ready to drop and the six-year-old's insanely grinning face and the hands turned to claws and the fingers turned to talons catching the green glow on sharpened steel.

Natalie fired the pistol upward even as she tried to leap aside, but Justin dropped with a loud hiss, the bullet struck only wood, and his steel claws raked her right arm, ripping the Colt from her grasp.

She staggered backward, lifting her left arm with the C-4 belt as a shield. Every Halloween when she was a little girl, Natalie had gone to the corner five-and-dime to buy "witch's claws," wax fingertips sporting three-inch painted wax nails. Justin was wearing ten of these. But the wax fingertips were steel and the nails were three-inch scalpel blades. Unbidden, there came the image of Culley or one of Melanie's other surrogates fashioning the steel thimbles, filling them with molten lead, and watching as the child plunged his fingers into them, waiting for the lead to cool and harden.

Justin leaped toward her. Natalie backed against the wall and instinctively kept her left arm raised. Justin's claws sank deep into the web belt, eight stilettos slashing through canvas, plastic liner, and the C-4 *plastique* itself. Natalie gritted her teeth as at least two of the blades punctured the flesh of her forearm.

With an inhuman hiss of triumph, Justin ripped the belt of explosives from Natalie's grasp and flung it over the railing. Natalie heard the dull thump from the hall below as twelve pounds of inert explosive landed heavily. She glanced at the floor, found the Colt lying between two uprights of the banister. She took half a step toward it but froze when Justin jumped first and sent the pistol spinning over the edge with a quick kick of one of his blue Keds.

Natalie feinted left and jumped right, trying to reach the stairway. Justin leaped to intercept her, forcing her back, but not before Natalie caught a glimpse of Culley pulling himself up the stairs, his massive body filling the stairway. He was a third of the way up. He had left a trail.

Natalie turned to run down the short hallway and stopped, sure that this is what the old woman had planned. God alone knew what waited for her in those dark rooms.

Justin moved quickly toward her, his fingertips a blur. Natalie completed her own turn in a single motion, bringing the Bentwood chair up with her bloodied right hand. One of the legs caught Justin in the mouth, knocking teeth loose, but the boy did not hesitate a second, advancing like the demon-possessed thing he was, hands flailing. The blades raked at the chair legs, ripped away the cane seat. Justin crouched and came in low, lunging for Natalie's legs and thighs, seeking the femoral artery. She thrust downward with the chair, seeking to pin him to the floor.

He was too fast. The scalpel-sharp claws missed her thighs by inches and he danced back before she could pin him. He feinted right, lunged left, slashed upward, danced back, lunged again. The soles of his Keds made soft squeaking sounds on the hardwood floor.

Natalie blocked each attack, but already her lacerated arms ached from fatigue. A puncture wound on her left arm felt as if it had been gored to the bone. With each attack she gave ground until now her back was against the door to Melanie Fuller's bedroom. Even with no time to think, a part of her mind insisted on generating an instant's graphic image of the door snapping open, of her falling back into waiting, flailing arms, into grasping hands and clacking teeth . . .

The door remained closed.

Justin crouched and ran at her, accepting the punishment of chair legs smashing into his chest and throat, swinging his arms wide in an attempt to get the blades into her hands, arms, or breast. His arms were inches too short to make the blows connect.

Justin sank his talons into the wood frame of the chair seat and tugged, pulled again, attempting to tear the Bentwood away from her or break it in half. Splinters flew, but the frame held.

Somewhere behind the wall of wild panic in her, a calm circle of Natalie's mind was trying to send her a message. She could almost hear it expressed in Saul's dry, almost pedantic voice: It's using a child's body, Natalie, a six-year-old's reach and mass. Melanie's advantage is in fear and fury. Your advantage is in size and weight, leverage and mass. Don't waste it.

Justin made a sound like a steam kettle overflowing and rushed her again, scrabbling forward, low to the floor. Natalie could see the top of Culley's bald head just appearing above the edge of the landing.

She met Justin's rush, extending the chair with both arms, putting her weight into it, pushing hard and stepping into the shove. The splintered chair legs caught him on either side of his throat and torso, slamming him back into the polished railing. The old wood of the banister creaked but did not come close to breaking.

Lithe as a mink, quick as a steel-clawed cat, Justin leaped up onto the five-inch-wide railing, caught his balance in a second, and prepared to leap *down* at her. With no hesitation whatsoever, Natalie took a broad side-step forward, gripped the chair like a Louisville Slugger, and followed through with a full-bodied swing that batted Justin off the railing like some flesh and blood wiffle ball.

A single scream issued from the throats of Justin, Culley, and uncounted voices behind Melanie's closed door, but the child-thing was not done.

Arching in midair, hair flying, Justin grabbed at the massive chandelier that hung six feet out and just below the level of the landing. Steel talons closed on the iron chain, Justin's legs crashed into crystal prisms, creating a musical chaos, and a second later he was clambering up onto the chandelier itself, balancing fifteen feet above the floor.

Natalie lowered the chair as she watched in disbelief. Culley's hand came to the top step and he continued to pull himself up. Justin's round face stretched into a terrible mockery of a grin as he swung the chandelier back and forth, his left arm extended, talons reaching for the railing that came closer at each swing.

In its day—at least a century earlier—the chandelier restraints could have held ten times Justin's added weight without complaint. The iron chain and iron anchor bolts still could. But the nine-inch wooden beam in which the hardware had been sunk had suffered more than a hundred years of South Carolina moisture and insects and benign neglect.

Natalie watched as Justin dropped out of sight, the chandelier disappeared, and a five-foot section of ceiling plaster, electric wiring, iron bolts, and rotted wood followed. The noise of the impact was impressive. Shards of shattered crystal struck the walls like grenade fragments.

Natalie wanted to go down to get the gun and the C-4 but knew immediately that they were buried by the mess filling the hall below.

Where were the police? What kind of neighborhood is this? Natalie remembered that many of the nearby houses had been dark the previous evenings, the neighbors away or very old. Her entry had been loud and dramatic enough for her, but it was possible that no one had yet noticed the car and figured out where the noise had come from. The car would be all but invisible from the street behind Melanie's brick walls. Two of the four shots she had fired should have been loud enough to be heard, but the heavy tropical foliage on the block muffled and distorted sounds. Perhaps it was just that no one wanted to get involved. She looked at her bloodied wristwatch. Less than three minutes had passed from the time she had come through the front door.

Oh, God, thought Natalie.

Culley pulled himself onto the landing, his pale, idiot gaze rising to meet Natalie's.

Weeping soundlessly, Natalie swung the chair at his head—once, twice, a third time. One of the chair legs snapped and ricocheted off the wall. Culley's chin banged on wood as his bulk slid five steps back.

Natalie watched as his bloody face came up, his arms and legs twitched, and he began moving upward again.

She swung around and battered the chair against the heavy door. "God *damn* you, Melanie Fuller!" she screamed at the top of her voice. After the fourth blow, the Bentwood chair came apart in her hands.

And the door swung inward.

It had not been locked.

The windows of the room were shuttered and shaded, allowing little of the predawn gray to enter. Oscilloscopes and other life-support equipment painted the occupants with pale electronic light. Nurse Oldsmith, Dr. Hartman, and Nancy Warden—Justin's mother—stood between Natalie and the bed. All three of them wore soiled white garments and identical expressions—expressions that Natalie had seen only in film documentaries of death camp survivors staring out through barbed wire at the arriving armies—round-eyed, slack-jawed, disbelieving.

Behind this last defensive line were the huge bed and its occupant. The bed was canopied with lace gauze, the view into it further distorted by the clear plastic of an oxygen tent, but Natalie could easily make out the wizened figure lost in the bedclothes; the wrinkled, distorted face and staring eye, the age-mottled curve of skull still fringed with thinning blue hair, and the skeletal right arm lying outside the covers, bony fingers clutching spasmodically at the sheets and quilt. The old woman was writhing feebly in the bed, reinforcing Natalie's earlier image of a sour-skinned sea creature dumped out of its element.

Natalie glanced around quickly, making sure that no one was behind the door or coming in from the hallway. To her right was an ancient dresser with a stained mirror. A comb and brush were set out carefully on a yellowed doily. Tufts of blue hair clung to the bristles. To Natalie's left, a clutter of food trays lay on the floor amid teacups, dirty dishes, soiled linen heaped in stacks three feet high, the tall wardrobe with doors open and clothing tumbled into the bottom of it, medical instruments lying around in the filth, and four long oxygen tanks propped on two-wheeled carts. The seals on two of the tanks were unbroken, suggesting they were the fresh replacements for the ones now bleeding air into the old woman's plastic tent. The stench in the room was beyond Natalie's experience. She heard a slight noise and glanced left to see two rats poking through the clutter of dirty dishes and sour linen. The rodents acted oblivious to the people, as if no human beings had been living here. Natalie realized that this had been the truth of the matter.

The three ambulatory corpses moved their mouths in perfect unison. "Go away," they said in a petulant child's whine. "I don't want to play anymore." The old woman's face, warped and elongated by the crinkled lens of the clear plastic oxygen tent, moved back and forth as the toothless mouth made wet smacking sounds.

The three catspaws raised their right hands in perfect unison. The short scalpels caught the green light from the monitor screen. *Only three of them?* thought Natalie. She felt there should be more, but she was too tired and too scared and hurting too much to figure it out. Later.

Right now she wanted to say something; she was not sure what. Perhaps explain to these zombies and to the monster behind them that her father was—had been—an important person—much too important to be wasted like a minor character in a bad movie. *Anyone—everyone—*deserved better than that. Something along those lines.

Instead, the thing that had once been a surgeon began to shuffle toward her, the other two followed, and Natalie contented herself with moving quickly to her left, breaking the seal and twisting the dial on the first oxygen tank, and throwing it as hard as she could at Dr. Hartman. She missed. The tank was unbelievably heavy. It hit the floor with a resounding smash, knocked Nancy Warden's legs out from under her, and rolled under the canopied bed, spraying pure oxygen into the room.

Hartman swung the scalpel at her in a swift, flat arc. Natalie jumped back but not quite quickly enough. She shoved a cart carrying an empty oxygen tank between the neurosurgeon and herself and glanced down to see the thin slash across the midriff of her blouse, already stained red from the shallow incision.

Culley crawled into the room, using his elbows for leverage.

Natalie felt the fury in her system reach new heights. She and Saul and Rob and Cohen and Jackson and Catfish . . . *all* of them had come too goddamn far to stop here. Saul might appreciate the irony of it, but Natalie *hated* irony.

With the adrenaline surge that allows mothers to lift automobiles off their children, businessmen to carry steel safes out of burning buildings, Natalie lifted the seventy-five-pound second oxygen tank over her head and tossed it directly into Dr. Hartman's face. The flow valve cracked off completely as the tank and doctor's body crashed to the floor.

Nancy Warden was crawling toward her. Nurse Oldsmith raised her scalpel and ran directly at her. Natalie tossed a urine-stained sheet over the tall nurse and ducked to her right. The sheeted figure crashed into the wardrobe. A second later the scalpel blade appeared, slicing through the thin fabric.

Natalie had grabbed a gray pillowcase and was wadding it up as she ran when Nancy Warden's hand shot out and clutched her ankle.

Natalie fell hard onto the threadbare rug, trying to kick the woman away with her free foot. Justin's mother had lost her scalpel but used both hands to hang on to Natalie's leg, apparently intent on pulling Natalie under the high bed with her.

Three feet away, Culley pulled himself into the room. His wounds had made his abdominal wall let go, leaving a trail of viscera that ran out onto the dark landing.

Nurse Oldsmith cut away the last of the sheet and swiveled like a rusty, street-corner mime.

"Stop it!" screamed Natalie at the top of her lungs. She fumbled the matchbook out, dropped it, struck one match while Nancy Warden pulled her a foot closer to the bed, and tried to ignite the pillowcase. It singed but did not catch. The match went out.

Culley's fingers seized her hair.

Her hands still free, Natalie lit the second match, held it to the matchbook, and pressed the short-lived flare to the pillowcase, resisting the impulse to let go when the fading brand burned her fingers.

The pillowcase burst into flame.

Natalie used a sidearmed toss to flick it onto the canopied bed.

Saturated by a jet of pure oxygen from beneath, the lace canopy, bedclothes, and wooden frame exploded in a geyser of blue flame that blasted straight upward to the ceiling and spread laterally to all four walls in less than three seconds.

Natalie held her breath as she felt the air become superheated, kicked free of the flaming woman who held her ankle, and stood up to run.

Culley had released her hair but had stood when she did. Now he blocked the doorway like some half-disemboweled cadaver rising in wrath from an autopsy table.

His long arms seized Natalie and spun her around. Still holding her breath, she saw the form of the old woman in the bed thrashing and writhing in a sheer blue ball of concentrated flame, her blackening body appearing to be all sharp-edged joints and angles—a grasshopper frying and changing shape even as Natalie watched—and at that instant the woman on the bed let out a single, overpowering scream that a second later was picked up by Nurse Oldsmith, Nancy Warden, Culley, the corpse of Dr. Hartman, and by Natalie herself.

In a final surge of effort, Natalie spun Culley and herself around and pulled herself through the doorway and onto the landing just as the second oxygen bottle exploded. Culley took the full force of the blast behind her and for a second the house was filled with the odor of roasting meat. His arms were forced open as they struck the wall together at the curve of the staircase and Natalie tumbled onto the stairs as the flaming man jack-knifed over the railing and fell into the carnage below.

Natalie lay head down on the stairs, face near the banister uprights. She could feel the heat from the burning ceiling and see the brilliance of the flames reflected in the riot of shattered crystal below, but she was too tired to move.

She had done her best.

Strong arms lifted her and she struck out feebly, her fists as soft and useless as cotton balls.

"Easy, Nat. I need one arm free for Marvin."

"Jackson!" The tall black man carried her in his left arm while he dragged his ex-gang leader along by the shirtfront. Natalie had confused impressions of a glass room with one wall smashed in, of being carried through a garden, of the dark tunnel of the garage. The microbus waited in the alley and Jackson lifted her gently into the rear seat, laying Marvin on the floor in the back.

"Jesus," Jackson muttered to himself, "what a day." He crouched next to Natalie, mopping away blood and soot with a moist washrag. "My God, lady," he said at last, "what a piece of work you are."

Natalie licked cracked lips. "Let me see," she whispered. Jackson put his arm under her shoulders and helped prop her up. The Fuller house was totally engulfed in flames and the fire had spread to the Hodges place. Through the gaps between buildings, Natalie could see fire engines, car roofs, and heads blocking the street. Two streams of water began to play ineffectively against the conflagration while other hoses were turned on the neighbors' trees and rooftops.

Natalie looked to her left and saw Saul sitting up, squinting nearsightedly at the flames. He turned toward Natalie, smiled, shook his head in sleepy disbelief, and dropped back to sleep.

Jackson propped a rolled blanket under her head and covered her with another one. Then he jumped down to slam the doors, and climbed into the driver's seat. The little engine started without hesitation. "If you tourists don't mind," he said. "I've got to get us out of here before the cops or fire persons get around to finding this alley."

They were out of traffic within three blocks, although cars and emergency vehicles were still rushing the other way toward the smoke.

Jackson got onto Highway 52 and headed northwest, past the park that overlooked the naval yards, then past the motel strip. At Dorchester Road he cut back to Interstate 26 and headed out of town past the main airport.

Natalie discovered that she could not close her eyes without seeing things she did not want to see and feeling a scream welling up inside her. "How's Saul?" she asked in a shaky voice.

Jackson answered without taking his eyes off the road. "The man's great. He woke up long enough to tell me what you were going to do."

Natalie changed the subject. "How's Marvin?"

"He's breathing," said Jackson. "We'll see about the rest later."

"Catfish is dead," she said in a voice not quite under control.

"Yeah," said Jackson. "Look, babe, a few miles up here beyond Ladson, the map says there's a rest stop. I'll get you cleaned up good. Get dressings on those two puncture wounds and some cream on the burns and cuts. Give you a shot that'll let you sleep."

Natalie nodded and remembered to say, "Okay."

"You know you got a big bruise on your head and no eyebrows, Nat?" He was looking in the rearview mirror at her.

Natalie shook her head.

"You want to tell me what happened in there?" Jackson asked gently.

"No!" Natalie began sobbing silently. It felt very good to do so.

"Okay, babe," he said and whistled a snatch of tune. He broke it off and said, "Shit, all I want to do is get out of this cracker town and back to Philly and it turns into Napoleon's goddamn retreat from goddamn Moscow. Well, if anybody messes with us between here and the Israeli Embassy, they'll be sorry bad asses." He raised a pearl-handled .38 revolver and quickly tucked it back under the seat.

"Where'd you get that?" asked Natalie, brushing away tears.

"Bought it from Daryl," said Jackson. "You're not the only one willing to finance the revolution, Nat."

Natalie closed her eyes. The images were still there, but the urge to scream was slightly less strong. She realized that—for a while at least—Saul Laski was not the only one who had given up the right to his own dreams.

"I saw a sign," came Jackson's deep, reassuring voice. "Rest stop coming up."

SEVENTY-SEVEN

Beverly Hills
Saturday, June 21, 1981

Tony Harod congratulated himself on being a survivor.
After the black bitch's unprovoked assault on him on the island, Harod had thought that maybe his luck had run out. It took him half an hour to unbend and he spent the rest of that insane night avoiding groups of security people who had the tendency to fire on sight. Harod had headed for the island's airfield, thinking that perhaps he could bluff his way out in Sutter's or Willi's private plane, but one look at the bonfire there had sent him scurrying back into the woods.

Harod spent several hours hiding under the bed in one of the Summer Camp bungalows near the amphitheater. Once a group of drunken security people actually broke in, ransacked the kitchen and main rooms for alcohol and valuables, and hung around to play three hands of poker in the living room before staggering back out to join their detachment. It was from their excited babble that Harod learned that Barent had been aboard the *Antoinette* when the yacht was destroyed.

It was getting gray in the east when Harod crept out and made a break for the dock area. Four boats were tied up there and Harod managed to hot-wire one of them—a twelve-foot speedboat—using skills he had not practiced since his street gang days in Chicago. A guard who had been sleeping off a hangover under the oaks took two shots at him, but Harod was already half a mile out to sea and there was no further sign of pursuit.

He knew that Dolmann Island was only about twenty miles from the coast and even with his limited navigation skills, Harod reasoned that it shouldn't be too hard to intercept the coast of North America if one headed west.

The day was overcast, the sea mirror calm, as if to make up for the night's storm and madness. Harod found a rope to lock in the steering wheel, dragged the canvas cover across the cockpit, and fell asleep. He awoke less than two miles from the coast, out of gas. The first eighteen miles of his journey had taken ninety minutes. The last two miles took eight more hours and he probably never would have made it if a small commercial fishing boat had not seen him and pulled alongside. The Georgia fisherman took Harod aboard long enough to give him water, food, and sunburn cream, and enough fuel to get him to the coast. He followed them in, between islands and wooded points that looked much as they must have three centuries earlier, finally tying up at a small harbor near a podunk town called St. Mary's. He discovered that he was in southern Georgia, looking across a delta at Florida.

Harod passed himself off as a landlubber who had rented his craft near Hilton Head and lost his way, and while the locals were reluctant to believe that anyone was so stupid as to get *that* lost, they seemed willing to accept the fact in Harod's case. He did what he could to cement bicoastal relations by taking his rescuers, the marina owners, and five onlookers to the nearest bar—a disreputable-looking dive sitting right next to the turnoff to Santa Maria State Park—and spending $280 on goodwill.

The good old boys were still drinking to his health when he prevailed on the bar owner's daughter, Star, to drive him to Jacksonville. It was only seven-thirty in the evening with another hour of summer sunlight remaining, but when they were almost there Star decided that it was too late for her to drive the entire thirty-five miles back to St. Mary's and began musing on the possibilities of getting a motel room out at Jacksonville Beach or Ponte Vedra. Star was pushing forty and expanding her polyester pants in ways Harod had not thought possible. He tipped her fifty dollars, told her to look him up the next time she was in Hollywood, and had her drop him near the United door at Jacksonville International.

Harod had almost four thousand dollars left in his wallet—he hated to travel without some spending money in his pocket and no one had told him that there would be nothing to buy on the island—but he used one of his credit cards to get a first-class ticket to L.A.

He dozed on the brief connecting flight to Atlanta, but it was obvious during the longer flight west that the stewardess who brought him his dinner and drinks thought that Harod had stumbled into the wrong section. He looked down at himself, sniffed himself, and could see why she might act that way.

His tan Giorgio Armani silk sport coat had avoided most of the blood being shed the night before, but it reeked of smoke, engine oil, and fish. His black silk shirt had absorbed enough sweat to keep a desalinization plant busy for a month. His summer-linen Sarrgiorgio slacks and Polo crocodile moccasins were, not to put too fine a line on it, shot to shit.

Still, Harod didn't appreciate some dumb cunt of a stewardess treating him this way. He had *paid* for first-class service. Tony Harod always got what he paid for. He glanced at the forward lavatory; it was empty. Most of the dozen or so first-class passengers were already dozing or reading.

Harod caught the eye of the stuck-up blond stewardess. "Oh, miss?" he called.

When she came closer he could see every detail of her tinted hair, layers of makeup, and slightly smudged mascara. There was a hint of pink lipstick on her front teeth.

"Yes, sir?" There was no mistaking the condescension in her voice.

Harod looked at her for a few more seconds. "Nothing," he said at last. "Nothing."

Harod arrived at LAX in the early hours of Wednesday morning, but it took him three days to get to his home.

Suddenly cautious, he rented a car and drove down to Laguna Beach where Teri Eastern had one of her hideaway beach houses. He had shacked up there with her a few times when she was between lovers. Harod knew that Teri was in Italy now, doing a feminist spaghetti western, but the key was still there, buried in the third rhododendron pot. The house needed airing and was decorated in Nairobi-chic, but there was imported ale in the refrigerator and clean silk sheets on the water bed. Harod slept through most of Wednesday, watching Teri's old movies on the VCR that night and driving up the coast for Chinese about midnight. On Thursday, he disguised himself with dark glasses and an oversize Banana Republic fedora belonging to one of Teri's boyfriends and drove back into the city to check out his house. Things *seemed* all right, but he went back to Laguna that night.

Thursday's newspapers had a short, page-six story on the elusive billionaire C. Arnold Barent dying of a heart attack in his Palm Springs estate. His body had been cremated and a private memorial service was being arranged by the European branch of the Barent family. Four living American presidents had sent their condolences and the article went on to tell of Barent's long history of philanthropic enterprises and to speculate on the future of his corporate empire.

Harod shook his head. There was no mention of the yacht, the island, Joseph Kepler, or the Reverend Jimmy Wayne Sutter. Harod had no doubt that their obituaries would pop up like late-summer flowers in the days to come. Someone was keeping a lid on things. Embarrassed politicians? The trio's long-term flunkies? Some European version of the Island Club? Harod didn't really want to know as long as it never again involved him.

On Friday he staked out his own house as best he could without calling down the Beverly Hills cops on himself. It looked all right. It felt good. For the first time in several years, Tony Harod felt that he could make a move without fear of bringing ten tons of shit down on his head if he took the wrong step.

Early on Saturday morning, before ten, he drove straight to his house, saluted his satyr, kissed the Spanish maid, and told the cook that she could have the day off after she fixed him some brunch. Harod called the studio head at home and then Schu Williams to find out what the hell was happening with *The White Slaver*—it was in the final steps of re-editing, getting rid of about twelve minutes that had bored the preview audiences— called seven or eight other essential contacts to let them know that he was back in town and operating, and took a phone call from his lawyer, Tom

McGuire. Harod confirmed that he was definitely going to be moving into Willi's old place and would like to keep the security on. Did Tom know of any good secretaries? McGuire could not believe that Harod had actually fired Maria Chen after all these years. "Even smart chicks get too dependent if you let them hang around too long," said Harod. "I had to let her go before she started darning my socks and sewing her name in my jockey shorts."

"Where'd she go?" asked McGuire. "Back to Hong Kong?"

"How the fuck should I know and why should I care?" snapped Harod. "Let me know if you hear of anyone who can take good shorthand and give good head."

He hung up, sat in his silent screening room for several minutes, and then went into the Jacuzzi.

Relaxing naked in the hot spa, considering going out to the pool to take a few laps, Harod closed his eyes and almost dozed. He could almost imagine Maria Chen's footsteps on the tile as she brought the day's mail in. Harod sat up, lit a cigarette from the pack by his tall glass of vodka, and leaned back against the hot jet of water, letting his aching muscles relax. *It isn't so bad when you keep your mind on other things*, he thought.

He was almost asleep again, the cigarette burning close to his finger, when he heard the sound of high heels in the access hall.

Harod's eyes shot open and he set the cigarette in his mouth and pulled his arms in, ready to rise and move quickly if he had to. His orange robe was six feet away.

For a second he did not recognize the attractive young woman in the simple white dress who entered carrying his mail, then he focused on the nymphet eyes in the missionary face, the pouting Elvis underlip, and the model's walk.

"Shayla," he said. "Shit, you scared me."

"I brought your mail in," said Shayla Berrington. "I didn't know you belonged to *National Geographic*, too."

"Jesus, kid, I've been meaning to call you," Harod said quickly. "To explain and apologize about that terrible mix-up last winter." Still not entirely comfortable, Harod considered Using her. No. This was a fresh start. He could do without that crap for a while.

"That's all right," said Shayla. Her voice had always been soft and dreamy, but now it seemed even more somnolent. Harod wondered if the poor Mormon kid had discovered drugs in the months she hadn't been working. "I'm not mad anymore," Shayla said distractedly. "The Lord got me through all that."

"Hey, great," said Harod, brushing cigarette ash off his chest. "And you were dead right about *Slaver* not being the vehicle for you. It's real schlock, light-years below you in class, kid, but I was just talking to Schu Williams this morning and he's been kicking around a project for Orion that you and I are perfect for. Schu says that Bob Redford and some kid named Tom Cruise have agreed to do a remake of the old . . ."

"Here's your *National Geographic*," interrupted Shayla, holding out the magazine and a stack of letters in his direction.

Harod put the cigarette in his mouth and reached for the mail to keep it from getting wet. The silver pistol that suddenly appeared in her hand was so small that it had to be a toy; even the five *pops* it made were toylike, sounding like a kid's cap pistol echoing off tile.

"Aw, hey," said Tony Harod, looking down at the five small holes in his chest and trying to brush them away. He looked up at Shayla Berrington and his mouth fell open, the cigarette bobbing away on the whirlpooled currents. "Oh, fuck," said Tony Harod and sat back carefully, fingers slipping and heavy eyelids closing as his face slid slowly beneath the agitated surface of the water.

Shayla Berrington watched without expression for ten minutes as the white-frothed water turned first pink and then bright red, clearing eventually as the jets poured fresh water in and the filters did their job. Then she turned and walked slowly away, posture perfect, head high, her polished high-heel shoes echoing above the sound of the water jets. She switched off the overhead lights as she left. The shuttered room remained quite dim, but scattered sunlight bouncing from the Jacuzzi threw random patterns of light on the white stucco wall, rather like a movie screen when the film has ended but the projection lamp still burns through random frames of imageless celluoid.

SEVENTY-EIGHT

Caesarea, Israel
Sunday, Dec. 13, 1981

Natalie drove her Fiat north along the Haifa Road, stopping frequently, savoring the view and the winter sunlight. She was not sure when she would pass this way again.

She was delayed by heavy military traffic on the stretch of coast road before she reached the turnoff for Kibbutz Ma'agan Mikkael, but was alone by the time she eased the Fiat uphill through the scattered stands of carob trees below the Eshkol estate.

As always, Saul was waiting by the big rock near the lower gate and came down to let her in. Natalie jumped out of the car to give him a hug and then stepped back to look at him. "You look great," she said. It was almost true. He looked better. He had never regained the weight he had lost and his left hand and wrist were bandaged from the most recent operation, but his beard had grown in as full and white as a patriarch's, a deep tan had taken the place of the pallor that had held on for so long, and his fringe of hair had grown long enough to curl almost to his shoulders. Saul smiled and adjusted his horn-rimmed glasses, just as Natalie knew he would. Just as he always did when he was embarrassed.

"You look great, too," he said, latching the gate and waving to the young Sabra who stood watching from his post along the fence. "Let's go up to the house. Dinner's almost ready."

As they drove to the main house, Natalie glanced at his bandaged hand. "How is it?" she asked.

"What? Oh, fine," said Saul, adjusting his glasses and looking at the bandages as if seeing them for the first time. "It would seem that a thumb is indispensable, but when it's gone you realize how easy it is to do without it." He smiled at her. "As long as nothing happens to the other one."

"Strange," said Natalie.

"What?"

"Two gunshot wounds, pneumonia, a concussion, three broken ribs, and enough cuts and bruises to keep a football team happy for a full season."

"Jews are hard to kill."

"No, I don't mean that," said Natalie, pulling the Fiat into the carport. "I mean all that serious stuff and it's that woman's bite that almost killed you—at least almost made you lose your arm."

"Human bites are notorious for becoming infected," said Saul, holding the rear door open for her.

761

"Miss Sewell wasn't human," said Natalie.

"No," said Saul, adjusting his glasses. "I suppose by that time, she wasn't."

Saul had prepared a delicious meal complete with mutton and fresh-baked bread. They chatted of inconsequential things during dinner—Saul's courses at the university in Haifa, Natalie's most recent photography assignment for the *Jerusalem Post*, the weather. After his cheese and fruit dessert, Natalie wanted to visit the aqueduct and take their coffee with them so Saul filled the steel Thermos while she went to her room and got a thick sweater from her suitcase. December evenings along the coast could be quite cool.

They walked slowly downhill past the orange groves, commenting on the mellow light and trying to ignore the two young Sabra men who followed them at a respectful distance, Uzis slung over their shoulders.

"I'm sorry about David's death," said Natalie just as they reached the sand dunes. The Mediterranean was turning to copper ahead of them.

Saul shrugged. "He lived a full life. The second stroke was mercifully quick."

"I'm sorry I missed the funeral," said Natalie. "I tried all day to get out of Athens, but the flights were all messed up."

"You didn't miss it," said Saul. "I thought of you often." He waved at the bodyguards, telling them to stay where they were, and led the way out onto the aqueduct. The horizontal light turned their shadows into giants atop the crenelated dunes.

They paused halfway across the long span and Natalie hugged her elbows. The wind was cold. Three stars and a fingernail moon were visible in the east.

"You're still leaving tomorrow?" asked Saul. "Going back?"

"Yes," said Natalie. "Eleven-thirty out of Ben-Gurion."

"I'll drive you," said Saul. "Drop the car off at Sheila's and let her or one of the kids drive me back."

"I'd like that." Natalie smiled.

Saul poured their coffee and handed her a plastic cup. Steam rose in the cold air. "Are you afraid?" he said.

"Of just going back to the States or of there being more of them?" she asked, sipping the hot, rich Turkish mixture.

"Just of going back," said Saul.

"Yes," said Natalie.

Saul nodded. A few cars moved along the coast road, their headlights lost in the glow of the sunset. Miles to the north, the battlements of the Crusader City glowed red. Mount Carmel was just visible, wrapped in a violet haze so rich that Natalie would not have believed the color was real if she had seen it in a photograph.

"I mean, I don't know," continued Natalie. "I'll try it for a while. I mean, America was scary even before . . . everything. But it's my home. You know what I mean."

"Yes."

"Do you ever think about going home? To the States, I mean?"

Saul nodded and sat on a large stone. There was frost in the crevices where the day's sun had not touched. "All the time," he said. "But there's so much to do here."

"I still don't believe how fast the Mossad . . . *believed* everything," said Natalie.

Saul smiled. "We have a long and noble history of paranoia," he said. "I think we fed their prejudices well." He sipped his coffee and poured more for each of them. "Besides, they had a lot of intelligence data they didn't know what to do with. Now they have a framework for the facts . . . a weird framework, to be sure, but better than nothing."

Natalie gestured across the darkening sea to the north. "Do you think they'll find . . . whoever?"

"The Oberst's mystery connections?" said Saul. "Perhaps. My hunch is that it would be people they already are dealing with."

Natalie's eyes clouded over. "I still think about the one . . . in the house . . . the one who was missing."

"Howard," said Saul. "The redheaded man. Justin's father."

"Yes." Natalie shivered as the sun touched the horizon and the wind came up.

"Catfish had radioed both of you that he 'put Howard to sleep,' " said Saul. "Assuming that was who followed you. When Melanie sent someone— probably the giant—out to murder Catfish, he almost certainly retrieved Howard as well. Perhaps he was still unconscious when the house burned. Maybe *he* was the one who was waiting for you in the back room."

"Maybe," said Natalie, wrapping her hands around the cup for warmth. "Or I suppose Melanie could've buried him there somewhere, thinking he was dead. That would explain why the number of bodies reported in the paper didn't come out right." She looked at the other stars emerging. "You know what today's an anniversary of? One year since . . ."

"Since your father's death," he said, helping her to her feet. They walked back along the aqueduct in the brief twilight. "Didn't you say you received a letter from Jackson?"

Natalie brightened. "A long one. He's back in Germantown. Actually, he's the new director of Community House, but he got rid of that old house, told Soul Brickyard to find another clubhouse—I guess he could do that since he's still sort of a member—and opened up a bunch of real community service storefronts along Germantown Avenue. He's got a free clinic going and everything."

"Did he mention how Marvin is doing?" asked Saul.

"Yes. Jackson's more or less adopted him, I think. He wrote that Marvin's showing signs of progress. He's about to the level of a four-year-old now . . . a bright four-year-old, Jackson says."

"Do you think you'll visit him?"

Natalie adjusted her sweater. "Maybe. Probably. Yes."

They stepped carefully off the crumbling shoulder of the ancient span and looked back the way they had come. Devoid of color, the heaped dunes could have been a frozen sea lapping at the Roman ruins.

"Will you be doing any photo assignments before you go back to graduate school?"

"Uh-huh. The *Jersulem Post* has asked me to do that thing on the decline of the big American synagogues and I thought I'd start in Philadelphia."

Saul waved at the two who waited in the lee of two pillars. One had lit a cigarette that glowed like a red eye in the sudden gloom. "The photo essay you did on the labor-class Arabs in Tel Aviv was excellent," he said.

"Well," said Natalie, a small trace of defiance in her voice, "let's face it. They're treated like Israel's niggers."

"Yes," agreed Saul.

The two of them stood on the road at the base of the hill for several minutes, not speaking, cold, but reluctant to go up to the well-lighted house and warmth and easy conversation and sleep. Suddenly Natalie moved into the circle of Saul's arms, burying her face in his jacket, feeling his beard against her hair.

"Oh, Saul," she sobbed.

He patted her clumsily with his bandaged hand, quite content to let that moment be frozen in time for eternity, accepting even the sadness in it as a source of joy. Behind them, he heard the wind move the sand gently in its ceaseless effort to cover all things that man had made or hoped to make.

Natalie moved back a bit, dug a Kleenex out of the pocket of her sweater, and blew her nose. "Damn it," she said. "I'm sorry, Saul. I guess I came to say shalom and I'm just not ready to."

Saul adjusted his glasses. "Remember," he said, "shalom does not mean good-bye. Nor hello. It just means—*peace.*"

"Shalom," said Natalie, moving back into the circle of his arms against the chill of the night wind.

"Shalom and *L'chaim*," said Saul, touching his cheek to her hair and watching the sand curl and scatter across the narrow road. "To life."

EPILOGUE

October 21, 1988

Time has passed. I am very happy here. I live in southern France now, between Cannes and Toulon, but not, I am happy to say, too near St. Tropez.

I have recovered almost completely from my illness and can get around without a walker now, but I rarely go out. Henri and Claude do my shopping in the village. Occasionally I let them take me to my pensione in Italy, south of Pescara, on the Adriatic, or even as far as the rented cottage in Scotland, to watch *him*, but even these trips have become less and less frequent.

There is an abandoned abbey in the hills behind my home and it is close enough that I sometimes go there to sit and think among the stones and wildflowers. I think about isolation and abstinence and how each is so cruelly dependent upon the other.

I feel my age these days. I tell myself that this is because of my long illness and the touch of rheumatism that assails me on chilly October days such as this, but I find myself dreaming about the familiar streets of Charleston and those last days. They are dreams of hunger.

I had not known when I had sent Culley out in May to abduct Mrs. Hodges exactly what purpose I would put the old woman to. At times it seemed hardly worth the effort keeping her alive in the basement of the Hodges place, much less all the bother of dying her hair to match mine and experimenting with various injections to simulate my illness. But in the end it was worth it. As I waited in the rented ambulance a block from my home during those last minutes before Howard drove me to the airport and our waiting flight, I appreciated how well the Hodges family had served me during the previous year. There was little more I could ask of them. Tying the old woman in the bed had seemed an unnecessary touch given her medicated condition, but now I honestly believe that if she had not been so secured, she would have leaped from the pyre and gone running from the flaming house, thus ruining the careful scene I had sacrificed so much to orchestrate.

My poor house. My dear family. The thought of that day can still bring me to tears.

Howard was useful for those first few days, but once I was settled in the village and sure no one was following, it seemed best that he have an accident far from me. Claude and Henri are from a local family that has also served me well over the decades.

765

I sit here and I wait for Nina. I know now that she has usurped control of all the lesser races of the world—the Negros and Hebrews and Asians and such—and that fact alone precludes my ever returning to America. Willi had been right as far back as those first months of our acquaintance when we had sat listening politely in a Vienna café while he explained in scientific terms how the United States had become a mongrel nation, a nest of grasping *under-people* waiting to overthrow the purer races.

Now Nina controls all of them.

That night on the island, I had stayed in contact with one of the guards long enough to see what Nina's people had done to my poor Willi. Even Mr. Barent had been in her control. Willi had been right all along.

But I am not content simply to sit here and wait for Nina and her mongrel minions to find me.

Ironically, it was Nina and her Negress who gave me the idea. Those weeks watching Captain Mallory through binoculars and the satisfying conclusion of that little charade. The experience had reminded me of an earlier contact, an almost random encounter, that distant December Saturday—the very day I had first thought Willi had been killed only to have Nina turn on me—during my farewell visit to Fort Sumter.

There had been the sight of the thing first, moving dark and shark-silent through the waters of the Bay, and then the surprising contact with the captain as he stood in the gray tower—they call it a sail, I know now—binoculars strung about his neck.

Six times since then I have tracked him down and shared those instances. They are sweeter than the random mind-matings that were necessary with Mallory. At my cottage near Aberdeen, one can stand alone on the sea cliffs and watch the submarine glide in toward its port. They pride themselves on their keys and codes and fail-safe procedures, but I know now what my captain has known for so long: It would be very, very easy. His nightmares are my manuals.

But if I am to do it, it should be done soon. Neither the captain nor his ship are growing younger. Nor am I. Both of them soon may be too old to function. So may I.

These fears of Nina and plans for such a huge Feeding do not come to me every day. But they come more often now.

On some days I rise to the sound of singing as girls from the village cycle by our place on their way to the dairy. On those days the sun is marvelously warm as it shines on the small white flowers growing between the tumbled stones of the abbey, and I am content simply to be there and to share the sunlight and silence with them.

But on other days—cold dark days such as this when the clouds move in from the north—I remember the silent shape of a submarine moving through the dark waters of the bay, and I wonder whether my self-imposed abstinence has been for nothing. On days like this I wonder if such a gigantic, final Feeding might not make me younger after all. As Willi used to say when proposing some mischievous little prank of his: *What do I have to lose?*

It is supposed to be warmer tomorrow. I may be happier then. But I am chilled and somewhat melancholy today. I am all alone with no one to play with.

Winter is coming. And I am very, very hungry.